Nos. 1 & 2.]   [One Penny.

LITTLE JOHN AND WILL SCARLETT

OR THE

OUTLAWS OF SHERWOOD FOREST.

EVELINE SAVES THE LIFE OF WILL SCARLETT.

LONDON: H. VICKERS, STRAND; AND ALL BOOKSELLERS.

LITTLE JOHN

AND

WILL SCARLETT;

OR,

The Outlaws of Sherwood Forest.

BY

THE FOREST RANGER.

" Come, lithe and listen, gentlemen,
    That be of freeborn blood,
I shall tell you of a good yeoman,
    His name was Robin Hood.

" Robin he was a proud outlaw
    As ever walk'd on ground ;
So courteous an outlaw as he was
    Has never yet been found."

LONDON :

H. VICKERS, STRAND.

LITTLE JOHN AND WILL SCARLETT

OR THE

OUTLAWS OF SHERWOOD FOREST.

THE FIRST MEETING OF ROBIN HOOD AND WILL SCARLETT.

CHAPTER I.

HARD KNOCKS.

WE are under the greenwood trees of famed Sherwood Forest.

The pleasant sun, which has been, during the day, vivifying and warming all nature, is setting, and darkness is stealing over the face of the entire surface of the forest, while already in secluded dells and thickets the shadows fall thickly.

A broken and discoloured light fell from the red sun on one of the richest grassy glades, surrounded on all sides by wide-branched, gnarled, short-stemmed oaks that made pleasant shade.

In one corner is a copse of beeches and hollies, which appeared made from an ambuscade, so gloomy was it, and so surely did the branches intercept the beams of the sinking sun.

All was silent, save where the birds still twittered on bough and branch, or a hare hopped lazily about, or perhaps a small herd of deer came running timidly through the forest.

Suddenly, however, the deep stillness of the spot was broken in a way least to be expected in such a lonely spot.

It was a person singing, in a rich and manly voice, one of the old ballads which were the work of either joyous yeomen of the day, or others, handed down to posterity by the rural ballad-mongers and inferior minstrels, who were the bards and historians of herd and husbandman, and which songs, besides cheering the fireside with rude rhymes and ruder legends, have, by transmission, proved useful in preserving to posterity many worthy characters who otherwise would have been forgotten.

Presently the singer stepped from the covert of the trees and looked around the glade.

It was solitary except from his own presence.

Halting a moment, as if to listen, he ceased his song, and then, hearing no sound, advanced on his way.

This man, who wandered all alone in that unfrequented forest, was young, and dressed according to the fashion, which was neither that of the lordly knights of the day, the steady franklin, nor the more simple yeoman.

It was foppish even for a young man, consisting wholly of silk,—

> "His doublet was all of silk, 'tis said,
> His stockings like scarlet shone—"

but there all idea of effeminacy ceased; for not only was the tread of the youth manly and erect, but he carried a good yew bow in his hand, while at his back was sword and buckler, not forgetting the hunting-knife, without which no man went in the days of which we speak.

Having assured himself that the glade was apparently abandoned to all, save the wild beasts of the forest, the stranger proceeded on his way for a few steps, until he reached the dark copse, when he was startled by a voice speaking close to him.

"Whither away, my master, and what do you here?"

The youth turned round and faced a man not much older than himself, slight, elegant, and well made, but wearing a suit of Lincoln green, having some dozen arrows stuck in his belt, and a six-foot bow in his hand. The features of the new-comer were singularly handsome, though browned by exposure, and revealed a remarkable mixture of command, habit of power, and sterling good nature.

"By what right do you ask, my friend?" said he of the silken doublet, with a tinge of irony in his voice.

"Enough for thee to know that I have a right," resumed the forester.

Quick as thought the youth strung his bow, and, adjusting an arrow, took aim at the rude questioner of his right to walk the forest glade. But he in Lincoln green making no hostile demonstration in return, a slight blush suffused the youth's cheeks, and turning round, as if in search of a mark, saw a buck at some distance, which, startled by their voices, was making off at a great pace.

Scarcely had the whizz of the arrow been heard through the air, when the animal gave a fearful bound, and then fell on its knees upon the sward.

"Right well shot," cried the stranger, with a look of genuine admiration; "if you would but practise, in a little while you might be fit to be yeoman of mine."

"I," cried the youth, hotly, "am no vagrant to take service under thee. Get from my path, and talk not such insolence, lest you get from me the hardest buffet you ever felt."

The man in Lincoln green smiled. The smile was ironical, and yet not altogether unpleasant.

"Talk not so largely," he said, "lest I blow my horn and show you that you have got into a hornets' nest."

"Blow you your horn or not, Sir Insolent," cried the youth, who was now in a passion, and whose face became red as the hair that crowned his brow, "it shall be your last."

And once again he fitted an arrow to his bow, the other, this time, doing the same; and there they stood, two as fine samples of English archers as man could have wished to see.

"Hold! one moment," suddenly said he in Lincoln green; "I have an offer to make."

"Speak quickly, for my arrow longs to taste thy best blood."

"Thou art a brave lad, and as we have no real quarrel, 'twould be a pity either should be slain. What say to take sword and buckler, and try our manhood in this open glade?"

"With all my heart," said the youth, casting away his bow.

In another moment the two men stood close to one another, with brows bent, with eyes fixed fiercely on one another, with buckler on the left arm, and sword firmly clasped.

"Now then—and beshrew me thank you for the thought," cried the silken doublet; "I fly not one foot."

Then began one of those apparently terrible hand-to-hand conflicts which were common in an age when guns were unknown—and when physical prowess was looked upon as almost the only merit in a man.

They were more sensible than the duel, as they did not at all necessarily end fatally, being oftener fought with quarterstaves than swords.

It was at once apparent that the men were well matched; for some time, though the forest rang with blows, and sword and shield clashed, and sparks flew madly about in the still night air—not a drop of blood was shed. At length, however, the forester in Lincoln green made a feint, aimed at the youth's feet, and then, whirling his broad sword on high, let it fall on the other's head with a force that might have felled an ox.

The youth staggered, and seemed scared out of his wit, but quickly recovered himself.

"Thou never lent a blow, stranger," he cried, "which might not be requited with a better—" and taking the forester by surprise, he hit him on the crown so effectually as to cause the blood to trickle down "from every hair of his head."

"God a mercy! my good fellow. I think you can work as well with the broadsword as the bow—what say you to a bout at quarterstaff?"

"With all my heart," cried the hot youth, throwing away sword and buckler, and taking from his feet where he had cast it the favourite weapon of the hour for friendly fights—albeit, such friendly fights often ended in angry words and broken sconces.

In an instant the forester was ready also, and then the combatants closed together, and in a moment proved themselves apt hands at this manly exercise. They were, to all appearance, almost equal in strength, courage, and skill, while, had any one been present, they must have supposed that four or five men were at work, so terrible was the clatter.

Again, as in the broadsword exercise, they proved equal for some time, aiming, parrying, and making feints without a blow telling, until the forester, thinking it high time to finish, rained his blows with such furious energy, that for a moment the youth was compelled to act only on the defensive, keeping his hands about a yard asunder, and covering himself by shifting his weapon with great celerity, so as to protect his head and body.

It was wonderful to see the way time was kept with eye, and arm and foot, the combatants all the while looking each other full in the face.

The forester stood back, and, as if to regain breath himself, assumed the defensive.

Only one moment.

Sliding his right hand to his left, he swung the heavy quarterstaff round, caught the youth on the side of the head, and sent him flying several feet before he fell at full length on the greensward.

The forester rose to help him up, but the other, mistaking his action, rose to his feet, and, regardless of the ringing in his ears, put himself on the defensive.

"No more," said the forester, gaily; "you have fought a good fight—and lest you think yourself worsted by a churl, know that my name is ——"

"What?"

"ROBIN HOOD OF SHERWOOD FOREST!"

The youth stood still, amazed and half incredulous.

"'Sdeath!" he cried, turning quite pale, "that we of all others should have fought!—for know that I am born in Maxwell town, and am called Young Gammel, or commonly Will—Will Scarlett—your sister's son."

"Will Scarlett?"

"The same."

"Then come to my arms, my boy."

And thereupon the old ballad says there was kissing and embracing good store.

"And now, my nephew, though, as you will hear in good time, I am not thine uncle—why have you come here?"

"In search of you, Robin—for I have killed a man."

"Wherefore?"

"That is a long story."

"Which you shall tell, Will Gammel, where there is salve for our wounds and provisions for our bodies."

The young man readily agreed, and both, shouldering their weapons, proceeded on their way.

Next minute they disappeared beneath the dark arches of the forest.

While they are reaching the rendezvous, let us explain how the son of a squire of no low degree came to offer his services to the outlaw of Sherwood.

CHAPTER II.

SIR GAMMEL.

To those who only judge England by what it is to-day, no idea can, in a few words, be given of that England falsely called merrie.

Miserable and wretched was indeed the true condition of the country, with every man's hand raised against every man.

The aristocracy was uniformly composed of marauders, tyrants, and sycophants—the usual characteristics of aristocrats—whose occupation was pillage, murder, and the ravishment of maidens; and for this reason is it that their escutcheons have long mouldered from the walls of their castles; that their castles themselves are but green mounds and shattered ruins; that the place that once knew them knows them no more; and that their very names are forgotten, except when brought to light by the exigencies of romance and history.

When kings are light, perfidious, and licentious, the lordly race will ape and exaggerate the vices of their superiors.

The middle classes were sullen, because, composed of Saxons, they were oppressed by their Norman conquerors.

To the house of one of the former we must now conduct our readers.

It is a large, low, irregular building, with several enclosures and courtyards, covering an extensive space of ground. It differed considerably from the ambitious edifices erected by the pirate barons, but was not the less prepared for attack.

It was defended by a deep moat or ditch, without which precaution it would not have protected its inhabitants an hour. This moat was further defended by a double line of stockades—such as were afterwards used by the descendants of these very men to defend themselves against the inroads of the Red Indians.

In a day when cannon was not yet invented, such a defence was sufficient for all ordinary purposes.

The interior was a mixture of barbarous splendour and Saxon simplicity, for Sir Gammel was essentially a Saxon, and a bitter enemy of the Normans, who lorded it over the land.

The huge hall, with its rough-hewn table, with its roof of beams and rafters, was richly ornamented on the walls with the spoils of the chase, and with a perfect armoury of days gone by, while all around were massive chairs and settees for Sir Gammel and his family.

A rare old English gentleman was he—fond of the chase, fond of his hawks and hounds, fond of his wife and stalwart children, and fonder, perhaps than all else, of his strong old English ale, which he would quaff in the largest flagons that silversmiths ever made.

But there was one thing that Sir Gammel loved even more than all we have alluded to—and that was his country.

Patriotism—staunch, sturdy adoration of English soil, and hatred of its piratical oppressors was his virtue.

In this belief he had studiously brought up all his children.

None was more thoroughly imbued with his father's spirit than his youngest son, William—from his ruddy complexion and red hair always called Will Scarlett.

Little time in those days was spent on the mental education of youth, much upon their physical.

Will Scarlett, then, at sixteen years of age could shoot, ride, use his quarterstaff with ere a youth in the land; but his rarest passion was hunting the wild deer and chasing the doe, in which his father initiated him.

But they needs must use discretion in the pursuit of their favourite amusement, as the Normans were without mercy on their inferiors.

The game laws, bad as they are now, are mild as milk in comparison with what they were under the sway of the Conqueror.

But Will Scarlett—hot, young, and impetuous—was not to be deterred by any such considerations from following the chase.

One morning early—having taken a respectful leave of his father and mother, and a more merry one of his brothers and sisters, who looked upon him as a mere youth—Will Scarlett took his bow, his arrows, and his hunting-knife, and went forth to kill a buck.

And not only to kill a buck, but to saunter through the grassy glades and woodland scenery of dear Sherwood Forest.

Within a few days Will had made a discovery.

Despite his happy home, despite the tenderness of his father and mother, despite that he was the petted favourite of his brothers and sisters, Will was dissatisfied. There was something wanting, and what that something was he was unable to say.

He was on the verge of that abyss which separates boyhood and manhood; on the verge of that precipice when purely innocent pleasures cease to flow, and passion, with its glow, its restless desires and burning thirst, begins to pervade the human frame.

He was in love—but with an ideal.

Secluded from all society save that of his sisters and their rather coarse Saxon handmaidens—girls able to have tried a bout at wrestling with him, the somewhat rude and unpolished lad, who had progressed in literature far enough to have read or heard of the nut-brown maid and certain other love ballads, had in his mind moulded an image of perfection which he would find difficult to realise.

But which of us in his time has not done the same, and is it not ever the most fascinating of our day dreams?

But we must allow Will's feelings to develop themselves in action.

The day was hot and sultry—the wind, when it did blow, came in scorching gusts that dried up the skin and parched the lips—and Will found that the deer had wisely retreated to the very deepest thickets of the forest in search of shade.

To follow them was an arduous and fatiguing task; so Will, having reached a spot where he knew they were likely to pass when the hottest part of the day was over, cast himself under the shade of an oak, drew forth refreshments, consisting of a venison pasty and a leathern bottle of ale, to which he began to address himself with an energy which spoke well for the appetites of the time, to which those of these degenerate days was as nothing.

From where Will Scarlett sat he had a good view of a large glade before him, and of a long grassy vista that, like a road, ascended a steep ascent to his left, Sherwood Forest combining every requisite of scenery that an artist could have wished for.

Soon Will was in a reverie, one of those sweet day dreams which come to the heart of youth—green oases in the stern desert of life—and raise us to the very heavens, so blissful are the self-created illusions they arouse.

Suddenly Will heard a rustle in the distant bushes about fifty yards ahead, and raising his eyes, saw first a fawn and then a doe emerge from the thicket.

To his surprise, the doe then halted and faced the thicket, while the fawn crept behind its mother.

Scarcely had this occurred, when a gaunt and hungry wolf leaped headlong across a fallen trunk, and flew at the doe.

In an instant Will was upon his feet, an arrow was fitted to his bow, and a sharp twang heard through the air.

The wolf fell dead, pierced through the heart, while the fawn and doe flew at their utmost speed over the green sward.

Will blushed, for it struck him he had done a foolish thing in killing a useless wolf, when he might have made a prize of doe and fawn.

"Never mind," he cried aloud; "I took the wolf for a Norman tyrant and the deer for their poor shorn and oppressed subjects, and I could not help it."

"Good brother," said a bluff, sarcastic voice near him, "an' thou speakest so, thy feet will soon be dangling six feet from the ground."

"Who speaks?" said Will, turning sharply round.

While he was idly meditating, so wrapped had he been in thought, a mounted rider had come up close enough behind him to witness his feat and hear his unconsciously out-spoken words.

It was a monk riding a mule.

The mule was a thin, gaunt, bony representative of his class—such was rarely even put to use as a sumpter beast.

But if the animal was gaunt and thin, the same could not be said of its master, for he was stout enough and—his cowl being thrown back in consequence of the heat of the day—brawny enough to have raised an idea somewhat averse to his extreme sanctity.

He was in the prime of life, with a close shaven crown, begirt, like a parish pound, with a bristly black hedge; his countenance was bluff, his eyebrows black, his forehead low but broad, his cheeks round and ruddy, while his chin was completely hidden by a black and curly beard.

There was a sly good-humoured smile about his face, which was the reverse of ascetic.

Altogether, Will thought he never had seen so jovial and ruddy a priest.

CHAPTER III.

AN ADVENTURE.

"A POOR monk," replied the other meekly, "in search of rest, food, and drink."

"Rest thou wilt find under yon tree, and if I have not quite finished my provender, thou mayest also find something to eat—but why speak so glibly, sir shaven cowl, of hanging? The sound is not pleasant to our Saxon ears."

"I merely warned thee as a father, of what would have been thy fate had Norman knight or his minions have heard you speak—a short shrift and a tight rope would have been thy due."

"Not before one or two of the hated race had fallen," cried young Gammel fiercely.

"So hot, my young cock!" laughed the priest; "take care they cut not thy comb. Ah! ah! venison too—I think I shall do thee a kindness in eating it all up, lest any keeper come by and is unmannerly enough to ask questions."

"Eat away," said Will Scarlett carelessly, as he cast himself on the grass, "there is plenty where that came from."

"You are a pretty out-spoken lad," cried the friar, who was making huge inroads upon the fat, lean and crust of the sturdy pasty, "and would, I believe, say as much to the beard of Lord de Beauclerk himself, our worthy Ranger, whom God defend!"

"Ranger me no rangers!" cried Will, hotly. "Who gave him such a post in Sherwood?"

"The good Prince John," said the friar, with a sly wink.

"Harkee, Mr. Monk, I know not whether it be your good pleasure to rouse my ire, but either you will leave off these encomiums of our hated oppressors, or I will drive you away with your head to the tail of yonder mule, which, by the way, you have this day stolen!"

"Stolen!—my face to the tail!" cried the irate friar.

"Yes, stolen, to answer your first question. Do you think that I do not know my own father's Dobbin, which, in consideration of his antiquity and many services, we had set in a paddock to graze the rest of his days—therefore I repeat—stolen!"

"Borrowed, young man," said the friar gravely, "and borrowed for a good purpose—the use of Mother Church. Would you have had a man of my inches walk a day like this? But the beast is slow and my weight too much, so take him back and no excuses."

Will could not but laugh at the man's solemn impudence, so that he was in no hurry to reply.

"And now, young man, that I have eaten with you, and drank with you, may I know the name to remember in my prayers."

"I am son of Sir Gammel."

"Whew! a goodly stock. I am proud to make your acquaintance, young sir."

Will Scarlett bowed, not ill-pleased at the evident compliment to his father's just popularity.

"And may I ask your name, Sir Priest?" he said.

"Hem! I am a poor friar travelling on the business of my order—but should you continue your ways, talking treason and shooting the king's deer, I have no doubt that we shall become better acquainted."

Will Scarlett was about to make an angry answer, when both their ears were assailed by a sudden series of appalling shrieks mingled with the fearful clatter of horses' hoofs, coming rapidly, to all appearance, in their direction.

Will rose to his feet, but the friar, stout, heavy, and just having completed a hearty meal, remained seated.

Will Scarlett had no need to go far to discover what was the cause of this sudden clamour.

A magnificent coal-black steed had taken the bit in its mouth, and was madly riding down the hill in such a way as to have defied the most accomplished rider.

In this instance the rider was a woman.

Even at that distance, Will could see that it was a vision of beauty.

But he scarcely paused to examine her then. His sole thought was to save the rider.

There appeared no prospect of reaching the horse in time to seize the bridle, and did the unruly beast continue his present pace across the open glade, the brains of the woman must be dashed to pieces against the low projecting boughs of the forest trees.

What was to be done?

The clamour of those thundering hoofs on the hill side, as well as the organ of vision, proclaimed that not an instant was to be lost.

Will made up his mind.

Again he adjusted an arrow to his bow; again it whizzed through the air.

The horse reared, stopped, and then continued on its way—but not so swiftly.

Quick as lightning, Will, the swiftest footracer in the country-side, bounded over the green.

Just in time; for as he caught up to them, the horse stumbled, fell, and the maiden was caught in the arms of the gallant young Gammel.

He saw a glance of deep and earnest gratitude, a smile ineffable in its sweetness; he drank in a draught of utter intoxication, and then—he felt a cold inert form in his arms.

She had fainted.

"Water! water! from yonder brook," shouted Will to the monk, who had risen, moved, despite his heaviness, at witnessing a scene of such sudden and startling interest.

"Nay, nay," he said, as he came up after a hasty visit to the crupper of Dobbin, "these dainty damsels are not to be brought to life by water, which might wash the colour off their cheeks. Here is wine—good vintage of the South—which I will warrant brings her back were her soul in purgatory."

"Give it here, then!" hastily cried Will; and taking the bottle, he let the liquor trickle into her mouth.

At first there appeared no power of swallowing; then suddenly the throat relaxed, a deep sigh burst from the pent-up bosom, and she opened her eyes to gaze at Will Scarlett with a look of utter bewilderment.

"What has happened?" she murmured, as if the terrible shock had bereft her of memory, "and who are you, gentle stranger?"

Will pointed to the dead horse, which lay on its side, with the arrow almost lost in its flank.

The girl shuddered.

"Poor Firefly," she murmured gently—"one of the gentlest and best of horses. What madness could have attacked the poor beast?"

The friar, meanwhile, had crossed over to where the animal lay insensible, and was examining the carcase.

"Humph!" he said; "there has been foul play here."

Will Scarlett assisted the girl to rise, and all three stood gazing with wonderment at what the quick eye of the hedge-priest had made out.

A number of small prickly boughs had been placed under the saddle, in such a way as gradually to work into the generous animal's flesh and drive him frantic, which fully accounted for the wild, headlong speed with which he had carried his fair charge.

"Who could have done this?" said the girl, thoughtfully. "Surely I have no enemies?"

"Even angels have at times," put in Will Scarlett, with a smile.

The girl blushed the colour of Gammel's hair, and cast down her eyes to avoid the ardent but respectful gaze of the youth.

"It is of no use now," she faltered, "devising of this cruel deed. To you, gentle sir, I owe my life. Can you add to the deep obligation I owe you—that of taking me where I can seek shelter with those of my own sex, until such time as I can return to my father?"

"My mother and sisters will gladly welcome you," said young Gammel, warmly; "and this poor nag must bear you, for want of a better."

"I cry you many thanks," she replied sweetly; "but the quiet horse is the more welcome now—I have had enough of runagates."

After a few more pleasant words and compliments exchanged, young Gammel contrived to seat the young lady on the monk's saddle—a spectacle at which the brawny friar made a wry face, but no remarks, except to wish them God speed, and decline, on the pretence of *physical weakness*, accompanying them.

And so the young couple were left alone.

The girl was thoughtful, and so was Gammel, who by this time had familiarised himself with the stranger's general aspect and features.

No pen-and-ink sketch can ever fully convey an idea of womanly beauty to the reader, scarcely can the glowing tints of artistic genius realize the intenseness of female loveliness; for everywhere is wanting the warm flesh, with its perfume of love.

Still, it would be to depart wholly from the precedent laid down "in the books" by the whole confraternity of historical romancists, did we not essay to give some outline sketch, however meagre, of a character who will play no mean part in our narrative.

Like all perfectly beautiful women, she was of medium height, the extremes of tallness and petiteness being opposed to all ideas of true loveliness. When we say, therefore, that she was formed in the best proportions of her sex, we indicate that though slight from youthfulness, there was full promise that that form would bud into full bloom as time progressed; while now, as she sat or walked, it was easy to see the lines of beauty everywhere, especially in the delicate waist, the upright bearing, and the admirably moulded limbs.

While her eyes were to all appearance of that varying colour which is so difficult to paint, so uncertain to realize, the fixed gaze of a lover would have soon discovered that they were a blackish-brown, enshrined beneath a graceful eyebrow of brown, sufficiently marked to give expression to the forehead. The eyelids, when lowered, were like a deep fringe that veiled the latent power that lay beneath—a power to strike with awe, as well as win hearts to love and all gentle feelings.

Her complexion was exquisitely fair, with the bright hues of health now quick returning, to make her cheeks not rosy, like one exposed much to the air, but of a pale pink, which was almost unreal in its admirable delicacy and changing power.

Her nose was not of the insipid Grecian cast, but slightly arched, indicating energy and vivacity of character, while to describe her lips were to exhaust all the rapturous similes of the poet, and then not to say enough.

They were made not to be described, but kissed.

Her hair was of that glorious intermediate hue between brown and flaxen which is no colour, and falling in artistic and fantastic curls over her neck, received but little additional lustre from the presence of costly gems that peeped from beneath the velvet hunting cap and feather she wore.

Round her neck was a gold chain that fell to her waist, where it was fastened to her girdle.

Her hunting dress was something like a riding-habit, close, and exhibiting her form to perfection, especially the bare arm, which, while holding up the reins, was made visible to young Gammel in a way that made him turn his eyes in another direction, lest he should forget himself and offend the lady of his heart.

CHAPTER IV.

A DISCOVERY.

THAT young Gammel was in love need scarcely be said. Young, ardent, with a heart overflowing with the milk of human kindness, it was not possible for him to be thrown into the society of so beautiful a girl under such circumstances, and not be stricken.

That morning, without knowing why, he had gone forth, heart oppressed and sore, longing for he knew not what, dreaming idly of something as yet not defined—ever looking forward never backwards.

Then had come this vision of beauty—and he had saved her life.

The life he had saved appeared to belong to him now.

At least he could not help fancying that it ought to be so. And yet it was useless for him to disguise from himself the fact that while he was but the son of a respectable country gentleman of old family, the fair apparition beside which he walked was doubtless some lady of high degree, to whom it would be the height of presumption for him to look up.

But though these thoughts might sadden and make him thoughtful, when has reason dashed the cup of love from our lips—when has youth ceased to be hopeful?

"Have we far to go?" said the girl at length, as if the silence had become painful.

"Yonder, lady, is the roof of my father, Sir Gammel's house. May I know whom I have the honour to introduce beneath his poor rooftree?"

The girl looked at him with a melancholy smile, in which was as much pity as earnest gratitude—for what maiden is blind to the evidences of such a sudden and tender passion as that conceived by William Gammel?

"Young and noble stranger, without hesitation you saved my life; but when you know who I am, perhaps you may repent."

"Never!" cried Will Scarlett, though a wild, strange fancy went like an icebolt to his heart—"never would I have seen so much loveliness perish without perilling my life."

"Had you known that I was Eveline, only daughter of the Ranger of Sherwood Forest," she replied, in quite a humble deprecating tone, as if she was quite ashamed of being not only so far above him in the social scale, but of the hated Norman race.

William Gammel stood still a moment with gaping mouth and staring eyes, as if utterly unable to realise the truth of the terrible statement he had heard.

No description, however elaborate, can convey to modern readers an idea of the utter detestation felt by the conquered for the conquerors, of the utter contempt of the vanquishers for the vanquished.

Then recollecting himself, Will bowed low, and taking the horse's bridle, led it hastily foward in the direction of Gammel House.

"You are not angry, young sir?" said Eveline, a little haughtily.

"Angry!" cried Will, looking at her with his honest English eyes—no! not angry, but sorry."

"Why sorry?" she asked, in a gentler tone.

"Do not ask me, lady, if you would not have me forget the respect due to your high degree and angelic loveliness."

Eveline blushed, but said nothing, and in a few minutes they were in the rugged pathway which led to the house, at the door of which they were received by the astounded relatives of the young man.

Will, with his strange companion, had been seen approaching from some distance. The Gammels could not make out the unexpected companionship.

A brief explanation, however, satisfied them, and though in their hearts they both regretted the circumstance of Will having connected himself in any way with a Norman girl, and still more that he should have brought her to share their hospitality, yet was their politeness more than a match for their prejudices.

It may, however, be surmised that, when Eveline insisted on only resting an hour, and then departing, they did not much repine, though in that brief time she much endeared herself to Will's sisters, so much so, that at length her objections were overruled, and Eveline consented to pass one night in the Saxon's house.

The girl was wildly anxious relative to her father, whose only child she was, and the darling of his heart. And yet she clung to her new friends with a pertinacity which she could scarcely explain even to herself.

Eveline, though a true Norman, without mixture with the Saxons in any way, was too gentle, true, and pure a woman to feel any animosity against any class. Still she had her native born prejudices, which in the case of the subdued race, had been warmly fostered by her parents and attendants.

She was singularly surprised to find Saxon men and women, not such swine as they were represented.

She discovered in Will's sister not only beauty, but refinement and delicacy.

No doubt, however, much of her warmth of feeling was traceable to her gratitude. We shall see.

CHAPTER V.

IN THE FOREST.

THE birds were singing matins when Will and Eveline —the latter having bidden a courteous adieu to her new friends—mounted a pair of sturdy nags, and followed at a respectful distance by two serving men on foot, took their way through the forest on the return journey to the proud castle of the Norman lord.

Across that forest, at a hard gallop, with such bogs, and ruts, and hollows as were in those days called roads, it would have been a day's journey; but some how or other, neither Will nor Eveline was in a mortal hurry.

Besides, their steeds were heavy, sturdy cattle, more used to walking than to trotting; while the footmen behind had also to be considered.

What wonder, then, that the young couple rode side by side, in earnest conversation, or in mute thought, as the case happened.

Theirs was the very first scene of love's young dream.

They were in that hour of happy intoxication when to live is in itself lovely, and when thought of to-morrow, with its sorrows and vexations, there is none. To sun himself in the flooded radiance of her eye, to watch for her smiles, to touch her hand was delight enough for Will; while for her, all she asked was to know him there, and hear the trembling accents of his voice as he poured upon her his thoughts and memories.

And so the morning passed, and the midday repose, and the afternoon journey, until the evening shadows fell upon forest, glade, and stream.

" How grand is this mighty forest," said Eveline at last, " and how beautiful is yonder tangled wood, where none should dwell but the wild boar and wolf; while here is the place for man and woman too."

" Alas ! " said Will, " a battlemented castle will soon be your abode."

" Always open to you ? " cried Eveline. " Surely you think not my father hard and ungrateful—at all events to the man who saved his daughter's life ? "

" I know not. We are all Saxon churls to him ; and I did but do my duty."

Almost impatient at the incredulousness of the young man, Eveline, with a pretty shrug of the shoulders, whipped her horse, and disappearing in one of the glades of the forest, invited him to follow, which he did, until the shadow grew longer and longer, and it was almost impossible to make way under the trees.

" Where are we ? " suddenly asked Eveline, with a shudder.

Will Scarlett started as from a dream, and gazed wildly around.

" Where are we, indeed ! " he repeated. " Heaven forgive me for thinking of other things and neglecting my way."

" Are we lost ? "

" We are off the track," said Will, musingly ; " as I intended to rest at the house of a friend of mine—but lost a woodsman cannot be in Sherwood forest. Gregory ! —Gurth ! "

But no answer came from the serving men.

Eveline, by a kind of instinct, moved close up to Will, and looked him full in the face. The young man was eyeing the forest with a strangely perplexed look, for, despite his assumed confidence, he really was quite at a loss to fix his whereabouts.

" Tell me the worst," she said, in a somewhat husky tone.

" That this darkness is deceptive, and that I have lost my way, dear lady ; but fear nothing while this arm has power to strike, and this heart beats in its bosom—you are as safe as in your own father's house."

" I believe you, Will Scarlett," she said, tenderly.

" There is now but one course to pursue," he continued, " and that is to trust to the instinct of our horses."

" You are right," cried Eveline, cheerfully, and next minute the reins were loose.

The good steeds no sooner found that they were at liberty to choose their own direction, than they seemed to gain new strength, vigour, and spirit, and, whereas before they had scarcely noticed the spur, except to groan at its application, they now pricked up their ears, hesitated one moment, and then set off of their own accord in a direction different from that which they had been following.

It was now a dark night, and great care had to be taken to avoid being unhorsed by the overhanging boughs of the trees, for which purpose Will Scarlett went first.

Suddenly, just as the horses were about to take a fresh start, he drew in rein.

" What is it ? " asked Eveline, in a low, hushed tone.

" A fire. I will leave the horse here, and go forward. It may be friends, but it may be foes."

And Will dismounted ; but quick as he was, Eveline was on the ground beside him.

" You will guard the horses ? " he asked of her.

" No ! they must guard themselves," she whispered, firmly ; " you are my true knight, and leave me not 'till you give me to my father's own dear arms.

" As you will, Lady Eveline—wait till I fasten the horses so that the poor beasts may eat and yet not wander."

The girl stood still while Will Scarlett did as he said, and then clutching her hand convulsively in his, walked beside him.

Who can say how much in that hour of doubt, and fear, and dread, her heart became wholly his, never more to owe allegiance to mortal man.

The light which had startled them was about two hundred yards a-head, on the top of a kind of slope of copsewood, which grew very thickly under the tall trees. This made the progress of the pair slow and tedious, the light on one or two occasions, vanishing from view and only re-appearing at intervals.

At length its full intensity became fully developed.

It was a large camp fire, round which were collected some half-dozen ill-looking ruffians, who neither wore the distinctive garb of any noble, nor the Lincoln green of the bold outlaws of the forest."

" Who and what are they ? " asked Eveline in a whisper.

" I know not ; but we must even play the eavesdropper," said Will, advancing slowly along one of the darkest and densest parts of the copse.

The young girl, whose heart beat high with emotions, followed.

In this way they came within hearing distance of the men, who, however, at that moment were only carousing and laughing.

" 'S death ! " cried one, " Hubert is long a-coming. Why tarrieth he ? "

" There may be goodly plunder abroad," said one.

" By my troth, it will then be something new. Since this springal, beardless boy, the men call Robin, I have not seen one good haul. The fellow secures every good prize—and hangs all knaves who slit a wizen or cut a throat."

At this moment Will Scarlett and Eveline were startled by steps close at hand, and next minute two masked fellows led a man, in the costume of a noble, into the circle of light, round which the bandits were collected.

Eveline clutched Scarlett's hand with intense energy, and with difficulty restrained a shriek.

Then she felt her warm lips close to his ear.

" My uncle," she whispered.

Scarlett pressed her hand in return.

The men who stood round the one who appeared a prisoner, were coarse ruffians, who, assuming the disguise of the patriotic outlaws made famous by history, did discredit and dishonour to the name of those who, driven to despair by the oppression of the feudal nobility, and the severe exercise of the forest laws, banded together in large gangs, and kept possession of the forests and wastes, setting at defiance the justice and magistracy of the country.

The man who stood unbound, but a prisoner in their midst, was of different character and appearance.

Past forty, thin, tall, muscular, and possessed of great strength, his athletic figure seemed to have retained none of the softer part of the human form, the whole having been reduced to brawn, bones, and sinews, which had sustained a thousand toils, and were ready for a thousand more. On his head he wore a scarlet and fur cap. His countenance, which was clearly displayed, was both repulsive and awe-striking. His naturally strong and powerful features, with high cheek bones, were burnt to swarthy darkness, while the projection of the forehead veins, the readiness with which the upper lip and its thick black moustaches quivered, showed the passion that slumbered in his veins. His keen, dark, and restless eyes seemed to always challenge opposition to his will, while now they expressed haughty displeasure.

He wore a long scarlet monastic mantle, with a white cross of a peculiar form cut on the right shoulder, this upper robe but part concealing a shirt of linked mail, with sleeves and gloves of the same, curiously plaited and inter-woven, as flexible to the body as those which are now wrought in the stocking loom out of softer materials.

The fore part of his thighs were also covered with linked mail; the knees and feet were defended by splints or thin plates of steel, ingeniously jointed into one another, and mail hose, reaching from the ankle to the knee, effectually protected his legs.

In his girdle he wore a long and double-edged dagger, the only offensive weapon about his person.

Such a man must have been taken at a great disadvantage to have become the prisoner of two ruffians armed with quarterstaves and short swords.

"How now, my masters," he said, fiercely; "what means this outrage?"

"We are minions of the moon—and ransom such as thee," said one.

"Knaves, but that I had alighted to examine my horse's foot, I would have sent both your souls to perdition ere you had laid hands on a knight of the True Cross."

"Ha! ha! ha!" laughed the robbers, scornfully; "bold blade."

"By my halidame, and you be not more respectful," continued the knight, in a voice of thunder, "you shall hang, ere forty hours, each on his own oak. But harken—I have a treaty to make which may suit your plans."

The robbers checked their rude laugh, and became at once respectful.

"Here is my knightly chain—he who brings it with this seal to my brother's castle shall have a thousand marks—on my faith as a crusader," and he kissed the cross hilt of his dagger.

"Long live the White Cross Knight!" shouted the ruffians.

"Now stay your sweet voices and listen," he said, fiercely.

"We listen."

"Yesterday there rode forth from Beauclerk Castle, with her own attendants, the Lady Eveline, my dear beloved niece."

This was said with a strange intonation of voice, which almost made Will Scarlett start, while Eveline shuddered all over.

"She was mounted on a coal black steed, which, taking fright in some mysterious way, carried her miles beyond the ken of her attendants."

"I saw her," cried one, eagerly, "go down the Beau-champ glade like a weird horse and rider."

"And I up the Ridged rock with headlong speed."

"And I."

"And I."

"'Tis well. I happen to know she did so ride," continued the knight, impatiently, "and this morning I came forth to search for her. You have just stopped me in my course."

"I can give you news of her," said Hubert, the chief bandit, motioning the others to keep silence.

"Ah!" cried the knight, with gleaming eyes, "what news?"

"I found the horse last night stone dead."

"Ah! but the girl? Speak, man—speak! What of her?"

"Of her I know nothing. The horse was shot through the flank, and stone dead; but some one had carried off the girl."

"Damnation!" cried the mailed knight, "she has escaped!"

"Sir Norman Malvoisin," observed the robber chief, "but just now you said you were in search of her ——"

"Body!" said Malvoisin, in a hollow voice.

———

CHAPTER VI.

THE COMPACT.

THE robbers looked at one another with astonished and meaning glances. They were not surprised to find a Norman noble a ruffian and a villain, but they had yet to learn the cause which made him so earnestly desire the Lady Eveline's death.

Eveline herself utterly overcome, and scarcely able to keep from fainting, was supported by the manly arm of Will Scarlett, while her head lay on his shoulder.

"Fools! dullards!" he said, avoiding as much as possible the inquisitive glances of the banditti, "know you not that this girl is my niece, and that the fond fool her father will leave her everything. His influence with the Prince is great, and her husband will inherit the fief of Beauclerk, to which I, as a man, am entitled."

"But, Sir Knight, art thou not a priest?" said the robber.

"Tush, man—such vows as mine have been broken, and give me but the broad lands and castles of Beauclerk and I will be no more a monk in name than in fact. I did think," he said, dreamily, as if speaking to himself, "of marrying the girl, but the trouble of getting a dispensa-tion and her own obduracy, made me change my course—for know you, my masters, I once loved the girl, as much as I now hate her."

There was a dead silence, and but for the intense interest with which the robbers listened to Sir Norman Malvoisin, they must have heard a low murmur at no great distance.

It was Eveline, who, caught passionately to the arms of Will, seemed to protest against the unholy statement of the knight, by allowing, nay, returning, his first pas-sionate kiss of love.

"To business," suddenly continued the knight, "the girl has escaped, but she must *never* return to see the battlements of Beauclerk. You mark me, my men."

"We mark and understand," said Hubert, "but the reward?"

"Two thousand marks more, when she is six foot underground."

"'Tis done!" cried Hubert, "what say you, my men?"

"One moment," put in a man, who had not as yet spoken. "I fear me 'tis too late this bout."

"Why?" shouted Sir Norman, turning angrily to the speaker.

"Because she may be safe in Beauclerk Castle by this time, for what I know."

"Explain."

"I was alone near the Three Tree bog, when she passed me, attended by one gallant on horseback and two sturdy varlets behind. Their way was towards your brother's castle, though I doubt their having reached it yet."

"Then they are in the forest!" cried the knight, "and must be taken dead or alive!"

The crusader stood in the full light, with his fierce countenance as it were fixed on Will Scarlett, who uncon-sciously played with his bundle of arrows.

"He is my uncle," whispered Eveline; "come."

Will Gammel said no more, but taking her by the hand, commenced the arduous task of extricating her from the vicinity of the banditti.

This was a matter of no small difficulty and danger, as the very slightest noise, a cough or word more than ordina-rily audible, a stumble, would bring upon them this horde of ruffians, now from cruel and mecenary motives at the beck and call of this recreant Norman knight.

Eveline's fate in that case there could be no doubt about.

That Will Scarlett, lad as he was, would act up to the honourable fame of his family, superadded to his personal devotion, there could be no doubt also.

But what could one armed man do against a dozen?

Prodigies of valour, it is true; but with but one end.

The night was still, not an owl even could be heard in the brakes, not a bat flitted in the dark sheen of that evening, sound was carried with intense rapidity, and as Will and Eveline, moving like people blindfolded, with outstretched hands and cautious steps, they could still hear the robbers talking.

By degrees, however, this sound ceased, and the young

couple took heart of grace and moved more rapidly and less cautiously in the direction of the horses.

In the direction of the horses!

Then what means that sudden and startling neigh a hundred yards to the left?

They have come in the wrong direction, and are leaving the horses.

But that shout! It is the bandits who, startled by the sudden neighing of horses in their immediate vicinity, have given way to their surprise, and then all is still.

The ruffians have dispersed in search of a prize, the value of which they can guess but too well.

Will looked around. To his left was a wide expanse of gorse and furze, while to his right was a dense low thicket, the branches of which swept the ground.

"We must hide till they pass," quoth Will, manfully, "and if they discover us, do or die. I have twelve arrows."

Eveline made no reply. Her heart was far too full for words, so, obeying the indications of his finger, she crept into the thicket, nor halted until they were both seated on a green bank under a huge but stunted oak.

Then Will peered through the boughs to watch the progress of the bandits. The fellows had lit up torches which they held on high, thus affording an admirable mark for the arrows of Will, had he chosen to have used them.

Then another shout proclaimed a discovery, and they saw the horses led forth from their hiding-place by one of the men.

A brief conference ensued, after which the robbers seemed to disperse as if in obedience to orders. It was quite clear that they were about to make a thorough search of the neighbourhood.

At this moment the moon, hitherto concealed, burst from her curtained bed of clouds, and flooded forest, glade, and heather with her bright and glorious light.

Will said not a word, but taking the girl's hand, turned away from a hiding place which could not serve them long against the diligent search of these interested ruffians.

"This is no place for us," he whispered between his set teeth; "there must be miles between us and them ere dawn."

"How shall I ever thank you?" replied Eveline.

"Lady, my life, my heart, my soul is at your disposal. Will Gammel will save you this night, or die——"

"And Eveline believes it," she began.

"Oh! what have we here?—staad, ruffians!"

They had suddenly come face to face with two men, who raised their long staves to strike.

"Our young master!" said the two men, with one voice.

"Hush! silence! Already have the knaves heard something—they are silent, and listen. Dost know of any place, not only where we can obtain shelter, but make a stand against a dozen ruffians, till morning shows us what to do."

"The house of John Neale is but a bows length from here," replied the man in a whisper.

"Then lead the way, in Heaven's name," cried Will; "if he be at home we will make a good fight."

Not another word was spoken. The missing serving men, who had been themselves wandering doubtingly about the fire, knew now the urgency of the case.

They made better use of their legs than of their tongues.

The way they guided the fugitives was along a path almost impassible, in which every now and then they sank up to their knees in mud. But trifles were not to be thought of when life was at stake; so not even the fair and lovely Norman girl, used to her palfrey or her litter, murmured or objected.

Suddenly the ground grew dry just as they reached an open space.

The serving men pointed upwards.

They had reached an open plat of turf, on the extreme verge of which was a rock rising abruptly from the gently sloping plain, and offering its grey and weatherbeaten front to the fugitives. Its sides were in part mantled with ivy, while in other places oak and holly bushes, whose roots found nutriment in the cliffs of the crag, waved over the precipices below. At the foot of this rock, and leaning to all appearance against it, was a commodious but rude hut, chiefly built of the trunks of trees cut close handy in the forest, and protected from bad weather by mud and moss being thrust into the crevices.

Without a word, Will hurried up the ascent and knocked at the door.

CHAPTER VII.

LITTLE JOHN.

FOR some few seconds there was no reply, and then there came a rumbling sound, as of a voice rising from deep places, which, by degrees, became articulate, as if the owner was rousing from slumber.

"Who knocks? pass on if ye be tricksters, lest ye get a drubbing."

"We are no tricksters, John Neale," said Will quickly; "open, for here is youth, beauty, and innocence, in danger from ruffians."

"Sayest thou so? Wait half a minute."

Then followed an interval, during which, the owner of the gruff voice was doubtless trussing his points to appear with decorum before a lady.

He then opened the door, and standing on one side, bade them enter.

All complied, though Eveline almost shrieked as the man doffed his cap.

Well she might.

Six feet six in height, stout in proportion, yet excellently well made, the man in his black buckram doublet, over which he was hastily passing a cassock of green, appeared a very giant, with arms and legs which, while for shape they might have served for Antinous, for size were surely moulded with those of Hercules. His head, not quite so large as to be fully in proportion to his body, was round and bullet shaped; the face being coarse, but with an irresistable good-humouredness about it, which was quite pleasant to see.

With hair black and matted, with beard and moustaches crisp and uncombed, with a capacious mouth, that as he smiled a welcome disclosed a marvellous row of white teeth, he looked one whom a timid maiden would rather have feared than courted; but Eveline felt no fear of him.

Will Scarlett had introduced her to the giant. That was sufficient guarantee for his good faith and honesty.

"And now, lad," said the giant, scratching his head, and looking round his room—but which, save broadsword and buckler, long bow and cross-bow, bolts for the one and sheaves of arrows for the other, had no furniture but a bed of leaves, a coarse table, and two stools—"now that I have opened, what can I do for the sweet young lady?"

"Give her and us refreshment, and then let her rest in thy upper room, while we as men devise how to keep out the ruffians."

The giant, who was evidently a man of few words, opened a hutch, and took forth a huge pasty baked in a pewter platter of unusual dimensions, flanking this with a huge leathern bottle of strong ale, beside of which he placed a smaller one of wine for Eveline.

It was no time or place for ceremony. All were hungry and weary, Eveline particularly, from excessive fatigue, feeling the want of sustenance.

"Eat and drink, lady," said Will Scarlett, with all the respect of an inferior to one of high rank, "for we shall want all the strength which God has vouchsafed unto us."

Eveline broke off a piece of crust, and filling a horn drinking cup, commenced her rude meal, after which, acknowledging herself sorely fatigued, she slipped upstairs and lay down, after Will Scarlett had seen that the window was small and narrow, and not likely to admit any intruder.

Will then descended, and in as brief a manner possible told his night adventures.

"The Lady Eveline," cried the tall forester, doffing his bonnet mechanically, "how came you with her, Will Gammel?"

Will briefly related the story of the accident to her horse.

"Heaven reward you, boy—you did a good deed," cried the burly yeoman; "and now who is this enemy that hunts her up?"

"Her uncle, Sir Norman Malvoisin, who would slay her that he may inherit his brother's fortune."

"The foul fiend seize him by the throat," cried the giant, tearing a badge off his cap; "that I should be a keeper of his—but keeper no more am I!!"

"Hark! hush!" said Will, hastily extinguishing the torch, and peering through a loophole, the outside of which did but just give passage to a bolt or arrow; "here they come."

EVELINE SAVES THE LIFE OF WILL SCARLETT.

All peered through chink and hole, and there truly could be seen a body of men advancing, carefully masked, as could be clearly distinguished.

They were examining the path by which the fugitives had come.

"Well, what say you," asked Will, sternly; "this is your house, John Neale, are we to give up this girl without a struggle?"

"Never!" said the giant, rising to his full height, and looking sublime in his enthusiasm. "I was keeper to the Deputy Ranger, and my name was John Neale; but here ends John Neale and home, if they drive me from house and home. I am also nameless, and yet men shall know me by thy pet name, Will Gammel."

"And that was"——

"Knowest thou not in our boyish days what you did call me, when I would lift you in my arms, and setting you astraddle on a tree branch, only let you down on hard entreaty?"

"LITTLE JOHN?" cried Gammel.

"Yes; and now let these knaves parley. We can then judge what to do."

"What ho! within there," cried the gruff voice of the chief of the bandits; "open, and quickly too, lest we burn the old hut."

"Go thy ways, thou drunken brawler," cried Little John, sternly.

"That voice should be that John, the deer keeper," re-plied one. "Open, in the fiend's name, we have questions to ask."

"Then ask them outside. No nameless ruffians enter my house at night, to eat my crust and drink my beer."

"Our questions are briefly asked and had best be well answered."

"Keep a civil tongue in your head, Sir night-walker, else you get more blows than you wot of now."

"The noble Lord Sir Beauclerk's daughter Eveline has been captured by three knaves, who are taking her to some hidden retreat there to ransom her. We have traced her here, and call upon you to yield her up to those who have a right and will conduct her to her father."

"The Lady Eveline, by her own wish and consent, has taken refuge, with her escort, in my poor house, where she is as safe as in her own father's home. Therefore go thy ways. I will not open my door."

A terrific rush took place at the door, which seemed for a moment to yield to their efforts.

The four men prepared, two their cross-bows, two the long, six-foot weapon, which then was the glory and delight of English hearts—the mainstay of British glory,—THE LONG BOW.

"Away, ruffians—away; the man who strikes, dies!"

"Batter his dog-kennel down," shouted a commanding voice, but scarcely were the words uttered, when twang went the bows and a loud wail or yell told the fatal character of the aim.

Two fell stark dead on the sward before the door, while two others with difficulty followed their flying companions. On discovering the strength of the garrison all had fled to cover.

"Ah! ha!" said the giant, who never before had fired a shot in anger, and whose life—he was two and twenty—had been passed in the, to him, congenial pursuits of the chase.

Dearly he loved the green glades of Sherwood, preferring often a lodging on the broad fern or damp grass to any under a roof or tree; dearly he loved the wild paths choked with tall rye grass, brambles and thick underwood; dearly loved he the brawling brook, that went meandering under massy and gnarled branches, until lost in the gloominess of the forest—and dearly too the tinkling of far-off sheep-bells, the music of the swineherd's horn, the bellowing of stags in the adjacent thicket, and the merry laugh of the woodpecker. But dearer still he loved his own home, to which it was already the height of his ambition to bring the smiling face of a woman to be its mistress and chief.

But now his hand has been raised against men, who, outlaws and ruffians as they were, still were under the command of one it should have been his duty and pleasure to obey.

He must even become a wanderer and an outlaw, for the nobles never forgave.

Such thoughts flashed through the young man's mind with the rapidity of lightning, as he saw the two dead bodies through the chinks.

But there was no time for reflection now—reflection was for leisure hours.

This was the moment for action.

"The knaves have left us, good Little John," said Will Scarlett in a whisper, "but to return. They are now at least ten. Fight we must—but though we may manfully overthrow and destroy half of them, in the end they must conquer."

"To what art coming, friend Gammel?"

"Would it not be wise to despatch Gurth and Geoffry to Beauclerk and advise the Earl?"

"'Twere well if we could—but how could they pass across this glade unseen? They would be stuck full of arrows ere they could reach a covert."

"Hist!" said Will, whose eye had never been off the spot where the robbers had disappeared. "The villains are preparing for a desperate rush."

Little John quietly threw open his door, and without allowing a glimpse of his tall body to be seen, surveyed the position of the enemy.

The moon illumined the whole of the forest glade, and open heath, while all around, the thick trees cast a circle of darkness in which the attackers were moving.

The gloom was deepest just under the rock where the shadows fell thick and heavy, and towards this part it was clear that the attackers were bound, hoping to get up to the hut unperceived.

They were all armed with cross-bows and heavy swords, and if allowed to approach the house would, now their panic was over, have quite as much advantage in the attack as the others had in the defence, as their wooden log-huts afforded no adequate protection.

There was close to the hut a projecting rock, where a small oak protruded from the high rock.

Brushing past the giant, Will Scarlett took up his post there, twelve cloth-yard arrows ready in his belt.

Though the young hero of Gammel had not yet attained to the perfection in archery which was to hand his name to the latest posterity in connection with Robin Hood and Little John, yet was he already expert in the extreme.

Under the guidance of his father he made his own arrows, which were admirably poised, and, in good hands, as sure and deadly a weapon as the rifle of the present day. Then peering low along the ground to where he knew the robbers were advancing, he deliberately waited until he could see the foremost man brushing slowly and cautiously against the cliff.

An arrow in an instant was fixed, and next instant sped on its way. A shrill cry proclaimed the correctness of the aim, and then, having no further motive for secrecy, the enemy let fly a volley of bolts, and rushed headlong forward.

They were nine, but only eight came up, and of these two were wounded.

But one of them was a knight, armed at all points, and wielding a huge battle-axe.

Will Scarlett and the two serving-men, after discharging their second volley, cast aside their bows, and seizing huge clubs, began to wield them with an energy which showed great practice in their use, while so devoted were they to the cause which they upheld, that no thought of their having to encounter each at least two men crossed their minds.

The robbers, men fighting only for the hope of pay, common ruffians, who thought only of plunder and debauchery, though willing enough to risk blows, were chary of their lives, and hence acted more on the defensive than those they assailed.

The object of the robbers being to force an entrance into the hut, all had made for the door; while, as the others were deeply interested in preventing the accomplishment of their purpose, they also stood round the entrance.

Why not, it will be asked, have remained inside?

In the first place, caged up in a small hut they could only use their shafts against an enemy advancing in front, while some of the attacking party might be employed in pulling down the simple fabric over their ears; secondly, they were genuine Englishmen, neither content nor willing to fight behind cover while they had an open glade upon which to stand and do or die!

Will, who laboured under the disadvantage of not being tall, though agile and sinewy from constant exercise and exposure to the breezy air, found three men upon him at once, armed with swords, while he used no weapon but his huge staff, which, however, he twirled about with such rapidity as to leave for some time no opening for the aim of the three ruffians. His aim was ever at their heads, and had not the bull-necked churls have been inured to heavy blows, the thwacks they received must have soon disabled them; but their skulls were thick, their heads were encased in leathern and steel caps, and the only sensation at first produced by the storm of blows was a ringing noise in the head that somewhat affected their coolness.

Now in all hand-to-hand fighting coolness and collectedness wins the day. The man who allows his enthusiasm or his passion to get the better of him is lost, for with the mental blindness produced both by excitement and rage comes both physical blindness and incapacity.

Will, keeping the one object he had in view—that of defending the hut which contained the lady of his heart—never swerved a foot from the position he had taken up, but making his staff describe circles in the air—*faire le moulinet* the French call it—now dealt a fearful blow with his right hand, then passing it to his left, sent another ringing volley of blows about their astounded pates.

This lasted for some minutes, during which the robbers lost their tempers, and, with a fearful array of curses, attempted to close with Will.

He saw their design, and never flinching, clutched the huge staff in the middle, raining upon them such a hail-storm as made them frantic.

"Die, dog!" shouted the foremost man, stooping and attempting a thrust at his heart.

One step back went Will, and shifting his staff so as to clutch the end, down it came like some mighty sledge-hammer, and ignoring such guard as the man's sword could make, struck him senseless to the earth.

But when Will turned to face the two other ruffians, he found that though the sword had not saved its owner, it had cut the quarterstaff, already cracked, right in two.

A loud ringing laugh proclaimed the delight of the two robbers, who, once more waving their swords, rushed quickly in.

"Come on," cried Will, throwing the broken staff with prodigious force into the first robber's face, "come on, a dozen such paltry knaves—have at you."

The foremost man, as if blinded by the unexpected blow, stumbled; while ere the other could effect his deadly purpose, Will was before him with his own sword waving in the moonlight, and ready for a fresh hand-to-hand encounter with the stout fellow now opposed to him.

Such was the perilous nature of the time of which we speak, that no man—nay, not even a town-bred merchant—could place any dependance on passing unscathed through life, unless able to defend himself against all comers.

This necessitated a universal training in the use of arms,

and, as we well know, even the citizens of London brought forth famous archers and soldiers.

One natural consequence of this was the extreme length of personal encounters. Where defence was reduced to a science, it became extremely difficult for one man to strike another in any vital place.

Hence we hear of hand-to-hand battles, such as that of Chevy Chace, beginning at break of day, and lasting "even when the evening bell rung;" hence we read that

"They fought until they both did sweat,
With swords of tempered steel,
Until the blood, like drops of rain,
They trickling down did feel."

So might it have been with Will Scarlett and the ruffian Hubert, for though the young man was animated by the highest and most chivalrous feelings, fighting with deliberation and coolness, yet the robber, though raging like a wolf at bay, was stouter built, stronger, and being a discharged soldier, well versed in the use of his weapons.

For some minutes there could be no perceptible difference seen, as both were trying in vain to throw the other off his guard in order to deal a fatal blow.

But neither was to be taken in by feints, and no one can say how long the contest might have lasted, had not a most unexpected incident have altered the complexion of affairs.

"Look out, Will Gammel, look out," said the earnest voice of Eveline, from the window above; "to thy left— to thy left!"

Quick as thought Will leaped to the right, just as the half-stunned and wounded robber let fly a shaft that, but for the noble maiden of the house of Beauclerk, would have been quivering in his side.

"Cowardly wretch!" he said, himself losing something of his coolness and temper.

With these words, utterly forgetful of his adversary, he rushed at the half-recumbent ruffian to cut him down, when Hubert, taking advantage of his one moment of unguardedness, lifted up his sword and rushed madly on to settle the conflict in one blow.

But a twang was heard, and a bolt from a cross-bow piercing his neck, with a yell he fell backwards, severely wounded.

It was shot by Eveline.

CHAPTER VIII.

SIR NORMAN MALVOISIN.

IT will be as well, before we narrate the issue of this fearful combat, to explain how Eveline Beauclerk came to the rescue of her faithful squire in this sudden and opportune manner.

Like all Norman girls of high degree, the Lady Eveline was not only an expert horsewoman, an adept in the noble art of venerie and hawking, but a good bowwoman.

Since her childhood it had been the delight of the grim baron her father to see her practise at a mark, and she had done so with such elegant bows and crossbows as the best and most skilled workmen in Chepe could make, until her aim was as true as that of many a bold forester of the woods.

And yet, despite the somewhat ruthless manner of the period, which reacted even upon the gentlest and softest of women, Eveline had never used her dexterity to the injury of even the savagest of birds.

When, however, the combat roused her from a deep and composed slumber, in which rosy dreams of love rather than of strife visited her mind's eye, she cast hasty glances around in search of some means of aiding her devoted follower.

It was a momentary impulse, that was as evanescent as the smile that had rested on her lips a minute before.

She would aid them as a maiden best should—with earnest prayer.

Casting herself upon her knees near the low narrow window, with her eyes fixed upon the combatants, she poured forth her whole soul in supplications to the Holy Virgin and all the saints of Heaven to guard and protect those who had engaged in mortal strife to defend her against her foes.

But in the very secret recesses of her soul, from a divine instinct which lurks in noble natures even when imbued with superstition, her prayer was to God himself, for that one being who, in the short space of two days, had become, as it were, a part of her existence.

Already she noticed the peril of Will Scarlett when he cut down the first ruffian, and with a shriek rose.

In the corner of the room was a crossbow. When Little John was a boy it had been his.

Eveline felt she could scarcely lift it, and yet such was her excitement, that when she essayed she was able to drag it to the window and fit a bolt.

Then came the attempted side shot at young Gammel. When she saw this, Eveline with a wild cry not only warned him, but with the utmost rapidity of action turned the wheel that served as a lever to pull the string and armed the crossbow.

Just in time, for Hubert has his hand lifted to slay —and if Eveline owes her life to Will, so does Will now to Eveline Beauclerk.

One eloquent glance upwards was all that the young hero had to bestow on Eveline, for now his eager eyes have taken in the state of the *mêlée*.

Gurth is on the ground, apparently dead, with the body of a robber lying across him. Gregory is sorely pressed by two ruffians, against whom, bleeding and weak, he is defending himself by means of sheer obstinacy combined with some skill.

He cast one imploring look at his young master. It was a mute but eloquent call, and quickly obeyed. With a bound and a shout—some Saxon war-cry or other, forgotten in these more polished days—he struck down the foremost man: the second fled.

All that has taken so many lines to describe has not taken above ten or fifteen minutes in action. But terrible as had been the fray already recorded, it was as nothing to the huge combat still going on at some distance between Sir Norman Malvoisin and Little John.

We have said that the tall forester was nearly seven feet high, and stout in proportion; but we may add that though he could fell an ox with his fist, and throw a bar twice the length of any other man, no maiden of sixteen had ever a tenderer or more sympathising heart.

His was one of the brightest characters mentioned in ancient story.

Utterly without guile, honest, straightforward, and manly, he was simplicity itself, and would not willingly have put out his giant strength to hurt the meanest thing that ever lived.

His heart was already heavy at having been accessory to the death of two men, however richly they had deserved it.

This accounted for the extraordinary tactics he adopted in his encounter with the mailed Norman knight, whose visor was now down, and who rushed at Little John with his battle-axe in hand, his dagger at his side.

For any one less certain of his strength than the forester, it would have been madness to have faced a mailed knight.

But Little John knew himself, and as the Norman came rushing at him, he lifted his quarterstaff to his belt, and using it as a lance in a tournament, the astounded military monk was, as it were, unhorsed by its striking his breast, and he sent reeling back many yards upon the sward.

There was something so irresistibly ludicrous in the way the knight pirouetted on his heel, that a grim smile illumined the round face of the forester—a smile that would have cost a less stalwart man his life.

To be thus bearded by a knave in Lincoln green—he, a belted knight, with all the newest appliances of art, both offensive and defensive—was maddening.

"Hulking slave!" he cried, rushing forward, and aiming a second furious blow at the giant, "dost think thou art in a bear-garden, and I Sir Bruin?"

"I wish, base and recreant knight," said Little John, once more tilting at him with his wooden spear, "thou wert anything half so honest."

The knight, who, despite his fury at the huge power of his enemy, felt that passion was simply misplaced, drew back this time of his own accord, and clutching his ponderous weapon with both hands, hurled at the forester's head such a blow as might safely have cut down an ordinary tree; but Little John, with as much coolness as if he had been engaged in a friendly bout, thrust his staff between the knight's knees, stepped aside with a jerk, and sending the mailed knight forward on his face, followed up his advantage by a shower of blows upon a part of the person not generally presented to the enemy in chivalrous encounters.

At length, bathed in perspiration, and actually weary from so much unusual exercise, the huge forester paused for breath.

The knight slowly rose, first on his hands and knees, and then wholly upright.

He stood leaning on his axe apparently suffocated with rage.

"By the holy rood!" he shouted, in a voice unearthly from rage, in accents choked with passion, "'twould be a mercy to kill thee outright? For for what thou hast done this night—hadst thou the fairest wife and most lovely children earth ever gave to man—thou shouldst die, and they too."

"But I have no wife, I have no child," replied Little John, "and now I have no home."

"The crows shall be thy sepulchre," cried Sir Norman Malvoisin, preparing to renew the combat.

"Beware, Sir Norman," said Little John, sternly, "for the foul wrong thou wouldst do. I should have slayed thee ere now, but that I have eaten thy brother's bread. But beware, least my patience be too long tried."

"What wrong, base churl and ravisher?" asked the knight, somewhat astonished at the words, and utterly heedless of the fray going on around.

"Dost think the very leaves upon the trees have not whispered over the whole forest, why you seek to capture your niece?"

"Why, base slave?"

"*That thou mayest murder her and take her inheritance,*" said Little John, in a tone of deep disgust.

"Thou liest in thy throat, base ruffian," cried the knight, making a hasty sweep of his huge axe in the air, in the hope of taking the giant by surprise, but, as before, in vain.

Had the tall forester desired to kill the Norman lord, he could easily have done so. His strength was so vastly superior to the man of five feet seven, that one or two heavy blows upon his sconce would have laid him low. But Little John was still a retainer of the house, and his coarse, good-humoured common sense seemed to indicate to him that forbearance was the right policy under the circumstances. He therefore merely raised his huge staff, and striking the knight upon the arm, made his armour rattle.

"The foul fiend, take thee, traitor and knave! Thou hast broken my arm," yelled Sir Norman. "But thou shall not live to boast of thy ruffian power."

And with an agility surprising in one so heavily clad, he sprang, dagger in hand, his left, at the forester.

But Little John caught him as he advanced by the throat, lifted him—with his armour, a huge weight—from the ground, and next minute hurled him, a heavy insensible mass, to a distance on the sward.

The battle was over—not an adversary remained!

"A victory!" quoth Little John, drily, as he wrung his matted hair with his fist, "that will cost us dear. The greenwood tree and the grassy glade is henceforth our only retreat."

"I know not," whispered Will Scarlett, as he dragged his follower, as it proved, only wounded, from beneath the dead robber; "the Earl of Beauchamp will own that we have done right, and see us harmless."

"You know not this Norman horde," said Little John thoughtfully; "they will stand by one another."

"But when his brother would slay his own daughter will the Earl fail us?" continued Will Scarlett, indignantly.

"You know not the world so well as I do," said the philosopher of two-and-twenty. "The Earl will take his precautions from what you have heard; but he may pretend to disbelieve you, and hang you, least you spread abroad the rumour."

"Tut, man! I will adventure all and deliver the daughter safe into her father's hands."

"Then let us indoors and rest awhile, for morning is not far distant, and this bout has recruited my appetite. What shall we do with these dead knaves?"

"Let them rot where they lie, as better men have done," cried Gurth, with a hearty execration.

"No, they be rogues all," said Little John, "but they shall have burial; an' no one else will help me, I will dig a grave myself."

"And I will aid thee," cried Will Scarlett, heartily.

"Too late," roared Gregory. "To cover!"

And setting the example, he rushed within the hut, followed by his companions, who closed the door just as a party of horsemen—soldiers armed at all points—dashed across the green right up to the hut, with a loud and appalling cry.

"Malvoisin! Malvoisin!"

"There has been foul treason here!" shouted one who seemed a kind of chief; "open there, within."

"Go your ways," said a hoarse, stern voice, "and take with you the body of a base and recreant knight, who but lately commanded a herd of ruffians and outlaws."

Several soldiers dismounted, having discovered the body of the knight, whose vizor was hastily removed and his visage exposed to the air.

With a huge sigh he seemed to return to consciousness, and in a few minutes, such was the iron endurance and power of the man, he was able to arise. As he did so, he glared around for some one on whom to wreak the first raw-edge of his dire revenge.

He saw, however, but a band of trusty followers, who crowded around him, with every mark of respect, deference, and sympathy.

"Who has done this foul and murderous deed, my lord?" asked the lieutenant, whose name was Robert Rosne.

"One, who—by the holy rood—shall never brag of it!" said Sir Norman, whose face was ghastly and livid. "Drag them forth, that I may scourge the whole gang to death."

The men all dismounted, and giving their horses to one to hold, rushed towards the hut, to be met by a shower of cloth-yard shafts, which, however, glanced harmlessly off their mail.

In a minute more they were thundering at the heavy oaken door, but without meeting with any response.

The follower who held the horses was squire to Robert Rosne, and not liking his vicinity to men who drew the long bow so manfully against soldiers in steel armour, was moving off to a safe distance, when a barbed arrow pierced the arm with which he held the horses, and nailed it to the quivering head of his own steed.

With an awful cry the animal fell dead, and dragged his wounded master down, the other horses rearing, neighing, plunging, and finally dashing away in every direction.

Sir Norman, who had been forced to seat himself in order to recover his strength and energy, saw all that passed with an amount of ferocious passion that was again nearly choking him.

He could not forget the ignominious flogging he had received at the hands of Little John.

"Burn the place down about their ears!" he cried, furiously. "Collect brands and brushwood. Let the knaves roast!"

Not a man hesitated to obey the ferocious behests of the knight, all rushing eagerly to collect fuel, which was to be found in abundance on the edge of the forest, one of the most ancient in England.

In a few minutes every separate member of the party returned, bearing huge bundles of dry underwood, brambles, dead branches, leaves, any thing that they thought would burn, the whole of which was piled up against the doorway.

"I give thee, Saxon churl and knave," said Sir Norman, advancing, and speaking in a loud tone, "two minutes to surrender."

"And thou would'st do this foul and wicked murder?" cried Little John from within.

"No parley, knave—I hold no words with such an arrant wretch. Come forth."

"Come and take me," said Little John, throwing the door wide open.

But all was dark inside, and none knew what they had to adventure against.

Not one of the soldiers but hesitated, and looked hardly at the yawning doorway, across which the moon shone.

"Drag him forth! Ten marks to the first man who brings out the ruffian."

Four of the soldiers rushed headlong at the doorway, but only two entered, the first being saluted in a manner that sent them headlong backwards.

Even men in armour are vulnerable somewhere, particularly about the neck; and these two received their death wounds ere they were able to see their assailants.

Then was heard inside a fearful tustle—a silent, awful struggle. Not a word was spoken; all that could be distinguished was a sound of heavy blows, of bodies hurled about; of groans of mortal anguish; with now and then a muttered oath.

It continued two minutes.

"Give light," said Sir Norman, taking a torch from one of the soldiers, who had just succeed in lighting it.

As he spoke he cast it at the pile of brushwood.

Up rose the flames with a roaring sound, followed by the crackling of reeds and brambles, and then by a huge belt of lurid flame.

Bent double, bleeding, scarcely able to crawl, the two soldiers came forth, and rushing through the flames, fell upon the green sward insensible.

With his fists the huge forester had so pummelled the men-at-arms, after repeated throws, that they went forth like whipped children.

"Come thyself, dishonourable knight," roared Little John, now fairly roused, "that I may pummel thy face, as I have flayed thy back,—so that thou shalt not sit except on silken cushions for a month."

In the vehemence of his passion, Sir Norman would have rushed madly at the forester, but his attendants restrained him.

The hut was in flames, the dry wood and moss had caught; and there, in the midst of the burning furnace, stood the broad, burly, erect form of the forester, leaning on his quarterstaff.

"Shoot him down with your bolts," yelled the military monk.

"Ha! ha! ha!" laughed the ex-ranger.

And he vanished from their sight, nor, though in five minutes the whole building was in flames, did a sound emanate from the interior of the doomed hut.

Sir Norman Malvoisin, as if determined to make sure of his niece's death, bade the surviving soldiers strip and bury their dead comrades.

A pit was dug by means of their swords, and then the soldiers retreated, after, at their lord's bidding, casting the dead outlaws into the flames, and stood gazing with awe at the funereal pile from a distance; nor did they proceed on their way until nought remained but a huge pile of smouldering beams and rafters, from which rose a thick, horrid smoke,

The dead bodies were being consumed.

The happy home of Little John was but a pile of ashes.

CHAPTER VIII.

EARL DE BEAUCLERK.

BEAUCLERK CASTLE, once the seat of a Saxon chief, and then called Hurlstone, was a complete fortress, with the central donjon or high square tower, such as may be seen in the ancient towers of London, with buildings of lesser height all around, which were encircled by an inner court-yard. Around the outer wall was a deep moat, well supplied with water. There were several towers on the outward wall, so as to flank it at every angle.

There was no visible access to the castle except through an arched barbican or outlet, which was terminated and defended by a small turret at each corner.

Above the lofty turrets glittered, at moments, the helm of sentinel or warder, for in those perilous days it necessary to keep a constant look-out.

In his baronial hall the earl walked up and down.

Its walls were covered with coarse crimson tapestry, while a huge iron lamp hung from the middle of the ceiling.

The baron, who strode angrily and fiercely from side to side, wore a cloak with ample sleeves trimmed with fur.

He had just risen from his bed and was chafing and fuming at the delay which took place in the discovery of Eveline. All the previous day men had been despatched to scour the forest in every direction, while Sir Norman Malvoisin himself headed a party of searchers.

But no tidings could be had of the lost young lady.

The earl was passionately attached to his daughter. This love for one so amiable and beautiful was the one green oasis in the desert of his character.

Grasping, avaricious, ambitious, a vassal who aimed at something more than kingly favour, the Earl of Beauclerk, Ranger of Sherwood Forest, had never spared man, woman, or girl who stood in the way of his desires or his hopes.

But he was a very child in the hand of Eveline.

There were fearfully dark rumours afloat with regard to the earl's wife. She had been a lovely, timid, gentle, innocent girl, who never could have regarded the rude Norman with any but feelings of dread and fear.

Their married life had been full of clouds.

Not even the humility shown by his wife could tame the tiger-like ferocity of this Norman lord.

Instinctively he felt that he was feared, not loved.

When he brought strange women, with braided hair, and foreign ornaments upon them, into his castle, the wife made no sign. Apathy and indifference fell upon her soul.

She had loved another, and being taken by actual violence as the bride of the shaggy-browed noble, had submitted to her fate like a martyr.

Then Eveline was born, and the girl subsided wholly into the mother.

One night there was a fearful uproar in the apartments specially affected to the residence of Eva of Beauclerk and her female attendants.

What occurred was never known; but next day a grave was hastily dug in the chapel, a coffin hurried into the hole, and then——*The countess was seen no more.*

Had the earl killed her in one of his moments of frenzied passion?

None dared say—but it was darkly hinted that the body buried was that of a man.

What, then, had become of the countess?

Even her apartments were closed, and a padlock put on the door, so that they were falling into ruin and decay.

Eveline was sent away to a nunnery to die or live, as it pleased Providence, while the earl drowned all remembrance of the past in revelry.

Strange women now peopled the castle, and the whole country rang with the story of the wicked earl who had murdered his wife, and placed harlots in her place.

But they only said these things in whispers, and then took care to keep their pretty daughters from being seen by himself or any of his lawless attendants.

Every year the earl mounted horse, and paid a formal visit to his child.

While she remained a child, his affection was of a very negative character.

But when at fifteen she budded into delicate womanhood, the scales fell from his eyes.

He took her home, invested her with the key of authority, and dismissed the strange women.

At all events they never came in sight of Eveline.

Three years had consolidated the earl's affection for his child, until it almost equalled his ambition and love of luxury.

He would have done anything to make her happy—in his own way.

He had been in a state of bitter anxiety about her ever since her disappearance in the forest; but knowing her to be a most accomplished horsewoman, he had less fear of the result than otherwise might have been the case.

The worst he feared was that she was prisoner of the outlaws, who would require a princely ransom.

But when he found that no tidings came at all, he began to fume and work himself into a terrible passion.

He was now a man of fifty, with short grey hair, a stout moustache, deep-set grey eyes, that rolled about in search of some one upon whom to let fall the hurried tempest of his passions.

An unexpected apparition delayed his call.

Gliding into the room with the mincing step of a Frenchwoman came a young woman of mature beauty, but exquisite charms. Her costume was foreign, and even Oriental—a freak of the earl's, who despised everything English, while the radiant brilliance of her eyes, the magnificent arch of her eyebrows, the admirably moulded aquiline nose, the bright row of white teeth, the richness and abundance of her purple black hair, which was the only covering at the moment for a neck and bosom of extreme loveliness, indicated that she herself was no native of this island, whose beauty is peculiar and great, but not voluptuous as that of more sunny climes.

She wore a kind of silken turban, with a tight-fitting jacket unbuttoned in front, and loose trousers to the ankles.

"What want you, Zorah?" said the noble, with a frown; "I wish to be alone."

"Methought my lord was ill, that he should rise so early—he is not wont to do so."

"Tut! I am a little feverish. This delay in finding my daughter frets me. Go to; you have done ill to leave thy couch—return to it."

"I cannot sleep, but would rather cool my brow upon the ramparts, an' you will accompany me," replied the young woman, with a witching smile.

Now the earl, despite his anxiety, was not a man to say nay for any length of time to a pretty woman who still retained any hold over him. When his daughter took her mother's place in his household, he had dismissed the "strange women," and put a stop to much riotous conduct—but there was always one favourite.

Eveline never suspected the presence of any woman in the castle, save her own handmaidens and the wives and daughters of retainers.

The loquacity of her attendants was checked by a very simple order of the baron. The man or woman who should betray his secret would simply have his or her tongue cut out by the roots.

So Zorah dwelt in the castle, known and recognised by all the household, but never daring to cross the path of the young heiress of the house of Beauclerk.

It will readily be believed that the recognised concubine of the earl looked with no pleasant eye upon the gentle maiden, whose presence alone seemed to prevent her being considered sole mistress.

Without knowing it, Eveline had a secret and bitter enemy.

It was, therefore, with very considerable satisfaction that Zorah heard of the strange and unaccountable absence of Eveline.

Judging the noble and virtuous maiden by her own standard, her first idea was that she had eloped with a lover; but on reflection, she came to the conclusion that some fatal accident had occurred.

To her it was a matter of total indifference which way it was. Whatever removed Eveline from the society of her father would consolidate her impure and immoral influence over the earl.

It was, therefore, with unqualified satisfaction that Zorah found a second morning elapse without any sign being given of the missing maiden.

They soon reached the battlements which commanded a splendid and extensive view across pasture land and meadow, forest and thicket.

At no great distance flowed the river which supplied the moat.

Under the walls of the castle, at about two bow shots' distance, was a ford.

As the two reached the ramparts and gazed below, a cavalcade came in view.

The earl shook with emotion, and clutched the girl's arm.

"Say—speak, wench, for my eyes grow dim, though not with age—who comes—is there a girl's kirtle amongst them?"

"No," said Zorah, after a keen examination of the party, "they are but men-at-arms, though thy brother Norman rides amongst them."

"Ah!" cried the earl, with a deep sigh, "then there is some bad news. These men come as if ashamed or sorry. A cowl will yet cover my grey head, for I have lost my child."

From one so rude, so hard, so cruel, these words, spoken with heartfelt anguish, came with additional force. The agony of a strong man is always a most terrible and painful sight.

Zorah eyed him with a look of scorn. Like all her class, she hated the man to whom she was bound by fear as much as for the wealth he had lavished on her.

"Ill news, my lord, always travels apace," she began, with her false smile.

"Tut! tut! girl—say you no homilies to me. Follow if thou wilt—I go to meet my brother."

And with a quicker step than was usual in one who prided himself upon his stately presence, the Earl de Beauclerk hurried to his reception-hall just as a horn sounded for the warder to open the barbican.

CHAPTER X.

SURPRISES.

EARL BEAUCLERK stood under his dais, bareheaded, and leaning on his two-handed sword.

He would, despite all he suffered, receive his brother like a noble.

Next minute the heavy step of the White Cross Knight was heard, his spurs ringing on the stone flags of the passage.

Then he swept into the hall, followed by his serving-men.

Zorah had followed, but had concealed herself behind the crimson hangings.

"I give you welcome," cried the earl, hastily; "what news?"

"None, my dear lord," said Sir Norman, with a hypocritical whine; "we have hunted hill and dale, we have scoured thicket and glade, we have hurried hither and thither until our bones ache, and have found nothing save the dead body——"

"Great God! of what?"

"Of the horse she rode."

"But if the horse has been found, where is the rider? Take five score of lances, and scour the forest; a thousand marks who brings her home dead—two thousand if they find her alive."

"If Eveline, my dear niece, be yet alive, it is with the outlaws of Sherwood forest."

"Then, by the holy rood, she is safe," cried the earl, striking his clenched fist upon the oaken chair; "there lives not a Saxon churl so base as to harm one who never hurt a living soul, and who many a time has begged off the knaves. Thou knowest, Norman, how sweetly she has intervened between us when we should have quarrelled in our cups."

"I know—I know," faltered Sir Norman, raising his hand to dash the huge drops of unbidden sweat from his brow. "Ha! what sound is that?"

It was a loud, joyous, merry series of notes from a horn outside, a challenge that made the earl, who had sank on his throne-seat, start up, and which made the knight shiver from head to foot as with the ague.

Next minute a servant-man burst in without any ceremony.

"My lady—my lady—safe under the escort of four yeomen," he said.

"Free quarters at sack and buttery for thy life!" cried the earl in a ringing tone, that sounded strangely different from his previous voice; "show them in—all."

Sir Norman Malvoisin moved to a window that overlooked the great court-yard, partly to convince himself by ocular proof of the astounding fact announced by the serving man, partly to hide the deadly pallor which overcame him, the lurid light in his wicked eyes, and the livid and rigid appearance of his lips.

He had come to the castle firmly convinced that Eveline and her brave escort had perished in the conflagration of the forester's hut, and that no witness he could not buy or crush would ever rise in judgment against him.

That he had been recognised by Eveline and her companions he felt not the slightest doubt.

What then was to be done? There was not an instant for reflection.

He must abide and brazen it out before them all.

At this moment he saw not only Eveline, but Will Scarlett and two yeomen crossing the yard.

It was no optical delusion, but them in the blood and flesh.

There was no choice for the dishonoured knight but to stand his ground and brazen out the accusation.

While with darkly bent brow and angry mien he resolved what to say, Eveline entered, and rushing across the hall, threw her white and glowing arms round her father's neck.

"I mourned thee dead, my darling," he said, forgetting all form.

"That I still live is owing to this brave youth," cried Eveline, turning towards Will Scarlett, who, with two followers entered the room as she spoke.

Little John, with that marvellous instinct which was so singular a part of his character, had remained without the walls.

Some how or other, he felt that he should be more useful out than in.

"May God forget me in my utmost peril," said the Earl, hotly, "if I refuse you, Saxon, any boon that you may have to require of me—so take time to consider what thou wilt ask."

If ever Will Scarlett deserved his name it was now, for the blood rushed in tumultuous floods to the very roots of his hair.

He, however, bowed low and said nothing.

His heart was in his mouth, and he could scarcely articulate.

"Wine, ho!—and now my child, retire—you must have need of rest."

"No, father—first hear of all the perils that this brave youth has endured—he is too modest to tell his own story."

"Thy will is ever law with me," said the baron, with a smile. "Take these serving men below some of you, and see they be blind drunk within an hour—as beseems Saxon hogs!"

This, for a wonder, was said in an inaudible tone.

"Come up, young sir," continued the earl, pointing to a table covered with drinking vessels, and overlaid with rich scarlet cloth, on which was set the materials for a breakfast that would startle a man for dinner in these more degenerate days.

Not even Eveline disdained to attack the pasty, wine, and strong ale.

But having heartily refreshed herself, she told her story.

But first the following singular dialogue took place between the young girl and Sir Norman Malvoisin, a dialogue that made Will Scarlett fume with rage.

"Come, uncle, and break thy fast. I hear thou hast been hunting all night in the forest; if so thou must be hungry."

"I am weary," stammered the White Cross Knight, "and would fain retire to my couch."

"Nay, thou shouldest hear my story," said Eveline, with a bland look. "There is much in it will amuse thee, nothing will annoy."

"Surely it will annoy me to hear of thy troubles," said the Norman knight. "I would rather leave you to your privity."

"I pray thee, Sir Knight," put in Will Scarlett, looking him full in the face, "join us and hear this noble lady's story, unless, indeed, there is some reason for thy not sitting down."

There was so dry a tone of sarcasm in the way in which this was said, that under any other circumstances would have caused an outburst; but the knight bit his lip, and then advanced to the table, on which menials were laying one of those solid breakfasts which justified our solid ancestors in calling themselves beefeaters.

For some minutes all were engaged in repairing the damages done to the human frame by fatigue, but after the lapse of a brief space of time, Eveline wiped her mouth and began her story, to which all listened with intense interest.

The Earl was now so delighted, that forgetting the temperance of a Norman baron, he quaffed huge silvermounted goblets of wine, that distracted his attention somewhat from the by-play.

Sir Norman Malvoisin drained cup after cup, in fear of what might be said, but according to a previous understanding between Eveline and Will Scarlett, not a word was said of the delinquencies of the uncle.

They thought to win him to repentance by forbearance.

As for William Gammel, he bent his head low to hide the blushes, which he could not restrain, as Eveline at every step of her narrative, poured forth his praises.

"By the holy sepulchre!" cried the Earl, warmly, "thou hast deserved well of me, Saxon. Let the feud between thy father and myself cease. I had not thought so much chivalry was in the soul of those who hate our sway."

"Sir Earl," said Will Scarlett, less hotly than he might have spoken, had not Eveline have given him one imploring glance, "you know us not. Where woman's honour and safety are at stake, we know no creed or country. For the meanest maiden in England I would

have wielded quarter-staff or bow. For your lovely daughter I would have died."

"Sayest thou so? Then art thou a gallant youth; but now methinks somewhat wearied. Go, sleep, and I will thank thee better to-night. Perchance thou mayest think by then of some boon adequate to a recompence of so much valour."

And the baron rose courteously as Eveline made her exit, and bade his own attendant show Will Scarlett to one of the best chambers in the castle.

"The boon the Saxon churl will ask," said Sir Norman Malvoisin, with a sneer, "will be one likely to be granted."

"What mean you?" cried the Earl, gaily; "the boy has done good service, and saved my girl."

"For which he will ask thy girl," said Sir Norman, coldly.

The earl started, clutched the two arms of his armchair—for such is a throne—and swore some fearful oath of the period, which to write were blasphemy.

"Brother of mine," he then added, after a moment's pause, "art sure of what thou sayest?"

"If you had seen the looks they interchanged you might know that what I say is true," urged the knight.

"And I have sworn to give him what he listeth," gasped Beauclerk's earl.

"A promise made in the exuberance of thy gratitude is no more binding than a daisy chain," urged the knight.

"I know not," said the earl, after some thought; and then he added, with that false smile which so well became his race, "some means must be devised to prevent his asking a boon."

"'Twere best he woke not," replied Sir Norman.

"I cannot slay the churl in my own chamber," said the earl, whose gratitude had all flown before the monstrous idea of a Saxon franklyn asking for his daughter's hand; "and yet I would not have him say I forfeited my oath."

"Leave all to me," continued Sir Norman, "I will send him forth unscathed, and yet having such a lesson, he will not dream of asking more reward than the smiles of one of Eveline's handmaidens."

"Be gentle with the Saxon knave, for he did save my child," said the Norman earl, with some touch of compassion in the tones of his rugged voice.

"I will," was the answer given by Sir Norman, who thereupon rose, and both crossing the hall, retired to their several apartments to seek the rest they so much needed.

Then from behind the tapestry came Zorah, her naturally pale face flushed crimson.

"Most false and recreant knight," she muttered, "I know your nature. You would slay that boy, worth a thousand of your vile race. Never did I see such complexion on man, never such eyes sparkle. His very hair is golden as the sands. It shall go hard but I will save him."

The woman's bosom heaved as she spoke with earnest passion, her step was quick and rapid, her form erect and dilated.

The hired harlot of a Norman baron had conceived in a moment an earnest and devoted passion for the handsome Saxon lad with the red hair and white and pink cheeks.

How to save him she knew not, but save him she knew she would.

CHAPTER XI.

A TRIAL OF A NOBLE HEART.

WHEN Will Scarlett left the presence of the earl, despite his courage and rapturous devotion to the lady of his heart, he could not prevent the terrible fatigues and excitement of the night from telling upon him.

He was, in plain English, utterly tired and weary.

It was, therefore, with no common satisfaction that he saw the chamber allotted to him opened, and himself left to rest.

Men never thought of taking off their clothes to sleep in those days; so Will Scarlett simply cast himself upon the rude couch that was provided for him, and whispering an ave and giving one thought to the chosen lady of his heart, fell into a deep slumber.

It wanted two hours of mid-day when the gallant young Saxon closed his eyes.

It was black dark when he awoke.

William Gammel had, when he retired, noticed that the bed on which he had cast himself was adorned with skins of forest beasts, and had felt that something soft was placed under, to give comfort and repose to the wearied limbs.

Yawning, and opening his eyes, he also cast out his arms—somewhat puzzled at the dreary blackness of the room.

He felt nothing but cold stone and straw.

With a wild cry of astonishment, he would have risen to examine into the mysterious and unaccountable change in the room.

His feet were fastened together by iron gyves.

A moment of consciousness was sufficient.

He was chained—a prisoner—in one of the cold and damp lower dungeons of the castle.

"Thou most false and treacherous earl!" he cried aloud; "is this thy reward? is this thy gratitude? May Heaven forgive you, for I cannot."

It was indeed a terrible awakening, and one which left no hope of escape or redress.

The earl, once his daughter restored to him, had doubtless repented of his promise; and to prevent the chance of his asking any boon that would tax his gratitude too much, had hit upon this cowardly way of silencing him.

"And yet," mused Will Scarlett, "he seemed sincere. Surely the father of one so lovely could not be so base a knave."

Then the unfortunate youth felt about, as if to convince himself that what he believed was true.

His hand touched a huge stone jar or pitcher, which, by a natural impulse, he lifted to his lips, and drank.

It was cold water, and seemed to cool and refresh him.

The truth flashed across his mind like electricity.

"It is the foul and recreant knight. Will Gammel is doomed, but he will die true to his God and his lady."

And folding his arms he resolved to abide his fate like a martyr.

But the hours passed and no change came, so that Will Scarlett began to think they meant to starve him; a thought which sent a chill to his very heart, no man, however brave, being able to endure the thought of this most horrible of tortures.

As yet he felt no suffering, though, after a long and refreshing sleep, and some hours of far from pleasant thoughts, he felt the cravings of nature.

Suddenly he heard a heavy step without, and then a key turning in a lock, followed by what appeared to be a blaze of light.

For a moment his eyes were utterly dazzled, and he could make nothing out, but in a moment more he saw that the intruder was Sir Norman Malvoisin with a soldier bearing a torch, a pitcher, and a platter with a loaf of black-looking bread.

The soldier stuck the torch in an iron ring in the wall, put the bread and water beside the prisoner, and retired without speaking.

"And this is Norman gratitude," said Will Scarlett, bitterly.

"Gratitude; what gratitude do I owe you?" asked the knight, who stood with a cold smile on his lips gazing at his chained victim.

"Did I not save thy niece from death? but I forget that because she would not contract incestuous marriage with you, she was doomed. Leave me, dishonoured knight; the sight of you is sickening!"

"Ah! you know that much. You have revealed that which it behoved me to know. Dolt—know you not that the secrets of the great are deadly poison to those who spy into them?"

Will Scarlett made no answer.

"Now, Saxon churl, mark well what I say. I have faith enough in you to believe that a solemn oath upon the cross would by you be held binding."

"A Saxon has but his word."

"I am willing to let you go, on this belief, if you will swear such oath as by you shall be held binding."

"And what am I to swear to?"

"Never to reveal to man, woman, or child any secrets of mine you may have discovered; and never to ask the earl to keep a promise rashly made in a moment of folly."

"Anything else, Sir Knight?" asked Will Scarlett, in a sarcastic and bitter tone.

"Never to seek speech of the Lady Eveline more."

"I swear, if God spares my life, to expose your villanies bare to the whole world. I swear that I will ride into the castle yard of Beauclerk, and there ask the baron who holds it to fulfil his sacred promise, and grant me the dearest boon that earth contains— his daughter Eveline."

"Insolent slave and braggart," said the knight, choked with passion; "you have in those words spoken your death warrant. But it shall not be said I gave you no choice. Say, shall my men-at-arms end thy wretched life, or will you lie here and rot?"

"As it shall please Heaven to direct thy false black heart!"

"I can stand thy jeers, churl," said the knight, coldly, "and will let thee live. And hearken, boy! you love Eveline—now mark me, while you lay here in chains, I shall be in your lady's chamber—for if she gives not up that dainty person of her's to me—she dies."

"Leave me, thou spawn of the evil one!" cried Will Scarlett, half leaping up to strike at the ruffian. "But Heaven will protect the innocent, and let thy wickedness recoil upon thy head."

The knight gave a grim smile. The licence of the times allowed so much of evil to be done, that he had some reason for doubting the power of any to shield the innocent and lovely. He appeared, however, to have had enough for the nonce of that dark and gloomy dungeon; for, taking the torch away, he opened the door and at once left the prisoner in total darkness.

Now hope is not easily extinguished in the human breast, so that Will Scarlett did not, because he was chained in the loathsome dungeon of a Norman baron, quite despond. Many men had been in worse plight, and had yet escaped. Fortune was fickle, and might reverse her ways at any moment.

The young hero therefore took his bread, ate it, and having washed it down with a good draught of water, fell back into a doze of thought.

It need not be said that his reverie had relation to Eveline.

How long he remained in this kind of brown study he knew not—but he was entirely lost to any consciousness of outward influences, when his attention was rivetted in a very singular way.

A strange noise was heard in the dungeon.

It was steady, regular, and mechanical, as if some one were turning a handle.

The dungeon was spacious, and being as it were the foundation of a heavy tower, had three large stone pillars to support its roof. Against one of these the prisoner was chained, while another faced him.

The singular noise proceeded from this direction, and Will Scarlett's whole faculties were rivetted upon the spot.

Presently a ray of light penetrated a chink in the stone pillar, which chink became every moment wider, until it revealed the form of a woman standing upon the upper part of a flight of stone steps, in the act of turning a handle, which had the effect of bodily moving a stone from its place.

Next minute Zorah stepped into the dungeon with a lantern in one hand and a basket in the other.

Will Scarlett stared wildly at the strange Eastern costume, at the full developed beauty, at the charms which her dress somewhat freely revealed. He was too surprised to speak.

"Take of this wine and meat," she said, fixing her eyes in earnest pity on the youth's face, "and then you will have strength to escape."

"Lady, how much I have to thank you, I cannot find words to say, though how you have found out my dungeon is a mystery, and your pity still more."

"I was behind the tapestry when you entered the banquetting hall—I was behind, too, when the Earl and Sir Norman Malvoisin plotted to escape granting you the boon you were promised—I know all."

And she looked into Will's eyes with a strange expression.

LITTLE JOHN JOINS THE OUTLAWS.

"Tell me what passed between the brothers," he said.

Zorah, while pressing on him the delicacies she had brought down, told him all that she had heard behind the arras.

"Ah!" cried Will, with a wild accent of rage that startled her, "I will yet outwit the Norman thief. Give me but my liberty."

"And what would you do?" said Zorah.

"Defy the knight to mortal combat, and take the earl at his word. *I love his daughter.*"

Zorah started back as if stung by an adder.

"Ungrateful boy! this to me, who, while the puny girl sleeps content in her dainty chamber, have braved the anger of the earl, and the horrors of the dank and murky passages by which I have made my way—and all for a smile from those brown eyes and a kiss from those ruddy lips!"

And speaking thus, the wild impulsive woman would have pressed him to her heart.

Will Scarlett gently repulsed her.

"I have but one lady of my heart, and rather than do evil unto her in thought, I would die."

Zorah was livid with passion. She rose—her eyes flashing with fearful light.

"You scorn my love. Be it so. For what you may expect from me, rot then in this lonely dungeon; I will not save you."

"I ask not help to be purchased at the price of mine honour and my fealty to my lady," said the sturdy Saxon youth.

The girl looked at him amazed and troubled.

"Thou art a gallant lover and a bold youth," she cried. "Rise—I will save thee, and thou shalt love me yet. Come."

"I am chained," said Will Scarlett, pointing to the iron gyves.

"Chained!" gasped the girl. "What is to be done? I had not thought them so cruel. But I must back and see if I cannot find hammer and file. Be not anxious. I may be delayed, but if I am alive I will come."

And before Will Scarlett was aware of her intention, she caught his head in her hands and snatched a kiss from his lips, that fairly overcame the brave youth's power of resistance.

Next instant he was alone and in darkness in the loathsome dungeon, where we must even leave him for the present.

CHAPTER XII.

A SOLEMN DETERMINATION.

WHEN Little John found that the Norman knight and his ruffianly gang of soldiers were intent on burning down the poor homestead which had long sheltered himself and his widowed mother Margery, his determination was at once taken.

"Let them burn; for, by the love I bear to strong ale and fat bucks, they have driven a quiet and peaceable man from his roof-tree, and they shall find it better to have loosened a nest of hornets. Come—ye all are good men and true?"

"All," said Scarlett, warmly—a sentiment loudly re-echoed by his attendants.

"By St. Peter, they think I own less sense than a fox, which has always two holes to his hiding-place."

And as he spoke, he hoisted a huge hutch from its place against the wall, and showed a large dark fissure, which appeared to lead into the very bowels of the mountain.

"Take them all in," continued Little John, "I will collect a few *hardes*, as these Norman thieves say, and follow."

With these words, followed by a taunting call to the ruffians without, Little John proceeded to collect such few things as he set value on, with which he presently also retreated to the cavernous hollow in the rock.

Following a kind of winding and narrow passage, which first trended downwards, the fugitives soon found themselves ascending, until they reached one of those singular vaulted chambers which have of late years been often discovered, and which in times past served as sheltering places now for the brave outlaw, now for the ruffian robber—at times for the wild beast of the forest.

Though the air was cold, yet the ground, of a gravelly nature, was dry, and all seated themselves, glad of rest after the fearful trials of that night.

Little John, with a bow and the huge two-handed sword his ancestor had wielded at Hastings, mounted guard at the entrance.

None were inclined to talk, even Eveline being silent, and fortunately sleepy; so that it was an hour or two after sunrise ere the party once more prepared to take the field.

Little John found a pitcher of ale and some cold meat with which to recruit the exhausted party, and this want attended to, went out to where the hut still smouldered—a black, shapeless, dilapidated mass.

He cast one look at it; a dark frown illumined his good-tempered face, and then the trial was over.

He never gave another thought to his own personal sufferings, but devoted his whole energies and powers to the requirements of others.

At some distance on the grassy plain grazed the horses which had been ridden by Will Scarlett and Eveline. These he chased into a corner and secured, though he had some difficulty in so doing, they having no particular desire to give up their liberty.

Then he went back and summoned his fellow sufferers to come forth, which they gladly did, the morning being bright and beautiful, the dew sparkling on the grass and bushes, and the birds singing lustily in the green forest boughs.

There is a charm in woodland scenery which singularly entrances the imagination, and, despite the terrors of the previous night and the anxieties she still suffered, Eveline could not but look around with a glance of admiration and keen enjoyment.

"There is something entrancing in the idea of a life in the forest glade," she said, as the cavalcade took up its march, "and I wonder not the bold outlaws — not the ruffians we have dealt with—but the men driven by oppression and game laws to seek a new life, cling with joy to the grassy haunts of this glorious forest."

"It has been my home since I was a little boy," replied Will Scarlett, "for I count not the hours spent in my father's house. From sunny morn to dewy eve, I have wandered through its myriad paths and never wearied."

"And I could do the same," continued Eveline thoughtfully.

There was a moment of silence. During the adventurous hours they had passed together, many of the barriers which existed between a Norman girl of high degree and the Saxon yeoman had been broken down, so that they had spoken with a freedom and absence of restriction which could scarcely have occurred under any other circumstances. But now morn had come, in all its sobering light and clearness, and both felt how soon a different state of things must ensue.

Eveline thought of her father, the haughty Norman baron, and of the mighty Baron Guiscard de Rollens, her high-born lover, upon whom, according to the custom of the age, she was to give her hand without any question of the affections.

His assiduities had hitherto produced mere indifference just tainted with dislike—now she hated him.

But still her father's word was pledged to him and she had tacitly agreed to accept his offer.

Will Scarlett, clearly as he saw his own feelings and guessed those of his fair companion, was too keen-sighted not to allow something for the influences under which she had been placed, and guessed how soon they would be tempered when once within the stern, cold, and battle-mented castle.

This state of mind on both sides caused the cavalcade for some time to be a silent one, as Little John strode in advance with quarterstaff and billhook, not only as guide but to clear away any impediments which might have stood in the way of the mounted travellers, while the pair of serving men appeared in no humour to indulge in their usual merry talk, but rather cast curious and anxious glances along the vistas of the forest, as if expecting every minute some one to cry, "Stand and deliver!"

But though they did catch one or two glances of suspicious-looking foresters, they received no interruption.

To those readers who only know England of the present day, and who judge of forests by what they have seen, it will be necessary to give a few words of explanation and information. Sherwood Forest, in the time of which we speak, rather resembled a vast primeval or virgin forest of the American continent than anything else to which we can compare it.

It covered all Nottinghamshire, with but a trifling exception, and had only one great thoroughfare through it, which, taking its start from the borders of Yorkshire, crossed at Radford the river Idle, passed the town of Mansfield, and ending near Nottingham, itself surrounded by wild wooded scenery, right away to the grassy banks of Trent river, itself bordered by a fringe of tall and beautiful trees.

It may readily, then, be imagined, that so vast a forest was full of winding and uncertain paths, which could only be followed by those who either were accustomed to their peculiar characteristics and sinuosities, or had the keen scent and quick instinct of the Red Indian.

Such were the outlaws.

But if the outlaws, whom unjust and wicked violations of every compact divine and human, drove to a lodging on the damp fern or grass, under overhanging trees with thickset stems and closely woven branches, the servants of the Ranger of Sherwood Forest were almost equally, if not quite as skilful.

In the case of Little John the faculty was marvellous. Born and bred in the forest, he had scarcely ever cared for towns. When five years old he had trotted beside his father, and learned to know every wild, leafy valley where the fallow-deer hid, and had gone on progressing in knowledge and power until now he crossed the forest by no given paths, but went straight for his mark with the certainty of a sleuth-hound.

It was not strange that Little John was thoughtful. To break up a home and throw off the harness of custom is always difficult and disagreeable, and the noble-hearted giant was quietly thinking of his future prospects, while with a careless eye he directed the motions of his companions.

Will Scarlett and Eveline, after some time of silence, resumed conversation, but they spoke only of past events and of the explanation to be given to her father.

There was one point on which they had a slight dispute. Will Scarlett would have exposed her uncle, Norman Malvoisin, and challenged him to deadly combat; but the gentle Eveline could not forget that he was her uncle, and judging others by herself resolved to spare him, in the hope that so much generosity would meet with its due reward of gratitude.

Will Scarlett had no such conviction, and firmly believed that so much disinterested mercy was misplaced, and would be the means of causing much sorrow and trouble.

But when did true man refuse his mistress's bidding?

The discussion, however, took some time, and did not end until they were on the extreme verge of the forest, with Beauclerk castle rearing its proud towers close at hand.

"And now, sir friend of mine," said Little John, halting suddenly, "if thou wilt take the advice of a fool, here thou wilt halt and let the lady go forward unattended."

"Never!" cried Will Scarlett, hotly, and then he added, in a milder tone, "why, my good Little John?"

"In yonder castle are pit and gallows, one of which will surely be thy guerdon of thanks for what thou hast done."

"Fie, brave forester," cried Eveline, the rich colour mantling to her forehead; "dost think my father a mere ungrateful hound?"

"I speak not of your father, noble lady, but of the knight whom we have so rudely used. He will surely be revenged."

"I pledge the name of Beauclerk and mine own honour, that who enters yonder castle in my train leaves in safety," cried Eveline, proudly.

"Lady," said the huge forester, with a good-humoured but quaint smile, "I would readily take thy word; but Little John will never be under a battlemented roof while there is a tree or hut or cave to shelter him. The forest is my home, and I feel out of place when away from it—*should evil be intended to my young friend here*. Besides, it will be better Little John were free than a prisoner, which I should surely be, for have I not lifted my hand against my master?"

"As thou wilt, brave forester," said Eveline; "and now for what you have done—and what you may yet do—receive my heartfelt thanks."

As she spoke she held forth her ungloved hand to the giant, who, stooping, kissed it respectfully, and then, turning with a warning smile to Will Scarlett, re-entered the forest, beneath the leafy arches of which he was soon lost.

CHAPTER XIII.

A FREE FIGHT.

THOUGH Little John was well aware that his life was at stake, he did not hesitate to take his way in the direction of a small village, inhabited by swineherds and others, and an appanage of the Norman castle. He was induced to this for more reasons than one.

In the first place, he knew that Sir Norman Malvoisin, and his immediate followers, were under the impression that not only he, but all his companions, had been burnt in the conflagration of the forest hut, so that no orders could have been given with regard to his capture.

Secondly, the stalwart forester stood in need of refreshment, which he could nowhere obtain except in the village at a small alehouse, frequented by the soldiers and other servants of the Ranger.

His chief motive, however, was to see and hear. Should any event of importance occur in the castle, it was not only possible, but most probable, it would be made the public topic of conversation among the retainers and servants.

In this course of action, Little John showed that wonderful discrimination which had much to do with his after celebrity. His plan was to hear all and say nothing.

In a few minutes he came in sight of what seemed a small straggling row of rude plank huts, covered with thatch, and nearly hidden by overhanging boughs. This was the village.

Entering a house of somewhat larger pretensions, Little John found himself in the presence of an aged matron, who welcomed him with a smile, and soon laid before him a foaming mug of ale and a hunch of bread and brawn, which he proceeded to discuss with all due solemnity.

The day being as yet young, there were no visitors, so Little John, having feasted the inner man, lay down upon a bench in a dark corner, and there did what giants, when fatigued and full of good cheer, are very apt to do, like other men—went to sleep.

When he awoke he found that it was getting dark, and that several men were conversing close at hand.

"By Satan himself!" said one, "I never saw my master look so white in all my life. He surely believed the maiden and all dead."

"And did not we see them burn with our own eyes?" added another in a doubtful tone. "Truly, it passeth my understanding."

"It will fare ill with this spark, young Gammel," continued the first speaker; "for though the Earl spoke him fair enough, the knight will surely not let him leave the castle alive."

"Then the foul fiend take him for the knave and coward that he is!" cried Little John, rising with a want of caution which was unusual on his part; "would that when I held the base craven's life in my hands I had taken it."

The first motion of the five soldiers who sat carousing within the alehouse was flight. Their terror was ludicrous and excessive, but no sooner had they gained the open air, than the recollection flashed across their minds, that, as Eveline and her three male attendants had escaped in the flesh, so also might Little John.

With which thought, after a hasty and whispered conference, they eagerly returned to the hut.

"By St. Dunstan," said the foremost of the band, "you did give us a fright, John. But here's to your health, and glad to see you safe out of the fix."

"By St. Nicholas!" cried Little John, who was now seated thoughtfully by the fire, his legs stretched out, and his hands rubbing his knees, "no thanks to you, who would have roasted not only me alive, but the noble lady to whom you owe allegiance and troth."

The soldiers exchanged meaning and significant glances. There was menace in these words of Little John, for were they twice the men of Sir Norman Malvoisin, did the earl hear of this murderous intent, they would perish on the gallows.

This their master had declared there was no chance of being known; but what could prevent it, now that Little John was known not only to be alive but free?

Nothing would prevent the stalwart yeoman from speaking his mind openly and freely, in which case the truth must finally come to the ears of the Earl.

In this case not all the power of the Norman knight could save them.

Their resolution was formed in a moment, and the five ruffianly soldiers understood one another at a glance.

"We did but obey the behest of our lord," said the chief, sullenly, "and have no account to give to any one else of our deeds."

"Think not to cheat the devil thus; and mark me, if anything should happen to Will Scarlett, look you all to yourselves, you, and your tyrant master," cried Little John.

"Look to thyself, fool!" roared the chief; and ere the bold forester was aware of their treacherous design, the whole five soldiers, to whom he turned his back, had flown at him—one at each leg and arm, while the fifth held him by the head, which he pressed backward.

For an instant, Little John was so astounded that he lost his presence of mind, and that instant was enough.

When he threw out all his giant strength, a strength that would have been sufficient to have hurled half a dozen ordinary men to the different ends of the room, he found that the soldiers had used their belts with such precision and accuracy as to render his struggle merely waste of time.

Without a word or murmur Little John submitted to his fate. Defeated, it was not his character to waste his breath in repining, but aware that for the moment his efforts were useless, he sank as it were an inert and helpless mass upon the ground.

"By the mass, 'twas well done!" cried one of the soldiers, scarcely able to believe in such an easy victory; "we have snared the big boar of the forest."

"And thou hadst kept a quiet tongue in your head, forester John," said the chief drily, "we might have quaffed a mug at thy expense, but when you talk so glibly you forget that we have necks to stretch, and that now you must swing to save ours."

Little John shrugged his broad shoulders, but made no reply.

"And now wilt thou walk to the castle, or shall we draw you on a wooden sledge?" said the chief soldier.

"I will walk if you loose my bonds," cried the mighty forester.

"I trow we had trouble enough to get thee down, my burly bully, not to wish to keep thee there," said the soldier grimly, "but you must even walk with the gyves."

"Which will be slowly enough," replied Little John, with something of his old humour. "Will it not, master Walter?"

"The more reason for departing early," said the chief addressed as Walter; "empty your cups, my men; an' we take our prisoner safe into the castle, I promise you good ale and beef this night."

The soldiers were ready, knowing right well that the reward would be even more substantial than beef and mutton, so, having paid their shot from money pilfered out of a pouch carried by Little John, they left the hut.

Little John, with the rapid instinct which was part of his nature, knew at once that his destination was not Beauclerk.

They turned their backs on the huge pile which frowned in the distance, and took their way west.

They were conducting him to the lonely tower of Goreleston, the wild and savage abode of the Norman knight; that is to say four of them, for one was despatched to the castle with the news of his capture.

This made matters more serious; for Little John, though never within the walls of the Tower of the Glen, had heard much of its horrors—for here Sir Norman Malvoisin ruled an absolute and unquestioned sovereign.

Though no one had ever escaped from its dungeons to tell the tale of its atrocities, enough had oozed out with regard to the conduct of the knight to make it a most undesirable residence.

Little John became even more thoughtful than ever.

For some time they passed through a portion of the forest, composed of moderate-sized trees, until at length they reached a deep lane running between two banks overgrown with hazel and holly, a dwarf oak in places casting its shadow over the path.

This was the entrance of the glen.

It was much broken up by the footmarks of horsemen and in the dusk of the evening looked something like a partially lit-up tunnel, so completely did the trees cover it with their umbrageous foliage.

Little John looked to the right, Little John looked to the left, as if in search of a fitting spot wherein to make a desperate struggle for that liberty and perhaps life which was rapidly escaping from his clutches.

A man may be as brave as a lion and yet have a prudent regard for his own skin. This was the case with our hero, who, while ready at any moment to sacrifice his life in a good cause, had no more desire to be flayed alive to please one of his Norman tyrants, than he would have had hesitation in dying for the defence of innocence or beauty.

His guards walked two before and two behind, so that could Little John have only got his hands free, there would have been very little difficulty about the matter. Four ordinary men were as nought to the valorous and powerful forester, but unfortunately his feet were so tied together as to admit only of short steps—a state of things which militated greatly against the two tremendous kicks in the rear which he had been for some time meditating.

Still something must be done, and Little John racked a brain, by no means unfertile in inventions, in vain to discover what that something was to be.

But he was helpless, and might have remained so, but for an almost involuntary exclamation of his own.

"By St. Nicholas, the patron saint of all good outlaws and honest thieves, I should be ashamed to be four men and keep one prisoner in gyves. An' you were men you would loosen my bonds and I would try conclusions with you all, ere I joined me to the followers of brave Robin Hood, the best of outlaws."

"Silence, if thou would not have thy mouth silenced with a gag. I would we were out of the shade of these infernal bushes," said one of the soldiers angrily. "This is a bad spot for thieves, and we should have but to slay thee if they stupidly came to thy rescue——"

"STAND—*move one step and you die!*" said a hoarse voice close to them, and in another instant six men with short swords by their sides, and armed with quarterstaves suddenly attacked the soldiers, who, however, brave, disciplined and stalwart men, made a ready and terrible defence.

Meanwhile one who had taken no part in the fray loosened the bonds which held Little John, who, with the roar of a bull let loose, flew at the soldiers, tripped up two and would

probably have brained the others, had not they in very terror at the fierce anger of their late prisoner, surrendered.

"Bring them along," said one in authority; "it is meet this affair were heard before him who has a right."

Little John made no resistance, though pretty well aware into what hands he had fallen; nothing could have happened more satisfactory or opportunely than this rescue. At all events, it took him from the hands of his fiercest and most deadly enemy, to place him in the power of men who, whatever their faults and errors, were driven to the life they led by oppression of the most grinding and galling character.

Darkness had now completely fallen over the forest and the narrow winding paths, overhung with clustering branches, were black as caverns.

The outlaws, however, by means of the marvellous instinct which characterises as well those bred in forest glades as it does the denizen of the forests, threaded their way through low leafy avenues, beneath which they could scarcely walk upright, so entangled were the branches of the oaks, with the accuracy of men following a beaten footpath.

An hour elapsed, and then they came suddenly, after ascending a wooded slope, to a vast thicket composed of oaks, yews, and hollies, and all other varieties of their forest trees, between the branches of which grew dense masses of underwood, impassable even to deer.

It was a wall of green.

This kind of wooded fortification they skirted, passing a clump of aged thorns, and then such a scene as was seldom witnessed in England fell upon their view.

Poets, painters, and romancists, to say nothing of travellers, have vied with each other in their endeavours to paint the wild picturesqueness of a Sioux, Camanche, or Iroquois encampment; but could they have given us even an approximation to the scene now witnessed it would have immortalised the fame of any one man.

Even by the fitful light of a placid moon, that now sailed in an ocean of azure, that they had entered upon a lovely semicircular glade, in shape almost as of a sylvan amphitheatre.

In the middle were three huge fires, one larger than the others, but at every one of them a fat buck roasting, supported by a triangle of powerful stakes. The odour, penetrating and subtle, even in the open air, of roasted venison, proclaimed the feast nearly ready.

Scattered over the sward in groups, chiefly lying on the ground, were numerous bodies of men, evidently waiting for the evening repast, conversing, whistling, or humming the simple ballads of the day in a low and cautious tone.

Many were more usefully engaged in examining their bows, tipping their arrows, and doing such other service as became a bold and valiant archer.

Others, again, were watching a game of quarterstaff, in which two stout men were engaged, who thought more of giving than avoiding blows.

Amid all this variety of action or repose, all lit up by the red and lurid glare of the fires, the seven outlaws passed, and only halted when they stood under a huge spreading oak, seated beneath which was a slight, elegant, and well-made youth, in conference with the chief of the band.

CHAPTER XIV.

ROBIN HOOD.

ABOUT twenty years of age, with a skin naturally fair, but browned by exposure to the healthful sun and wind of the woods, with a form that, reaching only to the middle height, was firmly knit and capable of great exertion, with limbs moulded like an antique statue, with a well-shaped head set firmly on his shoulders, with a bright smile revealing an exquisite row of white and well-shaped teeth, with a nose slightly aquiline and indicative of command, with a profusion of dark hair, escaping in rich masses beneath his jaunty feathered cap of green, there was no one who had ever heard of him who could mistake the presence in which they stood.

It was Robin Hood, King of Sherwood Forest, holding high revel in his sylvan court.

His lower limbs were encased in tight-fitting leggings of buckskin, while his shoulders were covered by a doublet of Lincoln green.

By his side was horn and hunting knife.

His other weapons—offensive and defensive—bow, arrows, sword, and buckler, lay at his feet.

"Well, Robert of the Mill, what have you here—a May-pole broke loose, or some foreign animal come to frighten our island folk ?"

"Neither, captain, but an honest lad, unfairly laid upon by four of Malvoisin's soldiers."

"Ah! he looks not like one who would walk tamely to the slaughterhouse," said Robin Hood, eyeing him with a keen glance—partly of admiration, partly of doubt.

"Give me but equal arms, and set the four knaves before me here, and you shall see how tame I am," said Little John, with a grin.

"Thy pleasure may be attended to," replied the captain of the outlaws, with a laugh ; "but first let us have a full report of the affair. Come hither, Robert of the Mill."

The sub-lieutenant approached, and a whispered conference took place between the subordinate and his chief, during which the latter continued to cast pleased and gratified glances at the man who, of all others, was to be handed down to the latest posterity as the dear friend and best lieutenant of Robin Hood.

"Ah! sayest thou so," suddenly cried Robin; "so you would join our band ?"

"If you be, as I suppose, Bold Robin Hood. I have walked here purposely to join you. Your knaves here would not have brought me so easily along, encumbered with four prisoners, had not I wished to see you."

"I am Robin Hood, then; what want you of me ?"

"To join thy band."

"Why ?"

"I am a man of few words," said Little John ; "and yet, that you may rightly understand me, I must speak awhile."

"You shall," cried Robin. "Supper is not ready yet; secure the soldiers of Malvoisin, and now, Big John, or Robert, or Thomas, thy story."

"My name is Little John," said our hero, with a sly look at the captain, a look so much made up of humility and pride and humour, that the bold outlaw burst into a roar of such laughter as rarely shook the arches of the forest, in which he was imitated by the whole band, who had crowded round to admire the huge mountain of a man before them, and to listen to his story.

"Little John," replied Robin Hood, when the excessive laughter had subsided, "by the holy rood, a goodly name. And if you be what you look and seem, it shall be a name known ere long in Sherwood Forest, wherever there are fat abbots to make disburse, or insolent nobles to chastise. Thy story."

Little John, thus apostrophised, related what the reader already knows, being listened to with marked attention by the whole band, not only from the intrinsic interest of the narrative, but from their great hatred of the Norman oppressor and tyrant.

But there was one thing evident to the least acute capacity among the thieves, which gave an additional zest to the story, and that was the excessive modesty with which Little John related his own share in the achievements.

A round of applause followed the cessation of the speaker, and then a marked silence.

"You have spoken well," said Robin Hood, "and but thy qualifications suffice, a brave member of our society you will prove."

"What need you of me ?" cried stout Little John.

"First, that you abjure all fealty and allegiance to any of the Norman race ; that you war with us upon the rich nobles and fat priests ; that you make all such pay toll who traverse our forests ; and that while you never take life without necessity, you aid and protect women, children, and all poor people of our own blood and race. Rise, Clerk of Copmanhurst, and do thy duty."

As the captain spoke, the burly friar, who had hitherto sat contentedly in the shade, rose to his feet, slipped on a cassock, handed the tall forester a bow, and then producing a dog's-eared missal stood ready.

"And this you swear on bow and book ?" continued Robin.

"I swear," said Little John, "on bow and book, which my mother's poor instructions show me the monk is holding upside down."

"Ah!" cried the friar, reddening with passion, while the outlaws could not restrain their laughter, "I did but do so to try thy learning."

"Enough, good Clerk of Copmanhurst," said Robin Hood, "do thy duty. In all things, Little John, you will obey the orders of your chiefs and hold to the laws of the community."

"Though I know them not, I dare swear to them ; for doubtless they are not such as kings and barons make for the ruin and destruction of the poor."

"They are not," replied Robin Hood, warmly ; "were the laws of the land just as merciful, could the poor hope for justice against the rich, could reliance be placed on the honour of prince, baron, or prelate, you had not seen so many brave and good men here. You have sworn ?"

"I have sworn."

"It now remains for you to prove what you can do with quarterstaff and bow. But this we will adjourn until the morning light tinges the green leaves of the forest. So now on with the banquet, and a merry cup to the advent of my Little John, who, considering his smallness, shall be my page and henchman to-night."

Amid the smiles of the outlawed patriots, the tall forester cast himself beside Robin Hood, who, lost in admiration at his stalwart and well-knit frame, passed his arm round his neck, pulled his hair, and took such liberties as a potent prince might with a huge pet bear or elephant, thus laying the foundation of an affection and brotherly love which was to cease only when death parted them.

CHAPTER XV.

THE TRIAL OF SKILL.

BRIGHT, serene, and lovely was the morning that broke upon Sherwood Forest, and tipped with golden light the tall tree-tops—the morning that was to witness the trial of skill appointed for every man who wished to join a band whose chief requisites were strength, endurance, a knowledge of bow, shaft, and sword.

The sun had scarcely penetrated to the green glade where the outlaws were assembled, ere they were on foot and showing the effect of their healthful mode of life by quaffing huge draughts of strong ale, attended by heavy morsels of pork and venison such as would alarm a prize-fighter in these modern days.

Robin Hood, seated on a log of wood placed for the purpose under his favourite oak, presided at a banquet of his officers, to which party Little John was already admitted, no one doubting that his prowess would entitle him to the distinction.

There were three requisites for a good outlaw—to use the sword and buckler, the quarterstaff, and the bow.

Now the huge stature and tremendous strength of the newly recruited outlaw, caused Robin Hood to reflect and the result was that he resolved to leave the sword trial to the last, intending, did Little John acquit himself well in the other trials, to leave that out, as he had no desire to witness bloodshed on so auspicious an occasion.

Breakfast being over the outlaws began moving towards the spot occupied by Robin Hood, not without glances of increased admiration, now that they see the forester in the broad light of day.

"Who here will try a bout with the long forester ?" said Robin, casting a hasty glance at the group of lieutenants.

All rose.

"'Tis well, my masters," cried the outlaw chief smiling, "but we must pick out the best match. Friar Tuck thou art too short, or methinks your broad shoulders should bear the brunt of this contest. But there is Much the Miller, whose head is up to Little John's chin—he must be the champion."

Much grinned—these encounters being as much enjoyed in those days as pugilistic contests are in our own.

Two quarterstaves were now produced, and being duly measured were found to be of the length alluded to in the old English ballad :

"I care not for length, bold Arthur replied,
My staff is of oak so free
Eight foot and a half, it will knock down a calf,
And I hope it will knock down thee."

Our ancestors, from good living, open air, and ample exercise, must have been hardy and sturdy to an extent we can scarcely realise, to have used such weapons in order to show off their skill; but they did, and not a day passed but the merrie outlaws took them up for pleasure or to settle any little difference that might have arisen.

In the present instance the contest promised to be an interesting one, as, though Little John was gigantic in his proportions, Much the Miller was six feet, stout, and a master at the weapon he now waved over his head with many a flourish.

"Art ready, my merry men?" asked Robin Hood.

"I am," each cried.

"Then when I drop my hand go at it, but when I cry enough halt, or I call you no good men."

And he dropped his hand.

The two men standing opposite one to the other, each scanning the respective appearance of his adversary, flourished their staves with an assumed indifference, which was but a feint to throw the other off his guard.

For a moment they essayed no blow, but looking into one another's eyes, sought to divine when and where the first blow would descend. Both, as it appeared, decided at the same instant, and both aimed at the adversary's head, while both struck so quick and alike, that the quarterstaves sent forth a loud crack and ring from the force of the concussion.

Next instant, Much, to his astonishment, ere he could use his own peculiar and extraordinary guard, received three blows, one upon his right shin, one upon his left, and then one upon his right cheek, which made him half dizzy and induced him to pour so vivacious an attack on his opponent as to compel him, in his turn, to use a rapid guard.

Then came a series of skilful manœuvres, in which each showed his offensive and defensive science so admirably as to call forth loud shouts of commendation and delight from the outlaws who stood or reclined around in anxious and interested groups.

At length Much, who was getting short of wind, began to play with redoubled rapidity to end the contest, but in this exhibited great want of discretion, as in a moment he received nearly a dozen blows, one of which, catching him on the jaw, sent him reeling back on the sward.

"Enough," said Robin Hood, warmly; "thou art indeed a brave lad, and none will readily quarrel with you here."

"I wot I won't," cried Much, grimly; "I have had friendly cuffs enough with thee, Sir Little John, and if my jaw be not broken, will gladly shake hands with thee."

"With all my heart, jaw or no jaw," said Little John. "I bear you no malice, my burly friend."

This caused a general laugh, so simply were the words uttered.

"And now for the shaft and bow," cried Robin Hood, "the day is waning, and men have other things to-day than play. Our larder and our purse are empty— we must replenish—cry 'Stand, sir, and throw us that you have about you—if not, we'll make you sit and rifle you.'"

The history of the long bow is the early history of England, for to it we owe much of our young supremacy. It was what the rifle is now. Even the Swiss gave way to us in this particular. Had we space we could here give wondrous instances of the power, precision, and long aim of the arrow; but we shall have many opportunities of illustrating this, the main and most picturesque feature in our narrative.

"A north-country mile and an inch at a shot," is a rhyming instance of the strength and skill of Robin Hood in archery—nor are there ample proofs wanting in the old prose chronicles of the time. "The Abbot of Whitby," says a Yorkshire tradition, "had heard that Robin Hood and Little John were famous for the distance as well as the accuracy of their shooting, and begged them after dinner to give him an example. He took them to the top of the abbey, whence each of them shot an arrow, which fell not far from Whitby Laths, in memorial of which the abbot set up a pillar where each of the arrows were found. The place where Robin Hood's arrow fell is still called Robin Hood's Field, and the place where Little John's is fell, called John's Field. The distance of these places from Whitby Abbey exceeds a measured mile."

Another ballad speaks with familiar ease of the doughty efforts in this way of the outlaws :—

> "Will Scarlett he did kill a buck,
>   And Midge he killed a doe;
> But Little John killed a hart of greace
>   Five hundred foot him fro.
> Joy on that heart, said Robin Hood,
>   Shot such a shot for me;
> I'll ride my horse a hundred miles
>   To find a match for thee."

On the present occasion it was not expected that anything very extraordinary would take place. The forest rangers, though good bowmen and true, had their living to get, and not their lives to defend. They were, therefore, generally good but not unerring shots.

Now Little John, though now an outlaw, had all his life been a ranger, and had never practised at any kind of mark with the patriots of the forest.

They made shooting the business of their lives, and were, therefore, accounted men of mark in this particular department of woodcraft.

A stout and burly outlaw called by the name of the Tinker of Tickhill, having been appointed provost of the games, the competitors were summoned.

About twenty of the leading outlaws stepped forward, but none of the chief, at which Little John frowned, though next instant a covert smile illumined his face.

"I'll beat the men first and the masters after," he muttered to himself.

The target was placed at the extreme southern end of the glade, a good long shot, such as was rarely needed in the fight or the chase, but which was generally adopted by way of arousing emulation and giving good practice.

The archers, one and all, took their station at the extreme northern end, the distance thus created making the shot more difficult and doubtful.

Each competitor selected three arrows, no more shots being allowed.

Little John took his bow, which had been recovered from the soldiers, and picked from his case three well-pointed shafts.

The provost of the games now placed the men in order, and, from perversity or humour, so lined them that the shortest man was at one end, and the line went ascending until it reached Little John, who towered a head above his fellows.

The archers then stepped forward in turns, and each man delivered his three shafts with that graceful ease which so much becomes a bowman.

About one-half struck the target, while the other half went so near as to be accounted good archery, considering the distance at which the mark was shot at.

All Little John's shafts struck the target.

The outlaws were not stingy with their applause, but shouted lustily to express their satisfaction.

Two of his arrows were declared to be within the inner ring, and this being the case with no other, Little John was declared the victor.

Robin Hood's eyes flashed with pleasure, and the hope of having a worthy competitor.

But three of the defeated wished to join in a second bout ; and when a second target was produced, there remained but one, Much the Miller, to dispute the final award.

"I will have a shot with thee, though my skull does ache," said the jolly fellow, "and if I beat thee not with the bow, I will shoot no more."

"Be not rash, Sir Miller," cried Robin Hood merrily, "for by St. Nicholas, the patron saint of thieves, and therefore doubly thy saint—thou miller and thief—for we have here a forester, with whom I may have to try conclusions myself."

Now, as young as he was, the fame of Robin Hood as a wondrous archer was already spoken of even in London. This was high compliment enough to make the ex-ranger blush, but in no wise diminished his anxious desire to win in a second contest with his late quarterstaff adversary.

Keenly examining the tips of his arrows and looking to the shafts, Much the Miller stood forward in that erect position which the action of drawing the bow requires, and which consequently does so much to promote the beauty of the human figure in either sex.

With all his outward confidence the outlaw was anxious.

He had received a good drubbing, and felt it in the marrow of his bones, so that the Miller was wrath and hoped and trusted to succeed in a trial where hitherto he had had few competitors able to defeat him.

He looked at bow and string, and then chose an arrow with an air of great discretion. Then he took his aim with great deliberation, measuring the distance long and carefully with his eye, holding firmly in his hand the bended bow, with the arrow notch placed in the string.

Then he advanced him a pace, and lifting the bow at the full stretch of his arm until the middle or resting place was to a level with his eye, shot.

The winged shaft with a loud whirr sped through the air, and even at that distance a heavy thud was heard as it lighted within the inner circle of the ring, but not in what we now call the bull's-eye.

The shot was, however, so good that even men accustomed as the outlaws were to good archery could not prevent themselves from giving a shout of applause.

But Little John said not a word. Without taking time to aim as Much the Miller had done, he drew his arrow to the head and sped it on its rapid flight with a careless confidence, which well became the good-humoured and jolly giant.

A perfect yell of delight followed.

At the other end of the line of shooting a small band of outlaws had collected under the shelter of some large oaks to watch the result of the shooting.

These rushed out, and with loud ringing voices proclaimed the result.

"Centre!"

"By my sore head, Sir Little John," said Much, with a frown, "but thou art Satan himself in guise of a man. Still, have at you!" and without another word he too let fly.

"Centre," again shouted the distant scouts.

"By the holy rood," said Robin Hood, "I must look to my laurels."

"I shoot no more, I fight no more, I quarrel no more with Little John," said Much, ruefully throwing down his bow and arrows.

Little John made no reply, but with three choice arrows ready prepared stood forth, and by an exercise of skill and ingenuity almost unparalleled in the history of shooting, sped them one after the other so quickly that all three had reached the goal ere the astounded outlaws had time to see what was the nature of the aim he was taking.

But when the result was announced, the forest rang again with a shout of applause such as was new to the oldest of those who had been outlying in Sherwood Forest glades since the days of their youth.

Little John had split each arrow in the target in twain, his own taking their place.

"By the pinfold and pledge of the Pindar of Wakefield," said Robin Hood, rising with a hot flush upon his cheek, "this is hot work. Since the old trees of Sherwood Forest gave shelter to its merry men, there has not been such shooting. I must even try a hand for the honour of the men in Lincoln green."

Now, much has been written and said of the celebrated shots of bold Robin Hood, than whom a more perfect archer never pulled a string; but each man has coloured his prowess to his own fancy.

Now, we prefer to give a picture of the gallant and patriotic chief, as he really was, and to relate his feats as as he really did them, to trying any new invention of our own.

We describe what really occurred on the green and grassy natural clearing.

The shot was one marvellous enough in itself to require no exaggeration in the description.

"Cut me two wands," said Robin Hood, taking his cherished bow from where it stood beside the oak tree.

An outlaw who stood by, and who well knew the requirements of the noble archer, went into the thicket and came forth a few minutes after with two upright peeled hazel sticks, not more than an inch in diameter.

"What wilt thou do with things we cannot see?" said Little John, grimly.

"Shoot at them, my gallant hawk," replied the captain of Sherwood Forest, laughing. "You know not what you can do until you try."

Two outlaws now took the wands and walked in a straight line, three score rods, when they planted them in the ground.

Little John stared with open mouth.

It was clear that Robin Hood was not about to let the adventurous stranger, who had bearded him in his own den, come off victorious before his own men.

Robin elected to shoot first.

The first time Robin shot at the pricke
He missed but an inch it fro;
Little John, he was an archer good,
But he could never do so.

"The devil himself cannot do it," said Little John, with a wry and puzzled face that was irresistibly humorous.

"Try again—first chance this time," cried the robber chief.

"I will try, but no shame to be beaten by Robin of Sherwood."

But though Little John took every pains this time, perhaps from his very over-nervousness, he missed his aim.

Then up stood again the perfect archer, and drawing his bow to the very steel point, Robin Hood let fly his arrow, and cleft the wand.

"By the mass of St. Peter's—and that is a big oath," said Little John, with a hearty admiration that utterly ignored his own defeat, "was ever such shooting seen? Proud am I, indeed, to serve such a master. I am thine, Robin Hood, for ever and a day."

Robin's reply is historical.

"A blessing upon thy heart," he said,
"Good fellow, thy shooting is good;
For an' thy heart be as good as thy hand
Thou wert better than Robin Hood."

Little John was about modestly to deny the soft impeachment, when a sudden end was put to the games.

CHAPTER XVI.

THE PAGE.

Low at first, and then becoming loud enough to be heard distinctly by all present, came the merry notes of a horn in the distance, sounding one of those forest airs which served as signals between the outlaws, as the hooting of owls and the cry of the whip-poor-will serve as signals with the redskins of the pathless wilds.

In an instant all were silent, and stood around their chief, awaiting calmly what might happen next.

In a few minutes a couple of scouts appeared, followed by an outlaw and a youth in the dress of a page.

The youth was evidently delicate and unaccustomed to the difficult passes and paths of the forest, for he could scarcely drag his limbs before him.

But his face was bright enough, sparkling eyes, rosy cheeks, and red pouting lips, proclaiming health despite his fatigue.

"What springal have we here," said Robin Hood, "that announces his coming by sound of horn? What want you, my little bantam of the forest?"

"I seek Robin Hood," replied the page, pertly, "and to him only will I tell my errand."

"Sirrah! and you mend not your manners, you may make acquaintance with the forest hazel," said Robin Hood as sternly as he could.

"Then does rumour belie thee, bold outlaws—but since thou dost talk so, I will show thee a passport thou *darest* not refuse to recognize, which shall e'en give me licence to talk to thee as I will," cried the page, audaciously.

"Who dares give pass or safe-conduct in my domains? Show me this magic safe-guard which Robin Hood dare not violate. Dost carry it about thy person."

"Marry, on my head," said the page, lifting *her* cap and allowing a flood of rich auburn hair to fall over her graceful shoulders in a way to betray a woman.

One instant was given to triumph, and then the girl's modesty conquered, and she cast her eyes upon the ground.

A marvellous picture it was to look on. Tiny, slight, but still elegant in form, the tight-fitting hose showed off rounded limbs that none could see unmoved, now they knew them to be those of a woman.

She was evidently a fascinating sylph-like creature, made for love and home.

Her complexion, which was of a clear olive colour, with the polish of marble and the softness of satin, was almost as transparent as amber, its whole surface being now suffused from the emotion she felt, which, quickening the circulation of the blood, gave an incessant play and animation to her countenance.

Dark, unconfined, and naturally curling, her profuse locks were so apt to fall over her face, that she had acquired the habit of frequently shaking them back, thus revealing for a moment a white and massive forehead—while, when she fixed them on the outlaw chief, all had admired her round, laughing, hazel eyes, which now were bent downwards with the bashfulness of girlhood. The dimples on each side of her face, however, revealed that, though thus modestly shrinking, as it were, beneath the shelter of her own hair, she was only kept from laughter by the gaze of so many of the ruder sex.

"A hit! a palpable hit," cried the outlaws, clapping their rough hands.

Robin Hood reddened with pleasure. Never did skilful courtier pay king a more artful compliment.

"Thank you, maiden," he said, with a swelling throat; "you have but done me justice. I war not with women—but for thy merry jest I will reward thee. Whatever boon you come to ask is granted."

"Thanks," said the girl, whose name was Rose, "then my errand is soon told. I come from Eveline de Beauclerk, to ask you to save your friend and her loyal lover, Will Scarlett, of Gammell Hall."

"By the rood!" thundered Robin Hood, while every outlaw clutched his weapon, "an harm happen to the lad who is foster-kin to me, I will make a pile of ruins of the castle, and hang the murderer on the top. Give me details."

But Rose could tell no more than that Will Scarlett had mysteriously disappeared, being, *it was whispered*, in the deepest dungeon of the castle.

The earl had, with a perfect air of candour, that Eveline believed to be not feigned, asserted that he had not seen or heard of Will Scarlett since he sent him to a bed-chamber.

But Eveline firmly believed that Sir Norman Malvoisin had either imprisoned or murdered him.

"In which case my lady will die," said Rose, who was but a handmaiden, weeping as she spoke.

"Dry thy tears," cried Little John, in a very peculiar voice—something as if indicating a wish to have a jolly good cry with her—"I've drubbed the knave once, and I doubt me he remembers enough of it not to risk another. Will Scarlett is my friend, and shall be restored to his lady, or my name is not Little John."

"And are you Little John, the brave forester?" said the girl, artlessly, as she looked upwards with evident admiration.

"I am," replied the giant, whom you might have knocked down with a feather at that moment. "What know you of me?"

"Only that you are brave, honest, and good, as you are big," she said, casting down her eyes.

"Now there speaks thy noble mistress. Lead on to the rescue. I long to dye the feathers of my shaft in the blood of his and her enemies."

"Hold!" cried Robin Hood, who had been reflecting. "This must be seen to. We are not enough here. Disperse, all save twelve, and seek your brave comrades. Collect every scattered troop, for I trow there is now game afoot that will have to be hunted hard; for Will Scarlett shall not die. These Norman knaves will stand at bay. Meet me at eventide at the blasted oak in Watling Street. Go!"

In a moment the forest glade that had been so full of life was still, the outlaws obeying the commands of their chief with a cheerful alacrity, that showed either great sympathy with the cause or an innate love of fighting, somewhat peculiar to our hard-headed but warm-hearted ancestors.

"Do you, Much, take six men and cross the road to Rotherham. Ned the Potter is there with twenty fellows, looking for a Norman abbot and his train. Bring them all on."

Much made no reply, but started into the forest, followed by six outlaws.

"Little John," said Robin Hood, "you are but a new member of our band, but you have proved yourself already fitted to command. Take these six men, and with their aid guard this maiden back to the castle. She must re-enter secretly, if possible, as upon her depends much of our success. She must communicate with you. Now go, and guard her from all evil."

"With life and limb," said Little John, heartily. "None shall harm her while I have a hand and heart."

"Bravely spoken," said Robin Hood. "Hasten, for the sun rises fast, and you have far to go—for the maiden is weary and may not be hurried."

"I will carry her," cried the forester, heartily.

"No, thank you," said Rose, retreating somewhat; "I can carry myself."

"As thou wilt," cried Little John; and beckoning her to his side, he entered silently beneath the leafy arches of the forest, leaving Robin Hood alone—monarch of all he surveyed.

The bold outlaw did not move for some minutes. He was devising some plan by which to outwit the Norman baron; but his usually fertile imagination was evidently at fault.

However, in a few minutes, after looking keenly around to see that he was not observed, he sprang up into the boughs of the huge oak tree, and disappeared.

Nor did Robin Hood re-appear any more during the whole of that day. Which way he went, and what he did, we shall soon see.

We must follow Little John.

CHAPTER XVII.

LIEUTENANT LITTLE JOHN.

THE brave forester started on his way with a due sense of his own importance and the responsibilities of his situation. When we say his own importance, we mean not to convey that Little John could by any possibility be conceited, but he was in truth highly flattered by the readiness with which Robin Hood had placed him in a situation of command, and resolved to merit the great confidence of the bold outlaw.

There was another feeling, however, creeping in upon the heart of the burly yeoman, though he was as innocent of comprehending it as a child.

This was love for Rose.

Now have you ever, be you man or boy who reads this veracious chronicle, seen the two great clear eyes of a young and beautiful girl lifted to your own, watching your every word with keen admiration, and not felt a something —you know not what—gnawing at your heart, that told you you should like never to have those eyes away from you.

Now this was the position in which Little John was placed.

He had seen the evident admiration exhibited in the eyes of Rose when she spoke of him from her mistress's not highly-coloured account, and that one look of undisguised pleasure was not easily forgotten.

Little John, man as he was, was still but a boy, and a *very weak one*.

Often the stronger we are in some things, the feebler we are with the female sex.

As they proceeded through the leafy arches of the forest, as they crossed brook and rivulet, it was a sight to see the burly forester lifting the tiny page in his arms whenever any obstacle more than common occurred to make the path arduous or painful.

Rose demurred at first, but brave as was her little heart, she was tired.

By degrees they got into conversation, but on the part of the girl it flagged, for she was really and truly weary.

Behind came the foresters, laughing and talking in their usual strain.

In this way they reached the end of a narrow trail, which opened upon a little path leading from the monastery of Jovault to Nottingham.

Suddenly Little John halted, and made signs to his men to do likewise. His eyes were brimful of delight.

He had seen something.

"Lie close," he said, "and watch me; but whatever betide, come not near. *I am going to rob a priest or two.*"

And the new fledged outlaw, with an enormous chuckle, shook his solid sides, as he pointed out *two* monks coming up the arched pathway.

The outlaws grinned. They were delighted to see their giant recruit at work

We have omitted to mention that on becoming a received outlaw Little John changed his dress, and assumed, instead of the livery of the house of Beauclerk, the bright Lincoln green which so became the forest.

SIR MALVOISIN CHASED BY THE GHOST.

He had also provided himself with a visor, which, as he debouched upon the rough, rutty, rude bridle-path, he took care to assume.

With a huge stride he presented himself full in front of the two monks, who looked at him with pious horror.

"Go thy ways," muttered one; "we want no masqueraders here."

"Prithee, fathers, pause in your disdainful progress. I am a poor man in want of many things," hypocritically urged Little John.

"Thou wilt get nothing but whacks here," said one of the monks fiercely, while both raised their staves to strike.

Little John, with a loud laugh, caught firmly hold of the sticks, wrenched them from the hands of the portly monks, and then with a buffet on their priestly ears, unhorsed them both.

The well-fed animals stood still, while their masters lay sprawling on the ground.

But in another instant both were on their feet.

They were sturdy, jolly fellows, well fed, and solid on their legs. They had no intention of giving up to one man.

But when they flew at Little John, he received them with such a ringing series of blows on their bald pates, that in a moment they were fain to cry for mercy.

"Sir outlaw, you are too many for us," they said, ruefully; "what seek you?"

"Whatever money you have in your possession, as, according to your own teaching, you only hold it for the poor."

"Money!" cried the stouter and older man of the party, with a quick, keen glance at his companion, "we have no money!"

"When I say that you have," drily replied Little John, "I freely give you the lie. An' you have none, I will apologise."

The monks turned red as turkey-cocks, as the bold outlaw spoke.

"Gently, my masters, stand back," said Little John, who was infinitely amused at his first essay in the art of lightening the pockets of his fellow-men; "if you do not want sorer pates than you have now, you will neither make nor meddle, while I search your valises."

And he took both valises or leathern bags from the horses.

The monks groaned with anguish, the perspiration pouring off their faces in huge drops.

Little John threw himself on the grass at the foot of a tree preparatory to an examination.

The monks clutched their short heavy staves or clubs.

"Would you, though," said Little John, carelessly. "Send a shaft through them, my merrie men, if they but move."

Motionless as statues, still as carved images, the monks stood with their uplifted sticks, not daring even to lower their arms, lest the unseen enemy should carry out the horrid behests of this huge robber, as they mentally designated him.

Their jaws fell, their staring goggle eyes were fixed on vacancy, and their bodies remained motionless, except that their knees shook under them.

"Oh! oh!" said Little John, turning the contents of one valise on the grass. "What have we here? A pasty that smelleth rarely savoury—venison, as I live, and white bread! Lord, that men of God should be so thoughtful of their bellies!"

"Worthy outlaw," stammered the elder priest, "we take this provender to a sick man."

"The cheese is excellent, I' faith, my fathers, you are not likely to starve; for here be hard eggs and a cold fowl, with a nice piece of brawn—all very good. But where is the money?"

"I wish it might choke thee and all thy belongings," muttered the priest.

"Ah, here we have it—a weighty purse indeed," laughed Little John, as he pulled out a leathern bag, and began counting the gold coin.

"It is not ours—it is the abbot's," said the younger priest.

"Who shall impose on thee seven dozen aves, and as many paters for thy falsehood?" cried Little John, sternly.

At the same moment he signed to his followers to advance, and, selecting a pleasant seat for Rose, handed over the provisions to the outlaws while he stowed away the money in a safe place.

The priests, utterly overcome by their feelings, sank on the green sward and blubbered.

Then Little John's heart failed him; and thinking they needed some consolation, handed them a moderate share of the provisions, to which the men in Lincoln green added some strong ale, which two of them had provided for the exigencies of the journey.

"And now, most reverend fathers, you may depart, but not as you came—for one of you must go on foot—this fat palfrey being needed for my young friend here who is neither so stout nor so sturdy as yourselves, my friends."

The monks were too overwhelmed at the loss of the convent money, too alarmed at the sight of seven stout outlaws, to say a word; and the elder mounting, while the younger walked, departed, if not better and wiser—sorer men than they had been half an hour before.

Meantime, Rose, nothing loth, was mounted on the second steed, and in this way the journey was continued.

CHAPTER XVIII.

HAND TO HAND.

WE left Will Scarlett in the deepest and most gloomy dungeon of the castle still doubtful as to his own fate, and unable to judge correctly of the intentions entertained towards him by Zorah.

Still, the consciousness that he had a friend who was cognisant of his true position was something, though he was fully aware that she would not communicate to Eveline, who he feared would regard his disappearance as either the result of cowardice or ingratitude.

There was still the hope that she might suspect the truth.

However this might be, the hours passed wearily enough, for to a strong and vigorous mind there is nothing so trying as utter inaction.

He could not walk up and down his cell, but lay there racking his brain with thought, until he was half stupified.

Then again sleep came to his aid and he forgot his woes.

When he awoke there was light in the dungeon, and Zorah was once more seated close to him, watching him intently.

"You sleep sound," she said, gently; "a prison has few horrors for you."

"I am an honest and innocent man—that is my shield," he replied.

The girl coloured violently; but without a word handed him some refreshments, after which she produced two files.

Will Scarlett scarcely thanked her, except by an elo-

quent look, and then both went to their tedious and arduous work.

The anklets were thick and solid; so, leaving these for a future occasion, they attacked the rusty links of the chain.

Zorah's efforts were feeble, but they prepared the way for the future operations of the prisoner.

One foot was free.

Zorah left off, for Will Scarlett now took her place.

The link wanted not a minute of being filed through when the door of the dungeon opened, shut again with a slam, and the Norman knight, torch in hand, stood before them.

He looked at the pair for a moment in utter amazement, but next instant his features changed their expression, and a coarse smile was followed by a loud laugh.

"So oh, my dainty maiden, because a red-haired Saxon takes up his lodging in one of my dungeons, you must make it a chamber of dalliance. What will my brother say?"

"I care not," replied Zorah hotly—*the file was still at work.* "I hate him and all his brood."

"Sayest thou so? 'Tis well. At noon I will have thee scourged from the castle gates. But now, by your leave, yonder doorway is your path."

"I believe Sir Norman Malvoisin," said Zorah, speaking loudly and rapidly with a motive, "to be coward enough for anything."

"Coward! base slave!" cried the White Cross knight furiously, advancing with clenched fist towards her. "Ah! what sound is that? An' you have tampered with my prisoner you shall surely die."

"No!" cried Will Scarlett, bounding to his feet and striking the other full in the face; "for I am here to defend her."

The noble staggered, so unexpected was the blow; but in an instant, recovering his presence of mind, and his brute courage rendering him even tolerably cool, he lifted his hand and aimed at the sturdy Saxon a reply to his attack which might, had it taken effect, have summarily ended this veracious chronicle.

But Will Scarlett was a master in all muscular exercises, knew both how to box and wrestle.

He warded off the blow, struck the astounded knight heavily between the eyes, and, ere he could recover himself, sent him sprawling by means of a common practice among wrestlers.

He lifted one foot, jerked it between his adversary's, and laid him flat on his back.

With an awful oath the knight rose, his hand searching for his dagger.

"Thy blood on thine own head!" he howled—for no other word can express his passion.

His astonishment may be conceived when side by side with Will Scarlett he saw Zorah, handing his enemy his only weapon, which, unperceived by him, she had plucked from his side.

One glance of the Norman's eye betrayed his intentions.

He would leave the cell and call assistance from above.

"No," said Zorah, and with a light bound she sprang to the door, turned the key, and took it out just as Will Scarlett renewed his attack on his enemy.

Partly encumbered by his armour, the Norman had no chance with the yeoman.

In another moment the knight was again upon the ground helpless, and Will Scarlett kneeling on his breast.

"Surrender!" said the young man, sternly, pressing the dagger to the other's throat.

"Never, Saxon churl—a knight surenders only to his equals. To your brakes and caves you outlawed thief, nor dare touch one of my blood."

"Now, by my father's faith," said Will Scarlett, "I have a great mind to end thy wicked life, but I am no murderer. Take the keys from his belt, Zorah."

The girl obeyed, and handed the keys to the young man, who, at a glance, selected the key of the padlock which fastened the cruel chains to the stone pillar.

"Unlock it," he said.

Zorah obeyed, and dragged the chains to where the knight was stretched utterly helpless on the ground.

Suddenly he made a mighty effort to throw his conqueror, but the sharp point of the dagger pricking his throat he gladly desisted, for, though he boasted loudly, no man was less inclined to part with dear life than Sir Norman Malvoisin.

Though the chains were awkward enough to manage, they were after one or two trials, passed securely round the prostrate knight, and secured by means of the padlock.

Then, a forester never being without a spare bowstring or two, the humiliated Norman's feet were easily secured.

Will Scarlett then rose.

"You have spared my life, sirrah" said the helpless knight, in tones of bitter hatred, "you have done ill, for I will have such revenge on you for this as shall make Sherwood Forest ring again. From this hour I wage war on you and all your race—your kith and kin, whom I will hunt down as I would the vermin wolves—so look to thyself, my madcap churl."

"You are privileged now," said Will Scarlett, sternly, "but if I catch you prowling about my father's home, I will pin you hip and thigh to your horse."

"Go too, braggart—and as for you, my dainty minion, I will have thee so scourged and punished, that the meanest hovel in the forest shall be held too good for thee, and thou shalt crawl from the sight of men the foul, tainted, painted strumpet, that thou art!"

"Ha! ha! ha!" laughed Zorah, it is true, with somewhat of a forced laugh—"a pretty position to threaten from. Look to thyself, proud knight, and beware lest thy bones bleach here when the rats shall have consumed thy flesh. *I have the key of the cell.*"

This was said in a low whisper, heard only by the knight.

A heavy dew of cold perspiration burst upon his forehead, while his face grew livid.

He spoke, but in a tone so hollow as to startle Will Scarlett.

"A boon! boon! you Saxon churl," he said.

"What boon?" replied Will Scarlett, surprised at the accent and the request.

"Slay me at once—use my own dagger to my heart, but let me not die the lingering death of starvation, to which this wanton fiend would condemn me."

"What mean you, Sir Norman?"

"She has removed the key from the dungeon gate."

"No, Zorah, I will not do this. Give me the key."

Zorah frowned, but gave it up. She could refuse Will Scarlett nothing.

The mode of entrance and exit adopted by Zorah soon showed to Will Scarlett that even in the lowest depths there is a lower deep, for when the pillar closed upon them they were on the top of stone steps cut in the solid rock, so slippery and slimy, so damp and oozing with water, as to convey a shudder to the frame.

On reaching the bottom one of the great secrets of the mighty castle stood revealed to them—a secret supposed to be known only to the master of the fortress and certain of his immediate and more trustworthy followers.

They were in a rude, vaulted chamber, in all probability a natural cavern, from which diverged numerous passages, both wide and narrow, in every direction.

"And now, young man," said Zorah, with a soft melancholy, as she handed him his weapons, "we part. Yonder is the way to safety. Follow the narrow path, and you will come forth in the forest."

"But you, fair lady," replied Will Scarlett, with a sigh.

"Will return to my bondage," she said, with a strangely proud humility.

"But the earl?"

"The earl owes you thanks for preserving his daughter. I will but say that, knowing the wicked intentions of the knight, I resolved to frustrate them, and all will be well."

"But could I not see Eveline before I depart," said Will, with downcast eyes.

"Fond fool," muttered Zorah; "but as you will. I can take you into the castle, but there my power ends."

CHAPTER XIX.

THE CHAPEL.

WITHOUT another word the girl turned up a wider path than that she had indicated to Will Scarlett, at the end of which was another flight of steps, also cut in the solid rock, on which the splendid pile of the castle was built.

Tripping up this with a rapid step, they soon reached a small square chamber in the rock, from which there seemed no exit. But Zorah merely pushed a stone, it

yielded, and they were in a large vaulted apartment, made by men's hands.

It was the celebrated chapel of the Castle of Beauclerk.

Will Scarlett looked around with some interest, and was much struck to observe that a whole tomb revolved on its axis as Zorah closed up the aperture through which they had just passed.

"This is the whole secret," she said, pointing to a knob in the brass ornamental work.

Will Scarlett examined it carefully.

"And now," continued the girl, speaking in a low and cautious whisper, "you must remain here. I will contrive to see Rose, the Lady Eveline's handmaiden, and I will tell her you are here. If she have a grateful heart she will come; and then you may forget Zorah, for you will see her no more."

"If I forget you, may I be forgotten. My nightly prayers," he replied, "shall be for you. But do me one more favour."

"What is it?"

"Give this key of the dungeon to one of the knight's private adherents. I would not have the man choke with passion ere the rescue arrives."

"It shall be done," said Zorah; "but hush!—some one is in the chapel, kneeling against yonder pillar. Hush! —move not until I have escaped—it is Eveline."

They had set their light down in a corner for fear some one might enter the chapel, and this precaution served them in good stead, as it enabled Zorah to glide away unobserved.

Will Scarlett now scarcely knew how to to act. He could see Eveline plainly enough keeling at the foot of a column, near which, by the pale light of the moon that streamed through a large stained-glass window, rose a brass crucifix.

She was utterly absorbed in her devotions, and the young Saxon's heart beat warmly, as the sweet persuasion pierced to his soul that she was praying for him.

There was, however, no time to be lost. At any moment some one might come and prevent an interview.

He had but one course of action to pursue—to speak.

"Lady Eveline! Lady Eveline!" he said, in a low, hushed way, concealing his natural tones.

"Who calls? who dares come here to pry upon my devotions?"

"I have news, lady—important news."

"That voice—'tis no delusion—tis he, my saviour and my friend!" she gasped.

Next instant she was clasped to his manly bosom. All reserve was for ever over between them.

"How is this I find you here?" asked Eveline, after the few first moments of silent rapture were over.

Now Will Scarlett felt slightly puzzled. He knew too well the position of Zorah in the household, not to be fully aware that it must be a secret from his fair mistress.

He, however, briefly told his story, winding up by stating that some domestic of the earl's had overheard the plot against him, and to thwart Sir Norman had assisted in his flight.

"And now, my bright, my beautiful," said William Gammel, "I must leave you—but, oh! star of my existence! am I to bid you an eternal farewell?"

"No!" cried Eveline, fervently, "let us hope for happier days."

"When you are married to your noble suitor," said Will bitterly.

"Nay; nothing will make me break my fealty to my vows."

"Then why not fly with me now? Once united to me by the most sacred and dearest of ties, all will be well. Your father is sure to forgive—hearken, dearest to the voice of love."

"No," said Eveline in faltering tones, "I cannot leave my father. I am bound to him by ties which cannot be broken thus easily. I am the only relic of a most unhappy marriage, and harsh and stern as he may be to others, me he loves, and were I to act thus rashly 'twould break his heart. Have patience, Will. My father believes me still the affianced bride of Sir Guiscard—let me disabuse his mind, and by degrees he may allow me to select the man of my choice. Do agree to this."

"If it must be so, then be it as you will. But I can never see you—months may pass without an interview. I shall live upon the rack."

"I shall ride often in the forest, and when I can, in your direction. You know, Will, I must pay a visit to your charming sisters."

"Thanks—from my heart thanks—but——"

"What?" said Eveline, noticing that he hesitated.

"If resolved to separate us they will put a watch upon you, and you may neither come nor send."

"I will meet you here. Come through the secret passages of the subterraneous vaults, and every Sabbath eve I will be there. But I had forgotten—I have sent forth a maiden of mine to tell Little John of your mishaps."

"Ever thoughtful and good," said Will; "but hush! some one comes this way."

Eveline said not a word, but pushing open the entrance of one of the side chapels, drew the young man after her just as Sir Norman Malvoisin entered the chapel followed by the earl.

CHAPTER XX.

AN APPARITION.

BOTH were intensely excited, but the knight was horrible to behold. Just relieved from his painful situation in the dungeon by the man-at-arms, who had received the key from Zorah, he had rushed to where the earl was in company with the prior of Jovaulx, and without any ceremony had dragged him out, telling his story by the way.

"Why, in the foul fiend's name, brother of mine, have you allowed this secret to be penetrated by ——"

"Hush! recollect where we are. Of that say nothing. I know my duties and my rights. But that this Saxon knave should have become possessed of so much knowledge is terrible."

"What have you done?"

"Sent Hubert and Regnold to scour the forest, and my eastern slaves to scour the forest from the forest entrance. If they find him, he dies."

"And well he merits such a guerdon," said the earl, hotly; "for it is not meet one of our serfs should know such a secret and live. And yet, brother, could you have spared this youth, I should have been glad, for he saved my child."

"For which he would have asked her as recompense, with the inheritance of all your broad lands," sneered Sir Norman.

"A man might do a worse thing than make a daughter happy," mused the earl; "methinks the girl looked at him with favour, and yet my word is pledged to Sir Guiscard."

"Mate a free hawk of the old race with one of these sottish Saxon churls?"

"We must not forget that there was an aristocracy before us, and that it will assert itself anew."

"Never."

"'Tis not worthy of dispute. We are now of one mind: the secret of the dungeon and the cave must be preserved. Do you think your men were in time?"

"I believe so. I was released almost immediately, and my first task was to open the secret postern to pass the Saracens. 'Twas to await their report I brought you hither."

"The knaves tarry," said the earl, impatiently; "do but these outlaws learn this way into our stronghold, we shall never hold our own. Hark! they knock."

A dull rumbling sound was heard behind the tomb already alluded to, and then it opened, and two men in the dress of an eastern clime came forth, holding a torch on high.

These men wore silver collars round their throats, and bracelets of the same metal upon their swarthy legs and arms, of which the latter were naked from the elbow, and the former from mid-leg to ankle.

Their dresses were characterised by silk and embroidery, while they were armed with crooked sabres, having the hilt and baldric inlaid with gold, and matched with Turkish daggers of costly workmanship.

They were simply negro slaves, some few of which seem to have been imported into this country by the crusaders.

Sir Norman spoke hastily in some foreign language, to which the others replied briefly, but with manifest regret and confusion.

"They have seen no sign of him. The villain has escaped."

"He cannot have gone far," cried the earl. "Take, then, a score of lances, scour the forest, and," he added, in a hoarse voice, "let him not live to bawl our secret."

"Bravely spoken, my brother!" said Sir Norman, with an infernal grin. "I will find him, never fear, if I hunt him to his den."

"No; once at earth, he is safe for the present. We may not envenom matters just now, when discontent is rife, by invading the privacy of any Saxon dwelling. The churls grunt enough already."

"Leave all to me; I will have my revenge, and yet not ruffle a feather of these savage island cocks," cried the knight, who strode out of the chapel, after giving orders to his Saracens.

In five minutes more, to the martial sound of a kind of trumpet, a score of lances were collected in the castle yard, with Sir Norman at their head—the slaves riding in the rear.

The soldiers were mounted on stout Flemish or Norman steeds, and armed with lance and cross-bow; a small battle-axe also hanging to their sides, in the ordinary fashion of the day.

But the slaves were more picturesque in their appearance. Each of them bore at his saddle-bow a bundle of darts or javelins, about four feet in length, having sharp steel heads—a weapon much in use among the eastern nations, and still known as djereeds.

The horses of these black attendants were apparently as foreign as their riders. They were of Saracenic origin, and consequently of Arabian descent.

Their fine slender limbs, small fetlocks, thin manes, and easy, springy motion, formed a marked contrast with the large-jointed, heavy horses of the Norman soldiers, bred especially to carry men-at-arms in all the panoply of plate and mail.

Nothing could have been conceived more picturesque than this cavalcade as, leaving the arched barbican, they rode down the sloping sward towards that forest it was their task to scour.

Meanwhile, Will Scarlett and Eveline were left alone; the latter trembling with mingled anger and fear, the former full of scorn at the villainous intentions entertained towards him.

"You have heard," said Will Scarlett, pressing the maiden to his side.

"I have heard. What, then?"

"What hope is there for us?"

"Will Scarlett, we are young. Let us be brave, nor repine because a slight stumbling block lies in our path. I cannot surrender up my father, because I have heard him use hot and passionate words—words which, though they burn my very soul, the tears of a loving daughter will wash out. Be patient, and feel that come weal come woe I am still faithfully yours—till death."

"I will believe you," said Will, as cheerfully as a lover ever can whose mistress will not run away with him; "and now must fain take my leave."

"No! I will accompany you to the outlet of the cavern. I shall need to know its windings."

Will Scarlett made no demur to this, and in another moment the two faithful, short acquainted lovers, had passed into the stone chamber.

Their only means of guiding their steps was the small lamp left by Zorah, which, after being trimmed up, gave a faint glimmer of light—just enough to prevent their tripping over the many loose stones from the roof which intercepted their progress.

The flight of steps which led from the chapel to the vaulted chamber was very steep and narrow, so that Will Scarlett walked first, lantern in one hand, while with the other he held the taper fingers of the proud Norman girl.

Suddenly both stood still in silent horror and alarm.

They had distinctly heard the click of the machinery that moved the tombstone above.

They were followed.

Both cast their eyes upward in expectation of seeing the flaring torches of men-at-arms.

All was still and dark, and yet from some strange instinct or superstitious dread both felt that *something* was behind them.

Have you never felt this strange sensation in the dark when ascending a flight of stairs, and hurried quicker to get over the sensation?

Eveline and Will Scarlett were in another minute in the

vaulted chamber, and concealed behind a pillar of lime-stone, in a niche of which the lamp was hidden.

Then they heard something pass.

It went by with a rustle as of flowing silk.

It had no footstep.

The strongest minds of that age believed in apparitions.

Unable to endure the horror of darkness, Will Scarlett suddenly pulled forth his lamp.

Then both saw something white disappear up the narrow passage which led to the forest.

But they also saw an awful face, livid flesh, glaring eyes and chattering teeth—and then it was gone.

" Let me go back," faltered Eveline.

" I will accompany you, dearest," said Will Scarlett.

" No, no !" continued the courageous girl, rousing her-self, " the weakness was but momentary. I have done no mortal sin that I should fear visits from those who have passed away. I have my rosary, my consecrated cross, and I will forward. How shall I learn to tread these passages alone, if I do not venture with you ? Methinks it was a coinage of the brain."

" We *both* saw and heard it," mused Will Scarlett, as they proceeded on their way.

But as nothing occurred of further moment, we at once bring them to the end of their journey.

CHAPTER XXI.

THE MEETING.

THE issue of the subterranean passage was in a dense thicket at the foot of the stony hill upon which the castle was built, and was, though narrow, lofty.

It was, however, on a steep ascent and so shaded by ivy and other vegetable growths as to be in little danger of discovery.

It was now the afternoon, while, bordering the pathway which led through the thicket, the trees were so thick and their boughs so interwoven that it was quite dark.

Presently the heads of Will Scarlett and Eveline might have been seen under the ivy in very close proximity.

They were bidding one another a long and fond farewell.

Their loving embrace was interrupted in a startling way.

" Surely something passed on the path. I did but bow my head a moment."

" Fell fast asleep," growled the other in a sleepy tone.

" Well, I may have nodded—but my ears were not asleep, for I heard a rustling on the path and then a deep sigh."

" 'Tis the youth escaping," said the other, " let's after him. We are fleet of foot, and then our cross-bows are sure. A hundred marks for him is pay worth trying for."

Then they saw two stalwart men at arms rise from under some deep underbrush and run along the pathway.

Will Scarlett hastily kissed his promised bride once more and then hurried after the ruffians.

By the care of Zorah he had found, on his first reaching the vaulted chamber, all his weapons. His trusty bow, his shafts his staff, were all in his possession, and clutch-ing these he felt himself a match for any two hired men-at-arms. At all events, he had resolved to defend himself to the last drop of his blood, though hoping to be spared to punish Sir Norman.

The golden sun was touching the tree tops with a magic pencil, and the bright and warm daylight was fading into the crepuscular evening, the leaves of the forest trees were of a rich brown hue, as passing through the dense thicket Will Scarlett came out upon an opening in the trees where the full force of day still lingered.

In the distance he could see the two ruffians hurrying along on the supposed track of the fugitive.

Will smiled, and but that gentle thoughts were in his head, would have sent two shafts after them to quicken their motions.

His duty to himself and Eveline was now to reach home as soon as possible, and be still until an opportunity was afforded of his claiming the promised boon in the face of day.

Born and bred in the forest, the son of the house of Gammel had no hesitation in making his way.

There were several pathways before him, but that which led most directly to his home was the same which had been taken by the two men-at-arms.

Gaily and jauntily then, Will Scarlett walked along, keeping his eyes, however, fixed a long way in advance, in case the ruffian soldiers should try an ambuscade.

It was a night for the minions of the moon, the forest glades at sundown at once being flooded with a light so bright as to indicate to the eye every bough and leaf.

The chaste planet sailed in a sea of azure dotted by stars.

For some time Will Scarlett had been descending a wood-clad slope towards a purling brook.

The opposite side was one of the finest and most mag-nificent specimens of English forest that could be seen. It was a mighty expanse covered by trees of vast growth, chiefly the glorious oak, with its gnarled and fanciful branches overspreading huge circumferences of grass-green turf.

Ascending one over the other like a terrace, their full grandeur became apparent to the eye.

But little time had Will Scarlett to examine the scene, his attention being otherwise engaged.

From where he stood he could see a well-known ford of the river, easily passable by horsemen, and having stepping stones tolerably close together for footmen.

On each side were low bushes. Now, behind a clump of willows, with their drooping garb of pale green, stooped the two men he had recently seen, in waiting for himself, in ambush.

Their cross-bows were bent, and their eyes fixed upon a pathway which led under the magnificent oaks, to the ford.

Will Scarlett laid himself flat upon the ground and listened.

There was the measured tread of a lady's palfrey, and with that the tramp of men approaching, all unconscious of their imminent danger.

The two ruffians evidently thought their prey near enough, for suddenly their bows twanged, and the short bolts sped through the air.

Will Scarlett heard a long shriek. It was that of a woman.

Swift as the very arrow he was about to let fly, it was fitted to the bow, and just as the villains aimed their second discharge, one fell with a bull-like roar, and then rising, ran away with the cloth-yard long arrow sticking in the least honourable, but most prominent, part of his person.

His shrieks indicated that the pain was excessive.

Suddenly he stopped, pulled forth the barbed shaft, and sank bleeding on the ground.

The other soldier would also have fled, but discharging a second arrow, which wounded him in the shoulder, Will Scarlett was, as it were, at one bound, upon him, striking him to the earth just as up came Little John leading the horse upon which rode the page.

" What have we here ? " said the burly outlaw ; " as I live, Will Scarlett ! This is good tidings, by St. Barnabas ! How escaped you ?—did the Norman earl relent ? "

" Thy questions are neither few nor easily answered," said Will Scarlett in reply ; " but this is worth knowing. Sir Norman Malvoisin, with two score of lances, is scouring the forest to take my life. I have promised the Lady Eveline I will return home and abide her influence with her father."

" Gammel House will stand a good siege," said Little John, drily, " and you will indeed be safest there. We will see thee on thy road. But what of thee, sir page ?——"

" Which page is the handmaiden—Rose ? " put in Will.

" You are right, and I would not any harm befel her. If the ruffian men-at-arms of Malvoisin be abroad, she is safer under our charge than journeying homeward."

" I would return to my mistress," said Rose.

" And so you shall, saucy boy," laughed Little John ; " but we must e'en escort our friend here first."

Rose making no further objections, the wounded soldiers were left to find their way as best they might, after nar-rowly escaping hanging to the nearest oak.

But Little John reproved the zeal of his followers, making use of some wise saw about tempering justice with mercy.

Again the cavalcade was in motion up the slope, shaded by the huge oaks and beeches—following a well-beaten path, flooded at intervals by streams of moonlight.

Half an hour brought them to the summit, after which the forest resumed its usual appearance of dense undergrowth surmounted by lofty trees, until at length again reaching a bottom, they were compelled to cross a marsh overgrown with bulrushes, water-flags, and aquatic plants.

A narrow causeway of a winding character was the only pathway; and upon this the whole party entered—Little John going first, then the palfrey, then Will Scarlett and the outlaws.

But at the same moment the air rang with a wild and furious cry.

"Down with the Saxon knaves! Strike, men, strike! Let not one cub escape to tell the tale."

At the same moment, Sir Norman Malvoisin and a party of his lances rushed from the deep shelter of a row of oaks, and came dashing through the bog at the astounded foresters.

The part acted by the several members of the band of outlaws was peculiar.

Little John spoke not a word, but took to his heels with a speed and activity that astounded his followers, the palfrey compelled by main force to follow.

Will Scarlett, after taking a backward glance to see how far the wood was off, stood firm and met the advancing men-at-arms with a flight of arrows that unhorsed one, sent three to the ground drawn down by their horses, shot in the breast, and put the whole troop in confusion.

"Strike, Normans, strike!" roared the knight as he dashed at Will Scarlett, waving in his hand a ponderous battleaxe.

Will Scarlett was active as well as strong, and skilfully evading the blow, he struck the knight a blow upon the head which startled him.

Then the horse, struck by Will Scarlett, reared, and but for the skilful horsemanship of the rider, he would have been thrown.

The outlaws, whose short swords were of little use to them against the lances of their foes, were compelled to act on the defensive, striking up the long spears with their quarterstaves—a process only possible from the awkward position in which the men-at-arms were placed, up to their horses' girths in mud and entangled aquatic weeds.

Meanwhile the knight, foaming with rage, returned to the charge; the mighty axe again poised ready for destruction.

The knight was a powerful man and well disciplined in the use of the weapons of a barbaric age—such as spear, lance, axe, and sword—while Will Scarlett, though admirable in the field as a quarterstaffer, full well knew that he could not long contend against the mailed Sir Norman.

His object therefore must be to unhorse him.

Leaping on one side, at the risk of sinking in the bog, Will Scarlett let fall a blow on the crupper of the horse, which made the noble steed plunge and rear in a way that forced the knight once more to look to his own safety.

But the young man followed up his advantage by whirling the club-like pole round his head, and bringing it to bear with such force on the rider, that both horse and master staggered, and then fell.

Several of the soldiers hastened at once to the assistance of their master, who rose foaming with rage, and so besmeared with mud as to be scarcely recognisable.

But his voice rang louder than ever, as again clutching his axe he advanced along the causeway on foot.

It was quite clear which way the battle was going. The soldiers, superior in numbers and arms, were pressing close upon the outlaws, all of whom were wounded, while one lay stretched at full length on the edge of the pathway, dead.

But they yielded not, and sullenly defended themselves with the determination of men who fight with a halter round their necks.

Meanwhile the weather had changed. The sun had long since gone down, and the moon which had erst been so bright was concealed by masses of dark and massive clouds, whence issued, shortly after the fight began, loud and terrible claps of thunder, attended with quick and successive flashes of lightning.

A fearful tempest had commenced.

The combatants, despite the desperation with which they fought, could hear the grating of branches of forest trees, while the clatter of heavy rain soon followed, which, mingled with the loud rumbling thunder—now near, now afar off—sounded like the grand but fearful rolling of the ocean.

The avenues of the forest grew darker and darker, and where the trees stood they formed a black impenetrable barrier.

"Strike, Saxons, strike!" roared Will Scarlett, above the din of storm and battle; "strike for your liberties and lives—blood is all the Norman tyrant seeks! Let him drink his own, or mingle it with the black waters of the marsh."

"The foul fiend take me, if you hang not on yonder riven oak ere the moon sets," said the knight, pressing onwards.

Scarcely had he spoken, when there came a lurid flash that seemed to fill the forest with light, followed by a deep and awful peal of thunder.

A mighty oak, which stood about fifty yards from the scene of combat, was struck, and rent into a thousand shivers.

Saxon and Norman cast a terrified glance around, gazing with awe and wonder at the sudden destruction, when, with a loud shout, there poured from the nearest thicket a score of lances, who, rushing up, at once overwhelmed and captured the outlaws and Will Scarlett.

As if waiting for the issue of the battle, the storm, which had exhausted itself in one mighty last effort, ceased, and the forest was once more still.

"Ah! we have the thieves," said the knight, remounting his steed, which had extricated itself from the bog, "and dearly shall they pay for their insolence. Drive them before you to dry ground, and choose a stalwart oak with a bough for each. Where are the Saracens?"

The soldiers, who were now nearly thirty in number, marshalled themselves ten in front, after which the prisoners, with a horseman on each side, then the main body, while the baron came last.

The causeway only admitted of four abreast, but as they approached the side of the marsh to which Little John had fled, the ground became harder and better, while tall bushes and small trees took the place of aquatic plants on both sides.

At that moment the blast of a horn was heard close to them, so loud, so near and startling, as to cause several of the horses to rear.

"Stand fast by the prisoners, cut down the knaves an' they would escape!" shouted the knight.

In an instant, and ere the echoes of the first horn had died away, another blast was heard in the distance, quite as loud and long; and ere the men-at-arms were able to see their antagonists, they were saluted by such a shower of arrows as scattered their forces, for the horses wounded, terrified, and startled, became for a moment unmanageable.

"Close round the captured thieves!" roared Sir Norman, riding full tilt at the outlaws.

But a deep and sedgy bog lay between him and the foresters, who now appeared on the skirt of the wood, full fifty in number, and all discharging with amazing rapidity a cloud of cloth-yard shafts, which made the horses plunge and rear in a way that fully occupied the attention of the men-at-arms.

"Spawn of hell!" shrieked the knight, whose passion had completely got the better of him; "let not a prisoner escape, scatheless! Cut them down—spare none!"

And as he spoke he rode back towards his men, who were fully engaged in quieting their horses, over which they had lost all control.

Not an outlaw was to be seen. The prisoners had escaped and the attacking band had vanished.

CHAPTER XXII.

WHAT SIR NORMAN MET.

IT would be hard to describe the fury of the knight when he found that the rescue had been complete, and that all that remained of the combat was the change of his band of gay men-at-arms into a sorely wearied body of besmeared ruffians, who crowded up together as if for protection against their angry master.

"The foul fiend seize the villains! But my punishment is but adjourned. If I burn Sherwood Forest down tree by tree, I will trace these outlaws and punish them, too. By the rood, they shall rue the day they crossed my path; but this is idle talk. My first task shall be to capture this insolent springal Will Scarlett. You know Gammel House?"

"We do."

"Disperse—go as you will—follow the most secret and private pathways of the forest ; but at daybreak be all of you in ambuscade around it. I will be there."

The men-at-arms made no reply, but not without casting strangely suspicious glances around, as if believing the outlaws were still in ambush, entered the forest one by one, and disappeared.

The knight, with his two Saracen attendants, who rode at a respectful distance, remained in the open glade.

Now the truth is, that Sir Norman Malvoisin had reason for remaining behind. What with the bruises he had received from the quarterstaff of Will Scarlett and the contusions which had ensued upon his fall, he was sore all over, and utterly unable to keep up with his men with that erect and manly bearing which became the flower of chivalry.

His plan was, however, despite his fatigue, to ride slowly forward, pushing in the direction of Gammel House as long as his horse could bear him or he sit in his saddle.

It was truly not a night for forest travelling, as, though one storm had passed away, another could be heard rumbling in the distance, while a faint glare of far-off lightning illumined the wood at intervals.

But there were passions raging in the bosom of the Norman knight which made him utterly indifferent to the war of the elements.

He was nursing his wrath to keep it warm, and hugging himself with the idea that his revenge would be swift and terrible.

Despite his brother's warning, he thought of nothing less than the destruction of the whole Gammel family, and scattering the ashes of their house to the four winds of heaven.

In his black heart there was no thought of mercy.

Silently and sullenly he rode along, only once now and then lifting his eyes to see that his steed was going in the right direction, communing with himself as to the best way to compass his revenge without compromising himself too much, or offending his powerful brother.

Devising thus, he advanced slowly until he came to the commencement of a long, picturesque, and pleasant forest ride, in which nature had displayed one of her marvellous fancies.

It was an avenue as complete, regular, and well proportioned as if it had been the work of an artistic hand. For more than a mile there was a road of green and grassy sward, fifty yards wide, bordered all the way on both sides by a row of magnificent oaks.

The spot was a favourite rendezvous of the chase, and the knight's way was directly through it.

The Saracens were a long way behind, and the knight in a wild reverie.

Suddenly his horse shied, thrust his fore legs wide apart, and stood stock still.

"So ho ! my sturdy steed," said the baron, rousing himself. "Art fatigued ?—a little way longer, and you shall have rest and food."

But though he jerked the reins and stuck his heels into the sides of his horse, it moved not.

"The fiend is in thee as well as in the accursed body of Will Gammel, whom Satan assoyle."

A loud mocking laugh, close in the knight's face, made him start.

At the same moment there was a quick flash of lightning, and the knight saw——

What did he see?

That he could scarcely have told at the time, though the memory never faded from his brain.

Erect, motionless, with bloodless face and lurid eyes, with livid cheeks and hollow jaws, sat upon a tall white horse, spectral and gaunt, the white figure of a woman, whose skeleton finger pointed directly at the knight ; while from her eyes darted rays of light that seemed to blind him.

Not if the yawning abyss of hell had opened beneath his feet could Sir Norman Malvoisin have felt and expressed more terror.

With a cry as of a maniac let loose, he drove his spurs into the sides of his noble steed, which plunged, reared, and then finally yielding to the mastery of man, started off furiously up the avenue.

"Hah ! ha ! ha !" shrieked the apparition behind.

The knight glanced fearfully over his shoulder, and

nearly fell off his horse, as he found the white gibbering face of the phantom woman quite close to him.

And such a face—one he knew too well.

'Tis said that our crimes are the scorpion whips that lash our consciences to frenzy. Certainly had not the soul of Sir Norman Malvoisin pleaded guilty to some awful crime, he had not felt such abject terror, such unmitigated horror as now convulsed him.

For the moment all presence of mind, all prudence, all feeling of native courage and resolution was gone.

His only object in life was to escape the foul fiend! which he believed was chasing him—but why in that fearful shape ?

On ! on ! went the horse and rider, each now apparently as eager as the other to cover the ground and escape the contact of the spectre.

On ! on ! close to the knight, now on one side, now on the other, rode the huge white steed, close beside the clattering hoofs of the Flemish stallion—*but itself giving no sound.*

Sir Norman had ceased to look back. The vision was too horrible, but he felt it was there.

The avenue is passed, the narrow paths of the forest, the scattered open glades, the occasional marshes are traversed. A brook intervenes. It is leaped, but still the Norman pursues his mad career, and still the white horse with its ghostly rider is close behind.

"A malison on the night !" muttered the knight ; "would but the day break, this hideous phantom must avaunt."

But still he spurred, and whipped and urged his steed. The poor animal went bravely on, but at every step exhibited fresh signs of distress.

This awful race could not last much longer. The steed tottered, his kness began to bend, and Sir Norman, in utter desperation, looked round to see if he was gaining on his pursuer.

The phantom was close to his elbow.

With a curse that waked the echoes of the forest, the White Cross Knight lifted his whip, struck his gallant steed between the ears, and bending his head low, pressed his knees into the animal's sides.

With a fearful cry, a neigh—but one of terror and pain—the noble animal leaped forward, fell, threw his master headlong against a tree, and next instant lay helpless by his side.

Like a storm-cloud—like a whirlwind—the white steed and rider passed on, and the Norman was alone.

The moonlight streamed from between the leafy boughs, the sky was unclouded, the wind scarcely sighed, when Sir Malvoisin sat up, and, gathering together his scattered senses, looked around.

"Have I dreamed a dream," he muttered, "or was it her ? Gone ! vanished—well 'tis past. Be still my beating heart—what care we for the beings of another world ? They cannot harm us."

And he rose to his feet, though scarcely able to stand upright.

Below him was a small turf-pit, in which lay his horse, quite dead, as a summary examination proved.

What was to be done ?

"Ah ! a light in yonder trees. Some cotter who dares show fire after curfew. I must crawl yonder and crave shelter, for I fear me I shall not sit saddle for some days."

Leaning on a stick he tore from a tree, the knight tottered forward, forced his way through a small thicket, and found himself in front of one of the better sort of houses, appertaining to the Saxon yeomanry.

Advancing as best he might to the oaken doorway, he struck it with his mailed fist.

No answer came though there was plainly a light within.

He knocked again.

"Who is without ?" said a thin, cracked voice—that of one aged and weak. "What want you ?"

"Shelter for one wounded and suffering. I can see thy blazing logs, good man ; open that I may warm myself."

"Art alone ?"

"Quite alone—my horse lies dead in your peat-pit close at hand."

Slowly the bolts were undone and the knight admitted. At sight of the noble all started back in affright and terror—such visits nearly always boding evil to those to whom they were made.

"Fear not, good people," said the knight, taking off

his helmet and exhibiting to view his livid face, " I have been set upon by thieves and escaped but narrowly. All I ask is refreshment and leave to rest in your upper chamber until my servants find me, or I have strength to take my departure."

No words were spoken. The inhabitants of the hut saw that the man spoke truth, and though as a Norman soldier—such they judged him to be—they felt an instinctive dread and horror of him; yet did hospitality overcome every other feeling, and in five minutes a smoking supper was on the board, with a flagon of ale.

The knight ate sparingly, but he gladly quaffed a goodly draught of ale, after which he asked to be shown his chamber; which was done and he entered it and lay down, seemingly without having taken a glance at those within the cottage.

But they little knew Sir Norman Malvoisin.

CHAPTER XXIII.

IN THE COTTAGE.

THE inmates of the forest hut were three: an aged man and woman, and a young girl of singular and almost matchless beauty.

Not sixteen, with fair golden hair that clothed her head and neck in a cloud of sunshine, with blushing cheeks rivalling the rose, a small forehead, soft round chin and dove-like eyes, that yet read your very soul, lips of ruddy hue, all but pouting to be kissed, she was indeed in her innocence, youth, and delicate loveliness, the very creature to strike the fancy of the lawless and licentious noble.

As the door closed upon the knight, the door of a closet opened, and one in forest garb stepped forward with brow as black as midnight.

"A curse on the fate that brought that man hither," he said. "Villain and murderer! But that he has eat of your bread and tasted of your salt, I would slay him as he lies. But I will take care he leaves not here unscathed; and yet," he added, "this lesson may suffice him. I have token of work to be done. Be it so. But as you value your lives and the honour of this dear child, despatch her ere morn."

"Who is the soldier?" asked Gilbert Hyde, fearfully.

"Sir Norman Malvoisin," said the forester bitterly.

"Merciful Virgin! save us," cried the woman. "Then this is no place for dear Becky Gammel."

It was, indeed, the sister of Will Scarlett, on a visit to her foster-mother or nurse, where she had been detained by the sudden storm.

"You are forewarned," said the forester, in continuation, "and beware of the wolf's fangs. Fare thee well! Commend me to thy brother."

With which the man in Lincoln green went forth into the dark and gloomy forest.

The old people, who had been detained up so late by the arrival of their forest friend, now determined to seek repose, in order to hurry Becky away in the early morn; for they now considered her nowhere safe but in her own happy home. We say happy, for believing in his escape, the outlaw, who knew all about the adventures of Will Scarlett, had given no hint of the dangers he had escaped.

All had arisen and were about to cover up the fire, when again they were startled by a loud knocking against the oaken door—a thwack that betokened a right sturdy arm.

"Go thy ways," said the old woman querulously, "there be wild folks abroad, and it behoves poor people to be careful."

"Good Mother Gerty, an' you open not to red-haired Will, you are no true woman," cried a laughing voice.

"My brother!" cried Becky, with the dove-like eyes.

All were too busy to note that while this conversation had been going on the door above had opened, and the pale ghastly face of the knight been protruded, as if prompted by curiosity to discover who it was had so rapidly followed him.

As soon as he heard what passed, a Satanic smile illumined his countenance.

"His sister!" he hissed though his clenched teeth; "ha! ha! The revenge will be sweet."

And he closed the door.

Meanwhile the party outside had been admitted, and proved to consist of Will Scarlett, Little John, the page, and four outlaws, all of whom were welcomed to the hut in the most affectionate and hospitable manner.

After the first few moments of sweet recognition on the part of brother and sister, the latter suddenly paused, and motioning for silence pointed up-stairs.

"What is it, my darling girl?" asked Will Scarlett, stroking down her golden hair.

"One lies sick up stairs we have cause to hate and fear," she said.

"Who, in Heaven's name?" asked Will.

"Sir Norman Malvoisin," she replied.

There was a silence as of death. All appeared overwhelmed with astonishment, when a few minutes later Becky told the manner of his arrival.

"He has cast himself into the jaws of death," said Little John grimly, "and he shall surely die."

"A mighty deed shall be done this night," added Will Scarlett, "that shall make our tyrants tremble."

"If you mean harm to the Norman," cried Becky, "it may not be. He has sought shelter of our roof-tree, he has eaten of our bread and of our salt, and he must depart in peace."

A deep murmur passed through the assembly, and then all acquiesced in the justice of the maiden's decision.

"We have but brief time for rest," said Will, after a moment's thought, "let us take it."

And setting an example to the others, he cast himself on the ground, and soon all slept—the page and Rebecca retiring to a small closet.

The old man and woman disappeared in some mysterious closet.

All was still and silent, for the whole of the party were fatigued and exhausted.

CHAPTER XXIV.

THE ABDUCTION.

THE crowing of cocks heralding the morn aroused the whole party, and despite their previous arduous journey, the travellers were up with the rest, ready to do justice to the good fare which the hospitable well-to-do yeoman had provided.

But none were laggards, all being desirous of reaching Gammel House as soon as possible; while Little John, who already felt the power of fascination universally exercised by the bold outlaw, longed to rejoin Robin Hood, the king of the forest glade.

About an hour after dawn, while the dew drops were heavy on the grass, and the trees sparkled in the rays of the rising sun, the cavalcade set out in very much the same order as before, except that on a pillion behind the bright-eyed page rode Rebecca Gammel.

Soon the golden rays of the summer sun fell brightly on all nature as they advanced, steeping the landscape in rich purple light, that blazed upon tree, upland, and wild heath, to say nothing of the hamlets, which, as if by common consent, were studiously avoided.

All nature appeared as if robed in her holiday garb, and Rose and Becky, chattering as they went, were never tired of listening to the sweet music poured forth from a thousand bills in glade, in thicket, and secluded den.

Travelling was necessarily slow through the dense forest, and it would be nearly sundown ere the house of Gammel was reached. A halt was therefore necessary at midday, both for man and beast.

A halt was therefore declared at a spot selected by Will Scarlett, where often he had come to listen to the dreamy voices of his soul and imagine that which now was a reality.

It was by the side of a little babbling brook, that ran over golden sand and shining pebbles, as clear, pellucid, and much sweeter than any filtered water that ingenuity has invented.

This brook was naturally in a valley, but a valley of a peculiar character. It was so secluded, retired, and lost to general observation, as to have been rarely visited even by the oldest inhabitants of the forest.

Passing by a winding path through high fern, six feet at least from the ground, a path made by Will Scarlett, this secret haunt of the timid doe and fawn, and, for what we know, of the fairies, was reached.

A green sward retreating about twelve feet from the bank, and extending thirty feet perhaps along it, lay before them, while to protect them from the ardent rays of the sun that promised to be intensely hot, stood a huge oak, such a one as for a thousand years has stood the brunt of the storm, and at last fallen in glorious old age upon the sward—we mean Herne's Oak.

LITTLE JOHN AND GERUTH ATTACKED BY THE NORMANS.

But the oak of Sherwood Forest—Will Scarlett's oak—was a thing of most marvellous growth and dimensions, so that its boughs waved over a vast expanse of ground, and might have sheltered a small army of footmen.

All were delighted, and Rose and Rebecca most, for the dell was full of flowers, and after snatching a hasty meal they left the men to take solid refreshment; while they, shaking the dew from many a sweet wild flower with their delicate feet, proceeded to gather a garland of honey-dropping woodbines.

The outlaws warned them not to go far, but had not the heart to put any further restriction on the gambols of the two children of nature, wandering to all appearance like a juvenile Adam and Eve in this terrestrial Paradise.

The outlaws and our two heroes had either more substantial appetites, or they enjoyed the repose, for they remained reclining on the sward, with good work for their teeth, not forgetting strong October ale, for nearly half an hour.

Then the forest rang with piercing shrieks that brought each man to his feet in an instant of time.

They gazed wildly and vacantly around, as if bewildered, and then rushed in the direction from which the shrieks came.

But as faithful chroniclers devoted to the fair, we must follow in the footsteps of Rose and Rebecca and explain the causes which led to this fearful interruption of the quiet and seclusion of that charming forest dell.

These two fair creatures were but children after all, just budding into beauteous womanhood, and had all the ways of children. Basking in the sunny rays that fell aslant the trees, they wandered hand in hand, a lovely and innocent pair, until they reached a spot which seemed suited to their fancy.

The earth was here still carpeted with turf, soft and smooth and curt as that of a lawn, but it was also spangled with flowers that perfumed the air with their rich fragrance.

It was a true ladies' bower, and not to be resisted by the two girls.

They sank down upon a bank and began a cheerful prattle—half wisdom, half nonsense—such as nature's innocents are apt to indulge in.

Singularly, they got to talking of men !

Girls of their age will somehow carry the male sex in their heads.

"What a great mountain of a man that Little John is," said merry Rose, with a laugh.

"But as good as he is big. I know him," replied Rebecca. "Hist ! was that a fawn moved ?" she added.

The girls' voices became instantly hushed to listen, but a moment's pause convincing them they were wrong, they continued their conversation—Rebecca telling stories of her brother, of Little John his friend, and prattling of home, until the ladies' bower echoed with the music of their laughter.

But what is it comes creeping along the ground, behind the screen of hawthorn bushes and tall gorse ?—creeping like some huge snake of the tropics through tne slime of morass and swamp.

On it glides over grass and thicket, through bush and briar, until at length it seemed to gasp for breath, under the long diverging stems of an ash, the boughs of which grew close to the ground.

Then it paused, as if to take breath ; and then the bushes were pushed aside with so much noise, that Rose and Rebecca could no longer be mistaken.

They raised their eyes and saw before them the hideous faces, goggle eyes, and protruding tongues of the two negro slaves.

Paralysed with terror for one moment, and then recognising the human character of their assailants, the two girls rose and made the forest ring with their shrieks.

One moment only ; for the next instant the Saracen slaves had thrown cloths over their faces, and throwing them across their shoulders bounded into the thicket.

In two minutes more, hot with furious haste, up came the outlaws—Little John first, Will Scarlett second, the rest clustering behind.

Not a word was spoken until they reached an open glade, at one of which they saw the negroe smounted, with the apparently insensible girls before them.

A man-at-arms, or rather, knight, with his visor down, but whom all, by his size and appearance, knew to be Sir Norman, was seated on a lofty war-horse, giving them directions.

When he saw the outlaws he waved his drawn sword in derision, and turned to flee.

Too late.

As he turned and bent forward to start his horse, the joining of his armour at the small of his back, yawned ; and, ere he recovered himself, an arrow, sped from the bow of Will Scarlett, was quivering a foot deep in his body.

With a hideous groan he fell forward—dead upon his horse.

But the Saracen slaves—faithful unto death—snatched the horse's bridle ; and, next instant, all three steeds, with their strange burdens, had disappeared beneath the leafy arches of the forest.

But none the less had Will Scarlett slain the Norman knight. All stood still—doubly horrified. Two girls had been carried off in the most cruel and inhuman manner, and then one of their party had taken the life of one of their haughty rulers.

"Be not downhearted, boy," said the giant, who himself was as weak as a child under the fearful infliction. "Go thee home. See thy father and mother ; tell them the truth, and then seek the shelter of the forest. By that time the scattered bands of our merry men shall be gathered together."

"I will," cried the young man, wringing the other's hand ; "but in the meantime what will be the fate of the girls ?"

"Fear nothing. If the devil have not taken Sir Norman to himself, he is not fit to think of ladies. Ere he is, we will burn his tower about his ears. Go !"

And thus the outlaws parted from Will Scarlett, who, anxious to reach home, started across the forest with a quick and angry stride that betokened a mind ill at ease.

It was long after sunrise that the wearied traveller came within sight of his paternal dwelling.

It lay in the valley below—he, at the moment, descending a narrow pathway soon lost sight of it. He was now nearly home, and he trod the ground like some haughty king.

Suddenly he was brought to standstill, in a most unexpected manner.

CHAPTER XXV.

GERUTH.

He had reached a kind of platform, whence three paths diverged—a platform so thickly studded with huge and ancient oaks, that, though the sun shone brightly, still the thickness of the foliage threw a deep gloom over all, though at no great distance patches of sunlight could be clearly seen.

The undergrowth was composed of thickets, brakes, and coverts, where the shadows never ceased playing at hide-and-seek.

"One step further homeward, and you die ! " said a gruff voice. " Join me, and speak not until you are safe by my side."

Will Scarlett halted, instantly feeling for his arms ; but, as if re-assured by the voice, glanced keenly round, took one look through an opening at the old hall, the little huts of the vassals which raised their heads humbly over fruit and flower trees, and then strode under the oaks, ascended a steep and rugged path to the left, to find himself next moment in the presence of the speaker.

"Well, good Geruth," said Will Scarlett, in a low whisper ; " and why may I not advance lest I die ?"

" Because, master mine, there be twenty men-at-arms lie in wait to kill you——" replied Geruth.

Geruth is worthy of a brief description.

He was tall, and of a stern, savage, and extremely wild aspect. His costume added to the fierce appearance which nature had bestowed upon him, he being habited in a close jacket with sleeves, composed of the tanned hide of some animal, on which originally the hair had been left, but which had been worn off in so many places that it would have been difficult to distinguish, from such patches as remained, to what forest beast the fur had originally belonged.

This strange garment—an improvement on the nakedness of our earlier ancestors—reached from the neck to the knees, and included all the body-clothing worn by men of his class. It was put on like a shirt.

On his feet were sandals bound with thongs of boar's hide, while a roll of thin leather, artificially twined round the legs, left the knees bare, like those of the Scotch savages of the same date.

In order that the jacket might sit close to the body, it was drawn in at the middle by a broad leathern belt, fastened by a brass buckle, to one side of which was attached a sort of wallet, and to the other a ram's horn, with a mouthpiece for blowing.

He also wore a Sheffield whittle—that is, a long, broad, sharp-pointed, two-edged knife, made in the neighbourhood.

In two words, he carried a bowie-knife, for truly there is nothing new under the sun.

Cap he had none, though his thick, coarse, matted hair —of a rusty dark red colour—fully supplied its place.

This man, who further wore the thrall's collar—a brass ring like a dog collar—leaned on a huge club.

Despite his rugged ferocity and sullenness, the glance he gave Will Scarlett was affectionate and devoted.

"What kind of men are they ?" asked young Gammel, thoughtfully.

"The men-at-arms of Sir Norman Malvoisin," said Geruth, " whom God confound, and their purpose is your death."

"How know you ?"

"The knaves lie in ambush all round. My infernal porkers—whom St. Withold curse—were alarmed by their presence, and scattered abroad. I was fain to go in chase, and so doing, heard men speaking. Then saw I their ambush, and curious to know their wants, listened. Your name mentioned redoubled my attention, and I heard the villains—may the devil draw their teeth—say how their master desired they should compass your death."

"Thanks, my faithful Geruth," said Will Scarlett, taking the serf's hand ; " the die is cast. I must join the outlaws."

"Then may my porkers starve if I do not the same," cried Geruth.

"It may not be, good friend. You are yet my father's swineherd—though free you shall be. Come some little way through the wood, so that I tarry not here. I have messages to give you for my father."

"By St. Dunstan," replied Geruth, " your word shall be law with me. But hark ! what comes ?"

"'Tis the Norman soldiers," said Will Scarlett ; " we must even flee. I have that to do which makes my own life sacred."

And without another word, the young hero, followed by the rugged swineherd, dashed up the path just as seven or eight dismounted men-at-arms came in sight, and hurriedly followed the same way.

"'Twas he! That accursed Saxon hog we saw skulking about has split on us. To him—to him!"

And with the fierce remorselessness of bloodhounds, the Norman soldiers took up the trail of their English foes.

CHAPTER XXVI.

THE TRAIL.

IT must not e supposed that the wondrous art of following a trail, which is ascribed as well by historians as romancists to the redskins of North America, is at all peculiar to that race of men.

Every tribe, when in its savage state, necessarily possesses the faculty.

We can hardly describe our ancestors at the time of which we speak as savages, but there were peculiarities about their position which necessitated the possession of a craft now useless.

If it was the business of the outlaws to hide in Sherwood forest glades, it was the business of the hired men-at-arms to track them.

We have given but a faint idea of the vast extent and peculiar nature of the huge wood, if our readers do not understand that to follow a man therein on chance was mere folly.

There must be a connecting link between the pursuer and the pursued.

This connecting link was the trail.

The moment the leader of the Norman soldiers found that their prey had escaped them, he halted.

He knew perfectly well that one so experienced in woodcraft as the man they were pursuing would not long follow a beaten path.

The object was to see where the quarry left it to plunge into the labyrinthine thicket.

The grim soldier, though hot with haste, was both experienced and resolute. He knew that his promotion and the favour of his lord depended on his success.

He determined, therefore, to proceed with the utmost caution.

The ground was drier than usual, no rain having fallen for some days; but beneath forest trees, the soil, principally composed of decomposed leaves, is always to a certain extent damp.

"Steady, boys, steady," said the lieutenant, whose name was Julian; "we have cute foxes to deal with. Keep all behind, nor let your zeal outrun your patience. We must track this vermin to its lair. I knew it."

He pointed to a small grass-plot which they had now reached, and on which were clearly footmarks.

"There is where the cunning swineherd trod, and here the youth."

He paused. Not a mark indicated which way they had taken thence, and as the path ceased, because the forest became open, it was difficult indeed to know how to follow the chase.

"Spread, and pass not a brake or thicket without examination," said the chief soldier, with a dark frown, "keep within sight if you can—but when I wind a call come all to me."

And as he spoke he touched his horn, which dangled at his side.

The soldiers, who were all to be partakers of the reward, obeyed with alacrity.

The chief himself, however, had different ideas from his followers. He was a man of huge strength and wondrous determination. His notion was to follow up the trail himself, and if possible, capture Will Scarlett single-handed, in which case the reward would all be his.

He knew every inlet and outlet of the forest, and he made up his mind to search it thoroughly.

At least he believed he knew. But the outlaws could have showed secret and lonely retreats that would have astonished him.

He did not wander up and down, through brake, covert, alley, thicket and glade, but went steadily forward to the centre of the forest, where it was popularly believed that Robin Hood held his court.

There could, he thought, be no other safe shelter for the fugitive.

He was soon in a wide valley, where the waters permeating the slopes of the neighbouring hills collected and made the soil swampy.

The soldier's eyes gleamed with pride and satisfaction.

There, deeply indented in the soil, were the marks of the two men's feet.

Without running, the man-at-arms increased his pace, until it was quicker than a walk.

The trail was clear, apparent and easily followed. The fugitives in their hurry to escape, made no secret of the way they took.

The grim Norman pulled his moustaches and then saw to his weapons. He had two tough customers to deal with, and he knew it.

But he was as brave as a lion, and felt every confidence in his own strength and courage.

By degrees the valley grew narrower, the trees larger, and then the ground, sloping upwards, was drier.

Suddenly the footsteps ceased. The trail had vanished.

What was to be done? Those he was pursuing were not sprites to have vanished into thin air, and yet after scrutinising the ground in every direction, he saw no hiding-place.

They must have gone up the valley, for they could not have turned back without passing within sight.

Cross-bow in hand, drawn and bolted, he advanced with excessive caution, casting wary glances to the right and left.

But after a march of a quarter of a mile, though the ground was soft enough to indicate footsteps, he saw no sign.

He at once determined to go back, but at the same time to make a circle.

He had been keeping to the right hand of the valley at the foot of steep clay cliffs.

He now kept on the other side in order to explore every secret covert.

But no place did he see where a child could have concealed itself without discovery. Grinding his teeth with rage, the Norman soldier continued on his way, until he came to the spot whence he had started.

A fearful oath burst from his lips.

There, on the soft sward, were the marks of the two men's footsteps.

They were following him.

With a wild impulse, that deprived him for a moment of reason, he wound a loud and spirited call, and then dashed upon the track.

In ten minutes he had reached the head of the valley, the trail being now once more clear and defined.

The Norman was bewildered. How had those who had been before contrived to get behind?

"There is witchcraft in this," muttered the superstitious soldier.

The less principled, the more ruffianly the man, the more superstitious.

But, then, superstition is a moral plague, which infects the wicked and the grossly ignorant.

It has no more similitude to religion than brass has to gold.

Just as he spoke aloud, he received full in his breast, just where the heart should be pierced, a cloth-yard shaft from some powerful hand, for though it could not pierce his armour, it made him stagger.

His eyes flashed with rage as he glanced around, but he could not make out whence the arrow had sped.

A large tree was close at hand, behind which he took refuge, peering all the while in every direction, and listening with charmed ears for the slightest sound.

But nothing could he see but the blue sky, the green trees, and the flowers. Nothing could he hear, save the warbling of birds, and the gentle rustling of the summer birds in the trees.

His head was bent on one side, as in the act of intense listening. In this attitude he stood like a statue.

Something glanced in the sunlight, and then an arrow pinned him to the tree by the ear.

The Norman's cries resounded through the forest, so sudden and exquisite was the pain.

CHAPTER XXVII.

HIDDEN.

THE Norman was no coward, and this unmanly exhibition of feeling was over in an instant. The cries had been torn from him by surprise more than anything else.

Next minute he had broken the arrow in twain, and hearing his men coming up, had wound another call.

"Whose pig was that squeaked?" said the facetious man of the party.

"This pig," replied Julian, sternly, "and had you a Sherwood arrow through your ear, you would squeak too, my fine friend."

The man-at-arms sprang to cover, making himself as small as possible.

The officer smiled grimly, but made no other remark, and his whole band now coming up, they received orders to charge up the valley in a line. They did so, but no further violence was offered.

Again the extreme head of the valley was reached, and the whole party were about once more to plunge into the forest, when Julian gave a significant sign.

The whole party stood stock still in the attitude of listening.

The chief pointed to one foot mark and then to another. They trended in different directions. One down the valley whence they had come.

Like a bolt from a cross-bow, Julian sped back. He saw the error he had committed.

He had looked on the ground when he should have glanced up in the air.

We must, however, return to Will Scarlett, and his friend Geruth.

The young scion of the house of Gammel had been wandering about so long that his limbs began to be distressed.

His flight from the Norman soldiers was, therefore, very slow. He could at times not forbear halting, and at last his sufferings became so great that he sank almost lifeless at the foot of a tree.

Geruth had his daily allowance of strong ale in a leather bottle, from which he made the young man drink. The powerful tonic roused him somewhat, but nature will assert its sway, even with the boldest.

"I must rest and sleep, or die," said Will Scarlett.

Geruth looked around for a place where securely to hide his young master, but none offered.

Then he looked upwards amid the gnarled branches and leafy boughs of a huge oak, the pride of that part of the forest.

Will Scarlett understood him, and rousing himself with the other's assistance, ascended the tree, crept into the the very heart of it's recesses, and sank at once into a perfect stupor.

He was both physically and mentally exhausted.

Then Geruth, wary as the fox he loved to hunt, removed every sign that might guide the Normans to the tree.

Then he climbed one himself, taking care not to shake down a leaf or bough.

And there he waited the course of events with the patience of an Indian.

He had not long to wait ere he saw the Norman soldier come up, and, after noticing that the trail ended, rush up the valley.

Geruth, the Saxon, descending from his tree, followed at a safe distance, from which he saw the Norman turn back at the head of the valley.

He had Will Scarlett's bow in his possession, and he could not resist the impulse. The swineherd was the huntsman of the family. He never missed his aim.

Drawing his shaft to the head, he struck the soldier full in the breast. Then seeking to avoid the armour, he pinned Julian by the ear, taking flight immediately afterwards.

At the mouth of the valley were some rough unhewn stones, behind which Geruth concealed himself.

He had previously run some distance on the soft grassy sward, and then had returned where the ground was hard.

While the Normans were coming up, he was retreating in the direction where Will Scarlett was concealed.

As soon as he reached the spot where he had given the Norman chief officer "the double," he ascended the tree, replaced all Will Scarlett's arms, and having seen that he was in a dead sleep, descended from the tree, and, as if careless of consequences, cast himself on the ground under a tree at some little distance from the great gnarled oak.

Here he was found by Lieutenant Julian, snoring a fit concert for his own pigs.

"Saxon beast," roared the Norman, clutching him by the collar.

"He—augh," grunted the thrall swineherd, "what cheer, eh?"

"If you wake not, 'i the minute, every bone in your body shall be broken."

"Am I not free to walk these forests without molestation from robbers?" said Geruth, yawning, and then leaping to his feet.

"Villain! where is Will Scarlett?" cried the exasperated soldier.

"Don't know no such chap," said the swineherd, rubbing his eyes.

At the same moment the whole body of followers came running up.

"Pick out a stout branch," exclaimed the Norman, "and hang me this lad. His blood will fatten many a good English oak."

"Sir soldier," cried Geruth, with a dark and ominous frown, "I am a Saxon thrall—men call me serf; but ere I would do the coward act you would sear your conscience with, I would black my face and turn Saracen."

The soldier looked him full in the face, with a cold sarcastic smile.

"Tell me where Will Scarlett is, and you may live for what I care."

"I will show you," said Geruth, with a deep sigh. "Follow!"

The Norman, delighted at his victory, smiled at the soldiers. He fancied his peculiar style of diplomacy most insinuating, and already felt the excruciating delight of grasping the great reward.

"Be quick, knave! and more than pardon—you shall have a guerdon."

"What guerdon, master?" said Geruth, humbly.

"Even ten marks."

"I never," said Geruth, with a low bow, "saw so much money."

And Geruth, too delighted to lead the ruffian soldiers away from the dangerous sleeping-place of his master, plodded through the forest—after the valley had been crossed—careless of what became of himself, so that his young franklin escaped.

This was all very well for half an hour, at the end of which Julian began to be suspicious.

"Slave, take care—you lead us right, or die!" said the Norman chief.

"I can but use my discretion."

"Knave, what mean you?"

"As I know not where Will Scarlett is, this way is as good as another."

"That word is thy death passport," roared the infuriated officer.

"Not if this prisoner is aware of it," said a cold, sarcastic voice.

They were in a deep grove of elms.

The evening was cool and bright, and the leaves quivered under the gentle influence of the coming night air; the birds, swarming in elm, oak, and beech, sang lullaby, just as, stepping forth with all the cool assurance of a practised outlaw, Little John stepped the way.

"One of the prisoners, by St. Mark!" roared the angry soldier.

"Silence! base and truculent knave."

"One for his heels," replied the giant, mildly.

When we say mildly, we allude to his words, for at the same moment he aimed at Lieutenant Julian's head a blow that, as he afterwards graphically expressed it, made him see seventeen evening stars—all at once.

Hitherto, Geruth had been silent, but by no means unobservant. With a swing of his fearful cudgel, he smote, not exactly hip and thigh, but thereabouts, two potent men-at-arms, who fell prostrate before him, like some hideous idols before a religious reformer.

The fight was now general, for the soldiery, finding their chief so rudely attacked, and two of their best men unseated by a blow from a swineherd, drew and charged promiscuously.

They were now eight to two, by no means to be considered short odds.

"Come on—St. Bothold protect me from such knaves," roared Little John, "I would I had the dressing of a hundred such."

"Take him alive—no torture shall be too much for this insolence," almost screamed the the Norman chief.

"Anan," said Little John, twirling his huge quarterstaff.

·"Catch'em alive oh—eh," laughed ponderous Little John. At which Geruth, as in duty bound, laughed.

Hard blows and knocks now rained upon all; but little interval was left for words, except now and then a stray execration or so.

"As I am a sinful man," at last said Julian, "these churls will beat us! An they do I turn Englishman, and forswear my native France."

"A likely boast," laughed Little John, "when every frog-eating Frenchman of you all would fain be English! But, no—the Pope said it—and it must be true: we English are not *Angles*, but *Angels*. Thwack!"

And while relating an old story about the origin of our national name, the tall forester hit harder with his quarter-staff than ever he could with his tongue—a usual circumstance with men of his size.

Strange as it may seem, the contest was not quite one-sided. The eight remaining Norman soldiers were well armed and accoutred, and brave. They were armed with short, sharp-smiting swords, while as yet Geruth and Little John had used nothing but their huge bludgeons, the modern term for quarter-staff.

It was the blood that did it: that blood, which, mixed as it has been, has yet made the Nelsons, Clives, and Clydes.

Hard at it they went, as if it had been play, for no Saxon in those days cared for a drubbing.

Two to eight.

Julian was as well prepared as any other man to receive the heavy blows dealt by Little John, but the mere fact of two Saxon outlaws standing erect against a squad of men-at-arms, moved the native of Caen to a degree of fury which it were difficult to describe.

"The foul fiend take the Sheffield ruffian!" cried Julian, "I would one of thy craftsmen's knives were in thy chitterlings! Where is thy vital part?"

"I have none," replied Little John, laughing.

"Have at thee, base slave!" roared the infuriated man.

"Where?"

As Julian spoke, he aimed such a blow at the tall forester, that had he been a man of less strength and height, he must have suffered severely; but as it was, the peculiar quarterstaff stroke, for which our hero was celebrated, took him aback.

Little John aimed full at his mailed head, and thanks to the Norman's leap, hit him—well! where he was not mailed.

"By the bones of St. Anthony!" shrieked the soldier, "and by the memory of the father and mother that bore me, thou shalt rue this day! Thou art a coward to take advantage of thy huge strength."

Little John looked at him with genuine amazement.

"Soldier," he said, with that sense of high gentlemanly feeling which was always the characteristic of him who,

> "Purveyed him an hundred bows;
> The strings they were well dight.
> One hundred sheafs of arrows good,
> The heads burnished full bright.
> And every arrow was an ell long,
> With peacock plume ydight;
> Ynicked too with white silver:
> It was a seemly sight."

"Soldier," said he, "thou canst not believe I would take advantage of thee—I hate thy race—but as thou wiltst. I will introduce a new order of chivalry."

"A new order of chivalry?" said the Norman grimly, "what order?"

"That of the P. R." said Little John.

"The P. R.?" laughed the Norman.

"Yes, the Primitive Resource of the Saxon," and he dealt the soldier a blow, that had his head have not been tolerably hardened must have finished his career, and for ever ended the glories of thatp eculiar institution pre-eminently British, which is still the glory of nearly every class of the community.

When Adam first viewed the garden of Eden, he could by no possibility have ever thought that one man would have been arrayed in enmity against another.

It must have been so gigantic an idea, so splendid a sensation, that enmity and hate must have been impossible.

To be a man.

To be a man—and the first man! No matter all the woes, the indignities, the sufferings, the wrongs which the descendants of our first parents have suffered, yet to feel that *we* are the lineal posterity of that god-gifted being, who was first place in that sacred paradise, which Satan thought worthy of invasion, is something.

Therefore, why should we quarrel, hate, or persecute?

Man, unfortunately, was born pugnacious.

No sooner had Little John intimated his intention of submitting the issue of the conflict to the weapons which belong to us in common with the wildest beast of the forest than all fighting ceased.

"A rare and good idea," said Geruth.

But, save the leader, not so thought the Normans. There was something in the very attitude assumed by the forester which made them uneasy, and yet was the soldier stalwart, brave, and active.

He stepped back, as if to survey his antagonist, and then, rushing at him, struck out.

The blow was warded off, and then the forester's ponderous fist hit the soldier one blow.

It was enough.

The Norman lay sprawling on the ground insensible, while his companions eagerly crowded round him.

Some minutes elapsed before he came to, and when he did, it was with a deep sigh.

"Where are the ruffians?—let them not escape," he cried.

But not a sign of Little John or Geruth was to be seen.

CHAPTER XXVIII.
A SURPRISE.

THE daylight had dawned upon the glades of the oak-forest. The green boughs glittered with their pearls of dew. The hind led her fawn from the covert of high fern to the more open walks of the greenwood.

Round the trysting-tree of the bold outlaws a large company was collected.

Suddenly a sentry challenged some one. Doubtless a satisfactory answer was given, for next minute Little John and Geruth stalked into the open glade.

"Where is the captain?" asked the new lieutenant.

"No man knows. Unless you see him in the body, not the best guesser of our band could say whether he is in the green wood or Nottingham town," replied Friar Tuck.

"He is sorely wanted here," said the tall forester, "for a great wrong has been done."

And as briefly as possible he told the story of the abduction of Rose and Rebecca.

The leaders of the band heard him with indignation, but great as was their hatred of the Normans and their cruelties, none dared to set the example of attacking the tiger in his lair in the absence of the chief.

Pending, however, his arrival, everything was done to prepare for the contest, while scouts were sent out in all directions to collect the scattered forces.

By mid-day three hundred good men and true were reclining in the opening of the forest, in the centre of which grew an oak-tree of enormous magnitude.

All were ready. Every man had, besides his bow and arrows and short sword, a huge quarterstaff, which he well knew how to wield.

"The day is passing swiftly," mused Little John to the bull-headed friar. "Would that our chief would come. This delay chafes me."

"Are the maidens pretty?" said the friar, with a jocose leer.

"Yes," replied Little John, blushing to the very roots of his hair.

"One especially?" asked Tuck, with a sly smile.

"One especially," continued the unsuspecting forester.

"I thought so," was the dry response.

The hedge priest was a practical philosopher, and from this brief cross-examination, knew that Little John was in love.

At this moment one of those murmurs which emanate from a crowd when their feelings have for a long time been pent up, rose on the air.

As Little John looked round, his delight was great to see two men enter the clearing.

They were Robin Hood and Will Scarlett, the former with irate brow and angry mien.

"Disperse!" he shouted, "disperse in bands of ten. Collect what force you can—let the lightest of foot scour the forest. The trysting place is Girlstone, on whose towers shall hang every Norman thief who is found within if harm has happened to the girls. Away!"

In two minutes more there remained in the outlaws' haunt but four men.

These were Will Scarlett, Geruth, Little John, and Robin Hood.

They delayed not long, the outlaw chief merely halting to give them from the general stores fresh arms, upon which all took their way to the general rendezvous.

All knew the serious character of the step they were taking, a step which would be sure to lead to a general attack upon the outlaws, who already had had to contend against one or two incursions, in which, however, the assailants had come off but badly.

Now, however, they might be sure a war of extermination would ensue.

Not one of the whole band, however, would have hesitated. The honour of English maidens was at stake, and that was enough for English hearts.

The journey was likely to be a long one, as, though in a straight line Girlstone Tower was not very far, they were compelled to make numerous detours.

But Robin Hood, whose knowledge of the forest was unequalled, took them by the shortest road.

At length the path became so narrow as not to admit of two men walking abreast, and began to descend into a dingle, traversed by a brook whose banks were broken, swampy, and overgrown with dwarf willows.

Here the outlaw called a halt, in order to refresh his party ere ascending the opposite slope.

With characteristic caution, he selected a spot a little way from the road, where, seated on the sward, they could see without being seen.

Suddenly they heard the sound of a horse walking slowly down the path. All listened attentively, while not a word was spoken.

All peered under the bushes which concealed them from view.

In another moment the horse and its rider came in sight.

It was a man in full armour, mounted on a black horse, large of size, tall, and, to all appearance, powerful and strong, like the rider by whom he was mounted.

His visor was down, so that not a vestige of his face could be seen.

"Some retainer of the late Sir Norman," whispered Will Scarlett.

Whether the rider heard them or not they could not say, or whether he thought the place a likely one for an ambuscade cannot be known; but at this juncture he spurred his horse and rode through the ford.

He leaped from his horse, and, lifting his visor, stooped to drink at the brook.

This act revealed the pale stern face of Sir Norman Malvoisin.

A loud incautious cry from Will Scarlett made him resume his visor, mount his horse, and instantly disappear beneath the leafy arches of the forest.

"Zounds!" cried Robin Hood; "I thought you had killed this man."

"Jesu Maria!" gasped Will Scarlett. "An' a man can live with a foot of English wood in his back, he must be the devil!"

"Or the wrong man," said Robin Hood, drily.

Will Scarlet struck his forehead.

"The foul fiend seize the villain! He was too ill to leave his bed, and, to deceive me, sent one of his men—who, poor wretch, suffered for his master's villainy."

"This is no time for reproaches," said Robin Hood. "Let us track the wolf."

No further word of command was needed. Grasping their weapons with fierce determination all hurried to cross the brook.

CHAPTER XXIX.

GIRLSTONE TOWER.

THE stronghold of the Norman soldier, where, when wearied of his brother's castle, he lived, to lord it, king of all he surveyed, was situated in a valley.

The outer walls stood on a pleasant ascent from a river.

It was a fortress of some size, with a donjon, or large and high square tower, surrounded by buildings of inferior height, which were encircled by an inner court-yard. Around the exterior wall was a deep moat supplied with water from a neighbouring rivulet.

Sir Norman Malvoisin, who had reason to provide against accidents, had made numerous additions to the strength of his castle, by building towers upon the outward wall, so as to flank it at every angle.

The entrance, as was the custom in castles of the period, lay through an arched barbican, which was defended by a turret at each corner.

Morning was glimmering over their grey and moss-grown battlements, when the two girls, who had sobbed themselves insensible, were roused by their black ravishers, who, when they found their white companion cumbersome, had left him to die in a secret nook of the forest, like a ravening fox in some obscure brake.

The prisoners were now compelled by their captors to alight, when one of the negroes wound a strange call upon a Saracenic horn.

The walls were immediately manned by archers and crossbow-men, who, however, showed no hostile demeanour, but proceeded to lower the drawbridge and admit them.

They were then led into a large room rising on clumsy but substantial Saxon pillars, where their guides, after motioning for them to refresh themselves, left them.

But they carefully locked the door behind them.

"Where are we, and what will become of us?" sobbed Rebecca.

"Well," said Rose, who, being a handmaiden and not a country girl, was bolder and more womanly than her companion, "we are in Girlstone Tower, the property of Sir Norman Malvoisin."

"That answers my first question," continued Rebecca.

"As to what will become of us," replied the disguised page, sternly, "I fear me much—death or dishonour."

All students of history know that until recently every Spanish lady wore——well how can we express our meaning to suit the delicacy of our modern nerves? We fear it cannot be done, and that we must speak plain English.

Wore, fastened to her garter, a small dagger, which every honest Spanish woman knew how to use to defend or to avenge her honour.

Rose, when assuming the costume of the stronger sex, did not forget to arm herself, and she now wore a small weapon of the kind alluded to, which she drew from its sheath and examined.

"'Tis sharp, and will do its work well," she said, manfully, as she passed her finger along it.

"But I am unarmed," exclaimed Rebecca; "you might have courage to slay yourself in the hour of peril: but how can you defend me?"

"There is but one defence against a soldier-monk," said Rose, gloomily.

"And—what is that?" asked Rebecca.

"Death!"

Rebecca started. At her age—so young, so beautiful—to die was horrible; and yet her fealty to some unknown lover never failed her. She would be the chaste English girl or perish."

"Will you kill me?" she said, in a voice sad, but, oh, how musical!

"If need be," replied the page; "but let us hope for better things. Think you, your brother or Little John will forget us?"

And, as Rose spoke, she blushed nearly as scarlet as her huge lover.

They now heard the great door creak, and next moment stood before them an aged sibyl, who gazed at them with a malignantly envious glance—such as only wicked old age can put on to youth and beauty.

"This way, my dainty ones," she cried, in a shrill treble; "two of you! My lord is greedy; ah! ah! ah! Bright eyes, golden locks. Look at me; when I came here I was as fair and young as ye."

"Then, take pity on us;" said Rebecca, imploringly.

"Pity," laughed the beldame; "why should I pity you, and what good would my pity do you?"

"Cannot you help us to escape?" continued Will Scarlett's sister.

"Who enters here leaves hope behind," she replied; "from hence there is no escape but through the gates of death. Follow."

As the girls had no wish to see their black captors, they thought it best to obey, and were led through several passages until they came to an apartment filled up with some attempt at ornament and magnificence, though decay and neglect had impaired the few ornaments with which the taste of some former owner had adorned it.

The once splendid tapestry hung down from the walls in many places, and in others was tarnished and faded under the effects of the sun, or tattered and decayed by age.

"Here my dainty lambs will stay until my lord's pleasure is known," said the hag, and without further comment left the room, which they distinctly heard her bar on the outside.

It would occupy many a page to tell all that passed between Rebecca and Rose; hopes, fears, devices, as to escaping their fearful fate, were all indulged in.

In vain, the next day's mid-day sun saw them helpless and forlorn.

CHAPTER XXX.

THE BANQUET.

They had been up some time, and were gazing through a narrow window on a deserted courtyart, when, with a loud crash, the door opened, and several servants appeared, bearing what appeared to be materials for a banquet.

Then the owner of the castle stood before them, in the full dress of the period in which Robin Hood flourished.

We give it verbatim from a characteristic picture by a great hand.

The knight's long and luxuriant hair was trained to flow in quaint tresses down his richly furred cloak. His beard was closely shaven. His doublet reached to the middle of his leg; and the girdle which secured it, and, at the same time, supported his ponderous sword, was embroidered and embossed with gold work.

He took off his velvet bonnet, and bowed with something like grace.

"Welcome to my poor castle, ladies," he said, with a wicked gleam in his eyes.

"Say us no welcome, sir, when we are prisoners and would fain depart," replied Rose, spiritedly, while Rebecca trembled all over.

"And so ye shall," cried the knight; "but honour my banquet first. It is plenteous, and one not often seen by such as ye. Sit down."

As Rose obeyed without many signs of fear, Rebecca was fain to do the same.

The knight, who was still suffering from his accident, and really both hungry and weary, from his adventurous jaurney, was for some minutes more intent on recruiting his strength than on making love; but when his appetite was satisfied, he pledged them both in a bumper.

"To your bright eyes and ruby lips," he said, and stooping forward he would have kissed Rebecca.

The poor girl shrieked, and, rising, ran from the table.

"Weak and silly fool," said the knight, sternly, "dost think thy childish ways will avail you here? I am lord and master of the house, and whoso comes within it is my slave. I tell thee, girl, I sue not twice—'twere better you came quickly to my arms and smiled, than have me punish you as others have been punished."

Rebecca could but weep. She was powerless to speak a word.

"And pray, most noble knight, what punishment was that?" asked Rose, defiantly.

"Dishonoured and weeping, they were cast to lowest menials."

"Coward and tyrant!" cried Rose; "God will forgive me."

And before he was aware of her purpose, she flew at him, clutched him by the throat, at which she struck with her short, sharp dagger.

But the knight, though taken by surprise, was as quick as she was.

Catching her uplifted hand in his, he wrenched the dagger from it, casting it to the ground.

"Wouldst thou? A pretty boy to carry such playthings. In Girlstone Castle we scourge naughty pages."

And the knight cast her from him with superb disdain.

"Now hussy," he said, addressing Rebecca, "come back to your seat and smile, or by the Heavens above——"

What further he meant to say was lost, for at that moment his attention was directed to the blast of a horn winded outside.

It was given three times, and then all was silent.

A moment after a discreet knock was heard at the door of the room.

"Who is without, and what means that horn?"

"'Tis a summons to surrender two damsels," replied the squire.

"Come in, knave, and let me hear who wants to thrust himself into a hornet's nest."

A squire entered, whose uneasy looks betrayed his apprehension.

"Who wound that horn?"

"A man in Lincoln green."

"Is he alone?"

"No, three hundred rogues stand behind him, all armed with bows and staves—a proper army."

The knight looked with an awful scowl upon the girls.

"This is some of your doing," he said, with an angry scowl.

"I did not know we had so many friends," said Rose, saucily.

"I will to the ramparts. Hang out my banner on the outward wall. I'll show these insolent yeomen what it is to defy their masters!"

And securing the girls in the room, he hurried to the walls.

The ramparts over the barbican were crowded by his retainers, who were gazing somewhat grimly at the array before them.

Close to the moat stood the one who had wound the horn—no less a personage than Will Scarlett himself, while at about two arrow-flights' distance, round a venerable oak, were congregated a host of some three hundred bold yeomen, in the centre of whom might be distinguished the lieutenants, known only from the others by a feather in their caps.

"What insolent varlet dares wind his horn under my battlements?" said the knight, making himself easily heard below.

"I, William Gammel, demand the instant surrender of my sister and a young lady named Rose, feloniously abducted by your slaves, and now present in this your castle."

"And were these wandering damsels within my walls, what, pray, my dainty youth, is to be my fate for refusing to give them up?"

"We will pull your tower about your ears, and cast you on the bonfire which we will make of it. We are no craven peasants of France, but English yeomen. So be advised, sir knight, and let thy prisoners free."

"Base slave, away, and tell thy swinish herd I am Norman Malvoisin, caring for nothing and fearing nothing. Lift but your hands to assail my house, and I will hang every tenth man of you as high as the oaks will let me."

"This night shalt thou rue thine insolence," said Will Scarlett; and then, as if controlling his feelings by a great effort, he added, "beware how you use my sister. If harm come to her, or the maiden with her, I will have flesh taken from thy bones with hot pincers."

"Thy sister, fool, is but now the harlot of my minions," said the Norman.

Quick as thought the outlaw's arrow was to his bow, and next instant might have been the titled ruffian's last, but that Will Scarlett recollected his vocation.

He was a herald, and might not forget his duty.

Not so, Sir Norman Malvoisin, who scorned to recognise his character.

Turning to where two men stood close at hand, he gave an order in a low voice.

They were arblast-men, with windlass and quarrel ready.

The arblast was a cross-bow, the windlass the machine used in bending the weapon, and the quarrel—so called from its square or diamond-shaped head—was the bolt adapted to it.

The men took steady aim at Will Scarlett. They took aim no more.

Little John and Robin Hood had been deeply interested spectators of the scene, standing near a tree a long-bow shot from the castle.

Intuitively as it were, they guessed the danger incurred by Will Scarlett.

Neither seemed to take deliberate aim, and yet so certain was their shot that both men-at-arms fell mortally wounded.

This appeared to be the signal for attack, the outlaws rushing forward and shooting so wholly together, that in a few minutes the soldiers had all sought cover, whence to assail the beleaguering foe with their large cross-bows and other such weapons.

For some minutes nothing could be made out but the whizzing of shafts and missiles, followed by shouts that rent the air, as outlaw or soldier, as it happened, fell.

This mode of attack was, however, soon seen to be unavailing.

"Withdraw a little," said Robin Hood, waving to his men, "now fifty of you put down your bows and take to axe and sword, while all you others keep the battlements well employed. We will attack the outer barrier of the barbican.

The outer barrier alluded to by the famous outlaw was a fortification composed of palisades, which were often the scene of severe skirmishes, as they must necessarily be carried, before the walls themselves could be approached.

Little John, apparently as a matter of course, took up a place beside his chief, Will Scarlett doing the same.

The archers again advanced, and in another moment there was no point at which a defender could show the smallest part of his person without receiving a cloth-yard shaft.

Under cover of this the forlorn hope rushed to the assault, and began hewing at the barrier with axes, while others tore up the piles and palisades. But they are seen from the battlements, a loud cry is heard, and, as a bugle sounded from amid the men-at-arms, a loud flourish of Norman trumpets is heard.

Tra la la! tra la la! tra la la!

A shrill tone of defiance, followed by the deep and hollow clang of the kettle-drums.

"En avant, Malvoisin! A la rescousse! A la rescousse!"

"St. George for merry England, and God defend the right!"

Such were the rival cries of the antagonistic forces as they met in mortal combat.

Now, the scene was indeed terrific. The outlaws, brave and undaunted, their weather-beaten countenances beaming with excitement, rushed in like a herd of wild horses, to meet an iron line of men better armed and better appointed than themselves.

In vain they wield their quarterstaves, in vain they thrust with their swords; the soldiers are encased in armour, they cannot be hurt, and then their numbers are equal to those of their assailants.

The men in Lincoln green are thrust back outside the barriers.

"Charge! charge!" shouts the ringing voice of Robin Hood; "if I stand alone—no retreat for me."

And waving a heavy axe over his head he rushed into the very midst of the Norman soldiery to find himself face to face with Julian.

"Surrender, false yeoman," cried the delighted Julian.

But he misjudged the slim youth who stood before him. Ere he could lift his own sword, the ponderous axe was crushing in his brain, and his form lay prostrate on the ground for ever.

The mêlée was now general, the outlaws in two parties, headed by Little John and Will Scarlett, supporting their leader, and thronging to the breach, which was disputed, man to man.

The conflict of two oceans, moved by adverse winds.

Robin Hood appeared everywhere, and his example was so contagious, that there appeared danger that the outlaws would enter the castle with the besieged.

A loud flourish of trumpets was heard on the ramparts.

The Normans took to their heels, and in a minute more were within the walls of the castle, the outlaws masters of the outer works.

This, however, for the nonce, was a barren advantage, as the castle was as far off being taken as ever.

CHAPTER XXXI.

THE FIGHT.

WHEN Robin Hood and Little John found that they were masters of the outer works, a signal agreed on was made.

Twenty fresh men from the rear came rushing up with large ladders that had hastily been constructed in the forest.

A terrific volley from the archers, replied to with energy from the battlements, followed. The air seemed swept by a cloud, and men fell killed and wounded on all hands.

Little John looked round. Shooting against stone walls left little hope of victory.

But now up come the ladders. The outlaws leap into the moat—they swim across—they plant the ladders under a pelting shower of stones, beams, and trunks of trees, which maim and kill dozens.

Fresh men take their places, but to be hurled back by the lances of the Norman soldiery.

Little John left them to try their fortune, while he, alone and unattended, approached the postern.

He wields his huge axe on high, and though the men-at-arms shower stones and beams on him, and shoot bolts, he heeds them not.

His ponderous weapon is in another minute thundering at the door.

The door shakes, and then gives way with a crash—it is splintered with blows.

All rush to this part of the battlements, the ladder-men being everywhere repulsed, and Sir Norman himself guides the defence.

A vast beam, which took three men to carry, is brought to be hurled down upon the brave and gallant outlaw.

"Look out, my Little John!" cried Robin Hood, "look out!"

The beam was tipped on the battlements—a dozen hands were put forward to impel it—a dozen arrows came whizzing through the air.

But though many fall, shattered and wounded, the beam falls too.

Too late! Little John is through the postern, and the beleaguers fly.

But the Normans, during the time that Little John had been pounding the door, had removed the plank which served as a bridge.

The outworks were taken, but the castle itself was still untouched. The outlaws had little fear of the ultimate result, but there was a great danger.

Some straggling follower might seek to enter the castle, and go for reinforcements.

Four score of Norman lances were within less than a day's ride, and three hundred could be mustered in twenty-four hours.

Whatever was to be done had to be done quickly.

Robin Hood was peculiarly fertile in resources. What was wanted was a bridge. Well, as they could not make one, they must do away with the necessity for one. He ordered his men to fill up the moat with earth and stones, and trunks of trees.

The whole force of the castle was now brought to repel this attempt; and Sir Norman, himself, though scarcely able to fight, headed his own men.

Robin Hood withdrew to a short distance, and quietly drew his good yew bow.

The knight was armed in proof, and had no fear of arrows; but Robin Hood rained such a shower on him, that his ribs were rapped as with a club, and, foaming with rage, he was forced to leave the ramparts for awhile.

His passion was something awful, and knew no bounds.

In another moment he caused his trumpet to sound a parley.

The fighting ceased, as if by enchantment.

"What terms ask you now?" said Robin Hood, advancing within speaking distance.

"The maidens, as pure as they came in, shall be yielded to you, so that you let us pass without let or hindrance," replied Sir Norman.

"I take your word," was the gallant outlaw's answer; "bring them forth."

The men in green unstrung their bows, delighted with their victory, and waited.

But the soldiery, though they had disappeared from the ramparts, showed no sign of coming forth.

Presently, however, the drawbridge fell down with a crash, and the whole force, headed by their chief, came rushing forth, their spears at the rest, and charged like a storm cloud through the midst of the astonished and astounded outlaws.

But no women were amongst them.

LITTLE JOHN SAVING REBECCA.

Scarcely had the treacherous soldiers made their desperate sortie, and ere the archers could fit an arrow to their bows, they understood.

The castle was on fire!

The remorseless and revengeful monk-soldier, rather than be cheated of his revenge, had set the pile a-blaze.

Robin Hood, Little John, and a dozen others, not forgetting Will Scarlett, rushed across the drawbridge, to find the postern closed.

The ferocious ruffian had cut off the only means of escape.

Not a moment was wasted in words. All knew that an instant of time lost might be fatal.

Robin Hood, resuming his axe, began slashing away at this second postern, while Little John, leaping into the moat, drew forth a huge beam, such as three ordinary men would have staggered under.

Lifting it on his shoulders, he ran furiously at the gate, which yielded slightly even at the first blow.

It was the ancient Roman ram peculiarly applied.

Thunders of applause from the excited outlaws encouraged Little John, who again retreated to have a second trial at the thick oaken postern.

"The ladders! the ladders!" shouted Will Scarlett, inspired by a sudden idea.

There was a general rush, the ladders were lifted up, and then the outlaws crowded up, one above the other.

At the same moment the gate yielded, and as Will Scarlett reached the battlements, he saw Little John rush into the court-yard.

A loud shriek warned them that they had not had a minute to lose. Little John and Will Scarlett seemed to recognise the tones.

The fire had now taken firm hold of the castle, which, being to a certain extent built of wood, and filled with old furniture, burned rapidly.

We must however return to Rose and her friend Rebecca.

They were soon aware that the attack on the castle had commenced, and never were two young women more grateful.

They felt quite assured that those without would not desert them.

Even if they did not capture the castle, they would so surround it that the Normans would be glad to surrender at discretion.

In the meantime they could have nothing to fear.

And yet the poor girls passed a most anxious time. They could have no conception of either the power or will of the besiegers to succour them, having besides, perhaps, an exaggerated idea of the strength of the fortress.

The prejudices of the multitude since the conquest of England by the Normans, were in favour of the invulnerability of the Normans.

They seemed to wrap them round with a kind of magic circle.

Would men, armed simply with bows and arrows and quarterstaves, be able to make any impression on stone walls guarded by deep moats?

It seemed to them to be as difficult to storm the clouds as the battlements of Girlstone.

Something of this feeling, mingled with thankfulness for their temporary release from the coarse attentions of the Norman knight, influenced their conversation, which was made up of alternate hopes and fears.

Presently they became fully aware that the summons which had called Sir Norman Malvoisin to leave the banquet was no idle one.

They could hear the noise within the castle occasioned by the defensive operations, which was soon considerable.

It became at length almost an unbearable clamour.

"What does it all mean?" said Rebecca, in a tone of great anxiety.

"They are attacked," replied Rose, "and what you hear is the rushing to-and-fro of the men-at-arms—hark to their heavy tread upon the battlements."

They could indeed be clearly heard on the narrow and winding passages and stairs which led to the different partizans and points of defence.

The voice of the knight, too, was clearly heard, giving orders to his followers or shouting out encouragements.

Then the uproar became confused, and the two young girls could make out nothing more than that a contest of some kind was going on to which they could but lend the assistance of their prayers.

And thus passed the weary hours, during which they suffered as much agony as is given to youth to endure in its hours of trial.

Then all was still—still as if no strife had ever desecrated that spot where, ere the Norman came, reigned peace and plenty.

Then thick volumes of smoke pouring into the apartment, made them aware of the new and fearful danger they had to encounter.

They were paralysed for a moment, and then gave way to the natural resource of women under the painful circumstances.

The old castle resounded with their shrieks.

"Ha! ha! ha!" was the reply, but whence they could not tell.

"Who is there?" cried Rose, who was a brave and ready-witted girl; "what art thou, and why that raven laugh at our misery?"

"Ha! ha! my pretty lambs," said a voice outside, "I was what you are now—a rosy-lipped, bright-eyed girl, and now I am an old woman, wearied of life and ready to depart. Sir Norman Malvoisin has fired the castle and we will burn together, my dainty ones."

"Mercy!" cried the appalled girls, "have mercy!"

"When had anyone mercy on me?" cried the hag, "I will have none."

"Woman!" said Rose, approaching the door—the smouldering and stifling vapour as yet filling the upper part of the room only, "you were young once, you were innocent; remember thy mother, and as you hope for Heaven's pardon for any sins you may have committed—release us."

"Avaunt! false fiend, I have sinned past pardoning; there is no mercy for such as I. The foul demon calls and I must go. I will not go unattended," continued the insane beldame.

A terrible shout was heard, and then the door flew open, and two men, blackened with smoke and bloody from contusions from rafts and beams, entered the room.

A wild, happy cry from the girls proclaimed them friends.

In the hurry however, a circumstance occurred which it was difficulty for either to explain after.

While Will Scarlett snatched up Rose, Little John lifted Rebecca, though there could be no doubt it was an oversight.

But like all brave and noble hearts, the forester was timid as a fawn in the presence of the woman who was mistress of his mighty heart.

Scarcely had the heroic foresters torn the young women from the burning apartment, than the fire, fanned by the wind, burst forth with renewed fury carrying away the roof.

The hag, foiled in her atrocious design, ran shrieking hither and thither.

"Get from the flames, you witch," said one of the outlaws, "though burning were too good for thee."

As he spoke, a huge stone, dislodged from above by the flames which split it to pieces, fell in a shower on the beldame.

Her stunned and lifeless body fell into the very thick of the furnace.

The whole tower was now in bright flames, which flashed forth furiously from window and loophole, and the triumphant outlaws were glad to sally forth, contented with their great victory.

They had, however, before the flames gained upon the principal chambers, collected a goodly heap of plunder, in the shape of plate, rich armour, and splendid clothing.

CHAPTER XXXII.

THE PALMER.

THE outlaws were well aware that so daring a deed as that which they had committed would not pass unnoticed. Already, the indignation of the ranger of Sherwood and the sheriff of Nottingham had been excited against them for the many robberies committed on wealthy knights and fat abbots, and both had vowed vengeance against them.

The prince, too, who reigned in England, heard with indignation of the existence of a power which his barons could not repress, and had vowed with many fearful oaths that, did they not soon capture and hang every outlaw in the forest, he would come himself and hunt them in place of deer or wild boars.

Wicked and evil as was King John, there were moments when he was brave enough, and it was not unlikely he would keep his word.

It was therefore determined by Robin Hood that his band should disperse for a while, and lie quiet in fortresses known only to themselves, while a few went forth as spies to discover the intentions of the Normans.

First, however, Rebecca and Rose were bestowed at Gammel House, the latter not venturing to return to the earl's residence, where now she had a bitter and relentless foe in the person of the soldier-monk.

In the days when Robin Hood reigned, England swarmed with mendicants; some real beggars, some imposters, but all willing to beg rather than work, and steal rather than beg—too often the case even now.

They were of all hues, all lands, all ages—pilgrims with a palm branch in one hand and a dirk concealed in their girdles; beggars with pikestaves to enforce the charity they solicited; tinkers, who mended pots almost as dexterously as they robbed the folds; shepherds, who carried stones in their scrips, and could convert their crooks readily into quarterstaves; monks, who served our lady less devoutly in the church than in the greenwood.

These motley bands furnished men and sometimes money to the sovereigns of Sherwood. No dexterous recruiting officer of our times ever surpassed him in singling out handy lads, on whose forehead nature had written soldier.

He knew a true customer at a glance.

The determined step, the resolute air, the tart answer, and the arrow-like sharpness of eye, marked him for the long bow or quarterstaff.

The whining tone, the lazy step, the supplicating air, the apparel well repaired, and the meal bags well filled, spoke to Robin as plainly as in words, that he looked on a wretch, rich and sordid, who had not the soul to enjoy the cash he had collected.

To one of these we must now introduce our readers.

Along one of the numerous winding and uncertain paths, which branched off on every hand, walked one whose costume indicated a begging pilgrim.

His coat was patched black, blue, and red; his palmer's hat was high-crowned, his hose and shoes were darned, mended above and below, and armed with broad-headed hobnails.

In his hand was a long staff.

> He had a bag for meal and a bag for malt,
> A bag for barley and corn;
> A bag for bread, and a bag for beef,
> And a bag for his little horn.

Though to all appearance old, he walked with a step that indicated no common strength, though his splashed legs, and dirty appearance, showed he had come some distance.

The path, which for some time had been through a plain of brushwood, soon led deeper into the woodland, and crossed more than one brook, the approach to which was rendered perilous by the marshes through which it flowed.

The palmer, however, seemed to know as if by instinct the soundest ground and the safest points of passage.

He soon, by his caution and attention, reached a wild but dry avenue, where, the sun being long since past the meridian, he halted to refresh himself.

Selecting a spot where one of the many forest springs bubbled and sparkled, he drew forth the contents of his wallet, which were miscellaneous and good, and proceeded to eat in a way that indicated an excellent and healthy appetite.

While doing so, suddenly the noise of horsemen attracted his attention—of horsemen, too, threading their way cautiously through the forest.

The palmer continued his meal leisurely and indifferently, as if a man of his character had nothing to fear.

Suddenly the party came in sight slowly, as men who were fatigued, peering about, too, as if uncertain of their road.

The foremost of the party was a powerful and athletic man, with huge bony shoulders and long muscular arms, almost out of proportion with the length of his body. He had fierce dark eyes, which looked out from under the shaggiest pair of eyebrows ever seen upon a young man. An habitual frown darkened his brow, while his upper lip had a perpetual and haughty curl.

He was apparelled in a beautiful suit of light ringed armour or chain mail, which shone like polished steel, and seemed flexible to every movement of the body, as if it had been wrought in the loom.

He had a flat-topped helmet, secured by a band of steel passing under the chin.

His arms were a long, straight, cross-hilted sword, battle-axe, and spear.

He bestrode a strong black horse, which seemed built for so powerful a rider.

Beside him rode a lady not more than eighteen years of age, girlish in her symmetry and beauty, but womanly in the expression of her face.

Rich flowing curls of auburn fell from under her pale pink gorget, fastened to her white and noble forehead by a band of gold.

Exposure to the air or some other cause had called up upon her face a bright colour that shamed the blush of the peach blossom; while her eyes, deep, unfathomable, and of a bluish grey, had a dreamy brightness which bespoke a character loving and determined.

She rode gracefully in her saddle, though it was evident she was either physically or mentally exhausted.

"Satan choke the knave who bade us leave the high road at the blasted oak," said the knight, aloud; "would I had him here, I would flay him with his own quarter-staff. The knaves grow insolent; they had need have their fore-claws cut, like their own dogs."

"Hush!" said the maiden, in one of those silvery voices which go to the heart, "yonder is one. Doubtless, if you are civil, Sir Philip de Beauvoisin, he will show us the way."

And she pointed to where the palmer sat intent upon his food.

"I will give him no chance," cried the irate knight; "by the holy rood, he shall."

"Hold!" said the young lady, with a look of pain; "you call yourself for the nonce my true knight. Will you not please me in one little thing?"

"I am now as ever your faithful and devoted slave," he replied.

And he bent his head over the saddle-bow to hide a cold sarcastic smile.

CHAPTER XXXIII.

EDITH.

SATISFIED, though he yielded with an ill grace, the maiden urged her palfrey forward, and reined it in close to the solitary wayfarer.

"Dost know the way to Nottingham, worthy palmer?" she said.

The man rose, looked fixedly at her for a moment, and bowed low.

"I know my way to Nottingham, fair lady, as I know every dell in the forest, few of which have not sheltered me in their turn," he answered, in a voice apparently tremulous with age.

"Wilt guide us? Thy reward shall be fair, and my thanks many."

"I will guide you, lady, for your thanks; but my pace on foot is hardly fitting for an armed party," continued the beggar, who had risen to his feet when addressed.

"Let not that be a hindrance," said the deep voice of the knight. "Hugh, bring the led hackney, and, as the proverb says, 'Set the beggar on horseback.'"

No one but the young lady saw the quick angry gleam from the palmer's eyes—an angry gleam that made her very heart leap, she knew not why.

"Nay, Sir Philip," she said, with an effort at playfulness, which cost her some pain, "this poor man is under my guardianship. I will have him respected."

The other rode hastily on to hide both a scowl and a sneer.

Meanwhile, the palmer mounted his horse, and drawing his rags and bags about him, took his place at the head of the small column, which he guided through the intricate paths, winding valleys, and picturesque glades with the ease of a forester who had dwelt there all his life.

"You know Sherwood well?" said the young maiden, dashing up to him, after they had travelled about an hour.

"Well; and therefore bid yon knight look to himself. He is where coats of Lincoln green are often seen, and fifty foresters might capture his men-at-arms if they look not out."

The travellers had now reached the verge of the deeply-wooded country, and were about to plunge into its darkest recesses, held most dangerous at that time from the number of desperate outlaws, whom hard poverty and cruel oppression had driven to despair, and who wandered through those vast forests in such formidable bands as to bid defiance to anything but an army.

Had the travellers been of the true English race they need not have feared so much; for the outlaws, whom the severity of the forest laws had driven to this roving and desperate mode of life, were chiefly peasants and yeomen of Saxon descent, and nearly always respected the persons and property of their countrymen.

"Ah!" cried the girl, warmly, "is it so? But surely they would not harm Edith Marian, the daughter of Athelston!"

"And art thou Edith the daughter of Athelston?" said the palmer, looking wistfully into her lovely face.

"I am."

"Then if this Norman knight will be guided by me, I swear to carry you all through unharmed," cried the palmer, solemnly.

"And what must he do?" inquired the girl, eagerly.

"Trust implicitly in me," replied the palmer, "and let me ride forward. Lady, I am a Saxon, and for your sake my countrymen will grant me a boon."

"Now, by the holy cross!" said the irate knight, "and thou wert not with me, I would ask nothing better than to face these churls. But their arrows might hurt thee, lovely one—and so even let the beggar have his way."

"No English shaft from English bow will ever harm me," cried the girl warmly.

The palmer nearly fell from his horse, but why or wherefore it would be difficult to say; recovering himself, however, he bade the whole party advance, until he was barely in sight, and then keep their relative distances, halting when he halted and riding on when he rode on.

The precaution of the rugged palmer was a good one, for ere ten minutes had elapsed, as they ascended a magnificent avenue of trees, skirted by a mass of under-wood, a splendid ambuscade for Saxon robbers, a cloud of foresters in Lincoln green burst forth, with arrows fixed to their bent bows.

"St. George for merry England!" they cried, "surrender ye all."

There would in another minute have been an encounter in which skill and discipline would have met with such fearful odds as to have rendered the adventure but doubtful.

"Saxons and fellow countrymen," cried the palmer in a ringing voice. "these people are under my guidance, and guard. This is her ye call the good Maid Marian, who saved your chief, Robin Hood, when in peril of his life."

"Long live Maid Marian, and long live Robin Hood!" shouted the outlaws, and next minute the whole party had vanished in the deep recesses of the forest.

"You have mysterious influence over these men, Sir Palmer," said the knight in a sarcastic voice, "which, in Nottingham, must be answered for."

"At your pleasure," was the cold answer of the phlegmatic palmer.

"Now, by our fair lady in heaven," said the girl, warmly, her eyes flashing fire and her bosom heaving, "this is not knightly. This good man, by declaring himself our guide——"

"Nay, that were poor safety for you," interrupted the palmer; "it was the fact that you once saved Robin Hood, when hard chased by his enemies, which was the passport to your safety."

"And pray how happened that?" said the still irate knight.

"I know no more than yourself," exclaimed Marian. "To my knowledge I ne'er saw the bold outlaw, who is a terrible man."

"Terrible to his enemies, gentle to his friends," was the palmer's reply.

"I would hear how the heiress of high degree, how the ward of the crown, affianced to the Earl of Nottingham's son, came to save the king of thieves," sneered the knight; "'twill be another reason for hunting him to his den."

"I know not the full particulars," said the palmer, "but what I know of the story you are welcome to."

CHAPTER XXXIV.

THE WARD OF THE CROWN.

BUT as we faithful historians are in possession of the full particulars, we think it better to give them in our own words.

At the time of which we speak, Robin Hood was, though from his skill as an archer, his infinite humour, his commanding qualities and consummate genius as a chief, the king of outlaws, but a very young man.

The adventure we are about to relate occurred nearly two years previously.

The heiress of the house of Athelston then, as a ward of the crown, inhabited the palatial convent of St. Vaux, situated within the forest, but almost on its extreme verge. Here she was educated as highly as it was thought necessary, for maidens to be taught, at a time when the knowledge of how to read lowered a man in the estimation of his fellows.

The convent, with its adjacent priory, had a magnificent garden, while on all hands without were beautiful and grassy glades, where the deer loved to roam and crop the green and pleasant herbage.

One reason for the abundance of game was the abundance of game-keepers, who watched with zealous care over the ground claimed by monks and nuns.

The whole was truly the property of the monarch, but powerful barons and rich religious communities arrogated to themselves a claim over certain select districts, and were as severe in the support of the game laws as the royal princes themselves.

These game laws were purely infamous, the present disgraceful state of the statute book on the subject being but a relic of ancient Norman barbarism.

A word on this subject, which is the key-note of the history of the times.

First, during the Roman sway all game was free to be hunted.

That was the law of nature.

The Saxon princes made some restrictions, but under their sway only useless wastes and untenanted wilds were set apart for the chase, while the laws were mild and the penalties trivial.

That was the law of the landed proprietor.

But when the brutal William conquered England, he destroyed villages and churches, made slaves of the inhabitants, and turning these stolen possessions into forests, guarded them by laws perfectly fiendish in their ferocity.

One extract from the laws, in which it says that his sovereign lord the king has this prerogative :

To have his places of recreation and pastime wheresoever he will appoint; for as it is the liberty and pleasure of his grace to reserve the wild beasts and the game to himself for his only delight and pleasure, so he may also, at his will and pleasure, make a forest for them to abide in.

Many and terrible were the combats the fearful forest laws caused between the rangers and those who pursued the game in the teeth of the law.

Especially in old Sherwood Forest, where the deer abounded.

The punishments inflicted by the proud and vindictive Normans were savagely severe.

In some cases, the offender, when detected, lost an eye or a hand.

In others, the law extended even unto death ; for was not the life of a Saxon churl of far less importance than that of an animal ?

These remarks will explain much that otherwise might be obscure in our story.

Despite shortcomings, the climate of England is sometimes both delightful and charming, while on the occasion to which we now allude the morning sky was both bright and clear.

It was spring, and the trees were clothed in their new bright vestments of green, while dewy diamonds sparkled in millions on the grassy turf ; the new ivy contrasting strongly with the antique leaves, clung gently to the trunks of huge oaks ; the winged choristers of heaven filled the air with music from bough of elm and beech and oak, while nature seemed redolent with brightness.

It was on the borders of a thicket that there stood three men, in the costume of rangers.

They overlooked whence they stood a large expanse of forest free from undergrowth ; but their task was listlessly attended to, for who would dare to trespass on ground sacred to the monks of the neighbouring monastery.

The foresters were seated, two of them on the ground, while a third leaned against a tree, whiling away the time in such conversation as was suited to their habits and feelings.

"Gilbert Frere will scarcely escape the loss of his hand," said one of them carelessly.

"And serve him right," replied another, lifting his hand to his chin ; "when I summoned him to surrender did not he set his hound at my throat ? Hanging to an oak bough were too good for him."

"Maiming will never cure him of deer-stalking," continued the other, "so thou mayest have thy wish. If caught offending a second time he shall surely die."

Scarcely had the words left the man's lips when a noble buck, as if unconscious of their presence, walked out to crop the young grass on a meadow at a considerable distance.

All examined him with a critical eye, and as their masters required a haunch or two, the ranger who stood upright prepared his bow.

But ere he was half ready the buck lifted his head with a frightened glance, leaped high and then fell dead with a marrow through his very heart.

The rangers leaped to their feet, looking earnestly in the direction the arrow had sped, but could make out not the slightest appearance of a human being.

"Some poaching outlaw," one cried, "he will surely come forth to claim his game ; so let us remain in ambush. 'Tis some months since we have caught a trespasser. This one shall not escape."

They had not long to wait long, ere from a distant thicket of May-thorn there advanced one who was a total stranger to the forest rangers.

He was a tall youth of about eighteen, somewhat

bronzed by exposure to the air, but with a naturally girlish complexion, so dazzlingly fair was it; his frame did not give the idea so much of strength as activity, so much of power to bound and leap as to endure; his walk was erect, his chest was thrown forward, while from his merry brown eyes there gleamed a twinkle of satisfaction at the marked success of so long a shot.

His nose was of the style called Grecian, his lips full and ruddy, his hair brown and hanging in waving curls.

The dress he wore was a doublet, cap, and fine hose of Lincoln green.

His arms were the bow and arrow, with a short sword.

"By the shrine of our lady, a proper youth!" said one.

"But one who must pay for the lot who have escaped," replied the head ranger.

And without further words, motioning his men to keep strict silence, he darted over the green sward with a noiseless step that scarcely seemed to brush the dew from the grass.

Like all who made hunting a trade he wore a buskin of leather, very much after the fashion of an Indian mocassin.

So intent was the handsome youth on examining his prize, that he heard not the keepers until they were close upon him, when their shouts made him start, and clutch his bow.

"Surrender, villain!" cried the foremost keeper, "for thou hast killed a deer within the forest."

"Villain thyself," replied the youth, coolly, putting his bow-string to his ear, and sending a shaft into the keeper's leg below the knee—"keep off at the peril of your lives."

But though the chief fell with a loud execration to the ground, the others rushed up.

"A buck is not worth three mens' lives," exclaimed the youth to himself, with which words he shouldered his bow, turned swiftly behind a tree, and took to his heels.

"Take him—dead or alive!" roared the head keeper, who was seated on the ground extracting the shaft from his wound.

The two forest rangers needed not twice telling. Their blood was up, and they would follow up the chase with all the energy of which they were capable.

Bounding like a deer, scarcely touching the ground, away went the handsome outlaw through brake and briar, across open glade, and down wooded dells, so rapidly that the rangers saw at once that they stood little chance of running him down.

Both were good shots, and both took simultaneous aim with fatal success, for two arrows could be seen sticking in his back as he finally disappeared from view.

The Normans smiled grimly. Their quarry could not run far with a cloth-yard shaft sticking in him, that they well knew, so they took up the chase with a loud and cheering cry that woke the echoes of the forest.

In a few minutes they reached the spot where the handsome outlaw had disappeared, and though they saw the arrows broken on the ground, they also saw marks of blood, which, with the impression of his footsteps on the green sward, enabled them easily to follow on the trail.

It led them direct towards the Convent of St. Vaux.

Surely the Sherwood robber was not going to take sanctuary!

The rangers smiled grimly. They knew the priests well.

So they continued on their way until the track ended at the foot of a steep wall, that of the convent garden.

But not a sign of the fugitive could be seen.

The keepers ran up and down like dogs that have lost the scent, searched a clump of oaks, and then confessed themselves wholly at fault.

They could, therefore, but return and report their failure to the irate and wounded head ranger.

He at once determined to demand permission of the abbess to search the grounds.

CHAPTER XXXV.

THE ESCAPE.

THE youth had truly been touched by the arrows, but the wounds inflicted were merely flesh wounds, from which, could he have halted to bind up a poultice with some of the herbs known to the outlaws, he would scarcely have experienced the slightest inconvenience.

As it was, the hurts, bleeding somewhat freely, the youth was not sorry to seek some sheltered spot where he might sconce himself awhile and bind up his wounds.

At first the fugitive scarcely noticed the way he was taking, but when the towers of the convent came in view his mind was made up. He was fast losing strength with the loss of blood, and he hoped and trusted that the pious ladies of the convent would not give him up to certain death.

No sooner did he reach the foot of the wall than he cast his glances hastily around. Not a soul was in sight, nor could he see anything to assist him.

The walls were high and apparently unapproachable.

But the outlaw's eye was keen and clear. There were some holes where probably scaffolding had rested, while some of the stones projected in a jagged and irregular manner.

With the agility of one of the squirrels which abound in the great Sherwood Forest, the young outlaw clambered up, reached the top of the wall, and aided by a branching tree, safely reached the ground.

It is needless to describe a convent garden in those days, as it was but a portion of the forest walled off. A few ornamental shrubs being added, with winding paths amid the thickets and trees.

After a few moments of repose, during which the young outlaw heard the hoarse voices of the keepers to his feet, uncertain what to do.

The noise he made startled some one seated at no great distance, and his eye fell upon the form of a beauteous girl habited in the rich garb of the noble and free.

Their glances met, and for one moment with mutual admiration. Then the maiden modesty and timidity of the young person overcame every other feeling.

"What do you here, sir?" she said; "fly ere I call assistance!"

"Lady," replied the outlaw, in a voice sadly musical, "I may not fly without repose. I have dared to climb yon wall to save my life from those who are raging for my blood."

"For your blood!" said the maiden, her cheek blanching, while she involuntarily advanced close to his side, at the same time glancing fearfully towards the convent.

"Lady," continued the youth, "for reasons I cannot now explain, save that 'tis for no crime. I am a Saxon outlaw; but now I killed me a deer, and three of the keepers would have ta'en me to certain death. I resisted, and so doing, wounded one of the rangers. Then I fled, and though myself wounded, determined to seek protection and shelter of the holy nuns."

"Hush!" said the girl, her eyes beaming and her cheeks flushing with emotion, "there is not one but would give you up at the first call. They are all Normans at heart. I alone have the will to save you; but what is to be done?"

And she stood irresolute, with her eyes cast upon the ground.

"Do not distress yourself, beauteous maiden. I will but retire to the bushes and staunch my wounds. Then will I again clamber over the wall, and escape by ways known only to myself."

A loud ringing at the convent gate startled them both. "No," said the girl, warmly, "you would faint in your present state and be caught, and your blood would be upon my head. This way: it shall never be said that Edith of Athelston ever deserted one of her race."

And, followed by the wandering outlaw, she led the way by a narrow path to the convent, opened with a key a small side door, and ushered the outlaw into a stone hall, supported by elegant columns in a foreign style of art.

"This part is reserved for ladies like myself who have not taken the veil. It is sacred as a sanctuary. I will go forth and learn what suspicions arise. Be of good cheer until I return."

The outlaw bowed low—too grateful for speech.

"I had forgotten your wounds. In yonder chamber you will find all you need: it is that of my Saxon handmaiden. If she comes say you await me."

And, without further delay, she closed the entrance to the hall, and went forth just in time to behold the two keepers, reinforced by all the convent servants, rush in the direction where they supposed the outlaw might be concealed.

The ward of the crown took not the slightest notice of

them, walking up and down at a distance, with her eyes fixed on the ground.

But she clearly heard the shouts, cries, and angry words of the foresters.

"The fellow is no witch," said one of the rangers; "here is where he crossed the wall, and here is where he sank down to rest. But, where in the foul fiend's name is he now?"

"We must search the trees," replied an officious servant.

"Tush, man! he could not burrow in such boughs as these; he is still within the garden."

And again the whole party dispersed—beating the bushes, trampling the walks, and obliterating every trace of the young man's footsteps.

"Well," suddenly said a rich, full voice—that of a woman in the pride of life—"have you found the impudent varlet?"

"No, my lady," replied one of the rangers, respectfully; "but we have seen his marks."

"Was no one in the garden?" asked the abbess, excessively annoyed to find that her high garden walls did not always keep out intruders. "Ah! my lady Edith, whence come you?"

"This instant from the house," replied Edith, meekly, glad to escape a falsehood, which otherwise she must have told.

"Then, of course you know nothing about it. Thanks! Now, good people, search the garden well. This insolent knave must be punished; though how, as he flew not, could he have crossed my walls?"

The ranger pointed to where he had glided down the wall, aided by the boughs of a picturesque elm—fragments of which were scattered on the ground—and then to the place where he had fallen heavily on the soft green turf.

"You are right. If he has not flown the way he came, he is within these walls. My servants and retainers will suffice to search—do you guard without. This night," she added, "the house shall be hunted over; and, if aid has been given to the outlaw, woe to the traitor."

The rangers made no reply, but bowed and withdrew, followed slowly and thoughtfully by the abbess, who cast one or two furtive glances at the Saxon maiden.

"She suspects me. He must escape ere vespers," she whispered to herself.

Had she suspected the real ideas of the superior, she might have felt something more of indignation.

"This rich ward of the crown refuses all Norman suitors: not the king's authority has been able to win her consent for wooing. She is too young—she wishes for time. What, if she have hoodwinked us all and has a leman? Soho! my simple daughter, this must be inquired into."

But the abbess never supposed the fugitive was in the young ladies' apartments, which were apart from those of the nuns, or dire indeed would have been the scandal.

Meanwhile Edith, having summoned her handmaiden, a hearty, rosy, merry Saxon girl, had provided the youth with all necessary refreshment. He had himself bound up his wounds, which were trifling, so that rest, good wine, and cheer would soon restore him to his wonted strength.

"And now, young sir," said Edith, "it is fit you should go. Your concealment in the chamber of a damsel of high degree can only be excused by dire necessity. But my chamber will no longer protect you."

And she told him all she had heard, to which he listened with the most profound attention mingled with the deepest gratitude.

"Lady," said the young outlaw, with a beaming smile, "you have done for one of the outcasts of the forest what few great ladies would have done, and I would not have a hair of your head, much less your fair fame, injured. I am ready to go."

"Not now," she exclaimed quickly, "you cannot escape except in darkness. The night will soon be here, and then go, and God speed you in safety!"

"So kind a wish from such fair lips will surely carry me through," said the outlaw gallantly.

"A truce to flattery," replied the lady, smiling, "you have an hour, perhaps. Tell me of the life you lead in the green forest glades."

The outlaw was delighted to talk of that which he loved, for to him the life beneath the greenwood tree had a charm which invested him as with a spell; to wander by murmuring brooks, to listen to the bellowing of the deer, and the barking of the fox, to hunt the former and destroy the latter, to practise with the bow and arrow, were things which filled his heart with gladness.

And he spoke therefore of them well and eloquently, and Edith listened with ears that drank in every sound.

Hers, too, was a free and ardent spirit, that chafed at being shut up within stone walls to please the fancies of a king, ready to give her hand to the highest bidder—to the nobleman who would make the greatest amount of sacrifices to obtain her.

Meanwhile a great change had come about. While they were talking, or rather while Edith was listening—for she could not rouse her courage to tell a stranger how much she sympathised with him and his feelings—the sun had set amid masses of dark and fiery clouds, so that night was gathering gloomily and rapidly over the forest.

"'Tis time I started," said the young outlaw, rising from a stool on which he had reclined at the maiden's feet, "and now brave damsel—remember. The outlaws of Sherwood Forest owe you a debt which one day they will repay. Come no further, the storm is about to burst—'tis safety to me, but may be peril to you."

And he bent low to kiss her hand, which, however, she gave him freely to press.

"Thanks. The day may come," she answered warmly, "when the daughter of Athelston may need and ask the aid of her countrymen."

The outlaw shook hands and then went out into the gardens.

Loud and terrible claps of thunder, attended with quick and successive flashes of lightning, told that the tempest, which had long thrown its threatening shadow over the sky, had at last burst forth.

He could hear the mighty forest trees without, all astir with their grating branches, and large heavy rain-drops clattered among the foliage, which mingling with the loud rumbling thunder, now near, now afar off, sounded like the grand but terrible rolling of the ocean.

The garden was in utter darkness, save when the blue and lurid flashes illumined it with scanty light.

The outlaw moved slowly. It was impossible to see three yards in advance of himself, so that the utmost caution had to be used not to run against any prowling spy who might be secreted along the pathways.

In this way, however, the outlaw reached the wall without let or hindrance, the fat and lazy servants of the convent preferring any shelter to being out in such a night.

"St. Dunstan shield me," muttered the outlaw, "if the storm continues like this the trees will be no shelter from danger."

He had reached the wall, and his strength much renovated by rest and refreshment, had no difficulty in climbing to its summit.

Just, however, as he was about to drop lightly down, there came a lurid flash that appeared to fill the whole forest with light, attended by a deep and awful peal of thunder.

But what the outlaw chiefly noted was, that under a large oak, at no great distance, stood the two rangers, who, at the same moment discovering him, plunged across the grass in the full conviction that they must capture their prisoner.

There was now an interval of total and extreme darkness.

Then came another flash.

Not a sign of the outlaw was to be seen, and the rangers were, under the circumstances, but too glad to give up the chase.

CHAPTER XXXVI.
NOTTINGHAM.

"And is this story true?" asked the knight, sarcastically, when the palmer had given a very brief outline of the narrative.

"That I saved a young man wounded and chased," replied the young lady, laughingly, "is true; but I never knew, nor has the palmer said, that it was Robin Hood."

"But it was," said the palmer, gravely, "most true; and when the young man was a few months after elected

King of the Outlaws, he made all his men swear to defend Edith of Athelston to the last gasp, to be at her beck and call by day and by night, to risk and lose their lives rather than she should be injured by prince, peer, or peasant."

The girl's eyes flashed brightly, but the knight was both angry and uneasy, to conceal which he made his horse curvet and jerk his haughty head and beautifully-arched neck.

At this moment they reached the summit of a wooded slope.

"Is yonder Nottingham?" said the knight, turning to the palmer.

"Yonder is Nottingham," replied the other.

"Then we need your services no more. We can find our way."

"Fie!" cried Edith, warmly; "the palmer leaves us not until he has tasted the hospitality of the guardian to whose house I am bound."

"But, lady——" began the palmer, with a low and humble bow.

"I will have no denial." said the wayward girl, gaily.

The ragged guide made no further reply, but bending his head low, retreated to the rear, where he kept his position until the cavalcade entered the ancient town of Nottingham.

We shall have other opportunities of describing this ancient city, in which many events connected with our history necessarily take place. Now we have more immediately to do with events which regard our leading characters.

Dashing up the streets at a more rapid pace than they had been able to attempt beneath the overhanging forest trees, the knight and his party soon halted before a house of splendid appearance.

It was then an old house, but not a trace of it now remains.

The whole cavalcade rode into a kind of court-yard, where, dismounting, the knight lifted Edith from the saddle, just as Sir Thomas Effingham, the haughty, insolent, purse-proud Sheriff of Nottingham, came bustling to the door.

"Give you good day, Sir Philip de Beauvoisin," he cried. "My service to your ladyship. Since the prince my good master commends you to my care pending your marriage, consider this house your own."

"I shall claim your hospitality a long time," said Edith, with a grave smile, "for I have no thought of marriage, nor should a maiden who has never been sued."

The sheriff would have made some quick reply, but the knight made a sign to the other to be silent.

This sign was seen by Edith, and caused her more alarm than even the speech of the imprudent host.

Next minute she was ushered to her chamber, where her baggage had preceded her under the charge of her Saxon handmaiden and other servants.

Scarcely had she thrown herself into a seat, with a view to repose, when in came a stout little fussy woman, richly dressed, with a good-natured look and a most voluble tongue.

"La, my dear young lady—and so you are here at last! You must be very fatigued; wilt have a drink of spiced wine—well no, you shall not. A bath? Yes—you shall—one ready in five minutes. Dinner will be served in half-an-hour—and then, while the men folk sit with their big wine flagons and talk of war and tournaments, we will look over the superb finery they have sent you for the wedding."

"Madame, I know not who you are, but surmise you to be Lady Effingham; but this I do know, that I am not going to be married."

"Lawk-a-day!" cried the stout lady; "and why not?"

"Because I have never seen the man yet whom I could select for a husband," was Edith's reply.

"But his royal highness the prince has, and his will is law."

"I am his ward," said the girl, spiritedly, "and he may take my possessions, but he cannot, and he dare not give my person against my will to a man I have never seen."

"The son of the Earl of Nottingham is no mean bridegroom."

The wicked Lord Richard?" gasped Edith. "Never.

I will die first. I pray you, lady, excuse me—I am fatigued, ill, out of sorts. I will not appear at the banquet to-day."

"But what will Sir Thomas say?"

"I have ridden far and fast," said Edith, imploringly, "and it would be cruel to force me to sit up when my head aches."

"Well, well," replied the good-natured woman; "you shall have your way now, though how you will gainsay the king is more than I can imagine."

"He is not yet king, and may never be," cried Edith, warmly.

"Hush! hush! I may not hear treason against my sovereign lord," and the worthy old lady waddled out of the room.

"And now, Rouna," said the young girl, with a wild animation which lent her form a grandeur and beauty which it had never yet displayed, "go to the offices; look round. There will be there feeding with the menials a palmer. Get speech with him, I care not how, but get speech. Bid him come here at once. I must speak with him at once. Go."

The girl, almost alarmed at her mistress's vehemence, hastened to obey, winding her way to the large kitchen hall, where the soldiers and servants were collected.

It was like all such rooms in those days, vast, with a huge fireplace, within which on benches under the yawning chimney, where scores of hams hung to dry, a dozen might cosily sit.

Most, however, were round the heavy oaken table, which groaned with good cheer, satisfying appetites which would alarm us now.

But in eating and drinking, our ancestors were giants in those days.

Rouna cast her eyes carelessly around as she joined the group of female servants and others, intent upon the dinner upstairs

But she could not see the palmer, until, happening to look in a dark corner, she espied him with a piece of bread and braun taking his solitary meal.

To glide close to him, to touch him on the shoulder, and to whisper, were to the acute serving-maid the act of a moment.

"Follow me, my mistress wants you," she whispered.

And without another word she glided to the end of the long passage that led to the state apartments of the house.

The palmer, with a slow and steady step followed, neither glancing to the right or left, until he stood in the antechamber of the room occupied by Edith of Athelstone.

It was a small apartment, lighted with a small iron lamp, and into which many doors opened; while in front of him were seven steps leading upward, at the summit of which stood the young lady herself.

"This way, palmer," she said, "I have much need of your advice."

With a low, meek bow, the palmer slowly ascended, and next entered the room to which he was summoned, the walls of which were covered with embroidered hangings, on which different coloured silks, interwoven with gold and silver threads, had been employed, with all the art of which the age was capable, to represent the sports of hunting and hawking.

There was a bed adorned with the same rich tapestry, and surrounded with curtains dyed with purple.

It was customary in England, as in France now, to receive company in a bed-room.

"Come hither, palmer," said Edith, hurriedly, as she seated herself in an arm-chair and pointed to a lowlier seat; "I summon you in haste, in that I am in trouble."

"In trouble already!" cried the other, much amazed.

"Yes, worthy man," she continued; "about that trouble I may have to tell you. But, palmer, tell me true: Are you friendly with the outlaws?"

The palmer looked carefully round, and appeared to listen with all his senses. Then he put his hand to his cowl, and, removing a mask, revealed to her astonished view the brown eyes, chesnut hair, and glowing countenance of the young outlaw she had saved.

"Art thou, indeed, famed Robin Hood?" she said, her own cheeks glowing a ruddier red than usual.

"I am; and ever at your service, in life as in death," was the solemn and earnest answer.

A deep silence ensued, during which neither spoke.

The king of Sherwood forest waited her pleasure, content to dwell upon her beaming countenance and glowing bust; while she, from some unknown feeling, hesitated to reveal her real sorrow to the youth. She had expected to tell it to an old man."

"Put on your mask," she said, after a time; "bold and brave as you are, this is no place for Robin Hood to be found."

The outlaw obeyed, and then again waited in perfect silence.

"Brave outlaw," she began, "my story is brief, indeed. My father, Sir Bosworth Athelston, being killed in the Holy Land, I became the lord of all his vast possessions, unfortunately; for I have become a ward of the crown. I need not add, that though I have ever lived in retirement, under the charge of worthy and godly nuns, rumours of the world have reached me.

"Many powerful barons and knights have sought to win my fief, and, as I must go with it, to win me," she added, blushing.

"'Tis like the Norman dogs and thieves," said Robin Hood, hoarsely.

"Lately, I was summoned here to meet the king, who is to honour the sheriff with his presence; but I fear I am sent for a most cruel and wicked purpose."

"And that is —— ?" asked the outlaw, his eyes gleaming through his mask.

"To marry me to the bad Lord Richard, son to the Earl of Nottingham," she replied.

"Whom God confound both !" he cried.

"Amen. But of this another time. I have sent for you to know if you will assist me to escape this—worse than death?"

"I will, at any price," was the calm response.

"Dost intend staying long in Nottingham?" she asked.

"Lady, I love to tread the daisies of my native glades, to lie beneath the oak and elm and watch the deer playing in the sun patches of the green sward—for I never kill but for food. I delight to wander by the murmuring brook, whence I quench my thirst—but my duty before liking. I am at your service."

"I will see the king," she replied, "and if my beseechings will not prevail on him to undo this great wrong, then will I put my trust in God and thee."

"I hope to fulfil the trust," said the outlaw proudly.

"Where shall I find you, and by what token?" was the answer.

"Send this glove," he replied, taking one from the table at hand, "to the widow Ann of the Lea, in the market-place, and I will be at your side in half-an-hour."

"And will guide me safely to the holy sanctuary, where I will take the veil rather than be coerced?"

"I will—but should ill betide me, take this little horn, gain the wood, wind it the best you may—and if, at the third blast, you have not friends around you, my power is forgotten."

At this moment Rouna entered, and the conference broke off, the palmer returning to the kitchen, from which he, however, soon made his escape, having heard quite enough.

An inroad had been decided on the fastnesses of the outlaws, in which not only the retainers of the Earl of Beauclerk were to join, but the posse comitatus, headed by the sheriff, with such royal troops as could be spared.

Scarcely had the palmer disappeared, when the bustling dame re-entered with a flushed and excited countenance.

"What is the matter, worthy madame?" said Edith politely.

"Matter! that the king is not coming—that there is a rising in the north, which he must fain quell, and that the Earl of Nottingham will not march until he sees his son married to thee, my fair wench. So make up thy mind. It will be all over before twelve of the morrow. Pray urge me not to stay—imagine the feasting I have to attend to."

CHAPTER XXXVII.

MARIAN'S FLIGHT.

NEXT minute the girl was alone, except that her maid stood apart awaiting her commands. She was stunned with the news.

For some minutes she sat gazing on vacancy, as if vainly striving to collect her thoughts.

"This most foul and bitter wrong shall not be," she cried. "Rouna, you have heard the news?"

"And fine news too, to marry off a noble maiden to a man she never saw."

"I will not wed him, though I die," she replied; "but my mind is made up. Though I forswear Edith of Athelston and become the maid Marian of the outlaws, they shall not find me here to-morrow."

The girl looked as if she thought her insane, but Edith was calm and collected.

"But how will you escape alone?" asked Rouna.

"You know the way to thy grandfather's hut?" asked Edith.

"I do, every step of the way," replied the Saxon girl, boldly.

"Thither we will fly, and at once. Give me a dress as near like thy own as possible. Not a minute is to be lost—the wicked earl may change his purpose once more."

The girl, who was both courageous and fond of her mistress, at once hastened to equip her in the garb of a serving maiden. Their fingers shook with anxiety, but at length the disguise was complete, and casting a cowl over her head, the noble lady, guided by the maid, descended to the offices, passed through the kitchen, and went out.

It had previously been arranged that Edith should walk slowly to the end of the town, even to the skirt of the forest, while Rouna with the glove, should seek the widow Ann of the Lea, and give the pledge to the rightful party.

She was then, with or without him, to rejoin Edith on the dark skirt of the forest.

With this resolve she threaded her way towards the market-place, where, alone at that hour, the populace congregated inside and outside the ale houses.

We will first follow the fortunes of the poor girl, driven by the wicked lawlessness of the times to abdicate her high position for a while, and seek shelter first in a peasant's hut, and then in a Saxon abbey, where she might hope for protection against even the rage of the prince who now ruled England.

In the days of which we speak even oil lanterns were unknown in the streets, which, rendering them to a certain extent unsafe, made them clear of nearly all passers-by soon after dusk.

The young girl, therefore, found no difficulty in leaving the town, or in crossing the narrow skirting of corn-fields which separated it from the forest.

Hers was a brave woman's heart, and yet it was not without something like awe that she approached the edge of that vast woodland tract which the fervid imaginations of our peasantry declared to be haunted, and of which so much was said over the cheerful and blazing fire on long winter nights.

Plucking up her courage, however, and resolved at any cost not to be taken by the servants of the Sheriff of Nottingham, she soon entered a deep ravine with an almost precipitous descent, the bottom of which once reached, she halted, fully aware that she could make herself heard by any she wished.

The spot selected by her as a hiding-place was one than which no wilder could have been found.

It was on the verge of a brawling brook, the precipitous banks of which were overhung with heavy hawthorns, while the darkness threw its blue dimness over the whole scene, making the trees that overhung trees, and branches rising above branch, look more like threatening piles of rock than anything else.

Seating herself on a huge stone under a stunted, stumpy oak, the young girl waited, listening anxiously for every sound.

But for some time nothing could be heard but the trickling stream.

The time that elapsed from her arrival in the glen seemed interminable, while the mind was filled with strange and peculiar fancies.

The young girl thought much of the bold outlaw, whose aspect was now indelibly impressed on her memory.

Suddenly, however, a shadow passed across the mouth of the glen, and she heard the voice of Rouna :

"Fly—mistress, fly—your escape is known, and Robin Hood is taken !"

THE ESCAPE FROM NOTTINGHAM.

For a moment the quick-witted girl was as it were paralysed, but next minute recovering addressed herself to the handmaiden.

"Return. I will conceal me in the wood. Heaven will have care of honest Robin Hood."

And without further words Edith, as for the present we must call her, seeing lights come dotting over the plain that intervened between Nottingham and the forest, disappeared within the trees, while Rowna glided along the skirt of the forest in the hope of escaping unperceived.

CHAPTER XXXVIII.

CAPTURE OF ROBIN.

THE wary chief of the outlaws had in every town and village round Sherwood some hiding place wherein to remain concealed when it suited his purpose to visit the ordinary habitations of men. It was necessary he should occasionally do so, in order to become acquainted with the various attempts which were continually made, not so much to conquer him by sheer force, as to entrap him by some artful trick.

One of these was the house of the widow Ann of the Lea, which on more than one occasion had sheltered the bold outlaw.

Thither, after parting with Edith of Athelston, he took his way, intending to abide an hour or so before he kept an appointment he had made.

He did so, and was received by the lone widow—her sons being absent—with her usual alacrity and glee.

The stout outlaw, still disguised as a palmer, threw himself on a rude couch, being by this time in need of repose, and, enjoying good and powerful health, was soon in a sound sleep.

But not of long duration. He had business to attend to which would not admit any long repose. At the end of three hours, after bidding the widow Ann fetch him if he was summoned by Edith, went out, directing his steps to one of the lone alehouses where he had appointed to meet Little John and Will Scarlett.

The public room of the alehouse was, as usual, a large kitchen, nearly full of soldiers, mixed with a few townspeople, the latter of whom made way for the palmer, who in this way reached an obscure corner, where he could remain an unnoted listener of all that took place.

The soldiers were, as usual, loud and noisy in their conversation, which had particular reference to the coming foray in the forest, of which they spoke very freely and merrily, though there were some who made wry faces enough at the prospect of coming in contact with the cloth yard shafts of the yeomen.

The townsmen said but little, though the glances they exchanged were gloomy enough. They suffered quite as much as the peasants from the insolence and arrogance of the soldiery, while every now and then some deed of violence or wrong sent some of them to recruit the out-laws.

"If this expedition be but carried out as well as it is planned," said one, "we shall be quit of these outlaws and the woods once more be safe."

"Humph!" cried a grey old soldier, "planning and carrying out are two."

"Pish! what can these Lincoln green yeomen do against men-at-arms, clad in steel—led, too, by knights in mail?" continued another.

"These same knaves in Lincoln green," added another, "have a strange way of picking off men, however pro-tected by shirts of mail. I would rather fight in open field against men-at-arms, then I would contend against fellows who skulk behind trees."

"They do not always skulk behind trees," said the palmer, in a half whining half sarcastic voice, "I have seen them fight fairly in the open glade."

"Hast thou?" replied one of the soldiers eagerly; "then I suppose you could lead us to their haunts, since thou knowest them so well."

"A poor palmer who oftener sleeps beneath a tree than a roof may see many things without being either an asso-ciate or a friend of the outlaws," continued the palmer discreetly.

"Thou liest!" roared the voice of one who stepped for-ward from behind the crowd of soldiers, "thou liest, Robin Hood."

All started to their feet with a perfect Babel of voices, as the man, a beetle-browed, dark-eyed fellow, stood sullenly forward.

"Man, thou art surely possessed," said the palmer quietly, "to take a holy man for a stalwart outlaw."

"I am neither possessed nor mistaken," was the bitter reply. "I am Hal, the weaver, whom thou did'st scourge with hazel boughs."

"I know thee now, knave," said the outlaw, raising himself proudly, "would that I had scourged to the death, cowardly hound!"

"You are, then, Robin Hood?" asked a subordinate officer, advancing.

"I am not what I seem," was the cold reply of the palmer. "If you believe yon cur, who was hunted from the forest for illusing a woman, why ask me?"

At a signal from the officer, two powerful soldiers clutched Robin by the arm, and tore off his disguise, when he stood before them truly a forester, his face beaming with haughty pride.

"You are my prisoner. To the lock-up with him, my men; let a dozen surround the cage and guard him, at the peril of their lives. The sheriff holds high festival—but in the morn his pleasure will be kuown."

Robin Hood made no reply to this, but looked keenly at his betrayer.

"Hal, the weaver," he said, "go you not in the forest, for as surely as you live by bread, so surely shalt thou die."

And he went forth with his escort, walking as proudly as any other captured king might have done in the midst of his guard.

The renegade outlaw, who, expelled the fraternity, had taken service in the train of the sheriff, shuddered visibly.

"You hate this Robin Hood?" said the officer, address-ing him.

"I do," replied the pale and almost repentant wretch.

"Then as you have served him, you must know his haunts—you shall be guide to-morrow," was the significant reply.

"Nay, heard you not what he said," cried the terrified renegade.

"Make that excuse to the sheriff," said the officer. "we have captured the chief. The rest will be easy work."

Had the soldiers not been so elated with their cap-ture as to think of nothing else, they must have noticed the significant looks exchanged between some of the towns-men when Robin Hood was captured, and how, one by one, they all left the room to return to their homes.

Among them were three men, whose close resemblance of face and figure proclaimed them brothers.

They were the three sons of the widow Ann of the Lea, and devoted adherents of Robin Hood.

They went forth into the night, which was now exces-sively dark, and gliding along the wall like shadows, soon reached the skirts of the town, where the plain commenced.

One of them, after looking keenly about, gave a low but prolonged whistle.

It was responded to from a small patch of heath close by.

"Art true men?" said the first brother, Andrew.

"Good men and true," replied a tall man, rising from the scanty retreat of the heather, "what is the news?"

"Bad. The chief is taken—betrayed by Hal the weaver."

"The foul fiend have him by the throat," answered the other, hotly, "but where have they put him?"

"In the lock-up," said Andrew of the Lea.

"We are but five—there are no others within call," said the tall man moodily, "but he must be saved or I must perish."

"All! all!" responded those around him, in low, hushed voices.

"Then follow," exclaimed the other, "what is to be done, must be done quickly."

And creeping back with the noiseless step of the red Indian, the outlaws disappeared in the shadows of the houses.

CHAPTER XXXIX.

WILL, THE TAPSTER.

THE prison into which Robin Hood was thrust, was a solid round tower of stone, somewhat ancient, having been the cage or lock-up house of Nottingham from time im-memorial.

It had several narrow loop-holes to admit light and air, while the ground was strewn with rushes and straw, by way of bed for prisoners.

The door was a heavy oaken affair, so that, guarded by a dozen men-at-arms, there could be no hope for the most sanguine prisoner.

The first few minutes of vexation and annoyance passed, however, Robin Hood began to cheer up.

Not that he had the faintest idea of any plan of escape, but because he was one of those brave and enduring hearts which never despond, never give way to the ordinary weak-nesses of human nature.

He heard the heavy bolt drawn, the key turned in the lock, and found himself in total darkness. He then quietly felt about, until he came in contact with a pile of rushes and straw, on which he cast himself to reflect.

This he did for some time with closed eyes, nor were his thoughts of the most agreeable character.

His very first idea was in relation to the Lady Edith, who might at the very moment be in peril, and need that assistance which he could not give.

Then, for a moment, gentler thoughts came upon him. Robin Hood could not deny to himself that the bright eyes and lovely form of Edith of Athelston had made a deep impression on him—an impression not easily to be effaced.

But of what avail could his misplaced affection? There were many mysteries with regard to his own birth, but he had every reason to believe himself an orphan, adopted by very humble parents; and as the thought flashed across his mind, his cheek flushed, the hot blush reached to his forehead, and a kind of strange shame filled his soul.

That the maiden had looked kindly on him, that she had smiled and spoken tenderly was natural; for had she not saved his life, while she herself expected an equally im-portant service from him.

A greater; for, with a true woman, honour is far dearer than life itself.

His task once accomplished they would meet no more. Edith of Athelston would marry some man of her choice in her own station of life, or she would retire altogether to the sanctuary of a convent.

In either case she was equally lost to him.

Robin Hood had totally forgotten his own forlorn and helpless position.

He was recalled to it by hearing his guard muttering about the cold.

He opened his eyes and gazed moodily around his prison, of which he could just make out the contour in the dim and flickering light.

He listened, but could make out nothing but half spoken words. Then came a louder call.

"Who goes there? Avaunt! we want no prowlers about here."

"Nor no hot spiced ale?" replied a voice, with a loud laugh.

Robin Hood pricked up his ears. His quick intelligence told him that something favourable to himself was about to happen.

"Is that Will the tapster?" said the soldier who had first spoken.

"Yes!" continued the other; "the captain sent me. He said it would keep out the cold, but that you must not go to sleep."

"No danger of that with this cold wind," was the growling reply; "but give us the ale—my inside is like a hollow lump of ice."

"And mine!" cried every soldier in unison.

The tapster advanced and began serving out the mixture.

"When was our captain ever so generous before?" said the first speaker; "'tis laced with foreign strong waters. Fore god! It is rare stuff!"

"'Tis in honour of the capture of the great outlaw. Ha! ha! the sheriff will give you something more substantial when he hears of it to-morrow."

This was said with a slightly peculiar inflection of voice.

"Oh! oh!" thought Robin; "then the sheriff is not yet aware."

The soldiers, meantime, made no response, but smacking their lips with intense satisfaction, soon finished the huge black-jack with which the tapster had come provided.

He then retired, after promising to return in about an hour.

Robin Hood listened with the deepest and most intense interest.

Will the tapster was one of his many confidential agents.

Gradually Robin heard the soldiers, muttering something about being tired of standing, seat themselves one after another on the ground around the tower.

Then came a chorus of the most unmusical of snores.

Robin rubbed his hands. The spiced ale was surely drugged.

"Hist! hist!" said a voice speaking through one of the upper loop-holes—a voice that thrilled to the very heart of Robin Hood.

"I hear, my faithful Little John," he answered in the same tone.

"I am going to drop in a knife and chisel. Can you reach to the beam on the roof?"

"No," said Robin, after a careful examination, "it is too high."

"Remain quiet, then—stir not," were Little John's next words.

Then some whispering followed, after which the outlaw heard somebody at work on the roof, in which he soon saw a hole appear.

By means of the gigantic stature of Little John, a confederate had ascended to the top of the cage, and was removing the roof.

Robin, though fuming at the inaction he was condemned to, stood still, watching the others progress with intense interest.

Soon the hole was enlarged sufficiently, and then a dark body passed through.

"All is now ready!" whispered the voice of Will Scarlett; "wait till I get out."

And something fell at Robin Hood's feet as the other spoke.

It was knotted cord, by means of which in another moment the outlaw had reached a thick cross-beam, from which he passed on to the roof. Will Scarlett was already on the ground.

Little John stood close to the wall, ready for his captain to step on to his shoulder.

At the same time a cry, or rather a yell, rose from the inn door, which was close to the cage.

"He is escaping! Treachery!—foul treachery! Up—up!"

It was the frantic voice of Hal the weaver, who had stepped out into the night air to cool his heated brow.

Then a strange shriek, an unearthly cry, rose over the stillness, and for a moment silence followed.

Then out poured the drunken soldiers to find the renegade outlaw writhing in the agonies of death, an arrow through his heart.

The captain rushed eagerly towards the tower.

"Ye base and idle knaves," he roared, kicking one with his foot, "up and account for this base desertion of your duty!"

But the man moved not, any more than a dead body.

"Drugged, as I am a living man!" cried the officer, throwing open the door of the tower, and peering in with fierce and angry glance.

No second one was required. The hole in the roof was quite sufficient.

But the fugitives could not be far off; so, rushing back to where the rest of the men crowded around the fallen and treacherous outlaw, he bade them follow.

CHAPTER XL.

MARIAN'S FLIGHT.

WHEN Rowna asserted that the flight of Edith of Athelston had been discovered, she made a mistake. She had learned by a visit to the Widow Ann of the Lea, that Robin Hood was not there, having left some time.

It was the loud shouts that proclaimed the capture of Robin Hood, which, deceiving and terrifying Rowna, made her apprehensive that the escape of her young mistress was known. Had it been so, the uproar would have been somewhat greater.

Edith had no sooner reached what appeared to be a secure hiding-place, than she halted, still hoping that the misfortune announced as having befallen the brave captain of the outlaws was a mistake, and that he ultimately would join her.

Almost utterly inexperienced in the ways that led through the forest, how could she possibly avoid capture, if tracked by the satellites of the Earl of Nottingham and the Sheriff?

Another feeling, too, unconsciously affected her. She had often thought of the handsome youth whose life she had saved, but never in the same way that she now did.

The danger to his life made her scan her own heart, and her heart told her how inexpressibly dear his was to her, and how their lives were bound up together.

With what delicious satisfaction Robin would have received this revelation!

But how often are two devoted hearts thus separated by timidity on the one side, and coyness on the other, until accident or irresistible impulse reveals the secret.

Wearied at last, and cold, Edith rose to her feet, and began walking up and down, having no desire to go to sleep in that dreary spot.

Suddenly she heard, or fancied she heard, footsteps close behind her.

Consulting only the impulse of the moment, she ran, dashing into a pathway that led through a thicket of pine trees growing close together.

"Stop!" said a gruff voice, "stop, or it will be all the worse for you."

But the girl was too terrified to be checked by that which proved her alarms to be well grounded, and dashing forward, increased her pace to a fast run.

All the while she could hear the heavy footsteps of a man crashing after her.

Fearing she knew not what, Edith again reaching the brook, waded into its midst, which brought her beneath a dark vista of trees, so thick and short a distance apart as to shroud her in total darkness.

This was fortunate, as it compelled her to slacken her pace, and thus to make no noise.

She at once knew that the ruffian was at fault, as she could hear him swearing, raving, and shouting to her.

He used the most horrible and fearful threats, some of which came to her ears.

But this only made her more careful; and so with a silent prayer she continued on her way, though some parts were so dark she could scarcely see.

At length the water, rising to above her knees, compelled her to land, which she did on a smooth, soft bank, where she sank a moment to regain her breath.

As she did so, beneath the sweeping boughs of the tall

and crowded trees, she caught sight of a distant light, as of that from a large fire.

Cold, wet, and even hungry, Edith determined to make her way to where the friendly blaze appeared to promise warmth and shelter.

She determined, however, to use the most extreme caution, as she was fully aware the forest contained ruffians who, under the pretence of belonging to the outlawed bands of Robin Hood, pillaged, robbed, and murdered. In these hands no maiden would be safe a moment.

Scarcely had Edith, holding her breath, began to take the direction of the fire, than she once more heard the heavy steps behind her.

No—they were at the side, slightly in advance of her.

She could hear the man muttering and swearing all the way he walked.

Was he advancing in the direction of the fire, and if so, what was she to do?

To lie down in the forest was to catch her death of cold, wet as she was, and without anything to cover her from the heavy dew.

At all events, she would keep on her way, using the most extreme caution not to betray herself to her invisible enemy.

In this way she soon came to a regular pathway, a hard beaten track, which widened as she advanced, but was so dark, it was scarcely possible to see her way.

Presently the pathway diverged into two tracks, along one of which she saw the figure of a man walking as one affected by liquor.

Suddenly he turned sharp round, and Edith had scarcely time to disappear behind a bush.

The man muttered something and continued on his way, while the young girl, her heart almost dead within her, followed the other path.

She could still catch occasional glimpses of the fire, the character of which was soon fully explained to her.

The path she had taken, neglected and partly overgrown by brushwood, had evidently been deserted for the other, as it suddenly ended in a thicket on the edge of a clearing.

This clearing had on its opposite side a semi-circle of huts or wigwams of a very curious formation.

They were entirely composed of poles about twelve feet high, tied together at the top in a bunch, and spreading out at the bottom, where the interstices were filled up by boughs and turf.

In front of them smoked and smouldered a huge pile of wood.

She had reached a village of charcoal burners.

No sooner did she make this discovery than her fears were somewhat allayed. Still, the man had pursued her with foul language and threats of the most awful description—threats expressed in language which few respectable women would now understand.

If we are not more moral than our ancestors, we have the outward signs.

She could see him plain enough now, crossing the clearing, staggering under the weight of two huge jars of ale.

He had himself evidently had his fill in the town.

His comrades saluted him with a mingled chorus of satisfaction at the sight of the strong ale, of anger at his delay in the town.

He tried to exculpate himself as well as he could, but his companions cut him short by catching hold of the jars, and pouring them out into pint blackjacks.

"Well, here's all our jolly healths," said one powerful-looking fellow, whose black face made him look quite demoniacal.

A loud shout responded to this ancient English custom, and then these hard-worked men enjoyed general conversation.

"Any news, Thomas of the Valley?" said one of the watchers.

"Robin Hood's taken, and likely to swing to a tree," said the messenger to the town.

An involuntary groan burst from Edith, who was listening to every word, and in an instant all were on foot, and the poor girl was dragged forth from her place of concealment.

"Eh!—a spy! I knew I heard sommat," said the half-drunken man, who had already terrified her. "Eh, lass, do you know how we serves spies?—eh."

"I am no spy."

"We pitches 'em into yon fire," he continued, with a brutal laugh.

They were all standing round her at some little distance, and Edith thought she had never seen so awful a collection of ruffians.

She was entirely in their power, and had nothing to expect.

Suddenly the last words of Robin Hood occurred to her, and putting the horn to her lips, blew three shrill blasts.

The men all started forward, as if to clutch at the little bugle.

"Stand back—ye shall only take it from me with my life."

"Be that Robin Hood's horn?" said one of them respectfully.

"It is."

"Then order us in everything, for we are your bounden servants."

"Can I trust you?"

"Our lives are at your disposition," said one young man, stepping forward. "Though charcoal burners, we own no monarch save bold Robin Hood, under whose protection we all live."

"Then give me some shelter, however rude—for I am faint, wet and cold," hastily replied Edith.

Scarcely were the words out of her mouth, than two girls, who had stepped out of a cabin of better appearance than the rest, hastened to her side, took her inside, and in five minutes had given her clean though coarse change of raiment, some milk and bread which she scarcely tasted, throwing herself utterly exhausted on a rude couch of leaves and skins, where, wholly overcome by the night's terrible exertions, she slept.

CHAPTER XLI.

THE FAITHFUL GUIDE.

THE sun-light was touching the tree tops, and the grey morn was merging into bright day-light; there was a rich purple tint on the dewy foliage, the trees cast regular and defined shadows, and the wind, now warm and balmy, sighed pleasantly through the trees, when Edith rose and found her new friends ready with a breakfast of coarse bread and milk, accompanied by venison steaks.

These made her smile, despite her sufferings and anxieties of mind.

"You have a breakfast for a princess." she said to the two young girls.

"We have a friend a keeper in the the forest, who sometimes gives us a buck," replied the older one, with a blush, and yet a merry twinkle of the eye which betokened little fear of their guest.

"Or a sweetheart who is a very good shot," replied Edith.

The girls made no reply, except to press the food upon their high-born guest, who, as much to please the untaught and unsophiscated girls, did her best to do justice to the repast.

This done, she resumed her own clothes, which were quite dry, and drew forth money with which to pay for her entertainment.

"We may not, lady. The captain of the outlaws would never forgive that one who bore his horn by her side should pay for shelter or food."

Edith blushed—why, they knew not.

"Then will I find other way to reward you. Can you give me a guide to the convent of St. Withold?—where, until better times, I would seek refuge."

"In what part of the forest is St. Withold?" asked the elder girl.

"I searcely know," said Edith; "but it is a good day's walk."

"One moment, lady," continued the girl; "there is one among us who will gladly for pay conduct you thither. He is a kind of mendicant, and does his rounds at every convent and monastery in the land. He has rested with us a few days, but now, being well, he is off again."

"I will pay him gladly," replied Edith.

The girl vanished, and soon returned with a man leaning on a staff, who wore the garb of those semi-monkish beggars, who go about living on the charity of the good-natured and benevolent.

He said, if the maiden could submit to his slow walking, he would guide her safely to the sanctuary she wished to reach.

"I will walk your own pace, good man," replied Edith, and perceiving that the man was ready, she once more thanked her entertainers, and followed in his slow and measured footsteps.

The forest was now lovely in the extreme, the day permeating even to the roots of the trees, and amid the under-brush and bush growth; the birds sang in every covert, and on every bough dashed or not with dewy spray. The way the mendicant took was at first beneath a rich growth of chestnuts, which perfumed the air with their bloom. He seemed to know the forest well, for though he walked but slowly he avoided all rude and rugged ways, selecting rather the green sward, as if careful of the young girl's delicate feet.

About midday he halted near a spring, and pointing to a green spot under a tree, advised Edith to rest herself, while he himself pulled out his wallet and began to eat.

The girl was healthy and hearty enough to be thankful that the charcoal burners had supplied her with food, of which she eat, having done which she advanced to the water to drink and wash her hands.

When she turned round her guide had disappeared. Not a trace of him was to be seen.

She accordingly seated herself to wait his pleasure, glad to repose a little, and fell into a reverie.

This was soon broken by footsteps at no great distance, and then a man of terrible aspect stood before her.

His face was of that villainous turn which belongs peculiarly to those who collect their income from the purses of others, while to this was added the confirmed aspect of a cut-throat.

While his skull, cheeks, and chin were covered with a profusion of matted red hair, there could be seen peering out from these a huge hook nose, worthy of the low class Jew, while his black eyes glared like carbuncles.

His body doublet was of goat-skin, while round his legs were trunks of the same.

He had naked legs, and sandals tied by coarse thongs.

He carried a cross-bow in his hand, and a short Roman sort of sword by his side.

Edith hastily rose to her feet and stared at him with all the firmness and coolness she could assume.

"Well, how like you me?" he said, with a loud laugh, "speak up, Jim of the glen is not cruel to the fair."

"I know you not, and this is no time or place for joking," she replied, "where is my guide? Surely you have not hurt the old man?"

"Hurt the old man!" roared the other in a tone of genuine enjoyment, as if he appreciated his own wit, "by no means. I love him as I do myself."

"Conduct me to him then, that I may continue my journey," said Edith.

The ruffian seemed to enjoy some exquisite joke, though what it was did not just then appear, for in his ecstasy he sat down on the bank and laughed until his sides shook.

"Come hither my dainty maiden," he said, "sit you down and I will explain all."

"I decline any conference with a stranger, and wish to know why you would detain me from continuing my journey. Where is the old man?"

"There is no old man," he answered with a leer, "being wounded and sick, I assumed a disguise. You wanted a sanctuary, I have found you one. Sit down or I will force you."

"Beware how you lay a finger on me," she said, with cold and steady firmness. "Robin Hood will avenge me well."

"Ah! you claim Robin Hood as a friend, do you?" he replied with a fiendish glance, "then the more reason for keeping you. I hate him; he is no true man, and would gainsay a poor man's right to live as he lives himself."

At the same time he glanced round amid the bushes as if he were half afraid the bold outlaw might suddenly appear.

Edith turned as for a place to flee to, but the wretch caught her wrist.

"Look you, my forest flower," he said, with an ignoble grin, "Robin Hood is by this time swinging to the sheriff's gibbet—but if he were alive I fear him not. I took a fancy to you the moment I saw you, and vowed you should be my loving wife. I have my cave close at hand—that shall be your sanctuary—while there shall be the sweetest

leaves for your bed, the daintiest venison for your food. What can you ask more?"

Poor Edith knew not what to do. To refuse the powerful and villainous ruffian, was to drive him to brutal violence—to pretend acquiescence was even more dangerous still.

She endeavoured to steer a middle course—the safest according to the poet, though, as a general rule, the poet is wrong.

"This, sir forester, is not the way a maiden should be wooed," she replied; "conduct me safely to St. Withold, and trust to my gratitude."

"Ah! ah! ah! oh! oh! ho!" cried the ruffian, laughing, "a fine for that speech—a kiss for a forfeit—it shall be the first of thousands."

Quick as lightning Edith drew his short sword, and smote him such a blow on the face just across the eyes as fairly blinded him, compelling him to put his hands to his face.

When he had wiped away the blood which trickled from his forehead, the girl was nowhere to be seen, though he fancied in the distance he saw the fluttering of her light garments.

With a fearful execration he commenced the pursuit, half inclined to shoot her with a cross-bolt.

But he believed himself to have a far surer revenge in store.

CHAPTER XLII.

FLIGHT.

MEANWHILE Edith, labouring under an agony of terror, flew along, though she really felt as if she could fall at every step. But she was none of those who faint at the slightest thing which alarms them.

She determined to do battle for her honour and her life.

She knew that he was after her in a very few minutes after she had struck the blow.

He had indeed done so, but he was for a long time at fault. Had Edith known sufficiently of the forest to keep straight in one direction, she might easily have escaped.

But, like a frightened bird, she ran in any direction which seemed open and clear.

In this way she doubled on herself, and when she thought herself far away from the spot whence she had started, was close to it.

Then she heard footsteps quite plainly, followed by the crashing of a heavy body through bushes.

By a kind of instinct she stood still in the hope of thus deceiving him, next moment stooping behind the wide trunk of a tree.

Soon she saw him glaring round like some wild beast in search of prey. He had not discovered her hiding-place as yet, but she could hardly hope to escape one whose trade was to track the wild beast to its lair.

Presently she saw his face illumined by a sudden light as of triumph, and knew she was discovered.

Losing all presence of mind, she now ran away, filling the air with her shrieks—shrieks that were heartrending in their intensity.

Guided now by an infallible medium, the ruffian ran over the ground with a speed which she, panting and breathless, could not equal for many minutes; when suddenly, just as she rolled down a green bank, fainting and nearly insensible, she heard her pursuer give vent to cries almost as piercing as her own.

But Edith, fearful of some ruse, as soon as she regained her breath, crept away, leaving the cruel forester to whatever fate had befallen him, which was not romantic but quite natural and proper.

At the bottom of the slope down which she had fallen was a stream, which she skirted a little while, until she found herself embedded, as it were, in a cluster of oaks, so cloaked by creeping plants, that she had to crawl under them ere she could reach the shelter.

Here she determined to repose until such time as she regained her composure.

Scarcely had she done so when she heard horses' footsteps in various directions, but all approaching her direction.

"Leave the fiend's cub to his fate. 'Tis the girl we must find. An' we go back without the Lady Edith or the archer Robin Hood, we shall gain but a sorry welcome."

Despite her danger, there was balm in these words. The bold outlaw who agreed to assist her to escape from the hateful bondage of a husband she detested was free.

She scarcely knew how much she did detest him until she had seen again the manly form of the king of Sherwood forest.

Now she felt as if death in any shape were far more welcome.

"She cannot have gone far," said one of the retainers, "here are marks of her footsteps—here she rolled down the bank."

"Egad!" cried the first speaker, "you are right. May St. Dunstan take me to his bosom if there be not a brook at the bottom. What if she fell in? Hold my horse while I descend."

And Edith heard the man-at-arms cautiously descending the slope. There was nothing for it but to trust to her hiding-place.

The least sound of an unusual character would betray her presence.

It appeared, however, that after rolling down the bank, she had made no trail; for the man was at fault, and continually muttering to himself, began beating the bushes just as he would have done to start game.

The hawthorn bushes and tall gorse, the stunted heaths, however, seemed to give forth nothing, and the man became angry, muttering all the while.

He was now in such close proximity to the unfortunate young girl, that between the boughs and leaves she could see him.

It was a dreadful moment, fraught with agony.

She saw his eyes fixed on the bushes, and felt sure that he must examine them, when her capture was certain.

Desperate cases have to be treated with desperate remedies.

Next instant the echoes of the forest were awakened by the tra-la-la of a horn.

The man started as if shot.

The tra-la-la was repeated, and yet a third time.

The sound was clear and distinct, but evidently blown by some youthful mouth.

The man-at-arms had been doubtful at the first as to the precise locality whence the sound came; but next instant he pushed aside the bushes and caught sight of the flying form of Edith.

In an instant he was after her, but before he could move two steps, two men in Lincoln green, armed with quarterstaves, stood in his way.

"Back! you ugly knaves," roared the man-at-arms, in order to attract the attention of his companions; "back, ye black-muzzled varlets." They were masked, and as he spoke he cut at them furiously with his sword.

But while one tripped him up with his huge pole, the other gave him such a cut or two over the back and sides as made him wish he had been more civil.

When he got up, and at his call, his companions rejoined him, all trace of outlaws and girl had disappeared.

When Edith found that her winding a call had brought assistance once more, she paused in her flight and waited the result.

In two minutes more they were by her side, and had led her out of reach of the Normans.

"Lady—you carry by your side a horn, which, albeit blown by no manly mouth, we know well. We are at your orders—what would you?"

"Be taken somewhere, where I can have repose and shelter until I can see your chief, if, indeed, he truly have escaped."

"Escaped!" cried one of the outlaws; "what mean you, lady?"

Edith told them all that was in her power to tell.

"You bring us bad and yet hopeful news, lady," said one of the outlaws; "but, be this as it may—it is our duty to see you safely housed first. Pray follow."

It was now night.

The path followed by the men in Lincoln green—one not easily to have been traced by the horsemen—was through a part of the wood thickly studded with oaks. Although the moon had already arisen, and shone brightly enough, the exuberance of the rich foliage cast a deep gloom over their path.

Sometimes, while passing through open glades, the light was as great as in the grey of morn, but next minute they were meandering through thickets, brakes, and coverts, where none could have seen a trail, save experienced foresters.

Then Edith would not refuse the assistance courteously offered by the outlaws, when she could scarcely keep her feet amid the jagged roots of the trees and the dense copsewood, through which they passed in darkness.

At length they reached the end of a long and winding path, and found themselves on the edge of a smooth and expansive opening, carpeted with delicious green; in the centre of which stood a millhouse, on the borders of a stream of pure water, that flashed bravely in the calm moonlight, and flowed with a low and pleasant sound.

CHAPTER XLIII.

MUCH THE MILLER.

In another moment the men were knocking at the front door, though not a light could be seen from any chink.

"Who knocks?" said a gruff voice, as if of one awakened from his sleep.

"Open! minions of the moon; there be hawks abroad."

"Sayest thou so?" was the answer, and next minute the door was opened by the sturdy miller, exhibiting a perfectly dazzling light.

He stared at the sight of the exhausted girl, whose pale haggard face and torn clothes did not wholly conceal her quality.

The men took him on one side and said a few words.

"Lady, I am at your command. What is there for your service?"

"Rest, my good man, rest; for I am utterly exhausted, and could lie me down on yonder settle."

"Nay, fair lady, I have a chamber will suit thee better. It was my mother's. My ancient beldame here," pointing to an old woman who sat spinning, utterly unconscious of what was going on, "will show you to it."

And while he gave instructions to the deaf old creature by means of signs, Edith briefly thanked him, and then retired to her chamber.

The outlaws, who had accomplices in almost every grade among the yeomanry, now held council and came to the conclusion that it was their bounden duty to defer every consideration to carrying out the wishes of their captain.

He never confided his own horn to any but one he wished to defend at any price.

They resolved then to remain in the mill-house all night, and when the exhausted girl was sufficiently rested, to remove her to one of their more secret fastnesses until further orders.

This decided on, all determined on rest, which they needed, and soon no sound was heard in the forest save the hard breathing of the men.

But all were up at cock-crow, Edith leaping from her couch with all the elasticity of youth.

A hasty meal had been prepared, sufficiently abundant, however; there being wheaten bread and brown barley cakes and venison, and eel pies in staring pewter platters, and brown vessels with yellow honey, nor any lack of milk and ale.

Suddenly one of the outlaws stepped to the window, his quick ear having caught some sound.

"This way, lady—not an instant is to be lost. That man must have followed us on foot and gone back to bring his fellows. Keep them dancing until we are snug."

"Put away all this feasting," said Much, by signs, to the deaf old lady.

Meanwhile the outlaw had pushed away a flour hutch, and thus revealed a ladder leading right down to the water's edge.

"Go down, lady, move not when you reach the bottom, nor make the faintest sound."

Edith obeyed, and was immediately followed by her two supporters. In two minutes they were crouching on the water's edge, concealed only by some willows.

Then they distinctly heard blows against the mill-house door, the neighing of horses, and the loud voices of men calling to the miller to open.

Then, under cover of this noise, one of the outlaws pulled a small wooden punt from under the willows, into which they motioned Edith to enter, which she did with a caution and deliberation that made the outlaws smile.

They followed, and began hauling the boat along by means of the bushes.

They had not gone a hundred yards, when a loud shout from one of the upper windows of the mill proclaimed them discovered.

"Lie down, lady," said one of the men, seizing a pole, and beginning to impel the unruly craft across.

But the moment they were in the middle of the stream, the force of the current drove them down towards the mill, where a weir would certainly upset them.

One of the men jumped up, and almost overturning the flat-bottomed craft, got out and began pulling it across by main force.

But this showed the horsemen where was a ford, and they came, one after another, to the edge of the water.

The first, taking a cross-bow from his back, levelled at the boatmen.

As he did so, a shaft from the opposite shore struck him right through the thigh, pinning him to the restive and now infuriated horse. A second shaft struck one of the foremost men-at-arms, right in his gorget. A third passed through the eye-hole of one of the men's helmets, killing him stone dead.

The other men retreated, especially as the boat was across; while rushing down the bank could be seen Robin Hood, Scarlett, and Little John.

CHAPTER XLIV.
THE INROAD ON THE FOREST.

THE daring of the outlaws, the escape of Edith of Athelston, and the incomprehensible flight of the outlaw chief from the custody of twelve Norman soldiers, so exasperated the sheriff of Notingham that he resolved himself to lead an expedition into the heart of the forest, to hunt out and finally destroy the whole daring band.

This resolve was heightened rather than diminished, when Earl Beauclerk, attended by Sir Norman Malvoisin, rode into the ancient city and demanded his co-operation. It was given with readiness, not that the fussy sheriff was a brave man, but that he trusted the warlike array which he would in part command, would so awe the outlaws as to prevent any chance of his falling into any personal danger.

The golden rays of a summer sun gilded the lofty and menacing turrets of Nottingham Castle, steeping the rock on which it stood in a rich golden light, and spreading a softened lustre over the distant Trent, that cast up flashing waters over many an overhanging oak which grew on the outskirts of merry Sherwood glades.

Tree and tower, hamlet and upland, wild heath and meadow, slumbered under the soft and tranquil beams of that glorious summer morn, and all nature came out in holiday array, and seemed listening to the music poured forth from a thousand hills, and from glade, thicket and secluded glen.

But what comes?

First belted knights, in all the gorgeous panoply of war, then squires bearing their pennons proudly in the bright sun.

Behind this some dozen score of men-at-arms, mounted on their huge Flanders horses, that seem weighed down by the load they carry.

Then a motley array of bow and crossbow men, who, in a combat like that to be expected, will be required more than any others to dislodge the daring outlaws.

The most enthusiastic of those present were well aware that the robbers, as they haughtily called them, would retreat to their most secret fastnesses, where mounted men could little hope to act.

But the great question arose where was their retreat?

The forest of Sherwood was of such vast extent that they might travel about for months as in a labyrinth if they had no clue.

But this clue they fondly imagined they had found.

On a strong roan palfrey, with downcast looks and pallid face, sat Will the tapster, whose complicity in the escape of Robin Hood being discovered, he had been given the choice between instant death and leading the whole party to the haunts of the outcasts.

In vain Will the tapster protested that he knew them not, that he never had visited the green glades of the forest, and that he had simply been paid to take the spiced and drugged ale to the soldiers. Nobody believed him.

He was accordingly placed under the escort of six powerful men-at-arms, with orders to kill him at the very first attempt at escape.

The young man, goaded almost to madness by this treatment, determined to lead them at haphazard, trusting that the brave yeoman he had served would do him a good turn. He had little doubt of the result of the expedition if the outlaws were only prepared.

Those who had planned this forest raid did not act without a regular plan.

In accordance with this, numerous advanced and outlying scouts were despatched into the forest to bring news of any concentration of outlaws, or any attempt made to oppose their advance. But with the exception of themselves, the barking foxes, and bellowing bucks, the vast solitudes were abandoned to their native silence.

"The rogues, methinks, have fled," said Norman Malvoisin; "they like not this array."

"Humph!" replied the sheriff, casting suspicious glances around from his grey glassy eyes, "I like not this stillness."

The Earl Beauclerk fixed his quick searching eye on the guide, who coloured.

"Rogue, an' you deceive us, you shall hang. Words will not save you," he cried.

"My lord," said the wretched man, "on my salvation I know not where Robin Hood holds his court."

"Holds his court!" laughed the sheriff, as if struck by the goodness of the joke; "the knave must have rare courtiers. 'Twill be a strange court-house when we hang a robber on every bough."

"We must first catch them," replied the earl, grimly.

For some time the conversation ceased, all being preoccupied by the strange silence of the forest, which appeared not even to be peopled by shadows.

Not a swineherd, not a ranger, not a living being of any kind for hours came within range of their vision.

Presently, however, just as they came to the crest of a hill, they saw before them a rude lonely hut, built of materials which the neighbouring forest had furnished, and thatched with reeds from the swamps.

"Egad! a house at last," said the sheriff, riding forward and striking the door with his lance.

The door of the miserable hovel opened, and a lad of about thirteen or fourteen came out, followed by an aged crone of some seventy years.

The boy was handsome and intelligent-looking.

"Boy," said the sheriff, in a commanding tone of voice, "know you the rogue men call Robin Hood?"

"I know the King of the Forest," replied the boy proudly, "by whose grace and kindness we live."

"Do we?" said the sheriff with a sneer, "then heark ye, lad. I have business with the fellow, and unless you lead me to him directly, I will fire the hut and burn this old witch in the flames."

"Burn grandmother?" said the boy with a frightened look; "Oh, sir, you would not be so cruel!"

"I am sheriff of Notingham," continued the magistrate, with a cold sneer, "and have hung dantier meat than you, my lad, beside burning many less hideous witches. Obey, or suffer the consequences."

"I know not where Robin Hood is now," whimpered the boy, "but I will take you to where he usually is when at home."

The old woman lifted her arms on high, as if deprecating the treachery and cowardice of the lad.

Her countenance bore some resemblance to that of the owl, her skin was ghastly, and her long beaked nose seemed to overhang her withered lips. Her eyes were large, round and grey, while her white hair had a feathery appearance.

"Accursed hag!" said Sir Norman, "seek not to move the lad from his purpose."

"Wrinkled dealer in darkness!" exclaimed Sir Thomas Effingham, "look but thy reason at me, and I will have thee scourged. Forward, boy."

The lad made no reply, but mounting before one of the soldiers, proceeded to lead the way.

"By ale and bread!" said the supposed old woman, casting off the disguise and revealing the brown face of an outlaw, "but the boy did it well, and now to give them a fair recepti...."

With which he darted into the forest, giving the cavalcade which had preceded him, a wide berth.

CHAPTER XLV.

THE AMBUSH.

THE boy seemed thoroughly to know his way, never hesitating a moment, but leading the invading force through a dark and dangerous part of the forest, which was in some parts almost impassible, from the dense and entangling underwood, and then diversified by small hillocks and patches of uneven ground, extending for a considerable distance beside a deep streamlet, the banks of which were occasionally broken and precipitous.

At length they came to the mouth of a valley, so densely wooded that it appeared impossible the horsemen could ride beneath the overhanging boughs.

"Is there no better way?" said the sheriff, sternly.

"None, noble sir. I know no other," he replied, meekly.

"Dismount and lead your horses," cried the earl, curtly; "the brave steeds are wearied. It will rest them."

As he spoke the forest echoes were awakened by the loud ringing blast of a bugle, and a storm flight of arrows poured upon the soldiery, killing and wounding several, and creating so much confusion that the sheriff ordered a retreat.

"On! on!" cried the fiery Norman Malvoisin; "strike, soldiers, strike," saying which, he uplifted his ponderous battle-axe and rushed up the valley, followed by the whole of his personal followers.

"Where is the young spawn of hell who led us into this trap?" cried the sheriff, who hardly knew whether to run away or follow the soldiery. "Hang him to the first tree."

But both the lad and Will the tapster had disappeared amid the undergrowth.

The bellicose magistrate foamed with fury and baffled vengeance, while up in the valley raged the battle.

The Norman soldiery were, as they darted up the valley, received by a fearful volley that took terrific effect, the archers selecting those parts which were most undefended.

But the mailed knights still advanced, everywhere driving the outlaws before them.

"Lead up your men, or be called craven," roared the Earl of Beauclerk. "Divide them, and clear the thickets to the right and left."

The sheriff thus summoned could but obey, and separating his posse comitatus into two bands, started them up the valley, he himself keeping in the rear.

Suddenly, however, there came from the adjacent thickets so galling a fire of arrows, that the magistrate was not ashamed to throw himself on the ground and cry for quarter.

His men, however, burst through the thickets driving the outlaws back by sheer weight and numbers.

In the van the fight was maintained with desperate vigour, the chief of the invading party pressing so close upon the men in Lincoln green, as to compel them to cease firing and take to sword and quarterstaff.

Foremost of all, with knit brows and faces that shone with excitement, fought Robin Hood, Will Scarlett, and Little John, each selecting a worthy antagonist.

Robin Hood, though wielding only his huge staff, opposed himself to the earl, whose fierce and terrible passions were raised to madness at being kept at bay by one who had no protection against his blows, and whose skill in the use of his ancient English weapon made him more than an equal antagonist.

Little John singled out his personal enemy, Sir Norman Malvoisin, whom, with one fearful blow, he cast to the ground, and resting his foot upon his body exclaimed—

"Yield ye—rescue or no rescue," he shouted.

This rather boastful position had well nigh been fatal to the tall forester, the soldiers of the sheriff now coming up with bent cross-bows.

Two of them took steady aim at the giant's head, and would have next instant ended his career, when a terrific volley from behind caused the most fearful havoc in their ranks.

Then a horn sounded, and, like magic, the outlaws were lost to sight in the thicket, leaving the ground strewed with the killed and wounded.

"Forward!" again cried the angry earl. "Let not the Saxon churls escape. Follow me."

And with the word, the earl, his men pressing close to him, all bursting with desire to avenge themselves, rushed up the valley.

But they were received with so fierce a shower of bolts and shafts, as to check their onward course, the said volley coming from behind a regular fortalice of wood.

The outlaws had cut down huge oaken and other trees, of which they had made a vast barricade, that promised to give even those experienced chiefs some trouble to overcome.

"Shoot them down!" roared Sir Norman furiously, as he himself snatched a cross-bow from the hand of a dying man. "Let not the base knaves show a finger."

The Norman soldiers were not bad shots; so that taking up favourable positions, they in their turn so harassed the yeomanry as to prevent their taking steady and deliberate aim.

In the meantime, the leaders held council with one another.

It was not their intention to carry on this desultory warfare. They knew that firing at one another from behind barricades and trees would last, in all probability, for days.

They must rush to the assault, and bear down the mass of outlaws who crowded behind the wooden fortress by the force of superior discipline, arms, and chivalry.

This decided on, the earl sounded a retreat, and in five minutes the whole Norman force were collected round their leaders.

"We waste our time shooting at knaves, who can hit a wand at a hundred and fifty paces; they must be dislodged by main force. Do you take one party, Sir Norman, and assault them to the left. You, Sir Philip, to the right. I will advance to the centre; and when I cry "Charge," do you support me."

The bold knights, whose fierce passions were roused to boiling heat by this sudden check received from men they were apt to look upon with scorn and contempt as unworthy to provoke their active enmity, sternly prepared for the assault.

They began to feel some kind of respect for the outlaws who could thus brave the men who, in the East, had known hundreds fly before their single arm.

The earl had noticed a spot where the arrangement of the boughs gave some chance of his scaling the rude barrier, and to this spot he rushed with the picked men of his band, men who could wield their battle-axes with any belted knight.

They were received with a cloud of arrows that laid several low. But the others but rushed more furiously on.

The earl caught hold of a large bough with one hand, by which he swung himself up, and confronted a powerful body of outlaws, amongst whom his terrible weapon fell with fearful power.

Two fell dead, their brains crushed in.

The rest hastily retreated, but only for a moment.

"Down with the Norman tyrant. St. George and merrie England!" cried the clear ringing voice of their leader.

And with a tremendous bound, he leaped to the gap and faced the mailed knight.

"Back or yield you knave," said the ranger, "quarter to all who ask it, save the leaders. Down, knaves, on your marrow bones."

"Ah! ah!" laughed the monarch of Sherwood forest. "Here are no slaves, but stout English hearts," and with a strength that seemed impossible in one so slight, he showered his blows upon the knight, warding off all his frantic endeavours to strike a blow with his axe.

But the soldiers pressed up.

"Charge!" shouted the earl.

Like stones cast from a catapult the two reserves came on, and the engagement became general.

There seemed little doubt of the result, for the Normans crowded up like bees, and despite the valour, endurance and vigour of the outlaws, they were driven back on all hands.

"Stand fast!" cried Robin, "stand fast, my men—the tyrants have done their worst. Have at you."

And with a quickness and power that nothing could evade, he struck the earl and hurled him back amongst his men—insensible.

At the same moment the outlaws, emulating their leader, made a dash at the soldiers, who were, after a heroic defence, once more glad to take shelter behind the nearest trees.

"The foul fiend fights on their side."

MAID MARIAN SAVES ROBIN HOOD.

CHAPTER XLVI.

THE FIRST BARRIER.

The cry of the Norman baron but expressed his genuine astonishment that men, without defensive armour, and using weapons of the simplest character, should be able to contend against men not only with the advantage of being iron-clad, but having also arms such as in those days were accounted to be perfection.

The haughty Norman baron, who in France had seen the peasants cower like sheep at the sight of one knight fully equipped, had yet to learn what the yeomanry of England could do in defence of the last remnant of their Saxon liberties.

This was, however, no time for reflection but for action, and the leaders, not taking any notice of the sheriff, who had kept prudently in the rear, seated themselves on a log, and there prepared to hold council.

They first, however, took off their helmets to wring the wet from their long hair and wipe their streaming faces, which they did in handfulls of long grass—other conveniences not being known to our simple and unsophisticated ancestors.

"These devilish outlaws fight like fiends!" said Norman Malvoisin, with a fearful scowl. "Our men showed their backs most valiantly that last charge. An' we defeat them not, there will be no law in Nottinghamshire save that of Robin Hood, whom Satan take as early as convenient."

"The fellow's impudence is inconceivable," cried the earl; "he must feel himself well supported thus to brave us. But the task once undertaken, must be carried out, even if we call up reinforcements."

"It would but ill become us to send for help," said Philip with a smile of scorn, "against a nest of stingless hornets."

"Stingless!" shouted the earl, with a forced laugh; "call you fork-headed shafts, a clothyard long, dull biters? I would, myself, we had never entered on this enterprise, but contented ourselves with hanging here and there a knave when good luck brought him to our sheriff's hands.

"Which, gramercy, I will do, please St. Michael, an hour after I enter Nottingham," cried the sheriff, magniloquently.

"Which you may never do an' you show your fat paunch so ready to the outlaws," sneered Sir Norman Malvoisin.

The sheriff looked wildly round. He was standing with his back to a large oak, and with a whole line in front of ' him, behind every one of which stood a Norman soldier. It did not, therefore, appear to himself possible the outlaws could see him ; so after a cautious survey, he allowed his fat and rubicund visage to relax into a smile.

"Sir Norman is pleased to be facetious," he said ; "I care no more for their bolts and shafts than I do for ——"

What, was never known, for at the same instant two arrows whizzed past, and striking the oak one on each side, pinned the boastful speaker to the tree.

"I'm dead," roared, or rather bellowed, the sheriff in such fearful and lugubrious tones, as fairly made an old owl in a neighbouring tree blink, while it scared the deer and foxes for miles around.

"Heaven have mercy on my soul ! My lords, take the tidings to my poor wife, and tell her that had I been spared I would have been a better husband. If I am saved this time, I will never ——"

"We want no confessions," said Sir Norman Malvoisin, grimly, while all the others smiled or laughed outright ; "nor do we want your worshipful self to set so bad an example to your men. You are more frightened far than hurt."

"More frightened than hurt," exclaimed the poor sheriff, quite overcome by the other's unfeelingness, "with two clothyard shafts through my arm, nailing me here like St. Augustin the martyr."

"Through your worshipful sleeves," said the brutal Norman soldier, plucking him away from the tree, leaving behind only a portion of his doublet ; "art thou convinced now of the danger of shewing thyself."

The sheriff appeared thoroughly convinced, for he slid to the ground, where he rather reclined than sat during the rest of the conference.

It was animated, but though regrets were expressed as to the expedition ever having been undertaken, no one flinched now, as to do so would call forth a loud cry of derision from all the chivalry of England, and especially from that cunning, bad prince John, who, in the temporary absence of King Cœur de Lion (pron. *Cur de Leon*), ruled the fair land of England.

"We must to the charge ; the knaves swarm the forest like bees in a hive," said the earl ; "and when the news reaches some who hate us, they will bring down an army on our flanks."

And a whispered order went through the whole of the Norman ranks, as the chief did not wish fully to prepare the enemy by sounding the charge.

The men now, as if fully aware of the valour and dexterity of those to whom they were opposed, used all the caution taught them by practice in the battle-field. Being all transformed to footmen, they closed up and advanced in line, shielded from bolts and shafts of the enemy by their bucklers.

The outlaws poured a tremendous shower of missiles upon the advancing mercenaries, but with scarcely any effect, their bucklers protecting them considerably from the arrows and bolts.

This filled the Norman soldiers with hope, so that they marched up to the barricade quite elated and joyous, as could be seen from the very springiness of their step and the grim smile on their countenances.

They soon reached the foot of the pile, and keeping as close together as possible, began scaling, led on and cheered by their knightly chiefs.

Their astonishment may be conceived when they met with no opposition, nor when they reached the summit could they see one single Saxon yeoman.

Even the killed and wounded had been removed from the field of battle.

No time, however, was lost, as they were in an exposed position. All dashed forward now with the impetuosity of men certain of victory and plunder.

Plunder was one of the most active incitements to the soldiers, who believed the outlaws to be in possession of untold wealth.

CHAPTER XLVII.
THE SECOND BARRIER.

ABOUT a hundred yards further on in the valley, the leaders of the attacking party were struck as it were of a heap with surprise by a new kind of defence which presented itself to their notice.

A line of trees grew very close together across the gulley. These had not been felled as in the former instance, but the openings between each were filled up with beams and shrubs, enlaced in such a manner as to form even a better fortification than that which they had, after so much exertion, and with such loss of life, succeeded in carrying.

Burning with rage, however, and half resolved to perish rather than yield before a troop of unmailed and undisciplined peasants, the Norman knights rushed forward with savage determination, and though assailed with a most staggering discharge of bolts and arrows, pounded at the defences with their huge axes until they saw the whole attempt was a failure.

"The demon of darkness take these hell-born churls !" muttered the earl between his teeth ; "this must not last. Cut the down yonder poplar," he cried ; "this barrier must and shall be taken."

This order was given after another retreat, the post of the outlaws proving even more formidable than the knights expected.

The order was obeyed, and in a quarter of an hour a heavy beam of wood lay before the fuming council of assembled chiefs.

"Mark you, Maurice," said the earl to one of his subordinates, "where the defence is highest between two elms. It is also there widest—do you and a dozen stalwart fellows lift me this beam, and while we charge have at that weak point."

"I see no weak points about these forts," muttered Maurice.

"I say not they are weak, my brave Maurice," continued the earl, with a dark frown ; "but that is our only hope—go."

Again the charge was given, again the Normans rushed to the attack, the battering ram taking up the centre and advancing on its human carriage with a rush against the wall.

The shock was terrific.

The men were hurled backwards with the tremendous force of the blow—but the wood pile gave way, and the whole Norman force, flushed with the idea of victory, poured in upon the outlaws.

The conflict now became a hand-to-hand one, the men of Sherwood having been taken too much by surprise to retreat in time.

The battle now was fought with a silence and determination that evinced a desire on both sides to conquer or perish ; it was fought too in good order, each party keeping to his own side, and advancing or retreating, which ever it might be, in line.

The outlaws fought with stern determination, To die with arms in their hands was far better than to be hung up to trees for the ravens to peck their eyes out.

The numbers were tolerably equal, though, if anything, in favour of the Normans ; a circumstance which would have ensured the defeat of the yeomen but for the unconquerable valour of their chiefs.

Ever foremost in the fight, Robin Hood, Little John, and Will Scarlett were ubiquitous. Did any part of the line yield, there they were, rousing the others by their example, and doing deeds of heroism that would occupy many pages to tell.

There was one huge fellow with a ponderous axe who seemed, on whatever part of the field he presented himself, to strike the outlaws with awe. He was quite as stout, and nearly as tall as Little John. His sheer strength, the power of his weapon, and his towering height, made every yeoman avoid him, and single out a more fitting foe.

He in one instance rushed at a point in the outlaws' ranks where more weakness than usual had been shown, and with a fierce and taunting cry, assailed them, not only with his club, but with all the insulting epithets which the inventive vituperation of the period had brought into common use.

"Fly not, swine, like your own vile pigs. I am a Norman soldier—fly not, let a dozen come on ; nor run away because my head towers an inch or two above you. Come on, churls."

This is but a very weak specimen of the language he indulged in.

"Lift thy head, Norman bandit, as high as thy power will allow thee, for, by my honest English troth, it is for the last time."

The Norman turned, and found himself confronted by the stern face and prodigious frame of Little John, who, exasperated at the other's insolence, had allowed himself to come out from his real character to answer taunt by taunt and boast by boast.

Hitherto the course of the huge soldier, Pierre by name, had been uniformly victorious; no man of ordinary girth could stand against him; he mowed his foes down like new grass, he cut them down like reeds, and in his craving lust for English blood danced with delight upon their corpses.

But now it seemed to the insolent marauder, one of the worst specimens of the free-lance ever seen within this fair island, that he had met with a worthy competitor, and he chuckled with delight.

He was a man knowing nothing, hoping nothing, fearing nothing.

His eyes actually glistened with savage pleasure as he took the measure of his new antagonist. Still he saw quite sufficient about his enemy to make him clutch his heavy battle-axe with something more of caution than he had hitherto exhibited.

"Ha! ha! and who art thou, to prate thus to thy betters?" he said.

The fight was hot. The wind whistled in the trees, the ravens croaked overhead, the owls hooted in their ivy-clad nests, the snakes rustled away through the grass in search of peace, while the fox and deer had long since fled; but Little John calmly leaned upon his heavy quarterstaff, as with a melancholy expression he gazed upon his ferocious adversary.

"Norman, I am one doomed to be the bitter enemy of thy race, and to exterminate all who dare come before me in wrong doing. I am no man of blood; surrender then, rescue or no rescue, and I will spare thy life.

The words were spoken so solemnly, with so much earnestness, that the man-at-arms, despite his courage was taken aback.

Only for an instant.

"Base Saxon churl! doest preach egg-wisdom to thy grandmother. Have at thee, knave and thief—my head or thine!"

"On thy head be it. I would willingly have spared thee," said Little John, who, to say the truth, had a pardonable weakness for big men.

"Have at thee thyself, huge bacon-side!" cried the Normandy peasant.

The ponderous axe described such a half circle in the air, as, aided by the man's own more brute strength, should have crushed two men the size and weight of Little John.

But the brave forester had no desire to fall beneath the blows of one, rightly judged by the outlaws to be truly worthy of the name of robber—for came they not to steal both our soil and liberties?

His mode, however of parrying the blow was peculiar. He did not really parry it, but quick as lightning struck the soldier such a blow with his quarterstaff on the descending arm as sent the axe flying, and forced the hired giant to howl with pain.

The outlaws saw the act, and shouted frantic cries of victory.

This one scene in the eventful drama restored the fortunes of the day, nearly lost, despite the heroic efforts of the outlaws.

"Demon from hell," said the Norman soldier, clutching at his sword with fingers that yet tingled from the blow, "thy base and churlish blood shall avenge that coward's blow."

"Wilt try these?" replied the Saxon with a grin, at the same time lifting up his brawny arms.

"If, base slave, you mean fists, no—try this," and as he spoke, he aimed a fearful blow at the forester's head with his long two-handed weapon.

But Little John was as active with his eye as with his hand. He gazed around, leaped about ten feet, snatched up a similar weapon to that clutched by Pierre, and ere a man might have counted an ave, their swords struck.

Little John had never used a heavy two-handed sword before. Any one who has not lifted one of these extraordinary weapons can hardly conceive how ponderous they are in their nature, and how difficult they must have been to use. But the tall forester was a master at a quarterstaff, that is, had consummate skill both in the science of attack and defence. The weapon, therefore was at once familiar to him.

And so the Norman found it to his unqualified astonishment.

The swordsman's art in those days as in this was a thing of itself apart, and was not to be learned in a day nor in many days.

Pierre le Norman was a professor, and had seldom faced the man who could resist either his herculean impetus or his skill.

He found that the simple stick with which English yeomen played, when fully understood, taught them all they needed to know.

The swords emitted sparks from the violence of the crash.

From the moment this battle of giants began, as if by one common consent, all further contest ceased. Outlaw and Norman mechanically rested, the chiefs forbidding the slightest interference.

Both sides were certain of victory, and looked upon the coming result as an omen.

A breathless silence followed, broken only by the fearful clashing and din made by the combatants.

The lookers-on gradually forgot the stake, and simply, with few exceptions, regarded the combat as one of gladiators.

It was certainly a magnificent and unequalled sight. The size of the men, the somewhat martinet style of the soldier, the rough energy of the yeoman, the quick blows, the sudden feints, both professional and original, the horrid blows, made men's hearts leap to their mouths.

It was quite clear that at the end of seven or eight minutes neither of the adversaries had the advantage.

The Norman had more science, but the Saxon more suppleness.

Such a state of things could not possibly last many minutes more.

Both were wounded, but with slight flesh wounds.

The Norman began to fume and to contract his dark and vicious brows.

"Diable d'Anglais!" roared the bull-like Frenchman, "this must not last. I were a laughing-stock to all Christendom didst thou give me but a serious wound."

"One!" said Little John, giving him a gash on the left arm, right above the elbow.

"Do that again!" shrieked the other, wildly striking out.

"Two!" said Little John, quietly; he had caught in that short time the exact gauge of the game and of his adversary.

"Kill me, but taunt me not!" yelled the Norman, with perfect frenzy.

"Three!" was Little John's reply, as lifting his sword high in the air, he brought it down full on the soldier's head, and clove it in twain.

"'Twas a brave soldier," he said, "and a pity he was a Norman."

The fight was hot, the wind whistled in the trees, the ravens croaked over head, the owls hooted in their ivy-clad nests, the snakes rustled away through the grass in search of peace, while the fox and deer had long since fled; but Little John calmly leaned upon his heavy quarterstaff, as, with a melancholy expression, he gazed upon his late adversary.

All animosity had fled.

CHAPTER XLVIII.

THE THIRD BARRIER.

A TERRIBLE tumult arose.

At first the knights and their followers were occupied only by the sense of defeat, as all rushed round the body of the stalwart soldier who had died so bravely in a bad cause.

Then came another and more fearful sensation over every man's soul.

Revenge!

"Normans, charge!—Revenge our brave brother!" they cried with one accord.

"A Malvoisin!"

"A Beauclerk!"

"A Beauvoisin!"

Such were the cries that rose from the followers of the different knights.

But no cry rose from the posse comitatus of the Sheriff of Nottingham. They followed in the rear, dispirited and dissatisfied.

But the outlaws had by no means played their last card. This attack of the soldiery in overwhelming numbers had been expected, and therefore provided for.

Robin Hood, during the whole of his varied and chequered career, proved himself as consummate a general as he was a good archer. In bush-fighting, such as characterised our forefathers in the early days of American-Indian warfare, he was unrivalled. He knew the value of every tree, of every bush, of every rock; and could turn them to an advantage which no common outlaw would have thought of.

And yet were all his men drilled with the most scrupulous care, and taught to provide against every possible contingency.

This perfect state of forest discipline was carried out by constantly practising his men, not only in the art of shooting with crossbow and longbow, in the use of the quarterstaff and sword, but in that of both hiding from and tracking the foe, in the science of ambushment, and other matters, by neglecting which many soldiers by rule have lost many a campaign.

Prizes were given to those who could best hide their trail and their persons, and it was held no disgrace to run from an overwhelming foe.

There were only three things bold Robin never forgave:— Cowardice, dishonesty, and ill-treatment of a woman.

This may appear a solecism, but it is nothing of the kind. The outlaws were not robbers in the common acceptation of the word.

They were victims of evil laws—outcasts from a certain society.

They turned upon their oppressors, and made them pay for their outraged hearths, their injured wives and children, their stolen property, their unjust decrees.

The outlaws levelled black mail on their tyrants and oppressors—that is the nobles, the wealthy clergy, and their joint adherents.

But to our narrative.

The Normans, rampant at the defeat of their champion, and yet exultant at the prospect of success, rushed forward with furious haste, but to find themselves checked by a barrier they had little expected.

That is to say, they saw it when they had recovered the first terrible shower of arrows and bolts, that laid many an incautious man-at-arms low.

They were now at the contrary end of the valley by which they had entered, and unconsciously were on the verge of one of the strongholds of the captain of Sherwood Forest.

There was a gentle slope, and at the summit of this a natural ridge, of which the yeomen had availed themselves to the full—aware that here they must do or die.

On the outside of the ridge the outlaws had dug a ditch, throwing the earth to their own side. In this earth they had thrust huge trunks of trees, in the form of a stockade, the beams being kept together by transverse poles, withes, and other contrivances.

It was one of those fortifications, however primitive, which are not to be carried in the face of a determined foe, except at the price of a great expenditure of time and life.

The Norman soldiery cast rueful glances at their chiefs, seeing which the knights once more collected themselves together.

No time was wasted in council. The Lord Ranger of Sherwood Forest assumed the command unquestioned in this emergency. None were inclined to dispute the dangerous rank.

"Retire!—form archers on each wing! Quick with scaling ladders—there are saplings enough. Three will do—quick! or these varlets will escape us. Sound trumpet and call—let it be 'Lay down your arms!'"

A brilliant fanfare was the reply, but the only response that came from the outlaws was one of bitter and unqualified defiance.

There was no surrender in the soul of men commanded by Robin Hood.

The Normans fumed with impatience. The courage of the soldiers seemed to warm with the occasion. They no longer felt that they were fighting against rebels and robbers, but against an insurrection of the good people of England, which it was—a perpetual insurrection against tyranny, oppression, and wrong.

The axes of the dismounted cavaliers were soon laid to the root of likely saplings, which, with withes and cord, were soon bound together—rude ladders, capable of bearing two men side by side—and with these in front, and bucklers to prevent their being shot down, the Normans advanced.

The crossbowmen, meanwhile, began shooting at all who presented themselves on the ramparts.

It has been said of some great battle, in which English bowmen played a notable part, that their flight of arrows made a shadow over the field, so rapidly did they ply their clothyard shafts.

Something of the kind took place now, while the Norman soldiers were obtaining a footing in the improvised dry moat.

They were soon there, and now began one of those gigantic struggles of valour against dogged obstinacy, the issue of which is always so doubtful.

But discipline seemed likely to have the day; the ladders were planted, the Normans crowded up, the outlaws rushed headlong to the rescue, but were mercilessly picked off by the soldiery in the rear.

Suddenly, however, whether from bad and hurried construction, or the weight of the crowded ladders, the stockade fell inward, crushing yeomen and men-at-arms in one confused heap to the ground.

For one moment.

Up, raging like wild beasts for each other's blood, the men of rival races rose, and another hand-to-hand encounter followed.

But fortune seemed to favour the law, such as it was.

The soldiery, reinforced every moment, stood awhile like a wall of iron, until every comrade was within the stockade, when they made at their enemies with a terrible kind of ravenous ferocity which better became wild beasts than men.

Robin Hood cast one wild, despairing glance around, and, resolved to die like a man, rushed at the earl, struck his axe from his hand, and then about to draw his sword fell backwards on the sward.

The ground was slippery with blood.

Robin Hood had glided in it and fallen.

With a savage cry of delight the earl rushed forward, kneeled on his prostrate foe, clutched his dagger in his gauntleted hand, and raised it on high.

"Die, Saxon thief!—too much honoured to fall by the hand of a knight!" said the Earl of Beauclerk, with cruel exultation.

At the same instant his arm, above the wrist, was struck by a bolt, the dagger fell from his hand, while a loud shout of uproarious joy from the outlaws proclaimed the triumph.

The soldiers looked up and saw nearly a hundred forms in Lincoln green, bounding over the green sward of the open glade to which they had obtained an access.

"A rescue! a rescue! St. George for merrie England!" shouted the outlaws.

"Wait, ruffians, wait!" said a grim and savage voice—that of Tuck.

But the soldiers did not wait, commencing, at sight of the terrible array of force, fresh and vigorous, against them, one of those panic flights often recorded in history but totally inexplicable.

The outlaws looked utterly bewildered, and Robin Hood slowly rising, rubbed his eyes to make sure it was not a dream.

"Safe! safe!" said a sweet, shrill voice, emanating from one in boy's clothes, and the youth was clasped to his arms.

"Marian! Maid Marian!" shouted the enraptured yeoman, and then all heartily greeted their boyish sons, but above all the wives and daughters, who, in this hour of peril, had come so fittingly and well to the rescue, proving women as usual to be our best and safest shield from danger.

CHAPTER XLIX.

LOVE.

WHEN Robin Hood, Little John and Will Scarlett appeared on the opposite bank of the river, to where stood the residence of Much the Miller, they were already aware that a foray would be organised against them on the part of the whole confederation of their enemies.

Robin, therefore, explained to Marian, that under the circumstances, she must, for a while, make his most secret haunt her home, until such time as he could in safety take her to St. Withold.

"I am in your hands, brave youth," she said, "and would not for the world injure you or yours. But once the enemy defeated or befooled, you will surely take me there?"

"On my word."

"And I know you would not deceive me," she archly added.

"Deceive you?—beautiful lady, I, who never deceived or injured woman—would least of all bring tears to the eyes of one I worship with veneration, one whom "——

Robin Hood blushed and stammered. He was in that most delightfully embarrassing state when a man dares not tell the love he really feels.

"I will place perfect and unquestioned faith in you," she said, with a smile.

Woman is an anomaly. The simplest, sweetest, and most innocent of the charming sex, are more than a match for any man in this particular.

They never fail to discover when a man's heart is unreservedly given to them.

It is one of the marvellous instincts of their instinctive nature.

Meanwhile, Little John and Will Scarlett walked behind, with something of a rueful cast of countenance. They looked at their leader, they heard his animated conversation, and they saw from the flush of the young peoples' countenances that they were becoming deeply interested in each other.

The consequence was, that while Will Scarlet thought of Eveline, the tall forester sighed deeply, and murmured the word "Rose."

At length Robin halted.

"My merrie men," he said, "'tis a pity that many of our fellows are dispersed—but we must do our best. Let every man in Lincoln green hurry to the trysting-tree, for surely will our foe now track us to our lair. I will hurry on by Watling-street, and send forward all I see. At every mile you walk wind your horn. You, Will, towards Gammel, and collect what bows you can; you, Little John, down the Glen-road. I will escort this lady to the cave, and then—heaven defend the right."

Without a word the whole escort vanished, and the two were alone.

And did the noble girl, the Saxon ward of the crown, feel no dread at being left alone with one under the ban of the law—with one accused by his enemies of every crime?

No.

She believed she knew him, and if so, could trust herself more readily in his hands than in that of most of the lordly knights and courtiers of the land, of whom a great historian has described the character in a sentence.

"As an instance of these bittter fruits of conquest, and perhaps the strongest that can be quoted, we may mention, that the Princess Matilda, though a daughter of the King of Scotland, and afterwards both Queen of England, niece to Edgar Atheling, and mother to the Empress of Germany, the daughter, the wife, and the mother of monarchs, was obliged, during her early residence for education in England, to assume the veil of a nun, as the only means of escaping the licentious pursuit of the Norman nobles. This excuse she stated before a great council of the clergy of England, as the sole reason for her having taken the religious habit. The assembled clergy admitted the validity of the plea, and the notoriety of the circumstances upon which it was founded; giving thus an indubitable and most remarkable testimony to the existence of that disgraceful licence by which that age was stained. It was a matter of public knowledge, they said, that after the conquest of King William, his Norman followers, elated by so great a victory, acknowledged no law but their own wicked pleasure, and not only despoiled the conquered Saxons of their lands and their goods, but invaded the honour of their wives and of their daughters with the most unbridled license; and hence it was then common for matrons and maidens of noble families to assume the veil, and take shelter in convents, not as called thither by the vocation of God, but solely to preserve their honour from the unbridled wickedness of man."

Such and so licentious were the times, as announced by the public declaration of the assembled clergy.

But if we were to say that the true woman's heart beneath that rich cloth dress did not beat more warmly, we should do injustice to her character.

It was impossible to know Robin Hood and not admire his noble qualities; and admiration, far more than pity, warmeth the heart of woman.

"Prithee why so silent, Robin?" she observed when, they had advanced through the forest about ten minutes without speaking.

"What should the simple yeoman have to say to the noble-born daughter of Athelston?" he replied sadly.

"That which any noble man might say to any woman," she added.

Still Robin remained thoughtful.

"Lady—Edith—Marian, and if the words I were to speak were such as tremble on my lips, which entwine around my heart and choke it—if the words which I could scarce contain within myself were to be those of love?" he cried wildly.

The girl stopped, looked him kindly in the face, and spoke.

"I should say Robin Hood—wait. I have known you but a little time—I am disposed to like. I should say, wait—because I am ward of the crown trying to free herself from bondage. I shall soon, I hope, be free, and then ——"

"What then?"

"Repeat what you have said unto me," she said, in quite gentle accents.

"Heavens!" cried Robin Hood, speaking to himself, "if I only knew the answer, I could live in peace."

"And would it give a man like you any comfort to know what answer a silly girl would give to the brave king of Sherwood?" she asked.

"Ah! if I could but believe, if I could but hope, that you would listen favourably to me, I should indeed be a king above all men!"

"And what question will King Robin Hood ask when Edith of Athelston shall be free?"

"Wilt thou, Maid Marian, be my loving, my adored wife?"

The answer was murmured, not said.

"Maid Marian will answer—yes!"

What followed is not so particular to this narrative to be recorded, especially as it did not occupy above five minutes.

When next they moved forward it was hand in hand, quite silent now, but neither of them disposed to break a stillness over which brooded a whole world of happiness and love.

And thus they reached the trysting place of the outlaw chief.

The young girl in astonishment and admiration gazed upon the wild scene before her, and although she had been accustomed to see armed men from childhood, still the bronzed countenances and the fine athletic forms, unincumbered by armour, that moved to and fro in the moonlit glade, struck her more forcibly than the sheathed figures she had so often seen.

CHAPTER L.

THE CAVE.

If there was one secret kept more religiously than another among the fraternity, it was that of the real abode of the outlaws of Sherwood forest.

But Robin Hood had no secrets now from the lady of his heart.

At one end of the glade, where stood the famous oak, was a thicket so dense that the light of day could not penetrate it.

But to the initiated there was a labyrinthine path which led easily through its intricate mazes.

Through this the bold outlaw led the young girl, holding her by the hand and walking cautiously; for the place was very dark.

Suddenly they descended a flight of steps and came in sight of the yawning entrance to a cavern, illumined by pitch pine knots.

Robin Hood led her in, still wondering at all she saw, until she found herself in a vast excavation, extending in every direction, beneath a hill, and capable of holding three times the number of the bold outlaws, their wives, and families.

We have hitherto only depicted the merrie men in the forest fighting and hunting.

We now introduce them in their home—where, in the hour of danger and difficulty, they installed those who were dearer to them than their own lives.

The cavern was perfectly dry and warm, well-ventilated and lit in the daytime through secret holes, artfully made, where none outside could detect them.

To prevent accidents, the roof was in various places supported by massive beams, placed horizontally, with others as pillars.

Robin had discovered it himself in its present state, and all who had seen it believed it to be the refuge of some of the bold Saxons, who would not yield to the tyrant and conqueror William.

Be this as it may, it was universally recognised as Robin Hood's cave.

There was accommodation for all, each man and his wife pitching their tent, or making their hut, according to their own fancy.

That of the chief was a handsome suite of apartments, adorned with the spoils of the chase—antlers, skins, and such like. To this apartment Robin introduced Edith of Athelston, appointing her, at the same time, as attendant one of the daughters of a favourite outlaw.

He then hurried to prepare for the defence of his home, by making barriers and collecting around him his valiant bowmen. And—

> Three hundred valiant men had this brave Robin Hood,
> Still ready at his call, that bowmen were right good;
> All clad in Lincoln green, with caps of red and blue.
> His fellows' winded horn, not one of them but knew.

Meanwhile, Edith, or, as the outlaws would call her, Maid Marian, made herself quite at home in the recesses of the cavern. She did not confine herself to the regal chamber of the king, but went forth to where the women sat round their charcoal fires, played with the children, nursed the babies, and, in fact, won every heart by the simple exhibition of her native good feeling.

She was often visited by Robin whenever he could leave his duty ; and these visits were to her ever delightful.

She began already to love that forest life which she scarcely understood.

And then, if there is heaven on earth, it is the ecstasy of love's young dream.

More solid happiness may be in store for us, but that is the one hour of real delight to the heart, both of man and woman.

Gradually, however, the visits of the outlaw-chief grew fewer and shorter, until they altogether ceased.

The conflict had commenced.

The roses left the cheek of Marian, to be replaced by the lilies.

She never could have thought until she knew him in danger how inexpressibly dear the Saxon yeoman was to her existence.

There were many youths in the cave of an age below that at which the King of Sherwood allowed them to be active members of the band.

These she formed into bands of scouts, and sent them forth to report progress.

We need scarcely paint the consternation of the women and children at the disastrous character of the news which was brought in.

Despair was in every haggard eye—fear blanched every cheek.

They all knew—that is, the young women—the outrages to which they would be subjected previous to death.

The Norman soldiers had an execrable reputation, which, on every occasion that offered, they appeared determined to keep up.

Loud cries and anxious prayers resounded through the vast cavern.

Maid Marian sat moodily on a settle near the outlaws' cabin.

Her eye glanced uneasily around.

The cavern was half lit, half in darkness, as the shadows fell.

Suddenly, just as a scout entered to announce the last desperate struggle, she leaped to her feet.

" My worthy women, and ye brave youths, the peril is great !'' she cried. "These brave men are fighting for us. Shall we desert them ? "

" No! no ! "

" The very sound of a rescue would be enough to scare the wary Norman tyrants. Let every woman don a spare coat of her husband's, snatch up crossbow or bow, and rush forth to save or perish with them. I can shoot my shaft—and so come ye all ! Maid Marian will lead you on ! "

A loud murmur of applause followed ; and in ten minutes more a body of a hundred women, girls, and boys went forth under the guidance of the gallant Saxon heiress.

Just in time, as we have already described in a previous page.

It is needless for us to describe the scene which followed—the rapturous happiness of those who were intrumental in saving, the deep grief of the others who found they had armed themselves in vain.

Forty-seven of the men of Sherwood Forest were dead—over a hundred severely wounded.

CHAPTER LI.

THE SHERIFF OF NOTTINGHAM.

It was with a sense of utter shame and confusion that the Norman soldiery and their leaders felt the necessity of sounding a retreat.

But there was not one man or knight, who did not feel the necessity of adopting this course after the sudden appearance of the rescue.

For about half an hour the three leading knights rode—as soon as they had reached their horses—helter-skelter through the wood ; the sheriff of Nottingham preceding them like a courier, without a word being said.

The whole of the Norman force had indulged in a performance which one would fancy from newspaper reports was the usual practice of armies.

They had skedaddled.

At length, however, the three chivalrous knights drew rein at the foot of a grassy mound, calling to the sheriff to stop likewise.

He, alarmed at the idea of being alone, tugged manfully at his horse and stopped.

The companions dismounted, and allowed their jaded steeds a feed.

" And so ends the raid that was to annihilate the power of the outlaws," said the Earl of Beauclerk, with a bitterness which only a brave man could feel, whatever the nature of his general moral qualities.

" The rot of Egypt eat into their bones ! " cried his brother ; " but I will not yield me. God's Malison on the knaves who came to the rescue ! "

" So say I ! " followed Philip de Beauvoisin, with a fearful oath ; " but had your coward knaves have had eyes in their backs they would have seen 'twas a miracle play of boys and girls, led by the madcap ward of the crown, Edith of Athelston."

" Is there witchcraft abroad ?—else how comes the girl in Sherwood Forest ? "

" She loves Robin Hood. Would you have me read the riddle of a woman's mind ? "

" Then is there a fair inheritance to be won ! " cried Norman Malvoisin, with an eager chuckle. " I will to Prince John and ask the reversion."

" First," said the sheriff, who had just recovered his breath—a reason why he had not hitherto spoken—" first kill the Earl of Huntingdon."

" Marry, thy run hast muddled thy brains, good sheriff," sneered Norman Malvoisin.

" How so ? "

" The earldom of Huntingdon is extinct, and no man dares take the title."

" And yet, if you take not care, the Earl of Huntingdon will marry both the fief and the girl," continued the sheriff, with a strange chuckle that made Earl Beauclerk shiver — he holding the lands of the nobleman now spoken of.

" Speak not in enigmas ! We are no sphinxes ! If Maid Marian, as these stalwart knaves call the wench, loves Robin Hood, how should the Earl of Huntingdon take her fief ? "

" Because," said the sheriff of Nottingham, rubbing his

nose with the left forefinger so slowly and deliberately as almost to drive the others mad—"because you ought to know if you don't——"

"What?—what?—what?"

"Robin Hood is——"

"In the fiend's name, speak!"

"Robin Hood is——"

"He may be in your lady's chamber for what I care!" roared Sir Norman.

"Nay, Sir Norman," urged the sheriff, "I allow no man in my lady's chamber save myself."

"Honest Robin Hood would do no hurt in your secret apartment," sneered the soldier.

"I allow no honest men in my apartments," said the sheriff, with ludicrous emphasis; "but you did interrupt, my lords. I was saying——"

They all felt a strong desire to laugh, but curiosity restrained them.

"You were speaking—at random we suppose—of Robin Hood, the bold, audacious outlaw, and the Earl of Huntingdon, long since dead."

"One and the same person," continued the sheriff, complacently. "Robin Hood is Robert Earl of Huntingdon—a fit mate for Edith of Athelston."

"All the fiends of hell forfend!" cried Beauclerk, with pallid cheek and livid lips. "The secret must be kept at any stake or price."

What was it that made the sheriff start?

It was a rapid snake-like glance exchanged between the three lordly knights.

He thoroughly understood them. He knew his life hung on a thread. For once in his life the paunchy magistrate was guilty of a stroke of genius.

"The secret is no secret. My wife knows it, and so does Robin Hood."

The stupendous lie saved him; and after a short conference on the subject, another topic was introduced.

"Where are our base knaves?" asked Philip de Beauvoisin. "So scattered, I fear me they may not be called together."

"Nay," said the Lord Ranger of Sherwood forest, "fear not. They are not far distant. The rascals know that not a Saxon churl but would gladly squeeze their throats, or cut their weasens. I will soon bring them up."

And taking a kind of bugle from his saddle-bow, he blew blast after blast, his knowledge of the Norman soldiery speedily being proved correct.

Not one of them had hurried far, being satisfied that their leaders when, like themselves, they had recovered their panic, would rally them.

All not killed or hopelessly wounded were soon collected round the knights.

"So," said the earl in a ringing voice—he had a right to speak, for his right hand lay inanimate by his side—"these are the wolves of Sherwood. Fools! had you but held your own five minutes I had given you rare sport. The phalanx of Roman warriors you fled before were innocent virgins! Ha! ha! base slaves; what say you now? Do you not all wish yourselves back?"

The soldiers hung their heads. Scarcely one of them but had after their flight a vague idea of the truth.

"Well," continued the earl again in a ringing voice—satisfied at the reproof, "no more of this. Next time keep your eyes open, and miss not a chance which may never occur again."

"'Twas a rare wench hit your lordship's hand," said an old trooper.

"Ah!" shouted the earl, with a dark scowl, "could'st point her out?"

"'Twas Edith of Athelston," continued the ancient man-at-arms.

"G—d's truth!" said the earl, with a fiery glance, "'tis a brave wench. An' Prince John gave his consent, I'd wed her myself. There were rare boys from such a conjunction."

"She is affianced to Robert, son of the Earl of Nottingham."

"To Robert, Earl of Nottingham—to the bold outlaw—to the Earl of Huntingdon?—if she were affianced to the foul fiend himself and I were to select her as my bride, who should say me nay?" cried the haughty baron—and then he added, as if he had said quite enough, "forward."

"Somebody shall hang for this," muttered the sheriff,

who was deeply in the interests of the Earl of Nottingham's heir.

And with these words the cavalcade resumed their march, or rather retreat.

The sheriff, like all bad men who have not courage to carry out their bolder designs, would make the bravest resolutions to do that which was not personally dangerous.

Somebody must suffer for this ignominious defeat.

The man had not a soul above a mean revenge; not being able to get at Robin Hood, he would hit at the outlaw through his friends.

We shall see how he carried out his designs.

CHAPTER LII.

SIR THOMAS EFFINGHAM.

TIME was when Sir Thomas Effingham was not Sheriff of Nottingham, but a plain goldsmith in the city of Nottingham, married, but unblessed with any of those pledges which usually are considered to set the seal upon matrimony, and to tie man and woman together by links which only death can loosen; by links we fondly hope may be renewed in a brighter and a better world.

The shop of the worthy goldsmith was in a leading street near the market.

He had no idea then that lucky speculations in wool, loans to an improvident and impoverished government, would raise him to the rank of a belted knight, living in a palace, and owning broad lands on all sides, besides those on which he held a claim.

The goldsmith was rich, but that was a circumstance he scarcely owned even unto himself, so distrustful was he of man, measuring every man's corn by his own bushel.

It was night.

The streets of Nottingham were deserted even by the watch, who snored cosily within some belated alehouse, as the worthy goldsmith turned in his bed and finding himself sleepless jumped out, opened his casement, and looked out.

In the nick of time for a man who was as curious as he was miserly.

Round the corner of a narrow street leading into that which the tradesman inhabited, he saw a shadow pass, a shadow that on close examination proved to be a man wrapped in a cloak, while his jingling spurs proclaimed his rank.

As the goldsmith opened his casement, the man looked up.

"Good man," said the stranger, "would'st earn a purse of gold?"

"Honestly I am always willing to make a penny," replied the goldsmith.

"If, as I surmise, thou art Thomas Beach," cried the stranger, in a somewhat sarcastic tone, "thou wilt fill thy purse honestly if you can—but first fill your purse. Open, and a thousand marks shall be yours."

The goldsmith made no reply. The very sound of the words *thousand marks* appeared to galvanise him. Without pausing to shut the window or to offer any explanation to his wife, who called for one from the bed, he dashed down stairs, entered his shop, and was about to open the door, when he heard a strange sound.

It was the clash of steel.

Peering through the chinks in his shop shutters—there were no windows—he saw that the stranger had put his back against the shop-door, and with a long Spanish rapier was defending himself against three masked ruffians who pressed him hard, striving to hit a kind of bundle he had under his left arm.

The goldsmith was sorely puzzled. He was not a brave man, he was not a hospitable man, he was not a good man.

But like a great many brave, hospitable, and good men, he loved money.

Something must be done. Desire is inventive. The goldsmith almost felt he had the thousand marks within his clutch.

Slowly withdrawing the two bolts which alone held the door, he shouted lustily.

"Keep up, worthy sir—here be two Norman soldiers with cross-bows will soon settle these arrant knaves—come on Hubert, fit thy bolt."

And at the same moment he opened the door wide, just

in time to see the masked ruffians turn the corner, running as if the foul fiend himself were after them.

"I thank you, honest citizen," said the other in tones of deep and earnest feeling, "for truly I was hard pressed. 'Twas not for mysel. I fought—no hired assassins would have stood before me—but for this innocent babe here. Go wake thy dame, and while she sees to this cherub, we, worthy Thomas Beach, will talk—*business*."

There was a magic in the word went to the goldsmith's heart. In five minutes he had not only made his wife and servant rise, but had set them lighting a fire.

The babe, still soundly asleep, was given into their charge, while the goldsmith put wine and ale before his guest.

He was a handsome man of thirty—fully caparisoned as a courtly knight.

He drank freely of the rich wine, which the honest tradesman fully intended he should pay for. Then he spoke.

"I am the Earl of Huntingdon," he said.

The goldsmith rose from his settle, nor could he be persuaded to sit down.

"I have broad lands and much wealth, but hitherto no heir. Why is it thought so? My words must be brief indeed. I have for more than a year been wedded to the sister of the Earl of Beauclerk, who, failing my issue, has a claim to my title and estates. The mortal feud between us has prevented my making my marriage public."

The man spoke bitterly, coldly, remorselessly.

"Well, sir, she was as women wish to be who love their lords. I, who never saw her but in secret, was summoned; but, as the malison would have it, all our secrecy was of no avail. She was in Nottingham Castle, here close by, on a visit; but the earl got scent of the way she was in, and suspected the truth. Hot with furious haste he rode, and burst into the chamber an hour after the child's birth. I had but time to escape with my son and heir, and such legal documents as proved his rank and title."

"But your wife, my lord?" gasped the agitated goldsmith.

"I had not left her," said the young earl, gloomily, "to their ferocious malice; but God has taken *her*."

"Dead?"

"Dead as yon buck," continued the bereaved husband, pointing to one which hung in a dark corner.

"I protest, my lord!"

"Protest me nothing. Coming out by the secret postern, I knew that I was followed. My mind was made up. I go to join the crusaders—such is my knightly vow—but in the meantime, I must have my chiid brought up in obscurity, until I return or he is of an age to defend himself. I knew not whom to trust, until I saw thy head at thy window. Look you, my man, put the infant to nurse, bring him up well, watch him carefully, and if his instincts be knightly, declare to him his own and father's name, and a dying man will bless you."

The goldsmith looked at him with a comical and doubtful glance.

"Take these thousand marks—this box, which proves on the most undoubted authority, his rank and title—keep watch over him and it—and I will forward, by safe hands, the same sum yearly. Wilt take the charge upon thyself aud keep it honestly?"

"Keep it!" cried Thomas Beach, clutching the gold with trembling fingers; "I should think I will."

"Send the boy at early dawn to some fresh woman, who has lately added a yearling to her flock, let her be strong and hearty—stint not money, good Beach—and when I return, the blessings of a father shall be showered on you."

"Eh?" said the goldsmith, with the gesture of a deaf man.

"And as much silver money as the boy weighs."

"My noble sir—good, excellent lord—was ever such a noble lord. The boy shall eat gold!" stammered the astounded artificer.

"Nay, rather good beef and venison," said the earl; "ar.d now, fare thee well. I must join the army ere three days. Do thy trust, and as thou dost it—so may God reward you."

He was gone.

The goldsmith sent the boy out to Gammel, to the care of a relative of Will Scarlett's called Hood, and thus did he fulfil the trust which was confided to him, though for many years the money was paid with scrupulous regularity.

CHAPTER LII.
THREE GALLOWS.

IT was no part of the policy of the belted knights to march through Nottingham with the ragged regiment of defeated tipstaves, constables, and soldiery. They knew that if the populace did not indulge in open jeer, they would in secret scowls.

The inhabitants of Nottingham as a rule were favourable to the outlaws.

And the sheriff knew it.

One half of the recruits who filled up the broken ranks of the King of Sherwood forest, had relations in the good old town.

There was then an undercurrent of popular favour on the forest side.

And the sheriff knew it.

What was to be done? His noble companions refused to march through Coventry—we mean Nottingham—with him.

As far as he was personally concerned, he would have sneaked into his princely home by a back way, but that was not to be thought of, and surrounded, as he was, by a whole horde of myrmidons.

He must strike a great blow.

The sheriff, once alone, scratched his wicked old head, but after some exertion, seemed to find nothing in it.

Like many other justices of the peace then and now, he called in the aid of his clerk.

Simon Longshanks was his name.

The clerk was no braver than his master, and not half so portly.

The generous wines of France, the March and October brewings of old England, had filled his corporate worship to the full extent of his skin.

The opposite was the case with his clerk, a lean, lanky, long-legged specimen of the genus—traitor.

Six feet high, and thin in proportion, with high cheekbones and staring goggle eyes, red hair, and black stumpy beard, it was impossible to mistake him for a cross between a thief and an assassin.

He was neither English nor Norman, but a little of both, with all the vices of the two races, without one of the virtues.

He had began as an Englishman, but finding his lynxlike qualities not appreciated by honest men, he had gone over to the enemy.

He was a low, cringing, hollow-hearted, scrivenous clerk.

He would gladly have kept out of the foray, but as the sheriff's law was very defective, and he liked to hang, draw, and quarter on principle, he never stirred without his walking law-dictionary.

Simon Longshanks was therefore bound to bring up the rear in all expeditions against either the outlaws or any other men.

He, now that the spires of Nottingham could be seen, was in the van.

"Very foolish business this, Simon," said the worshipful.

"Very," dryly replied Simon.

"Is it?" asked Sir Thomas Beauchamp Effingham, with a cold sneer, "and pray if it is who prompted, who invented, who advised it?"

"Your worship asks me a question which I r—r—r—e—l—ly cannot answer."

"I'll pound your carcase to a sack of bad flour, an' you say that again," cried irate Sir Thomas.

"Why your worship."

"So you did not prepare it?"

"I?"

"You did not promote it?"

"I?"

"You did not invent the expedition?" roared the furious magistrate.

"Not I."

"Lying knave!" said the sheriff, striking him with his whip; after which, having unburdened himself to his satisfaction, he went on.

A dead silence prevailed for some minutes.

"If you don't tell me what to do," continued Sir Thomas, "to get me out of this scrape, I'll trip you up by the heels."

"Hang somebody," said Simon Longshanks, emphatically.

A LUCKY SHOT.

"That is all very well," replied the sheriff, rubbing his hands; "but who shall I hang?"

"Anybody."

"No; the prince blamed me last time because it was the wrong man. As if it mattered! If the fellow had done nothing, he soon would. Let me see—who did the fellow who was shot by Robin Hood say were his accomplices?"

"John, Stephen, and Andrew——"

"Well!"

"Sons of the Widow Ann of the Lea."

"So! thou art right, Simon Longshanks. It was as thou sayest—they shall hang——"

A glance of ferocious glee illumined the face of the traitor as he mentally made up the items of the warrant to arrest the three brave and devoted friends of the defrauded Earl of Huntingdon.

The man was naturally a coward, but armed with the authority of the law, he could be brave enough.

He determined accordingly to execute the warrant himself.

CHAPTER LIII.
THE THREE BROTHERS.

THE sons of the widow Lea were mechanics, but like most Englishmen of that day—equally true now—fond of sport.

Many a journey had they made in the forest with bow and arrow. During one of these excursions, they had met with Robin Hood, and enjoyed his hospitality—never refused to the poor and needy.

They at once accepted him as the hero of their imaginations, and were on all occasions ready to serve him.

It was ever after the outlaw chief's habit to stay with them during all his visits to Nottingham—visits of not unfrequent occurrence.

Robin rarely trusted to spies, preferring to see everything for himself.

The three sons of the widow, stalwart and tall, were seated on a bench outside the rude hut they inhabited, with their mother, chatting and laughing.

They had heard of the defeat of the forces under the ranger with an intense satisfaction they scarcely cared to conceal.

It was the talk of the whole town, which, the partisans of the Normans excepted, was delighted at the event.

Presently, one lifting his eyes from the ground, saw a party of constables advancing, with Simon Longshanks behind them.

"What ill-natured knavery is abroad?" said the elder brother.

"Hush, John! let not the scoundrel hear you, or he will find some rascal's trick to be avenged."

"He comes close this way," said John.

As he spoke the constables made a rush at the three young men.

"In the name of the law," shrieked the the clerk, "I arrest you as aiders and abettors of Robin Hood!"

The youths were so astonished that they were manacled before they could offer the least resistance Besides, the force was overwhelming, and could not been have successfully opposed.

"You shall suffer for this, varlet," said the eldest son. "This is some foul trickery. What know we of Robin Hood?"

"Only that he lodges in your house when in Nottingham," sneered Simon.

The three brothers exchanged glances. They had been cruelly betrayed. They made no remark, however, but walked moodily along, surrounded by the tipstaffs.

The sheriff was in his audience hall, and no sooner saw the crowd approaching than he took his seat—a look of gratified malice in his grey twinkling eyes.

His was the mean soul panting for petty vengeance on those who could not turn round.

The audience hall was crowded in a moment by the populace.

"Well, whom have we here?" asked the justice, with affected indifference.

"Please your worship," says clerk Simon, "three knaves known to have harboured that notorious thief and robber, Robin Hood."

"Sayest thou so?" cried the sheriff. "What is your answer, base churls?"

"We have nothing to say, except that the statement is made on the unsupported evidence of the greatest liar in all the shire."

The clerk smiled grimly. He could afford to be spoken ill of by men whose necks were in his hands.

"I have the dying denunciation of one of Robin's own men," put in Simon.

"Ah!" cried the sheriff, as if he heard the statement for the first time. "Let it be read."

Simon read it out, and the three sons of the widow Lea turned somewhat pale as they heard the circumstantial deposition of the traitor.

"Treason, by my knighthood!" said the sheriff. "Treason against our person and that of our lawful king! Let three gallows be erected. This is Saturday. On Monday they shall hang, though I put on the rope myself. Keep them fast."

The men, who knew the magistrate too well to look for any mercy, were removed, sullen, but silent. It is true that they had all man's instinctive love of life, but they were brave, and prepared to meet their fate like sainted martyrs.

The crowd dispersed also without much noise—all fearing to show the genuine detestation they felt at the barbarous decision of the sheriff.

But there was one exception in the person of their mother, who came rushing up with frantic gestures and cries.

"Give me my boys! What have they done that ye should chain them like dogs? I will pass."

"Get thee away, witch," said Simon Longshanks, "or perhaps thou mayest hang with them."

"Hang!" gasped the poor woman.

"Yes. I go now to order the gallows to be erected," sneered the clerk, as the constables disappeared with their prisoners within the walls of the gaol.

One glance, however, passed between the mother and her sons. It was but a glance—and yet how eloquent.

She understood them instantly, and without waiting to exchange a word with any one, made her way in the direction of the forest.

Meanwhile, the prisoners remained loaded with chains in the principal cell. They were not separated, as the room was full, and the other cells fully occupied. They had,

therefore, the poor consolation of bemoaning their misfortune.

"Mother understood us, I think; and if she but finds Robin Hood, 'twill be a chance."

"He is brave and generous, but even if there be time he will scarcely dare attack the sheriff in Nottingham town," replied John.

"I know not. The king of Sherwood has devices we dream not of. He never yet deserted a friend in his last extremity."

In such conversation the time wore away, and the evening sun set on the last night they were to spend upon this earth.

CHAPTER LIV.
THE HANGMEN.

It is Monday morning.

Though the light yet scarcely shed its rays fully over the earth, there was a hollow murmur in Nottingham market place.

The workmen had been all night erecting the gallows in full view of the prison.

The sleep of the condemned had been broken by the sound of the hammer and the saw.

All Nottingham was on foot, filling up every corner of the market-place not occupied by the soldiery and constables.

There was a low and whispered conversation on all hands, but though nearlye very one spoke of rescue, no one offered to be leader.

As the morning advanced people began to collect round the gate of the prison, anxious to catch a sight of men whose misfortunes had elevated them to the rank of popular heroes.

They were also general favourites with their class, being jovial and honest men.

Dark scowls, therefore, greeted the sheriff as he came forth from his house, and no man said "God bless him;" but, on the other hand, no outward manifestations of dislike were attempted.

His power was limited only by his will.

He was surrounded by a powerful escort, with which he rode up to the gates of the prison.

The three prisoners were brought forth, and formally delivered to the sheriff.

"Where be the hangmen?" said the magistrate, sternly.

"There are but two, Sir Thomas," said the governor, bowing low.

"I must have three. The knaves must swing together."

"Murderer and assassin!" cried John of the Lea, in a ringing voice. "I call you to the judgment seat to answer for this cold blooded atrocity."

"Silence! or ye shall be gagged. Who will serve as third hangman?—pence thirteen is the hangman's fee."

"That, will I," said a man in the garb of a butcher, coming forward and touching his cap.

"Forward, then, silly old man," cried the sheriff, and the procession formed, the amateur hangman keeping close to the sheriff's horse, as if afraid of the mob.

And well he might be—hundreds resolved, in their own minds, to punish him for his avarice and cruelty.

The prisoners, their hands pinioned behind their backs, walked with manly strides towards the awful scene of their coming doom.

Aware that from man they could expect nothing, they were silently communing with their God.

Suddenly they came in view of the three gallows, and a cold shiver passed through their frames.

They looked despairingly around at the huge multitude, and everywhere met sympathetic glances, but no cheering ones.

All hope then departed from their bosoms.

"Now, then, be swift," said the brutal magistrate. "If ye know a prayer, say one."

The lips of the doomed men moved, but no utterance came forth.

"Do your duty," the sheriff continued.

"And I really am to hang this man?" cried the butcher, with a curious glance at the sheriff.

"Didst not offer it?" cried the justice; "ah! what have we here?"

And he pointed suspiciously to a little horn the butcher had in his hand.

"It is a horn," said the other slowly, "which I got from a friend of mine; and were I to set it to my mouth, it might blow small good to thee."

"Blow and crack your wind, saucy fellow—wind it as loud as you please—but hang me this man, or you shall change places with him!"

The butcher looked keenly round, and then gave forth a blast that made the sheriff of Nottingham almost fall from his horse.

"Close up," roared the magistrate, "a rescue! turn them off!"

It is almost impossible accurately to describe what followed.

At the first sound of the horn two hundred men in Lincoln green who had approached unheeded, came bounding forward, with arrows bent to the head.

The first city hangman, more expeditious than his fellow, had Andrew of the Lea ready for execution.

Nothing stood between him and death but a tall stool.

The hangman when he heard the voice of the sheriff kicked it away.

Andrew swung in the air, but only for a second.

An arrow cut the cord clean in two and sent the man heavily to the ground.

It came from the bow of Little John.

The confusion was awful, but no fight occurred.

The outlaws overpowered and disarmed the officials in less than a minute.

"The gallows shall not be tenantless," said the butcher—who was no other than Robin Hood; "hang me the hangmen and the sheriff."

The magistrate gave a fearful cry, and fell stupidly inanimate in the arms of two powerful outlaws.

Then suddenly wrenching himself from his guardians, he threw himself at the outlaw's feet and filled the air with such lamentations and supplications as moved the very tipstaffs to smile with contempt.

"It was no doing of mine," he said at last.

"Of whom, then?" sternly inquired Robin Hood.

"Of my clerk, yonder," continued the sheriff, pointing to where Simon Longshanks was sneaking off; "if anybody deserves hanging it is he."

The outlaw looked on the magistrate with a smile of utter contempt.

"Dost think we are such base and cruel knaves as you? I hang no man—but let any come to harm who are my friends, and you shall be found, even on the judgment seat. Come."

And after administering a smart drubbing to the clerk he left the town, accompanied by the three brothers, who now openly and avowedly joined the band.

CHAPTER LV.
MARIAN.

THE outlaws were allowed to retire unmolested to the forest, though the furious sheriff was already revolving in his mind how to organise such an expedition as, without subjecting him to any personal danger, should wreak dire vengeance on his enemies.

But such an expedition could not be organised in a day, and the haughty magistrate retired to his house, there to hide his mortification and defeat from the eyes of the amused mob.

No sooner was the forest reached than the men dispersed, going to their several posts.

Robin Hood, Little John, and Will Scarlett kept together.

The chief was moody. He had made a promise to Edith of Athelston which it was time for him to fulfil.

He was to escort her through the forest to the convent of St. Agnes, for her there to take sanctuary until such time as she should be of age.

They were affianced now. It was impossible for two such ardent and noble hearts to be deceived.

They loved one another and could not conceal the fact.

Maid Marian, after the fight, formally presented her hand to the bold outlaw, and solemnly vowed to be his and his only.

But she stipulated that this interval should be passed in a convent where she would be free from the persecutions of her suitors.

"But why part at all? Are you wearied of the forest?" urged Robin.

"Robin, the wife of the noble hearted Earl of Huntingdon must be above suspicion. You have no mother or sisters here, and 'twere unmaidenly for Edith of Athelston to be living in the house of her future husband."

The outlaw flushed crimson. The word seemed to send a thrill of happiness to his heart.

"You are right my bright, my beautiful! You shall to the convent at once—this very day."

Edith's eyes beamed with a sad delight, but such is the heartfelt gratification one naturally feels in doing that which is right, the pleasure conquered the pain.

Every preparation was made for their immediate departure, Robin promising himself the satisfaction of a long and lonely walk, the intricate passes and pathways of the forest not allowing horses to be generally used.

But they were doomed both to be disappointed.

About an hour before the time fixed on for their departure the outlying scouts brought in an old woman crying bitterly.

At first, so torn, dilapidated, and dirty was she, that the bold outlaw did not recognise her.

"What news! what news! thou silly old woman!
  What news hast thou for me?"
Said she, "Three squires of Nottingham town
  To-day are condemned to die."

"What have they done, old dame to deserve this?" asked Robin Hood. "Have they burned parishes, or murdered priests, or injured virgins?"

"They have done neither," said the old woman, "not burned villages, murdered priests, nor harmed virgins—and yet they must die!"

"Now what have they done?" said Robin Hood then,
  "Old woman now tell to me."
"Oh! it's for slaying the king's fallow-deer,
  And bending their bows with thee.
Dost thou not mind, Robin," she said,
  "Since I made you sup and dine?"
"By the faith of my body," quoth bold Robin Hood.
  "You tell 't in capital time."

No sooner did he recognise his generous and devoted hostess, but his mind was made up. All private feelings were bound with him to give way to duty.

He explained the matter to Edith, who at once urged him to action. She would remain in the cave until his return, praying for victory.

"Nay, walk in the forest," said Robin Hood, "but never lose sight of the trysting tree—so you may always find your way back."

Maid Marian was soon grateful for this advice, as the crowd in the cave, the noisy children, their gambols and cries were intolerable.

When the heart is to full for utterance, when the soul is attuned to love, the silent solitudes of the forest are more suited to the mind than the voice of man or woman.

Marian wanted to be alone, to think of him, to recall his words, and dream,—wicked girl—of the kisses he had given her, and the memory of which she treasured with all her heart.

With this feeling she took her way across the lawn-like glade, and entered beneath the dark shade of the forest trees.

Marian was sad though happy. She was alone, and he whose voice vibrated to the most secret chords of her being was away. She felt a deep weariness of soul, a depression of spirits unaccountable.

She had a strange dread of something, she knew not what—a fear of something going to happen, which often takes such firm hold of the imagination it will not be driven to flight.

Thus it was that for awhile she wandered hither and thither, wherever there appeared an open path. And yet should Edith of Athelston have been more mindful of the outlaw king's advice, for the sun was touching the tree-tops, and the bright laughing daylight was rapidly merging into the softer twilight; the foliage was assuming its rich purple evening mantle, the shades of the vast trees grew longer and longer, while no sound save the soughing of the wind in the trees could anywhere be heard.

At last she began to feel weary, so she seated herself on a fallen tree such as were to be seen on all sides, and gave way to reverie.

Covering her face with her hands, she fondly conjured up the image of Robin Hood.

Thus she sat, perhaps an hour, when reflection coming to her she opened her eyes, and found to her great astonishment that night had closed in.

At first she was not alarmed, but after a minute or two she recollected that she had taken no notice whatever of the way she had come, simply wandering as her fancy directed her, and following the mazes and intricacies of the forest mechanically.

But now what was to be done?

That she had utterly lost her way she knew, which, in the gloom, was a very serious thing.

In the first place, she did not know in the least the direction she should have taken, and was not sufficiently learned in woodcraft to use moon or stars as a guide.

She arose from her seat and glancing round, tried to decide upon which of the many tracks she should select, but memory was of no avail.

She had never noticed the way she had come, her mind being upon other thoughts intent.

And yet something must be done, for the sun was dropping rapidly behind the trees, and the forest was becoming thoroughly dark.

With a kind of desperate determination which was part of her character, Maid Marian, who had her bow and arrow with her, took the most beaten path, hoping and trusting it would lead to some hut where, for promise of reward, some one would lead her into the right way.

Not only was it very annoying to lose her way, but very dangerous, as though safe from the outlaws, she was not from the wolves which prowled about in packs.

She had not walked more than for a few minutes, when she discovered how far she was in error in her course, by coming to a vista of trees so thick and such a short distance apart, as made night hideous.

She fairly sat down, and took refuge from despair in a flood of tears.

This, however, was a very temporary remedy, and presently, drying her face, Maid Marian rose, and again retracing her steps, strove to fall into the right track.

CHAPTER LVI.

MARIAN'S ADVENTURE.

UPON the Monday morning which so nearly terminated the career of the three sons of the widow—a morning which arose in unclouded splendour, and ere the sun was much above the horizon, there might have been seen, crossing the forest, a knight in black armour, mounted on a black horse, large of size, tall, and, to all appearance, powerful and strong, like his rider.

He entered the forest on leaving a small road-side hostelric, and by the pace he rode at, seemed either not in a hurry, or to have great thought of his beast.

He appeared to know the forest pretty well, and evidently hoped to cross the forest in one day; but if so, his purpose was baffled by the devious paths through which he rode.

It was quite evident he did not wish to be observed, as he avoided all frequented paths and took the road that led through the heart of the woodlands.

It thus happened that night was fast approaching, so that he looked around him in search of some place to pass the night.

In romances of chivalry, knights errant are represented as rather preferring to pass their nights beneath the canopy of heaven, dreaming of their mistress's eyebrows.

In real life, however, men require better accommodation, and more substantial fare.

Our knight appeared of our opinion, for he gave vent to one or two hearty curses at the prospect of a night in the open air, and then prepared to start again.

The place where he had paused proved to be a spot deeply involved in the woods, through which, indeed, there were many open glades and some paths, but such as seemed only formed by the numerous herds of cattle which grazed in the forest, or by the animals of chase and the hunters who made prey of them.

The sun, which had served during the whole day to direct the traveller in his course, had begun to set behind the Derbyshire hills; so that if he was to find the comforts of a bed and a supper he must soon discover them, or bear the pains of fatigue and hunger with an oak tree for a canopy.

The knight, after a few minutes, finding the beaten path lead him to no definite spot, not even to the humble hut of a swineherd, or a charcoal burner, did what he should have done at first, under the circumstances—trust to the sagacity of his horse.

There must have been no immediate opportunity for the animal to shew his talent for extricating his master from his difficulties, for the animal, after, on feeling the rein loose, pricking up his ears a moment, subsided into the same jog-trot pace which he had kept up all day, and which, with a man in full armour, in such a place, was all that could be expected.

Presently, however, he appeared to assume new spirit and strength, as if he had alighted on some discovery; and whereas before he had scarcely replied to the spur, except by a groan, he now of his own accord assumed a more lively motion.

The knight, who had been half asleep from sheer fatigue and apathy, roused himself and looked about him, in the hope that they had reached the vicinity of some village.

But nothing was in sight, though the horse kept straight on.

Suddenly, however, a small and glimmering light caught the traveller's eye, and knew that he was somewhere in the neighbourhood of his fellow creatures.

As in a straight line the fire appeared close at hand, the knight dismounted, and fastening his horse to a tree, pushed his way through the bushes—his olfactory nerves now saluted by the welcome odour of roast meat.

Presently he was close to a small clear fire, before which a portion of a fawn was roasting, held up by a wooden spit and two forked pieces of wood.

But, despite hunger—despite the pleasant sensation which came over him, as he stooped to turn the meat—the knight had eyes only for one thing, and that was the solitary hunter whom he had thus opportunely discovered.

It was a young and beautiful girl—in a word, Maid Marian—fast asleep.

She had killed a fawn, after a whole night and day in the woods, and in the act of cooking it had fallen asleep.

CHAPTER LVII.

MARIAN'S ADVENTURE—(continued).

THE knight saw that the girl was no ordinary tramper, but some lady of condition, who had lost her way in the woods.

He was well assured, also, that she had become too sleepy to resist the impulse, and had fallen while in the act of cooking.

With a gravity that was ludicrous in a mailed knight, he began turning the meat and trimming up the fire, with something of the air of a campaigner who had been used to it.

Presently the roast was done to a turn, and the knight touched Marian gently on the shoulder.

She woke with a start at beholding the black knight, but his voice, soft, sweet, and commanding, at once reassured her.

" Fear nothing, lady! for though my trade be war, yet does my knightly vow compel me to protect and serve all such disconsolate damsels as I may find in such peculiar circumstances as your own."

" I have been two days lost in the woods," she replied, timidly.

" I am nearly as badly off as yourself," continued the knight, " and consider myself lucky to find you and your provisions, to which, if you will allow me, I will do honour, without further talk."

Nothing more was said, for both felt exhausted and hungry, and the meal proceeded for some time in silence, the knight simply lifting his beaver to enable him to use his jaws.

Then Marian pointed out a spring, which had induced her selection of the spot, and the knight, who carried a cup at his saddle side, where holsters are now, fetched it full of the sparkling fluid, and handed it to the young girl.

" I pledge you," she said, with one of her brightest smiles.

" Would that we had more generous fluid," said the knight, with a merry laugh, to which Maid Marian responded.

"And now," he continued, "what say you, lady? how shall we pass the night? We must fain do so in the same chamber, with the heavens for a roof. But first tell me how this mishap befell."

Maid Marian, convinced in her own mind that she was in the hands of a knightly man of honour, did not hesitate to comply.

She was the soul of innocence and candour, and told her true story, even to her compact with Robin Hood.

"By my halidame!" said the knight, after a few moments of deep thought at the end of her story, "and Robin Hood be really the son of the Earl of Huntingdon he is the child of a noble father. I knew him well, and now methinks he said, when dying, he commended his child —to the—to me." He corrected himself.

Maid Marian looked curiously at him. There was something in his voice which had a familiar ring, and yet—no it could not be—it was impossible.

The one she took him for was far away in a foreign prison.

"What means that look?" he said, somewhat coldly and haughtily.

"Nay—it was but the shadow of a thought," she stammered.

"Nay, lady, say I. Be frank. You know me," he cried.

"I have my suspicions, and if it be true, then is Edith of Athelston blessed indeed, for justice shall be done."

And she cast herself at the feet of the knight with clasped hands.

"Edith of Athelston!" cried the knight, taking off his helmet, and showing to her view a head thickly curled with yellow hair, high features, blue eyes, remarkably bright and sparkling, a mouth well formed, having an upper lip clothed with moustaches darker than his hair, and bearing altogether the look of a bold, daring, and enterprising man, with which his strong form well corresponded.

Maid Marian uttered a cry, and again falling on her knees, would have kissed his mailed hand.

"Rise, maiden, and prove to me that a woman can keep a secret. You only in all England know that I am here. If you betray me not, even to this outlaw lover of yours, you shall be free and he shall be Earl of Huntingdon, despite all his enemies."

Maid Marian could not reply—her heart was too full for words, but she bent low with deep respect.

"And now, fair lady," he said, "while I lead my horse, seek you some sylvan bower where to rest those dainty limbs. Put thyself out of sight, for beauty like thine is apt to tempt even a belted knight—and I am one of those who, when I woo, like not much maiden coyness. 'Tis waste of time."

Maid Marian blushed to the eyes, for she saw the knight look at her with glances more ardent than respectful.

The knight, however, strolled away to where his horse stood, and having seen to his wants, returned to the fire from which the ward of the crown had disappeared.

The knight smiled grimly, and then, throwing himself upon the sward, was soon fast asleep.

It was daylight when he awoke, to find Maid Marian preparing a morning meal from the remains of the evening feast.

She courtesied with a heightened colour, to which the black knight added by giving her a salute.

"Egad! this king of outlaws is a lucky fellow," he said, "to win one so fair. But a truce to idle talk. I must once more trust my horse, on which you must ride with me to the nearest village, where, no doubt, the knaves who herd with these robbers will guide you where you may hear of this saucy varlet who dares take the title of king, while his true king liveth."

"To whom he is a devoted and attached subject," cried Marian.

"Ah! he herds not then with the adherents of my—of the Prince John, who would feign reign?" cried the knight, merrily.

"Richard the Lion-hearted, is his and my king. We know no other."

"Bravely spoken, wench, and now to horse," replied the knight, and fetching his steed he made a seat of his cloak, and putting her on it behind him vaulted into his saddle and began his journey.

The animal, refreshed with his night's rest and a good supply of nutritious grass, as well as a hearty feed of corn, walked along as if proud of his extra burden. He was a noble steed, and had carried his master through many a well-fought field. The additional load was as nothing, especially as the rider in no way endeavoured to force his pace.

CHAPTER LVIII.

THE ENCOUNTER.

IT was a curious sight to see that tall broad-shouldered knight, large of bone and strong of person, mounted on his mighty black charger—made as if on purpose to bear his weight—with his vizor raised to admit freedom of breath, yet keeping the beaver or under part closed, so that his features could be but imperfectly distinguished.

Still his ruddy embrowned cheeks could plainly be seen, and the large and bright blue eyes that flashed from under the dark shade of the raised vizor.

The whole gesture and look of the man expressed careless gaiety and fearless confidence.

Maid Marian, bashful and blushing, held to his waist, particularly in places where the ground was rough and broken.

All the time the knight kept up a merry round of conversation, saying many things that made the maiden blush, even though the talk of the day was usually rather coarse, and yet not going beyond what the manners of the hour thought gentlemanly.

Some hundred years ago we called things by their names, as most Frenchmen do now, and thought ourselves no more indelicate than those who indulge in inuendo.

Suddenly he felt Maid Marian's arms clutch him violently.

"What ails you, maiden?" he cried, somewhat impatiently.

"I saw, methinks, company in yonder brake that are on the look-out," she whispered.

"Ah! were they knaves in Lincoln green?" he asked, closing his vizor.

Just in time; for half a dozen arrows at the same moment sped through the air and struck him on the breast.

They all, however, fell harmless to the ground.

"By my faith," cried the knight, "you are right, wench! Slip to the ground and hide in yon thicket. I have work to do here."

And as he spoke a dozen horsemen came charging down upon him at full speed with levelled lances.

Maid Marian had scarcely time to glide off and conceal herself in a bush, whence she watched the fight, ere they were upon him.

But though four of their lance heads touched his breast, they splintered as if they had been driven against a tower of steel.

The black knight stood firm and erect as a rock.

"Have at you!" he shouted, as he rose himself in the stirrups. "What want you? No pastime here, but blows."

"At the foul tyrant!" roared the men-at-arms, all of whose faces were concealed by vizors.

"Ah!" said the knight, "'tis foul treason, then? St. George and merry England defend the right!"

Then began a combat which must have been seen to be appreciated. The black knight, wielding a ponderous battle-axe, struck down a man at a blow, until the attackers began to retreat before an arm that wielded so heavy a weapon with such ease.

But still, treachery appeared likely to prevail, for the men-at-arms came crowding up so rapidly as almost to overpower the knight by sheer numbers.

Maid Marian, meanwhile, suffered agonies. She knew too well what hung upon the issue of this fight, which appeared to her a premeditated assassination.

What could she do?

Suddenly she recollected what she ought to have thought of twenty hours before—the horn which had been confided to her by Robin Hood.

A tra-la-la of considerable strength then sounded and for a moment checked the fury of the combatants.

"Ah! my masters," cried the knight, "are you frightened?"

No more words were said, the mailed warrior being now closely pressed by the enemy, who feared that succour might come.

All the time Maid Marian kept up the music of her horn. But not for long, as in five minutes a band of yeomen burst from the wood, and effectually stopped the unequal contest by one volley of their grey-goose shafts.

All who were not disabled fled.

Robin Hood then doffed his cap to the knight, after which he turned to Maid Marian.

He had suspected the cause of her absence, and was close upon her track, which he had followed steadily, though since her mounting he had been sorely puzzled.

"Thanks, my good men," said the knight, looking upon the men in Lincoln green with something of curiosity, "'twas a rude encounter, and but for your coming up might have ended badly. What ask you in return?"

Robin Hood turned round and surveyed the knight curiously.

"What can you do for us, sir knight?" cried the outlaw.

"Nothing now—but the day may come when my aid may be useful. Edith of Athelston will guarantee my power, and I guarantee thee the well."

Robin Hood advanced quickly to the side of the knight, took off his cap, and whispered low.

The knight simply nodded his head, and with a wave of his hand would have ridden off.

"Sir knight," replied the outlaw, "you have been kind to one very dear to me, and an occasion like the present may not often occur. My trysting-tree is not far distant, and if you will delay your journey so that I may put something before you on my festive board, I shall ever be proud of the remembrance and grateful for the condescension."

"I will not say thee nay, thou king of outlaws and prince of good fellows. Lead on. My time is my own for an hour or two," cried the knight.

The outlaw bowed, and led the way up a fine avenue of trees to where a huge oak-tree stood not more than a mile distant.

Robin Hood had many trysting places, and never took any strangers to his secret and most cherished haunt.

A sylvan repast was soon served up, to which the knight, Maid Marian, and the captains of the band sat down, the men eating apart.

Good wine and venison made up the repast, to which the black knight did ample justice, proving himself a good trencher man as well as no niggard at a sparkling cup.

A merrier man the outlaws thought they had never seen, for after emptying a flagon or two he began in a rich, melodious voice, to troll forth songs that filled the sylvan audience with delight.

No one was more pleased than Friar Tuck, who grinned and laughed, making the most horrible contortions of countenance.

"Thou art amused, mad priest," said the knight, graciously.

"I, faith, 'tis rare singing," replied the clerk of Copmanhurst.

"Thou hast a singing face," cried the black knight;" "troll us a ditty."

The outlaws laughed. They all well knew the jolly friar only wanted to be asked.

His song was, however, the wind-up of the entertainment, the black knight pleading important business, and starting on his journey, one of the outlaws serving as a guide; while some twenty others, under orders from Robin Hood, served as his escort—a circumstance quite unknown to the other, who was, if anything, too foolhardy.

As has been truly said, the knight errant of romance—useless but brilliant character—was revived in him, and never with more personal glory.

CHAPTER LIX.
ON THE WAY.

ROBIN HOOD was now left to the society of Maid Marian, and painted to her in glowing colours what he had endured since he had discovered her absence.

At first he thought she had wilfully fled from him, but soon, by a visit to the forest, found out that she had lost herself.

When he reached the scene of her encampment, his amazement was great to find her in the company of a warrior.

A cursory examination had shown the bed of boughs and leaves on which she had reclined, so that he knew she was on friendly terms with whoever she had met.

He now begged hard for a short prolongation of her stay, which he was the better able to urge that two young couples about to be united by the friar desired to be honoured with her presence.

"I wish I could persuade you to be my own," he added, with an amorous glance.

"Nay, in the chapel of some holy house must Edith of Athelston be wedded to Robert Earl of Huntingdon. Urge me no further, my mind is fully made up."

Robin Hood sighed, and tried to look very penitent, but in this he failed.

It was agreed then to have a week's festivities, after which, Maid Marian was to accompany Robin Hood to the convent, there to stay until such time as she had formal consent to marry—the marriage of a ward of the crown being prohibited under very heavy penalties.

It was a happy week, and Maid Marian acknowledged that nothing but her innate sense of right and duty would have made her leave—but she desired to be respected as well as loved.

All turned out to witness her departure.

Robin Hood had so arranged their journey that it should occupy two days—they hoping to rest at the mansion of a friend of the outlaws.

Now all in the band knew the motive which made their captain refuse an escort.

He wished to be alone with the girl of his heart.

But two ventured to disobey his orders and these were Little John and Will Scarlett, who determined, without trenching on his privacy, to be at hand in case they were wanted.

It can be readily understood the lovers did not hurry. They walked along hand in hand, conversing by the way, and every now and then halting when the spot was a pleasant one, and so beguiling the time as young people will.

They did not speak of love. Who does when their very soul is full of it? But their very silence was eloquence.

Robin told stories of his early life, comic adventures with fat abbots and rich traders, Maid Marian listening with a wrapt attention which is incense to a man's soul.

In this way the day passed, until they were within about a mile of the obscure little village where he hoped to lodge.

The evening was close at hand when they descended a hill, at the foot of which was a brawling stream.

Suddenly Robin Hood halted.

"We are followed," he said, "some one is on our track."

"Friends or enemies?" whispered the young girl, without a tremor in her voice.

"Enemies! I heard the clash of steel," replied Robin.

Both stood still and listened, though Marian herself was half inclined to think her lover too cautious; but in a few minutes she herself was aware of the truth.

She distinctly saw six men-at-arms come over the crest of the hill, their eyes fixed on the ground.

They were following the trail.

Robin placed his finger on his lips to command the most perfect silence, while a dark frown settled on his face.

Then emphatically he selected an arrow from his belt, and was about to fit it to his bow, when Marian stopped him.

"For my sake do not. They are merely servants of my guardian, and as such doing their duty."

"For your dear sake there is little I would not do," replied Robin, in a whisper; "we must even fly."

The outlaw sighed as he made use of these words, but putting his grey goose shaft back in its place, caught the young girl in his arms, and without a word, began a headlong course down the slope, making his presence as obvious as possible to the soldiers.

This lasted about three minutes, when Robin Hood reached the river's banks, and still retaining Maid Marian in his arms, began leaping along the stepping-stones which supplied the place of a ford.

In this way he soon reached the other side, where, panting and out of breath, he halted.

"Put me down," said Edith of Athelston, softly.

"I fain must, dear girl," replied Robin Hood, ruefully, as he sat her down upon the grass at the foot of a tree, "as I must defend this pass."

"Let me be queen to-day," continued Edith; "let us

rather seek shelter in the village than shed blood uselessly. These men are but the hired retainers of the earl of Nottingham, and do their duty. Come."

The bold outlaw smiled, but never thought of arguing the point with one to whom he owed the most perfect obedience.

During the period that had elapsed since the presence of the soldiers in the wood had been recognised some time had elapsed.

It was now night.

As they stood on the banks of the river and looked down stream, its clear surface, glistening brightly in the moonlight, could be seen plainly as at noon-day, until it disappeared from sight in a sweeping bend.

From where they stood it seemed more like a lake than a river, the forest apparently closing round so as to hide the bend altogether.

Not a ripple was heard along the shore, and but once while they watched did a zephyr hurry over its bosom, crinkling the surface as it passed, and rustling the tops of a few trees along the bank as it went on, and was lost in the wood beyond.

Far as the eye could reach on every hand, the forest stretched miles and miles away, until it was lost afar, like a sea of gloom in the sky.

While still they stood watching, concealed behind some bushes, the soldiers came in sight, running towards the banks of the river.

At sight of the stepping-stones they halted, as if aware of the presence of a dangerous enemy on the other side.

"I could hold this ford against a hundred such," said Robin.

At the same instant the call of a night-bird rose from amid the trees on the opposite bank.

"Against a thousand, with such allies," he added, with a merry laugh, and turned upwards without another glance on his way to the village.

CHAPTER LX.

IN THE COTTAGE.

THE village towards which Robin Hood had directed his steps was both small and obscure.

One straggling street, with a score of plank-huts covered with thatch, was all it had to show, and to one of these residences the outlaw directed his steps.

It was rather larger, and more important-looking than the others.

It had once, despite its being composed only of one story, been an extensive low building, and although the outer defences had long since fallen to decay, it still bore a few traces of its former strength.

The half-filled fosse, together with the dilapidated barrier of pointed oak piles, plainly told that there was a time when its owners had dared to dispute the entrance with the boldest foemen.

Where the ponderous drawbridge had once fallen was now a solid embankment of earth, broad enough for a modern highway, and bearing the marks of wains and oxen which had recently passed to and fro with the produce of the earth.

Even the dry moat had fallen back to its original state, and instead of forming a wall for the imprisoned waters, had thrown out hazel and thorn, sloe and furze, as fresh and green and beautiful as when, traversed by hart and hind, it formed part of the lonely forest.

It appeared as if the hand of nature were passing over the scene, and blotting out every record of battle and bloodshed with the beauty of her own works, as the ivy creeps over the mouldering turret that is blackened by the fire of the oppressor.

These buildings were, in the inside, in comparison with those of the present day, naked in their simplicity.

There rudeness was something perfectly primitive.

The floors were composed of clay and sand, while the principle hall was not so well furnished as a village kitchen.

But there was salt to all these drawbacks—open-hearted hospitality.

Few men knew or cared to know who owned this ancient Saxon castle, and yet were there few men more worthy of being known.

Of pure Saxon blood, Nicholas Gammel retained all the characteristics of his race, adding thereto the most intense and genuine hatred of the Normans.

It was as an enemy of the oppressors that he welcomed Robin Hood, and, once her name announced, proffered his home to Edith.

"There be night-hawks abroad," said the king of the outlaws, after the first hearty shake of the hand.

Nicholas Gammel looked at the forester in some surprise.

"I understand you," replied Robin; "but this, the lady of my heart, forbids me to use violence. I would fain use stratagem."

He then explained the true state of matters.

"As you will," said their host, with a courteous bow to the lady; "then follow me."

From the hall to a kind of back-yard was but a step, and then about ten paces back was a thatched hut of two stories.

"Go yonder. I will see your enemies and speed them if I can, though it goes against my heart to meet them with aught else but bow and lance."

"The day may come," replied Robin, with glistening eyes, "when we may so meet all our enemies."

Nicholas Gammel made no verbal reply, but clutching the outlaw's hand, returned towards his own house, at the front door of which loud knocks were now heard.

"A brave and noble nature," said the outlaw, as he lifted the latch of the cottage and went within.

This house had sheltered Robin Hood more than once before, and belonged to the foster-mother or nurse of the owner, an old woman, but still retaining her intellect.

She expressed no surprise at seeing the outlaw and his friend, but eagerly set before them refreshment, which both declined at the moment, being bent on watching the movements of their pursuers.

But Nicholas Gammel appeared to have hoodwinked them completely, as no more was heard for same time.

The supper, then, after a time was welcomed, and the lovers gladly availed themselves of the good woman's hospitality; anxious, however, to retire to rest as soon as possible, so as to start early in the morning.

Suddenly Edith started and turned deadly pale.

"What is it?" cried Robin Hood.

"A man looked in at the window—such a face! I never saw anything so black and hideous."

At the same moment the latch was tried, but the outlaw had barred the door.

He took up his quarterstaff, and, with a dark frown, approached the door.

Maid Marian looked beseechingly at him.

"For my sake, be careful," she said.

'Tis said conscience makes cowards of us all; but surely love does not. If a man ever feels brave at one time more than another, 'tis in defence of the woman that he loves; and yet, when pearly-eyed beauty looks upward at us, and asks in melting accents that we should be careful of ourselves, who can resist her?

Robin Hood felt that his life was valuable, now that she looked upon it as hers.

"I will—but beshrew the knaves, they must have a warm reception."

The words were scarcely spoken, when there came a loud thwack at the door.

Robin signed to the old woman to speak.

"Who is this beats so loudly at my door-post?" she said in her cracked voice.

"Men-at-arms, in search of a strayed maiden," replied an imperious voice, that Edith of Athelston knew too well.

It was that of the knight who had handed her over to the sheriff of Nottingham.

The lovers exchanged a glance of anguish. They had, it appeared, seen only a small party of those who were in search of them.

Marian laid her small hand on the outlaw's arm.

"Defence is useless," she said, "and I would not harm befall you for a king's ransom."

Robin Hood mused a moment, and then, the others still knocking at the door, stooped low and whispered.

A smile came upon the face of the girl, who then went to the door.

"Who knocks?" she said. "'Tis past curfew, and I may not open."

"Edith, herself!" shouted the knight. "Open, lest I break the door."

"I know you not," she replied.

"Open! I say," he replied. "No malapert wench shall keep me waiting."

And as he spoke a heavy beam of wood was hurled at the door, which shook on its hinges.

"Leave my door alone," said the cracked voice of the old woman. "Why should decent folks be kept waiting? I don't care if—if you be Robin Hood—it's nothing to me. Coming, good gentlemen—coming."

And the ancient beldame rushed up to her door, and, drawing the bolts, threw it wide open.

The men-at-arms and their leader rushed in, while the old woman went out as if glad to escape from the scene she expected would follow.

Robin Hood stood with folded arms in a dark and obscure corner.

"Hang me the varlet to the rafter," said Sir Philip de Beauvoisin, fiercely.

Two of the soldiers made a rush at the outlaw, who gave a screech that startled them.

"You wouldn't hurt a poor old woman who has done no harm?"

"Out! out! scour the village, the ruffian has escaped," cried the Norman chief; "and as for you, detestable and damnable hag, fire and faggot shall be thy shrift."

The men-at-arms, themselves furious at being out-witted in so outrageous a manner by the daring outlaw, rushed to obey their leader, but too late.

Robin Hood was in the forest, far out of the reach of any hired soldier.

The rage of the knight was something dreadful to behold. He foamed at the mouth, he cursed and swore at his own men, at the old woman, at all the Saxon race, and wound up by ordering them to fire the house.

The thatch, as usual, was very dry, and a torch to it would have soon put the house in flames.

One of the men stirred the embers, and having lit a small handful of sticks, approached the thatch.

An arrow pierced his brain, and he fell at the knight's feet a corpse.

The knight swore a fearful oath, but gave no further orders as to fire.

"So my dainty cousin," he said, turning in a taunting way to Edith, "I find you wandering in Sherwood Forest with a robber for your guide. Belted earls are not good enough for you! But I have found you. Say, will you go quietly to a convent, or shall force be used?"

"My wish," replied Edith haughtily, "is to retire to St. Agnes until such time as I am released from my position as ward of the crown."

"Which, wench, you can only do by wedding Notting-ham's heir."

"The king is good and generous, and I have his promise," said Edith.

"What king?" sneered the knight, "surely you put no faith in the generous impulses of King John?"

"I know no such person. My king is the brave and chivalrous Richard."

"Much good he can do thee. Let him release himself from prison, and then he may reverse the orders of the prince—which are, that you yield your fief and become a nun, or marry his adherent, the son of the Earl of Nottingham."

"I am content," said Edith, with a smile, which made the knight thoughtful.

"Surely the lion is not loose!" he muttered to himself, but took care none should hear him.

He then gave orders for palfreys to be brought up, and mounting himself, with sarcastic courtesy helped his lovely kinswoman to her saddle, placed himself by her side, and, despite the lateness of the hour, rode on towards St. Agnes Convent.

CHAPTER LXI.

STRATEGY.

WHEN Robin Hood escaped from his deadly foes in the disguise of the old woman, he contrived, in the confusion which ensued on opening the door, to snatch up his bow and arrows, with which, standing under an oak at no great distance, he watched the progress of events.

Quick as a flash of lightning his cloth-yard shaft was fixed and sped, when he saw the soldier about to put his flaming torch to the thatch.

Another arrow would have ended the days of the brutal knight, but that Robin Hood recollected he was a relative of Edith of Athelston.

He forebore, then, and leaning his back against a tree, watched her depart with some such feelings as sways a man when he sees all he values on earth carried to the grave.

"Shall I ever see her again?" he asked himself, bitterly.

"What chattering old woman have we here?" said a loud and ringing voice close to him; "and what does she with the bow and arrows of good Robin Hood?"

The outlaw chief turned round with a melancholy smile.

"Were my temper different," he said, "good Little John, I might have played with you—but I am too sad to joke."

"Our captain!" cried in one voice Little John and Will Scarlett.

"Aye, and only escaped from hanging by means of these old duds. But come into the village while I resume my dress. There is work to be done ere morning."

The lieutenants made no remark, but unhesitatingly followed their leader into the Saxon village.

The inhabitants of the Saxon village were all herdsmen and labourers on the lands possessed by Nicholas Gammel, the uncle of Will Scarlett.

Their reception was, therefore, warm in the extreme.

The men under the command of Sir Philip de Beau-voisin had not molested Nicholas Gammel, as they had at once traced the fugitives to the hut, and were ignorant of the fact that they had passed through the franklin's residence.

Had they known this he would have suffered severely.

But there was no selfishness in the heart of Nicholas. No fear of offending the Norman tyrants influenced his bosom.

The outlaws were received with open arms, and every facility given to Robin Hood.

What he chiefly wanted was the services of messengers to apprise his men of his wishes.

These were found in a moment, and being despatched, the outlaw, accompanied by his two favourite lieutenants, started on the trail of the ravishers.

It was not difficult to follow, from the simple fact that Robin Hood knew the direction they had taken.

They started at a rapid pace, fully aware that the horsemen, if they pressed forward, would clear the skirts of the forest before morning.

But the dark shades of night rendered this extremely improbable, as the intricacies of the path could not be followed at any pace but a walk.

Scarcely a word was spoken, the three men walking in Indian file, the captain leading the way.

This continued until midnight, when just as they reached the banks of a small stream they heard the neigh of a horse.

All stood still and listened with charmed ears.

A murmur of conversation at once attracted their attention, and at no great distance.

The noise proceeded from the vicinity of the river, and proved to be two men—the night-watchers of the party—who were talking somewhat loudly for sentries, to keep themselves awake.

With all the caution of Red Indians the three outlaws crept towards the group, and soon saw that all the rest of the party were asleep—Marian in a small bower of branches and bushes, the rest under a large and spreading elm.

There is a power in such men as Robin Hood of conveying ideas by a glance, and the outlaw exercised it.

Little John and Will Scarlett fully understood him.

They held back ready for any emergency that might occur, leaving him to act alone.

The ground over which Robin Hood had to crawl was turfy and soft, so that by moving with the undulating motion of a snake he made no sound whatever.

The sentries had their backs to the bold outlaw.

His eyes were never off them.

The position was precarious and terrible. In order to reach the spot he desired he had to pass between two rows of sleeping soldiers and within five yards of the watchers.

A cough, a sneeze, a stumble, would utterly ruin all.

Once the conversation of the sentries ceased. They had heard something uncommon.

Fortunately they did not look into the camp, but around and about.

THE WARNING ARROW.

Like all experienced night sentinels they were recumbent, in which position every object within range comes into view.

"It was a hare, I trow," said one, "disturbed by the fire."

The conversation continued, and Robin Hood, who had lain like a log, once more advanced in the direction of Maid Marian.

The greatest danger now lay in her waking with a start, and this Robin Hood felt.

His heart throbbed violently as he approached her.

At length he was near enough to gaze into her face.

She was sound asleep, as still and calm as an infant. The outlaw chief looked at her for a moment with perfect rapture.

Then he stooped and kissed her on her two pouting lips.

She did not move for a moment, but lay, as it were, in silent ecstasy.

Then she opened her eyes and looked him full in the face.

She knew before she opened her eyes who it was, and smiled upon him with her own bright smile.

Robin Hood made a sign to her to imitate him, and began crawling along the ground as before.

Maid Marian followed him, imitating his movement exactly, nor did they utter even a whisper until both were hid beneath the overhanging undergrowth.

CHAPTER LXII.

TEMPTATION.

WHEN Sir Philip de Beauvoisin awoke in the morning and found that the ward of the crown had escaped, his astonishment and fury knew no bounds.

He raved and stormed at his men like a madman, until at length, reason resuming its sway, he dispatched them on all sides in search of her.

This proceeding, we need scarcely observe, proved of no avail. The fugitives had many hours' start of them.

Nothing remained to be done but proceed on his journey without her, and wait until such time as the spies which he employed in the forest were able once more to put him on her track.

Towards the evening they came in sight of the convent, and as men and beasts both required refreshment, the knight determined to cast himself on the known hospitality of the abbess.

The monastic establishment was situated in a green and fertile valley, while all around was astir with life; flocks and herds were bleating on the skirts of the forest, along which floated many a wild and woodland sound, and near which might be seen many a picturesque hut and rural grange.

The setting sunbeams gilded the deep-dyed windows, rich with the figures of saints and warriors.

The party halted at the gate, which was readily opened by the porter, who then bade an ancient man lead the knight to the parlour, while he guided the soldiers to the kitchen, whence arose a most savoury odour.

The abbess, a dignified woman, with a fine aquiline nose, curled lip, and lofty forehead, received the knight politely, but at the same time somewhat coldly.

"My poor house is at your disposal," she said; "do you wish to stay the night?"

"If you do not find the charge too burdensome," he replied.

"My house is open to all, to the rich and poor alike. A poor lamb took refuge here to-day of whom you know something."

The knight started, as the abbess fixed her piercing eyes upon him.

"Of whom I know something? May I ask her name?"

"Edith of Athelston."

"But this is witchcraft. She was on foot, and in my company, but this morning," was the reply of the astonished and much puzzled knight.

"She came on a grey palfrey, escorted by some Saxon yeomen."

"Rogues all—followers of Robin Hood."

"That matters not. She claimed my protection and leave to rest her weary limbs under the shadow of the cross."

"But she is a ward of the crown, and under the charge of the sheriff of Nottingham, to whom it was my wish to lead her."

"The sheriff is no fit guardian for a timid maiden."

"You do not mean to give her up, then?" asked the soldier, speaking in a voice that trembled with suppressed passion.

"Certainly not," said the abbess, calmly; "and now that we understand each other, I crave your leave to retire. Refreshment shall be served you, and an apartment prepared."

Before the angry knight could reply she had left the room.

"May all the curses of the foul fiend alight upon her," said Sir Philip; "by the mass, I have a good mind to drag her out by force. And yet, 'twere too bold. The Prince is in no good odour with the church, and the scandal might do harm. Have her I will."

It was easy to come to this determination, but far more difficult to carry it out.

In those lawless days the one sanctuary that was respected was the interior of priories and convents. In rare instances did kings even dare to violate them.

It required some resolution to venture on the only course by which he had any chance of success, and that was cunning and trickery.

While these thoughts were in his mind, an aged servant woman, not in the garb of the church, entered with a kind of tray, which she sat before him.

The knight looked at her keenly, and thought her a fitting instrument at once.

"Would'st earn a handful of rose nobles, ancient mother?" he said, abruptly.

The old woman started. Such an idea had never presented itself to her senses before.

"And what should an old woman like me do with gold?"

"Forswear service, and live at thy ease in some neat cot," replied the tempter.

"'Tis true. My bones are not so young as they were—and pray, good sir knight, what am I to do, to earn a handful of rose nobles?"

And the old woman's eyes glistened as he repeated his offer.

"A truant relative of mine has, from some mistaken notion, taken sanctuary here. The abbess refuses me speech with her. If you would contrive to enter her cell unknown to any one, this purse is yours."

The old woman trembled violently.

"But they would kill me if they found it out," she said.

"Pish! Where am I to sleep?"

"In a corridor where rooms are provided for noble visitors."

"And she—where have they put her?"

"In the same corridor, but with a door locked between."

"And the key ——"

"Hangs at the girdle of our lady abbess," continued the woman.

"That key I must have, or else no gold. Her bunch is large, and she will not miss it."

"I will try—I will try," mumbled the crone, in whose bosom the miserable love of gold had nearly conquered her fear of consequences.

And without another word she left the room, leaving the knight in a state of anxiety mingled with hope.

He knew the convent well, and was aware that at the end of the gallery devoted to the more honoured guests was a stairs leading to the courtyard.

His idea was to bid his soldiers be ready in the grey of the morn, when everything is indistinct, and the porter, half-asleep, would not notice very carefully what occurred.

He hoped to envelope the slight form of Edith as completely in his cloak as to stifle her cries, and thus carry her out before she was missed.

Once out, he felt certain of being forgiven by the prince.

Ruminating on his plot, he continued eating his evening meal with as much relish as if he had been thinking over some honest and pious device to do good.

These Norman tyrants, from whom some people are so proud of being descended, were the most case-hardened ruffians that ever wore coat of mail.

When not cowed by the most abject superstition, they lived without fear, and committed every possible crime without remorse.

Having finished his meal, and drained a large goblet of wine, he turned towards the door, and descending to the courtyard, summoned one of his men, to whom he gave the most minute directions, one of which was by every means in his power to induce the porter to drink.

In this way, by using his key, they could leave unperceived.

This part of his plans being communicated to his lieutenant, he returned to the room above, where he found the old woman shaking dreadfully, but with the key in her hand.

"And now, worthy sir, go to thy chamber, and give me the gold, with which I will presently leave the house, and hide my head in some small village; for they will scourge me to death an' I stop here."

The knight threw her the purse, and clutching the keys as if they had been a treasure, strode to his apartment, glad to seek repose early that he might awaken before dawn.

CHAPTER LXIII.

THE WARNING.

MEANWHILE the unconscious object of his avaricious designs was in her chamber.

She had been taken direct to the convent by Robin Hood, and had thrown herself under the protection of the good abbess, herself a Saxon, and who had taken to the conventual life to escape the brutal violence of a Norman baron as well as for gentler reasons.

The worthy dame had seen troubles herself, and sympathising with Edith, promised her at once aid and protection, even if she had to go direct to the king for it.

When the time came for her to retire for the night, early in all convents, the lady abbess conducted her to her apartment herself.

It might be considered to be situated in an outbuilding over-looking the forest, though, for protection, the windows were closely barred.

There was quite an air of comfort about the place, which at the period was unusual. The furniture was massive and good, the huge chair in which, when once alone, Edith cast herself, containing timber enough to manufacture a dozen such articles in the present day.

The arras was rich, and represented a stag-hunt painted with some taste and skill; whilst two tall candles, like those offered on the altar to the virgin, stood on the table before, in solid silver candelabra.

Edith had no inclination for sleep. She was in that

young stage of love's dream, when it is happiness to think even of the being of one's choice.

She sat for more than an hour without moving, and then, as if weary of the monotony of her position, rose, and going to the window, looked out upon the night.

It was clear and starlight, though the moon had not yet risen.

About thirty yards out on the sward was a clump of oaks, and as the young girl cast her eyes in that direction she discovered the figure of a man, who, however, instantly disappeared.

But the eye of affection is not easily deceived.

It was Robin Hood.

Her cheek flushed with pleasure, and for an instant the idea flashed across her mind that she would wish him good-night. Her native modesty, however, prevailed, and with a deep sigh, she returned to her seat.

Again she closed her eyes and thought, but this time nature appeared to assert herself, for presently her head was bowed on her shoulder, and the gentle heaving of her bosom showed that she slept.

Clouds crossed the sky, the sky became overclouded, broke again, and flooded forest and plain with light; but still she moved not, sleeping as calmly as a baby on her mother's breast.

At last the dawn began to break, and still she slept as soundly as ever.

Suddenly a whizzing noise was heard, something came in at the window, and then an arrow might have been seen sticking in the arras, a kind of letter hanging to its shaft-end.

But such is the soundness of slumber which belongs to youth, that even this failed to awaken her.

A minute more and the door opened slowly, giving passage to a man who glared upon the sleeping girl with intense delight. One great difficulty was overcome, since he found her dressed.

On the table was a scarf that had served to shield her swan-like throat.

This he clutched, and by a dexterous movement converted into a gag. Next instant the struggling but helpless girl was concealed from view by an ample cloak.

As if she had been an infant he carried her along the corridor, whence he rapidly gained the court-yard, where his men were collected with the gate wide open.

The porter was dead drunk in his lodge.

The knight waited not a moment, but leaping on his horse, led the way across the glade at a gallop.

A loud shout made him turn, and there he saw a party of men in Lincoln green, running at the top of their speed for the convent.

Robin Hood, pale with indignation and rage, led the van, and soon was at the open gate ringing with terrible violence.

In five minutes, servants, nuns, and abbess, none of them fitted by dress to face a dozen bearded yeomen, came rushing forth.

"What is it?" cried the head of the flock, gasping for breath.

"The foul and felon knight has just departed, taking with him the ward of the crown," was Robin Hood's angry cry.

"Impossible! I have the keys," replied the abbess, and then casting her eyes around at the half-naked nuns, she continued, "retire, my daughters, retire at once, while I inquire into this matter, and why the gates are open at this hour without my permission."

The frightened flock, some young and pretty, huddling their clothes around them, re-entered the house, as did the abbess, who, however, soon returned with a mantle thrown around her, and the news that two of her keys had in reality been stolen from her bunch, and that Edith had in truth been carried off.

"And what is this?" said the abbess holding up the arrow she had taken from the arras.

Robin Hood blushed.

"As soon as I found out the outrage that was about to be attempted on Edith of Athelston, I shot an arrow through the only window where I saw a light, hoping to alarm the inmates."

"But how came you to suspect this most foul crime against the laws of mother church?" asked the abbess, curiously.

"An old woman came rushing suspiciously forth from the convent at dark, and I desiring to know what the cavalier wanted who had just before gone in, she became frightened and dropped a purse of gold, on finding which I suspected something was wrong, and assuming a fierce and angry mien, so frightened her that she confesses all—and here she is."

The abbess said not a word, but fixing her eyes upon the wretched and trembling crone, seemed to look her through.

"So," she said after a pause, and with a voice that was terrible from its cold distinctness, "you are the vile caitiff that has betrayed and sold her mistress. Away with her to the vaults beneath the chapel. She shall have sentence presently. And now, sir yeoman, what purpose you?"

"To find Edith of Athelston and restore her to sanctuary," said the outlaw chief.

"You have acted like a brave and ready-witted fellow already. Go, and fortune go with you—you have my blessing."

Robin Hood doffed his cap and bowed low.

"Ere I depart grant me one boon, noble lady," said the outlaw.

"An' it be in my power."

"Be not too hard upon the poor old woman. The gold was a great temptation."

"I was never spoken of as cruel," said the abbess mildly; "and am not going to begin now to earn such a reputation. I thank thee, however, for thy Christian friendly feeling. Bread and water for a week shall be her punishment—then she shall go forth from this with her ill-earned gold."

"Which, for that purpose, I must render up," cried Robin, taking it from his pouch.

CHAPTER LXIV.

THE FLIGHT.

SIR PHILIP DE BEAUVOISIN was a man of the most unbounded ambition and unbridled passions.

He would never allow any one or anything to stand in his way when he thought he could cope with it.

His determination to make Edith his wife was a sudden whim or impulse, which had since grown to be a passion, which wholly carried him away. He resolved both to win her love and revel in her beauty.

As soon as they were fairly in the forest and out of sight of the convent, he took off his cloak and removed the gag.

Edith had never lost her senses. She was magnificently beautiful in her anger.

"Release me, unmanly lord!" she said. "For this base insult you shall suffer, if I crawl to the foot of the throne."

"Give the lady a horse," said Sir Philip, without taking the slightest notice of her speech.

Not wishing to enter upon a struggle with one of the men-at-arms, Edith allowed herself to be transferred to a kind of pillion made with the man's cloak, and rode in silence, musing on what was likely to be the termination of this unexpected adventure.

As yet she had no suspicion that the knight was acting for himself. She believed him to be taking her to the house of Sir Thomas Beauchamp, and hence had little fear.

She had resolved to die ere she gave her hand to the husband selected for her by a crafty and subtle prince.

Sir Philip, meanwhile, was well aware that the outlaws were not only good shots but fleet of foot, so that if they would escape their assaults they must hurry.

He, therefore, suddenly gave the word to use whip and spur, and dashing among the entangling trees with all the speed that could be made, drew Edith unwillingly after him.

Presently, however, the underwood became so thick that the party were compelled to rein in their horses and look around for a path somewhat more passable.

Though nearly breathless from the rapid motion of her steed, which had called a colour to her cheek that fairly put to shame the rosy tint of the bramble blossom, Edith looked around at the grim soldiers with a countenance which they, rude as they were, could not but gaze on with admiration.

"This is not the road to Nottingham—whither would you bear me? Is this the act of a gallant knight, or even of a brave man?"

The knight made no reply, being busily engaged in looking around for some pathway.

As he he did so voices became audible at no great distance, and Edith, hoping for rescue, began to scream at the top of her voice.

The voices immediately seemed to approach, bnt, at a signal from the knight, the men-at-arms forced their heavy and powerful steeds through the bending beds of hazels, wild sloes, and every variety of shrubbery, which speedily rose again to an erect position, and concealed the heads even of the tallest horsemen.

A couple of soldiers, obeying a whispered order, drew a bandage across the mouth of the unfortunate girl, and thus stifled her cries.

The pursuers seemed at fault, and presently heir voices died away in the distance.

"Coward!" said Edith, when the bandage was once more removed. "Before the king will I proclaim you a cruel-hearted churl—unworthy to wear spurs. But faugh! words are wasted on such as thee."

And she turned to follow the man who appeared to act as guide.

The knight, fully aware that the outlaws would soon get on their trail, now took council with his lieutenant, and after a few words it was agreed to divide, the knight going on as to Nottingham; while two men, with the female prisoner, started by the most secret and winding paths to go forward to their destination.

Edith soon found this out, and felt for the moment somewhat relieved by the other's absence.

A new hope also arose within her bosom.

"Ye are the servants of one whose deeds little honour his name," she said; "but let that pass. Lead me straight to the convent whence I have been torn, and not only do I pledge myself to forgiveness, but will pay rich rewards in money and lands."

The two men shook their heads. They had a rude sense of fidelity to their lord; but what chiefly decided them was the fact, that, hide where they would, where could they conceal themselves from the vengeance of the Norman chief.

Edith said no more, but drawing a veil over her face, seemed content to abide by her fate.

The men kept on at a slow and methodical pace through the most circuitous and difficult paths, always using the greatest caution, which seemed to increase as the twilight darkened.

Soon after crossing a dark and gloomy ravine that still exists on the sight of Sherwood Forest, they came to a place where it was less wooded; and after crossing a gentle ascent of green sward, saw before them a kind of fortified farm-house, such as have existed in all countries in lawless times.

At a loud summons from one of the men, a kind of drawbridge was lowered, and the two entered though a wide doorway into a yard, where pigs wallowed in plenty.

Calling to a rough kind of woman, in the costume of a farmer's wife, the first soldier bade her take Edith to her room, which she was by no means to leave until her master's pleasure was known.

The room to which our young heroine suffered herself to be led was long and low, with a chilly aspect, that was partly relieved in a few minutes by a wood fire blazing on the hearth.

And here we must leave the young girl, and see what was being done without for her release.

CHAPTER LXV.

ROBIN HOOD PUZZLED.

THE artful measure of Sir Philip de Beauvoisin, dividing his troop and then riding forward at a trot, deceived the outlaws—even Robin Hood being taken in.

He kept on in pursuit, therefore, of the larger party, only coming up with it when in sight of a large village, where the wearied soldiers put up at an inn or alehouse, glad indeed to get any refreshment.

The king of the outlaws was never without means of disguise; so, hastily browning his face and assuming the garb of a swineherd, he pushed into the village at the opposite end by which the others had entered, and entering the alehouse by the back door, speedily ascertained the truth from a stout, rosy-cheeked Saxon lass, who readily took a kiss in full payment.

Robin Hood was sorely puzzled. Edith surely could not have escaped from their clutches.

Then a horrid feeling came over him—a dread that something fatal had happened.

Had they murdered her and buried her in the forest.

But he could not believe this possible, so dismissed the very suggestion.

What was to be done? It was now quite dark, and both he and his followers were weary and footsore. They could travel no more that night. His only plan was to send them into a secret covert of the forest, while he watched the knight and men-at-arms.

They were soon glad to seek rest; upon which Robin returned to his men, bidding them camp as well as possible, keeping within horn-call, in case he needed their services.

As he came up to the inn he remarked the clatter of a horse's hoof, and saw in the distance one of the men riding away.

Now this puzzled Robin much, but there was no help for it—the man was gone. All he could do was to wait and watch, which he did from a hayloft into which he crept.

Now all men are mortal; and the outlaw, musing on his mistress and racking his brain to guess what had become of her, suddenly fell into a sound sleep, from which he did not wake until late the following morning.

The knight and his train had been an hour gone.

The young man had every inclination to tear his hair; but as that would simply have availed nothing, he changed his mind, and, making minute inquiries as to the course they had taken, started once more in pursuit.

But the trail was well concealed, and the outlaw wandered about for some considerable time without any definite result being produced.

Meanwhile, events were occurring in a different part of the forest which had considerable influence over the fortunes of all concerned.

On the borders of a certain bubbling brook—a stream of clear, sparkling, crystal water, which ran laughingly over glittering pebbles—sat a young man, neither tall nor short, but rather stout, habited in a low wide gown with wide sleeves, on his head a cowl with a point behind, his waist girt with a belt of long grass, to which was attached a rosary, while by his side was a huge crabstick quarterstaff, and before him an amount of provisions, eatable and drinkable, fit for about three ordinary men.

The man was devouring his meal with some such zest as the hungry beggar in Gil Blas, and had just lifted up his huge leathern bottle to his mouth for the second or third time when his attention was attracted by the sound of tinkling bells.

Looking keenly in the direction of the sound, the friar at once saw that it proceeded from a mule upon which sat a priest belonging to one of the neighbouring monasteries who was slowly making his way through the forest.

The jovial friar at once proceeded to conceal his bottle, which held some four quarts, under a bush, and then rising and leaning on his staff, awaited the coming of the portly personage borne so sedately by the sleek and sure-footed animal.

The priest, who was either wrapped in deep thought or nearly asleep, did not perceive the stranger until quite close upon him, when, rousing himself with a start, he dug his heels into the sides of his mule, as if anxious to avoid contact with the other.

These wandering mendicant friars and hedge priests were much dreaded by their more stay-at-home and opulent brethren, as they were apt to presume upon their superior strength to levy unwelcome contributions.

But the sturdy friar had no intention of allowing any such proceeding.

He caught the mule by the bridle.

"Unhand me, brother," said the priest, in a thick pursy voice. "I am in haste, and cannot pause a minute."

"Thou goest marvellous slow for one in haste," replied the other, in a sarcastic tone. "I only ask you to look at this cool and shady nook—at this venison pasty, and while thy tired mule recruits himself, request that you will do the same."

The priest had travelled since morning, the nook was shady and pleasant, the pasty was capacious, and he was hungry.

"It would verily be a sin," he said, in a gentler voice, "to refuse so hospitable an offer. 'Tis true that the body can only be mortified by fasting and penance; but there is a time for all things, and when on a journey we are allowed to taste both of good sirloins and smoking haunches."

And as he spoke, the goodly priest was getting rid both of the food and his appetite in a way that seemed to indicate one not much given to abstinence.

Still between the mouthfuls he contrived to sermonise a little.

"A long voyage in the open air does give us such appetites as can only be appeased by food; but when within the cloisters it is our duty to pray and fast lest we forget the higher duties which appertain to man."

"As I live chiefly in the forest," replied the friar, with twinkling eyes, "I am absolved from much fasting. I always find hunger produce bad thoughts, and apt to mingle in my devotions; so I endeavour as much as possible to keep down the feeling."

"But if you live in the forest, what are thy duties, brother? You surely do not confess the wolves and bucks?" asked the priest.

"Nay, but men and women nearly as savage. I have a hermitage some miles away where poor folk come for absolution. I go about to the scattered hamlets, and, lest the young folk should live in sin, marry them."

The priest had paused in his attack on the pasty.

"Hast had enough of that?" said the friar; "and now taste this"—dipping into his capacious wallet—"'tis powdered beef and salad. 'Twill give thee new appetite."

"Hast ever a goblet I could dip in the stream? Were I to wash the pasty down with a goodly draught, maybe I might taste the beef and salad."

"Water!" said the other, his nose reddening with indignation, "would'st spoil such pasty? This is the stuff—October ale of the oldest brewing—taste that."

A slight hesitation on the part of the priest, who hardly understood such hospitality on the part of a hedge priest, was conquered by the bottle being thrust into his hand.

He placed it to his mouth, nor took it away until he had thoroughly satisfied himself as to its character.

"A good drink enough, and not too strong," he said, smacking his lips. "I think after that I could taste the powdered beef."

All restraint was now gone between the two men, and they laughed and talked like old acquaintances, until the meal being finished, both leaned against a tree in a state of perfect beatitude.

The friar said nothing for a few minutes, nor had a chance, the priest speaking first.

"Your patients are generous," he said, "an' you live this way every day in the week."

"There is a worthy keeper whom I whilome served," replied the friar, "and he rarely kills a buck but he sends me a joint."

"Does he the brewing of thy ale?"

"Nay, an excellent miller of my acquaintance sees to that," replied the friar; "and now I think of it, I put down to cool just now a small flagon of burgundy, in the hope some passing stranger might join me, and need a cordial after meals."

The priest smiled paternally as from the river the friar drew a stone jar, some of the contents of which he poured into a horn.

"Taste, and say if ever you put your lips to finer," cried the friar.

"And pray who may be the friend who gives such liquor to a mendicant friar?"

"I have a butt and a buck a year from Sir Gammel," replied the hedge priest.

The other made no reply. He was too busy in tasting to speak.

"Beautiful!" he cried, enthusiastically.

The friar pledged him, but whether from habit or the hardness of his head, the deep potations in which they were indulging had no effect on him, though the priest's face was crimson, his voice thick, and his cheeks covered with perspiration.

"And pray," said the friar, in a tone of mock humility, "where was my brother going in so huge a hurry?"

"Marry, thou dost well to remind me of it, though methinks I need a little more rest. Marriage is a thing that may be deferred, while 'tis criminal to hurry the servants of our Master."

"Marriage! so you were going to buckle some franklin to his rosy-cheeked wench?"

"Franklin me no franklins," cried the priest, indignantly, "I move not for such. Sir Philip de Beauvoisin is a liberal lord, or else I had not moved."

It was with extreme difficulty that the friar kept down a shrill whistle.

He began to have a burning desire to know more.

"And, pray, upon whom does Sir Philip intend giving the honour of his alliance?"

"That is his secret. My orders," hiccupped the priest, "are to hurry to the grange in the glen, and there unite in holy wedlock this noble knight to some lady unknown."

The friar made no instant reply. He was evidently revolving something important in his mind.

"It must be!" he suddenly cried, and looked once more at his companion.

He lay open-mouthed upon his back fast asleep.

The friar smiled grimly, and rising, went first to the water, to which he stooped, or rather lay down, drank a good draught, dipped his head into the stream, and rose refreshed and invigorated.

Then he stripped the sleeping priest of his goodly cassock and other essentials, and casting off his own ragged apparel, clothed himself in the other's garb.

He then, forgetting to leave behind him the sleeping man's well-lined portmanteau, mounted the mule and rode rapidly off beneath the gloomy vista of the forest.

CHAPTER LXVI.

SHADOWS OF EVIL.

EDITH of Athelston remained for some hours unmolested, and her door being well furnished with bolts on the inside, after a slight meal, went to bed in search of that rest which is more to health and strength of mind than all else beside.

When she awoke, after a long refreshing slumber, she could tell from the noise without how much the garrison of the grange had increased in numbers.

This made the poor girl shudder, for she had no doubt whatever but her persecutor was among them.

She began, from her being taken to this solitary and out-of-the-way retreat, to have some faint suspicion of the real nature of his designs upon her; and as she did so, her cheek blushed with fear and horror.

She too well knew the indifference of the Norman nobles to the feelings of women, and had very little hope.

But she made a silent resolve in her own bosom rather to suffer death than the foulest outrage on a woman's feelings—union with a man she hated and despised.

Worse than that—separation from all she loved.

The morning meal was brought in by a young girl, with bright eyes and rosy cheeks, who curtsied as she spoke to the high-born maiden.

There was a look of honesty about her face which gladened the heart of Edith.

"Canst thou explain, young girl," she said, "why I, a free-born maiden and a ward of the crown, have been dragged from my secure retreat in a convent by lawless marauders, and confined I know not where?"

"I cannot say, fair lady," replied the other, in a soft and pleasant voice, "except that I have been sent to wait upon you until your marriage takes place."

"Marriage with whom?" cried Edith, at this confirmation of her worst fears.

"Gramercy, I know no more than that our lord and master came here this morning, and hath said that he expects a priest presently, about mid-day, when the old hall is to be turned into a chapel."

"Girl!" said Edith, sadly, as she took up a knife and concealed it in her bosom, "I loathe and hate this man, and before I will wed him, will die. But be not alarmed—there is succour at hand, I hope. I have friends in the forest——"

"The outlaws?" cried the girl, with a look of blank amazement.

"Hush!—speak not so loud. They are already in pursuit, and may rescue me before the fatal hour of a struggle which can only end in my death."

"Death for one so young and beautiful?" replied the girl, sadly.

"Death is welcome when nothing else stands between us and the horrors of a hated union," was the gloomy answer.

"I am but young and foolish, and my power extends but little; but this believe, I am wholly at your service. I will return anon, and tell you all I know."

This was slight, though it might be some consolation to the prisoner. A friend, however humble, is still a friend; and hence the avidity with which men cling at times to the singlehearted devotion of a dog, most true and faithful of all animals.

Edith sank upon a kind of couch, and lay still wrapped in thought, until suddenly she was interrupted by the sound of footsteps approaching her door.

The sound of knightly spurs proclaimed what kind of visit she had to expect.

Drawing herself up haughtily, she turned towards the window and looked out.

Then came a knock at the door, of which taking no notice, it was speedily opened, and Sir Philip de Beauvoisin entered.

"Methinks," he said, "you show little courtesy to your host."

"To my jailor," she replied, turning round with so queenly an air as to make him doff his beaver.

The man, with all his ruffianism, had learned really to love her in his way.

"Maiden," he said, repressing every sign of anger, "'tis folly for us to quarrel, who will have to pass together the remainder of our lives."

"Is this, then, my dungeon, and art thou my keeper?" she said, in freezing tones.

"Lady," he answered, with that lofty courtesy which belonged to the courtiers of the time, "it is useless for you to misconstrue my meaning. I love you. Never have I seen woman to match you, either in whiteness of teeth, or brilliancy of eye, to say nothing of thy rich and peerless form, fitting you to mate with the highest in the land."

Edith turned away with a bitter and scornful glance, but without making any reply.

"I love you, and would woo as knight and noble should; but if you treat me as a churl, I shall even woo as churls are used to do," he added.

"Churl!" she cried; "and what else do you call the man who can descend to steal a hapless maiden from the very bed chamber in which she has sought refuge, under protection of the holy virgin, against the unholy devices of lawless ravishers?"

The knight walked up and down the room impatiently ere he replied.

"Words are the weapons of women and children, therefore will I waste none. Let it suffice that, having won thee at the point of the sword, I would not give thee up were death and the devil to stand in the way."

Edith looked keenly at him. She saw he was moved.

"Sir Philip you were not always thus. I have heard that once you were much beloved, and loved in return a noble lady, who became your bride—that happy were your days and hours in her company—that then befell some sore trial."

"What demon prompts you to recall that which I have long since forgotten? I was then a youth, not unattuned to soft emotions—enough; she died, and with her death ceased in me all the gentler feelings which the witchery of her sex can rouse in the bosom of weak man. I would wed me now a rich and lovely bride as I won my spurs at the point of the sword."

"There are richer and handsomer women within England's shores than I can ever be; why not seek one who will appreciate your worth?" said Edith, gently.

"And why cannot you?" he cried.

"We mould not our feelings at our will. Besides, if you would know the truth, I love another."

"'Sdeath!"

"And, were these unholy nuptials to take place, would fly to him at the first hour of freedom," she forced herself to say.

The knight ground his teeth.

"I have wasted too much talk already," said the knight; "hear me. My decision is irrevocable. Wife or leman choose, an' you will not have the blessing of holy church, you shall still be mine. Choose, then, between the bride of honour or dishonour."

"The bride of death before either," she murmured, as with angry glances he strode from the room and closed the door, and fastened it on the outer side.

In modern times such enterprises as that which the knight had undertaken, would have been simply impossible; but in the days of which we speak the highest love was that of the bow and spear, and the highest powers, those of king and church, were forced to wink at the reckless manner in which the Norman knights lorded it over the multitude.

It was a common thing for men to take unwilling brides, maidens of high lineage and wealth, who, to escape a worse fate, were fain to say an unwilling yes at the altar, and who ever after lived a life of helpless misery—the slaves, not the helpmates, of their husbands.

Edith knew this, and had she been of the gentle, vapid, and insipid specimen of woman kind, often found in a time when women were generally uneducated she might have submitted to her fate without a murmur.

But she had a noble heart and vowed fidelity with all her soul to him she had made lord paramount of her existence and her love.

She had hoped at one moment to move the tyrant's heart but now knew better.

He was as much made of iron as the armour he wore upon his back, and as impregnable.

Still she did not wholly despair, and so, not to add physical to mental weakness, accepted slight refreshment each time it was brought in.

She had, during this time, the advantage of the society of Elfrida; so the Saxon girl was called whose prattle amused her.

From her she heard that the knight was chafing with many oaths and much violence at the delay in the arrival of the priest, who was expected at mid-day, and had not, now that evening approached, showed himself.

The baron was venting his rage, and ill-humour on his men, at whom he cursed and swore with an indelicacy he had never shown before.

Edith was sufficiently a judge of human nature to be aware that this petulance arose from a sense of wrong much more than from anger against the holy man, whoever he might be.

Suddenly a loud knocking was heard at the door without, and rushing to the window, they saw a mounted priest hastily admitted.

We will, however, return to the knight and record what passed.

CHAPTER LXVII.

THE INTERVIEW.

EDITH rightly judged that there is a small green oasis in every man's heart, and hit that of Sir Philip with true feminine sagacity.

The memory of his young wife had come upon him like a vision of the past, he would fain have utterly forgotten.

Despite his great love for her, he had not been so kind to her as he now wished he had, and the scorpion whips of conscience lashed with the most intense and searching vehemence.

He resolved, by way of compensation, to be kind to this young creature he was about to force to his bed and board, as if any man who had allowed his evil passions to grow upon him can control them.

The force of sudden and ungovernable impulse will overthrow them all.

But there was another feeling gnawing at his heart, a desire to give up his present enterprise, ask forgiveness of Edith, and grant her liberty.

Pride here intervened and suggested his becoming a laughing-stock.

No; be would pursue in his evil course come what will, even if he had to break that stubborn heart he fancied so akin to his own nature.

Wishing to divert his own thoughts, he first called for wine, of which he quaffed huge goblets, imprecating and cursing his servitors in a way that would, now-a-days, startle a Whitechapel thief.

No restraint of any kind was then laid upon the tongue, which spoke with unbridled and blasphemous license.

The slow, fat, and lazy priest came in for a portion of his invectives.

If he had come before, the thing were done, and the haughty

maiden turned into the submissive wife, only too glad to do the bidding of her lord and master—and so the insolent knight truly believed.

But it was sundown when the priest, his mule covered with mud and perspiration, entered the court-yard, where the knight rushed to greet him, but was so much astonished for a moment he could not speak.

"A murrain on him who sent for me, and a murrain on those who sent me. By St. Nicholas, patron of thieves! here has a quiet priest been chased up hill and down dale by a part of filthy outlaws, who, but that I dodged them, would have stuck me with arrows, and all because I would not stop and be robbed," said the priest, rubbing his bullet head with his cossack.

"By St. Ignatius!" cried the knight, scarcely able to prevent himself from laughing; "so the insolent thieves have troubled you, whom God confound."

"Trouble me, noble sir—I would not have such another ride for a thousand marks," replied the priest.

"Come in and have some refreshment," said the knight, quite pacified by the other's simulated indignation; "you must surely need it."

The priest groaned and followed the knight into his hall where, after protestations that, but for his excessive heat and the terrible trials he had endured he would have preferred bread and water, he sat down and ate a copious meal.

The knight meanwhile walked up and down in deep thought. Now that his passion was cooled, he was at a loss how to proceed.

He knew the church to be nearly as venal and remorseless as his own class, except those recruited from the Saxon race, but he wished if possible to keep up appearance before the world.

How was this to be done?

He could not say, but resolved when the ghostly adviser had concluded his meal, to take advice from him as to the course to be pursued.

Presently, turning round, he saw the holy man in a state of complete beatitude murmuring a slight prayer thanksgiving.

"And now worthy father," said the knight, "I wish to have talk with thee."

"I am perfectly refreshed," said the priest, "and ready to do thy bidding."

The knight seated himself, and drawing his settle close to that occupied by the churchman, began an elaborate account of his reason for being married in this way.

"But the maiden is coy and hard to please," he concluded. "I am, however, resolved, and should she persist in her obstinacy, will have no mercy. Now you, who understand how to give good advice can, if you will, soon convince her of the sin and folly of resistance. Marriage is a holy institution and should not be despised."

"Amen!"

"Go thou, therefore, to her, and if you do succeed, there is no boon thy monastery can ask I will refuse; as for thyself, thou shalt die a fat abbot as surely as thou art a jolly priest," he added.

"I will do thy bidding even now," said the churchman, rising, "if the lady be visible," he added.

The knight shouted to one of the men to call Elfrida, who presently came.

"Conduct this holy man to the Lady Edith, and bid her receive sensible and ghostly advice of one who is able to render it," he said.

"This way," replied the Saxon girl, who tripped out of the hall and along the passage which led to the lady's chambers.

"One word," said the priest checking the maiden by the arm, "art sure we cannot be overheard?"

"Why?"

"Because I come as a friend and would not be betrayed," replied the priest.

"You will not be overheard; the walls are of solid oak," said the girl, rather surprised.

"And so are these," grinned the priest; "and for thy bright eyes and pretty face thou shalt have the kiss of grace and peace."

And before she could resist he had succeeded in stealing a good long hearty kiss, which seemed quite to delight the sacrilegious churchman, and certainly did not offend the laughing girl.

"Here, please you, lady, is the priest come to see you," she said, throwing open the door and letting him go in first, to hide her blushes.

Edith turned slowly round and looked the man reproachfully in the face, but all sternness vanished from her face on the instant.

"Friar Tuck!" she cried, clasping her hands with intensity of joy. "Then am I not wholly deserted of man."

"Nor of woman, either," the waiting-maid cried; "and this is the impudent Clerk of Copmanhurst!"

"Hast found it out already?" said Edith, with one of her old cheerful smiles.

The maiden retreated, suffused with blushes, nor spoke any more for some time.

"I am alone, unfortunately," replied the friar, ruefully, "and in great danger, for this knight thinks I have come to marry you unto him."

"How came that about?" asked Edith, somewhat disappointedly.

The friar, in his dry humorous way, told his story, adding, however, incidents of which our readers are not yet aware.

"Coming along, I met many of the brethren and despatched them in all directions for Robin Hood, Little John, or Will Scarlett, as it might happen, and then bade them come on here and surround the grange in every direction."

"More bloodshed!" mused Edith, in a sad and pensive tone. "Why was I ever born?"

"To be a happy wife and mother," replied the jolly friar; "but now to business. I must back to Sir Philip, and I must take with me some consolation or he will scout me. I wot of his passionate nature before to-day. Not that I fear him, but twenty men-at-arms are more than a match for a poor friar."

"What would you have me say?" replied Edith of Athelston. "I cannot lie."

"I want you not, good and brave young lady," said the friar; "but I, a priest, will invent some story for you, for which I will give myself absolution when I have done penance therefor. At all events be sure of respite until mid-day."

"Heaven reward you, for I cannot. Hope does return to my breast. Good-night!" she cried, "and may Heaven have you in its good keeping! Elfrida, show him a light to the end of the passage."

The girl blushed somewhat, but nevertheless obeyed. Her surprise was great, therefore, when the friar drew her to a settle, and made her sit down.

"What now?"

"A word in thy ear."

"Two if you keep your distance."

"You heard how I changed with the priest?"

"I did."

"And do you know the consequences?"

"No."

"He will follow me here."

"Well?"

"He will tell his story."

"But the knight believes you the true man."

"His belief will not last many minutes."

"What then?"

The priest looked at her with a strange expression, and then jerking his head sideways, pointed to his neck.

"Poor fellow! would he hang you?"

"He would, like a dog."

"Poor fellow!" said Elfrida, nestling closer to the burly friar, whose youthful countenance pleased her.

"As certain as I am a friar."

"Are you really?" she said, with a pout.

"Well, half and half—but of that anon. Now you can save me."

"How?"

"When I have seen the knight I shall ask leave to retire to some quiet spot to my meditations. I will come into the yard, and you—leaving the soldiers to stuff themselves with sodden beef, and undried bacon, and salted eels—wilt come forth and show me some safe hiding-place. Dost know of any?"

"Art a true man?"

"Prove me," said the friar, by way of interlude, trifling with her lips, which were bright and rosy.

"I will trust you," she replied, putting faith in a style of argument which has deceived more women than any out of books.

"That is a good girl," he added; "and now hie you to the lady, tell her I need your services, and then come forth. I will to the knight."

And with slow and methodical steps he moved in the direction of the hall, where the knight awaited him.

"Well," he said, "have you shrived this maiden and learned the secret of her will? Does she decide to be the lady of my heart and wide domains?"

"She will attend your pleasure at mid-day. There were a few words of haughty denial, but soon I talked to her, and after one or two floods of tears, she resigned herself and made me the promise."

"By my knightly cross but thou art a brave priest," said Sir Philip de Beauvoisin, "and shalt never rue this day. Hast a good stiff head?"

"Why asks your worship?"

"I am no great winebibber like those Saxons who swill like their own root-eating pigs, but I will try thy mettle this night."

This was awkward, but Friar Tuck thought it best to submit.

A couple of flagons were soon on the table, and the amorous knight began quaffing rapidly. Excitement soon did its work on one not used to potent liquor, so that the friar was soon relieved by seeing the soldier carried off to bed by two of his own men.

He then quickly glided into the yard, where he found the girl awaiting him in no very good humour, which, however, he restored in the way he generally found most useful in young girls.

She took him by the hand and leading him across the yard, opened the door of a large disused stone kitchen, across which she carefully led him, until opening another, she made him start at a spectacle by him totally unexpected and not overwelcome.

It was a supper for two neatly laid out, and consisting of cold capon, some salt eels, with goodly store of ale and mead.

The friar had supped, while the wine he had consumed was no moderate quantity. Still he knew the girl would be annoyed at a delicate attention usually paid by all classes to the priest now being refused. He therefore resigned himself, and at once sat down to the meal with an appetite such as only forest air could have left him.

"And now my pretty one, that we are alone here, as cosy as a pair of wood-pigeons, wilt tell me why you think me safe here?"

"You are safe here for the present," said the girl, "because I have locked all the doors; but thy night's hiding-place will not be so comfortable, unless, indeed, you sit up until morning."

"Well, I don't know," replied Friar Tuck, "the temptation would be great, but I know not what I may have to do to-morrow."

The girl rose, and showing what appeared to be the hearthstone, showed how, by touching it in one spot, after pushing it an inch, it gave way; and while one side went down and the other kept up, it disclosed a small cellar, boarded over, however, and with some very dry trusses of straw.

The friar made a wry face, and looked at a pile of rushes in a corner.

"Then art thou a false and wicked man!" said Elfrida, indignantly. "Though as thou wilt, I will go down into the pit where many a Saxon prince has escaped the destroyer, and yet is not good enough for a hedge priest."

"I will go down," replied the friar, ruefully, and straightway returned to the table and continued his meal, thankful, by any means, to postpone creeping into such a den.

CHAPTER LXVIII.

THE TRUE PRIEST.

MORNING had broken about an hour, and its heavenly choristers had sung matins, and yet not a sound was to be heard within the grange.

The knight, when his men were on secret expeditions of this character, had every reason to relax discipline, and allow as much carousing as they liked.

They took advantage to the full of their permission, and lay late. Besides, they knew their master unusually affected himself.

Not a sound could be heard, save a chorus of full round snores.

Then came a loud banging at the gate, followed by a faint and plaintive cry, both which were repeated several times, ere any response came from the heavy sleepers within the fortified farm.

At length one rose, and yawning, spoke,—

"Who knocks, ere the moon hath really risen in the sky?" he said, dreamily.

"A holy servant of God, who hath been waylaid and robbed, both of his clothes, horse, and money, by a knavish hedge priest," was the doleful answer.

"Ah!" said the man-at-arms, in a more sprightly way, ready always for a joke. "Was thy horse a mule?"

"You are right, my man."

"A brown mule?"

"A brown mule;—but open, for surely the knave who robbed me is within."

"He is," replied the warder, who harshly opened, as he heard the knight asking the cause of all this clamour.

"A priest, who says the one who came here last night is an impostor," replied the man-at-arms.

With a roar, as of an angry lion, the knight burst from his couch, and rushed, half-dressed, down to the courtyard.

"Say thou liest," he cried, clutching the man by his throat, and shaking him as though he were a child, "or, by the mother that bore thee, I will throttle thee and throw thy carcase to the hounds."

"I tell no lie," growled the man; "open the door thyself."

"Mighty well! Dost beard me—dost fling saucy words in my face?"

Like many other passionate men, his anger blinded his reason, and made him reject the only proper plan for ascertaining the truth.

"Open, in Heaven's name," said a piteous voice, "lest I die at your door."

The knight let go his follower, and rushing to the gate, unbarred it; the priest, having in his terror crawled across the moat, fell forward.

So ragged, so weary, so torn, so bespattered with mud, his clothes ragged, he was not to be recognised as the spruce churchman who had been deluded to drink the strong ale and stronger wine of that arch deceiver and dissembler, Friar Tuck.

"Pray forgive me, my lord," he said, in broken accents; "that I came not is no fault of mine—a ragged fellow, in a friar's garb, did set upon me and rob me of my mule and my portmanteau containing a change of vestment. I have hurried as much as possible, but in the dark, and hope I have not arrived too late."

"Thou hast not, my worthy friend," cried the knight, a set and fierce purpose gleaming in his eyes. "I'll have this unfrocked knave hanged up by the ears and whipped to death—the base born churl, the serf's mongrel, the dissembling, cheating friar! What ho! is he not found? Drag him from his lair."

The men, who were all awake, rushed in all directions, but not a trace of him was to be seen, though mule and portmanteau remained.

"The scum of Satan is hidden somewhere," said the knight, who, finding his men made no progress in discovering his retreat, assailed them with every degrading epithet he could think of, to which, however, they were too much accustomed to pay the least attention.

"Ah, ah! where sleeps that Saxon handmaiden? I saw the liquorsome rogue's eyes twinkle as he looked at her. Hunt them up!"

The farmer's wife who had charge of the grange led them across to where Rose slept, but ere they knocked at the door the girl came forth, more rosy, fresh, and blooming than ever.

"Where is that villain priest?" roared the knight, while the men rushed in to search the place.

"I know nothing of him. I pointed him out the chamber appointed for him last night, and he should be there now."

"Well?" cried the baron to the soldiers.

"There is no priest here."

"Didst hope to find him in my chamber?" said the girl, with a flaunt.

"It would not be the first priest who had made vigil in a wench's chamber," cried the knight, coarsely; "but the hunt is but deferred. Go, churchman, and frock thyself afresh, for I shall want you within the hour; and, saucy

ROBIN HOOD'S CATTLE.

one, go bid my lady prepare herself. The hour of her wedding has arrived."

Elfrida, with a conscious look, escaped, and hastened to the room occupied by Edith.

She had risen, and was anxiously awaiting an explanation of the sudden hubbub which had arisen.

"What is it, my good girl?" she cried.

"Oh, lady, such a mischance! The one last night was not the right one—and the right man's come—and my lord is in a terrible passion—and you are to be married in half an hour!"

The girl was so confused, she knew not what she said.

"Am I?" she said, in a half-unconscious way. "Am I? Where is the other priest?"

"Safe!" replied Elfrida, in some little confusion; "quite safe!"

But Edith's thoughts were far away.

"Heaven surely will not allow this sacrifice," she murmured; "but were it so, I shall true and faithful be to my noble Robert. I should have been proud to be thy bride, 'tis true; but that is impossible. Welcome death, which alone can now protect an English maiden against the cruel violence of the wicked. Go forth, Elfrida, and warn me when this bridegroom cometh."

Elfrida bowed and went out.

"'Tis but one thrust," said the young girl, looking at the rude Sheffield blade with something of awe, "and all will be over."

Then she kneeled in prayer to the Virgin to release her from this strait, or forgive her the terrible deed which now she was meditating.

The time flew fast, and soon the unhappy martyr of iniquitous oppression heard the coming of her enemies.

The door opened, and the knight, with two of his retainers and Elfrida as witnesses, ushered in the priest.

"Good morrow, fair damsel. I see by the bloom upon your cheek that you are pleased the hour to consummate our union has arrived."

"False knight, or rather cowardly caitiff, the roses on my cheek as you call them are the life-blood of my indignant soul. I scorn and loathe thee as a thing unmeet to live—a burden on this earth! To you, priest, I appeal—dare you be an actor in this outrage?"

"Maiden, I understood you had given your consent to this very proper union."

"Who told you so lied!"

"Bandy no words," cried Sir Philip; "free or against your will, you become my wife. Proceed with the ceremony."

"And see me fall dead at your feet," she cried. "Cruel or avaricious priest, proceed if you dare!"

And waving aloft the knife she had secured, she pressed it to her snowy bosom.

"Daughter," said the priest, who was impatient to have the scene over that he might rest, " put down that knife. The crime you meditate is the foulest known to mother church, and one she never forgives."

The knight looked at her with perfect awe, mingled with admiration, and seemed scarcely to know what to do.

"Silly fool! dost think I do not understand such coyness? Put up that knife."

And he made one step towards her.

As he did so, the loud and startling summons of a horn was heard without, and with a shriek of delight Edith fell on her knees.

"What is it?" said the knight, fiercely, as a retainer came rushing in; " who dares invade my privacy?"

"Pardon, Sir Philip, but some three score of men in Lincoln green demand instant admission, or say they will fire the grange. What answer shall I give, my noble lord?"

"Tell them go hang!" yelled the knight. "What; dare they beard the lion in his den? Give them a volley of bolts —stay, rouse up the girl at all events; the girl shall be mine by church and bed ere they enter. Proceed."

"St. George for merrie England!" shouted twenty voices, and the door burst open, bringing twenty outlaws headed by Robin Hood and Friar Tuck.

His secret lair had an opening on the moat through which he had let in the outlaws, who at once overpowered the garrison without the loss of a life.

The first thing the friar did was to gather up his stick in a scientific way, and shower a fearful volley of blows on the person of the knight, who, unarmed and without armour, could only attempt to ward off the attack with his hands. In vain! the friar was merciless, and at length the haughty knight fell from exhaustion.

Robin Hood, who, despite all present, had caught his Marian in his arms and cordially embraced her, now bade him desist.

"I'll teach you to fill my ears with your villainies," said the friar, scarcely able to speak from want of breath. "Wilt try an even bout with me?"

"No, slave, but I will find thee even wert thou in the bowels of the earth, when thy punishment shall be a warning to all Saxon knaves."

"Beware!" said Robin Hood, with a dark frown "lest you tire even my patience—go; but by heavens, beware how you once more fall within my clutches!"

The discomfited knight, whose arms, with those of all his followers, had been removed, hastened to obey, for he trembled now at the searching eye of Edith.

He had seen the warm caresses she had lavished on the handsome outlaw.

It was pouring molten lead upon his brain.

He said not a word, but stalked forth so humiliated, so discomfited, so miserable, as never man had felt before —at all events, no man more so.

His sufferings were, however, purely mental—those of the body he scorned.

In ten minutes more, amid the jeers of the rough yeomanry, they rode unarmed through the forest.

It is needless to recount the happiness which swelled the bosoms of both Robin Hood and Maid Marian, as he always would call her, at this sudden and almost miraculous deliverance; and many were the congratulations which were poured upon Friar Tuck for his opportune meeting with the priest.

But Tuck was too busy to attend to such trifles. He had bidden Elfrida, wonderfully devoted to his will on so short an acquaintance, provide a solid breakfast for himself and the unwilling churchman, whom once more, by threats of using his powerful crabstick, he intoxicated and cast upon the ground to sleep off his heavy inebriation.

The friar then searched his valise, and found therein no less than one hundred and twenty rose nobles, which he speedily transferred to some secret pocket about his person, all the while inveighing against the abominable avarice of the church.

In the meantime the outlaws, having taken hasty refreshment, were summoned to depart, as Edith felt that she should now neither be safe nor in a creditable position until she was restored to the abbess, who would know how to avoid stratagem.

Robin Hood and his ladylove now mounted on one horse, and again, unattended, rode through the forest.

We say unattended, but not unfollowed, as the whole party of outlaws, divided into two bands, kept upon his skirts.

When Robin proposed that Edith should mount before him on a splendid charger which remained at the Grange, she blushed, and hinted something about the priest's mule, but the outlaw looked so reproachful that she yielded.

And now, as they passed slowly through the narrow and intricate paths of the forest, she confessed in her own soul the rapture she felt at being held in the arms of the only man she had or ever could love.

Robin often tenderly but respectfully pressed her to his heart. She was seated sideways before him, with her right arms round his neck, so that their eyes and, we believe, lips met more than often—forming a pleasing interruption to a conversation in itself deeply interesting.

But why record the tender words uttered by these lovers, who spoke of the past, the present, and the future with equal delight; if Robin Hood told her that she was the highest, proudest, and most priceless gift on earth, she answered that she felt honoured by the love of so noble and generous a man; if he spoke of the sacrifice she made leaving the wide world of fashion and renown, as the act of a peerless soul, she laughed, showed her white teeth, and blushing, drew her head to her, would have kissed his forehead, a proceeding which the daring young lover would never allow, but met her half way, and silence reigned for we know not how many minutes.

And thus, bathed in a cloud of glorious happiness, flooded with love and joy, living in a world of their own, some island, perhaps, of the sunny south, where aught save eternal sunshine was unknown, and where the soft blue waves bathed golden sands, and where the sky was ever fair, and the flowers and trees and fruits sufficed for man, they were awakened suddenly to the ordinary things of this world, by reaching the confines of the valley in which the convent was situated.

Here occurred an event which showed the discretion and delicacy of the outlaw's heart.

Dismounting, the captain of Sherwood forest made Edith fast on her pillion, and respectfully led the horse to the gates of St. Agnes.

They were readily admitted, and their story excited at the same time the indignation, delight, and admiration of the abbess.

"I thank you much, sir yeoman, and as for you, my gentle lamb, ere a month is over I will take you to the feet of Prince John himself, and obtain his consent to your complete freedom from any ties but those which that affection which the heart may induce you to make—unless you have a vocation for the church."

"Nay, lady, my heart is already given, though I would not have it known," said Edith, blushing deeply.

"May I ask?" pressed the abbess, gently; " your secret is safe with me."

"Robert Earl of Huntingdon."

"My God! thy ways are indeed mysterious—but, child, if he lives he is a man of fifty!"

"Nay, I speak of his son."

"His son? Did he then marry—and was that the reason?" gasped the abbess.

"He secretly married."

"My younger sister—whose soul God rest," cried the deeply agitated abbess; " but tell me all the story— but first let us thank this yeoman, and send him on his way."

"Nay, mother," said Edith, warmly, " this is Robert Earl of Huntingdon—known now as Robin Hood."

The abbess almost shrieked, but recovering herself, made both sit down and tell their story, which, indeed, Robin would have never known but that garrulous Sir Thomas must needs, when on a visit, tell Sir Gammel, not suspecting the deep interest that worthy felt in the King of Sherwood Forest.

"This must be seen to, but all in good time," said the abbess, when the story was completely unveiled to her. "For the present my child, you are quite safe—as for you, Robin, as we still must call you, be advised by me. I am told thou art too free with the property of mother church. I know how you men have been driven to this sorry life by bad laws and the cruel execution of them; but an you would hold your head up once more among your fellows, be ruled by my advice."

Robin bowed low, and soon after took his leave—not without, in Edith's ear, "Every Saturday, in the garden."

CHAPTER LXIX.

IN THE FOREST.

THE nature of Robin Hood was peculiar. One of the principal characteristics of the man was a love of such adventures as most men would have avoided.

Ever since his meeting with Will Scarlett, however, he had been so occupied by his private affairs that the ordinary course of his life had been interrupted.

He now, however, as he walked under the greenwood-tree, after leaving Edith to the charge of the good abbess, reflected upon his idleness.

He wanted some occupation to drown thought, the more that the coffers of the corporation required replenishing. Many a fat abbot and insolent Norman had passed lately through the forest without paying the usual toll to those who claimed to be the lords of its intricate pathways and secret fastnesses.

But first it was needful that he should return to the trysting-tree, and there hear the reports of his lieutenants and their men, as well as listen to and adjudicate on any differences which might have occurred between any members of the band.

Shortly after leaving the convent the two favourite lieutenants, Little John and Will Scarlett, came up, as if quite by chance.

"My friends," he said, with a slight frown, "why do you watch me in this way?"

"We have kept within call. The wood is not so clear of stray rogues that you could afford to be alone."

Robin Hood smiled, and then held out to each a hand.

"Thanks!" he said; "I know you well. Would all had such true and trusty friends!"

The tall forester laughed grimly, in his honest, hearty way, while Will Scarlett simply smiled.

His heart was far away, though he walked beneath the sun-lit glades of the broad forest.

But Robin Hood was determined that neither he nor his men should be downcast, so exercising that vivid power of humour which was a peculiar trait in his character, he soon cheered the spirits of young Gammel; and before half an hour they were as merrie as the merrie green wood, with its bright green leaves, its fair flowers, and its blithe singing-birds.

Robin Hood would carol a ditty, or cut a joke, or tell an anecdote, and always in such excellent style as would have made a priest laugh, much more those who knew and appreciated him so well.

In this way the rest of the day soon passed; and as the shades of evening fell upon the forest, the outlaws halted, selected a secluded spot shaded by trees, lit a fire, and were soon sleeping that sweet and genial sleep which is seldom earned but by exercise in the open air.

At break of day the three foresters bold were up and stirring, and before the sun was midway in its course had reached the vicinity of the trysting-tree, where their presence was hailed with the usual enthusiasm.

The rest of the day was spent in the usual sports—shooting at marks, playing at quarterstaff, winding up with a supper, which, for sumptuousness, rivalled any the Sheriff could have put before his guests.

Then sentries were appointed, and each man retreated to his appointed sleeping-place for the night.

The following day was devoted to business. Each outlaw gave an account of any little adventure which had occurred to him, paid in whatever money or other valuables he had acquired. Others made complaints, on which decisions so perfectly equitable were given as even to satisfy those who were punished; and then, finally, the usual monthly distribution from the general treasury took place.

The band was then divided into small detachments and sent forth to seek their fortune, with the strictest injunctions to spare the poor and the Saxon, but to ransom the rich and the Norman without mercy.

Then Robin Hood, after a long and private conference with Little John and Will Scarlett, took up his bow and arrows, fastened a well-filled purse to his girdle, and started on an expedition which he had planned more than once, but had never, hitherto, found leisure to put in practice.

He started in the evening, wishing to reach the high road to Nottingham early in the morning, as it was market-day, and he hoped to learn news from some of those who were bound to the mart.

The outlaw, though he carried his trusty weapons, did not wear his usual garb of Lincoln green, but a dress similar in shape, though more suited to a keeper of the forest, with the addition of a baldric and badge of silver; while his face was as brown as a hazel-nut.

In this way he might readily pass for the forest keeper of some knight or prior, or even of royalty itself, which employed men innumerable to guard the game and enforce their cruel laws.

Thus accoutred, just as twilight had deepened on the forest and over the narrow winding paths overhung with clustering branches, the disguised outlaw started on his way, never swerving to the right or left, except to evade impassable obstacles, so thoroughly did he know the intricacies of his own domain.

He proceeded rapidly, considering the obstacles he met in brake and copse, in covert and underwood, nor halted until it was quite midnight, when, having selected a secure and sheltered spot, he sought rest.

CHAPTER LXX.

A NEW FRIEND.

WHEN the outlaw shook himself, and, rising, prepared to continue his journey, it was broad day. The night march of the forester had fatigued him.

"I have been a laggard," he said, as casting his eyes around for some sign of water, he prepared to sluice his face ere he indulged in his morning meal.

Just as he did so, a noble hart cleared a natural hedge of brush at a bound, followed by a staghound, which, ere it had advanced twenty yards on the highway near which the bold outlaw had slept, had the animal by the throat.

Robin Hood drew within his covert to watch who the owner of the hound might be. In moment the bushes were pushed on one side, and a youth of about seventeen, well dressed, but in the garb of a franklin, with bow and arrow, came rushing forth, and, bounding to where the noble dog had pinned the game to the ground, cut its throat in true sportsmanlike manner.

"We have caught you at last!" roared a voice close at hand, and from what appeared an ambush, forth came three men in the garb of royal rangers, who ran towards the youth.

"Stand back!" he said fiercely, as he drew an arrow to the head. "Stand back, I say, at your peril! I have a right. This is a stray deer, and in the purlieus."

The men halted an instant, as if uncertain how to act.

"This is a royal hart," replied one, after a brief consultation with his fellows; "and, purlieu or no purlieu, you must go before the Lord Ranger of Sherwood Forest."

"That will I not—the Norman tyrant!" said the other, hotly, "Rather will I perish in the struggle."

"Have at thee, then" cried the rangers; and they rushed in.

Their astonishment and amazement was great when, instead of the flight of one arrow, another came whizzing from the wood, which sent the foremost keeper headlong to the ground.

The youth had missed his aim, but he had also nearly missed his chance of defending himself, so surprised was he to see a man with a mask and short cloak come bounding over the road, waving a quarterstaff.

But the keepers were upon him both, hoping to disable him before his accomplice could come to his assistance. But though slight in appearance, he was evidently skilled and brave, for taking from his back the favourite English weapon, the quarterstaff, he was able to keep the keepers at bay for a few minutes, when the heavy weapon of Robin came into play with such force, as soon decided the contest.

The keepers, feeling themselves overmatched, took to their heels, and left the outlaw and his new acquaintance masters of the field.

They now had time to turn their attention to a scene of horror which was taking place close at hand.

The man who had been wounded by Robin Hood, only slightly, with a view to render the contest more equal, had striven to rise and assist his comrades.

The staghound, with a savage roar, had immediately flown at him, and planted his sharp teeth in his cheek and jaw, thus effectually keeping him down.

Now began one of those contests which are almost as difficult and painful to describe as to witness. The man, despite his wound, wrestled with his antagonist with desperate strength and courage, and grasped the hound in his turn by the throat with such force as to cause the eyes of the noble animal to almost burst from its sockets.

In this position the two rolled over—now the man, now the dog, uppermost.

But loss of blood began to tell upon the ranger, and his hold relaxing, the dog became his master.

Drawing a long breath, the savage hound swayed his shaggy head to and fro; with his jaws besmeared with blood, still tugged at the unfortunate man's throat.

At this moment the others fled, and both Robin and the young stranger turned to view the fearful combat.

The youth, with a bound, was upon them, and clutching the hound by the ears, forced him, more by words than by strength, to let loose his hold, though his deep, ferocious growling showed how reluctant he was to part with his victim.

They might, however, have left him alone, for the man gave a convulsive shudder and expired.

"Poor victim of infamous laws," said Robin Hood, gazing thoughtfully at the dead man; "but we may not stay here in safety. These rangers have comrades in abundance along this road."

"'Tis a sad morning's work," said the youth, gravely, "but forester, whoever thou art, my life is due me at your hands. You are right in saying these men have comrades, who, if they find us, will revenge themselves. I have shelter at no great distance that these knaves wot not of. Nay, I will take no denial."

There was something in the youth which seemed to please the bold outlaw, for he was

—— A brave young man,
As fine as fine might be;

and as, if he continued his present life, he would surely need his protection, he determined to see a little more of him.

"Lead on, my gallant hunter—I follow," he said.

The youth pushed through the thicket by which he had first appeared, not before, however, he had hastily cut several joints from the deer, which he divided with his companion, and then began the descent by a rapid slope into a picturesque valley.

They both walked at a rapid pace, the dog running on before, apparently as fresh as if nothing had happened.

The path for some time was marked, but soon the young man diverged into thickets so close, into coverts so dark, with dank and mouldering undergrowth, that Robin Hood was lost in admiration.

"You know the forest well," said he, with a smile.

"I have dwelt here since boyhood—since my father's death, and all my time nearly has been spent in exploringit."

"You love a forest life?"

"Love a forest life!" cried the youth, with glowing and sparkling eyes, "indeed I do, and, but that I have a widowed mother who looks to me as her only stay, would never care to enter house again. I live now in the forest more than in the homestead which my father left me, and were I alone in the world, should long since have sought to league myself with bold Robin Hood."

"Ah! sayest thou so? But 'tis a rude life and one not suited to so fair a gentleman as you. 'Tis well for outcasts driven mad by the laws, but not for such as own houses and lands."

"And how long are houses and lands safe from the paw of these dishonest descendants of a race of robbers," said the youth, bitterly.

"True—but still you have them."

"My mother has; and I have some hope of adding to them—but what safeguard have we against the greed of any of our oppressors, stripping us of all at his will?"

The youth was right. A Norman looked out for a handsome piece of land, he rode over it, saw that it lay lovingly in the lap of his own estate. He coolly slew the male possessor, and then married the female owner; or at best forced the unfortunate Saxon to sell it for some wretched sum that precipitated him from comfort to penury.

With such conversation as this, which the fearful state of the period rendered common enough, they continued on their way, crossed a brook by picturesque stepping-stones, and began another ascent.

It was steep, and continually, as they went up, they were compelled to hold by the boughs and roots of trees, until at last they came to an almost impenetrable thicket, into which they, however, pushed themselves, until they reached a fallen tree, which, however, retained sufficient vitality from such roots as remained to send forth a mass of green boughs at its upper extremity, which lay against a precipitous bank.

Along this trunk the dog ran and disappeared.

The youth followed, but more slowly, as the trunk was slippery, and a man needed to clutch bushes and branches in his progress.

Robin Hood imitated his every movement, even when he stooped and crept in at a hole something resembling a fox's, which opened into a passage, along which it was impossible to advance, except on the hands and knees.

Soon, however, the earthern corridor enlarged, and the outlaw found himself in a chamber, about ten feet square, very dimly illumined, but which soon was made clearly visible to the eye by the presence of a torch.

A more sylvan retreat it could be scarcely possible to imagine.

Fond of the chase, and compelled by the decrees of the law-givers of those days to abstain from indulging openly in his favourite amusement, this young man had, both for the purpose of concealing his predilections and of secreting himself when hotly pursued, found out and furnished this natural cavern.

He had first found it when quite a boy, nutting in the woods, and had even then kept it secret, as it was his delight to believe the place only known to himself.

When his Nimrod propensities came upon him, the place became his head-quarters altogether, he being forced at times, when hotly pursued, to lie concealed several days.

Hitherto, he had contrived to conceal his personality from the keepers, who little suspected that the somewhat simple-looking son of the Widow Dale, who hung for hours over a harp in his mother's hall, was the poacher they had so often pursued.

His garb was different when hunting from what it was at home, when

The youngster was clad in scarlet red,
In scarlet fine and gay,
And he did trip it so over the plain,
And chanted a roundelay.

The lad was careful to keep up the incognito he had commenced, as he well knew the ruthless character of the gamekeepers.

They would vent on his mother whatever grudge they owed him.

It was with this view, then, that his bows and arrows, his crossbows and bolts, all save his quarterstaff, were left in the cave, which was further adorned by many trophies of the chase.

"A right good lair," said Robin Hood, gaily, as he surveyed the place with sparkling eyes.

"Aye, and many a pleasant evening have I spent in it."

The dog gave a low growl, or rather moan, and then was silent, upon which the youth hastened to creep to the entrance of the cave and look.

Presently he returned, and after making signs to his companion to speak low, whispered that a large party of rangers were scouring the forest in every direction, and had reached to within a very short distance of the place where they were concealed.

Robin Hood nodded his head, and pointed to his bow, after which the two men seated themselves in solemn silence, and waited the result.

They could hear the men calling to one another, swearing and uttering the most terrible threats against the wretches who had not only killed a forester, but slain a royal hart within the forest.

Robin's brow grew dark as he heard the words, for in the whole course of his career, if there was one thing would irritate him more than another, it was any reference to those laws which he hated with all the indignation a free man feels against oppression.

Then both were silent, for discovery would have been fatal; for if they could defend the narrow entrance against all comers, yet there would be nothing easier than either to bury them alive or to burn them out.

But the men passed, and after some hours the outlaw,

being anxious to continue his journey, bade farewell to his young friend, after promising to visit him at his mother's on his return, there to make further acquaintance.

Little did they suspect the important result to both of that meeting.

CHAPTER LXXI.

THE BUTCHER.

BETTER to avoid the outlying rangers, Robin descended the slope of the valley to the stream, reaching which, he waded up it some distance, well knowing that three miles above was a ford, leading from a small village of humble swineherds to the main road to Nottingham, which he reached once more at eventide, putting up this time at a scotale or alehouse, where he purposed passing the night.

It was a place frequented by drovers, butchers, and such-like, on their way to market, and therefore tolerably well appointed in such food as men looked on as rich in those days.

Those who had money to pay could have either real milk with the rich hue of the primrose and the cowslip on it, with eggs, or huge rashers of streaky bacon, or venison, or beef, brown jars of the real ale of old England's best produce—humming ale.

Robin was not surprised, then, when he found the place crowded, not only on the inside with men, but on the outside with cattle, guarded by boys.

These had halted until daybreak, few in that region caring to travel by night.

Robin Hood entered the hostelry as quietly as possible, and glided, without fuss or pretension, into a seat, where an attentive and jolly hostess soon saw to his wants.

At first all seemed too busy eating and drinking to indulge in conversation, which, however, in an English house of entertainment, is rarely wanting; but the first rage of hunger being appeased, all let loose their tongues with one accord, and the place became a Babel.

As none in authority appeared present, all appeared to join in complaining of the authorities, both general and local. The game forest laws were worse than ever. One had had his hand cut off for simply defending himself against the brutality of an officer of the court of oyer; another was in prison, who would surely be hanged, unless powerful intercession were made; and then the forest was more and more being considered royal property.

"What makes meat so dear?" cried one—a citizen of Nottingham—"so dear that none but the rich can have it, except on Sundays?"

A young man—half butcher, half drover—looked up, and, after a glance round the room, spoke.

"If you go on planting forests and building cities, where is a man to graze his cattle?" said he. "Besides, there be men who bring beasts from France, which all have the murrain, and give it to ours. But be that as it may, meat is dear because it is scarce."

"I have not had a pound within my house this ten days," said the citizen, who, however, now that he was on a journey, was making up for domestic abstinence.

"Say you so?" cried the butcher; "well, perhaps you may find it cheaper soon. I have heard meat was dear at Nottingham, and have driven my cattle many miles, which I dare swear will benefit my purse and satisfy your stomachs, which do so crave for food."

The company laughed, and the subject went on.

Robin Hood said never a word, but thought deeply. He had set himself up as a redressor of the wrongs of the poor, but here was one which for the moment beat his ingenuity.

Had he have been a Wat Tyler or a Jack Cade, he might have easily formed the nucleus of a revolution that, assisted by the mass of discontented persons then suffering in "merry England," might have overturned the existing order of things, and restored the country to a milder sway.

But those two brave but unfortunate patriots were patriots on a larger scale than the outlaw of Sherwood Forest, who turned against the unjust laws of his land as much for love of the life he now led as from hatred to his foes.

Besides, during the whole course of his career, Robin Hood had an aversion to shedding unnecessary blood.

He would fight to the last gasp in defence of those he loved or those who were dependent on him; but no one more readily subdued his anger—when he struck a blow in anger—when the need was passed.

The good outlaw—living well, and enjoying, with his men, plenty of good cheer—naturally thought his countrymen of Nottingham very ill-used by the butchers. He might, it is true, send them in a load of deer, or he might threaten the dealers with his vengeance, but that would not make meat plenty.

In times of scarcity the masses are always too ready to blame the dealers, who, if they sold at ordinary rates, would only sell to such as would rise upon their price, to make profit.

Robin Hood had sense enough to know that when a thing is rare it will surely be dear.

What, then, was to be done?

Suddenly a merry thought flashed through the brain of worthy Robin Hood, and he resolved on the spot to carry it out.

He called the butcher on one side, and intimated his wish for some conversation with him.

"Good master butcher," he said, "dost know Nottingham town?"

"Not I, i' faith!"

"Nor the Nottingham people?"

"Still less."

"Well, you must know, they are very hoggish and jealous of strangers. Now, you are a total stranger, and when the butchers see that you have come into the market to undersell them, they will unite to rob you, and you are likely to lose some of your cattle."

The man scratched his head.

"Are there no magistrates?" he said.

"Yes; there is a shallow justice, one Sir Thomas Beauchamp—but he is of no use. Robin Hood, they say, fooled him the other day, and took from him three of his men he was going to hang."

"Egad! a capital story," cried the butcher, laughing; "tell us how it happened."

Seeing that he was a simple fellow easily amused, Robin Hood complied, and the two sitting down together became great friends.

"A fine fellow that," he laughed, when the other had finished; "but what am I to do?"

"Can we not strike a bargain?" continued Robin Hood. "I have friends in Nottingham who will protect me. So if you will sell me thy drove of horned cattle, I will pay thee in a lump, and all will be saved."

The butcher was delighted, as he was becoming very rueful at the prospect of a quarrel in open market with the other butchers. A bargain was therefore struck, and behold next morning Robin Hood on a fine horse, in the dress of a butcher, with a long whip and two attendants whom the other had lent him.

The parting between the outlaw and the butcher was characteristic.

They had pledged one another in a cup, and the King of Sherwood had paid the money, when the following brief dialogue ensued,—

"Hearkee, friend, how travel you back with so much money?"

"On a nag the hostelry will lend me."

"Do you expect to escape the men who cry 'Stand and deliver?'"

"I have never been attacked—and, then, Robin Hood's men do not waylay such as us."

"Nay, be not too sure of that. There are rogues in Lincoln green who, if they dreamed your purse so well lined as it is, would stop you—so put this cap on your head—and if any stop you, point to it, and say Saxon yeoman robs not Saxon churl, and so Robin Hood told me!" he added.

The butcher looked at him with open mouth, but before he could articulate, the bold outlaw was off.

"I'fakes," grinned the countryman; "and so that was Robin—a rare good fellow—should like another bout with him. His money is as good as any other man's."

Then, as if rather doubtful of his own axiom, he proceeded to ring it somewhat carefully, but found it all perfectly sound.

CHAPTER LXXII.

AN OLD SOLDIER.

ROBIN now began to ruminate.

Twice he had imposed upon the sheriff of Nottingham, and twice successfully; but experience teaches most men, and it was not likely that he could a third time so thoroughly disguise his voice as to take in the magistrate, stupid as he was in some things.

He determined, therefore, on another plan.

With that love of daring and audacity which characterised him above everything, the outlaw originally intended to have gone straight to the sheriff, and asked for his protection; but, with a smile, he dismissed an idea which might militate against the carrying out of his plans.

While these thoughts were passing through his mind, he still intently watched his cattle, which, far from advancing like a herd of wild bulls, went at a slow and leisurely pace, as if well aware that the end of their journey was the slaughter-house.

Several parties of traders, one or two knights, with their attendants, passed him on the road, a tournament being talked of as probable; but of these Robin took no notice, fixing his eyes on his cattle, hallooing and slashing his whip, as if he had been a driver all his life.

While this was going on, he was overtaken by a tall man, in the garb of a foreign soldier, somewhat ragged withal, and who carried a very heavy armoury about him. He had crossbow and bolt, sword, and target, a knife of large dimensions; while, to assist his walk, apparently, he leaned on a huge stick, like a young tree.

His face was so bearded, his eyes so shaggy, that very little of a face—browned or rather bronzed from exposure to a tropical climate—could be seen.

His aspect was truly that of a terrible ruffian, with the power and the will to do an injury to any one.

Robin Hood eyed him askance, but it being his cue to quarrel with no one, and really fearing no one man, he gave him an answer to his good-day, uttered in a tone of voice which seems peculiarly to belong to big men, both ruffians and comedians.

"At the pace you go, friend butcher," he added, "most foot passengers must pass you."

"Some have."

"Hast seen anything of a rough fellow in ranger's clothes, with a silver badge in his cap, and in his baldric a bow and sheaf of arrows—a rather proper man of his inches, but one I would gladly catch up to?" said the big man.

The butcher looked sideways at the soldier, who himself gazed forward with an affectation of indifference somewhat ill assumed.

"I saw," said the outlaw, with a deliberation which, could his face have been seen, would have been comic to a degree—"I saw some such fellow, a proper-looking man enough, but an arrant knave and coward."

"Eh?"

"Yes! the varlet was saucy, and I sent him on his way with a good lash round his body," continued the pretended butcher.

"Then 'tis not the man I seek. He could have drummed the soul out of your body," cried the soldier.

"Could'st do it thyself?" sneered the false butcher.

"If wilt come off thy horse, you shall have as sound a drubbing as ever fell upon drover's carcase," replied the soldier.

The butcher made no reply but seemed to shake, but whether with apprehension or not could scarcely be told, but the other thought so.

"Art afraid, my jolly meatsman?" cried the huge fellow, twirling his staff in the air.

"What terrible eyebrows!" murmured the butcher to himself—"they are enough to frighten a fellow."

The soldier rolled them about in a most ferocious manner.

"What teeth!" added the butcher.

The soldier gnashed them and pulled his mustaches.

"What a stick!" continued the butcher.

The other whirled it round as if it had been a feather.

"Wilt defend thyself?" he cried, with comic passion.

"No, Little John, I won't!" screamed the other; "a pretty masquerading jest this! What on earth does it mean?"

"Robin Hood, by all that is glorious!" said the other.

"Yes; but why assume this monstrous disguise?" cried Robin Hood, when his laughter had ceased.

The tall forester bent his head. In his earnest desire to be at hand, should his chieftain want him, he had assumed what he thought to be a perfect disguise. To be thus found out at the first glance!

"Be not downcast, my good John," said Robin, smiling, "'tis impossible to hide thy big body from one who knows thee well. I had but to look into your eyes to recognise their good-humoured and good-hearted glance. Now you are here, however, you may remain, as, in this new trade I have undertaken, you may be useful; only, as the men are suspicious of our long talk, be not too familiar. We shall not enter Nottingham till early morn, as I wish the beasts to have rest. Towards even, the first open glade that offers, we will drive the beasts off the road and rest—we shall be almost in sight of Nottingham spires."

Little John made no reply, though a broad grin overspread his features at the sight of Robin Hood driving his cattle forward with all the art of the most experienced grazier or butcher.

Few words were exchanged between them, as the oxen were somewhat restive at times, and Little John, though not affecting to do so, was intent on saving his leader as much trouble as possible, by intervening his huge person when the brutes would have turned backwards or gone off into the forest.

Thus the day passed and the shades of evening spread over all nature.

The animals were driven into the glade, a couple of fires made for the two assistants to watch by with their wiry dogs, and then Little John and his chief were alone.

Robin Hood now explained his intentions, which the lieutenant listened to with undisguised alarm. He could not forget how easily his own subterfuge had been discovered, and he trembled, lest the same should happen with his captain.

But Robin Hood reassured him, adding, however, that even if the danger he fancied existed, he would still run the risk.

To this the lieutenant had nothing to say, as nothing was further from his thoughts than disobedience to orders.

It was then arranged that on entering the town the two should part, as the long forester's reputation was spreading abroad, and the fact of his being in company with the supposed butcher might excite suspicion. He was, however, to hang about and watch the progress of affairs, so as to be ready if he really was required.

They then rested so as to be afoot at early dawn in time for market.

CHAPTER LXXIII.

CHEAP MEAT.

As in all genuine old English towns, market day was a great day in Nottingham, and people rose betimes in order both to attend to business and pleasure.

There were those in Nottingham town who always were up earliest of all, and those were the poor, who came, with greedy eyes and open mouths and haggard looks, to prowl round, in the hope of some unexpected change.

They scarcely did expect it; but the very faintest doubt kept them up.

Now close to the market-place was a large hostel, frequented by the better sort of people, travellers of note, the larger graziers, and supported even by the gentry on great occasions, such as fairs and the like.

It was kept by one Michel de Brandon, who, being a well-to-do Norman, was also sheriff-deputy to Sir Thomas Beauchamp.

Now cunning Robin Hood knew this, and expecting a disturbance in the market, resolved to have a powerful ally to back him.

He drove his whole herd of cattle into the market, secured them in pens, left them in the charge of his men, and then, having selected one fat bullock, the flower of the flock, drove it right up to the door of the inn.

The sheriff, as a landlord is apt to do, was standing at his own door, viewing the preparations for the day's business, and calculating all that he should make out of the motley crowd, there being in his large house accommodation for every sort of company.

"A fine bullock, my master," he said, with admiration expressed in his corpulent countenance.

"Thinks your worship so?" cried bold Robin: "then is it yours. I am a young man and a stranger here, and fear me the regular butchers will do me a mischief. But I am sure, by your worship's right excellent countenance, you will see me righted."

The man coloured with pleasure. He was a good judge of cattle, and knew the bullock to be in prime condition.

"By the holy rood," he said, "I will see justice done thee—and that is a big oath. Fear nothing—you have my word. Go into the market, and see to your business. I will follow."

People were not very nice in those days, and meat was often eaten a very short time after it came from the slaughter-houses.

The two men, during Robin Hood's absence, had been busily engaged with the slaughterers, and when he returned, his stalls were already garnished with meat, which looked exceedingly well, though too fresh.

Then, amid an uproar of voices, followed by a shout of joy, the outlaw announced his intention of selling his beef at one third of the usual rates.

The hubbub that followed was something wonderful to behold. The poor shouted, danced, jumped, or ran away to tell the glad tidings to their children and wives, who came up in troops, scarce able to believe their ears.

The regular butchers raised a clamour of execration, when Robin Hood, jumping on a block, proclaimed silence. Curiosity on the part of both butchers and crowd gained him a hearing at once.

"I came here this day freely of my own accord to sell my beef, hearing that you have been starving for want of it, and I mean to sell cheap to the poor; but to all who by their appearance I judge to be able to afford meat every day, I shall sell it dearer than the regular price. No, no," addressing himself to a burly man, who pushed forward for a sirloin, "worshipful sir, there is too much beef in thy gizzard already. Make way for those to whom it is a holiday treat; to such only do I sell."

A roar of applause, of laughter, of shrill cries rose upon the morning air, which might have been mistaken for one of those which in modern times emanates from an election mob in the same town of which we speak.

The butchers were puzzled. They could not make the new man out. They began to think him either a lunatic, a thief, or some prodigal who was hurrying through his estate as rapidly as possible.

But they soon found that all but the poor, rare customers of their own, indeed, were turned away by their rival, and that none but those whose appearance almost vouched for their poverty were served. This quieted the apprehension of a riot, though the noise round Robin Hood still went on increasing rapidly as the news spread over the town.

Many a man and woman, and child, blessed Robin Hood that day, when they sat down to their meals; and no one knows but the poor how hard it is to live for ever on coarse bread and beans, without the hope of really nourishing food.

At length the market was over, and Robin, at some considerable loss, had disposed of all his meat. He now thought it high time to retire, but his fellow-tradesmen would not have it so.

They had began by hating him; they had ended by admiring him.

The worst that any thought of him was that he was some young spendthrift, with more money than wit, enjoying the fun and humour of prodigality.

There were such fools in those days as well as now.

As Robin was paying his men, and fastening the remainder of his money in a bag, several of the head butchers came up, and in rather a smart speech, apologised for their seeming rudeness at first, which arose wholly from misapprehension.

Robin graciously replied that the matter was quite forgotten.

"Thou art a jolly fellow!" said one, "and to show in good old Saxon style that you bear us no malice, we invite you to join us at a banquet, which is being prepared at the hostel, at which, as often is the case, Sir Thomas Beauchamp, will graciously take the chief seat."

Robin could not help laughing in his sleeve at this announcement, but readily answered that he would join them with pleasure. As for the honourable gentleman who was to grace the banquet with his presence, he had always understood that he was a very honest gentleman, and therefore would be glad to see him.

This important matter settled, the crowd dispersed, after fixing the hour of dinner, which was to take place shortly before noon.

Now, the truth was, that a rumour of what occurred had reached the High Sheriff of Nottingham, who was curious to see this young prodigal butcher, who thus wasted his money, fancying that perhaps he himself might make something out of him.

Sir Thomas Beauchamp was still the same grasping tradesman he had ever been.

CHAPTER LXXIV.

THE BANQUET AND THE SALE.

THERE was no particular restriction as to numbers at the banquet, except that a man should be able to pay his score, so that by the time the dinner was ready the room was crowded, Little John taking care to make one, not at all easy as to what mad-cap trick Robin Hood might play when the wine began to flow.

For some time, the sheriff sending word he would be with them anon, and not to wait, in true English style the viands kept all men pretty quiet, which was not surprising, when we remember the huge platters full of victuals which our hearty and stalwart ancestors could put away.

But soon the beer began to flow, to say nothing of the wine which Robin ordered up, forbidding the landlord to take money from any one but himself.

"I will pay all," he cried, "so drink and be merry to your hearts' content."

The shout which followed was tremendous, and while still its echoes lingered in the old hall, Sir Thomas Beauchamp entered, upon which the company rose to salute him with becoming honour.

The sheriff looked curiously at Robin Hood, whose face was flushed with drink, and then shaking him by the hand, seated himself next to him, on his right hand.

"I have to thank you, sir," he said, "that you have come to Nottingham at such an opportune time. The king's poor subjects thank you heartily."

"I need no thanks," replied Robin, modestly; "I would do more if I could."

The sheriff was silent a moment, revolving some plan in his head.

"I suppose," he began, "that from selling your cattle so cheap, you are desirous of realising all your property, and retiring to foreign lands?"

"No, worshipful sir," said Robin; "I have but sold the surplus of my cattle thus cheaply, as my land was overrun by them."

"Land!" cried the sheriff; "is it far from here?"

Robin made no reply.

The roaring, shouting, laughing, and drinking continued all the while, everybody talking at once, so that the sheriff and the young butcher were able to talk unnoticed.

"Young sir," said the sheriff, gravely, "you are not what you seem to be?"

Robin peered curiously and rather comically into the other's face.

"No! I noticed it from the first. There is something of nobility stamped in your countenance, which proclaims you no ordinary butcher or grazier," continued the insinuating sheriff.

Robin only bowed.

"I am quite sure that you wear a coat that belongs not to you, and that you are far above cattle dealing or keeping."

Robin could not reply. He was literally convulsed with laughter.

"Now how many cattle may you have to dispose of?" he asked again.

Robin Hood mused.

"May be six hundred, may be a thousand. I never count them."

"The prodigal fool!" thought the sheriff, and then he added aloud, "Wilt sell them, and for how much?"

"I would not be hard with your worship," said the butcher, thoughtfully, "and would say six hundred marks."

"Three, and it is a bargain."

"Nay, I should lose—these butchers here would give me fairer prices," said Robin, speaking rather loudly.

"Nay, silence. I will buy the whole—nor haggle over a score head or two. Put money in thy purse, young man. Any day a raid of free lances may carry off your cattle, or the murrain seize them—but the money you can secrete."

"True," replied Robin, as if relenting.

"Say it is a bargain, and I will pay the three hundred marks down as soon as I see the cattle."

"But they are some distance off."

"Good youth, an' you will keep our bargain secret, I will ride with thee at once, settle the business, and return to our friends."

"I do not engage," said the pretended butcher, slowly, "to sell you the cattle for three hundred marks, but you may bring the money with you—who knows but what it may tempt me?"

And he smothered a laugh, as, taking advantage of a loud chorus, he gave the company the slip, followed by the avaricious sheriff, who took him to his own house, there to take horse and prepare the money for his purchase.

Tradition has it that Sir Thomas Beauchamp, his lady wife being away from home, had on a visit a pretty lively little lass, his niece, whom he left to entertain Robin while he booted and spurred.

Now Robin always dearly loved a joke, and would never let a pretty, willing lass come near him without making her pay toll with her lips, which the wenches of those days were very willing to do.

So, when the worshipful knight returned to his hall, where he had left Robin, he found him kissing the little maiden, who was nothing loth.

Surprise choked his utterance for a moment, but it also gave him time to reflect.

He did not wish to offend the young prodigal, so he resolved to stifle his jealousy and indignation.

"Hem—ah—hem!" he said; "art ready, master butcher?"

"I was but wishing farewell to thy charming niece," replied Robin, turning round, without the slightest hesitation or confusion.

The sheriff bit his lip, and bade the girl retire to her chamber.

But Robin, with something of malice, took her hands, bowed respectfully, and then kissed her again.

"Excuse me, lady, but I may never see your face again."

She looked sadly down at this, which so exasperated Sir Thomas, that, with a furious glance at her, he caught Robin by the arm.

"We shall be late, young sir."

And so reached the porch, where their horses awaited them.

They mounted, and, riding gently, soon were out of Nottingham town.

"Wilt tell me, good· youth, how far and in what direction lies your property? I know most about here."

"I neither wish my name or property mentioned, for various reasons," said the prodigal butcher, gravely; "some of which you may comprehend when you reach the spot."

The avaricious justice made no reply, though fairly puzzled, especially at the direction taken by his companion.

He had nothing, however, to fear. The butcher was but one man, and close behind them rode half-a-dozen armed servants.

They soon left the high road, and rode by lonely paths in the direction, certainly, of several notable estates owned by men of various degrees, but all of whom the sheriff knew right well by name and face.

An explanation, however, offered itself to him. One of them *might*, perchance, have died, and a prodigal son have suddenly taken possession.

"Art not afraid of riding alone across these woods?" he asked, abruptly.

"I—why so?"

"Dost not know that that fearful villain Robin Hood is abroad, and spares no man, little or great?" replied the sheriff, glancing fearfully between the trees as they rode past.

"I care not how soon I meet him," said the butcher, with a laugh; "I am told he is a right good heart, and

ransoms the rich that he may relieve the poor, even as I have the poor of Nottingham."

"Ha! ha! ha!—a good joke," said Sir Thomas, with a forced laugh; "but this is a lonely place. If thy land be much further, I would fain return, and come another day. Night will be upon us."

They were close to the mouth of a vast grassy meadow, forming an open glade in the forest.

"Behold my land, and behold my cattle!"

The sheriff peered suddenly forward, and saw, indeed, a large prairie, with some two or three hundred deer grazing here and there in groups.

"Young sir, you do but jest with me. Show me thy cattle, or my servants shall bind thee, and take thee back to Nottingham for condign punishment. I do suspect me thou art a traitor loon."

"Sir Thomas Beauchamp, I did say that I would show my land—I show you some hundred acres of it," said the outlaw, loftily.

"Sirrah, it is the king's," cried the other, angrily.

"I make it mine," continued the other, "and yonder are my droves of cattle."

"They are the king's deer," roared the maddened sheriff.

"I make them mine."

"Then, in the foul fiend's name, who art thou?"

"I AM ROBIN HOOD!"

"I thought so, foul robber and murderer! Seize him!" cried the sheriff, backing his horse towards his serving-men.

But Robin wound his horn, and from the wood came Little John, Will Scarlett, and their fellows, who speedily surrounded and made prisoners the whole party.

"Welcome to Sherwood, Sir Thomas," said Robin, with a lofty bow; "and now, my merry men, a right royal banquet—the very best the wood affords, for the knight will pay liberally."

"Pay?"

"Yes, pay as I paid the score at the hostel in Nottingham. Did I not say Robin Hood ransomed the rich that he might relieve the poor, and when they know how generous you have been, will not every meat-eater in the town bless your name to-day?"

The sheriff groaned, for he knew that his three hundred marks were clean gone.

The outlaws, with a shout of delight, surrounded the party of prisoners and led them, trembling, horror-stricken, and filled with the most revengeful thoughts, deep into the fastnesses of the forest.

Meanwhile, Robin Hood, Little John, and Will Scarlett took a short and secret cut to the appointed rendezvous to prepare for the reception of their guests. The path was a most unfrequented one, and they therefore met with none of the scouts who usually were stationed at stated intervals in the solitudes, and who were bound by their rules to challenge every passer by.

It was a kind of blind trail, where only one man could walk abreast, and from the dense underwood that formed an impenetrable barrier on either side there remained but little doubt that these paths had been made by the outlaws and were known to them alone.

It was after about three hours of good walking that the outlaws arrived at a small opening in the forest, in the centre of which grew an oak of enormous dimensions, throwing its twisted branches in every direction. Beneath this tree four or five yeomen lay sleeping on the ground, while another, the sentinel, walked to and fro in the moonlight shade.

Upon hearing the sound of feet approaching the watch instantly gave the alarm, and the sleepers as suddenly started up and bent their archers' bows.

Six arrows placed on the string were pointed towards the quarter from which the travellers approached, when their guide, being recognised, was welcomed with every token of respect and attachment, and all signs and fears of a rough reception at once subsided.

This was one of the subsidiary trysting trees of the band, but was, perhaps, as well concealed as any.

"Up! up! my merry men—arouse the wenches from the huts—roast and boil, and lay a goodly spread, for the Sheriff of Nottingham sups with ye to-night."

A murmur of astonishment arose, followed by a roar of laughter, and then one rushed to a small village hut, utterly concealed in a secluded bottom from all mortal ken, to arouse the women and such of the outlaws as, being off duty, were enjoying the calm pleasures of domestic life.

FRIAR TUCK DISCOVERED AT HIS DEVOTIONS.

But Robin Hood knew his men well, and was well aware that at the announcement of such an invitation as he had given, all his merry yeomen would crowd to the front, all too pleased to exchange the chance of sleep for the certainty of pleasure.

In a few minutes everybody was at work, and soon the beautiful little forest glade or prairie was blazing with fire, while fat bucks were hung up to roast; a pig was cut in quarters, and hares and pullets thrust into pots, while bread was put in piles ready for the feast.

A square space was stuck round with pine torches, and within this were set rude stools, logs of wood, and other apologies for a seat, while in the centre were placed flagons, horns, and cups for the beer and wine.

Scarcely were the preparations made when the tramp of horses was heard, and there came shortly in sight the whole body of outlaws with their mounted prisoners, none of whom could help glancing with satisfaction at the feast prepared for them.

"Welcome!" cried Robin Hood, now clothed in the garb of the forest king, though with a half smile upon his face; "welcome, Sheriff of Nottingham, to the greenwood and to our rural feast. Come, my merry men, give him a hearty welcome."

The outlaws, who knew their chief's meaning at once, as soon as the sheriff alighted joined hands, and forming a circle, began in a loud and ringing voice, one of the rude but expressive ditties of the day.

SONG OF THE OUTLAWS.

As free as the wind is the life that we lead,
That sweeps without let over mountain and mead ;
We own not a tyrant, no foeman we fear,
Our home is the greenwood, well stocked with red deer.

The king lives by tollage—we toll whom we please;
He collects in the cities—we under the trees;
But he showeth no favour, nor misseth a door,
While we stop but the rich and molest not the poor.

No baron, nor abbot, nor monk 'neath a hood,
Shall pass heavy laden through merry Sherwood,
For we lessen their burdens by taking a toll,
And lighten the body to better the soul.

We lack not a stoup of good berry-brown beer,
We lack not a pasty well lined with fat deer,
We lack not an arm, when the tyrant does wrong,
To succour the weak, and strike down the strong.

There are eyes in the hamlets, and hearts by the Lene,
That brighten and beat for the outlaw in green,
When in the blue twilight he steals forth alone,
And lists for a footstep more dear than his own.

Then drink to the arrow, the bolt, and the bow,
That can strike down a coward, or level a foe ;
For we own not a tyrant, no foeman we fear,
Our home is the greenwood, well stocked with red deer.

The sound of this song waking the echoes of the forest was peculiarly effective, but it produced a most disagreeable effect upon the sheriff, who sank on the sward, wiping his brow with his hand, and staring at the moving circle as if he had been in the very Pandemonium himself.

Suddenly Robin Hood made a signal, and the circle broke up at once to allow those to pass who carried the viands to what may be described as the head table.

This done, the whole of the outlaws fell to, not forgetting the wants of their prisoners, entertaining them with right good cheer, as the outlaw entertained his guests.

All was jollity and merriment, save that the sheriff did not eat. He, however, made up by drinking a quantity, in which he was peculiarly conspicuous.

His followers were nowhere backward in this, quaffing the humming ale with rare gusto, until one by one they fell with their heads on the grass, and so, ere midnight, not a man-at-arms was awake.

The sheriff had been an hour asleep.

When the choristers of morn awoke them, they were alone, their horses grazing near at hand, but not a sign of outlaws could be seen.

On examination, it was also found that the pockets of no man contained a stiver.

The outlaws were strict in exacting payment for the entertainments they gave freely to all and every one.

With a dark frown, the sheriff rose and mounted his horse, returning to Nottingham, a better, and, it is to be hoped, a wiser man.

But the secret could not be kept, and soon all the town rang with this merry jest of Robin Hood.

CHAPTER LXXV.

THE FORLORN LOVER.

THERE wanted two days to the eventful hour when the chief outlaw was to visit his own dear Marian. He felt a great desire to keep moving.

True, there were many travellers now crossing the forest, on their way to the tournament, but they travelled chiefly in large and powerful bodies, only to be attacked at a great expense of life on both sides.

This Robin would not allow. But had he not have been merciful by nature, he must have been also aware that such wholesale hostilities on his part would soon have arrayed the constituted authorities against him, and compelled Prince John to have marched against him even with an army.

He accordingly sent his men out in their usual detachments, made half-a-dozen rendezvous, and then departed to pay a visit to his young friend of the cavern, in whom, by a kind of prevision of the future, he took the deepest interest.

The way was familiar in the extreme, and as the outlaw-chief never cared to be idle, and was also at times fond of solitude, he trod the heather and the sward with a proud consciousness, not only of enjoyment, but of pleasure, as he advanced carolling, swinging his quarterstaff, and even now and then stopping still to laugh from sheer exuberance of spirits.

Robin Hood had a presentiment that the youth he had assisted to escape from the keepers, and with whom he had been an accomplice in what the law treated as the worst form of murder, would soon join his band, and it was with something of a personal feeling that he undertook this journey.

He was anxious, also, to know if he had evaded the keepers.

Robin Hood judged according to his own ideas that the youth would ere this have contrived to leave the cave, and visit his mother, whom he professed himself unable to abandon many days together.

His course was, almost in a direct line for the Saxon village of Worlfton, leaving the cavern to the left.

He started at daybreak, but such was the difficulty then of making his way through the forest, that it was the next morning before he came in sight of the home of the widow.

It was a fortified farm, as he expected, with a few of the usual poor huts about it.

Robin Hood was about half a mile distant, on the summit of a slope, when he came in sight, and was about to descend the hill, when he heard footsteps.

With his habitual caution, he stepped aside, and looked keenly about.

> Among the leaves so gay,
> There he did espy the same young man
> Come drooping along the way.
> The scarlet he wore the day before
> It was clean cast away,
> And at every step he uttered a sigh :
> Alack and a well-a-day !

Now, Robin Hood was too seriously and recently in love not to understand these signs.

The youth was in love, but still, why so very downcast and low-spirited ?

He determined, however, to have his joke, come what would ; so putting on his mask and assuming his deepest and most threatening tones, he addressed the youth appearing before him with startling suddenness.

"Young man," he said, "hast thou any money to spare for my men and me ?"

Robin Hood had expected a blow, and was ready for it. His astonishment may then be conceived at the answer he received from the youth who had fought so valiantly a few days before.

"I have but five shillings and a ring, sir," he replied, sorrowfully, "which I kept carefully for my wedding, for——

> Yesterday I should have married a maid,
> But she was from me ta'en
> And chosen to be an old man's bride,
> Whereby my poor heart is slain—

Saith the old ballad."

> "Now what is thy name," said bold Robin Hood ?
> Come tell me, and that without fail.
> "By the faith of my body, then," said the young man,
> "My name it is Allan-a-Dale."

Robin Hood, at this, unmasked, and the other seemed for a moment to rally at the sight of his stalwart defender.

"Come and sit down," said Robin Hood, "and let me hear the exact truth in this matter. Perhaps I may help you."

Allan-a-Dale brightened up, though scarcely daring to hope.

"I love the daughter," he said, "of a neighbour. I have not known her long, having met with her by accident in the forest. I was chasing the wild deer about six months ago, when I got led away to a district of the forest which was unknown to me, but no great distance off.

"As a rule, I did not hunt that way, it being near the residence and within the territory of the Saxon, Sir Gammel——"

"A right worthy neighbour," smiled Robin.

"Suddenly, I lost sight of the deer and pausing to hear which way it had gone, was transfixed by the sight of a young girl.

"She slept.

"Her beautiful eyes were closed, but her half-open lips revealed a double row of pearls, and gave passage to a respiration as regular as the soft breathing of a child, and perfumed as the odoriferous violet.

"Her hair fell on her shoulders in rich auburn curls, which now and then were lifted by the wind and revealed her swan-like throat.

"I could not restrain an exclamation.

"She awoke, and would have fled, but that I knelt and begged her pardon for disturbing her, telling her how unwittingly it was.

"Then she smiled upon and forgave me."

"Like a sensible girl," cried bold Robin Hood.

Allen-a-Dale smiled a sickly smile.

"Well, she saw that I was tired and asked me to her home. She was a niece of Sir Gammel's, and was a kind of ward of his with some property, but not more than would be mine at some future period.

"This encouraged me to pay my addresses, which, I must say, were graciously received by the guardian and the young girl. All went merry as a marriage bell, when a Norman ruffian, a man knighted for services in Palestine, though originally a squire of Sir Philip de Beauvoisin's, saw her. She took his brutal fancy, especially when he learned that she had worldly gear, but she repulsed him with scorn.

"He threatened.

"She laughed in his face, but she forgot *her* widowed mother. The knight played upon her feelings, talked of rank, and position, and court, so that at last the dame was induced to withdraw her consent, and to-morrow at eleven o'clock she will be wedded to him from his tower of Shattelstone, at yonder church."

And he pointed to a spire that rose afar off in the valley beneath.

"That he shall not, even if Robin Hood forbid the banns," cried the outlaw.

"Robin Hood will have to come in force, then, for the Bishop of Bayeux comes with a rich train, and the knight is attended by some twenty men-at-arms."

"Sayest thou so?—then there will be sport withal. Now cheer you up, Allan-a-Dale, and to-morrow you shall kiss your bride, though a thousand bishops said you nay—on the faith of Robin Hood's word."

The youth started back, coloured with pleasure, and doffed his cap.

"And thou art Robin Hood?"

"That am I, verily, and I doubt not, if I blow blast loud enough, we shall find that obstinate Little John not far off."

With which words he blew three peculiar mots, and before the echoes had fairly died away the tall forester came rushing from the covert, quite astonished to find no enemy to pound with that huge flail-like staff, which, in his hands, was so ponderous and terrible a weapon.

"Where are they?" he cried.

"There is no one to exercise thy wrath upon," said the outlaw chief, laughing; "but as I thought you were lurking about, I sounded my horn. Thou art as soft-hearted a fellow as ever loved a damsel, or broke a head, so hearkee."

And he briefly told the story of Allan-a-Dale.

"By'r lady!" cried the giant, with glistening eyes, after wringing the other's hands with tremendous violence, "what can I do?. A proper youth, a most proper youth! A curse and murrain on the whole race of Normans and their masters."

"Do you collect fifty of our best men, and take up your post in sight of yonder church. Let any enter, but when I wind my horn, enter ye also; ye shall see some fun. I and this worthy youth will hie us to the hermitage. We may want the friar's help to-morrow, and 'twill be a good resting-place. Besides," said Robin, with one of those merry laughs which so well became him, "I shall want one of my disguises."

Little John smiled, shook his chieftain's hand, and then without a moment's hesitation departed on his journey.

Robin Hood now bade Allan-a-Dale follow him and they would not only find shelter for the night, but find, as he said, a mad priest, who would be useful to them during the events of the following day.

The young lover was already too much impressed in Robin Hood's favour not to be ready to obey him in everything. He felt, too, an exhilaration of spirits in walking through the greenwood forest, which in itself was a kind of happiness.

Little was said, the two not having yet those interests in common which go so far to make up the subject matter of all conversation.

Soon the path they travelled was so narrow as not even to admit of them walking abreast, and began to descend into a dingle traversed by a brook, whose banks were broken, swampy and overgrown with dwarf willows.

"Yet two miles," said the outlaw, " and we shall be at our journey's end."

CHAPTER LXXVI.

THE KNIGHT AND THE FRIAR.

WE, however, must precede him.

We hope that none of our readers have forgotten the mysterious knight whom Robin Hood befriended after he had aided Edith in escaping from the wood.

We must, at the risk of rendering our readers impatient, return to him, and narrate an adventure familiar to all students of old English lore, as told in the erudite but somewhat monotonous ballads of the early period of English literature—but, if familiar, necessary to the course of our narrative.

The knight made numerous journeys, some short, and some long, putting up now at hostelries, now in castles, but chiefly in Saxon priories, where he was always well received and treated with the bland courtesy which appears the heritage of the churchman from the earliest days to those of the Jesuits.

He was again on the move, entering the forest fearlessly and unhesitatingly, like some knight errant of old, caring not for outlaws or ruffian robbers, men-at-arms or knights of high degree, ever pursuing the even tenor of his way, ready to sleep beneath an oak and feed on acorns and water, or to seat himself at the richest board in Christendom.

But whether in hostel or priory, never did he show his face to the vulgar or curious.

He was now all accoutred for battle, and started with every appearance of a desire to cross the forest ere nightfall, the business he was upon being now almost come to a head.

But though accustomed to the way, it was not easy to travel through those woods without mistaking one path for another, so that it happened, when man and beast were tired, he only found himself on the borders of the West Riding of Yorkshire.

The knight, who wore richer armour than on the previous occasion, had been dreaming, for he had at last allowed his horse to lead him as he listed, so that, when he at last looked up, he found himself in a spot quite strange to him.

The feeble tinkle of a bell, as if swung by the wind, also attracted his attention.

He was on a kind of lawn at the foot of a precipice which rose abruptly in front of him, dotted, however, with a rich verdure of ivy, oak, and holly bushes.

A rude kind of structure, half hut, half cavern, presented the appearance of considerable strength, while near at hand a rude cross, formed by means of a fir pole and a transverse bar, with the ruins of a small chapel, indicated a hermitage.

The chapel, when entire, could not have been more than sixteen feet long by twelve wide; resembling those so well known to the wayfarer in foreign parts, as being dedicated to the Virgin by pious sailors.

Its low roof rested upon four concentric arches, which sprang from the four corners of the building, each supported upon a short and heavy pillar. The rests of these two arches remained, though the roof had fallen down betwixt them; over the others it remained entire. The entrance to this place of devotion was under a very low round arch, ornamented by several courses of that zig-zag moulding resembling sharks' teeth, which appear so often in more ancient Saxon architecture. A belfry rose above the porch on four small pillars, within which hung the green and weather-beaten bell, the feeble sound of which had been some time before heard.

The whole of this peaceful and rustic scene lay glimmering in twilight before the eyes of the traveller, giving some assurance of a lodging for the night—since it was one of the duties of hermits who dwelt in the vast solitudes of the forest to exercise such hospitality as they could to belated or bewildered travellers.

The horseman at once dismounted, and, with a fist which would probably have felled an ox, struck the door violently.

No answer came.

The knight repeated his summons with renewed vigour, and this time with something like success.

"Whoever thou mayest be, pass on," was the answer in the feeble tones of an old man, "and do not thus thoughtlessly disturb the servant of our Lord and St. Dunstan—whose name be blessed!—when at his vespers."

"I would not, holy man," replied the knight, "I would not wish to annoy or pester thee in any way, but I am a poor wanderer and have quite lost my way, so that thou really must open and give me such comfort and food as thy house affordeth."

"Comfort and food. There are but logs for bed and roots for food—so pass on, traveller—for you have already made me miss two paters, three aves, and a credo, which, for my sins, I have to repeat on my knees until daybreak."

"But the night is dark, the wood intricate, and my horse tired—or I would go on; there is no place within reach."

"Follow the road."

"The road!—what road?"

"Nothing can be easier to find. Follow the path through the wood until you come to the Blue morass, then you will reach a swampy ford, which will only reach to thy horse's back—if the late rains have not swollen it—then, when thou shalt have reached the opposite bank, which is extremely difficult to be climbed, by reason of its precipitous sides, follow the path which hangs over the river; but here be careful, as I understand from some of my penitents that it has lately fallen in in sundry places—then keep forward till you come to the Devil's Dyke."

"The devil and all his imps take thee for a godless hermit," cried the knight; "fords—morasses—broken paths! Dost think I'm a will-o'-the-wisp? I tell you what, an' you wish not broken bones, you will quickly open. I give thee fair warning, most inhospitable priest, that unless thy door be stronger than usual, it will be stove in less time than it will take thee to say an ave."

A short silence prevailed, and thinking the hermit meant to defy him, the knight struck the door so violently with his foot as to make the very staple shake.

"Friend wayfarer," said the hermit, in a gruff tone, "spare thy strength—which you might have done all along, since you had but to lift the latch and enter, which now thou mayest do, and welcome."

But the knight had already heard the bolts withdrawn.

"And now thy voice is merrier, though, truly, thou liest," said the soldier, entering.

What caused the hermit, whom we shall soon recognise, to take all this time ere he opened, will presently be seen.

The hermit now stood upright—a stout, large, strong-built man, with sackcloth, gown, and hood, bound by a rope of rushes.

In one hand he held a torch of pine, that flared in the wind, while in the other he clutched a quarterstaff, so thick and heavy that it could well be called a club.

He looked angrily at the intruder, and appeared about to resent his intrusion, but when his eyes fell upon the lofty, erect, gigantic frame, and golden spurs of the knight, he gave him a surly kind of welcome.

"'Tis not my wont to open after sunset to any but those whose voices I know," he said; "there being so many robbers and outlaws abroad who give no honour to St. Dunstan or our Lady."

"I should think," replied the knight, in a tone which was slightly sarcastic, "that the poverty of your cell was your great safeguard against the inroads of such men. Methinks it would require one or two to dare contend with those sturdy arms, more made for wrestling, methinks, than to count beads."

The hermit turned away to hide a palpable grin.

"And now, most hospitable Clerk of Copmanhurst, in the vulgate called Friar Tuck," said the knight, "where will thou put my horse?"

The hermit dropped his hood, and exhibited the astonished features of the chaplain of the outlaws.

"Thou art the knight who did befriend Edith of Athelston," he said, holding out his hand and shaking the other's mailed fist; "take off thy tin-pot and sit down to such poor fare as my cell affords."

The knight, however, insisted on seeing to his horse, and the friar, muttering something about his cell being sometimes turned into a hostel, pulled forth a goodly bundle of forage.

"The abbot of St. Joveau did stop here last week in the thunderstorm," he said, apologetically, "and his servants left this behind."

The knight took it from his hands and went forth into the open air to his horse, which he placed beneath a portion of the rock quite sheltered from wind and rain, covered him with his own cloak, placed the food before him, and went in doors, the friar all the while holding his torch on high.

"And now, my good friend," said the knight, "are we likely to have more visitors?"

"The night promises rain and wind," replied the friar.

"Why?"

"Because my helmet wearies me. I have a vow that I will not take it off before more than one man at a time, until I take it off in triumph in the presence of the assembled court, after the tournament."

"None will come, and I am but one man," said the friar.

The knight at once unhelmed, and showed the countenance already described.

The friar could not but admire it, and looked rather ruefully at the scanty fare—dried roots, acorns, parched pease and water—which he had laid before him.

The knight smiled.

"I will not say, sir knight, that the carnal desires of the body do not impel me to seek for other food; but such is the fare which is allowed by the canons of the Holy Church."

"Such horse provender and horse beverage," said the knight with a smile, "may suit one who has made saintly vows, but to one who has ridden five and twenty miles since sun arose, across this forest, it is but miserable diet."

"There speaketh the flesh and the devil," replied the hermit, putting three pease in his mouth, and drinking about a teaspoonful of water; "this beverage is from the well of St. Dunstan, and hath most marvellous powers."

"It should, to give thee such an array of muscle," smiled the knight. "There are few men, fed on beef and venison and good foaming ale, would contend with thee in a wrestling match, or go about with thee at quarterstaff. Come, hath not your cell some private hutch or inner room that hath as many secrets as the cell of an amorous nun?"

The monk blushed crimson, while his speech was tart and almost angry.

"I am a poor man, living in a desolate wilderness, saying masses and living, as by rights, on parched pease and water."

"And quite right. But when you entertain such churchmen as the Abbot of St. Joveau—whom Heaven forgive for his treachery to his true king—he eats not such desert food. The last time of his visit did he not perchance leave some scraps behind which might suit the stomach of one who could rather digest half-a-dozen pounds of venison than champ yonder roots?"

The friar looked at him with a strangely quaint smile.

"Thou hast, I fancy, been used to defile thyself with wine and meats, even as Solomon, instead of restraining thyself to the pulse and water of the children, Shadrach, Meshech, and Abednego."

"I have in the Holy Land endured hunger, thirst, and hard fare, enough to satisfy a life-time, to say nothing of some months of prison. Come, sir priest, shall I search for myself?"

"No!" said the hermit, rather hurriedly, "my mind is usually so bent upon my monastic duties, that it had slipped my memory—so unsuitable it is to me—of a good pasty that the said abbot's purveyor did leave as a kind of payment for the poor hospitality he enjoyed."

"I knew it. There is something in the air," said the knight. "I could sniff it afar off, as the war-horse does the battle-field."

The hermit rose with a look of reproach, and went to a kind of secret cupboard, whence he produced a vast pasty of unusual dimensions, which had that crisp appearance which betokens that it has not been long cooked.

"The odour is delicious," said the knight; "but I dare be sworn the abbot did a miracle, for by some spell it hath kept almost hot since last week."

The monk mumbled something, but what it was the knight could not hear.

But he placed a platter before him, bidding him, with rather a rueful countenance, fall to.

"And now, most worshipful friar, hear me. When I have devoured this pasty I shall want something to drink. Bethink thy somewhat oblivious memory if that same purveyor to the abbot—a guzzling, gorging priest as ever lived—did not, in honour of St. Dunstan, leave thee something with which any lay traveller like myself might wash down this generous food."

"There is a stoup of wine and a flagon of ale," stammered the hermit, scarcely able to keep his gravity; "but they were as completely forgotten as——"

The knight stooped, picked something from under the table, and held it up to the discomfited friar.

"Did the Abbot of Joveau leave this kirtle and hat, which belong to a woman, I trow?"

"A penitent, who for her sins has sometimes to walk all this way to be shrived. But harkee," he said, changing his tone, " I trow it is not the act of good-fellowship to pry into my private affairs."

" Good hermit," cried the knight, laughing, " I knew the pie was hot, and it does thy fair penitent great credit." He had cut it open and was allaying his hunger in a way that threatened to leave very little for any future guest.

" I am a soldier and a man of honour—what passes within these four walls is a secret between us two, and therefore be not afraid. I can see it all—some old and ugly female sinner, to propitiate thee to pardon her sins, did intend to sup with thee to-night. Bring her forth, if she be not so great a fright she will scare me from my meal."

" Old and ugly women," cried the hermit, irately, " never entered within these four wall:. 'Tis true a penitent of mine did—mistrusting my abstinence, and believing the stories told by minstrels and others—bring me this good cheer, and was about to take her departure when you alarmed her and she ran away. Come forth, my dear," he then added; "'tis a knight and a soldier, who will not hurt thee."

With eyes cast upon the ground, with blushes that reached to the very roots of her hair, with an air of confusion that added, if anything, to her true Saxon beauty—came forth Elfrida.

But the knight simply bowed with lofty courtesy.

" And now, mine host, I have been, I have said, in Palestine and many other strange foreign parts, and I have always observed it as a rule to make mine host assure me the viands are not poison by seeing him eat of them himself. Come, help thyself and this damsel here, whose supper I truly have interrupted."

There was no sneer, no look, no inuendo in the knight's speech or manner, and next minute the friar had filled the girl's platter, and himself thrusting his hand into the pasty, was endeavouring to make up for the time which his professions of abstinence had made him lose.

There was no false modesty about appetite in those days. Women did not eat hearty lunches in secret and have delicate mouths in public, but sustained the wants of nature openly and honestly.

Observing that the knight sat with his side to her, his head almost turned away, Elfrida soon recovered her sprightliness, and enjoyed her supper as best she might.

Soon the ale flowed, followed by the wine, and, the ice being broken, all restraint vanished.

The hermit set the example of a song, and soon the cell, supposed popularly to be that of an anchorite, became the scene of a carouse, more suited decidedly to a scotale-house than to the place where it was enacted.

But the hypocrisy and license of religious houses in those days was something not to be described.

The reader must go back to the chronicles of the times, or to the pages of history, where necessarily the scalp-knife lays bare the truth with regard to nunneries and monasteries.

And rely upon it, nothing ever said in story is exaggerated on this point.

The knight and the monk had sung each a solo, and then, finding their voices agreed, had indulged in a duet.

Elfrida, after some hesitation, had agreed to do what she could towards the amusement of the company, when there came such a knocking at the door as fairly made all start.

The knight caught at his helmet and put it on, the girl siezed her kirtle and hood and retired to the innermost recesses of the cavern ; while Friar Tuck, in a nasal tone, asked who dared to interrupt him in his holy songs.

" Open, mad priest !" said an authoritative voice. " Wouldst bring all the keepers in the forest about thy ears ?"

Friar Tuck at once knew the voice and hastened to open, when, with somewhat of an air of ill-humour, Robin Hood entered, followed by Allan-a-Dale.

At the sight of the knight the outlaw stopped and doffed his cap with every mark of profound respect.

" Welcome, my brave yeoman," said the knight, with dignity—" welcome ! Having lost myself in the woods, I have craved hospitality of this jolly priest, and have made him so far forget his monastic vows as to join me in pasty and ale, also in a song."

" Which he loves better than matins. But I hope some of the good things are left, for both myself and friend are hungry."

Friar Tuck lost no time in attending to the wants of the new-comers ; but the festivity having been interrupted,

the knight, after a short conversation with the leader of the outlaws in a low tone of voice, retired to a couch of sweet hay and fern leaves.

The others did the same after a very brief delay, and soon no sound was heard in the hermitage but the heavy respirations of the various sleepers.

At early morn the knight rose, thanked the monk for his hospitality, and rode away, after receiving minute directions from Robin Hood as to the way he was to take.

CHAPTER LXXVII.

THE MARRIAGE CEREMONY.

THE lieutenant was early at his post. The mother of the victim who was to be immolated at the altar of Mammon and wantonness lived within sight of the church where the sacrifice was to be consummated, and could see from her own window the spire of the holy house thus to be desecrated.

She passed a restless and almost sleepless night, devising, as all must do under the same circumstances, how to escape from a connection hateful to her senses and repugnant to her best feelings.

The blushing, conscious maiden, rising from her couch to adorn herself on her wedding morn for the man who has won her young affection, is a picture the most blunted natures must admire.

It makes the heart even of the old feel young again, if even but for a moment.

But if we use our peculiar privilege and enter the chamber of the young girl to whom Allan-a-Dale was so devoted, we shall find a very different spectacle.

Ella, the Saxon girl, was fair, very fair—a pretty, light, brown-haired girl, with a broad but low white forehead, over which the brown hair, with a warm tinge in it, curled in a pretty, fantastic way, as if indignant at being drawn into straight bands. Her eyes were large and blue, with large, dark pupils, that looked like little wells of clear water, at the bottom of which one should have found truth.

Her mouth was small, red, and very pretty ; her chin round and well-formed, but without a dimple ; and her neck, which was very graceful, was of that indescribable whiteness which is only seen in the flesh of women, and which no poetical simile—such as alabaster, marble, drifted snow, or lilies—can convey an idea of.

She had just risen ; but now her eyes were red, not with weeping, but from vigil.

Ella was a good, pure, and virtuous girl, but without the energetic will of Edith of Athelston.

She no more thought of escaping from the clutches of the Norman knight by any act of volition on her own part, than she would have thought of flying from her chamber window.

Her hope was in the devotion and ingenuity of her lover, in whom she had that unbounded confidence which is one of the sweetest charms of love's young dream.

She made no attempt to dress herself. There was time enough for that when she was summoned.

Her mother and maids would see to that quite soon enough—for herself, she wished the day were a year long, that if she must yield to fate, it might be put off as long as possible.

Slowly she walked to her window and looked out.

At no great distance down the valley was the little village, with its church spire.

The cottagers were just lighting their fires, for a veil of thin smoke half obscured the scene—for a moment only, however, a light breeze springing up and scattering it over the forest.

The beauty of the scenery, the pureness of the air, could not be without some effect on Ella, but it was a melancholy one.

Soon she was examining everything around minutely, with streaming eyes.

Every well known spot reminded her of him.

There was the style leading into the village churchyard, where often they had sat engaged in innocent prattle.

There was the shadowy oak on the edge of the forest, with its rustic seat, where he had told his love.

There was the garden, in which, with the approval of her mother, she had so often walked, his affianced and much-beloved bride.

With a cry of anguish, she retreated from the window, and, falling back into a chair, wept bitterly.

But after the first pang was over, she rose again.

"I must not thus give way," she said, washing her eyes with cold water, "I must be calm, very calm and resolute. I must not show this discourteous knight that I fear him in the least. I must be brave, very brave."

And again she went to the window and peered out.

A thrill went through her heart as she saw a procession moving in the direction of the church. It was the bishop and his train who were about to take up their quarters in the humble abode of the parish priest.

It was, as a spectacle, rather fine, as churchmen in those days travelled not only with guards, but with servants, cooking apparatus, bedding, and provisions, the fare they required to keep up their portliness not being found in every house.

How long the maiden watched, how long her eyes were fixed on the spot, the church, she never knew; but her reverie was broken by a sharp knocking at her door.

Slowly and wearily she dragged herself towards the spot and opened.

Her mother and two tirewomen entered.

"Ella, what is this?" cried the foolish and ambitious mother. "Why is your face so white—your eyes so red? You have risen many hours."

"I have not closed an eye all night. I could have rested nowhere but in my coffin."

"Girl, let me hear no more of this nonsense. You are to be wedded to a noble gentleman this day; an' you look as you do now. he will turn from you at the altar."

"I wish to heaven he would!" said poor Ella.

The mother made no reply—not naturally hard-hearted or cruel, she had simply been led away by the sophistries of the Norman knight and the prospects of his advancement in high favour with Prince John.

She could not see that the land which was to be Ella's was indeed that which he most coveted, though he did entertain a kind of coarse passion for the girl herself.

Had she possessed no money or other pelf, he would certainly not have sought her in marriage.

Ella made no resistance, suffering herself to be attired with a kind of languid indifference which was painful to behold.

But oh, woman! As the mysterious ceremony proceeded, and the girls showed awkwardness or want of taste, her female instincts became aroused, for she exerted herself to set everything off as carefully as if she had been about to meet the man of her love.

The mother smiled.

She believed that something more than mere harmless female vanity was aroused.

She believed that her pride and ambition were aroused at the idea of holding her head high with the first noble ladies of the land.

She little knew her daughter, a delicate flower made to blush unseen—to wither with too much exposure to the sun.

Ella would have adorned a cottage, a humble, a placid home. She would have been out of place in a palace.

She had one ambition and no other—to be the happy wife of young Allan-a-Dale.

This not being possible, it seemed very little matter to her what happened, as she soon must die.

There are natures like this, which combat not with the resolutions of others, but fade away and perish.

It was about eleven when the elaborate process of getting-up the bride was concluded, and just then a messenger from the knight came to inform them that all was ready, and that nothing was wanted but the presence of the bride.

Ella turned ghastly pale, and had not her mother forced wine through her parted lips, she would have fainted.

It was a painful and sad spectacle.

The mother turned away half in compunction, wondering if indeed she were doing right; but pride, that caused Lucifer's fall, overcame every other consideration.

In ten minutes more the bride, attended by her own servants and six comely maidens, who were her friends, walked in slow procession to the church.

CHAPTER LXXVIII.

A CHANGE IN THE BRIDEGROOM.

IN the church a somewhat large congregation was collected. There was the knight himself, who, in comparison with Ella, "was both grave and old," though "wealthy," and around him numerous friends and acquaintances.

Then there were most of the neighbours for miles round, who, knowing something of the story, had come out of curiosity.

Then there was the bishop, a rare sight in a small parish church, and therefore all the more highly appreciated. He was a comely and portly man, and conversed affably with knight and priests.

The good man had made an excellent breakfast—the venison collops being done to a nicety.

This had put him in the best of humours.

The talk was trivial enough and not worth recording, when suddenly a kind of scuffling sound was heard, and a wandering minstrel, with his harp upon his back, pushed his way towards the altar and made a profound obeisance to the bishop.

"What hast thou here?" the bishop then said;
"I prithee now tell unto me."
"I am a bold harper," the other replied,
"The best in the north countrie."

The bishop, who was a tasteful man and very fond of music, brightened up and at once requested the minstrel to give them a taste of his quality.

"I see the bridegroom, but where is the bride?" replied the minstrel, boldly.

"She will be here anon. Let not that trouble you."

"I play for love of fair ladies," said the bold harper, "and wait until I see the finikin lass who is to wed this reverend greybeard."

"Thou art an impudent varlet," laughed the bishop, who, fortunately, was in a good humour, "but thou shalt have thy will. But here she comes."

"An' I had not something else to do," cried the knight, angrily, "I would slit thy nose."

"Take care I slit not thine," replied the minstrel, coolly, but in a loud voice.

The knight turned angrily round, the bishop frowned; but conceive their astonishment when the harper addressed them in fierce and indignant accents.

"This is no fit match, worthy bishop, to which you are about to lend yourself," he cried; "but since we have come to this holy church, the maiden shall chose her own dear."

"Sirrah, you shall pay for this," said the bishop, wrathfully; "but still all shall know that thy impudence is without cause, I will address the maiden."

"Hum!" said the knight, with a little cough.

"Young girls will be young girls," observed the mother, with the deep conviction of having made a remarkable statement.

"I adjure you, lass," said the bishop, who did not notice these asides, "to tell me the truth. Are you here of your own accord or not?"

"I am not."

The bishop fell back a step, somewhat disconcerted, but the knight and mother came to his aid.

"It has been settled six months," said Sir Guy de Lussac.

"Good sir—noble sir," added the mother, "this is but maiden modesty. You should have seen her dress herself this morn, with smiles and blushes. *Say yes, or have my curse.*"

Now, the curses of wicked people have about as much importance as pellets of paper, to do harm, but the curse of a parent is always dreaded by a good child.

Ella trembled violently.

"Speak girl," said the bishop, "be not alarmed. I am sure Sir Guy de Lussac will make you an excellent husband, and——"

"Tra-la-la!" resounded through the church, waking up the echoes of the corners and chapels in a way that startled the congregation.

There was the minstrel on the altar steps, sounding his horn with calm persistence.

"Turn the pestilent knave out of the church," cried the bishop, irately.

The servants rushed forward.

"Back! here comes more company," shouted the minstrel, casting off his flimsy disguise, and standing before the astounded company, a bold outlaw.

At the same moment the church was filled by archers, headed by Allan-a-Dale, who, having handed Robin Hood his bow and arrows, rushed to the side of Ella, who stood bewildered and trembling, unable to realise the scene which had just taken place.

"What means this outrage, this sacrilege?" cried the bishop, lifting his hand on high as if to pronounce a malediction. "Away—go—lest the heaviest curses of the church fall upon and crush ye all!"

"We believe not such mummeries, invented for your own base and wicked purposes," said Robin, who, with many of his men, had been awakened to a sense of Romish imposture by personal contact with priests and by the preaching of certain missionaries of the truth, who even then, in secret and dark places, began to expose the darkness and degradation into which the church of the gospel had fallen; "so talk not thus to us."

The bishop, purple with rage, the more that he observed a smile on the face of several, looked around him to compare numbers.

"Will ye allow this desecration of God's temple? Are there no men here to prevent this place being made a den of thieves?" he cried.

But none moved; the archers, with bent bows, commanded every position.

"Sir bishop," began Robin Hood, sternly, "I am master here, and my will is law. I come to prevent a great wrong. This girl is being hurried into a hateful marriage by a wicked and avaricious knight and an ambitious and silly woman. She has told you plainly this mating is against her will."

Robin Hood looked wistfully at the bride, upon whom all eyes were fixed.

"Tell the truth," he began. "For all your dress shines like glittering gold, is not your heart sad, and would you not gladly say no?"

"I gladly would," she cried, glad of the opportunity. "I hate this man."

A loud cry of joy and applause ensued.

The knight fumed, the bishop wished himself well out of the scrape, while a dark, lowering frown settled on the face of the disappointed mother.

Then Robin took his friend by the hand, and led him to where Ella stood.

"This is thy true love," bold Robin, he said,
    "Young Allan, as I hear say,
And you shall be married in this same hour,
    And sicker I swear and say."

The bishop turned his back and whispered to the priests around him.

"I tell thee, impudent varlet," he cried, resuming his position, "that none here shall marry them. Besides, they have not been asked three times in church, so that no servant of God dare unite them. Go thy way in peace, satisfied to escape without condign punishment, which thy insolence and sacrilege so well merits."

"Not asked!" cried Robin Hood, with a smile, "we'll soon remedy that. Here is my clerk, who shall ask them not three but seven times in the church, lest the three times be not enough."

Little John, to whom he nodded, stepped into the choir, and with a very red face and a voice that trembled somewhat, began asking them slowly and deliberately.

The people began to laugh.

So says the historian of the day, who seems to think the whole affair a very good joke, though more delicate critics, will necessarily find much to blame.

The clergy veiled their faces, kneeled, crossed themselves, and would have gladly left the church, but that sharp arrow points, pointed at their bodies, made them fearful to move.

The bishop alone kept up his haughty demeanour, looking on scornfully and with looks which plainly indicated how terrible would be the vengeance he would take, if opportunity offered, for this gross outrage on mother church, before whom most men were wont to tremble and bow the knee in all humility.

"And now," said Robin Hood, who stood inflexible and stern amid all the confusion and uproar, "come forth holy friar—and finish this business. The bishop will lend thee his trappings."

The jolly friar, somewhat abashed at the presence of the bishop, came forth with something of a sheepish countenance.

Two stout outlaws stepped out as if to borrow the bishop's coat and mitre, but he laid them down in a dignified kind of way which even awed bold Robin Hood himself.

But, as soon as he saw the burly friar putting on the prelate's grand robes, his countenance cleared up, and a joyous burst of laughter relieved him from the slight feeling of compunction which, against his will, had come over him.

Friar Tuck himself, however, was not comfortable. He had some little remnant of respect for the priesthood in which he had been reared, and felt that he was acting in an unwarrantable fashion, which only his great love for his chieftain would justify.

He, therefore, somewhat hurried over the ceremony, saying not a word more than was absolutely necessary.

And so in a very few minutes Allan-a-Dale and Ella were man and wife.

"Who gives this fair maiden away?" said Friar Tuck, at length.

"That do I!" cried Robin Hood, "and let me add, he that takes her from my friend Allan-a-Dale shall buy her dearly."

Ella blushed, and would have kissed her mother, but she turned haughtily away.

Allan took her hand gently and led her from the church, at the porch of which a stout palfrey awaited her.

Then the outlaws closed round them to escort the happy pair to Robin's woodland palace in Barnesdale forest, there to make merry.

There was no safety now for bride or bridegroom under the maternal roof-tree.

The bishop watched them go with an eye which spoke volumes, but for some time he said not a word. His bosom swelled with fierce and terrible emotions.

"Sir Guy de Lussac," he said, addressing the knight in deep hollow tones, "what intend you to do?"

"Do?" cried the other, "the fellow is the foul fiend himself; do what we will we cannot trap him."

"Can ye not?" said the churchman, in colder and more thoughtful tones; "then most holy mother church help you. Murder, robbery, treachery of the basest kind, are recorded of this fellow; but now he has placed himself out of the pale of civilisation—*leave him in my hands.*"

"But you will want assistance," said the knight, "command me for one. Never will I rest until this foul outrage has been revenged—speak, my lord."

"I accept your offer. Disperse, good people—and take warning by these knaves who triumph for a moment, to fall into the bottomless pit. Ye have heard such awful heresy, that all who would not be tainted by it must fast an extra day for three weeks—which doing, I give you absolution for the horrors which have polluted your ears—go!"

The congregation bowed low, a sigh seemed to escape their bosoms, and then all retired in good order, amazed as well as amused—that they could not prevent.

"And now, Sir Guy de Lussac, the wedding dinner shall not be wasted—I and these holy fathers will take the place of the fair bride and her pretty bridesmaids; over the meal we will devise some means of punishing this bold outlaw and most insolent heretic."

The knight smiled grimly at the enforced exchange of guests, but the latter part of the sentence pleased him—for his soul yearned for revenge.

Few men under the circumstances but would have been actuated by similiar feelings.

But let us quit awhile these scenes of strife for something gentler.

CHAPTER LXXIX.

THE LOVERS' MEETING.

WOMEN'S occupations were few in those days. In the position in society occupied by Edith of Athelston they were confined to embroidery, the lute, singing; unless, indeed, she chose to spell over some almost undecipherable manuscript best left unread, being either some foolish romance of chivalry or minstrel's poem, neither edifying to mind or morals.

Now Edith of Athelston liked embroidery very well, so she did music, and sometimes she liked a song; but she yearned ever to have her foot upon the grassy turf, a roof of green overhead, and to enjoy the liberty and pleasures of the forest.

Convents were so often the refuge of noble maidens against the violence and coarseness of the times, that the good abbesses were compelled to provide in some measure for the amusement of the fair damsels.

Edith did not feel at all inclined to share in all the vigils and prayers which were incumbent on the nuns; she, therefore, looked about her for some occupation befitting her tastes and habits.

Close to the garden in which the nuns worked, or took exercise or recreation, was the private garden of the abbess—a lovely glade stolen from the forest and walled in, with its green sward, its fine oak trees, and every other sylvan attraction, to which were added flowery and odoriferous shrubs.

Here the good abbess allowed Edith to walk freely, as she was conscious that confinement was not good for her, while neither had she any desire to drive the roses or lilies from her cheeks until after her interview with Prince John.

The man who ruled England in the absence of her lawful king was notorious for his admiration of the fair sex, and often would grant to the tearful eye of a woman that which he would refuse to any other suppliant.

Now 'tis all very well to walk in a beautiful garden and dream of those we love, but even such pleasant employment is apt to become monotonous.

Edith found it particularly so; so made her maid search the wing appointed for the residence of young ladies to see if anything worthy of her offered.

"There is a pretty bow and a sheaf of arrows," said the girl; "but that is of no use."

"The very thing of all others I shall like," replied Edith, with a blush; "bring them."

"Certainly, lady."

"Is there a target?"

"Yes, lady."

"Bring that also, that I may try my skill," continued the young girl, quite elated.

Edith almost looked upon this as an omen. Dreaming always of the forest glades, of the happy life led by Robin Hood and his foresters bold, she instinctively longed to excel in those accomplishments which best became one likely to share the fate of an outlawed and persecuted man.

It was not as Robert Earl of Huntingdon that the girl loved him, but as plain Robin.

Of a vigorous intellect, fitted to shine in court or castle, in hut or cavern, Edith, in the first burst of her bright womanhood, preferred the wild life to the constrained, fictitious, and slavish existence forced as a rule upon her sex.

Made much of when quite young, treated with scant courtesy when in the bloom of early wifedom, the first sign of declining charms transformed them into household drudges or slaves, while younger favourites took their places.

What wonder, then, if there were more charm in being the wife of one in a humble station, than to be the temporary toy and plaything of a noble, cast aside with the first loss of her bloom.

Many such ideas passed through the brain of the young girl as she awaited the return of her attendant.

The handmaiden soon arrived, and, with sparkling eyes, Edith seized the bow.

"I shall be very awkward," she said, with a laugh, "and cannot bear to be looked at. You can rejoin the convent servants."

The Saxon attendant curtsied and retired, wondering much at her mistress's taste.

A small easily managed butt, doubtless provided for the amusement of some noble lady, was soon erected at the end of the lawn, and Edith looped up her petticoats the better to be able to run to the target.

Then she strung her bow and commenced.

At first she was very awkward, for though she had had some little practice with the crossbow, the standard weapon of old England was unknown to her.

She, had, however, a determined will, and was not one of those who easily give up.

A whole hour did she practice, ere she began at all to satisfiy herself.

Her arrow then struck the target. She had made a very tolerable shot.

"Good!" said an admiring voice, near at hand.

Edith let fall the bow, and, with a roseate blush, which seemed to paint her whole face in its flood of pleasurable emotion, she fell into Robin's arms.

Now the good abbess had given them free permission to meet once a week—in the parlour!

That was the objection; in the parlour where the noble guests received their friends, always sat either one of the nuns or the lady abbess herself.

In such a case, what can any one say or do, except whisper a few unmeaning trifles, or exchange an occasional sly glance or pressure of the hand.

But they had need of more full communion than this. They wished to converse without restraint; so Edith had consented to the audacious proposal of Robin to meet her every Saturday, during afternoon prayer, in the garden.

Edith wondered how he was going to do it; but she knew not either the physical powers or invention of Robin Hood, who had carefully examined the place during his watch on a previous occasion, and marked down one bastion that supported the high wall, where not only was the ivy thick, but under the ivy the holes many.

What more did one so sure-footed as Robin want, once he had made this important discovery.

He watched his opportunity, found no one was looking, and easily ascended to the summit.

To descend was easy.

When men and women love, meetings of this kind are very similar; the conversation is all of self at first; each has his or her feelings to pourtray, emotions to record, adventures to relate, until at last, the past and present being exhausted, they come to speak of the future.

Then commences sweet communion.

The future is always bright and sunny, in our thoughts and in our dreams. We never are, but are to be blest. Such is the happy ordination of nature.

But any record of the murmured words, any attempt to give even a small portion of the talk they indulged in, would be idle until towards the last.

"And so, my bright, my beautiful," he cried, "you were consoling yourself for my absence, by practising archery."

"I wished to fit myself to be an outlaw's wife," was her proud reply.

Robin Hood did not answer for a moment. He was musing.

"True," he said, "this dream of rank may never be revealed, and then repentance, when too late, may cut you to the heart."

"Never! If I cannot be Countess of Huntingdon, I will be queen of the outlaws—I will be Maid Marian," she continued with a sweet and earnest smile.

"And so you shall. They love you already, and for my poor sake will obey you in all things—so you shall learn to use the bow—let me teach you a lesson or two, which you may practise during my absence."

To this Edith laughingly acquiesced, and for about a quarter of an hour all thought was given to the noble art of bowcraft, which so mainly assisted to make England what she is.

Then came a sound of steps at no great distance; one hasty embrace and he was gone.

"My lady abbess asks for you," said the handmaiden.

"Tell her I wait on her," replied Edith. "Go forward and announce my coming."

The girl obeyed, while Edith slowly followed, stilling the tell-tale beating of her heart, to meet the worthy abbess, who, however, merely wanted her to join in a little extra festivity which that excellent women allowed herself on Saturdays after prayers.

The woman was exemplary in her conduct, and good in her heart, but like many other good and exemplary people, she had no objection to a well-spread table.

MAID MARIAN'S FIRST SHOT.

CHAPTER LXXX.

THE SPY.

MEANWHILE, with a light and springy step, the outlaw walked onwards, not exactly himself aware of where he was going.

He was for the nonce too happy to reflect or plan. He moved in an atmosphere of sunshine, so that he could scarcely see. Its very dazzlingness blinded him.

The general direction he knew, as his idea was to scour the forest in search of some of his men, with whom to pass the evening, not caring to walk that night as far as any of his own more immediate haunts.

Love has various effects upon various men; some indulge in solitude, there to muse upon their fair one's charms, but Robin Hood was essentially companionable, and would rather find a boon companion, upon whom to spend his exuberant spirits than waste them all upon the desert air.

And still as he walked he sang, though not in a very loud tone, some of those ditties which the wandering minstrels of the age had rendered so popular.

In this way the portion of forest which he proposed to traverse was soon crossed, and yet not a sign of any of his people had he met with.

Night was coming on, and the bold outlaw began to think he should spend his evening alone, when he came upon a spot which then, and during his whole life, was a favourite resort.

There was a remarkable group of stones or rocks near a place called Haddon Hall, surrounded on all sides by trees and dense underwood, popularly believed to be Druidical remains; and here the outlaw resolved to halt for the night, being disappointed in his idea of finding company, alone.

The stones were in a deep dell or hollow that could only be reached by a narrow pathway, overshadowed by trees, and here Robin Hood thought he should like to build him a sylvan palace for his future wife, in the belief that here they would be free from any of the ordinary annoyances of the world.

It was, indeed, in the soft twilight, a charming spot, and well worthy of the outlaw's predilection.

And now we shall see how love will blind a man, and how little notice he takes of external things when the heart is full and the mind occupied with thoughts and feelings that wrap us round as with a cloud.

On ordinary occasions no one could be more observant than Robin, but in the present instance his vigilance relaxed.

As he made his way through the forest, ordinary attention would have made him aware that he was followed, that his footsteps had been dogged ever since he left the convent.

Whoever it was made no attempt to come up with him, but rather kept in the background, as if anxious to escape observation. When Robin stopped he stopped; when Robin advanced he did the same, and always so stealthily that it was nearly impossible for the keenest ear to detect a sound.

Once or twice the outlaw had entertained a slight suspicion, sufficient to make him halt and listen, but his ears heard only the chattering jay, or merry laugh of the woodpecker; the other showing marvellous skill in concealing his presence.

The English yeoman had none of that instinctive power which appears to appertain to American hunters, who can *feel* the presence of pursuers when they are miles behind!

The outlaw, however, omitted none of the precautions essential to be observed by men who war with the world. He paused some moments ere he descended the rude pathway into the dell, and when at last he reached his usual halting-place, he stooped behind one of the stones and peered slowly and cautiously round.

Not a sound met his ears, not a sign indicated the presence of any enemy.

Robin accordingly ensconced himself in his usual place, made a fire, and, having given up some little time to thoughts of the absent, cast himself on the ground, with his cloak around him, to seek rest, of which he was much in need.

Like all men who live in the open air, he slept easily, nor did he wake for some hours, when the hooting of an owl induced him to shift his position somewhat, as one does naturally when disturbed by any unusual sound.

He then laid his head again upon his earthern pillow, and would next minute have gone off once more into the land of dreams, when he heard something which made him lift his head and listen attentively.

It was the heavy breathing of a man at no great distance.

In another minute the outlaw was moving up the path with the slowness of one who knew the importance of surprising the intruder.

At the very head of the dell he nearly stumbled against the body of a man, who had evidently fallen fast asleep while in the act of watching.

Robin Hood stooped.

He was no outlaw, neither was he a retainer of any of the great prelate with which Robin Hood had recently had differences.

What was he, then—a common robber, or a spy hoping to making money by revealing his haunts?

Whichever was the truth, it behoved him to assure himself; as were spies allowed to roam the greenwood, their band would easily be broken up—their chief reliance being in the inviolability of their secret fastnesses.

With a dexterity which indicated some practice, the chief of the merry men pulled some cord from his pouch, and quietly tied the man to the tree against which he was already leaning, not forgetting to secure his hands.

He then walked quietly away, and resumed his couch, sleeping none the less soundly for the propinquity of his neighbour.

But a little after daylight he was roused by loud cries, oaths, and expostulations, which he at once knew proceeded from the mouth of the captive, whose surprise and indignation at his humiliating position may be more readily conceived than easily described.

With a grim smile, Robin Hood walked in his direction, and stood for a moment facing him with a look in which auger was blended with contempt.

One glance in the daylight was enough. He was a retainer of the Bishop of Hereford.

"I say, you yeoman in Lincoln green, are you going to leave off this joke?" he said, at last.

"Joke!" said Robin Hood, sternly, "I think you will find it no joke. How, in your part of the world, do you serve spies?"

"Spies!" cried the other, with a cold perspiration bursting out upon his forehead; "what know I of spies?"

Robin Hood, who had been contemplating him with a look of superb contempt, started from his half-musing and apparently careless attitude, and lifting a bugle-horn to his lips, blew a loud peculiar blast, which made every dingle and dell ring again with their doubling echoes.

Scarcely had they died away, when four archers came running up to their chief, to whom they bowed low.

"See here, my merry men, a spy whom I found last night prowling round the dell. What is the punishment which our laws provide for such crimes?"

One of the outlaws, with a grim smile and grimmer frown, took a stout rope from his pocket, and pointing to a branch overhead, made a significant jerk with his thumb under the man's neck.

"It is but just. We molest not such as these; why will they not leave us in peace? Hang me this man up for the crows to feed upon—'twill be a warning to the next."

Robin turned away as he spoke, as if to shut out the horrible spectacle of the wretch's execution.

The outlaws untied him from the tree, and binding his arms in the approved style, prepared to carry out their chieftain's orders with the utmost calmness.

"Sir yeoman," said the bishop's retainer, in a tone which was expressive both of anguish and determination, "my body swinging from a bough will do thee no good, especially as I shall carry a secret useful to you with me."

"I care not for thy secrets, knave," replied Robin Hood, "which you may invent to save thy wretched life."

"I invent nothing. That which is to happen is the fortune of war. I but do the bidding of my master; but as my game is played out, if you will give me my life, I will tell you something which will be of service to you and to your men."

"Out with it!" said Robin.

"But have I your word?"

"If you tell me honest truth you shall have pardon," cried the outlaw, who never intended to hang him.

"Sir yeoman, if you be, as I have no doubt, bold Robin Hood, know that the Bishop of Hereford will not forgive the slight you have put upon him. He and Sir Guy de Lussac have resolved to leave no stone unturned to find you. He bade me follow you at a distance, promising me house, land, and money if I would discover your secret places, and enable him to capture you."

"And this is the truth?" quoth Robin Hood.

"The whole truth, my masters."

"I will believe you—and so go. But tell the bishop to beware. As certainly as he comes into the forest he shall have a welcome which he will never forget. Let him face me like a man, and not try to trap me by surprise and treachery."

This was spoken with dignity, at the same time that it was uttered in a tone of deep indignation.

"I will faithfully record your words; but the bishop is very angry, and will never rest until he meets you," said the retainer.

"The sooner the better," cried Robin; "but warn him that he comes not empty-handed, or he will get no victuals from the merry men."

The baffled spy bowed low, in token of his thanks to Robin Hood, and went on his way, rejoicing at having so easily escaped from men who bore with his people but an indifferent reputation.

Robin Hood was wrapped in deep thought for some time; after which he gave minute directions to his men, who were then despatched in different directions to carry orders to various detachments of his band.

CHAPTER LXXXI.

THE BISHOP OF HEREFORD.

WE must pass over two whole days, during which nothing occurred noteworthy to those whose history we are recording, and carry our readers to a different part of the wood.

In the neighbourhood of the various towns which here and there dotted fair Sherwood were pastures where fed sheep belonging to different landholders and farmers.

One of these was directly on the road which led from the city of Sheffield, where the Bishop of Hereford was temporarily residing, to that part of the forest where the sylvan retreat of Robin Hood was situated.

It was a charming forest glade, with here and there a tree; but chiefly consisted of cleared land, upon which the grass grew in rich abundance most grateful to the animals which are so useful to man, both for food and clothing.

About three hours after dawn, in the very centre of the glade, under a pair of oaks which so intertwined their boughs as to be like one tree, was collected a rude group of men—some six or more—engaged in preparing a feast.

They wore the primitive and coarse costume of shepherds, of which an untanned sheepskin coat, with the wool on, was the most conspicuous characteristic.

Their faces were bronzed by constant exposure to the weather, while their features, as a rule, were gaunt and fierce.

Upon the present occasion, however, there was an unusual sparkle in their eyes as they watched the feast which the youngest and best-looking of the party was in the act of preparing.

He wore the same rude costume as the others, but his features were more regular, and his cheeks plumper and fuller than those of his companions.

He had but just skinned and dressed a fat buck, which he was now busily engaged in roasting whole before a splendid fire; an occupation which appeared to afford his companions the most intense satisfaction, though an eager desire to begin was depicted on every countenance.

But the young man took no notice whatever, pacing round and round as the wooden spit revolved with its savoury load.

The fire was good—the cook knew his work; so that after the lapse of some time, during which a very large quantity of wood was consumed, the roast began to emit a most agreeable odour.

The shepherds began to smack their lips with anticipation and impatience.

At this moment the noise of horses was heard close at hand. The shepherds rose to their feet, and would have fled; but not only did the words of the youth restrain them, but far more effectually, an armed party of men, at whose head rode the proud and haughty bishop.

He looked at them with a fierce and awful mien.

"What is all this, my masters?" he said, with the velvety softness of voice which is alarming to those who understand it. "For whom do you make such a feast, and of the king's venison, verily? I must look into this."

"We are shepherds—simply shepherds!" said the young man, meekly. "We keep sheep the whole year round, and as this is our holiday, we thought there was no harm in holding it on one of the king's deer, of which there are plenty, and to spare."

"No harm!" sneered the bishop.

"None!" said the youth, while the others exchanged terrified glances, "since they live wild in the forest."

"Indeed, my fine fellows," cried the prelate; "indeed, my mighty fine fellows; this is the way the forest laws are obeyed? But the king shall know of your doings; so quit your roast, for to him you shall go, and that quickly."

All the shepherds, save the one who served as cook, fell on their knees, crying for mercy.

"Oh, pardon! pardon!" they said, "oh pardon us, we pray; for it ill becomes a holy bishop's coat to take men's lives away."

The bishop, however, looked sternly at the men, he having always been a bitter enforcer of the game-laws.

"No pardon! no pardon!" was his cold reply. "Therefore, make you haste; for I swear by St. Paul, before the king you shall go."

The young shepherd who had acted as cook peered curiously—almost comically—into the bishop's face, as he placed his back against a tree.

"And this, holy father," he said, "is your reply?"

"Seize me this insolent, knave!" was the answer. "He at least shall pay for all the others."

But the shepherd leaped back, drew forth a small horn, and setting it to his mouth, made the wood ring.

The bishop and his men closed together, fully suspecting what would happen.

"'Tis that pestilent knave, Robin Hood," whispered the bishop, biting his lips till the blood came.

But his astonishment may be conceived, when from all parts of the wood there poured forth the men in Lincoln green, headed by Little John, Will Scarlett, and others of the noted leaders of the outlaws.

The bishop's guard would have made resistance, but the prelate, who had some regard for his own person, forbade them, and surrendered at discretion.

His alarm, however, was great indeed when he found that Little John was before him, rolling his eyes, twisting his moustaches, and making altogether such fearful grimaces as might even have intimidated a bolder man.

"So," he said, "this is the Bishop of Hereford—this is the cruel churchman, who robs the poor, and oppresses the weak. Do you cut off his head, Robin, while I go dig him a grave."

The prelate fell back appalled. He looked at his men. They had been disarmed, and there was no hope there. He must fain humble himself; though, perhaps, if he had but seen the merry twinkle in Robin's eyes, he might have been less particular.

As it was, he spoke in a soft and whining voice.

"Pardon me, good sir; had I known you were so near, I would have gone another way," he said.

"No pardon! no pardon!" replied Robin Hood.

The bishop turned ghastly pale. He little knew the bold outlaw, who had not only no pleasure in shedding blood, but while loving to enjoy the terrors of those he captured, never took life except in self-defence.

When large parties of rich nobles, or priests and abbots, with their guard, were to be attacked, he always took care that the attacking force should be overwhelmed by numbers, thus, in general, avoiding a useless contest.

"Sir outlaw!" mumbled the late, haughty priest, "you have misjudged me. I sought but to frighten these shepherds, whom, for your sake, I will freely pardon, and hold from harm."

"Well said," cried Robin, looking the bishop full in the face, "but how shall it fare with myself and followers if I let you go? will you incite the prince to persecute me—yes or no?"

"I am not ungenerous," said the bishop, evasively, "and never forget a favour."

"'Tis well, then," continued Robin Hood, with a gay laugh, "we may yet be friends—but this night thou shalt sup with me in merry Barnesdale in the clear moonlight, and taste my red wine and ale."

The bishop made a wry face but said nothing, being quite assured now how the matter would end.

Robin now bade the hungry shepherds fall to, and then retreat into the forest, to a pleasant and retired part of which it was the intention of the chief to take his guest.

It was the trysting-place of Hart-hill Walk.

The place of rendezvous was an aged oak, with a throne of turf erected under the twisted branches, upon which Robin seated himself, giving the bishop one near him.

A feast of venison collops, wine, and ale was soon spread out, and even the prisoners did justice to it, so powerful was nature in them.

But the prelate was all the while uneasy, and anxious to be away.

For some time he turned over in his mind some means of escaping, with as little injury to his purse and person as possible.

At length he came to a resolution.

"I wish mine host," he said, with a grim smile, that but ill became his saturnine features, "that you would now call a reckoning; it is getting late, and I fear that the cost of such an entertainment will be high."

Robin Hood bowed courteously.

"I never interfere in these matters. Here, Little John, what say, will you be tapster?"

"That will I, noble captain. Give me thy purse, sir bishop, and I will settle the reckoning."

The churchman dearly loved his gold, but he knew he was completely powerless.

"My purse is in yonder portmanteau," he said, with a deep and reluctant sigh.

Little John rose with extreme gravity, and opening the portmanteau, spread the haughty dignitary's cloak upon the ground, and then opening the purse proceeded to count out the contents, which proved to be three hundred pounds.

The bishop watched him with dark and saturnine smile, mentally determined to devote his every energy to the extermination of a body of men who had no respect for holy mother church.

"Art satisfied?" he said, tartly; "or do you really in gravity mean to take all?"

"I am as grave as a father confessor," said the king of Sherwood forest. "I know 'tis a round ransom, sir bishop, but ye have rich abbeys, much wheat and barley, with every fruit of the earth, not forgetting wood. We have not given you the sweet wines you love so well, but the fare has been homely and good.''

"I object not to the fare," said the bishop, demurely, "but to the price paid for it. I thought if you were robbers, you had some Christian charity in you.''

"If we have not Christian charity as you understand it, we have divinity—expound, oh friar, the laws of the woods to this most reverend father.''

Friar Tuck, who rarely was absent from a feast, stepped forward, half drunk, half sober.

"Holy father," he began, "welcome to the greenwood. *Deus faciat salvum benignitatem vestram.*''

"What have we here?" cried the irate priest, "what mockery is this? 'Tis but a hedge priest I see—avaunt, *excommunicato vos!*''

"It is useless to be angry, holy father. I have but to tell you that this is St. Andrew's day, and you cannot pass without paying tithes.''

The bishop turned away, leaving the money on the ground, and signed to his men to mount their horses and attend him, which they did.

And terrible was the vow of vengeance which the bishop muttered against all.

How he kept his vow we shall presently see.

CHAPTER LXXXII.

THE FOUR BEGGARS.

FOR some days the outlaws remained in comparative idleness, resting and enjoying themselves; but it was not in the nature of the chiefs to be long without seeking those adventures on which their existence mainly depended.

Driven from the pale of society, and deprived of the means of living by honest labour, they were compelled to support themselves and their families by levying contributions on the public.

Robin Hood, Little John, and Will Scarlett, accordingly one morning agreed, after dispersing their men in different parts of the forest, to take each different routes, with an arrangement to meet at a given spot on the following day, when all hoped to have some good news to communicate to the other.

We will, in the first instance, follow in the footsteps of the tall forester who, though so recently inducted into his post of a lieutenant, was already extremely popular with the men.

One plan of the outlaws was to post detachments of archers in such positions that when wanted they could easily be found, and as these posts were chiefly near roads where the wealthy, on whom they preyed, travelled, it may be readily understood how it was, that at sound of horn there was in general always a party ready to come to the rescue.

John had assumed a disguise which was a favourite one with the merry men.

It was a palmer's weed, with a staff and coat and bags of each sort.

The only visible weapon which he carried was a staff, but this was long and thick, and until the introduction of firearms no more useful means of attack or defence could have been placed in the hands of a man so powerful and active.

The tall forester having bade adieu to his comrades, took his way under the leafy forest, with a steady and measured tread that well became his portly and powerful figure.

The direction selected by him was towards the high road so often alluded to, it being his hope to find something there worth the trouble he was taking.

But the way was long, the paths intricate, the day warm, so that Little John made but moderate progress, though at twelve he was a long way from the general rendezvous.

According to the usual custom of the time, the sun reaching its meridian was the signal for a halt, which the outlaw made on a solitary and deserted spot.

For some time, to avoid the noontide heat, he had been following a wild bridle path, one of the many which ran through the forest, and were in some places almost dark with the overhanging branches.

The hazel copse, from which he at last emerged, skirted the sides and bottom of a deep valley or glen, that was hemmed in by high banks on either hand, and so precipitously steep, as to be all but inaccessible to human

footsteps; and what with their approaching each other so closely, and the gloominess of the intermingled branches overhead, the spot was so dark as to give the appearance of deep twilight.

A rapid rivulet also coursed through the steep and dusky glen, dashing downwards with a gibbering, melancholy sound, and showing here and there white masses of foam.

No other sound could be heard save the rustling of a few hollies and blackthorns, which shot out from the clefts and fissures of the bank.

But Little John only cared to know that the place was secure and solitary so hastily devouring his mid-day meal, he cast himself on the sward to take his mid-day nap, of which, being a very early riser, he was particularly fond.

The outlaw, however, never gave more than an hour to this luxurious refreshment, and from habit woke to his time, sat up, and prepared to resume his journey.

But his surprise was great, when he heard voices at no great distance, voices of men either in loud converse or altercation.

He rose to his feet, and clutching his trusty staff, crept slowly through the bushes towards the river.

In a few minutes he came in view of a group which somewhat startled him.

It was composed of four sturdy beggars, well known to the tall forester; beggars who haunted the purlieus of the forest, waylaid the charitable, and even at times levied their contributions as much by insolence as entreaty.

But what made Little John stare was a remarkable change that had come over them all.

One who pleaded incurable deafness and dumbness as an excuse for asking the assistance of the charitable was listening to the conversation without the slightest hesitation.

Two others, reputed blind, were gazing around with keen and intelligent eyes, that could see as plain as the keenest hawk or bustard.

The fourth, who was used to hobble on crutches, was making up for his usual inactivity by dancing with the utmost zest round a tree.

All had just partaken of a copious and luxurious meal, as might be seen from the fragments; and were now solacing themselves with wine from huge bottles, which they contrived, when carrying on their trade, to conceal beneath their loose coats.

The dancer had a number of bells fastened to his cap, which made a merry jingling by way of music.

"Enough of that, Diccon," said the deaf man; "you split my ears with your noise.''

"Ah, ah! my merry master; you are the child of a miracle. Where be your deafness now?''

"Where your lameness has gone to," replied the other, laughing.

The blind men laughed too; and the dancer, probably tired of his exertions, seated himself on the grass.

"And now," said one of the blind men, after a short pause, "allow me to call your attention to the articles of our association.''

"With pleasure.''

"Once a month on this green sward we meet to report our progress, dine, and divide whatever fortune may have thrown in our way—which then belongs to us by right, and goes to the support of our wives and families.''

"Exactly.''

"I have been fortunate this month," said the blind man, who seemed by right of prescriptive rascality to be the leader of the band. "By virtue of my infirmity" (this was said with an ignoble grin) "I am admitted to many houses, where no secrets are kept from me. I slept, a week ago, at Sir Gammel's, and *saw* his worship lock up a number of gold pieces, taken by sale of swine, which in the night I appropriated, and left in the morning utterly unsuspected. They are in my wallet.''

"Oh, oh!" thought Little John, "here is a pretty rascal. I'll make you see presently.''

"I have not been without my luck," said the second blind man. "Left in the chapel of St. Joveau, I contrived to hide away good store of gold and silver plate, which I sold to Isaac of York, for a fair price, and there it is in my wallet.''

The other two men had similar exploits to relate, but which need not be particularised here.

"'Tis well!" said blind man number one; "ye have

all been good men and true; no risking necks and broken bones, like the foolish outlaws of Sherwood forest. Now then pour out all you have on to my cloak, and I will apportion it out into four parts."

"Five!" said a terrible voice close at hand, and the tall outlaw stood before them.

"What is there to do, sirs?" said Little John;
"Why ring all those bells?" said he;
"Whose dog is a hanging! now let us be ganging,
That we the plain truth may see."

The beggars exchanged startled glances.

"There is no dog a hanging," said the first beggar; and then he added, in a significant and threatening tone, "but there is a man will soon be dead, who will afford us bread and cheese, and possibly one poor penny."

"We have brethren in London," said the second beggar, fiercely; "so we have in Coventry, in Berwick, and Dover, and all the world over, but ne'er a crooked carle like thee."

At the same moment he jumped up, clutching as he did so a stout cudgel.

"Stand back, thou crooked carle!" he said, "and take that crack on the crown."

"A fight! a fight!" cried Little John; "and before I leave I will have a bout with you all."

The four sturdy beggars were already on their feet, with their cudgels ready for action.

"Fight one, fight all!" exclaimed Little John, with great glee, and to work he went.

The men were clearly accustomed to the work, for they began in a scientific way, but they were ill prepared for such a pelting and pitiless shower of blows as Little John rained upon them.

It was done with such terrible rapidity as to admit of no warding off.

Little John first settled the deaf and dumb man, making him run manfully; the two blind men he made to see more stars than ever studded the firmament; while he that was lame he made to run with unexampled rapidity.

In five minutes the beggars took to their heels—one running east, another west, yelling as if Satan himself had been at their heels, eager for his prey.

Little John, after one of his silent but hearty laughs, seated himself on the grass, and began counting out the contents of the wallets, in which he found more than he could possibly have hoped for, even after hearing their stories.

There was six hundred and three pounds.

"If I drink water while this doth last," he cried aloud, "then may I die an ill death."

The spoil was speedily put away about the giant's person, who then in the highest spirits started on his way, leaving the beggars to reflect on the instability of all things human, and of gold in particular.

Little John's intention was to reach a small ale-house, near the village of Papple, and there pass the night, quite satisfied that he had done enough for one day, though had anything tempting have been cast in his way, he would, in all probability, not have rejected the opportunity.

"Oh, my begging trade, I will now give over," he cried, "my fortune hath been so good."

And singing merrily, so as to wake the echoes of old Sherwood, he started on his way, thinking no more of his valuable load than if the gold had been a pound of feathers.

CHAPTER LXXXIII.
EDWIN.

SCATTERED over the forest, here and there, were numerous huts, chiefly inhabited by swineherds and others of the poorer class, though on occasion they were the residences of families who owned patches of property, which they farmed on their own account, the said land being their own property sometimes, at others, being leased to them by larger owners.

All these persons were rigorously restricted from shooting the king's deer, and, if found, were punished with the most fearful severity—a severity which was the main origin of the bloody character of our laws until a very recent period.

Though the Normans have died out root and branch, their code remained years in the statute book.

It was a code of blood.

It would be out of place here to enter into any detail of the clauses which allowed keepers to pursue stray deer over the purlieus or cultivated lands, and all the vexatious privileges by which they were reclaimed.

The boundaries were difficult and almost undefined, consisting of a tree, a mill, a hut, or any other object, perhaps a mile apart from the next mark; and the imaginary line between these was too often left to the decision of some tyrannical officer.

Pasture lands were at this time almost wholly open, or at best but indifferently enclosed; so that one may easily guess the many altercations that took place between the keepers and those who wandered into the forest in search of stray cattle.

If a man was found armed, or stationed in any suspicious part of the forest, or with the marks of blood upon him, or carrying a cord, or followed by a dog which had not had its fore-claws struck off—he was amenable to the laws.

We are within an arrow's flight of the dense forest.

The sun had long sank amid masses of dark and fiery clouds, and night was gathering gloomily over the forest.

Loud and terrible claps of thunder, attended with quick and successive flashes of lightning, told that the tempest which had long thrown its threatening shadow over the sky had at last burst forth.

The huge forest trees were all astir with their grating branches, and large heavy rain-drops clattered among the foliage, which, mingled with the loud rumbling thunder, now near or afar off, sounded like the grand but fearful rolling of the ocean.

An aged man and an aged woman sat cowering over a rather large fire, always welcome at night in the damp regions of the forest.

They sat peering at the flickering flames, buried in their own sad thoughts.

Something had cast a gloom over their souls.

They listened between the crashes to every sound from without, and it needed no conjurer to say, from their continued and startled glances towards the door, that they expected some one who came not.

"'Tis a terrible night," said the old man, "and I would that Edwin were not abroad."

"'Tis a wilful lad, a wilful lad," groaned the old woman, "and I fear me will get into trouble."

"Scarcely to-night, except from the tempest," continued the aged speaker; "'tis the tempest I am fearful of now."

And rising, he went for the hundredth time to the door, and peered out into the darkness.

As he did so there came a red lurid flash that seemed to fill the forest with light, attended by a deep and awful peal of thunder, which striking an oak on the edge of the forest, rent it into a thousand shivers, and scattered the riven branches far and wide around.

The old man stood petrified, gazing with fearful wonder at the sudden destruction and the huge white splinters, which were visible in the darkness.

As he did so he heard a rustling close at hand, and two men stepped forward.

The old man, considering the hour and the lawless character of the forest denizens, would have closed his door; but the men darted forward, and one put his pole in such a way that the door could not close.

"Ah! thieves, villains—what means this?" shouted the enraged Saxon.

"'Tis I, father, with a friend," was the eager reply.

"My son—my dear son!" cried the old man, and the two men were dragged in and the door made fast.

The youth whom the fond grandmother and grandfather had been so unhappy about was a tall, slight, wiry chap of eighteen, with some promise of increased bulk as he grew older, but with a peculiarly shrewd expression of countenance.

"St. Dunstan shield us!" said the old man; "what hast been doing in the wood such a night as this? Surely you have not been to Gaffer May's to-night?"

The youth blushed, though why, except that Gaffer May had a pretty daughter, it would have been hard to tell.

"Nay, not half so far. I was seeking practice with my bow when this good archer came up, and the storm threatening, we hastened hither in search of shelter."

"Thy bow wilt bring thee into trouble," said the old man, shaking his head.

"How so?"

"You know the forest laws—and if caught touching the king's deer, will suffer loss of thy hand at least."

"Nay, good grandfather, I fear not the keepers. I take good care never to practice but when I am safe. But no more—we are hungry. What can we have to eat?"

"There is bacon and some eggs, with a few of the old pickled eels," began the old man.

"The nights are long, and the moon has been clear. Hast never enough meat for a venison collop?" said the stranger, in a deep, commanding, but pleasant voice.

The old man trembled.

"Dost think we want to bring the vengeance of our masters on us?" he said.

"I am an outlaw, a bitter enemy to our masters, and one who chooses to claim the deer as my own; so fear not me. I absolve you beforehand for anything of the kind you may have done."

"Bring out the pasty and fear nothing," laughed the thoughtless youth.

"A wilful child will have his way, though he die for it," replied the antiquated personage who owned the house. "Sit down; your supper shall be put before you."

And soon it was, proving very satisfactory to and good men who had toiled for hours in the forest.

As soon as it was consumed, it was hastily cleared away, lest any other visitors were to arrive, and the whole party prepared to make their arrangements for the night.

The old people retired to an inner room, while the youth and the outlaw prepared to make themselves as comfortable as they could.

The grandson of the old people had met the outlaw in the forest, and had been caught by him shooting a buck, which he did in such good style that he obtained the applause and commendation of the archer.

The buck shot, however, had not been brought home, but secreted high in the branches of a tree, to be used as wanted.

Death had been the result had the dead carcase been discovered in the house.

Just after they had secreted the animal the storm began, and the stranger gladly accepted the offer of the youth to attend him to his home.

CHAPTER LXXXIV.

GAME LAWS.

THE night was not quite spent, a semi-darkness brooded over forest and upland, when the inmates of the hut were violently aroused by an angry knocking at the door.

Both started up, and Edwin wou'd have opened, but his companion, more cautious, peered through the chinks.

"'Tis seven stout forest rangers, with one I know well at their head, for a man as brave as cruel. Young man, will you trust to me?"

"With my life."

"Conceal me, make no resistance, and offer to take the men to where the dead deer is hidden. Be brave and circumspect, and before six hours you shall be free, and the keepers so punished they will not trouble thee again."

The youth seemed to hesitate.

The outlaw whispered a word.

The young man clasped his hands, while a wild light of enthusiasm and pleasure shone in his eyes.

The old people came in to know the reason of the noise. Edwin bade them first hide the stranger, and neither by word or deed betray his presence. All will be well. I shall be taken away, only to return in a few hours."

The old people, terrified but passively obedient, placed the outlaw in a dark corner behind some faggots, just as the door was assailed again with extreme violence.

"Coming! coming!" cried the old woman, beside herself all the while with terror.

"You'd better, ere we fire your old battered hut," said a gruff and insolent voice.

The door was at once opened, and the keepers tumultuously rushed in.

Edwin remained standing up with flushed face and folded arms.

"So, my pretty springal," said the fierce keeper, clutching him by the arm, "we have caught you at last."

"Why he's as innocent as a babe unborn," whined the old woman.

"Silence, midnight hag!" shouted the keeper, "lest I burn thy old barn about your ears. Wilt answer, boy?"

"What ask you?"

"You shot a deer last night?"

"I did."

The old people clasped their hands at this frank declaration, while the rangers exchanged meaning glances.

"You did, did you?"

"I did, and will do it again whenever it so fancies me. They are wild beasts intended for our sustenance and not for the mere amusement of the great," replied Edwin, hotly.

"Soho! we talk treason do we? bind his arms."

This was done expeditiously.

"And now, unless you produce the deer at once, I will set fire to this thatch."

"I will produce the deer."

"Ah! where is it?"

"Near the Black Mass pool, where I fell it during the storm," said Edwin, undauntedly.

"Every cock crows on his own dunghill!" laughed the keeper, "we shall see if you will be so impudent before the justice."

"Justice!" said Edwin, "where is there a justice in all wide England?—faugh! talk not of justice."

"Marry! an'you speak thus you will hang as a traitor——bind his hands and forward."

The followers of the ranger obeyed, and the brave and gallant youth was dragged forth, leaving the old people to lament their sudden and terrible loss.

"Fear not, my good people," said the outlaw, stepping forward, "there is one in this forest will see that no harm comes to the lad, but ye must agree to part with him for a while—even until this quarrel blows over."

"But shall we see him sometimes?" whimpered the poor old woman.

"You shall see him safe, sound, and free this very day, but only for a short time," was the reply; "and now, fare ye well for a while—I go to save him."

"Thanks, noble sir!" they cried.

But ere they had uttered the words, the stranger had quite vanished from their sight, walking towards the forest at such a pace as to indicate anxiety to keep the others in sight.

The man in Lincoln green, who had so earnestly promised to rescue the poor victim of the vile feudal laws, had himself only a very vague idea of how it was to be done.

The part of the forest he was in was not one frequented by Robin Hood and his bold outlaws, except by such a chance occurrence as that which had made him take shelter in the hut.

Still he was not without hope that he should be able to muster force enough to attack the rangers, and thus obtain a rescue of the youth, who else would suffer some dreadful and cruel punishment.

One thing he was particularly anxious to do, and that was to reach the Black Moss pool before, or as soon, as the keepers, who there might be induced, by the sight of the fat and juicy buck, to make a halt, when they might, while feasting, be easily surprised and overcome by even an inferior force.

But no man, however brave, could hope to cope with seven stalwart rangers, except by lying in ambush and slaying them all one by one, a proceeding strongly repugnant to the feelings of nearly all the outlawed patriots, who, could they have but obtained decent liberties for England, would have returned to their posts as decent members of quiet and industrious society.

But no Norman understood any other meaning in relation to liberty save that of licence.

It must be remembered that nearly all those who obeyed the sway of Robin Hood were men who, having transgressed some abominable mandate of the Norman tyrant, had been proclaimed throughout the district, and not having appeared at the given time, were declared outlaws, whose punishment, if caught, was death.

What wonder, therefore, that they should betake to the forest, repel force by force, and defy both the Normans and their laws.

They did not, however, confine themselves to attack on the barons or their followers.

Imitating the petty tyrants of the hour, they levied tolls upon travellers, confining themselves, however, to the rich and powerful, and often secretly executing more daring plans than the Norman, with all his retainers, dared to attempt.

Hence such expeditions as we have already recorded, and which were executed with such remarkable impunity.

Taking his way under the leafy canopy of the trees, the outlaw hurried away, taking from sheer instinct a much quicker way than that which had been followed by Edwin, under whose guidance the rangers had to move, in order to discover the deer which, when found, was to cause his conviction of the crime of which he was accused.

Still, the pathway followed by the outlaw was not a very straight line; as so many rivulets had to be crossed, so many thickets to be avoided, it was doubled in length, nearly always the case in forests which have not been cleared by the hand of man or the action of fire.

Fretting and fuming at what appeared perilous delay, the archer soon came in sight of a village, one of the very humblest of its kind, but still, as usual, not without its small ale-house, as might be seen from the buck which hung over the doorway.

The man was thirsty from his walk, and therefore determined to refresh himself with a drink.

He hastily made his way in the required direction, and was checked on the threshold by the sound of a merry voice, which gave forth, with great glee, an extract from a ditty ascribed to that day, but which some say is much older.

> Drink! drink! drink!
> Both layman and priest have a part in the feast,
> The church and the cowl, the bowman and bowl.
> We'll merrily, merrily troll,
> With a hey down derry;
> We'll ever more be merry.

A grim smile passed over the other's face as he slowly entered the inn, where, with some half-dozen peasants about them, all listening and drinking their ale, sat Friar Tuck and Little John, who were, doubtless, spending some of the money which the huge forester had taken from the four sturdy beggars.

They were so intent on their favourite amusement—the favourite amusement in those days of all the Saxons, high and low, which in part accounts for their subjugation by the temperate Normans—that the outlaw entered the room unperceived even by the landlord.

"I say," said Little John, "that Robin Hood is a man—yes, a man; and I don't care who knows—the friend of the poor and of the oppressed—the enemy of the tyrant and the Norman."

"And of all fat priors and greedy bishops," chimed in Friar Tuck.

The rustics, who had been drinking strong ale until they almost began to forget their sorrows and their fears, gave a faint chorus of applause—very weak and feeble it is true, but clearly demonstrative of the real feelings existent in their bosoms.

"If there were ten men in merry England like the king of Sherwood, we should have our own again," continued Little John; "and Saxon churl would set his foot on Norman neck—and that's the honest truth."

"Dominus—pax vobiscum," muttered the drunken friar, not knowing what he said.

"These be dangerous words, my friends, and hawks abroad," said a stern commanding voice. "You run your own necks into a noose while making such supreme asses of yourselves before these churls, whose backs will suffer, perhaps, for listening to you."

The two boon companions turned fiercely to the insolent intruder, with half anger, half fear.

Their gaze was met by a clear eye and a compressed lip, that made both shiver.

"When the ale is in the wit is out," said Little John, speaking quite humbly.

The friar only made a wry face; and then his countenance was gathered up in such a way as he thought might best express the most profound contrition—his eyes being turned up and the corners of his mouth turned down, like the tassels at the mouth of a purse.

There was, however, a ludicrous humour in his eye which belied his pretended fear and repentance.

"But a *little* good ale giveth wisdom, while, if you *tuck* in too much, words escape your lips which you may afterward repent. Give me the bowl, good giant, and let me drink to our better acquaintance and more discretion."

Little John rose, and handed the huge jug to the strange outlaw with manifest satisfaction.

As he did so his head was bent low.

The outlaw whispered two or three words.

He then drank, rose, left some change for one more jug of ale, and went forth.

The friar also rose, went into the yard behind, stripped off his gown, and appeared in a close black buckram doublet and drawers, over which he speedily passed a cassock of green, and hose of the same colour.

He then stepped to a stone basin, in which the waters of a fountain as they fell formed bubbles which danced in the sunlight, and took a draught, as if he intended to exhaust the spring.

He then rose, refreshed, clear-headed, and quite sober.

CHAPTER LXXXV.
ROSE LEIGH.

WE must, however, return to young Edwin, who, with mingled feelings of hope and doubt, continued on his way with his captors.

He was truly a brave and valiant youth, almost to rashness; but he was young, and loved those sunny hours of life which never come twice, and which cease the moment we plunge into the restless turmoil of the world.

He loved to tread the wild heather under the warm rays of a lovely summer morning; he loved to listen to the sweet music of the thousand and one rills of the forest; he loved to hear the feathered choristers sing their early matins; but, above all, he loved to sip honey from the lips of the girl he loved, and to hear her softly whisper, "I love you."

It was, therefore, with some anxiety, he walked along with his savage captors, who, besides carrying out the laws they were appointed to execute and defend, were fond of wreaking private vengeance on their personal enemies.

The chief keeper, a man of about thirty, and of a sullen and saturnine character, had taken into his head to honour with his affections the same girl as Edwin.

He had long been on the watch to catch him napping, and it was with profound delight that he heard from one of his spies of the act by which Edwin had become amenable to the laws.

Hate and jealousy were added to his professional feelings.

Had Edwin been aware of the private reasons the keeper had for hating him, he might have been more cautious; but he was neither careful to conceal the favour in which he was held by Rose Leigh, any more than he was as careful as he ought to have been ere shooting the dun deer.

It was entirely his personal sentiments which made him tie the youth with a rope, as escape was in any way neither easy or probable from seven men.

"Sir ranger," said Edwin, civilly, "if you will loose my arms I shall walk the easier and the quicker."

"Just so."

"And I promise that if you will remove these bonds I will faithfully lead you to the Black Moss."

"Humph!"

"My word is my bond," said the youth.

The keeper looked at him keenly, as if to assure himself of the other's truth.

Edwin looked all candour.

"Harkee, friend," he said, drawing the other close to him, while the men mechanically dropped behind, "on one condition I will not only loose your arms, but give you leg bail."

"The condition?"

"You know Rose Leigh!"

"I do."

"Give her up—and never see her again."

"Ah! sits the wind in that quarter?" cried Edwin, scornfully; "but it is useless to discuss—I will never, never give her up—never—never!"

"The law will separate you—for as sure as you go before the court of Eyre, you hang."

"I will die true to the lady of my heart."

"Bah! you once dead, she will prefer a live man to a corpse—and before a year is over we will merrily dance at our wedding," said the keeper.

"I spit upon you," cried Edwin, now comprehending the trap into which he had fallen.

"As you will, my fine springal, a short shrift will be thine. At the foot of the gallows tree you will repent."

And he stepped back, signing to two of the rangers to seize the other's arms and urge him forward.

About mid-day, with the sun shining merrily, with a balmy, placid wind replacing the storm, they reached the Black Moss pool, near which, in the branches of an oak, the youth had concealed his buck.

He quietly pointed out the oak, into which one of the rangers climbed, and at once cried out that no buck was there.

Edwin uttered an exclamation and looked the astonishment he really felt at this discovery.

"What means this, fellow? Do you fool me with tricks?" cried the irate keeper, lifting his quarterstaff.

As he spoke an archer in Lincoln green stepped from behind the oak and confronted the party.

"How now, my master, what have we here? Is this lad a thief or murderer that you bind him thus? A little more kindness might be shown when you have him safe."

"Mind thy own business, sir archer," replied the keeper, with a grim smile, "else I may mind mine enough to make me take thee off to prison with this young rascal, who hath been killing deer within forest bounds."

"But where is the deer?"

"Ah! I verily believe thou hast it," cried the ranger, angry at the other's imperturbable coolness in the presence of such overwhelming force of armed men.

"If you think so, come and take it. I care no more for thee than for thy rascally employer, the head ranger of Sherwood Forest, under whose evil deeds the shire groans, and the dark dungeons beneath his lofty castle are wet with the tears of his victims."

"Stand by the prisoner. Secure me this insolent knave, who so foully speaks of the man whose bread we eat."

He, at the same time, aimed a terrible blow at the outlaw's head with his quarterstaff, but the outlaw bounding on one side, and by a dexterous movement of his foot, overthrew his adversary, at the same time felling a second ranger to the ground with his stick, by striking him on the head.

The quarterstaff in the outlaw's hand speedily created a circle, the rangers being taken by surprise; but rousing themselves, they prepared to dash at the one terrible robber who dared to confront them; when, with a joyous cry, Little John, Friar Tuck, and a couple more of the band, came on the scene.

With a dexterous jerk of a long whittle, or wood knife, one of these cut the prisoner's bands.

The youth at once snatched up the head ranger's quarterstaff, and the *melée* became general, ending, however, in a very speedy flight on the part of the keepers, who were no match for men whose whole life was spent in practising the use of this terrible weapon.

The victors paused to take breath, and looked at one another in amazement.

The battle had been nothing like so serious or well contested as they had expected.

What now was to be done?

The outlaw, whom we need now scarcely introduce to the reader, turned to Edwin.

"Have you any idea who I am?" he said, with a smile.

"Speak, man!"

The youth kneeled gracefully.

"Thus I swear allegiance to bold Robin Hood, king of Sherwood Forest."

"Rise," said the captain of the outlaws, with dignity. "I have but done what I would to the poorest or the meanest in the land. What think you of doing?"

"I know not."

"You may not return home."

A shade passed over the countenance of Edwin.

"But I seek not to win one so young as a permanent follower. You must keep out of the way for awhile until this affair is forgotten—then you may return. But first you must visit your worthy parents. I have so promised."

The youth bowed his head. Alas! he was not thinking of them so much as of the girl of his heart.

Treason, it is true, to the old people who had replaced his parents, but treason which belongs essentially to human nature.

Rest and refreshment taken, the whole party started on the return track, soon to find that the rangers, having after their flight reunited themselves in one body, were making rapidly in the same direction.

"What can this mean?" said Edwin.

Robin Hood frowned.

"No good, I fear," continued the young man.

"I fear not, good youth," said the outlaw, "but speech will mend nothing. Forward. Life may hang on a mere thread."

And leading the way, the outlaw chief advanced at as rapid a pace as the nature of the ground would allow, all too slow, however, for the impatience of the anxious youth.

He knew the vindictiveness of the ranger well, and now that he alsok new him to be a rival, he feared he knew not what.

There was agony in this doubt.

His impatience was such that it was with difficulty Robin Hood could restrain him from advancing alone.

He was like a madman.

"Be patient," said the outlaw, calmly, "be a man. Alone you can do nothing."

Edwin groaned aloud, but made no reply.

They had advanced to within a quarter of a mile of the rude hut of the old people.

Edwin bounded like a stricken deer.

"What is the matter?"

"Smell you not the smoke borne down upon us by the wind?" replied the agonized youth.

No answer was given, but the whole party, guided by the long, low stream of pungent vapour which descended the valley, advanced with as much epeed and as little noise as was possible under the circumstances.

It was night.

CHAPTER LXXXVI.

THE FIRE.

THE chief ranger, baulked in his personal vengeance, and defeated in his official capacity, moved away from the scene of conflict with his sore and discomfited followers, breathing the most horrid imprecations on the outlaws, and murmuring vows of revenge on Edwin, which he fully intended carrying out.

The sweetest revenge of all he must defer, he knew, for some time, as Rose Leigh. engaged to Edwin, would not surrender at discretion; but the ranger's experience of women told him that in most instances absence is a sad trial of their constancy.

Women live a good deal on admiration, and care not to be admired at a distance.

They love soft words, and soul-stirring speeches, and, especially in an age when writing was nearly unknown, such things could not be communicated from a distance.

The ranger, William Thurston by name, was a bit of a cynic, but we fear that, take women all in all, he was right.

How few are faithful to the memory of the absent!

But we have said this sweet revenge must be deferred until a future period.

What his dark soul panted for was instant satisfaction for the injuries received.

In his own mind a man is always the injured party, however bad his own actions.

"A murrain on these cursed yeomen!" said William Thurston to his men. "Were I the king I would burn down the forest rather than it should shelter such arch thieves."

"How would our trade flourish?"

"That is true; but while this wood lasts they will never be exterminated. They know every fastness, dell, and cave twice as well as we do. Many an accursed dance have they led me, for which I hope yet to take revenge. But now my thoughts are how to be even with this springal," cried the ranger.

"Burn the hut over the old witch and her mate," was the brutal reply of his follower.

"By our master's sword and baldrick," continued the ranger, "the idea is a good one. But we may not burn the old people; 'twould rouse the whole country. But we can, by way of a reminder, slit their ears for them," he added, with a grin.

"I care not a jot which, so you be satisfied, Master Thurston," was the careless reply of the follower.

No more was said.

A FOREST ENCOUNTER.

They had made up their minds to one of those brutal actions which in our own day find a parallel in the wholesale evictions of cold-blooded and avaricious landlords.

The greed of vengeance is great. Once the idea formed in their minds, they were eager to carry it out.

Besides, there was another reason.

The outlaws might take it into their heads to pursue them, in which case no time was to be lost.

With grim determination on their countenances, with a fierce gleam in their eyes, they hurried on.

One might have said, a hungry band of wolves in pursuit of some noble game.

They reached the cottage a little more than a quarter of an hour before the outlaws—the bruised and wounded being unable to advance at so rapid a pace as the others.

There was the house in all the peace and tranquillity of even, and within it two prayerful, hoping hearts.

The rangers knocked loudly at the door.

The startled old woman, with trembling hands, hurried to open the door.

She expected to see Edwin.

"The ranger!" she cried; "oh, where, where is my child? Give him back to me, and I will bless you."

"I hope the young ruffian is food for crows by this time," was the brutal reply. "I left him with six inches of steel and two clothyard shafts in his body."

"Thou liest!" shrieked the aged woman; "or if thou speakest the truth, may Heaven begrudge thee six feet of earth for thy bed. May the curses of an old and childless woman ——"

"Accursed hag," cried the ranger, turning slightly pale—for like all ruffians, even the most irreligious, he was superstitious—"I did but jest with thee; the lad is safe enough, and 'tis because he is safe that I am here."

"Thank God!"

"And now, Giles-a-Godfrey, do you set fire to this heath-hag's hut. Be quick, ere those devils are on us."

The old man, who had heard all, now tottered out.

"Spare my home—the home in which I was born, in which my children, now all in heaven, saw the light. Spare it, as you wish that in your dying hour God may spare you."

"Silence, thou mate of a she-wolf witch!" cried the ruffianly soldier. "Fire the hut."

The attendants had entered, taken embers from the hearth, and placed them in the thatch, which being quite dry, and the wind fanning the flames, was soon in a complete blaze.

The old woman seemed frenzied.

"Thief, liar, oppressor, tyrant, murderer! you shall rue this day," she cried, imprudently. "I have friends in the forest, and as surely as you dare show thyself in the forest, so surely shalt thou share the fate of Rufus the Red; for thou art as evil minded and cruel as any Norman tyrant of them all."

"Pitch the old hag headlong into the blazing pile," roared the infuriated ranger; "no mercy on the delectable and damnable witch! Away with her, I say, to fire and faggot."

Two men clutched the poor old woman, who was still upon her knees, and dragged her towards the flames.

The scene was awful.

The burning house, the hot and lurid flames rising to the vaulted heavens, the black smoke driven by the howling wind, the crackling and hissing sound of the dry wood of hut and furniture, some of it a hundred years old, the imprecations of the rangers, the shrill cries of the old people, made up a scene worthy of Pandemonium.

The old woman was raised in the men's arms.

One instant more and the awful deed would have been done, a deed of devilish malice.

Whizz! whizz!

Two arrows, sped by some unerring aim, came hurtling through the air, and the wretched supporters of the aged woman fell dead upon the sward before the burning house.

"Damnation!" roared the ranger, "escape who can, and the foul fiend take the hindmost!"

And with these words, at a pace which must almost have astonished himself, he led the flight.

When the outlaws and Edwin came up, none were near the blazing house, save the old people and the officers still writhing in their death agony upon the sward.

It was indeed a sight to see the meeting of the old people with their darling grandson, all that was left of seven tall sons and three lovely daughters.

The aged woman wrapped him in a long embrace, and then seating herself on a log, watched the progress of the flames.

Nothing could be done to save the hut, which was too far gone towards utter destruction.

"Nay, take not on so, mother," said the youth, kneeling at her feet, "you shall soon have a larger and a better one."

"'Tis possible, my son, but here have I lived since the day when Gaffer Drew there took me to his happy home; the very chinks that time had made in its battered walls were dear to me; every crevice in which the sunbeam beat brought soothing remembrances to my heart, that never left me all alone; the very smoke that had blackened the rafters brought back the tongues of other days to my ears, a language of past ages, that seemed to babble beside my hearth, nor left me altogether desolate. I lived upon the food of memory.

"Come, mother, take not on so—you shall have another home, and you shall have me there, and see my children playing around your knee. Come, these good foresters will shelter us awhile;" and the young man, using both his hands, raised her up.

"Edwin," said Robin, "I know of a cottage untenanted, which the good owner will freely let you have. It is some distance from here—but so much the better; these villain rangers will have more difficulty in finding you."

Edwin spoke the thanks of the old people, whose hearts were too full to speak theirs.

"I had not thought," murmured the old man, dashing his hands across his eyes, "that the burning of my old hut would have cost me a tear; but such is our love for that which has been familiar to us, that like our ancient liberties, we value them not until they are gone. Then when we feel that they can never return, we are heartsick."

"True, my worthy friend," said Robin Hood, cheerily; "but now we must even move to where we may have shelter. There is a ruined tower in a dell close at hand, where we can pass the night. Follow."

And while some of the outlaws and Edwin supported the tottering steps of the aged couple, he led the way slowly through the forest, by ways which perhaps few men could have found in the dark.

The spot selected by the outlaw was as near as was consistent with safety, which selection was made with a view to avoid any unnecessary fatigue to the old people.

CHAPTER LXXXVII.

THE CAVERN.

DURING the Norman invasion of England, the tyrants, pirates, and robbers, who made this successful expedition, were in the habit, when they did not take possession of the castles of the conquered people, of dismantling them and leaving them in ruins.

It was to one of these that the outlaws were taking their way to pass the night in comfort.

Let us precede them.

It was a tower.

From the first floor to the second (third from the ground) was a way by a stair in the wall five feet wide.

The next staircase was approached by a ladder, and ended at the fourth story from the ground.

Two yards from the door at the head of the stair was an opening newly cut, accessible by treading on the ledge of the wall, which diminished eight inches each story; and this last opening led into a room or chapel ten feet by twelve, and fifteen or sixteen high, arched with freestone, and supported by small circular columns of the same; the capitals and arches Saxon.

It had an east window; and on each side in the wall about four feet from the ground was a staircase, with a hole and iron pipe to convey the water into or through the wall.

This chapel was in one of the buttresses, but there was no sign of it without, for even the window, though large within, was only a long narrow loophole, scarcely to be seen from without.

On the left side of this chapel was a small oratory, eight feet by six in the thickness of the wall, with a niche in the wall, and enlightened by a like loophole.

The fourth stair from the ground, ten feet west from the chapel-door, led to the top of the tower through the thickness of the wall, which at the top was only three yards.

Each story was about fifteen feet high, so that the top of the tower was seventy feet from the ground.

The inside formed a circle whose diameter was about fourteen or fifteen feet.

In the lower story was a low entrance to the vaults, which were extensive.

In a remote part of these was a well, an essential matter in a tower which might have to stand a long siege.

It was now dry and full of stones, though probably on their removal water would have been found.

We are thus minute in our description, as here took place one of the most murderous conflicts in the whole history of the eventful life of Robin Hood.

The owl was hooting in the trees, which waved sadly in the breeze, when the outlaw and his party came in sight of the dismantled and ruined tower.

They were all tired and weary, and glad of rest.

It was not the first time that Robin Hood had visited it, and lain even days concealed from his enemies.

There was one hiding place little suspected by any, and to which we need not here allude.

On the present occasion, for many reasons, the outlaw led the way to the cavernous depths of the lower dungeons.

They were dry, and on many a previous occasion grass and fern, and dry leaves, had been carried in to provide them with beds.

Very little preparation was required, and, save that a fire was lit to keep off the bats and cheer the place up a bit, no other was necessary or required.

The old people went into a kind of niche, and, utterly exhausted by the fatigues of the day, soon enjoyed the delights of slumber.

The stalwart outlaws, also, took to their rude beds, with the air of men who, having done their duty, require repose.

Robin Hood and Edwin alone remained seated by the fire, which cast its ruddy glow around, and seemed even to cheer up those dark, cavernous, and gloomy vaults.

Edwin was a young lover, and in danger of seeing the girl he loved taken from him by the arts of a crafty Norman, who had the means of cajoling the parents of his beloved.

This drove sleep from his eyelids, and made him even to decline reclining on the rude couch prepared for all.

His thoughts were far away, in the kitchen of a large farm-house, where he had spent so many and pleasant evenings.

Robin Hood sat by the fire, wrapped in deep thought. He, too, had his gentle images; but on the present occasion they were driven away by dark shadows, by gloomy forebodings, by the sense of ill coming.

Philosophise as we may, there is something in this second-sight of the soul which we cannot explain.

A cold sinking of the heart.

A nameless dread.

A desire to hurry over the next few hours.

What do these generally portend but some coming ill, which we cannot ward off, or even foresee?

A cold, convulsive shiver, passed through the frame of the outlaw, as if, according to popular tradition, somebody had been treading on his future grave.

He glanced at Edwin. The lover had at length fallen to sleep.

The outlaw fancied that it might be the cold and chilliness of the night which affected him.

He rose to select some dry wood from a pile at some distance, intending to cast them on the glowing embers.

He stood still, a statue of silence.

Voices clear and distinct fell upon his ear.

The eye of the outlaw brightened; for now he felt that he had to deal with mortal foes or friends.

He glanced at his companions. They were all in sound sleep, and not likely to awake.

He took his bow and arrows, felt for his short sword, and walked slowly and methodically towards the mouth of the vaults.

Then, stepping with the caution of a hunter in pursuit of the wild and skeary deer, he ascended by means of several large stones that served as steps, until where he stood was on a level with the floor of the tower.

There he paused and peered in.

A fire had been made hastily in the centre of the ruin, a warm and glowing fire of charcoal, beside of which sat a man with a large cloak around him.

His back was slightly turned, and he bent over the embers in the act of warming his hands.

It was impossible to see his face without moving, which Robin Hood now knew to be dangerous.

Not that the outlaw feared any one man.

But outside the door he saw the gleam of men-of-arms, and heard the neighing and stamping of many horses.

What were they doing?

It was not a night halt, for the men-at-arms sat grimly on their steeds, ready to start.

What, then, could it be?—a rendezvous. If so, between whom?

Robin Hood was strangely puzzled.

Suddenly the crouching figure lifted his head, and the outlaw almost fell back with astonishment when he recognised—*the Sheriff of Nottingham.*

CHAPTER LXXXVIII.

THE TRAITOR.

ROBIN HOOD, however, held his breath, for he knew that the man was about to speak.

"Godfrey!"

"Sir!"

"Will this lurking knave come?"

"He promised me by all that was sacred he would," said the serving man.

"You are sure he said he had a personal reason for what he was about to do?"

"He said he hated not only the life that he led, but the men he was compelled to associate with."

"He did."

"The rascal may be detained, so let us even wait his pleasure. Unload a sumpter mule and let the men dismount. While he tarries we can but refresh ourselves," was the answer.

A cold shiver passed through the frame of Robin. He began to suspect what it meant.

One of his men was about to betray him. There was, then, another Judas in the camp.

The stern outlaw could scarcely repress a deep and loud sigh, but he choked it ere it came forth.

Stepping up one more step, he cautiously seated himself—prepared to wait even all night.

One thing, indeed, he was grateful for.

Providence had brought him to that spot just in time to discover and defeat this foul conspiracy.

The varlets brought in wine and other refreshments, to which the sheriff at once began to pay due attention.

Scarcely, however, had he swallowed a mouthful, when the same servitor announced the arrival of the man.

Robin Hood peered with his keen eyes into the lower chamber of the ruined tower.

A man entered.

He was a short powerful man, with a bow in his hand and a sheaf of arrows by his side.

His dress was a green doublet, extending to about the same length, or somewhat shorter, than a modern frock coat, and not unlike it below the waist, while the collar was furred.

Part of his under-garments were concealed, as the doublet fitted closely. His lower extremities were encased in long buskins, not unlike modern overalls.

He wore a fur cap made of the skin of some beast of the chase. He also carried a short pointed sword and hunting-knife—the latter without sheaf. These were stuck in a rude belt, on which were certain hieroglyphics suggestive of the chase. On his back was strung a huge quarterstaff.

On his face was a visor.

"Welcome, yeoman!" said the sheriff, pointing to a large stone which might serve the purpose of a seat.

The man bowed.

"There is no need to conceal your face from me," continued the servant of the crown.

"I am only masked because of your men," said a deep hollow voice that made Robin's heart leap. "Are we quite free from interruption?"

"Quite."

The man slipped off his mask, and placed it on the stone which served the Sheriff of Nottingham for a table.

Robin Hood could scarcely refrain from sending an arrow through his heart.

It was the stolid and somewhat heavy countenance of Thomas the carter that were revealed to view.

"I understand," began the magistrate, "that, weary of a life of crime and rapine, you are ready to make your peace and gain the clemency of a wise and kind government, by giving up to punishment the accursed leader of this permanent rebellion in the forest of Sherwood."

"So I have said."

"You further stipulate for reward?"

"I do."

"The amount?"

"Sir Sheriff," said the traitor, gravely, "I run great risk; and should my part in this be ever discovered, even were I to hide hundreds of miles away, they would find me out."

"Doubtless."

"I ask, then, this: I engage, in the first place, to place in your hands Robin Hood——"

"Accursed Judas!" muttered the outlaw.

"Then Little John——"

"Traitor!——"

"Then Will Scarlett——"

"Oh, most venomous scoundrel."

"Which done, you will have no trouble in dispersing the band, which, deprived of its leaders, will break up. I can then easily indicate the various haunts, and you can, at your leisure, exterminate the whole tribe."

"And the reward?"

"My lord, no man in Sherwood Forest can do what I have undertaken to do but myself. They have implicit confidence in me—I leave, therefore, the reward to your sense of justice."

"I will give a thousand marks for Robin Hood," said the generous sheriff, musing.

The royal private proclamation offered three.

"I accept," said Thomas the carter, with sparkling eyes.

"Five hundred each for the other two."

"I accept."

"When can it be done?"

The traitor mused.

"The moment it is done I must flee far away. I dare not even show myself in Nottingham. Let your scouts await my signal, and when I send word the bird is caged, come riding in hot haste where I shall direct. Bring the money with you, as I must put the seas between myself and the band at once, for years."

The sheriff made some objections, but after some further discourse, all was agreed on, and the magistrate rose to go, evidently delighted to leave that wild sylvan retreat, to which nothing but his duty would have tempted him even to pay a flying visit.

Thomas the carter remained seated where the sheriff had left him, in such a hurry as to have abandoned his wine flasks and dainty meats.

He then turned round, and a broad humorous grin crossed his hitherto stolid features.

"Fool," he said, shaking his fists at the retreating body of royal satellites and servants, "we will have the money, while—

Unto the end of time the tales shall ne'er be done
Of Scarlett, George-a-Green, and Much the Miller's son;
Of Tuck, the merry friar, who many a sermon made
In praise of Robin Hood, his outlaws, and their trade.

Dost think Thomas the carter, though he may look like a fool, would betray his beloved master?"

A deep sigh was heard from the dark entrance to the cavernous vaults of the old tower.

"Eh! what?" cried the startled carter; "have we ghosts about, or do rats sigh like mortals?"

A low laugh followed.

"Be it spirits from the lower regions, or goblins from fairy land, have at you!" cried the resolute outlaw.

"Thomas the carter," said a solemn voice.

"Who calls?"

"Wouldst thou cheat the king of fifteen hundred marks, when for that you should give up three of the arrantest rogues in all Christendom?" continued the deep, hollow voice.

"Arrant rogue thyself, come forth; or if thou wilt not, I will give thee such a drubbing as will not soon be forgotten in thy family," replied Thomas the carter, angrily.

"And yet thou hast agreed to betray three rogues in buckram," continued the secret speaker.

"Spy I hate, ghost I fear not—so show thyself, derider of all that is good;" and as he spoke he seized his quarter-staff, and rushed upon the supposed spy.

"Thomas," said quite another voice.

"Robin!"

"The same!" said the king of the outlaws, stepping forth and shaking his follower heartily by the hand; "but you gave me a rare fright when I first heard you speak."

"And," cried the honest fellow, "did you, for one moment, suspect me of treachery?"

"Frankly, I did," said Robin Hood, in his usual open way, "and you did it so well that any one might have been deceived."

Thomas the carter looked dumbfounded for a moment; and then, seeming to see some sort of compliment in the speech, appeared more satisfied.

"And now," continued Robin, "wilt explain? Little John and the friar are below, but as the rosy wine is here, we may as well talk without disturbing them. How came it about that you met this high sheriff?"

"Master, I will tell you, though you be never so angry," said Thomas the carter, blushing.

The Normans called him Thomas à Carter; the Saxons Thomas the Carter; the outlaws indifferently.

"Fill a bumper of the sheriff's wine," replied Robin Hood, merrily, "I promise not to scold thee."

Now, as Thomas the carter was almost as modest a man as the tall forester himself, it may be as well not to allow him to tell his own story, but to narrate it in our own words.

CHAPTER LXXXIX.
THOMAS THE CARTER.

IF there was one thing these jolly outlaws had in common with all those who, having rebelled against their country's laws, seek to replenish their pockets, it was their love of good cheer.

All who steal—a fico for the phrase — *convey* the *wise* it call—winning their money easily, spend it freely.

The men in Lincoln green were no exception to the rule.

Not only were the outlaws fond of those glorious banquets under the greenwood, which Robin was himself in the habit of indulging them in, but they liked to pay sly visits to the ale-houses and scot-ales alone, either for the liquor, or quite as often for the sake of the bright eyes of the land-lady or chamber-maid.

Our forefathers were sad love-makers.

Now Thomas the carter was, despite his somewhat vacant countenance, as fine a specimen of humanity as any within twenty miles of the famed Hollybush tavern.

He was tall, stalwart, and strong—he had a rare shock-head of his own, and stood five feet eleven in his—we were almost about to say stockings, but such things were unknown—feet.

Now if there is one thing which a certain portion of the fair sex thoroughly admire in ours, it is size, strength, and power.

No woman ever ventures to henpeck a man she respects; though not respecting, she may love.

Now Thomas the carter was a huge admirer of the better half of creation, and albeit not very faithful to his female cousins, was tolerably regular in his visits to his favourites.

Still, every man who indulges in a perfect harem of sweethearts has always one who is the sultana.

So it was with Thomas the carter.

And his sultana was the buxom, black-eyed, jovial widow of the Hollybush.

Thither, his task for the week over, and his holiday round, the bold outlaw took his way, always gladly received and treated to the best of everything at bed and board.

Now it chanced that three days before the evening on which took place the interview with the Sheriff of Nottingham, Thomas the carter took his accustomed walk up Watling Street, in the direction of the Hollybush, situated in that celebrated locality.

It was only an ale-house, other houses of entertainment being almost unknown out of cities; but it was kept so well, so cleanly, so neatly, that many honest franklins would go there to enjoy their flagon of ale, and listen to the news of the day.

Not that there was much news. Luckily, news and newspapers came in with pipes and tobacco, without which they are hardly to be appreciated by anybody.

Still the English race, when warmed by malt and hops, will find some subject to talk about.

Now, our ancestors were huge bibbers, both of the strong October, and of the French wines, which, in those days, were ten times as cheap, as they ought to be now, a penny fetching a good quart of Burgundy in a flagon.

Of course, under a tyrannical government topics of conversation are limited, as no man is safe from arrest one moment.

This was particularly the case during the absence in Palestine and prison of King Richard, and during the government of the country by Prince John.

Any ill-natured allusion to the powers that were put you at once in the power of the meanest village constable, which satisfactorily proves the correctness of the theory of Young England, that we ought to return to the manners and customs of the olden times.

Now Thomas the carter was used, in the costume now of a ranger, now of a drover, now of a plain yeoman, to visit the kitchen of the Hollybush, where the gossips collected, and there to sit listening to the conversation, rarely joining in it, but waiting for the auspicious moment when, the house being closed, he sat down to enjoy his supper and *tête à tête* with the buxom widow.

Now it happened on the occasion to which we refer Thomas the carter did talk awhile, as long as those present were known to be honest Saxons, and spoke rather freely to men whom he knew, of the dire oppressions and vexations of the law.

Suddenly, however, there was heard a noise without, and several cavaliers alighting, came bustling into the room.

They were retainers of the Earl of Beauchamp and the Sheriff of Nottingham.

Thomas the carter, and indeed all the Saxons present, at once relapsed into utter silence.

The soldiers passed up the room to an empty table, and seating themselves, called for wine.

The summons was answered, not by the buxom landlady, but by Thomas the carter himself, who had at the first call slipped out of the room and put on the apron of servility.

He well knew the insolence of these pampered soldiers, and was by nature jealous.

He bowed low, and asked their pleasure.

"Wine, booby, wine! Dost think we drink beer—fit swill only for Saxons and swine?" said one Norman.

"Wine you shall have, good sir," replied Thomas the carter, with a sudden humility not shared by others in the room, who darkly frowned at the insolence of these hired marauders.

The new tapster withdrew, and soon brought in two pitchers of very good Burgundy, with sundry tasty knick-knacks which might whet their appetite for drink—the Normans not keeping up to the conquered in this particular.

The Normans of Normandy have not retained the character of their ancestors—*they* drink inordinately.

The soldiers did not even thank their waiter, but began mechanically to pick at the numerous salt things he had put before them.

The tapster lay down on a bench and closed his eyes, as if waiting for further orders.

He heard every word they said.

"And so, another great expedition is to be organised against the Saxon outlaw," said one.

"Yes, truly; so I have heard."

"But they have all as yet been failures."

"This," continued another, "will be better managed."

"Of what use is an expedition marching about in a large body, while the outlaws play hide-and-seek?"

"True; but the remedy?"

"Four expeditions will start at once," said the loquacious confidant.

"Humph!" said one more sceptical than the others, "what we want is a guide."

"Guides are indeed that which is essential to success," observed the other, musingly; "but where are they to be found?"

While this conversation had been going on in a low tone, all the Saxon franklins had risen and taken their departure.

The tapster alone remained.

He sat up and gazed warily around.

"My masters, if you would *pay* him, I wot of the guide you want."

The startled Norman soldiers looked at the man, whose stolid countenance, however, seemed to indicate truth.

"Ah!" cried one, "you have been listening."

"Heard every word."

"Frank as a fool," laughed one of the retainers of the Sheriff of Nottingham; "but now, sirrah, since you have listened, either a cord or a purse—choose."

"I choose the purse," he said, with a foolish laugh.

"Well chosen!" cried all.

"And now about this guide?" said the man in authority.

"I can find you one who knows every haunt of the men in Lincoln green," continued the tapster.

"His name?"

"That I may not tell."

"How know you him?"

"He is a bit of a relative of mine—an honest outlaw enough; but tired of his trade, where he gets more blows than money."

"Ah!"

"Robin Hood, who is choleric at times, beat him soundly the other day with his quarterstaff."

The soldiers exchanged glances.

"Well?"

"He vowed revenge."

"Cans't find him?"

"I can."

"When?"

"If any cared to meet him who would pay him well, I would undertake he should meet any agent of the sheriff in a sure place," continued the tapster.

"Why not come to Nottingham?"

"You see," said the tapster, scratching his head, "the outlaws be woundy suspicious. If he went direct to Nottingham, they might follow him; but if one or even an armed force would meet him, as it were, by chance, no one would be the wiser."

"There is some truth in this, knave; but how know we that you are not playing with us?"

"Anan!"

"How know we that you will not deceive us?"

"You pay me and him, and we won't deceive you. What he and I want is the gold, the reward," grinned the tapster.

A whispered conference took place, and it was finally agreed that the meeting should take place, as the supposed traitor proposed, on the fourth night after the present evening.

The soldiers, completely taken in by the stolid cupidity evinced by the serving-man, rode off in great glee, after paying their score without any murmuring; though all declared that the villanous tapster had made them drink more than was good for them.

It was a sight to see the luxurious enjoyment evinced by Thomas the carter, as, over a tasty supper, enlivened by the bright eyes of the buxom widow, he planned in his own mind the trick he would play the persevering sheriff who had vowed their destruction.

We must not judge the men by the standard of ordinary times. Now, when lawless men band together to rob their fellows, the general feeling of society is decidedly against them and with the government.

But these men were more in the position of the Polish rebels of to-day than of bandits.

They were driven to the forest life they learned to love by the bitter cruelty of their conquerors.

CHAPTER XC.

ARCHERY.

ROBIN HOOD laughed heartily at the *ruse* by means of which his faithful and attached lieutenant proposed to fill the treasury of the outlaws, and having duly congratulated him on his ready wit and ingenuity, led him inside the cavernous depths of the vaults; and, all the wearied party still sleeping soundly, the two made choice of corners, and sought relief and repose in slumber.

No cock crowed at early morn to wake them, and nature having been exhausted the previous day, they slept well.

It was somewhat late, then, when they rose and prepared for departure.

Robin Hood dismissed all his friends, urging that in his journey with the old people the presence of so many would render all suspicious.

He determined to guide them to their destination alone.

Blithely and merrily now did he and Edwin start on that summer morning through the sun-tinted glades of Sherwood Forest.

It was a novel journey to Robin Hood, for never before had he sauntered so slowly.

They were all happy, and though the day was fine, lovely, and pleasant, Sherwood was not more merry with its bright green trees, its fairy flowers, and full throated choristers, than were the young people.

Youth is love.

And love shows itself in many ways. At times it makes us melancholy enough, at others it but rouses within us some dormant sense of enjoyment which can only be satisfied by song.

The new friends, as they waited the pleasure of the old people, indulged, therefore, in witty sayings, in lively ditties, or in duets suited to their several voices—not ill matched.

The venerable parents of Edwin looked and listened with glistening eyes. It was their pleasure to see the grandchild of their old age happy.

And thus the time passed, until about mid-day they found themselves on the confines of a village where a halt had been decided on, but which, to their great astonishment, they found in an uproar.

It was crowded, or rather its outskirts were, which was the reason of their being involved in the mob almost ere they were aware of it.

One glance satisfied them all that the occasion was festive.

There was music, dancing, quoit throwing, while all the

village girls were in holiday attire, belles of the buxom order, with ruddy cheeks, rosy lips, and limbs that, in our degenerate days, would rather do honour to a man than a woman.

Roars of laughter burst from the motley crowd as the strangers, unperceived, joined it on the outskirts.

"A rare wench—what a leg!" said one, with a loud guffaw, that showed his eye teeth.

"What has she done?" asked Robin.

"Run a foot-race," replied the bumpkin, still laughing, "and won it too. 'Tis a bonny lass, and cared not what one saw of her sturdy limbs, so she got the prize."

"Any more such races to be run?" asked Robin, gravely.

"No—now it's the shooting match."

The archer's eye twinkled. No allusion could ever be made to his favourite pastime without rousing in him those instincts which made him the greatest bowman that ever lived.

The outlaw now saw that what he had imagined to be a mere village festival was a regular gathering of the whole neighbourhood.

On a raised platform sat men who wore the garb of knights, and women whose dress denoted their nobility.

Round about stood franklins, yeomen, and others, while the crowd was made up of the more common herd.

On inquiry, Robin Hood, who it must be remembered was in disguise, learnt that to the best archer a prize was to be awarded, consisting of a bugle horn, mounted with silver, and a silken baldrick, richly ornamented with a medallion of St. Hubert, the patron of all sylvan sports.

"Wilt shoot?" whispered Edwin, whose eye glistened at the mere mention of the sport.

Robin nodded.

"What shall I do with the old people?"

"Take them to yonder shed and let them have refreshment. Then join me," replied the outlaw.

And he sauntered to where the competitors for the prize were collecting.

They were about twenty in number, many being rangers and under-keepers in the royal forests, who wore the regal livery; others were rangers who served other masters.

Robin Hood eyed them keenly.

Not one was known to him.

With a slouch like that of the swineherd he looked in his present costume, the famed archer strode forward into the circle where the various competitors stood.

The judges on the platform, the women, the yeomen, the spectators all smiled, while some even laughed.

"Wouldst try thy skill with these merry men?" said a portly knight, who filled a rude arm-chair.

"Yes," drawled Robin.

A loud shout of derisive laughter greeted this reply. The skill of every marksman for miles around was so well known—and every known one was present—that this determination of a mere peasant was looked on as mere bombast.

"And so thou shalt, my bully," said the knight cheerily, "never mind the insolent babble."

"I don't," drawled Robin, in the broadest of Yorkshire dialect.

Again the crowd laughed, not at him but with him this time. So changeable is a mob.

The competitors now began to examine their bows, none more keenly than Robin, who heard names bandied in the crowd which made him well aware that he had his work cut out for him.

The favourite appeared to be one, Ned of the Hill, a tall and stalwart youth of good proportions.

Now it was the intention of Robin to watch them all, and reserve himself for the last.

"Now then," said the portly knight, addressing the outlaw, "show thy skill."

"No," replied Robin, in his assumed tone. "I shoot last or not at all—the best man for me."

"As you will," cried the judge. "Begin."

And amid renewed laughter, the competitors commenced.

A target had been erected near the forest skirts, the distance being such as to afford a fair shot.

The archers having arranged their order of precedence, were to shoot three shafts in succession.

One by one the yeomen and rangers, stepping forward, delivered their shafts right yeomanly and bravely.

Of nineteen arrows shot in succession nine were fixed in the target, and the others ranged so near it that, according to the distance of the mark, they were accounted good archery.

Of the nine which hit the target, two within the inner ring were shot by Ned of the Hill, who, amid loud acclamations, was pronounced the victor.

"You forget me," drawled Robin.

The winner cast a contemptuous glance at the swineherd.

"Do you really wish to shoot with me?" he asked, in tones which mingled indignation with contempt.

"I do."

"Let him shoot," said the judge, sternly this time, "but be quick, for yonder a buck and a bowl of wine awaits you. Harkee, master swineherd, if you win I add twenty nobles to the prize, but if you but waste our time, I will have you whipped off the course as an impudent braggart."

"I am quite willing," said the swineherd, with such confidence as almost staggered Ned of the Hill, and at all events determined him to shoot his best in order to retain his reputation; "but an your worship pleases, an I shoot twice at his mark he must shoot once at mine."

"Agreed! agreed!" cried all.

As the judges began to have some suspicion that the contest was to be real, the former target was removed and a fresh one of the same size placed in its room.

Ned of the Hill, who, as the conqueror in the first trial of skill, had the privilege of shooting first, took his aim with great deliberation, long measuring the distance with his eye, while he held in his hand his bended bow, with the arrow placed on the string.

At length, when all were becoming impatient, he made a step forward, and raising the bow at the full stretch of his left arm, till the centre or grasping place was nigh level with his face, he drew his bowstring to his ear.

The feathered shaft whistled through the air and alighted within the inner ring of the target, but not quite what is called plum centre, announced the marker.

The cool observation of the swineherd electrified the whole of the spectators.

"Ah, Master Ned of the Hill, you did not allow for the wind, or that had been a better shot."

"Beat it," said his adversary, angrily.

"I mean to," drawled Robin.

With these words, and not appearing to take the slightest trouble about aim, the swineherd stepped forward and let fly his arrow without, apparently, even looking at the mark.

The shaft buried itself in the target fully an inch nearer the white spot than that of Ned of the Hill.

A terrific shout from the spectators woke the echoes of the forest glade.

"By the light of heaven," cried the old judge, "thou hast a worthy competitor!"

"The foul fiend take him!" muttered Ned of the Hill, who was, however, not too proud to take advantage of the hint given to him by the stranger.

He was even more careful than before, and this time was rewarded by success.

He hit the centre.

The populace again shouted, for the archer was well known to them all, and was rather a favourite.

The women smiled upon him most graciously.

"Wait a notch," broadly said Robin.

This time he took some semblance of aim; and when his shaft was loosened from the bow it lighted upon that of his competitor, which it split to shivers.

There was for a moment a dead silence, and then the clamour was awful. Men could scarce believe their eyes.

"Such archery was never seen since a bow was first bent in England," said the knight. "Who art thou?"

"A poor swineherd, who, having nothing else to do, does practise daily with my yew bow," said Robin; "and now, if your worship will permit, I will put up my mark—that which I shoot at in the forest."

"Not a buck, I hope?" said the judge.

"God forbid!" cried Robin, with such a look of pious horror as made the whole crowd in his vicinity laugh.

"Set it up then."

"One moment," continued Robin; and casting down his bow and arrows, he walked to the skirt of the forest, where he paused at a willow bush, and then slowly returned with a willow wand about six feet in length, perfectly straight, and rather thicker than a man's thumb.

Recollect that what we are relating is historical, and has often been told before.

This wood began to peel with the utmost coolness, remarking in a loud voice at the same time, that to ask a real archer to shoot at a common target was to insult his skill.

"As for myself," he said, "I would as soon shoot at King Arthur's round table as at yonder wooden shield. A child of ten years old could hit it. But he who hits this mark at five score yards, him I call an archer fit to bear bow and quiver."

"'Tis folly," observed Ned of the Hill, angrily. "I will not shoot. If yon master swineherd, who shooteth as if the devil were in his jerkin, can cleave that rod, I yield you the buckler."

"Art, then, faint-hearted?" said the judge.

"Not faint-hearted; but one might as well shoot at the edge of a pared whittle, or at a wheat-straw, or a sunbeam, as at a twinkling white streak."

"If you shoot not, you lose the prize."

"I care not; but I do not believe he will try. He does this but to vaunt us."

"I will try," said the swineherd.

He now bent his bow anew, no true archer ever leaving his bow bent even for five minutes. But this time he even seemed anxious, for he took care to put on a new string, because he thought the other was not sound, having been slightly frayed by the two former shots.

He now took aim, with great care and deliberation, while all around held their breath.

The late victor, Ned of the Hill, watched him keenly and anxiously.

The arrow sped on its way.

It split the willow rod in two.

"'Tis the devil or Robin Hood!" said the ex-victor, with an angry glance, when the shouting of the populace gave him an opportunity for speech.

These words fell like oil on the waters. The falling of a glove might have been heard.

"And if I be Robin Hood?" he answered proudly, in his natural tone of voice.

"I give thee my hand!" cried the defeated candidate, with pleasure dancing in his eye.

"Well spoken," said the portly knight; "and though as a justice of the peace, I should take thee to him who would stretch thy neck with a cord, as provost of the games I award you the prize, and invite you to share our venison and wine, with perfect safety for the day, and two hours' law from the hour you choose to depart."

"Sir knight," replied Robin Hood, "I thank you for your courtesy and hospitality, which it were churlish to refuse; but as to the prize, I cannot accept it, for I take it as unfair for one to shoot, except in jest, who never yet was beaten."

"I cannot accept."

"You must, if even as a gift."

"As such I will," replied Ned of the Hill, "and it shall ever remind me that I had once the honour of shooting with the famed archer, Robin, than whom no stronger hand or truer eye ever directed shaft."

The populace, mad with delight, shouted their applause, and a few minutes later the outlaw of Sherwood Forest sat down to a banquet, which lasted until evening, when uniting himself to his comrades, he continued on his way.

It was long indeed before those who witnessed this remarkable feat forgot to speak of it, or to boast of how, in amity and friendship, they sat down and junketed with the bold outlaw.

CHAPTER XCI.

A NEW HOME.

THE sun had climbed high into the clear arch of heaven on the second day after the scene above recorded.

The travellers followed a road which skirted a kind of wooded meadow land, beyond which rose the forest in the distance, gloomy and grand, and towering like a huge mountain range beside the sky.

Here and there the tops of the tallest and remotest trees fell back, as if upon the clouds, and wore a deep black tint, that would have seemed terrible, had it not been softened by a blue mistiness, which also overhung the mingling purple that sprang from the darker masses.

This, again, had diffused its hues into a sloping bank of branches of a deepish green, that spread far abroad until it caught a broad, mellow, and sudden flood of sunshine, that gave to the tops of the lower trees the appearance of a field of waving golden foliage.

It was a spot redolent of peace and quietness; though, let a very paradise exist, man will often contrive to make a hell of it.

At the bottom of a dell was a rude cottage; neat and clean, despite its simplicity, and with a small garden in front.

The old people were in raptures at sight of it.

"And are we to live here?" said the old woman.

"As long as you like, and rent free," replied Robin Hood, with a hearty laugh.

The husband and wife seemed scarcely to regret the house they had lost.

"There is one thing I must tell you," continued the outlaw; "that is, it is tenanted by one who does not know my name, and one I wish not to know it."

"What appellation does he give you?"

"Plain Locksley. But be not surprised—he will not live with you. The house is my own, and in the absence of other tenants I have allowed him to dwell there."

While this conversation was going on they were approaching the house, against the door of which the outlaw chief began to rap with his staff.

It was opened readily.

It was not easy for the companions of the outlaw to prevent a start of surprise. The tenant of the house was a short thick-set person, apparently not more than four feet high, and measuring nearly as much across the shoulders, which supported a large round bullet head of remarkable shape.

His eyes were large and dark, and had a peculiar expression, the pupils of each being lodged in the furthest and most opposite corners, and therefore enabling him to see distinctly on each side at once without moving either eye or head.

A long black beard fell in wild disorder upon his breast, while his hair had the appearance of a lion's mane, all tossed, disordered, and uplifted, as if by rage and combat.

It would have baffled any one save an artist to convey a proper notion of the formation of his nose and mouth; for the latter might well be compared to the arch of a bridge, filled in with white piles—for such appeared the huge spanning upper lip, that revealed some of the most formidable grinders in Christendom, while the nose spread over him like a huge buttress that would fain cover the wall it supports.

His sole weapon was a cudgel.

Any one who had seen the smile with which he greeted Robin Hood would have guessed how faithful and attached he was.

But he was on trial.

Robin Hood had saved him from the mirth, blows, and jeers of a mob; and had placed him in this house to reside until he should think proper to reveal the mystery of his name.

"Well, master mine, you have come back to see Wamba," he said, showing his white apparatus of grinders.

"Yes, good Wamba; and bring friends with me. Have you been well all this time?"

"Well."

"Short, as usual."

"Yes, master."

"I like plain speaking. Come in, my friends."

And they were conducted into the hut, which promised to be their home for some time.

There was a fire on the hearth; and the dwarf, without a moment's hesitation, proceeded to prepare a repast for his visitors, who were not sorry to see him so pleasantly employed.

This operation duly performed, the outlaw took the dwarf out into the open air, for the purpose of having a conversation with him without being overheard.

"Wamba," he said, "you recollect the circumstances under which we became acquainted?"

"I do."

"And you are still grateful for the little service I rendered you?"

"Deeply grateful."

"Then you will do me a favour?"

The dwarf's eyes glistened, and reaching out his hand—his arms reached to his knees—kissed that of the outlaw, with the rude affection of a bull-dog.

"What is it?"

"I want this hut!"

"It is yours, master; I but lived there to please you; but where am I to go?"

"Wouldst like to go back to your village?"

"Never!—they baited me like a bull—they treated me worse than a dog. I will never go back."

"Wouldst like to follow me?" said Robin Hood, with a smile.

The dwarf fell on his knees.

"Until the grave calls me to itself, I swear to serve with all true fidelity and faith," he cried.

"I believe you, my lad; but as it is right you should know whom you serve, I must tell you that I am Robin Hood, of Sherwood Forest—the noted outlaw."

"Ha! ha! ha!" roared the dwarf, laughing a deep chuckle peculiar to himself. "Danged if I didn't think so. Who but Robin would have opposed a dozen men? Master, I am yours all the more; who should be an outlaw if it be not Wamba?"

"You shall be."

"And may I stop a fat priest?" asked the dwarf, with glittering eyes.

"You may."

"And drub a Norman soldier, or two?"

"Yes."

"Ha! ha! ha!" said the dwarf, cutting mad capers, "this is good—this is good. The priest spurned me from the church as too ugly to pray; the Norman soldiers kicked and cuffed me; and Wamba can now return the compliment—ha! ha! ha!"

And the little man laughed until his sides ached—his eyes rolling frightfully in their sockets all the while.

Robin Hood could not help laughing, though he was sorry to see the man so revengeful.

He turned away then, and informed his tenants that they were now formally inducted, and soon after took his leave, it being his day for visiting Maid Marian, who was never absent from his heart or thought one moment.

He, however, promised to return soon, bidding Edwin in the meantime to be very circumspect, as the rangers would omit no opportunity of being avenged for what they had endured at their joint hands.

Edwin promised, though there were projects in his head which were not consistent with great prudence.

But when is prudence and love united in the same person?

CHAPTER XCII.

THE STURDY BEGGAR.

ROBIN HOOD was welcomed at the convent in the usual way, and, strangely enough, doubly so in consequence of his companionship with Wamba.

The door porter had been dismissed for drunkenness and other bad conduct, so that they were in immediate want of another janitor who could be trusted.

Wamba demurred at first, but when Robin Hood told him that that house contained all that was dear to him in life, he joyfully assented to the arrangement.

This settled, the outlaw, who was anxious to get news of the Bishop of Hereford, hastened on his way.

Now it was that Robin met with an adventure which somewhat surprised him, and which, if only for its originality, merits a place in our narrative.

Thinking of her whom he had left behind, and of the happy future which he so ardently hoped for, the bold robber did not notice that he was taking anything but a straight path toward his trysting tree.

He wandered along, unconscious of time or place, until the lengthening shadows of the trees made him aware that the night was fast approaching.

He mechanically looked about him for a place where to pass the night, but started to find himself in a part of the forest he had hardly ever visited, simply because its morasses and thickets were so inhospitable as not even to tempt the game to visit it.

Now, thinking of Marian and the happy future, Robin Hood had totally forgotten the present.

Not a bit or drop had he provided himself with.

Now we know that in ancient times it was the custom of knights errant to wander about doing wondrous deeds, fighting dragons, rescuing maidens, and defending on all occasions the distressed and unhappy—and then, when night came, they would sit them down under some tree, and there sigh over the memory of their mistresses while their horses were feeding near.

Now, though the said knights travelled for months through dark and gloomy forests, never a word do we hear of their eating, which, considering the labours they endured, may at least be considered rather wonderful.

But Robin was of no such ethereal nature, and rightly judged that beef and bread were necessary to existence.

But repining was of no avail, so drawing his belt tight round his body, he ensconced himself under a thick bush and went to sleep, probably to dream of fat bucks and venison pasties.

But fatigue is an excellent bed-fellow. The outlaw, therefore, did not awake until daylight, when it is not surprising that he felt somewhat famished.

There was nothing, however, in that neighbourhood which could afford him refreshment, so looking up at the sun, and taking mental bearings of the right path, he hurried on his way.

It was now in vain that thoughts of love assailed him. He did not turn from his path one moment.

About eleven of the clock, he was hurrying up a hill-side quite faint and weary, when——

But let the poetic chronicler of the time have his say for one moment:—

> He met a beggar on the way
> Who sturdily could gang,
> He had a pikestaff in his hand
> That was both stark and strang.
> A clouted cloke about him was
> That held him frae the cold,
> The thinnest bit of it, I guess,
> Was more than twentyfold.

Now when Robin Hood caught sight of him, he noticed that he had a meal bag suspended from his neck, that he had three hats on his head, and a noble pikestaff in his hand.

Now it was not the outlaw's habit to interfere with these men, who, however, were generally sturdy mendicants, as rich as they were sordid and ill-looking.

But on this occasion the bold outlaw was urged on by no ordinary motives.

He was hungry, weary, and faint.

Robin could have sworn that the fellow was wealthy, and that within his cloak was goodly lining.

"Tarry, tarry, my friend," said Robin, "tarry there. I want to speak with you."

But the beggar "heard him as if he heard him not," and continued faster on his way, though he cast rather a startled glance over his shoulder.

"Tarry, lest I teach you manners," cried the outlaw, angrily.

"Nay, my good man," cried the mendicant, "it's far to my lodging-house, and, besides, it's growing late. If they have supped before I come in, I shall look a pretty fool."

The outlaw increased his speed.

"Thou art a sordid, mean fellow," replied Robin Hood, angrily. "I see plain enough if you get your own supper, you care not about my dinner. So, at a word, either give me a good meal, or lay down thy clouted cloak, loose the strings of thy pocket, let me grope for thy gold, and take what may serve my turn. Nay, an thou art sulky, I shall soon see if thy beggar's skin can resist an arrow."

The sturdy beggar, evidently of Scotch birth or extraction, smiled grimly.

He was a tall, gaunt fellow, with high cheek-bones and a sinister smile.

"You had far better let me be," he said; "think not that I am afraid of thy bit of a crooked tree."

"Wilt try a bout?"

"Neither do I fear thee a whit, for all thy sharp nips of sticks. I know no use for them so meet as to make pudding pricks."

Now Robin was not easily put out of temper, but he was hungry, and this contemptuous allusion to his bow and arrows, uttered with insolent sarcasm, angered him.

With the utmost rapidity he put an arrow in its right place, and placing his finger in the right place, drew it a span, but no further.

ROBIN HOOD FOUND WOUNDED.

To use the picturesque language of our forefathers, "the beggar with his noble tree reached him so round a rout, that both his goodly bow and broad arrow in flinders flew about."

Robin Hood stood still, struck dumb with amazement and horror; nothing of the kind had ever happened to him before.

"Have at thee, knave," he said, in a really angry and choking tone of voice.

His quarterstaff was on the ground, and stooping, he snatched at it with the intention of chastising the bold beggar man.

But the canny Scotchman, a North countryman, was too quick for him, and this second effort of Robin Hood also proved vain.

The beggar dealt him a fearful blow on his hand with his huge pikestaff.

Weak, angry, with his right arm disabled, and his bow broken, Robin Hood was now at the mercy of the mendicant, who was, however, not in any way disposed to be merciful.

The outlaw staggered, while the mendicant laid on him with his pikestaff so heavily as to make him fall down in a swoon.

"Come, stand up, man," the beggar said;
  "'Tis shame to go to rest.
Stay till thou get thy money told;
  I think it were the best.
And syn go to the tavern house
  And buy both wine and ale,
Thereat thy friends will crack good carouse;
  Thou hast been at the dale."

With this jeering speech the canny Scotch beggar started on his way, singing some ditty of the time with great glee.

Now the combat had not been unheard, and scarcely had the north-countryman disappeared, when three outlaws hurried up, who were horrified to find their leader lying for dead upon the ground.

Two of them were common fellows, new acquisitions to the band; but the third was Much the Miller.

Kneeling down, the alarmed and attached friend of the

chief threw water from a bottle on his face; and this soon bringing him to his senses, they eagerly inquired how this had happened.—

He replied,—

> "A beggar with a clouted cloak,
>   Of whom I feared no ill,
> Hath with his pikestaff clawed my back;
>   I fear 'twill ne'er be well.
> See where he goes out oure yon hill,
>   With three hats on his head;
> If e'er you loved your master well
>   Go and revenge this deed."

The outlaws required no second asking. They were too glad to do his bidding.

CHAPTER XCIII.

THE STURDY BEGGAR AND THE TWO OUTLAWS.

ROBIN HOOD, however, called them back a moment, to warn them to beware of the cunning knave, who was a master of the pikestaff, as well as a master of dissimulation; but the two men scoffed at the very idea of fearing one man, being each in the habit of encountering one without any hesitation.

They had lost sight of the north-country beggar, but were fully aware of the direction he had taken.

They tightened their girdles and started off at a trot, with the full determination of giving the audacious vagabond a lesson which he should long remember; so severe an assault on their beloved leader being held by the outlaws to be inexcusable.

The bottom of the valley was soon crossed, and then the opposite slope. When on the crest of the hill they saw him leisurely pursuing his way.

A word passed between them, and then separating, each man took a different path towards a brook which he must needs cross in about ten minutes.

The sturdy beggar, quite delighted with his morning's work, and chuckling at having overcome one so renowned—for he had at once recognised Robin Hood—pursued his way without any fear or doubt.

He little suspected what was in store for him.

The pathway was open and clear, being a green forest glade dotted with flowers.

Near the brook it became, however, so narrow as scarcely to admit of the passage of one man, and the trees were here so interlaced as to make the winding pathway quite gloomy.

The beggar, however, pushed himself through, as one who knew his road well.

He had reached to within ten yards of the stepping-stones by which the brook was crossed.

Suddenly from opposite sides two men were upon him unawares, and had him down ere he could use his mighty weapon.

They took from him his pikestaff, and then, with many a cuff and kick, seated him on the ground near a tree, binding his hands despite his powerful resistance.

Then they stood over him to consult what should be done. One was for beating him within an inch of his life, the other would have slain him on the spot.

"Trounce him," said the first outlaw.

"Cut his throat," said the second, scowling at the man with a fierce and angry look.

"For God's sake, noble gentlemen," said the mendicant, "harm not a feeble man who never harmed any one in all his life!"

"Thou liest!" cried outlaw number one.

"And I too say thou liest, false loon," added the second, "for all thy whining oaths, for we know that thou hast nearly slain the gentlest man that ever yet was born."

"Nay."

"Silence I say! We will not punish thee now, but we will lead thee back; and lest you play any tricks, we will bind thee fast. And he shall decide whether thy false throat shall be cut, or your carcase dangle from a tree for ravens to fatten on."

A further short conference took place between the outlaws as to how they should make him march, during which the canny north-countryman, casting his eyes hypocritically down upon the ground, thus muttered to himself,

"It is true I am in a sad plight," he said; "but were I once more upon my feet, with my pikestaff in my hand, they should find it a harder task than they imagine to take me anywhere but where I pleased. Let me see, now; there are wiles in all trades, and more in mine than in any other, and an I use some of my own well, I may yet get out of their hands."

He thought a few minutes, and then, just as the outlaws turned to him, spoke.

"Brave gentlemen, good gentlemen, be merciful to a miserable man. What I did I did purely in self-defence; but if you will be indulgent, I can be liberal."

"With what is already ours!"

"How so?"

"Every penny you have will be forfeited."

"But what will be your share?"

"It will be in our monthly division of profits."

"Fools! why not have it all yourselves? If you set me fair and free, going back and saying that I have disappeared, I will give you a hundred pounds, about which nobody need know anything."

The outlaws looked uneasily at each other. It was truly a sore temptation.

The old vagabond improved his advantage.

"All the savings of long years of labour," he whined, "are gathered in this clouted cloak—hid up wonderfully private—in the bottom of my poke."

The forest outlaws stepped on one side.

In every society, in every congregation of men or women, there are bad and good. We have heard that evil-disposed girls are sometimes found in boarding-schools.

Now, these were mercenary and low minded ruffians, who had contrived, by trickery and mock bluffness, to gain admission to the band.

They were compelled to behave themselves in such a way as not to be found out.

The present, however, was not the first occasion on which they had deceived their comrades.

But never so great a haul had been thrown in their way.

A hundred pounds.

"Well, what shall we do?" asked number one.

"Take the money and let him go."

"He will split upon us, as sure as we live."

"But we can take his money," observed the other, "and then slay him."

"But Robin Hood?"

"We can tell him that we were obliged to kill him—dead men tell no tales."

The two outlaws having agreed upon this act of atrocious villany, turned with a smiling face to the beggar.

They then informed him that for present pay they were willing to pardon him his offence against the band.

They then loosened him, and he at once spread his cloak upon the ground as if to search for the money.

He first drew out a bag, and loosening its neck, he thrust both hands into its depths.

Then jumping suddenly upright, he dashed in the faces of the astounded outlaws two handfuls of finely ground meal.

The effect was blinding.

Like lightning the sturdy beggar clutched his staff, and began to belabor the two men as unmercifully as he had Robin Hood.

"What! must I dust the meal off your clothes? if my pokes have blinded you, I shall knock it out of you"

The outlaws rubbed their faces, which only made matters worse. Besides, they had laid down their staffs.

Their only resource was to run, the beggar running after them to some distance, after which he walked back, picked up what belonged to him, and started off at a rapid pace out of so dangerous a neighbourhood.

Meanwhile, crest-fallen and half repentant at their intended villany, the delinquents returned to where Robin Hood lay still incapable of rising to his feet.

"Ah!" exclaimed Robin Hood, laughing, "You have sped well—you have been at the mill."

He then demanded an explanation, which the discomfited outlaws gave in as favourable a way as they could.

Not a word about the money.

Robin Hood looked grave.

"We are shamed for a year and a day," he said, gravely; "but it may not be helped. I am ill, my friends, and must seek some house where I may be nursed."

He then directed them to make a rude litter and carry

him to the hut to which he had admitted Edwin and his grandparents.

It was near at hand fortunately, and, we need scarcely say, was opened to him with pleasure and satisfaction.

A bed was prepared, and the patient undressed and put in it.

CHAPTER XCIV.

WILL SCARLETT.

WE have too long neglected Will Scarlett not to return to his fortunes.

His desire to see his beloved Eveline became a kind of wild dream. He could not live without it.

Various plans passed through his brain, but none of a satisfactory character.

He knew that he should long since have heard from her but that she had no trusty messenger through whom she could communicate with him.

At last he took Friar Tuck into his confidence.

The burly priest's eyes twinkled with pleasure.

" I have a friend," he muttered, as if speaking to himself, " whom I have not seen for a long time—a client of mine, whom sometimes I do confess."

" A man ?"

" Nay—a woman," cried the friar ; " verily the head she-cook of the noble earl's."

" Then hast thou admission to the castle ? "

" Aye, truly, even to the larder itself," smiled the priest. " Now, as I have not been for some time—the earl admits me to shrive the women and maids but once a month—I can take you as a novice whom I wish to take my place, I being about to remove to distant parts."

" That will do. But the dress ? "

" We have all dresses in our wardrobe. But you must dye that carroty beard of thine, and keep thy cowl well on thy head, or they will betray you at once."

" Anything to see her," replied the outlaw, " to learn my fate, to realise my misery or my happiness."

This agreed on, the dexterous friar soon had his young friend attired in a becoming manner, nor could any one, not in the secret, have suspected the deception.

There were, however, two unfriarly things about them which, if known, might have caused suspicion, but in those days, and in the depths of that vast forest, even this might have been deemed excusable.

Under the girdles were tucked long and pointed daggers, while in their hands were long staffs.

But then they were pilgrims.

It is remarkable how the mere fraction of hope reacts on mind and body.

No sooner was the expedition arranged, than Will Scarlett felt his spirits revive, and when, with a sprightly step and hopeful eye, they stepped out—the stout hearted sturdy-limbed friar and the handsome young novice—they could not refrain from singing for very joy and lightness of heart.

Again was beautiful Sherwood Forest brighter and greener than usual, again did its fair flowers seem more sparkling and greener than ever, again the song of the feathered choristers was more sparkling and lovely—because the heart that loves is ever attuned to heavenly harmony.

It was impossible to be dull in the friar's company. He had ever a ready joke, a witty saying, or if his originality failed him, he had but to call memory to his aid, and his companion was delighted with him.

Half the charm of existence is companionship, without which no happiness is possible.

Will Scarlett could not even think of love in the society of the blithe priest.

We cannot answer for the wisdom or propriety of the priest-outlaw's anecdotical repertory, but it made people laugh, and in all ages and in all times laughter has been held to be conducive to fatness.

On that whole day, without any rest, except an hour at noon, they advanced on their road, both being good pedestrians, and reached at nightfall a small dell, where they agreed to camp under the trees, rejoicing their hearts in addition with a comfortable fire, which is always welcome to sleepers in the open air, even in the warmest summer nights.

Friar Tuck said he knew of an hostelry at no great distance, but the night proved so dark, that it was thought best to resort to their old habit of outlying in the forest, a habit which grows upon man and gives him that dislike to towns and cities which is the common characteristic of the gipsy, the prairie hunter, and the dark-skinned savage of North America.

As they intended starting at daybreak, they stretched themselves on the green sward soon after dark, and fell into a sound slumber.

But not for long ; heavy rain soon began to fall, accompanied with the crash of distant thunder, which speedily woke them.

They were, however, too experienced in woodcraft to mind this, as their halts were always selected with a view to such contingencies.

They merely yawned, stretched themselves, and went to sleep again, little heeding the pattering of the rain, or the loud roar of the tremendous artillery of heaven.

When again they woke the moon was rising, and threw her chequered and silvery light over the forest.

The disguised priests were refreshed, and accordingly at once proceeded to breakfast, a meal which at all times has been grateful to Englishmen, whether it consisted of beef, venison, or bacon, washed down by huge draughts of beer, or the more effeminate meal of the present day.

By the time they had concluded the moon was sufficiently high in the heavens to enable them to thread the tortuous and difficult paths which they had to follow.

Rising and clutching their cudgels, they pursued their journey through the wild and gloomy avenues of the forest.

Man in the darkness of the night is little disposed to converse, the air is raw and cold, and he instinctively closes his mouth, wraps his clothes around him, and advances in moody silence.

But soon a morning of sunshine and beauty followed a night of storm and darkness ; the earth seemed refreshed and beautified by the heavy showers, and the sky looked calm and clear as the face of a lovely woman lit up by the first smile that breaks in upon days of sorrow.

Now the friends unloosed their tongues, nor ceased until the usual mid-day halt was declared in a lovely open glade at no great distance from the main road.

Here, the air balmy and warm, the two friends indulged in a hearty meal—so hearty, as far as rosy wine was concerned, that it necessitated a slight nap, from which, however, they were speedily aroused by shouts and unexpected noises.

Rubbing their eyes, and looking around them, they found that they were no longer alone.

The glade, at some distance, was occupied by citizens and artisans, who, at a respectful distance, were gazing at a number of menials—some holding in the leash tall, deep-chested stag-hounds, limbed like antelopes, yet strong enough to tear down a wild boar.

Every now and then they bayed loud and deep, like the hollow bass of an organ, or strained at the leash, and snuffed up the morning air, while they watched with anxious and attentive eyes for the long-expected signal.

It was a spirit-stirring and pleasing scene, that made the blood race gladly through the veins.

What could it mean ?

" 'Tis the livery of the Earl de Beauchamp, of Eveline's father," said Will Scarlett.

" Ah ! "

" What is to be done ? "

" Mingle with the crowd, and when the cortége returns, enter the castle with the servants."

" 'Tis well ; but what comes yonder ? "

" 'Tis the hunting party."

" But what hunting party ?" cried Will Scarlett, his face crimson with delight. " I see but her ! "

The cavalcade was passing close to them, having ridden up and turned a corner while the monks were still speaking.

At its head rode Eveline, pale but beautiful, her lovely countenance being proof even against the sorrow which racked her heart and filled her soul with doubt and fear.

The earl and his brother, Sir Norman Malvoisin, rode beside her, while behind came the usual attendants.

The hour was late to begin a chase, but it had chanced a messenger from Prince John had detained the earl, who, his business once despatched, was determined, at all events, to have half-a-day's hunting.

There was no time to lose, and when the earl came up to

the spot where the hounds were tugging at the leash, he gave the signal.

The attendants led them forward, and when they had gained the skirts of the forest, and were set free, hill and wood and vale and river returned the deep baying of a thousand echoes.

No one can say how old merry Sherwood Forest then was; but be that as it may, its hoary oaks never shadowed a gayer assembly than that day sped through it with whoop and halloo, nor did its dells and dingles ever ring with wilder or more cheering sounds.

Here and there might be seen the forms of strong and stately stag-hounds emerging from beneath the green foliage of the hazels, or half buried amid the rustling fern; while others elevated their high heads above some wild furze-bush that was covered with its golden flowers.

But Eveline!

She had joined the cavalcade very much against her will, pleading a woman's hereditary excuse, an headache.

But she had obstinately refused to follow the chase, as this would make her seriously ill.

She would remain at the rendezvous with the two women who had followed her, and such menials as were not needed, and there watch the eventful occurrences of the day.

A certain number of domestics and vassals were employed to rouse the deer, and their shouts might be clearly heard as they narrowed their circle in the wide woods.

The earl and knight awaited the propitious moment on horseback, while Eveline, leaping lightly from her saddle, seated herself thoughtfully on the grass under a large tree.

Will Scarlett could see her plainly, they having approached nearer by degrees, and his heart was in his mouth.

Should he be able to speak to her—to hear once more the music of those sweet lips?

He could hardly hope for such good fortune, and yet had he fully made up his mind to try.

Then the shouting came near, and presently a panting heart appeared—a fellow of some six summers—and shot by tree and bush like glancing lightning.

He shook his antlered head aloft, and soon crossing the glade at right angles from the group of hunters, kept his stately course along a small stream; when reaching the widest part, he plunged his reeking breast into the stream, gained the opposite bank, shook his noble head, paused a moment to listen, and then dashing into the dense thicket was lost to view.

Now came the baying hounds, who ran straight in the direction of the royal hart.

As soon as the last had passed, the horsemen put their steeds on their mettle, and dashed after the chase.

The footmen slowly followed, to catch even a glimpse of a chase, always popular in Old England.

CHAPTER XCV.

THE MARRIAGE.

EVELINE scarcely noticed what was taking place, so wrapped was she in her own thoughts.

Her handmaidens looked keenly at her. This melancholy was becoming habitual, and not one of those present could give any explanation of its cause.

They little suspected how near that cause was at the very moment of time.

The two monks, deserted by the crowd, now became conspicuous objects in the glade.

The handmaidens exchanged glances. There was a copious repast close at hand, which Eveline had not forgotten, but which such robust damsels as the girls of those days were not likely to drive from their thoughts.

They exchanged a few words, and then one of them resolved to speak.

"Lady," she said, in a respectful tone, "yonder stand two priests, one of whom might bless your meal, when it shall please your ladyship to indulge in it."

Eveline started as from a dream.

"What saidst?"

The girl repeated the above sentence.

"I fancy, Brenda, you think more of your own creature comforts than of ghostly benedictions. But spread out the dinner and bid the holy men approach."

A sign brought the two monks to where Eveline was seated under the greenwood tree.

"Welcome, holy fathers," she said, with a languid smile; "my handmaidens feel the cravings of hunger, but would fain you should ask a blessing on their meal."

"It is our duty and shall be well performed," said the deep bass voice of Friar Tuck.

The girls required no twice telling, but hurried to where the sumpter mule stood under a tree at some distance.

"Lady, a boon," said the friar.

"What boon?"

"I have news for you, and would crave that you start not."

"News, from whom?" cried Eveline, her cheeks blushing crimson.

"From Will Scarlett."

"What news?—is he well?—is he safe?—when shall I see him?" she cried, now blooming and with flashing eye.

"Lady, he is well, quite well—calm yourself and show no sign of surprise. He is here."

Eveline became for a moment deadly pale, placed her hand upon her beating heart and closed her eyes; then, with that wonderful power of self-command which is so valuable to the sex in all affairs of the heart, she recovered herself.

"Take this burly friar," she said to the girls, as they came up with the provisions, "to yonder tree and treat him well. I wish some converse with this priest, who may minister something to that sickness of the soul which sets like a spell upon me."

The girls obeyed, having first placed a luxurious meal, for the time, before their mistress.

They then retired to enjoy their own dinner, the artful friar inducing them to spread it where they could neither see nor be seen by the happy pair.

The lovers were alone, and we cannot say that for some moments they spoke.

There is a means of showing delight at reunion far more eloquent than words.

"And so, my angel, we meet again," he said at last; "alas, but to part again!"

"Let us hope for happier days," she answered; "lately my father has ceased to persecute me on the score of marriage, though I fear me this lull is but the forerunner of the storm."

"I have not known a happy hour since we parted," replied Will Scarlett; "and was on my way in this disguise to visit you at any risk when this fortunate chance threw me in your way."

"'Twas fortunate; but we must not remain long in converse. The girls with me are not in my confidence, and should they suspect anything, will betray me. The earl pays well."

"Alas, I am poor!"

"What matter? If but fortune favours, you will be lord of rich domains; so sigh not."

"You mean, my adored, then, to keep your faith with me?"

"No other shall ever wed me, though it may chance I may not be your wife."

"Little comfort," said Will, ruefully.

"Wouldst have me wed another?" she replied, with a sly smile.

"No; but I almost wish this meeting had not taken place."

"Why, my most noble lover?"

"Because you will not let me come to the castle."

"Who forbade you?" she answered, with a radiant smile.

The only answer to this was a kiss upon her rosy lips, which made no more resistance than was due to maiden coyness; and then the conversation turned upon their future plans.

At last, however, they were recalled to recollection by the merry laughter of the other party.

The chase still continued.

The shadows of the trees, however, at length began to slope eastward; for the sun had left his high station in the centre of the sky, and was fast journeying to the west.

Just then, with mouth black and dry, tongue hanging out, and sides panting with such force that they seemed to stretch his leather coat almost to bursting; his light, elastic vigour changed to a heavy, weary gallop, his eyes glaring savagely, on came the jaded hart.

"Go. You know the arrangement. I shall expect you in my chamber, where no man ever entered. Who knows but there may be news which may change my weak resolves?"

Will Scarlett rose, and hastily summoning Friar Tuck, hurried at once on the way towards the castle.

He did not go far, for he soon found that his companion was hopelessly drunk; and though he allowed Will Scarlett to lead him like a child, there could be no chance of his going far.

He therefore led him, through a narrow and intricate path, into a dense thicket, where, finding a convenient spot, he allowed him to cast himself on the ground; and in a few minutes a running fire of snores from the capacious nose of his ghostly fellow traveller indicated that the friar was fast asleep.

Will Scarlett was delighted at this, as it enabled him to sit down calmly and review the events of the day.

Perhaps the young man had never tasted more pure enjoyment. It was like a fairy dream for him to be openly loved by a maiden of such high degree; not with that lawless love which made many in that age surrender their hearts, *par amour*, to some handsome face, and then marry for station and rank, but openly and avowedly as his future wife.

There was no sting of remorse in his or her love, as there always is with illicit passion.

They loved sincerely, purely, devotedly, and for life.

The man whose love is exhausted by a few years of possession knows not what love means.

Will Scarlett looked forward to the days when, having, perhaps for military service done to the crown, been elevated in rank, he should see a green old age, with his children around him.

But he thought more of the present than of the future—the present, ever delightful to the happy.

At length, however, he fell asleep, nor woke until the beams of morn illumined the eastern sky.

Friar Tuck still slept heavily and soundly.

Will Scarlett was impatient to be off, and being slightly vexed at the friar's inebriation, under the influence of which he might have spoken too much, gave him a somewhat hearty whack with his heavy oaken staff on a part of his person least liable to injury.

The friar leaped up with a roar, and, clutching his pike, aimed a fearful blow at Will, who, however, easily parried it.

"Art mad, Friar Tuck?" he said, laughing heartily.

"'Tis well you spoke," was the half angry reply; "who would be awakened from pleasant dreams thus rudely."

"You have slept ten hours at least," continued Will; "but no wonder. The damsels in yonder glade must have heard rare matter from you in your cups."

"Cup me no cups, except a cup of wine. I talked of nothing but kisses—kisses of grace and peace. But that is neither here nor there. Give me a horn of stiff October."

"We've left the bags behind us," cried Will, with a start.

"Heart of grace!" cried the friar, "this comes of keeping company with a man who is in love."

"By St. Dunstan!" replied Will, mocking him, "this comes of keeping company with a man who drowns all memory in the wine-cup. Who had the bags?"

"That had I; but let us forward. Perchance we may find some scotale-house, or even"—this said with a wry face—"we may fall upon some sparkling stream where I may cool my tongue, which is wondrous hot and dry."

Will made also a grimace, for the sight of Eveline had driven all thoughts of food from his mind.

There was no help but to advance, and this they did as rapidly as might be, the friar especially feeling his lips glued together with thirst, and bending his burly head every now and then to listen for the plashing of a brook, for which sound he several times mistook the sleepy rustling of the gloomy foliage.

They journeyed forward silently, neither caring to exchange his thoughts with the other.

As they advanced the friar grew ravenous, and his imagination expanding, he conjured up shapes of haunches and sirloins in the boles and branches of the trees.

He grew angry, and could have quarrelled with his companion for not bringing his bow with him, when some of the game in which the forest abounded could have relieved their wants.

But it was not so, and the reverend father had already muttered some very choice interjections, which sounded somewhat like the oaths of the period, when they came upon a clear and crystal stream, into which he soon plunged his head, nor lifted it up for full five minutes.

"Ah!" he said, smacking his ruddy lips, "I knew not before that water could be so sweet. It was like malvoisie. But, now I look about me, we are near the end of our journey."

Will Scarlett brightened at this, and truly in half an hour they came to a roadside inn, which commanded a view of the earl's castellated residence.

The young man sighed as he entered the hostelry, for he knew that an hour must be wasted there, the friar not being likely to move under that time.

But he could not deny that repose and refreshment were necessary. He was mistaken, however, for the friar, fo sundry private reasons, did but take a hasty mouthful and a goblet of ale, and then signified his willingness t proceed.

CHAPTER XCVI.

INSIDE.

THE drawbridge of the castle, when they reached it, being down, they had little cause for complaint as to any delay in admitting them.

The moment the friar's voice was heard the wicket opened, and a rubicund face protruded itself.

"Ah, the blessing of St. Dunstan on you!" cried Tuck; "'tis you, my worthy friend Tristam."

"Welcome, jolly Tuck—merriest of friars. But why two? canst not shrive the women thyself?"

"I have chance of promotion," said Tuck, with a wicked wink, "and this young man, who is related to me by blood, I would fain introduce as my successor in case of my becoming abbot."

"Go to!" laughed the warder. "You know your way to the buttery. I will crack a horn with you anon."

The friar made no reply, but crossing the yard with his arms crossed upon his breast, with a firm step and meditative look, soon brought Will Scarlett to a kind of kitchen, before the sparkling fire of which sat a young girl attending to the roasting of some pullets.

"Hem!" said Tuck.

The girl turned hurriedly round, and displayed the features of the ex-page Rose.

"And where is Margery," said Friar Tuck, "with whom I would hold spiritual converse?"

"She will be here anon," replied Rose, whose eyes were all the while fixed on the novice; "are you Will Scarlett?"

"Did you then take me for Little John?" replied the young man, merrily.

"No," blushed the girl, "but no nonsense. I have a message from my mistress."

"Speak it."

"Strangers have arrived at the castle—strangers of note and distinction, and she fears, from ominous looks, their coming bodes no good to her. But her father will make her greet them, and she may not have speech with you until this evening. Margery has strict orders to treat you well. None come here save a few servants, but if they should, yonder is Margery's bedroom, to which you must retire. Farewell, my friend, and hope for the best."

But Will was too fond of his little sister, as he called her, to let her part thus.

He caught her to his bosom and gave her a hearty and manly kiss ere she was aware of it.

"Fie, for shame!" she said, reddening all over her pretty and speaking countenance, "am I to give it to my lady?"

Will Scarlett looked dreadfully sheepish at this home-thrust.

"Wilt tell?"

"Never kiss and tell," she laughingly replied, and then ran away, leaving the lover a little uneasy.

He need not have been. Many a girl has been bribed to espouse a lover's cause with her mistress, by means of a judicious kiss, where money would have been refused.

But we must leave Will and the friar to the care of Margery, and follow in the footsteps of Rose.

The girl tripped along winding passages, vaulted arcades, up and down winding stairs, until at length she came to a corridor into which a number of doors opened.

From one of these the earl came forth, full dressed for a banquet.

" Is that my daughter's tirewoman ? " he said in his usual haughty and commanding tones.

" Yes, my lord."

" Where is my daughter ? "

" In her chamber."

" Go forward, and bid her be ready to receive me in ten minutes. I have matter of high importance for her ear."

The girl curtsied and then ran away.

The earl bit his moustache as he watched her.

" These jades are all conspirators," he muttered ; " for that matter, so are all servants. But these young ones always take part against the father. I had expected to hear from that young springal, and Malvoisin says I shall soon, and to some purpose. There is but one course to pursue, lest he carry out the idea that my brother lends to him."

And the knight re-entered his apartment, whence he shortly emerged, and walked in the direction of his daughter's chamber.

A slight, imperious knock caused it to be at once opened,

There sat Eveline dressed for the coming banquet, very pale and very sad, gazing out of the window into the court-yard below.

Rose was folding up some articles of dress.

" Leave us, hussey. I would be alone."

Rose's face flushed, but she dared not reply, knowing the earl's impetuous and fierce ways.

She contented herself with flouncing out and slamming the door after her.

" An impudent jade that, who must be corrected."

" She is a very good girl, and loves me."

" Humph ! then tell her to show more civility to her lord and master," was the reply.

" I will chide her."

" 'Tis well you should," said the earl, sternly, " and now to the business of our interview."

" I listen, father."

" For some time you have been sad and melancholy ; you eat not, but mope about, caring for nothing. Now can you explain to me what all this means ? "

" I cannot, father. I suppose I am not well," was the gentle reply.

" So I thought, and, as your father, have taken upon myself to find you a physician."

" You are very kind. Father Ambrose is leech enough for me."

" You mistake me, child. When a young, high-born lady of eighteen grows pale, becomes thin, neglects her food, and joins not in the amusements of her age, there is but one physician."

" And that is——"

" A husband ! "

" A husband ! " she faltered.

" Yes, miss," he said, mimicking her voice, " do not pretend to misunderstand me."

" I am very young to think of marrying."

" Young !—your mother was two years younger."

" Could she have known her own mind ? "

The earl frowned darkly. He had married his wife for her estates and money, without a thought of love, and we have already alluded to the dark rumours which existed relative to her end.

He was silent a moment, ere he could recover himself enough to speak again.

" Who has dared tell you any such base falsehood ? " he cried.

" None has dared whisper a word to me anent my mother," replied Eveline.

" 'Tis well they have not. She was a woman quite, and so are you. I had hoped that as you did not like your former suitor, someone else might have met your fancy."

" I am, perhaps, difficult to please ; but——"

" It is too late. I have reasons for your immediate marriage, and this day a noble knight, Sir Walter de Mont-gomery, recently from Normandy, has asked for your hand, which I have duly promised him."

" Promised without my consent ? " she cried.

" Consent ! " laughed the earl. " Who ever asks the consent of a silly girl who knows not her own mind ? I say, my consent is given, and as the knight wishes to return at once to his possessions in Normandy, before

settling down in England, the ceremony must be has-tened."

" My father, keep me at home. I will not marry with-out the consent of a parent," she began.

" Without the consent of a parent ! " roared the infu-riated earl. " Why, the girl is mad, and, to cut short a col-loquy which is becoming painful, know that I have fixed your wedding-day for to-morrow."

" Father, have mercy—I cannot ! " she cried, with her face suffused with tears.

" I have spoken. Now prepare to meet your destined bridegroom."

" Spare me this morning. I will obey you in the evening —but now I am so perplexed, so weak, I should faint."

" I excuse you this morning," he said, slightly touched at her grief, " but to-night you must be in presence of your future husband."

" I will."

With a haughty stride he now left the apartment, to communicate the result of his interview with his daughter to the Norman knight.

The earl's real reason for this sudden resolve he had not even alluded to.

He wished to marry again, and with this view desired to get rid of his daughter, who was ever a living reproach unto him.

The banquet went off very well, but did not last very long, as the Normans were abstemious.

They then adjourned to a court and played the games of the hour, which, of course, were rough enough.

At sunset the great banquet of the day took place, and at this were present several visitors.

Nothing was wanting to complete the number of guests but the presence of Eveline.

In a lofty and courteous tone the Earl de Beauchamp bade an attendant summons his daughter.

There was some considerable delay ere the man returned pale and trembling, his knees shaking from terror.

" What ails my daughter ? "

" Gone—clean gone—she and Rose, and the two strange friars," cried the bewildered serving-man.

The earl swore an oath so fearful that we cannot even allude to it here.

" Let me not disturb you," he then said, rising. " I will but give orders for a search. The foolish maiden," he added, recollecting himself, " is coy and will not face her future husband."

With which words, which provoked a smile from the ladies, he went out.

But all his questions, imprecations, and inquiries were utterly vain.

Nobody had seen either Eveline or Rose, while the terrified warder who had admitted the two priests, declared they must be the devil.

He had let them in, but no one living soul had seen them afterwards.

This was but adding fuel to the flames, and the earl swore a round oath that if all were not found—daughter, Rose, and the two vagabonds who had entered in the dis-guise of holy men—somebody should suffer.

He then ordered a minute search of the castle, while men were sent out to scour the forest in every direction, and confidential men to scour the passes.

Then, with a courteous smile, the wily noble returned to his expectant guests.

CHAPTER XCVII.

EVELINE'S CHAMBER.

WHAT had happened was in reality so wonderful that we gladly leave the banquet hall and return to the chamber occupied by Eveline.

As soon as her father departed a calm, resolute expression might have been seen upon her face, a calm determination which boded no good to him.

Then she wiped her eyes and summoned her trusty Rose to her side.

" Where is Will ? "

" In the buttery kitchen."

" Go fetch him."

" At once ? "

" Yes."

The girl turned to go.

"And mind you be careful. His discovery by my father would be death."

"Trust to me, my dear lady. Your interests are mine," was the warm reply.

"I believe you, and I hope you will be rewarded in the way you wish best."

"I hope so too," said the girl, with a tell-tale blush that was very pretty.

Then the brave little girl, who had so surprised Robin Hood by her pertness and ready wit, made her way in the direction of the buttery kitchen.

She did not take the same way as before, but by a series of dark and unfrequented passages near the ruined part of the building, which few but a devoted heart would have followed in those superstitious days.

In this way the buttery kitchen was soon reached, where a spectacle met her view which rather shocked the simple, innocent girl.

Friar Tuck with his arm round Margery's waist, whispering something in her willing ear.

On any ordinary occasion the right-minded confidante of the lady of the castle would have said something rather cutting.

But she could not afford to make any fresh enemies for her dear mistress.

"Ahem!"

The pair started; and Margery was at once very busy at something about the fire, while the burly priest lifted up a huge horn of ale and drank it.

"Where is your friend?"

"In the room yonder."

"Thank you."

And Rose tripped away, in secret very indignant. She need not have been at all.

In every country where an ambitious priesthood, to divide its servitors from the rest of society, has imposed celibacy on the clergy, such things are.

In England, in France, in Spain—everywhere the Roman priesthood had sway—the notoriously favourite lovers of women were their father confessors.

This simply by the way to excuse somewhat the amorous tendencies of Friar Tuck, who, however, always made love to the cook.

Rose found Will Scarlett seated by a kind of loophole, watching the passing clouds. Any such idle occupation suits your true lover.

"Will!"

"Rose!"

He started up as he spoke, with a beaming eye and hopeful countenance.

"Am I wanted?" he faltered.

"Yes—at once; but we must be very cautious. You must not speak a word, and in all things obey my directions. The castle is full of servitors."

"Your will is law, my little sister, whom soon I hope to see the wife of Little John."

"Fie!" blushed Rose; "I don't want to marry a man-mountain."

"He can the better protect you," said Will Scarlett, with laughing eyes.

"He might beat me."

"Little John?"

"Men are such brutes."

"The bravest, the biggest, and the gentlest of mankind," replied Will, putting his arm round the girl's waist; "but now one kiss and we will go."

"I'll tell him, if I don't her," was her reply when the affair was over.

"Don't," said Will Scarlett, with a comical grin. "Now lead the way."

"But tell me, master novice, what means the real friar by making love to the cook?" she asked, with something of indignation in her tones.

"Cupboard love, my dear. 'Tis a way they have got."

Rose shook her head, but made no reply; leading the way through the kitchen without so much as a glance at the cook or priest.

They now turned down a narrow, dark, and damp flight of steps, which seemed to lead to the vaults below, and which made Will Scarlett shudder at the memory of the past which now stood vividly before him like a picture.

They were compelled to go slowly, as they dared not carry a lantern.

Rose led the way, when necessary holding the other by the hand.

At times they were compelled to grope against the wall with their hands.

At last they came to a long vaulted corridor, at the end of which was a large door.

"Where does that lead to?" asked Will.

Rose gave a frightened glance, sidling up to Will with a convulsive shudder.

"What is the matter?"

"That part of the house, half in ruins, is haunted," she said. "No one would enter within its precincts for the earldom of Beauchamp."

"Why haunted?"

"Terrible things have been done there, of which it is death even to speak."

"Indeed! but what comes here?" whispered Will Scarlett, suddenly.

Rose clutched his arm, and bit her lips till the blood came, to prevent a shriek.

"I know not," she gasped; "but, by my duty, I will wait and see."

With these words she drew him into a kind of dark and gloomy niche.

What they had seen was a twinkling light in motion near the ground, as if a lantern were held low in a man's hand, now throwing the light forward, and now backward.

It soon became quite evident that it was about to pass close to them.

They held their breaths.

Whoever it was came on towards them with slow and measured steps, his eyes fixed on the ground, apparently in a deep and earnest reverie.

Rose clutched Will's arm.

"Father Ambrose."

This was an explanation to Will, who knew that such was the earl's chaplain.

But what was he doing there in that lonely and secluded passage?

They could not surmise, and dared not interchange opinions on the point.

The old man, who was what might be called handsome, with a fine aquiline nose, curled lip, and lofty forehead, looked both hasty, bold, resolute, and crafty; passed them without lifting his eyes.

Under one arm was a bundle.

At the door of the haunted part of the dwelling he put down the lantern, and pulled out a key.

Even Will Scarlett shuddered.

The door opened, the priest took up his lantern, and going in, closed the door behind him.

"What means this?" asked Will Scarlett, in a low and earnest tone.

"I dare not think. Come, my mistress will be impatient—let us go."

And the girl sped quickly along this corridor, ascended another flight of steps, and then reached her mistress's door, which, after a gentle knock, she pushed open.

CHAPTER XCVIII.

THE INTERVIEW.

WILL SCARLETT entered alone, and found Eveline awaiting him with a flushed face, a hot, feverish eye, and a mien of great excitement.

"Dearest," he said, springing to her side, "tell me what has happened."

"Happened!" she replied, with an abruptness quite startling; "I am to be married to-morrow."

"Married!"

"Yes."

"Who to?"

"To one Sir Walter de Montgomery, of fair Normandy, who I have not seen."

"And do you, Eveline," said Will Scarlett, "intend me this terrible wrong?"

"Am I not bound to obey the commands of my own father? Answer me."

"In all things reasonable, but not to sell yourself body and soul, which to carry out such a marriage is to do. There is no more obedient son than Will Scarlett of Gammel, but my father could not force me to marry."

"You are a man."

"I am—and one to whom you have plighted your troth," was Will's answer.

"But even to-day I told my father I would not wed against his consent."

"Dearest, that must have been said on some condition," cried Will.

"I did say," faltered Eveline, with a roseate blush, "if he would leave me free from this great sorrow, I would never marry against his consent."

"If!—that is enough, dearest. Recollect, to-morrow you will be too late for repentance. Your father will force you to wed a man you loathe—my heart beats with horror when I think of it—while here I stand, loving you truly and tenderly, and, as you would have me fain believe, beloved in return. Why, then, should you stay to suffer worse than death, when I promise to love, cherish, and protect you in a quiet, happy home, unless this splendour tempts you?"

"Oh, Will!"

"'Tis a cold, cheerless home where love is not seated by the fireside," he continued. "Come darling—let us fly ere it be tood late, and we part for ever."

"I am his only child; he loves me in his way," she sobbed, leaning on his shoulder.

"If he truly loved you, he would leave you free to choose your mate."

"And so he would if——"

She paused and blushed.

"If what, dearest?"

"I would choose in our own peculiar circle," she whispered.

"I know," said Will, with a choking sensation at the heart, "and does my darling hesitate because of that; or does she think me venal enough——"

"Hush! perish the thought! I know you for nature's true nobleman, the things he intended should be looked up to above all—an honest man; but still, forgive a daughter who has to leave a father. If she leaves him, what will he do?"

"Marry again."

Eveline turned deadly pale.

"What mean you?"

"'Tis the talk of the whole castle that he is about to bring home a young bride."

"And he wants me out of the way. My darling Will, I am yours for ever."

And she fell into his arms at once, without any further hesitation.

"Let us lose no time, my beloved," cried the young lover; "but call Rose, and flee!"

"Could we not be married first? Is your friend a true priest?" she asked.

"Yes. He belongs to the noted priory of St. Hubert, albeit not very attentive to his duties. But why waste time now in vain delays, when every minute is as precious drops of life-blood?" cried the impatient and impetuous lover.

"Waste time?" said Eveline.

"Dearest, we can be married to-night, at the first chapel we meet with."

"I would be married in my father's chapel, if it could be done, and leave the protection he has driven me from on my husband's arm," was her gentle reply.

"So it shall be," replied Will, opening the door and beckoning Rose.

"What want you?" she asked.

"Go fetch the priest to the chapel. Bid him be careful. It is a question of life or death!" said Will; "and then prepare thyself for a journey through the forest."

Rose ran quickly away to hide the radiant glance of delight which this intelligence gave her, for now would she not soon see Little John again?

The lovers now—Eveline having attired herself in a garb suited to the forest, while Will kept guard in the maid's place—entered the corridor and made for the chapel, which was abandoned by all on this festive occasion.

Here both knelt and prayed for protection in their perilous adventure.

It was an earnest and fervent prayer, such as any Christian might have sent up to the footstool of all Power, and surely was heard and recorded.

Presently they rose, as Friar Tuck and Rose entered the building.

"Already," said the hedge-priest, with something of respect in his manner, and with a tone becoming the occasion, "are my services required?"

"They are, and quickly. No time is to be lost, lest we be pursued. We leave within a moment."

"I am ready. You shall be bound as fast as Church can bind in a moment," he replied, and pulled out his missal.

"HOLD!"

The voice was solemn and imperious, and the whole four turning round, beheld Father Ambrose leading by the hand the white lady mistaken by Sir Norman Malvoisin in the long walk for a veritable ghost.

"What want you?" cried Will Scarlett, putting his hand to his sword. "I will only part from her with my life. By what right do you cry *hold?*"

"By the right of a parent. I am her mother, boy!"

And she held out her long thin arms to clutch her long-lost child.

In a few moments she pushed her away.

"And now, my child, listen. I know all. There is nothing you do that is unknown to me. I can explain nothing now. I will soon, however, join you to part no more. But I wish you to marry with a mother's blessing, and to be wed by the regular chaplain of the house of Beauchamp. Nothing can then ever affect your fair fame, for your marriage will be entered in the official register of our house."

The lovers knew not what to say. The event was so startling, so inexplicable, that they felt like one in a dream.

The mother alive!

Eveline never for a moment doubted her word, her looks of gentle love were enough.

"But, mother, why have you been reported dead? why have you concealed yourself from me?"

"For your good, child. I am universally believed dead—why come to life? But proceed with the ceremony. We may not tarry here. To the altar, my children."

"But," said honest Will Scarlett, "does your ladyship know that I am but a yeoman?"

"Honestly spoken, lad. Do you love my daughter?" smilingly replied the pale woman.

"Then take her. When you know my fatal history you will understand my feelings."

No more was said, and the ceremony was now commenced in earnest, Friar Tuck, out of politeness, being admitted to take a part in the solemn service, a condescension on the part of the father confessor which the clerk of Copmanhurst was not likely easily to forget, and to which he ever alluded in grateful terms.

It was soon over, and the trembling girl received her husband's kiss—sly girl—as bashfully as if no such endearments had ever passed between them before.

But then it was with modest pride, for she was his, and only his, for life.

"You, Father Ambrose, bring the book," said the lady.

The confessor went to a large steel coffer, opened it, took out a book with large clasps, and opening, entered in the quaint writing of that period the fact of the marriage between Eveline and Will Scarlett.

All signed their names—Rose and Will by means of a mark, the wife of the Earl of Beauchamp and Eveline in a delicate, distinct female hand.

The book was then closed and returned to its proper receptacle in the coffer.

"Now follow," said the lady. "You, Father Ambrose, I thank. We shall meet to-night."

The confessor bowed, and with a blessing on the young people went his way.

The Lady of Beauchamp now led the way behind the altar, and pushing aside a thick oaken panel, disclosed a dark and gloomy passage, into which, however, all entered at her bidding, advancing with due caution by her direction.

They heard her close the panel, and then all within was pitch dark.

At the end of the passage, however, was a faint ray of light, that acted as a guiding star.

When it was reached they found themselves in a kind of vaulted chamber or cell, probably a clerical prison when the castle was first built.

Here again a secret doorway was opened, and the whole party passed through to find themselves in a vast room completely tapestried with black, without a door or window to let in light or betray the presence of a lamp with several burners, that hung suspended from the ceiling by a silver chain.

THE TWO TRAITORS.

"My children," said the countess, pointing to a substantial repast, "sit you down to your wedding feast. Child, there is an alcove in your bedroom where I have for years, when I have been sane, spent most of my time. There I heard your innocent secrets. Maidens love to talk them over with their confidants."

Eveline blushed deeply, while Will Scarlett looked roseate red with pleasure.

"From my faithful and attached friend the chaplain," she continued, "I heard of my husband's intentions towards you. My mind was at once made up, and I resolved you should wed the lover of your heart who had gallantly saved your life."

"Thanks, madam."

"Thanks, mother."

"Now be seated, all. Thanks to the waste and extravagance of my husband's retainers, there is ample store of provisions," she continued, with a wan smile; "and if they do think the holy father a somewhat hearty eater, it is not uncommon."

"Penance and much fasting," put in Friar Tuck, demurely, "do cause us to need much refreshment; for what we lose by the one we make up by the other."

No one controverting this sentiment, the meal commenced.

The countess ate a mouthful, and drank one glass of wine to their happiness.

"Listen, children," she said. "Rely upon it the pursuit will be hot and strong. Every effort will be made to track you out, but none will suspect you of hiding in the castle. One night, then, will be spent in the home which one day will be yours. Yonder three doors lead to as many cells, where you can find shelter as you list. My duty is to keep watch and ward. There will be rare uproar in the old castle to-night."

None but were glad to hear these cheering words, as, once the first brunt of the search over, they were much more likely to get off clearly and surely.

CHAPTER XCIX.

THE ESCAPE.

ANOTHER day had sped and gone, another evening had come, and the married lovers prepared for their departure, under the guidance of the Lady Alicia de Beauchamp herself, who wished to see them safely out of the old castle.

They did not go the same way, as some one might be in the chapel, and from the altar they must cross it in view of the grand entrance.

In these old troublous times, men were in such everlasting antagonism with each other, that every huge castellated mansion, resembling rather a town than a simple residence, was full of so many holes and hiding-places, that their own master often really knew not of them all.

The tradition was lost.

Now a man so astute as the earl would be very likely to suspect something of the kind, and in consequence to post sentries in every likely place.

It behoved them all, therefore, to be extremely cautious and circumspect.

The unused part of the castle was in itself vast in its dimensions, and it was wonderful the galleries, corridors, and unoccupied apartments they traversed.

The number of stairs they ascended and descended appeared endless; but at last they found themselves once more within the confines of the chapel.

They entered cautiously, stepping with the lightness of antelopes and the cunning of foxes.

As they expected.

A sentry walked up and down, with a partisan in his hand, exactly opposite where they stood.

He seemed to hear a faint sound, for he halted a moment and listened.

All was still as death.

He resumed his walk, and the whole party glided like shadows to the secret door in the tombstone, so constantly used by Lady Beauchamp, as to glide noiselessly on its hinges,

Next instant it had closed upon them, and they were descending the steps to the dark and winding passage which the vagaries of nature, assisted by the patience of man, had cut so far through the solid limestone.

A torch was now lit, and the whole party hurried through the passage, which was damp and cold, and seldom trodden by human foot. Here were pools, the drippings of the roof; there damp mould and mosses; there again a wet slimy bed of mosses and short dank grass.

It was the vegetation of darkness and of desolation. No sun ever penetrated those gloomy regions to warm, invigorate, or fertilise.

It was as the valley of the shadow of death.

At length a cool blast of air, coming in puffs, proclaimed that they had reached the vicinity of that opening where, if any, danger was to be apprehended.

Lady Beauchamp waved her hand for utter silence, while she reconnoitred through the low hawthorns and stunted trees, which effectually concealed the entrance.

All stood still, aware that now their fate was probably about to be decided.

Will Scarlett and Friar Tuck had received bows and arrows from the lady of the castle, to whose forethought they owed whatever success they hoped for.

She turned quickly back with a bitter smile upon her pallid countenance.

"What is it, mother?"

"The entrance is guarded," she replied; "but fear not, I have it in my power to save you. But I do not wish to part from you yet. Follow my directions."

"Implicitly."

"When you hear the men-at-arms flee, turn to the right until you come to a solitary oak."

"I know it," said Friar Tuck, who was, indeed, well acquainted with this part of the wood.

"Take a straight line to one blasted by lightning, to the right of which is a path."

"Yes, my lady."

"Follow that until you reach a small moated farm," continued the countess, "and, saying you come from Lady Alice, abide until I return."

"But are you not running into unnecessary danger?" cried Eveline, warmly.

"My child, you forget that I am the Hag of the Woods, from whom all men turn."

And as she spoke she cast her white veil back—she was all in white—and pushing through the brambles, or rather gliding through them, went out.

She made no sound.

Then loud cries of terror and alarm were heard without. The brave retainers of the castle, who would have fought a dozen men, were fleeing from a woman.

Will Scarlett took his bride by the hand, and followed by Rose and the Friar, plunged into a small thicket, and there concealed themselves.

In a few minutes they had lost even the sound of their enemies' cries.

Not a moment was lost in obeying the directions of the unfortunate countess.

They had luckily no open glade to cross, for they were still in sight of the battlements.

The oak appointed as the guide was easily selected from those around it.

It was immense in girth and branches, and probably a thousand years old.

CHAPTER C.

A FAIR FIGHT.

LEAVING the fugitives to pursue their way, we return to Robin Hood.

The blows which he had received, though not dangerous, were exceedingly painful.

There was little hope that the bold outlaw would be able to go forth for some days.

Edwin and the old people were unremitting in their attentions to their benefactor.

The old woman was somewhat learned in simples and "yarbs" for wounds.

Every day Robin began to mend.

The day appeared not far distant when he would be able to resume his forest command.

He earnestly longed for this hour, as inactivity is the abhorrence of such minds.

The chief solace of his illness was the society of Edwin,

with whom he could talk of a forest life, of hunting the wild deer and chasing the roe, and of Marian.

Both were in the heyday of youthful passion, and this subject was everlasting.

Edwin would speak rapturously of his humble village belle, while Robin would enlarge on the unequalled loveliness of his young lady of high degree.

This was a solace which would not have sufficed any less romantic mind.

But both found a somewhat sad pleasure in the subject, for in both cases their love seemed equally hopeless, equally unlikely to terminate well.

At last Edwin confided wholly in the outlaw, and told him his plans.

Robin Hood lay on the bed convulsed with laughter.

There were, however, other distractions for Robin Hood in the numerous visits he received from his lieutenants and outlaw friends.

Little John was unremitting in his attentions, and would have remained altogether, but that Robin Hood made him captain-in-chief for awhile.

About ten days after Robin Hood's mishap, and when good living began sensibly to repair the severe loss of blood which he had sustained in the fight, an occurrence of an unusual character diversified the monotony of his life.

Little John appeared at the head of a detachment of ten men with a prisoner.

It was the sturdy beggar who had wounded him so severely.

The cannie man looked pale as death. The eyes of the outlaw chief glistened.

"Ah! ah!" he said, seating himself on a bench before the hut; "so we have found the hard-hearted thief who refuses the honest man a crust."

"Pardon, my lord and master," cried the terrified beggar; "I did but defend my own."

"Defend thy own, foul loon?" said Robin Hood, darkly.

"I did but ask for food."

"I thought your worshipful sir did want to take the savings of my old age."

"Sirrah, I war on the rich."

"But the two cruel men you sent after me would have taken all I had," he murmured.

"Ah! ah! I see them yonder," cried Robin Hood, who, like many other great generals, never forgot faces. "Stand forth, you Greenham and Fenton."

The outlaws, with something of a rueful countenance, obeyed his orders.

"Now, you north-country beggarman, tell your story—and tell it truthfully."

"I will, my lord."

And he did, retailing the whole adventure with a humour which made all laugh.

"What say ye?" asked Robin.

"'Tis false."

"Your faces betray you. You know the penalty. Any of the band of Brethren of Sherwood Foresters of England found guilty of appropriating public moneys to their own use, shall suffer death, and I, grand Forester of England, condemn you."

The two outlaws fell on their knees, and in abject tones begged for their lives.

Four armed men, two with noosed ropes, approached them sternly.

"Stay," said Robin, with ineffable contempt. "And these men were of my outlaws."

"Hang them."

"These men I trusted."

"No mercy!"

"Mercy! mercy!"

"These men have been admitted into the secrets of my band," he said, adding to himself, "fortunately not into any secrets of great importance."

"Master, shall we string them up?" cried their late companions, impatiently.

"No! they are not worthy to defile rope or tree, but an they are ever seen in the forest or within its purlieus, let a cloth-yard arrow end their lives."

The crestfallen ruffians rose.

"Stay, my masters," said Robin, sarcastically; "you go not thus. Strip off their Lincoln green."

It was done.

"Take their bows and break them on their backs; and

now scourge them from my sight. They stink in my nostrils."

The order was obeyed with alacrity, the sturdy beggar looking on with awe and admiration.

"And what shall we do with this gudeman?" said the greenwood sovereign, turning to his late assailant.

"Hang him!" said Little John.

"Hang him!" repeated the outlaws.

"What sayest thou why sentence should not be passed upon thee?" asked Robin.

"Everything. In the first place I would fain live, if but to sing of your justice."

Robin smiled.

"What next?"

"All that I have seen has so delighted me, that if you will but forgive me the ugly blow I gave, I will throw down my old poke with its money, and join ye."

"But first, sirrah, we must have a *fair* bout at quarter-staff."

"Any time. I have lived too long in the forest not to be prepared to defend my own, and this feeling alone made me hit out. Besides, I knew you not at first."

"What say you all?"

The outlaws murmured somewhat.

"Wilt fight now?" asked Little John.

The sturdy beggar scanned his sturdy proportions with a grim attentive smile.

"Thou hast bone and sinew," said the beggar; "but hast thou the real science?"

"Try."

"I am ready."

A smile irradiated the countenance of Robin, while even the men grinned.

The quarterstaffs were handed up, and the two men placed themselves in position.

They were very different in size, but both of sinewy and stalwart frame.

Little John had the advantage of height, the sturdy beggar was more lithe.

Little John flourished his staff over his head, and looked at his adversary with something of disdain.

He promised himself thoroughly to avenge the treacherous blow his chief had received.

"Now, my man, an you are ready, begin. I hope thy shock head hides a good skull."

"A better head than thine, and more in it," said the beggar, "as you will see if you hit it."

"Play!" said the good-humoured giant, somewhat nettled at the other's coolness.

"Play!"

"And fortune favour the bold," cried Robin.

"Amen!"

The two men now seemed to see nothing but themselves. Both were intent and anxious to succeed, as these contests among the common sort of people were as much thought of as tournaments among the higher classes.

With good reason.

Nothing better developed the bone and muscle of the people. The beggar began his attack by a quick flourish of his staff, as if to throw his man off his guard, but this feint did not succeed.

Little John was ready.

The sturdy beggar made a rapid and clever feint at his shins, intended for his head.

It was stopped.

Then making him see more stars that there are in the heavens, and before he could rightly comprehend how it was accomplished, he himself received, first on the side of the head and then on the shins, two such thwacks, as, for an instant, made him unconscious where he really was.

He, however, was soon brought to his senses by a loud laugh from the outlaws.

The fight now waxed hot and furious, for both were master of the science; still, though the beggar could hit terrific blows, he could not guard so well as the giant.

From this cause he received six blows to the other's one, which state of affairs could not last.

He began to think that he had found more than his match—a fatal surmise.

In all fights the first requisite for success is personal confidence.

Without that, all is lost.

He was, however, a really brave man, and would not think of giving in as yet.

Robin Hood saw how it was.

"Hold!" he cried, in an imperious voice.

The combat ceased as if by magic, the two perspiring, palpitating combatants gladly leaning on their sticks to regain a supply of wind.

They were reeking with sweat and utterly out of breath.

"You are a bold player," said the captain of the outlaws, "but better men have succumbed to Little John."

"Little John!" grinned the beggar, "hang me if I buy a pig in a poke again."

"What mean you?"

"I thought you some big lubberly lout, with more bone than skill—an I had known thee for Little John, I would sought me an easier match."

"Well said," cried Robin, "and now I induct you of the band of bold outlaws. Swear him in."

This ceremony duly performed, the sturdy beggar freely cast his money into the treasury, which, if he served faithfully, would support him and his for life.

The organisation of property in Sherwood Forest was really practical communism.

It could only be practicable under the peculiar circumstances of their life, when, from being outlaws, private possessions were simply valueless.

This business thus satisfactorily adjusted, the outlaws took their departure, leaving Robin Hood for a few days longer an inmate of the hut.

Before, however, Little John left, it was arranged that the return of the outlaw chief to his trysting-tree should take place under an escort of the whole band.

A resolve which had mightier results than any one of them expected.

CHAPTER CI.

THE BISHOP.

THOUGH this is not the place to explain the peculiar plans of young Edwin, we may mention that they were connected with the rescue of Rose Leigh.

The youth had still faith that, despite his misfortunes, she loved him.

Faith!

The dearest, most priceless, and best diamond in all the crown jewels of love.

To assure himself of the true state of affairs it was necessary for him to take a journey towards the town of Nottingham.

Robin Hood also was extremely desirous of hearing of the sheriff of that ilk, who had as yet shown no design of carrying out his plans with Thomas the carter.

What was he waiting for?

Probably for reinforcements; it might also probably be for a warrant from royalty.

The Sheriff of Nottingham was a wary man, and therefore not easily deceived.

Perhaps he suspected the connivance of the outlaw was merely a trap.

In four days Robin Hood hoped to be well, and he longed to be up and doing.

He was quite as impatient of solitude as the wildest panther of the hills.

It must not be supposed that all this time he had forgotten his lady-love. Several messages had passed between them by the connivance of the good abbess.

He was, however, naturally impatient to assure her in person of his complete recovery.

How he longed to have been nursed by her through his painful and disagreeable illness. He could in imagination fancy her hand upon his heated brow.

He could fancy, as he half dozed, her warm, perfumed breath fanning his cheek.

We cannot say that these sort of reflections were wise for a man in a fever.

But a man in love may not keep them down.

It was the dusk of the evening, the birds everywhere were on the wing in the direction of their night haunts.

Darkness was falling slowly over forest and glade—slowly but surely.

It would soon be night, when nought would be heard save the hoot of the owl.

Robin, feeling quite himself again, sat on the rustic seat before the sylvan hut, thinking not of the morrow, but of the happy day when Marian, casting off all the restraints of society, would become his bride.

He was so far gone in a deep reverie as to be insensible to all around.

Suddenly he was aroused to a sense of existence by a voice close at hand.

"What ails the boy, that he runs so?" said the aged grandfather of Edwin.

Robin looked up, and saw the youth rushing over the plain like a madman.

"In! in!" he cried, in frantic tones.

In two minutes more he was close by the outlaw's side, speechless and out of breath.

"What is it?" asked Robin.

"The bishop."

"What of him?"

"The bishop," panted Edwin, "led by those rogues you scourged, is close upon us."

"Merciful heavens!" cried the old people; "oh, good sir, escape!"

"Impossible," said Edwin; "they have taken their measures too well. The hut is quite surrounded."

Robin muses.

"What is to be done?" cried the old woman, wringing her hands with genuine sorrow.

"My friends," said Robin, "I am willing to give myself up without a struggle, rather than harm shall befal you—but if taken, he will hang me."

"Hang!"

"A fat churchman is the last man who forgives," said Robin Hood, quietly.

"Can anything be done?"

"If I could but gain twelve hours all would be well," continued the outlaw.

"But is that to be done?" asked Edwin, with a sharp, scrutinising glance.

"A woman alone can save me, because a woman alone he would not harm.

"I will do anything, even give my life," said the grandmother.

"All we have to do is to change clothes. In the dusk of the evening, and in the delight of capture, they will not examine too closely. When a prisoner, be silent as long as you can. By morn, so help me Heaven, you shall be free!"

There was not a moment's hesitation on the part of any. All felt there was a duty to perform.

Robin took the gown of grey, giving up his mantle of green; he then brought out her spindle and twine, while she took in hand his bow and arrows.

The transformation was easily made, and in the dusk few could have detected the cheat.

Scarcely had the ludicrous transfer been affected when up dashed the proud bishop.

The supposed archer stood in close proximity to the spinning old woman.

"Surrender, villain!"

"I surrender, my lord," said the full, rich voice of Robin Hood, "the more that I am sick; but harm not these good people who were forced to give me shelter in my illness."

"But that I think thee villain enough even to maltreat an old woman," replied the bishop, furiously, "I would burn their house down. But beware ye, lest again ye harbour ruffians and thieves."

"We main do it," whimpered the old man—Edwin was concealed in the thatch—"these foresters take or leave just as they please. Poor old people like us cannot say them nay."

"I dare say, old man, there is some truth in this, so I forgive you and give you my blessing."

The old man kneeled in earnest, for a bishop's blessing was really no mean thing.

"Now bind me this King of Sherwood on a horse, and we will ride quickly to Nottingham town," cried the bishop, "lest the coppice knaves try a rescue."

With these words, and having seen the capture duly secured, the portly bishop led the way, anxious, now that he had succeeded, to return as quickly as possible.

The guides he had brought with him, the scourged rogues, knew the forest well.

But they could not control the power of fatigue on men and horses.

About midnight all gave in, and a halt was necessarily declared.

A spot was selected capable of easy defence, which, however, scarcely seemed necessary, when we note that the bishop was attended by one hundred armed men.

Still, an exaggerated fear was always entertained of the prowess of the yeomen.

As soon as the halt took place, the old woman was taken off her dapple white steed and tied to a tree.

The bishop, who

> For joy he had gotten him bold Robin Hood,
> Went laughing all the way,

had the supposed outlaw tied to a tree close in sight.

Four sentries were placed over him.

On pain of instant death, these sentries were to keep the captive in sight.

This settled, the bold priest, under an awning, went cosily to sleep, to dream of the high reward and immense credit he would surely obtain at court for having rid the purlieus of Sherwood of the boldest and best outlaw it ever possessed.

He slept until dawn.

He was then rudely aroused.

"My lord, my lord, we are attacked!" said a voice in his ear.

The bishop sat up, and rubbed his eyes.

"What is it?"

The retainer pointed to a close column of a hundred yeomen, led by a stalwart chief.

"Who dares attack us?" he asked. "Who dares range the greenwood so freely?"

"'Tis a hundred yeomen led by one Little John," replied one of the spies.

"Ah!" cried the bishop, "another column led by a rogue who dares to wear a cassock."

"Friar Tuck."

"The knave!"

A third column appeared in sight, still a hundred strong, led by a sturdy yeoman.

"Who dares come this way?" again asked the bishop.

"Much the Miller."

The Bishop of Hereford swore a round oath, as another column of two hundred men—picked men of Sherwood Forest—came in sight.

"Two hundred men?"

"At the least."

"Who commands them—my eyes are dim?"

"ROBIN HOOD!" screamed the horrified and alarmed ruffians who had, as they thought, betrayed their chief.

"Then, in the foul fiend's name, whom have we here," cried the bishop, turning round, with a dark and gloomy scowl upon his face, "that has dared trifle——"

"I am an old woman," said the dame, with a chuckle, "as I shall presently prove."

"Hang up the witch!"

"They are about to attack, my lord."

"Attack," murmured the poor bishop, seating himself and wiping the cold perspiration off his brow, "attack!—woe is me that I saw this day—woe is me! It is of no use fighting against the foul fiend. Surrender or fight, I will have none of it."

Of course this was tantamount to an order to lay down their arms quietly, and an officer at once advanced to announce the fact to the outlaws.

"Stack them, and not one man shall be harmed," said Robin Hood, in a stern, commanding voice, "unless, indeed, evil has occurred to the poor old woman."

"She is quite safe," replied the lieutenant, with the most perfect politeness.

Prisoner or in his haunts, Robin Hood was merely the bold outlaw, but once victorious no prince could have been addressed with more profound respect.

"But you have not let the spies escape, surely," said the outlaw, looking keenly around.

The officer was about to point out where they were crouching, when two arrows were heard to hurtle through the air, which, however, missing their intended mark, wounded slightly two of the outlaws in the rear.

Before they could repeat their infamous attempt, they were secured by their late comrades.

But before justice was done to these ruffians, we must explain how it was that Robin came up just in the nick of time.

CHAPTER CII.

THE WITCH.

IT was night, and the silvery moon rose above a scene which, for splendour and genuine beauty, could scarcely be rivalled.

We are in one of the oak glades of the forest.

Far and wide, wherever the eye can reach, oak trees, and for the rest green grass.

But on the occasion of which we speak there is an active addition to the scene.

Round twenty large camp fires recline some five hundred men in Lincoln green.

They have the canopy of heaven for a roof, the trees as shelter from the storm. They are variously occupied. Some, as was natural where so many pair of human grinders were ever ready for the feast, were engaged in roasting fat bucks, hares, and birds for the evening meal, always doubly welcome in the open air.

Some were thoughtfully examining the progress of the cooks, as if impatient at their delay,

Most, however, thinking of the next day's review, were examining their arms and accoutrements, eager to look as well as possible in the presence of their beloved leader.

Their bows were fitted with new strings, their quarter-staves were duly pared of all excrescences, and every due attention paid to that neatness of costume he so much admired.

Some were sharpening the points of their arrows, or substituting a good for a damaged feather.

Some simply were stretched full length on the ground humming tunes, thinking of their sweethearts, or, which was the case with more than one of them, of nothing at all.

To while away the time others were practising single-stick, not in a soft and gentle way, but with hard blows and knocks that would have certainly stunned most ordinary men.

Here, however, these things were looked upon as a matter of course, and excited little notice.

In one corner, seated by themselves, without taking any part in the active proceedings, were Little John, Much the miller, and with them Thomas the carter.

Where they sat they were able to command a view of a slope which ascended from a neighbouring stream to the oak copse or glade, which served the outlaws for a sylvan amphitheatre.

They were in conversation, Little John telling some stories of his own personal experience, in which successful wrestling matches were most noteworthy.

Hitherto the worthy fellow had been too modest to propose anything of the kind to the outlaws, fearful they would look upon his strength as a drawback.

But Much scouted the idea, and said the noble game was by far too much neglected in the camp.

It was agreed that at the first forest festival a friendly fall should be tried.

Suddenly Little John checked all further conversation, and by a peculiar whistle caused all the outlaws to sink, as it were, into the ground, so quickly did they disappear.

It was like magic.

"What is it?" whispered Much the miller, who was a trifle or so superstitious.

"Well," said simple Little John, "an it be a witch I shall not wonder; it comes in so strange a guise, one cannot say if it be of heaven or the other region."

"Whereabouts?"

"It passes one of the watch fires," continued Little John, in a low whisper, "and what puzzles me above all things is, how has it past the sentries and the watches?"

The awed lieutenants looked and saw something in the shape of an old woman in grey clothes, a coatee as it were, and strange head-gear, who walked with huge strides, followed in the rear by an active and alert stripling, who could scarcely keep up with her.

"Shall I shoot her?" said Little John, in a tremulous whisper.

He had never been so frightened in his life.

Round the camp was a chain of sentinels, through which, on no former occasion, had anybody succeeded in passing. Were they all asleep, or intoxicated?

"No. An it be a witch, no arrow is any good unless it be tipped with silver."

"I will even tip mine, then, with the needful dross," said Little John, quickly.

Next minute he had a clothyard arrow to the string, and was about to bend.

"Who keeps watch and ward here?" then said a deep, commanding voice, "art *all* asleep—or afraid?"

A terrific shout of laughter, and then a cry of welcome, that shook the welkin, was the response to this sudden discovery of the true character of the suppositious Witch of Endor.

"Ha! ha!" said Robin Hood, as his lieutenants crowded round him, the whole of the band forming a respectful circle, "wert afraid, my bully boy?"

"I thought you were an old woman, and a very ugly one," replied Little John.

"Hast eyes only for the pretty ones?" said Robin, laughing merrily; "but a truce to joking. By the agency of an old woman, I have just escaped hanging by the neck——"

Profound silence.

"Those knaves whom I scourged from the band betrayed my illness to the bishop——"

Loud shouts of execration.

"The bishop, too glad, came, attended by a hundred horsemen, to the hut ye wot of, and captured—who think you?"

No one could tell.

"An old woman, who at this moment of time is riding beside the most worshipful bishop disguised as Robin Hood."

Loud shouts of laughter greeted this new merry jest of their beloved chief.

"When the bishop finds out his woeful mistake, he will be furious; and I ask which one among you will allow the old woman who saved your chief's life to suffer—will any of you?"

"None! none! To arms to save the old woman."

"There is another task to be performed, and that is to punish the sordid traitors who betrayed me to the prelate."

A grim murmur of approval greeted this part of the chief's speech, and all rose.

A hasty mouthful replacing the promised feast, the whole band was soon in motion.

First, of course, a new suit of garments was found for the forest chief, who disrobed himself amidst loud laughter.

What endeared Robin to his numerous and devoted followers was quite as much his love of fun and humour as his strict justice and integrity, his love of truth, and undaunted courage.

Now commenced one of those forced marches of which few but Englishmen are really capable.

Nothing is so trying to the body and mind, nothing causes more physical endurance.

Tramp! tramp!

Always on the move, each man striving to keep up with his neighbour, some to distance him, all to reach the distant goal in time to save the old woman who had so generously devoted herself to save their beloved chief.

But many also were actuated by an earnest desire to see justice done to the forest Judases.

Revenge is a fearful passion, but one which is as strong as any which actuates man.

We have seen the result.

The forest king motioned to his followers to bring him a log for a throne, and then the two trembling culprits were immediately brought before him—so white, so wan, so miserable, they had to be supported by some of their ancient comrades to prevent them from falling prostrate on the sward.

"Wretches, base and sordid knaves! because I would not suffer pettifogging thieves and cold-blooded assassins in my band, you must needs betray me. That even I could have forgiven. But in your reckless desire to slay me, you have wounded two of my men. Such knaves deserve not to breathe the same air with honest men. To the tree."

It was now the turn of these two poor forlorn knaves to kneel and pray for life.

"No!" said Robin Hood, sadly. "I forgave you once; forgiveness now were suicide."

He made a sign, and one or two of the gang, more expert than the others in this particular, caught them by the arms, and gagged them, despite their furious cries

A couple of convenient trees were then selected, and the cords being cast over strong boughs, the wretched men were, as newspapers now say, launched into eternity.

A shudder pervaded the whole assembly, Robin Hood himself remaining some time to hide his emotion.

"Now for the bishop," he at length said, in a loud and stentorian voice.

The worthy prelate, who had witnessed the elevation of the spies and traitors with the most profound indifference, now sprang to his—not feet—but knees, with a rapidity and success which made a goodly portion of the assemblage laugh outright.

He was deadly pale.

"Avaunt, bold traitor! I know thee for bad enough, but thou darest not assail mother church," he cried.

"I dare do anything for which I have just cause," replied Robin Hood, sternly.

"Hast thou no fear of Heaven," continued the bishop, "if not of men's laws, which you despise?"

"I despise no just laws, and I fear and reverence those of Heaven," continued the outlaw, proudly.

"Then," said the bishop, rising with alacrity, "you will allow myself and friends to depart."

"I will, on payment of due ransom. You have dared to use the services of two of my discarded men, to try and do me harm—you must pay for it, if not in person, in money. Strip the bishop of every rose noble," he added.

None made any resistance, and the outlaws had the satisfaction of seeing that their expedition to rescue the old woman had proved an eminently lucrative one.

Five hundred pounds was the plunder taken in money, to say nothing of the gold and silver plate carried by the sumpter mule.

"And now may we go?" said the prelate, sullenly.

"No," replied Robin Hood, gravely; "it is not often we have the honour of a bishop amongst us. We would fain you would chaunt us a mass, God wot, under the trysting tree."

"Sacrilege!"

"Sir bishop, I and my men, by cruel and unjust laws, have been driven to a life we in the main abhor; but we chose it not, therefore it is not dishonest. We are good men and true, and quite ready to accept the consolations of religion, if honestly offered us."

"You are in earnest?"

"Quite in earnest."

"Then lead the way, in Heaven's name," cried the bishop, whose anxiety was not so much to discharge his religious duties as to get fairly out of the clutches of the outlaws.

Robin Hood needed not twice telling, but led the bishop to a beautiful spot, at no great distance from the green glade itself.

A short delay ensued, and then a rude altar of earth was upreared for the use of the prelate.

To his surprise and secret mortification everything that he needed was also upon the altar.

They could not have done it better in a cathedral.

The bishop bit his lip, but when he saw the mute and humble attitude of the outlaws his heart smote him.

"These men are not what they seem," he muttered to himself; "they are misjudged."

He was right, and many other men and women, too, in this world are not to be so judged.

Appearances are ever deceitful.

The whole vast party of men, soldiers, and outlaws kneeled on the sward at a given signal.

They all listened devoutly and anxiously to the words of the proud and haughty churchman.

Not a word or sign made known any levity of feeling or doubt as to his powers.

"Thanks, my lord bishop," said Robin Hood, heartily; "my men are truly delighted, and as for myself, I hope this may be the seal of everlasting peace between us."

"Amen."

"And now that we have ministered to the spiritual, what say you to refresh the physical?"

"I know not," said the bishop, blandly—he was very hungry, not having yet breakfasted; "I know not, for Robin Hood is said to charge somewhat heavily for hospitality."

"On occasions," said the outlaw, drily; "but my lord bishop has paid already. Come."

Nothing loth, the burly prelate accepted the invitation, and when he did begin, ate certainly as if he had not tasted food for about a week or more.

Robin Hood was profusely hospitable; the venison was good, the wine excellent, and he himself doing justice to the good cheer, both were soon merry enough.

But the outlaw, who well knew that it was good to be merry and wise, seldom, therefore, except on great occasions, exceeded the bounds of moderation, either in eating or drinking.

He reminded the bishop, therefore, that it was time to move, if he would reach his abbey in time.

But the meat was good, and the wine was strong, and the bishop very obstinate.

The open air and exercise, he said, acted wonderfully upon his digestive organs.

He had never enjoyed anything half so much in all his life, and only wished his wine-bearer could find him such wine as he drank under the greenwood tree.

Soon the bishop became maudlin, and as this was a state of things which Robin detested, he rose.

"Boot and saddle!" he cried, and a dozen bugle-horns resounded through the forest.

The bishop was lifted on his palfrey and tied on, a man riding on each side.

Thus departed the powerful cavalcade that had entered the forest bent on the utter destruction of Robin Hood and the merry men in Lincoln green.

It was a long time before the escapade of the haughty bishop was forgotten.

It was a thorn in his side all his life.

CHAPTER CIII.

ST. MARY'S.

ERE we relate the progress of Robin Hood's love, and tell of the innumerable dangers and extraordinary adventures it caused him to encounter, we must enter upon the narration of an entertaining and curious episode with which he was connected.

Close to the Abbey of St. Mary's, where now the bishop is sleeping off his deep potations, is the village of Faddle.

It is a moderate-sized hamlet belonging to the abbey.

All its inhabitants are tenants or serfs of those proud and haughty monks.

There is no pretence or affectation of Christian humility about the clerical power.

They live for greed of power, for mere enjoyment, to rule and confound the world.

They have not much changed, even in these more enlightened, and civilised times.

One of the chief houses in the village is the farm-house of one John Leigh.

It belongs to a well-to-do farm, one that makes quite a warm man of its owner.

Now, John Leigh was proud of his farm, proud of his acres, proud of his cattle—but of one thing prouder still —his daughter.

She was the pride of his eye, the delight of his heart, and the mirror of what another was he had loved so dearly.

Unfortunately, John Leigh was a tenant of the abbey, though why unfortunately, it would have been hard as yet for him to say.

But the evil time was coming.

He was punctual with his dues; as punctual as in his respect to mother church herself.

Somehow, this particular autumn his crops had not been so good, certain of his cattle had died unaccountably, and hence his rent was a little behind.

But what would this matter?

The churchmen were not greedy of gain, they surely only wanted their own.

He would lay his case before the almoner on the first fitting occasion.

Well, to be sure, to-morrow was quarter-day; he would step up and see the worthy almoner.

With this idea, he had been standing outside his own door, he went inside.

There was Rose Leigh.

Shall we describe her?

Well, what need we say more than that she was of middle height, very fair, with rosy cheeks, white teeth, a laughing smile, and general appearance of happiness.

Her contour was faultless.

No ridiculous whalebone and canvas confined the bursting beauties of her bust.

But she was not insipid: gentle and tender, with a fund of good sense and a certain amount of will, her great need was somebody to look up to—to love.

"Well, Rosy dear, let me have a jug of ale; I be thoughtful like, and when I'se thoughtful I foinds nothing loike ale to sharpen the wits."

"Or take them away altogether."

"Ho! ho! ho!" he laughed, in quite a stormy kind of way, "but thee's right. Too much is good for nobody— still I wants to think, and think I can't without."

If John Leigh had only lived a little later, since the discovery of tobacco!

Rose Leigh tripped to where a large barrel of genuine October stood and drew a foaming mug.

"Drink, lass, drink!" said the jovial farmer; "thee knows I like it better."

The girl just sipped and laid the foaming mug beside her father on a table.

He took a long and powerful draught. As he did so, his faculties suddenly seemed to brighten up.

"What's become of Edwin?"

Here was a sudden fiery face with a vengeance, but no audible reply.

"I say, lass, hast lost thy speech? What's become of Edwin?" repeated the father.

"I don't know."

This was spoken quite in a whisper.

"Not quarrelled, I hope? not taken offence at thy mother's ways, eh?" cried the fond father.

"No! He stops away of his own accord, and so he can stop away altogether now."

"Eh, lass! thee says that in such a way, I've a great mind to saddle Dobbin and go fetch the young rascal."

"Father!"

"He may be ill, you know."

"Ill?"

"Or his parents may be ill, and Edwin was ever a good son," said the father.

"He was."

"And a good son makes a good husband, Rosy."

"I suppose so."

"Well, never thee fatch thyself about un. If he don't come to-night, I'll ride over to-morrow and see what's become of him."

"There's a darling father."

"Ride over and see that ne'er-do-well, poaching vagabond Edwin?" said a shrill voice. "None of your empty-purse vagabonds for me. Let me see you!"

"Dame, our own purses are not so full that we should talk of our neighbours'," said the farmer.

The dame, a portly, but vixenish likeness of her daughter, seated herself and began to whimper.

"That I should live to hear John Leigh say that! I that brought him a hundred golden guineas, two cows, a drove of pigs, and what not besides, as my dowry; to think that it has all been squandered and wickedly wasted, and that we may yet have to beg our bread in the highways and byways—oh! oh! oh!" and the good woman went off into a series of little shrieks.

In modern times we should have said hysterics.

The farmer, with a groan, left her in charge of her daughter, well knowing from long experience that nothing he could say or do would be of any service.

He was a wise man and well-drilled husband.

In the meantime, other events were occurring within the abbey of great importance to Edwin's fortunes.

It was in the ancient Abbey of St. Mary's, then a celebrated sanctuary, but now—

Let its poetic historian speak.

"Time hath left the deep traces of his destroying hand upon its crumbling walls; and the passing footsteps of bygone years, as they hurried on in their march to eternity, have worn away the quaint carvings from column, cloister, altar, and shrine. Where the setting sunbeams then gilded the deep-dyed windows, rich with the figures of saints and warriors, and all the emblazoned pomp of barbaric heraldry, now waves the monumental ivy with a solemn motion, as if it kept time to the sobbing wind that moans mournfully among the ruined battlements. The deep and mellow voices of the friars, who then chanted the holy vespers, have died away; even the high and arched roof, which gave back the rolling echoes, is gone; the vaulted and pillared aisles, where the sounds were prolonged or lost, are fallen; and the long green grass waves in the silent choir.

"Little did the peasant then dream, as he went whistling under the deep shadow of the lofty walls, and eyed the huge granaries and out houses well filled with the fruits of the earth, that in a few more years neither garner nor threshing-floor would be seen, and only a few walls and patched-up wings left to point out what had been."

We enter the large vaulted cell of the almoner, where he doles out his petty charities and receives his large rents.

He is seated in a huge chair of quaint formation.

The almoner is about forty, strongly built, dark, with a visage exhibiting saturnine qualities, but above all the most intense and selfish sensuality or rather voluptuousness.

Before him stands the brutal ranger who fired the hut of Edwin's grandfather and grandmother.

He has been speaking of the game which he and his fellows have brought in.

"It is well. When the bishop has recovered from his mishap, there will be need of all."

"Anything else, holy father?" he asked.

The almoner looked keenly at him.

"I have seen the white-faced little Agnes."

"Well?" said the almoner, with a strange glow on his face and fire in his eyes.

"She will be at the dark postern at eight of the clock," was the quiet reply.

"You are sure?"

"These demure ones never fail."

"You are observant, sirrah. I have myself truly observed that more dependence is to be placed on these quiet ones. You shall be rewarded."

"A boon! a boon!"

"Dost want more money?" cried the almoner, a shade of displeasure crossing his swarthy countenance.

"No."

"What then?"

"You have not forgotten, Edwin, the poacher."

"I have not."

"He eludes my grasp."

"Well?"

"Still I mean to punish him."

"For which you shall not be forgotten."

"But without seeing him I have the means of punishing him," replied Hubert, with downcast eyes.

"How so?"

"He loves——"

"Whom?"

"A maiden."

"Any one I know?"

"Rose Leigh."

"Ah!"

"My father knows her."

"I have seen her."

Yes; and insulted her, and been refused by her, scorned, and laughed at.

"Edwin loves her?"

"He does."

"She loves him."

"I knew not that. Well——"

"I love her."

"Indeed!" thought the almoner; "and I hate her."

"Now if her marriage with me could be brought about, my revenge upon the insolent poacher would be half completed."

The priest reflected. Rose had called him an old man. This was a deadly insult, and one a voluptuary never forgives. Should he revenge himself thus?

He pictured the girl to himself.

He felt he could not hope ever to corrupt that pure and virtuous soul.

His revenge, however, lay before him.

"In what way, Hubert, can I help you?"

"You have influence with her father."

"He adores his daughter."

"With the mother?"

"Humph! I have, but John Leigh is not a man to be ruled by wife."

"He will not pay his rent to-morrow——"

"Ah!" cried the almoner, and he drew a long breath "sayest thou so? Then we have him."

And a savage gleam of long-deferred vengeance flashed from his lurid eyes.

"Leave all to me," said the almoner, quietly; "leave all to me. You have faithfully served me, and I will do what I can for you in return."

The ranger bowed low and left the apartment.

Two proper villains.

We need not here dwell upon the profligacy of the church. Every historian and historic novelist has done it over and over again. Celibacy was but a blind; and more ruin, desolation, and sorrow was spread through the land by these abandoned men than by as many free lances or debauched retainers of a noble.

Hubert, it will be seen, hunted other game besides deer, for the almoner of the Abbey of St. Mary's.

CHAPTER CIV.

THE INTERVIEW.

IT was morning. The almoner sat in his easy chair. He had just breakfasted on the fat of the land, as idle priests only can breakfast.

His arms were folded over his broad chest, which should have been that of a soldier.

But the church was chiefly recruited amid those who disliked bodily exercise.

The almoner's only weapons were cunning and duplicity.

He was waiting to receive the dues and rents of the numerous abbey tenants.

A book was before him in which to enter their payments.

Gross as he was, the man knew the value and influence of learning; he was, therefore, a tolerably good scholar. At all events, he could read and write.

A servitor announced a tenant.

"Show him in."

John Leigh entered with a proud and manly step.

"Welcome, Farmer Leigh," said the priest, in an unctuous tone, "always first at audit."

"I strive to do my duty."

The priest turned to the page of the book which contained John Leigh's name.

He read out the items of the rent-charge.

"All right, holy father," said John Leigh, heartily.

"Shall I sign thy quittance?"

"One moment, father. Here is money in this bag, but not quite all," he began.

"Go on," said Father Thomas, in the same oily, silky tone. "I think you said not all?"

"Your reverence is right."

"Explain yourself."

"I know not if my land be worn out or tired of giving good crops," said the farmer, "but somehow or other, everything this season has been half-crops; and then the murrain in the cattle, and, somehow or other, after overhauling every rose-noble in my drawer, and leaving myself a pauper, I have but half the rent."

"Farmer Leigh, I hope this is not the effect of idleness or drink?" said the priest, severely.

"No man, your reverence, ever called me idle," was the manly reply, "and I drink not half so much ale as many a holy father."

The monk looked at him askance, but detecting no hidden meaning, let the hint pass.

"I can, therefore, no wise account for my misfortune. Your reverence will perhaps give me time. I will work early and late to redeem my debt."

"Farmer Leigh," said the priest, kindly, "take yonder settle and sit you down."

The jolly farmer joyfully acquiesced. This was at all events a promising beginning.

"I have in the twinkling of the eye discovered the cause of all your disappointment."

"Sir?"

"You are not so young as you were; tut! tut! man, I know—hearty still, and ready to work—yes—but the farm wants young blood; it wants a fresh life in it."

"Sir reverence!"

"In fact, you want a son-in-law to aid you in your arduous labours."

"It never struck me."

SIR RICHARD OF THE LEE.

"It often has me. You have a most charming daughter, whom it is your immediate duty to marry. There are plenty of wolves about in sheep's clothing, and the sooner a young girl has a natural protector, the better always for herself."

"The excellent—the worthy man!" thought the farmer; "how they are calumniated."

"Marry your daughter to an honest and industrious man, and instead of leaving your farm at times to the mercy of hirelings, you will have one about whose glory and duty it will be to look after your interests just as if they were his own."

The priest spoke in glowing terms.

"Your reverence is right, and this very afternoon I will ride over to a young friend of mine, who has, I fancy, won my daughter's affections, and who, I know, loves her."

"His name?"

"Edwin."

"The excommunicated poacher!"

"Sir?"

"Silence! Dare to breathe the reprobate's name in my presence! A low, common, sacrilegious thief, who has not only dared to kill the royal deer, but to insult, deride, and maltreat the joint keepers of the chief ranger and the church," continued the almoner, in solemn tones, that bespoke his real conviction of the heinous character of the crime indicated.

"My most revered father!"

"Would you defend him?"

"I would defend him, an please your reverence," said the English yeoman, sturdily.

"Speak!"

"These same keepers did waylay and nearly murder him, prevented only by the intervention of some honest yeomen."

"Thieves! robbers! outlaws!"

"I did hear, so please your reverence, they were simply honest yeomen. The rangers, finding they could not slay the youth, in sheer wantonness burnt his father's hut. This is the truth."

"They did well. Now, mark me, John Leigh, this scoundrel, who will soon be within the clutches of the law, is no fit mate for your daughter. But mate them an you will," he added.

"But——"

"Listen."

"I do."

"Mate them an you will, and the consequence shall be,—you will be expelled from your farm, the excommunication of the church showered upon you, and your family driven forth beggars on the wide world."

The farmer bowed his head.

"Do as I bid you, and the deficit this quarter shall be forgiven you—I will be answerable for you, and you leave this place with my cordial blessing."

The farmer stared.

"What, holy father, would you have me do?" he asked, really quite bewildered.

"I have selected a son-in-law," said the priest, unctuously and coaxingly.

"Father!"

"A worthy fellow."

"Father!"

"An excellent fellow; most devoted to mother church, and useful in every way."

Oh! Sir Pandarus of Troy, why art thou not here to listen?

"Name him, holy father."

"Hubert the forester."

"Hubert the Red Hand!" burst forth the farmer, "the accursed of hill and valley, of forest and glade, and thicket, of earth and heaven, fit tenant for the lowest depths of hell."

"Stop, how dare you, a layman, utter thus a curse in the presence of a servant of the church?" cried the angry priest. "Stand, while I curse you myself in——"

"Pardon, father, I forgot myself. I will listen calmly to what you have to say," said the farmer.

"'Tis well, I forgive you. Remember my words, and either prove yourself an obedient or a disobedient son as you will. You have your choice—now go."

And the priest waved his hand.

But the farmer humbly laid down his money, which the almoner thereupon entered in the large book, and sent him away.

The worthy farmer left the room, stooping low and bowed down with bitter care.

What had become of his resolution to take Dobbin and ride over the lea in search of Edwin?

He dared not look his daughter in the face, and yet he must, or ruin stared him in the face.

He walked slowly towards his home, and paused on the threshold of the door.

He scarcely liked to enter.

At length he made up his mind.

He started as if an arrow had struck him when he had done so.

At a window sat Rose Leigh, looking thoughtfully, pensively, but prettily, out of window.

Near the fireplace was Hubert the Red, in a spick and span new suit of uniform, talking in a most insidious manner to the good dame.

Farmer John Leigh clutched his stout cudgel, rage at his heart, but one thought restrained him.

The priest!

Hubert no sooner saw the farmer, than he rose with a profound bow, and hastily apologised for his unexpected intrusion.

"No apology, Master Hubert," said the farmer, coldly; "I see you are making yourself at home."

The ranger grinned, Dame Leigh looked astonished, while Rose was overwhelmed both with fear and astonishment.

She knew well her father's utter dislike and thorough contempt for this very man.

What could it mean?

A dull, heavy foreboding, such as a sailor feels long before a storm, struck a chill to her very heart, as if she foresaw some let or hindrance to her bright young love.

Her father sauntered her way, and threw his hat upon a settle.

"You are not hospitable, my dear," he said, sarcastically, "let us have dinner."

Hubert glanced askance at the farmer. He saw that the priest had been at work.

His heart bounded with unholy joy as he surveyed the youthful proportions, graceful attitudes, and blushing charms of the farmer's pretty daughter.

In imagination he already claimed them for his own.

The dinner was stiff and ceremonious, the farmer being silent and thoughtful. He had *not* made up his mind to sacrifice his daughter, not he, brave heart.

But as yet the good man really did not know what he was to do to get out of the scrape.

His ideas were limited, but they were founded on honesty; above all on truth.

As if satisfied with breaking the ice, Hubert of the Red retired very early.

Farmer Leigh drew up to the fire, with a fresh jug of foaming ale.

"Shall I saddle Dobbin?" said the girl, with an innocent, happy smile upon her face.

"Saddle Dobbin!" cried the father, testily, "in Heaven's name, why saddle old Dobbin?"

"To ride over the lea," she whispered.

"Listen to me, dame and daughter," he cried suddenly, "I must speak out or die. There has come upon me a blow to-day, which I know not how to ward off."

"Father!"

"Husband!"

"I am a plain man of few words, and if you interrupt me shall never tell my story," he began.

"We will listen."

And they did, while he told a plain, unvarnished tale of the true state of affairs.

"Oh, father!" cried Rose.

"Hoity toity! a pretty thing for priests as ought to have nothing to do with marriage, a marrying off people in this way," cried the indignant matron.

"Thanks, mother."

"But what is to be done?" asked the farmer, when the first burst of feeling was over.

The women were silent. He spoke in such a piteous woe-begone way, so unlike his former self, that they had not heart either of them to say a single word for some minutes.

"All I can see is that Rose must marry the fellow," said the dame, philosophically.

"If nothing else will save papa, I will consent," whimpered Rose; "besides, Edwin don't seem to care much about me."

And so for the moment this momentous question was settled.

CHAPTER CV.

ROBIN HOOD'S RESOLVE.

THOUGH Robin Hood was fully aware that he possessed Marian's love, yet until possession gave fruition to his hopes, he could not believe it possible that so much happiness could be his.

It was with him, therefore, a stern necessity to occupy himself constantly.

It was the only way to drown that care which proverbially is said even to kill animals.

The only occupation which suited him was trials at archery, or forest adventures.

But there were few even of his own band who would try to shoot against him, except as a pure matter of honour.

"I have shot against Robin Hood" was a passport to the admiration of all.

The merry outlaws had had one of their annual meetings for the distribution of treasure, and for the usual manly games.

All, then, had retired to rest within the confines of the cavern.

It was a stormy evening, chill and cold; the wind came in sharp, fitful gusts, whistling, now and then sighing, through the young green leaves and old boughs of the huge trees.

The sun had long gone down with a wild aspect, deep red clouds clustering about him, and, as he sank behind the trees, long streams of grey mist rising, to give evidence of a stormy night.

Soon the storm burst, and even within the cavern could be heard the wail of the tempest.

The trees, riven by the wind, tottered and fell; the old green column that had stood through the storms of past centuries, smitten by the lightning, crumbled a heap of ruins, and the fitful lull of the storm was ever broken by the wind's wild sobs, as, like groaning giants, they came again and again to the contest.

Robin Hood, after some thought, slept soundly. His previous agitated thoughts and the howling of the wind made him sleep.

Sleep! the weird sister of death, the symbol in life of the great coming shade that will for ever numb and paralyse joint and sinew. Away in that misty future whose portals Death guards and opens, the soul gazes on a new world, inscrutable but expected; down in this the body rests in its nightly collapse, and rises with its old senses freshened, quickened, to work away its travail, until the long hour comes, and then there is an end. The worm riots and the maggot crawls, the frail and polluted tenement moulders and crumbles with its initial element, but the Immortal has gone forth, trembling, doomed, it rises a star, or sinks a fiend. The resurrection after sleep is the hope in life, the resurrection after death, the promise of immortality.

Robin dreamed, and his dream, as that of lovers ever is, was of the loved one.

It was a quaint, peculiar dream, and one the outlaw long remembered.

A fairy palace stood on a hill shining with gold and diamonds, emeralds and rubies, and all manner of flashing precious stones.

In the midst stood Marian.

He was advancing towards her, a thousand voices bidding him enter.

But on the threshold of all this splendour, lay a grinning skull, bowing and mocking at him, wild words shaking themselves out from between its loosened teeth, and there it gibbered and danced about in the broad light of all these countless, priceless gems, and the astonished dreamer could not pass.

Death itself seemed to stand between the lover and his beloved Marian.

And yet the glorious voices called him still, in rich and musical strains.

Robin awoke.

"What means this?" he cried, the heaviness of sleep not quite cast aside; "do angels suddenly visit us in our dreams, and warn us? Do fiends from the nether world come forth to mock and laugh at us? What means this? Will I have to cross the dread threshold which the bravest man shrinks from ere we can finally be united? A something tells me 'tis so—and that Robin and Marian were not for happiness here."

He rose and looked around the vast and gloomy cave, dimly lit by torches.

"And these are the ancestral halls to which Robert Earl of Huntingdon must bring his noble bride," he said, bitterly; "and these rude men and women be her companions. But what oh! I am growing dull and sentimental—I must drive these cobwebs from my brain, or I shall become a woman and wear petticoats. Tra la la! tra la la!"

And he wound a gentle strain on his bugle, waking, however, the echoes of the cavern.

Next minute every man and woman was on foot, no dressing being required.

Our ancestors slept on a bed in the garb of the day simply loosened.

No one needed any intimation of what was required, but as the storm had not yet abated, the whole of the party began to prepare for breakfast inside the cave.

As this was a morning for business the first meal of the day did not take long.

When it was over Robin Hood sauntered forth to the mouth of the cave.

The glorious sun was now high in the heavens, and the earth steaming with savoury vapours, while every stem and leaf and bough had its own sparkling gem.

The men rushed forth and surrounded their chief seated on his sylvan throne.

As soon as silence was proclaimed, the young outlaw rose with a grave smile.

"I take my stand in Barnesdale Wood," he said, "and here I sit; nor will I go to dinner until some one of you bring me some bold baron or unasked guest, either clerical or lay, who is able to pay all the expenses of our joint table."

The outlaws laughed, but as they knew that when Robin Hood said a thing he meant it, they were somewhat puzzled how they were to bring a prisoner soon enough.

Little John, above all, whose cavernous stomach required constant replenishing, scratched his head.

His answer to the speech of his noble chief is strictly historical.

"Where shall we take, where shall we leave, where shall we abide behind? Where shall we rob, where shall we reave, where shall we beat and bind?"

"There is no force," said bold Robin Hood, "can well withstand us now; so look ye do no husbandman harm that tilleth with his plough. But mind also that you touch not yeomen good and true, nor even knights and squires if they show themselves good fellows; but beat and bind bishops and archbishops, and be sure never to let the Sheriff of Nottingham there out of your mind."

"Your words, noble and illustrious captain," said Little John, smiling, "shall be our law; and you will forgive me for wishing for a wealthy customer soon—I long for dinner."

"So soon shall I," said Robin, gaily; "so now go, and one hour after mid-day I hope to witness your safe and happy return."

The whole band dispersed, and Robin himself, not to be disturbed by the women and children, who were flocking round, retired to a secret bower, where no one would think of invading his privacy, there, like a knight-errant, to meditate on Marian.

Little John, Much the miller, and one other stout outlaw, took their way towards a high road leading in the direction of the celebrated town of Sheffield.

Little John had a frown upon his face. The simple-hearted fellow thought that he must avert a great misfortune from the devoted head of his beloved and venerated leader.

To go without one's dinner Little John regarded in the light of a misfortune.

"I say, Much," he began, twisting his huge moustaches, "what think you?"

"Considering you have asked me no questions, I cannot say," was the reply.

"This freak of honest Robin's?"

"It is not my business to think."

"Well, I think it's very—no, I won't say foolish—very—no, I won't say absurd—but decidedly very wrong of him," said Little John, unwilling for a moment to blame his chief.

"He knows what he is about. Hang me if you shan't disguise me as a knight, and I'll pay, rather than honest Robin shall go hungry," cried Much the miller, enthusiastically.

Little John wrung him by the hand with a grim smile. The idea was not a bad one.

They had now reached a fit place for an ambush—one that had served before.

It was a spot where a stream of clear and pellucid water crossed the road, which descended with an abrupt slope on both sides. Trees quite overhung the way, their branches touching.

The outlaws seated themselves within a thicket, upon a fallen trunk of a tree, and beguiled the time with conversation, jest, and anecdote.

They were too wary to indulge in the popular ditties of the day.

"I wonder how poor Robin's stomach is?" said Much, after nearly three hours.

Little John looked ruefully at him, as if he thought such remarks no joke.

"Well," he said, slowly, "I am sorry to say that he must feel very queer."

Much laughed outright, a clear, ringing laugh, which his superior officer checked by a frown.

"Hist!" suddenly exclaimed Little John, after a few minutes; "I feel my thumbs prick."

"What is it?" asked Much, whose ears were generally very sharp and quick.

"By the pricking of my thumbs, something earthly this way comes," said the giant, in a hollow whisper. "I clearly heard a horse's tramp at the top of the glen. Silence, all of ye!"

All listened attentively and the slow, measured tread of a horse was distinguished.

Little John stepped forward and gazed up the slope of the hill.

"By St. Barnabas!" said the big forester, ruefully, "this man will not pay for dinner."

"Why not? if I may ask," exclaimed Much, "it seems to me a knight."

"Aye, but the most miserable wretch that ever one saw in that garb."

Truly, the man was not very pleasant to see, being in sordid array.

He was, it is true, in the costume of knight, but the romaunt of the days shall speak :—

> All dreary then was his semblaunt,
>   And little was his pride;
> His one foot in the stirrup stood,
>   The other waved aside.
> His hood hung over his two eyes;
>   He rode in simple array;
> A sorrier man than he was one
>   Rode never in summer day.

"By the bones of St. Dunstan !" cried Much, who was a judge of horseflesh; "I know not which is most dreary, the horse or the horseman that rides him. Surely the man is demented !"

"Or in love," sighed Little John, with a huge sigh, "which is the same thing."

The knight had by this time reached the bottom of the slope, and next instant he and his steed, a broken-winded and bony beast, had crossed over.

"Halt !" cried a deep voice, breaking the deep silence of the forest.

The knight looked up and saw two powerful men at his horse's head, while a third stood at some distance with an arrow drawn to the very head.

"What want you, my masters ?" he said, in a low voice, so doleful as to be ludicrous.

"I greet you well," replied Little John, somewhat rudely, "and welcome you to the greenwood. Our master has refused to touch his dinner these three hours, expecting your arrival. So come quickly, lest he be angry."

The woeful knight looked at the three men as upon three lunatics.

"It is impossible, since I know not your master and he knew not of my coming."

"Nevertheless he expects you, and as dinner is ready we may not tarry, but go."

"But," said the bewildered knight, who made no attempt whatever to defend himself, "if I may be so bold, who is your master, and why this pleasantry ?"

"Our master is bold Robin Hood, the King of Sherwood Forest," they replied.

But nothing surprised the woeful knight, who scarcely moved a muscle.

"E'en Robin Hood ! Ah ! Robin Hood," he said, carelessly; "he is a good yeoman and true, and I accept his invitation with all my heart and soul. Forward then at once."

The man exhibited neither surprise nor annoyance, nor any sign of fear.

Put it which way they could, it was impossible for them to make it out.

But in their own minds, the three foresters had not the slightest doubt that at all events his sordid and miserable appearance was but put on to disguise his real wealth and substance.

This was a stale trick in the forest, and one that was no longer of any avail.

The two chief foresters now walked one on each side of the woeful knight, while the third outlaw led the way along the narrow bridlepath, with which he was well acquainted.

This soon brought them to Watling Street, where they were joined by other outlaws.

As soon as ever any of the men in Lincoln green caught sight of this rueful Don Quixote of a by-gone age, they left their watch to follow with the stream and see how Robin Hood got a dinner out of him.

The knight appeared utterly unconscious of the interest he was exciting, and moved vacantly forward, as if utterly without volition or will.

He scarcely could have been aware that, just before he reached the trysting-tree, he was the central point of attraction of nearly two hundred pair of curious eyes.

Suddenly he was compelled to halt, and lifting his eyes, saw Robin on his sylvan throne.

The outlaw chief, without allowing the smile that was just upon his lips to be seen, rose and welcomed the traveller with considerable dignity, and much greater cordiality.

"Welcome, sir knight; we have waited long for you, but here you are at last."

"Gramercy," replied the woeful one; "you puzzle me much ; but I will gladly dine."

"You shall, and right well, as you are entitled to," said Robin, with a covert smile.

The woeful one now dismounted, and was offered a ewer to wash his hands, which he did with evident satisfaction, quite glad to clear himself of the dust and dirt of the road.

"Dinner," cried Robin, and as he spoke a long stream of men and women appeared groaning under the weight of copious and multifarious dishes, such as in those days were admired.

CHAPTER CVI.

THE PRICE OF A DINNER.

It would be turning our narrative into a catalogue to tell all that the woeful one saw before him, but we will allow the old minstrel to say his say,—

> Of bread and wine they had enough,
>   And nombles of the deere ;
> Swans and pheasants they had full good,
>   And fowls of the revere ;
> There failed never so little a bird
>   That ever was bred on brere.

The feast was right good, and the knight, though he still retained much of his taciturnity, was not quite so woebegone and miserable. The good wine warmed his heart, while he ate as if his abstinence from food had been at least of a week's duration.

Then he wiped his mouth, and seated himself beside Robin under the oak.

"You seem happy, sir outlaw," he said, with a deep sigh ; "happy under the greenwood."

Little John, Much, and one or two of the other chiefs now sauntered up to see the fun.

"You see, sir knight," replied Robin, "that we do not live so very miserably."

"On the contrary, you have given me a princely dinner, and I thank thee heartily for it, Robin; and if ever it should chance you come by my castle, I promise you I shall repay it."

"I am not accustomed to make such exchanges, sir knight," said the outlaw chief, "nor do I ask any man for dinner. I vow to heaven, as it is against good manners for a yeoman to treat a knight, that you must pay for your entertainment."

The woeful knight blenched not, but a quiet smile illumined his countenance.

"I have nothing more in my coffer," he said, with a deep sigh, "but ten shillings."

Robin stared at him with a half doubtful, half comic look. He had never seen so cool a customer before. He then made a sign to Little John.

In those days and under such circumstances there was little ceremony.

The tall forester proceeded with great dexterity to examine into the stranger's finances.

"The knight speaks truly," he cried, dolefully; "there be ten shillings, which will scarcely pay our expenses. Never mind, at all events, captain, you have dined."

"Ten shillings are but little use to me, my friend," continued he of the woeful countenance ; "'tis all I have in the world, and yet you are welcome to them."

The outlaw chiefs exchanged glances. The man puzzled them more and more.

"And pray may I be so bold," said Robin, sarcastically, "as to ask the name of the knight who has been so sorry a steward of his inheritance as to be in this plight—for surely ten shillings is but a poor sum for a man to travel with ?"

"My name, please you, worthy Robin Hood, is Sir Richard of the Lea."

"Then, in the name of Heaven, how is it you are so sadly distraught ?"

"'Tis a sad story, but a true one," replied the knight ; "if you will give me shelter for the night, I will defer my journey until to-morrow, and tell it."

"I shall gladly give you hospitality," quoth bold Robin, "so now for your story."

The lieutenants placed themselves in easy postures, and

prepared to listen to a narrative which at best they expected to be some doleful ditty or imaginary tale made up for the occasion.

Sir Richard of the Lea, as he announced himself in sonorous tones, thus spoke.

THE KNIGHT'S STORY.

I am fifty-one years old, and during thirty of those years have been a happy husband.

I have, as sole fruit of this long and happy union, one only boy.

His name is Robert, and for his sake his mother and myself have never thought any sacrifice too great. He is as brave, gallant, and handsome a young man as any.

He is fond of manly sports, and never passes a day but what he is out in the forest with his hawks and hounds; for hitherto all my possessions have been his.

His habit of roaming the forest began at a very early age indeed.

Before he was twelve, he was wont to range the wooded glades with his bow.

About seven years ago, and when he was fourteen, an adventure occurred to him, which, though I do not and shall not ever regret it, has been the main cause of my present troubles.

He had shot a fawn and was coming home, when he heard a gentle sobbing close to him.

Hurrying in the direction of the sound, his astonishment may be conceived when, at the foot of a tree, he saw, tattered and in rags, the dearest little girl that the imagination can picture to itself. She was, though weeping, a lovely vision to behold.

She was not more than ten, tall, and graceful in the extreme: had long golden hair hanging in clusters round her neck — clusters where the god Cupid far too often nestles.

"What ails you, child?" said my boy, whose name is Arthur, "and what do you here?"

"I am hungry and weary, and have been lost three days in the woods."

My son put no further questions, but busied himself preparing some hasty refreshment for the child, after which he heard her short and simple story.

She was the daughter of respectable and even wealthy parents, her mother she said being a Norman, her father a Saxon.

Her mother was sister to a petty Norman knight, Sir Guy de Lussac.

Her mother and father died rather strangely and suddenly the same week, leaving the whole of their property to Sir Guy de Lussac in trust for the child.

It was not quite clear, from Heloise's account, what the uncle's designs were, but at first he treated her with great kindness and consideration.

Four days before, instead of proposing a ride, he proposed a walk, which the girl gladly joined in, loving nothing more than the green forest glades.

They came into the forest, the girl merry and happy, the uncle sullen and thoughtful.

He never spoke, but the nervous twitching of his mouth indicated deep designs.

A great dread came upon the young girl's soul, and she was afraid.

Gradually she moved away from him and when he halted hid herself.

"Where is the little wretch?" he said wrathfully, and then he added, "'tis but one blow, and 'tis over. I cannot and I will not give up the estates to her."

Then little Heloise became convinced that she had been brought into the darksome wood to be murdered by her wicked uncle.

The instinct of preservation is strong within us all. The girl determined at once to escape from his clutches, and slipped away with a footfall as light as a fawn. The man's angry voice calling her only strengthened her determination to escape.

Soon she was in a dense thicket, and though once or twice she thought she heard him call, she coiled herself under some dense bushes, and lay quiet and still.

When next she remembered anything she had just woke out of a refreshing sleep.

It was dark, and she was alone in the gloomy and stupendous forest.

But Heloise was a brave little girl. She knew herself to be innocent and good, and felt that scarce any one would harm her save only her uncle.

She waited, then, eating a few berries which she knew to be good, until daylight.

As soon as she could see she retraced her steps, with a very vague idea of what she was going to do, but with an earnest desire to get out of the forest, and find some charitable soul to shelter her from her one enemy.

But little girls do not understand woodcraft, and once lost in a forest, nothing is more difficult than to get out of it, as I have myself often experienced.

With water to drink and berries to eat, she wandered about, now marching bravely on, now seating herself in tears, until she met with my son.

As soon as she had refreshed herself, Arthur took her by the hand, and led her on.

In two hours they arrived at my residence, and my wife and myself were surprised to see our boy walk in with the ragged little girl.

"Mother," he said, "you have often wished for a daughter—here is one!"

We looked, I suppose, our utter astonishment and surprise at the words.

"Heloise," cried the shrewd and clever boy, "you tell your story yourself."

She did, and its truth, simplicity, and candour quite won our hearts.

"Child," said my wife, when she had done, "consider this your home."

And so it has been ever since, and we have had truly an angel in the house.

I suppose it is needless for me to tell you that when they grew up, and he was a handsome man and she a lovely girl, budding into womanhood, they loved.

And we approved of their mutual affection, which reminded us of old days.

They were to have been married a little more than a year ago.

It was my full intention then to denounce the felon knight, and endeavour to obtain from the king restitution of her lands and hereditaments.

My house or castle is not far from St. Mary's Abbey, and there one day came Sir Guy de Lussac on a visit to the abbot and almoner.

Some devil put it in their heads to speak of Heloise, and the scoundrel at once surmised the truth, though he said nothing, I believe, at the time.

He contrived, however, to call suddenly on me as a neighbour.

He saw Heloise, and recognised her at once. The recognition was mutual.

Nothing, however, was said—Sir Guy being too cunning, Heloise too terrified.

The very next day, a hind working in the fields came rushing in, to say that two mounted and armed men had carried off my girl, gagged and bound.

Arthur had a splendid black charger—few could ride, none could beat.

He mounted it at once, and followed by several armed men, whom he soon outstripped, dashed in the direction taken by the ravishers.

They had not a quarter of an hour's start, and so soon were caught up to.

The retainer he unhorsed with one blow of his lance, and then, rushing impetuously forward, the head pierced the felon knight through and through. When Arthur had released Heloise from his grasp the cruel uncle was quite dead.

Now this was called a murder, and for this deed my son was arraigned, tried, found guilty, and condemned to death, without hope of mercy.

The Norman knight, Sir Guy de Lussac, was most highly connected.

Our dismay, our despair, may be conceived, when this result was known.

We petitioned the crown for mercy, and mercy was granted unto us.

But I was to pay a fine, which I could not raise on my whole estate.

By the aid of friends I succeeded in getting together nine thousand and six hundred pounds out of ten thousand, the gross amount of the penalty.

I could do no more.

At last I bethought me of the almoner of St. Mary's, who lent me the money on mortgage—and now

> My lands are sett to wad, Robin,
> Until a certain day,
> To a rich abbot here beside
> Of St. Mary's Abbaye.

And now, the day being at hand that I am to pay or lose the whole of my property, the abbot and almoner who covet my estates, insist on the money or the land. They must have the broad acres, for of the four hundred marks I have ten shillings, and no more. I and my children, once so happy, must even turn beggars, and I, in my old age, hold out the hand that hitherto has given, not taken.

Thus spoke the woeful knight, without any interruption from Robin Hood or any of his lieutenants. The story to them was as interesting as a romance.

The historian of the day says in conclusion of his lay—

"Little John wept, Will Scarlett's eyes were moist, and Robin, much affected, cried 'Fill us more wine: this story makes me sad too.'"

CHAPTER CVII.

THE OUTLAWS' DECISION.

THERE was silence for some time, the knight brooding moodily over his misfortunes, the band of outlaws devising each man within his own thoughts.

"And what has become of the property belonging to Heloise?" asked Robin.

"Until we prove her identity, it has gone to the crown," said Sir Richard, "but had I money to prosecute her claims that matter were soon settled."

"And the abbot and his friend will not wait?"

"Not a day."

"Hem!" said Robin Hood, "but hast thou no friend, sir knight, who would give security for the loan of four hundred pounds?"

"None," sighed the other, sorrowfully, "not one friend have I, save the saints."

Robin shook his head, as if he thought the proffered security rather doubtful.

"The saints are but middling security in the matter of money," he said, scratching his head; "you must find better before I can help you."

"Then," cried the knight, ruefully, "I have none other —the very sooth to say—except that it be our dear Lady, who never failed me a day."

Robin smiled at the knight's simplicity and earnestness. He was pleased.

"Sir Richard," he said, heartily, "I am satisfied, and will lend on that security. Little John, count out the money."

A murmur of approval went round the assemblage of outlaws.

Robin declined any thanks, and bade his treasurer add to the money "three yards, and no more, of each colour of cloth for his use."

Little John is said to have counted out the cash with the accuracy of a perfect miser, but as his big heart was really touched at the knight's misfortunes, he measured out the cloth most liberally—calling his bow an ellwand, and every time he applied it he skipped, as the ballad avers, "foots three."

> Scathlock he stood still and laugh'd,
> And swore by Mary's might,
> John may give him the better measure,
> For, by Peter, it cost him light.

"And now," said good Robin Hood, "give him a grey steed instead of his hack."

The grey steed was at once forthcoming from the mysterious stores of the outlaws.

"And now a new saddle," continued the prince of merry men, with a laugh.

"And now," said Sir Richard, in a tone which expressed more than words, "now that you have overwhelmed me with your liberality and generosity, tell me when and where I am to repay it."

"If it please you, sir," replied Robin Hood, "on this day twelvemonth, and the place shall be this good oak."

"And so be it," said the knight, who thereupon rode away in the direction of St. Mary's Priory.

"There goes a happy man," said Robin Hood, with a benignant smile.

"A brave man too, and a good father," added sagacious Much the miller.

"And an honest man," put in Little John, emphatically, "or my name is No-go."

"We shall see twelve months hence," drily observed Robin Hood himself; "I hope so. But now away all of you. The feast is over, and as we cannot afford to give four hundred pounds away every morning, find me some fat abbot or baron, who shall amply repay us. I walk to St. Mary's. I wish to know why my friend Edwin tarries so long."

"May I attend you?" asked Little John, in a beseeching tone; "I will keep behind."

"My dear Little John," said the chief, kindly, "your society is too agreeable to be rejected. Come, take your staff and follow—something tells me we may need them."

They said no more, but just as the band dispersed glided into a thicket and were soon lost to view.

"I wonder what Will Scarlett is doing all this while," cried Robin.

"Making love," replied Little John, with a deep and heartfelt sigh.

"Which is as much as to say that you wish you were in his place?"

"No—no," said Little John, with a huge blush; "you are quite mistaken."

"Ah, my little pigmy," smiled the chief, "it is of no use deceiving me. I am a sufferer myself and can feel for you. Little Rose, the handmaiden, the pretty page with the golden hair, has conquered where all else have failed."

Little John made no reply, but burst forth with a bacchanalian song by way of drowning care.

Robin Hood laughed, and then began to muse as he went off love and Marian.

But events are occurring in connection with Edwin and Rose Leigh which require us to precede the outlaws by a few hours.

CHAPTER CVIII.

THE HOME FARM.

A GREAT change had come over the Home Farm since we left it awhile.

The farmer himself was miserable, unhappy, and churlish. He rarely spoke except to give orders.

Rose — pale, disconsolate, and thoughtful — wandered about the house doing nothing. There were several causes for her sorrow. In the first place, she felt herself bound to marry the forest ranger, to save her father—but, then, why did not Edwin come?

She tortured herself with all kinds of reasons, and at last became jealous.

Surely he would not be so long away if he had not found some other ladylove.

This is the almost universal reasoning of women under the same circumstances.

But of what use would be his coming now that she was affianced to another?

The heart of woman is ever a mystery—a mystery which no one man will ever wholly solve. It would be almost a pity if he did, as 'tis after all the one charming mystery of man's life.

There was one person in the household who was, however, but slightly affected. Indeed, she appeared unusually gracious and happy under the circumstances.

The almoner, who was her father confessor, had called upon the dame, and won her quite over.

Hubert of the Red Hand, despite his abominable reputation, despite his notorious bad character, had at all events one friend he could count upon.

Father Ambrose told the dame that the church had absolved Hubert.

What could she want more, for his sins had been forgiven him?

She accordingly gave him every opportunity of enjoying the society of Rose, which otherwise would not have been easy, as the young girl, whenever she could, retired to her chamber on his arrival.

She literally hated the sight of the man, and shuddered to be near him.

It was a fearful struggle for a young girl to carry on, and now that her own mother was against her she had very little chance.

Hubert had come early on the occasion to which we refer. The farmer had an interview on the previous day with the almoner, who had hurried the marriage.

The dame, under pretence of business, had retired, and left the lovers together.

Rose was seated at her spindle, which she plied industriously, in order that she might look upon the ground and not at the hated man near her.

"Rose," said the deep, husky voice of the keeper, "a word with you."

"I am listening to you," she answered, in a low, hushed tone.

"This is Monday. This day week I leave for Nottingham."

"Ah!" she cried, a bright light illumining her speaking countenance.

"You seem pleased," he added, in a sarcastic tone that jarred upon her nerves.

"Yes—no—that is, it is a matter of indifference," she stammered.

"It is a matter of considerable consequence to you," he replied; "for as I do not go alone, we must be married on Saturday next at the very latest."

"Married—Saturday! No, surely this is a jest," she cried.

"No jest, as you will find. Hearkee, Rose. I love you well, and, if you choose to be kind to me, I will be so to you; but if you play the disconsolate, it may happen that our wedded life will not be of the smoothest," he said.

"Once a wife, I shall know a wife's duties," she answered, humbly.

"'Tis well. A sulky wife makes but an uncannie household," was his reply. "Now all is settled, I will go give such directions as are necessary. Cheer up, lass," he added, in a heartier tone, "and you shall be as happy as the day is long."

Before she could reply he had left the apartment. The poor girl burst into tears—the last hopeless refuge of woman in the direst distress.

"Hoity-toity, what's the matter now?" cried her mother, bustling in; "in tears! and what is it all about? Because it is going to be married. I didn't waste any time when I was married in such nonsensicals—it's what we all must come to."

"Mother," said Rose Leigh, simply, "I am ready to marry a man I love."

"And so you do not, cannot, love this man?" asked her mother, tartly.

"I hate, I loathe, I abhor him!" was the reply, "I would sooner die than link my fate to one who is a monster of cruelty, brutality, and a drunkard besides."

"I really don't know what's to be done," said Dame Leigh, who really loved her child, "but you see Father Ambrose has absolved him, and says he's quite a reformed character, and only wants a good wife to make him quite a pattern."

"Mother! mother! you should have seen his eyes just now; they glittered like a snake, as he threatened me with the future if I did not smile on him."

"Threaten!" cried Dame Leigh, hotly, "threaten indeed—a man threaten a woman! You are quite right, Rosy. He is a brute, a wretch, and you certainly shall not have him."

"Then must we leave the farm for the open fields on Sunday next," said the farmer, who came in as she spoke. "I have no further delay."

The two women looked bewildered, but Rose dried her eyes, and spoke in the resigned and determined tone of one who meant to be a martyr to duty.

"Father, for eighteen years have you fed, and clothed, and nurtured me; you shall not be turned from your home in your old age, if I can help it. I will marry Hubert of the Red Hand," she added, with a pardonable deep, long-drawn sigh.

As she said these words the door of the house was darkened, and a hearty, strong, Saxon girl, of about twenty, sunburnt, footsore and with a bundle, peered in.

"Does any one want a hardworking girl, who can do any kind of odd chores?" she said in a loud, coarse, but not unpleasant voice.

"No!" replied Farmer Leigh, "I have more than I can afford to pay now."

"But while this wedding is going on we shall want help," said the dame.

"Well, well, have it your own way," said the farmer, who really did not like turning the girl from the door.

It was now time for the mid-day meal, and as in those days men did not allow sorrow to spoil appetites which were not easily injured, the suddenly inducted handmaiden proceeded, under Rose's directions, to lay a table in the kitchen.

All dined together. The family at one end, the servants at the other.

The girl was evidently very awkward, pushing Rosy about in a most stupid manner, running against her, catching hold of her waist as if to prevent herself from falling; but she loaded the table, and when the men and women came in, dropped on a seat close to Rosy, close to whom she sidled as if fearful of the strangers present, who certainly did stare at her in a very rude manner.

"Do sit a little further," said Rose, almost ready to laugh; "what is your name?"

"Gurta," replied the handmaiden, who then began to eat with an appetite which, had it attracted the attention of Dame Leigh, might have cost her her place.

The dinner consumed and cleared away, all went to their occupations, leaving Rosy to further explain her duties to the young girl.

Now took place an event which so startled Rose, that for a few minutes she could not speak, much less scream, as she felt inclined to.

As soon as the door was closed upon the labourers and the master and mistress, Gurta advanced close up to where Rose stood, preparatory to clearing the table, caught the sylph-like figure of the young girl in her arms, and kissed her half-a-dozen times upon the lips.

"Mad!" suddenly exclaimed the young girl, gazing wildly at the supposed lunatic.

"No, Rose, not mad, but very unhappy to hear you say you would marry Hubert of the Red Hand," said a clear, ringing, manly voice.

"Edwin!" she cried, and without hesitation the kissing was renewed.

Then, after two or three minutes, she disengaged herself from his arms.

"Oh, Edwin! why is it you have stayed away all this time?" she said.

"Long enough to enable you to get another lover," he answered.

"We are not safe here. Come to the orchard. There are apples want picking—and there I will tell you all that has happened."

And Rose led the way to an orchard in the valley, which could have told many a soft tale of love could its leaves have whispered.

Here she explained the true state of the case to young Edwin, who heard her story with mingled indignation and alarm.

It in some degree altered his plans, but it did not for one moment discourage him in his hopes of himself wedding the girl of his heart.

Then he briefly told his plans to Rosy, who at first hesitated and cried—and hesitated again—and then finally laughed and gave way.

It was a pleasant sight that evening, when all else had retired, to see the affectionate attitude of the two girls beside the kitchen fire.

They sat with interlaced arms, whispering low, and occasionally stopping to speak awhile the silent language of love.

CHAPTER CIX.
THE WEDDING.

As the week advanced great changes took place. To the astonishment of all, Rose lost her pallor; the clear, red and white cheeks were again as charming and seductive as ever, while even the farmer seemed resigned to his fate.

Dame Leigh could hardly make it out, but so it was.

The marriage was arranged to take place at the farm-house itself, the almoner condescending to come down himself to perform the ceremony.

It was a lovely evening. The hearth was swept, the wedding feast laid out, the guests were collected in the house, and none were waited for but the three most important personages, the bride, bridegroom, and the holy priest.

Hubert of the Red Hand had gone to the abbey to fetch the priest.

The bride was said to be in her chamber with her new but favourite servant, Gurta!

Some one else had gone in with them, but who it was no one could say.

There was a strange brightness in the eye of the old farmer, which must have been caused by some very deep emotions.

Dame Leigh was one mass of finery, which she had raked out for the occasion.

Suddenly the door opened, and Hubert of the Red Hand, followed by the priest and his assistants, entered the room, all rising as he did so.

The father, in the meekest of tones, gave his blessing all round.

He then bade his companions prepare an extempore altar in the huge room, where he could say mass previous to the marriage ceremony.

"And now," he said, when all was ready, "bring forth the bride."

Two young girls went to the bedchamber, whence next moment they issued with Rosy, dressed bravely enough, and closely veiled.

She shrank timidly and shuddering into a chair, without a word.

A kind of gloom settled over all. It was quite clear to the meanest of the churls present that this was a forced match on the part of the girl.

But what was any one to do, when parents and priest were satisfied?

The ceremony commenced, and during its continuance not a word was spoken. At length the priest bade the bridegroom and bride stand up.

The ceremony continued, and Hubert approached his trembling bride.

He glanced down at the hand he was soon to take in his for ever.

A cry of horror escaped from his lips, as with *his* hand he tore the veil off the bride's head.

The clamour was fearful at this act of unparalleled rudeness.

The supposed bride was a half-witted lad, devoted to Rosy Leigh.

"Damnation!" roared the bridegroom, whilst all others laughed; "'tis mad Diccon. What means this trickery? Speak, you vagabond."

"Miss Rosy run'd away with Edwin," mumbled the boy; "tell me come here—such fun."

"Is any one else cognisant of this sacrilege?" asked the priest, severely: "do you, Farmer Leigh?"

"I know nothing of it—it's come on me like a thunderbolt," replied the sturdy yeoman; "but I will say I admire the girl's sense and spirit."

"You shall suffer for this," said the almoner, forgetting himself, "to-morrow."

"Here is a receipt for a year's rent in advance, from my lord bishop," replied Farmer Leigh, demurely.

"Ah!" said the priest, biting his thin lips, "I am not wanted here, then."

"But they cannot be gone far," cried Hubert, hotly; "my men are without. If I am to be jeered at others shall suffer as well. This Edwin is but an excommunicated poacher."

And the ranger went furiously forth in pursuit of his enemy and rival.

Meanwhile the lovers who had eloped, after giving, from Robin Hood, money to pay the rent, had taken their way down through the orchard in the direction of the forest, where they had decided to be united by Friar Tuck; marriage in those days, among the humbler classes, not being looked upon as so serious an affair as it is now.

They had planned the trick upon Hubert of the Red Hand in order to screen the father from any consequences, as well as to punish the insolence of the forest keeper. Farmer Leigh knew that some plan had been hit upon by which to put off the marriage, that was all, and that he should next see Rose as the wife of Edwin, in whose honour and truth he had every confidence.

They had about twenty minutes' advance, but well knew how little this would avail them did they not throw the ranger off their scent.

They were necessarily seen by several hinds and shepherds, so that their route was known.

Edwin chose one that took them towards the cell of the clerk of Copmanhurst by a circuitous pathway.

It was not quite dark when they started, so that they were able to travel for some time with great rapidity; but at the end of an hour they were compelled to move but slowly, as they could scarcely see their way.

They were now on the verge of a dense thicket of bushes and fern.

Voices suddenly fell upon their ears. It was the rangers in pursuit.

Edwin placed his finger on his lips, led Rosy into the thicket, and disappeared, just as the savage ranger came up with his followers.

He passed, but to halt about a couple of hundred yards further.

"They cannot be far," he said, in his most brutal accents; "we will pass the night here, and track them in the morning."

And so he did, making a fire, and snatching such repose as was possible to one whose mind was intent upon disappointed lust, hatred, and vengeance.

He, however, slept towards morning, and the sun had some time risen ere he awoke.

He now looked around him, and addressing his followers, bid them cautiously scour the neighbourhood in every direction.

He himself went back, prying into every place which could by possibility be a hiding-place, with all the patience and endurance of the sleuth-hound.

At length he reached the fern thicket, and his eye lit up with a savage fire.

He saw where they had entered beneath the shelter, and following the trail, soon stood transfixed with rage at the sight he beheld.

With her head pillowed on the young man's breast, Rose slept soundly. Never had she, perhaps, looked so lovely, for she was happy.

He, too, slept soundly, his dreams telling him nothing of the fearful peril in which he stood, or of the demon who stood over him with glaring eyeballs, that devoured every detail of the picture before him.

"Up, shameless hussey!" he cried, in a voice hoarse with passion; "up, in time to see your leman die!"

With a start and shriek Rose woke, and in an instant was on her feet, while Edwin, rolling over, avoided the blow aimed at him, and next instant was, pikestaff in hand, ready to do battle for the lady of his love.

"Put up thy quarterstaff," said Hubert, grimly—"we are six here, and if you once commence, no quarter shall you have. Surrender! lest you see this ——" (he used an opprobrious term) "scourged before your face."

"Have at you, knaves!" replied Edwin, placing his back against a tree.

Rose stood behind him, pale, but blushing at the wild thoughts which rose in her bosom.

The ranger rushed in, but slight as he was, Edwin had great dexterity. He hit some hard knocks.

But in two minutes he must have been overpowered, when two rangers were shot dead, and then, with a shout, in rushed Little John and Robin Hood, the former of whom dealt upon the back and head of Hubert of the Red Hand a series of blows that soon felled him to the ground.

The rescue was complete.

Edwin and Rose Leigh were free, and the latter, pale and shamefaced, could scarcely thank the outlaw for his opportune arrival.

"And now," said Robin Hood, sternly, "what shall we do with these arrant knaves?"

"It is my opinion," replied the giant, looking askance at the wounded keeper—"it is my deliberate opinion that such vermin only cumbers good mother earth. Hang him up!"

"I say, friend John," put in the keeper, with a grim wit which rather became the ruffian, "it is *my* deliberate opinion that if it were your own case you would not be in so great a hurry to adorn the branches of an oak tree."

All laughed, even Little John condescending to unbend, though, as it were, under protest.

"Now, good Robin Hood," said Rose Leigh, with a blush, "will you leave him to me?"

"An' that I will with pleasure," the king of the forest replied; "what shall be his fate?"

"To dance at my wedding," was the prompt reply.

THE WIFE'S SECRET.

"Wedding!" cried Robin, with affected astonishment, "not married yet, and pass the night in fern beds with young men! Fie! fie! for shame!"

"Robin," said Edwin, stoutly, "an you with your own fair Marian had been chased by six ruffians, you might have done worse than have sought shelter in a bed of fern."

"Bravely said," responded Robin, with something of a sigh; "and now, since your bonny bride wishes it, Hubert of the Red Hand shall dance at your wedding."

The ranger rose, and there was something in his look made all start.

"Rose," he said, "you have been generous and good to one who to you has been but a persecutor and an enemy. Your generosity is beyond all thanks; but if you will seriously forgive me, never again will I be your enemy. But you must forgive me really, and prove it."

"How?"

"Do not ask me to dance at your wedding—it is too much punishment!"

"Go free, Hubert," she said, with much emotion; "I believe and trust you."

"You may," replied the man, bluntly; "and hearkee,

Master Edwin, I am a rough one, I know, but now you have won your prize, I promise that it shall not rankle at my heart. But if you will take the *advice of a friend*—odd as the word may sound on my lips—keep out of the clutches of the almoner. I give you all good day."

And the ranger, with something manly in his gesture, moved away, leaving the assembly much amazed.

"I don't understand these sudden conversions," cried Little John.

"Well," replied Robin Hood, "you are a great heathen—but it is real. The man is touched, as who would not be, by Rose's generosity."

"I shall be watchful, though," said Edwin; "the man means well, but it may not last."

"And now, young people," cried Robin, "the word is, haste to the wedding. We shall find Friar Tuck at home just now—and I have my day to spare. To-morrow I and Little John go in search of Will Scarlett."

No objection was made to this proposition, and the young lovers, looking intensely happy, were left behind, while Robin Hood and Little John led the way singing and laughing, so as not to intrude upon the joyous couple, who were in the full freshness of their young and happy love.

About mid-day the hermitage of Friar Tuck was reached, and luckily for Edwin and Rose, the priest had been muddled over night, so much so as to be unable to rise until late.

When he heard the story his reverence laughed, washed his head, and put on his cassock.

The ceremony was not long about, and when finished was quite as binding as ever any Gretna Green marriage.

Fondly and tenderly the young couple pressed close to one another, hardly yet, however, realising that, happy as we may be in the future, that is really the happiest moment of our lives.

Fame, renown, wealth, prosperity, every blessing that Heaven can shower on us, never equal, in the enjoyment they give us, the one proud, glorious feeling of satisfaction, pleasure, and delight, that fills the soul when she—the one woman of our love—is ours..

There was dancing on the greensward that night, and right joyous merriment.

The outlaws got all the women of the forest together, and by the aid of such rude instruments as were known in those days the fun and frolic went on until morn.

Long before, however, Edwin and Rose were nowhere to be found.

CHAPTER CXX.

WILL SCARLETT AND EVELINE.

'TIS morn : the winds are hushed, and the very heart grew cheery to see the heavens so bright, and to behold the stars dancing, as it were for joy, in their spheres.

As the sun first began to tinge the bright blue sky with roseate hue, Robin Hood and Little John were on foot.

They were uneasy about the long stay of Will Scarlett, and thought him in trouble.

Like the noble and attached friends they were, they determined, at any risk, to discover the cause of his absence.

As they started, there seemed no sound abroad, save where, towards her secret den, the she-wolf sped, while now and then a deer might shake the wild briar or the rustling grass as it hurried through the tangled thicket.

Robin Hood was thoughtful.

He had no time to lose, for Much the miller had already started on his seeming errand of treachery, a task Robin required all his best energies to aid.

He wanted, however, the co-operation of Will Scarlett, and besides, he wished to know his fate.

*   *   *   *   *   *

Let us precede him, and discover what Will Scarlett is doing.

We left Will Scarlett and Eveline standing under the huge boughs of an oak, whence in a few minutes, however, they took their departure alone.

Friar Tuck was eager to regain his hermitage, and did not care about the circuitous route about to be followed by his companions, who wished to meet the countess.

The lovers did not attempt to restrain him. Like all those upon whom the sunshine of affection smiles, solitude was their most earnest desire and wish.

They took an affectionate leave of the burly priest, and then continued on their way rejoicing.

The path they had to follow lay through a part of the wood thickly studded with huge oaks.

Despite the circumstance of the moon shining brightly, the thickness of the foliage threw a deep gloom over their path.

They observed the directions of the countess implicitly.

They could not too often speak of the delight they found in the fact of one parent having consented to their union.

This was a salve to their consciences which they little expected, and which sanctified their young affection.

It was with deep pleasure also that they knew her to be alive, and many were the conjectures they indulged in as to the reason which had induced her to live secluded so long.

But the principal part of their discourse, necessarily had relation to themselves.

They were in the first wild intoxication of love's young dream—the honeymoon of life.

They spoke of the days to come as days of endless joy.

In this way they advanced but slowly, until at last they entered a more than usually dark path, which quite startled the gently-bred girl.

But a manly arm supported her.

" Do you really feel unable to advance ? " said her husband, in his tenderest tones.

" If we have much further to go," she replied, in a faint voice, " I must have rest."

" Then will we go no further," said Will Scarlett; " my wife shall be the outlaw's bride at once."

Eveline smiled. The romance of love was strong within her, and what he said must be right.

Seeking for a spot totally sheltered and so placed that there was no fear of observation, Will Scarlett soon found one.

When Sherwood was a vast, almost primeval forest, it had twice as many rivers, streams, and brooks as it has now-a-days—when they have disappeared.

Were every tree, hedge, and bush cut down all over England, it would soon be barren.

Rivers would become streams, streams brooks, and brooks would be dried up altogether.

Navigable rivers known to history have vanished from the face of the earth through mere ruthless destruction of trees.

With such an abundance of water permeating the whole forest, Will Scarlett soon reached the bank of a small branch stream, with high banks.

Having selected a fitting spot on which to erect a kind of tent or hut, he first lit a fire, which soon burnt cheerfully and brightly.

He then cut three or four poles, which he fastened together at the top, and against these he laid boughs, and again piled leaves and grass over the whole.

A good armful of fern made an excellent and perfumed bed within the tent.

Eveline felt her spirits rise, and as she sat beside the bright little fire recovered her elasticity of mind.

Then Will Scarlett waited upon her with as much attention and courtesy as any belted knight.

The thoughtful priest had provided them with food.

Their little supper was quite a festive occasion, not unmixed with happiness.

Hunger is a rare luxury after all. The researches of Ude and Soyer have never found anything to equal it. No epicurean dainties can match the exquisite pleasure found in its gratification. A night in the mountains or forests, drinking in the very breath of life—the pure, clear, bracing air—a breakfast from the glowing embers and a draught of water from the icy brook, are worth more than all the exquisite dishes that ever man invented. It needed no urging, therefore, for Eveline to satisfy the cravings of her keen appetite.

In after life she might feast from silver spoons on tables groaning with costly luxuries, but that delicious meal from the hot coals, that smoking venison, the forest bivouac and the forest appetite, she could never forget.

But they knew that early dawn must see them rise, so soon they retired within the tent.

*   *   *   *   *

The fire burnt low, the wind blew keen and sharp, so much so as to awaken Will Scarlett.

Eveline slept well after the unwonted excitement and fatigues of the previous two days.

Will Scarlett crawled silently from the tent, and picked up some pieces of wood to replenish the fire.

As he did so his quick ear caught the sound as of a footstep on the banks of the stream.

Retreating into the darkness, he drew his bow and arrow to him and watched.

The night was intensely dark in that secluded and sheltered spot, so that Will Scarlett was compelled to trust almost wholly to his sense of hearing.

On ordinary occasions this would not have been a task of great difficulty.

But Will Scarlett was desperately in love, and had just awakened from a sound sleep.

He listened with bated breath.

All he could make out was a slow and stealthy tread at some distance on the banks of the river.

It came in his direction, without, apparently, any pretence at concealment.

Will Scarlett lived in an age of superstition.

It could be no enemy, he thought, who walked slowly and deliberately to where an armed man lay camped.

If not a man, what could it be' as he had no friends in this immediate neighbourhood ?

Unused to walking, she was weak, faint, and nervous.

Nearer and nearer came the steps, crunching the dried wood, and casting pebbles and dirt into the stream.

"A drunken man," thought Will.

Standing out of the glint of the fire, Will Scarlett cast on some dry grass and leaves.

A great flare discovered the advancing object to be a huge figure with vast horns.

Will's heart for a moment stood still. Every wood in those days had its legend of some Herne the Hunter.

The outlaw gave vent to a low laugh as he launched his arrow full at the creature's breast.

Next instant he had cut the throat of as fine a buck as he could have wished to see, which, as these curious animals will be, had been attracted by the fire, and led by it to its own destruction.

The smaller deer of America are commonly trapped at night by fire, during the day by gaudy rags.

Will Scarlett returned to his couch, delighted that fatigue had kept Eveline from waking.

CHAPTER CXXI.

IN THE FOREST.

It was rosy morn, all nature smiled, and to say nothing of the loveliness of that early hour in the forest, the very air rang with music as the young lovers rose.

It was a lovely morning. The sun had risen from its nightly course radiant with beauty, kissing the dew from the tiny cups of the myriad flowers, tinging with gold the emerald leaves of the forest, and gilding the crests of a thousand little billows that were just waking to life in the shaded pools of the mountain streams.

It was a morn of wondrous loveliness, a scene that the eye might willingly rest upon for ever, while the soul drank in its freshness till satiated with the very excess of beauty.

But let us dismount from Pegasus, and flow on in simple prose.

Eveline was naturally astounded to behold her lover's night capture, which before she was afoot he had artistically cut up, and, when their morning meal was over, concealed in some tree branches out of the reach of wolves.

Then, when ablutions had been performed in the stream, the happy pair continued on their way.

It was now, however, necessary to be cautious, as they might at any moment be pursued, or meet retainers of the earl, who would certainly consider it their duty to restore Eveline to her father, in the hope of a rich reward.

Will Scarlett knew pretty well the direction he had to take, and preferred rather to follow the windings of the valley through which the stream ran to seeking the actual pathway which led to the habitation indicated by Lady Alice.

He hoped soon to strike into such depths of the forest as might make pursuit almost impossible.

Even though the young girl walked slowly, a considerable portion of the way was soon got over, and Will Scarlett felt his heart grow lighter and his step freer as he felt the most dangerous distance to be got over.

But in order to escape observation they had come by a most difficult and arduous road, one that surely Eveline had never travelled before.

But her outlaw-husband was by her side.

When the narrow trail caused her to shrink back from the dizzy brink on the one side until she brushed the perpendicular wall of rocks on the other, when the descent became deep, when the path was cumbered with loose stones, when an overhanging branch threatened to sweep her over a precipice, when the rocky bed of the branch stream was deep and the current strong, when more than usual danger lurked around her in any form—he pressed still nearer to her, warned her of the danger in deep, earnest whispers—whispers whose undertone was more like the lower notes of a flute than a human voice—and held her firmly with his strong arm.

And amply was he rewarded by either a smile, a pressure of the arm, or a kiss.

"We shall soon be at the end of our journey," he said.

"I hope so," she replied; "and yet I am very happy. I never before felt this glorious exhilaration of spirits."

"My own dearest!"

"This, my husband, is to live. Cooped up in my father's castle, poring over embroidery, reading a missal, or sitting in fine clothes to listen to the unmeaning nonsense of fops and fools, or the insolent love-making of courtly profligates, was not to live; but to wander where the deer climb, where the eagle builds his nest, where the wolf skulks and the hunter clambers—that is to live!"

Her eyes flashed, her cheeks glowed, a heavenly radiance was in her eyes as she spoke.

They were on the summit of a hill with a dense clump of forest before them.

After one glance at the waving tops of oak and elm, and larch and pine, they slowly descended to the plain.

As they did so they came in sight of a small road, either a swine track or a cross road between two highways.

Will Scarlett halted, and signing to his companion to be still, listened.

As he did so a dark and ominous frown crossed his handsome countenance.

"What is it?"

He silently pointed with his hand in the direction of her father's castle.

"We are pursued."

"Art sure?"

"I have both seen and heard. It was only for an instant that I caught sight of him, but that was enough. He wore the dress of one of your father's retainers."

"Let us hide."

"Hiding will not suffice," said the outlaw, sadly. "My dearest wife, our position is a peculiar and a desperate one. Evidently this man, whom others follow, is on the right scent. He must be stopped."

And, with a stern look of settled determination, Will Scarlett fitted an arrow to his bow.

Eveline sank behind a bush.

"Cannot his life be spared?"

"Eveline," replied the young man, gravely, "the hand of every man is against us. I fear me you are too gentle and tender for this rude life of ours. I must, in justice to ourselves and to your mother, prevent this horseman's further progress."

And on the moaning wind came clearly the clatter of the horse's hoofs.

Eveline made no reply.

Did she regret? No.

She only felt how horrible was this everlasting warfare between man and man.

"Heaven rest his soul!" she said, audibly.

Will Scarlett gazed at her fondly and with intense admiration; then, seeing that she was well concealed, himself took up his post behind a tree, hiding himself with the dexterity and calmness of a redskin.

Eveline, from womanly curiosity, raised her head.

She was alone.

Like a frightened bird, she was about to rise to her feet, when a low whisper checked her.

"Be still."

She cowered down, covering her head with her hood, and placing her hands over her ears.

But she could not shut out that horrid clatter of horse's hoofs, coming nearer and nearer.

Her heart palpitated with wild emotion.

Every moment she expected to hear his death-shriek—his last, agonising cry.

It was to Eveline a bitter foretaste of the drawbacks in the forest life of an outlaw's bride.

The horseman is evidently close at hand.

There is a slight rustling in the bushes close at hand, and then the whirr of an arrow.

A fearful yell, a piercing shriek, followed.

Eveline started up, unable to contain the emotion that was swelling her heart to bursting any longer.

For a moment she could see nothing; her sight was so dizzy, and her brain in such a whirl.

"That cry?" she whispered, clutching Will Scarlett's arm; "what was it?"

"It means," said her husband, with a laugh, "that your father has one horse less in his stables. That was his death wail you heard. It is strange indeed to those who have not seen this noble animal in his death agony. But the man lives, and, if I mistake not, is a bold, determined fellow. We must continue our journey, for, be assured, he is not alone."

Eveline's spirits at once revived, and, taking her husband's hand, she followed him through the wood; and in an instant the two had disappeared behind a group of hawthorn and furze bushes forming a brake, close to a cluster of beech trees.

They now walked slowly and with precaution, anxious that in no way should their presence be made known.

They thought not, at all events they spoke not, of refreshment, however, of which both stood in need.

Their only thought was to reach the end of their weary journey.

Suddenly Will Scarlett stood quite still, with his fingers on his lips.

As he did so, Eveline clearly caught the sound of footsteps in their rear.

"We are followed!"

"By the man I spared," replied Will Scarlett, bitterly.

"Do not blame me, my love," she whispered.

"I will not if you are brave," he said, with a cheerful smile; "and even now, if I can help it, I will not slay him, but he must not follow. Hide there."

And he pointed to a hollow tree, shaded by bushes.

He then secreted himself, taking care to make a great crashing of bushes first.

He had scarcely effected his purpose, when a man-at-arms emerged from a thicket, peering carefully around.

The sun was already touching the tree-tops, and the bright daylight was fast merging into the softer twilight.

There was already a rich autumn tint, which evening always gives to the foliage.

The shadows of the tall trees were already longer, more decided and deeper.

There was no sound save the sough of the wind in the trees.

The man appeared puzzled, and for a moment stood still.

He was an ill-looking fellow, with prominent nose, glaring eyes, black hair, armed with cross-bow, sword, and now with a huge staff he had cut in the wood.

"Where the foul fiend has the cowardly assassin hid himself? I heard him but this moment!" he muttered.

"Here I am," replied Will Scarlett, stepping out within a yard of his pursuer.

"The devil!"

"No—only an honest yeoman," said the outlaw, sarcastically.

The man-at-arms looked keenly at him. He was young, slight, ruddy, and exhibited no great signs of forest experience. It surely could not be this springal that had shot his horse through and through with a clothyard arrow.

"Harkee, my master," replied the man-at-arms, "honest or not, a word with you."

"Two if you please."

"An you crack jokes with me, I will crack thy pate," was the angry reply.

"Two can play that game," jeered Will.

"Sirrah, I but ask you a civil question. I have some time been following a rascal, murderer, and thief, who has stolen my master's daughter, and now, in an attempt to murder one of his servants, has slain my horse. I know they passed this way—hast seen them?"

"None have passed since I have been here."

"An you quibble, I shall think you the malefactor," cried the angry man-at-arms.

"What then?"

"Wilt answer me truly?"

"I will."

"Art thou the man who shot my horse?"

"Yes, and would have shot thee had I pleased," was Will Scarlett's quiet answer.

"Then art thou the thief who stole my master's daughter? Have at thee, traitor!" he cried.

And he at once aimed a blow at Will, which that youth guarded so coolly and easily as to make the other furious with disappointment and astonishment.

The soldiers of the Norman oppression, bred to the use of regular arms, were seldom a match for the merry English yeomen in the management of the national weapon.

This man, however, was fond of the exercise, and had had many a bout with some of the Saxon tenants.

He, therefore, prided himself on his science, and expected an easy victory. His surprise, then, was great, when he found that, instead of defeating the other, he himself could never give a blow, but received so many that ere ten minutes he was sprawling on the ground, and in two more bound to a tree while in a state of insensibility.

CHAPTER CXXII.

CAMP FIRE.

TAKING advantage of his victory, Will Scarlett was about to rejoin his companions when he suddenly heard other horses rein in.

He lifted his finger, and pointing to a hollow at some distance, bade Eveline go there.

He then threw himself beneath a cluster of hawthorn, bushes and tall gorse.

As he did so he saw three men-at-arms, one of whom was alighting.

Probably the fight had been heard, and he was about to see what was the matter.

The two horsemen trotted back in the direction of the dead horse, but probably to bring up stragglers.

Will Scarlett determined to meet the intruder.

Like all true deer-stalkers and hunters, many a time and oft, when hunting in the forest glades of merry Sherwood, he had practised hunting and crawling serpent-like beneath the stunted heath and gorse, in order silently to approach the deer.

Like all true deer-stalkers and hunters, then, he excelled in this difficult accomplishment.

Will Scarlett took a careful note of the place to be reached, and then began.

His progress was slow, as now, as well as when hunting, his chief object was stealth.

But habit is second nature, and Will Scarlett got over the ground three times as quickly as an ordinary man.

Presently he reached a spot suited to his purpose.

It was a narrow pass between two oaks whose boughs almost touched the ground, but where, in a stooping posture, a view along a clear vista showed the captured man-at-arms tied to his tree.

Will Scarlett stepped behind one of the trunks with the rapidity of lightning.

He could see the second man-at-arms advancing along the forest, himself crawling.

Will smiled grimly.

He must pass beneath the lowly, leafy arch of those sweeping oak boughs that nearly touched the ground.

The man was coming on, leaving a trail behind like that of a serpent.

The man every now and then raised his head, and peered forward in the direction where the fight had taken place. He seemed inclined to rise until he saw the passage under the oak.

He advanced upon his way, and bent his head low, to peer under the low boughs.

"That's Hardinge!" he muttered. "By the saints, a prisoner, if not dead! Oh!"

A fearful thwack on the part of his person most exposed to blows drew this exclamation from him—a thwack followed by others in such rapid succession, that he could, for a minute, only roar and struggle impotently on the ground.

Then he would have risen.

But in his haste to jump up he engaged his neck in such an awkward position in the boughs, he thought some giant hand held him by the throat.

"Have mercy!" he cried.

Not a word was said, but the blows fell thick and fast upon him all the time.

"Good master demon," he moaned, "have mercy! Paternoster—ave Maria—*damnation!*"

"Swear not," said a hollow voice.

"Mercy!" repeated the man-at-arms.

"Hast ever mercy on churl or yeoman?" continued Will Scarlett, unmercifully continuing his chastisement "I am the avenger of the wood. That for Rob of the One Hand, who lost it by thy lies."

"Oh!" shouted the ruffian, as an unusually hard blow fell upon him; "I'll have his other."

"That, then!" was the answer, as another, of fearful violence descended; "and now, good John of the Saddle, thou wilt not ride this month in chase of the merry yeomen of Sherwood Forest."

Saying which, Will plunged into the forest, as the cracking of the bushes indicated the arrival of a rescue.

It was quite dark.

But the cries and moans of the man who had received such severe chastisement soon brought them around him.

Not one but laughed at his ludicrous position, from which they speedily disengaged him.

They would have seated him on the grass, but a cry of agony escaped him.

"Leave me to die," he said, and threw himself flat on his face. "Leave me, I say, to die."

An officer bade him grimly to die and be ——, but to explain his adventure.

"I caught my neck in the branches, and the foul fiend took the opportunity to discipline me for my sins," groaned John of the Saddle. "Lambert is yonder, and will tell you more."

About an hour later the whole party was sleeping round a camp fire, except four sentries, who guarded every avenue to the extensive bottom, or alluvial valley, into which the fugitives had descended.

They had forgotten that, half-insensible as he was, Lambert had the use of his eyes and ears.

CHAPTER CXXIII.

THE ESCAPE.

AGAIN another morning broke pleasantly and cheerfully over the forest.

And yet, radiant as was the beauty of nature, lovely the mantle she clothed herself in, she could not keep man from rapine, slaughter, and thoughts of evil.

The men-at-arms, leaving their wounded companions in the camp, had completely encircled the valley, and were now beating up every bush, as they narrowed their circle towards the centre.

The sentinels declared that not a sound had been heard during the night.

The birds, then, surely could not have flown.

Suddenly the whole party met on a little greensward, in the centre of the valley.

The officer pointed to a rude bed of leaves.

"There is the form—the hare cannot be far off," he cried. "Beat up the bushes."

All rushed out, without method or place; but though in turn they clearly visited every place where a hare could have been concealed, they found no trace of the fugitives.

The officer glanced up into the trees under which they had slept, but there they were not.

"We must scour the forest until we find them," said the officer, with a dark frown. "I, for one, cannot return without the daughter of our house."

"I should think," replied one of the soldiers, drily, "the earl would almost not find her."

"Why, sirrah?"

"There were two slept on yonder bed," continued the observant man-at-arms.

"Dolt! idiot! ass!" roared the officer—"dost think I am blind?—but rather cut out thy tongue than whisper this to our lord and master. Our business is to find our lady; what she has been doing is nothing to us."

The soldier bowed his head and made no remark. The officer then bade his men bring the wounded men to this secure and comfortable spot, and leave them there until they were able to mount their horses; two of which they contrived to leave them, grazing about the rich bottom.

The rest then departed towards the highway, in order to make such inquiries as they could about the fugitives.

Scarcely had they done so when a bugle sounding the outlaws' tra! la! la! aroused their attention. In hot and furious haste they dashed in pursuit.

But ever as they advanced the bugle sounded further off, until they grew mad with vexation.

It seemed as if the forest were alive with beings of another world, that took pleasure in tormenting them.

"Well, John of the Saddle," said Lambert, when they were left alone, "this is a pretty start."

"Start! don't talk to me of starts and saddles; I shall never sit in one again. I'm black and blue with bruises," he said; and groaned as he said it.

"I'm little better," cried Lambert. "The fellow must have been the foul fiend himself."

"I'll foul fiend him whenever I catch him—the base, cowardly ruffian," added John of the Saddle, who then groaned again in evident pain and suffering.

Then came a kind of silvery, merry laugh, floating on the air, which made them shudder.

Their cheeks blanched, and they gazed wildly on each other's faces.

"Did'st hear?"

"What was it?"

"A laugh."

"Was't human?"

"That I know not; but this I do know—I never yet heard of a laugh without a laugher."

And both were silent, looking warily around in every direction in the hope of discovering the solution of the mystery.

Had they but have elevated their organ of vision a trifle, they might probably have discovered the secret.

The tree which formed the centre of the bottom was a large oak, so overgrown with ivy and other parasitical plants that the original trunk was all but concealed. Being old, the upper branches were spare and thin, which at once assured the officer that no one was concealed within them.

But the trunk had been more than once the refuge of Will Scarlett, when out on his poaching expeditions.

When a boy he had climbed in search of an owl's nest, which he found in a cavernous hollow of the trunk, quite sufficient to conceal a person of ordinary size.

From this hole the charming but pallid visage of the earl's daughter peered down upon her father's followers a smile irradiating her face at their comic disgrace.

* * * * * * *

But let us recount things as they happened.

When Will Scarlett fled before the band of armed retainers he had little difficulty in finding Eveline.

She had scarcely ventured beyond the skirts of the dark thicket in the valley-bottom.

Having rejoined her, he led her silently into the deepest hollows, and hastily made up a couch, upon which the husband and wife lay in uneasy slumber for a few hours.

It was considerably before daylight when they arose.

Will Scarlett then explained his plans. He told Eveline of the hiding-place in the tree, where he wished her to lie secreted while he led the pursuers on a false trail.

Every moment increased the confidence of the wife in her husband—and she agreed to remain.

Will, who had made this his retreat fifty times, swung himself into the tree, and lowered a rope ladder, by which means Eveline was able to ascend without difficulty.

He saw her safe inside, replaced the ivy, and then ascended to a higher branch.

At the back of the oak the forest was so dense that the trees thrust their boughs one into the other.

Nothing was easier than to step from one tree to another, and this the young outlaw did for about two or three hundred yards, when he slid down, cast himself under a bush, and slept till dawn of day, the light alone making him jump, to his feet.

Then he listened attentively, and ere long heard the men-at-arms marching through the wood.

He wound his bugle, and then darted with rapid steps down a green and pleasant slope, where he hid himself.

Again he sounded his bugle, and often in such opposite directions that the pursuers became bewildered.

Then the sound which hitherto had guided them ceased, and they were at fault.

Will Scarlett, satisfied with his cunning trick, now took his way straight back to the trysting-tree.

As he approached, to his extreme mortification he found that a guard had been left.

He could distinctly hear their voices.

Other steps, too, were in the wood, and turning quickly he saw two horses, bridled, saddled, and caparisoned.

These he caught at once and tied to a tree, after which he approached carefully.

A burst of laughter nearly overcame him, as he saw the two men-at-arms bemoaning their wounds.

A merry thought suggested itself, the more that he wanted their room instead of their company.

"Hooray! come on, Robin, Little John—here are some of the villains—lay on, my hearties, and leave not a whole bone in their bodies;" and saying this he dashed forward through the thicket.

As if by a miracle the wounded men bounded to their feet, and made off in an opposite direction.

They had not gone far, however, when they both fell down in a swoon or faint.

When they came to all was silent as the grave, save

where they saw Will Scarlett and Eveline walking slowly away upon the horses they counted on to escape from their predicament.

Futile oaths and curses escaped their lips.

But the young lovers, delighted to have found a suitable means of transport, having reached an open glade, set their horses to a trot, taking care to enter beneath the arches of the forest in the different direction from that they wished to follow.

CHAPTER CXXIV.

THE COUNTESS'S STORY.

ABOUT mid-day, having been compelled to make continual rounds to avoid dangers, difficulties, and supposed ambushes, the happy couple reached the small house to which the countess had directed them, and where she, not unsuspicious of what had occurred, eagerly awaited them.

The moment they rode up to the door the gates flew open, and as quickly closed again.

They were clasped in the arms of her who would have died to save her daughter.

A council of war was held, and various opinions expressed, but Will Scarlett firmly, yet respectfully, insisted that for the present there was no possible safety for Eveline but in the stronghold of Robin Hood.

"Amongst the outlaws!" said the countess, sadly.

"Madam, these outlaws are better men than their persecutors. They have been driven to their fastresses by great cruelty and oppression, for which they retaliate only on the foe which has caused them misery. Our chief, the defrauded Earl of Huntingdon," he continued, "is nobility itself."

"Earl of Huntingdon!" cried the countess, "what mean you?"

"Such indeed, madam, is Robin Hood."

"Well! well! there is no time now for me to hear this story. I own that you are right for the moment, but hope that soon you may hold your head up proudly as any noble of them all, for my daughter is the earl's sole heiress."

Will Scarlett's cheek flushed, but he made no reply.

"And now, my children, ere I leave you to work for your interests and my own, allow me to claim your attention to the short story of my life, which will explain much that otherwise appears mysterious."

The young people gladly acquiesced, and seating themselves near her, listened to her narrative with profound and rapt attention.

THE COUNTESS'S STORY.

I have a story to tell of myself, which, at first blush, may surprise you.

Listen, however, to it in detail, before you blame me.

My father was one of the richest and proudest of the Saxon lords who made their submission to the Norman.

He was haughty and ambitious, and could not brook any society less elevated than that of a court.

He was also allied to one or two Norman families by various marriages.

His castle, a magnificent structure, was splendidly appointed, though he himself did not often honour it with his presence preferring the atmosphere of courts, of jousts, and tournaments, to that of his home.

I was fifteen, and brought up under the charge of an old nurse and a worthy priest, who, between them, taught me to embroider, read, write, and sing ballads in commemoration of deeds of valour and heroism.

Thus passed my early days.

I seldom saw my father, and when I did, not under favourable auspices, for he said I reminded him of his wife, of whom it was notorious he had been excessively fond.

He was never unkind to me, always generous, and I never lacked rich clothes or costly presents.

This he did partly from kindness, partly from pride.

But my heart yearned for some other show of affection; for kind words, for smiles; and these, it appears, it was not in his power to bestow upon me.

Well, I have said that I was fifteen, when one day, standing with my nurse on the battlements of a tower, listlessly admiring the prospect below, my eye was caught by the flash of spears entering the valley below.

"Your noble father," said my nurse.

I scarcely moved. It was seldom he sent for me at all the first day, and then only for a moment.

But I could admire the warlike array of the cavalcade, the prancing horses, and the gay flags and banners that shone in the summer sun.

The armed party approached the drawbridge; and then I first noticed that beside my father rode a youth in gay habiliments, whose countenance I could not rightly make out.

Next minute the whole body swept into the courtyard, while I retired to my chamber, to be in readiness if by any accident I happened to be summoned.

My handmaidens soon made me fit to be called to my father's presence, though I scarcely expected it.

My surprise, therefore, may be imagined when, shortly after, I was called to join the banquet.

At fifteen, though slight, I was as tall as now; and as I entered the hall my father started.

"Alice," he said, with some emotion in his voice, "you have grown quite a woman."

I bowed.

"Take your place at the head of my table," he continued. "Knights and friends, this is my daughter."

There was a flutter of compliments, but I heard nothing, such a buzzing had taken possession of my head.

By degrees, however, as the conversation became general, and no one noticed me, I grew less confused, and went through the ceremony of the meal without any mistakes.

I even ventured to look around me.

But on the bearded and moustached knights, though manly and handsome enough, my eyes fell listlessly.

At length they alighted on a face which moved me much, and which, alas! I shall never forget.

It was a youth about my own age, with raven-coloured hair, black eyes, a high forehead, a countenance beaming with intelligence, though sad and pale.

Our eyes met.

I blushed, and he lowered his.

My father, who, unknown to me, had been watching us, smiled good-humouredly.

"Alice, this is the son of an old friend of mine. His name is Theodore de Neville. His parents are dead, and so I have brought him here awhile to be my page."

The youth bowed low.

"And now, Alice, we have to speak of weighty affairs. Send up fresh flagons of wine. Take Master Neville with you, and induct him into the mysteries of the castle; as far as you know them," he added, with a grim smile.

Children, that was the happiest day of my life, for then it was I had my first taste of love.

Not that he or I knew anything of the master-passion of the world, but its spell was upon us.

We, however, were most innocently happy.

I took him down into the garden, whence a splendid view could be obtained of the country round; and there, like children as we were, we laughed and prattled, were merry, and were happy.

I found that Theodore de Neville, or, as I called him from the first, Theodore, was to remain with me, as he was not to accompany my father until after a great expedition to the north.

With what rapturous delight I heard this—I, who hitherto had only had companions in the shape of my nurse and father confessor!

Youth, however, longs to mate with youth.

Like to like, at all ages and in all times.

Two days later we were left alone, and now began hawking expeditions, hunts, rambles in the forest, every kind of amusement in which the young and happy are apt to indulge.

This lasted three months, when—I must speak the truth, children—we began to be sad.

We were as much together as ever—we scarcely ever parted company, but we spoke little.

At times we would remain seated, one beside the other, for an hour, without a word.

We both became pale, and our appetites failed us. The good priest, who was like a leech, did minister to us; but it was not in his power to do any good.

Our favourite stroll was to pass through a small postern gate, cross a stout plank, which was cast over the moat, and descend by a sloping hill-side to the most unfrequented part of the forest—unfrequented because of its tangled thickness and its bad reputation.

In earlier days we should have avoided this spot, but both of us on one occasion seemed to long to fly from our fellow-creatures, and bury ourselves in utter solitude.

As we advanced, the wood became denser and denser; the rank weeds and creeping parasites so interlaced and entwined themselves with the thick underwood, that progression was almost impossible.

The peculiar and ever varying gloom had in it something awfully appalling.

Now it was a light only rescued from darkness by a shade: and now it was a dull, lurid semblance of light, like the atmosphere before a thunderstorm a thousand times intensified.

Now we came with a start of surprise upon a little patch left bare by the fall of some sylvan king, where the bright sun streamed through in all his glory.

At length we seemed unable to go further, but halted on the dry bed of a stream.

We seated ourselves, still silent and thoughtful.

Somehow or other, I did not dare look at Theodore, while his eyes were averted.

Suddenly he put his arms, as he was wont, round my waist.

I started, like a guilty thing, blushed, and almost fainted. He let go his hold.

"Alice!" he said, in a tremulous voice, "Alice, my own dear, this must be love."

Love!

Like a mountain torrent, swollen by the rains of heaven, a flood of feeling came gushing o'er my soul.

My pallor vanished, and my face became crimson.

"Alice!" continued the page, after another brief silence, "this is love; I feel that that which in the pages of the past I have scanned is now within my soul, and that my soul's idol is here before me. I know that it is wrong—I know that you are rich; I poor—you powerful; I a waif by the roadside. I love you!"

I could not speak, I could not reply, my eyes were cast upon the ground; I drank in the delicious music of his words, and then I raised my eyes.

"I know not if this be love," I said, blushing, "but I know I am very happy."

Hours passed, and yet we discussed, innocents that we were, the everlasting question; while our eyes, our hearts, our souls, were overflowing with love.

Suddenly the bushes parted, and a man of the most venerable aspect I ever saw came forth.

His dress denoted a hermit.

"Yes, my children," he said, in solemn tones, "this is love—and I knew it. If you are in the same mood in a week I will marry you."

We sat amazed, awed, trembling.

Now, be it recollected that we were but children, that we were in the heyday of a youthful passion, utterly ignorant of the world's ways.

"We may never be able to return," said Theodore, warmly, "why not wed us now?"

"And wilt thou be faithful unto death?" asked the man, fixing his piercing eyes on him.

"Faithful unto death," he replied.

"And you, girl of woman born?"

"Yes! But it is not meet to marry thus," I cried.

"You will never gain your father's consent," said the hermit, sarcastically.

I reasoned no more; but led away—mind, I do not excuse myself—by my boy-lover, I entered the hermit's hut, and there was duly united.

Children, how the next three months passed I cannot say, so happy were we.

Then came the thunder-claps.

CHAPTER CXXV.

THE COUNTESS'S STORY (continued).

MY father returned from his expedition, and took Theodore to London.

He secondly announced to me that ere long he would return with my affianced husband.

Now that we were married, and something of reason guided our actions, Theodore and I both saw the full depth of the abyss into which we had rushed.

During my father's life the marriage could never be avowed, especially as we casually heard that the hermit who united us was half crazed.

That, however, did not invalidate our marriage, as he was a recognised priest, and who the church has united none may part.

Theodore was to return shortly with my father, and then we hoped to hit upon some scheme to avoid the awful peril which menaced us.

From that hour the sunny brightness of my life departed from me.

I could not have another moment of happiness, living in doubt and despair.

The absence of my beloved husband, no more to hear the music of his voice, to be pressed to his heart, was bad enough.

But where were we drifting to?

I knew not.

Alas! I ought to have known, as just before I expected my father's and husband's return I knew that I should be a mother.

There was joy unutterable at the first blush, there was unutterable woe at the second.

My husband's rapture I could understand, my father's anger I dreaded to think of.

And yet all must come out now.

It was wicked, hopeless, to conceal the truth from my father under the circumstances.

I was worn to a skeleton when they came.

My father was startled by my illness, which interfered with his projects, but believing it a slight indisposition, he said nothing.

My husband was frantic with joy when we met, but soon he, too, saw the danger.

He never hesitated.

He at once decided on telling the truth.

My father was wont of a morning, when no equals in rank were present, to take his morning meal in a small room overlooking the garden.

We were poor contrivers.

We had not the courage to go to him; we contrived he should come to us.

We walked up and down in a most tender attitude under his very window.

For some time we were not interrupted.

Then we heard a fearful oath, and the knight, with rubicund face, distorted countenance, and eyes glaring with fury, stood before us.

"Shameless one, away! as for you, base hound, my huntsmen shall chase you from my castle with their whips—away, I say."

"Sir Percival," said my husband, quietly, "you are speaking to your lawfully married son and daughter."

My father's anger was checked as if by magic art, though he stilled champed at his moustaches.

"Oh!"

This word seemed torn from him by wild horses.

"Lawfully married!" he repeated, "and pray by what hedge priest?"

"Father Ignacius, the hermit, late abbot of Wartbury, Sir Percival."

I afterwards found that this statement struck my father to the heart.

The marriage was legal and binding to the last degree.

"And pray how long has this precious marriage taken place," he continued, still calmly, but with a fearful gleam in his eyes I could not look at.

"Long enough for us to expect an heir in a few months," was my husband's reply.

Cold drops of sweat stood upon my father's brow. His face was corded with emotion.

"Forgive us, father," I said, in the tenderest accents a daughter can assume.

"I must think over the matter," he said, coldly, "give me until to-morrow."

"Then you are not angry?" I said.

"Angry? oh no."

"Sir Percival, if the devotion of a life-time to yourself and her can compensate for the indiscretion into which love has led me, command me," said Theodore.

"Theodore de Neville," said my father, hoarsely, "when your father died, poor and homeless I found you. I brought you here, and the reward is that you steal away the old man's daughter. No words, sir—actions shall prove. You say I can command you."

" You can."

"We meet again to-morrow," he replied, and strode away without another word.

We were astounded. We had expected violent reproaches, threats, partings, my husband to be expelled the castle.

And now he left us together.

We were totally unable to make it out. My husband, who was ever of a sanguine temperament, believed that when the first storm of passion was over, he would forgive us, while I could not bring the same flattering unction to my soul.

And yet what could it mean?

We passed the day half in agony, half in hope, and awoke at daybreak to ponder and think again.

We shared the same apartment openly that night. This I thought a master-stroke of policy.

I confided the fact of my marriage and its consequences to my handmaidens.

I believe this was wise.

We were summoned to join our father at his early meal.

He was cold, but courteous and polite.

When the domestics had retired he quietly and calmly addressed us.

"Theodore de Neville," he said, "you, a boy, have in defiance of all the rules of hospitality and honour, married a child who knew not her own mind."

"Sir."

"Hear me out, and you shall speak your fill."

My husband bowed.

"Last night, or rather yesterday, you told me that to make up for this great wrong you were at my command."

"Yes."

"My commands are simple—very simple. You are not even a squire. Go forth into the world for three years, and there win your spurs with some renown, and on your return I will welcome you cordially, acknowledging your child my heir—or return unennobled, or without gold spurs, and take your wife into obscurity, where none shall say she is child of mine."

He looked at me. I see the love-light in his eye now. My father's looks were on me.

"Decide for me, my husband, my lord, my master," I cried.

"I will, and honour shall be my choice. Sir Percival, I accept the ordeal, and, by heavens! within the three years you shall hear of me—or I shall be dead."

My father looked at him with something, I thought, of half admiration in his glance.

He muttered something inaudible.

"You will take care of my wife and child?"

"I will."

My husband turned to me.

"When do I leave?" he asked.

"To-morrow," said my father, with something of a lowering frown; "my chaplain will write letters for you to court. You see I give you every chance."

And he went out muttering.

The words he used—my maid heard him—

"Curse the earl—curse my vow, curse everybody, for 'tis a noble boy."

I little comprehended the meaning when she told me.

Next day, my husband went—the parting was—no—away the memory!

CHAPTER CXXVI.

THE COUNTESS'S STORY (continued).

DIM is the recollection for some time of what followed his departure.

My father was not unkind, but he was thoughtful and rather cold.

He seemed to have some scheme in his head, which tormented him.

I heard more and more every day of the enormous wealth of my father, and of the dowry he could give me.

I was happy, for let my husband but win his spurs, land would be at his command at once.

How I blessed my stars that the good old father who had educated me taught me to write. My husband was too fond of manly pleasure to devote much time to such pleasures, but still he could write a little, and could read more.

I wrote to him several long epistles.

To one of them I received a hopeful and cheerful reply, that made me happy for many a long day.

Then approached the hour when I was to be a mother. How I longed for the moment to arrive. Everything that I could desire was provided for me—nurses, leeches, attendants of all kinds—but I wanted the presence of one.

I was ill and low-spirited.

But still I held up in the hope of giving to my lord a son, for somehow or other, I would always fancy it must be a son—the heir to the proud honours of my father's house.

It was born.

It was a son.

My joy knew no bounds. Even my grim father smiled when it was shown to him.

In a month I was well, though they would not allow me to nurse my own child.

It was given to a stranger, who could never love it as I could love it.

At the end of a month I was quite well.

Then my father came into my chamber, stern and cold, and as severe as ever.

He waved me to a seat, and seated himself beside me.

"Alice," he said, with his old gravity and haughtiness, "I come to explain much that may appear to you strange and peculiar in my conduct."

"Explain!" I cried.

"It may sound strange," he said, "from a father to a daughter, but it is necessary."

"Then I await your pleasure, sir."

"You must know, in the first place," he began, "that I am under greater obligations than I can ever repay to the father of the present Earl of Beauclerk."

"I did not know."

"I can never fittingly repay them; and yet, four years ago, he showed me an infallible means of doing so."

I lowered my eyes.

"That was, to give you, when of proper age, to his son, the present earl," he continued.

"I am sorry."

"I promised, and, by my knightly vow, I swore that no other man should ever be your husband."

"Father!"

"What, then, I felt when a miserable page stole your affections and married you, you may conceive."

"But you have forgiven him," I gasped.

"Listen."

"I am all attention, sir."

"At first I could have killed him, and would, but that he cleverly let me know you were to be a mother. That alone," my father said, in a hollow voice, "saved his life."

"But you forgave him."

"For a time."

"But your compact?"

"Is at end."

I was brave for my husband, brave for my child; and I determined to hear unto the end.

"At an end, sir? It has not begun. You must wait until the three years are over and my husband returns."

"You have no husband," he said, moodily.

"No husband?" I gasped.

"Here is a bull of the Pope annulling an irregular and clandestine marriage," my father continued, casting a parchment with heavy seals on the table.

"I will not obey it—he is my husband—no one shall tear him from me!" I cried.

"Alice," said my father, in a cold and bitter tone, "not only will you cease to speak, or even think of him as your husband, but you will, in four months, marry the Earl of Beauclerk."

"Never!"

"Dare you defy me?"

"I dare do that which any woman would for her husband and child," was my reply.

"Your husband is dead, and his bastard is in my power," was the cold-hearted reply.

I fell insensible, and was dangerously ill for days.

I then learnt that my husband, on his way to Palestine, with other crusaders, had been wrecked in the Channel; and everybody on board lost, save the pilot.

My child had been taken, Heaven only knew where.

My father renewed his importunities.

They were vain.

THE STAG AT BAY.

He used threats—threats against the life of my innocent boy—and I yielded.

What cared I? My husband was dead, my child taken from me for ever. If I yielded, it was to be cared for and educated well; if I refused, speedy means would be taken to rid the world of a useless burden.

I grew pensive, melancholy, sad.

My women said it became me; and when the earl came in all his splendour to woo, he professed himself delighted with my appearance.

But I knew from the first that he only wanted my wealth and possessions.

There is no mistaking real love, when once one has loved truly.

But I must hurry on. The rest of my story is bitter and cruel enough.

I had been married a year. I was peaceful and calm, if not contented. There is a state of mind when we are quite as impervious to sorrow as to joy. I was in that state. My new husband was neither kind nor otherwise; he was simply indifferent.

There was one reason made him always treat me with a certain amount of consideration.

My father came regularly to see me every three months. It may seem strange to you, my children, but no sooner had he fulfilled his vow than all his old kindness returned; and I felt that in him, at least, I had a kind of guardian.

There was another reason.

My father had given me a large dowry, but it was in his power to alienate the whole of his other property from my husband.

My husband loved money above all.

Well, again I expected to be a mother. This time my feelings were blunted. I felt very different from when the father of my child was adored and beloved by me; but, at the same time, I regarded my future offspring with a kind of sober affection which I had sense enough to know would soon ripen into love.

My husband's great passion was the chase.

Weeks, to say nothing of days, were occupied by him sometimes in hunting.

When he went I was left solely to the society of my women, and a worthy young priest, my father confessor, Friar Ambrose.

He was my husband's chaplain.

The confessional had put him in possession of the whole truth, but during nineteen years he has solemnly kept my secret, fatal as it was.

He never breathed a syllable of it to any one.

Alas! why delay my story?

My husband started, one day in August, to course through the forest.

I was in my chamber.

The day was hot, and not feeling inclined to wander through the gardens of the castle, I entered the neglected apartments now in ruins.

I had not been there long, when one of my handmaidens came to say a palmer from the Holy Land wished to speak with me on matters of vital importance.

I trembled and turned pale.

"Show him in."

A something instinctive told me he brought news of him.

I was in a vaulted chamber, massively furnished. It had been the residence of the dowager countess, lately deceased, and nothing had been done to it since her departure.

The room was half dark.

I seated myself in a high-backed arm-chair, to wait the coming of the palmer.

He came tottering like an old man into the room, and muttered something inaudibly.

"Leave us!" I said.

The girl who had guided him obeyed.

"What have you to say, palmer?" I asked, observing that he was shaken by strong emotion.

"What have I to say, traitress?" he replied, in tones I knew too well.

"Theodore!"

"Alive!"

But how unlike the accents. Mine all joy, and delight, and pride—his all anger.

He cast away his priestly garb, and stood before me a belted knight in all his manly beauty.

He was pale, but oh! how handsome.

"Traitress! is this the reception I was to meet with; and but one little year and a half of the three gone?"

"Theodore!" I cried, solemnly, "before you condemn me, hear me. I claim the right of the worst criminal, not to be condemned unheard."

With proud and knightly courtesy he handed me to a chair and listened.

I saw at once that he fully believed me, and ere I had finished, my cause was won.

"Angel—injured angel!" he cried, "and this explains all—my supposed death—the bull—the fear of losing your child. Ah! woe is me—all false."

"How mean you?"

"My death—false!"

"But the bull?"

"False—false—no man on earth can be divorced after marriage, except he was 'sibb' as the Scotch say—too nearly related."

"But my child ——"

"Is being brought up befitting his rank."

"Merciful heaven!" I cried, "tried like this, what am I to do?"

"Follow your husband, and abide by his decision."

I cowered at his feet.

"What is it?"

"But his child ——"

"Where—when—what?" he gasped.

"Is yet unborn."

"Wretch! then am I lost indeed! But no," he cried, raising me to my feet, "you are not to blame; forgive me, and hear my prayer."

He kneeled beside me.

"I care for no honours now," he said; "all I ask is obscurity in which to rear up my son. Come with me—let us fly to the uttermost part of the earth, where none shall know or care for us, and there seek the nepenthe of oblivion. We can yet be happy. Neither of us has sinned either in the sight of God or man, and sin alone is evil. Come, my wife, my soul!"

"Ha! ha! ha!" cried a hoarse voice; "who calls the Countess of Beauclerk wife?"

It was the earl, who rushed in sword in hand.

"I do," replied Sir Theodore de Neville, proudly;

"and if, proud earl, you choose to hear how, I will explain."

"I have heard all—know all—dare all. I have been foully tricked by your father—foully tricked by you, woman —and worse than all by you, whoever you may be."

"Sir Theodore de Neville ——"

The earl started, and turned deadly pale.

"Ha! So—at one fell swoop I find the son of the bastard, who would have claimed my estates, and he who has debauched and ruined my wife. Have at you—away woman. Be not in a hurry—you shall soon share his fate —have at you, I say."

Sir Theodore snatched up his sword, and the combat began; but I fainted.

When I came to I was in bed in the ruined chambers, with you, my darling, by my side.

When I could understand anything, Father Ambrose gently informed me that my young husband was dead and buried.

Then I resolved to die too; and when a good constitution struggled against my will I persuaded Father Ambrose to pass me off for dead.

And so to the world I have been for many days. I will tell you more, my children, another time; this is all of my story you now need know.

The young people heard her in amazement; but wishing to obey her in all things whom they truly honoured, were silent.

Next morning, ere they rose, she had departed.

CHAPTER CXXVII.

THE MILLER OF TRUMPINGTON.

MEANWHILE, Robin Hood and Little John, very anxious to know what had become all this long while of their friend and comrade, Will Scarlett, were on their way to the neighbourhood of the castle of the Earl of Beauclerk, in the vicinity of which they had every reason to believe tidings of the missing outlaw would be found.

Both were themselves too much in love not fully to sympathise with any trials to which the young red-haired Gammel might have been put in trying to rescue his lady from the clutches of rivals—to blame him for any holiday which he might take upon himself.

They were simply anxious to know if he were safe, or if he were in danger, desired to aid and assist him with their good bows and staves.

As there was nothing that the two chiefs, the captain, and the lieutenant, loved more than a stroll together in the forest, they trod the sward like little kings; nor hurried they; winding their way through green glade and pleasant valley, over hill, down in dales where the dun deer grazed, until at noon they found a pleasant place to repose from the heat of the day, and to take such refreshment as hearty, sturdy men required after plenty of exercise.

Then, again, with many a quip and crank, with many a laugh, and many a song, they advanced, until the lengthening shadows of the trees proclaimed that evening was coming.

"I think me," said Robin Hood, looking round like one who knew his localities, "that we shall have good cheer to-night."

"How so?"

"I have not walked this way exactly for a year or so; but near here should be the house of the jolly miller of Trumpington."

"Oh, oh! I've heard tell of him; he will give us pudding and roast-meat, and good ale. Whither away?"

"You are as tall as a ship's mast, and should therefore look out well. Look across yon bush to the other side of a stream; what see you?"

Little John lifted himself on his toes, held by a bough, and obeyed his captain.

"What see you?"

"A ruined mill."

"Yes, yes; they neglected it. 'Tis human nature. They did not want it," said good Robin. "Next."

"A ruined house near it."

"Ah! Look again, good Little John—a ruined house quotha?"

"Yes—and a small cabin near it."

"Follow me—there is some knavery here," cried the monarch of Sherwood Forest; and with a dark frown upon his brow, he hurried, followed by his tall companion, towards the ford which led in the direction of the ruined mill.

*   *   *   *   *   *

But who was the Miller of Trumpington, and whence did Robin Hood take all this interest in him?

We shall see.

The bugles sounded at early dawn before a palatial mansion near the forest, to call forth its denizens to a splendid chase, and far and near the common herd collected to witness the start.

Beneath the windows of the moated mansion minstrels were collected singing a roundelay, in which the deep voices of rangers and falconers joined chorus, a verse of which will suffice :—

> Waken, lords and ladies gay,
> The mist hath left the mountains grey,
> Springlets in the dawn are streaming,
> Diamonds on the brake are gleaming;
> And foresters have busy been
> To track the buck in thicket green.
> Now we come to chant our lay—
> Waken, lords and ladies gay.

The head falconer was in attendance, with falcons for the knights and tiercelets for the ladies, if they should choose to vary their sport from hunting to hawking.

Seven stout yeoman-keepers with their attendants, called Ragged Robins, all meetly arrayed in green, with bugles and short hangers by their sides, and quarterstaffs in their hands, led the slow-hounds or brachets, by which the deer were to be led.

Ten brace of gallant greyhounds, each of which was fit to pluck down singly the tallest red deer, were led in leashes by as many squires.

The pages, squires, and other attendants of feudal splendour, well attired in their best hunting gear, upon horseback or foot, according to their rank, with their boar spears, long-bows and cross-bows, were in seemly waiting.

A numerous band of yeomanry, called in the language of the time, retainers, appeared in livery coats ; they were the tallest men of the surrounding villages, with each a good buckler on his shoulder, and a bright, burnished broad-sword dangling from his leathern belt.

For a trifling gratuity they were bound bail as rangers for beating up the thickets and rousing the game.

On the green without were the peasantry, a motley collection enough to see.

Soon came forth the hunting party, a gallant array of lords and ladies, flushed with excitement and ready for the chase.

In their midst rode a youth—he was scarcely more—in rich costume, to whom all paid the most profound respect.

But, except a jewel and feather in his looped cap, there was little to distinguish him from the others.

At the sight of the hounds his eyes beamed with pleasure. Like all his race, he was particularly fond of hunting.

At a signal from him the hunt set forth in good order towards the forest.

The huntsmen having carefully observed the traces of a large stag on the preceding evening, were able, without loss of time, to conduct the company, by the marks they had made upon the trees, to the side of the thicket in which, by report of the chief huntsman, he had harboured all night.

The horsemen spread themselves on each side, along the cover, walking until the keeper entered, leading his bandog, a large bloodhound tied in a band, from which he took his name.

The cover having been thoroughly beaten by the attendants, the stag was soon compelled to abandon it and to trust to speed for his safety.

Three greyhounds were at once slipped upon him, whom he threw out, after running a couple of miles, by entering an extensive furzy brake, which extended along the side of a hill.

* "Tayout ! tayout !" shouted the huntsmen.

The horsemen now dashed up, headed by the youthful noble in rich costume, and a number of slow hounds being cast off, they were sent with the prickers into the cover in order to drive the game from his strength.

---

*Tailliers-hors—in modern phrase, Tally ho !

This object was soon accomplished, and afforded another severe chase of several miles in an almost circular direction, during which the gallant animal tried every wile to rid himself of his persecutors.

With rare instinct he crossed and recrossed and traversed all such dusty paths as were likely to retain the least scent of his footsteps ; he laid himself close to the ground, drawing his face under his belly and clapping his nose close to the earth lest he should be betrayed to the hounds by his breath and nostrils.

It was a buck of the first head.

Now it chanced that when the young knight so fair to see was far ahead of his companions, all the hounds save one became at fault.

The tracks of the deer had been partially successful, but what finally deceived the hounds was that a hart of the second year arose, and 'ere the error was discovered, the whole hunt swept by—horses, cavaliers, ladies, hounds and all.

The young man smiled cheerfully and went on.

The buck was gamesome enough, but at length it began to feel that flight was useless.

Then, when all was vain, and he found the hounds coming fast in upon him, his own strength failing, his mouth embossed with foam and the tears dropping from his eyes, he turned in despair on his pursuers.

They were but two, the dog and the horseman.

The dog flew at the noble stag's throat, at which the young knight swore a round oath, but there were no huntsmen with familiar voice to call him off.

With that, taking a cross-bow from his saddle, he discharged a bolt at the stag, leaped from his horse, drove the dog howling and yelping into the wood, and then finally despatched the deer with his short hunting sword.

Such was stag hunting in the good old times of merrie England, as people forgetful of truth and consistency are apt to call them.

CHAPTER CXXVIII.

LOST IN THE WOOD.

With eye elated, with a hot blush upon his cheek, with a noble and lordly mien, the young man gazed at the victim of his day's sport.

"A goodly buck," he said. " I wish my lords were here to see. A finer never graced a board."

He looked around for a place to secrete it, but none offered, save a bough, to which he proceeded to hang it by a leather thong, at a sufficient height to keep off the wolves.

He then listened for some sound of the hunt, but nought could he hear, save the deep baying of the refractory hound, darting through briar and brake to rejoin its companions.

The young man looked glum. He certainly had no wish to spend a night in the forest.

It was something to which he had never been used, and bred as he had been, a thing he could hardly imagine.

A dead, ominous silence, brooded over the forest.

The young noble stood irresolute ; and then, taking from his side a handsomely mounted bugle, sounded a call.

But though he blew till he was hoarse, no one came to his assistance.

" I must e'en take fortune, fickle jade, for my guide, and mount my horse," he said.

This he did ; and slowly and carefully endeavoured to retrace his steps.

But it is one thing to dash through the forest with buck and deer, and another to find one's way out alone.

The more the young nobleman sought a road, the more astray he seemed to go, until at last in a mood of melancholy and uncertainty he gave the reins to his horse.

The animal was utterly exhausted, and wandered, all alone, up and down, until they came to a path.

Here the young nobleman drew under a tree, determined if within an hour nobody came by, to rest him there.

It was evening.

The knight waited, and waited, and looked up and down the pathway, until what with weariness and hunger and vexation, he was nigh falling asleep.

Suddenly his horse made a movement, and there in the gloom he saw a miller on horseback.

" Pray miller, my good man, tell me the way to Nottingham town, for I have lost my way," he said.

"Sir," quoth the miller, "I mean not to jest.

> Yet I think what I think, the sooth for to say,
> You do not ride lightly out of your way."

"Why, in heaven's name," said the nobleman merrily, "what dost thou think me—passing judgment on me as you have done so brief?"

"Good faith," said the miller, who was not only well armed, but also tolerably well provided with pelf, "I have no intention to flatter you; and if you wish the honest truth from me, I guess thee to be but some gentleman thief.

> Stand thee back in the dark, nor light not adown,
> Lest that I presently crack thy knave's crown."

"Good sir," said the nobleman, stifling to keep down a most uproarious fit of laughter; I am not a thief, but a true gentleman, I have lost my way and seek for a lodging."

The miller looked at him, keeping a tight hold of his staff. He had not been used to see knights in the woods without armour, and the hunter's clothes were torn and dirty.

"Thou a gentleman?" exclaimed the miller, snapping his fingers; "why all thy whole estate hangs upon thy back, and thou hast not one penny in thy purse. Yet, after all," he mused, "thou mayest be a true man; and if thou really art, I will give thee a night's lodging."

Master miller, you are not the first by many, with whom second thoughts have proved the best.

"I am, indeed, a true man," said the nobleman, "and have ever been—and there's my hand on it."

The miller's suspicions were not satisfied, and he drew back a little.

"My friend," he observed, "I shake no hands in the dark. I must know a little more of thee before we cross palms; but come on quickly—we are no great distance from my house—and horse and I would be better for food."

The nobleman thanked him courteously, infinitely amused with the roughness of a class he was little personally acquainted with.

Descending by a path to a well-known ford, the miller crossed a small river, quickened his pace, trotted about a mile briskly up its banks and then came in sight of a mill and mill-house, the door of which flew open at their approach, emitting a strong but not unwelcome odour of puddings and "seething souse."

It was, moreover, so smoky that the young noble would, under any other circumstances, have hesitated to enter.

But he had lost his way, was tired, hungry, and glad to obtain any shelter, however rude.

A stout woman, and gawky lad with a rubicund countenance and red hair, welcomed the master.

They cast shrewd glances at the young nobleman, whom the miller surveyed; and for all the smoke there was enough light to illumine the other's countenance.

Upon which the miller spoke.

"I like well thy countenance, thou hast an honest face. With my son Richard this night shalt thou lie."

The motherly woman, who owned obedience to the rule of the man of the mill, put in her word.

> Quoth the wife, 'By my troth, it is a handsome youth;
> Yet it is best, husband, to deal warilye.
> Art thou no runaway? Prettie youth, tell.
> Show me thy passport, and all shall be well.'"

The other smiled a smile, that had been rarely without its effect, ere he spoke. He also bowed low.

"I am but a poor courtier," he said; "and have during the day's hunt ridden out of my way; I can assure you that any kindness you can show me will be amply repaid."

The miller now drew his wife apart, leaving the young hunter with the son, Richard, who asked him to recount the incidents of the day's hunt, which he did partially, to the great delectation of the lad, who listened with open mouth.

Meanwhile the miller, who had the greatest opinion of his own discernment, whispered his wife secretly—

"It is not often that I make a mistake, though in the dark I did, from very thought of my money, take him to be a gentleman thief, yet did his very voice misdoubt me."

"A soft, pleasant voice, i'faith."

"It is now my feeling; and it seemeth to me that this youth is of gentle kin, both by reason of his apparel and eke of his manners," he continued.

"He is gentle as a lady."

"To turn him out were certainly then a great sin," he continued.

"I would not do it for the world."

But the miller's last argument showed how the other's meekness had gone to his heart.

> "Yes," quoth he, "you may see he has some grace,
> When he does speak to his betters in place."

The good woman blushed rosy red as she recollected his bow and smile to her.

With all the dignity of her position, and the suavity of a hostess, she addressed the noble lord.

"Young man, thou art welcome; and as thou art welcome, thy lodging shall be of the best. I will give fresh straw to thy bed, and spread good brown hempen sheets upon it."

The nobleman, who had quietly removed his diamond buckle from his cap, thanked her cordially, and said in his merry way that she was as good as a mother to him, at which the dame laughed and slapped him on the shoulder.

"Supper before bed," said the jolly miller. "I have ridden from good Nottingham town, and this gentle here seems to have dashed far enough through bush and briar."

Wives were not accustomed in those days to show in public much of that latent authority which most of them possessed; the dame, therefore, without a demur, served up the supper, which the historian of the day—doubtless a hungry friar—has described with a minuteness which we always find in monastic records.

> Then to their supper were they set orderlye,
> With hot bag-puddings and good apple-pies,
> Nappy ale, good and stale, in a brown bowl,
> Which did about the board merrylye trowl.

For some time the party eat in silence. Gifted with appetites such as Homer gives to his heroes, they did not find time for talking.

It is some excuse for the priests, that most great poets, and even great prose writers, love to pause occasionally, and allow their heroes and heroines to prove themselves men and women by eating and drinking.

At length, however, to quote the greatest poet save one—when the rage of hunger was in part appeased—they found time to look at one another.

Richard wanted some more details of the day's hunt, of who was there, and all about it.

But the miller was not ready to listen to any long speeches—so cut the matter short.

"I drink to thee, good fellow, and to all who are ruled by petticoats, wherever they be," said the miller, and winked at his wife good-humouredly ere he took a pull at the bowl.

He handed it across.

"And I pledge thee faithfully, mine host," said the nobleman; "and thank thee for this welcome. But let me mind manners and drink to thy wife and son."

"Prithee, friend," said Richard, drily, "talk less and drink more—you detain the bowl."

At which specimen of his son's wit the miller and his wife laughed heartily.

The ale was strong, the ale was good, and the social miller, only by vocation suspicious and doubtful of his fellow-men, opened his heart more fully.

He looked at his wife and then at the stranger.

"This ale does put an appetite under the ribs of death," he said. Wife, fetch me forth Lightfoot."

"Husband—"

"Fetch me forth Lightfoot, I say, and of his sweetness a little we'll taste."

Upon this the obedient dame went to a kind of rude cupboard and brought forth a hare and fair venison pasty.

"Eat," quoth the miller, "but, mind, no waste."

All resumed their supper, the fresh viands seeming to have revived their appetites.

The miller and his family made considerable inroads upon the second course, but the noble hunter was not much behind them.

His eyes glistened, a merry twinkle settled round them, and a smile moved his lips.

"This is dainty Lightfoot, indeed," he said, with his mouth half full—"I never before eat so dainty a thing."

"I am sorry for you," said imprudent Richard, the son, "for it's no dainty here, sir—we eat of it every day."

"Indeed!" replied the nobleman, drily. "And, pray, in what town, then, may it be bought?"

"Bought!" exclaimed Richard, with a loud laugh. "Why, we never pay a penny for it—more fools if we did: we find it running everywhere beside us in merrie Sherwood."

"But," said the nobleman, affecting to taste it again carefully, "I think me it is venison."

All the family laughed heartily, the miller patted him on the back, the good wife poured him out a fresh flagon of ale, while the son looked at him with undisguised contempt.

"Each fool," quoth Richard, "I should think, full well might know that."

"I was not sure."

"Never are we without two or three in the house—all very well fleshed and excellent fat."

"So I observe."

"It is true—and *I shoot 'em ;* but, prithee, wherever you go, say nothing ; for above all things in the world we would not—no, not for two-pence—the king should it know."

"Doubt me not," said the young nobleman, demurely, "*the king shall never know more of it from me.* But my kind and excellent host, I would fain retire, as I must be up early and seek my way. I may be wanted."

"I will guide thee," said Richard.

"No bed yet," cried the miller ; "I never go sober to bed, myself, and surely I will not let a guest."

The young knight, who was soberly inclined, smiled, but gave way to hospitable wishes.

For once he thought it might do him no harm.

Then the miller brewed a noted provincial compound of ale and wine, popularly called "lamb's wool," of which, having freely partaken, he allowed the tired hunter to seek repose upon his fresh straw and sheets of brown hemp.

He often said in after life that never on any occasion had he slept sounder or more comfortably.

It was bright morn when he descended to the kitchen, and there found his untiring hosts, with a breakfast quite equal to the previous night's entertainment.

"Ere I eat, my good Richard, how about my horse?"

"A good man is kind to his beast," said the miller.

"I 'fakes," continued Richard, "I've seen him to ghts ; and a splendid bit of horseflesh he is, to be sure. Just look at him?"

The nobleman went to the door, and there, saddled and caparisoned, and champing his bit, was the glorious steed ; but around it were a dozen gaily-dressed courtiers.

The noble drew back.

Richard went out.

"It is," cried one.

Then all rode at Richard, and one caught him by the collar.

"Wretch, what have you done with the king?"

"King," said Richard, "I aint seen no king—what like is a king?"

"I am here," said the youth, stepping forth ; "release my young friend, my bed-fellow of last night."

"Sire, booted and spurred," answered a grave old man, "we have ridden the forest all night, and just now, seeing your horse without its illustrious rider,—"

"Enough. Thanks, Fitzhugh—thanks all—your king is your debtor."

All the courtiers dismounted, and, kneeling one after another, kissed the young king's hand.

"Which," says the old chronicle, "made the miller's heart start. He thought at once of his rough welcome, the perilous secret of the venison party, and of the gallows."

The young king could not but enjoy his embarrassment for a moment, though half inclined to laugh.

His natural sense of dignity, and his regard for the feelings of his host, prevented him from breaking out.

The miller spoke not, but stood "fearfully trembling ;" his wife thrust her apron into the corner of her eye, while Richard stood with open gaping mouth.

Then Henry II. drew his sword, but while so doing "nothing he sed."

The miller, who thought his last hour had come, "down did fall, crying before them all—doubting the king would have cut off his head."

The courtiers had to bite their lips to avoid laughing in the honest man's face.

"Thy name?" said the king, gravely.

"John——"

"Well?"

"Cockle, please your reverend worship."

A murmur, suppressed at once, of laughter, went round the circle.

"Rise, honest Sir John Cockle," continued the king, "and many thanks for thy rude but hearty welcome."

Thus saith the ballad :—

> But he his courtesie to requite
> Gave him great living, and dubb'd him a knight.

The miller, overcome by the king's generosity, caught his hand, and wet it with his tears.

"And now, my friends," said the amiable young monarch, father of Richard Cœur de Lion and John, "I hope you have provided yourselves."

This was addressed to his courtiers.

"That we have not," said Lord Fitzhugh.

"If your gracious majesty will allow me," cried the miller, starting to his feet. "there is ample store——"

"Of venison," whispered the king.

"Sire," replied the miller, blushing ; "I will find salt eels, and swine, and bag-puddings."

"Give them all thou hast—thou hast thy king's pardon ; and my Lord Chancellor here shall see to the land—so feast them as you will."

"Dame! dame!" began the miller.

"Lady Cockle, if you please," said the king ; "let your girls wait upon my lords—I go into breakfast."

The miller, with a proud and happy glance, watched the king sit down at his humble board, and then proceeded to raise extempore tables outside.

An hour after the king and courtiers rode away, the monarch and his lords equally amused and pleased.

To describe the raptures of the Miller of Trumpington, would be a task of some difficulty.

"And I called him gentleman thief!"

"And he kissed me, sweet prince."

"And I was his bedfellow," whimpered Richard.

CHAPTER CXXIX.

MILLER OF TRUMPINGTON—*(continued).*

Now Sir John Cockle and his lady were truly raised to a dignity of which they scarcely understood the value; but strange to say, they never received from the venerable Lord Chancellor, Fitz Hugh, that investment of land which alone made knighthood valuable.

Did they murmur?

No.

Honest hearts and true were the old couple. They had been treated with kindness by their young king ; he had honoured their house, and made them the envy of their neighbours. What if, in the hurry of business, he had forgotten his promise, or if his advisers had withheld the promised reward?

At all events, he had supped with them, had laughed at their rudeness, had treated Dickon as an equal, and shown himself, when revealed a king, no prouder than before. That was quite enough for these simple specimens of the old English race.

We are not approving of blind loyalty, but only alluding to a characteristic of our countrymen.

The memory of princes is usually treacherous, especially when benefits have been conferred by subjects.

Not so with Henry II.

Immediately after the events recorded in the previous chapters, he was forced to start for Westminster—then a distinct city from London—and in the intervals of public cares—when talking with his favourite courtiers over their sports and pastimes—he would declare that the miller of Trumpington's sport was the best, and would often vow that he would never rest until he had him with his wife and son to court.

This was so often repeated that at last the lords and knights ceased to look upon the king as serious.

Well, on a summer's day, the miller was seated in front of his house with a jug of ale, his wife was spinning, and his son practicing at a mark, when there came forth from the forest a well-accoutred squire, booted and spurred, who, riding up to the door, took off his bonnet.

"Have I the honour to address worthy Sir John Cockle and Lady Cockle?" he said politely.

"I am Sir John Coclke," said the miller, turning as rosy as an apple with pleasure.

"I bear you a message from my lord the king," began the squire.

"Worthy sir, the king himself has deigned to enter our poor home—will it please you come in and refresh yourself after your long ride," quoth Lady Cockle.

"I shall be proud humbly to imitate my sovereign," said the astute messenger; "but let me first obey orders."

"Certainly," cried the miller.

"I bring you a command from his majesty," continued the messenger, "to attend at his court of Westminster without delay—you, your lady and son."

"I don't understand the jest," cried the miller; "what are we to do at court?"

"To be hanged at least," said Job's comforter, Richard, remembering his own tattle in the matter of Lightfoot.

The squire-messenger smiled.

"Not so, indeed," he said. "The king loves you and has provided a great feast for your sake."

Then Sir John Cockle, the jolly Miller of Trumpington opened his heart.

"Then," he said, "by my troth, my gentle messenger, thou hast contented my worship full well. Hold! Before we enter the house, *here are three farthings* to quit thy gentleness. I cannot thank you, too much for these happy tidings which thou dost tell. Let me see; hear then me; and tell to our king, we'll wait on his master-ship in everything."

The messenger bowed gravely, took a mouthful and a horn of ale, on which he rode away, leaving the whole family in considerable perplexity.

The miller was a prudent man, and no sooner was the squire's back turned than he began to reckon the expense as well as the equipment suitable for this journey and visit.

"Here come outlay and charges, indeed," he said grimly, "but we must appear with dignity, though all we have gathered should go. We have need of new garments, of horses and servant men, of bridles and saddles. This will be a salt matter."

When was woman ever at a loss, and when does her native wit come forth more brightly than when her husband is at fault? With a hearty slap on the shoulder she addressed him.

"Tush! Sir John! Why should you fret or frown? Nothing of all this is at all necessary. I know his worshipful majesty better than you do. At all events, you shall be at no charges for me. I have already made up my mind. I will turn and trim up my old russet gown; with everything else as fine as may be."

"Wilt do?"

"Yes—and you shall put on you the best you have; and Dickon too. We can no more."

"Will the king like it?"

"Ay, better than if we were to try and ape the finery of all the courtiers we saw at our door."

"I leave it all to you, Lady Cockle."

"Then on our mill-horses swift we will ride," she continued; "with pillows and pannels, as we shall provide."

"And so it was decided; and in this stately sort they rode towards the court; their jolly son Richard on a huge mill-horse, foremost, as if he had been a courier.

He, youth-like, must do something to distinguish himself—for he set up, for good hap, a feather in his cap.

Travelling was slow in those days, but every journey has its end, and at last they reached Westminster, where, being expected, they were at once admitted.

None of the courtiers expected them to have good sense enough to come in their own costume, which raised them in the estimation of the sensible ones, though some said it was trickery, and that they played off on this visit a little of the wit and art of the clouted shoe, appearing as they did before King Henry and his courtiers in rough country trim, abating not one jot of rustic manners or dress.

But the king smiled, for the contract was to his majesty's liking, and the game was kept up with much spirit.

"Welcome, Sir Knight," said the young monarch, courteously, "and welcome to your gay lady; and welcome, too, to thee, my young squire."

"A bots on you," cried the rustic; "and do you know me?"

"How, indeed, should I forget thee?" continued the king, with the most imperturbable gravity; "for thou wert my bed-fellow, well I wot."

Now, though Richard's answer delighted the courtiers hugely, and nearly convulsed them, it was of a nature too rustic for these columns—and for that presence, thought Sir John Cockle, for he angrily interfered.

"Ah, knave!" he cried; "hast thou no more manners?"

"The queen! the queen!" was now the cry, and put an end to the discussion.

It was indeed the queen, who, having heard the story oft, and having received her husband's commands, spoke most kindly and graciously; though she could not help gravely enjoying the embarrassment of the good miller's dame, who stood as stiff before her as the queen of spades, while she dropped a courtesy at every word.

To end a scene which was evidently becoming too much for both sides, the king bade a domestic of high position show them their apartments, where they remained, overwhelmed with astonishment at all they saw, until they were summoned to dinner.

This dinner scene was the crowning glory of the visit.

Sir John, Lady Cockle, and son, sat at the top table with the king, and the merry monarch, desirous of putting his humble visitors at their ease, and also wishing perhaps to divert himself a little, had directed his courtiers to drop for the nonce all etiquette, which, if preserved, he knew would alarm the miller.

At first the good man was a little startled and shamefaced, looking at all with a doubting air; but soon, the king pressing him to eat, and eating himself, his natural joviality got the better of his rustic modesty, and he burst forth in his true colours.

He did not seem much to relish the viands, perhaps, because, being chiefly French, he did not understand them; but he ate and drank all that was offered, wine, ale, and beer, without a word, until his countenance became quite flushed, his eyes sparkled, and he was quite at home.

Then quoth Sir Cockle, breaking silence and addressing the king, "I will pledge you in a pottle—were it in the very best ale of all Nottinghamshire."

"Aha!" said the king, with a sly smile, "you are too much for me, my worthy knight. But now I think of a thing—I would, indeed, we had some of your Lightfoot here."

"Oh! oh!" cried master Richard, with a reproachful glance at the king, "full well may I say it—'tis rank knavery to eat it, and then to betray it."

"Thou sayest true, friend, and speakest like an oracle," cried Henry II.; "but be not thou angry—let us have a cup of wine together; cup-bearer, pour to us."

"Stay till I have dined—stay till I have dined," cried the miller's son, letting the wine stand. "I make but small way among these twatling dishes of thine. One good black-pudding were worth them all."

"Aye, marry would it, my man," replied the monarch, remembering his own hearty supper at the miller's house; "then I wish indeed we had one here."

"I have one," cried Dick, readily, pulling at once a large black-pudding out from his huge hose.

King, queen, courtiers, could contain themselves no longer, and the whole table burst into one uproarious laugh, which was not over when Richard had finished his humble addition to the meal—which he seemed truly to enjoy.

Presently, the banquet over, all rose and followed their majesties to their great hall, where they witnessed various sports and pastimes, the king keeping Richard near him, and amusing himself infinitely with his quaint sayings and utter rustic simplicity.

All round stood the favourites of the monarch, to whom the novel scene was a great change from court life.

A number of very handsome ladies stood in a knot apart.

"Come Dickon," said the king, addressing the young rustic, "you are a vigorous lout—if thou wishest to wed, look round among my ladies here and choose thee a wife."

Richard turned and surveyed, with some disdain, the plumed groups of mincing and bridling madams.

"Why!" he exclaimed, "my own love, Jugg Grumball, with the red head, is worth them all."

This was convulsive; and the king, being afraid that he should himself be ill with laughter, now closed the audience.

"Sir John Cockle," he said, "I am now called by state affairs to leave you; but ere we part," he continued, taking a parchment from venerable Lord Fitzhugh, "know that here, at my court of Westminster, I make you overseer of Sherwood forest, with three hundred pounds yearly—the first in this box out of hand; and now take heed you steal no more of my deer. Once a quarter in every year let me see you—and now, Sir Cockle, I bid you adieu."

And the worthy man, overwhelmed and delighted, retired with his family from the king's presence.

Such is the veritable and true history of ye miller of Trumpington.

CHAPTER CXXX.

TWENTY YEARS AFTER.

FROM that hour until the king's death Sir John Cockle enjoyed his happy honours. The post of one of the overseers of Sherwood forest was, in his case at all events, but a sinecure; so that he carried on his mill, bought land with his yearly three hundred pounds, and was, at the epoch of the monarch's demise, a well-to-do yeoman, owning his own broad fields and meadows.

Then he and his dame died, leaving the whole of his property to Richard and his red-haired wife and children.

They, too, prospered, as long as King Richard reigned in England, but soon he went to Palestine, and John was regent in his absence.

The licence and violence of the Normans under this prince we need not recapitulate. We have already alluded to them in different parts of our narrative.

It is sufficient for our purpose to say that about six months previous to the day on which Robin Hood and Little John descended the valley towards the mill of Trumpington, a Norman, with full power from Prince John, expelled Richard from his possessions, burnt his mansion, destroyed his mill, and left him nothing but a wretched hut for himself and family.

And here Robin Hood found the once blithe and hearty Richard, cowering with his wife, sons, and daughters, over a miserable fire.

After the first greetings had taken place, Robin Hood asked the name of Richard's persecutor.

"Sir Norman de Malvoisin."

"Now, by my father's head," said Robin Hood, which with him was a large oath, "this man and I must square accounts. He is a most greedy and unconscionable knave. Cheer up, Dickon. You have the parchment safe?"

"I have."

"And you would not be afraid to plead your cause before Prince John himself?" asked the outlaw.

"I was not afraid to sit at the same table with his father," replied Richard.

"True," mused Robin; "the Prince is not all bad. Be of good cheer, my hearty Dickon; all will be well yet. I have a friend or two at court, and we'll e'en try an honest Saxon with a king's sign manual against a Norman robber. And now to roost—we must be early on our way."

Somewhat cheered by the confidence with which Robin Hood spoke, Richard Cockle retired that night within his poor home comparatively a happy man, and slept while Robin passed many hours of the night in devising how he was to act in order to fulfil his promise to the son of Sir John.

At cock crow, he bade the miller's son adieu, promising to return in a few days and report what plan he had hit upon to restore the once jolly youth to his own.

Then, with bold Little John stalking by his side, he went on his way in the direction of Earl Beauclerk's castle.

* * * * * * * *

When the young married couple parted from the countess, and once more began to traverse the forest beneath the greenwood trees, neither were in a very great hurry to reach the end of their journey.

Will Scarlett was as loyal and full of fealty to his chief as he had been at any time, but we must recollect that he was in the first flush of a happy honeymoon.

There was another reason why Will Scarlett took a somewhat oblique direction towards the trysting tree.

There could be no doubt that in every part of the forest where horsemen could penetrate emissaries from the earl would be on the lookout, while even in the densest thickets

men, urged on by the love of gold, would try to hunt them down.

Will determined, then, to go by ways scarcely known to any of the rangers, ways which he had become familiar with when a boy, and which, when shown them, even surprised the outlaws themselves.

Thus then wandered, now through obscure thickets, now beneath dense clumps of oak, now hastily crossing a path or road, which they did rapidly, until a little after mid-day they halted in the centre of a dense copse, which, while wholly screening them from view, gave them a complete command of a cross-road between Gammeltown and Nottingham.

"Have we far to go, my own dear Will?" said Eveline; "I feel to long to be under the protection of a brave band of bowmen. Every moment I feel as if my father or my uncle were coming up in chase."

As if as an echo to her words, there came at that moment a tramp of horses on the wind.

"A troop of soldiers," whispered Will.

Eveline turned deadly pale.

"Remain still—breathe not—stir not," he continued; "where we are, no horse can come; and if we are still none will suspect our presence."

Eveline crouched behind a thick nut-bush and said nothing.

She was in the bright heyday of love's young dream, and to have it rudely driven from her, was more than she could bear to think of.

"But who comes—and what is the meaning of this pace?"

This was muttered to himself, as he stepped upon a fallen tree trunk to peer out upon the road.

True, it was a troop of horse, but at its head rode one who seemed bereft of sense.

His feet were out of the stirrups, his jewelled cap had flown far away, his hair streamed in the wind, while his horse, maddened, dashed forward at a fearful pace, which those behind vainly tried to compete with.

Just in the skin of the horse's neck was a cloth-yard arrow, that had nigh drove the animal mad.

"By heavens!" said Will Scarlett, with a grim smile, "it is my noble father-in-law. I may not let gentle Eveline see him. But why that arrow in the horse's neck—surely no friends of mine can be about?"

He waited until the sound proclaimed the earl and his companions out of sight and then advanced his head.

There was the earl, under a large tree, mounted on a fresh horse, alone.

He had dispatched his men forward, and was probably waiting for other reinforcements.

What was to be done?

Will Scarlett owed the earl no good grace, and personally, after all he had heard of him, might have cared little about making free with his noble father-in-law's life.

Those were not days in which consanguinity much affected men's actions in the world.

But young Gammel had the most intense respect for Eveline, for her wishes, even, if she had them, for her foibles.

He would not, therefore, have harmed the earl personally, and as he had no coadjutor just then, he really knew not what to do.

To continue on his way towards the trysting tree he must cross that road. To do so in full view of the earl was simply madness.

Will Scarlett smiled. In his own mind he was firmly convinced that the shot which had so startled the earl came from Robin Hood. Will was not ashamed to be an imitator.

Concealing himself from Eveline, he fitted an arrow to his bow, and measuring the distance with an accuracy only to be obtained by long practice, shot an arrow into the horse's neck, so surely and yet so gently as to produce no immediate dangerous effect.

Just as Will Scarlett expected, the horse, the moment he felt the barbed point, began to rear and plunge dreadfully, and so suddenly withal as nearly to throw his rider.

With fearful imprecations the furious earl checked him for a moment, but the barb working in, the horse soon became unmanageable and then darted off at a fearful rate —into the forest.

Will smiled, and taking Eveline by the hand, crossed th road, and when not only was he in a thick covert, bu heard no sound of the galloping horse, gently wound a mot.

It was answered in the same tone, and in five minutes more Robin Hood and Little John came up.

Both doffed their caps with profound respect.

"Robin Hood and Little John, allow me the proud satisfaction of presenting you to my wife—Eveline, daughter of the Earl of Beauclerk."

Both heartily congratulated the lovers, and then the chief of the outlaws drew Will aside.

"The forest is alive with armed men," whispered Robin, "and they will ere long, if we contrive not some plan, encircle us. They have some clue to your being in this part of the wood; and to-morrow they will be in sufficient force to beat us up like game."

"What is your advice, captain? For myself, I take my wife home to Barnesdale, or die."

"I do not despair," said Robin; "but this I know, that what is to be done must be done to-night. As soon as darkness sets in we will try how fortune favours us."

And he returned to where the unsuspicious Eveline was in conversation with the forest giant.

Now that these two new defenders were near her, she felt no fear of the future.

A retreat was beaten into one of the darkest and gloomiest of the thickets, where all remained until the shades of evening fell upon the forest.

"Not a word—not a cry—not a whisper!" said their young leader; "our lives hang on our silence."

No sooner had they left their place of concealment than the reasons for his precautions became apparent.

Every here and there they saw watch-fires scattered over the forest, while every few minutes sentries challenged one another to look out.

To the left were three distinct fires, which made Robin Hood swerve to the right, where the men-at-arms were not quite so much on the alert.

Slowly they pushed along, beneath an avenue of oaks, keeping right in the shadows, until once more, on turning a corner, they came upon a blaze of light, two hundred yards distant at most.

"Like a hunted hare," whispered Eveline.

"Hush!" said Robin Hood; "be still, as you love your life. Await me here."

This to Will Scarlett and Eveline, while he led Little John away to where he heard low moans at no great distance.

He had not gone far when he discovered whence they came.

On the greensward, under a lofty oak, lay a man.

He was dead or insensible.

Robin Hood stooped.

It was the earl in a swoon.

This is what had happened.

When the earl's steed took the bit in his mouth he flew away through glades, tearing through the roughest coverts, brakes and thickets, so that, had not the earl been a first-rate horseman, he must have been immediately overthrown.

As it was, however, his ride was not doomed to be a very long one.

Darting under an oak-tree, a bough struck the baron across the breast and cast him to the ground insensible.

Robin saw that he was coming to, and at once determined on his line of conduct.

Drawing his hunting-knife, he placed the point at the nobleman's throat.

The earl slowly opened his eyes.

"One word—one sound," hissed Robin Hood in his ear, "and you are a dead man."

The earl was brave enough, and would have faced death in the field without hesitation.

But this was to die like a dog.

He looked keenly at Robin Hood, and even by that dim light saw that he was determined.

Robin continued,—

"Rise and walk slowly forward. I will hold your arm. When challenged by the sentries tell them what you please; but attempt to betray me and that instant you die."

Robin made a rapid sign to Will Scarlett and to Eveline, which the former understood.

Robin on one side, Little John on the other, pressed the earl forward.

Eveline and Will Scarlett brought up the rear, walking so as not to be observed by the prisoner.

"Who goes there?" suddenly said a sentry.

Robin pressed the earl's arm nervously.

"All's well," he said, "keep good watch and ward. 'Tis Herman of the Turret."

"Yes, my lord."

"I shall return shortly," continued the nobleman.

The sentry bowed respectfully and walked away.

In this manner the whole chain of sentries was passed, and a part of the forest reached where Robin believed himself safe.

But trust the earl he would not.

He bade Will Scarlett forward with Eveline as rapidly as possible.

The earl was then suddenly gagged by Little John, at a sign from his chief.

Despite his struggles, he was secured and left to take his chance under the greenwood trees.

The outlaws then hurried away, quite sure that the earl would leave no stone unturned to have his revenge.

CHAPTER CXXXI.

THE MARRIAGE.

THE earl, however, acted in a very different way from what they expected.

When he found that his daughter had really left him, for the society of the outlaws, his feelings took quite an unexpected turn.

He determined to be revenged on the girl he had hitherto so much loved.

For some time he had contemplated marriage with the daughter of a neighbour, whose wealth was almost equal to his own, a proud, haughty Norman lady, whose ambition was gratified by the idea of wedding one so highly placed in the favou rof the prince.

Her name was Rosabelle d'Ambricourt, and her father a brother-in-arms to the earl.

Eveline's father determined, on his return to his castle, furious and foaming, that his runaway child should never, come what would, wrest any of his fortune from him.

If Providence gave him other children, they should be the sole heirs of his wealth.

With this feeling gnawing at his heart, he hurried on the marriage with such haste that a week after his unsuccessful pursuit of Eveline all was ready for the ceremony.

A large number of his friends and acquaintances were present to do honour to the occasion.

The earl never once mentioned his daughter's name, though her elopement was the public talk.

As no allusion was made to any marriage having taken place, none ventured to allude to her absence.

She was looked upon as a very naughty young lady indeed.

Father Ambrose was absent from the castle. For many years there had been a coolness between the earl and himself; but the confessor knew too many secrets to be trifled with.

An abbot of high rank attended to sanctify the marriage ceremony.

The whole of the party was collected in the chapel.

The earl was radiant.

The bride was cold and haughty, but rarely beautiful, of the true Norman type.

The earl placed the register of the house of Beauclerk in the hands of the priest.

He slowly opened it, and glanced his eye at the last entry in the book.

He started and looked strangely at the earl.

"What see you?" asked the earl.

"But nine days back another marriage was celebrated in this chapel," said the friar.

"A marriage?"

"Yes."

"What marriage?"

"That of your daughter with William Gammel, son of old Sir Gammel."

"D——n!"

"It is signed by Father Ambrose."

THE SHERIFF'S TRIAL.

"The traitor!"

"With the formal consent of the Countess of Beau-clerk," continued the abbot.

Had a thunderbolt fallen the earl and his friends could not have been more surprised.

The bride turned ghastly pale.

"What countess?" she said.

"My wife has been dead seventeen years," gasped the earl.

"Here is her signature"

"A forgery."

"No," said the quiet voice of Father Ambrose, as he stepped from behind a stone pillar, "it is no forgery, I declare."

"Fiend!" cried the earl, "what mean you? What is your object? Why disturb my wedding day with your tricks and mummeries."

"I come here to prevent a fatal crime," said Father Ambrose, solemnly.

And he led the pale and white woman forward, who, to the earl, and to the whole world besides, had been dead seventeen years.

He looked wildly and madly round.

"Vile monster!" he cried, "will you explain, ere I cast you into the moat? Who is this woman who lowers at me thus?"

"I was your wife," said the countess, sadly, "until you murdered him who was my love."

The earl seemed scarcely able to support himself, his looks were haggard and wild. He really thought himself dreaming.

The company exchanged looks.

The bride stood haughty and unbending, a look of settled scorn upon her countenance.

"There is a mistake here," said an old man of venerable appearance, coming forward, "which I alone can clear up."

It was Alice's father.

The earl looked first at him, then at his daughter. He was evidently fast losing his senses.

"Alice is mistaken," he said coldly, "she was never the wife of the Earl of Beauclerk."

A sigh could have been heard, the assembly was so still.

"When she accepted the hand of the earl her first husband, Sir Theodore de Neville, was alive," added the old man.

" Father ! " cried Alice.

" I sinned my child. I had promised you to this man —and I preferred a crime to betraying my promise. I knew your husband was alive."

" Then this marriage can proceed," said the earl, beginning to recover his assurance.

" I have nothing to say against it," said the father, in a sarcastic tone, " but since Alice is not your wife, all the fortune you were to inherit at my death goes to the son of Theodore de Neville."

The earl ground his teeth with passion.

" Fair Lady Rosabelle," he said, turning to the haughty Norman beauty, " this scene is not interesting to you. Wilt retire with your friends, while I unravel this mystery ?"

" I came here to be married," replied Rosabelle, coldly.

The earl's face was radiant in a moment.

Alice's father quietly placed in the abbot's hand the proof of his daughter's marriage with Theodore de Neville, and then taking his daughter's arm, disappeared from the chapel with Father Ambrose.

" And my son ?" whispered Alice.

" I am taking you to him," replied the old man ; " he is a noble boy."

The widow of Theodore de Neville stooped and kissed her father's hand.

   *   *   *   *   *   *

The marriage ceremony proceeded, but the bride was cold and haughty.

Pride, stubborn unbending pride, alone enabled her to go through with it.

She would not, after her marriage was announced, allow the world to talk, but this day's exposure did not promise any great happiness for the household.

Eveline and Will Scarlett little suspected the strange events which were taking place in Beauclerk Castle, events which left them free to be happy in their own way.

We shall see the issue of their elopement as we proceed —we have now to do with more pressing events.

Thomas the carter has started to lure the credulous Sheriff of Nottingham to the forest, under the impression that he is about to capture Robin Hood.

We must shortly follow in the burly outlaw's footsteps.

CHAPTER CXXXII.

A FESTIVE SCENE.

EDWIN and Rose, with Will Scarlett and Eveline, now fairly belong to the band, and Robin Hood has determined, while waiting for a report from Thomas the carter, to hold u. der his trysting-tree high festival in honour of the newly-married people.

Robin Hood never did anything by halves, and by his directions masters of the ceremonies were appointed, and to them was given the management of the festive arrangements.

The morning was balmy and rich, the sun warm, and even glowing, the thin vapour that rose from the moist earth soon vanishing into thin air, and leaving all bright and clear.

Robin Hood, on this occasion, as King of Sherwood Forest, was richly dight in crimson, while around him stood his lieutenants in their holiday costume of Lincoln green, somewhat more rich and elaborate than that which they wore upon their forest adventures.

They took their way from the cavern under the arches of the leafy wood, winding their way among the giant trees, which were profusely and pleasantly decorated with garlands.

The fanciful spirit of the chief had caused deer to be caught, and to be held prisoners here and there on the road, their fawns frisking about them.

Soon the short interval between the cave and the trysting-tree was passed, and they entered the greenwood glade.

Here the trees were decorated in the most liberal and ornamental style, such as might have well become Christmas.

A circle of poles, from which hung festoons of flowers and green boughs, indicated the place where the dancing was to take place ; then there were targets and rings for quarterstaff play, and alleys for quoits, a favourite amusement with the merry men of Sherwood Forest.

We need scarcely say that the cooking preparations were on a scale of magnitude commensurate with the numbers who were expected to partake of this Homeric feast.

Venison and pork and feathered game were roasting before huge fires, while some were busy rolling casks of ale and beer and wine into fitting positions.

From the village near which Sir Gammel resided all the young people had been invited, and it was to them a matter of amazement to behold the preparations.

And now, heralded by rude music and escorted by a bevy of gaily-dressed youths and maidens, the bridal procession advances, halting only when before the rustic throne on which sat Robin Hood.

The heroes of the day now formally presented their wives to the merry monarch.

Robin Hood, whose respect for the fair sex was beyond all powers of description to convey, rose, and descending the steps of his rustic seat, took a hand of each lady, which he pressed within his own, and then drew them to a seat beside him.

At a signal the games commenced.

In an instant every light-footed dancer had selected his partner, and was tripping it lightly on the fantastic toe upon the green and springy sward.

In the open air, with no close ball-room air to injure the health, a more glowing and invigorating pastime than dancing cannot be conceived.

It opens the heart, it exercises the muscles, and it brings the sexes into pleasant contact.

The girls from the village, who at first were shy of the bold outlaws, lost all their timidity at the first fling, and from that time laughed and joked as freely as any.

Then the cooks gravely announced that the repast was ready, and could any pen do justice to the scene that followed, it would have been worthy of the pains. But it will suffice to say that a merrier meal never was partaken of beneath the waving tree-tops, under the shelter of the huge forest giants.

Again they are up.

No time is lost.

All are eager to resume the games, and while the great majority of the elders simply move on one side to drink huge draughts of ale or wine, the younger rush to dance, to play quoits, to shoot.

Will Scarlett had now resumed his wife's arm, and was walking round, proud and happy as he looked up into her face, and anxious that all should, if possible, share his pride and happiness.

He had a good word, or a smile, or a shake of the hand for everybody.

Edwin and Rose did the same, and though not equally known, were greatly admired.

Friar Tuck was the life and soul of the feast ; under pretence of his holy character he stole kisses in abundance, every now and then, however, returning to his favourite corner to quaff a horn of strong ale, after which he returned to join the throng with additional heartiness.

On one occasion, when he had just laid down his huge flagon, a whole bevy of girls and boys surrounded him, and before he had the least suspicion of their meaning or intentions, they made a ring about him, caught hold of hands, and ran round with such hearty good will and such extreme rapidity that the friar began to see more stars than there are in the heavens.

But the friar was a man of resources ; so, suddenly, he plumped down upon the green sward and closed both his eyes.

" Go on," he said ; " you will be tired before I am. Go on to your hearts' and souls' content."

Then the girls tumbled him over and rolled him about, and kissed him and pinched him and thumped him until he was glad to rise again.

Then they wanted all to be confessed.

" Nay," said the friar, with a wink at the foresters around ; " I shrive such pretty ones always one at a time."

" Oh, the wicked man ! " cried the merry, light-hearted girls, again taking up their circular dance, which they continued until the clerk of Copmanhurst fairly roared for mercy.

They were a little tired themselves, or they might not have granted it so easily.

There now came a most interesting part of the day's amusements.

Among the guests was a man of huge stature and powerful frame, called Donald Doubletree, a Cumberland man, famed in all the country round as a wrestler.

He had challenged Little John to a friendly match, and this was to come off two hours after dinner.

The place selected for the wrestling was an enclosure of some extent, which, on ordinary occasions, was used by the outlaws for their merry dances and games, as well as for such like trials of strength.

Here, to make the gaiety all the more, they had erected a kind of Maypole.

The spot was admirably chosen, being covered by a perfect carpet of greensward, even and beautifully turfed, and, therefore, excellently suited for the purpose to which, on the present occasion, it was to be applied.

The greater part of the holiday-makers now began to collect around the scene of action.

The effect was pretty much the same as must be presented at a great prize fight, only that the monotony of the scene was diversified by the presence of the fair sex, who in all countries like excitement and displays of courage.

Who crowd the arena when a bull-fight is to take place in sunshiny Spain?

The ladies.

Who are the chief spectators when any man is about to risk his life for the amusement of the public?

The ladies.

On the present occasion the contest was not so dangerous as those we allude to, but it had, however, its chances.

Donald Doubletree stepped into the ring in a slight doublet and hose that showed off his manly limbs and powerful proportions to great advantage.

Little John was not behind him, retaining only his short under tunic and hose.

A finer specimen of humanity never stood six feet ten in his bare stockings (we say this from habit, in those days stockings not being known).

They shook hands heartily, the bout being perfectly friendly on both sides.

The spectators began betting freely, and it was noticed that most of the villagers and townsmen supported Donald, while the outlaws backed Lieutenant Little John.

Then all was still, the contest exciting the most intense interest.

The adversaries began by laying hold of their antagonist's shoulder and elbow with a firm grip.

Then each essayed his strength.

Both stood firm as rocks, their muscles swelled by the unusual tension.

Neither gained the slightest advantage over the other this bout.

But Donald was really rather taking the measure of his man than doing anything else.

He was a practised wrestler, from a distant county ever famous for its men of mark.

He made several feints.

Then he attempted a terrible jerk with his foot against Little John's leg.

All his strength and science were thrown into this last effort.

He might as well have tried the same experiment on a firmly rooted iron statue.

Little John never budged an inch.

A tremendous cheer burst from the outlaws. The backers of Donald Doubletree looked grave.

Again half a dozen feints were made on both sides, each striving to take the other by surprise.

Then Little John threw all his strength into a great final effort.

It failed, for though the Cumberland man yielded for an instant, he soon recovered his position.

Then the giant outlaw had recourse to his peculiar tactics. Letting his hand fall from his rival's elbow to his hips, he suddenly dropped on one knee, and exerting all his huge strength, lifted the other right-up, and cast him over his head—the man, utterly helpless, falling heavily to the ground on his back, his head indenting the green sward.

Anywhere else but upon greensward he must have been killed.

Little John stood erect, with his usual modest air, despite the frantic shouts of his adherents, not even by a smile indicating any unmanly triumph over his fallen antagonist.

"I had not thought," said Donald Doubletree, rising, and rubbing his head, "there had been a man in England could have done it. But, there is my hand, and I will take another time for my revenge."

"Now, if you like," replied Little John, in his quiet and indolent way, something like that of a Red Indian.

"No, try someone else. I will quaff ale the rest of the day, unless you have set your mind on it."

"No—anybody else?"

But all were scanning the make, the sinews, and the muscles of Little John.

None answered.

A burst of music now recalled all to the dance, which was kept up, with other amusements, to what, in those days, was considered a remarkably late hour.

Then, when legs were weary, and mouths began to yawn, and eyes to dim, the cavern was re-entered.

The revels were over.

But one natural result of the festive day's events soon followed.

Many of the outlaws had been smitten by the fair girls who came to visit them; and, on the other hand, many of the girls were taken with the merry men.

As they whirled lightly and gladsomely round in the dance—as they looked in the flashing eyes and merry features of their partners—they could not help wishing that they might be partners for life.

Ere many days were over, the jolly friar found himself called upon to marry some thirty young and happy couples, so that the race of Sherwood outlaws was not likely to become soon extinct.

CHAPTER CXXXIII.

THOMAS THE CARTER.

IF there was one man more than another the outlaws took a delight in tricking and annoying, it was the worshipful Sheriff of Nottingham.

To him on such an errand was now bent Thomas the carter.

He was habited in the ordinary garb of a forest outlaw, mounted on a sorry enough jade, with a large bundle behind him, and a long wooden case containing his bows and arrows.

There was a quiet sedateness in the man's face, which showed how much he enjoyed the task he had undertaken of his own accord.

No fear of the result or of discovery filled his mind with aught of discomfort.

The stupidity of the purse-proud Sheriff was matter of notoriety.

Anybody could deceive him; and to deceive him, therefore, was no great merit.

But the results were, at all events, satisfactory enough.

His money was quite as good as any other man's.

Thomas the carter necessarily took his time, as the steed he had selected, though strong and sturdy, was made rather to carry weight than for speed.

He, however, arrived during the evening of the second day in Nottingham town, and at once presented himself at the sheriff's gate.

Orders had previously been given that he should be at once admitted.

He had been daily expected.

A plan had been for some time concocted between the Sheriff of Nottingham, the Earl of Beauclerk, and Sir Norman Malvoisin to entrap Robin Hood, but the details had been adjourned until the devices of Thomas the carter were known.

By the most false representations, the sheriff, who well knew that Robin's title to be Earl of Huntingdon could be easily proved, had obtained a royal warrant to take the bold outlaw anywhere they could, and execute him on the spot.

Robin Hood had been most abominably libelled to the prince who then ruled England.

He was described as a murderer.

But a dispassionate historian, whose words are gold, says:—"I disapprove of the rapine of the man; but he was the most humane and the prince of all robbers."

He was described to the prince as a mere ordinary thief,

preying upon poor and rich alike, but always fleeing before any display of superior force.

"He and his men," says a contemporary, "were most skilful in battle, whom four times their number of the boldest fellows durst not attack."

But princes seldom hear the truth, even the most affable being deceived at times.

But, even though the conspirators were fully in possession of the authority to take Robin Hood, there occurred simultaneously to all a slight difficulty.

It was easy to say take, but how was he to be taken?

First catch your fish.

After long conferences between the parties interested, it was decided that the offer of Thomas the carter was the only one desirable.

To march into a forest, the brakes, thickets, and fastnesses of which were so intimately known to the bold outlaw, was simply folly; as, if the invading army were too large for him to face, he had but to retire and conceal himself in some of his impenetrable retreats; or, if the force against him were not enough to alarm himself and men, then, with his forest tactics and superior knowledge of the means of defence, the invader would stand but little chance.

Thomas the carter, as he walked towards the audience chamber, gathered his thoughts together, in order to prepare for an encounter of wits with the sheriff.

His utter astonishment and surprise may, therefore, be conceived when he found himself confronted with the two Norman knights.

He was not, however, a man to be daunted by any display of force, but determined to play his part well.

With a low bow, he stood cap in hand before the grandees collected to meet him.

"So, sir outlaw," said the earl, "you have agreed to guide us to the trysting place of Robin Hood?"

"No!"

"How now, knave?"

"I say—no!"

"Explain."

"I promised, for a sum of money and a free pardon, to put the worshipful sheriff in the presence of Robin Hood, and to show him his secret haunts."

"Well, sirrah?"

"But I shall do it my own way."

"How so?"

"I have a neck."

"To be stretched."

"Exactly; and knowing Robin Hood as I do, I have no wish to fall under his displeasure."

"Traitor!" began the sheriff.

"No traitor, but one with a due regard to the preservation of his neck. If I led the whole army prepared to invade the outlaws, he would hang or shoot me, if I were only above ground."

"Let us hear what you have to propose," said the Earl of Beauclerk, sternly.

His detestation of the outlaws was so great that he had left his young and newly married bride, to concoct their destruction.

"I would have the worshipful sheriff here," began Thomas the Carter, "disguise himself as an outlaw."

"If I do may I be ——"

"Hear the man, Sir Thomas."

"And walk with me to where I can point out how the outlaw may be surprised. Then his worship can return to lead you to the spot, while I amuse the outlaws and keep them from suspicion. Thus I shall win my reward and save my neck, should any outlaws escape."

"'Tis well," cried the earl.

"But, my lord," began the sheriff, who was purple with excitement and passion, "I like me not this expedition through the forest. It savours too much of danger to my person."

"Art afraid, Sir Thomas?" asked his superior, the high sheriff, sternly.

"No."

"Then the matter is settled. At early dawn you will start, and we will follow at a reasonable distance—and now let us to the banquet-room."

To this motion no one made any objection, Thomas the carter being told to seek the offices and secure a place for the night as best he might.

The jolly carter found no difficulty in so doing, as being of an exceedingly versatile disposition, he soon ingratiated himself with the servants, who gladly gave him bed and board.

CHAPTER CXXXIV.

OF THE WALK WHICH THE SHERIFF TOOK WITH THOMAS THE CARTER, AND WHAT CAME THEREOF.

THE unfortunate sheriff, who now cursed his stars that ever he had been so deluded, would gladly have found some excuse to avoid carrying out his own plans.

He did not dare openly to disobey his superior officer, but a sleepless night was spent in racking his brains for some plan by which to evade his engagement.

But the morning came as it comes even to the condemned criminal—without an idea of escape.

The sheriff rose with a groan, which quite startled his spouse.

"What aileth thee, my dear?" she said.

"I know not exactly," he dolefully replied; "but I wish it could be made to appear I was ill."

"Why?"

"That someone else might be found to enter the forest in my place."

"Aye! and be called coward?"

"Nay—but I much misdoubt this outlaw. He may lead me into danger."

"The outlaw," replied the provoking wife, "seems to me a very honest fellow, and would, I am sure, do my husband no ill."

"The foul fiend take him and all connected with him," said the sheriff, as he huddled on his clothes and left the room.

He had appointed early morn for the preparations for his masquerade.

He found Thomas the carter waiting for him in a room below, with the two suits of outlaw's garments ready spread out upon a table in formidable array.

"Sirrah," said the sheriff, angrily, "why have you played me this scurvy trick?"

"What scurvy trick?"

"What means this dragging me into the forest?" cried the other, fiercely.

"Your worship wishes to capture Robin Hood?"

"I do."

"You cannot get him to come to you."

"I suppose not."

"Then you must go to him. Your worship has no other means of getting at him."

"But will you see me safe?"

"I will; not a hair of your worship's head shall be hurt. You shall have full protection, and I swear your personal safety shall be my most earnest care."

"I take your word, my worthy fellow," said the sheriff, somewhat mollified.

Then, with the assistance of the jolly outlaw, he proceeded to dress himself in the forest garb; and when his toilet was ended, it would have been difficult to have discovered much discrepancy between his costume and his real character, except that he was a trifle obese for one leading an active life in the woods.

When he presented himself at the morning meal, his wife first setting the example of mirth, the table was soon in a roar, the earl mischievously enjoying the other's secret annoyance.

"I think, dame, an you were to attend to your guests, instead of indulging in unseemly laughter, it would be wiser and more decorous," said Sir Thomas, with a dark frown.

"Ah, ah, my dear old duck! but you do look so comical. Now do say, Stand and deliver," cried the merry dame.

"I' faith, not I."

"Do."

"I will not."

"Fie, for shame!" continued the dame, with a secret look of intelligence, the nature of which husbands know generally; "but for that contradiction you must now. Come now—be not an old silly, but speak up at once."

"Stand and deliver!" cried the sheriff, in a gruff and angry voice, that made all scream with laughter.

The earl, however, saw clearly that if the joke were carried too far, they might lose the co-operation of the worthy magistrate ; he, therefore, skilfully turned the conversation to the details of the expedition, which was, once for all, to root out the glaring insolence of the outlaws, who, had they but robbed the poor and middling sort of people, leaving the rich alone, might have flourished to this day, for what the nobles cared.

It was their bold defiance of the Norman invaders that made them so obnoxious to the wealthy.

Their courage all feared ; while in case of a tussle for the monarchy between Prince John and Richard Cœur de Lion, no one could doubt which side the outlaws would take,—when they would be worth their weight in gold to the opposite side ; for

> Of these archers brave, there was not any one,
> But he could kill a deer his swiftest speed upon,
> Which they did boil and roast in many a mighty wood,
> Sharp hunger the fine sauce to their more kingly food.
> Then taking them to rest, his merry men and he
> Slept many a summer's night under the greenwood tree.

The great source whence the outlaws were recruited was the violence of oppression of the Normans.

The merry men were nearly all Saxons ; many of them individuals who had been defrauded of their birthrights and family possessions, by Norman spoliation ; scarcely one in the band but had been a sufferer through Norman avarice or wickedness ; and upon the Normans they retaliated whenever it lay in their power ; succouring when opportunity offered, those who were oppressed and trampled upon ; feeding and clothing, aiding the poor, and levying contributions upon the rich. There were two classes from whom the poor suffered—indeed, the whole British public generally—the wealthy landholders, who at that time were nearly all Normans ; and the church, who left no means untried or unpursued, to squeeze money from both the rich and the poor, to swell their already enormous and simonious incomes.

And as upon the landholders and the church, Robin chiefly made war, these two classes were necessarily his bitter enemies.

As soon as the dame found that the conversation was turning to business she left ; and, a few minutes later, the sheriff, with slow and reluctant steps, went forth by an obscure back-way which opened directly on the vast forest.

Now anybody who is afraid in the dark, and has been compelled to traverse long passages in utter obscurity—any one at all timorous and superstitious, who has been obliged to cross a churchyard at midnight—may be able to understand the feelings of Sir Thomas, as, in company with Thomas the carter, he entered beneath the waving boughs of that mighty forest, in which a hundred thousand men might have lain unperceived and unsuspected.

And yet the forest glades were pleasant enough ; the trees were green, and the sward soft to the tread ; and the birds were singing merrily on the dewy boughs.

But the sheriff had at no time much of an eye for the beautiful.

On the present occasion the lovely forest seemed to him to teem with things horrible and ghastly.

He glanced at every thicket.

If the thief does fear that every bush conceals an officer, here the officer did fancy each bush a thief.

" Have we far to go, good outlaw ? " he said, in a tone of deep humility.

" To Barnesdale."

" When shall we arrive ? "

" May be to-night, but more likely to-morrow."

" At what inn, then, shall we sleep ? "

" Inn, quotha, inn ? Well, well, an your worship wishes it, we will find an inn," said Thomas the carter, with a grim and somewhat suspicious smile.

The sheriff certainly did exert himself to get over the day's work as fast as possible ; but though he could not walk very fast, yet was the exertion so great that he literally larded the ground with fat as he walked.

The perspiration poured off him in streams.

Every now and then he would stop to take breath, but a word from Thomas the carter sent him off again.

" Quick, your worship, or we shall never reach this hostel of mine ; an we walk briskly we shall be there by nightfall."

And the sheriff, terribly alarmed at the idea of spending a night in the open air, moved his fat legs and obese body as rapidly as in him lay.

Thomas the carter wickedly and maliciously enjoyed the fun.

At mid-day they halted half an hour for refreshment. The outlaw was inclined to have taken more time, but the knight, in great trepidation, urged him to go forward.

The yeoman laughed inwardly at the other's hurry, and, rising, again guided him through the intricate paths and winding ways of the forest—paths and winding ways which the sheriff could no more have found again than he could have followed an Indian trail over the vast and trackless prairies of the West.

Night drew near, and the sheriff began to look uneasily about for the expected hostelry, when suddenly they came to a small stream, sparkling in the evening light—a murmuring rivulet, which,—

> Wanton and wild, through many a green ravine
> Beneath the forest flowed. Sometimes it fell
> Among the moss with hollow harmony,
> Dark and profound. Now on the polished stones
> It danced, like childhood, laughing as it went ;
> Then through the plain in tranquil wanderings crept,
> Reflecting every herb and drooping bud
> That overhung its quietness.

" How now, sirrah," cried the panting sheriff, " where is this same inn you wot of ? "

" 'Tis somewhere hereabouts," replied Thomas the carter, scratching his head, " and yet——"

" What, you sorry knave ? " exclaimed the knight, becoming choleric and valiant.

" Let me but think," continued the outlaw ; " yes—we must cross the stream, which here is only above our ankles, and then we shall be there."

The sheriff groaned. Wading in cold water of an evening—he, who never at any time liked cold water—was to him one of those minor miseries of life which for the nonce made him as wretched as if he had been next day about to be led out to execution.

But needs must, as the proverb says, when a certain person pushes up behind.

Thomas the carter entered the water, which, far from being only ankle deep, was up to the thigh, and cold water too.

" A curse on Robin Hood and all his gang," muttered the sheriff ; " would that I had never heard of him."

" Did your worship speak ? "

" No, his worship didn't."

" How like you this forest life ? " said Thomas, as he plunged into a hole up to his waist.

" The curses of Satan on you, fellow ! " cried the sheriff scarcely able to speak for shivers ; " hast sworn my death ?—is this the way you keep your word ? "

" We shall reach mine inn soon," said the outlaw, " and then we shall be comfortable."

The other made no reply. He was desperate, and hardly seemed to care what became of him.

At length, however, the stream was crossed, and the two stood before a small gloomy-looking hut, near the huge wheel of a deserted mill.

" What place is this ? "

" Once the village of Hachleg," said Thomas, coldly, until one day the Norman tyrants, whom the saints accurse, came ; and because a joint of venison was found in each house, set fire to every hole-thatch, and sent men, women, and children into the ranks of the outlaws."

" How escaped this lonely hut ? " whispered the now more than ever terrified sheriff.

" It was mine ; and just as the fiends were about to commence its destruction, Robin Hood came up and drove them away, with the loss of a dozen men."

" I recollect. It was the first of his many misdeeds ! " said the sheriff.

Meanwhile, Thomas the carter had opened the door of the hut, and was in the act of striking a light,

CHAPTER CXXXV.

NIGHT IN A HAUNTED MILL.

THE hut was entirely bare of furniture.

Every vestige of anything suitable to human habitation had been removed ; but on the ground were piles of dry grass and ferns, which promised a comfortable bed enough.

But the sheriff was cold and wet.

Thomas the carter took no notice, but began at once to build up, in the comfortable fire-place, what promised to be a roaring wood fire.

The sheriff fetched some logs himself, and bestirred himself as much as his corpulence would allow him.

He then selected one for a seat, and as soon as the wood crackled and blazed on the hearth, felt a glow of satisfaction come over him, no wise decreased by a hearty pull at his flask of strong waters, without which the luxurious ex-merchant never travelled.

He then, with something of a genial smile, offered it to Thomas the carter, who, however, producing from a secret recess a jug of old October, said he preferred a pull from that to anything else which could be offered him.

Peace and goodwill, however, were now fully restored between these strange and somewhat ill-assorted companions.

A hearty meal was the next thing, after which the sheriff, declaring himself fatigued, proposed to retire.

"Sleep, Sir Thomas," said the outlaw; "I will take a turn in the forest. There may be prowlers about, and it is as well to know if there be night hawks abroad."

"Leave me here alone!" cried the sheriff, turning deadly pale. "I won't be left."

"Sir knight, I go for our mutual advantage and protection. Close the door and lie down, nor open to any save me. There is, however, little fear of any disturbing you."

"Why?"

"Because this house is haunted."

"Holy Virgin!" gasped the knight—like most of his class, as superstitious as cruel and wicked, "let us away!"

"Where?"

"Anywhere."

"But in the night there walk abroad many ghosts. The forest, they say, is peopled by them," said Thomas the carter, in a low whisper. "This house is haunted by no fearful spirit. I should gladly see her an she be as the troubadours describe her."

"How so?"

"'Twas a maiden upon whom some lawless knight set his eyes, and being a Norman, to wish and to have is the same thing—God curse them all! This is the description given of her *before* the knight saw her. There was, says the poet,

A sweet disorder in the dress
(A happy kind of carelessness);
A lawn about the shoulders thrown
Into a fine distraction;
An erring lace, which here and there
Inthrals the crimson stomacher;
A cap neglectful, and thereby
Ribands that flow confusedly;
A winning wave, deserving note,
In the tempestuous petticoat;
A careless shoe-string, in whose tie
I see a wild civility.

What she may be like now I know not, for I have never seen her; perhaps your worship may be more fortunate."

And the outlaw, drawing the door to, went forth into the night, leaving the sheriff shaking with apprehension in the hut adjoining the ruined mill.

"Now if Heaven but gets me free from this trial, and I once more lie upon the marital couch, Robin Hood and all his gang may rule the forest for me. *Pater noster, qui es in coelis, sanctificatur nomen tuum!* A murrain on the earl, who has made a catspaw of me, and sent me forth, through brake and briar, to sleep on a fern bed in a haunted hut."

As he spoke these words aloud, he looked around with a fearful and terrified glance.

"My time has surely come," he muttered; "for my sins have I been brought here to be murdered or frightened to death by ghosts—oh!"

This little shriek was caused by the sudden going out of the flames, which left the hut in darkness.

"*Libera nos quæsamus Domine, ab omnibus malis,*" he continued, mumbling all he knew of pater and ave.

The wind began to sigh around the house.

"Oh Lord! if I escape with life I will cause a mass to be said every day for three years."

The hut was now in total darkness, and the mighty sheriff was too much afraid to get up and put on fresh wood.

He lay shivering and moaning on his fern bed, too much agitated to go to sleep.

He had never in his whole experience passed such a night before, and he could almost understand the feelings which are experienced by criminals the night before their execution.

Having to preside at such ceremonies, however, had never yet interfered with his slumbers.

The sheriff vowed that in the execution of his duty he would in future be a little more merciful in his dealings with the violaters of the law.

Such resolves, however, are generally written in sand.

While these ideas were passing through the unfortunate magistrate's brain, he heard the latch of the hut distinctly rise.

And as it rose his hair rose also, while his teeth chattered fearfully.

He half opened his eyes, and then, to his horror, remembered that he had forgotten the injunction of Thomas the carter to bar the door.

He clearly saw it open and a dark figure peer into the hut, after which it entered, slowly followed by a second.

Then they closed the door.

"Ah!" said a gruff voice, "this is better. The night is awful; and under the greenwood tree is pleasant enough at times, but not when it blows."

The weather had indeed changed during the last hour. It had become both stormy and sleety; it blew a hurricane, and the sky was like a vault of lead.

"Little chance of catching those two spies on such a night," responded a second voice.

The sheriff, who had crouched up close to the wall, now shivered as with the ague.

"But why does our noble captain, Robin Hood, think the two men who were seen to leave Nottingham together spies?"

The sheriff felt a fearful faintness coming over him.

"Dost know who they were?"

"One is said to be a much-trusted outlaw," said the first speaker, "and hence our chief's displeasure."

"What will be his fate?"

"He will be strung up without judge or jury," replied the outlaw, quite coolly.

"And the other fellow!"

"Well," said the man, in a kind of slow, hesitating way, that sent a shiver to the very bones of the listener, "I should say that he would be skinned alive, or roasted, or some such trifle as that."

"Inhuman monsters," thought the sheriff. "Domine exandi ora lionem meam—*mea culpa, mea culpa, mea culpa!*" he added, muttering inaudibly.

"If, however, it should turn out to be the Sheriff of Nottingham, then it will be altogether a different thing," said robber number one.

"How so?"

"Well, you see, he is such a cruel, lustful fellow, that Robin would put out his eyes and cut off one of his legs; thus leaving him to wander about a dreadful example of God's justice on the man who has oppressed the widow and the orphan."

The agonies endured by the half-insensible listener to this fearful threat cannot be described.

The rack was nothing to it.

Breaking on the wheel appeared a trifle in comparison to what his mental sufferings were.

"By our Lady!" suddenly said one of the men, "there is a fire! Some one has been here!"

And with his quarterstaff he stirred up the embers, threw on fresh fuel, and once more lit up the dark corners of the haunted hut.

The sheriff now decidedly thought that his last hour had come, and closed his eyes with a silent prayer.

The men, however, never turned their eyes towards him, but went on making up the fire.

Had he seen the leers on their faces, and the comic glances they cast obliquely in his direction, the Sheriff of Nottingham might have understood the real nature of the case.

The two outlaws knew all the time he was there, and it was not their cue to discover him.

The abject terror he must experience was by far too good a joke to be lost.

Presently one of the men rose, and opened the door.

"'Twas but a squall," he said, "and it is quite over. We had better cross over and watch the path to Barnesdale. We can shelter from the storm under the hanging oak."

"As you will," replied the other; "it would be rare sport to catch the villains."

And the two men went out, closing the door behind them, and laughing heartily, though not loudly, at the fright they had given to the sheriff.

"Now may every curse that priest can call up with book and candle fall upon the knaves!—may boils blister them to the very bones!—may hot pincers take off their flesh!" said the sheriff, passing his hand over his reeking brow. "This is, indeed, most damnable! Accursed be the hour that I was born! But I will not stay here to be murdered. I will, even in the darkness of the night, venture forth into the forest; for verily, do I know that spirits are less wicked than men."

With these words, the sheriff scrambled up, and though he was scarcely able to stand, moved toward the door.

He was just about to raise the latch, when the door seemed to open of itself, and Thomas the carter came in, looking terribly frightened.

"What is the matter?" gasped the poor sheriff, now utterly overcome.

"The devil's the matter—everything's the matter!" replied Thomas, bluntly.

"Explain yourself, my friend," continued Sir Thomas, in his humblest tones.

"Robin Hood, in some strange way, has conceived an idea that I am betraying him."

"I know it!" gasped the wretched man, clinging to the arm of the strong outlaw.

"How should you know?" said Thomas the carter, with quite a bewildered look.

The sheriff, with many "ohs" and "ahs" and other interjections, told his story, to which Thomas the carter listened with terror.

"There is something wrong somewhere," he said; "and yet how can it be?"

"Did you confide your intentions to any one?" asked Sir Thomas.

"I trusted no one. But let us not be alarmed. I know the merry men and their ways well. Keep a bold front if we meet any of them, and all will be well."

"A bold front when men talk of skinning you alive!"

"Nonsense! they couldn't mean it. But I am tired, and seek repose that we may be under way by daylight."

As really there was nothing else to be done, the sheriff sighed and returned to his couch, where he passed the night in such agonies as only himself could conceive or understand.

CHAPTER CXXXVI.

THE CAPTURE.

BEFORE dawn Thomas the carter was up and stirring.

The moon now shone like a silver shield in the cloudless firmament, and the morning star glittered like the finest jewel in the light above the horizon.

But Sir Thomas was less and less inclined to notice the beauty of nature.

He thought of nothing but how, as speedily as possible, to get home to his wife.

Though a little shrewish to him when at home, she now, at a little distance, appeared an angel of light.

He had given up all idea of seeking the haunt of Robin Hood, and told Thomas the carter that if he would but see him safe home to Nottingham, he should have the reward.

Thomas the carter seemed himself to think that this was, under the circumstances, the best policy.

They took their way then by one of the most unfrequented ways to be found in the forest.

They did not cross the stream, but skirted its other bank.

The path, which in former and more peaceful days had led to the once happy, now deserted village, was entangled and choked up, so that their progress was slow.

An hour after sunrise they came to a small clump of oaks, where the road was freer and clearer.

They were about to pass on, when six outlaws stepped suddenly forward.

Sir Thomas fell on the ground and began raving, clutching, swearing, and kicking all at once.

A good hard buffet or two speedily aroused him.

When he stood up he found that the outlaws were in whispered but not unfriendly conference with Thomas.

Their backs were turned to him.

He thought it a good opportunity to run, and, with a nimbleness quite extraordinary in a corpulent man, ran towards the oak thicket.

"Stop!" cried a stern voice.

Sir Thomas darted behind a large oak and peered at the outlaws.

One of them had fixed an arrow and pulled it to the head.

"Keep where you are," said the outlaw, sternly. "I know you not, save that you have run away, which looks ugly. Show me but a limb, or a portion of one—the tip of your nose—aye, even an eyelash—and I will send an arrow at you."

With a fearful shiver the poor sheriff leaned against the tree, and never moved.

Suddenly he heard the men advance, and next minute heard them speak.

"Ye may be true men both, but this bout you go before Robin Hood, who will know what to do."

And ere he knew what, the sheriff was being hurried along in the very midst of his captors.

In this way, silent, hopeless, and half dead, the ex-merchant, who would have gladly exchanged places with the poorest apprentice he had ever starved or pinched, was taken along, until, suddenly halting under the full blaze of a noontide sun, he seemed to open his eyes for the first time, to find himself face to face with Robin Hood seated in state, surrounded by all his officers and an array of some five hundred outlaws, among whom the astounded sheriff recognised a number of citizens, and especially a large band of villagers from the estates of Sir Gammel.

"Well?" said Robin, quietly.

"An please you, captain, we found these two men skulking about in the garb of merry-men, and seeing they are but sorry knaves, brought them before you."

"I know them not," replied Robin, gravely; "but yet I fancy I do. One, I have heard, is of the band, while the other is a spy. Let them prove themselves yeomen, and they go free; an they are not, hang them."

"What proof?" asked Little John.

"There is a mark yonder. Give them a bow, and each three arrows—that shall decide," said Robin.

Thomas the carter took his bow in his hand with a quiet stolidity which was very droll to all who knew him.

The sheriff clutched his as if it had been a hot poker.

"An you like not the trial," said the merry monarch, "you have only to speak. Open confession is good. He who is not the yeoman must hang."

Thomas the carter's only reply was to look at the target and shoot three arrows in rapid succession, all of which hit the target very near the centre.

"Now, sirrah," said the captain, sternly, "beat that, or you will surely hang."

The sheriff knew not how to hold a bow, much less how to shoot; and it was ludicrous to behold him trying to look as if he was quite used to the weapon.

He tried to adjust the arrow to the string.

It fell upon the ground.

"Hang him up," said Robin Hood; "hang him up as a spy and a false traitor."

"Who dares lay hands on the Sheriff of Nottingham?" cried the magistrate, wildly.

A tremendous shout greeted this announcement.

"Then our eyes deceived us. It is indeed our old and valued friend. Welcome to our trysting tree. But what, in Heaven's name, want you here?"

"Yon fellow promised to give you up to me," he blurted out, with angry violence.

"You lie, in your teeth!" said Thomas the carter. "I told you I would bring you here, and then you could bring up your men if you knew how."

"Betrayed! betrayed!" cried the unhappy dignitary. "What is to become of me? Speak."

"Sir Thomas," said Robin, gravely, "were I a severe man I would do unto you as you would do to me; but, as it is, I will detain you until first your friends withdraw from the forest, and you pay me a ransom of a thousand marks."

"A thousand pounds!" cried the infuriated sheriff; "you might as well ask me for a king's ransom."

"As you will, Sir Thomas; but you leave not my charge until you have prevented the advance of the attacking army, and also until you have paid the ransom fairly fixed upon one so important as yourself."

The sheriff groaned, and was handed over to a guard; while preparations were being made to repel the invaders.

*   *   *   *   *   *   *

Meanwhile, the Earl of Beauclerk and his brother were slowly advancing to the rendezvous where they had appointed to meet the sheriff after finding out the true haunt of the outlaws.

They were a powerful band of some six or seven hundred men, armed with every appliance for attack and defence known to modern warfare.

But the mysterious character of those they had to deal with at once demoralised the men. They, with the song writers of the day, were decidedly of opinion that these men possessed some magic power against which it was impossible to contend.

They, therefore, as soon as they were beneath the leafy arches, began, like the sheriff, to look about them with a certain amount of anxious awe highly characteristic of a credulous age.

At length, however, the scene of rendezvous came in view, and the whole body entered with pleasure on a green and grassy sward, where the light came down in floods.

A halt was at once declared, and a spot selected for an encampment.

The side of the open glade opposite to that by which they had entered was a semicircle of dense thicket, almost impenetrable to cavalry.

Towards this the earl and his chief officers moved, as being more sheltered and pleasant.

Then piteous cries assailed their ears.

"Keep back, for the love of God, keep back, if you would not have me stuck as chockfull of arrows as St. Francis the holy martyr! Keep back, I say."

"Who speaks and cries in such a frightened way?" said the earl, imperiously and angrily.

"All that is left of the wretched Sheriff of Nottingham," was the lachrymose reply, "who, if you come nearer, will be made the butt of six hundred outlaws armed to the teeth, who line every bit of yonder copse."

The earl and his attendants stood still, but not so much because the Sheriff of Nottingham had made his appeal, but because he dreaded the effect on his men of a steady discharge of arrows that, killing and wounding a large number, would probably cause a panic.

"What is desired of us—what would you have us do?" said the earl, in a loud voice.

Before the unfortunate sheriff could reply Robin Hood stood forward with a low bow, and waved his hand as a sign that he wished to be heard.

The chief ranger of Sherwood Forest signified his assent, though inwardly fuming with rage.

"What is your will?"

"My lord, the Sheriff of Nottingham, basely taking advantage of the supposed treachery of one of my fellows, has come here to kill, destroy, and plunder the people who live under my protection."

The earl made an impatient movement.

"Who live, I say, under my protection," replied Robin Hood, proudly. "The fair land of England is held in durance by foreign nobles, and only in the forests is there freedom and liberty for the Saxon. Those who are oppressed fly to me for shelter, and I give it them. While I live such protection shall never be refused."

The earl bowed haughtily.

"The sheriff is now my prisoner, and so he remains until this expedition is for the nonce abandoned, and a ransom of a thousand marks is paid."

"You will not dare, insolent yeoman."

"Earl," said our hero, rising almost a foot in stature, "when I please, I will beard thee in thy den; not as Robin Hood, but Robert Earl of Huntingdon!"

The earl and Sir Norman stood with open mouth, gazing at the audacious outlaw.

"Pay the money; it's all true, and I knew it," murmured the sheriff.

"May the devil choke you!" said the earl; and then he added in a lower tone, turning to his treasurer, who, as was customary in those days, attended their masters to the field, "pay the money."

"But you will retreat?"

"Half a day's march," said the earl.

Robin Hood bowed, with a sarcastic smile; and in ten minutes more the sheriff, exhausted and ready to faint, was once more among his fellows.

————

CHAPTER CXXXVII.

THE RESOLVE.

HALF a day's march—for the earl, as a belted knight, kept the promises publicly given—from where this scene took place was a position almost marked out by nature as a military camp, and which, subsequently, antiquarians have declared to have been a Roman camp during that people's military occupation of Great Britain.

It had a kind of natural rampart all round, with trees growing thickly on all sides.

Here the army halted, and, lighting fires and erecting hastily constructed huts of boughs, proceeded to prepare for the night's encampment.

The sheriff had recovered his equanimity, and with it his ordinary ferocious malignity.

A wicked thought had entered his mind and played round his lips in the shape of a sensual smile—a smile of sensual cruelty.

"I told you, my lords, that I had discovered many reasons why we can never outwit these outlaws. They are not only very fiends themselves, but the whole forest population is with them. I saw in the camp twenty young retainers of old Sir Gammel."

"Ah! what then?"

"Let the villagers be punished with fire and sword, that will teach them to aid and abet such ruffians."

"Thou sayest well," said the earl; "but let not a breath of this escape your lips. I must pay a promised visit to my young wife—we are scarce wedded a fortnight—and will then join you. This would be unwise to approach with so large a body of men. This is Monday,—say that on Thursday, in four divisions, at daylight we march upon the spot. Remember," he added, with a dark frown, "none must be spared to tell the tale—not even the household of Sir Gammel. Such an example is much wanted."

This was agreed to; and minor details being settled, the three men betook themselves to rest.

Scarcely had they done so, when the thicket behind them opened, and the face of Robin Hood, livid and ghastly, peered out upon them.

"But that I can have pleasanter revenge," he murmured, "I would slay you all as you lie. I, too, will remember, and by St. Dunstan, there shall be no quarter given or taken on that day, when we shall see who are best at hard knocks, Saxons or Normans.

And he quietly withdrew with the cautious and noiseless step of a Red Indian.

*   *   *   *   *

It must be remembered that the kingdom of England was at this time in a most distracted state, and that the prince who ruled was continually besieged with accounts of ravages, and outrages, and robberies, so that the earl had a roving commission to put down by the strong hand all who were against the royal authority.

*   *   *   *   *

The villagers who owned the famed old knight Sir Gammel as their landlord and master, had, ever since the youthful days of Heny II., been in secret league with the outlaws, who on all occasions were ready and willing to befriend them.

Sir Gammel, a hearty and jolly sportsman himself, as a rule neither made nor meddled with anybody.

He hunted the wild deer, he went forth hawk in hand to enjoy old English amusements; but as a man owning large possessions, and having a family, he abstained as much as possible from doing anything which might bring upon him the anger of the crown.

He was never happier, however, than when in the midst of his friends and tenants overlooking their sports and pastimes.

Thoroughly Saxon and English, he above all things encouraged archery, the art to which England owed so much of her greatness.

ATTACK ON THE FIRST BARRIER.

A match was on between the most celebrated of the village bowmen.

All the males able to carry arms were collected on the village green.

A target had been set up, and the most skilled marksmen were practising.

Many a good shot had been made, and many words of praise bestowed, when two men in Lincoln green appeared in their midst.

A tremendous shout arose.

"A Robin Hood! a Robin Hood!"

"A Will Scarlett! a Will Scarlett!"

But Robin gravely waved for them to be silent and listen to his words.

"My friends," he said, addressing the knight in the first instance. "I come to warn you. Practice every hour of your lives, for ere five or six more mornings are over you will have to do battle for your very existence."

Dead silence prevailed.

Then Robin Hood told them of the abominable plot concocted against them by the Sheriff of Nottingham and the Earl of Beauclerk.

"My precious father-in-law!" half whimpered Will Scarlett.

"Eh?" said the old man.

"Egad!" cried the youth, blushing crimsom, "never thought on't; didn't think of asking father to my wedding. Well, Sir Gammel, I have the pleasure to come of introducing you to my wife—Eveline."

The excitement with regard to the threatened attack was, however, so intense that this announcement, which at any other time would have created great excitement, passed without notice.

All stood round Robin Hood, listening to what he had to say. His words were few, but thoroughly to the point.

"Prepare to defend yourselves—collect all your friends, and I and one hundred of my men will be here to aid you."

Sir Gammel rose.

"I have never lifted hand nor lance against the Norman foe—but this time my house shall be my castle, and I will give it freely as the stronghold whence we will launch our deadliest bolts upon the enemy."

A tremendous hurrah followed, and the whole of the men present separated to prepare for a defence which they knew must be desperate in the extreme.

CHAPTER CXXXVIII.

PREPARATIONS FOR DEFENCE.

IN all the petty conflicts which took place between the conquerors and the conquered in the good land of England the stern Norman pirates, whose descendants ruled the land, were pitiless when success crowned their efforts.

Every device of cruelty and wickedness was carried out to intimidate other people from rebellion and resistance.

But that old British spirit which has survived so many centuries of kingly and priestly misrule was not to be put down by intimidation and bluster.

Englishmen could die, but not voluntarily wear the yoke which their rulers and taskmasters would fain impose upon them.

The tenants and dependents of Sir Gammel knew well that did they basely surrender, or die defending their houses and homesteads, the result would probably be the same.

Murder and rapine stalked ever in the train of the hired mercenaries of the ruling powers.

A noble defence was therefore the only hope they could have of ultimate escape.

One and all resolved that the contest should be one to be remembered in Sherwood Forest.

Robin Hood took care that there should be an ample supply of arms for all who could carry them.

The women and children were removed to the secret recesses of the forest.

The men had thus nothing to distract their attention, while the hope of rejoining their wives and little ones would add strength to every arm and fill every heart with a hearty glow.

It was a painful sight to witness the parting of husbands and wives, and sisters and brothers, of parents and children.

Parting is indeed sweet sorrow when there is a reasonable hope of being reunited.

But here some who parted could not but know that they met for the last time.

Robin Hood, who, apart from his severity to such of his foes as were obstinately bent on his destruction, was the tenderest hearted of men, could not but view the tearful separation with deep emotion.

He, however, had counselled it, and from the very best and most unselfish of motives.

Whenever such scenes presented themselves to his view, he thought at once of Marian, who, naturally enough, was ever present to his heart's best and noblest reflections.

Then, the graceful tribute to human nature paid, he was again the brave and skilful soldier.

Under his advice such of the villagers' valuables as were easily removable were taken to the forest, so that, should the worst come to the worst, none might hesitate to make a hecatomb of the whole of their remaining property.

Then every available means of defence was resorted to. Every avenue, road, or path to the village was guarded by means of huge barricades of felled trees, earth, and stones, upon which men mounted guard day and night, in order to give notice of the approach of the enemy.

Scouts, too, were sent to outly in the forest, while spies were forwarded to Nottingham itself.

But the enemy was perfectly quiescent, not a sign being given by them of any intended attack.

So confident were the leaders of the strict secrecy with which their plans had been laid, that they never even thought of inquiring whether the villagers expected the expedition.

It was therefore the impression of the earl and his subordinates that the very terror of his name would induce the Saxons to lay down their arms and surrender at discretion.

In order the better to conceal the supposed secret foray from Sir Gammel and his dependents, it was given out that a great move to the north had been ordered by the prince.

And thus a week passed away.

The villagers knew well what they had to expect. It was not their first lesson with regard to the tender mercies of the Normans, whom they hated with good Saxon hate.

They therefore not only entrenched themselves as well as was in their power, but laid in an ample stock of provisions.

Robin Hood superintended everything, even to the making of arrow-heads, the sharpening of spears, swords, and other weapons of defence, in which he was indefatigable.

Now all was still. Everything for which human foresight could be prepared had been done, and the villagers, who had hitherto been kept up by excitement, began to relapse into apathy.

Their nerves were unstrung, and it needed at last a goodly supply of ale from the hall to keep up their spirits.

Inaction was wearing them out.

Robin Hood suddenly recollected that the barricades would be all the better if ditches were dug in front of them.

Everybody acquiesced, and with right goodwill the whole of the defenders rushed to the spade and pick-axe to remedy such a notorious deficiency.

A plentiful supply of beef and beer enabled them, however, to get through this task in a day, and the whole body, from sheer want of something to do, would have again relapsed, when the outlying scouts and spies came in to say that the vanguard of the Normans was all but in sight.

Earl Beauclerk, satisfied that a band of about a hundred men at arms would excite less attention than a detachment of seven hundred headed by himself, had sent forward one Gaultier de Simon, a Norman soldier of fortune, to kill, slay, and burn all who resisted, reserving to himself the right to appear on the scene should the villagers be supported in their struggle by the outlaws of Sherwood Forest.

The man who led this band was a true Norman soldier of fortune, with all the *fanfaronade* of a Frenchman, and the ridiculous contempt which a regular trooper is too apt to feel for undisciplined masses.

Such men allow nothing for the inherent and sterling bravery of the true Anglo-Saxon.

He advanced as gaily at the head of his men, armed with crossbows, lances, and other weapons of the day, as if he had been going to parade.

In his approach to the village not a living soul met his eye, and judging from the supposed utter ignorance of the unfortunate villagers, he fully expected to take possession of their homesteads without a struggle.

His idea was that they were scattered abroad, pursuing their ordinary every-day avocations.

With this idea, it was with a perfect chuckle of self-satisfaction that he threaded the woodland glades.

He never even thought of sending skirmishers forward to inquire into the true state of affairs.

His advance was something similar to that of some stubborn martinets in the British service, who marched to attack Red Indians in an American forest as they would disciplined troops.

The Norman did not despise Saxon valour, but he believed it thrown away in a contest with such men as he commanded.

As soon, therefore, as the forest was passed and the upward road to the village was clear before them he sounded a charge, and rode headlong forward to complete his triumph.

He was within twenty yards of the first barricade before he had an inkling of the truth.

Then, as he would have formed his men and examined into the nature of the defences, a fearful shower of arrows, bolts, and stones—cast by means of rude leathern slings —showed him how terribly he had been deceived.

With twenty men unhorsed, and with the horses prancing wildly in confusion and dismay, nothing was to be done but sound a retreat, which very much resembled a flight.

Only, however, for an instant.

The man was courageous, and the moment he saw the error of self-confidence into which he had been led, a man of resources.

Horses he saw at once were not only useless but an incumbrance.

All his men were ordered to dismount, leave their horses in a secure place, and act as infantry.

Two mounted men, however, were ordered off to warn the earl of the fact that the villagers were fully prepared.

Then Gaultier de Simon made his arrangements.

A scout or two soon made him aware that every arrangement had been made for a desperate defence.

Every known avenue to the village and hall was fortified, rudely but effectively.

Champing his grey moustaches with rage, and cursing the villanous traitor who had brought about this *contretemps*, the veteran soldier lost no time in preparing to remedy the inevitable evil.

His plan was, in the first instance, and until numbers were on his side, to storm one barricade, and thus effect, if possible, a lodgment inside the works.

For this purpose he divided his hundred men into three bands, two of which, armed with crossbows, he placed one on each side of the barricade to fire upon the Saxons; while with the other fifty he purposed charging the enemy.

It was a soldierly and bold arrangement, as the villagers at once perceived, and would necessitate the most vigorous measures to repel.

The Norman soldiery, in whom there existed very much of the *esprit de corps* which belongs in general to all disciplined troopers, were furious at the losses they had already sustained, and burned to avenge their killed and wounded comrades.

No sooner, then, was the signal given than, with a loud and ringing shout, they rushed to the charge.

They were met by a terrible volley from unseen hands, Robin having directed proper loopholes to be left at every barricade around the whole of the village.

But wounded or not wounded, the hired mercenaries, with a courage and recklessness worthy of a better cause, hurried to the foot of the barricade, crossed the ditch, and began clambering up the defences.

While some engaged in hand-to-hand encounters with the enemy, who now appeared on the summit of the fortifications, others, with their bill-hooks, began tearing asunder the logs and trees of which the rampart was composed.

A terrible conflict ensued, in which blows were dealt with heartiness and goodwill, accompanied by execrations and taunts of a nature that proclaimed the mutual ill-will of both parties.

The Normans at length succeeded in tearing away enough of the rampart to effect a breach, and through this prepared to rush in steady line, lance to the rest.

The villagers, snatching up their killed and wounded, were about to retreat, when a huge figure bounded into their midst, crying to them to hold.

"Little John to the rescue!" he shouted.

"A Little John! A Little John!" responded his fellows, and the fight was renewed.

Little John, himself wielding a huge quarterstaff or club of oak, dashed down the points of the spears levelled at him, and struck down several of the enemy's best men.

Taking heart, the villagers one and all who were in charge of that barricade poured a deadly volley of shafts and bolts upon the Normans, and then again rushing to the rampart, cast huge stones, logs of wood, and other missiles, with such fury that the battered, wounded, and disheartened men-at-arms retreated, despite the outcries of their chief.

A tremendous volley from Sir Gaultier de Simon's crossbowmen alone prevented the retreat becoming a perfect flight.

The fight of the first barricade was over.

CHAPTER CXXXIX.
THE FIGHT CONTINUED.

NOT a moment's time was lost by the Saxons in patching up the old rampart as best they might, all being roused by the sight of a hundred disciplined soldiers driven back by men comparatively inexperienced in the art of warfare.

Robin Hood, however, who had watched this conflict, leaning on his longbow, bade them remember that only the most desperate heroism would save them, as this was but the vanguard of the invading army.

He had been watching intently the conduct of his allies in the presence of the enemy.

As yet not an outlaw had fired a shot.

Robin knew what was coming, and kept the whole of his merry men as a reserve.

He had not the remotest doubt of the result; for even if the Normans were temporarily checked, their overwhelming numbers must eventually win the day.

He wished, however, to punish them as much as possible before he retired into the forest with the survivors of that once happy English homestead.

While these thoughts were passing through his mind the Norman soldier of fortune had formed his men into a column, and was rushing at the barricade with the determination of a man who would win, or die in the attempt.

Robin Hood at once saw this, and bade everybody retreat to the second rampart, which was not thirty yards from the other.

He knew that, were the first feeble barrier defended against the raging Normans, it would cost more than it was worth.

The men-at-arms were astounded at their bloodless victory, and stood irresolute.

"Down with the Saxon dogs! death to them—man, woman, and child!" cried Sir Gaultier de Simon.

"Thou hast thyself sealed thy own death-warrant," said Robin Hood, as he heard these words.

And he fitted an arrow to his bow.

Waving his sword on high, and bidding his men follow him to the charge, the dauntless soldier rushed forward, despite the deadly volley of shafts and bolts, to almost the foot of the barricade, followed by nearly all his men.

Many dropped by the way.

"Charge!—down with the Saxon churls!—let not one live to tell the tale of their insolence!" he shouted, as his men flew to the foot of the earthen and wooden rampart.

"Die in thy sin, foul-mouthed villain!" said Robin, suddenly appearing on the summit of the barricade.

At the same moment Sir Gaultier fell into the arms of his men, pierced by an arrow through the brain.

Before the Normans could recover the sudden shock of this loss a general sortie of nearly the whole garrison took place, preceded by such a terrible flight of winged weapons as, with their previous losses and wounds, fairly dispirited the men-at-arms, who fled in all directions.

Mounting their horses, in ten minutes more the whole of the invading party were galloping back, without their veteran leader, to report themselves to their chief commander.

Robin Hood, as soon as the backs of the discomfited men-at-arms were turned, gave directions for the first barricade to be repaired and strengthened.

He formed no illusions.

He knew that this first victory presaged ultimate defeat.

* * * * * *

The insolence of the Norman conquerors was only equalled by their cruelty, and Robin Hood was determined, before he led away his friends into the secret fastnesses of the woods, to teach the lawless soldiery that if the Saxons were not exactly prepared to make reprisals, they were able to avenge themselves in a manly and valorous manner that should ring through the land, and encourage others to go and do likewise.

With the keen eye of an experienced general, the King of Sherwood visited every defence, suggested improvements, and then, day being on the wane and night approaching, posted sentinels at every point where an attack might be apprehended, and then retired with his lieutenants to the house of Sir Gammel, there to hold a final conference as to future operations.

The worthy knight, having drawn the sword and thrown away the scabbard, had given up his house entirely, as the citadel of the fortress, and even, says one who has made himself the historian of this exciting period, using his furniture in blockading and strengthening the weaker parts of the hall. The principal staircase, which had been made movable for occasions like the present, and which was outside the house, was removed, and rendered available to be thrust from the uppermost windows, should flight become actually necessary, and present a means of escape that way. They had all resolved to fight from chamber to chamber and room to room, and had so contrived their defences as to hold each for a length of time against vastly unequal numbers; and ultimately, if compelled, to retreat to the forest, and in its intricacies shelter themselves finally from the cruel ferocity of their enemies.

Sir Gammel, ever mindful of his duties as host, had spread his hospitable board with a profusion of such luxuries as were within the means of a well-to-do Saxon gentleman.

All the villagers and outlaws were equally well provided by their camp fires.

The meal was eaten almost in silence, as most were wrapt in their reflections, none of a very pleasant or satisfactory character.

Brave they all were, yet bound to earth all by some pleasant tie, that made them thoughtful when about to face death where his grim scythe would surely collect a goodly harvest.

"My friends," said Sir Gammel, when nothing remained on the table but huge brown jugs of ale and flagons of wine, "I pledge you all—victory to the Saxons, death to the Norman tyrants!"

The toast was drank heartily, but silently.

"I thank you," replied Robin Hood, as he set down his cup; "and will take advantage of this moment of quiet to say a few words about the contest we are engaged in."

All set down their cups.

"The Normans are approaching in overwhelming force, and unless some miracle occurs must prove victorious. Even if we drive them back, they will return in double numbers—so that in any case all here are doomed to destruction if they remain within the precincts of the village."

"All! all!"

"My advice then is, to defend the place to the last gasp—to do battle for every house and homestead; and when at last the Norman bandits are momentarily struck with a panic which I have in store for them, to retreat to the woods, where I offer all that hospitality which you have hitherto accorded to me and mine. Your life will be that of all the merry men; but I can only give you that which I have."

Loud cheers responded to these words, and without a dissentient voice it was resolved to hold out to the very last moment.

"I have another word to say," put in Sir Gammel, "I am a belted knight, and as such have some claim to be heard. Younger, I would have asked to lead you, as a leader is above all things necessary to our hopes of success—but my bones are old, and though my will is good, I am not active enough to be at your head. Let us all obey good Robin Hood, our best and sincerest friend, and I, for one, shall do so whether as private, petty officer, or lieutenant."

One cry, that made the rafters ring with the echoes, responded to this appeal.

Robin briefly thanked the knight, and accepted the responsibility, after which he bade all but the sentries retire to rest, which order being instantly obeyed, he summoned Little John to accompany him in a scouting party to the woods.

CHAPTER CXL.

OUT IN THE WOODS.

ROBIN HOOD felt too keenly all that devolved upon him to care for much repose that night.

He knew, by his scouts, that the enemy had united their forces and were at no great distance, quite ready to attack with the first blush of dawn, even if they did not try a night assault.

Before he left the precincts of the camp he visited every post, put two sentries at each, and then, after an earnest caution to them to be vigilant, glided forth into the open glade, accompanied by his stalwart companions.

They took their way diagonally across the plain, where some scattered trees protected them from observation.

It was well they were cautious, for no sooner did they reach the summit of a small swell in the plain, than the watchfires of the advancing foe became clearly visible.

The night air was sharp and keen in the forest, so that the soldiers had erected either tents, or had constructed hurdles with boughs and furze, to protect them from the blast, while wood had not been spared to make cheerful blaze under the forest trees.

The long line of fire showed at once the force of the foe.

That they were commanded by one used to war could be seen by the chain of sentinels walking up and down on the side towards the village.

The rest appeared slumbering.

About the centre of the camp, and about a hundred yards from where Robin stood, was a tent, which doubtless contained the persons of the commanders.

"Had we all our merry men here," said the outlaw chief, thoughtfully, "I would soon rout this hired rabble."

"A night chase would be rare sport indeed," replied Little John, with a grin.

"Aye—rare sport did Englishmen all think as we do, and rising in their might, drive these pirates into the sea, and bring our fair island back to the days of freedom and justice—to the state in which good King Alfred left it."

Little John sighed.

"'Tis useless remaining here," continued Robin, after a short pause; "we must outflank the knaves, and find out their intentions if we can. Come, my friend."

And gliding back into the forest, Robin Hood made a long circuit to avoid the sentinels, and thus got upon the other side, where no sentinels had been posted.

This enabled them to actually enter the camp unperceived.

Robin Hood clutched Little John's arm, and as he did so trembled violently.

He pointed around.

There were the watchfires, there were the distant sentries on the other side, but not a man was to be seen in the camp.

"Come," said the outlaw chief, "the villains have outwitted us—now, an the saints guard not our people they are lost!"

Utterly regardless of the men-at-arms posted so obviously to mislead the outlaw scouts, Robin Hood plunged into the forest, closely followed by Little John.

Ten minutes' hard running brought them to the skirt of the forest, in sight of the first barricade.

A dark, silent, and stealthy column of armed men, supported by a powerful reserve, were crossing the greensward, and were within fifty yards of the rampart.

Not a sign came from the village.

Robin Hood strained his eyes in vain to catch a glimpse of the sentries he had posted.

But he knew where they were seated, and, with a calm decision which was the leading feature of his character, drew an arrow to the head and fired.

Scarcely had the arrow whizzed through the air when a sharp cry rose from the barricade, and then from all parts of the camp the alarmed sentries sounded the note of alarm.

But the Normans were not to be discouraged; they had approached thus near under cover of the night, and they were determined to try what a sudden rush upon the sleepy garrison would avail.

Robin Hood was necessarily compelled to remain a mere spectator of the event for the moment.

The enemy, finding themselves discovered, rushed at the barricade with loud and hearty war-cries, discharging their crossbows and then using the lance, a weapon in the use of which they were exceedingly expert.

The shower of arrows that met the foe was proof enough that the outlaws were now in the fray.

But only one volley was practicable, as the fight was now hand to hand—a regular melée.

Robin Hood and Little John, re-entering the forest, took a path known only to the villagers, by which, beneath overshadowing trees and over rocky, uneven ground, they were able to gain the interior of the village.

The fight raged hot and strong at the first defence. Nearly the whole of the garrison had rushed to partake in it.

This was just what the chief of the outlaws expected; and anxious to parry any attack which might be made elsewhere, he first went the round of all the rude defences.

Lucky was it that he did so.

About a hundred yards from one of the barricades was a narrow ravine, at the mouth of which were no less than two hundred men, creeping upon the village with the stealthy crawl of Indians.

The fight was hot on the eastern side, the outcries of both parties woke the echoes of the forest, the shrieks of the badly wounded, writhing in mortal agony, filled the air, and then clear and shrill came the tra-la-la of a bugle, which seemed to exercise a magical effect upon both parties of combatants.

The Normans hesitated, and looked at one another as if they expected it was a reinforcement.

The outlaws, on the other hand, at once retreated from the barricade, leaving the villagers to fight their own battle.

The silent column of the enemy, quite ignorant they were discovered, still advanced slowly.

A perfect shower of shafts and bolts soon undeceived them, and drove the whole in confusion to the rear.

But rallying at the cry of their leaders, they again rushed in, and a fearful hand-to-hand encounter ensued.

The outlaws had the advantage.

They were on the summit of a height; and, after pouring their volley of missiles upon the heads of the men-at-arms, were able to deal heavy blows, with axe, quarterstaff, and bill, upon the heads of the advancing foe—remorseless, and therefore treated remorselessly.

Robin watched the fight.

He was too good a general to throw in simply the strength of his arms, when it was his head was required to plan.

Every faculty of his brain was put in play to judge the powers of both parties in the skirmish.

And he saw that his own men were to be depended on, for, no matter what the odds, not one of them flinched.

On the contrary.

With a loud rallying cry, the outlaws suddenly made a sally with such irresistible vigour as to drive all before them.

The fight was over for the night.

CHAPTER CXLI.

A SHAM RETREAT.

THE villagers and their associated friends, the outlaws, were clamorous with delight. With a loss of three killed and twenty-one wounded, they had vanquished in fair fight above their own number of disciplined soldiers, killing over a score, and wounding a hundred.

All were in high glee, and were almost ready to believe that the worst of the affair was over.

But the chief of the outlaws knew better.

He was well aware that the combat had only in reality commenced.

The royal troops would not accept that repulse as a defeat, but would see what the daylight would produce.

The outlaw chief, therefore, exercising his right of command over the men, again ordered them to seek their rest, and posted—this time outlaws all—double sentries at every post.

Then, and only then, he sought repose himself.

It was with something of a melancholy feeling that the patriot chief retired to rest.

To him bloodshed was above all repugnant, and *never* resorted to, except in self-defence.

It mattered not to him that men were Normans or Saxons; they belonged to the human race, and it went against his feelings to take their lives.

But in the present instance they were acting from stern necessity, and though his feelings as a man might have made him spare the enemy, as a soldier he knew that the more were killed the severer would be the lesson.

What, then, was his astonishment when next day not a sign of any enemy was to be found.

The villagers, in their premature haste, would have at once accepted this as victory, but Robin, fortunately, was able to control them.

He sent out some of the cleverest men in the band as scouts, who quickly proved him to be right, by reporting that the Earl of Beauclerk had simply retreated three miles, and it was reported had despatched messengers to Prince John for reinforcements.

Robin Hood's lip curled as he heard this news; though it seemed to make him the rival of a monarch, he was not elated.

He knew what was to come far better than any of those for whom he was devoting himself.

He assured them that what they had seen was but a prelude to what was to come.

If seven hundred men could not conquer them, a thousand would be brought, and if a thousand could not do it, two thousand would be found.

Everybody, after a little thought, became convinced that Robin Hood's view was right, and all agreed to be guided by him in everything.

The utmost attention was paid to the wounds of the sufferers, provisions were hastily collected, while from many quarters came staunch Saxons, who, after depositing their offerings in the hands of their friends and relatives, volunteered their strong arms for the fray.

Every one was accepted.

Then the barriers were further strengthened by means of trees and stones, while a good supply of the latter were piled up as weapons in case of need.

And still the enemy came not.

But Robin did not allow his people to be idle; every spare hour in the day was devoted to practising at a target.

The outlaw chief himself set the example, and roused them to honourable emulation by his wonderful skill.

Having done this he stood by as a kind of judge of the sports.

The villagers, however, were never weary of seeing Robin himself displaying his skill.

For him to hit the centre of the bull's eye without appearing to take aim was a common shot.

In this Little John began to emulate him, he being now an accurate and powerful archer, on several occasions quite equalling his chief in his aims.

Robin Hood, however, whenever his lieutenant hit the bull's-eye, followed, splitting Little John's arrow in twain.

Little John somewhat warmly offered to do the same, and on one or two occasions succeeded.

The outlaw of Sherwood Forest procured a willow wand and displayed to the admiring spectators his most complete feat of archery.

He took a willow wand and stripped it of every leaf but one, which he left at the extreme end.

He then stuck it upright in the ground.

The leaf fluttered in the wind.

He then walked with his lieutenant a hundred and fifty yards distant.

"Now hit that leaf," said Robin.

"I would do anything that mortal man can compass," replied the lieutenant, stoutly; "but this is impossible."

"Then you will not make the attempt?"

"I do not say that. I will try, but I shall fail, as every one else must who makes such a trial."

"It is easy."

"Then will I make an effort, that I may see Robin Hood fail for once."

"I will shoot after you," said Robin, quietly.

Little John with a very bad grace selected one of his best arrows, and took long and careful aim.

The arrow whizzed in the air.

"A hit! a hit!" cried some.

"No," said the chief, "it was no hit, though a very good shot—see now, all of you."

Next instant the leaf was cut clean off the wand to the admiration and delight of all spectators.

Little John apologised to his commander for doubting him, and declared that in future he would never believe anything impossible which he undertook to do.

The chief smiled in reply, and then said he would show them another specimen of his skill.

A similar wand to the previous one was firmly planted in the earth, by Robin's direction, a leaf hanging about a foot from the point; a thin strip of cloth was fastened to the top of the wand and to this was tied a small pigeon: he stood two hundred yards from this target, and while the spectators could count ten, he cut the leaf off, then the strip of cloth, freeing the bird, which he shot ere it had flown five yards. Little John, accustomed as he was to archery, was astonished at Robin's skill, and the villagers were perfectly amazed; but their admiration was raised to even a greater height when they saw him, from the same spot, split the wand, and do with similar ease several feats of archery apparently incredible. The villagers congratulated themselves upon having such an ally, for the importance of a sure aim, at particular moments, was evident to all; and when Little John explained to them, as many had a previous opportunity of judging, that he was almost as expert at all other manly feats, their respect for him was raised in a vastly increased ratio.

While indulging in these manly exercises time wore on, and daily expectation was roused as to the arrival of the enemy.

They were not left long in doubt as to the intention of the Earl of Beauclerk.

CHAPTER CXLII.

ATTACK ON THE HALL.

It was about ten days after the last skirmish that the scouts brought in a positive report.

A perfect army of soldiers, cavalry and infantry, were approaching in hot haste.

The villagers, now well drilled, were quite ready to meet them. Not a man flinched or hesitated.

The last finishing stroke was put to the fortifications, and then again they waited.

It was a warm morning in June that brought the vanguard in sight of the village.

The scouts had signalled their march since daybreak, so that the garrison was fully prepared.

Robin Hood, surrounded by his lieutenants and aids-de-camp, addressed them in a short and pithy speech; after which an earnest prayer, also short, was said, reverently enough, by Father Tuck.

Then each man went to his post.

As the outlaw chief expected, the enemy divided themselves into several parties, one of which was led by the earl in person, the second by Sir Norman Malvoisin, the others by subordinate officers, royal and local.

They evidently hoped in this way to worry and distract the Saxon villagers.

But not a sign of confusion was given.

The enemy marched up straight for the breastworks of earth and trees, to be met by such a fierce and well-sustained fire of bolts and shafts as fairly staggered them.

The first attack was a failure; but after drawing off his men a minute or two, the earl resolved on a desperate charge.

All the horses, which, frightened by the arrows, plunged, reared, and kicked, in a most ludicrous manner, were sent to the rear as worse than useless.

There was no chance of success but for a determined charge of footmen.

The Earl of Beauclerk sent his emissaries round to every leader to warn them of his determination.

"The village must be taken at any cost," was his cold and stern command; "no quarter to be given."

Then, himself cased in armour, he made his men close up behind their bucklers, and advance.

A powerful reserve awaited the moment when their services might become useful.

The Normans, cheered lustily by their fellows, now advanced, despite a fearful shower of missiles, which, however, to a great degree, fell harmless on their broad shields.

The barricade was at least ten feet high, but the soldiery, furious at the havoc committed by the bowmen on previous occasions, were not to be daunted.

Helping themselves with hand and bills, they were soon, with some loss, upon the summit of the rampart, face to face with the Saxons, in hand-to-hand conflict.

Little John commanded here, with about seventy men. At first he had but a hundred against him, but fifty more were advancing.

The uproar was awful.

In addition to the noise of the fight itself, both parties shouted their favourite war-cries until they were hoarse.

The Saxons appeared, however, likely to be overpowered by the mere weight of numbers.

Little John in vain rushed from place to place, doing prodigies of valour.

He could not make up for the fact that the disciplined soldiers were two to one, and animated by the most rancorous hatred of the Saxons.

The earl, who fought in the ranks with a huge broadsword, at last was before Little John.

"Ah! ah! accursed Norman!" said the outlaw; "thou seekest thy fate!"

"Have at thee!" cried the earl, waving his terrible weapon on high, and letting it fall directly on the shoulder of the giant, who met it by a guard, and then retaliating, struck the knight to the ground.

"So perish all England's tyrants!" shouted the tall forester, plying his mighty staff right and left with never-failing success.

But though the huge strength and desperate personal valour of the outlaw did wonders, he could not but see that his gallant band, each man contending against two, was becoming disheartened and demoralised.

On every side lay the bodies of dead or dying men, the latter of whom could not forbear from uttering groans of mortal anguish, such as pain will draw from the bravest.

"Up, Saxons! Down with the Norman knaves—beat them from the ramparts! Tra la la!"

The rush made by all at the soldiery was in this instance a feint, while the notes of his bugle sounded a retreat, which was made in good order, the men of the next line of fortifications covering it by means of a murderous discharge.

They were readily admitted into the inner circle, and there were able to repose themselves awhile, while fresh men prepared to do battle with the Normans.

The combat a moment after was hot and furious as ever; the Normans, warming to their work, showed that dogged and determined valour which gave them so wide a reputation in Europe, and which, in after years mingling with that of the Saxon, had so much hand in making the modern Englishman.

Despite pits and holes—despite showers of shafts, both stones and beams—they bounded like demons to the assault; clambering up the defences, and engaging in hand-to-hand combats, in which the weapons of nature were used as often as those provided by the human ingenuity.

On every side the conflict now raged madly. The royal troops, elated by numbers and the prospects of victory, poured in their forces with a determination that was irresistible.

On every side the first barrier was carried, and the outlaws and villagers compelled to concentrate their forces in the centre.

Robin Hood was flushed and excited.

He was fully sensible of the responsibility that devolved upon him.

His heart bled to see the work of devastation that was going on around him.

"Little John," he said, calling his huge lieutenant on one side, "where is Will Scarlett?"

"Yonder, by his father's side."

"Call him."

Little John put his finger to his mouth, and uttering a peculiar whistle, the young man was speedily at his side, inquiring his wishes.

"It is I want you," said the chief.

Will Scarlett bowed, and waited the commands of his leader in silence.

"This day will decide our fate," said Robin, "and what that will be no man can doubt. Numbers are overcoming us; and yet, rather than yield, would I perish under the burning rafters of your father's house."

"Amen!" said both.

"But we have all many reasons for living, and if we can give these Normans a proper lesson, will gladly once more seek the shelter of the forest. Do you make your way by the secret path in the hills; scour then the glades, and collect every man you can find. With these be ready yonder," pointing to an elevation about half-a-mile off; "and when my bugle sounds the retreat, advance you with such force as you have to the rescue. The fight will then be over."

Will Scarlett made no reply, but with a respectful inclination of the head, left his chief, to obey his orders.

Scarcely had he taken his departure, when the battle recommenced with double ardour.

The Normans were elated by victory.

The Saxons fought doggedly but without hope.

But they made a most fierce and determined stand at the second barrier.

In vain.

The Normans, many of whom had fought against the Saracens or Moors, rushed on in close and serried masses that were irresistible.

Again they reach the summit of the second barrier; but here a terrific opposition awaits them.

Not only do they find themselves opposed to a close column of sword and quarterstaff men, but, from a mound behind, the bowmen ply them with continued flights of arrows, by which many a tall man is laid low.

Sir Norman Malvoisin is here in his element. Wielding a two-handed sword, he mows down the enemy as a mower does grass.

Nearly everybody gives way before him.

Robin Hood, whose eye was everywhere, saw this, and at once decided on his course of action.

With a pale brow he fits an arrow to his bow, and watches his opportunity.

The knight was in the act of lifting his fearful weapon in the air, when the arrow sped and hit him under the arm, in the side, a terrible shot.

With a fearful exclamation he falls to the ground.

A loud shout of triumph from the Saxons rings through the air, a wail of fury from the Normans responds to this, and then again the struggle continues.

But despite heroic deeds of valour, which need Homer to chronicle, the outlaws are compelled to retreat this time upon their last barrier, the most extensive and best fortified of all.

It is higher, partly from natural causes, and has a deeper ditch or moat.

This carried the day is lost, for the house of the good old knight cannot long stand a regular siege.

The retreat to the central point of defence was effected without difficulty, from the tremendous volleys which were poured upon the Normans from the barriers.

Robin Hood, who seemed to bear a charmed life, was the last man within the ramparts.

Unknown to him, his men kept a watchful eye on all who aimed in his direction.

A dozen shafts were sure to strike the man who took deliberate aim at the person of the chief.

It often puzzled the King of Sherwood Forest how it was he escaped while others fell in heaps around him.

The inner barrier gained, there was a slight pause in fighting.

The Norman chiefs were holding council.

Hitherto they had been victorious.

But now they had a much greater difficulty than ever to encounter. The barrier was only attackable at the two ends, as a deep trench had been cut beneath it, completely preventing them, without making ladders, from scaling it. At each of the ends a high screen of woodwork had been run up, and behind this was stationed a strong body of the best archers.

To have advanced rashly and attacked this would have been sheer madness, as it must have involved the loss of a great many lives without any good being gained.

They halted, therefore, and the whole party of Norman chiefs assembled to learn what plan of attack would be the most wise.

The earl was, as a rule, reckless of human life, but he had on the present occasion not only a victory to win, but an account to render to his royal master of the men he had asked for.

Nearly sixty were already dead, while more than two hundred were disabled.

This, too, in a contest with a far inferior force of outlaws and undisciplined peasants.

"Yonder Robin Hood, as the knave calls himself," said the earl, "is the foul fiend himself. Here is my brother half dead, a fifth of our forces *hors de combat*,

and we not a whit nearer our mark than ever. What is to be done?"

Sir Norman being in the hands of the rude leech who accompanied the army, this question was addressed to one of the royal officers in command of a detachment.

He was a grizzly warrior, who had seen much service in the East, as well as Europe.

"We must either continue the assault," he said, "or starve them into submission."

"The latter plan is not feasible," replied the earl. "The peasants round about are all in league with them, and would supply them with provisions by some secret way unknown to us."

"Secret way," mused the soldier. "'Tis quite possible where a village is so surrounded by trees; but may we not discover this secret way ourselves?"

"'Tis known only to the Saxon knaves, if any such way exist," continued the earl.

"I know not. There be some gallants among your fellows who probably have had friendly relations with some of the village lasses, and might know."

"A hundred marks to who so shall guide us," said the earl. "If any know, that will tempt them."

The officer bowed, and retiring, the proposition was soon spread abroad through the ranks.

A saturnine-looking individual, about thirty years of age, stepped out from the ranks, and said that he had, while standing with the reserve, noticed an outlaw creep from a thicket, which he supposed would contain the clue to whatever secret way there was.

As he spoke, he pointed towards an almost impenetrable thicket, through which it appeared impossible to make any way.

But for that very reason, this was the most likely spot to lead by some unknown way into the village.

A couple of hundred men, under the leadership of Simon Guiscard, the Norman royal soldiers, were at once detached in that direction.

But the conference had been watched.

The wave of the hand of the Norman soldier had been rightly interpreted.

Robin Hood had quietly adjusted an arrow to his bow, and ere the column had marched ten yards, the man who had volunteered as guide was dead upon the ground.

The others, however, made for the thicket, which, however, after being searched over and over again, showed no clue to whatever maze or labyrinth existed.

Another attack was therefore absolutely necessary.

The earl at once divided his men into two parties, each under the command of royal officers.

He retained the supreme direction himself.

There was no help for it but to take the two ends of the barrier by a regular assault.

As soon, therefore, as his dispositions were made, the word was given, and the men flew to the attack.

They had provided themselves with long bill-hooks, with which they pulled down the boughs and shrubs.

Death again reigned triumphant.

Again the groans and cries of dying and wounded filled the air, accompanied by shouts and execrations.

The combatants were at one time so mixed up that it was difficult to strike with safety.

Then an awful shriek arose, and the barrier gave way beneath the weight of friend and foe, and some hundreds of men were precipitated into the moat.

Robin and his lieutenants at once recalled their followers to the inner circle, where back to back they were to do or die.

But, in the meantime, Sir Gammel had entered within the walls of his mansion, whence he and some choice retainers poured an incessant and galling fire upon the invaders.

A temporary lull in the combat took place.

The outlaw chief now looked around.

Enough had been done for glory.

Enough had been done for honour.

He sounded his bugle three times.

Ere the last notes had died away amid the reverberating echoes of the hills, the large majority of the besieged had disappeared, while a small and devoted band, led by Robin Hood himself, had effected an entrance into the stronghold of the village.

Ten minutes later the outlaws, who had, as it were, vanished into the ground, were seen issuing from the very thicket indicated by the unfortunate Norman who had paid so dearly for his shrewd guess.

The fury of the earl knew no bounds, as to pursue the outlaw into the forest was folly.

The siege of the hall, too, promised to be an unsatisfactory affair, as it was a stoutly built house, defended by a band of heroes.

It was, however, impossible to endure the disgrace which would accrue to them if they did not make the attempt, and though it necessitated great loss of life the earl ordered his men to the charge.

Then came anew the sound of Robin Hood's bugle, warning the Normans to be wary and cautious.

At the same instant there appeared in the rear of the Normans not only some five hundred outlaws, but hundreds of peasantry from all parts.

A cloud of arrows darkened the air, and fell like hail upon the invaders.

Then from all parts of the old hall, which had sheltered the worthy Gammel family for years, burst flames and smoke.

The Normans turned to face the more numerous foe, who at once retreated to the cover of the woods, where they kept up a galling fire.

While this was taking place, Robin Hood and his select party of heroes retreated from the hall.

An hour later the Normans might boast of a barren victory, indeed. They had destroyed a happy village without taking a single prisoner, and at a terrible loss of life.

The outlaws were safe from pursuit in the deep and green fastnesses of the forest.

The earl and his officers had no choice but to return whence they came, to report an undeniable discom-

CHAPTER CXLIII.

MAID MARIAN.

ABOUT ten days have elapsed, during which Robin has been busy providing for his new subjects.

There are many unsuited to the life of an outlaw. These Sir Gammel sent off to his distant estates, of which, fortunately, the ranger of Sherwood Forest was ignorant. The rest are spread abroad with different detachments of the band.

The young chief now thought it high time to give himself a holiday and attend to his own affairs.

Appointing Little John and Will Scarlet to the supreme command in his absence, Robin Hood started on his way to visit the abbess and her fair charge.

Robin saw around him young couples enjoying the height of human felicity in wedded life, and began impatiently to hail the day when he might claim a bride.

He panted for the hour when he might present his subjects with a queen.

As on all former occasions, when about to pay a love-visit, Robin Hood arrayed himself in his best.

Though as little of a fop as anybody could be, he knew the value of personal appearance.

A woman, however noble-hearted, thinks none the less of a man because he dresses well.

On the present occasion, however, it would have been difficult for his best friends to have known Robin Hood.

He wore the complete dress of a roving knight, but without any device upon his shield.

His arms were the lance and sword, with the usual dagger of mercy.

A fine and stalwart figure did the noble youth look in the habiliments of the rank to which he properly belonged.

Of course we need not observe that Robin was mounted upon a splendid steed, that bore his master's weight with ease.

Robin started early, with a view to reaching the convent before curfew, when it was always difficult to obtain shelter.

With what view had Robin selected this costume?

Merely to let the lady of his heart see him to advantage? No.

There was a tournament on at Ashby de la Zouche, and Robin meant boldly to appear in the ring.

He had not forgotten a squire, but his selected squire he had directed to meet him at a certain rendezvous.

There was another reason.

The abbess was about to take advantage of Prince John's presence at the tournament to present Marian to him, and obtain, if necessary, by bribery, permission for her to select her own husband.

As a knight, Robin Hood would be able to form one of the escort.

There was no real impropriety in Robin's assuming his post. Believing himself the son and heir of the Earl of Huntingdon, he could assert his undoubted right.

Musing of the future, and allowing his steed to go pretty much his own way, Robin took no note of time, so that it was mid-day before he became conscious how slowly he was proceeding.

Suddenly he looked up to examine into his own whereabouts.

He was not far from the ruined tower, where had taken place the interview between the Sheriff of Nottingham and Thomas the carter.

Deceived by the similarity of many of the forest glades, Robin had unwillingly taken a wrong direction.

He was nearly as far from the convent as ever.

He was about to dash his spurs into his horse's sides in order to make up for lost time, when he was loudly hailed.

"Stay, sir knight. I am a stranger in these parts and would fain know my way."

The voice seemed familiar, but when Robin turned round and gazed upon the huge figure of a man in complete armour, mounted on a coal-black steed, both travelled-stained and dusty, he failed to view a familiar form.

"Where would you go, sir stranger?" replied Robin, courteously.

"I would fain rest at some hostelry to-night, or rather at some priory. To-morrow I have far to travel."

"Fair sir," said Robin, "I am bound to the convent of St. Agnes, where I have business. The lady abbess is somewhat a friend of mine. I will guide you thither. I know that if you be true knight you will be welcome."

"Truer English knight I may say never fought in Palestine," replied the other, heartily, "so let us forward. The keen forest air of England has given me an appetite.

"It will be too keen ere we reach St. Agnes Convent," laughed Robin; "if you are not provided I am. It will be an hour after curfew ere we reach the end of our journey."

"Then do I say amen to our taking a snack in the forest. Yonder is a pleasant shade, this July day, and whatever you may have in that wallet of yours will be welcome."

Robin rode quietly up to the spot selected by the stranger, and ere ten minutes had elapsed, the two were seated upon the green sward, with helmets off.

Both ate heartily of the provisions provided, though both were keenly intent on examining the other on the sly.

The strange knight was a handsome man, much bronzed by exposure to an eastern clime.

His whole visage was commanding in the extreme.

Presently Robin produced a leathern bottle of very choice wine, with which he filled a silver tankard to the brim.

No sooner was it full than he rose, and with an air of the most proud and yet deferential respect, kneeled, tankard in hand, to the astonished knight.

"How now?" he said, with a dark and angry frown.

"Welcome, my liege, to England," was the quiet reply. "Pardon me if my respect has overcome my discretion."

The strange knight smiled, took the tankard, drained it to the bottom, and returned.

"Pledge me!" he said.

Our hero obeyed.

"And pray who are you, who seem to take a wandering and unknown soldier for his absent king?"

"There are not two Richard Cœur de Lion's," replied the outlaw, respectfully. "As to who I am, since your majesty asks the question, I must answer. People call me Robin Hood——"

"An outlaw!" cried the king, gravely, "in this garb!"

LITTLE JOHN REACHES THE PRIZE.

"My liege, I say that men call me Robin Hood; but when I stand in your presence at court, it will be as Robert Earl of Huntingdon."

"'Fore God!" said the good-natured monarch, "your wine is good, let us hear your story. I will take one cup more, and then you can talk as we ride."

"As your grace please."

"Hearkee, though, Master Robin, I am secret. Not a soul but yourself as yet knows of my return. I wish to judge of certain things for myself before I reveal myself. Call me, until I bid you do differently, the Black Knight, as I will call you the Disinherited."

Robin readily agreed to this, of course, and then, as they rode along, briefly related all he knew of his history.

"By Heaven!" said the king, when he had finished, "'tis a strange story, with truth upon its face. It shall be inquired into. And now let me ask you, know you that there is a wish upon the part of certain traitors and hired mercenaries to keep me from my throne?"

"I have heard so," said Robin.

"They fear my justice. They need not do so. I am indeed too easy. But, be that as it may, if I require your men can I rely on them?"

"On every English heart," cried Robin, heartily.

"Thanks," said the king, in a gratified tone of voice. "That sounds well. If I need them you shall not find me backward in summoning them. I may then more easily pardon any of their infractions of laws which I must respect and administer."

"All would return to their homes, and to a lawful state of society, if not oppressed."

"We shall see," said the king. "And now let me hear all you can tell me of news. I have been long away, and much will be novel to my ears."

"In the forest," replied the outlaw, "we hear but little; but such rumours as I know of your grace is welcome to."

The king nodded his head by way of assent, and Robin Hood told all he could, bearing, however, more lightly on the misdeeds of Prince John than might have been expected.

"But rumour," said the king, bitterly, "tells me that my brother is head of the malcontents; and that, did they put him on the throne, he would not be unwilling."

Robin looked at his horse's head.

"Speak out, man."

"I have heard such reports, but know not what to think of them."

"Well, well, rumour may exaggerate," said the king; "at all events, I will not prejudge the case. Let what passes between us be secret as the grave, and I will never forget the hour when chance brought me *once more* in the presence of Robin Hood."

"We have met before, my liege?"

"In Friar Tuck's hermitage. I have been sometime in England journeying to and fro among my own friends; for a month I have been ill, but now I am quite recovered, and woe to those who have sought to betray me."

And for a time the king rode on in moody silence. He was thinking naturally enough of that brother whom he had left regent of his kingdom during his absence, and who, upon authority he could not doubt, had abused his generosity and confidence.

What was he to do?

To punish one so near to him was not part of his nature; and yet he could not allow such black-hearted treachery to be passed over altogether.

The hatred of brothers is proverbial, but the heart of Richard, though so large, was not large enough to find place for any such feeling.

His was a noble and generous nature, bordering somewhat on the eccentric, it is true, but chivalrous and honourable to the last degree.

Robin Hood respected his silence and his thoughts, and to leave them full swing, he rode somewhat ahead as guide, the forest being unfamiliar to the king.

The king suddenly, however, seemed to awake from his torpor, and changing to the opposite extreme, burst forth with a merry drinking song.

Robin turned round with a smile.

All trace of the king's vexation had passed away.

In this way the day passed over, and night came on long ere they came in sight of the convent.

The heart of the outlaw-chief bounded within him as he saw the roof-top of the house which contained all that he loved in the world.

They were soon before the door, and then rang loudly.

The porter came at once, and put his head to the loop-hole.

"Who is there?"

Scarcely had Robin Hood's voice made itself heard than the door flew wide open, and the dwarf was embracing his knees.

No disguise could conceal the person of his benefactor from the grateful dwarf.

"That will do," said Robin; "go tell the abbess a noble knight and his humble follower ask hospitality for the night."

The porter closed the gates, and hurrying away, soon returned with directions to make the guests welcome and comfortable. The abbess would see them in the morning.

It was a jolly sight to see the dwarf, as soon as he had led them to a couple of chambers specially provided for guests, attending to their creature comforts.

Had they been a troop of horse he could not have been more anxious to pile the table with provisions.

The supposed knights had agreed to sup together, which was most grateful to Robin Hood's feelings, he not being able that night to see his own dear Marian.

"I prithee, Master Robin," said the king, when, after supper, they sat over some hot-spiced wine, "why so dull?"

"I am not dull, sir knight," replied Robin, "only rather thoughtful."

"Art in love?"

"I may say that I am, and that the lady is in this house."

"A nun?"

"No—a ward of the crown. Edith of Athelston by name."

"My Lord Earl of Huntingdon will need his golden spurs to win such a prize," said the king, with something of a sneer.

"I will win *her* or die!" replied Robin, heartily.

"Well, well, win her and wear her if you can. Richard, your king, will not say you nay."

"Will my king aid me?"

"I will, by my knightly oath!" was the chivalrous monarch's eager answer.

"Many thanks!" cried Robin, rising; "and now, if I may be allowed, I will take my leave."

"Nay—no one will hear us here. May we not troll a lay to our lady loves?"

"An your grace pleases."

The king, whose voice was clear and mellifluous, at once began one of those love songs for which he had so great a liking.

He gradually drew Robin out to imitate him, and thus the night passed jollily enough, until twelve o'clock warned them that they were breaking into another day.

CHAPTER CXLIV.

ROBIN BECOMES " SIR ROBERT."

At early dawn Robin Hood arose, and moving past the king's chamber with an amount of caution which showed his desire that he should sleep soundly, descended into the garden, a favour which he was able to enjoy through the instrumentality of the grateful dwarf, now living at the convent in the height of comfort and luxury.

The porter waited for him at the bottom of the stairs, opened the door, and begging he might come away when summoned, left him to pursue his own way through the enclosed grounds.

Robin Hood was well aware that his arrival had been made known to Maid Marian; and as she was under no such restrictions as the nuns, he was quite hopeful that she would be there to meet him.

When we speak of early dawn, we speak figuratively; as, though it was about the hour of daybreak, it was still nearly dark, the clouds being dense, and the sun—if indeed, arisen—not yet able to pierce their black and piled up masses.

Robin, aware of the chilly state of the morning, had wrapped himself in a cloak, also drawing over his eyes his fur cap.

He did not wear his armour, as being unsuited to a meeting with a lady of his heart, but a handsome curt costume, many of which were to be found in his wardrobe.

With quick and almost hurried steps, he strode round the garden, examining every avenue, especially those usually frequented by the noble Saxon maiden.

But she was nowhere to be seen.

Robin Hood forgot, perhaps, that however impatient a man may be in these cases, a maiden must preserve her maiden modesty.

To creep out in the dark to meet a lover was by no means the part of a crown ward.

Women of rank, if they have their privileges, have also their strict duties to conform to.

The outlaw chafed somewhat at the delay, but in his heart of hearts could not blame her.

Ah! there she is.

He has caught the flutter of female garments; and stepping lightly on the sward, hastened in the direction where he had espied her.

But she is not alone, he finds, when about to bound over a low hedge and surprise her.

She is accompanied by a man of tall figure and most commanding presence.

A chill went to the heart of the honest outlaw, as it struck him that his king had betrayed him.

With a cold and haughty stride he entered the pathway. The man looked up; the woman, who wore a nun's dress, and had cast off her hood, tried to conceal her face.

It was neither the king nor Marian.

"Who are you and what seek you here?" said the man, laying his hand upon his sword.

"Who I am matters not!" replied Robin Hood, trying to avoid a smile; "but I may say that I am in this garden on a somewhat similar errand to your own. For a moment I took the lady for the one I expect."

"You expect the Lady Marian," said the nun, in a low, trembling tone.

"I do."

"She will be here directly. The abbess was with her before daybreak to tell her the news. If you be him I wot of you will not betray one wicked and sinful as I am."

"Nay, Agnes," said her lover.

"Lady," replied the outlaw, approaching nearer, "do not for one moment think that to love is sinful or wicked; the crime, if any, lies at the door of those who immure young girls in these fearful prisons, before they know their own minds, and make them take oaths which they do not comprehend."

"I have taken no oaths," she faltered.

"Then—but first, fair sir, do you mean this tender girl honourable treatment?" asked Robin.

The stalwart youth whom he addressed—he was not more than twenty—seemed struck by the other's manner, and instead of showing any signs of anger, bowed courteously."

"Agnes de Treherne was my affianced little wife at fourteen—while I was absent in Normandy her uncle, on her father's death, placed her here, intending to compel her to take vows which she abhors. By great good chance I have discovered her retreat. My one and only aim is to take her hence—in one hour after she shall be the wife of Sir Ralph Tressilian."

"I believe you. Lady, what is your desire?"

"I know not—advise me; you seem wise and good."

"Do you love this man?" he whispered.

"I do."

"Then how can you perjure yourself by taking vows to God which are insincere and wicked?"

The girl looked up into his face and saw honesty and truth written in every lineament.

"I will trust you—do with me as you please."

"We shall repose here until the day after to-morrow; during that time Sir Ralph here must find you a page's dress—well fitting and suited to disguise you. Then, when we start, I shall have a whole party of followers around me, amongst whom you must contrive to mingle; once in their society you will be safe."

"Thanks!" burst from both their lips.

"Be careful," he replied; "part soon, or all our plans will be vain—see where my own dear approaches."

The lovers disappeared behind a row of rare evergreens, imported from foreign parts, while Robin Hood hastened to fold his beloved Marian in his arms.

All love meetings are the same, so that we will not inflict upon our patient readers any details.

It must suffice that they parted mutually happy, in the hope of soon being reunited for ever.

By desire of Richard, the abbess was informed of the rank of her other guest, upon which she ordered such a breakfast as was rarely seen in a convent.

To this meal sat down the king, Robin, the abbess, and the Lady Edith of Athelston, whose beauty quite astonished and delighted the monarch.

Under pretence of encouraging conversation, all domestics were excluded as soon as the meal was laid.

But under no pretence, in addition to the danger of such a proceeding, would the monarch allow any ceremony.

"I' faith, Master Robin," said the kingly crusader, laughing, "since, like other wandering knights I wot of, you will keep your higher titles private, I knew you not for such an arrant robber as you prove to be."

"How so?" cried our hero, with a grim smile.

"What else is it but robbery to steal from court one of the brightest jewels of the crown, and immure it here to waste its sweetness on the desert air?"

The young lady blushed rosy red. and murmured something about not caring about courts.

"Disloyal and arrogant maiden," said the king, with a comical frown; "but we shall soon be able to compel you to leave the forest."

"How so?" asked Marian, in some alarm.

"By restoring the Earl of Huntingdon to his rights," replied the good-natured monarch.

"'Twill be the generous deed of a good and valorous king, my liege," said Marian, bending low, as if to kiss his hand; which the courteous knight evading, advanced his cheek, which she lightly touched; "but I do not think that it will be at all conducive to my happiness."

"How so?"

"My happiness is in the forest, hanging from the boughs of the trees, in the soft rain, in the dew on the open grass, the clouds that float about in the blue heavens, the birds that sing in the woods, the sweet springs where I have slaked my thirst. and in all the other glorious gifts that come from God's providence."

"Quite poetical, I declare!" laughed the king. "Is this your teaching, Master Robin Hood?"

"No, sire," replied the monarch of Sherwood Forest, quite rapturously. "It is her own fancy."

"Then, by Heaven, she is bound to be an outlaw's bride!" cried Richard, heartily.

In such talk the meal-time passed away; after which the two men retired to the monarch's chamber, where they remained for some considerable time in secret conference.

Then, on the intimation by Robin Hood that he had a large band of followers at no great distance, King Richard agreed to avail himself of their services to carry secret messages and missives to such of his sturdy and staunch retainers as he thought might be safely trusted with the news of his arrival.

Robin no sooner received the intimation of the king's wishes than he sauntered forth to the front of the convent, and there rang a merry peal upon his bugle, which was answered by the rushing forth of a dozen merry men from the wood.

Robin quietly selected those he required, gave minute directions to one or two others, and then re-entered the convent, where his will appeared to be very much like law.

The king at once gave his orders, and then challenged the monarch of the forest to a trial of skill in manly sports in the convent garden, a challenge which Robin accepted with a smile.

He had meant to bring it about somehow himself, as he wished for instruction from the king in matters which he knew nothing of, and upon which he sorely desired information.

At the king's express command the whole of the nuns and novices were allowed to view the sports from certain summits where they could see without being seen.

The Lady Edith of Athelston, with the lady abbess, stood close to the two knights, one as having taken no vows, the other by virtue of her office.

Robin Hood fully intended that Marian, as he always would call her, should show her prowess in the presence of her king, for which purpose he had bidden Gra'h bring her bow and arrows.

The noble outlaw, after two shots at the target with an invariable good fortune which elicited loud applause from the warlike monarch, prepared for other illustrations of his extraordinary skill.

"Had I had such archers in Palestine," cried Richard, with cordial admiration expressed in his tones. "I would have done battle with twice as many infidels as ever dared show their faces before our valiant troops."

"That is nothing," said Robin, smiling.

"Canst do more?"

"Any of my men can do as much," replied the outlaw.

"Fore gad, then!" observed the king, "no wonder my valiant Normans have been kept at bay—as they deserve. But what more canst thou do?"

Robin, without any ostentation of manner. then repeated the two wand trials which had so puzzled Little John.

"A marvel!" said the monarch, when the trial was over, "a marvel, ladies! Never since England was England did such noble feats of archery astonish the land."

The lady abbess bowed, Marian blushed with delight, while Robin looked for some other means of showing his wondrous skill.

As he did so a flight of crows passed over head at a great distance, some of the laggers being at a seeming unapproachable distance.

Two were making neck and neck efforts to get up with the main body of the birds.

Robin Hood watched his opportunity, and took steady aim at the unsuspecting prey, which was nearly perpendicularly over his head.

Next instant a whirring noise was heard, and the birds fell at the monarch's feet.

"'Tis all but incredible," he said.

Robin bowed low, and then stepping behind a tree, brought forth the bow and arrows belonging to Marian, to whom he handed them with high bred gallantry and courtesy.

"Behold my pupil," he observed, with a smile.

Maid Marian blushed, the king laughed, while the lady abbess stared in wonder.

"She is an apt scholar, dear lady," said Robin, addressing the latter, "and understands at a word what is said to her."

The lady abbess shook her head.

Meanwhile, the noble Saxon girl had nerved herself for her task, being resolved not to shame her teacher.

The outlaw, while she was preparing, walked across the green, and brought the target nearer, neither the girl's bow nor her practice enabling her to shoot the same distance as her teacher.

Then the outlaw stood aside and watched while the girl, with a nerve and precision that was truly wonderful, delivered twelve arrows in succession, five of which hit the bull's-eye, while seven came within two inches of its centre.

"Well done! No wonder you hit hearts so truly," cried the gallant monarch, "when you are a perfect Diana, not only in beauty, but skill!"

The Lady of Athelston laughed and blushed, the allusion being understood by her, whose education had been attended to with a care and assiduity that did not often fall to the lot of girls in her time—generally mistress only of lower accomplishments.

Robin now came up.

The king seemed more inclined to banter compliments with the lady of the outlaw's heart than to continue the sports.

But though Robin had too much faith in his king to feel the slightest jealousy, he had a secret object at heart.

"My liege," he said, kneeling, "a boon! a boon!"

"What, my gallant yeoman?"

"I crave to break a lance with your grace on horseback on this sward."

Richard Cœur de Lion laughed aloud.

"Hast ever tried?"

"Never."

"And wouldst try with me?"

"There would be no disgrace in defeat in such an encounter," replied the young chief, proudly.

"Robin," said the monarch, gravely, "I am gay and thoughtless, but my knightly vow forbids."

"Why, my liege?"

"I may not run in the lists with any but a knight," said Richard; "and you——"

"I am Robert Earl of Huntingdon!" interrupted the bold yeoman, with a proud glance.

"True! true! but still no knight," urged the king, with a good-humoured smile.

Robin knelt, with a significant and even beseeching glance at the other's sword.

"You have a purpose in this?"

"I have. To enter the lists at Ashby de la Zouche, and, if needs be, to defy all suitors for the hand of the Lady of Athelston."

"It's rank impropriety," said the king, at the same time that he drew his sword. "And now listen: as an outlaw, you remain simple Robin Hood: as one of my nobles and councillors, rise, Sir Robert, Earl of Huntingdon, and what else baronies your enemies have dispossessed you."

If ever a woman's smile was sweet Marian's was, as the two took a hand of the king, and respectfully kissed it.

"My liege and merry England unto death!" cried Robin, and then, at a signal, the court-yard portals opened, and men appeared with armour, horses, and spears, blunted at the end, so carefully that accident was almost impossible.

These men were some of the most trusty of the outlaws, and of this Robin having assured the king, he allowed one to act as his squire.

Both were soon clad in armour, and in a few words certain rules being explained to the outlaw, they vaulted into the saddle and rode as far from one another as possible in the garden.

A tall forester, with a baton in his hand, as soon as he saw both ready, gave the signal.

Like centaurs the two men sat upon their horses, to

the great admiration of the nuns, whom this spectacle was by no means calculated to make contented with their lot.

Then on they rushed, the king's powerful frame making all shudder for the slighter youth.

The horses swept along with an ardour equal to that of their masters.

In mid career the two knights met, striking each his lance upon the other's shield.

No harm was done.

Again they took up their posts, and again they started, this time both aiming directly at the other's breast.

The shock appeared terrific, Robin's lance was shivered on the monarch's breast, he never flinching, while Robin was thrown heavily back on the ground, to all appearance insensible.

Next instant, however, he was on his feet again, and about to vault into the saddle.

"No more, Sir Robert," said the Black Knight, gaily, "we are overmatched—my weight and that of my horse are too much for you. I will, however, give you, ere we part, such instructions as may enable you to hold your own against any ordinary man."

"Thanks," replied Robin, as he assisted the monarch respectfully to alight, "my gratefullest, most humble thanks."

"What merry shouts are those without?" then said the king.

"'Tis a statute fair," replied the lady abbess; "the tenants of the convent and neighbours hold it in a field hard by—'tis said to be somewhat noisy."

"My lady abbess," continued Richard, "this exercise has made me forget my matin meal; if there be some cold pastry in the pantry, such as a certain friar once gave me, and the miller of Trumpington gave my father, I would fain take a mouthful, and then under your escort, sir outlaw, there would be no harm in seeing how my subjects disport themselves in my absence."

Robin bowed, while the abbess hastened forward to order some sort of lunch that should better befit the rank of her guest than cold venison pasty.

CHAPTER CXLV.

A STATUTE FAIR.

THERE is nowhere an Englishman of the humbler classes is happier than when he is one of a meeting, where the two sexes are thrown together for the purposes of amusement. At all events, this was true, some centuries ago; the puritanical element having somewhat modified our society, while the dissolute conduct of the wretched King Charles the Second, by disgusting the virtuous, gave a great blow and heavy discouragement to popular sports.

The present meeting was supposed to be for hiring labourers, selling sheep and pigs, and other purely agricultural matters.

That, however, was hurried over, in order that the populace might come to what was rightly considered the real business of the day—that is, the amusements.

Morris dancing, foot-ball, racing by men and women —the latter without much regard to decency, which, like all other refinements, is much the effect of education— were the most popular games, though there was a couple of fellows in a corner of the field, who, having arrived late, were preparing what probably would prove even more attractive to the masses.

This was a greasy climbing-pole, with on its summit, by way of prize, a fat leg of mutton.

The dancing had been going on some time, when the two knights, accompanied by the Lady of Athelston, on a splendid palfrey, and the abbess in a kind of chair on the back of a mule, with some twenty mounted followers, rode up to a corner of the field, where, without interfering, they could witness the sports.

All doffed their hats and continued their games.

The chief part of the crowd was composed of peasants, labourers, small farmers, and their wives and daughters generally; while on the outskirts stood many men in the livery of the different noble houses who dwelt within the forest, and a larger mixture than was ordinary of yeomen and others in Lincoln green.

They were, however, spectators of revels which were a little beneath their pride and manhood.

But when the girls who had entered for the race prepared to run, they too became interested, and many an eye sparkled with pleasure and admiration at the sight.

The prizes were articles of dress, and the course was staked out right round the field.

There was a first, a second, and a third prize, for which all were eager to compete.

The girls began to strip.

Our readers might think we are about to speak of a brutal prize-fight, or hearty English foot-race by men.

By no means.

When we say began to strip, we speak advisedly, though we are alluding to Saxon maidens, and not savages.

These races were always run in one garment, recently introduced in dress—the smock.

The smock was loose, as usual, about the neck and bosom, and scarcely descended to the knees.

While standing still the rosy-cheeked but not blushing damsels revealed more of their massive beauties than was quite consistent with modern notions of modesty.

We leave to imagination how much this dress was calculated to conceal when every other feeling was forgotten in the wild ardour of the race.

"'Tis most unbeseeming," observed Maid Marian, blushing for her sex. "I would fain retire."

"Nay, fair lady," said the monarch, with a sly glance at Robin, and speaking with the freedom of the day—in the best society not far from license—"'tis a good old English custom, and, i'faith, promotes marriage, and happy marriages too, for few of the lads need be taken in as to shape of limb after seeing his lass run a race in a smock."

"Your grace," replied Robin, in the same bantering tone. "speaks like an oracle—a very oracle."

"'Tis without precedent and shameful," pouted the lady.

The abess had a thick veil, and seemed unconscious of what was going on around.

"Nay, Lady Edith," continued the monarch, gravely, "though we have not dipped much into ancient lore, we have heard the worthy priest who taught us to write our names tell of a country I think he called Lakmedon."

"Lacedemon," smiled Edith.

"Right, fair wizard; where the youths and maidens run races together in the garb of our first parents, Adam and Eve, to say nothing of wrestling and other games; and he spoke of the result as good, the race being hardy, comely, and soldierly."

"The climate was warmer, perhaps," observed Robin Hood, a little, only a little, curtly.

"Perhaps so—but, i'faith, the lasses have started, I know it by the shouts and laughter."

The king was right, though the start was a false one, no less than three of the competitors having fallen, from the very suddenness of the signal.

This had brought out the guffaws of the yokels, who were infinitely delighted at the exhibition, making comments on the fair more picturesque than refined.

And now, again, eleven girls, models of solid beauty and strength—all ignorant of corsets or any contrivance to spoil the shape and dishearten maternity—stand ready, their eyes fixed on the starter, who, this time, has intimated that his signal will be final.

Away!

'Tis away!

Denuded of all superfluous clothing, and soon in the ardour of the race lifting the slight tunic which decency had left upon them, the girls, unimpeded in their progress by dress, dash along at a pace incomprehensible to modern ideas.

They seem to fly.

For a long time, too, they keep close together, and though every one on the course has his favourite, none can tell who will win the day, so equally, so evenly do they run.

Loud shouts, in which delicacy is utterly forgotten, burst from the lips of the crowd, each man calling his pet by some epithet more characteristic of her physical charms or defects, than any given appellation.

On! on! they press, panting as they fly, and a third of the course is run, when a tall, slight girl, with golden hair, blue eyes, and a roseate complexion, takes the lead, quickly followed by one nearly as tall, but not so slight.

Though the others keep up for form's sake, it is now manifest that without a very great change one of these is sure to win the leading prize.

But there are three prizes, so that those in the rear still press forward, certain that a reward, however slight, remains to be contended for amongst them.

Would that to us were given the graphic pen with which Homer paints the games in which Ajax and others of the Greeks took part, that we might do full justice to the contest between Madge and Margery, for so were the two light-footed maidens called.

To describe their charms, almost full-blown—they were between seventeen and eighteen—would need also the pencil of a Phidias, the glowing imagination of a Martial.

Suffice it for us to say that now, nearly neck and neck, the eager competitors tear along, regardless of anything but success—that they are within forty feet of the goal.

Still they are neck and neck, a position which Margery, the stouter one, only keeps up by superhuman exertions.

It is quite clear that she must lose, as being more encumbered with her smock by reason of her stoutness, it interferes more, when in sudden desperation she makes a heroic resolve.

Down go her arms, down goes the garment, one leap and she is free; next instant she is in advance with a bound, and ere the assembly is hardly aware of what she has done, she sinks victorious at the feet of the umpire, huddling over her person, with instinctive modesty, the clothes she has so recently cast away.

A terrific shout that made the welkin ring, followed by bursts of laughter, reward her triumph, to which Madge, however, objects, on the score of her having discarded what in modern parlance is delicately called the chemise.

"Thee canst do the same," said Margery, hotly, "and I will run the race over again."

"That's fair!" shouted some of the young men.

Madge, however, shook her head as she proceeded to robe herself, content to take the second prize, and to retire with the other competitors to a tent, where they could resume the decent mien and costume of the Saxon peasantry.

It must steadily be borne in mind that these were strictly virtuous girls—in time to be faithful wives and affectionate and devoted mothers.

We are simply recording in a plain, unvarnished way, the manners and customs of a bygone age.

The king laughed heartily, Robin grinned somewhat, while the Lady Edith averted her eyes during the whole race towards the convent and the forest.

A movement in the crowd aroused her from a dreamy reverie, as it roused all.

"They are moving to the climbing-pole," said Robin.

"Let us follow," continued the king, "fore gad! these sports quite warm me. I feel I am indeed in merry old England once more when I see the people so happy."

"Happy, indeed, if they were never oppressed or injured by those who should defend and guard the poor."

"Robin," said Richard, quietly, "it may not be in the power of one man to remedy the evils of a year, nor am I of the stuff to make a code of laws like your Alfred; but while I live I promise you justice shall be done, and that the meanest hind shall have as solid justice and patient hearing as the boldest baron of them all."

"They are hard even for a prince to rule," mused Robin Hood, in a low, cautious tone.

"They are," said Richard, with startling emphasis; "but while I am king I will be king, and they shall know it."

Nothing further was said, as they were now sufficiently near the other part of the field, by reining, to see the new sport without in any way putting the people out of the way.

Not only did their horses give them an advantage,

but the crowd instinctively left an open space on that side.

The pole was now firm and erect. On its summit was lightly fastened the coveted leg of mutton, to reach which, however, was by no means an easy task, as the wood was well greased, making the trial a very serious matter to any but a very old and experienced hand.

The owners of the pole were a couple of astute Yorkshiremen, who found the instrument and the prizes; and hence were allowed to form the ring—that is, to take a certain small coin from all intending competitors on condition of always keeping a prize on the summit.

The pole was high, stout at the base, and naturally tapering at the top.

All eyed it with doubt, as on more than one occasion the cunning Yorkshiremen had erected and kept it up for hours without any one succeeding in reaching to the summit.

But nearly all of those who had thus been baffled had been quietly practising on a pole of their own during the intervening months.

A dozen competitors paid their money.

The first three trials were failures, though the climbers evinced considerable agility.

Then came a wiry youth, who stepped into the ring with a confident air that startled the owners.

They were terribly anxious to take money, but had no idea of giving anything for it.

They exchanged uneasy glances as, with an ease and grace betokening long practice, the young man ascended.

It was with the activity of a monkey.

Hand over hand, and leg after leg, he slipped up, without once halting to take breath.

Soon he was two-thirds of the way.

The faces of the speculators grew mottled, while the lookers-on cheered lustily.

The climber continued steadily on his way until within a foot of the leg.

He looked down triumphantly, and for the first time since his ascent opened his mouth.

"Get another leg of mutton ready," he said, with a laugh, "for this is mine. Hurrah, my lads!"

He had taken one hand from the pole to wave joyfully to the multitude below, and as he did so the other relaxed its grasp, and down he was at the foot of the treacherous pine ere he knew what had happened to him.

The frantic delight of the avaricious owners of the lost prize it is not easy to describe.

"Wilt thee try again, my lad?" said one of them, hoarsely, as he tapped him on the shoulder.

"Hands off!" replied the crestfallen candidate. "No, I will not try just yet. It's my deliberate belief that there's witchery about that pole."

"Good words—good words!" said the man, irately; "witchery is a statutable offence, and to charge a man with it is a crime. Who goes next?"

Several responded, but of all those who had paid not one succeeded in reaching even so far as the first.

"Now then, art all afeared?" cried the speaker of the two owners; "the pole aint half so greasy as it was—try again—faint heart never won nothing that I hearn of—try, try!"

"I will try," said a huge, stout, powerful man, who towered over the heads of even reputed tall men.

The owner of the pole eyed him with something of a sarcastic smile as he took his money.

"Well, what are you grinning at?" asked the man.

"Nothing."

"Oh, yes, you're grinning like a bear leader—out with it, man. Do you think my chance but poor?"

"Your worship is rather stout."

"True, my buck of the woods; but then, you see, I have not to climb so far as other people."

And as he spoke he put his hands about four feet higher than any one else had done.

"A proper man," said the king, admiring his form and stature; "truly a proper man—who is he?"

"Little John—my lieutenant."

"Whew! a man of sinew; but what is the Jew-Yorkshireman chaffering about?" asked the king.

"You seem certain I shall fail?" asked Little John, ere he made any sign of moving.

"It looks like it, master."

"Will you put anything on besides the mutton?"

"Hum," began the Yorkshireman, feeling in his pocket; "have you any money to lose?"

"I'll break thy pudding head if you ask impertinent questions; but I'll wager thee a golden mark I bring down the prize," observed the giant.

"Done!" said the Yorkshireman; "wilt hold the stakes?" addressing his companion and confederate.

"No," laughed Little John, "that's not fair; here's Margery of the smock, who won the race, a stout girl, and well-made, who shall hold the money, and if I win I'll kiss——"

"Will you, sauce-box?"

"If you bring down that mutton," said a commanding voice that caused all to keep silence, "I will add a purse to the winnings."

All turned and recognised the Black Knight as the speaker, though as nothing but his chin was to be seen none could recognise his countenance.

"Thanks," cried Little John; "consider your purse gone, sir worshipful."

And with a grasp that seemed about to crush the pole, he hoisted himself up with an activity and lightness scarcely to be expected from his powerful limbs.

The king and party looked on with admiration, the crowd with wild delight, the Yorkshiremen with awe.

If he succeeded, their day's winnings would be wholly gone—and more too!

They exchanged words in whispers, mutually blaming one another.

"Why did you bet?"

"Why did you let me?"

"Dolt!"

"Ass!"

Meanwhile, more slowly as he advanced, but with what appeared a certainty, the stalwart outlaw continued to ascend until he reached the thin part of the pole.

"I say, you Yorkshire, your cursed pole won't bear my weight," he suddenly exclaimed; "if it breaks, and I bring the leg down, I win certain."

"Break your neck if you like," muttered the owner, while the crowd applauded loudly.

Pausing, as if to try the strength of the sturdy pine, the giant forester continued until the whole pole was grasped in his stout hands.

Then, with a grave obeisance to the crowd, upon which he looked down admiringly, he stretched out his hand, took hold of the mutton, slung it by a loop to his wrist, and descended amid loud and reiterated plaudits.

The Yorkshiremen were white with rage, and would have disputed the bet, but that they knew that all would be against them.

"Curses light on the brawny Saxon ox," muttered one, while Little John, beckoned by Robin, went to receive the congratulations of his party and the king's purse.

The outlaw hesitated.

"Take it," said Robin, in a whisper; "he is one who may give a purse to higher than thee; whilst thou must unseen kiss his hand."

The burly giant was never slow to take a hint, and at once obeyed, taking the purse and seizing his opportunity to kiss the monarch's hand.

He then returned to his fellows, and found the Yorkshiremen cursing their ill luck.

"Here, you measly Yorkshiremen," he said, taking the money from the girl's hand, and pocketing his own, "I don't want your greasy coin. Come, all good lasses, to the booth, and let us see if clean limbs and fat calves know how to trip it. Come all; the winner pays all—and I'm thirsty."

This announcement smoothed all animosities, and as there was a copious meal prepared for all who were inclined to pay, all present accepted the offer of the bold outlaw, and hurried to prepare for the sports of the evening by laying in a goodly supply of solids and fluids.

How they ate, and how they drank, and how they danced, and how Little John kissed all the girls, and made sly jokes to the runners in the foot-race, and how they laughed and boxed his ears, and were supremely happy, this veracious chronicle hath not time or space to record, especially as we have matter of more moment to relate.

The knightly party returned to the convent, where they too refreshed the inner man, retiring to bed early, in order to be ready for the morn.

It may be amusing to show how in much later times such a departure from decency attended another part of our domestic manners.

"There is a vulgar error that if a woman who has contracted debts previous to her marriage leave her residence in a state of nudity, and go to that of her future husband, he, the husband, will not be liable for any such debts. Now this opinion is probably founded not exactly in total ignorance, but in a misconception of the law. The text-writers inform us, that 'the husband is liable for the wife's debts *because* he acquires an absolute interest in the personal estate of the wife,' &c. (Bacon's *Abridgment*, tit. 'Baron' and 'Féme.') Now an unlearned person who hears this doctrine might reasonably conclude, that if his bride has no estate at all he will incur no liability; and the future husband, more prudent than refined, might think it as well to notify to his neighbours by an unequivocal symbol that he took no pecuniary benefit with his wife, and therefore expected to be free from her pecuniary burdens. In this, as in almost all other popular errors, there is found a substratum of reason. In Burn's *History of Fleet Marriages* p. 77, occurs this entry:—'The woman ran across Ludgate-hill in her shift;' to which the editor has added this note:—'The *Daily Journal* of 8th November, 1725, mentions a similar exhibition at Ulcomb, in Kent. It was a vulgar error that a man was not liable for the bride's debts if he took her in no other apparel than her shift.'"

CHAPTER CXLVI.

THE CAVALCADE.

BUT Robin Hood, while solicitous for his own happiness and settlement in life, never forgot others.

He had contrived to enlist the sympathies of Marian in the novice's case, which made the matter easy.

At daybreak he was therefore in the garden, and in receipt, from the hands of the young lover, of a plain kind of youth's dress, more resembling that of an attendant on a squire than that of a page.

This Maid Marian took from him at an upper window, by means of a cord, and then Robin retreated into the house.

About four hours later, having tasted of the convent hospitality once more, the cavalcade started, the supposed page keeping among the outlaws, who were disguised as men-at-arms, under the particular charge of Will Scarlett, who was the lieutenant for the nonce.

The procession was one of mark, as the abbess, with the Lady Edith, to avoid attracting attention, occupied a litter borne by mules, while in front were the armed servants of mother church.

On each side of the litter, a little in the rear, rode the two knights, and behind came the retainers.

It was a party that might have excited the cupidity of any Norman tyrant near whose castle they might have passed, though, perhaps, the display of force might have made the boldest hesitate to attack so stout a band.

Of the outlaws there was no fear.

Quite the contrary, for by the strict injunctions of Robin Hood large parties secretly hovered around in case of need.

The day was pleasant enough, and the paths selected by the outlaw chief so winding and peculiar that the slow pace at which the party moved was quite a relief.

For the greater part of the journey, until the usual mid-day halt was declared, the king and the outlaw conversed in earnest whispers, not only with regard to the state of the country, the humour of church, nobles, middling, and common people, but much as to the wants and requirements of the humbler classes.

The monarch listened with pain to the outlaw's summary of their sufferings, their oppression, and their general hard treatment by the nobles; but even his noble, but prejudiced nature could not sympathise with Robin's denunciations of the game laws.

He was willing to modify them, but that was all.

"A king has burdens and trials enough, and whoso knows them, except it be for the honour of the thing, would never covet a crown. But once a king, with peremptory duties, it seems to me that there are rights which justly belong to the first man in the realm, and to

rule over the wild beasts of the land is surely a simple one."

"I doubt not your grace is right; all I complain of is the hard and cruel laws which protect the royal pleasures."

"Wert thou not thyself a king," said the monarch, smiling. "I would say, beshrew thee for a false courtier. I would my learned chancellor heard you. 'Tis not my wish, however, to deny that, as administered, the laws are severe. During my reign they shall not be unjust."

"I have full and entire faith in your grace," said Robin; "but the forest is badly administered."

"I deny that, since it covers the sins of so many of my subjects in arms against the law," laughed the king.

Robin smiled, and fully aware that his arguments on this point would not convince Richard, changed the subject.

This was in the afternoon, when, indeed, within an hour or a little more they might desire shelter.

"Is there any chance of hostelry by the way?" asked Richard, who, when there was no necessity for roughing it, loved his ease as well as any man.

Robin shook his head.

"There is little chance of our sleeping, except under trees, this night," said the outlaw.

"But those towers we saw but a quarter of an hour since?" observed the king.

"They rise over the castle of Lord Julian Fitzwalter," replied the outlaw, with a significant glance.

"Ah," said the king, in a hoarse voice, "'tis the castle of that traitor, is it? the knave! I verily believe but for his evil counsels and the bad courses he has led my brother into, there would have been no evil intent towards me. By God's truth I will sleep there to-night, if I blow my trumpet and hang out my banner before the walls."

Robin bowed, for he knew his companion was angered. In a minute or two more he spoke.

"My lord is absent at court. His lady holds the castle, and is to join him, the country-side says, at the tournament."

"Ah!" mused the monarch, "that alters my plans. Send forward a trusty messenger to say that the abbess of St. Agnes, with a crown ward in charge, on her way to the court of Prince John, craves shelter for the night. Mention two humble knights from Palestine; but let that be, as it were, an after-thought."

"It shall be done."

"This young lady—for Fitzwalter married after I left—knows me not," said the king; "we shall therefore sound her. But, for better precaution, I will plead a knightly vow not to take off helm, or corselet, until I have visited a certain holy shrine; that will leave all the talk to you. Mind, Robin, you sound this woman well—I would fain, if I could, find Julian honest—else he dies on the block."

Robin now withdrew to where his men rode in the rear, and selecting Edwin as his trumpeter, sent him forward to prepare the lady who held Fitzwalter's castle for the coming guests.

When the procession came suddenly upon the open ground in front of the castle, they could see that though the walls were ostentatiously manned by soldiers, the portcullis was up and the drawbridge down.

"The villain holds rare state for a petty noble who has risen solely by my mistaken favour," said the king.

At that moment all were silent, for suddenly there burst from the castle gates a small party, headed by one upon whom every eye was instantly fixed.

It was a vision rare in those forests.

It was a young lady, the natural loveliness of whose very striking features was enhanced by the animation of the chase and the glow of the exercise, from which she had but just returned.

She was mounted on a beautiful horse, jet black, unless where he was flecked with spots of the snow-white foam which embossed his bridle.

She wore a complete hunting dress, well fitting to the shape and form.

Her long golden hair streamed in the breeze, having, in the hurry and excitement of the chase, escaped from the confining bands that bound it.

She rode towards the party without hesitating, guiding her horse over some broken ground with such admirable address and presence of mind as to rouse feelings of admiration in every bosom.

All had a good view of her uncommonly fine face and form, which was half girlish, half womanly.

Her features were all but perfect: a mouth somewhat over-sized, with lovely teeth, and eyes so concealed by lashes as to be unfathomable, somewhat baulking the spectators.

"Welcome, my lady abbess, welcome," she said, with a ringing laugh; "this visit is a decided pleasure. Welcome, also, ye truant knights errant, from the far East—thrice welcome to my lady's bower, where, believe me, I am dying of *ennui*."

All made suitable acknowledgments, and then the whole party entered the castle, except Edwin, to whom Robin Hood, more cautious than his monarch, gave certain directions which will appear as our narrative proceeds.

CHAPTER CXLVII.

THE LADY FITZWALTER.

THE young lady to whom Lord Julian Fitzwalter was married, was one of those women who, born to all appearance for love and the gentler sentiments of humanity, had in her several qualities essentially French, which kingly profligacy has contrived more than once to introduce into this country.

She was fond of intrigue, both in love, in war, and diplomacy.

For some time she had been the brightest ornament of the court of Prince John, where scandal was rife as to the intimacy of the royal favourite's wife with the temporary sovereign.

But Lady Fitzwalter bore such a serene brow, looked so pure and innocent, was so utterly above all calumny, that she actually looked it down.

She was ambitious, and wished to see her husband placed on the highest pinnacle of power next the crown.

Hence her desire, well known, to behold the prince become king, and hence in part the devotion with which she served his interests.

As the conspirators who wished to deprive Richard of an earthly crown, and, if necessary, to give him a crown of immortality, had pretty well made up their mind to proclaim the unpopular prince at once, it was necessary to have everything in readiness in case of failure.

For this purpose, and also to see to the strengthening of the castle in case of siege, the Lady Fitzwalter had visited her husband's residence, the gift of Richard.

All her diamonds, ready money, plate, and valuables were first packed up ready for shipment to Normandy.

This was in case of failure.

The castle was strengthened, troops called in, and every art used to make it impregnable.

This was to overawe the country round.

To this brief introduction we may also add our own remark, that Richard scarcely knew into what a hornets' nest he had fallen.

No sooner were they within the castle walls than the drawbridge was hoisted for the night.

Then all the party were led to their several chambers preparatory to joining the Lady Fitzwalter at a banquet.

The king retired to his room with a temporary squire from among the outlaws.

Robin retired to his room with Will Scarlett, and at once closed the door, visited the arras, and then addressed his lieutenant in a low and cautious tone.

"Will," he said, with far more of solemnity than he was wont to assume, "can I trust you?"

"With your life."

"I know it, Will—but I have that on my head worth a hundred of my lives," continued the outlaw.

"Impossible!"

"'Tis even so."

"What is it?"

"The honour and life of England."

Will Scarlett looked at his chief as if he really thought him demented.

"Stare not so, my good Will. But 'tis a shame to doubt thee for a moment. I will tell you all. Dost know the knight who rides in our train?"

"I know him for a burly, jolly fellow," said Will; "as strong as an ox, and as generous as a king."

"'Tis even Richard King of England, my good Will."

"May God assoilze us!" cried Will Scarlett; "you jest."

"'Tis even so. Against my counsel he has entered what may prove a hornets' nest; be it our task to see him safe out of it, for the glory and good of merry England."

"My life, my blood, are yours and my king's."

"'Tis well, my honest Will," said Robin, pressing his hand warmly; "now listen. Let not our men drink, and take injunctions from the abbess to her retainers to be cautious. Say that we start betimes, and when we get to the tournament all will be free to junket as they please. Find a place where they can all lie down together, and keep you guard on your king's life the whole night."

"I will."

"At the first hint of danger," continued Robin, who now saw that his room looked by a loophole towards the forest, by a larger window into the courtyard, "I will be there."

"I hope and trust no danger may arise."

"My only hope is in the king's discretion. If he betrays himself, all is lost, for I mistrust that woman's eye; besides, 'tis utter ruin to her to let King Richard reign."

"Why came he here—why did you let him?"

"'Tis ill jesting with men who rule over millions," said Robin, quietly; "now go."

Will Scarlett, deeply gratified at the trust put in him, retired, and went down to rejoin his men, whom he found in a separate refectory with the convent men-at-arms, waited on by some clumsy boors.

He at once saw that the position was a good one, and fully intended to keep it.

Meanwhile, Robin having arrayed himself for the evening by putting a silk tunic over his armour, beneath which he concealed a dagger and pointed sword, went without ceremony to the monarch's chamber.

Finding the services of his squire no longer necessary Robin Hood at once dismissed him.

"Why so grave?" asked Richard.

"Your grace," said Robin, speaking in a low faint whisper, "I mistrust this woman—her known partiality for your brother should of itself warn you."

"Tut! tut! man," said the king, reddening, "how know you this?"

"Your grace will not believe rumour. But this I ask, my liege—trust me."

"I will."

"You are, your grace, brave even to rashness, and look danger in the face for the pleasure of overcoming it. But I have the heart of England in my charge. If I discover treachery—if I know that evil is intended, may I use my own resources—may I act as my judgment may best dictate?"

"You may, my noble-hearted Robin—but listen. I have glanced around, and there is not soldier or officer who knows me here. The Lady Fitzwalter was in a convent when I left for Palestine—I shall robe as you do. 'Tis misery to talk and eat in a helmet."

Robin Hood bowed low, and made no reply. He saw at once that the open-hearted and somewhat amorous prince was struck by the charms of the beautiful equestrian.

To oppose the king's wishes he knew would be futile, but he resolved that no harm should accrue to him while under his charge, unless indeed he lose his own life.

A loud note from a trumpet without made Robin start, and with a hasty tread he followed the monarch, not to the banquet-hall, but to a terrace that overlooked the court-yard.

After some delay, the drawbridge was again lowered, and once more a dozen men-at-arms crossed the bridge, headed by young Sir Ralph Tressilian.

The youth smiled as he bowed low to Robin, and then started, while his face became crimson.

Richard that instant turned away to the hall, where he saw the ladies assembling.

Robin hastened below to meet Sir Ralph Tressilian.

ROBIN HOOD AT THE TOURNAMENT.

"My generous friend," he began, panting for breath, "surely that is——"

"A name not to be mentioned here. Art thou loyal?"

"To my heart."

"Then this way—for he has, I fear, need of loyal hearts when this castle holds a hundred men-at-arms in the service of Lord Julian Fitzwalter."

And drawing the youth behind a pillar, in a few words he told him all, and asked and obtained a solemn promise of profound secrecy and dissimulation.

"I believe that even against the rankest treachery we can now defend him," said Robin; "hasten to your room, and join us at table. Be sober."

"And Agnes?"

"Will sleep in a closet in the Lady Edith's room, probably in her bed," said Robin.

"'Tis well."

And the two men parted mutually satisfied with each other.

CHAPTER CXLVIII.

THE BANQUET AND ITS RESULTS.

THE profusion, confusion, and abundance of American banquets at the commencement of the present century, have been made the subject of much comment and ridicule not only on the part of partisan writers, but of American writers themselves.

But if they were to go back to the early history of England, especially to the times of the Saxons, they would find that their boards literally groaned under the weight of the dishes, some of them of the most fantastic and extraordinary character, such as stuffed swans, and other strange and foreign luxuries.

It was a great matter of reproach on the part of the poorer classes that the aristocracy and church lived on the fat of the land.

It would seem that the poor themselves had but little to complain of, if we believe the ballad-monger, who says,—

I'll tell thee what, good vellowe,
  Before the vriars went hence
A bushel of the best wheate
  Was zold for vourteen pence,
And vorty eggs a penny
  That were both good and newe;
And this I say myself have seen,
  And yet I am no Jewe.

But then it must be recollected what was the value of money then and now. At that period the treasures in silver and gold of the American continent were unknown, so that gold brought quite six times as much as it does now.*

The table of Lucille, Lady Fitzwalter formed no exception to the general custom, for though, as a rule, the Normans were more sober than the Saxons, they were equally fond of display.

And here, be it noted that, as everywhere else, the relative sobriety or drinking habits of the two peoples necessarily influenced their character. The moderate Normans were ferocious in the extreme, the wine and ale bibbing Saxon s generous and tender-hearted.

Lucille received her guests with a winning courtesy which almost for a moment disarmed the suspicions of the outlaw chief.

The guests were the Black Knight, Robin Hood, Sir Ralph Tressilian, the Lady Edith, the abbess, and the Lady Fitzwalter, who was attended by her chaplain, a grave, beetle-browed and saturnine monk, whose visage was by no means prepossessing or pleasant.

He, however, said grace in a mumbling kind of way, after which he remained silent, apparently absorbed in his own thoughts, though whatever viands were set before him he ate with a phlegm almost comical.

The coquettish beauty who presided over that board had placed the king on her right, Robin on her left, leaving the ward of the crown to be amused by Sir Ralph Tressilian, who contrived, at all events, to amuse himself by asking on the sly questions about the lady of his heart, who, as was natural with a young lover, was never out of his thoughts one moment.

"Well, sir knight," said the Lady Lucille, gaily—her eyes swimming in their own liquid brightness, "what say you of merry England after your sojourn in the land of the pagan?"

"I thought it well enough yesterday," replied the somewhat amorous monarch, with a glance of deep meaning; "but I now verily believe 'tis Paradise."

"Why?" asked the lady, bending her eyes on the silver plate before her, in rosy confusion.

"Lady," whispered the king, taking her hand under the shield of the table, "pardon me if my admiration makes me rude; but had I known there was such beauty in England, I had remained to have done battle with Fitzwalter for it."

The lady laughed, though without withdrawing her hand, an act warranted by the freedom if not the license of the times, the more that under that calm and placid exterior, Lucille concealed the passions of a Messalina, the soul of a Lady Macbeth.

But in the gay monarch's speech one thing surprised and somewhat startled the lady.

The stranger called her husband Fitzwalter.

"Did you know my lord before you became a crusader?" she asked.

"Did I know 'my lord?'" he replied, with something of a sneer, and then meeting the warning eyes of Robin Hood, he added—"yes, but we were never friends. I suppose I instinctively guessed he would some day stand in my way. But what is done cannot be helped."

The lady laughed, and for some time the dinner proceeded with much of that style of conversation which the French so characteristically describe as *badinage*.

Some-how or other the conversation turned to some of the events of the Crusades.

"Does this cruel robber," said Lucille, showing her white teeth, and with a smile the meaning of which was not easily to be understood, "who has way-laid our good King Richard, intend to confine him for life?"

Both the monarch and Robin slightly started and exchanged glances.

"I should hope not," put in Robin, severely; "'tis pity, if it be really known, that his princely brother does not either ransom him, or demand him at the lance point."

There was a strange glitter in the eyes of the Lady Fitzwalter.

"There are those in England who do not wish his return," she said sarcastically; "Richard is not the only prince in Christendom."

"For my part," replied Robin Hood, with a heartiness which nearly convulsed the monarch, "I don't care who is king so that somebody is—and if anybody would knock that big, bony Richard on the head, I for one am ready to throw up my cap for King John."

"You speak the thoughts of many," said the lady, gravely, "though few speak so plainly."

"I am a blunt man."

"Well, and I a ready spoken woman. An Diccon come not back quick, he will find a Jack upon the throne; and a Jack, too, who once there, will not be ready to yield even to his brother."

A dark shadow passed over the Black Knight's face, but it vanished instantly.

"'Tis dry talking, this," he said; "for my part give me music, wine, and bright eyes, and I will kneel to any monarch. Shall we try yon harp, fair lady?"

"With pleasure," replied Lady Lucille, who, like all voluptuous women, was passionately fond of music, which soothes the soul naturally to soft emotions—rarely to powerful ones.

She rose.

"I will but give some orders to my maidens, and I am your humble servant to command. They shall dance a saraband, and play on the lute—do anything to please your worships.

She bowed with a gracious smile to all, a most meaning one to the Black Knight, and went out followed by the priest.

"I will, your grace, but see to our men," said Robin Hood, with a finger on his lips, "and return anon."

Giving the king no time to object, he darted from the hall just in time to see the priest draw the lady on one side to a kind of vacant chamber, stopping her in her course to her own private apartments.

CHAPTER CXLIX.

THE EAVES-DROPPER.

The honour of England and the life of a king were at stake, and the outlaw never for one moment hesitated.

The passage down which the lady had gone appeared one almost portioned off for herself, so that he had little to fear from interruption.

The priest, apparently to listen for any eavesdroppers, had left the door ajar.

With all the stealthy stillness of a naked-footed savage, Robin glided to where, through a narrow chink, he could both see and hear.

"A truce to homilies," said the lady, in a haughty tone; "I am not in the habit of receiving warnings from my father confessor. 'Tis enough that he should know of my sins at the proper time."

"Daughter, I am neither severe nor prudish; in my great love for you and for your house, I overlook much that should rightly shock me," began the father.

"You dare not blame me, knowing what is in your own heart," said the Lady Lucille, with a smile that made the priest's blood tingle and rush to his head.

"I know not what you mean," he replied, speaking vacantly, however, like one who with a deep and powerful sentiment in his heart, is forced to crush it within him; "I come here to warn and save you."

"That is, you are as usual insanely jealous," said the lady, with a cynicism which revolted Robin Hood.

"Heaven knows how pitiless you are, Lucille, since you discovered my dreadful secret. But it matters not. My sinful thoughts are mortified enough by reality for me to win forgiveness—in this case you wholly misunderstand me."

---

* The two following items will interest the young student of history:—

In 1299 the price of a fat lamb in London, from Christmas to Shrovetide, was 16d. (Stillingfleet's *Chronicum Rusticum*, p. 66.) Three years afterwards the price of a fat wether was 1s., and that of a ewe 8d. (Dugdale's *Hist. St. Paul's Cathedral*); and in 1309 there is a notice of an extravagant price given on occasion of an installation feast, when 200 sheep cost 30*l*., or 3s. per head (W. Thorn, in the *Decem Scriptores*). The reader will not much err if he multiplies these sums by 15, as expressive of their proportionate value at the present day.

The following is comparative:—

		s.	d.		£	s.	d.		s.	d.	
In 1350	wheat	1	10½,	an ox	1	4	6,	labour	0	3	per day.
1450	„	1	5,	„	1	15	8,	„	0	3¾	„
1550	„	1	10¼,	„	1	16	7,	„	0	4	„
1600	„	4	0½,	„	—			„	0	6	„
1675	„	4	6,	„	3	6	0,	„	0	7½	„
1760	„	5	9¼,	„	8	10	0,	„	0	11	„
1795	„	7	10,	„	16	8	0,	„	1	5¼	„

"How so?"

"Do you know who the new victim to your charms is? are you aware whom you have added to your triumphal car?"

"No; is he somebody then?"

"Richard King of England."

The lady stood speechless and pale with astonishment, her countenance meanwhile a mystery.

Gradually her colour returned, and with it all her most cunning and wreathed smiles.

"You are sure?" she asked.

"Certain."

"What a coincidence," she continued, laughing like a young girl at some frolicsome joke, "both—ha! ha! ha!"

The priest groaned.

"But we must be serious," she added, pacing up and down the room. "Now is a moment by which to make or mar ourselves for ever. 'Tis which king shall reign. You must advise me, father, but hear me first."

"I am all attention."

"Personally I prefer the Crusader," she said, with a glowing smile; "he is handsome, generous-hearted and noble, but he is a king; and will he forgive my husband, without whom I am nothing at court? I hate, or rather despise, John."

"And yet people say ——"

"No matter. I am, above all, an ambitious woman, and to win power would sell my soul, if needed."

"Lady ——"

"Listen, I tell you. We are so pledged to the prince that I really cannot decide until my husband knows the truth."

"But the king will not stop here."

"Father, I am chatelaine of this castle," she answered, with a singular smile, "and pledge myself he shall not leave until I have an answer from my husband. Besides," she continued, with a look which made the monk turn pale, "dost think he would not linger in Capua a week were I to choose it?"

"Woman," said the priest, in a hollow voice, "I understand you but too well; but sin if you will, I will not hear again your unholy records of wicked indulgence. Go get thee another confessor!"

"Tush, man!" laughed the abominable woman, "you couldn't find it in your heart to leave me. But that matters not. Do you write to my husband—explain all; tell him that which way he chooses to go, that way will I go. In the meantime, by cunning or force, I will detain the masquerading monarch here. Our soldiers are all devoted to my will, and surely I can find a woman's reason for making him stay. Let the despatch be clear but short; and send it away to-night by a trusty messenger, telling him to ride for life and death. I must return to my guests."

The father bowed meekly, Robin backed in a dark and gloomy corner, and the beautiful but erring woman came forth, with a strange light beaming in her blue and lustrous eyes.

Ah! they were lovely indeed, and might have beguiled a stronger-hearted man than ever was King Richard.

The Lady Fitzwalter said truly, that she loved not Prince John. She had never really loved any one yet, and if she could be said to know the real and genuine force of a passion which in her had been hitherto a luxurious impulse, she had begun that night to feel it for the Black Knight; and now that she knew him to be her rightful monarch, her imagination, vivid and warm, became proportionably inflamed.

She re-entered the banquet-hall a perfect queen of beauty, and advanced to where the monarch eagerly awaited her.

Her eyes were beaming with sparkling light, her cheeks flushed, and her whole mien that of a woman under the influence of strong and almost uncontrollable feelings.

"Has your friend played us truant already?" she said, with a languid smile.

"Nay, my queen of beauty," replied the king; "but as we have a long march before us to-morrow, he is chivalrous enough to see that the horses are taken care of and the men not too much indulged by your generosity."

The Lady Lucille smiled, and seated herself on a couch near the gay and thoughtless monarch.

The apartment was a large one, and, now that the banquet-table had been removed, appeared larger than it really was.

It was badly lit up, as in those days were even royal palaces—but for the time it was bright.

A kind of rude couch occurred in the alcove of every window, and to one of these the king and lady had retired.

Maid Marian thoughtful and musing, occupied one to herself.

The abbess had retired to a distance to count her beads, or feign to do so while she thought of other times.

Sir Ralph Tressilian had left the room, probably in search of the little page who watched alone in Marian's chamber.

Soon Robin Hood, having made his rounds, returned to the banqueting-hall, bringing the young knight with him.

One glance told the outlaw how far gone was the monarch in the toils of this new Circe.

It was quite clear that whatever might be the ultimate designs of the abandoned and immoral woman, her first design was so to entangle the king, that he would desire nothing more than to protract his stay.

Richard scarcely noticed the entrance of his new friend, so absorbed was he with this syren, one of whose hands was in his, and both of whose eyes looked fondly up in his face.

The loyal-hearted outlaw felt so much indignation he could scarcely disguise it. His thoughts he afterwards put into words.

"If wife of mine could look even a king in the face that way I feel I could have hit her."

And this from a man of Robin Hood's known gallantry was saying a great deal.

He passed down to where Marian sat awaiting him, and making no allusion to the subject at the moment nearest his heart, spoke gaily but in a low tone, of the coming events at Ashby.

Marian smiled as she listened to the young knight's fervid aspirations; Robin, now that the royal sword had been placed upon his shoulder, felt half an earl.

"But my gentle lord," said the Lady Edith of Athelston, "art sure that returning to a sphere to which, though born, you are not accustomed, will give you happiness. For my part I cannot understand quitting the greenwood glades, with their natural music, to dwell in halls amid a heartless crowd that neither cares for you nor anything else but the pursuits of self."

"My darling preacher," replied Robin, gravely, "the merry greenwood is probably my destiny. But if my right to my father's home and estates be proved, my duty to my king, to say nothing of that to my name, will compel me to reassume my title. But never will I be a hanger-on at court while there is a blade of grass on the sward, a leaf on the green trees of Sherwood."

"Then why ever leave them?"

"My own sweet Marian," cried Robin, "do you know were I once Earl of Huntingdon, under King Richard, what would happen?"

"No."

"I would ask for the rangership of Sherwood Forest," he answered; "and he could not refuse."

"Well?"

"To how many thousands of suffering and oppressed people could I not then give happiness!" he cried.

"True, true," said Marian, with a sigh; "and we must always, I know, sacrifice ourselves to the happiness of others. Would, however, we had been born in a humble sphere."

What answer might have been given by the bold outlaw we cannot say, as the Lady Fitzwalter suddenly rose and clapped her hands thrice, after a recently introduced Eastern fashion.

She was answered in an Eastern fashion.

Half-a-dozen pages first hurried in, and stuck torches round one end of the long banqueting-hall, thus shedding a resplendent light on that portion of the magnificent room, while the other was left in gloom.

Then came a band of music, said for its day to be unrivalled in power.

The first rude melodies they played caused the monarch to smile and arouse himself from his amorous lethargy.

His pleased look, however, changed into a blank look of speechless astonishment.

From a side door, tripping fantastically like modern ballet girls, came a troop of dancers, who ranged themselves upon the lighted part of the room.

They were nearly all dark.

Their costumes were as singular as their general expression. Their dresses, striped with gold, were fastened round their bodies in such a manner as accurately to define their figures; their waists, as flexible as reeds, were encircled by silver bands; their naked shoulders shone resplendently from the corsets which imprisoned their glowing busts; their arms waved slowly round their heads as the music struck up; their heads trembling with all the symptoms of wild passion, which was expressed with remarkable truthfulness by the graceful attitudes and modulated movements of their bodies; their fingers, moving rapidly, seemed to testify to the various phases of eager enjoyment, and confused songs and wild, melodious music added still more to the mysterious effect of their gestures.

The abbess had retired; Robin and Marian gazed with unaffected surprise and some admiration; Sir Ralph, who had returned, with ecstacy; while the king, who alone, save the luxurious countess, knew the meaning of the dance, was spellbound with breathless curiosity and amazement.

"Are we in fairyland, or are we in Palestine, where the pagan monarchs do carry such a troop in their train?"

"They are a party of Hungarian dancers, sent over by the King of France as a present, or loan, to Prince John, who, not wishing them to appear at court, has sent them here."

"Oh!" said the monarch, with a slight cough, remembering his own individuality as well as his assumed character. "Well, I must say, they do much credit to the French king's taste."

They were gipsies, Normans, Saxons, the cream of all the female companies of jugglers and tambourine-girls who went round the country, collected and drilled by an able master, and were one of the means brought to play by the favourite, Fitzwalter, upon the senses of his luxurious master, Prince John.

He little expected that they would ever perform the same office for the lion-hearted king, who, like most brave men, was passionately fond of the fair sex.

We always doubt old Napoleon's native courage when we come to know how cold-blooded he was to women.

But not so the English monarch, who, by his previous amorous conversation with the lady of the castle, being attuned to soft emotion, took the liveliest interest in the ardent poem of voluptuousness of which these women were the delineators.

For the spectators, the magnificent windings of the arms; the head rolling upon the shoulders as if abandoned to its own weight; the expression of the eyes; the imperceptible balancing of the body; that hurried, tumultuous, convulsive trembling of the whole frame; the fingers, in which every active principle of life seemed to have taken refuge—were like some mysterious elf music, of which, at all events, the king understood every note.

"'Tis passing strange," he observed, when these houris retired, "how your ladyship should have contrived so bright a spectacle on so short a notice. Some of the girls are really beautiful."

"You are a crusader, and fond of Eastern loveliness," she said, with a strange sparkle in her eyes. "Would you like to know them better?"

"Faugh!" replied Richard, with undisguised contempt. "How can a man have eyes for any woman where you are?"

"Flattery," whispered Lucille, with a deep sigh.

"No flattery. But why repeat what I have said until you must weary of hearing. Ah me, we poor crusaders stand little chance beside your idle courtiers, whose trade it is to mince and talk!"

The wife of Lord Fitzwalter looked at his stalwart limbs with a smile, and then bent her eyelashes on the ground, after a glance full of meaning at the Black Knight.

He caught her hand, and whispered something in her ear.

She blushed, hesitated, and then nodded her head.

The king at once rose, and moved towards the table, where the wine cups stood, and filled himself a rich goblet of Burgundy, which he drained off at a draught.

The lady of the house having also risen, Marian prepared to follow her, after a whispered word from Robin.

"Will any of you, gentle sirs," asked Lady Fitzwalter, in her most dulcet tones, "take spiced wine ere you sleep?"

"That will I," cried the monarch.

"One of my handmaidens shall bring it when you shall have retired," replied the chatelaine. "Will you, sir disinherited?"

"Nay, lady," said Robin, heartily, "nothing hot for me. Here is a stoup of Burgundy would make a saint thirsty; if your ladyship will allow me, I will take it to my chamber?"

"An you will be your own attendant," said Lucille, laughing, "you are welcome. Good night, and pleasant dreams."

And as Sir Ralph refused anything, she retired, while the three knights took their way to their several chambers.

CHAPTER CL.

WATCH AND WARD.

ROBIN HOOD and Sir Ralph, without any extraordinary show of outward respect, attended the monarch to his chamber door; and there, with a low obeisance, his majesty, who had drank deep of love and wine, dismissed them rather cavalierly on the threshold.

Robin bowed low, but made no remark, save that he pulled Sir Ralph by his sleeve, and bade him enter his room, which was separated from that of Richard by a thick stone wall.

"What is it?" asked Sir Ralph.

"That infernal Jezebel!" said Robin, in a low tone of voice, "has bewitched his grace. The cup-bearer with the spiced wine will be herself—that I know."

The young knight smiled, as if he thought this a venal offence at a time when chastity was little regarded.

"I know what you would say," continued Robin Hood; "and were this a mere passing amour, I should sleep in peace. But this painted, deceitful cockatrice has but lured him on to make him tarry here, while she, another Dalilah, shall betray our Samson."

"Nay."

"I have overheard the whole plot, and three hours since a messenger went from the serpent wanton to her worthy husband to ask which king he will serve. She is ready for either, or both."

"You amaze me."

"Well I may."

"Can such deceit exist?"

"Aye, woman is difficult to judge," continued Robin; "but this one bears the stamp of all her infamy upon her brow. Where his grace not so infatuated he must have seen it."

"But what are we to do?"

"Keep watch and ward," replied Robin, gravely.

"How?"

"I have arranged to prevent any evil coming to the king by any machinations that I know of; but this female fiend may have other designs, and it behoves us to be on our guard. In a few minutes she will probably be here, bringing in disguise the spiced wine, and then who knows she may not let murderers in?"

"You are right," whispered the youthful knight; "in everything command me. I am yours."

"Put the light in the fireplace, and screen it well," said the outlaw, "and then I will examine the door—we may see through that."

Scarcely had the king of merry Sherwood given these directions than he motioned to Sir Ralph to be still.

Footsteps were gliding down the passage, the soft pattering footsteps of woman.

Robin at once saw that the hinges were not well put on, or that he could see plainly enough.

As he expected, it was the Lady Fitzwalter, who, with a taper in one hand, passed, with nothing to disguise her but a flowing veil over her head.

On a tray was the spiced wine and two glasses.

She entered the room, and Robin clearly heard the bolt of the door pushed inside.

"Now, Sir Ralph," said Robin, cautiously opening his own door, "I leave the life and liberty of England in your hands. If there be treason afloat, die at your post ere you yield. I have work to do to-night."

"Trust me," replied the young knight, heartily.

"I shall not be long absent; but one loud cry from yonder window will summon me at once to your aid."

And clutching his dagger and sword, Robin passed forth into the corridor on his way down to the court-yard.

He had careful note of every minute detail of the household arrangements, and thus easily reached the court-yard without meeting a living soul.

All had retired to their several apartments, or if soldiers and tambourine girls did indulge in revelry it was in some remote corner where their late orgies could not reach the ears of their masters and guests.

Not a light was to be seen save in the kind of lodge where the porter lay, a fellow whose task it was to attend to the gate at night; and in the guard-house devoted to the outlaws and the retainers of the abbess.

Robin went first to the latter, tapped in a peculiar way, when the door was opened, and Will Scarlett stood before him.

"Well," said Robin Hood.

"All's well," replied the lieutenant, "the royal soldiers sleep or drink with the dancing-girls, an idle troop of hussies from horse-fairs."

"And the porter?"

"Sleeps as sound as Burgundy, and ale, and hippo-cras can make a man," continued Will Scarlett.

"Medicated wine is not a bad night-cap," said the outlaw. "Take thy sword, bring yon cord, and come."

The two men closed the door of the guard-house, and glided across the wide court to the porter's lodge, the door of which they found was ajar.

The man lay on a wide wooden settle, fast asleep; his keys nervously clutched in his hands.

"Better not tie him after all," whispered Robin, as, without much difficulty, he unloosed his grasp on the bunch.

Will Scarlett merely nodded.

"This is the postern key," he observed, as Robin examined the bunch. "I know it well."

Asking no questions, Robin Hood followed his guide through some cloister-like passages, entered a small garden, and then both seemed to disappear under the shadows of the ramparts.

They were within a dark and gloomy archway, at the end of which was a door.

Robin soon found the keyhole, and the door flew open, grating on its ponderous hinges.

The moat presented itself before them.

It was narrow, but deep. This, however, was provided against; for under the archway was a plank, with a cord fastened to it—a strong and serviceable cord.

The plank was lifted on high, and then, by means of the cord, gradually lowered to the other side.

A low whistle from Robin Hood met at once with its echo on the other side.

Robin crossed to where Little John stood erect, still, in the shadow of the ramparts, and all unnoticed by the sleepy sentinels, who, it being time of peace, slept chiefly at their watch.

Little John, who never wasted words, handed a large sealed packet to his chief.

"Thanks! Are your men ready?"

"Quite."

"Come then," said Robin, who returned swiftly the way he came, and held the door while two hundred shadows, as it appeared, glided into the garden specially reserved for my lady and her friends, and took their post beneath the crowded trees.

Then Robin held a whispered conference with Little John, after which he and Will Scarlett returned to the courtyard.

Everything was just as they left it.

The porter still slumbered heavily, so that the keys were restored to him, though cast on the ground at his feet.

When this was done the outlaw found his own men and those of the abbess waiting in the courtyard.

They stood still and motionless, like statues in the night air.

Robin locked the guard-house and put the key in his pouch. Then he led his men into the interior of the castle.

All trod like men who knew the important duty on which they were detached.

Their chief led them to a room close to the banquet-hall, containing surplus furniture and lumber.

Within this he bade them retire, bolt the door, and open only at the sound of his voice.

Then Robin returned to his own apartment, where he found Sir Ralph, with drawn sword, keeping watch and ward.

Nothing suspicious had occurred, and the lady was still in the royal chamber.

"'Tis well!" said Robin, "but we must now disturb the ladies. I have need of them."

Sir Ralph was so utterly in the hands of the outlaw chief, his confidence was so unlimited, that he made no remark.

Robin glided into the passage, listened attentively, went down some distance, and returned with Lady Edith, and the novice, both of whom were dressed.

They entered the chamber, the door was closed, and then Robin pulled forth the packet given to him by Little John.

It was a despatch, tied with silken strings, and sealed.

Robin broke it boldly, and handed it to Maid Marian, who, after some little study, read it aloud.

It was in Norman-French, which she had to translate.

It was addressed to Lord Fitzwalter, and plainly repeated the message given to the priest by Lady Fitzwalter.

"Thanks!" said the outlaw, while Sir Ralph listened, awestruck at her duplicity. "And now, fair ones, go slumber; I am sorry to have kept such bright eyes from their rest so long."

It was no time for courtesies, and the young women glided away without a word, glad indeed to obtain some sleep.

"The deceitful, beautiful fiend!" said Sir Ralph; "but are we quite safe from her toils?"

"Quite safe," replied Robin Hood.

The two young men now indulged in a draught of wine; after which, both seated themselves in chairs to converse in whispers.

For these devoted watchers of the night there was yet to be no sleep.

CHAPTER CLI.

THE EXPLANATION.

At a later hour than was usual, the whole of the guests of Lady Fitzwalter sat around her table in the banquet-hall.

Every luxury known in those days was set before them, and, to a certain extent, was done justice to.

Richard sat at her right hand, conversing gaily and freely with his beautiful hostess.

The Lady Lucille answered him with her usual beaming smile; but still, there was uneasiness in her manner.

"And now," said the monarch, when the meal had been protracted almost beyond reasonable bounds, "'tis sorry thanks for your noble hospitality to say it; but the hour of parting has come."

"Parting!" replied the lady, with a start and a languishing side glance at Richard. "I had thought you my guests for several days. I had ordered a new dance for this evening."

"Indeed!" said the good-natured monarch, avoiding, with something of a displeased mien, the grave looks of Robin. "I would, then, that our journey could be delayed."

"Why so eager to be gone?"

"Foregad!" cried Richard, with a view to try the generosity of his new friend. "You must ask my companion."

"'Tis to you, then, I must turn?" said the Lady Lucille, with a winning smile. "Why are you in a hurry?"

"I am in a hurry," said Robin, in a cold, stern, and ringing voice, "because I have no wish to await the result of your message last night to the court of Prince John."

"Ah!" said the lady, momentarily confounded.

"Sdeath," said the king, rising.

"So," she continued, "we have traitors here!" and then she added, with flaming eyes, "Who dares address me thus?"

The king interrogated Robin with his eyes. The outlaw nodded.

"It is my place to speak," said the monarch, in his loftiest tones. "Then you knew me, madam?"

"Yes, your grace—who for one moment could mistake that lordly presence—for whom else—" and she whispered a word or two.

"Yes, yes," said the king, colouring; "but wherefore this midnight despatch?"

"Despatch—I sent none," she said, with the coolest effrontery.

"But you ordered one to be sent," replied Robin Hood, coldly—as he handed the open parchment to Richard; "the seals are broken—but my men are rude and ready."

The king read it through with a dark and lowering brow, and then turned to where a moment before the Lady Fitzwalter stood—but she had retired.

Next instant she returned, all her smiles again upon her face.

"Most noble knights," she said, in a way that intimated her wish to conceal the monarch's rank, "I cannot let you go until my husband comes to greet you."

"And these men-at-arms," observed Robin, grimly, "are to detain us, if we would not stay?"

Behind the Lady Fitzwalter came some twenty of her chosen soldiers.

The king leaned upon his drawn sword, a livid circle round his mouth. He felt utterly ashamed of the folly and weakness which had led him into a trap.

"Madam——" he began.

"One word, sir knight, of the Black Shield," put in Robin Hood; "we will treat as equals."

And as he spoke the armed men from the lumber-room poured into the banquet-hall.

"Who dares thus invade my private chambers?" cried Lady Fitzwalter, livid with rage.

"It does not become your grace," whispered Robin to the King, "to banter words with this woman. Allow me—Lady Fitzwalter," continued the outlaw, "I have only to say that I heard every word you spoke to the priest; but that is no affair of mine. If you would know who and what I am—I am Robin Hood, king of Sherwood Forest, and this castle is now mine."

"Audacious varlet!" cried the furious chatelaine, who despised the small force commanded by the outlaw, knowing her own numbers; "seize him! There is a reward of a thousand marks for him, dead or alive."

In another instant there would have been a fray, despite the intervention of the warm-hearted monarch, when another actor came upon the scene.

"Hold!" cried a loud voice. "Down bills and bows, down pikes and swords, or there will be broken sconces and bloody conks ere you sav an avo."

They turned, and there stood Little John, leaning on his staff with a look of sarcastic humour in his eye.

"What hulking ruffian is this who lords it in my hall?" exclaimed the countess, furiously. "Cut him down."

The tall forester waved his hand, and a dense crowd of yeomen, armed to the teeth, rushed and disarmed the retainers without a blow.

"Hurrah!" said Little John, "the castle's all your own."

And the men did give a shout that made the very rafters ring.

Then, at a sign from Robin, all retired, save those who had been at the breakfast table.

"And now," spoke Robin, addressing the king in a low voice, "what commands have you?"

"First, my noble friend," said Richard, taking his hand in his, "my thanks for your watchfulness and devotion."

"Tut! tut! I did but my duty."

"Well, tell me all."

Robin Hood briefly related the events of the night.

"This woman is an incarnate fiend. What is to be done with her?"

"May I advise?"

"Let this appear a raid of outlaws. My men will carry her off, with the priest, and detain them while they are dangerous, under pretence of ransom."

"And you will do that?"

"I will."

"Would that I had many such friends," said the king, averting his head from where the lady stood, endeavouring still, by coquettish arts, to draw his attention.

But without another look Richard left the room to arm for the journey.

Half an hour later, secured, and even gagged, before they could communicate a word to any one, the guilty woman and the priest were hurried off into the deep recesses of the forest.

Half an hour later the same cavalcade departed, that had entered the castle the day before.

The soldiery, domestics, and dancing girls, left to themselves, and afraid to face their master, pillaged the castle, and dispersed in all directions with such valuables as they could collect.

In this way, not a soul remained who could communicate to the favourite of Prince John what had happened.

The thoughtless monarch who, in dalliance with a beautiful woman, had so nearly betrayed his secret and his person to the hands of his enemies, was for a time sad and thoughtful, but after a time he became the same open-hearted and free-spoken person he usually was.

That was to be his last day in the company of Robin Hood for a while, so that they had much to say; and when the moment came for parting, the farewell was more cordial and real than often takes place between monarch and subject.

They understood one another; and, on his part, Richard had the most unbounded confidence in Robin Hood.

The Black Knight had to visit a monastery, to meet some tried friends, and, at a cross road, left.

The outlaw pursued his way towards Ashby-de-la-Zouche.

CHAPTER CLII.

THE WRESTLING MATCH.

As we hope and trust that our readers do not read these pages wholly for amusement, but will willingly be reminded of their studies, we here put in a few words illustrative of the state of England, which was indeed sufficiently miserable.

King Richard was supposed to be abroad, a prisoner, and in the power of the cruel and perfidious Duke of Austria.

His dungeon even was not known.

Prince John, in secret league with Philip of France, Cœur de Lion's mortal enemy, was using every species of influence with the Duke of Austria to prolong the captivity of his brother.

The legitimate heir, failing Richard, was Arthur Duke of Brittany, son of Geoffry Plantagenet, the elder brother of John.

For this purpose he was strengthening his faction, in order to dispute the succession.

Light, profligate, and perfidious, John brought round to his faction not only all those who justly dreaded the resentment of Richard, but all such lawless resolutes as the crusades had turned back on the country, accomplished in the vices of the East, impoverished in substance, and hardened in character.

The nobles, fortified within their own castles, and playing at petty sovereigns over their own dominions, were the leaders of lawless and oppressive bands to put the outlaws to shame.

To maintain this force of legalised banditti, and to support their own extravagance and munificence, the nobility borrowed of the Jews at usurious interest, which gnawed into their estates like consuming cankers.

Under these circumstances, the people of England suffered deeply for the present, and had yet more dreadful cause to fear for the future. They always in the end bore the burden, and have from time immemorial, until the present day.

Once, when Cromwell released them from despotism, they had an opportunity, but they threw it away.

To add to their accumulated miseries a most dangerous contagious disorder spread over the land, made more virulent by wretched lodging and worse food.

It was under these gloomy auspices that the grand tournament was announced; and, despite the severe distress and discontent, poor as well as rich, vulgar as well as noble, were sure to rush to see the grand show, in presence of which the lower orders might forget their troubles, and the rich the gloomy clouds on the political horison.

Prince John, it was rumoured, would himself preside with perfectly regal magnificence, to prepare the populace for the day when they were to throw up their bonnets, and cry "Long live King John!"

The locality selected was the town of Ashby, in Leicestershire, and thither the party, guided by Robin Hood, made their way.

To hope for ordinary lodgings was out of the question, but the abbess was able to secure a reception at one of the convents in the neighbourhood for herself and the Lady Edith of Athelston.

Robin, fortunately, had friends in the neighbourhood, and with them he deposited both his armour and accoutrements, while he strolled about in the costume of a humble retainer, in order to look around him and listen to and observe all that was going on.

A word or two as to the ground.

On the verge of a wood, which approached within a mile of the town, was an extensive meadow of the finest and most beautiful green turf, surrounded on one side by the forest, and fringed on the other by straggling oak-trees, some of an immense size.

The ground, as if fashioned on purpose for the martial display which was intended, sloped gradually down on all sides to a level bottom, which was enclosed for the lists with strong palisades, forming a space of a quarter of a mile in length, and about half as broad.

The form of this enclosure was an oblong square, save that the corners were considerably rounded off, in order to afford more convenience for the spectators.

The openings for the entry of the combatants were at the northern and southern extremities of the lists, accessible by strong wooden gates, each wide enough to admit two horsemen riding abreast.

At each of these portals were to be stationed two heralds, attended by six trumpeters, as many pursuivants, and a strong body of men-at-arms for maintaining order, and ascertaining the quality of the knights who proposed to engage in the martial game.

Tents were placed in all directions for refreshments as well as for armourers, farriers, and other attendants.

The exterior of the lists was in part occupied by temporary galleries, spread with tapestry and carpets, and accommodated with cushions, for the convenience of those ladies and nobles who were expected to attend the tournament.

A narrow space between these galleries was to give accommodation to the yeomanry and spectators of a higher degree than the mere vulgar, who, as usual, had to shift for themselves, and had selected some large banks of turf that had been hastily thrown up.

In the centre of the eastern side of the lists was a throne and canopy for the prince—opposite him was another, for what purpose will be seen.

Robin marked these peculiarities as he strolled about one of an idle crowd, for the morrow was to see the commencement of the tournament, and already great numbers of people were coming in.

Satisfied with what he had seen, and thinking with some anxiety of the morrow, the outlaw strolled away to an inn of the better sort, where he had an appointment.

They had been now two days in Ashby, and Robin seemed quite at home. Nodding familiarly to the innkeeper, he passed up a rude staircase, knocked at a door, and entered.

It was an apartment rude, as such apartments were in inns in those days; but it was the abode of happiness, for there side by side sat young Sir Ralph and his blooming bride, Lady Agnes Tressilian. A complaisant and perfectly qualified priest had united them on the very evening of their arrival, in the presence of a noble friend of the young knight's, and Robin Hood, who contrived, in some fashion, to sign his name Huntingdon.

Few in any rank in society could then make more than their mark.

But they were not ignorant for all that; some shrewd, clever, well-informed men of the present day have not mastered the mechanical power of writing.

Indeed, a nation which is satisfied to know that its masses can read and write, as one or two boast they can, is none the more advanced.

It is what you give them to read that breeds the result.

Robin came to know their designs for the next day, and the young knight at once said that before he entered the lists he would see his wife to a seat becoming her rank.

Robin shook his head.

"You have two enemies—your friends, who wish you to marry elsewhere; her friends, who, for the sake of her wealth, do not wish her to marry at all. Better bide your time, and wait until a just prince sits on the throne of England."

"But I am married," said the girl, artlessly. "Who now can touch me?"

"You are a child, and know not the power of rank and money. If the church is paid to do it, it would snatch you from beside the baby in its cradle, if it died. When did you ever know churchmen have bowels of compassion?—never!"

"Robin!"

"I speak truth. The greatest enemies of human progress, of the happiness of the people, are the priests, who, under pretence of watching after their interests, rob and plunder them. The day will come," continued the patriot of Sherwood Forest, "when men will hail the religion of Christ as all in all, and scout the priests as ignorant pretenders, mountebanks, quacks, and charletans."

The young couple stood amazed and horrified. Though by their own act somewhat emancipated from priestly rule, yet the free-thinking words of Robin alarmed them.

"I see too much of them; I know them too well," said Robin, sadly, "not to curse them as the worst instruments of tyranny the world ever knew. But a truce to this: if you will be advised by me you will go to the tournament not at all, or in the garb of a peasant girl, and in company with our worthy host."

Now Lady Agnes Tressilian was as good as she was pretty, but she was vain and thoughtless, as became her age and education. She was now in the full fresh dignity of matronship, and cared not to look up at those of her own rank from amid a crowd.

Seeing which way she desired the decision to be made, Sir Ralph supported his wife.

"I shall say no more. Mine is mere advice, and may signify nothing; but blame me not if you are parted for ever."

And with these ominous words Robin went out of the room, leaving the married lovers in some little consternation. But they were in the first fresh heyday of the honeymoon, and the gloom soon passed away.

The outlaw, scarcely angry with the happy young couple for disregarding his warning, descended the stairs and went into a kind of shed at the back, where the common sort—"the mere vulgar," as historians complacently call them—were collected, drinking ale at a great rate.

Here he heard many home truths, principally complaints against the oppression of the upper classes, and clearly saw that as far as the masses dared to pronounce themselves, they were all heartily sick of their ruler, Prince John.

Hearty wishes for the return of Richard were heard on all sides. But people seemed to regard this as almost a hopeless affair, and there mused sorrowfully how to escape the villanous oppression of the disorderly gangs which infested England.

His own name was frequently mentioned with applause, and a hearty, genial admiration which was very pleasant to hear from the lips of the unsophisticated multitude.

"Well," said a stout, strange-looking fellow, with something of the cut of a seaman about him, "I've heard tell a good deal about this fellow, but I never saw him. People say that money might be made by catching him."

"Like to catch you at it." "Poor man's friend." "Wish there was more like him." "He's the man for us."

Such were the murmurs which passed round the room as the fellow said these words.

"Now I don't know that. The man's a outlaw, which, to my idea, is something very much in the style of a pirate. I've served on board king's ships, and when we gets hold of any of those sort of people we ain't particular whether we scuttle their ship and let 'em down, or shoot them with arrows, or hang 'em. For my part I don't care a rose-noble for Robin Hood, and if I saw him would say the same."

"So you've been on the sea, old one-eye?" said the outlaw, alluding to a patch over his left orb of vision.

"I have, stripling; and mind who you're talking to, or I'll undertake to teach you manners."

"My worthy soldier of the navy," continued the outlaw, with something of a swagger, "I think you are given to boasting."

"Boasting! Curse you, who are you?" spluttered the seaman; "why, if I were not ashamed to touch such a whipper-snapper, I'd pitch you over my head."

"Wilt try?" said Robin, quietly.

"Thou art but a boy."

"I've lived on the borders of Sherwood Forest some years," continued the outlaw, "and people who have seen him say that Robin Hood is very much of my size and make."

"Haw! haw! haw!" laughed the sailor.

"So if you would try your hand on one of the green-coated men of the forest, you'd best begin with me."

"A challenge! a challenge!" said the mob.

"A challenge!" growled the sailor; "and when I've broken his neck, what then will you say, my fine fellows?"

"That is no business of thine," said the outlaw, whose juvenile appearance always puzzled everybody. "I am ready and willing to have a bout with you on the meadow behind; and if these good people will come and see fair, I'll roll a cask of ale out and pay for it—eh, worthy Tristen?" he added, addressing the host, who had just peered in for empty mugs.

"Your word is as good as your money, Master Locksley," said the landlord, nodding familiarly; "Diccon and Harry shall broach the cask."

In another moment the whole party were on the meadow behind the house.

Well and truly do the multitude love such exhibitions as this, in which the physical characteristics of our race are brought into full play.

The two men stripped, and as they did so comparisons unfavourable to Robin Hood were made.

The seaman, who wore a short cloak, dropped it from his shoulders, and extending his long brawny arms with a look of determined resolution, offered himself to the contest.

But Robin was nothing abashed by the muscular frame, broad chest, square shoulders, and hardy look of his stout antagonist.

But, at the same time, the outlaw was a little uneasy at the number who flocked to see the contest.

He had no fear of the common people, but he had every reason to dread that amid the motley crowd some officious knave of a keeper might recognise him.

Apart from this feeling, his manner was as calm and apathetic as a Red-Indian's.

"Art ready, master yeoman?" said the seaman, scornfully; "hast said thy ave?—an it be not thy last, there is no faith in these bones and sinews."

"Do we fight to the death?" quoth Robin, quietly.

"An thou wilt."

"Nay, I shall throw thee as hard as I can," smiled the outlaw "but I hope the devil will take care of thy neck."

The man laughed aloud, while the crowd applauded.

"I am ready," he said, tauntingly.

"Come on, then."

In the first struggle which took place the seamen appeared to have some advantage, and in the second close neither could be called decisive. But it was plain he had put his whole strength too suddenly forth,

against an antagonist possessed of great endurance, skill, vigour, and length of wind. In the third close the yeoman lifted his opponent fairly from the floor, and hurled him to the ground with such violence that he lay for an instant stunned and motionless.

A loud cry rose from the crowd.

"I say, fellow," said a keeper, coming forward, "this passes a joke. You must stay to answer for this before the prince—nay, I will take thee."

A loud cry of execration, general and warm, greeted this interference, and the outlaw waved the man aside.

"The man is stunned," quietly observed Robin, clutching his quarterstaff, "and if you touch me but with your finger, I will lay thee by his side, catchpole though you be."

"In the name of the gracious prince who rules," spluttered the keeper, "I command you to aid me to seize this man."

"Seize him yourself," roared the crowd, delighted to bait one of the minions of the law.

"Put up your bilboes," growled the sailor, as he rose rubbing his bloody sconce, "the man threw me fairly. I little thought there was a churl of them all could throw one who has tried back-falls in Dutchland and France. Give us your hand, my hearty, and may we meet again. I like an honest, straightforward chap like you."

Robin laughingly gave his hand.

"As for you, Mr. Catchpole, you'd better move. My bile is up, and if you don't move precious quick I'll make a rantipole of you. Quick, march."

The keeper withdrew to a distance growling. But he saw that the whole crowd was against him.

"And now," continued the seaman, as every man filled his mug with beer, "the name of my conqueror?"

The outlaw was on the verge of the meadow, the forest was within twenty yards.

He smiled as he glanced at the greenwood cover.

"My name," he said, with a proud humility that always became him, "is Robin Hood, the outlaw."

Amazement kept all quiet an instant, and then a shout such as seldom burst from the popular voice filled the air.

"Eh! what?—ah!—did he say?" blustered the keeper, now reinforced by an armed posse of companions. "I thought I heard——"

"Whatever you thought you heard keep to yourself," said the seaman, clapping the other's bonnet so roughly as to fix it over his eyes.

"Murder! violation! robbery!" roared the catchpole. "Seize that fellow! A thousand marks for the outlaw Robin Hood!"

The rangers and keepers rushed in, but Robin Hood and the seaman were already beneath the leafy arches of the forest, where, though the officers followed, there was little hope of capturing them.

CHAPTER CLIII.

THE TOURNAMENT.

MORNING broke on the day of the tournament, and from all parts of the country spectators flocked to occupy their respective stations.

Squires, pages, and yeomen in rich liveries waited round the throne of Prince John and his attendants.

Round the one facing him were also trains of pages and young maidens, the most charming that could be selected, gaily dressed in fancy habits of green and pink.

Among pennons and flags bearing wounded hearts, burning hearts, bleeding hearts, bows and quivers, and all the common-place emblems of the triumph of Cupid, a blazoned inscription informed the spectators that this seat of honour was designed for *La Royne de la Beautte et des Amours.*

The crowd was so dense, even of those who claimed to have seats or standing-places within the ring, that confusion was not to be avoided.

Quarrels arose as to the places each was entitled to hold. Some of these disputes were settled by the men-at-arms, with very brief ceremony, by means of the shafts of their battle-axes and pummels of their swords, which soon convinced the most refractory.

ROBIN HOOD CARRIES AGNES FROM THE VAULT.

But when the rival claims of more elevated persons were concerned the heralds or marshals intervened.

Gradually, however, everybody found their places, and the whole multitude waited the commencement of the sports with the impatience of children.

The entrance of Prince John, attended by a gay and numerous train, consisting partly of laymen, partly of churchmen, as light in their dress, as gay in their demeanour, as insolent and lustful in their looks as their companions, attracted all eyes.

Fur and gold were not spared on their garments, and the points of their boots, out-heroding the ordinarily preposterous fashion of the time, in some turned up so very far as to be attached not merely to their knees, but to their very girdles, which effectually prevented them from putting their feet in the stirrups.

The prince himself was well mounted, and splendidly dressed in crimson and gold, bearing upon his hand a falcon, and having his head covered by a rich fur bonnet, adorned with a circle of precious stones, from which his long curled hair escaped and over-spread his shoulders. He rode into the ring on a grey and highly mettled palfrey, caracoling at the head of his jovial party, and laughing loud with his train, and eyeing with all the boldness of royal criticism the beauties who adorned the lofty galleries.

Beside him rode Lord Fitzwalter and Sir Hugh Fitzurse.

"And where is the fair Lady Lucille?" said the king, addressing his new favourite.

"I know not—she should have been here yestere'en—I will send a messenger. I fear me she is ill."

"By the bald scalp of Abraham!" cried the prince, "I hope not. But who have we here?"

And he pointed to where Edith of Athelston and the blushing Agnes sat together.

"I know not—they are quite strangers to me," replied the young nobleman. "They are rare beauties, any way."

"Do you know them, Fitzurse?" asked the prince.

The knight, a saturnine man of five and forty, with heavy beetling brows and thoughtful mien, looked direct at them.

"Foregad!" he said, turning somewhat pale, "I know not who the superb beauty is, but yon blushing little minx is my niece, whom I thought safe in a nunnery. This is rank sacrilege and must be looked to. I will have the wench taken away at once."

"Nonsense, man," replied the king, examining the blushing Agnes with one of his insolent leers; "let there be no scandal this morning, but do it quietly just as the sports are over."

"As you will, my liege," said Sir Hugh Fitzurse, "the minx shall, however, sleep in a convent to-night. It puzzles me how the abbess has allowed this. I saw her but this morning."

"Gramercy! then the girl has but come to see the tournament. Let her enjoy herself for once."

"But the hussey is in full costume—that of a knight's lady, foregad!" said Fitzurse, whose passion was the greater that he knew very few words would overthrow his hold upon Agnes.

His brother's will distinctly stated that, were she immured in a convent, his guardianship was to cease, as it was his hope and desire she should wed with Sir Ralph Tressilian.

In default of which, at the age of twenty-one, she was to be free to choose between convent and husband.

Did she freely choose a convent, or did she die before she was one-and-twenty, the estates and money went to his brother.

This no one knew but the knight and his confederate, the priest Leon, a learned man, who had shelter in his house for keeping the secret.

In the meantime the prince had taken his seat, and had given a signal to his heralds to proclaim the laws of the tournament.

It had been an arranged thing, previous to the tournament, that three Norman knights should challenge all comers; these were Sir Norman Malvoisin, Sir James Falconbridge, and the youthful Earl of Falaise, a handsome knight of three-and-twenty, who, it was said at court, was one of the aspirants for the hand and broad lands of Edith of Athelston, the Saxon ward of the crown.

The rules were simple.

First. The three challengers were to undertake all comers.

Secondly. Any knight proposing to combat might, if he pleased, select a special antagonist from among the challengers, by touching his shield. If he did so with the reverse of his lance, the trial of skill was made with what were called the arms of courtesy; that is, with the lance at whose extremity a piece of round, flat board was fixed; so no danger was encountered, save from the shock of the horses and riders. But if the shield was touched with the sharp end of the lance, the combat was understood to be à l'outrance; that is, the knights were to fight with sharp weapons, as in actual battle.

Thirdly. When the knights present had accomplished their vow, by each of them breaking five lances, the prince was to declare the victor in the first day's tourney, who should receive as prize a war-horse of exquisite beauty and matchless strength; and, in addition to this reward of valour, it was now declared he should have the peculiar honour of naming the Queen of Love and Beauty, by whom the prize should be given on the ensuing day.

Fourthly. It was announced that on the second day there should be a general tournament, in which all the knights present who were desirous to win praise might take part; and being divided into two bands of equal numbers, might fight it out manfully, until the signal was given by Prince John to cease the combat. The elected Queen of Love and Beauty was then to crown the knight whom the prince should adjudge to have borne himself best in this second day, with a coronet composed of thin gold plate, cut in the shape of a laurel crown.

On this second day the knightly games ceased; followed the next day by feats of archery, of bull-baiting, and other popular amusements of the populace.

In this manner did Prince John endeavour to lay the foundation of a popularity, which he was perpetually throwing down by some inconsiderate act of wanton aggression upon the feelings and prejudices of the people.

The lists now presented a most splendid spectacle. The sloping galleries were crowded with all that was noble, great, wealthy, and beautiful in the northern and midland parts of England; and the contrast of the various dresses of these dignified spectators rendered the view as gay as it was rich; while the interior and lower space, filled with the substantial burgesses and yeomen of merry England, formed, in their more plain attire, a dark fringe or border around this circle of brilliant embroidery, relieving, at the same time setting off, its splendour.

Then rose on high a shrill blast, and the barrier at the end was crowded with knights anxious to compete with the three challengers.

But as all could not try their fortunes, lots were drawn, and three stalwart soldiers entered the lists, proclaiming, by the way they struck their shields, that they selected arms of courtesy.

A murmur of regret from all quarters proclaimed that the audience thought this child's play; but the champions took no notice, riding about the lists freely and unconcernedly, except that one and all sought to exhibit the paces of their steeds and the grace and dexterity of the riders.

There was a pause, and then the two parties formed, each of the challengers facing the knight who had touched his shield.

Then came a flourish of clarions and trumpets, and the whole six started at full gallop. They met, and the wisdom of the selection made previous to the tournament was shown, by the three nameless knights being unhorsed and rolling on the ground.

They at once retreated on foot, their arms and horses forfeited to the victors.

It would not serve our purpose to record the general events of the day—but, in general, we may mention that at the fourth round the challengers still remained the victors; after which there seemed no anxiety on the part of any to face the victorious and triumphant Normans.

Sir Norman Malvoisin had been the most prominent victor of the day. Perfectly recovered from his wounds, and passionately fond of the public sports of that day, which were but prize-fights on a different scale, he had remained hitherto like a solid statue on his horse, having overthrown three knights and foiled a fourth.

Sir James Falconbridge had unhorsed two, as had the Earl of Falaise.

Ten minutes of deep silence had elapsed, during which the heralds vainly strove to incite the other knights to face the challengers.

No one cared about rushing to certain defeat.

Prince John looked haughtily round to enjoy the triumph of his favourites, but a sullen silence pervaded the assembly, the three Normans being hated cordially by the multitude.

A low murmur went through the crowd when they saw that the sports were about to end without one of the challengers being defeated.

The prince was consulting his councillors as to terminating the day's sports.

Then upon the still air came the sound of a trumpet, sounding in notes of defiance.

The multitude gave a loud and spontaneous huzza.

The crowd of knights outside the barrier gave way as a man of middle height and slender form, in a suit of steel armour, and mounted on a noble steed, rode into the lists.

With a grace and elegance that won him many plaudits, he saluted the ladies, and then caracoling past, bowed to the prince.

The old knights and nobles ceased lamenting in whispers the decay of martial spirit, and speaking of the triumphs of their younger days; while the dames and demoiselles brightened up visibly.

The day was at last becoming promising, there being always something exciting in mystery.

Now no one could form the slightest conception as to who the stranger could be.

No one seemed able to recognise his figure, or his horse, while his shield bore no device at all.

The knight rode slowly across the lists, until he reached the three shields of the challengers.

Even they looked anxiously to see whose shield he would touch—and how he would touch it.

The unknown halted before that of Sir Norman Malvoisin, and then, lifting his lance, struck the shield with the sharp point of his lance, firmly and with decision.

A long breath was drawn by all present.

"Egad!" said the prince, "'tis a daring gallant. Who can it be?—some of Richard's ragged lot, I expect."

"At all events, not Richard himself," whispered Fitzwalter; "he could not put his carcase in that coat of mail."

Meanwhile Sir Norman, startled at the audacity of this comer, had, with his usual insolence, sought to terrify the new comer by big words.

"Your worship is aware," he said, tauntingly, "that you have challenged me with sharp weapons?"

"I come to fight, not to play, Sir Norman."

"Then art thou nearer death than ever thou wert," replied the other, angrily.

"I am ready—which is more than a dark oppressor of the poor and the weak ever was," replied the stranger.

"Ah!" said Sir Norman, with a dark scowl, "who have we here who talks so glibly?"

"An honourable man, with a clear conscience and sound heart, which is more than you can say."

"Fore gad! you are insolent," said Sir Norman, who at once began to prepare for the combat, while the stranger rode quietly back to his post, amid loud plaudits.

The way he had bearded the Norman tyrant had excited deep sympathy in the crowd.

Sir Norman selected a fresh steed, a fresh lance, and a new shield, as he wished to give the Saxon, as he judged him to be, a good lesson, such a one as he might not forget, and that might teach others to be more cautious.

In a few minutes the two antagonists stood opposite one another in the lists, which enabled the public to compare their appearance.

Looks were decidedly in favour of Sir Norman Malvoisin; his herculean frame, stout horse—an immense brute—bore no comparison with the slight frame of the Unknown.

But there was no time for much discussion on the matter, as no sooner did the trumpets sound than challenger and challenged dashed from their posts with lightning-like speed, and came in collision exactly in the middle of the lists.

Both their lances were shivered, and so terrible was the shock that both steeds fell back upon their haunches, nearly unseating their riders.

But as in each case they were consummate horsemen, they brought up their animals by the use of bridle and spur, when, glaring at each other fiercely through the bars of their visors, they rode back to where their squires stood in readiness with fresh lances.

Hitherto the proceedings had been so one-sided, as to have been tame to the spectators, who now gave a loud and ringing shout, the ladies waving scarfs and handkerchiefs until it was seen that the second encounter was to take place.

The silence which then prevailed indicated the deep interest felt by all in the issue.

It was deep, dead, breathless.

Again the trumpets sounded.

The two combatants, taking careful aim, dashed forward, and again met in the centre of the oval, each striking his adversary full in the face.

The lance of Sir Norman shivered; but that of the unknown stuck in the bars of the helmet.

Next instant knight and steed rolled on the ground in a cloud of dust.

"Have at thee, recreant," shouted Sir Norman, as he rose to his feet; "think not you have yet defeated the best knight in Christendom."

And, amid terrific acclamations for the Unknown and jeers for the Norman, he rushed forward with his drawn sword.

The victor leaped to the ground, and had placed his hand upon his sword when the marshalls rode up and stopped the encounter.

"To-morrow," said Sir Norman, with a demoniacal glare at his antagonist.

"To-morrow—if you are sufficiently recovered," replied the other. "It took your worship a week to recover from the drubbing Little John gave you."

Suffocated with rage at the repartee, and the grins and acclamations of the crowd, Sir Norman retired, musing as to who the audacious knight could be, and what means he might have of carrying out his revenge.

The victor then, riding briskly forward, tapped the shields of both the other knights.

A murmur of unqualified admiration greeted this bold act, bowing to which, the knight opened the beaver, or lower part of his helmet, riding back to his post as he did so, and calling for a bowl of wine.

"To all good English hearts, and to our valorous king," he drank amid tremendous shouts, that made Prince John turn pale, and look inquiringly at his co-conspirators.

"Some one of Richard's besotted lances returning home," said Fitzurse, coldly; "one may know that by his loyalty."

The prince made no reply; but wished he could find the disinterested loyalty that would be true and faithful to royalty when under a cloud.

Sir James Falconbridge the stranger unhorsed at the first turn, while the Earl of Falaise's horse proved so restive, that the stranger lifted his lance when he could have struck his adversary, and prepared for a second encounter.

The earl bowed courteously, and saying that, accepting no favours, he accounted himself defeated, whereupon the stranger was declared the victor of the day.

A perfect shriek of applause greeted this wondrous and unexpected result.

CHAPTER CLIV.

THE QUEEN OF BEAUTY AND LOVE.

FOR a moment the conqueror of such renowned warriors and knights sat still upon his horse, as if he had been turned to stone, and was then about to ride from the lists, when the marshals stopped him, saying that he must advance and receive the prize of victory from the prince.

"What name shall we announce as that of the victor of this day's tourney?"

"I have vowed to announce my name only at the last," replied the Unknown. "I believe that is allowable?"

"Perfectly so," said the polite marshal, who rode off to inform the prince.

He and his courtiers made a wry face at this; but there was no help for it, as it was quite within the habits and practices of chivalry.

Slowly and quietly the cynosure of all eyes rode up to the throne, and received from the mouth of the prince his hollow congratulations on his victory.

Then the horse, a splendid and noble creature, was led up to him for acceptance.

In another moment he was on his back and riding round the lists, his eyes fixed keenly on the galaxy of beauty around him.

Many a heart beat high, many a lovely demoiselle, who would have given her best jewels to be selected, tried to look demure and indifferent, while glowing with hope, as the knight, through his visor-bars, seemed to scan every feature of their countenances.

The heralds rode behind to hearken for his choice.

Suddenly the Unknown reined in his steed.

He had received from Prince John, as one of the prizes of the day, a coronet of green satin, having around its edge a circlet of gold, the upper edge of which was relieved by arrow points and hearts, placed interchangeably, like the strawberry leaves and balls upon a ducal crown.

All eyes were fixed on the gallery before which he halted.

Next minute the coronet was placed at the feet of Maid Marian.

The heralds then proclaimed Edith of Athelston the Queen of Beauty and Love.

Terrific was the applause from the crowd at his selecting a Saxon, while the nobles exchanged glances.

What did all this mean.

But this was no time to inquire too minutely into the causes which had led to the result. It behoved the prince, as he left the ground, to hail the queen of a day, and press her to take upon herself in the morning the rank which the victorious knight had bestowed upon her.

Blushing rosy red, and revealing new beauties at every word, Edith accepted the position most gracefully, though, in her heart, infinitely amused at the evident discomfiture of the prince and his favourites.

She then rose to leave the gallery, closely followed

by Agnes, who, now the excitement was over, was anxious to the last degree to escape from observation.

They reached the entrance of the grand stand, as we should call it now, in safety, and there stood several of the retainers of the convent to escort Edith.

A party of sullen-looking men, in a livery which Agnes knew but too well, were beside them.

Agnes shrank back terrified.

"Lady," said one of them, advancing, and speaking less gruffly than might have been expected, "your uncle waits for you. He saw you in the gallery, and cannot allow you to lodge anywhere but in his own house."

"Where is my husband?" said the unfortunate girl.

"Husband!" laughed one of the attendants, "the young lady is demented. This way, miss."

"A truce, insolent knave, to your jests," said Edith, sternly; "this fair young creature is a friend of mine, and I will allow her neither to be insulted nor ill-used. Make way—I answer for her; go tell her uncle so."

"Here comes Sir Hugh."

Edith and the crowd who had been standing listening to this parley now turned, and saw the grave and morose knight advancing, surrounded by his men-at-arms.

He tried to look serene and pleasant, but the attempt was a pure failure—he did but grin like a monkey.

"He will take me!" gasped Agnes, in a whisper, "I cannot resist. I trust in you and Robin Hood—Robin Hood, the friend of all the injured and oppressed!"*

Edith pressed her hand.

Sir Hugh pushed his horse right up to where his niece stood beside Edith.

"Pardon, Queen of Beauty and of Love," said Sir Hugh, doffing his cap with courtly grace, "pardon me for disturbing you; but in your company I see a truant niece of mine, of whom I would ask a question or two."

"Certainly," replied Edith, glancing everywhere in the crowd for Robin Hood and Sir Ralph.

But they were together in the tent of the former, who was disrobing and receiving the ransom of the knight's arms and horses.

"How came you to leave your convent?" said Sir Hugh, in a stern and commanding tone.

"To see the tournament."

"In what company?"

"That of my husband, Sir Ralph Tressilian."

The uncle looked black as night. Married, and to the man, above all others, he feared!

---

* Did Robin Hood ever really exist, or is he a mere coinage of the brain, is a question we are repeatedly asked by persevering correspondents.

As we have no desire to mislead our readers, we at once emphatically say to this question—Yes.

The first distinct mention of Robin Hood is by Fordun, the Scottish historian, who wrote in the fourteenth century. He says:—"There rose among the disinherited the famous brigand, Robert Hode, with his accomplices, whom the common people are so fond of celebrating in their games and stage-plays, and whose exploits, chanted by strolling ballad-singers, delighted them above all things." Upon these ballads, adapting themselves, generation by generation, to the changes of language, rests the historical evidence of the individuality of Robin Hood, beyond this mention by Fordun. But this evidence is quite sufficient.

A theory has been set up by some enthusiastic interpreters of song and legend, that Robin Hood and Little John, and many a nameless outlaw, were great heroes, who had been defeated with Simon de Montfort, at the battle of Evesham, in 1265. Others make out Robin Hood to have been an Earl of Huntingdon. He is the Saxon yeoman, Locksley, of Walter Scott.

According to Thierry, the whole of the band that ranged the vast woodland districts of Derby, Nottingham, and Yorkshire, were the remnants of the old Saxon race, who had lived in this condition of defiance to Norman oppression from the time of Hereward, the same type of generous robbers and redressers of wrongs as the famous Cumberland bandits, Adam Bell, Clym of the Cleugh, and William of Cloudesley.

Mr. Charles Knight, in his "Popular History of England," accepts Robin Hood as a real personage, and considers that there may have been a succession of Robin Hoods during the long term of Norman tyranny; but, whoever he was, and in whatever reign he lived, Robin Hood is the representative of a never-ending protest of the people against misrule. In the Robin Hood ballads the detestation of the oppressor was long kept alive; and, having put aside the exaggeration of these ballads, we feel that we are in the natural regions of poetry, surrounded by adventures that might have been real, and by men that have human hearts in their bosoms, when we read of the stories of "the gentlest thief that ever was." Fuller, who places Robin Hood amongst his "Worthies," says:—"Know, reader, he is entered on our catalogue, not for his thievery, but for his gentleness."

But he was a cunning courtier and a shrewd dissembler.

"Child, if you are indeed married, my service to you and your husband. In the meantime, you must to my house, where, if Sir Ralph will follow, I shall know how to entertain him."

Next instant Agnes was seated on a palfrey, and after a meaning glance at Edith, rode away beside her false and cruel relative.

Edith made the best of her way to the house where the abbess awaited her, cold, stern, and as much changed as if she had been another woman.

"And you had some hand, it appears, in this sacrilege," she said, harshly.

"What sacrilege?" cried Edith.

"Stealing away a child whose vocation was heavenward," said the abbess, coldly.

"No more vocation for heaven than either you or I," replied the girl, hotly.

The abbess crossed herself, looked horror-struck, and then smiled.

Edith pretended not to see the smile, and quietly told Agnes's story.

"Alas!" said the good woman, whose sympathies were soon won for the young and happy, "'tis much as I expected. The young and innocent are always sacrificed for the avaricious and greedy. But this Sir Hugh is powerful. I know not what may be done."

At the same moment Robin Hood and Sir Ralph entered, the latter pale and with a red flush in the middle of his cheek.

"I wonder you dare enter here!" cried the abbess, with a look as dark and gloomy as was in her nature.

"Have you, too, turned against us?" said Robin, "then, indeed, we are lost."

"Don't believe a word she says!" exclaimed Edith, "she thoroughly sympathises with your trouble, and will do her best to ease it."

The young men caught each a hand, and pressed it to his lips. Sir Ralph had found Robin's warning but too true, and was now well aware that his wife was in the clutches of one who would part with her only when forced.

"There was a will strongly in poor Agnes's favour," he observed, "and which fully accounts for his conduct. If Agnes either enters a convent or dies, he inherits."

The abbess shook her head mournfully at this manifestation of worldly wickedness.

"Enters a convent or dies," mused Robin, "the most satisfactory would be for her to die."

Sir Ralph started.

"My friend," he said, "what mean you?"

"Nothing—nothing, an idea. But we will talk of it presently."

A domestic entered, and handed a letter to the abbess. It was from Sir Hugh's chaplain, saying that Agnes was ill both in body and mind, and would gladly see the abbess.

When the servant had withdrawn she told them her message.

"Go," said Robin, earnestly, "see her, and give a promise that you will send her a leech. Leave the rest to me."

The abbess was of too gentle and yielding a disposition to make any inquiries, so agreeing to all the outlaw told her, she went out on her expedition.

Then the outlaw, whose fertility at expedients was well known, had a long conference with Sir Ralph and Marian, who listened with charmed ears.

They heard all he had to say, and even then could scarcely believe his proposition possible.

It appeared, however, to be the only feasible one.

Much as they feared the results, both were fain to agree to it, and to let Robin Hood carry out his plan without any let or hindrance.

Now Robin had matured his ideas the instant he had heard that Agnes was ailing.

He had a double object in view, but this he did not think proper to explain to anybody.

There were few towns within fifty miles of his own head-quarters where the outlaw had not some friends. His deeds of kindness and generosity had been so many, that everywhere he went he found men devoted to his interests.

With a simple yeoman's cap on his head, a cloak over his shoulders, and yet with a trusty sword and dagger by his side, Robin sallied forth into the open air.

He had some distance to go, and, despite his great fatigue from the events of the day, he never hesitated one moment, but leaping on a fresh horse, dashed out of the crowded little 'town in the direction of a hamlet hid in the bosom of the forest.

He knew his way well, and before twenty minutes were passed came in sight of a small knot of houses, the first of which was larger than common.

It was the abode of Simon Sheepshanks, a learned herbalist and apothecary in great request among the rich and great.

He was said to know the secrets of all the plants which grew wild in the forest, and to be able to distil from them the finest remedies for all known diseases.

Robin tied his horse to a bush, crossed a rude kind of garden in front of the cottage, lifted a latch, and entered.

He was in the "physician's" laboratory; as usual, in those days, presenting a mixture of stuffed birds and animals, crucibles, jars, bottles, fire-stoves, and sundry things which it would take a whole page to describe.

The man himself was thin, pale, and cadaverous. He was a man of about fifty; thin, light, active; with a twinkling grey eye, somewhat too full of moisture; and a number of those long radiating wrinkles which, we believe, are called crows' feet.

His general complexion was white; of that dry and somewhat withered appearance which long habits of dissipation sometimes leave behind, when dissipation is not combined with drunkenness.

But his dissipation was unremitting study, from early dawn long into the watches of the night—more injurious than dissipation.

In his every glance there was a quick, sharp, prying expression.

"Welcome!" he said, in something of a subservient tone, which his intercourse with the insolent great had accustomed him to, except such weak minds as were to be ruled by pertinacious effrontery. "What happy conjunction of Mars and Venus brings to my door the prince and pattern of outlaws?"

"I' faith, no broken bone nor illness of mine," said Robin, laughing, "though I have this day tilted in my first lists."

"Didst feel thy overthrow much?"

"Marry, as I am the victor," continued the outlaw, merrily, "I have no falls to speak of."

"Victor!" cried Simon Sheepshanks. "You, a Saxon yeoman, fight in the lists, and overthrow three first-rate Norman knights! Oh, Robin! they'll tear off your spurs, scourge you from the ring, and then hang thee, lad."

And the good-natured Saxon leech fairly blubbered.

"Canst read?" said Robin.

"Boo—oo—oo!" sobbed Simon.

"Read that,"—handing him a parchment. "Read it out, man."

"*This is to give notice to all men, that the bearer, Robert Earl of Huntingdon, was duly knighted by me, and is a fit and worthy person to enter the lists against even a crowned prince.* RICHARD."

"Richard King of England!—Robert Earl of Huntingdon!" cried Simon. "What has all this to do with us?"

"Only that I am Robert Earl of Huntingdon," said the outlaw, proudly; "as many have yet to learn to their cost."

"My gracious master," exclaimed the somewhat watery-eyed physician, "what can I do for you?"

"I am in haste, my worthy Simon, and another time will tell thee more. Remember, a word may undo all. You shall live to see me in my castle yet, and then I will never forget my old friends."

"You have done for me enough already. What can I do for you?"

"Have you any drugs that will mimic death—that, given to a young and innocent girl, will blanch her cheeks, whiten her lips, glass her eyes, still the beating of the heart, and make men think her truly dead?"

"I have," said the leech, drily.

"Give me some."

"For what purpose, Robin?"

"For a good, a noble, a just purpose—to make a recreant Norman knight give up a pilfered inheritance!" cried the outlaw. "You shall know all another time. Give me the drug, and one that will revive the patient at will."

Without another word, the "physician" proceeded to compound two mixtures (liquids), which he placed in two small stone bottles—the one white, the other brown.

"This, Robin," he said, pointing to the white one, "given now, in an hour will so counterfeit death that not even blood would flow from a pricked wound. Take this lancet—it may be of use to you. In this brown bottle is a compound that in ten minutes will chase the black demon from the human frame and light it up once more to life and sunshine. Be careful not to leave any one too long under the influence of the first."

Robin promised, thanked him, and withdrew, leaving a purse upon the table, which the leech put away with a sigh.

"Not from you, Robin, can I refuse, but I wish you would believe in my unselfish devotion and friendship. But bah! what friendship can there be between a belted earl and a poor student, who studies how to save the human life ye brave men are so fond of taking?"

CHAPTER CLV.

AGNES IN DANGER.

WHEN Sir Hugh Fitzurse came into possession of the person of his niece he was for a time so overcome by fury and surprise that his reasoning faculties were entirely gone.

Married! and to a brave and popular soldier—her cousin—one who must know something of the will.

What was to be done?

Part from her he would not at any price.

This he was determined on, even as the wicked uncle in the famous nursery story of the Babes in the Wood.

But how was he to contend against the influence of the young knight, if he could prove their union?

In those days the marriage of a novice was common enough, the greedy church exacting only pecuniary fines.

As with the present High Priest at Rome, anything could be done in a church which traded in indulgences and invented miracles, much more clumsily, however, than spirit-rappers and such like impostors.

His first act was to summon the abbess, to whom he read such a lecture that the good woman was quite put out; albeit, she gave him rather a severer lesson than he expected.

But now his difficulties seemed to increase. Under the circumstances, he at once resolved to take counsel of his confessor, who was sufficiently cunning and unscrupulous to serve his purpose.

On entering his house, Agnes, who, gentle creature, was flushed and feverish, was given over to a kind of housekeeper to be cared for.

This woman received strict orders to be kind to her but under no pretence, however, to allow her to leave her room.

Agnes, as soon as she was alone, began calmly to review her situation, and knowing full well the great power and influence of her uncle, began to entertain exaggerated fears of what might occur.

The worst to her was to be separated from the young husband of her love, just as she had tasted the happiness of wedded life, where true affection unites a man and woman in bonds to last as long as life.

The woman brought her cooling drinks, which alone she could take, and then advised her to lie down.

Meanwhile the knight had sent for the priest Leon, with whom he held a long conference.

In those days principle was a thing scarcely understood, men being divided into three sets of thinkers—those who believed, those who did not, and those who hardly knew whether they did or did not.

Of one class were those who, admitted behind the pale of the church, living with its dignitaries and high priests, had seen so much hypocrisy, deceit, and profligacy, that, confounding the men with religion, they rejected all they taught, and were, in consequence, hardened infidels.

Then came the bigoted and superstitious, who were scarcely any better, for if the former sinned from utter recklessness, they sinned fully prepared to confess and obtain absolution when needful.

The masses, who were simple enough to pay respect to the priests, and to worship from an inherent feeling of piety, had about them a bluff sort of honesty, rarely to be found where the regal, noble, and clerical powers combined to make them dissolute and dishonest.

Sir Hugh Fitzurse was a man of the most cold-blooded nature, avaricious and ambitious to the last degree.

He clung to Prince John, because he knew the king's brother would support him in many unjust deeds, by which he had become possessed of property.

"This girl has flown high," he said, after a while: "this Ralph Tressilian is a brave and wealthy youth. whom the prince has long wished to win: did he but know this he would soon tear this fluttering dove from me. What is to be done?"

"You know the tenor of the will?"

"I do, man—but why talk to me thus? If the case gets to the Court of Eyre I'm ruined."

"She must become a daughter of the church or die," continued the priest, "to make you heir."

"Well?"

"One or the other must be accomplished."

Sir Hugh looked keenly at him; his bronzed cheek was somewhat flushed. Cold and selfish as was that man's heart, there was yet a remnant of the old sensation left; this child, wife of the young and gallant knight, was his brother's child. To condemn her to a nunnery was a kind of death, and yet that he could reconcile himself to.

But to imbrue his hands in her blood!

"I would to Heaven she were taken away," he said, pettishly, "my great trouble would be over."

There was a discreet knock at the door, and then the aged female attendant, already alluded to, entered hastily.

"The young lady is taken very ill," she said, "and begs you will send for the abbess."

The knight and priest exchanged glances.

"Certainly, my good Madge," said the former, with every appearance of heartiness: "will you write a line, father, to invite her? It will be necessary—she is an imperious dame.

The priest acquiesced, and hastily wrote. The old woman retired and sent the letter.

"If she be really ill," said Hugh, in a low, hushed whisper, "all may yet be well."

"You are right, my son—and the silver candlesticks you have so long promised to the shrine can be paid," he added, with a low hypocritical bow.

"Certainly, father."

"And now, my son," he continued, after a moment's thought; "when the abbess has been, we will ascertain how ill she is. If her dissolution be certain, and these sudden attacks often end suddenly, you can easily withdraw all kind of suspicion from yourself, and even gain credit for great generosity."

"How so?"

"Give the will to the chancellor at the festival to-night—it is for him to record it."

"But the excuse for hiding it?"

"You wished no adventurer to know of her wealth, and hence persecute her with futile attentions. You can say all kinds of handsome things about hoping she will live long to enjoy her good fortune; when she dies you will come into your rights without a murmur."

"If she be really worse I will do it. But, Father Leon, if once the will is made known she must not recover."

"Leave that to me, Sir Hugh."

In a very few minutes they heard that the abbess had gone into see her, and both waited somewhat impatiently the moment of her departure.

The abbess remained more than half an hour, at the end of which time she entered the room with a grave and sorrowful mien.

"Well," said Sir Hugh.

"You have much to answer for, Sir Hugh," said the abbess, coldly. "I hope you may win forgiveness from Heaven."

"What mean you, madam?"

"The girl, ill as she is, solemnly swears that she entered my house against her consent, by force; that in her father's last hours he bade her choose between a husband and the church, and that she chose the former."

"Good lady abbess," said Sir Hugh, with every evidence of the most profound respect, "the poor girl speaks truth. My brother wished her to take time, however, and I placed her with you for a year, determined at the end of that period to dedicate her to the church, or marry her, just as she herself chose."

"Then have we wronged you," replied the abbess, who, without guile and cunning herself, could not believe it to exist in others; "but I fear me any regret is now too late—the child is very ill—and I am now hastening away to send a learned leech to her, who may prognosticate her real illness.

"You do well," continued the knight, "and I beg you to receive my thanks."

The abbess bowed and left the room.

"Heaven is on your side," said the sacrilegious priest, crossing his hands on his bosom.

"Say, rather, the devil," cried Sir Hugh, impatiently; for, sooth to say, he was much ashamed of the part he was playing.

"This leech must be seen to. If he saves her ——"

The knight looked at him with a strange smile. The man he had purchased was more wicked than he had believed.

"We will hear his report. I suppose the thing of herbs and simples has his price."

"All men have," observed the priest.

Sir Hugh had seen too much of the world not to know that in most cases this was true. But, like most other men of his calibre, he judged all men by the experience of his narrow circle of selfish, profligate, and ambitious men.

To while away the time, the two accomplices entered a small banqueting room, and there agreed to abide until the leech should come.

CHAPTER CLVI.

A THING OF SHREDS AND PATCHES.

IT was not long before the domestics announced the arrival of the apothecary, who was at once introduced to the presence of Sir Hugh and the priest.

About middle height, not at all stout, his frame might have betokened less poverty than his dress and visage, the latter of which was white, wrinkled, and pinched; while his clothes were not only of the humblest, but the most ragged character.

He appeared either utterly oblivious of the outer man, or could not command the means to obtain better apparel.

There was, however, a roguish twinkle in his eye that seemed to indicate at bottom a jolly fellow.

"You come from the lady abbess?"

"I am so honoured."

"You know your duty?"

"To see a young lady sick unto death."

"'Tis well. Go to her: and when you have seen her, return—I am anxious to hear your report."

The drug dealer retired with a low and humble bow, following the old woman to the apartments of the young girl.

Agnes was lying on a couch dressed as she had been during the tourney. She was flushed, hot, and feverish, but not more so than was explained by extreme anxiety of mind.

She looked up languidly, and with a pout, at the thing of shreds and patches that gazed at her.

"Why have you brought this man here?" she said, querulously; "I have no money, palmer."

"She is ill," put in the leech. "My good dame," he added, addressing the old woman courteously, "if you would order these herbs to be warmed gently without boiling, we will soon get rid of this fever, when I believe all may be safely left to your excellent care and judgment."

"I will do it myself," said the gratified dame.

"I won't take any of your stuff," cried Agnes.

The thing of shreds and patches shook his head at the

dame, smiled benignly at Agnes, and advanced towards her as the beldame left the room.

"Get away."

"Lady Agnes Tressilian," said a voice that thrilled to her heart, "I never expected to be treated thus cavalierly by you."

She sat up on the couch, and looked at him with mute wonder and astonishment.

"Who and what are you?"

He smiled, and something in his smile reassured her.

"My name," he said, in a whisper, "is Robin Hood. I come here to save you from your uncle, and if you will but obey me in all things, to-morrow you shall be safe in your husband's arms."

"I am your slave," said Agnes, rapturously; "command, and I will obey."

"Agnes," continued Robin Hood, with his eyes fixed upon the door, "we are playing a bold and dangerous game. One act of hesitation on your part, and all is lost."

"Try me—anything to take me back to my husband."

"Your uncle, now that you cannot be cloistered, wishes your death," he began.

"My death?"

"Even so—because it will give him all your lands and riches; if he cannot compass it, he will be your bitter enemy, and make it difficult for your husband to regain you."

"Well?"

"The only plan by which we can defeat his machinations is for you, to all appearance, to be dead."

"How so?" said Agnes, now pale enough.

"Drink this potion—leave all the rest to me. Quick, for I hear the woman coming."

Agnes looked at the stone bottle with pardonable horror.

"For his—for your husband's sake."

She took it and quaffed it to the last drop. Robin held her hand in his, and watched her with admiration and deep affection.

"I trust in you wholly," she whispered.

"You may. May your waking be a happy one! I will give you some warm drink; then turn as if sleepy."

Madge entered the room and brought the drink, a substance very much resembling the *tisane* of the French doctors, whose faith in common herbs is great.

"Now sleep," said the leech, gravely.

Agnes drank, turned her head, and closed her eyes.

The leech took the old woman from the room with a grave and sorrowful mien.

"The child," he observed, "is worse than she looks. This sleep is doomed to be her last. Be not cast down or surprised, my worthy dame, for not all the skill of every learned man in the world could save her. At midnight she will have breathed her last. Be prepared, for I see that you are good and gentle."

The old woman seated herself, overwhelmed with the excess of her emotions.

She had not seen the charming young girl without feeling a deep interest in her fate.

There was another reason, of which none knew, that influenced her feelings.

"Merciful Heaven!" she cried, "the poor child that drew her first nourishment from this aged breast. 'Tis the cruelty of her villain uncle has done this. Heaven forgive him!—I never will."

Robin looked keenly at her; her sorrow was evidently genuine. But, with every disposition to be generous and believe in people's good qualities, the outlaw recollected that she was a salaried servant of the enemy.

"We are all in the hands of Heaven," said the leech, "I must go prepare Sir Hugh for this heavy loss."

"Gain—a gain he has plotted for for years," answered the woman, in a low tone; "how know you he has not poisoned her?"

Robin started, and almost coloured.

"Judge not too harshly, lest we be judged," he said, gravely, "had she been poisoned, it had not escaped me. But," and he looked the woman full in the face, "if you do feel pity for this child, hope for the best."

There was a light in the woman's eyes he could scarcely mistake or doubt.

"Why did you not make yourself known to her?" he said.

"She never knew me after a year old. I have ever since been with her uncle. She never probably heard of me."

"'Tis a pity. But what is done cannot be helped. Be at hand to compose her limbs should the worst happen. I must away."

And leaving the horrified woman, really overcome with grief, he went down to where the knight and priest eagerly awaited him.

The knight was pale, the chaplain stood apart in the shadow to watch the leech.

"Well," said Sir Hugh.

"I wish I had been called in sooner," said the thing of shreds and patches, in a querulous tone.

"Why?"

"I might have saved her."

"Saved her! what mean you?"

"That ere midnight the girl will be a corpse," was the cold and phlegmatic reply.

Sir Hugh turned deadly pale, and pressed his hand upon his heart, and gasped forth something inaudible.

"Is there then no hope?" asked the priest, mildly.

"None. I leave now to announce to my lady abbess that she may prepare for the funeral to-morrow."

"Art sure?" said the knight.

"Quite. The attack is one that almost baffles my experience. I think the heart is stopped, but she will, I say, be a corpse ere midnight."

And the leech went out, with a low and humble bow to both the knight and priest."

"Well, Sir Hugh," said Leon, "why do you not hasten to the festive scene, deposit the will with the chancellor, sealed as it is—saying that you fear its contents must now be made known?"

"You say well," cried the knight, "but this is most sudden. I almost wish I had not interfered. This girl's death will sit heavily on my conscience, heavier than I could wish—but what is done is irrevocable."

And with this cowardly salve to his own conscience, the knight went forth to the castle of Ashby, where declaring his niece's serious state, he begged the chancellor to relieve him of the burden of the will, which, for reasons he explained, he hitherto had kept secret.

The chancellor gladly acquiesced, as out of all such transactions, regular or irregular, he made his penny.

But neither had any idea what an explosive compound that will was doomed to be.

CHAPTER CLVII.

THE GREAT DAY OF THE TOURNAMENT.

THE daylight had dawned upon the glades of the oak forest. The green boughs glittered with all their pearls of dew. The hind led her fawn from the covert of high fern to the more open walks of the greenwood, and no huntsman was there to watch or intercept the stately hart as he paced at the head of the antlered herd.

The abbess had been informed of the death of Agnes at midnight; and as the uncle had no wish to blazon the marriage with Sir Ralph Tresilian, she was allowed, without let or hindrance, to remove the body of the noble girl, as a novice belonging to her convent.

The good abbess had not been admitted into the secret by Robin Hood, and therefore acted in perfect good faith.

Before dawn the body was removed to a small vaulted chapel in the church of Ashby-de-la-Zouche.

The place would have been quite dark, but for the red and smoky light from a couple of flambeaux or torches.

There were the usual arched roof and naked walls, a rude altar of stone, and a crucifix of the same material.

Before this altar was placed a bier, on which was the body—pale, waxen white; and by its side kneeled three priests.

The ceremony was, however, brief; and then all retired, preparatory to the final obsequies, which were to take place the next day.

The abbess shut herself up in her apartments, to muse on the instability of human happiness, while Edith of Athelston, though she had received a mysterious hint, hesitated to take upon herself the prominent position of Queen of Beauty and Love.

But she was overruled.

The concourse of spectators was even greater than it had been the day before, the single encounters having only whetted the popular appetite.

This day was to be given to a general *melée*, in which all the knights could take a part.

Sir Norman Malvoisin was too bruised and injured to take the lead, as expected.

The duty devolved then upon the young Earl of Falaise.

Great was the expectation of the crowd, and hence the enthusiasm with which they rushed to get good seats and positions whence to see the contest, which resembled more a real battle than any mimicry possible in modern times.

The two leaders—for the Unknown, as a matter of course, was selected to lead one side—rode first into the lists, and took up positions opposite to one another; while the heralds proceeded to settle the terms on which the other knights joined the combatants.

It was naturally decided that each party should be equal numbers, and the heralds carefully counted the noble candidates as they appeared for either side.

All knew the perilous nature of the encounter which was to take place; an encounter far more dangerous than single combats, but, nevertheless, more frequent.

Many knights who did not feel sufficient confidence in themselves to stand in front of a single adversary of high reputation, were, nevertheless, desirous of displaying their valour in the general combat, where they could make their own selections, and probably meet with those with whom they were somewhat of an equality.

There were on the present occasion some forty knights on each side, ready for the conflict, all, to judge from appearances, valorous and experienced men; though the show of rank was on the side of the earl, many gallant knights disdaining to follow an unknown leader.

It thus happened that the unknown led some whose horses and caparisons did not bear comparison with those of the Normans; one of these was a gigantic knight, mounted on a black horse, large of size, tall, and, to all appearance, powerful and strong.

The man himself was in black armour.

About nine o'clock the whole plain was crowded with horsemen, horsewomen, and foot passengers.

It might have been remarked that a much larger proportion of them were yeomen armed than had been seen on the previous day.

Then came a flourish of trumpets, marking the arrival of Prince John, while a second heralded the approach of the Queen of Beauty and Love.

She was surrounded by a bevy of beauties, whose loveliness, however, only made her own shine the more resplendent and bright.

She took her seat amidst a burst of music, half drowned by the loud shouts of the "swinish multitude," as the insolent Normans loved to call the people; while the hot sun shone fierce and bright on the polished arms of the knights.

Then the heralds proclaimed the conditions and laws of the second day's tournament, which, as explaining the manners of the day, may justly be transferred to these pages.

The champions were, by these laws, prohibited to thrust with the sword, and were confined to striking. A knight, it was announced, might use a mace or battle-axe at pleasure, but the dagger was a prohibited weapon. A knight unhorsed might renew the fight on foot with any other on the opposite side in the same predicament; but mounted horsemen were in that case forbidden to assail him. When any knight could force his antagonist to the extremity of the lists, so as to touch the palisade with his person or arms, such opponent was obliged to yield himself vanquished, and his armour and horse were placed at the disposal of the conqueror. A knight thus overcome was not permitted to take farther share in the combat.

If any combatant was struck down, and unable to recover his feet, his squire or page might enter the lists and drag his master out of the press; but, in that case, the knight was adjudged vanquished, and his arms and horse declared forfeited. The combat was to cease as soon as Prince John should throw down his leading staff

or truncheon, another precaution usually taken to prevent the unnecessary effusion of blood by the too long endurance of a sport so desperate. Any knight breaking the rules of the tournament, or otherwise transgressing the rules of honourable chivalry, was liable to be stripped of his arms, and, having his shield reversed, to be placed in that posture astride upon the bars of the palisade, and exposed to public derision, in punishment of his unknightly conduct. Having announced these precautions, the heralds concluded with an exhortation to each good knight to do his duty, and to merit favour from the Queen of Beauty and of Love.

And now,

> The heralds left their pricking up and down,
> Now ringes trumpets loud and clarion.
> There is no more to say, but east and west
> In go the speares sadly in the rest.
> In goeth the sharp spur into the side;
> There see men who can joust and who can ride;
> There shiver shaftes upon shieldes thick,
> He feeleth through the heart-spone the prick.
> Up springes speares, twenty feet in height,
> Out go the swordes to the silver bright.
> The helms they to hewn and to shred;
> Out burst the blood with stern streames red.

It was a magnificent sight to one who could divest himself of all idea of the fearful nature of the strife to follow—the champing steeds, the gallant champions seated like statues in their war saddles, waiting alike with impatience the signal for the combat.

The lances of the good knights were held upright, their bright points gleaming in the sun, and their streamers flaunting in the breeze.

Laissez aller!

Such at last was the cry from the voice of the herald in a loud and anxious tone.

The champions were drawn up two deep, and, as the trumpets sounded the charge, all in the first row dashed their spurs into their horses, a cloud of dust arose, the thunder of hoofs, the clanging of shields was heard, and the rivals met in the centre of the lists.

The rear rank waited.

The front rank of the northern band was commanded by the unknown victor of the day before.

The rear rank was commanded by the Black Knight, his prodigious form and the secret assurance of the captain having won him this indisputably.

For some minutes it was hard to distinguish anything but a confused mass of combatants. The dust from so many horsemen darkened the air, and it was a minute or two ere the spectators had any idea of the results of the encounter. At length, however, the fight became visible, and it was found that about half of the knights on either side were dismounted, some by the superior ability of their opponents, some by their superior weight and strength, which in several instances had borne down both horse and man.

Some lay still upon the ground, as if they would never open their eyes more to the glad light of the sun.

Others, on both sides, who had received wounds by which they were disabled, were stopping their blood with their scarfs, and trying, as far as in them lay, to extricate themselves from the tumult.

As for the still mounted warriors, whose lances had been almost all broken by the fury of the encounter, they were now hard at it with their swords and battle-axes, and exchanging buffets and blows as if honour and life depended on the issue of the combat.

Now from the rear came as many of the second row as was needed, the ranks of the Unknown, however, leaving a reserve, as more of the followers of the Earl of Falaise had been thrown than of the other side.

The noise and tumult was now something terrible. Each party shouted its peculiar war-cries; the horses neighed; the knights cried lustily to one another, and such a hubbub and confusion prevailed that none could tell who was the victor, or even recognise the men in the *melée*.

The champions on both sides fought with the blindest fury; their blood was at fever point, and all felt as if they were on a real field of battle.

Now the victory seemed to lean to one side, then to the other, as the tide flowed.

The clang of blows, the shrill blast of the trumpets, the groans of those who fell heavily, were distinctly heard.

ROBIN HOOD AGAIN VICTORIOUS.

The armour in which the combatants had come forth arrayed, as if to escort some fair princess to her wedding, was now defaced by dust and blood, indented and cracked by the strokes of sword and battle-axe.

The gay plumage, shorn from the crests, drifted upon the breeze like snow-flakes.

All that was beautiful and graceful in the martial array had disappeared, and what was now visible was only calculated to awaken terror or compassion.

The interest was now intense. The ladies strained their eyes to discover the true state of affairs.

Suddenly the general combat ceased, as if by enchantment, as the well-known forms of the two leaders were distinguished in hand to hand conflict.

They fought as if some instinct on both sides had told them how deeply their interests were opposed.

All the fury which mortal animosity, joined to rivalry of honour could inspire, animated them.

The conflict was long, doubtful, and on both sides almost equally creditable, when suddenly the trumpets sounded a charge, and the heralds cried the stereotyped words,—

" Fight on, brave knights. Man dies, but glory lives. Fight on—death is better than defeat! Fight on, brave knights, for bright eyes behold your deeds."

The warriors, who had hitherto taken no part in the fray, and those who had reposed, now dashed into the midst of the lists; a fearful encounter again took place; once more a cloud of dust arose, and then, just as the feelings of the audience were wound up to the highest pitch, the dust cleared away.

The fight was over.

The Earl of Falaise lay prostrate on the ground, with the Unknown's sword at his throat.

The Black Knight, after unhorsing two, was receiving from them the homage of defeat.

The day was finished, and the bright Norman cohort, despite its force, its splendid array, and show of early triumph, was utterly routed and defeated.

The prince, with a scowl, gave the signal, and loud and long-continued acclamations greeted the victors, who rode or walked to their tents to array themselves as became gallant knights ere presenting themselves before the Queen of Beauty.

Prince John would now gladly have left the field, but the minor sports were to be carried on, and the politic though wrong-headed and worthless pretender to sovereignty had no wish just then to offend the sturdy yeomanry, who in any great contest would play, necessarily, so leading a part.

The ground was cleared, targets were set up, and it was announced that while the knights took refreshments, an hour would be given to the archery competition.

There was a murmur of satisfaction on all sides at this announcement, as all who were feverishly impatient to hear the names of the victors felt it would be at all events a pastime.

The number of competitors was about fifty, as even many who were not reputed good shots were glad to try for such a prize as a bugle-horn mounted with silver, and a silken baldric.

The first shot, however, lessened the number to a dozen, among whom suddenly appeared Robin Hood, in the dress of a forester.

No one had noticed him leave his tent.

The favourite of the day was one Hulbart, a well-known shot, who in the service of the crown had won golden opinions both as a diligent enemy of poachers, and an admirable shot.

Of all the competitors, he and Robin alone put every arrow in the bull's-eye—and each man shot ten.

Prince John, who now sat on horseback between the throne of the Queen of Beauty and the targets, leaned forward to gaze at the competitors.

As far as he could judge, one of the victors was in the royal uniform, the other in that of a plain yeoman.

He beckoned them up, and Hulbart and Robin Hood stood in presence of the prince.

"You shoot well, my masters," said the prince, with a keen glance at both; "who is to win?"

"Well," replied Hulbart—a somewhat forward and conceited fellow—grinning the while, "an please your grace, I never was defeated yet."

"By St. Hubert," cried Robin, jollily, "but you will have to cry small this time."

"You talk big, fellow," said the prince.

"I say no more than I mean," replied the forester, drily.

"You must know that Hulbart has never been defeated," continued the prince, who wished to propitiate the large body of royal rangers.

"That is because, though the best bowman of Leicester and Staffordshire, he has never tried conclusions with the men of Yorkshire."

"Where do you hail from?" asked the brother of King Richard, with a suspicious glance.

"From Sherwood Forest."

"I thought so. Look to him close, men-at-arms. I have a strong suspicion the fellow is an outlaw or a braggart. Let him shoot—if he loses he shall be scourged from the lists and taken to prison to await the proof of his identity; if he wins, by God's truth! an he were that plucky varmint, Robin Hood himself, he goes scot free, on my word as a prince."

The outlaw looked strangely into the other's eyes, while a shout of such good Saxon applause as did not often greet the Norman prince made John aware how much he had done in those words to restore his popularity.

"Your grace," said Robin, "must let us after the target trial choose our own marks—I will shoot mine let him shoot his. The Queen of Beauty"—with a low and profound bow he said this—"will, I am sure, assist a poor Saxon yeoman."

"With the greatest pleasure!" cried Edith of Athelston, with a deep blush.

"Foregad!" said the prince, laughing, "thou art an impudent varlet."

"Nay, my liege," replied the Queen of Beauty, with a meaning smile; "we are bound to care as much for the requests of the meanest of our subjects as if they were the noblest and most powerful in the land."

Dead silence prevailed a moment, and then a cheer so deafening as to be heard a mile broke the stillness; none save the haughtiest minions of the tyrant forbore to applaud this novel sentiment of the Queen of Beauty.

Prince John bit his lip until the blood came, astounded as he was at the cheering.

But he made no remark.

Robin had exchanged two words in the meantime with the Queen of Beauty.

The target was now examined by both, after which the two retired to their posts at the end of the ring.

Hulbart shot first, hitting the bull's-eye so exactly as to leave no space for Robin.

The outlaw smiled as he pulled his bow to his ear, took careless aim, and shivering the ranger's arrow in two, sent it flying on all sides, and took its place in the centre.

"The foul fiend take the knave!" muttered John, "this will never do. The Yorkshire thief, an outlaw I am certain, will beat the other. Shoot knave, shoot!" he roared, "or it will go ill with thee!"

"Shoot first," said Hulbart, sulkily, addressing Robin

The arrows had been withdrawn from the target, and the outlaw took his usual aim, sending his arrow again into the bull's-eye, when it was followed by that of Hulbart, the two so close and tight together that none could declare the winner.

Prince John's brow lightened.

Robin then indicated his mark in a whisper to Hulbart.

"Never," said the ranger, with a start; "if you do that I give you the bucklers, or rather I yield to the devil that's in your jerkin, and not to human skill. A man can but do his best—and I shoot not where sure to miss."

"Thou art not sure to miss; the bull's-eye is still there—shoot at that," replied the yeoman.

"I will for my conscience sake, and because you shall not crow over me," said the ranger.

Both now keenly examined their arrows, while the spectators looked on amazed.

What was to be the target now?

They were soon made aware of this by the Queen of Beauty and of Love descending from her throne.

In her hand was a small silver ring, about an inch in diameter, with which she stood by the target, holding the ring between her fingers exactly in front of the bull's-eye, about two yards distance.

"Higher!" said the far-off voice of Robin Hood.

The ring was lifted higher.

"In the devil's name—no!" said Prince John, more gallantly than politely; "this cannot be. Your precious person cannot be endangered thus."

"I have no fear of the yeoman," said Edith of Athelston, quietly, "and as queen of the hour I claim obedience—shoot."

Hulbart, astounded at the calmness of the Queen of Beauty, and awed by the death-like stillness that prevailed, took as steady aim as he could and shot.

The arrow passed within three inches of Edith's outstretched hand, and buried itself in the target to the right of the centre.

Robin stood a moment still and motionless. He took his aim with settled calm and deliberation. The vast crowd awaited the result in breathless silence.

The arrow parted from the bow, whizzed through the air, passed through the ring, and struck the bull's-eye.

Frantic shouts succeeded this demonstration of skill, while Prince John frowned darkly.

"Fetch me this man," he said, "that I may know who carries certain death in his hand."

An inferior officer, called the Provost of the Games, who had superintended the archery sports, rode up with a flushed and heated countenance.

Again all listened with bated breath.

"Please, your grace——"

"Where is the winner?"

"Please your grace," stammered the provost, still without having gained his breath, "he's gone."

"Gone! how dared he leave without receiving his prize?"

"Please, your grace," continued the other, "he said Hulbart was to have the prize, to remember by it the day when he was defeated at bowmanship by Robin Hood."

"Ah!" cried the prince, hotly, "has that arch traitor dared to come here? a thousand marks——"

"Safe conduct, safe conduct!" shouted the crowd, without caring for the black looks of guards and soldiers.

"True, true!" said the cunning prince. "I had forgotten. I promised the man his safe conduct. Let him go."

A roar of applause, not often heard from English throats in those days, burst from the multitude.

"Long live Robin Hood! Hurrah!" was the cry.

"Long live Prince John! Hurrah!" was added in much fainter tones.

A flourish of trumpets, loud and repeated, now announced that the victorious knights were prepared.

The conquered stood in a row on foot, their horses and armour in the hands of pages to hand to the conqueror.

The Queen of Beauty and Love had regained her seat; Prince John and his favourite councillors were on horseback in a group around her.

The Unknown rode up, supported by all the party able to sit on horseback.

A dense mass of archers in Lincoln green were now congregated at the northern end.

At their head might have been seen Will Scarlett and Little John.

The prince took no note of this, or of sundry other suspicious preparations.

The Unknown rode up to where the royal party awaited his coming.

"You are the winner," said the prince, carelessly, "and have a right to receive a crown or chaplet of honour."

The champion bowed low, while loud shouts of exultation and admiration rose from all sides.

He moved his horse so as to face the throne on which Edith of Athelston sat, and lifted off his casque.

A wild cry of rage from some, of uproarious joy from others, greeted him.

Everybody had recognised Robin Hood.

The prince, who was livid with passion, turned towards the marshals, while Robin waved for silence.

"I came here as a knight and belted earl," he said, "to claim the chaplet of honour. Who dare say me nay?"

"Knight—belted earl?" began the prince.

"Pause, prince," said our hero, sternly, "here is the proof."

And he handed the parchment signed by Richard.

The prince turned ghastly pale, looked wildly around—he saw the writing was recent—and then recovered himself.

"This looks like the writing of my brother," he said, slowly, "but it is recent; who can prove that it is genuine?"

"That can and do I," put in a voice that made more than one tremble.

At the same moment the Black Knight advanced slowly, bare-headed, towards the throne.

Simultaneously there was a clattering of horses' hoofs, advancing in such numbers, and so rapidly, as to shake the ground before them.

At their head was the Earl of Essex, High Constable of England.

The archers came slowly behind.

"My liege—my brother!" stammered Prince John, white as death, while every courtier trembled—the people were stunned, and all for a moment was confusion.

"'Tis Richard King of England, who, because he would to-day fain fight in the tournament unknown, came thus poorly attended. But let not us interrupt the ceremony. Conclude it, I have journeyed far, and would retire.

The courtiers deserted Prince John, and would have crowded round Richard, but he waved them back, with a dark frown.

The air rang with shouts; the more that for a moment none could believe their eyes and ears.

Edith at once placed the chaplet on the victor's brow, who then was invited by the king to share the banquet prepared for the conspirators.

But the conspiracy was broken up. Some of the worst fled. One or two—Fitzwalter especially—were arrested for high treason, and afterwards pardoned by the generous monarch

Thus ended the tournament known in history as the "Gentle and Joyous Passage of Arms at Ashby," where four knights died shortly after leaving the field, thirty were desperately wounded, of whom six died afterwards.

CHAPTER CLVIII.

AGNES RECOVERED.

IMPATIENT as Robin Hood himself to be again in the woods, we pass over the royal banquet, where the

outlaw was received as Earl of Huntingdon, subject to a suit in the Court of Eyre, which the monarch ordered should be carried on without delay.

The banquet was dull and constrained, and soon none were left but Richard and his friends; the discomfited prince retiring, on a visit to his mother, and his immediate followers dispersing.

With a breath Richard had broken the conspiracy like a reed.

The monarch was very grave, and evidently glad to be alone with his trusty advisers.

This Robin saw, and soon retired with Ralph, without asking one or two favours, which, at a more propitious moment, he would certainly have wished to secure.

One was the recognition of Sir Ralph's marriage; the second, a formal release to Edith as a crown ward.

But as state affairs might occupy the king for several days, the outlaw—as we shall call him until he is really and truly recognised by law—determined to leave the affairs of Maid Marian in the hands of the abbess, while he and Sir Ralph placed Agnes in a position to claim her property under her father's will.

With this view the two men shifted their garments, changing them both to those of simple franklins, travelling armed and accoutred, and then taking three horses, tied them in a convenient place, and there left them.

They had secured an entrance to the church, the boozy sacristan being quite open to receive a bribe.

He gave them the key, and by its means they were soon inside. They were forced to move with extreme caution, as to have lit a flambeau or torch would have been to call public attention to them and their intentions.

They groped their way towards a door that led to the vault-like chapel in which Agnes lay.

They soon found it, and, as they had previously learned from the drunken priest, on opening the door, they also found that the monks who had been paid to watch all night had left the torches burning, and had retired either to feed or sleep.

This saved them much trouble.

Robin Hood led the way calm and fearless, while Sir Ralph, not without some doubts, and much of the superstition of his age, followed him.

It would be difficult but curious to analyse his feelings. He had the fullest confidence in Robin Hood; but, at the same time, it seemed to him impossible to feign death, as he had been told by the outlaw, Agnes appeared to do.

It is doubtful, such is the besotted ignorance which accompanies a religion into which no one is allowed to inquire out the priests, that Sir Ralph, somewhere in a corner of his soul, had a glimmering idea that his friend was about to raise the dead.

Now, with all his love and tenderness, Sir Ralph had no wish to make a life companion of one who had passed the mysterious threshold of the grave and then returned to earth.

He felt very much as weak and silly children do when passing through a churchyard at night.

The light seemed, however, to rouse him.

Still he glanced fearfully at the bier upon which lay something covered by a pall.

He glanced at it uneasily, and with strangely mixed sensations, while he could not be but astounded at the calm countenance of Robin Hood.

The outlaw pulled down, or rather lifted, the pall.

"Is she not lovely?" said the outlaw; "beautiful, even in this sleep of death, from which it seems cruel to wake her."

"Surely she is not dead," whispered Sir Ralph Tressilian, in an appalled tone.

"Dead! certainly not, or I were not here to commit the sacrilege of gazing on her mortal remains. She, in a moment, will revive; but not here; we must take her to the sacristan's hut. The shock were else too great. Go first, and lead the way."

The lover literally trembled, and as he saw Robin take her up in his arms, though he would gladly have relieved him of his burden, shook so he could not.

But his nervousness and agitation came now from hope.

The solemn, earnest tones of the outlaw chief were not to be mistaken.

Robin, lifting her as if she had been a child, carried her through the church, Ralph closing all doors.

They were soon in the open air, and then in the sacristan's hut, where burnt a light.

The whole clerical party were in the refectory of a neighbouring monastery feasting.

There was a small fire on the hearth, while Robin, a man of precaution, had brought with him a small wallet.

He placed the young girl on the sacristan's rough couch, and bade Ralph open the wallet.

The knight smiled, and his colour came, as he pulled forth a capon, some wine, and white bread.

"What is this for?" he said.

"My dear Sir Ralph, if you had been asleep for thirty hours, you would wake with an appetite like a hunter——I am sure the Lady Agnes will."

He then gently opened her mouth—the teeth were slightly set—and poured the contents of the brown bottle down her throat.

She was pale as a corpse; a livid ring was round her eyes and mouth; her eyes were set as in death, and scarcely the learnedest leech could have told she had not passed the Valley of the Shadow.

Then there came on the cheek a little red spot, so small as scarcely to be seen, which, however, faintly and gradually spread until the whole face became of a pinky white.

Then there was a deep sigh.

The colour became warmer and warmer, sigh succeeded sigh, and then the bright orbs, that most of all indicate life, opened and were cast wildly round a moment, to beam next instant with unaffected happiness.

"My husband!"

"My wife!"

And, regardless of the outlaw's presence, they cordially embraced.

"How long have I been asleep?" she asked, after a pause.

"Twenty or thirty hours," smiled Robin.

"I recollect—I was to die. Was it so?"

"Everybody believes you dead," replied Robin, laughing, "and must believe so for a day or two, when Ralph will take you to court in triumph. Now for Tressilian Hall."

"But I am so faint, I cannot stand," she murmured.

"Hungry, my lady," said the outlaw.

Agnes nodded her head in such a comical way that her husband could not help laughing.

The supper was then placed before her, and to induce her to eat the others joined her.

Talking and hearing explanations, the young girl recovered her strength and spirits.

A cup of wine, highly spiced, revived her wholly, and then mounting their horses, the three left Ashby-de-la-Zouch, striking through the forest by a well frequented road leading to a large town. This they travelled until nearly dawn of day, when Robin gazed curiously around.

The spot through which the travellers were riding, and which was a wide piece of forest ground, one might have supposed, from the nature of the scenery, to be as common to all lands as possible; but no such thing; and those who gazed upon it had no need to ask themselves in what part of the world they were.

The road, which, though sandy, was smooth, neat, and well tended, for that time, came down the slope of a long hill, exposing its own course to the eye for nearly a mile.

There was a gentle rise on each side, covered with wood; but this rise and its forest burden did not advance within a hundred yards of the road, leaving between a space of open ground covered with short green turf, except where it was interrupted by some old sand-pits, with here and there an ancient oak standing forward before the other trees, and spreading its branches to the wayside.

To the right was a little rivulet, gurgling along the deep bed it had worn for itself amongst the short grass, in its way towards a considerable river which flowed through the valley at about two miles distance; and on the left the eye might range far amidst the tall, separate trees—now, perhaps, lighting upon a stag at graze, or a fallow-deer tripping away over the dewy ground as lightly and gracefully as a lady in a ball-room—till sight

became lost in the green shade and the dim wilderness of leaves and branches.

They were near a small town, Robin could see, by the road, and by the sight of a distant tower. Here it appeared the knight was known, and so easily obtained shelter for the day.

It was nearly evening when they resumed their journey; Sir Ralph pleading fatigue on the part of his wife, and caution on the part of himself, for thus reversing the order of things.

Robin Hood smiled, and sighed, and thought of Maid Marian.

As they proceeded the purple of the evening died entirely away, and a grey dimness fell over tree, and stream, and hill.

Star by star looked out, grew brighter and brighter, as the wandering ball on which we travel through the inconceivable depth turned our hemisphere from the superior light, and at length all was night.

In the lapse of ten minutes more, the road—which, winding about between the hill and the stream, was forced often out of its true direction—had conducted them to a steep bank overhanging a wider part of the valley, and here Sir Ralph Tressilian divined—for he could scarcely be said to see—that a scattered but considerable village lay before.

Up and down the sides of the hill a hundred twinkling lights in cottage windows were sprinkled like glow-worms amongst the darker masses of orchard and copse-wood, and now and then, as the travellers advanced, a bright glare suddenly flashed forth from some opening door, and then again was as speedily extinguished; some watchful dog, too, caught the sound of horses' feet, and, after one or two desultory barks, set up his tongue into a continued peal.

His neighbours of the canine race took the signal, and —not at all unlike the human species, ever inclined to clamour—yelped forth in concert, whether they had heard or not the noise that roused their comrades' indignation, so that the village was soon one continued roar with the efforts of various hairy throats.

They, however, paid no heed to these signs of watchfulness.

"Yonder stands Tressilian Hall, and these are my tenants," said the young knight, "but I do not want them to see their young mistress until they see her in state."

Robin Hood smiled. The travelling only at night was now clearly explained.

CHAPTER CLIX.

ROBIN HOOD AND THE POACHERS.

By this time it was as dark as could well be desired. It was not exactly Egyptian darkness, for there was nothing in it that could be felt, but the sun was entirely gone, and the last fringe of his golden robe had swept the sky some time. The moon was not yet up, so that the stars had the sky all to themselves; but though they were shining as brightly as they did many thousand years ago, when they were first sent glittering into the depths of space, they did very little to show the travellers their way.

But Sir Ralph Tressilian knew it well, and guided them directly through the village to where they could see the lofty turrets, two in number, of the young knight's Saxon home.

It was a moderately sized castle, with large grounds, and, what was rare in those days, a reserved park with deer and other game, which the juvenile Nimrod preserved carefully.

The castle was surrounded by a moat, standing, however, principally on its own ground.

Sir Ralph Tressilian had been two years abroad in foreign parts, during which time his mother had resided with her own friends.

She had now been summoned in haste to receive him in his ancestral halls, which she had hastened to put in a state fit for their lord and master.

The grounds, however, had been neglected; there were long tufts of grass in the walks and on the road, some of the trees which had been felled were rotting in the long, dank grass, while the fences which had been placed to keep the deer within proper bounds lay flat upon the ground, overturned and broken.

Sir Ralph bit his lips as he noticed these signs of neglect, but made no remark, and in a moment more was sounding a horn at the entrance.

He was at once admitted, and the three were ushered into the presence of the mother of Sir Ralph, a lady of little more than forty—and a very handsome woman for her years, feeling those years as light as a young king s crown.

She received them warmly, and after the usual greetings, saw Agnes to her apartment, that she might rest herself and change her dress before supper.

Sir Ralph showed Robin to a room, where in a very short time the friends were together, gazing out upon the reserved park and the forest beyond.

"There is no part of England where deer abound more freely," observed Sir Ralph.

"Then why pen them up in an enclosure?" said Robin.

"'Tis our custom; we like to see them in the park, where they are happy enough, well fed and cared for. We seldom kill them, though I am told the idle lads about prefer taking my property."

"Your property, Sir Tressilian?"

"There spoke the outlaw," cried the knight, laughing; "yes, my own private property, brought at great expense from an estate in Normandy, where my uncle collected them."

"That is different," observed Robin; "you were saying——"

"The lads prefer my deer to the forest bucks; so that I expect to have work with poachers ere I am many days older."

"I hold all deer," quoth Robin Hood, "that run wild in the forest to be as much my property as the king's; but animals which you have brought from foreign parts, and which you feed yourself—that is different. Shall we visit your keepers anon and see if much poaching is about?"

"With pleasure," laughed the knight; "dost want to turn keeper awhile?"

"I should like the amusement for a night," replied Robin. "I would gladly see what stuff these lads are made of."

The young host again smiled, and led the way down stairs, where they found the ladies and the evening banquet awaiting them. The two ladies were already fast friends.

The banquet was rich and hospitable, and lasted some time, after which the two men rose, to enable the wife and mother to make better acquaintance.

They made their way to the courtyard, where they were sure to find the keepers.

Sir Ralph, it appears, knew their habits, for they were seated round a fire in a kind of guard-house.

From soon after sunset until about nine o'clock there had been a slight refreshing rain, not one of those cold autumnal pours which leaves the whole world dark and drenched and dreary, but the soft falling of light, pellucid drops that scarcely bent the blades of grass on which they rested, and through which ever and anon the purple of the evening sky, and as that faded away, the bright glance of a brilliant star, might be seen among the broken clouds.

Soon after nine, however, the vapours that rested on the eastern uplands became tinged with light; and, as if gifted with the power of scattering darkness from her presence, forth came the resplendent moon, while the dim clouds grew pale and white as she advanced, and, rolling away over the hills, left the sky all clear.

It required scarcely a fanciful mind to suppose that in the brilliant shining of the millions of drops which hung on every leaf and rested on every bough; in the glistening ripple of the river that rolled in waves of silver through the plain; in the checkered dancing of the light and shade through the trees; and in the sudden brightening up of every object through the scene which could reflect the moon's beams—it required scarcely a fanciful mind, we say, to suppose that the whole world was rejoicing in the soft splendour of that gentle watcher of the night, and gratulating her triumph over the darkness and the clouds.

The men rose and touched their caps to their master.

"What think you, Keldon," said Sir Ralph, addressing the head keeper; "will the boys be prowling to-night?"

"Very likely, sir."

"The rain has gone off."

"Yes, Sir Ralph, for the night, if I know anything of weather."

"Then 'tis time you were in the park. This noble gentleman here, a dear friend of mine, and one who could teach woodcraft to you all, will lead you; and as he reports you, so will I reward you."

"We are ready, master," said the keeper.

Sir Ralph smiled, and turning away, left Robin to manage as he should think proper.

"Shall we start, sir?" asked Keldon, who, with his companions, had taken their crossbows and staves.

"Yes; but mark me. I go out to-night more from curiosity than anything else; if we can capture one or two of these lazy knaves who prefer a tame deer to a wild buck we will do so. But no bloodshed for me. If they mean fighting leave them to me. I'll undertake to make them as quiet as fawns."

In the present day nothing can be more beautiful or more thoroughly English than a gentleman's park; while then, when it was only a portion railed off by royal favour from the splendid forest, it was even more grand than now. There were the grassy slopes, the groups of majestic trees, the dim flankings of forest ground, broken by savannas and crossed by many a path and many a walk.

The moon was within half an hour of her rise, when the keepers, headed by Robin Hood, entered the reserved ground; and before they selected a hiding-place it shone full into the park, and poured her flood of splendour over the wide slopes glittering with the late rain, along the winding paths and between the broad trunks of oaks and beeches.

The autumn was not so far advanced as to make any very remarkable difference in the thickness of the foliage; but still some leaves had fallen from the younger and tenderer plants, so that the moonbeams played more at liberty upon the ground beneath, and the trees themselves had been kept so far apart that any one standing under their shadows—except in the thickets reserved as coverts for the deer—had a view far over the open parts of the park, and if the eye took such a direction, could descry the castle itself on one hand, and the village on the other.

At the same time, though a person thus posted under the old trees—either beneath the clumps which studded the open ground, or the deeper woods at the extremes—could see for a considerable distance around, yet it would have been scarcely possible for any one standing in the broad moonlight to distinguish others under the shadows of the branches, unless indeed they came to the verge of the wooded ground.

This became more true as the moon rose higher, and the crossings and interlacings of the shadows in the woodland were rendered more intricate and perplexed, while the lawns and savannas only received the brighter light.

The keepers had their regular watching places, while Robin selected one for himself, a signal having been agreed on by means of which they might reunite.

Robin had his bow, quiver, short sword, and dague, which having seen to (he could not tell whether he had to deal with lawless ruffians or reckless youths who came into danger from mere love of venison), he crouched under a tree and waited.

He was infinitely amused at his task. Accustomed himself to shoot deer in the open day without fear of any one, Robin had never had occasion to prowl about deer-stalking by night.

He was so fond, too, of the open air and open air amusements, that the being out of itself was a pleasure, and the time passed quickly enough, simply ruminating.

At a little before eleven, the outlaw raised his head. The moon was now high in the heavens, and he could hear a rustling, scraping sound as of one thrusting himself through a hedge.

Then a youth of about twenty, simply dressed, with a bow in his hand, sauntered into the open glade.

He gazed calmly around, and then, as if convinced the coast was clear, whistled low and cautiously.

In a few minutes he was joined by a whole band of youths armed, some with the long, some with the cross-bow.

"What say you, sir?" asked a keeper, who had crawled up close to Robin.

"Wait until I give the signal," was the dry reply.

He could now see the whole party creeping stealthily along, and he himself prepared to follow, with the keepers behind.

Once or twice he noticed that the guide stopped and listened, and once or twice spoke a few words.

"Did you not hear a noise out there to the left?"

But when, after listening some minutes, no sound could be distinguished — though they gave breathless attention with bended head and listening ear — they proceeded.

Robin followed.

A light breeze stirred the tree-tops, and a leaf would now and then fall through the branches, but nothing else was to be heard; and as the poachers passed the end of many a vista and moonlit alley, and looked cautiously out, nothing that could excite the least apprehension was perceivable, and they moved on, gaining greater courage as every step familiarised them more with their undertaking.

They now turned more into the heart of the wood, following paths with which none of them seemed very thoroughly acquainted, and the perplexity of which often caused them to halt, or to turn back, in order to reach the spot which they had fixed upon as the scene of their exploits.

The keepers were now able to follow with ease.

"Be careful," said Robin, in a low tone, "not to be provoked to fire without my orders. Appear when I call you, and be surprised at nothing which may occur, however strange."

The men bowed and followed.

The lad who had at first reconnoitred soon, however, led them right; and taking a small footway towards the east, they found themselves suddenly upon the edge of an opening in the wood, through the midst of which ran a stream of clear water.

There was here a space of about five acres without a tree; but on all sides were deep groves of old chestnuts, and to the east were some thick coverts of brush-wood.

It became necessary now to ascertain the direction of the wind, lest the deer should scent their pursuers, and take another road; and for this purpose the lad who acted as leader wetted his finger in the water, held it on high, till he discovered by the coldness that ensued which side it was that the wind struck.

As soon as this important point was known, he placed his comrades in separate stations, each by one of the old chestnuts, in such a manner and at such distances as would render it impossible for the deer to cross the open space without receiving one or more shafts from one of his party.

Robin, who had secreted himself with great judgment, saw that this sport was not unfamiliar to the youth, who, indeed, appeared to have the skill and knowledge of an old sportsman.

As soon as his companions were properly disposed, and he had himself taken up a position in a most favourable spot, he took a beech-leaf, bent it in the middle, and applied it to his lips.

A quick, sharp percussion of the breath upon the bent leaf instantly produced a noise exactly resembling the cry of a young doe.

After calling this way once or twice, he ceased, and was all attention.

Robin smiled grimly.

But no rustle followed to indicate that any of the horned dwellers in the wood had heard the sound.

Again the low cry rose upon the night air, and then in the bushes beyond a slight sound was heard.

Again the poacher repeated his cry, and there was at once a rush from the brushwood.

Then again all was still.

The poachers waited with bated breath; the watchers looked on with absorbing interest.

Then, not from the bushes, but from the opposite chestnut trees, which the low wood joined, trotted forth at an easy pace a tall and splendid deer, bearing his antlered head near the ground, as if trying to scent out the path of the mate whose voice he had heard.

As soon as he came within full moonlight, he stood at gaze—as it is called—raising his proud head and looking steadfastly before him.

Then turning to the right and the left, he seemed striving to see the object that he had not been able to discover by the smell; but as he was still too far distant for anything like a certain shot the youth once more tried a solitary call on the leaf.

The deer trotted on quite fifty yards, when the clang of the bow was heard, and the deer fell dead upon the spot.

"A pretty good shot, my springal," said Robin Hood, advancing into the open glade, "worthy of an outlaw."

The youth stood astounded, and then rushed towards the yeoman.

"Death to the spy—to the river with him!"

"Beware, my hot-blooded youths," continued Robin, putting his bugle to his lips, "one blast and ye are all lost. Which is your chief or leader?"

The youth already alluded to stepped forward.

"This expedition is of my organising," he said, a little sullenly, "and I am ready to take the blame. Who are you?"

"A new keeper," said Robin, drily, "now tell me, my masters, are you not pretty fellows to come here shooting a man's private property, that which he has bought with his money, and fed with his food, when the forest is open to you and a deer more or less there is not missed."

"And the laws?"

"The laws," laughed our hero, "why there's no law against shooting a deer unless you are found out. Now hearkee—if you will take my word, I make a solemn engagement. Lift that deer, attend me to the castle in the morning, present, in honour of his wedding, this deer to Sir Ralph, and promise to shoot no more without leave, and I engage that you shall have free pardon, and permission to shoot a deer once a year."

"Ha! ha! ha! a pretty trap!" cried several of the youths.

"No trap," said the outlaw, with a shrill whistle, "if I wished mischief, these men you see now coming would soon turn a scene of peace and goodwill into a bloody one. They are powerful men, well armed, and the law is on their side—take my word, and surrender to me, and not to them, before they come up."

"To whom should we surrender?" said the leader, quietly.

"Hush! listen; not a word to them on your lives! They know me not. I am Robin Hood of Sherwood Forest!"

With a cry of joy and pride the whole party threw their arms at the foot of the outlaw.

One, the leader, had realised the fond dream of his life.

"'Tis well," said Robin, and then addressing the keepers, "'tis as I wished. Touch them not—they have my word. Lift up the deer, young fellows, and follow."

To the utter astonishment and bewilderment of the liveried servants of Sir Ralph, the poachers quietly raised the deer, and with unbent bows, followed Robin without a murmur.

"These men must be lodged—not as prisoners, but as my guests—until the morning, when Sir Ralph shall decide their fate. Have you a room where they can feast at will? and hearkee, Keldon—deer's meat all—cram them with venison. If they starve for a year, let them feast to-night."

The keeper, much surprised and astounded, declared that there was a vaulted guard-house seldom used, but where a roaring fire could be made.

"Make it," said Robin, as they entered the court-yard, and proceeded to hang up the deer in a shed, with the arms which the poachers had carried.

The youths of the village were as in a dream. They could hardly believe their senses, and at times thought they were wilfully and madly rushing to their own destruction.

But now a pile of crackling wood blazes on the great hearth. The cellarman is induced to bring in good ale. Keldon acquaints the sleeping cook that his master's guest has some friends to supper, on which all that the larder contains is put in requisition.

The youths began to rub their eyes and look about them for some way of escape.

But Robin gave them no chance.

"Eat, drink, and be merry," he said, "if to-morrow you die."

"No such jokes," said the leader, drily; "if you are Robin Hood—I have trusted you."

"And you have done well. Were none of you at the tournament?"

"The first day——"

"Then you saw the Unknown unhorse the knights?"

"We did; and were told the unknown knight proved to be the exiled Earl of Huntingdon."

"His son, better known in merry England as Robin Hood of Sherwood Forest."

A low murmur of applause rose from the young men, who now began to feel at ease, and devoted themselves with diligence to the good things before them.

Meanwhile Robin and the leader conversed in a low tone. The outlaw saw that he was a bold and fearless youth, with undoubted intellect, and took a pleasure in drawing him out.

The poaching expedition in the park was quite an uncommon thing, he said; he knew that much was said about the continual disappearance of the deer, but as to that the villagers were not to blame.

"Who then?"

"The keepers."

"How so?"

"They kill the deer regularly and sell it to chapmen, who take it away to Sheffield. Then, because we lads once a year or so take a moonlight walk, we bear the blame."

"Canst prove this?"

"Every old dame in the parish knows it."

"But the proof?"

"I could trap the head keeper any night," said the youth, gravely; "but I like not the task."

"If you speak truth, he is a villain and knave, who, to hide his own cheating and rascality, accuses the innocent, I would gladly aid in his exposure."

"But he may suspect."

"No. I will tell you. To-morrow you shall all be discharged with a severe reprimand, pardoned only on account of your lord's bringing home his young wife. Then at eventide I will meet you. Where do you live, and what is your name?"

"I live at the end of the village, the last house on the right hand, and my name is Walter Allen."

"Then, Walter Allen, to-morrow night we will meet to concoct measures to expose the trickery of Master Keldon. Now good night—'tis past the midnight hour, and I must rise betimes."

With those words Robin retired to his couch.

CHAPTER CLX.

DEER STEALING.

IT was very little more than break of day when the outlaw was again on foot, and bustling about the castle.

Sir Ralph, himself a tolerable early riser, knew very well that his friend had some object in view in being thus soon about, so joined him shortly.

Robin, with a slow and demure smile, beckoned the knight to follow him to the picture-gallery, and there frankly related his experiences of the preceding evening.

The knight listened with intense surprise, and not without some manifestations of amusement at Robin Hood's decided sympathy with the poachers.

But when he heard the accusation brought against his keepers, his brow lowered, and his countenance grew black as midnight.

"Something of this I did suspect," he said, quietly; "when I was a lad, in my father's time, I know it was so. But we will see; your suggestions are good. After breakfast I will receive these youths in the hall, scold them well, and then send them away pardoned on account of my marriage. To-night I will myself join you and see if indeed this accusation be true; arrange any meeting these lads may appoint."

Robin Hood made no attempt to prevent him from joining in the expedition, but left him, to let the poachers know what had occurred.

Walter Allen was delighted, and promised in all things to obey the outlaw chief.

"And now," said Robin, "when you are dismissed, go quietly to your homes—but mind one thing, at the hour we are to meet, let all be ready to follow."

"So it shall be," replied Walter Allen.

Robin now returned to pay his respects to the dowager and young Lady Tressilian, who both were more and more charmed each hour with his frank and manly ways.

The breakfast was soon over, and then Sir Ralph, exchanging a glance with Robin, adjourned in company with his mother and wife to the hall of justice.

Robin went forth and directed the keepers to bring in all the poachers, unarmed, but with the carcase of the deer.

Keldon and his party were too delighted, and at once hurried to command the presence of the youths, all sons of respectable yeomen and franklins, who were on a frolic rather than a wilfully destructive expedition.

The young knight, composing his face to a look of gravity above his years, and looking so stern that Agnes scarcely knew him, took no notice of the culprits as they entered the hall.

Robin Hood stood near him and made no sign, delegating to the head keeper the duty of charging the poachers.

Keldon told the story as energetically as he could, but in a very different way from what he would have told it if the outlaw had not been present.

Sir Ralph heard him in ominous silence.

"Well, my masters," he said, slowly, "what excuse have you to give for trespassing on my grounds and killing my deer?"

"None!" replied Walter Allen, respectfully. "It was a mad frolic, very foolishly conceived, and very wrongly carried out. We are not, we trust your worship to believe, in the habit of taking our neighbours' goods; and if, therefore, your worship will overlook this mishap and allow us to lay the buck at your lady's feet—to whom and all her future progeny we wish every happiness—we shall remain your obliged and faithful servants until our dying day."

"'Tis cool impudence, varlets!" began Sir Ralph, looking black as thunder, in order to stifle a desire to laugh, "to offer me that which is mine——"

"Nay, my gentle lord!" said Agnes, with a spirit that well became her gentle nature and appearance, "they offered it to me. What will you say if I accept the gift?"

"That I never deny you anything, and yet you are but encouraging these youngsters in their unlawful pursuits."

"No!" said Walter Allen, stoutly. "I, for one, will, when I want a deer, try the open forest—no meddling with park deer any more for me."

"On this condition," continued Sir Ralph, "I am willing to overlook this breach of the law. Go, then; but remember, that whosoever comes before me on a charge of unlawfully appropriating that which is not his to touch shall surely be severely punished."

The youths made no reply, but held down their heads and retired, glad to get off; when, had Sir Ralph given them up to justice, they might have run fearful risk.

The keepers retired, with a very poor idea of their master's leniency, which they were sure would produce bad results; and, as they said this, they thrust their tongues into their cheeks, and winked at one another with a strange and meaning expression.

Towards evening Sir Ralph and Robin Hood announced their intention of riding over to a distant neighbour's to make arrangements for a great deer hunt on the morrow.

This was done with a double purpose. It would enable them to keep the appointment with Walter Allen, and would throw the keepers off their guard.

If they were really guilty of the malpractices ascribed to them, they would certainly take advantage of their absence and of the night being dark.

They both mounted gallant steeds, and rode away at a rattling pace through the village.

Their pace was kept up as long as they could be seen and heard from the castle; after which they halted, rode down a narrow lane into the forest, and put their steeds up at a roadside alehouse.

The landlord was a tenant of Sir Ralph's.

He was a sturdy, honest, straightforward Saxon yeoman, and had known his master since the latter was a boy.

"I am on some secret business to-night," said Sir Ralph, "and would not have these horses seen. Have you any one in the house?"

"Two men from Sheffield, with a cart, who generally put up here once a week," he replied.

Sir Ralph and the outlaw exchanged glances.

"What do they deal in?"

"Why," said mine host, scratching his head, "that is a matter I can never make out. They come in the daytime, rest awhile, take their meals, and then leave after curfew. I never could make them out."

"It's my opinion," put in the knight, in a low voice, "that they are agents of the knaves in Sheffield who deal in stolen venison."

"My lord!"

"Don't think I suspect you; but, to be frank with you, Wandal, we are out after those who for some time past have been destroying my deer, and 'tis most probable these men are the delinquents. Show us a room where we may lie quiet until they move."

"But Walter Allen?" whispered Robin.

"True. I had forgotten. Wandal, dost know a youth named Walter Allen?"

"Do I know the best singer, harp-player, and morris-dancer in all the district round? Certainly."

"Go then, or send to him, to say, he whom he was to meet to-night is here, and that he is to join him alone."

"I will but show your lordship to my best room, and bid my dame see to these carters, and then I will go myself."

They entered the house, called for refreshment, to be civil to the landlord, and then bade him go on his way.

"Tell him," said Robin, "all he undertook last night must be carried out, though he come alone."

The landlord bowed and left the room.

The voices of the carters, who were somewhat influenced by drink, could plainly be heard, though their words were not very plain; and every now and then one of them indulged in a snatch of song.

"Though I cannot go as far as you do, good Robin," said the knight, after some brief discourse, "I can scarcely blame those who, in defiance of the forest laws, shoot a buck for their own use; but that these knaves, whom I pay to guard my deer, should rob me is intolerable."

"They all do it. Half that is laid to the charge of honest men is done by the fellows who report them. I once knew a ranger, high in the graces of the Earl of Beauclerk, who sold his half-dozen head a week; being careful to send them up in wagons towards London, where his roguery could not be traced."

"I would hang such a fellow without benefit of clergy," cried Sir Ralph, hotly.

"And I," said Robin, "would hang no men but murderers and foul traitors."

"And what call you these fellows?"

"My dear Sir Ralph, you and I will never agree in our view of game, which is really no more your property than it is that of the poorest hind. If this country were crowded with people, if there were more towns, and all the land was required by man, the game would die out, and all would be sold; but while there are wild beasts, not tended by the hand of man, I hold them to be the property of all."

"You say truly, that we shall never agree," replied Sir Ralph, gravely. "Your ideas will not suit this land."

"There is the pity. The nobles and gentry have power enough already, have land enough, castles enough, cattle enough, to leave to the poor and miserable the fowls of the air, the beasts of the field, and the fishes of the sea and brook."

"I' faith you are a good advocate," laughed Sir Ralph; "but, prithee, hush. Here comes our host and the youth you wot of."

While he was still speaking, Walter Allen entered, cap in hand, bowing in the usual fashion of the day.

"Sit you down," said Sir Ralph, with one of his pleasant smiles. "I hope the worthy dame your mother is well."

"Quite well," replied Walter.

"Drink, then, to her health," continued the young knight, filling him a cup full of sparkling wine.

Walter, somewhat confused and surprised, drank, however, without hesitation.

He was too much of a genuine Saxon to refuse a cup of good honest liquor.

"And now to speak of these malpractices of my keepers," said the knight.

Walter hesitated.

"It somewhat ill becomes me—" he began.

"Tush, man!—young men will be young men. I should enjoy a moonlight deer-stalking myself; but these men eat my bread and take my wages. Their conduct is unpardonable. Speak out."

Thus admonished, Walter Allen told the knight that during his minority the deer had at first, under the stern but honest rule of his father's late keeper, multiplied to such an extraordinary extent that it became necessary to thin them.

This, however, was done openly, and the bucks, does, and fawns sold for the benefit of the estate.

Then came Keldon, who, bringing with him an excellent character, was allowed to choose his own subordinates, and to act, after the departure of the Dowager Lady Tressilian, exactly as he pleased.

He at once began his midnight pranks in the park, and under pretence of the most thorough severity to the villagers, kept off all poachers and invaders of the preserves.

But he was watched, and though from fear of his power none liked to inform against him, there was not a villager but guessed at his lawless proceedings.

Every week a mysterious cart came from Sheffield, was driven close up to the park hedge, where a gap had been purposely made, and here the trade was done.

"At what hour?"

"One or two hours after curfew," said Walter.

"Then take thee a cup more. Where are thy fellows?"

"On the skirts of the wood."

"Take them a skinful of ale; send them to a safe ambush in the wood, where they may overlook the rogues, and then do you return and guide us."

Walter Allen obeyed, and was soon back in attendance on the knight and his friend.

They all now spoke in an undertone, lest they might be overheard by the so-called drovers. The young knight made himself familiarly acquainted with the gossip and wants of the village, which he stored in his mind for future use, being determined to show himself to his humble friends and tenants a landlord of the new and rare school, a fine old English gentleman of the good old Saxon time.

When mine host announced that the drovers would soon be moving, the three men issued forth from the inn, and took their way to the point of observation which, by the advice of Walter Allen, they had selected.

CHAPTER CLXI.

ROBIN HOOD AND THE POACHERS.

ABOUT a quarter of an hour later, three men were sitting under a high sandy bank upon the extreme edge of the village common.

The broken ground, with its high bank, covered on the top with furze and brambles, with here and there a thin birch-tree or a hawthorn hanging over it, might either have afforded a very pleasant shelter on a warm, hot, sunshiny summer day, or a comfortable, protected nook against the cold wintry wind.

Why it should have been selected particularly, however, as a place of repose at the time we speak of, would be more difficult to say, as the night was bright and clear, with scarcely a breath of wind stirring the calm, sweet air, and the moon was clear in the sky, without even the favourite thin veil of a white cloud.

There was, however, one thing to be remarked in regard to the spot, which was, that from the little dingle, or old sandpit—for that had most probably been its origin—there wound away a deep gully or ravine to the spot where two roads crossed at the angle of Tressilian Park.

ROBIN HOOD AND MAID MARIAN PURSUED.

The angle of the park hedge and fence itself was about two hundred feet distant; but the gully, with its high banks and peculiar shape, formed a sort of speaking-trumpet, or Dionysius's lug, which enabled any person sitting in the sandpit to hear all that passed upon either of those roads much more distinctly than the distance would have permitted under any other circumstances.

All such little particulars and features in the face of the country round, the capabilities of every spot of ground, and the nature and quality of every inch of earth were always keenly marked, noted down, and remembered by Walter, who, whatever might be the truth with regard to the park, was an inveterate poacher in the forest, thus eking out a very slender patrimony.

All his topographical researches were then made, and the results remembered in connection with the birds and beasts and creeping things in which his natural affections chiefly centred.

His knowledge of the dingle and sandpit just mentioned had been acquired while prowling about in search of forbidden fruit; he knew its *embouchure* on two roads and the facilities it afforded for hearing even a light step upon either of them, and had consequently directed his choice on the present occasion, when, as he observed, he wished to have all his eyes about him.

In the rear was the forest.

Presently they heard, first, the sound of people's feet walking along the rough and gravelly road just outside the park hedge. There was a murmur of voices speaking too, but neither in a low nor hurried tone. It was the sound of persons conversing quietly and leisurely.

"Can that be our venison thieves?" said Sir Ralph.

"Yes, sir; and if you take note, there comes the rumble of the cart and horses behind them. They are so used to this affair, as a matter of course, that they have no fear."

"The rogues!"

"With your worship's permission I will get nearer. A shrill whistle will bring my men; will your worship follow?"

"All well," said the knight.

"I'll creep on them in a minute," said Walter.

"Take care," said Robin, "or they'll see you as you get over the bank in the moonlight."

"Never fear," was Walter's reply.

At the same moment, gliding up the bank as if he had had no corporeal existence at all, Walter thrust himself through the furze bushes on the top, crawling on his belly like a serpent; so that the method of his passing was scarcely perceptible even to his companions in the pit below.

Then taking advantage of every swell and knoll and bush, he crept along, guided by the noise of the feet upon the road, till he reached a spot opposite the angle of the park, where the sound of feet ceased entirely, and it was evident that the two men had stopped.

As soon as Walter Allen had ascertained that such was the case, he began gliding on again towards the spot where he calculated that they must stand; from time to time pausing, raising himself a little on his elbow, and looking over every bank and knoll that happened to be in the way.

At length he obtained a sight of the end of the road, and a more wild or romantic spot could certainly never be seen than that which lay before his eyes at that moment.

From the road up to the base of the park hedge was a soft, broken bank of yellow sand and turf, crowned with oaks and chestnuts, similar to those within the park itself, and on the opposite side was a rude and irregular piece of woodland ground, the inequalities of which cast the trees, wherever it was adorned by them, into every fantastic position.

Between lay the rich-coloured, gravelly road, running away from the eye down a steep descent, while the other road was seen crossing it between the common and the wood.

"That youth should have been one of us," mused Robin.

"What do you mean by us?" said Sir Ralph, smiling.

"I meant an outlaw."

"But you are no longer one. The king——"

"Has enough to do to quiet his refractory nobles, without offending two or three powerful aristocrats to please me. I mean to go on with my cause in the courts, where, please God our good king lives, I may win the day. But until right is done I remain an outlaw."

"It appears a rare life," mused Sir Ralph.

"Bring Agnes to spend a month with us when I am married," laughingly observed Robin.

"Done!" said Sir Ralph. "That is a bargain."

These words were spoken in some such tones as might have been used by redskins on the war-trail, so low, so cautious, and observant were they.

The moon was now shining bright upon the heath and upon the transverse road; but the other highway down into the valley was darkened by the thick wood and tall trees on the one side, and by the bank, the park hedges, and the beeches and ashes on the other, so that there was nothing to be seen on that road but profound and deepening masses of foliage, here and there streaked and marked by the white boughs and large branches of the trees, and the yellow line of road itself becoming more and more indistinct as it plunged into the shadows.

At the end of the wood, however, just opposite to Walter, the beams of the clear, mellow moon poured in among the trunks of the beeches and oaks, and tipped the soft, mossy undulations of the ground, or the rugged banks of yellow sand, with pure and golden light.

By the time he had reached a spot where they could see without being seen, the two men whom he was watching had seated themselves under those very trees amongst which the moonlight was streaming, and apparently awaited some addition to their party.

Suddenly there was a low, cautious whistle, that made Walter Allen start, for he feared it might bring up the knight and his friend.

But he little knew Robin Hood, who laid his hand upon his friend's arm, and restrained his impatience.

"That is one of the keepers," he said.

Scarcely were the words spoken, when a lad leaped the park hedge.

"Is that you, Mark?" said one of the two men.

"Yes," replied the lad. "Keldon says you must wait here. There's no fear—we're a mile from the house, and all are in bed."

"Good," said the butcher, "it's just as well I've brought a good skin of ale. That will pass the time. I'm glad he has sent you, Mark, because for all your whey face you can sing a song."

"I must sing a little low," cried the other, laughing; "for the road is close;" and without further asking he burst forth with his song.

The green leaf, the green leaf, there's nothing like the green leaf,
  So said the wild deer under the bough.
To corn-fields and cities, and man's dwellings leave grief;
  There's nothing like the green leaf on all the earth, I vow.
The glad lark in the sky carols forth his gay strain;
  Hovering, quivering in the sunny light;
But when his merry song is done, down, down he drops again,
  Under the green leaf to pant with delight.
The green leaf, the green leaf, there's nothing like the green leaf,
  So said the wild deer under the bough.
Lo! the little villager, with her bonnet tied in haste,
  Stealing through the copse by the lone river's tide;
What makes her beating heart break the riband round her waist,
  Lo! through the green leaf Harry by her side.
The green leaf, the green leaf, there's nothing like the green leaf,
  So said the wild deer under the bough.

"That's a good song," said the butcher, laughing.

"Hark!" cried the youth, "here comes Keldon."

The sharp ear of Walter Allen had already told him that quick steps were crossing the park.

Next instant the forms of three keepers, headed by Keldon, might have been seen issuing from the gap in the hedge.

Walter Allen gave a shrill whistle, followed by a hearty laugh, and then sprang on the summit of the cliff-like elevation, from which he overlooked the prowlers.

"Ha! ha! ha!" he said, in a loud, ringing voice; "this is the way to put down poaching in Tressilian Park—ha! ha! ha!"

"Rascal!" cried Keldon, furiously, as he fitted a bolt to his crossbow, "come down out of that, or I'll shoot thee like a dog."

"Two can play at that game, Master Keldon," he said, as he quietly put an arrow to his bow; "but I don't mind coming down, if so be you've anything to say."

And with a bound he was on the road beside them.

"'Ware hawks!" cried the late singer; "the whole village is upon us—run."

"Too late, my game-birds," said Walter Allen, wielding his quarterstaff; "down with your arms, or I'll beat you all to a jelly."

The keepers were seven, strong and determined men all, while the youths of the village, though ten in number, were neither so well armed nor so stout. The keepers at once resolved to fight, wondering excessively what could be the motive of their assailants.

There was a terrible crash of quarterstaves as the rival parties met; and then each man singling out an opponent—the village youths only putting forward seven at first—there appeared likely to be as pretty a bout at singlestick as any hearty Englishman would have wished to see.

"Hold!" suddenly cried a commanding voice, while Sir Ralph and Robin Hood came up, panting and eager, "Down with your arms, knaves, or it shall be the worse for you."

"Who is it talks so big?" cried Keldon. "By the holy mass, Sir Ralph!"

"Yes," said that gentleman, as the keepers and the receivers let fall their cudgels, and were secured without another blow by the villagers. "I've caught you at last. Away with them to the castle. Hanging to a tree is too good for them. They shall be handed over to the tender mercies of my Lord Chief Justice of the Court of Eyre."

The men were all so dumbfounded at this sudden and unexpected event that they could not speak, but allowed themselves to be led away without a struggle or a murmur.

They were secured in the guard-house, and the venison made over to the villagers.

Next day not a vestige of the keepers or their confederates could be found. Mysteriously enough, they had escaped from their lock-up room; though it was shrewdly suspected that they had been released by Sir Ralph, with a caution.

At all events, they were seen no more, nor were any appointed in their places; the village youths being selected to watch in their places, with permission to kill occasionally for their own genuine wants.

At the end of a year the game had largely increased, instead of diminishing.

CHAPTER CLXII.

AT COURT.

NEXT day Sir Ralph, his lady, and mother, in a handsome litter carried by four mules, with female attendants and men-at-arms, with bright pennons waving, departed on their way back to court, fully determined to bring the will to an issue, and to force Sir Hugh to disgorge the money and property of which he had so iniquitously deprived his niece.

Robin, who had the king's own assurance that he would not leave Ashby-de-la-Zouche until his affairs were settled, mounted his steed gladly to return to Maid Marian, who was never absent from his heart.

He was not alone.

Walter Allen had become so warmly attached to him that he declared he could not leave him.

Robin Hood was secretly charmed, for it was not often that he took so sudden a fancy as he had done to this adventurous youth.

They rode side by side a great part of the way, conversing of forest life, Robin Hood giving such a glowing description of it as clearly to prove that he did not much wish for the change which was to transfer him from a chief of outlaws into a knight who owed suit and service to a sovereign.

Walter Allen listened with profound attention and deep and lasting interest.

The dream of his young existence had been to share in the forest glades the dangers and delights which belonged to the free, unfettered, and entrancing life of a hunter, a woodsman, and an outlaw.

It was late in the evening when the party reached Ashby, and took up their quarters at a friend's house, the town being now no longer so crowded as it had been during the tournament.

A trusty messenger was sent to obtain words with the Earl of Essex, who sent word that he awaited their pleasure.

All were arrayed in their best, Robin assuming the costume of his rank; and thus, escorted by their attendants, they reached the palace occupied by King Richard.

The earl awaited them in the entrance-hall.

"His grace expects you. He has just ceased giving audiences; but he will give you one."

And the earl, who was perfectly well aware of what his heroic master owed to those present, smiled good-humouredly as he ushered them to the presence-chamber.

The hall was magnificent.

On a kind of seat a little raised above the others, and hence called a throne (some people fancy kings and queens always sit in state, with a globe in one hand, a sceptre in the other, and a dozen pounds of metal on the head) was Richard, in a rich and flowing garb, chatting with Maid Marian, who stood, in company with other ladies, to his left, while the other courtiers stood a little further off, content to listen.

Man seems really born to worship man, if we judge by the inane outward loyalty he is so fond of testifying, without regard to the merits of the individuals.

We ridicule the Chinese, the Japanese, and other semi-savage nations for their kou-tou's, their bended knees, and head scraping the mud before royalty—we are little better.

We are afraid there are few things Englishmen and Englishwomen would not do to be honoured by a word from royalty.

The fulsome adulation, the servile flattery in which we too often indulge, ought to make us more indulgent to our savage and ignorant neighbours.

The monarch saw at once who entered, and so did Sir Hugh Fitzurse, who, being one of those time-servers—too common—who worship the throne, and not the man in it, had remained at court, utterly deserting his former employer.

He turned ghastly pale.

"What is it?" said the king, who noticed that he wished to leave unseen.

"My liege——"

"Speak up, man!"

"I am ill."

"Why glare you so?"

"See!—see!"

"Well, what then?"

"It cannot be flesh and blood!"

"Eh—then," cried the monarch, "what is it?"

"'Tis she—my niece!"

"Yes, uncle," said Agnes, curtseying as she came up to him. "Lady Agnes Tressilian, at your service."

"Oh, this is the little lady who pretended to die," cried the king, laughing. "Pray, how was it you ventured on such a very rash proceeding? I am curious to know."

"My liege——"

"Come nearer. Art afraid of us?"

"No."

"Who, then?"

"My uncle."

"S'death!"

"Silence, Sir Hugh! Speak up, girl—you are safe here from a hundred uncles."

"Then, please your grace, I had a good reason for dying."

"How so?"

"I knew there was a will."

The knight's cheek blanched.

"You did?" he muttered.

"I knew there was a will——"

"Fire and furies!"

"Leaving all my father's estate to me."

"Hell and damnation!"

"But——"

"Proceed, my pretty one."

"If I died, all the property went to my uncle, as it did if I became a nun."

"Oh!"

"Now, as I had no vocation for a nunnery, and the will would not come forth any other way, I was forced, in order to bring it out, to die."

Richard bit his lips, but in vain. A peal of laughter he could not restrain burst forth, in which the whole court joined.

"Jade!" muttered Sir Hugh.

"This is some of thy tricks," said the king, with a sly look at Robin Hood.

The outlaw only bowed.

"And did the will appear?" continued the king.

"I have it, my liege," said the chancellor. "Sir Hugh Fitzurse gave it into our own hands."

"Then see justice done. Que justice soit fait," said the king, warmly. "Glad to welcome you to court. Strike up music."

This was so evidently said to prevent Robin Hood from addressing him, that the outlaw would have fallen back, abashed and pained.

"I will speak with you in private," whispered Richard, "as one king should with another. You, Maid Marian, and Sir Ralph and wife, sup with me in an hour."

The outlaw drew back, and the court broke up into groups—the king drawing round him the Earl of Essex and some of his most tried followers, leaving the younger courtiers to amuse themselves as best they might.

Presently the king rose, when all became mute, until the monarch had retired, when all followed his example.

A page intimated to Robin and his party that they were to follow him.

They did so, and soon found themselves in a small chamber, where a supper was laid out, and where the king awaited them.

"Now, my friends," he said, when the page had retired and the door was closed, "fancy ourselves in the forest once more, and forget my state. Let me be happy while I may."

All bowed, but though the conversation was free and dégagée enough, yet all were too wise and polite to forget that the lion, however tame, had claws.

To a certain extent, however, etiquette and ceremony were cast aside until the end of supper.

Then the king's brow became overcast a moment.

All were silent.

"Robert Earl of Huntingdon," he said, addressing our hero, "I have recognised you and continue to do so. But I find your claim repelled and disputed strongly—

still I have put it in the hands of my chancellor, with strict orders to see you righted with despatch. This, too, I have decided, that if your claim is not recognised within a year, if the law proves too slow, then I will act as chief judge, and under my sign manual call you to my court, re-installing you in all your possessions and rights. Art satisfied?"

"Most noble king," said Robin, bending the knee, "I thank you from the bottom of my heart. Really I covet not rank and wealth, save to give me fair claim to the hand of this, the lady of my heart, and *Royne de la Beaulte et des Amours*."

"Foregad! there comes the disagreeable part of my communication," said the king.

"Your grace!"

"My king!"

"Now do not look daggers at me; I'd sooner you'd stick me with one Robin; while if Maid Marian looks so reproachful, I must even cut off a head or two to settle the matter."

They held down their heads.

"Where mean you to live while waiting the decision of the courts?" asked the king.

"In the forest."

"Well then," said the monarch, with a dry smile, "if I were Robin Hood, and my king for state reasons could not openly give me Maid Marian, I should marry her to-night, to-morrow I would run away, and when I came up to London to hear my cause finally tried, I would bring with me a big, bouncing heir to the title and estates."

"My liege," began Robin, "may I ask for explanation?"

"You may. Now listen. Here am I just returned to a kingdom on the verge of a civil war. Now if I openly offend the Earl of Nottingham, his son Robert, Sir Philip Beauvoisin, and their party, I drive them into the arms of my brother and his friends. They say I promised this young lady to Robert; if I did I forget it. But do you settle the matter by getting married, on hearing which I will sequester the young lady's estates until you appear to answer for your contempt. I will take care that all shall go well. In six months I hope to see the kingdom so pacified that I shall not be obliged to treat my unworthy barons with so much tenderness. For if I cannot by then quiet their turbulence, and have England in peace, the block and scaffold shall cool their courage. Is it well?"

"Well, my liege," cried Robin, "only too pained am I that you have need to ask me; only too glad at any price to take this fair hand."

"Well, Edith of Athelston, what say you?"

"To-night?" she murmured.

"Yes—why not? I give you away and sign the contract. You have me there, Robin, and can expose my duplicity if you will, a duplicity but thinly veiled under the said reasons of state. Come speak up, Maid Marian."

"An you will."

"Foregad!" cried the king, "one would think I was forcing the young lady's inclinations."

"Marian," said Robin, taking her hand, and speaking in a low, hushed voice, "am I to be blessed or not?"

"Take it an you will have it," she replied, merrily. "I suppose this is no time for maiden coyness!"

The king smiled as he turned away, and next minute they were ushered into a small chapel, where the Bishop of London—a stout adherent of the king's—the chancellor, and the lady abbess, awaited them.

The chancellor, all being settled beforehand, read out a document which released Edith Marian of Athelston, from all obligations as a ward of the crown, and left her free to choose a husband where she listed, but this document to be kept secret for one year.

Having been signed by the monarch, it was handed in a small box to Edith, and the ceremony, which was by no means a long one, was soon over.

The party then bade the king farewell for a time, and left, with the intention of making the best of their way to the house inhabited by Sir Ralph and Lady Tressilian, who were to accompany them to the forest.

Robin, to satisfy his outlawed friends, fully intended having a grand wedding, and being united once more in the holy bonds of matrimony by Friar Tuck.

CHAPTER CLXIII.

IN THE WOOD.

IT was arranged that the next evening, about curfew time, the small party of friends should commence their journey, a portion of which, before they struck into the forest fastnesses, could be performed on horseback.

All were ready dressed in peasant and yeoman costume. The Dowager Lady Tressilian had taken her departure in a litter for home.

Robin, about half an hour before the time for starting, went to a back window to look at the night.

The moon had risen high over the wood, and every object around might be seen almost as clearly as in the daylight. The huge oak-trees, the tangled brushwood below, and the wide sweeping amphitheatre of hills, with their sides scattered with occasional woods and thickets, and sometimes broken with cliffy banks, were all seen in the clear moonlight, till they faded away in the intense blue sky at the horizon.

Robin's heart expanded with delight as he reflected that soon he should once more enjoy the solitude of the wood softened by the moonlight.

He was about to leave the window, when his eye fell upon the form of a man running towards the back of the house.

He was making signs to Robin.

"Who is it?" asked the outlaw.

"Walter Allen. Come to the hall. I have important news."

Robin hastened to descend to the hall, where he found his new recruit. The youth had been to the alehouse on purpose to pick up rumours. He had heard that the king had left, and that Sir Hugh Fitzurse and young Nottingham, whose given name was Robert, had been all day in conference together.

One of their men—the alehouse was full of them—said they meant to have the two girls, Agnes and Edith, if they fled the country for it.

"To upset that will," said Ralph, "Sir Hugh would stick at nothing—her life is not safe."

"They are sending out men to guard every avenue of the forest—while a large body is to follow whenever you start."

"Many thanks," cried Robin, shaking him by the hand; "but we'll outwit them. Sir Ralph, let your men escort the *empty litter* on the road. When attacked, let them bluster awhile, and finally give in and fly—leaving the litter only in the hands of the scoundrels. Do this, and then join me here."

Sir Ralph obeyed, went out into the courtyard, gave his lieutenant pointed and strong injunctions.

Ten minutes later a litter, closely guarded, and closed against the night air, issued from the courtyard, and began its march towards the forest.

As it did so, a man who had been watching the doorway, at once went off in the direction of the market-place.

A quarter of an hour later, a troop of horse, double in number, passed at a trot, and took a road which would enable them to head the fugitives in a solitary place within the forest.

Meanwhile, Robin Hood, his wife, Agnes, and Ralph—as they were now plainly called—accompanied by Walter Allen, had crept out the back way, and made for the forest, where a brook entered beneath its leafy arches.

The path he took lay above the stream, which was seen pouring on beneath its high banks, sometimes catching a single solitary beam, where some obstruction cast the impetuous waters high into the air to overleap it; sometimes, in deep and rapid currents, rushing on dark and shadowy, and only streaked here and there by a wavy line of light; sometimes, where the bank sloped down, or the trees broke away, pouring on like the gushing tide of silver in the full moonshine.

At length, however, he came to a spot where a small old stone bridge, with grey buttresses, crossed the river, marking the precise point of separation between the parishes, and then turning to the right, he walked on to where a little embankment, long since disused and broken down in many parts, likewise distinguished the limits, which had been strictly kept in former years.

Proceeding thus, he intended to have gone through the greater part of the chase, but as he was beginning to climb the higher hills, he heard the sound of crackling, as of wood burning in a not very dry state, and fancied also that his ear caught the sounds of a human voice.

With his curiosity excited, he turned in the direction from which those sounds proceeded, and after pursuing the little path through the little brushwood which led towards the spot, with as noiseless a step as possible, he suddenly came in sight of a scene which he certainly had not expected. It seemed to them all not a little picturesque, indeed, but its effect was probably aided by the suddenness with which it burst upon them.

A low bank of yellow sand, and somewhat procumbent at the top, covered in many parts with thick vegetation, brambles, and broom, and underwood of various kinds, formed a little amphitheatre in the wood, at the bottom of which lay about a dozen yards of green turf. This turf was strewed with hillocks like molehills, but all covered with the same green garment, and forth from the side of the sand-rock, at about three or four feet from the ground, welled a little stream of very pure water, nourishing the turf below and wandering away to join the river. At the distance of two or three yards from this source was, now burning brightly, a large fire of wood, with the flame blazing high, and the faint bluish white smoke curling up amongst the brambles in forms as graceful as imagination can conceive. Before the fire, superintending the revolutions of a wooden spit, constructed with great ingenuity, so as to turn round and round with a temperate degree of velocity, was a boy in the garb of a peasant, with large nailed shoes, which ill became the size of his feet, and an ankle and leg somewhat unworthy of such a pedestal. On the spit before him, by no means unskilfully trussed, was the goodly form of a well-fed fawn, and while one man was standing by, and from time to time giving directions to the youth who was acting the part of a cook, another was seen sitting calmly under the bank.

This one was quite an idler, for he was stretched out, doing nothing but watching the others with a half grim, half good-humoured smile.

His garb was the full Lincoln green, while his bow and arrows were cast on the ground by his side.

He seemed infinitely amused by the way in which the lad attended to the cookery.

To one accustomed to the forest the way of doing it was certainly truly awkward.

But boys are seldom anything at cookery.

"I don't believe," said the big man, good-humouredly, "I don't believe you ever cooked a fawn before."

"Well?"

"If I hadn't a skinned and trussed him, I believe you would have cooked skin and inside and all."

"I didn't know."

"Ha! ha! ha!"

"Just you be quiet," said the other man, grimly, as he notched an arrow, "or I shall have to chastise thee for thy impudence."

"Ha! ha! ha!" laughed the big man.

"I suppose you think I couldn't?" replied the other, with something of pique in his manner; "because you are such a great big mountain of a fellow you take liberties."

"And who should," said the boy, "if not our friend here?"

"Oh, everybody takes his part," pouted the first young man, "men, boys, girls, and all. You must get up early to get over him."

"The early bird gets the worm."

"I'll example you with thievery."

The big man laughed, and began to sing:—

"Jolly, jolly rover, here's one who lives in clover.
Who finds the clover? The jolly, jolly rover.
He finds the clover, let him then come over,
The jolly, jolly rover, over, over, over."

"Hist!" whispered Robin, smiling, "they are friends of mine. I must teach them to be more cautious. *How now, Master Poachers?*"

This was said in a loud, gruff voice, and the man, who was sitting under the bank, leaped up.

"Who wants a broken head?" he cried, elevating his vast stature to its full height. "If there be one, let him come forth."

"Nay, nay! Master Little John," said Robin, "two can play at that game. You seem snug here."

"Robin Hood!" cried the tall forester, joyously, while the others rose, revealing the ruddy complexion of Will Scarlett and the blushing beauties of his wife.

The whole party of fugitives now stood round the fire, and were mutually introduced—Will Scarlett's astonishment at finding Robin Hood married being something really wonderful to see.

"Married!" he said. "Well, I never!"

"Ha! ha! ha!" laughed Little John.

"If you don't be more cautious," quoth Robin, quietly, "we shall find a *halter* pretty quick, which may make our visit to the *altar* less pleasant than you might imagine. The wood is alive with men searching for our blood. Eat quick, and then away to the nearest shelter you can find."

All were still, seating themselves round the fire, from which the fawn was soon taken, and divided amongst the party, who ate in silence; while Robin Hood explained to his lieutenants the danger in which they were placed.

"We must give them leg bail, till we find some of our companions," said Will Scarlett.

"I'm for fighting 'em!" put in Little John.

"I wish you'd get a wife," said Robin Hood, drily; "You would have a little more consideration for other people."

Little John held down his head, with a somewhat rueful expression of countenance.

"I know every inch of ground about here," said Walter Allen, "and can take you where you need fear no soldiers."

"Well spoken, my little game-cock," put in Little John; "well spoken. I say, for one, follow the leader."

"Is't far?" asked Robin.

"Four miles."

"I will, for the sake of the women."

"The way is rugged," said Walter, "very rugged; but once over it, we may be hid for days."

"Egad!" replied Robin, gaily, "I will go, if it be only to see what others know about the forest more than myself. Lead on."

"I am ready."

"But first, Little John, do you put on a mighty armful of brush, so that the fire may make a smoke that may draw the uncouth enemy here. It will puzzle their noses to follow any further."

"True, captain, true," said the tall forester; "and I will put on plenty of green boughs to tell our own folk none of the merry men are here."

"As you will," laughed Robin.

Walter Allen struck up the side of a steep kind of embankment, nor stopped until he reached a level sort of platform, whence a magnificent view of the green ocean of verdure could be distinguished.

It waved, green and pleasant, under the moon, and with the soft and pleasant breeze.

Close to them was a dense mass of trees that, what with underbrush and trunks, formed one of those thickets which are scarcely penetrable, even by the game of the forest.

But Walter Allen, by nature a woodsman, seemed intuitively to find a path, which, however, none could follow, except in Indian file—one by one.

This continued about half an hour; during which time not a word was spoken, each being too busy to talk.

At last the trees began to get thinner, the light became lighter, and presently they stood above a deep valley, on a ledge of rock.

The valley was, some distance across, on the opposite side, green and grassy; but on this with precipitous cliffs, which forbade much vegetation.

All cried a halt, and Robin Hood surveyed the scene.

Next instant he waved the women back, and called his comrades to his side.

Deep down in the valley below, moving slowly, was the cavalcade of horsemen they had sent in advance.

The litter, supported by its two mules, went at a snail's pace, while the horsemen crawled.

But they seemed keenly on the look-out for any attack that might be made upon them.

"They have missed their way," said Robin, "and taken a wrong turning. But it will not save them from the enemy."

And the outlaw pointed to where, along a white and

winding road of sand, the spearsmen of their enemies were advancing at a hard gallop.

The men-at-arms were below them about fifty feet, and not much further off.

"Tell them to fight," whispered Robin, "and we'll give the knaves a lesson."

Ralph stooped, and creeping under a bush, put his head over the edge of the cliff.

"Rose—in—cross," he said, in a shrill, sharp tone.

"Sir?" cried the lieutenant, with a start, while every head was lifted upward.

"Fight. The enemy are close at hand. We shall help you," was the quiet order.

The men-at-arms formed at once in a line before the empty litter, with their spears at the rest.

Like a whirlwind the cavaliers of Fitzurse and Nottingham came round the corner and dashed forward.

"A Tressilian! a Tressilian!" shouted the defenders.

"A death to all Tressilians!" cried the assailants.

Both sides set spurs to their horses, the ground resounded with the thunder of their hoofs, the lances were lowered, when—whizz, whizz—and, while still the combatants were apart, five arrows struck as many men or horses, and five warriors were *hors de combat*.

The rest dashed on with loud execrations, and a fierce and terrible *melée* took place, which, however, thanks to the swiftness of the arrow flight from above, soon ended in the utter discomfiture of the servants of Sir Fitzurse and Nottingham.

"Surrender, rescue or no rescue!" cried Robin, standing on the verge of the cliff; and then he added, "Tressilians, fly—fly for your lives!"

"Robin!"

"Look, Sir Ralph. This is but the vanguard," replied the outlaw. "Yonder comes the main body."

Five minutes later a cavalcade of knights and soldiers came up to find the battle-field strewed with killed and wounded; but the litter in their hands.

Fitzurse and Nottingham advanced to it with mock politeness in their manner.

"Pray, ladies, favour us with a sight of your transcendent countenances," said young Robert, Nottingham's heir, "that we may not mistake you for milkmaids."

And he pulled away the heavy curtain.

"*Mort de ma vie!*"

"Empty!"

"Deceived!"

"Betrayed!"

"Ha! ha! ha!" shouted Little John, rising, and standing, like Cyclops of old, upon the shores of his desert island; "ha! ha! You have the nest, but the birds have flown, my hearties. A pleasant journey to you."

As he spoke he waved his hand, and laughing heartily at the horsemen as they plunged about in search of a way upwards, darted into a thicket after the fast retreating forms of his companions.

CHAPTER CLXIV.

THE EYRY.

WALTER ALLEN kept along the top of the ridge, but without showing himself to the enemy for some time, when he mounted higher up among the hills, where the climbing became exceedingly steep.

At last he stood upon the summit of a hill which overlooked a glen so darkly overgrown with trees that one might, to all appearance, have walked upon them.

The way was now down a rock half shingle, half fixed stones, down which it was difficult to climb.

Still all moved onwards, conscious that for the moment their safety wholly depended upon their young guide.

They were soon in the densest thicket any of them had ever seen, and in hearing of a waterfall.

Five minutes later they were on a verge of a rocky abyss—at the bottom of which rushed the mountain stream, which below flowed so calmly.

The other side of the gap was about seven feet away.

"Are we to leap this?" said Robin Hood, drily.

"No," replied Walter Allen; "but I must."

He then, with the nimbleness and agility of a monkey, clambered up a pine tree that grew on the edge of the

abyss, and leaning over until some of its boughs hung over to the other side of the mysterious and gloomy gulley.

As soon as he was high enough, he ran out upon the end of a branch, slid off until he hung by his hands, and then dropped on the opposite side.

"Bravo!" said Robin Hood, "well and excellently done. But how are we to follow?"

Walter Allen moved away, and in a few minutes reappeared with some long poles, which he laid across, and then rapidly covered with short sticks and boughs, that left after awhile a very tolerable bridge.

"Welcome to the eyry,"* said Walter Allen; "when Simon Dyke swore I killed his brindled cow, and I struck the rantipole† knaves who came to arrest me, I hid me here six months, and never liked a bed made under a roof of man since."

"And a famous eyry it is, my rantipole runaway," cried Robin; "but are we to lodge, or did you, on the bare ground?"

"Nay," cried Walter Allen. "I dare swear there is goodly living here. It is not a week since I and some of my band made merry here. We don't like curfew hours, and oft come here to turn night into day."

"Band?" said Robin, laughing.

"Aye, aye!" replied Walter, blushing. "I call them so because I am their leader. Here we are."

And turning a kind of narrow ledge, they found themselves in the entrance of a large cavern.

Walter Allen began to strike a light; and having done so, very sedately and deliberately lit a pine torch or two, and invited his friends to enter the eyry.

It was a large cavern, the sides chiefly stone, but, in parts, earth; though any certainty on this point was prevented from the quantity of black pine smoke which covered the roof and sides. There were half-a-dozen niches with sweet smelling turf and grass, and many signs that the cavern was frequently inhabited.

"Oh, oh!" said Robin Hood, "we have rivals in the woods. This is indeed a splendid robbers' cave. My belief is, Master Walter Allen, you and your friends have been playing at outlaws."

"No," replied the young man, gravely, "not playing. I cannot leave my mother, because she is poor; but were I once able to send her to the home of her parents, out of reach of my enemies, I would become an outlaw in earnest."

"Why?"

"I love."

"Oh! oh!"

"With all my heart and soul, one placed some degree above me, and whose supposed father guards her with jealous care."

"In love, my little bandit?" said Little John, with a huge grin. "I thought that was a passion for men."

"I know it's a passion of giants. If rumour tells the truth, a very small girl has stolen your heart. But, friend Little John, I *am* a man, or else you would not be here."

"Ha! ha! ha!" said the tall forester; "give me your hand. I like you; and when we've had supper and some of that ale stowed yonder we'll talk."

"Supper?" cried Robin.

"Yes. Do you call that snack a meal? Not I!"

"You are a very cormorant," said the outlaw, smiling, and seating himself with Maid Marian by a goodly fire of half-burnt wood that Walter Allen was making in a large and yawning chimney.

"Now," continued the King of Sherwood Forest, "if you had proposed some hot spiced ale to drink my lady's health in, I should understand you."

All laughed; and Walter Allen contrived to satisfy all parties by bringing forth the ale in one hand and a huge chine of pork and a hunk of bread in the other.

The ale was heated, the toasts were drank, and then each married couple retired to their own apartment or niche in the cavern; leaving Walter Allen and Little John to enjoy the pleasures of social intercourse, which they did to their own great satisfaction until a late hour, when they curled up by the fire and went to sleep.

All were up early, but none ventured forth, as they

---

* *Eyry*, a place where birds of prey build their nests and hatch.
† *Rantipole*, wild, roving, rakish.

were aware that a thorough search would be made of the woods that day by the enraged and baffled knights.

They had no fear of this cavern being discovered.

"None know it but Saxons," said Walter Allen, "and I know none who would betray it. Many a time and oft have the keepers chased us hitherward, when as boys we had been snaring hares, or getting eggs, or capturing birds; but if we once crossed this gully they were off the scent."

"'Tis a notable and splendid retreat," cried Robin, "and I promise myself more than one visit to it."

Meanwhile, all were preparing to pass the day in such guise as they thought best.

Robin Hood and Maid Marian, as the newest married, were the dullest of the group, having eyes only for one another, and sitting as close together as possible—he pretending to fashion arrows, while all the while he was listening to her talk, and looking full into those great dreamy blue eyes.

Sir Ralph and Agnes were nearly as bad, though as they had no arrows to make, they were compelled to talk openly.

Will Scarlett and Eveline were as merry as larks; but then, be it remembered, that they were old married people—they had been married three months.

Walter Allen and Little John, already sworn friends, were thrown entirely on one another's resources.

As soon as a hearty and substantial meal had been consumed, these two moved to the platform in front of the cavern, whence they could look down the narrow gully, which, about a hundred yards distant, widened into a valley, and was finally lost in the wooded plain.

The opposite side of the ravine to where they stood was precipitous, with huge trees growing to the very brink—trees, as Walter Allen well knew, not easily reached.

"I believe some boy bird-nesting among yonder trees first saw the mouth of this cavern," continued Walter Allen.

"You are right there, my lad; but hist! stand back! there are hawks abroad!"

Both listened attentively, and made out that there were indeed men in the wood. They were a long distance off, but they were evidently approaching.

They moved back into the dark entry.

Not a word was spoken for some minutes, during which they could distinguish voices clearly calling one to another as they advanced.

"Why call you them hawks?" said Walter Allen.

"Well," said Little John, musing, "because most of the hawks and owls are averse to the trouble of constructing nests for themselves. Thus, the brown falcons take possession of the old nests of magpies or squirrels, to which, as far as I can make out, they never add any fresh materials, nor take any pains to repair damages or render them tidy."

"Indeed!"

"Yes; and if we don't mind, these hawks will serve us so—they are on the right track, and if we are not careful, will take from us not only our nest, but our nestlings. Let us confer with Robin."

CHAPTER CLXV.

THE CHASE.

THE exact state of things was explained to the outlaw chief, who at once sent the women into the rear of the cavern, and invited the men to join him near the entrance, in order to consult as to their future proceedings.

Walter Allen was thoroughly of opinion that there was not the slightest apprehension of discovery, as for years he had known all the keepers of the forest search for them in vain.

"But the pitcher, Walter, goes hundreds of times to the well ere it is broken," replied Robin Hood, smiling; "and it is our duty to take every precaution that wisdom can suggest."

"Hist!" said Little John.

All were silent.

They could now distinctly hear the men calling to one another, while above all rose the voices of the chiefs urging them on.

Nearer and nearer, until their words could be distinguished.

"They are here somewhere," said the stern Sir Hugh, "and they must be ferreted out. They can't have leaped this gully."

"One never knows where to look for these outlaws," said Robert, son of the Earl of Nottingham.

Robin exchanged glances with Walter.

"My opinion is," said Sir Hugh, after a pause, "that some of the most agile of our people descend into the gully, and follow the stream until it reaches the forest again."

"Well?"

"If they have waded down, and then landed, we shall find their tracks on the bank."

"Truly. The hounds would then be useful."

"Hounds!" said Robin.

Walter nodded.

"True," continued Sir Hugh. "If you like," he added, sarcastically, "you can step across this chasm and investigate yonder rocks. I shall send some of my men up into the tall trees. They will obtain a good view."

"We shall have to fight," said Robin, quietly; "the villains will find out our quarters."

"Nay," said Walter, with a smile, "we need not fight unless you like, Robin Hood."

"Well, we can easily run away," he continued, and then, in somewhat of a theatrical way, said—

"I know each lane, and every alley green,
Dingle and bushy dell of this wild wood;
And every bosky bower, from side to side,
My daily walks and ancient neighbourhood."

"Were we men alone," replied Robin, "I should say fight. But, under present circumstances, the better part of valour is discretion."

"Then follow me," said Walter.

Robin followed.

The youth took his way towards the darker depths of the cavern, following a narrow passage, until they reached a chamber illumined from above.

In one corner stood a rude ladder.

"Ascend," said Walter.

Robin climbed to the top, and found himself at the mouth of a narrow passage, which descended a few feet, forcing a man to advance downwards.

Robin crawled forward, and soon, cautiously putting his head out, found that the exit was guarded by several bushes growing on the side of a hill, to all appearance only suited to the climbing powers of a mountain goat or chamois.

At the foot of this steep decline was the forest.

The outlaw chief drew back, and returning to the ladder, descended beside Walter.

"We must leave that way."

"Yes. Art ready?"

"No. At any risk we must wait until night. These incarnate fiends number over a hundred, and will guard every avenue and pass in the woods so that a deer should not pass."

"They will."

"By night I care not for them. If we pass through their camp, we must escape. Every hour our danger increases."

Walter Allen at once yielded to the opinion of his leader, and with him returned to where their friends and companions were congregated together.

The noises continued, men beating the bushes could clearly be heard, while heavy bodies forced their way through the thickets and bushes.

Then came a loud, clear hollow ringing through the air; it was a stentorian call, and then all was still.

"What's that?" asked Walter.

"Look up," replied Robin, as he pointed to the tall trees on the opposite bank.

On the bough of a large oak was a man in the garb of a forest-ranger, pointing directly into the mouth of the cavern.

A ragged oak grew on the right bank of the gulley, nearly opposite to their position, which, seeking the freedom of the open space, had inclined so far forward that its upper branches overhung the stream.

Amid the topmost leaves, which scantily concealed the gnarled and stinted limbs, a dark looking man was nestled.

"It's Quentin Dick," whispered Walter Allen, with clenched teeth; "the worst ruffian in the country."

The man kept shouting to his companions, who could hear him, however, as yet without seeing him.

"What is it, Quentin?" said an authoritative voice from the ledge above, whence his position could be seen.

"Well, Sir Hugh," he cried, "I believe I've found——"

An arrow at this moment pierced his side, he slipped, caught at the branch, and swung in mid-air, supported only by his hands—

> His limbs with horror shake,
> And as he grinds his teeth, what noise they make!
> How glare his angry eyes, and yet he's not awake!
> See what cold drops upon his forehead stand,
> And how he clenches that broad bony hand.

Dead silence prevailed, the pursuers as they came in view seemed to hold their breath, the leaves and bark of the oak flew in the air, and were carried away by the wind.

The cries in the forest now wholly ceased, and all eyes, those of friends as well as enemies, became fixed on the hopeless condition of the wretch who was dangling between heaven and earth.

The body yielded to the currents of the air, and though no murmur or groan escaped the victim, there were instants when he grimly faced his foes, and the anguish of despair might be traced in his dark lineaments.

Walter Allen stepped out of the cavern.

"Quentin," he said, in low, stern accents, "say you repent—that you wished you had not winged the arrow that slew my brother John, and I will forgive you."

"Ha! ha! ha!" cried the ruffian, clutching with desperate energy at the bough; "ha! my nimble legged colt is that you? Repent, eh! I left not a stick standing, and planted an arrow in the boy's side——"

Before he could finish his sentence a second arrow struck him, and as it did so, one hand of the ranger lost its hold and dropped exhausted to his side.

A desperate and fruitless struggle to recover the branch succeeded, and then the forest ranger was seen for a fleeting moment, grasping wildly at the empty air.

It was over.

Again dead silence prevailed, and then loud and angry cries rose from the forest.

"Silence!" roared Sir Hugh.

All obeyed.

"We have the knaves now, and if we smoke them out or choke them, they shall not escape. Axe-men to the front. Cut me down all those trees, so that they fall across the gulley."

"Ah," said Robin, between his clenched teeth, "they will have it, will they? Then they must."

"But they will choke up the mouth of the cave."

As he spoke, he could hear the heavy fall of the axe against the trunk of the opposite oaks.

"Now is our time," said Robin.

"Yes," replied Walter, "but the secret of my cavern is gone for ever. It will never again shelter me."

"I will find you a dozen such caves."

"You may find me a cave, but not this cave," said Walter, with a smile; "but come."

Not a word was spoken until all were in the inner apartment of the cavern, where the outlaw cried a halt.

"As each man and woman reaches the open," he said, "glide down the slope and enter the forest; there I can defy them—give me but an hour's start."

Little John ascended the ladder first, it creaking under his weight, then one by one all sought the light.

Robin Hood and Walter alone remained.

The latter dragged a huge pile of brush, wood, and leaves to the foot of the ladder.

"They shall not find the exit. That will delay them an hour. The smoke will wind all round the hill and deceive them thoroughly."

Robin nodded and ascended.

Walter cast his torch into the midst of the pile, and hurried up to escape the smoke and flame.

Next instant he was on the hill side, down which the whole party were climbing with a care and caution which proclaimed its steepness.

But in a very short space of time they were once more beneath the leafy arches of the forest, where Robin Hood once more trod a king—monarch of all he surveyed.

Without a word, but in obedience to a sign from Robin, Little John now took up the leading position.

His feet were gigantic in their proportions, compared with those of any other of the party.

His weight, too, made him leave a heavy trail.

Robin now bade everybody tread in his steps.

"No," said Little John, suddenly stoping.

"Well?"

"I will go last. Do all you tread in Robin's, and then I coming last, will tread out your marks."

"Good," said the outlaw, approvingly; "I thought I should make something of you."

Little John grimly smiled, and next minute was in the rear, his huge quarterstaff resting on his shoulder, and his eyes looking over the heads of the others.

All were too full of apprehension for words. The pursuers had too much at stake not to be desperate in their exertions to capture the fugitives.

'Tis true that Robin had a final appeal to the king, but after what had occurred he wished to avoid this until driven to it by the full force of circumstances.

But for Agnes there was scarcely any hope.

Death awaited her if once in the clutches of her uncle, who would have no mercy.

Death alone could give him a certainty of those estates which he so coveted.

Sir Hugh Fitzurse was a double traitor. His pretended adhesion to Richard was simply a trick arranged between himself and Prince John.

They had no idea of giving up their treacherous endeavours to displace Richard.

They only meant to bide their time, and when that brave and generous prince least expected it, to rise in arms and proclaim a pretender to the throne.

The chief hindrance to the immediate carrying out of this plan was the habits of tergiversation characteristic of the prince.

But Sir Hugh Fitzurse had determined that, could he but secure to himself the property which he wrongfully coveted from Agnes, he would at once push Prince John to an open revolt against his brother's authority.

Any attempt on his own part to deceive King Richard he was perfectly aware would be utterly vain.

Robin Hood, from what he had seen of the man, knew as well what was passing through his mind as if he had heard him speak aloud.

He was, therefore, sternly determined not to be taken, for his own sake and for the sake of his friends.

For some time he proceeded on his way in silence. No effort was made to walk very fast, as this might have attracted attention on the part of their pursuers.

Suddenly the outlaw waved his hand for all to halt.

A loud ringing cry rose in the air, which the king of the merry men knew very well never proceeded from any of his followers.

They were not apt to be so free of their lungs, when their profession made secrecy desirable.

Again the shout was repeated, and the fugitives peering through the bushes, saw a man on horseback breaking through the interstices and intricacies of the straggling trees, and dashing wildly through the forest.

Behind him came two others riding, and then half-a-dozen more, all to every appearance searching every avenue of the forest.

Robin waited not, but signing to his followers, led them rapidly on one side across a green and grassy dell, which having traversed in safety, they glided beneath the underwood, now through thickets and coverts, and then resting between the widely spreading branches of an elm or oak, as occasioned served.

The women exerted themselves to the utmost of their ability to assist Robin in his task, and though they really began to feel faint and weary from their efforts, they strove to conceal it.

But the outlaw chief knew it and saw it, and did all that was in his power to lighten their path, remove difficulties and cheering them, by holding out encouraging hopes.

The women smiled, but it was a cold and cheerless smile, despite every effort they made to appear cheerful.

Suddenly having quitted the mazes of a deep thicket, they reached an open glade; this they rapidly traversed, and as they were about to dive into the recesses of a covert of young trees and underwood, they were startled by finding themselves face to face with half-a-dozen men at arms.

ROBIN HOOD IN DISGUISE VISITS OLD CARTER.

"Ha! ha! knaves!" cried one of them, an officer, "these are the men we seek."

The shock was so sudden, the surprise so great, (they had halted behind a row of chesnuts) that Robin could only put an arrow to his bow.

"Keep off, villains," he said, after moment's pause; "what would you, assaulting peaceful yeomen on their journey through the woods?"

"If you are peaceful yeomen," replied the soldier, quietly, "you can have no objection to await the coming of our chief, Sir Hugh—therefore I must detain you."

"Sirrah," said Robin, "we care neither for you nor your master, though if he be a Norman we scorn him the more. We are journeying across the wood."

"Taking a quiet obambulation," added Little John, dryly.

"Oaf, idiot, dolt!" cried the angry soldier, "if you give me any of your insolence, I'll obambulate you."

"Keep your distance, or by the mass your life shall pay the forfeit," said Robin, sternly.

"Upon them—take them dead, or alive!" cried the loud and ringing voice of Sir Hugh, in the distance.

The men-at-arms charged, and as they did so, four fell from their horses, while a fifth as he came up was hurled backwards by Sir Ralph.

"Follow!" cried Robin, snatching up Maid Marian and dashing into the nearest thicket.

At the same moment Sir Hugh, whose spies had detected the movement of the party through the wood, rushed up followed by a dozen retainers.

They saw at once the fearful devastation caused by the outlaws.

A shout of rage and angry surprise from Sir Hugh quickened the pace of all, many dismounting and following in pursuit.

All the male fugitives, aware that now was coming the supreme struggle, had lifted up the girls that they might obtain some rest.

It was now that the outlaws' thorough knowledge of a forest's intricacies served them in good turn, for what they lost in speed from the weight they were carrying they gained from knowledge of the path.

Robin kept on at a rapid pace, avoiding instinctively those places where the path was entangled by briars and by thick clusters of young trees.

At a single glance of his eye he saw the openings which offered a facility of passage, as well as those which had the advantage of being surrounded by shrubs and trees which might screen them from notice and yet not interfere with their advance.

But still the shouts, cries, and execrations of those in the rear could be distinctly heard.

They were powerful and active men.

Robin Hood felt the big drops of perspiration settling on his brow.

He felt that not much longer could he stand that killing pace.

Without a word he put Maid Marian on the ground beside him.

"We must fight."

All followed his example.

Every arrow was drawn to the head, and as the pursuers came in sight, they were launched with deadly aim.

A furious cry of rage and despair was the reply.

In an instant Robin had led his party down a dark and gloomy dell, where it was not easy to follow.

This ravine was soon crossed, and the whole party were once more in the open forest.

Not a sound was heard.

Close at hand was an elm-tree, with a trunk of tremendous dimensions.

It was flanked by a thicket or copse, crowded with young trees of all species, thickly interspersed with underwood, shrubs, and tall gorse.

Into this the outlaw rushed, followed by his companions, and there sought on the soft ground that repose of which they stood so much in need.

It was some considerable time ere any body could have supposed that they were not alone in the forest.

Soon, however, they again heard the shouts of men in pursuit—though in the distance—and could hear them tearing the branches aside as they dashed onwards.

Robin signed to all the others to lie close while he watched.

About a hundred yards from where they stood, was one of the many bridle-paths leading through the forest.

This the outlaw knew well, and hence his desire to overlook it carefully.

Still the clamour continued, though now it was clear the whole party were at fault.

Suddenly a horseman rode at a leisurely pace along the green pathway, his eyes fixed intently on every bush and tree.

"I tell you," said Sir Hugh, "if the knaves went down that black-looking galley, they are lurking somewhere hereabout. Dolts! fools! cowards! will not the reward I offer satisfy you? Let me but see them dangle freely from an oak bough and command the money."

The retainers to whom he was speaking, and yet who could not see him, were heard beating the bushes, and coming, guided by the horseman, in their direction.

The savage instinct of the Norman knight had guided him well, and he walked straight towards the elm.

Robin's eyes glistened.

His bow was in his hand, and a dark frown for a moment settled on his brow.

He had for a moment a great mind to lay the speaker low. He had no particular goodwill towards him, and yet he was a man.

The arrow sped then, and struck the horse in the skin of the neck, wounding, but not injuring.

The steed pranced furiously, while the choleric knight uttered curses not fit for our pages.

The horse stood upon his hind legs, curvetted, plunged, and reared, and then ran away; but not very far from the direction which the outlaws wished it not to take.

Robin dropped his bow.

With outstretched hands he stood directly in the way of the furious animal, which simply swerved a little, passing within ten yards of the fugitives.

The knight cursed loud and strong, which so enraged Little John, he could not help giving him a taste of his quarterstaff as he passed.

Now no Gilpin's horse ever was madder. Away it flew up hill, down dale, dashing through glades, tearing through coverts, brakes, and thickets; now grazing the knight's legs against the trunks of trees, then putting his head in danger of a blow from a straggling branch.

The fugitives were quite ready to avail themselves of this opportunity, and speedily took their way in the direction of one of their securest fastnesses, though there was now no hope of their reaching it that night.

It was long before this adventure was forgotten in those parts; for, of course, the Norman men-at-arms were the very first to speak of their master's discomfiture.

The exploits of the outlaws made the Nottingham woods dangerous for a time to their sovereign, and he removed his roving camp into the forests of Yorkshire, where his name is still associated with bank and brae, and hill and dell, and glen and stream. Nay, the well out of which Robin and his chivalry drank found such favour in the eyes of one of the Carlisle Howards, that he erected a handsome stone arch over the spring, where passengers used to halt and drink, and bestow alms on two old people, who, as late as half a century ago, found it profitable to abide by the well and keep it in order. It may be found about four miles north of Doncaster, in a small hollow close by the highway, with its arch still in good order, and its water pure, but the attending spirits are departed, and the spring is left with no other protection but the fame of Robin Hood.

We are of those who would gladly see such heroworship preserved, and would gladly record that this old custom had been revived. Did any again see to the fountain, and plant it round with fine trees in honour of the gallant outlaw, we should cry with the poet :—

> Hail old patrician trees, so great and good!
> Hail ye plebeian underwood!
> Where the poetic birds rejoice,
> And for their quiet nests and plenteous food
> Pay with their grateful voice.

CHAPTER CLXVI.

A NIGHT CAMP.

WEARY, footsore, and hungry, the hunted fugitives were glad, indeed, to halt for the night on the first spot which afforded them the promise of a shelter.

The outlaw chief avoided every village and hamlet, quite certain that not one but would have its roystering party of Norman men-at-arms, too glad to catch at the reward, which Sir Hugh, in his desperation, had offered for the apprehension of the abductors of his niece and violators of the sanctuary of the church.

The spot was one not easily reached.

They had to scramble up a steep ascent of shingle and rolling stones, to slide down an almost perpendicular cliff, wade a rapid stream, and then cast themselves weary and exhausted under a dark and gloomy cliff.

All sat down by one accord, and seemed to think that to move any further was impossible.

The women were glad to throw themselves helplessly against the cliff.

"How like you forest life?" said Robin Hood, moodily, speaking rather to himself than Marian ; "is it not delightful, charming? Might not man or woman either be happy here?"

"Robin," cried Marian, rising from the ground, "I am very tired, or I would get up and box your ears. This is not a specimen of true yeoman's forest life, but rather of what we have to suffer from the insolent oppression of our Norman tyrants.

"Good," said Robin, smiling.

"Very good," repeated Little John.

"Excellent well," added Sir Ralph, sarcastically.

"Pardon me," continued Maid Marian, holding out her hand. "I had forgotten you were Norman. But I was about to say, if I had a broiled venison steak, a cup of good ale, and a roof of the humblest thatch over my head, I should be as happy as a queen."

"And I as a king," mumbled the giant.

"Which means," said Robin, "that you are hungry, thirsty, and tired.

"Yes."

"And hungry and thirsty you shall not be long," cried Robin heartily. "Do you, Little John, make a fire under the shadow of yon oak. We shall then better see what is to be done."

The oak referred to by the outlaw was a huge and vast tree overhanging the whole stream, and as all round trees grew in the greatest profusion, it was not by any means a dangerous experiment to enjoy one of the cheapest of heaven's blessings during a night in the open air—a warm fire.

The order was soon obeyed, and in ten minutes the wearied and exhausted fugitives were seated round the cheerful and crackling blaze.

But, though this was pleasant enough, it gave no indication of food, for want of which the whole party were scarcely able to carry one leg before the other.

Robin, while the fire was making, was washing his feet in the stream.

In ten minutes he rose, to all appearance fresh and ready for renewed trials of his endurance.

"How far is Hockley-in-the-Hole?"

"A mile."

"Thomas the carter's father keeps the ale-house?"

"Yes."

"Then I'll have, god wot, supper for you all in an hour," said bold Robin Hood.

"Amen," groaned Little John.

"Not for thy sake, fat paunch," said Robin, "do I travel to-night. I could not carry food enough for thy ungodly stomach in my best of moods."

"I will come and carry it myself."

"Good."

But Robin Hood did not move. Taking from the fire a number of charred pieces of wood, he dipped them in water, and then proceeded deliberately to daub his face and hands until he was to all appearance one of the regular charcoal-burners of the forest.

He then cut himself a faggot of dry wood, hoisted it on his head, and striding in the stream, followed by Little John, made as rapidly as he could for the village with the picturesque name of Hockley-in-the-Hole.

Little John knew the neighbourhood well, though, as he was not in general very fond of putting himself forward, he had hitherto said nothing.

"We're running into a trap," he said, as soon as they were quite out of hearing.

"I know it."

"Eh?"

"What am I to do?"

"Avoid it."

"When you are hungry what do you do?"

"Eat."

"When you are thirsty?"

"Drink."

"And tired?"

"Sleep."

"If ever you have a wife who is all three, what will you do, Master Little John?"

"Find her food, drink, and house room—or die."

"Come along—that's exactly what I am going to do."

"Hem!" said Little John.

"Well?"

"I have an idea."

"Out with it."

"Bill the charcoal-burner—he who people say shot at Prince John—lives down below. I know him. If you mean to go into the village, borrow clothes of him. I will stop with him and watch."

"It shall be done. Where is his house?"

"Come on shore, and I will show it you."

Robin did as he was directed, and scarcely did he stand upon the bank, ten feet lower down, when the whole scene came in view.

On the extreme edge of a point, jutting out into the river, was a ruddy, glowing fire, which a man stirred with a long stick.

His face was clearly seen by the lurid glare of the hot flames.

It was dark, gloomy, and thoughtful.

"Prince John stole his daughter?" asked Robin.

"Yes."

"Pity he did not shoot him to the heart. Were it prince or king, bishop or lord," hissed Robin, "he should die who harmed child of mine."

"Amen!"

"Curst Will will swear you are his best friend if you talk this way. Listen."

As he spoke the low, prolonged howl of a wolf burst from his lips.

The charcoal-burner stood still leaning on his stick.

Again the prolonged howl of the wolf was heard from his direction.

Then Little John raised his hand to his mouth, and produced an imitation of the frightened screech of a heron pursued by a falcon, with a clearness and accuracy that was amazing.

"It's long since I heard that so well done," said Curst Will, "come in, my old hearty—I'm glad to see you."

The two fugitives now advanced, and Little John, after a hearty shake of the charcoal-burner's hand, introduced him to Robin Hood, who at once saw that the man, however rough and uncouth, was thoroughly to be trusted.

He explained to him his desire to enter the village unsuspected by any.

"You ain't going to take John, here, with you, then. He's as well known in Hockley as the hangman in Nottingham."

"No."

"I will attend you, then," said the charcoal-burner, "there are many of my trade about here, and they won't suspect you in my company."

"Have you got anything to eat?" asked Little John, "its all very well for you fellows to be going down to the ale-house, while I stop here starving."

"There's no need to starve in Sherwood Forest. In yonder hutch you will find some brawn and oatmeal cake."

"Ah! ah!" laughed the tall forester, "you hav'nt derogated, Curst Will! By St. Barnabas, but here is a jug of ale—do you drink first, Robin."

The charcoal burner smiled at this summary way of dealing with his property, but both he and most men of his class would have done much for Robin Hood.

The ale was drank, the outlaw was disguised as well as possible, his only weapon being his knife, and thus accoutred they started on their journey.

Curst Will was by no means the saturnine and sulky companion his name might have indicated; he did not speak of himself, but on any other subject he was pleasant and communicative enough.

He had lived long in the neighbourhood, and knew every turn and winding of the forest.

"Are you far from any Norman residence?" asked the outlaw.

"Yes, some distance, but aroint the evil dogs, no place is too lonely or too humble for them to spy out. But that I live for vengeance, I should have left this part of the country long ago."

"Hast been injured by them?"

"To my heart's core," said Curst Will.

"Well, no man can say what may, or what may not happen. If you ever need a shelter, a tree home, come to the forest. Robin Hood will always give you a welcome."

"I may some day, but not yet, not yet. I have that to do must be done, ere I can leave this neighbourhood."

"As you please. But do not forget my offer."

"That will I not, but yonder is the village, and here is the ale-house. Mum! there are archers about. Follow me."

CHAPTER CLXVII.

THE ENGLISH VILLAGE.

MODERN peasantry know nothing of the luxury of being landholders.

It was very different before the rapacity of the newly enriched contrived to destroy the small tenancies.

It is a fact that within the last two hundred years almost every acre of land in this country, except the large entailed estates of the aristocracy, has quite changed hands. There is quite a different race and class of men now living on all the small possessions of land, or on what has been formed out of those small possessions, but the greatest and most rapid and striking alterations of this kind have taken place within the last fifty years. The French Revolution, in fact, introduced an English Revolution, which, if it did not shed so much blood on the British soil, thoroughly altered the title and holding of property, and pressed the blood as perfectly out of thousands of oppressed hearts.

That possession of small portions of land by the people, which now so strikingly distinguishes the people of the Continent from those of England—which makes, indeed, poverty so different a thing there and here—

would seem at one time to have been almost as general here as anywhere. If we still go into really old-fashioned districts—into those which the modern changes have not yet reached, where there are no manufactures; into the obscure and totally agricultural nooks—we see evidences of a most ancient order of things. The cottage, the farmhouse, the very halls are old, the trees are old, the hedges are old, everything is old. There is nothing that indicates change or progress. There is nothing, even in furniture, that may not have been there at least five hundred years; there is much that induces you to believe that eight hundred years ago it existed. In common labourers' cottages—before the late rage for old English furniture, which led the London brokers to scour the whole empire, penetrate into every nook, and buy up all the old cabinets, hall tables, old carved chairs, carved presses, and wardrobes, and retail them for five hundred per cent. profit, besides importing great quantities of similar articles from Holland, Belgium, and Germany —most persons have seen old, heavy, ample arm-chairs with pointed backs, in which one might imagine an Alfred or an Edward the Confessor sitting, with the date in great letters on their backs, of 1300 or 1400. There are plenty of houses so ancient that in the roofs and woodwork the ends of the great wooden pegs with which their framing is pinned together are not cut off. But without, how old is everything! The trees are dead at top and hollow at heart; there are ancient elms and oaks standing, whose shadow is said to have covered it's acre of ground, but which have now neither head nor heart; huge hollow shells, so capacious, that whole troops of children play in them, and call them their churches, and whole flocks of sheep or herds of cattle seek shelter from the summer sun in them.

The old villages, too, are lost, as it were, in a wilderness of ancient orchards, where the trees produce apples and pears totally unlike any now grown in modern plantings. The villages are surrounded by a maze of little crofts, whose hedges have evidently never been set out in any general enclosure, for they do not run in regular squares and straight lines, but form all imaginable figures, and with the true line of beauty, go waving and sweeping about in all directions. They are manifestly the effect of gradual and fitful enclosure from the forest in far-off times, many of them long before the Conquest, when this dense thicket and that group of trees were run up to and included as part of the fencing. These old hedges have often a monstrous width, occupying nearly as much in their aggregate amount as the aggregate amount of the enclosed land itself. They are often complete wildernesses of stony mounds, bushes, and rank vegetation. The hawthorns of which they are composed are no longer bushes, but old and widespreading trees, with great gaps and spaces often between them, having ceased to be actual fences between the old pastures, and become only most picturesque shades for the cattle. In the old crofts still flourish the native daffodils and the snow-white and pink primroses, now extirpated by the gathering for gardens everywhere else.

Such, there is no doubt, were our villages generally, all over the country, formerly, and for at least a thousand years. The whole country seemed to lie in a long and sunny dream. So little did population seem to increase, that rarely a house was built. The army and the distant towns took up the small surplus of people that appeared. So little did land seem wanted, that the forests and wastes lay from age to age unchanged. Every man had his little plot, or could enclose it for a small annual acknowledgment, and the rural race lived on with little exertion and no care.

The first shock to this state of things was the Reformation. The breaking-up of the monasteries at once turned on the country a vast number of monks and nuns nearly destitute of means of existence, and a still vaster number of poor people, who had to be supported on the third of the church revenues given expressly for the poor.

The people—greedy courtiers, gamblers, commissioners, and speculators—who got hold, by a variety of means, but seldom by any honest ones, of the church and abbey lands—rose, or wished to rise, into the ranks of the aristocracy. They would have their halls, their parks, their chases; their children would no longer

learn trades—they, too, must be provided with land; and hence came the growing jealousy of all encroachments by the poor on waste lands—nay, the violent disposition to encroach, on one plea or another, on the small proprietor. Then, in fact, began those scenes so well described by Goldsmith in his "Deserted Village." Every one of these *novi homines* would have an establishment like the ancient aristocracy.

> The man of wealth and pride
> Takes up a space that many poor supplied—
> Space for his lake, his park's extended bounds,
> Space for his horses, equipage, and hounds.
> The robe that wraps his limbs in silken sloth
> Has robbed the neighbouring fields of half their growth;
> His seat, where solitary sports are seen,
> Indignant spurns the cottage from the green.

Robin Hood—if our readers will pardon this digression—assuming that slouching walk which belongs to those who labour in the open air for their daily bread, followed the charcoal-burner into the house.

It was crowded with men-at-arms, who had halted here to pass the night.

The woman of the house and her daughter were waiting upon the soldiery; but the landlord, a sturdy Saxon, was away in a kind of shed, working away at a coarse kind of shoe, probably more with a view to be away from the Normans than from any very great desire to be industrious.

The charcoal-burner entered the shed, the outlaw following, and leaning listlessly against the doorway.

The Saxon looked up rather angrily, but when he saw the face of Curst Will he smiled, and spoke in his own dialect.

Will did the same, and mentioned the name of his visitor, upon which the proud father of Thomas the carter looked up with a pleased and gratified glance.

Then, with an affectation of carelessness, he left off his work and closed the door.

"Do you know why these men are here?" he whispered.

"After me?"

"Yes. They have orders to keep every avenue, and search all suspected persons who pass."

"Indeed!"

"I saw one fellow look oddly this way just now," continued old Carter.

"Then I'd better be moving."

"Hist!" said the old man: and then he added, in a loud tone of voice, "A cup of ale?—yes, my masters; and some swine?—directly."

And he pushed open the door, leaving the charcoal-burner and outlaw together.

The soldiers, whatever their ulterior objects, were now too fully employed in satisfying their appetites to take much notice.

They had been out half the day in the wood.

The landlord passed through their midst, glancing at the empty goblets and leathern bottles, until he reached a kind of store-room, the door of which he closed behind him.

His wife was in the store-room.

"What is it?" she said.

"Not a word. Curst Will has brought one here we must oblige, though at the peril of our lives."

"Hoity, toity! a drinking tinker, like himself."

"Hist, woman! 'tis our Thomas's best friend, Robin——"

"Holy Virgin! if they find him they will sack and pillage and rob—oh, Lord!"

"Silence! They will not suspect him. Give me food for him and his friends, who are hiding from these bloodthirsty hounds. I see the hutch. Now go to these Norman pirates, and keep them amused with your gabble."

The wife, hardly knowing what she was about, left the room; while old Carter passed a load of provisions through a narrow window into a dark yard at the back.

He did not forget ale, knowing that it was as necessary as food to the fugitives.

Then he again passed through the public room.

"Well, old sourchops," said one of the men, "won't you join us in some of your own swipes?"

"He! he! he!" replied old Carter, with a grin.

"My master, you are funny. Never refuse a good cup when any one else pays for it."

The soldier laughed at this, and then allowed the inn-keeper and cobbler to leave the room.

He found Robin and Curst Will still standing waiting, and pointed to a narrow door leading to the yard.

The shoemaker then reseated himself, and appeared wholly absorbed in his work.

His eyes were fixed upon the ground.

" Be careful," he muttered, without ceasing his work. "The stuff you want is in the yard. Take it, but don't come back this way. There's one knave whose eye is this way now."

Curst Will and Robin made no reply, but glided into the yard, which was completely dark.

The charcoal-burner, however, appeared gifted with the sight of a cat.

He moved, with stealthy steps, to where the ale and provisions stood, divided the load with Robin, and moved towards the rear of the hut, which was not ten yards from the forest.

They were in another moment beneath its shadows, on their way to rejoin Little John.

They had not gone a hundred yards when they heard a great cry.

Their absence had been discovered, and no doubt had excited suspicion.

Still they did not hear that they were followed in the wood.

Robin was too anxious about his wife and friends to be very curious as to what was just then occurring in his rear.

He pressed forward then, in the footsteps of Curst Will, who threaded the forest with the *sang froid* and phlegm of a Red Indian runner.

They soon were within hailing distance of Little John. But Will suddenly halted.

He drew his companions behind a tree.

" What is it?"

"Something suspicious."

Robin glanced across the stream to where the charcoal-burner's hut and fire could be clearly distinguished upon a spit of land.

The outlaw examined the whole scene keenly.

" I can't make it out."

" Do you see Little John?"

" No."

" I do. He is, to all appearance, asleep, out of the range of the fire."

" Well?"

" It is'nt likely he would get away from it a cold night like this."

" True."

" Then my firm belief is he's tied and gagged, that we may not be warned."

" True," said Robin, putting down his part of the provisions.

"They've taken him asleep, and tied him," said Will. " Ah! I saw an eye peer through a chink, the light fell full upon it. They are in my hut."

A short pause ensued, during which time the outlaw and his companion concealed their bundles, and then, secreted by the bushes, ascended the stream until they could no longer see the fire.

They then waded across the stream, climbed the opposite bank, and, with the stealth of snakes, crawled towards the charcoal-burner's hut.

Soon they were in full view of it.

But they were on their hands and knees.

A distance of some six yards separated them from where Little John was tied to a tree, his strong arms secured by ropes, and his mouth gagged.

Robin signed to Curst Will to remain still, but ready to act on occasion.

The tree to which the tall forester was attached was a large one, and cast a heavy shadow.

In this line, the fire making all bright elsewhere, Robin, lying flat on the ground, began to crawl.

His motions were slow, and made with the most profound caution.

He never advanced a half-foot without pausing to listen. The men in the hut did not stir.

At length Robin lay recumbent on the ground, with his head close to the trunk of a tree.

He whispered low, but distinctly and clearly.

" Little John—don't move, look, or speak. Whatever you do, don't be in a hurry to use your arms."

As he spoke he cut the cords which bound the tall forester, leaving the gag slightly attached.

Then he retreated the way he came, and once more concealed himself in the bush.

After about five minutes he rose, and speaking aloud to Curst Will, began shaking the bushes.

" Come along," he said, " I am sure this is the way."

And he and Curst Will burst from the cover.

Three men-at-arms rushed at them from the hut, armed with short swords and provided with cords.

Robin Hood and Curst Will stood quite still.

" That's the wrong way," roared a voice with the emphasis of a bull.

At the same moment Little John, leaping up, kicked one man right into the stream, while upon the others he rained heavy blows with his cudgel.

" The fiend! the fiend!" they cried, and plunged after their half-drowned companion.

Curst Will quickly lifted up a brand, flung it into the thatch of his hut, and in an instant it was in flames.

" Why?" cried Robin.

" I know the evil knaves," said Curst Will; "they shall not have the pleasure of destroying it. But let us hasten away—the rascals have run nimbly, and will be upon us ere we expect them."

All acquiesced, and again the stream was crossed, and the provisions secured.

Not a word was spoken, as every ear was bent to catch the faintest sound.

But until they came to where their friends had been left no further alarm was heard.

CHAPTER CLXVIII.

SIR HUGH.

THEY found Maid Marian and the others exceedingly anxious about them, which, as they had been some considerable time, was but natural.

Robin at once cautioned them as to the danger of their position.

Not a word was to be spoken above a breath.

The spot selected for a halt, it will be recollected, was under a sort of bank, with trees and brushwood overhanging the river.

It was quite dark, and in this was their chief security. A fire would have been certain to betray them.

All ate and drank in silence, and then thoughtfully and moodily sat staring at the river, which flowed by with its soft and placid murmur.

" How feel you, Marian?" said Robin, after the meal was over; " can you walk?"

" Must we?"

" If we remain here until dawn we shall never escape them. Our only chance is the night."

" Then let us be moving," whispered all.

As Curst Will was best acquainted with this particular part of the wood he took the lead, and at once led the way in the direction of the village.

They were too well satisfied of his feelings to doubt him for a moment.

Suddenly he halted.

A loud crackling of flames, lamentations of women and children, the stern shouting of soldiery arose from the hamlet.

" The wretches are illusing and pillaging the Saxons," cried Curst Will.

In another moment, by pushing through the bushes, they came in sight of the village.

The ale-house and adjacent huts were in flames, while round about were mounted soldiers urged on by a ruthless officer to continue their work of destruction.

The Normans were fifty well-armed men.

" Would that I had two dozen of my yeomen," said the outlaw chief, with a stern smile.

At the same moment he unstrung his bow. All his companions, save Ralph, did the same.

The chief was a burly man in armour, who, with loud execrations, was urging his men to continue the abominable work of destruction.

" To h—— with all who give shelter and food to outlaws. Death to the knaves who aid and abet men under the ban of the church," he cried.

A whizzing was heard through the air, and four arrows struck the chief.

Two pierced his coat of mail, and felled him to the ground.

"The outlaws! the outlaws!" roared the men-at-arms, who, scarcely able to tell whence the attack came, galloped furiously up and down.

"Charge them! Down with the sneaking wolves!" cried the Norman leader, sitting up. "Thrust the Saxon churls into the flames!"

A second volley of arrows was the response to this brutal order, and then, to augment the confusion, the outlaw chief sounded his bugle.

It was answered.

Loud and ringingly did Robin ply it now, and ere ten minutes were over, a large detachment of outlaws, who had been searching for the fugitives, from information received in Ashby-de-la-Zouch, came up.

One volley was enough.

The men-at-arms fled, taking with them their wounded, and the yeomen in Lincoln green were masters of the field.

But Robin Hood knew the danger of delay when the wood contained such bitter enemies in overwhelming force.

He bade such of the villagers as were compromised to secrete themselves in the forest until the ruffians had retired, while he, at the head of his gallant band of fifty outlaws, retreated to one of his fastnesses capable of defence.

Here he proposed to hold out until reinforcements came up, and while he sent a trusty messenger to inform the king of what was taking place.

Curst Will was determined for the present to share their fate, though he was by no means willing permanently to give up his private way of vengeance.

With such a party as he had now around him, the King of Sherwood had little fear of being attacked at night in the forest, so determined, for the sake of the women, to halt at once.

But though he had every desire to make the women comfortable, the outlaw neglected none of those precautions which are so essential in this peculiar kind of warfare, to protect the smaller party from attack.

About a mile distant on the summit of a hill, called by some Moulse Coombe, was a space devoid of trees, though overgrown with bushes, which was popularly said to be the remains of an old Roman camp.

At all events there was a ditch, a solid mound of earth, round the whole hill top, and four steep mountain sides to overcome, ere the camp could be attacked.

Here the outlaw then led his party, tents, or rather huts, were hastily erected, provisions drawn forth, and then the whole party, wearied and fatigued, lay down to rest.

When we say the whole party, we do not include the sentries, without whom no cautious leader would have taken repose.

But though four tried archers walked beneath the shadows of the trees on the verge of the forest, Robin Hood himself did not long remain within the rude brush hut that served him for a tent.

He crawled out, and quickly roused Little John and Will Scarlett, to hold a council of war.

With all the gravity of Indians the two lieutenants settled themselves round a small fire in a hollow.

Robin Hood did not speak for some time.

"Sir Ralph ought to be here," he said, after some thought. "He is as much interested as we are."

Will Scarlett went to his hut, and at once aroused him.

Sir Ralph, half asleep, came to the hill-top.

"What is it?" he asked.

"Be seated, all," said Robin; "I wish to take council with you all. We are in great peril."

"Yes."

"Sir Hugh Fitzurse once dispossessed of the property, would not be able to win it back, even at the expense of her death."

"Death!"

"Well," said Robin, "we must put things plainly. Your great object is to escape his clutches."

"Certainly."

"I am equally intent on defending my Marian."

"Of course."

"I have called you together to consult, therefore, as to the best means to be employed."

"We trust to you."

"In the multitude of councillors there is wisdom," said Robin.

"Flight is our first resource."

"Hum!" said Robin.

"Listen. For myself I say that doubtless, ere morning, our fort will be surrounded by a powerful, well-armed, and disciplined body of men, against whom we shall have to defend ourselves by every means in our power. Flight, therefore, would be wisdom should we be able to decide that the women can move like men and soldiers."

"Agnes is exhausted," said Ralph.

"So is Eveline," said Will Scarlett.

"And so is Marian."

"Then flight," said Little John, "is out of the question."

"Exactly," continued the outlaw; "and therefore it is that I wish to take such precautions for our defence as shall seem wisest, discreetest, best, to all friends."

"I'm ready," said John.

"I know you all are; but it must be plain to you if Sir Hugh Fitzurse and Robert of Nottingham come to the charge with anything like vigour, and overpower us with numbers, we must, in the end fall, when our bones will surely whiten this old hill-top."

"Humph!" said John.

"Very likely," added Ralph.

"True as gospel," observed Will Scarlett.

"My opinion, then, is, that our only hope of escape is a rescue; for which reason I propose to fortify this spot with all convenient haste, until it is capable of lasting at least one day. In the meantime scouts must go forth, collect our men, and, with such force as they may command, burst upon the Norman assailants."

"Good!"

"Excellent well!"

"I would go, myself," continued Robin Hood, "but I feel that I am wanted here. Who will volunteer? There is Much the miller, Thomas the carter——"

"Nay," said Will Scarlett; "I and Little John will go this bout. Do you but hold out till to-morrow night, and there shall be help enough, in God's name."

"Thank you. What says Little John?"

"Nothing, except that he's ready to obey orders."

"'Tis well. Now hearkee. As soon as you have found some of the merry men, take them and send them to yonder height," pointing to a wooded mound at about a mile distance. "One of you should then command there."

"That will I," said Little John.

"As soon as we have fortified this place I will have a beacon made you shall see, when fired, at any distance. Let no succour come until that is fired; but when it is in a blaze, be quick, for you will all be wanted."

Little John and Will Scarlett knew that no promises on their part were needed. They simply rose, crossed the open camp, and buried themselves in the forest.

"We must now begin our fortifications," said Robin. "These knaves may attack us ere daylight."

A light, tremulous note on the bugle roused all the party; and the outlaw's orders being given with brevity, all flew to obey commands so necessary to their own safety and well-being.

The object was to fell such trees as did not form a line round the old Roman camp, leaving on the summit of the hill all such bushes as were useful and advantageous to the bowmen.

However rude these logs and boughs were piled, they would impede men in armour and confronting such shots as the outlaws were known to be.

But in the centre of the space enclosed by the old ditch and earthworks a second defence was made. It was made with faggots piled up about six feet from the ground, and kept together by stakes struck through them into the soil.

This of itself was a formidable rampart.

As long as the outer works could be defended this was to serve as a shelter for the women.

About an hour before dawn all was completed, and the yeomen lay down to repose.

"We shall have it stormy," said Ralph.

"No," said Robin Hood. "'Tis true there were clouds in the sky when the sun dropped below them yester evening, but there was also a streak of yellow light, near to the line of the mountains, that our wise people say is a sign that the sun will rise in beauty to-morrow."

"Perhaps so," replied Ralph. "I am not very learned in weather signs."

"Hist!"

"What hear you?"

"Stoop low."

Sir Ralph Tressilian did so, and heard distinctly the low, heavy tramp of men in a body moving with extreme precaution.

"They come," he said.

"Do you," continued Robin Hood, "remain here with twenty men, while I sally upon these fellows, and teach them that, whatever else they may do, they cannot surprise us."

At the same moment the outlaw gave a low whistle, that brought round him all the men he required.

He then crept to the edge of the wood, crawled beneath the rude defences, and advanced some distance down the side of the slope, halting as soon as the heavy tramp of the advancing soldiers could be clearly heard.

At the place they had now reached, the bushes and undergrowth had disappeared, and a wide glade, stretching over hill and hollow, swept away from both sides of the track further than the eye could reach.

The trees, standing wider apart than usual, were, if possible, of a more majestic character; their wide and massive tops were so thickly interlaced, that not a single sunbeam, moonbeam, or ray of starlight found its way among the gloomy arches below.

The merrie men stood in this way in impenetrable gloom, so that by simply closing up to the trees their enemies could perceive nothing of them.

The column of assailants that now advanced to attack them in those still hours of morn when man is most influenced by heavy sleep, was about a hundred in number.

A low, subdued order was given by Robin.

Every man fixed an arrow and loosened two more.

The column of assailants was not more than fifty feet from the outlaws.

"Strike!" roared Robin.

A flight of arrows poured at the same moment into the very thick of the soldiery.

The confusion was intense. Oaths, cries of savage anger, curses loud and deep, burst from all. The fact of their enemy being unseen unmanned them.

A second, a third volley ensued.

The men-at-arms took to their heels, despite the loud and angry cries of their chiefs.

The surprise was a failure.

Robin Hood and his victorious followers retired to the old Roman camp, well aware that they had only obtained a short respite from their merciless foes.

CHAPTER CLXIX.

THE FIRE.

SUCH provisions as were in the encampment were now brought out, and found to be sufficient for two hearty meals, in which the whole was divided.

Robin had too much confidence in little John and Will Scarlett to believe he needed to reserve his victuals.

Especially when it is well known men fight not well upon an empty stomach.

This important domestic arrangement being settled, the whole band was divided into four troops, which were severally detached north, south, east and west, to wait for the advent of the enemy.

The women were placed within the frail citadel of fagots cut from the tops of the forest trees, that had been felled for the ramparts.

They were here safe from the arrows and bolts of the enemy.

But whatever they might have felt inwardly, none of these noble girls showed any fear.

They knew too well the terrible stake for which their husbands were about to do combat.

Agnes was as thorough a Saxon as any of them, while she knew her husband's truth and honour.

Besides, if fighting against Norman foes, he was doing the bidding of his lawful king.

The archers, whose numerical force was so vastly overcome by that of the enemy, took up positions which commanded the best view of the four ascents.

They were in themselves in the garrison's favour, as before the intrenchments could be reached the enemy must in some places crawl on their hands and knees.

It was some hours before any sign of hostility could be distinguished.

Then it came warmly and suddenly.

From all sides the Normans pressed upon them.

In silence until warned by a murderous discharge that they were discovered.

They were led by chosen chiefs, and were Robin Hood saw in numbers so great as to be overwhelming.

With stern and settled mien, Robin and three others descended into the old ditch.

On all sides four volunteers did the same.

They were armed with bow, arrows, quarterstaves, and knives, with short Norman swords.

The archers from above plied their arrows with incessant activity.

The Normans replied by their crossbows and bolts, and then rushed to scale the wooden ramparts.

Robin Hood and the other concealed outlaws were ready for them. Leaping up, they shot their arrows in their faces, and then used their quarterstaves, with the determination of men who fight for liberty and life.

But numbers in all contests, were there is almost equal bravery, must ultimately prevail.

The outlaw chief saw that he was utterly overpowered. He looked up almost despairing at the heavens.

The sun indicated mid-day.

A desperate expedient suggested itself.

He looked about him. No Norman had, as yet, gained the inside of the camp.

But his comrades were wounded, some severely.

He blew one blast of his bugle.

In three minutes more the outlaws were in full retreat, next moment they were within the fortress of faggots and stakes.

A small fire burnt low in the centre.

Robin bade his men give the Normans one warm welcome. He then glanced at the wind.

"Close up all," he said, as he saw that a desperate volley had taken effect upon the Normans.

The outlaws retreated to where he stood. A number of burning brands had been cast on the fire.

"Light up!" cried Robin Hood, setting the example. "Light up on three sides only."

The women, cowering under the fourth, showed the one that was to be spared.

It was that to windward.

Next instant the dry and dead wood, pine-knots, and other fuel of the kind first catching in flames, the green wood sent forth a strong and pungent odour.

A cloud of smoke poured upon the Normans, followed by the roar of incessant flames.

The outlaws looked aghast.

The moment this fuel was exhausted, they were at the mercy of the soldiery.

"'Tis a beacon fire," said Robin aloud, "prepare to hold out better than ever. We shall have assistance soon. See! see!"

And he pointed to where a dense column of smoke rose from a distant hillock of the forest.

And the attack of the Normans had ceased.

Bewildered by this startling occurrence, the soldiery had retreated to the woods to wait the result.

The outlaws were not even attacked on the side where there was no fire.

Perhaps the Normans thought it a voluntary snare.

By no means.

It was only fear drove them back.

They were afraid that the desperate men in Lincoln green, thus surrounded by their foes, were about to set fire to the forest.

The fearful flood of smoke, of sparks that whirled down the sides of the mountains confirmed this idea.

The whole body of Norman soldiery had rushed down the declivity to take fresh orders from their chief.

Sir Hugh Fitzurse, Robert of Nottingham, and a select body of men were collected together at some distance, the overwhelming force they had sent against the foe, making them really ashamed to lead them on, as one knight was generally considered more than a match for a host of footmen.

They expected every moment to see the sturdy yeomen brought prisoners to their feet by the powerful body of soldiery that had been sent against them.

"These yeomen are stubborn dogs," said Robert of Nottingham, "audacious dogs."

"Aye, and will be more audacious still," added Sir Hugh Fitzurse, "if we allow this springal who calls himself Earl of Huntingdon to escape."

"Aye, indeed. Does not this prove how weak Richard is? Who else would take a man's word in a matter so important to himself."

"True," added Sir Hugh, in a low tone; "it only proves that if we knights and barons would rule the roast, we must side with a prince we can trust."

"True, I say—but how suddenly the conflict has ceased. What is the meaning of it?"

The chiefs of the invading party, had selected a kind of rocky terrace, on the summit of a cliff, surrounded by a dense belt of forest, to await the issue of the conflict.

Both rose from the stones on which they sat.

At the same moment immense volumes of smoke rolled over their heads, and whirled in eddies around.

"They have fired the wood."

"Curse the fiends!" continued Fitzurse, "we must flee."

At the same moment they heard a roaring sound, like the rushing of furious winds.

They turned to flee.

It was clear that the wind, which was rather high, had carried the sparks and flames into the forest, which, at that time of the year, contained great quantities of dry brush and under-growth.

"Fly! fly! for your lives!" roared voices in the wood.

But though Sir Hugh and the son of the Earl of Nottingham, with their companions, would gladly have done so. They soon saw that it was impossible.

The platform of rock was both high and perpendicular to leeward, while to windward it was completely surrounded by the dense forest.

At first the Norman leaders had seen nothing but immense clouds of white smoke that had been pouring over the summit of the mountains, actually concealing the progress and ravages of the devouring element.

But now a crackling sound drew their eyes towards the outline of smoke, and they perceived the waving flames shooting forward from the vapour, now flaring in the air and then bending to the earth, seeming to light into combustion every stick and shrub on which they breathed.

The Norman soldiers turned pale and red.

Upwards all was flames, to the north and east the rock was precipitous.

To the south was a narrow gap, leading towards the places below.

But here lay not only a line of brambles and other shrubs, but a collection of the tops of trees, old and dried right across their course.

With one accord all made a rush in that direction, when an eddying of the warm currents of the air swept a forked tongue of flame across the pile, which lighted at the touch, and the whole body were at once opposed by the surly roaring of a body of fire, as if a furnace had been glowing in their path.

They recoiled from the heat, and stood back out of reach of the smoke, looking with a kind of stupid interest at the flames, which now had made of the hill side one sheet of living flame.

The rock was examined, but no means of descending was visible to any.

"We shall be choked," said Fitzurse, in a surly tone; "a pretty rabbit's death—smoked in our warren."

"The flames cannot reach us," replied one of the soldiers, "if we can keep our insides clear."

And he pointed to the surface of the rock.

The extremely thin covering of earth over the rock on which they stood naturally supported but a scanty and faded herbage, and any trees that might in former days have found root in the fissures had already died during the great heats of one or two summers.

Round the edge of the terrace were one or two retaining still a slight appearance of life, bearing a few dry and withered leaves, that were drained of their nourishment, while others were mere wrecks.

These flared and roared terribly as they successively caught fire, filling the air with a pitchy smoke that threatened to choke the party on the rock.

By the advice of one of the men all lay down, and thus got rid of the worst of the huge volumes, which, though beat down upon them by the eddying winds, soon found their natural level in the air.

It was a scene of utter desolation and woe.

The air seemed quivering with rays of heat, that quivered round the parched stems of the trees.

The roaring of the flames, the crackling of the furious element, with the tearing of falling branches, and the thundering echoes of prostrated trees, caused altogether an awful and terrible din.

Dark clouds swept over head, adding additional horror to the scene.

Then came a lull, as if the destructive element had done its worst.

A lull strangely broken in upon.

There was a loud tra-la-la from the very summit of the hill.

Was that an echo?

No.

The notes of the bugle were repeated from half a dozen different parts of the forest.

The Normans rose.

The trees no longer crackled, the bushes no longer hissed; the fire, which had been confined to a dry strip from the ancient Roman encampment to the spot were they stood, was now dying away.

There were no flames, but the smoke that rose from the smouldering trunks was still black and dense.

Still, from the burning element they were saved, the question being simply one of time.

A cold, chilly blast next struck their faces. It was simply the wind veering round, and, by contrast, appearing quite cold and icy.

Where were their companions?

Robert of Nottingham, taking a long and refreshing breath, took his bugle and sounded a mot of alarm.

It was answered from below the mountain, quite from the plain.

Then came a taunting echo from above.

The chiefs exchanged glances.

Their men had fled in all directions, while they, in all probability, were at the mercy of the outlaws.

They seated themselves and waited.

Nothing could be done.

The wind became colder and colder, the heavens were covered by black and angry clouds, and then in five minutes more the rain came down in torrents.

The Normans sat with their backs to the storm, which, at the end of half an hour, was over.

The forest now scarcely smouldered, and the whole party rising from the ground, prepared to force their way through the smouldering embers.

At the same moment some twenty bowmen, armed to the teeth, appeared on the platform, and demanded their surrender.

The Normans sullenly obeyed, and were then, after being disarmed, led them up the hill.

At the summit they found Robin Hood, surrounded by four hundred men in Lincoln green.

The Normans, nothing abashed, looked insolently around.

"What means this, fellows?" said Fitzurse.

"It means," replied Robin Hood, with a stern and angry look, "that you are my prisoners, and that I will not give you up except into the hands of such persons as King Richard, his grace, may appoint."

The Normans hung their heads and whispered.

"Robin Hood," said Fitzurse, with as much assumed ease as he could put on, "if you will let me go scot free I will pay ransom."

THE MORRIS DANCE AT ROBIN HOOD'S WEDDING.

"That will not suffice."

"Hear me. I will sign any document that may be prepared, relinquishing all claim on the lands and rights of my niece, Agnes Fitzurse."

"Lady Agnes Tressilian," said Ralph, slipping forward, "my honoured wife."

"Do you accept this pledge?" asked Robin.

"Yes; as soon as parchment can be prepared he shall sign it; and then let him go—hang himself, if he will," added Sir Ralph.

"What offer you?" said Robin, addressing the son of the Earl of Northampton.

"I ask my affianced wife," he replied, with a haughty and angry look.

"And who may that be?" said Robin Hood, with a meaning smile.

"Edith Marian of Athelston."

"My wife," replied the outlaw, as, amid loud and long-continued cheers, Maid Marian stood forth.

"Wife!" gasped the young nobleman; "wife! Hast dared to wed a ward of the crown?"

"I dare do anything that does become a man," replied Robin Hood, haughtily.

"Married!" he repeated, with pale face and quivering lips. "Marian," he added, turning to her with a sad and sorrowful face, "what is done cannot be undone. But the day will come when you will repent this."

"Never!"

"So now you think. I loved you, though you knew it not, but preferred to woo you through my father, certain that, once my wife, your duty and my affection would have made our home a proud, a glorious, and a happy one. Instead of this, a ward of the crown, under the tutelage of regal authority, you have gone through some idle ceremony with one whose head bears a price, and who, whatever his courage and good qualities, is still an outlaw."

Robin Hood and Maid Marian exchanged glances.

"A word with you, Master Robert of Nottingham," said the merry monarch of Sherwood Forest.

The young man advanced, and conversed with Robin and his wife apart.

"On your honour as a man, and your faith as a Christian," said the outlaw, "will you keep a secret?"

"I will."

"Will you swear it on the crossed hilt of this sword?" continued Robin Hood.

"I will."

Robin waited while the other drew his sword, lifted it to his lips, and swore a solemn oath to keep any secret which might be confided to him.

"Then let me tell you," said Robin, showing one parchment; "here is the release of Edith of Athelston from all wardship to the crown; and here," showing another one, "is a second, as the proof of our marriage, celebrated by the Bishop of London, and witnessed by King Richard himself."

"Damnable traitor!" roared the Norman, and, ere any one guessed at his foul intent, he struck at Maid Marian with his sword, "you never shall enjoy her."

But the girl, who, surprised and astounded, had never taken her eyes off him, leaped on one side.

The young man fell prostrate on the sward, floored by a terrible blow from the quarterstaff of Little John, the lieutenant.

"Die, dog!"

"Nay, leave him," said Robin, who was deadly pale; "he shall be given up to trial by the laws."

They lifted him up, but he was dead. A burst of furious passion had killed him on the spot.

"You saw this, Sir Hugh," said Robin, mildly.

"I did, and am much surprised. It was indeed rank treachery," replied the knight.

"You will report it as such. As soon as you have signed the parchment, and paid my men your ransom, you can remove the body. All can see that his own passions slew him."

The knight stepped up to where Sir Ralph and Friar Tuck, with great difficulty, had written, in very few words, on a piece of parchment that which they had agreed to. Sir Hugh signed, though manifestly with an ill grace; for which, however, no man, or woman either, in that company cared one brass farthing, as there were ample witnesses to the deed, and the signatures well known.

"And now," said Sir Ralph, sternly, "I bid you adieu. But recollect that I hold you accountable for any harm that may befall me or mine. I have the king's promise to befriend me, but I shall know also how to defend my rights."

"And I shall know how to maintain mine," replied Sir Hugh Fitzurse, who thereupon, with his fellows, left the ground wholly to the possession of the outlaws.

A scornful cheer followed them; and then the whole party of men in Lincoln green took their way down the slope of the hill, not at all desirous of any more fighting that day, but rather wishing to enjoy such repose as the presence of women seemed to require.

That night they once more camped in the greenwood; but the next day they reached the cavern, where, during the years it had been occupied by the outlaws, it had been so much restored and improved, as now to contain a perfect subterraneous town.

It was well warmed; the forest supplying them with some such an inexhaustible supply of fuel as the coal districts do at the present moment.

But in those primitive days coal and porter were not patronised, for no other reason than because they were black.

The outlaws, however, knew well enough what good things were, and took care to have an endless supply of ale, if they did of nothing else.

Had they but known of tobacco, we believe they would have thought themselves in Paradise.

END OF BOOK I.

BOOK II.—ROBIN HOOD MARRIED.

I have heard talk of Robyne Hode,
    Hey down and hey down a;
And of brave Little John,
Of Friar Tuck and Will Scarlett,
Locksley and Maid Marion,
    Hey down, derry down.

CHAPTER I.

THE FOREST WEDDING.

WE have already said that Robin Hood, though quite satisfied that his real marriage should take place on the sly, had no intention, however, of baulking either himself or his friends of a jolly wedding.

In the olden times, when people were happy and did not feel too much the hand of the oppressor upon them, a merrier-hearted crew than the English people could not be conceived.

Even when poor, dependent, and suffering from want of the real necessaries of life, there is a tendency to joviality about them, which is shown on every occasion that is afforded them.

Now, of all occasions to bring about a jollification, a wedding is the most suitable.

Some people have so great a tendency that way that they will be jolly at a funeral.

This, however, is bad taste.

As soon as the young people were reposed from their fatigues it was agreed that the ceremony should take place.

All the wits and ingenious sprites of the confederation had for days been racking their brains to find suitable devices for the occasion.

Friar Tuck was both chaplain, bishop, and master of the ceremonies ; everything being under his directions.

Robin Hood gave no heed to what was going on. He was still in that happy fools' paradise of the honeymoon; when really a man can think of nothing but his love.

They were truly a happy couple.

> With every morn their love grew tenderer,
>   With every eve deeper and deeper still ;
> He might not in house, field, or garden stir,
>   But her full shape would all his seeing fill.
> And his continual voice was pleasanter
>   To her than noise of trees or hidden rill ;
> Her lute string gave an echo of his name,
> She spoilt her half-done broidery with the same.

It was early morn, and the green forest glade, already so often referred to in these pages, was crowded by a perfect multitude.

There were present all the outlaws in the forest, gathered to do honour to their chief and queen.

With men, women, lasses and children, there were over a thousand.

The deer of the forest suffered pretty extensively for all this unusual collection of people.

They were slaughtered without any very great regard to regal or manorial rights.

Swine, too, were killed in abundance.

The whole were in holiday dress ; the outlaws in bran new suits of Lincoln green, the women in their short petticoats and kirtles.

At one end of the arena was a rude altar of turf, adorned with a great array of candlesticks and holy utensils.

Friar Tuck was arrayed in full canonicals, and looked, with his rubicund face, leering eyes, and hypocritical pretence at gravity, a perfect specimen of the priest who believes not that which it is his trade to preach.

But Friar Tuck was no worse than many of his fellows—no worse than many in modern times, who make religion a mere cloak to hide their vices and the pocket which they are eternally filling from those of other men.

All the girls had been busy making garlands, and every tree was festooned with flowers, while myriads of coarse lamps, with pork and venison fat, and rude wicks, were stuck about the trees ready for the evening.

At eleven of the clock—dreadfully late in times when breakfast was taken at daybreak, dinner at ten, and supper at four—the wedding party, escorted by a select division of the merry men, came towards the altar.

Robin Hood wore bright scarlet, Maid Marian a rich court dress, that in which she had been privately married.

They looked, indeed, a happy and a handsome couple.

The jolly friar received them with all the dignity of which he was capable.

The vast audience formed the two-thirds of a circle in such a way that all could see.

Then the hedge priest began the ceremony, which, with a due regard to the feelings of the spectators, and the state of the coming repast—the odour of which assailed his nostrils—he made rather short, and, before the whole of the merry men, Robin Hood and Maid Marian were made one.

The shout that greeted this announcement made the forest ring again.

Then followed the feast, to which all having done due honour, some turned to quarterstaff, some to quoits, some to wrestling, some to shooting, while those who had lasses with them crowded round the music, and prepared to join in the somewhat complicated morris dance.

Robin Hood and Maid Marian commenced, and it was a pleasure to see them tripping on the greensward, running in and out, clashing swords, ringing bells, and performing every item of this dance recently introduced from among the Moors.

Then, having broken the ice, the king and queen sat them down on their sylvan throne and surveyed their subjects.

The older men were collected apart, paying more attention to their gullets than to the games.

The leader of these was Friar Tuck, who, having put about three pounds of solid meat under his belt, was now busily striving to wash it down with as many quarts of good old English ale, a beverage the priest preferred even to the most generous liquors of France and Spain.

Every now and then there came from this quarter a burst of song.

Like all men half seas over, they became at once musical, liquor of any kind seeming to dispose a man to sing, whether he owns a voice or not.

As for Friar Tuck, he owned a most melodious voice of his own, and elevated or sober, was always ready with a ditty or a stave either about love or wine, two subjects on which the worthy priest was never tired.

Soon Will Scarlett's wife and one or two others of the young maidens, or matrons we must now call them, wearied of the dancing, and came round the throne, they and their handsome and stalwart husbands forming by no means an inappropriate court for the monarch of Sherwood Forest and his lovely queen.

It was at this moment that a general silence took place near where the friar sat, he having called it to sing his favourite and standing song, when roused to boisterous merriment by the red, red wine, or foaming ale—

> You may talk as you please of your candle and book,
> And prate about virtue with sanctified look,
> Neither priest, book, nor candle can help you so well
> To make friends with the world as the jolly bottle.

"Chorus, my lads. Out with it!" shouted the singer, and the whole crew set up an uproarious cry as they joined him—

> Sing heave and ho, and trombelow,
> The jolly bottle is the best, I trow.
> Then take the bottle, it is well stitched of leather,
> And better than doublet keeps out wind and weather.
> Let the bottom look up to the broad arch of blue,
> And then catch the drippings, as good fellows do.
> With heave and ho, and trombelow,
> 'Tis sinful to waste good liquor, you know.
> The soldier he carries his knapsack and gun,
> And swoons at the weight as he tramps through the sun,
> But, devil a loon did I ever hear tell,
> Who swore at the weight of the jolly bottle.
> So heave and ho, and trombelow,
> The jolly bottle is a feather, I trow.

"Bravo!" shouted Robin. "Well sung, my jolly clerk of Copemanhurst. Now, silence for Maid Marian!"

A crimson blush passed over the features of the young girl at this sudden call.

But she was not one of those who, having a good voice and knowing it, would hesitate to comply with the wishes of one she so loved and honoured as her husband.

A dead silence prevailed, and then in rich and mellow tones, that went to the very heart, Maid Marian sang one of the ballads of the time, with a feeling and exquisite grace that excited general admiration.

What it was tradition has not told us, though we would gladly have given it a place.

The eyes of the outlaw chief sparkled with pleasure at the cheerful readiness of his wife.

The outlaws themselves were enraptured.

These men, no mere vulgar robbers collected together for the mere love of lucre, but patriots, outcasts, and victims of society, were many of them born to adorn a higher station.

They had hearts and feelings far superior in many instances to those of their oppressors.

That day was long remembered by the foresters, who looked forward to it as the commencement of a new era in their somewhat erratic and peculiar existence.

The festivities were kept up until sundown, when bonfires were lit, lamps blazed; and after a short enjoyment of the striking landscape thus produced, the whole party retired to be ready to resume their usual avocations.

CHAPTER II.

OUR LADY "DOUBLES THE COST."

A WOODLAND life, sleeping under trees, and camping round the bivouac fire, appears doubtless very romantic and very pleasant to all; and would be if there were not such trifling drawbacks as colds and catarrhs, rain, drizzle, sleet, and snow, which are apt, while bringing on rheumatism and aches and pains, to detract somewhat from the beauty and charms of a sylvan life.

There can be no romance in connection with sneezing; no enjoyment with rain trickling down one's back; no delight where a damp bed of leaves is the only couch at night.

Living in caves is all very well, but doubtless a house is better.

Now whatever ideas Maid Marian had formed of a woodland life, they doubtless were somewhat damped by the reality—the truth never comes up to the conception in anything.

No human enjoyment is equal to what we think it is to be.

But Maid Marian was true to her word, and pending the great surprise which the outlaw chief was preparing for her, by building a sylvan palace—which, as we shall see, he did near Haddon Hall, in Derbyshire—determined to share his bed and board in cave, tree, or wheresoever he lay:

She accordingly made her home in the green glades, dwelling in bonny Sherwood, queen of the forest, as Robin Hood was king.

Now it happened on a day when the honeymoon was over, and the king was settling into a steady married man, that he and some of his lieutenants sat under the great oak of Barnesdale devising of many things, and speaking with gusto of their many exploits and valorous deeds in forest and dale.

Robin had come to the trysting oak with a purpose, though he had said nothing to his companions.

The ladies stood at no great distance, enjoying their own topics of conversation, which were varied enough.

Presently Robin signed to them to approach, and seating Maid Marian beside him, began.

"There appears to me," he said, "not one man among you all who guesses why I have come here to-day, instead of roaming through the forest—nay, not one."

Little John scratched his ear, Will Scarlett stroked his fiery red moustaches, Allan-a-Dale hummed a tune, and Much the miller took hold of his nose with his hand and sagaciously pulled it, and then all shook their heads.

"There's nothing in them," said Robin.

Marian laughed.

"Now I should have thought Friar Tuck," continued the outlaw, "would have had a better memory."

"Of what?"

"Of four hundred pounds."

"A new horse," said Little John.

"Nine yards of cloth," said Will Scarlett.

"Sir Richard of the Lee," added Much the miller.

"Waste of time thinking of him," said Allan-a-Dale.

"Why?" asked Robin.

"Man is an ungrateful animal," said the priest, "and is only too glad to forget favours. He looks forward. What is it to me that I dined well yesterday? 'tis to-day I think of first and then to-morrow."

"Bravo, Clerk of Copemanhurst!" said Robin, "for there thou saidst the truth."

"Now what is all this about?" asked Maid Marian, "you speak all of that which I do not understand, which in a lady's company is truly very ill manners."

All bent their heads low as if accepting the reproof.

"Well spoken, Maid Marian mine!" cried Robin, "and now thou shalt hear the story and be the judge."

"That will I with pleasure."

Then the outlaw, merrily and blithely, told the story of the woeful knight, who had but ten shillings when he came, and nathless went away with four hundred on the security of his word and that of the Holy Virgin.

"Was it not very silly of me?" quoth the outlaw in conclusion.

"No!" cried Maid Marian, with flashing eyes, "you were right, even if the money be never repaid; but I have better faith, and insist that ere the sun sets the knight will be here true to his word, as a soldier and man of honour."

"Gad sooks!—buss me!" said Robin, warmly, and suiting the action to the word, he drew the maiden's head towards him and kissed her, a style of proceeding injudicious, to say the least, before company, but which was very common in those undegenerate days.

"Spoken like a true woman.

"Go we to dinner?" said Little John,
  Robin he said nay,
"For I dread our Ladye be wroth with me;
  She hath sent me not my pay."
"Have no doubt, master," quoth Little John,
  "Yet is not the sun at rest,
For I dare say and safely swear
  The knight is true and trest."

Robin smiled on his big lieutenant, and said that neither he nor any other should abide there, but rather take his bow, and with Will Scarlett and Much the miller, scour the wood in the hope of finding some baron or bishop with gold in their purses.

The three stout lieutenants at once obeyed, and bidding a detachment of their followers keep them in view, but without even showing themselves, they went on their way, hoping, however, to meet the knight, and thus obviate the necessity of any farther hunting through the wood.

They took the sun as a guide, a common practice with the outlaws, and made in as straight a line as possible, until they came to the very verge of Barnesdale Wood, where the high-road divided it from another district.

Now, while Little John and his two companions stood watch in the woods of Barnesdale, the former, who loved his dinner quite as much as any fray, soon began not only to be very impatient, but to entertain very considerable doubts about the hour of payment being kept.

We all know that if there is a moment when an Englishman is grumpy it is just before dinner.

A man who would lend you money under the influence of roast beef, Yorkshire pudding, and sound October, will button up his pocket an hour earlier and look both savage and disagreeable.

If you want to be well with your friends neither disturb them when feeding, nor seek them when hungry.

"I begin not to believe in this knight," said Little John, in a gruff and surly tone.

"Why?"

"The jack pudding ought to have come earlier."

"He went late and may be expected late."

"A man should pay his debts in the morn."

"Why so?"

"Because then it's off his mind and off the mind of his friends."

"You're hungry, John," said Much.

"What then?"

"You are hungry and it makes you bad tempered," continued Much, laughing.

"In the humour to crack your crown, you bawling, blasphemous, uncharitable dog!"

"I say, John—what's up? I'm not now in the humour for play."

"Work then"

"Hang, cur, hang," cried Much, flushing in the face, and looking as if he should soon come to crown cracking; "you rascally insolent noise-maker—hang, for you'll never drown."

"I'll warrant you against drowning, you wide chopp'd rascal!"

"And you'll be hanged yet, though every drop of water swear against it, and gape as if it would englut you."

"Hearkee, you pair of bears—you rugged untamed unicorns!" said Will Scarlett, choking with laughter, "wouldst fight when, if that's your game, here come fifty odd armed men who will give you your bellyful."

Little John's good humour returned like magic. We have said he liked his dinner, almost as much as he did a fray—and here was a fray ready made.

Looking in the direction hinted by Will Scarlett he saw his meaning.

For as they look'd in Barnesdale Wood
  And by the wide highway,
Then they were aware of two black monks,
  Each on a good palfraye.
Then up bespake he, Little John,
  To Much he thus gan say,
"By Mary, I'll lay my life to wad
  These monks have brought our pay."

But this was not all, for close behind these two black monks, as the balladmonger called them, were fifty armed men, to attack whom seemed, indeed, a serious task for three outlaws, with their guard at a distance that permitted not of their being called up in a moment.

They were, however, men who knew no fear, and the task was undertaken without any hesitation.

"My brethren twain," said Little John,
  "We are no more but three;
For an we bring them not to dinner,
  Full wroth will our master be.
Now bend your bows," said Little John,
  "Make all your press to stand;
The foremost monk, his life and his death
  Is closed in my hand."

They then stood forward across the highway, three outlaws against fifty men-at-arms and two black monks.

"Stand, churl monks!" said Little John. "How dared you to be so long in coming when our master is not only angry, but fasting?"

"And pray who may be your master, sirrah?" said the astonished monks.

"Robin Hood," quoth Little John.

"I never heard any good of him," exclaimed the monk. "He is a strong thief."

The three outlaws with this waxed exceeding wroth, called him a false monk, and bade them stand and deliver.

All this time the men-at-arms were coming leisurely on, little thinking who the yeomen were.

One of the monks clapped his hand beside his saddle-bag, seized a ready-prepared crossbow, and aimed steadily at Little John, shouting to the cavalry to come up.

Much at once drew his bow, and with one shot killed and unhorsed the audacious monk.

He then seized the surviving monk and the sumpter horses, while the outlaws, pouring from the wood, slew or dispersed the armed men.

Having thus effected a capture, the merry men, who, unfortunately, regarded human life with very great contempt, retired hastily into the forest, nor drew rein or halted until they came to the trysting tree where Robin Hood awaited them.

The monk had never spoken once, expecting every minute to be hanged, at least, as he knew the hatred borne to his cloth by all save the superstitious and ignorant.

But Robin received him graciously, welcomed his dismayed guest, caused him to warm himself, and, sitting down with him to dinner and passing the wine, began to converse merrily.

"Who are you?" he inquired at last, "and whence comes your reverence?"

"I am a monk, sir, as you see," was the surly reply, "and the cellarer of St. Mary's Abbey."

The lieutenants of the outlaw chief pricked up their ears.

Robin Hood bethought him on this of the knight and his security.

He exchanged a meaning wink and shrewd look with his merry men.

"I have great marvel," then Robin Hood said,
  "And all this livelong day,
I dread our Ladye is wroth with me;
  She hath sent me not my pay."
"Have no doubt, master," said Little John,
  "Ye have no need, I say;
This monk hath got it, I dare will swear,
  For he is of her abbey."

The outlaw chief on this smiled and looked exceeding grave.

"That is well said, Little John," answered Robin Hood. "Monk, you must know that our Lady stands security for four hundred pounds. The hour of payment is come. Hast thou the money?"

The black monk upon this swore roundly that he now heard of this for the first time, and that, moreover, he had only twenty marks about him for travelling expenses.

"We shall see that," said the outlaw, gaily, "for I marvel that our Lady should send her messenger so ill-provided. Go thou, good Little John and examine, and report truly."

Little John spread his mantle down,
  He had done the same before;
And he told out of the good monk's mails
  Eight hundred pounds and more.
Little John let it lie full still,
  And went to his master in haste;

" Sir," he said, " the monk is true enough,
  Our Ladye hath doubled our cost."
" I make my avow to God," said Robyne;
  " Monk, what said I to thee ?
Our Ladye is the truthfullest dame
  That ever yet found I me.
I vow by Saint Paule," said Robin Hood, then
  " I have sought all England thorowe,
Yet found I never for punctual pay
  Half so secure a borrowe."

The monk looked sullenly on, but said nothing, as few
words, under the circumstances, were the wisest.

Little John—a fellow of infinite humour—enjoyed this
scene of profit and fun, and stood ready to fill the monk's
cup when Robin ordered wine.

" Monk, you are the best of monks," said the outlaw ;
" when you return to your abbey, greet our Lady well,
and say she shall ever find me a friend ; and, for thyself,
harkee, thine ear : a piece of silver and a dinner worthy
of an abbot shall always be thine when you ride this
way."

" To invite a man to dinner, that you may beat, bind,
and rob him," replied the monk, " looks little like courtesy."

" It is our usual way, monk," answered Robin, drily ;
" We leave little behind. Now thou mayest go."

And the black monk, nothing loth, mounted his palfrey
and rode off rejoicing.

CHAPTER III.

SIR RICHARD'S ADVENTURE.

The sun was now about to set, and the outlaw chief
was beginning to fear that Sir Richard of the Lee would
fail him, when scouts came in to announce his immediate arrival.

The knight had been on his way to the trysting tree
since morning, with the four hundred pounds in his
pocket, and a noble present for the liberal outlaw.

The present was suited to his character, and is graphically described by the poetic chronicler.

He purveyed him an hundred bows,
  The strings they were well dight ;
An hundred sheafs of arrows good,
  The heads burnished full bright.
And every arrow was an ell long,
  With peacock plume y-dight,
Y-nocked too all with bright silver.
  It was a seemly sight.

In a few minutes more the knight and his array rode
up, and Robin Hood rose to greet him.

" You were late in coming," he said, with a smile ;
" so our Lady, who was your security, sent and paid it
double."

The knight looked strangely at the outlaw ere he
made reply.

" Had I not stayed to help a poor yeoman, who was
suffering wrong, I had kept my time."

" For that good deed alone, sir knight," said Robin,
" I hold you fully excused ; and more, you will ever
find me a friend."

The knight shook hands, and then moved to where
dinner was provided.

Robin Hood was indeed delighted with the present
brought by the knight, which was duly divided among
the best men of the band.

Then, after dinner, he begged Sir Richard would tell
him of his adventures by the way, which the knight did.

*   *   *   *   *

It was early morn when Sir Richard of the Lee left his
castle, destined to play so great a part in the history of
Robin Hood, on his way to redeem his promise to the
outlaw.

He had been detained to the last moment through the
proverbial dishonesty of the priesthood.

The abbot of St. Mary's had raised difficulty in the
restoring of his lands and the receipt of the redemption
money.

Thus, in part, was it that the sun was down, and the
hour of payment stipulated with Robin expired when the
good knight arrived at the trysting tree.

He was attended on his way by a party of retainers,
who carried the presents for the outlaws.

In those days it was impossible to move quickly, as the
roads were badly kept, full of holes, and more resembling
the tracks through a Canadian forest and American wilderness than aught else we can compare them to.

Travelling was little practised, except by the rich,
who could afford to have large escorts, while the pack-
men and carriers led their horses through pathways that
would have astonished a Spanish muleteer, who will
make his beast, at a pinch, hold on by his teeth.

The road was winding, the day hot, so that at about
mid-day they were glad to see a village at no great distance, where they could have a halt, that must be conducive to the refreshment both of man and beast.

It was a picturesque wayside village, with an ale-house
facing the green, which, in those days, so much con-
duced to the health and happiness of the boys and girls
of the locality.

As the cavalcade neared the place, it became clear
that something more than usual was afoot, the green
being crowded by the village beaux and belles in holiday
array.

Sir Richard of the Lee bade one of his men ask what
was the matter, and learned that a sailor-looking fellow
was about to wrestle for a prize.

All the best wrestlers of the neighbourhood had collected to compete for the somewhat valuable prize which
had been given by the lord of the manor.

It was a fine horse, saddled and bridled, with a pipe
of wine.

Then came this sailor fellow, upon whom all frowned,
none being inclined to let the horse or wine go out of the
parish.

" Is this a public wrestling match ? " he asked.

The peasants murmured.

" Yes," said the representative of the lord of the
manor, emphatically.

" Then I will ride away on that horse, and mine host
here will buy the pipe of wine ; what say you, my hearties ? "

" Then it was," put in Sir Richard of the Lee " that
I resolved to abide and see fair."

" You did right," said Robin ; " the more that that
sailor is a jolly fellow and one of my band."

" Oh ! " said Sir Richard, " now I understand."

The knight having come to this decision, commanded
all his men to arm themselves and follow him to the
green, where his rank at once gave him the seat of
honour.

The wrestling commenced. The sailor stood on one
side, having elected to wrestle only with the victors.

The man was not inclined to throw away his strength
upon his inferiors.

In every village neighbourhood, as everywhere else,
will be found men of all sorts and all characters.

The bold, the brave, the braggart, and the confident.

But there is always the peer.

However much vanity and self-love may deceive the
majority, the victors stand forth known, almost beforehand, to the public gaze.

Theirs is the privilege of success.

The very habit of conquests makes them confident,
and to feel sure to win is half the battle.

The girls nudged one another as two perfect athletes,
youths who had never yet been defeated, prepared for the
contest.

It was noisy and tumultuous enough at first, as all
save the sailor went in.

Thirty wrestlers, fifteen couple.

As many falls.

Fifteen now retired to resume their ordinary dress,
and drink somewhat copiously to hide their bitter mortification.

When, however, primed with Dutch courage, they
returned to the green, the sense of humiliation soon wore
off.

They were true Englishmen, overwhelmingly attached
to the sight of these personal struggles, which have done
so much to keep up the prowess of English lads and the
love of English lasses.

The fifteen selected their antagonists, one naturally
remaining out.

The result was a very fair contest, in which again
only seven victors remained.

The odd man made still four pair.

Neither of the two chief champions of the ring had as

yet been thrown, nor had they been as yet opposed one to the other.

Soon, however, all others had retired.

They now stood opposite one to the other, with a horn of ale in hand.

They were refreshing themselves after the tiresome contest.

They were both eager for the fray.

They were double rivals.

Rivals in love, rivals in emulation.

In a few moments the cups were handed to their attendant sprites.

They were respectively named Richard and Thomas.

"Well, and what do you make of the moon?" jeered Thomas, as he saw his adversary accidentally glance at that luminary, visible in full day. "She's a good'un to keep secrets."

"Is it, Mr. Jackpudding?" cried Richard. "What says the proverb? ' Wit's in the wane when the moon is full.' Dost trust thyself out under her guidance?"

"A word in your ear," replied Richard; " if you give me any of your impudence, look to your jacket, you d——d impudent oxdriver. Come on."

Thomas was square shouldered, compact, and muscular; the firmness of his gait, his long and easy stride, as he moved across the green, showed he was no mean adversary, though for symmetry Richard was preferred.

They clutched one another, and the struggle commenced—a struggle which promised to be of some duration.

But public expectation was deceived. Richard had been from the first the favourite, but now he appeared in the hands of Thomas to stand no chance.

He was hurled to the ground, and picked up scarcely sensible.

Loud shouts greeted the victor, who was about to claim the prize, when the sailor dashed down his cap.

"Eh?" said Thomas.

"I'm ready," said the sailor.

"Don't be a fool. I've licked the best man in the country round—why do you want to risk your neck?"

"You may find yourself mistaken," continued the sailor, drily. " I've never found my match but once, and he was the very devil."

The young man turned round with a surly, and yet self-satisfied look.

"If you must, you must."

"Take breath and another wet."

"Not I."

"Then have at you."

Now Thomas made no such silly mistake as to despise his adversary. He had seen too many defeated by such tactics. On the contrary, he determined to try his utmost.

Despite his late tussle he was by no means blown.

He sprang forward, clapped his hands, one on Nathan's left shoulder, and the other on his right hip.

"Art ready?" he said.

"I am."

"Then down with you, if you were a ball."

And as he spoke, the champion put forth his utmost strength, but moved not the other.

"Same to you," said the sailor.

As he spoke he exerted his strength to the utmost, and with consequences that no one expected.

By magic, as it seemed, the heels of the astonished champion were suddenly seen flying in the air, his head aiming at the earth, upon which it suddenly descended with extreme violence.

The man lay insensible.

A loud cry arose from the mob.

"He has killed his man—down with him."

"Come on," roared the sailor.

The defeated champion rose, wiping the blood from his pale and livid face.

"Scoundrel," he said, "this is some sorcery. Secure the wretch—my flesh burned when he touched me."

"Hold!" cried the knight; "are ye truly Englishmen to set thus unfairly on one? This fellow hath fairly won the day, and if you would knavishly cheat him of his prize, hands off, for I, Sir Richard of the Lee, will not stand by and see him ill-used."

The villagers looked at one another, while the defeated swain, after again rubbing his head, spoke out.

"Well, sir, what business had this fellow here, a interfering with other vokes affairs? But if so be you thinks he has fairly won, well he has."

And in this surly and unsatisfactory manner the palm was yielded to the sailor, who, after thanking the knight, mounted the horse which was rightfully his, and rode off, leaving the pipe of wine to his churlish opponents.

The knight then, recollecting his rendezvous, also rode forward, with what success we know.

CHAPTER IV.

AN OLD HOSTELRY.

WE cannot say that during the early part of the married life which Robin Hood led he was quite as devoted to the interests of his band as before, but this was excusable.

There was, however, some fear that Hercules was for ever going to be reclining at the feet of Omphale.

Little John and Will Scarlett began to complain that they enjoyed but little of the society of their chief, when rumours arose throughout the whole kingdom of expected risings and movements in certain quarters to change the personage of the sovereign on the throne.

At this moment we again take up our story.

For some time, under the mild and beneficent rule of the lion-hearted king, England had indeed been Merry England, which epithet, though so commonly applied to this land, rarely was deserved, and never could be, while tyrants, oligarchs, and priests monopolised the property of the soil, and treated the people with more abject contempt than the animals of the field.

It will never be so again until the tillers of the earth shall be fed and housed like human beings, and enabled to educate and prepare themselves for the truly high destinies of the English people.

But do not, in your hurry to lay the blame, put it on the wrong shoulders.

Why are the labourers, the drudges, who make the wealth of those who feast sumptuously every day, kept in such abject subjection and poverty?

Not by the tenant farmers.

By the greedy aristocracy, the monopolists of the soil, who the more they have the more they want.

Let them let their farms at fair rents, and labourers can then be paid.

Digression enough.

Near where the wide forests waved their green boughs, near the lair of the fawn and the burrow of the cony, stood, in those days, a neat and cosy inn, kept by one Luke Simon, aided by his pretty daughter Margaret.

The house was constructed of wood, and was but of two stories; but those who think at once of some of those wooden edifices they have seen about must not suppose that it was on that account at all devoid of ornament, for manifold were the quaint carvings and rude pieces of sculpture with which it was decorated, and not small had been the pains which had been bestowed upon mouldings, and cornices, and lintels, and door-posts by the hands of more than one laborious artisan.

Indeed, altogether, it was a very elaborate piece of work, and had probably been originally built for some superior purpose than that which it now served.

It was then old, having evidently been constructed long before; for there was strong proof, in the forms of the windows and the cutting across of several of the beams which traversed the front, that at the period of its erection the use of glazed casements in private houses was not known.

Glass had now, however, been introduced; and though cottages were seldom ornamented with anything like lattices, yet no house with the rank and dignity of an inn, where travellers might stop in rainy and boisterous weather, was now without windows formed of manifold small lozenge-shaped pieces of glass, like those still frequently employed in churches, only of a smaller size.

It was a gay-looking, cheerful place, no matter whether the weather was fair or foul.

The upper story of the house projected beyond the

lower, and formed of itself a sort of portico, giving a shelter to two long benches placed beneath it, either from the heat of the summer sun or the rain of the spring and autumn. And it need not be said that these benches formed the favourite resting-place of sundry old men on bright summer evenings; and that many a time, in fine weather, a table would be put out on the green before the house, the bench offering seats on one side, while settles and stools gave accommodation on the other, to many a merry party round the good roast beef and humming ale.

Before the door of the inn spread out one of those pleasant open pieces of ground which generally found room for themselves in every country village in England; on which the sports of the place were held; to which the jockey brought his horse for sale, and tried his paces up and down; on which many a wrestler took a fall, and cudgel-player got a broken head.

There, too, in their season, were the merry May-pole and the dance, the tabor and the pipe. There was many a maiden wooed and won; and there passed along all the three processions of life—the infant to the font, the bride to the altar, the corpse to the grave.

It had all the things pertaining to its character and profession. It had a dry, clear, sandy horse-road running at one side; it had two foot-paths, crossing each other in the middle; it had a tall clump of elms on the south side, with a well and an iron ladle underneath.

It had a pond, which was kept clear by a spring at the bottom; welling constantly over at the side next the road, and forming a little rivulet, full of prickle-backs, flowing on towards a small river at some distance.

It had its row of trees on the side next to the church, with the priest's house at the corner. The surface was irregular, just sufficiently so to let some of the young people, in any of their merry meetings, get out of sight of their elders for a minute or two; and the whole was covered with that short, dry, green turf which is only to be found upon a healthy, sandy soil.

And now that we have introduced the outward scene of our present action, let us proceed.

It was now in the spring tide of the year—somewhere about that time which Chaucer alludes to when he says,—

> Whanne that April, with his shoures sote,
> The droughte of March hath perced to the rote,
> And bathed every veine in swiche licour,
> Of whiche vertue engendred is the flow'r.

It was also towards decline of the day, and the greater part of the travellers who visited the inn for an hour, on their way homeward from the neighbouring towns, had betaken themselves to the road, in order to get under the shelter of their own roof ere the night fell, when, at one of the tables in the low-pitched parlour, the beams of which must have caused any wayfarer of six feet two to bend his head, might still be seen a man, in the garb of a countryman, sitting with a great black leather jug before him, and one or two horns round about, besides the one out of which he himself was drinking.

People in inns were not over highly fed in those days. A slice of brown bread, which had been toasted on the embers, was the only solid food which he indulged in, probably because he could afford no better, if we may draw inference from his dress, which, though good and not very old, was poor and homely—plain hodden grey cloth, of a coarse fabric, with leather leggings and wooden soled shoes.

His costume, however, was by no means the most peculiar thing about him. He had a peculiar characteristic, which, though few would consent to part with, most men would rather be without.

In a word, he had a hump.

It was not exactly upon either shoulder, it was not exactly one of those large knobs which are so designated, but there was a general and peculiar roundness above the shoulder-blades which fully justified any one in calling him hunchback.

In no other respect was he an unseemly man. His legs were stout and well turned, his arms were brawny and long, his chest singularly wide for a deformed man, and his grey eyes large, bright, and sparkling.

His beard, moustache, and hair of an odd colour. They might once have been dark brown, but though not grey, there was a saddened look about them which was not easily explained.

There was a good deal of fun and sly merriment about the corners of his mouth and under his eyelids but his nose was the point of all, being red and sunshiny.

It seemed like one of those mountains which, by reason of its being higher than the land about, caught the sunshine morning and evening, and hence glowed with the rosy hue of morning before the rest of the country obtained the rays.

It had the purple brightness of the vine.

This man sat sopping his bread in the contents of his jug, and from time to time looking down into the bottom of the pot with one eye to see what was left.

He never, however, stirred from his seat, nor even turned his head, though there *was* a pretty girl in the room, who looked at him from time to time.

But the peasant did not flatter himself. He knew this girl Trina would scarce consider a grey-haired peasant a man.

Once or twice, however, as involuntarily he caught her glance, his eyes sparkled, and one might see that, at all events at one time of his life, he had had sweet things to say to all the black eyes he met with.

The man was evidently in deep thought, and his thoughtfulness was so evident that he puzzled the girl.

Presently, through the open door of the hostelry, might be heard the sound of a trotting horse or two.

"Trina," he said, in a voice the marvellous richness of which made the girl start.

"Master—what would you?" she replied, rising with a smile, and laying her left hand gently on his hump with the familiarity of a girl to an old man.

"Well, divine compound of woman and serpent," he continued, "take away the jack; somebody's coming."

"Why take away the jack?"

"Wouldst have any roisterers see a hunchback peasant drinking wine of Bordeaux?"

"Is it painful?" she asked, demurely.

"What!"

"This," touching the hump

"No," said the peasant, showing a row of brilliant white teeth. "Give me a good tankard of ale. How does the room smell?"

"Like a friar's cell," replied the girl, laughing.

"How so?"

"Grape juice well fermented, and a brown toast beside."

"Get thee gone, slut. What should you know, girl, about friars' cells? Ah's me! there's no girls now."

We should particularly wish to know when there were girls, for we always found every sage generation making the same remark.

The girl brought the ale.

"Bring it here, girl; but spill some first on the floor—it will flavour the room afresh."

"Shall I bring you a sprig of rue, jackanapes?" she replied; "that will give out odour enough. Put it in thy posset when thou get'st home; it will sweeten thy blood and whiten thy nose."

"If you don't spill the ale about as I tell you," he said, in a voice so strangely at variance with his appearance as to thrill to the maiden's heart.

"Hoity—toity!" she said, "I should like to see you do it."

"Would you?" cried the peasant, glancing round the room to see that they were not overlooked.

And as he spoke he rose.

"Spill some," he said, sternly.

"I won't!"

The girl had the tankard in her hand, and the peasant, seizing her in his brawny arms, carried out his threat, thus effectually compelling her, in self-defence, to spill the ale.

As soon as the man had carried his point, he seated himself again. The girl, whose cheek was crimson, at once set down the tankard, and with her pretty brown fingers, still wet with a portion of the ale which had gone over, bestowed a buffet on the side of the peasant's head, which made his ear tingle for a moment, and then carefully wiped her mouth with the corner of her apron, as if to remove every vestige of his salute.

"Did I bite you?" said the seductive voice.

STRUGGLE FOR A KISS.

Trina turned with a start and a smile. The voice had for her an inexpressible charm.

But her womanly instincts overcame every other feeling.

"You do it again, that's all!" she said.

"Wait till I catch you," replied the hunchback, who seemed to possess several qualities appertaining to deformed persons.

He was witty, merry, saucy, and vivacious; we shall see if he was, as is too often the case, malicious.

Scarcely had the girl left the room when a horse galloped up to the door.

A great change took place in the appearance of the man. His neck became more bent, his shoulders were thrown more forward. He untied the points at the back of his doublet, so that it appeared somewhat too loose for his figure.

He drew his hair, too, more over his forehead, suffered his cheeks to fall in, and by these and other slight and almost imperceptible operations, contrived to make himself look fully fifteen years older than he had done the minute before.

Enter thereupon a tolerably portly, well-looking man, of somewhere about forty, in the costume of one who traded from town to town.

He was, there could be no doubt of it, a chapman, alias a bag-man, alias a commercial traveller, alias the representative of &c., &c.

The hunchback went on sipping his ale.

The chapman, in his good and useful but sober costume, walked up to the fire and slacked his boot.

"What's the news from Aldgate?"

"It stands where it did."

"And Traitors' Gate?"

"Is still near the Tower."

"A King's ransom."

"For an outlaw."

These words, rapidly exchanged, were spoken without the two men looking at one another.

No sooner, however, was the somewhat complicated pass-word exchanged, than the chapman walked to the same table occupied by the hunchback and sat down.

At this moment Trina entered to take orders.

"A stoop of wine, my pretty girl," he said, "and bid your rascals take care of my horses. Yonder pack is heavy," pointing to one at the door, "and I will have it brought in. What are you drinking, ploughman?" he added, taking the liberty to taste—"thin ale. Come, my man, take a cup of something better to cheer you. Bad times, arn't they? A stoop of wine for the neighbour, good girl."

"Thank you," replied the hunchback, in a voice that made Trina start, it was so harsh.

"Some of the gang coming up close behind," continued the chapman, who called himself Paul Drux; "I rode on to warn you. They halt here to-night."

"Will they know me?"

"No."

"Then I stand their brunt."

"You are a man and a soldier. But we may not confer here," added the chapman.

"I will see to that. Let us avoid one another when the knaves come. I will, as soon as I hear them, retire to my corner."

The chapman nodded. The girl came in with the two stoops of wine.

The sound of horses galloping was now plainly heard, and then the tumult of a powerful body of soldiery halting before the inn.

The chapman took up a dark corner. The hunchback glided into a back room.

Next instant the inn kitchen, best room, and landlord's private sanctum were all flooded with soldiers.

As if wishing to make way, the chapman rose, yawned, and left the room in search of a bed.

The soldiers, several officers, lieutenants, and inferior officials, alone crowded the kitchen.

The men were satisfied with a *hangar* or shed of some extent used to shelter horses. Here they were amply supplied with ale and other liquors.

The commander, a stout, thick-set Norman, had ample supplies of money, and, to the landlord's delight, paid cash.

"A soldier has only two ways of paying," he said; "down on the nail or not at all. Which will you have, old lanky chops—rations or free quarters?"

"As your honour shall see fit to command."

"Well, I shall pay. 'Tis my lord's money, and I am bidden to do it."

The landlord bowed to the ground, and set the best of everything before his guests.

He was only too glad to hold himself wholly at their disposal.

The soldiers sat down; the chiefs near the door of the back room, and these began conversing freely enough of matters which were treason.

There was to be a meeting of all the discontented chiefs at the castle of Pontefract.

There, in secret, the prince was to join them, and devise of things for the great benefit of the nobles and commons of England.

They were there, it was evident, expecting a nobleman who was always called "my lord;" but who was not farther designated.

It was a sight to see the hunchback in merry converse with some inferior men in the back-kitchen, drinking in every word.

The waiters came and went; one of them, a lame boy of excessive ugliness, serving with great alacrity.

He was about twelve, lame, and short, but as active as a kitten.

He laughed loudly at the sallies of the soldiers, drank their wine, and then stood stolidly by, listening to their conversation, which he devoured.

"What's your name?" suddenly asked one Dufraisse, a Norman lieutenant, with one eye, and a countenance seamed and marked with all sorts of scars.

"Fly-by-Night."

"Well, Mr. Fly-by-Night, curse you for an impudent whelp! Keep away, or I'll flog the skin off your back, slit your nose and ears, and kick you to your father the devil."

"Nunky!" cried the boy, "why you're my uncle."

"How so, sirrah?"

"You said my father was the devil. I'm sure you must be his brother."

Exit Fly-by-Night on his hands and head.

"I'll skin that young rat alive," said the irate Dufraisse.

"Tush man," replied the chief, a grizzly soldier of two score and ten, by name Sir Guy de Lussac, "we must humour these churls. Bid the men put out their lights, plant sentries round the house, and let none in or out."

Dufraisse rose grumbling.

He went out into the great yard at the back and bade the main body of the soldiers retire to rest.

He then strolled back towards the inn, keeping in the shadow of the hangar.

Suddenly he halted.

Not a dozen feet from him stood the hunchback and Fly-by-Night in earnest conversation.

The man was giving minute directions to the boy.

He spoke in the pure Saxon dialect, and though many words fell on the ear of the listener, he understood not.

But he heard enough to make out, *Pontefract—Prince John—the King—and guard all roads.*

"Whew!" ejaculated the Norman. "This must be looked to."

But at the same moment Fly-by-Night mysteriously disappeared, while the hunchback moved towards a side door of the inn.

The soldier returned by the way he came, and found the chief part of the revellers lying down in various corners to enjoy rest and sleep.

The hunchback had, by the narrow side entrance, gained noiselessly the foot of the stairs, and was about to enter the room, when he heard startling words.

"There's mischief afloat," said Dufraisse.

"Well."

"That accursed Fly-by-Night——"

"Pish!"

"Has just started, sent by a hunchback fellow about the house, with some message to whom, or its character, I know not; but I heard dangerous words."

"What words?"

"*Pontefract—Prince John—the king—Guard all roads.*"

"H—l and d—n! This comes of speaking over wine. Have you posted sentinels at every point?"

"Yes; and bade them bring in every straggler through the night, allowing none to enter or to leave."

The chief, Sir Guy de Lussac, walked up and down with a dark and frowning brow.

"I will find this infernal spy. I give you command until the midnight hour. Then call me. See that all the sentries are at hand."

Dufraisse went out and returned with the intelligence that they were within ten feet.

CHAPTER V.

TRINA SAVES ROBIN HOOD'S LIFE.

The hunchback now knew that he was in a dangerous and difficult position, from which alone his utmost courage and resolution could extricate himself.

He heard the order given, which was decisive of his life peril.

"Find the infernal spy," said the chief, "the vagabond hunchback. He shall swing as a new sign to-morrow. But make no noise—alarm not the house, but keep such watch as may prevent a mouse from leaving the house unmarked."

"Shall we search the house?"

"I want not any disturbance *now*, but at daybreak it will little matter; then every inmate shall come before us."

This was enough for the deformed peasant, who ascended the stairs leading to the only upper story, there hoping to find, if not the means of concealment, the means of escape.

All were as yet too busy in the rooms below to notice him in his progress.

He was able, therefore, by disguising his steps, to walk about with ease.

He opened every door and peered in.

None suited him until he came to one at the end of a dark passage.

It was small and neat; the first glance showed it was a woman's, and that woman Trina.

The peasant paused, as well he might, the intrusion being one that was scarcely warrantable.

But his life was at stake, and no man but is justified in using even unusual methods to save his existence, which is given to him but once.

The peasant entered and closed the door behind him.

Except the narrow window, which gave a flickering light, the room was in total darkness now.

A stream of moonlight fell upon the bed.

The peasant felt about with consummate caution and coolness. His object was to find a hiding place.

There appeared none.

In one corner, however, was a recess, against which were hung up a number of dresses, rude, it is true, but when worn by a blooming beauty, pretty and becoming enough.

The peasant passed within this recess and seated himself on an oak chest.

His arms were at once folded, his head bent forward, and his thoughts busy.

He soon forgot his danger, his position, and even the necessity for caution. His mind was far away.

Presently reality resolved itself into doubt, and doubt into dreams.

He was fast asleep.

Fast asleep in a young lady's bed-room, who might be momentarily expected to retire.

But this man, whatever he might be in reality, was one accustomed to trials and privations, plots and counterplots.

His was a cat's sleep.

A handle was on the door, and he was awake in an instant. Every sense was as acute and real as ever it had been.

There was no intermediate moment of stupidity between waking and sleeping with him.

"Good night, Trina," said the gruff voice of the landlord.

"Good night, father."

"Fast bind fast find," continued the old man; "there be queer lads about. I shall lock thee in."

"Law, father, I can take care of myself!"

"That's more than I can do, it seems. There's that confounded wine-bibbing hunchback left two stoops unpaid for. Hang him, say I!"

"Why hang an honest man?"

"Honest man—then why didn't he pay?"

"Father, he'll come again. He left for some reason which he had no time to tell us of—so sleep sound, and, believe me, the money's all right."

"You speak as if he was one of your galivanting sweethearts, Trina," said her father.

"Sweetheart—not he; but an he be not worth half the young ones, my name ain't Trina, that's all."

"Good-night," said the landlord, gruffly.

The door was closed, and the hunchbacked-peasant and the pretty girl were locked up in the same bedroom.

Now we do not care how moral and virtuous a man may be, the position is, to say the least, unpleasant.

The peasant did not at first know what to do.

Trina approached a small rude table, set down her lamp, and seating herself on a stool, began to undress.

Now this was decidedly trying.

The peasant peered through the hanging dresses, and saw that the kirtle had been cast on one side.

It was time to act.

Her back was to him.

He stood in the room.

Death was in a false step—that he knew.

With the stealthy step of a wild cat—he had taken off his heavy shoes—he strode across the floor.

Next instant his hands were pressed in a peculiar way over the girl's nostrils and mouth.

She tried to shriek.

There was a gurgling sound—nothing more.

"Trina," he said, holding her firm, "I do not want to hurt you. But my life is in danger, and I have a perfect right to protect it. Do you understand?"

She nodded, though trembling.

"I never did hurt woman or child in my life, and rather than harm you, would surrender to the bloodthirsty Norman troopers. But will you listen to me calmly?"

She nodded.

"You will not scream?"

She made signs that she would not.

"And now forgive me for using the least violence at first. But women who scream at mice and spiders could not but scream at the sight of an ugly man in a bedroom."

Trina, who was now as red as at first she had been pale, put her finger to her lips.

"Speak low."

"I will, my good girl."

"Why are you here?"

"The chief of the troopers wishes my life."

"Why?"

"Can I trust you?"

"I think you can," said Trina, a little piqued.

"I will."

His eyes had a peculiar glitter in them, a merry roguish twinkle.

"One moment, he added, with a joyous smile; "help me one moment."

"How?"

"To get rid of this burden," pointing to his hump.

The girl stared.

"I am not the first man," said the peasant, with a smile, "who has made himself look more than he is. There, put your hand behind my frock and untie the knot you will find. I will unfasten this one in front."

So saying he loosened a little cord and tassel that was round his neck, and with the aid of his bewildered companion, let slip from his shoulders a large pad containing a number of articles, some hard, some soft, but which altogether had been so arranged as to give him the appearance of a deformity that nature had certainly not inflicted upon him.

As soon as this was removed, he threw off his loose frock, put aside a most artistically contrived mask, and exhibited himself to Trina, the handsome but sturdy youth, nature had made him.

Trina's eyes sparkled with satisfaction, though she strove to hide her emotions.

Her first idea was a lover.

"Who are you?" she faltered.

"Can I trust you?"

She caught his hand, pressed it to her heart, and looking him full in the face, spoke:—

"With your life."

"I am Robin Hood."

She could not speak.

Romantic, reared in a situation to hear all the ballad and love songs of the time, Trina, though surrounded by lovers, was too vain of her own charms to have as yet cast an eye upon any one with more favour than another.

Her heart beat violently, her breath came and went, her bosom heaved, and her pallid cheeks were crimsoned with delight.

Her hero, the dream of her youth, was before her.

The outlaw watched her with a keen and observant eye. Though young, he lived in a time when gallantry was the trade of every man, and when a virtuous woman had to fear every outrage; when to break hearts, deceive and betray, was the amusement of an idle hour.

Some such relics of the past do still exist, but they are regarded with all due aversion and disgust, despised by all who are not worthless themselves.

"Trina," said the youth, "you are a good girl."

"I hope so."

"I have trusted you. Lest you make any mistake as to my motives, understand that I am married."

The girl trembled, and though semi-nude, leaned on the shoulder of the outlaw.

A tear dropped on his hand.

The revulsion was so sudden.

The outlaw passed his arm round her waist, and lifting up her head, kissed her cheek.

Shade of Maid Marian, appear!

It was only fraternal.

But none the less very dangerous.

"You are a brave girl, and one lover more or less will not make any difference," he whispered.

"I never had one," said Trina.

"That shall soon be remedied. But now, dear girl, will you for a while talk business?"

"Go on."

"I have come here on important business. I did not expect that so many troopers would attend the persons I have to watch, or my gallant band would have been near. The worst of it is that a lad, who has attended me during this excursion, has been seen by one who knows him as an outlaw, and they accordingly suspect me. In the morning the house will be searched."

"You must fly."

"How?"

"Ah! the door is locked. The window."

"Is narrow enough—and then every avenue is guarded. Every corner has its sentry."

"What is to be done? Will they harm you?"

"Hang me to the first tree."

The girl turned ghastly pale. Despite all he had said, she had taken for him one of those sudden likings which are so dangerous.

"How can I hide you? But they will not search my room."

"You do not know these hired ruffians, these free lances imported to raise revolt while the king is in Normandy."

"But there is no place to hide you."

"Let us consult," he said, and trimmed the half-expiring lamp.

Soon perfect stillness pervaded the whole house, and when the cock crew at early morn, all was still silent.

It was about half an hour after dawn, when the noise of people moving might have been heard in the inn—a bustling movement of soldiers and others.

Then a heavy tramp was heard in the corridor leading to Trina's room.

The door was slightly opened.

Not a sound was heard.

"This is my daughter's room."

"Fast bind fast find," laughed a gruff soldier's voice, as he noticed the father unfasten the door.

"Exactly."

"Who is there?" said Trina, rising from her couch on the ground, a mere pile of ferns, with rough bedclothes spread over.

"It's only a form," replied the father drily.

"What is?"

"They're searching the house. You don't happen to have such a thing as a hunchback about you?"

"What mean you, father? Are you mad?"

"Not I," said Luke Simon, with a loud guffaw, "only you see that I have had to show these gentlemen all round the house."

"I must look in," observed the officer, grimly.

He put his head in and looked round; the girl sat up, with her clothes half round her.

"You are not men," she said, angrily.

"Duty is duty," replied the veteran, with a smile, as he crossed the room, and peered into the recess.

It was empty.

"He then retired to the passage.

"Get up, Trina," said the innkeeper, in a somewhat husky tone, "I am busy, and want you."

He then closed the door, but did not fasten it. Trina leaped from the bed, bolted it on the inside, and hastily slipped on her garments, blushing deeply.

"Make haste," she presently whispered.

As she spoke Robin Hood, somewhat pale and woebegone, crept from the inside of the fern, between which and the wall he had been lying.

He had indeed been near death—if not from the brutal soldiery, from the infuriated father, who would not have waited for any explanations.

The girl, assisted by Robin, who appeared quite expert at this kind of thing, was soon dressed and tripping down stairs.

In about ten minutes she returned.

All were busy getting their meals.

Her father was waiting on them.

She took Robin's hand—she sighed deeply ; he kissed her fondly and tenderly.

"I shall never see you again," she whimpered.

"I will come often."

The girl brightened up; not that she was badhearted, or if she had known Maid Marian, would have injured her ; but it was to her something to believe in the love of the great hero of the hour.

From that moment he was doubly her hero. She had saved his life at the risk of reputation, life, and honour.

The only further remark we have to make about this adventure is, that the bold outlaw never told his wife of it.

The girl led him down, showed him the back way—by means of which he soon reached the forest with his bundle—and re-entered the house, not quite so lighthearted as she had been the night before.

CHAPTER VI.

SIR ALURED MEETS THE FORESTER.

THE commander of the party of free lances was evidently waiting for some one—it could very well be seen.

He seemed, though the morning was fine, in no hurry to depart.

It was a public inn, and, as such, open to all who thought proper to enter it.

And yet would the soldier have gladly rid himself of Paul Drux, but for one thing.

He had the most stringent and positive orders to molest no one, but rather to render the populace friendly to their aims.

This Paul Drux puzzled him.

He was a simple, quiet fellow, to all appearance, and, by his costume, a trader.

He might easily be a spy.

Warfare in those days was never carried on without them, so that all parties suspected each other.

"I say, you sir," at last observed the impatient Norman, "your business is but a lazy one."

"Very," said Paul Drux.

"What on earth are you waiting for?"

"For your escort."

"Fire and furies! what mean you?"

"Between this and Pontefract are sixteen miles, much frequented by outlaws. I purpose following respectfully in the rear."

"Hearkee, friend chapman. If you are truly a huckster you are quite welcome to our protection. But if I find you are a spy I'll hang you, as sure as my name is Longley."

"Spy of what?" asked Paul Drux.

"Never you mind. That's my affair. We understand each other," muttered the officer.

"Do we?" said Paul Drux.

At this moment a new comer entered the inn.

It was a man clothed in a close-fitting coat and hose of Lincoln green, with a sword by his side, a narrow buckler on his shoulder, a sheath of arrows under his left arm, and a leathern bracer just below the bend of the elbow, carrying a pole about six feet long.

He wore in his cap the badge of some nobleman.

His countenance was swarthy and weather-beaten. With a rough salute to the officers, he passed through the kitchen to where Trina was drawing beer.

He put a coin in her hand, and seated himself at a coarse wooden table.

"Anything to eat you can find, and a jug of ale," he said, in a kind of gruff but jolly voice.

"You must wait," she replied, tartly, "until your betters are served."

"My betters, Trina?" he whispered in a voice so different as to make her first start and then blush roseate red.

There was no reply, but in a few minutes the remains of a noble venison pasty was put upon the table, flanked by brown bread and a flagon of ale, the universal drink of man, woman, and child, in those unsophisticated days, when the Chinese were philosophers in pigtails, and drank tea till they scalded their insides.

The ranger eat with the appetite of a man whom nothing disturbed, and when he had finished, passed out again as carelessly as he had come in, and was soon sunning himself in the April sun before the inn door.

He was, to all appearance, quite unoccupied, though now and then he gave a hasty glance up and down the road.

Soon, as he expected, he heard sounds.

Lifting up his eyes he saw a party of men, evidently of rank, coming along at a brisk pace, their horses foaming as if they had undertaken a long journey.

The forester, who had no inclination to play the ostler, strolled round towards the back of the inn.

There was a large pool at some distance, partly surrounded by thorn bushes, partly shaded by trees.

Here the man found Paul Drux, throwing lumps of brown bread to a number of ducks and ducklings.

"Lively amusement," said the forester.

"Innocent," replied Paul Drux.

"There's Lord Saire, Lord Mentressa, Sir Hugh Fitzurse, just come up," continued the forester.

"Aye—then it must be meant for soon," said Paul Drux, quietly. "What shall I do?"

"Enter Derby—the castle if you can. I will not be far off. The George and Blue Boar is a fine inn, and there I and Fly-by-Night will await your reports."

"My friend," said Paul Drux, the chapman, in a tone of some sadness and melancholy, "how can it be that England should never be without civil wars?"

"Because king and nobles have little to lose and much to gain. They lord it over all, certain that yeoman, franklin, and churls——"

"But the remedy?"

"The remedy," said the forester, raising his eyes quietly to heaven. "I have thought of it many times. In the long watches of the night, beneath the twinkling stars, it has come to me like a dream of such bliss as makes my heart bound within in wild delight."

"Tell it me."

"There is but one. Let the kingly race return whence they came, let the nobles follow, or if they remain, dismantle their castles and be quiet. The people then might till their land, hunt their deer, improve the face of the land, while the traders could move through the country without fear of molestation. Public affairs there must ever be, especially as England has foes. Well then, let the best men be sent to meet and confer upon the wants and wishes of the nation; make laws, and execute them. This is my remedy, chapman, and until it is carried out, now or hereafter, there will be no real happiness in merry England."

Paul Drux heard him with wonder and awe. To do without a monarch and his attendant nobles was an idea so awful, at the first blush, that he could not realise it.

"There may be some truth in it," he said, with a sigh, "but it ain't worth talking about. It won't come in our time."

"If the commons of England were of my opinion it would. But now we must part. Our worthies are suspicious, and will soon be on the look-out for a stout forester."

With these words the man flourished his stick and quietly moved off in the direction of the forest.

Paul Drux returned to the inn, attracted by the sound of preparation for departure, which could now be clearly distinguished.

The new comers had mounted, the men-at-arms were in line on the road, the sumpter horses and camp followers were congregated in a group in the rear.

Paul Drux, who had no attendant, hastened to discharge his bill, and by the aid of the hostler, harnessed his two horses.

Then, with a humble mien becoming his station, he took his post among the suttlers and others.

The whole party moved onward, the chiefs riding in front in earnest conversation, one trumpeter, acting as a look-out, alone preceding them.

It was a gallant array, and though not so formidable, much more picturesque than anything in modern times.

As soon as the last straggler was out of sight of the inn, a number of archers left the skirts of the wood, and came across in search of refreshment.

There was Little John, Will Scarlett, and many others with whom the reader is familiar.

In a few minutes they were joined by Robin Hood, who, for this purpose, left the forest.

As soon as their appetites were appeased, they paid their reckoning and entered the forest, each man, however, taking different directions.

We must follow in the track of Robin.

He took his way for but a short distance through the forest, crossed a couple of roads, and then again came back to that by which the gentlemen had arrived and which led towards London.

Where the outlaw halted the road was extremely narrow, between high banks, which were further overhung by trees. Some of these were short and stunted, but thick with boughs. One in particular, an oak that had seen many days, was so covered with ivy that little of its original character could be seen.

Into this the forester clambered, fixing himself in a situation that allowed him to see without being seen.

He was even thinking deeply, though now and then he would lift his eye vacantly towards the road.

Presently he heard the measured trot of horses.

His head stooped, and he looked keenly along the highway.

A man in some military guise, followed by two armed servants, came along.

The forester watched them closely.

In a few minutes they were in the dark and gloomy hollow roadway.

The servants were some distance behind.

The forester began to whistle.

As soon as he heard this undoubted evidence of the presence of man he drew rein.

"Whoever thou art," he said, "come forth. If you be a true man you shall be welcome."

"There be true men in country, and true men in London; but the truest man of all is now in Sherwood Forest."

"Ah! then you know a Lion!"

"I have heard him roar, Sir Alured," said the forester. "Keep your horse still, and I will join you."

With these words he swung himself from the overhanging oak to the ground, and stood beside the horseman.

"Ride forward to where there is an oak by a pond." continued the forester. "Send horse and men forward to the inn. When you are alone I will join you."

Sir Alured bowed and rode forward, his servants still too far behind to make out even the fact of an interview.

As soon as he saw that his companion was safe behind the trees he set spurs to his horse, sounding a *mot* as he did so.

The servants came trotting rapidly through the dark and gloomy gully, where, as a matter of prudence, it was necessary to bow the head, to avoid the fate of Absalom.

When they reached their master he was dismounting by a pool, and next instant stood on the greensward.

"Forward! You will find an inn some miles forward. Wait there till I come. Look to yourselves. I know you will; but do not forget your horses."

The servants made no reply, but bowed low and departed quickly.

Next instant the forester was beside the traveller.

"Sir Alured," he said, gravely, "I know you and I trust you, but I have a duty to perform to others. You must give me your honour as a true man and good knight never to reveal anything you see or hear within the forest."

The knight gave the promise without the slightest hesitation.

This being done, the bold forester led him through one of those narrow lanes, so common in the forest, where only one person could advance at a time.

This path continued for about half a mile, and opened out into one of the wildest parts of the forest, through which there seemed to be no track of any kind.

It was not one of those spots properly called coverts —which name was only applied to woods so thick that the branches of the trees touched each other—but, on the contrary, it was a sort of wild chase, scattered with fine old oaks, and encumbered with an immense quantity of brushwood. There were patches of green grass to be seen here and there, indeed, and once or twice a sandy bank peeped out amongst the bushes, while two or three large ponds and a small silver stream appeared glistening at about half-a-mile's distance from the spot where the horsemen issued forth from the lane.

It was as lovely a forest scene as ever the eye rested upon, for the ground was broken, and a thousand beautiful accidents diversified the landscape. Every here and there a tall mound of earth, sometimes covered with turf, sometimes rounded with brushwood, would rise up, bearing aloft a graceful clump of trees, while the setting sun, pouring its long horizontal rays across the wild track, cast lengthened shadows over the ground below, and brightened all the higher points with gleams of purple light.

Beyond, again, at the distance of not less than two miles and a half, and considerably lower than the spot where the two journeyers stood, reappeared the thicker coverts of the forest, rolling like the waves of a deep green sea in the calm and mellow rays of the departing day; while a slight mist here and there marked out its separate lines, growing fainter and more faint till some distant objects, like towers and pinnacles—they might be clouds, they might be parts of a far city—closed the scene, and united the earth with the sky.

Here all trace of a road ended, but without the slightest hesitation the forester led the way onward, threading with unerring steps the different green lines which separated one mass of brushwood from another, guiding his companion under one tall bank, and round another high mound, between the boles of old oaks, and across the dancing stream, without even once meeting a check or having to pause in his whole course through the woody labyrinth.

At length, however, the sun went down, just sufficed to show Sir Alured his way, as they had reached the lowest spot of the chase, and approached a clump of several acres of thick covert. There was a path at one angle by which the forester and his companion entered; and winding on in darkness for some way, for the trees excluded the whole of the remaining rays, they at length emerged into an open space in the centre, where they could again see, though faintly, the objects around them.

CHAPTER VII.

THE FOREST BIVOUAC.—HADDON HALL.

THE wind was from the south, sighing softly through the trees—the sun had gone down about half-an-hour—the moon was rising, though not yet visible to the eye, except to the watchers on castle towers, or the lonely shepherd on the mountain. The night was warm as midsummer, though the year had now waned far, and in the sky there were none but light and fleecy clouds, which scarcely dimmed the far twinkling stars as they shone out in the absence of the two great rulers of the night and day. It was one of those sweet evenings which we would choose to wander through some fair scene with the lady that we love, looking for the moon's rising from behind the old ivy-clad ruin, and re-peopling the shady recesses of wood and dale with the fairy beings of old superstition, though they have long given place to—to use Rosalind's term—"a working day world indeed."

Such was the night when, under the brown boughs of the wood, with yellow leaves overhead and long ferns around, sat a party of some seven or eight men, dressed in the green garb which we have already described in another place. Their bows rested against the trees close by, their swords hung in the baldrics by their sides. Some horses were heard snorting and champing at no great distance, and a large wallet lay in the midst, from which Fly-by-Night was drawing forth sundry articles of cold provision, together with two capacious leathern bottles, and a drinking cup of horn.

The merry jest went on around the green table, where their viands were spread. The torch stuck in a hole in the ground, shed its light upon the various faces in the circle and upon the sylvan repast; and a song from one of the foresters cheered the minutes.

Suddenly a horn sounded low, clear, and distinct, close at hand.

The party was at once on foot ready for any encounter, and as they rose, it was difficult not to be struck by the stature of one of the outlaws.

This man, though nearly as tall as Little John, was still wanting about an inch or two.

His mien, however, was that of one who was equal in strength and energy to any who might be brought before him.

His face, during the festivities, was merry and light to a degree that amounted almost to carelessness.

Now, as he listened to the notes of the horn, a frown settled on his brow—a brow made for thought.

It is a great and pleasant faculty of those whose avocations compel them to much thought, that they can throw care off at will, and be as merry, light-hearted, and thoughtless—more so—than those to whom nature has not vouchsafed any other characteristics.

In a moment more Sir Alured and the forester stood amongst them.

"Welcome, my hearty ally," said the tall man, heartily; "whom have we here?"

"Sir Alured de Montemart," replied the knight, bowing.

"'Tis well; let us sit apart. Here, Fly-by-Night, come and be my torch-bearer."

The ill-favoured boy came forward with a laugh.

He stood beside the one who had commanded him, while Robin Hood and Sir Alured, at his desire, seated themselves nigh him on the sward.

The young knight respectfully handed despatches to the tall forester.

He broke them open.

"London," he said, reading little bits aloud here and there. "London is loyal and ready. The Earl of Essex commands a large army, which is hurrying by stolen marches towards Nottingham. Secret levies are being made by all my friends. Foregad, I wish the rebels would come to blows this time. I should then be able to unmask my enemies, and punish them as they deserve."

"That your grace is too generous to do."

"What now, my sturdy councillor? what now, my minion of the moon—what, if you were king, wouldst do?"

"My lord, an I were king of England, and felt in my conscience that I was as you are, a good king, as kings go in this world, rather than I would allow my faithful and suffering commons to be harassed, alarmed, and disturbed, from the machinations of evil men, I would even make every taken chief a head shorter, especially he for whose pretended benefit these evil things are done."

"Would'st take thy brother's life?"

"If he acted like a traitor and an ingrate, the law should do it for me."

"Thou art a rude *galliard*," said the king; "but now for the present. None know of my sudden return to England?"

"None, save your trusty councillors; these men around, and Sir Alured here."

"Then all is well. Sir Alured must share our hospitality to-night; before morn he shall have despatches for the earl. In a week we will be in the field as becomes a king."

The monarch, however, seemed inclined to conclude the meal, which the forester had interrupted, and as Robin Hood had, with Sir Alured, had a long walk, neither were they loth to join in the homely festivities of the night.

The meal, however, was despatched rapidly, and then all such as had horses mounted and made their way through the forest, under the guidance of Robin.

Half-an-hour's journey brought them to the first habitation which had been discovered since the inn had been left behind, a habitation which the King of Sherwood had erected, in order, during his movements towards Nottingham and Derby, to be able to have a home to give shelter to Maid Marian and the ladies of her sylvan court.

This building was of very peculiar architecture, consisting of round stones piled upon one another, and cemented together, being what is popularly called rubble, while the windows and doors alone presented hewn stone, lintels, and transoms, with short small columns supporting each.

A quantity of ivy had grown over the walls, which, with the trees that grew around, rendered it not easily distinguishable even by day.[*]

Here Robin Hood halted, giving two notes or, as they were called, mots upon his horn.

He then had recourse to an instrument in use during many centuries in England, and which served the purpose of a knocker.

It consisted merely of a large ring, with sundry notches in it, and a small iron bar hanging beside it by a chain, which being rapidly run over the indented sur-

---

[*] The books say—"The favourite resort of Robin and Little John, and their comrades, when they desired to enjoy the wine of which they had deprived some luxurious abbot or sheriff, was a remarkable group of stones or rocks, near Haddon Hall, in Derbyshire, where the outlaw is believed to have built a sylvan palace, and reigned lord of all, in spite of the Norman strengths of Haddon and Chulsworth. Two stones rise above their neighbours, and here an old tradition says that Robin sat on one and Little John on the other, delivering judgment on litigated matters of forest law; while another tradition, still older, asserts that Robin leaped or stepped from the summit of one to the other to show his wondrous agility, and that in consequence the stones have ever since been called Robin Hood's Stride."

face, produced a sharp and unpleasant sound, that soon called the attention of those within.

The door was soon opened, and leaving most of the party in the outer hall, Robin Hood and the monarch, with his messenger, Sir Alured, followed a long, dark passage, until they came to a large room at the back.

This was well lit up, and was hung round with tapestry.

Here sat Maid Marian, who, despite the presence of the monarch, rose and threw herself into her husband's arms.

After a few whispered words, Robin Hood's wife retired to order the latest meal of the day, to which, however, justice could not be done, until such time as the monarch had finished his conference with his new minister and councillor, Robin Hood.

The door of this secret chamber was locked, a map was laid on the table, from which King Richard proceeded to explain to his deeply interested auditory his plan of campaign.

"If they mean to fight—they shall fight," he said. "That rampant Earl of Beauclerk will never rest until he has dragged my brother into the mire."

He now pointed to the centre of the approaching insurrection, the strings of which were being pulled by his brother and his selfish advisers.

He then pointed out the army of the Earl of Essex.

"These rebels, if the news we hear be true, are drawing to a head; but they cannot fight under a month. You, Sir Alured, will take despatches to your father, the noble earl, and bid him advance slowly, recruit his army on all sides, and be ready at any moment."

"Yes, my liege."

"I will remain here. Robin will give me house-room, and in this disguise I may even shoot a few of my own deer."

"Certainly," laughed Robin.

"Who will take messages to Paul Drux?"

"Fly-by-Night."

"Ay, that will do."

"Anything else, my lord?"

"There must be a messenger found for Northumberland."

"Will Scarlett is ready."

"For the good Bishop of London, who holds within his palace a party of my best friends."

"Friar Tuck's the man."

"True, my droll hermit of Copmanhurst," said the king, laughing; "and now to write despatches."

The outlaw made a wry face here, as that was beyond his province; but Sir Alured, being a scholar, was able to assist the monarch, himself more fond of wielding the lance or battle-axe than the pen—perhaps the more dangerous weapon of the two.

The task was brief, and the gay monarch laid down his pen."

"And now, friend Robin, for the most difficult task of all—for one which I ought to perform myself, only that just now I may not play the knight errant."

"What is it, my liege?"

"Listen, both."

"With all our ears."

"You know that at the first news you sent me of this cruel and wicked rebellion, I left Normandy in haste."

"Certes, my lord."

"My task there was nearly over, and in two days all would have been settled."

"That we understood, my lord."

"But what you do not know is, that I bade my admiral, Sir Roland Sansterre, follow me in all haste, but secretly, with such lances and bows as his fleet would bear," continued the king.

"'Twas well done."

"If he acts wisely. Now I have bid him rendezvous at Scarborough, and there await orders. Now, what I want is a trusty, acute, clever messenger, who can not only carry a letter, but bide his time, excite no notice, and when the fleet arrives, give verbal directions to the admiral. Where shall I find him, Robin?"

"I am your man," cried the outlaw.

"Wouldst leave thy forest?"

"Certes, my lord."

"Thy wife?"

"Well," said the outlaw, smiling, "it's not the pleasantest of things to do, but duty calls."

"'Tis well, my brave and honest friend. Now, you must remember that on these men may rest my crown, so if you succeed in finding them, bring them on as fast as they may march to join me."

"Where?"

"Here."

"'Tis well, my liege. I will start at daybreak."

"Thanks. But in the meantime I and my lieutenants, Will Scarlett and Little John," said the king, smiling, "must not be idle. How many bowmen can you promise me on a pinch?"

"I have seven hundred of my own, and each man of them can find four friends."

"If that be not over three thousand, then never believe me again," continued the monarch.

"'Tis so; and they will fight, my liege; for the person of the prince and the leaders of this revolt are as much hated as your Majesty is loved."

"'Tis their own fault, Robin. If these turbulent barons would but cease their tumults, England might be great and happy, keeping war alive only with our enemies beyond the sea."

"What of the Scots and Welsh?"

"Robin," said the king, with flashing eyes, "were my nobles but united and patriotic, my secret dream should be carried out—ah, that it should."

"Which, my lord?"

"That of making this island one great and powerful kingdom, before which all others should bow the knee."

"'Tis a rare thought, and worthy of a mighty king," said the outlaw, musing.

"But it may not be. Business is over, and my walk since our forest meal, with this dry talk, has quite prepared me for Maid Marian's supper table."

"Meat and drink in moderation," said Robin, quietly, "are strength, if not courage; and hunger is a sad lamer of strong limbs."

As Robin Hood spoke he lighted a small silver lamp at one of the candles which hung in a large polished brass sconce against the wall; and bidding them follow, he led the way through another of those long narrow passages which occupied so much space in all ancient houses.

No door appeared on either side till a sudden turn to the right brought them to the foot of a heavy wooden staircase, the steps of which seemed to be composed of solid blocks of wood piled round a common centre.

There was a rope on either hand, fastened by stanchions of iron let into the stone-work of the wall.

At the top was a large vestibule, lighted from one end and containing three doors.

The centre of these Robin Hood opened.

The sight that met their eyes somewhat astonished his Majesty and Sir Alured.

The room was a small low-roofed chamber, covered with dark-coloured painted cloth, instead of arras, but well lighted, and with a blazing log on the hearth, which was needed in that old dwelling, notwithstanding the month was nearly May.

Although the furniture was ancient, even in those times, yet everything was most comfortable, according to the usages of the day. The floor was thickly strewed with dry rushes, and a table was in the midst, on which a pretty handmaiden was arranging in haste a number of dishes, and plates and drinking-cups.

In a chair was a fair lady, amusing herself with an old embroidery frame, while on two seats, lower than hers, were two young girls about the same age as their mistress.

Such was the court of Maid Marian, Queen of Sherwood Forest.

Such was the home which Robin Hood had appropriated and repaired, now that he was married.

CHAPTER VIII.

CAPTAIN CANTAGREL MEETS HIS MATCH.

THIS course of proceeding being determined on, Robin Hood determined himself (as we have said) to be the king's messenger, as no one could better act as leader and guide than he himself, should he be so fortunate as to fall in with the earl and his fleet.

There was a certainty that, from the information sent

by Paul Drux,' those who had gone into Wales to raise these recruits and hirelings for the rebellious prince and nobles, could not return under three weeks.

Prince John, all knew, would avert as long as possible any rash encounter, while the slow way in which the Earl of Essex advanced made the confederate and traitorous barons believe that he was afraid of them.

There could, therefore, be no danger in Robin Hood absenting himself for awhile, especially as he left to command the now large bands of English outlaws, not only his trusty lieutenants, Will Scarlett and Little John, but the king of England himself.

The outlaw provided himself only with the suit he wore, his bow and arrows, hunting knife, a goodly purse of gold, and, secreted carefully away, his credentials from the king, in which he was spoken of as Earl of Huntingdon.

From where they were located to Scarborough,* was in those days no mean journey.

But Robin was not sorry to see new country, and so buckling a thick cloak behind him, in case of wet, and a portmanteau of disguises, he mounted his horse and went on his way rejoicing, as during his king's residence in Sherwood Forest, he was forcibly kept from laying abbot, baron, or any one else under contribution.

Guide posts there were none, but on such rude maps as the men of those days could make, and one of which was entrusted to his care, the king had marked the different *étages* of his journey.

This was enough for Robin, who had a tongue in his head and knew how to make men speak whether they required to be bribed or to endure the *argumentum ad hominum.*

It was early dawn when he started on his way, having a very vague idea of where Scarborough was, but with a settled determination to discover it, if no unforeseen accident prevented him.

The king had advised him that there were several large towns to be avoided, and Robin Hood therefore made up his mind in his quiet way that all had better be left on one side, as apt to bring him into many a false position and uselessly dangerous scenes.

He was well mounted, but though willing to travel as quick as a king's messenger with vital interests at stake, should, he by no means intended to blow his horse until the proper time came.

His charger was a lean grey horse, that might bring him many a flout or laugh in Yorkshire; but if no beauty, had, like some women, hidden qualities that were far superior.

The outlaw trotted on then in silence; he wished to attract no attention, and to interfere with nobody, so that nobody interfered with him. His reputed character of a nobleman's servant travelling on his master's business was tne best he could assume, as at inns it promised the entertainers money, and hence the traveller was without any fear treated with the attention he sought and deserved.

It was some time after mid-day when he halted at a road-side inn, which, being near four villages, was called the Chequers, and was also not honoured by any acquaintance of Robin Hood.

Here the outlaw had his horse groomed, took a meal, paid for it, and was about to depart, when a second traveller made his appearance from the inn, a strong, well-built man, in the garb of a priest, but armed also, and looking, to judge by his thews and sinews, like one who might have set more men at defiance.

"Do you travel northward?" he asked.

"I do."

"May I claim your companionship until the next resting-place? I know the road well, and it is not the best reputed in the world," said the soldier-priest.

Now Robin Hood did not like his looks, did not like his voice, and had, in fact, a general vague idea that he did not like the man at all, having met him somewhere before.

---

* This rare and curious incident in the life of Robin Hood is contained in a ballad called the " Noble Fisherman," and was found by Ritson in the collection of Anthony à Wood, with the following prose heading:—" Showing how Robin won a prize on the sea, and how he gave the one-half to his dame, and the other to the building of almshouses."

He was not, however, at all desirous to be uncivil, or to arouse suspicions.

"I am for the north to-day," he replied, "and, if it please you, we can travel together. But I am not afraid of half-a-dozen robbers. Besides, I know these parts, and never travel with money—of my own," he added, aside.

"Many thanks," said the ecclesiastic, who now mounted his steed, placed upon his pillion a small but somewhat weighty portmanteau, and trotted off beside Robin Hood.

Now the outlaw at once had his suspicions.

In the first place the man was a priest, which to Robin Hood was no recommendation, as he knew them as a rule to be guzzling, gormandising gluttons, with nothing spiritual about them, and no love for any but themselves, and a favourite lady-penitent or two, to whom for a short time they were particularly attentive.

A great many of them, too, were hired spies of the rebel army; and against this contingency it was that Robin Hood was most anxious to guard.

Not by avoiding him.

By no means.

But by being jovial, and thus throwing him off his guard.

Robin, however, was fully aware with what an astute class of men he had to deal.

He took his measures accordingly.

They conversed as they went on the usual English topic of the weather, which topic once broached, our nationality stands revealed before the whole world.

The priest rather thought there would be rough weather, but the outlaw knew not, and said so.

"If the times were only as good as the weather," he said, "there would be hope for England yet."

"What ails the times?" asked the priest.

"Out of joint," said Robin.

"If they are out of joint they should be mended."

"True."

"It only remains for us to know who are the right men."

"Too many tinkers."

"Tinkers!" cried the priest.

"Yes, every second knave you meet fancies he could cure the land of all the evils it was ever subjected to."

"You are a wit, my master."

"No."

"What part do you hail from?"

"Sheffield."

"Whither away?"

"Which way the wind blows."

"How is that?"

"Am I not a gentleman's attendant, and must I not go the way that he bids me? His breath is my wind."

"Aye, aye, sir—you are pleased to be merry. But I would know if we are to be comrades after our halt to sup to-night?"

"Can't say."

"How so?"

"Don't know which way you are going."

"Well, my friend," said the priest, with a smile, "I may have my reasons too."

"Then keep your way to yourself. I ask no man his road, nor tell mine; not that it is of the slightest consequence, but it is a way I have got."

"And a very good one too. Let us forward. The air is keen enough, and I shall not be sorry to empty another flagon to our better acquaintance."

"Guzzler!" mused Robin.

"I picked a bone or two for dinner," continued the priest, with the air of an injured man; "but seeing you ready, left them; so that a pasty will be welcome."

"Guts!" thought the outlaw.

"'Tis not my way to think much of creature comforts, but when a man is travelling he should keep up his strength to the utmost."

"Hypocrite!"

"The innkeeper where we shall halt is a friend of mine," added the priest, "so that we shall be treated well."

"Oh!" said Robin.

And so, for want of element, the conversation flagged.

"Any robbers in these parts?" began Robin, after a pause of some duration.

"Many," said the priest, drily.

A PERILOUS ADVENTURE.

"Have you ever met one?"

"One."

"Well—and what happened?"

"Killed him."

"Oh!" said Robin, who really could not tell whether the man was a mere braggadocio or a true man, and so began telling, as they approached a gloomy forest, some tales of Sherwood well calculated to startle a nervous person.

Among other anecdotes, he told of unfortunate travellers, who, having fell among thieves, incurred that calamity from associating themselves on the road with well dressed or entertaining strangers, with self-offered guides, or sham priests, who cheered their journey with tale and song, protected them against the evils of over-charges and false reckonings, until at length, under pretext of showing a near road over a desolate common, he seduced his unsuspicious victim from the public highway into some dismal glen, where suddenly blowing his horn, he assembled his comrades from their lurking-places, and displayed himself in his true colours.

They were now in a narrow road between lofty trees, that made deep shadows in a dark place.

"Hearkee, stranger," said the priest, suddenly, "I don't quite understand you, my master. Do you or do you not know me?"

"What mean you?"

"Do you know my name?"

"I only know you as a companion."

"Then you are utterly unaware of my name?"

"I am."

"What was your object then in telling that story?"

"To while away the time."

"So," smiled the other, grimly, "and now, my joker, that we have come to the dismal glen, out with thy purse, and if I take thy money be thankful for thy life."

Robin Hood replied by a roar of such laughter, as fairly threatened to unseat him.

"What are you laughing at, churl?"

"Are you really now a knight of the road?"

"I am."

"So am I."

"None of your silly jokes, or, as sure as my name is Cantagrel, it will be the worse for you."

"Cantagrel!" said the outlaw, calmly, "then I am sorry for you, for I have sworn, by the true cross on which God died for us, that if ever I did come across that rascal knave, that foul disgrace to England, he should die."

"Who and what are you?" cried the other, somewhat startled.

"Robin Hood."

"Gad sooks!" said the other, turning of a deadly white, "then this is no place for me," and he clapped his heavy spurs into his horse.

A bolt from the outlaw's crossbow soon checked the steed, which fell, throwing his master headlong on the ground.

Ere he could rise he was pinioned, hands and feet.

Captain Cantagrel was an outlaw, but driven forth from society for crimes for which he had ten times deserved and merited death.

Since he had collected a band of ruffians about him he had made all England ring with his atrocities. The cruelties of which he was guilty are scarcely to be told, but his most fearful crimes were directed against women

The countenance of Robin Hood was stern and cold. Not a shadow of compunction or pity was on it.

He took some halters from the other's steed—horse-stealing was his favourite amusement—fastened them together, and passed a loop round the ruffian's chest, under his armpits. Then he strung him up to the bough of an oak, so that his feet were a yard from the ground.

"I say, Master Robin," he said, with a ghastly laugh, "when is this joke going to end?"

"Joke!" replied the outlaw. "I wish to Heaven it were a joke, or that I had never met you. When I heard of how you treated pretty, plump Jenny, of the Up-stream——"

The man shuddered. His crime here was abhorrent to human nature, and in his hour of need it came home to him.

"I vowed that if I ever met you, at board or in bed, in house or in the field, on foot or on horseback, I would kill you with my own hand, and thus I keep my vow."

Speaking these words, he drew an arrow and took aim.

The forest resounded with the shrieks, yells, and imprecations of the ruffian.

His body had whirled round.

Robin would not hit him in the back.

He waited until his breast was in view, when an arrow flew from his bow, and pinned the wretched ruffian to the trunk of the tree.

The man brandished his arms with frantic gestures, while his eyes rolled in horrid wildness, then he writhed an instant in his passing agonies, and then his head dropped lifeless on his gored breast.

Robin Hood, with a deep sigh, proceeded to examine his valise, which contained money and papers.

The money he left, but the papers he took, suspecting them to be of importance to his cause.

Then he rode off.

An hour later the sheriff of the county rode by on business with his javelin-men and bow-men, attended by some gentlemen of substance and rank.

"What have we here?" cried the sheriff.

"'Tis that rank scoundrel, Robin Lythe, called Canta-grel," said the head javelin-man, in amaze.

"Ah! then has somebody done us a good service."

"Cut him down," said a noble gentleman.

They did. He was quite dead. The arrow had gone through and through his heart, and between the peacock feathers that winged it on its way was found written—

"*Robin Hood.*"

"Fore gad!" cried the sheriff, "but this is rare indeed. But I ever knew the outlaw of Sherwood to be a better man than this ruffian. What ho! bring that valise here, and put that gold back, my men."

The valise was instantly put at the sheriff's feet, and gold, silver, and other valuables found.

"Said I not so? There is some secret in this. The Sherwood outlaw has slain him and disdained to touch his money. You fellows will be less nice. Bury the bandit, and then share the money. Share and share alike; or if I hear of any big bullies taking more I will, on evidence, strip them of all. Follow in a quarter of an hour. Come, gentlemen, dinner waits."

And the portly sheriff rode away at no very quick pace; and, as he went, he hummed lightly to some old forgotten air :—

> And this is the end of Robin Lythe
> And his knave, Gaudelyne.

But his knave, Gaudelyne, appertaineth not to this our narrative.

CHAPTER IX.

SCARBOROUGH TOWN.

Now Robin Hood continued on his way, anything but in a pleasant mood.

He was musing on the folly of making rash vows, which, once made, an honest man feels compelled to keep.

Truly the death of this Captain Cantagrel, as the fellow Robin Lythe was called, sat heavily on the outlaw's conscience.

It was no part of his nature to kill or slay at all, much less in cold blood.

He was moody, then, and dull, and was glad when, seeing a large town in the van, he was able to turn aside towards a village, where a very plain ale-house gave him all the shelter he required—a cup of good ale, a round of beef, and a fragrant fern bed.

There was a jolly fire too.

Before this Robin sat drinking his ale, with a toast in it also ; and dreaming.

His elastic mind had cast off melancholy, and he was now busy with plans against the rebels and in favour of his king and country.

It is not our province to relate all the adventures which befell him on his way.

Suffice that at last he was within a mile of Scar-borough, on the borders of a small forest.

There was a charcoal-burner, who also sold ale by the roadside. Here Robin left his horse, his travel-stained garb, and habited himself in the dress of a fisherman.

That recent acquisition to the outlaw band, the sailor, had made it.

Then he walked on until he came to the summit of the cliffs near the town.

The outlaw rubbed his eyes in amazement.

At what?

The sea.

Many may be surprised at this, but to a man with a soul, the first sight of the illimitable ocean is ever bewildering.

It excites awe and wonder.

In Robin's days his countrymen were timid sailors ; they seldom made a voyage in the winter months ; they rarely went out of sight of land, and had exhibited but symptoms at least of that audacity, tempered by skill, which has since given them the command of the ocean.

A few fishing boats.

That was all.

The fleet were not in sight, so that the outlaw had to make up his mind to do something.

He would become a sailor, not that he felt any very particular fondness for salt water, but it was for the sake of variety.

It was a change from the woodside, chasing the fallow deer, and wandering beneath the leafy arches of the forest. Hence was it he is said to have sung :—

> The fishermen brave more money they have
> Than our merchants two or three ;
> Therefore will I to Scarborough go
> A fisherman brave to be.

Our forefathers appear to have been rare hands at improvising—so at all events says tradition.

> "So," quoth Robin Hood, "I'll to Scarborough go,
> It seems a very fine day ;"
> And he took his inn at a widow woman's house,
> Adown by the waters grey.

Now, it so happened that the sailor, as he was always known in the outlaw band, had recommended him to a widow, who not only let lodgings, but owned a coble of her own.

The widow, after he had rested and dressed himself, looked at her lodger, and seeing him personable and promising, inquired who he was, and what was his trade.

Robin was sitting outside her house, looking with endless admiration on the great salt sea.

"I am a poor fisherman," replied Robin, with a down-cast look, "and in my country I am called Simon of the Lee."

Now the outlaw used often grimly to observe that these wanderings about, these disguises and assumptions of other people's names, were sadly destructive of his morals.

They compelled him to tell more stories in a day than he could have wished to have told in a lifetime.

But there was no help for it.

The life of a secret messenger is no pleasant one, and once undertaken must be carried out.

> "Simon," she said, "if thou'lt be my man,
>   Round wages I'll give thee;
> For I have as good ship of my own
>   As any that sails the sea."

It appears that in those days seamen must have been scarce, as any landsman seems to have been accepted without discussion. At least, so we are left to judge from the present narrative relative to Robin Hood, which bears upon it the stamp of truth, except that, by the poetical license, the outlaw walks from Sherwood to Scarborough "on a very fine day."

But this is a geographical error.

Such trifles are never noticed in ballads or romances of chivalry, where heroes and heroines go three months at a time without eating or drinking, a contingency against which we honestly provide.

Robin having accepted the liberal offer, entered at once into the service of the buxom widow, and joining his new comrades, they plucked up the anchor, and sailing till old England grew dim in the distance, cast their baited hooks into the sea, and began to catch fish.

These men who accompanied Robin Hood were all experienced in their trade, and took it for granted that their companion was the same.

But alas! poor Robin, he was utterly ignorant of the whole mystery of fishing, and when others dropped their baited hooks in the water, he dropped in a naked hook and a bare line.

Awful mistake!

The outlaw should have reasoned better, for when he did not take them by force even a monk was not to be caught so easily as all that.

His new companions, who were jealous of the stranger, did not allow this to pass unobserved.

> "It will be long," said the master then,
>   "Ere this lubber thrive at sea;
> He shall not have one fin of our fish,
>   For in faith he's not worthy."

The new fisherman heard their conference, and wishing to enjoy himself, let them think him even a greater lout than he was, as is well depicted in the ballad,—

> "Oh, woe is me," said Simon, then,
>   "And the day that I came here;
> I wish I were in Plympton Park
>   Chasing the fallow deer.
> For every clown laughs me to scorn,
>   And a lubber they me call;
> But if I had them in Plympton Park,
>   I would put scorn upon them all."

But though the sailors laughed at him, they attempted to do him no injury, and when their take of fish was considerable, proceeded to give him a fair share, which they cooked and broiled on board.

They, however, all the while kept their hooks out, moving on under scarcely any sail at all, when suddenly the sky became overcast to the eastward, and a heavy squall with hail, sleet, and snow, came pouring down upon them.

The sailors seem to have been as brave and experienced as seamen as they were sharp as fishermen.

The sea rolled mountains high, and Robin Hood, to his utter amazement, felt sensations which he was never able to describe.

He never could find words to paint what he endured for some considerable time.

Then the billows went down, the sea became calm, and the boat turned its prow homeward.

But the moment for Robin to assert his superiority even at sea was at hand; if he failed to arm his lines and bait his hooks, and caught nothing, while his companions laughed at his ignorance, his looks brightened as he saw a French rover bearing down upon them, for he had not forgotten to bring his bow and arrows.

But as Robin's face brightened, that of the master and those of the other men sank.

> "Oh woe is me," said the master then,
>   "And the day that I was born,
> For of all the fish we have caught this day
>   There is every fin forlorn.
> For your French robbers upon the sea
>   Will not spare us a man,
> But carry us to the shores of France
>   And cast us in prison strang."

The simulated fishermen looked on, watching the sea-rovers with interest, perhaps with a kind of secret sympathy.

Surely had he have been educated to it, Robin Hood would have delighted in a life on the ocean wave.

But a French prison, and French diet, which was looked upon as something fearful, was by no means within the list of pleasant probabilities.

"Master," he said at last, "do not be afraid; give me my bow and arrows, and not one Frenchman will I spare."

There was a general smile among Robin's companions at this, for they rated his skill at the bow by his skill in fishing.

The master, who was in a very bad humour, thus roughly answered him,—

> "Now hold thy tongue, thou long lubber,
>   Thou art but brags and boast;
> If I should cast thee overboard
>   There's but one lubber lost."

This was rather too strong even for the good temper of the great outlaw of Sherwood Forest.

> Simon grew angry at these words,
>   An angry man was he;
> But he took his bent bow in his hand,
>   To the ship hatch then went he.

But Robin Hood soon found that a ship's planks afforded no such steady footing as the greensward of Plympton Park.

He stood with difficulty, and drew an unsteady string.

> "Come tie me to the mast," he cried,
>   "Against any object fair,
> And give me my bent bow in my hand,
>   And I'll no Frenchman spare."
> He drew his arrow unto the head,
>   And he drew with might and main,
> And to the first Frenchman's heart straightway
>   The clothyard shaft is gane.

The sailors gave a great shout, and seeing some hope of escape from the dexterity of Robin Hood, stood to their tacks and sheets, the master himself cheering.

Success brought security, as the Frenchmen began to drop before his deadly arrows. Robin's footing grew firmer and his hand quite steady, and he requested to be unbound, that he might despatch his shafts more readily and rapidly.

> "O, loose me from the mast," he cried,
>   "And for them take thou no care;
> But give me my bent bow in my hand,
>   And I'll no Frenchman spare."

This request was at once complied with, and Robin Hood then shot so fast and so well, that when soon after they boarded the rover, they found all the crew transfixed with arrows.

The master and the men could have fallen down and worshipped him.

Twelve thousand pounds in good red gold, and a ship well appointed and fit for sea, was the reward of the victors.

By the universal custom of the time, the prize and all it contained was Simon of the Lee's.

Robin had long forgiven the harsh words of the master and the slighting laughter of his comrades.

> "One half of the ship," said Simon then,
>   "To our dame and children small:
> And the other half of the ship I'll bestow
>   On you, my comrades all."
> But up bespoke the master then,
>   Says "Simon, now list to me;
> You have won the ship with your own hand,
>   And you shall the owner be."

A pleasant picture this of the generosity and honour of an English sailor in the olden time.

> "It shall be as I said," quoth Simon then;
>   "With this gold for the oppress'd
> An habitation I will build,
>   Where they may live at rest."

And for this purpose, that of an almshouse, Robin Hood gave the whole of his share, and other money afterwards.

The almshouses were built, the residue of the money invested, and but for bloody civil wars and sanguinary conflicts, in which everything peaceful and good was destroyed, we might at this day have seen the children of the poor fed and clothed from the bounty of an outlaw chief.

Many men ten times worse than Robin have been canonised.

It is scarcely needed here to relate the delight and joy of the widow, with whom Robin Hood, now very anxious, determined to remain three more days ere he took his departure.

CHAPTER X.

SIR ROLAND SANSTERRE.

POOR sailor as was the outlaw chief, he was easily able, from the conversation of the fishermen, to understand that a series of contrary winds had detained the fleet.

Not that he said a word of his secret, but obtained his information in a casual, careless kind of way.

One morning, when the wind had shifted, and not a boat could put out, the wind being dead on shore, the fishermen suddenly signalled a large fleet, which those who had experience among them said was coming directly towards Scarborough.

The sailors and others exchanged alarmed glances, and consulted for nearly an hour on what was to be done.

At last, as the huge body of vessels neared the shore with a spanking breeze, they came to the conclusion to run inland and hide, as it might be Danish pirates for what they knew.

"Fear nothing, my men," said Robin, appearing amongst them in a kind of travelling courtier's dress, "it is the fleet of our good King Richard, to await which I have been here all this time."

The astonishment was now general, as all recognised Simon of the Lee, but they also readily believed.

In a few minutes more all doubt was at an end.

The vessels came to an anchor close to the shore, with the flag of England flying, and then a boat, all silver and gold and tapestry, put out, and with ten rowers dashed for the shore.

It contained officers of rank, who, one and all, landed hastily, and ascended the strand.

"Sir Roland Sansterre?" said Robin, courteously advancing.

"Yes," said the other, eyeing the stranger with suspicion.

"I have despatches from his grace," whispered Robin.

"Then lead us to the first house, for I am in haste to know their contents: you must read them," addressing a stout warrior with grey hair.

"That will I," cried the stout warrior, who was about forty-five, who then fell forward and embraced mother earth; "that is my first touch of English soil for twenty years."

In a few minutes the distinguished party were in the house, and shut up in a rude room.

Robin took forth his despatches, and, at a sign from the admiral, handed them to the stout and handsome soldier, who undid the parchment, read it, turned white, red, blue, all colours, looked at the signature, the back of the letter, the contents, and then sank on the nearest settle.

"Am I d——d, demented, blind, or has the foul fiend run away with me?" he cried, looking askance at Robin.

"What is the matter? Is it not genuine?" asked the admiral.

"Genuine—yes. This is the Lion's signature."

"Well?"

"Listen."

"*To my most trusty and well-beloved cousin, Admiral Sir Roland Sansterre, greeting:—*

"*The bearer of this despatch is Robert Earl of Huntingdon, who will give you, by word of mouth, our orders, to which conform as to our own personal words.*

"RICHARD."

"Has pandemonium broken loose," continued the stout soldier, "or am I on English soil?"

"That despatch was given to me, Robert Earl of Huntingdon, by my liege, with verbal instructions of the utmost importance."

"'S'death, sir! if you are Robert Earl of Huntingdon, who the devil am I?"

And he stood with folded arms before our hero.

Robin almost gasped for breath.

"If"— he stammered "if I have no right to bear the title, it can only be that I stand in the presence of my honoured and beloved father."

"Gad!" said the soldier, "I suppose that's it. Are you the boy left with the honest jeweller of Nottingham?"

"Yes; but who is now the dishonest sheriff of the same place."

"I see his mother in his eyes—come to my arms, my son! Excuse me. D——n it! this cursed climate is just as bad as ever. It makes a fellow's eyes water."

And the father and son, without any further explanation, embraced.

Robin then turned to the admiral and fully explained the position of affairs, the king's hopes, the difficulties he had to encounter, and the progress made by the rebels.

"We will go every man to his assistance," said the admiral; "let all the vessels be drawn up on the beach. If defeated, we shall not want them; if victorious, they are safe with our English brothers."

And the orders were given at once.

It was night ere they were all collected on the shore, when the admiral commanded horse, foot, and sailors to camp for the night, as all needed repose after the cramped and awkward way in which they had been confined on board ship.

The officers of highest rank were invited to a kind of banquet, of which our heroic outlaw was the life.

He had so much to tell them.

The Earl of Huntingdon, an exile from his native land for twenty odd years, was delighted with his son.

"But how have you managed," he said, during a pause in the conversation, "to keep your existence secret from the bitter enemies who persecuted my youth?"

"I have lived in the forest."

"But they know you now."

"Lived in the forest?" said the admiral, a jolly soldier and sailor, a devoted adherent of the king, a noble of ancient family, one essentially a friend of the people; "eh? then, you have seen this pet outlaw of his grace's, the brave, the handsome, the jovial, honest English heart, whom men call Robin Hood?"

"I have seen him."

"Why do you smile?"

"Yes—why do you smile?" repeated his father, who was so happy to find a son, when he thought himself childless, and his rights gone from his family for ever.

"I am Robin Hood," said the outlaw, with a modest smile.

"The devil!" began his father.

"I thought so," cried the admiral; "give me your hand, for though, as the young Lord Huntingdon, I respect you, as the brave Englishman, Robin Hood, I love you. Why did you not speak before?—your counsel is worth its weight in gold."

And the brave admiral shook him heartily by the hand, followed in this by all the company.

An hour later the father and son were alone, entering minutely into explanations.

At dawn of day the little army was on the march in the direction of the king and his enemies.

Many and many a year was to pass ere England ceased to be the battle-field of vanity, ambition, and crime.

'Tis not long since old men could remember the last occasion when a base and vile race of kings made their last attempt to establish despotism and bigotry through the British Isles, and when they were driven away, not because the new royal family was any more lovable, but because they were not quite so bad.

As usual, John Bull paid the piper.

But at the time of which we speak bloody engagements, rebellions, executions, and military murders were the order of the day, and failed to rouse even a passing remark.

But we must return to Sherwood Forest and its mighty king, who, however, in this forced holiday from state affairs, is said to have enjoyed himself immensely.

CHAPTER XI.

WAR'S ALARMS.

But at the moment of which we write King Richard was no longer concealed in the forest.

He had come forth and taken up his stand in the open fields.

His tent was pitched upon a height, and there he sat in the outer tent, in company with the Earl of Essex, and several other noblemen.

On a table before them were some of the rude maps of the period, and they were all measuring distances and tracing out lines.

Richard was grave and thoughtful.

To his right lay, in profound slumber, the gallant army of Essex; to his left, other levies of his friends.

But the rebel lords, finding that Richard was in England, had gathered together a mighty force, with which they were hurrying forward by forced marches to attack the king ere he could be reinforced.

They were more than twice his numbers, their leaders desperate men, who fought as with a halter round their necks; the men brave, resolute, and well disciplined.

Every now and then messengers who, having the password, were allowed free ingress and egress by the chain of sentries, came into the tent with news.

But none of it was satisfactory.

"We shall fight at a rare disadvantage," said Richard, thoughtfully. "I would not care were it an ordinary field. but here we shall battle for my crown and life."

"Life, my liege!"

"Dost think, Essex, if they can slay me they will risk the wearied clemency of their outraged sovereign? We conquer or we die to-morrow."

"Then we must conquer!"

"Ah, truly," said the king, "that we must, if we can. But knaves though they be, we have brave Englishmen to deal with. Well, see to the sentries, my lord. I will take rest to-night. At break of day we march to meet these rebels.

"Is the prince with them?"

"He is."

"What of him to-morrow?"

"Heark you, Essex," said Richard, with a lowering brow, "if the fight goes against him, he will be with us before the battle is over, offering to betray his followers; but let him not come in my sight, for, by the holy rood, I swear——"

The king paused.

"What, my liege?"

"Well—no. Let him be taken to Hereford Castle, and there confined. I could not see him."

And the monarch went into the inner tent, allowing the folds to fall behind him, to pass the night alone, well aware that he was safe in the hands of his followers.

At break of day the army was in motion to meet the foe, which the spies said was now twenty miles distant.

The lion heart could have awaited them where he was, but he had no wish to appear to fear them, so started forward on his way to meet them half way.

There could be no more showy sight than the march of a feudal army.

They had not as yet assumed all the splendour of later days, when the surcoats of the knights were embroidered with their arms; but even now those arms were emblazoned upon the banners and on the shields, while the richest colours that the looms of France, Italy, and England could supply, were to be found in the housings of the horses, and in the pourpoints and coats of the knights, and in the beautiful scarfs called cointeses, which, passing over the right shoulder and under the left arm, fluttered like many tinted streamers in the air with every breath of wind.

It was truly a gorgeous sight, as indeed, before the fight is over the panoply of war.

A large body of horse archers and men-at-arms went first, and behind these came the king with his staff, and then the main body of the army.

Sunshine, the bright sunshine of a summer's day, was over the whole, mingling the ingredient of its own loveliness with everything in the landscape.

Still every now and then, over the bright blue sky, floated a light cloud like a flying island, casting here and there a deep shadow, which hurried speedily onward, leaving all shining behind it, like those fits of gentle pensiveness which come at times even upon the happiest spirit, scarcely to be called melancholy, but seeming as if a shade from something above us flitted over our minds for a moment, and then left them to the sunshine and the light.

The vanguard was commanded by Sir Alured, who had cast off all disguise, and assumed his rank as the nephew of the Earl of Essex.

He had advanced some distance to reconnoitre, and now halted on a small hill.

On one hand, rising tall and blue, was a beautiful range of hills, with many a lesser hill springing out from the base, wooded to the top, and often crowned with an embattled tower.

On the other side were high grounds running down in the direction of another range covered with magnificent trees, and bearing up innumerable castles, while here and there the spire of a church peeped out, or the pinnacles of an abbey.

Too calm, too beautiful, for a battle-field.

The large space between these two points was filled up by rich slopes, green meadows, corn-bearing fields, and long lines of forest, some of which remain to this day.

Everywhere could be seen towers, towns, hamlets, brooks, and rivers, offering a confusion of beautiful forms and splendid colouring.

From this height the enemy's army became visible a little before mid-day.

In the van were slingers, with their staves and leather bands.

Behind there were the light foot pikemen, armed with short spears and oncins.

The slingers carried no defensive armour, but the latter were protected by a pectoral or breastplate of steel scales hanging from the neck, and a round steel buckler on the arm.

These were what we call irregular troops. All was confusion amongst them, as they ran on preceding the rest of the army, somewhat in the manner of modern skirmishers, only with less discipline and skill.

Then behind these came those on whom the battle mainly depended—the regular troops, consisting of various bands of heavily armed spearmen, with much longer lances than the former, and defended by the steel cap, or *chapel de fer*, the long oval shields, and thick stuffed haquetons, so stiff and hard as to resist the blow of sword or dagger.

The uniform was irregular and according to the fancy of their special chiefs.

Some of these bands, according to the taste or means of their leaders, were furnished with the same pectorals of scales that were borne by the lighter spearmen; while some had short hauberks of steel rings set edgewise.

Some had no other armour for the body than the hauqueton already referred to.

Marching, however, in regular order, with their spears leaning on their shoulders, and their steel caps glistening in the sun, they presented a fine martial appearance, and were, in fact, a very formidable body to attack.

Behind the array of pikemen came the bands of archers, the pride and glory of the English army.

In general they were covered with the hauberk and the steel cap of the times, but—upon what account it is difficult to be discovered—each wore above his armour a sort of leather cuirass, ornamented with four round plates of iron.

Their arrows were in a belt at their waist, their bows unbent in their hands, while each man had his anclace, or short dagger, hanging from his neck by a cord, and many of the bands were also furnished with a strong broadsword of about two feet in length.

Again behind these came crossbowmen and horse archers.

From where he stood Sir Alured could hear every now and then the stirring blast of the trumpet.

It was a glorious sight, and riding onward at the head of his men, he bethought him of what a country like England could have done were all this chivalry, now pitted one against the other, united.

At this moment a voice roused him.

" 'Tis a glorious sight, and a splendid host," observed the king; " but I would rather see the village girl tripping away through the fields, with the long ears of corn around her; I would rather see the labourer reaping yonder rich and early barley ; I would rather see herds reposing in the shade."

" And so would we all, my liege."

" Ah !" cried the king, " what have we here, that rides with such hot and furious haste ?—another !"

As he spoke two mounted messengers came in sight, one to the right, one to the left.

In a few minutes they were spurring up the hill, nor halted until they handed despatches to their sovereign. The noble staff rode up and waited.

" This from Sir Ralph Tressilian, commonly called Paul Drux, some time a prisoner in Derby Castle, but now free. He does not promise much, but to-morrow three hundred lances will be added to our force."

" 'Twere well added," said the Earl of Essex, drily, as he surveyed the mighty host that were spreading out upon the plain below, as if inviting them to battle.

" Ah !" cried the king, glancing round to see that none but intimates were within hearing, " this from Robin Hood, who, with Sir Roland Sansterre and all his force from Normandy, is but a day's march behind. Good news, i'faith !"

" Good news indeed," said the earl, who never took his eyes off the enemy, " and so good that I would decline battle until the aid came up, or was near at hand."

" You would not retreat ?" said the king, hotly.

" No, my liege ; but I would retain my vantage ground ; if they attack, let them ; but, for all their bravery, the rebels are weary. They will gladly rest a night."

" But a charge would settle the matter."

" No, your grace," continued the earl, " they are more than two to one, and well commanded. The force we expect will make us a little more equal."

" I am a pretty king," said good-natured Richard, laughing, " to be led thus by my lords. But I suppose in the multitude of councillors there is wisdom—let it even be as you will, Essex."

The brave and loyal gentleman bowed to his king, and then rode away to take such measures as were necessary in the presence of so superior a force.

He was, however, right when he said the rebels, after their forced marches, would be glad of a rest, for as soon as their spies informed them that the king's army had halted they were seen to disperse, light camp fires, and devote themselves wholly to repose and refreshment.

Thus passed the day.

The king chafed somewhat at his enforced idleness, but a little after dusk he owned to the earl how wise had been his discretion.

A little after dusk there came to the camp Little John, Will Scarlett, and seven hundred of the choice bowmen of Sherwood Forest and its environs.

This in itself was a reinforcement of no mean importance, as, though battles were generally won by the heavy men-at-arms, the winged messengers of death, scattered by such hands, often had much to do with the fray.

Should the admiral and Sir Ralph but join them ere daybreak, there could scarcely be a doubt of the result.

But where was Robin Hood? where was Sir Ralph? We have too long neglected the latter.

CHAPTER XII.

THE CAMP FOLLOWERS.

WHEN Paul Drux journeyed with the detachment of rebels it was in the humble mass of attendants that he mixed himself.

He had, doubtless, his reasons for avoiding the company of the haughtier chiefs and knights.

However this might be, in company with the camp followers he had no need to complain of dullness.

A more jovial, reckless or improvident crew were rarely collected together.

Knowing actually nothing of the intentions of their masters, they surmised a great deal.

What they could not surmise on any known ground they contrived to invent.

Paul Drux was too cautious to ask any questions, but his very dullness and want of curiosity caused him to be deluged with voluntary information.

It went in at one ear and out at the other, so little did he pay attention to servile gossip.

In this way he at last reached the town where so much was going on that Paul Drux was anxious to know.

No sooner did he get within the walls than he contrived to give his escort the slip. He had no wish to be subject to the constant companionship of the army sutlers.

A small out-of-the-way inn at the back of the castle served his purpose very well, as being near the forest, and out of the beaten track.

Its owner was a small farmer, who sought to add to his other means of existence the profits on his ales and wines.

Here the packman deposited his load, giving as a reason that he wanted to be near no such plundering crew as the camp followers of the army.

" There, friend," said mine host, " thou spakest like a sensible man. God forbid I should see anything of such *franc lurons*. They would drink me dry and never say thank you, much less pay. What does it all mean ?"

" That wiser heads than yours or mine wish to know," replied Paul Drux, with a sapient look.

" Where's King Richard all this time ?"

" Nobody knows—but he'll turn up when least expected," added Paul Drux. " Catch him asleep !"

" That's just my opinion, dang it."

" Well don't talk too much about it, neighbour, here come some ugly customers," said Paul; " give me a brown crust and a tankard ; I will sit yonder. My pack is well hid ?"

" All right."

" Then I care for no man."

As he spoke three ill-looking knaves sauntered into the ale-house, and called lustily for ale.

The landlord, a stalwart person, with a resolute countenance, assumed, however, a very pliable manner.

" Coming, folks, coming," he said, all the while at tending to the wants of his first customer.

" Thieves !" whispered Paul Drux.

" Eh ?"

" Camp followers ; be careful."

The landlord only nodded, and hurried out for a jug of ale—of which he brought down a gallon pitcher, and setting it before the three men, asked for the reckoning without letting go the handle.

" Reckoning !" said one black-bearded fellow, stroking his heavy moustache, " what mean you? We know not what we may have yet—set it down."

" Quick reckoning makes long friends—pay as you have is my way," said the host.

" Oh," said one of the fellows, " that's your idea, is it ? Well, here's your money—but this is not the way to bring custom ?"

" Don't want your custom," cried mine host, gaily, " I've enough of your betters."

" Surly brute !" muttered one of the three men, as mine host, after pocketing his cash, moved away.

Now Paul Drux had noticed, during the march, these very three men casting many a coveting eye upon his pack, and was at once satisfied that they had followed him with evil intentions.

He determined, therefore, to be wary and to keep a strict eye upon them.

Pretending not to see them, he went on with his frugal meal, looking up every now and then at the castle which towered overhead.

The three men whispered together in a very low tone, and every now and then pointed towards the apparently unconscious pedlar.

Suddenly one of them rose and approached Paul.

" Art deaf, friend ?"

" No."

" Dumb ? "

" No."

" Then what are you ? "

" A peaceable man, who wants nothing to say to bullies or ruffians," said Paul.

" Spy ! "

" Thief ! "

" Scoundrel ! " shouted the three men, each in his turn, " have at you, knave ! Back to the camp you go with us—where is that big pack of yours, which I daresay is as chuckfull of treason as its master ? "

" Hands off ! " cried Paul Drux, stepping into the middle of the room, with his staff in his hand.

The three men drew forth their short swords.

With a scientific twirl, which smacked somewhat of a pupil of the outlaws, Paul hit every man a blow ere he was ready to parry.

The three camp followers howled with rage, and then all three flew at the packman.

He defended himself with energy, but the ruffians were experienced old *reitres*, and in a few minutes had inflicted wounds upon him which bade fair to weaken his defence.

" To the *rescousse !* " shouted mine host, darting into the room, followed by his wife and the Maritornes of the inn, one armed with a huge spit, the other with a broom, while he whirled a huge cudgel in his hand.

The ruffians had their backs turned to the reinforcements, so that one got a pointed blow in his rear that made him prance again, while the other two staggered under two heavy blows on their sconces that made them cry for quarter.

" Quarter, you knaves ! " roared Boniface, " down with your weapons and then clear out—I'll have no such rampaging bully-boys here."

The men surlily lowered their weapons, but refused to depart the inn, alleging their wounds, one of which the stout man swore would unfit him to ride on horseback for a month.

" And serve you right. But if you would stay here, just give me your swords."

The men, who were completely cowed, did as they were bid, and retiring to their corner of the room, proceeded to finish their ale, which all in those days considered a sovereign remedy for all evils of the flesh.

Paul Drux retired to have his wounds dressed, and came back no more to the public room where this encounter had taken place.

It was a pity, however, that he could not have heard the conversation of these doughty heroes, for, from the brave way in which he had defended himself, they began to have some suspicions as to his really being a wealthy chapman.

" That fellow is more used to staves than yards of cloth," said one; " 'twould be well to denounce him as a spy."

" Aye, thou sayest well. Shall two dog him while the other goes fetch the guard ? "

" The devil is in the fellow," said the other ; " I would rather not remain. But we can bring help and take him in his sleep. Sir Hugh Fitzurse will reward us well."

This was agreed on, and some minutes later the three ruffians took their departure.

In the meantime Paul Drux had found that not only was mine host a faithful subject of King Richard's, but one devoted to the outlaws of Sherwood Forest, whom he looked upon as men of spirit.

The chapman then confided to him that he was a confidential agent of the king's, acting in conjunction with Robin Hood, and that hence he had the greatest objection to being taken before any officers of the rebel army.

" Will you trust me ? " said mine host.

" You look an honest fellow—I will."

" You have done well, Sir Ralph," continued the innkeeper, with a smile, " your disguise is very well, but I knew you directly you spoke."

The young knight looked confused and vexed.

" And this is what Robin Hood calls a safe disguise," he said, with a dissatisfied air.

" My good master," said the host, " Robin Hood nor no other man can disguise a voice, and yours is so like your worthy father's was that I knew you the moment you spoke."

" You knew my father ? "

" I was his body servant in many a foreign land. It was only at his death that I retired here."

" Your name ? "

" Roger Doone," said the man, smiling.

The knight shook him heartily by the hand.

" You seem, Roger, to have a better memory than I have. Of course I know all about you now. I was very little then, but, if I remember rightly, you taught me to ride ? "

" Yes."

" And to hold a lance ? "

" Yes."

" And to use the crossbow ? "

" I did."

" Then I am most delighted to see you. But now to business. Know you aught of what is going on here ? "

" I know that it will not be safe for my honoured master to pass the night here. Those vagabonds will surely return, and 'tis my opinion that the sooner you are housed the better."

" Where ? "

" If you will shoulder a crossbow, and make believe that we are going out to try our fortunes with our crossbows, I will show you."

" Many thanks, Roger."

" Is your pack valuable ? "

" Aye, that it is. I was forced to play the chapman thoroughly, so have silks and satins, and furbelows and lace, all from the great mart of London, which, when I resume my knightly garb, I pray you accept for your wife, and that buxom lass who made such good use of her broom handle."

" My wife's sister," said Roger, laughing. " Well, an the pack is to be mine I'll doubly hide it."

And with these words he left the room.

A few minutes later the pack was carried into the woods by the stout lass and a serving man, the harness of the two horses piled on top.

Then the horses, their feet slightly hoppled, were driven forth to seek food for themselves.

The landlord returned now with a pair of crossbows and a well replenished wallet.

" Now, Sir Ralph, though I don't expect the ruffians back before night, 'tis best I should be here when they come."

Sir Ralph Tressilian assented to this, and two minutes later the young knight and his stout middle-aged attendant went forth.

Casting their eyes warily about, they could see nothing suspicious.

They went then on together, and followed a narrow and entangled footpath which the occasional passage of anglers or woodcutters had traced by the side of a stream.

This continued for about two miles, when the path ceased, and the two men halted before a steep rock.

Roger Doone now explained the nature of the concealment in which he wished to place Sir Ralph.

" People call it the outlaws' den, and the frantic priest who was condemned to death for saying that the Bible was more than the Pope said that its dwellers were like the conies in Holy Scripture, a feeble people that make their abode in rocks. But he hid there six months, and glad, until he escaped to foreign parts."

" Where is it ? " asked Sir Ralph.

" Follow me."

And with this he began to ascend the rock, striding with his hands from one precarious footstep to another, till he got about half way up, where two or three bushes concealed the mouth of a hole resembling an oven, into which the stout landlord insinuated first his head and shoulders, and then by slow gradation the rest of his long body : his legs and feet finally disappearing, coiled up like a huge snake entering his retreat, or a long pedigree introduced with care and difficulty into the narrow pigeon-hole of an old cabinet.

Sir Ralph had clambered up and looked into the den with something of a rueful countenance.

But honest Roger Doone came out, and bade him do as he had done.

The knight somewhat ruefully obeyed.

The cave was very narrow, too low in the roof to

admit of his standing, or almost of his sitting up, though he made some awkward attempts at the latter posture.

"I hope the worthy priest did not remain here wholly for six months."

"No; he crept out at night; sleeping and reading by day—for he had some rare manuscripts."

"I must make the best of it," grinned Sir Ralph. "When shall I see you again?"

"Early i' the morn at latest. But if the knaves stay about, my little girl that's ten years old will bring you victuals and drink. This wallet contains enough for to-night—but keep your bow to your hand. There are few know this place, and, if I may be bold enough to advise, answer no man save myself, and no woman either, save Greta or the stout lass that hurtled the rebel knave."

"As you say, my worthy host."

"And now I will go back to the house and see if I cannot bamboozle the knaves on to a wrong scent."

And Roger Doone soon disappeared, leaving the knight to his meditations.

As the cave was dry, and filled with clean straw and withered fern, it was not so uncomfortable as might have been fancied.

This premised, we leave the soldier to his watches and follow Roger, only remarking that from the mouth of the cave the knight had a full view of the castle, and even of the inn across the forest tree-tops.

CHAPTER XIII.

SIR HUGH TEMPTS BRIAN DE FALAISE.

ROGER DOONE was a good man and true.

But, like a good many other very worthy persons, while entertaining a very sincere regard for his young master, the churl had also a very sincere love for himself.

That if Sir Ralph were discovered in his house in disguise he would suffer was too much in accordance with the manners of the times to doubt.

We know what soldiers too often are now that they are not only disciplined but strictly subordinate to the civil power, of which they are merely the humble servants, not to be fully aware what ruffians and tyrants they could be when left to their own personal devices.

The burning of his house, slaughter of himself, and ill-usage of his women, would have been but a natural consequence of any such discovery.

But if nothing suspicious were found, Roger knew too well the tactics of the rebel chiefs and lords not to be fully aware that he was safe.

Both sides were appealing to the sympathies of the people.

All can do this with hearty goodwill when they want to get anything out of them.

They are then the source of all legitimate power, the bold peasantry, their country's pride; while at another moment they are the common people, the fustian, the raving mob.

Ainsi va le monde.

Roger Doone kept open late that night. A good many country folks were there, and some camp followers, but not the three who had assaulted Sir Ralph.

The women folk were busy serving the customers, while Roger, with his back to the fire, was conversing with some of his own particular cronies.

Suddenly a heavy tramp of horses was heard.

A slight flush came over Roger's face.

"Sit still, all," he said, "'tis but the night patrol. I bear the blame for being open after curfew, but there are so many gentlemen of the army here I could not well do otherwise."

"Surround the house, and cut down who dares try to leave it," said a stern voice.

"Body o' me!" quoth Roger; "who's this?"

Ere the words were well passed his lips an officer of rank, in a full suit of armour, entered, accompanied by several of inferior rank, behind whom came the three discomfited camp followers.

"Who owns this house?"

"I do, Sir Hugh," said Roger, with a low bow.

"Humph—you know me, knave."

"I have often seen you with his grace the prince."

"Well, that matters not. Here are three fellows who say they followed a spy to this house, and when they would have arrested him and brought him to my camp you and your household did assault and ill-use them."

"I trow my dame did stick her spit where it may have incommoded yonder black-bearded thief, since most men like to sit down awhiles; but they deserved all they got," cried Roger, heartily.

"How so, knave?"

"I am no knave, your worship, but an honest inn-keeper, and follower of my lord the Earl of Beauclerk."

"Ah, but that will avail you little if you reset spies."

"I know nothing of spies, Sir Hugh; I only know that an honest gentleman, with a pack of some value which he wanted to sell at to-morrow's fair, was having some refreshment, when three cowardly loons wanted to rob him, and though we did not allow that, contrived to rob me as it was."

"How so?"

"No sooner was their ugly backs turned than the traveller turned upon me, told me I kept a disorderly house, threatened me with the provost, and rode off there and then, declaring that he would find some shelter where he was safe from thieves."

"Well, you fellows?"

"The man lies. We thought not of his pack."

"A false and wicked lie," said the shrill voice of the landlord's wife; "you asked for the pack, and wanted to search it. If I had my will of you, for driving away a man who, besides being a good customer, would have given us belike a handsome fairing, I'd strap you all up."

"Silence, woman," cried Sir Hugh, grimly; "there are enough of men here without your clatter. Women are all very well in their way, but an your tongue ran like a mill always, were I your good man I would try the ducking-stool."*

Roger's wife looked daggers, but, afraid to irritate the soldier, retired with flashing eyes, which were not rendered milder by the laughter of her neighbours.

"Let the house be searched, and as I apprehend these knaves have misled me, a stoop of your best wine, landlord, and roll a cask of ale out for the men."

"Certainly, Sir Hugh."

And the knight, while some of his lieutenants searched the house from top to bottom, drank his wine, which he condescended to praise highly.

But the search brought nothing. Traveller, pack, and horses had disappeared, leaving not a trace behind.

"'Tis well," said Sir Hugh; "I trow these fellows have been mistaken. But I have myself suspicions of this chapman, and will leave half a dozen troopers with Master Hardy here, to watch if he should return. Take your reckoning, man, and you, Hardy, mind you keep your fellows within bounds. We are in arms for the rights and liberties of our country, and should respect the commons, our allies and friends."

With which bit of theatrical gag, very common in the mouths of insurgent leaders in all times, Sir Hugh Fitz-urse left the house and rode off.

The six troopers and their lieutenant remained behind, as did the three camp followers, between one of whom, the dark-bearded man with the uneasy seat, and Sir Hugh a very meaning glance was exchanged at parting.

The knight had scarcely got out of sight of the inn, when his true nature was revealed.

"That base Saxon played his part well," he said to a young officer; "he little thinks I know who the spy is. But both shall hang, both shall hang."

"'Tis the young spark who married your niece."

"Yes!" said Sir Hugh, "it is, and one on whom I have vowed the bitterest hatred and revenge. But I must be cautious. This Roger Doone is a tool of his—but I will have him. Spy or no spy he dies. I will not trust him in the hands of my lords, his rank and relationship to me might make them merciful. No—he shall hang as a spy to the first tree, and lie in a nameless grave—then, my saucy niece, we will see who stands between you and a convent."

---

* A chair in which scolds are tied and put under water. At the top of a wide open space, opposite the infirmary at Manchester, was formerly a pond called the Daub Hole, now to be traced by two fountains. At this pond was the ducking-stool used to punish scolds and bad characters. At one end of a beam was a chair, in which the victim was tied firmly, the middle rested on a support as in the game of seesaw, so that the executioner had only to lift and lower the extreme end to drench the unfortunate.

A WELL-TIMED SHOT!

The young soldier made no reply.

"Brian de Falaise," he continued, after awhile, "I have been a friend to you."

"You have, my lord, indeed; when play and ill-luck reduced me to poverty and disgrace you lifted me by the hand, and put me on the road to fortune."

"Well, art willing to serve me?"

"I am."

"Then take this matter in hand. You know my real wishes—act as seems you best, When we reach the camp use this purse;" and he handed him a heavy one. "I give you three days' holiday. Go about it how and in what way you list, but do my bidding."

"I will, my lord."

"An you do, my gratitude shall be eternal, and my memory good."

"I will so contrive this matter," said Brian de Falaise, with a grin, "that your lordship shall never have reason to forget me, or regret the mode of my conducting the affair."

"'Tis well; the matter then is settled."

Brian made no reply, but drew back somewhat, leaving the old knight to his meditations.

It was two hours after curfew when they reached the camp, but the leader held a long conference in his camp the lieutenant whom he was about to speed on his errand of villany.

CHAPTER XIV.

THE CAVERN.

We cannot say that Sir Ralph Tressilian bore his confinement in the cavern much like a philosopher. On the contrary, we must acknowledge that, being somewhat wearied of his meditations, and with gazing eternally at the same view, he opened the wallet, ate a hearty meal, drank far more of Roger's good Burgundy than was his habit, and then, drawing his cloak round him, went sound asleep.

Under the circumstances it was really the very best thing he could have done, a deed to be highly commended and approved by all sensible men.

The day had given way to twilight, and twilight to moonshine, when Sir Ralph woke, much refreshed, but also very weary of his warren.

Seeing that it was quite dark, he ventured forth, and not daring to walk up and down, lest he might have been watched, wrapped his cloak closely about him and gazed about, happy even to breathe the fresh and balmy air.

In a straight line he was not half a mile from the castle, while that he was not so far from the outposts of the rebel camp was quite clear.

A heavy sound sank on the night wind down the woody glen, and was answered by the echoes of the banks.

A second, third, and fourth time the signal was repeated, fainter and fainter, as if at a greater and greater distance.

It was obvious that a party of soldiers were near, and upon their guard, though not sufficiently so to detect him.

But there was a deep fog or mist in the air, which, hanging low over the trees, precluded all danger of his being seen, so that at length he was able even to walk about.

But he kept his eye in the direction of the spot where the picket was established.

Presently, however, by one of those sudden changes of atmosphere incident to a mountainous country, a breeze arose, and swept before it the mist and the clouds which had covered the horizon, and the night planet poured her full effulgence upon a small and blighted heath, skirted under with copse wood and stunted trees, upon which a troop of horse were encamped.

The men lay round their camp fires, the horses were feeding, but four mounted sentries both kept guard and the animals too.

Sir Ralph at once retreated into his hovel, nor did he again leave it, towards morning a heavy sleep leaving him in happy insensibility to the cares and troubles of life.

The sun had just risen in the sky, the balmy breeze of morning was waving the tree-tops, and the birds were making merry as they rushed about in search of food, when the soldier again crept forth from his hiding-place, and feeling the want both of a drink of sparkling water, and having also a desire to perform his ablutions, crept down the steep side of the hill towards a small stream that ran at its back.

It must be understood that he did not descend the rock on the side facing the enemy, but where nothing was to be seen but the dense and waving forest.

Sir Ralph had drank, washed himself, and was standing upright leaning on his crossbow, when he distinctly heard steps in the forest, and steps, too, somewhat hurried and rapid.

He concealed himself behind a hollow tree and waited.

Soon he saw the girl who had acted with such energy in his behalf at the inn emerge from the forest, and take her way deftly and carefully towards his place of concealment.

Anxious to meet and confer with her, he was about to clamber up the hill, when he saw the girl halt.

She looked fearfully about her.

With her short petticoats, pretty ribbed hose, smart shoes, and straw hat with waving ribbons, with her basket on her arm, and her head on one side in the act of listening, she made quite a pretty picture.

Sir Ralph halted himself and listened, as his policy was to reveal himself only at the last moment.

Then a black-bearded fellow, with a heavy spear on his shoulder, a crossbow on his back, a sword by his side, and a knife in his girdle, stepped right before the girl.

"Whither away, my dainty one?"

"Sir, let me pass."

"No hurry, my darling."

"I am in a hurry. I have a long way to go in. I cannot stop."

"Hearkee," said the man, gruffly, as he caught hold of her arm with his great fist, "we shall be either good friends or thorough enemies. You will do wisely to make me a friend."

"I don't know."

"You will have the more pleasure in making my acquaintance."

"I will scream."

"And bring my fellows down upon you. Now listen! You are carrying this basket to the spy."

"I am not."

"Let us examine. I have a nose for good things, and if there be not a venison pasty and a couple of bottles of wine in that pannier, my name is not Gilbert Short-shanks."

And the man leaned forward to snatch at the basket.

At the same moment he gave a wild roar, and clapped his hand behind, running away wildly, as he did so lugging at an arrow—which arrow, says Peter Cunningham, drily, "hindered him from sitting easily at dinner for some months after."

The girl, laughing with all the hearty goodwill of a Saxon maiden, ran away, nor stopped in her course until she and Sir Ralph met at the mouth of the cave.

The knight relieved her of her burden, and then bade her stoop.

"Was it you fired?"

"Yes. Not a word. Creep into the cavern—the fellow will be back with a dozen in a moment," he continued.

The girl obeyed.

Sir Ralph, guided by the directions of Roger Doone, now pulled a whole curtain of ivy and blackberry bushes, that had been parted, over the mouth of the cave, which completely concealed its mouth.

He had scarcely restored the screen, which made the hole quite dark, when loud cries were heard in the valley below, cries of soldiers calling to one another as they scoured the woods.

They cursed and they swore, and used all kind of threats to induce the girl to come forward—to no purpose, of course.

Then the young prisoners heard an officer command his men to camp on the open glade where their comrade had been wounded.

"The girl cannot have gone far; and as for the outlaw knave who shot at Drake, I'll hang him as safe as I find him. My troop will want a trumpeter this month—the fellow will not mount a horse in less time."

The girl of the inn could hardly repress a laugh, while Sir Ralph himself smiled grimly.

"Well," he said, "since we are likely to stop here all day, we had better break our fast."

"But my brother will be running his head into danger," said the young woman.

"Not he—he is cautious enough. All we have to do is to be still until darkness sets in, then we may venture on a round through the forest. Ca... me at the back across the stream to the in...

"Yes."

"Then unless we are attacked," said Sir Ralph, "all we have to do is to remain quite still, and pass the time as best we may."

To begin, Ralph, reclining on his side like a Roman epicure, pulled forth the dainty fare contained in the basket, and urged the girl to eat, which, however, she declined.

"I had a hearty breakfast," she observed, "before I came out. I daresay I shall want dinner presently, but can eat nothing now."

The meal concluded, the provisions were placed on one side, and the knight and maiden of low degree solaced themselves by long and intimate conversation.

During the hours which passed ere the day was run Sir Ralph was surprised at the charms of conversation which this poor girl possessed.

Though, like most Saxon girls of her day, hers was the voluptuous kind of beauty, yet was she very pretty; nor did the knight, like the gallant knight he was, fail to tell her so.

Upon which the girl, as in duty bound, blushed.

The longest day—and neither of these young people were ever heard to say that this was the longest day of their lives—will at last pass away, and at last the sun set with a lowering sky, that spoke of a coming storm, a sign which was rather a pleasant one to Sir Ralph.

Still could they hear the sentries, or rather scouts, in the valley below; and when at last they crawled from their den, they distinctly saw the whole party—twelve truculent-looking troopers—seated on the ground round a blazing fire.

Sir Ralph looked upward at the sky.

"Shall we go at once, my fair guide," said Ralph, taking the girl's hand in his, "or shall we wait until it is late?"

"'Tis best go forward ere the moon rises," she said, without any effort to disengage her hand.

Very naughty and very improper truly, but we are describing the manners of seven hundred years ago.

"'Tis well. Go on—lead the way; I follow you to the death!"

The girl smiled as she turned round to the back of the cave where for twelve hours they had been ensconced, except when now and then one crept out to gaze at the fire in the valley, and began descending a narrow and almost imperceptible pathway in the direction of the forest.

They walked slowly, taking care to make as little noise as possible; but in some places the descent was so steep that the young man more than once came in contact with projecting stumps and branches that overhung the pathway.

As a large stone was jerked forward by one of his feet, and rolled down the steep ascent, the loud conversation of the troopers ceased, and the girl clutched hold of Sir Ralph with sudden terror.

"Move not for your life!" she whispered.

Sir Ralph only replied by pressing her hand, and the pair of fugitives remained still and motionless.

They could hear the soldiers moving about in every direction, but none came close to them.

At the end of about ten minutes they ventured to advance, this time still more cautiously than ever.

At the bottom of the descent, and, as it seemed by the side of the brook (for Sir Ralph heard the rushing of a considerable body of water, although its stream was invisible in the darkness), they again halted.

"This way," said the girl, as soon as they made out that no other sounds could be made out.

The young man took her hand, and followed into a dense thicket.

For a quarter of an hour they moved in utter silence along a path which the girl could have only followed by a kind of instinct.

Then they came to a small and rudely-constructed hovel.

The door was open, and the inside of the premises appeared as uncomfortable and rude as its situation and exterior foreboded.

There was no appearance of a floor of any kind; the roof seemed rent in several places; the walls were composed of loose stones and turf, and the thatch of branches of trees.

The fire was in the centre, and filled the whole wigwam with smoke, which escaped as much through the door as by means of a circular aperture in the roof.

An aged crone, the only inhabitant of this forlorn mansion, appeared busy in the preparation of some food.

She lifted her eyes from the low stool on which she sat.

"Eh, Lucy, is that you—and with a man? What want you here?"

"You must go up to the house, and bring brother Roger here."

"And why cannot you go yourself?"

"Because, Bridget, there are those in the wood who will use me ill. Come, Bridget, for the love you bear your little Lucy, go."

"And this gold piece shall be your guerdon," said Ralph.

"Eh, sir?" cried the woman, rising and clutching nervously at the gold, "you don't mean the girl any harm?"

"Certainly not," replied Ralph, while both he and the girl laughed and blushed.

The old woman, whose limbs appeared marvellously more lissom since the present of money, now busied herself putting on an old hat and a red cloak; after which she asked for a message.

"Say to Roger that he is to come here. Tell him when he is alone; and mind that no soldiers follow you."

"Follow me," grinned the toothless old hag, "what for should they follow me? But never mind, my pretty one, I know what you mean, and the old folks must have their jokes."

With this she went on her way, leaving the young people in the old hut, which, however, with its fire, being by no means a safe retreat when enemies were near, they retreated to a thicket hard by, and there waited until the old guide returned with Roger.

CHAPTER XV.

THE PATROL.

THE owl was hooting in the dark forest, and no other sound could be heard save the soughing of the wind, as Ralph and Lucy sat on the greensward.

Suddenly, however, they heard both voices and footsteps.

"Where are you?"

"Here," said Ralph, heartily, as he and Lucy approached the fire.

"A pretty long stroll of it you have made, sister mine," said the innkeeper, a little pettishly.

"I suppose I might have been murdered and buried in the forest, ere you had looked for me," she replied, pertly.

"Hush!" said Sir Ralph, "we have no time to lose. Listen."

And he explained briefly what had occurred.

The innkeeper scratched his ear.

"Why did you not remain in the cave?"

"Well," said Ralph, laughing, "I'm not an old man, and Lucy here is a pretty girl, and I didn't know how you or her sister might like it."

"But she could come home."

"Alone? Certainly not, my worthy host. One encounter with forest ruffians was enough. But now what is to be done? I am not doing the king's will here. If I am to be out in the woods, I may as well go back to Sherwood."

"There is a watch on my house," mused Roger.

"But can you not point out some inn in the town where I can go, in some other disguise?"

"There's the Dun Cow, this lass's brother keeps it. He's a true man."

"That will do well, and then Lucy here will have a good excuse to bring you news."

"True," said Roger Doone; "but the disguise?"

"You must open my valise; there is the dress of a forest ranger in that."

"Capital. Lucy must guide you right round the castle, so that you enter the town by the other side; but we must be stirring. All the houses will be closed."

Ralph Tressilian was quite ready, and soon the three entered the forest, leaving the old woman to her hut.

They were not long, knowing the forest as they did, in reaching a point within a hundred yards of the inn.

Roger now left them, as he had reason to believe the comrades of the wounded trumpeter had set a watch for the girl who had been the cause of his inglorious wound.

He returned shortly, and with a warning to be careful, and a promise to be round in the morning, left the young knight to the guidance of Lucy, who was truly nothing loth to be cast so intimately into contact with a young nobleman so superior in manners and conversation to the clodhoppers she was accustomed to.

In a dense thicket Sir Ralph changed his clothes, hid the old ones where they could easily be found by any one who knew where to look, and then went forward, joining Lucy, who awaited him in the deep shadow of the castle.

They had many a detour to make, many a sentry to avoid, many a patrol to hide from.

One of these halts was peculiarly dangerous; the soldiers of the night-watch caught a glimpse of them, so that they had hours to hide under a half-ruined archway beneath the ramparts.

It was nearly daybreak when they reached the Dun Cow, and the host was not stirring.

When he heard, however, that it was a friend of King Richard, and the son of Roger's old master, he bustled about, and soon found Sir Ralph a comfortable bed, which both his fatigues and his necessities made him keep until evening approached.

It was nearly dusk when he went down stairs, and sat down to his first meal at seven o'clock in the evening.

Lucy waited upon him with unvarying good temper and kindly assiduity.

It is half a fortune to a man to be young and handsome and noble—with the women.

Intellect and honesty are shining lights, but they probably make too much glare.

The commoner ones are more easily distinguished by the fair sex.

Once the meal over, and assured by the girl that his disguise was admirable, for even she herself hardly knew him, Sir Ralph Tressilian sallied forth to look about him.

All the principal streets of the old town were thronged with personages of various conditions and degrees, towards the evening of one of those soft but cloudy summer days when the sun makes his full warmth felt, but without the glare which dazzles the eye when he shines unveiled upon the world.

The street to which we must for a moment conduct the reader was narrow, so that not more than three or four horsemen could ride abreast, and yet it was one of the best in the town.

But in reality the space for passengers was much wider than it seemed; for, as was then very common, especially in that part of the country, one-half of the ground floor of the houseswas taken up by a long, low arcade, which sheltered the pedestrians from the rain at some periods of the year, and from the heat at others.

The same style of architecture was common recently in Paris, and is peculiarly characteristic of Genoa.

From the first floor of these houses projected long gilt poles—just high enough to allow a tall horse, mounted by a tall man with a lance in his hand, to pass, without striking his head or the weapon he carried—and suspended from these poles appeared many of the various signs which are now restricted to inns and taverns, but were then common to every mansion of any importance.

Down this street, and underneath numerous symbols of swans and horses and eagles and mermaids and falcons and doves, and all those heterogeneous mixtures of birds, beasts and fishes which the fertile fancy of heralds ever compounded, were riding, at the time of which we speak, various groups of horsemen.

Ever and anon the progress of one party or another would be stopped by some man, woman, or child, darting out from the arcade at the side.

About an hour after Sir Ralph left the Dun Cow he was standing listlessly watching the busy throng, and picking up information from threads and patches of discourse which fell upon his ears, when he saw a group advance towards a second-rate inn, the Maypole, near which he was standing, which was unnoticed by any of the good people of the town.

There were four human beings and four beasts, two of some value and strength, the others, thin, vicious-looking brutes.

The latter were mounted by two ill-favoured-looking knaves enough, fellow-labourers in the same vineyard, that is, lower servants of some man of note.

The man mounted on a good horse was Ralph's own body servant.

Beside him rode a female form, covered with a thick veil, which shrouded the face, so that it was impossible to see whether there was beauty beneath or not, although the figure gave indications of youth and grace which were not to be mistaken.

Ralph knew by instinct that it was his wife, and was about to rush forward, when a hand was laid upon his shoulder.

"The woman interests you," said a slightly sarcastic voice.

"Woman, Lucy!" replied Sir Ralph, impatiently, " it is my wife; what she can be doing here is a mystery to me."

"Wife!" said Lucy, shivering all over.

"Yes, my poor girl," continued Ralph, without noticing her emotion, "and her being here is the sign of some foul conspiracy."

"Wife!—you never spoke of wife," continued Lucy.

"Hush, Lucy! we shall be heard. I have said my wife—my young, innocent, and beautiful wife—trapped here by some abominable treachery."

"Why think you so?"

"I know Sir Hugh Fitzurse. He suspects my presence here, and has dared to play some vile trick to carry out some abominable plot. Lucy, will you help me to save her?"

"Sir Ralph," said Lucy, who, having taken such a sudden fancy to the handsome young knight, was some-

what astonished at his coolness after his making love to her by the hour, " you seem to have faith in me?"

"Girl, I had forgotten," he cried, turning pale. "I have no right to expect aid from you. Go—denounce me, for I will perish rather than harm shall befall her!"

"Hush! I am a foolish, vain girl, and not so good as I ought to be; but my heart is in the right place. Say not one word more, but command me. On my salvation I will do everything I can to aid the lady."

"I believe you, Lucy," said Ralph; and then he added, lowering his eyes, "but ——"

"She shall never know that a whisper of gallantry ever passed your lips to me. Why should she suffer for my folly?"

"Lucy, I know not how to thank you."

"Command—I obey."

"Well. The stout well-dressed man who entered last is my own servant; the other knaves are I fear me, hired cut-throats. Go you in and speak to Gilbert—tell him I am here, and would speak to him yonder"—pointing to an archway opposite.

"I will."

"Ah!"—drawing back in the shade—"there goes one of the villains to announce his news to his employer. Make you haste."

Lucy made no reply, but with a slightly burning cheek entered the Maypole, where she was well known.

Sir Ralph, in an agony of mind difficult to describe, waited, leaning against the inn stable wall.

As he did so his eyes fell upon a new arrival.

Jogging along upon his mule, with his legs hanging down easily by the side of the animal, and his fat stomach resting peacefully upon the saddle, was a jolly friar, clothed in grey, with his capuche thrown back—the sun not being troublesome—and a bald head, the glistening smoothness of which had descended by tradition even to Shakespeare's days, and was recorded by him in his "Two Gentlemen of Verona."

In fact, it looked like an ostrich's egg, peeping out from a narrow ring of jet-black hair, scarcely streaked with grey.

His face was large and jovial, which, in sooth, was no distinction in those times between one friar and another; but there was withal a look of roguish fun about the corners of his small grey eyes, and a jeering smile, full of arch satire, quivered upon his upper lip, completely neutralising the somewhat sensual and food-loving expression of the under one, which moved up and down every time he spoke, like a valve, to let out the words that would never come in again.

Indeed, he seemed to be one of those easy-living friars who, knowing neither sorrow nor privation in their own persons, appeared to look upon grief and care with a ready laugh and a light joke, as if no such thing in reality existed. His rosy gills, his double chin, and his large round ear, all spoke of marrow and fatness; and, indeed, at the very first sight the spectator saw that he was not only a well-contented being, but one who had good reason to be so.

The friar looked at the ranger in green.

The ranger in green started and stepped forward to speak to the friar.

Just as he did so the serving-man sallied from the yard on horseback, and the friar, by some mismanagement, contrived to get his mule's hind-quarters towards the servant, who was riding by, and by a touch of the heel, given apparently to make the beast put itself into a more convenient position for all parties, he produced a violent fit of kicking, in the course of which the horseman received a blow upon the fleshy part of his thigh, which made him roar with pain.

The seat upon the vicious beast's back was no easy one, but yet the fat monk kept his position, laughing heartily, and calling his mule a petulant rogue, while he held him by the left ear, or patted his pampered neck.

"Though you be a friar," said the man, "I've a great mind to dust your jacket. If I have not broken my leg, it is not your fault."

"Eh?" said the priest, rolling quietly off at the side, and looking up to his companion, saw the wry face of the other.

"I'll punish the rogue; he shall have five barley corns less than usual for supper."

"Give me any sauce and this stick——"

"Away!" said a deep and commanding voice; "how dare you insult the worthy priest?"

And Ralph, waving his staff, advanced.

"Nay, if there be two, I'm off," replied the serving-man.

"Thanks, my son," said the priest.

"No need, Friar Tuck," whispered the other; "I am Sir Ralph Tressilian—my wife is inside, go you in, and I will follow—every moment is precious."

The astounded friar made no reply, but handing his horse to an obsequious attendant, went in, followed by the man in a ranger's dress.

The Maypole, though a second-rate inn, was large and divided into many rooms; so that, seeing the strange servant who had attended his wife taking refreshment where he could watch the foot of the staircase, the two passed on to where they saw Lucy in conversation with Sir Ralph's own body domestic.

"Oh, sir," said Jukes, quite trembling with terror at what the girl had told him, "you don't think I had anything to do with this matter?"

"Certainly not," replied Sir Ralph; "but there is no time for talk. Do you go out and saddle the horses."

"Where mean you to go?" asked the friar.

"I know not."

"Then see my horse is fed," replied Friar Tuck, "and get a wallet of provender, and I will guide you all. My business is with you, Sir Ralph."

Jukes promised to do whatever he was ordered, and this once settled, Lucy, who had taken off her hat and made herself look like one of the numerous chamber-maids of the establishment, watched her opportunity—the house being crowded with guests—and then slipped up stairs with the forester.

The room occupied by Lady Tressilian was known to the girl, and in a moment Sir Ralph knocked at it.

"Come in."

The girl and supposed ranger entered.

Agnes looked at them in some surprise.

"What may be your will?" she said, in her usual soft and amiable tones.

"Agnes."

"That voice!"

"Come to me, darling."

And regardless of the presence of Lucy, who looked on with a pale and sickly smile, they heartily embraced.

"But how is it you have come away from home?" asked Sir Ralph. "I implored you to remain with my mother until these troubles were over."

"Why write to me to come?"

"Heavens! have you the letter?"

"Certainly."

And she hastily drew it forth, handing it to her husband.

"This is a base forgery. There is not an instant to lose. Hearing of my absence, your wicked uncle has devised this plot to separate us for ever. We must fly directly."

"But the lady will be known," said Lucy.

"True," cried Sir Ralph; and then, seeing that Agnes looked inquiringly at her, he added, "this is the sister of good Roger Doone, my father's old servant."

"Come, lady, there is no time to lose," continued the girl, who then drew her into a kind of dressing-room, whence they soon emerged, Agnes turned into a charming chambermaid, while Lucy made rather an awkward lady.

A few words were exchanged. Lucy bade Ralph leave her as soon as possible, for that she was sure Sir Hugh was coming, and then appointed a meeting at Roger's for the next day.

Ralph went first, and descended the stairs as if he had been visiting somebody in the upper rooms.

In this way he reached the little side room where Jukes and the priest were.

They were hard at work at a chine and flagon.

Agnes came tripping down, with a rather dull imitation of a chirrup.

The starveling servant looked up, but either his intellects were obfuscated by the beer he had been drinking, or he had no suspicion.

The friar paid the reckoning from a purse handed to him by Sir Ralph.

They then strolled out as if to look after their steeds.

The stable-yard opened into a street, where a couple of horsemen could barely march abreast.

But here stood the means of freedom.

A waiting-man who knew the friar, and who had received a good fee, had brought out the three horses belonging to the travellers, with a fourth, which was to be hired and returned on the following day.

All mounted, the ostler touched his hat, and the party rode away.

They only walked their horses, affecting to be in no hurry. The friar conducted them through numerous winding streets, until they were on the outskirts of the town.

A turfy common lay between them and the forest.

A loud clatter of hoofs was heard in the distance.

"We are chased," said Friar Tuck; "follow me. There is a ditch or two, but they must be leaped."

They were half across the common.

A glitter of armour and lance heads was seen, and then a dozen men-at-arms dashed in their direction.

"Yoicks! yoicks!" shouted the foremost man.

"Tally-ho!" replied the fat friar.

And the fugitives dug their heels into their horses' sides. First rode the burly friar, his mule when put to it using her heels to some purpose; behind him came Sir Ralph leading his wife's palfrey; behind again was Jukes, who looked over his shoulder every now and then, well aware that the enemy were gaining on them.

They now approached a wide ditch, used to drain the flat surface of the common; and Friar Tuck, bidding them all follow his example, dashed through and up the steep bank on the other side.

They were now screened by bushes and then by a thicket from the pursuers.

In a moment more they were walking around the thicket at a slow and cautious pace.

The men-at-arms dashed furiously by, spreading over the plain by order of their chief.

Friar Tuck turned again to the ditch, waded through, and trotted along the soft banks for about two hundred yards, when, the ground rising, the banks of the drainage-cutting became high and far apart.

At this instant the enemy uttered a shout, and then came tearing wildly down upon them, to be brought up by the ditch.

"Surrender!" shouted a loud voice.

"Come and take us, my hearties," said the friar.

A volley of bolts replied to this sally, but they were fired too hurriedly to hurt.

In ten minutes more they were in the forest, which everywhere in England in those days sheltered the oppressed and weak.

The clerk of Copmanhurst confessed himself too weary with his days' journey to go far, but urged that if they were to go fifty miles they could not be safer.

He therefore threaded the wood for about half an hour when they came upon a valley, where the whole party were compelled to alight and lead their horses.

After about ten minutes of this laborious work, they came upon a small clearing, in the midst of which was a ruined tower of three stories.

It was one of the old Saxon strongholds.

It was situated upon a high woody bank, showing a bold craggy front to the river.

It was one of those many small fortalices which had not been without their use in restraining the license of the Normans.

The friar dismounted from his mule, the others did the same, and then all entered the ruin.

Luckily it had a roof to the ground floor and the first story, where a bed of fern was at once made up for Agnes.

A fire was then lighted, round which the whole party sat, Agnes reclining with her head on her husband's lap, while he and Friar Tuck conversed in whispers.

Jukes, with professional gravity—he aspired to the dignity of butler at home—laid out an excellent supper.

Friar Tuck, with an eye to the evening's entertainment, had himself selected the menu.

There was a chine, a moderate-sized pasty, a couple of roast fowls, some white and brown bread, excellent English cheese, and one or two little knicknacks, such as a jolly priest would only have thought of.

The conference between Friar Tuck and Sir Ralph ended as soon as the meal was ready.

All did justice to it, travelling being the best whet to an appetite that yet has been discovered.

The wine and ale were excellent, but to this the young knight and his wife paid but moderate attention.

"Enjoy yourself, good clerk of Copmanhurst," said Sir Ralph, laughing; "I want a clear head for to-morrow's work."

And he ascended the rugged stairs, which almost yielded beneath his step, to the chamber he was to occupy with his wife.

It was a ruined room in a ruined tower, with no windows or door, and but a pile of fern for a couch.

But they were young and they loved.

True love is as a cloak.

The friar and Jukes, who were equally convivial, drank a silent toast to their happiness, and then gave way to the jollity of the hour.

"What think you of the wine?" said Tuck.

"Good liquor."

"Ah! ah! did you ever taste better out of the spare tankard which the butler hideth behind the cellar door?"

"Never better," laughed Jukes, after an attempt to loo demure and staid.

"Leave me alone for choosing; these knaves of land-lords know that it is no use giving me bad stuff. Here's to our better acquaintance."

Then taking a deep draught he poured forth, in full mellow strains, the well-known old song,—

> In a tavern let me die,
> And a bottle near me lye,
> That the angelic choir may cry,
> God's blessing on the toper.
> &c.,   &c.,   &c.

After one or two more glasses, and one or two more songs, the priest and serving man replenished the fire and lay them down to rest.

CHAPTER XVI.

FLY-BY-NIGHT.

THERE are some days of life when everything appears to combine to heighten the hues of happiness; when not only the sensation in our own bosoms, and the circumstances of our fate, are all bright and cheerful, but when every external object, every feature in nature's face, seems to smile, and every sound to be in harmony with our feelings. But such hours are too precious to be many; blessed is that life which can count two or three of them; and it has been often remarked that, as at some seasons of the year, a peculiarly fine day generally announces the approach of storm and tempest, so do one of these bright intervals in our cloudy existence precede a period of sorrow, trouble, and disaster.

An hour after daybreak, on as sweet a morning as ever dawned on the magnificent scenery of the forest, Sir Ralph and Agnes stood by the side of their horses ready to mount and depart.

Love gave its sunshine to each heart.

Agnes's bosom beat high with pleasure at this reunion with her husband.

The young husband was scarcely less joyful.

The yellow morning light spread sweetly overhead; the old, grey Saxon building rested calm in its ivy robe behind them; every blade of grass was sparkling with a thousand diamonds; every air wafted the breath of the sweet forest flowers; every tree was tuneful with the song of the birds. It was like some happy dream, when imagination, stripping life of its stern realities, revels supreme, and decks the brief moments of sleep with all the boundless treasures of her airy kingdom.

It was true that the young couple were about to part, but then Agnes was only going into the forest to one of the many haunts of Robin Hood, where Ralph could rejoin her as soon as his duty to the king was performed.

"And mind," said Agnes, as she mounted, "I saw some very bright eyes and smiling faces in the old town; don't let any of these laughing girls wean you away from me."

"Not a thousand of them," cried Ralph, something of a blush rushing to his embrowned cheeks, "would win my love from my darling wife."

And Ralph, like a good many others, spoke very truthfully, for few men count some trifling infidelities as anything, especially when their love remains unchanged.

Half an hour later Friar Tuck put Sir Ralph, or, as he now called himself, Luke Tangel, in the right road; and with somewhat of a sad heart and downcast mien, he rode away towards the city occupied by the rebels.

Ralph knew very well that he had a difficult and arduous task to play. Sir Hugh Fitzurse, furious at the defeat his nefarious designs had received, would of course be on the look out, and knowing or believing that Sir Ralph had ventured into the enemy's camp as a spy, would avail himself of this circumstance to have him treated with indignity and insult.

The young man knew this, but such was his devoted loyalty to his king, which the ignorance of the times confounded with loyalty to one's country, that he never hesitated a moment.

He knew Sir Hugh well, and knew that from him he had nothing to hope save the worst.

He was determined to keep a keen watch on the knight and all his attendants, but especially on Sir Hugh, whom he meant next time they met to examine so keenly that no future tricks might be played by him.

In the words of the poet, he might have exclaimed:—

> Which is the villain? Let me see his eyes,
> That when I note another man like him
> I may avoid him.

It was no part of Sir Ralph's policy to enter the town during the day, but he had every desire to speak with Roger Doone, who might, he thought, have heard some news of the rebels.

It was quite clear to Sir Ralph that they were drawing to a head, and that if he would serve his king, he must make haste and collect all the information that was to be obtained, with which to start and join the royal forces.

But the young knight did not wish to do so without being of more use than as a collector of useful information.

With this view he had bade Jukes, as soon as Agnes was housed with Maid Marian, or Will Scarlett's wife, or any other trusty friends, to ride homeward and collect every lance, bowman, and slingman loyal to the king, which were to join him in the Hawks Hill plain, near Derby.

The young man would readily have carried his courage abroad, being decidedly of opinion that—

> One drop of blood drawn from the country's bosom
> Should grieve thee more than streams of foreign gore:

but rebellion was rife within the land, and it behoved all good men and true to join the better prince of the two.

For many centuries before and after England was, indeed, a battle-field.

The story is printed in her blood.

About a mile from where the castle towered above the plain Ralph drew rein to gaze around.

What he hoped for was to see some path which might lead him to Roger's inn, that lay, he knew, under the tower over which floated the flag of the insurgents.

As he did so his ears caught the sound of a trotting horse close at hand.

Not knowing what it might be, he drew his cap over his eyes and loosened his sword in its sheath.

Then came a tall horse in view, with something perched upon its back.

It was doubtless human, for it had hands and guided the steed, while above all was a human head of large size and somewhat strange shape.

The whole was wrapped in a cloak.

As the strange being came near Sir Ralph he halted, and turning his horse, prepared to go the same way as the supposed forester.

"How now?" said the so called Luke Tangel, "what want you? Surely you are not a highwayman?"

"I'm a boy," replied the other, chuckling as he leaped up, and stood on the horse's back like an enormous ape, so extraordinary was his agility and such the pliancy of all his limbs.

The arms, too, like those of the Simia tribe, were of

an extraordinary length, and seemed longer than the whole body.

"Then what are you?" cried Ralph.

"Ho! ho! Sir Ralph, ho! So you don't know me, you wicked wanderer. You have been feasting in the forest."

"How now—who are—what are you? Do not jest with me, or I may break every bone in your body."

"Oh! Mr. Paul Drux," grinned the imp. "I don't like that Paul Drux—a scurvy master of wickedness. I'll carve his pink cheeks for him; and if I find him I'll roast him before a slow fire, baste him in his own fat, and serve him up to you as a barbacued pig."

"'Tis Fly-by-Night," cried Sir Ralph; "why where has the demon of darkness come from?"

The boy laughed heartily, for he was really full of fun and good humour, and of him when he was older, it could truly have been said:—

A merrier man,
Within the limit of becoming mirth,
I never spent an hour's talk withal.
His eye begets occasion for his wit;
For every object that the one doth catch
The other turns to a mirth-loving jest,
Which his fair tongue (conceit's expositor)
Delivers in such apt and gracious words
That aged ears play truant at his tales.

"Yes, truly, Fly-by-Night," said the boy; "and here have I been running up and down the country by day as well as by night, and could not find you. It seems you wander in the woods with cherry-lipped damsels. But that matters not. Where do you lodge?"

"I have no place to lay my head," replied Sir Ralph; "but could I but see Roger Doone I might hear news."

"Then this way. I came from thence, and he sent me to ride on this road in search of you. There was rare talk of you in the camp last night—oh! oh!"

"What said they?"

"Wilt like to hear?"

"Speak, urchin."

"You know Sir Hugh?"

"I do—the knave!"

"Well fear him."

"Why fear him?"

"He is a pestilent knave, and I would ever be on my guard."

"I know him, that is enough."

"You have seen cruel proof of this man's strength," replied the boy, gravely; "if you saw yourself with your eyes, or knew yourself with your judgment, the fear of your adventure would counsel you to a more equal enterprise."

"How so, my little man?"

"This fellow is a great chief, holds sway with the prince, and if you fall in his way will hang you."

"How to avoid it?"

"Wilt, being a wise man, take counsel by a fool?"

"Art thou the fool?"

"There are many men as mad as I."

"That I believe. But why enter the forest here?"

"For a fool's reason—because I hear a troop of horse dashing along the road, and because this is the way to Roger Doone's house."

Sir Ralph made no reply, but leaping a wide ditch, entered beneath the cover of the forest, and drew rein in a thicket whence he could distinguish the great road and all who passed.

To his deep gratification it proved to be a patrol of men-at-arms wearing his wife's uncle's scarfs and colours.

"Is not a fool sometimes wise?" said Fly-by-Night, as he handed a packet of despatches to the young knight.

"Yes, truly," replied Sir Ralph, who opened the king's letter, and there read his anxious desire that all his friends should join him as speedily as possible, with as many men as he could.

The rebels were becoming very daring, and must be taught a lesson.

"Lead on, my lad," said Ralph. "Here is matter to think on. I would be in the town to-night, and the day after to-morrow we start."

"Alone?"

"No. At the head of a bold band of lances," replied Sir Ralph, as they drew rein in sight of the inn.

CHAPTER XVII.

SIR HUGH.

IT was now decided that the knight should wait on the skirt of the forest, while Fly-by-Night went forward to the inn to see how matters were progressing.

That the soldiers had not left could be seen at a glance, as half a dozen of them were playing quoits at the side of the house.

"The storm is up, and all is on the hazard," said Sir Ralph. "Go forward. I will abide here. Sir Hugh shall give me ample satisfaction for these deep shames and great indignities."

Fly-by-Night, perched upon his big horse, like an imp, rode across the space between the forest and the hostelry.

Sir Ralph dismounted, gave his horse a good halter's length, and waited.

About half an hour elapsed, and then the disguised knight started, as he saw that a dark figure was creeping along the edge of the wood at no great distance.

These days of civil wars made a man above all suspicious, as friends and enemies are, during such convulsions, not to be distinguished one from the other.

Well might Sir Ralph cry out:—

What stratagems—how fell, how butcherly,
Erroneous, mutinous, and unnatural—
This deadly quarrel daily doth beget!

The supposed yeoman armed his crossbow.

"Who comes?" he said, in a hoarse voice.

"Lucy."

The arm fell to his side, and next moment the buxom sister-in-law of Roger Doone was greeted in a way that left her little to desire.

"And so you are safe back?" she said.

"Thanks to that imp of Satan, Fly-by-Night. But what news?"

"I must tell you."

* * * * * *

When Lucy remained at the Maypole, after the departure of Agnes, she was patient enough for a few minutes; but when she reflected that the young wife of Sir Ralph was safe, she thought it just as well to see to her own safety.

She had risen, therefore, with the intention of leaving the apartment, when a considerable clamour below stairs made her aware that her intended flight was too lately conceived.

Then she heard Sir Hugh ascending the stairs, in loud talk with the two servants who had decoyed Agnes from her home.

"This is the door, my lord."

"'Tis well—wait here. I want no announcing."

And he thrust the door rudely open to face Lucy, who stood with folded arms in the middle of the apartment.

"Where is Lady Tressilian, as she calls herself?" asked Sir Hugh, in a gruff and angry voice.

"I don't know."

"How now, hussy?"

"I'd have you know, sir, I am a respectable girl. My father is a Saxon franklyn, and my brother, Roger Doone, who keeps the Derby Castle——"

"Curse you and the Derby Castle too! Where is the Lady Tressilian?"

"Do you mean the young lady who came with those servants awhile ago?"

"Yes."

"Well this was her room, but it isn't now."

"Why, in the foul fiend's name?"

"Because her husband told her this place was not good for her."

"Husband?"

"Yes—husband."

"Girl, tell me the truth. How knew her husband that she was coming here?"

"Saw her in the street."

"Curses light on the fools! Where have they gone?"

"Well, sir," said Lucy, as if communing with herself, "I heard them say, that until the times were better they would put their property under the guardianship of the crown, while they took refuge with Robin Hood."

"Ah, curses on them! Where is the rascal monk, who kicked and illused my servants?"

"His mule did, sir."

"Well, where is the friar?"

"Gone, sir."

"Where?"

"I know not the holy friar's movements, except that he eat a whole dish full of as fine stewed eels as ever were cooked, worthy of the Wye, whence they came, whose waters have no mud to give them a foul flavour."

"Pshaw!" cried the irritated knight, "you do but flout me; if I thought you had any hand in this, I'd have you stuck in the pillory, my saucy madam; but beware how you give aid to spies and traitors. There are provost-marshals for women as well as men."

And the knight darting out of the room found his two varlets in the passage, whose astonishment at receiving a hearty kick and shower of abuse, may readily be imagined.

"My lord."

"My gracious lord."

"Silence, ye crop-eared knaves. Where is my niece?"

"In there, sir—have you not spoken to her?"

"No, animal."

"But we saw her in."

"And she has seen herself out again. Where is Jukes?"

"We cannot find him, and supposed he'd gone to stare about the town."

"He's given you the slip, ye numskulls. Look you that she be found in three days, or I'll find an excuse to hang you."

And with an angry step he went down stairs, mounted his horse, and taking no notice of the bowing and scraping of the landlord, rode back to his quarters in a towering passion.

There he found Brian de Falaise, who reported that the knight had not shown himself in the house of Roger Doone.

"No, sir!" said the irate commander; "I daresay not, seeing that the fellow can scarcely be in two places at once. He has baulked me again, but he shall rue the day—yes, he shall rue the day!"

"How so, my lord?"

"Art blind?"

"My lord!"

"And deaf?"

"No."

"Surely one would think you all were, since this man moves about in Derby, defying my power and my desire to see him."

"I have never seen him," said the lieutenant, quietly, "which, perhaps, accounts for my not so easily hunting him up; but be assured everything that can be done shall be done, and that once he is in my clutches he does not leave them easily."

"'Tis well," observed Sir Hugh, who did not wish to offend or anger his subordinate; "do as you say, and you shall have a double reward. This man stole a maiden from the arms of the Church."

"A goodly change—from the cold cloister to a husband's arms," cried Brian.

"Nay; 'tis ill jesting, Brian, with holy Church. I have vowed to restore my niece to the convent, where in sackcloth and ashes she may expiate her evil deeds. 'Tis this that troubles me more than the inheritance she has robbed me of. Be, therefore, on the alert, good Brian."

"I will," he said, and went forth muttering something which was inaudible to his employer.

The words we cannot repeat, but their meaning might be worse conveyed than in a quotation.

> This holy fox,
> Or wolf, or both, for he is equally ravenous
> As he is subtle; and as prone to mischief
> As able to perform it.

But Sir Hugh heard him not, nor did Brian de Falaise reveal his true sentiments to any one.

* * * * * *

Such was a little more than Lucy could tell, but which, as it is important to our narrative, should be known at once to the reader.

"And now, how fares the business of the house?"

"Too well," said Lucy; "we have more knaves than we like about—soldiers and others."

"Do they talk of me still?"

"No."

"I warrant the knaves are sly enough. But this hiding work is very useless. I had better ride away to the king's camp at once."

"You are in a hurry to leave?"

"By no means, Lucy," said Sir Ralph; "but I have a written summons from King Richard to join him as soon as possible; but I would fain remain three days longer."

"Is the dwarf to be trusted?"

"Yes."

"You know what I mean," replied Lucy, looking down on the ground.

"I do not."

"Is the boy to be trusted with so foolish a secret as that a Saxon girl, old enough to know better, is perilling herself, soul and body, for one who will forget her when his back is turned?"

"Lucy," said Sir Ralph, seriously, "circumstances, accident if you will, have made us more intimate in a day than we might have proved in years, but if you think I ever can forget your devotion and kindness you are mistaken. You know that, being married——"

"Say no more! Silence! I should not have been your wife even if you had been single. Lords mate not with lasses. I did not expect it. 'At Christmas I no more desire a rose, than wish for snow in Mag's new-fangled shows.' Enough of this. What is to be done is to secrete you for three days, collect all the information we can for you, and speed you then on your journey."

"That is it."

"Do you leave your horse to Fly-by-Night. The other nags have been caught and sent down to the Maypole, whence this one came. Now follow me."

Sir Ralph, who knew that he might depend on this girl, with whom, as many a young man does without thought, he had trifled, without any regard to the injury which might accrue, followed, without a word.

They skirted the forest.

They passed the front of the house.

By making a long detour they came to the back of the inn.

The stable-yard, barn, and loft lay in view.

The pair crept across the ground which intervened between the forest and the stable-yard wall.

A low ladder leaned against a small swinging platform.

Lucy ascended, and opened a narrow door that served to fill the loft with hay.

Sir Ralph followed.

The night was not afar off, but light enough remained to see plainly.

The hay was piled nearly to the roof, though in some places large quantities had been removed.

In one place only a bundle or two had been taken away, while the ostler selected a spot where the fodder was easier of removal.

Lucy pointed to a square space at the end of the loft, where a man might easily repose in comfort.

"There you could hide in safety."

"True, but three days of such a life would be rather dull," said Sir Ralph.

"I will send Fly-by-Night."

"Lucy."

"Sir."

"I wish this were the cave in the sand-rock, you couldn't then leave me thus."

"I wish I had never seen it."

"Come now, be cheerful. Send Fly-by-Night to me now; but when you have done your household duties—"

"Well?"

"You will bring me some supper."

"I will. But be cautious. These soldiers prowl about in every corner."

And Lucy glided away, and soon regained the house, leaving the young man alone.

"Heigho," he said, with a sigh, "'tis a pity, but how can one help it? The girl is very charming."

A few minutes later the young knight heard footsteps in the loft.

He felt for his sword.

"Oh! oh! Master Ralph," whispered a well-known voice.

KING RICHARD IN THE BATTLE.

"This way, Fly-by-Night."

And in a few minutes the agile little dwarf was with him.

"Well, what cheer?" asked the knight.

"Very little. The public-house is pretty full of soldiers."

"I know that."

"There is a sly officer fellow who seemed half to suspect me, for he asked me some strange questions. I fooled him though—he got nothing from me."

"That's right," said Sir Ralph, after some reflection, "and now, that we may throw him off the scent, do you take your horse, trot down to where you left me, and catch my horse, which take to the Maypole, pay for the loan, and bid the host take the best care of my two horses. Here is money, with which also make merry, and collect such news as you can. To-morrow saunter down this way, and we will see what can be done."

Fly-by-Night willingly assented, and when Lucy came to bring the knight his supper she found him alone in the hay-loft.

CHAPTER XVIII.

SIR BRIAN DE FALAISE.

NEXT day at an early hour the soldiers were removed from the inn, a rumour getting afloat that the army was about to move to the southward.

As soon as Sir Ralph and Lucy discovered this they settled that the former should regain the house, where he could remain in safety by keeping a good watch.

If any danger was to be feared he could always retire to his hole in the loft.

Ralph was not sorry to make this change, as though a night in the loft was not without its advantages, a day would be dull enough.

He, therefore, got rid as much as possible of the disorder of his dress, and walked to the house.

There was no one there but the household, and a drover who had come in for his pint of ale.

This man had a large whip in his hand.

Sir Ralph seated himself at the same table, it being nearest to the fire.

The drover finished his ale and rose.

"A word with you, Sir Ralph," said the man in a low tone, "believe me, I am your friend."

The astonished young man started and put his hand to his sword.

"Sit down," continued the other, calmly "and hear what I have to say—then act as you please. I am a soldier and a gentleman."

He cast off his drover's frock and some other parts of

his disguise, and stood before the other a smart young man-at-arms.

"We have both been mumming," said Sir Ralph, with something of a dark frown and bitter smile.

"My name is Brian de Falaise," continued the other, "an unworthy lieutenant in the levy of Sir Hugh Fitz-urse. This worthy gentleman, who hates you with a hatred which is only equalled by his avarice, has employed me to trap and murder you—hear me, my friend."

And then Brian de Falaise told him the whole of the foul conspiracy.

"Now, Sir Ralph," said the soldier of fortune, "the proposals he has made to me absolve me from all allegiance and gratitude. I swear by all that is sacred and holy that I wait but to save you, and then hie for the king's army. Whatever you may want to know I can tell you. Is it then a bargain? Shall we outwit this holy fox?"

"Sir Brian de Falaise," observed Sir Ralph, "you astound—you surprise me; would I could trust you!"

The other drew his *dague* from his belt.

"On the cross of my dagger of mercy I swear to be faithful and true."

"Enough—we are brothers. Much more than Sir Hugh could ever do, I will, if we escape."

"Then, by the holy rood, 'tis settled. Now listen. The knaves who were here have only drawn off as a trap. They will be here anon. Their mission is to waylay and slay you; your head will pay them better than your body. Now my advice to you is—share my apartment in the castle. I am in favour with the earl who commands, and once there, you are safe. Sir Hugh will believe that you have fled, and I can then prepare for our joint departure."

"I am in your hands."

"'Tis well, Sir Ralph, and Heaven's worst malison on me if I deceive you. But we must be cautious; Sir Hugh is powerful and cunning, vindictive I need not say. We must act with circumspection."

At this moment Lucy entered with a breakfast that, in these days, would have alarmed a ploughman.

She started as she saw Sir Ralph in conversation with an officer.

"'Tis well, my dear," said Brian de Falaise, laughing, "all friends. I will breakfast with the gentleman."

Lucy came up rather sadly and put down the loaded platter.

"Could you not throw off this dress?" said Brian, after a moment's thought.

"I could dress as a *reitre*."

"Then do it at once, for if my men return they will suspect nothing."

Roger, who had been watching the interview with some anxiety, at once produced from the pack the dress needed, and Ralph was not long changing.

In ten minutes he was again in conference with Brian, and the two eating breakfast as if they had known one another all their lives.

Sir Ralph had contrived a five minutes interview with Lucy, who was not best pleased at the change affairs had taken.

The wilful, thoughtless girl had hoped to retain him near her until his final departure.

But Ralph contrived to appease her by the judicious use both of flattery and promises.

He then took with him such necessaries as were part of a gentleman's wardrobe in those days, and, having his horse brought to the inn door, rode out towards the castle with Sir Brian.

They did not as yet seek the town.

Having bidden his men remain on the watch round the inn, the soldier of fortune accompanied his new friend into the forest, where he remained with him in earnest discourse until night closed the conference.

The young Norman became delighted with Sir Ralph's picture of the character of King Richard.

One more devoted adherent was made to that chivalrous monarch, who, had he been less of a knight-errant and more of a politician, might have consolidated the government of England, and broken the neck of an insolent nobility.

The aristocracy, unless tied down by laws made by the commons, are the greatest curse a country can endure.

People say, deliver us from the Pope and wooden shoes.

We say, deliver us from an aristocracy, which for all useful purposes is dead long since.

Deliver us from game laws and game law makers.

Amen.

The young men, in defiance of the restrictions which an arbitrary government had put upon the pleasures of the chace, shot a buck and took it into the Dun Cow.

There they supped.

CHAPTER XIX.

IN THE TRAP.

THE sun had declined about two hours and a half from the meridian, but the day was still warm and bright. The month of May, in the olden time, indeed, was a warmer friend than at present, if we may believe the ancient tales and chronicles; and in good sooth, the seasons of the year seemed to have changed altogether, and the weather to have become chilly, whimsical, and crotchety, as the world has grown older.

There are no vineyards to be found now in Northumberland, and yet many a place in the northern counties retains the name to the present day, evidently showing to what purposes they were formerly applied.

It is rarely now in England, too, that we have any title to call it the merry, merry month of May; for very often, cold and piercing are the winds, sad the sleet and rain, and for one of the bright and glorious days of summer we have a multitude of the dark and shadowy ones of winter.

Perhaps one cause of this change may be that which has brought about many another evil in the land, namely, the cutting down of those magnificent old forests which sheltered the breast of England like a garment, and stopped the fierce winds in their career over the island. Indeed, we know that the destruction of the woods in other countries has produced such effects, and there is every reason to believe that here also the climate has greatly suffered, though other benefits may have been obtained.

However that may be, the month of May at that time in England was indeed a merry month, replete with sunshine, and the whole world full of the warmth and the tenderness of youth. It is true, indeed, that in the early part of the month April would still look in, with tear in eye, to bid the earth good-bye, and such had been the case on the morning of the day of which we have lately been speaking.

In the old castle, which, according to the account of Leland, was one of the largest and finest specimens of the military architecture of feudal times, were numerous courts and various detached buildings, so that the number of persons which it could contain was immense, and even when several hundred men were within the walls, many of the open spaces and passages would be found silent and solitary.

Thus on that evening, the chief court, the halls, and the corridors around it, were crowded with not less than seven or eight hundred persons, but as one turned one's steps to other parts of the building the throng decreased, the passers to and fro became fewer and more few, and at length nothing presented itself but untenanted courts and empty arcades.

The young free-lance, as soon as Ralph was ready, rode with him in the direction of the castle gates.

No one stayed them or asked any questions, as the uniform of the lieutenant was known.

When they came to the market-place Brian de Falaise trotted forward at a more rapid pace than before.

He had seen Sir Hugh Fitzurse eyeing them closely; but being one of the staff of the insurgent earl, was unable to leave him, as the chief held him in conversation.

The young officer did not like the glance of his patron Sir Hugh.

Still there was now nothing to be done but to go forward and enter the castle, which they did without any difficulty.

"There appears no attempt made to keep any one out," observed Sir Ralph.

"By no means," said the other, drily, "the objection is to one's leaving sometimes."

The young knight smiled grimly, and the two new friends, reaching the great court-yard, gave their horses to one of the many hundred attendants to lead to the stables.

They then went into a dark corner, where was the opening of a dark passage, which, traversing one side of the keep, open under cloisters, passed through a large mass of buildings, receiving no light but that which poured in at either end; they reached a narrow staircase which they ascended until they came to a spiral staircase.

Ascending this, they entered a wide corridor with many doors in it, one of which Brian de Falaise opened with his private key.

It lead into a chamber, which was superior to what Sir Ralph Tressilian expected, comprising, as was usually the case with those assigned to noblemen of high rank, a bed-room for himself and an ante-room, across the entrance of which one or two gentlemen attendants usually slept, thus barring all dangerous access to their lord during the night.

"You are well lodged," said Ralph.

"Sir Hugh Fitzurse owns these apartments," replied Brian de Falaise; "but the old fox likes not to be cooped up within the castle. He has his apartments in the town."

"I understand."

"So, to lodge me the cheaper, I keep his castle residence warm for him. There are one or two secrets of his in my noddle, which he would not willingly have known, so he is chary of giving me offence."

"He is a hard man."

"He is indeed, and if I read his glance or scowl just now aright, I shall not be long for these parts. Will you ensure me pardon and employment in the king's camp?" he added, abruptly.

Sir Ralph hesitated.

"Understand," said Brian de Falaise, "that I am no more a rebel, than being an officer of Sir Hugh Fitzurse, I have obeyed orders."

"Then, on my word as a knight, you shall ride into the king's camp in safety and shall fight under my banner."

"'Tis well. When will you be ready to start?"

"To-morrow at midnight."

"Umph! I will be prepared. Who comes?"

And rising, he opened the door, to admit Lucy and the hostler of the inn, with a goodly supper, which the young soldier had ordered to be sent.

Lucy looked vexed to find the knight with company, but hid her discontent as much as possible.

The soldier of fortune drew the ostler on one side to give him some directions.

Sir Ralph then bade the young woman look out for the dwarf, whom he expected would come with some message from Robin Hood.

"Bring me the message if you can," he said, tenderly, "if not, you can send him."

After a whispered conference the two parted.

"I had some provision here," observed Sir Brian de Falaise going to a cupboard and drawing forth wine, "we will make a night of it. I will remain late in case Sir Hugh should think proper to visit me—in which case I can secrete you."

Sir Ralph acquiesced, and then the two young men, as freely as if they had known one another for many long years, proceeded to discuss their evening meal—which finished, they stirred up a fire, always welcome in such old buildings, and seated themselves, with a settled determination to enjoy themselves now, come what might to-morrow.

It was midnight when the young man left Sir Ralph; and it was an hour past midnight, the sentries had just been relieved upon the castle wall, and Sir Ralph sat by the window, looking out into the depth of night, and gazing at the far twinkling of the stars.

The mind was occupied in the same manner as the body, for it was looking forth into the dark night of death, and marking the small bright shining lights from heaven, that tell of other worlds beyond.

Sir Ralph had full confidence in the young officer, but he knew the malignant and interested hate of Sir Hugh Fitzurse to be such as to make him clear-sighted.

The hint of Sir Brian de Falaise was not thrown away. Resolved that he would not be murdered in cold blood, he secured the door and clutched his dagger, which was the only weapon left him.

His thoughts were far away in the forest glens where his wife was secreted.

Light and somewhat fickle, as all men were in a day when it was considered a duty to make love to every pretty woman, Sir Ralph was devotedly attached to his wife.

His little flirtations and intrigues had nothing to do with the heart, and it was balm to him to believe that, come what might, Agnes would mourn for him when he was gone—aye, that she had promised to love him and be his beyond the grave.

Of such things were his thoughts as he gazed forth on that solemn night; but suddenly something, he knew not what, called his attention from himself, and he looked down from the window of his chamber upon the top of the wall below.

The distance was some thirty feet, the night was dark, for the moon had gone early down, but even in the dim obscurity he thought he saw something like a man's head appear over the battlement.

In a moment after, with a bound as if it had been thrown over by an engine, a human body sprang from the top of the wall, ran forward to the tower in which he was confined, and struck the stonework with its arm.

The next instant, without any apparent footing, he could perceive one leg stretched upwards, while the hand seemed to have obtained a grasp of the wall itself, and then the rest of the body ascended to the height of about four feet from the ground, sticking fast, like a squirrel swarming up a large beech-tree.

A long thin arm was then extended far overhead to a deep window just beneath that at which the young knight stood, and by it the whole body was drawn up into the aperture of the wall, while a sentinel passed by with slow and measured steps. As soon as the soldier was gone, the arm was again stretched forth in the direction of the casement from which Ralph was gazing down, and the hand struck once or twice against the wall in different places, making a slight grating sound, as if it were armed with some metal instrument. At length it remained fixed, and then the head and shoulders were protruded from the opening on the window below, the feet resting upon the stonework.

Then came one of those extraordinary efforts of agility and pliability of limb which Ralph had never witnessed but in one being on earth. By that single hold which the fingers seemed to have of the wall, the body was again swung up, till the knee and the hand met, and the left arm was stretched out towards the sill of the casement above.

Although the figure appeared to be humpbacked, and, consequently, in that respect, unlike the dwarf Fly-by-Night, Ralph could not doubt that it was he, and reaching down as far as possible, he whispered "Take my hand, Fly-by-Night."

In an instant the long, thin, monkey-like fingers of the dwarf clasped round his as if they had been an iron vice, and with a bound that nearly threw the stout young soldier off his balance, Fly-by-Night sprang through the window into the room.

"Ha, ha!" said he, in a low tone, "who can keep out Fly-by-Night?"

"No one, it seems, my good boy," answered Ralph; "but what come you here for? I fear I cannot descend as you have mounted."

"Here, help me off with my burden," rejoined the boy, "and thou wilt soon see what I come for. But we must whisper like mice, for tyrants have sharper ears than hares, and keener eyes than cats. Here's a priest's gown and a hood for thee, and a chorister's cope, for thou art just the height of the earl's confessor, and I shall pass for his pouncet-bearer. Here's a ladder, too, not much thicker than a spider's web, but strong enough to bear up the fat friar of Barnesdale."

"When saw you Lucy?"

"I went to the inn late, and told her that I came from Robin with news for you. I saw at once she favoured you, Sir Ralph," he added, with a sharp twinkle of the eye, "and did not hesitate to ask news."

"Well?"

"She gave me your message," continued the boy, "and we then arranged that she should come hither, but her brother said it was too late."

"And what said Lucy?"

"It was never too late to do a good action."

"Well?"

"The girl has a good tongue of her own, and spoke sharply to her brother-in-law, saying she was not slave of his."

"And what answered the brother?"

"That she was free; but if she went at that hour the soldiers would take her for some light o' love, not to say your leman, like which it looked much."

"Well?"

"The girl turned gravely to her sister, and said she would not stay in the house with Roger to be insulted."

"Brave girl!"

"Then she gave me a message to bring you. You were to beware of Sir Hugh, who, though reconnoitering with the prince, had sent men to inquire for you there, who said that they had good reason to believe Sir Brian de Falaise was playing his master false."

"You came then?"

"The castle door was open and I walked in, asking for Sir Brian de Falaise in whose rooms I knew you to be."

"Go on."

"I easily got in the castle, but could not ascend here. The courts were so crowded that I easily hid myself, and when all the passers-by were still, contrived to find out your room and to climb as I have done."

"It was a bold deed."

"Robin ever prepared me for such events, and provided me with all that could under any circumstances be needed; so here, my lord, I am, and quite ready to start as soon as you like."

"But why all this precaution, Fly-by-Night?"

"I will tell you. Lucy sent me first; but I have just seen Sir Brian de Falaise, and he is in custody. Sir Hugh is furious, and the knight whispered that you should put as many leagues as possible between the knight and yourself in the morning."

"He has suffered for his good nature."

"Well, the knight rated him more for a fool than anything else, in bringing you here instead of to the tents, and said that he should remain under arrest until you were disposed of."

"Any more?"

"'Death will be his portion,' said the young free-lance, 'if found in the castle to-morrow. I have led him into a nice trap. But if he suffers I will kill Sir Hugh and die.'"

"Poor fellow—he meant well," continued Ralph, "and we must make the best of it. As for you, if I live, boy, I will reward thee. If I die, thy heart must do it."

"No thanks to me," replied Fly-by-Night, in a somewhat trembling voice, "no thanks to me, good knight. It is all Robin's doing, though I was glad enough to have a finger in the pie, and he, great cart-horse, could no more climb up that wall than he could leap over Lincoln Church. But come, come, fix these hooks to the window, get the gown over thee, and then let us look out for the sentinel—he will pass again before we have all ready.

"But there are sentries in the outer court too," said Ralph. "How shall we manage if we meet with any of them?"

"Give them the word," said Fly-by-Night. "I waited, linging as close to the wall as ivy to an old tower, till I heard the round pass and the word given. It was, 'The three leopards.' But there he goes now—let us away—quick!—he will soon be back again."

Letting the ladder, made of silken rope, gently down from the window, Ralph bade the dwarf go first; but Fly-by-Night replied, "No, no, I will come after, and bring the ladder with me. I have got my own staircase in the four daggers that I fixed into the crevices. Go down, holy father, go down, and if that book be a breviary, take it with you."

"It may serve as such," said Ralph, "but, ere I go, let me leave them a message; and taking a piece of half-charred wood from the fire, he wrote a few words with it upon the wall. Then approaching the window, he issued forth, and descended easily and rapidly to the battlements.

The dwarf seemed to have some difficulty in unfastening the hooks of the ladder, however, for he did not follow so quickly as Ralph expected, and, whether the sentinel had turned before he got fully to the end of his beat, or his pace was more rapid than before, ere the boy began to descend the soldier's steps were heard coming round from the other angle of the wall.

Ralph gave a quick glance up to the window in the tower, and saw that the dwarf was aware of the sentry's approach, and also that the ladder hung so close to the building as not to be perceptible without near examination. His mind was made up in an instant, and folding his arms upon his chest, he drew the hood further over his face, and walked on to meet the sentinel with a slow pace, and his eyes bent upon the ground.

The moment the soldier turned the angle and saw him, he exclaimed, "Who goes there? stand! Give the word!"

"The three leopards," replied Ralph, in a calm tone.

"Pass," cried the sentinel. "Your blessing, holy father! This is a dark night."

"Dominus vobiscum," replied Ralph; "it is dark indeed, my son. But no nights are dark to the eye of God;" and turning with the sentinel on his round, he added, in a clear voice, as they passed under the window, "you did not see my boy upon your round, did you? He was to come hither with the books, but marry, he is a truant knave, and is doubtless loitering with the pages in the earl's ante-room."

"I saw him not, holy father," said the soldier. "Is the earl still up?"

"Ay is he," answered Ralph, "and will be for an hour to come." And on he walked by the side of the sentinel till they were out of sight of the window.

"The boy is marvellous long in coming," observed the pretended priest.

"Shall we turn back and see, good father?" asked the soldier.

"Oh, no," replied Ralph; "this is the way he should come, for he had to pass round by the court, unless, indeed, he goes up the steps at the other side;" just as he spoke the sound of quick feet following was heard, and the man turned sharply, once more exclaiming, "Who goes there?"

"The three leopards," said a childish voice, very unlike that of Fly-by-Night; but Fly-by-Night it proved to be, dressed in his white cope and hood, and bearing a small bundle.

"Thou hast been playing truant," cried the knight, "and shall do penance for this."

But he did not venture to carry far his pretended reprimand, lest some mistake between him and Fly-by-Night might discover the deceit; and walking on by the sentinel to the top of the flight of steps which led down into the great court close by another of the towers, he there wished him good night.

The guard at the bottom of the stone stairs heard the conversation between his comrade and the priest above, and without even asking the word, walked on beside the knight and the dwarf, and passed them to the sentry at the gate.

The large wooden door under the archway was ajar, while several of the soldiery were without, telling rude tales of love to some of the fair girls of the town, who had ventured upon the drawbridge even at that late hour, to lose their time and reputation with the men-at-arms, for human nature and its follies were the same, or very nearly the same, then as now. At the end of the drawbridge, however, was a sentinel with his partizan in his hand, taking sufficient part in the merriment of the others to make him start forward in alarm at the sound of a step, and show his alertness by lowering his weapon and demanding the word. Ralph gave it at once.

In another minute the boy was running forward to the town gate, and knocking at the low door under the arch. At first there was no answer, and the dwarf, after knocking again, shouted loudly, "Ho, Matthew Blunt! Matthew Blunt! open the door for a reverend father, who is going forth to shrive a sick man."

"To shrive a harlot, or a barrel of sack!" grumbled an angry voice from within. "I will get up for no one, and if I did, I would not open the gate wide enough at this hour of the night for the fat friar of Barnesdale to roll his belly out."

"'Tis neither he of Barnesdale or Tuck," cried the boy, "but a holy priest come from the castle."

"Then he had better go back whence he came," replied the warder; "and unless you move pretty quick, my jackanapes, you will get something on your jacket that will soil thy garments for many a day."

"I go forth," said Sir Ralph, in a deep voice, "to see Sir Hugh Fitzurse on business from the earl. Shall I have him called up to tell you your duty? Perhaps when your ears are slit you may behave better."

At these words the burly old man came forth, grumbling and saying that his lantern had gone out.

"You must give me the word," he growled.

"The three leopards."

"You've got it pat," said the warder, and with provoking slowness he undid bolt after bolt, and then threw aside the heavy wooden valves.

They were free.

They moved in silence some little way, and then more freely chatting of what had occurred with an increase of life and spirits that was natural in their position.

Fly-by-Night led the way, taking the road towards the old inn, where horses could be found, and where there might be news of the lances expected by Sir Ralph.

Now Fly-by-Night was a rogue in grain. The boy loved fun for its own sake, and was as wide awake and artful as many a man of experience in the world.

After the conversation which had passed between the brother and sister-in-law, the young sprite knew how to form his own conclusions.

"We won't disturb Roger," he said, with a sly wink of the eye, "unless it be needful. I will wake Miss Lucy."

Now Sir Ralph scarcely heard him; his thoughts were far away; but when he saw him plant a ladder to the side of the house and tap at a window, he drew his cloak around him, and waited the result.

The wooden shutter was soon opened, a low whispering was heard, and then all was still.

Fly-by-night came down.

"Well?"

"She's a-coming."

"Who?"

"Miss Lucy."

The knight started. He had almost forgotten her existence, thinking of ambition and a higher love.

"What of her, boy?"

"I thought she'd be pleasanter company than Roger," said the dwarf.

Sir Ralph made no reply. It was to him a matter of great annoyance to have his attentions to the girl thus noticed. But explanation would only make matters worse.

The door was opened.

Lucy peered out.

"Call your brother at once," said Sir Ralph, in a quick whisper, "or he may be angry."

The girl nodded and at once went up stairs.

In ten minutes more the landlord was down.

"I am sorry to disturb you, Roger," he said, "but as I am going away for some time, I wished to thank you for your kindness. I shall not forget it."

"Welcome as flowers in May, my lord. You and yours have done me good service. But why have you left the castle at this hour?"

Ralph explained.

"Ah, then you have done well. Sir Hugh Fitzurse would else have contrived to shorten you by a head had he found you."

"Hush!"

"Hist!"

A noise of prancing horses, and of voices speaking loudly, was now heard close at hand.

"I will sell my life dearly," said Ralph, clutching under his black robe the hilt of the anlace, a sharp knife which he had secured.

The horsemen drew rein and one man entered.

It was Sir Brian de Falaise.

"This is, indeed, glorious," he cried, taking the young knight by the hand; "keep that pious garb a little while; as soon as we have taken an early breakfast—'tis three—we shall be on our way."

"But these horsemen?"

"My children," laughed the free-lance "won't part

with me. If you muster well we shall take a goodly reinforcement to the camp."

Roger at once bustled about, called his men, and in a very brief space of time, as should be at a well-conducted inn, had provisions for all.

The men-at-arms did not dismount.

They might have need of their horses at sudden warning.

The sun in the month of May rises soon after four, but the first glimmer of dawn is sooner still; so that, would they depart ere the light, it was necessary to hurry.

The bill was paid liberally, Sir Ralph shook hands with Roger, and then all mounting, rode away.

Sir Ralph and the soldier of fortune rode side by side; the men two by two; Fly-by-Night with the soldiers, in low conversation with one of the men in a cape and hood.

They did not hurry.

It was their plan to appear a patrol on duty.

They did not intend proceeding very far, but to camp in the forest at the place where Sir Ralph had made his rendezvous with his men.

CHAPTER XX.

IN THE WOOD AGAIN.

WITH the poet we say:—

Honour to the old bow-string !
Honour to the bugle-horn !
Honour to the woods unshorn !
Honour to the Lincoln-green !
Honour to the archer keen !
Honour to tight Little John !
And the horse he rode upon !
Honour to bold Robin Hood !
Sleeping in the underwood !
Honour to Maid Marian !
AND TO ALL THE SHERWOOD CLAN !

Still it is not in our power, in a narrative which embraces historical events, to keep always beside our heroes. The subordinate characters and their adventures are quite as necessary to the full comprehension of our history as even the story of what Robin did himself.

We shall not, however, detain you long from Robin, of whom we have still many a wondrous tale to tell, not the less interesting because connected with the sheriff of Nottingham.

"Lyth and lysten, gentil men,
  And herken what I say :
How the proud Sheryfe of Notyngham,
  Dyde cry a full fayre play.
    *   *   *   *

"He that shoteth 'alder' best,
  Furthest, fayre, and lowe ;
At a payre of fynly buttes,
  Under the grene wode shawe.
"A righte goode arrowe he shall have,
  The shaft of sylver white,
The heade and the feders of ryche rede gulde,
  In England is none lyke.
    *   *   *   *

"But take out thy brown swarde,
  And smyte all of my hede ;
And gyve me wounds dede and wyde,
  No lyfe on me be lefte.
I wold not that, said Robyn,
  Johan, that thou wert slawe,
For all the golde in mery Englond,
  Though it lay now on a rawe."
  (A LYTELL GESTE OF ROBIN HODE.—The Fyfth Fytte.)

"Forthe he yode to London toune,
  All for to tel our kynge.
    *   *   *   *

"Toke he there his gentyll knyght,
  With men of armes strong,
And lad hym home to Notyngham warde,
  Ibonde both fote and honde.
    *   *   *   *

"Up then sterte good Robyn,
  As a man that had be wode :
Buske yeu, my mery younge men,
  For Hym that dyed on a rode.
And he that this sorrowe forsaketh,
  By Him that dyed on a tre ;
And by Him that all things maketh,
  No lenger shall dwell with me."
  (IBID.—The Syxte Fytte)

Still we must hasten on, and as soon as possible connecting the dispersed threads, bring our characters together.

Robin, it must be remembered, has gone to Scarborough in search of reinforcements.

We shall find him anon.

The spot indicated by Sir Ralph for a trysting-place for his levies was one selected with a soldierly eye.

It was a ruin, one of the many which the Normans had made in once happy England.

But it was surrounded by such a dense mass of yews, oaks, and other trees that, but for treachery, a small army might have lain there without any fear of discovery.

Fires were allowable.

They did not here betray the presence of a camp, as they might have done on the prairies.

Charcoal-burners were dotted all over England, and naturally more in the forest than anywhere else.

Their columns of black, grey, and white smoke rose in the air at all hours of the day and night.

Sentries were placed, however, one on top of the ruins, two in trees.

They overlooked in this way every possible path.

The rest of the men hoppled their horses, and then made camp fires, while others went forth to try their luck upon the forest deer.

Sir Ralph and the soldier of fortune, who for his trade was not only a right joyous fellow, but an honest one, seated themselves apart in conversation.

Fly-by-Night stole away into a thicket and disappeared for some considerable time.

Sir Ralph and Sir Brian de Falaise spoke of Robin Hood, of his merry jests, of his happy life; and the former, who since his connection with the outlaw, had come to love the wild and seductive existence of the woodsman, told many a pleasant tale of Little John and Will Scarlett to his pleased listener.

About two hours after mid-day the whole of the party, after a hearty meal, sought repose in slumber.

The air was warm and balmy.

There was nothing to tempt them to keep awake.

Sir Ralph, for awhile, thought cheerfully and pleasantly of his coming reunion with his wife.

Then he too slumbered.

He was in the land of dreams.

Dreams, which are the bright creatures of poem and legend, which sport on earth in the night season, and melt away in the first beam of the sun, which lights grim care and stern reality on their daily pilgrimage through the world.

Suddenly he was roused by a tap on the shoulder.

"What is it?"

"A fat priest," cried Fly-by-Night, "some black plague or other, as dull as any wicked dew my mother ever brushed with her feet on unwholesome fen, declares that as there is another in company he will speak with him."

"Bring him hither," said Sir Ralph, drawing his cloak around him, and assuming something of the attitude of a forest outlaw.

A priest on a mule, with his hood over his eyes, appeared guarded by two soldiers.

"What seek you?" asked Sir Ralph.

"To go untouched through the forest."

"Who and what are you?"

"A poor priest."

"No house of God would own so corpulent a knave; none of thy vile race are recognised."

"I am an honest Saxon," cried the other, hotly.

"Humph!"

"A true man, and if you will doff your jerkin, I'll pound your impudent carcase as full of holes as a honeycomb."

"Wilt thou do that or eat thy dinner?"

"Buffet thee, and eat my dinner afterwards," continued the other, indignantly.

"Fie! fie! master Tuck, you are but a boaster, I fear me."

"You know me?"

"That fat paunch is known everywhere."

The clerk of Copmanhurst dismounted quickly, and despite the presence of the laughing soldiers, advanced fiercely towards Sir Ralph.

The knight dropped his hood, and held out his hand.

"Oh! oh!" laughed Tuck, "what have we here? A false priest, indeed, and one who shrives ladies bravely."

"What news of my lady?"

"She is well."

"And my men?"

"Will be here at dawn."

"We should wait."

"Yes, and bait."

"That shall your mule, and you too. So come, sit down, and tell us all the news."

Now Friar Tuck was the very best of chroniclers, that, as a travelling priest, being a part of his means of livelihood, so that he had much to tell him; and the laugh, and the joke, and the song went round for some time with the hedge priest's favourite bottel, as he always pronounced bottle.

Towards evening all selected their posts.

Fly-by-Night intimated to his new master that he had erected him a hut.

In the interval between their arrival, and during the siesta of the afternoon, the devoted little imp, who loved Robin Hood's friends almost as much as he loved the outlaw king himself, had with his neat fingers made a rude kind of wigwam for his master.

It was in the thicket, quite away from the general camp.

The small open glade, with the low fire burning, the red embers sending a genial glow around, the hut of sticks and boughs, the open part of which was to the fire, made in the darkness of the night, a picturesque scene enough, and one which singularly struck Sir Ralph Tresilian, who more and more every day was learning to love the wild forest life of the outlaws.

There is, indeed, a charm in the forest, which even those who, like poachers and charcoal-burners, see it under every disadvantage, find does bind them to the life.

Sir Ralph, from association with Robin Hood, had begun almost to wish himself an outlaw.

As he passed along the path leading to his forest hut, with Fly-by-Night running before him like a huge mastiff or hound, he could, having something of an artistic eye, but be struck by the little secluded camp which the dwarf had chosen.

But he was puzzled to see one of the troopers patrolling up and down in a cloak and hood.

It was a short, thick-set fellow.

"What does he want?" asked Sir Ralph.

"He! he!" grinned the dwarf.

At this moment the hood was thrown back, just as the knight and trooper met face to face.

It was Lucy.

The young soldier stood transfixed with astonishment.

"You young rascal," he cried, turning round to chastise Fly-by-Night.

But the mischievous imp had disappeared, leaving only a low laugh behind him.

"Ralph!"

"Dear Lucy!"

"Are you angry?"

"Angry, no," said the soldier, drawing her to his side; "not angry—but sorry. This is most unfortunate, what will your sister and brother say?"

"I don't care."

"But Lucy dear, what will my wife say?"

"I don't care."

"But dear girl, we shall get into sad trouble."

"You should have thought of that before."

"True," said the knight.

Quite true.

Before we commit ourselves beyond recovery or retreat, we should always look a little a-head.

There is no proverb of more universal application than that which says—look before you leap.

"Well, you are right, Lucy, so the best thing to do is for us to talk the matter over seriously. One word with that little sinner, Fly-by-Night."

And he called him aloud.

The dwarf came, with a penitent look.

The knight drew him on one side.

"You young imp of evil," he said, "you know who this is?"

"Yes."

"And you know who is coming to-morrow."

"Yes."

"Who?"

"Your wife."

"Well, if they meet, I'll break every bone in your body," said Ralph, heartily.

"All right, master,"

And the imp retired, after receiving other and minuter orders.

Next day, when the whole party rode forward among the free lances, archers, and men-at-arms, was a kind of page, with short curly hair, who was not much noticed.

CHAPTER XXI.

BATTLE FIELD.

WE left King Richard and his brave army encamped upon the field, the meeting of the monarch and the rebels being marked only by some skirmishes of outposts.

Day, however, soon broke.

The country was for the most part open, but there was a small wood and some rising ground to the right, a rivulet running along across the patch of common land which the road now traversed, and a cultivated field with its hedgerows on the left.

About a quarter of a mile from the point at which the highway issued from between the banks was a stone post, marking the spot where three roads, coming down from some slight hills in front, met and united in one, along which the king marched.

For nearly the same distance beyond, these roads might be seen crossing the common, and then, plunging amongst woods and hedges, they all three ascended a gentle slope opposite.

The day was by no means so bright as the preceding one had been.

There were clouds in the sky.

The air was close, heavy, and oppressive.

The horses were either languid or impatient, and everything appeared to portend that the sun would go down in storms.

A small advanced guard had been sent forward to reconnoitre the country in front, and the head of the column of the army was about a hundred yards behind.

The king was calm and serene.

His helmet hung at his saddle bow as he surveyed the field.

The advanced guard fell back suddenly to announce that the enemy were pressing up in great force.

The monarch calmly gave his orders.

The wood alluded to was lined with archers, under the command of Little John and Will Scarlett.

In front of them were men-at-arms, with other archers and slingers to keep the ground between a hedge and some scrubby bushes and hawthorn trees.

Having given these and other orders, he slowly rode along towards the wood, giving orders as he passed his officers, and ranging his men with a shrewd eye in the proper order of battle.

The slingers, as usual, were thrown forward about a hundred and fifty yards in front of the rest of the army.

They were closely supported by the pikemen.

It was their custom to take advantage of every bush and brake which might give them shelter, while they discharged their missiles at the enemy.

The sturdy lines of English archers and regular spearmen were behind.

Then, despite the grim occasion, rose from all hands cheerful sounds, leaders shouts, repeated blasts of clarion and of trumpet.

The whole royal army hung like a thunder cloud on the edge of the slope, and the calm but preceded the breaking forth of the tempest.

Suddenly a quiver went through the ranks.

Then some men ran forward, slinging large balls of stone and lead.

Those behind followed up in irregular masses.

Then a whole flight of arrows from the rebel army darkened the air.

Then onward came the forces of the insurgents, and the arrows, quarrels, and bolts on both sides began to make fearful havock, for the dogs of war were let loose.

It was a terrible sight.

The arrows from the Nottingham bows did fearful execution among the crossbowmen.

One went down quick after another as they hurried forward.

Their ranks became thinner and thinner.

Then they were scattered to the right and left, as the horsemen charged with levelled lances.

The bowmen aimed at man and steed, and the confusion was fearful.

The royal army, overweighted by that of the rebels, despite deeds of heroic valour upon the part of king and his nobles, began to yield.

It was now that the brave outlaws did gallant service to the cause they had espoused.

Their arrows were shot in unceasing showers, while any who escaped their flights were struck down by weighty quarterstaves.

Then many of them, with long lances, kept the cavalry at bay, and, despite heavy and furious charges, held their ground.

But Richard, who raged about the field like a lion, indeed, resolved to conquer or die, saw that in other parts numbers were gaining ground over courage and valour and loyalty.

It was indeed a regular melee in all its fierceness: knight against knight, man to man, where hurry and confusion were triumphant everywhere.

Again the clang of arms, the blasts of the trumpet, the shouts of the combatants, the galloping of horse, the groans of the dying, and the screams of men receiving agonising wounds, offered to the ear of heaven a sound only fit for the darkest depth of hell.

Suddenly there was a pause.

The rebels withdrew.

It was to leap afresh like a tiger.

King Richard, surrounded by his glorious staff, and standing now in the centre, prepared for the last desperate struggle.

The sky was dark, the wind was cold, the sun had vanished from that desperate field.

"Down with the tyrant," shouted the rebels, as they charged anew.

"Death to all traitors," roared the royal troops, in feebler because fewer tones.

The scene which ensued it would be vain to attempt describing.

The king fought like a madman. His heavy battleaxe crushed foemen at every blow.

But the day was going.

Treason was triumphant.

The recreant prince and his party were winning.

Ah! ah! ah!

A sudden pause takes place.

Bugles, fresh and joyous, sound on every hand.

Then, while Richard with a mighty oath dashed at the enemy in front, there poured upon the battle ground the large reinforcement led by Robin Hood.

Also the five hundred lances, spearmen, and archers, led by Sir Ralph Tressilian.

The rebels were struck with amaze; the panic was general on all sides.

The sun at the same moment touched the edge of the horison, shining out beneath the edge of the stormy canopy that covered the greater part of the sky, and blending its red descending light with the thunder drops which were now pattering thick upon the plain.

The whole circumambient air seemed flooded with gore, and the clouds on the eastern sides of the heavens, black and heavy as they were, assumed a lurid glare, harmonising with the whole scene, except where part of a rainbow crossed the expanse, hanging the banner of hope. light, and peace in the midst of strife, destruction, and despair.

Such was the scene at the moment of the last dire shock of battle, and fierce and terrible was the encounter, as soon broken into separate parties, they fought hand-to-hand, dispersed over the plain.

Then the news came that the rebel chiefs, headed by Prince John, had sought safety in flight.

The king at once ordered the trumpets to sound the recall, and bade his tent be pitched on the banks of a small rivulet.

In ten minutes more he was receiving the congratulations of his lieutenants.

"Ah!" he cried, as Robin stood a little aloof, "thou art there, my hearty Robin. Always in at the death. I owe you once more my crown."

"He did aid you much, my liege," said Sir Roland

Sansterre; "but for him we had never arrived in time."

"Has he not won his spurs, and should he not at once be proclaimed Earl of Huntingdon?" cried the king.

"Not while my father is alive," said Robin.

"Eh—what?"

"You are wanted," said one, touching the outlaw on the shoulder; "but they bring him here."

As he spoke the ranks opened to give passage to some who, on a rough litter, bore a wounded knight.

They laid him on the ground, where in a moment his head and shoulders were supported by the knee and arm of Robin Hood.

Deep in his breast, piercing through and through the steel hauberk, was buried the head of a broken lance, and in his right shoulder was a clothyard arrow.

"A priest," he murmured.

A monk stood forward, and all the noble group bared their heads, while Robin turned to hide a tear, which, despite his manhood, stood upon his brown and weather-beaten cheek.

The father smiled on his son, and then began what appeared to be his confession *in extremis.*

The good man, who saw that he was dying, murmured over him in haste the hurried absolution of the field of battle.

But no good soldier who does his duty need care for the presence of priest.

The power of absolution, not the form, is elsewhere than on earth, no *man* having leave to pardon or condemn.

Human power ceases on earth.

The countenance of the earl was pale, the dull shadow of death was upon it; the lips were colourless and the nostrils widely expanded, as if it caused an agonised effort to draw his breath; but the eye was still bright and clear, and—while the man of God repeated the last words—it rolled thoughtfully over the faces of all around, resting with an anxious gaze upon those with whom he was most familiar.

"Draw out the lance," he said to the king's physician, who took the place of the monk.

"If I do, my lord," replied the leech, as they were popularly called in those days, "you cannot survive ten minutes."

"Enough to bless my son, and leave him to the charge of my king," replied the dying man.

"Enough, my brave companion of many a well-fought field. I had thought you perished at Ascalon. Fear nothing for this good and brave Englishman. Your recognition of him is the last link in the chain of evidence, and I call on you all to remember it."

"Thanks. Now draw it out, for I cannot breathe. I would speak a few words to Robin. My liege, 'tis my last request—make this man obey me."

"Draw it," replied the king in a husky voice.

The physician, pale and trembling, unwillingly, and not without a considerable effort, tore the head of the lance out of the wound.

Very little blood followed.

He bled inwardly.

Robin stooped close beside him.

"Your mother calls me," suddenly exclaimed the earl; "Robin, my boy, let me carry her a kiss from the child she never saw—do your devoir!"

And as he said this, and the lips of the son he scarcely knew touched his cheek, he fell back a corpse.

"A brave soldier," said Richard.

And his epitaph was written.

The same night he was buried on the field, a portion of the army moving forward at early dawn, in pursuit of the enemy.

But it was needless.

The rebellion was crushed.

The monarch no sooner discovered this than he was all eagerness to return to France to prosecute his designs in Normandy.

He took a kind farewell of Robin, and then rode in hot haste for London.

There for the present we leave him.

How frequently in real life, as upon the mimic stage, the most opposite scenes that it is possible to conceive, follow each other in quick succession. Often, indeed, are they placed side by side, or only veiled from the eye of the spectator by a thin partition, which falls with a touch, and all is changed. While revelry haunts the saloons of life, anguish writhes in the garret, and misery tenants the cellar. Pomp and pageantry, and splendour occupy the one day, sorrow, destitution, and despair the next; and, as in some of our old tragedies, the laughter and merriment of the buffoon appear alternately with tears and agony.

If it be so with human life—if in this fitful spring-day of our being, the storms and the sunshine tread close upon the heels of each other, so must it be with everything that would truly represent existence, even with a tale like this.

We must change the scene from the battle-field where the noble earl fell, and many others with him, to the life in the forest wild, which, with that on the ocean wave, is so dear to every Englishman.

CHAPTER XXII.

THE SHERIFF AGAIN.

THE death of Robin Hood's father, though it gave him a perfect right to the title, and enabled him to prosecute his claims in the law-courts with more assiduity and certainty of success, did not the less affect the bold outlaw.

It is true that the parent to whom he owed existence had been but little known to him, but enough had passed between them to endear the brave soldier to the equally brave son.

Robin, therefore, on parting from the king, repaired to the forest and lived some little time in retirement, and probably would not have been heard of for some time, had not his scouts let him know that the audacious and yet prudent Sheriff of Nottingham was bent on one more trial of his fortune in capturing the outlaw.

The Earl of Huntingdon's dying declaration had been signified to him.

He was to appear in open court.

The sheriff, who had been bought over by the other side, was perfectly furious.

Unfortunately for our hero at this moment, King Richard had already embarked for Normandy ere he heard of this.

The good this king might have done was marred by his restless desire for battle.

No wise king, a useful lawgiver to his subjects, ever puts himself in the front of war.

He's the head to conceive, while others find the hands to execute.

Robin Hood was in Yorkshire with half his men, when the news first reached the foresters.

They learned that a large force of javelin men, troopers, and royal soldiers, provided by the prince, would attack them, even in their strongholds.

The fact was that the Sheriff of Nottingham had heard of the absence of the chief of the outlaws, and shrewdly surmised that if he could destroy those who were left, the task of putting down the whole of the freebooters of the forest would be the easier.

Besides, his opinion of men was very summary. Rogues all—was his motto, and it was very hard if after breaking up the haunts of the merry men, some one or other did not turn informer.

So true is it that evil men are always the first to think evil of others.

The sheriff, as usual, did not take the command of the vanguard, giving that to a brave Norman.

He rode a good fair distance behind.

Now Will Scarlett and some of the other chiefs were at the rendezvous when they heard of this new attempt against their peace.

All heard it from their friends in Nottingham, who were many and in varied positions.

But, bless their eyes, it was the girls, the bonnie lasses of the town, who chiefly looked to the safety of the merry men.

They did not write letters, but they sent messages to their lovers by their cousins and brothers.

So they concerted together to give the sheriff as good a reception as could be got up in the time.

The spies, with one accord, announced that the army would march in the direction of the old trysting-tree.

THE LITTLE BIRD WAKES ROBIN HOOD.

And so it did, the royal and county forces being seven hundred in number.

The outlaws could not muster half that number, a great many having perished in crushing the rebellion, while Robin had taken a heavy detachment into his temporary place of retirement.

But courage and bravery will always compensate with Englishmen for want of numbers.

They also took care to avail themselves of the facilities which the forest afforded of being defended.

The royal and other troops were led by a grizzly old soldier of fortune, who having been in the Holy Wars, and having served many masters, was now one of the many ready tools found by Prince John to carry out his behests.

He utterly despised such men as forest outlaws.

Under these circumstances he rode in front of his men, without a scout or vanguard to see whether there were enemies in the woods.

A guide, a kind of hind, half Saxon, half Norman, kept in front, peering about as if really fearful of what might happen.

He was better aware of what the outlaws could do than the boastful soldier.

"Well, sirrah!" quoth Mondidier the Norman, "are we ever to see these same thieves?"

"I dare vow, my lord, that I am leading you as well as I know, and that, for my part, I would rather not see them."

"There spoke a craven heart."

"Nay, sir soldier."

"Hearkee, friend swine," said the Norman; "here have we been walking up and down the forest glades until my men are growing weary. I have in my train those who carry well-greased ropes, and if you play me any tricks you shall hang from the first acorn-tree that I find."

"Sir, I play no tricks."

"Show me these dastard outlaws."

"I cannot show but you can feel them," was the quick reply.

And ere the soldiers were aware of it there came such a shower of arrows as that which darkened the sky at Cressy, which startled the men-at-arms and committed dreadful slaughter.

"To your arms!" cried Mondidier. "To your arms! Cut me down the traitor guide!"

The men prepared their crossbows, but not an enemy could they see.

"Charge me these coward knaves, who dare not show their faces," said the chief.

But ere he could reorganise his broken ranks there

came a second and a third volley, each arrow telling with a dreadful precision of aim, without the assailed soldiers knowing from whence the shafts came.

A general panic seemed to seize the whole party.

"Stand, soldiers! stand!" roared Mondidier. "Wouldst flee before such coward churls? At 'em! Charge, soldiers! charge!"

At this moment an arrow sped with deadly speed and aim, and striking Captain Mondidier in his thigh, pierced to the horse itself, which began at once to prance and caper.

"The foul fiend assists the hand that did it," roared the Norman soldier, galloping in the opposite direction to that in which he had been riding before. "Where is the rebel churl?"

"Here," said a voice, and a second arrow pinned him to his steed.

Now the Norman captain was not mortally, nor even dangerously wounded; but the pain was galling enough, while the utter impossibility of extracting it himself at the moment made him quite frantic.

At the same instant the outlaws, after a fourth and rattling volley, burst, true merry men as they were, from their coverts, with great shouts, and, sword, pike-staff, and bill in hand, cut everything down before them.

The Norman leader was by no means an exception himself.

It was not a retreat, but a panic, seized the troop at this sudden and terrible attack; so that they fled, without striking any further blow, in the greatest disorder to Nottingham, with the loss of nearly half their men.

The victory was bloodless to the victors.

The rage and fury of the sheriff when Mondidier and his party retired in confusion on the rear-guard can be more easily imagined than described, but that of the Norman captain was perfectly frantic.

A soldier, with trained and disciplined troops, who had bravely conducted themselves in many a well-fought field, it was to him incomprehensible how men armed only with bows and unused to regular warfare could put them in danger and fear.

But so it was; and when the outlaws collected the bodies of those who had fallen in the engagement, and in the night bore them right through the town and laid them down before the house of the sheriff, bidding him give them such Christian burial as he would obtain if he came to them, the two men—the sheriff and his wounded guest—were perfectly mad with rage.

"Who and what manner of man is this Robin Hood?" said Mondidier, as the sheriff sat with him to pass the weary time away.

The arrows had been drawn from him with some difficulty, and what from loss of blood and the fever which naturally ensued, he was very ill.

"Man!" cried the sheriff; "why, call him not such—rather say that he is the devil himself."

"You have seen him?"

"Several times."

"And not caught him?"

"No."

"But how?"

"My blood boils to think of it."

"Tell me."

"I will not keep secret my adventures with this arrant knave, who has troubled me since he was first born."

"Speak—I am all ears."

The sheriff began, nor did he in his narrative spare himself, as he rather thought the adventures creditable to him, while showing the rascality of the outlaw.

"A brave rascal."

"Eh?"

"Yes; and were he not an enemy of the king's, I should say a man to lead an army."

"Ah! Robin's no such enemy of the king's after all," put in the sheriff, with a wise look.

"Man!"

"It's true."

"Explain yourself."

"Evesham battle might not have been won had he not turned up at the right moment."

"Strange!" cried the suffering soldier; "well, it's no

use talking any more about him. Give me to drink, and then play me a game of dice."

"With pleasure, my friend. But who comes here?" he added, as a knight in armour entered unannounced.

CHAPTER XXIII.

SIR GUY OF GISBORNE—A TRAGICAL AND HUMOROUS ADVENTURE OF ROBIN HOOD.

"Ah! my good sheriff, I heard you were playing the good Samaritan. Who is your wounded friend?"

"I, Sir Guy."

"What?—Captain Mondidier, as I live!"

"The same."

"Who put you in this strait?"

"Robin Hood."

"Curses light on that name!"

"How so?" asked the sheriff.

"I've travelled through the forest three days, and if I saw a fine herd of deer, this discourse followed:

"'Whose deer is that?'

"'Robin Hood's.'

"'Whose forest glade is that?'

"'Robin Hood's.'

"'What old tower is that?'

"'Robin Hood's.'"

"Sooth, my lord," cried the sheriff, "the man who answered you thus must have been of his gang. But if you will take refreshment I will tell you all about him."

"I have fifty stout men-at-arms at my back, and have called to spend a day. If you will order something for an early meal I will cast me the dice with Mondidier, whose fingers are itching to win some money. Canst sit up?"

"Robin Hood is famed for depriving men of their seat," said Mondidier, grimly.

And he described his wounds.

"Par le sang dieu!" cried the soldier, "this is a bold ruffian. While the sheriff is out we'll e'en have a throw; but I am curious to hear the story."

They played for about ten minutes, when Mondidier was obliged to lean back.

His wounds were too much for him.

The sheriff bustled in, followed by servants with a table already laid.

The knight, who had travelled since daybreak, seated himself and enjoyed his repast, while the sheriff told his story, culminated by his last disaster.

"So," said Sir Guy of Gisborne, laughing, "this man has taken your money, violated your seat of honour, insulted you grossly, kissed your wife before your face—and yet he lives."

"I wish he didn't."

"He is not a magician."

"I fear he is."

"Tut, Tut, man, that is your folly."

"He has never been defeated."

"He is not immortal."

"Something like it."

"I say it is the weakness of those who attack him, that makes so much of this man."

"Sir Guy," said Mondidier, hotly, "I am an old soldier, and I have seen some service. Fore gad! I had seven hundred good men and true, and as I live by bread, these Saxon outlaws defeated us with half that number. They seem to me the very spawn of hell."

"Were this outlaw the foul fiend himself," said the knight, as much bully as soldier; "if I made up my mind to tweak his nose, or pull his tail, or cut off his horns, I'd do it."

"Sir—"

"I fear nor man nor devil."

"Forbear!" cried Mondidier," I know not what you might do to his Satanic Majesty from whose contact all the saints in heaven keep us—but I am certain you would not match with Robin Hood."

"I tell you, sir, that I would."

"Well," continued the sheriff, who, at home at his own table, and with plenty of wine before him, was exceedingly pot-valiant, "you don't know this King of Sherwood Forest. Even King Richard yields the palm to him in the woods."

"Is he a friend of the Lion's?"

"He is."

"I hate him."

"Why?"

"Richard has stripped me of every manor but my old one of Gisborne, for my part in the proposed change of government."

"He will give some of them to Robin if his trial goes right," sneered the Sheriff.

"What trial?"

"'Tis said that Robin's real name is Robert Earl of Huntingdon," added the officer.

"Ah!"

"But earl or bandit, no one ever yet faced him and lived."

"'Tis well I have come this way, that I might hear of this bold braggart. I will face him, 'an he were ten times an outlaw, earl, or devil!"

"I fear me, Sir Guy, you may have reason to repent your audacity," said the sheriff."

"Repent my grandmother! You know me not. Why, ere a week is over, you shall have his head sliced off, and put on yonder dish. I wonder much, coming as I do from foreign lands, to find such fear of a mere robber among Englishmen."

"I thought you had been away a long time, or else you wouldn't talk with such temerity."

"Temerity! ha! ha! ha!" laughed Sir Guy, filling a full bumper of claret, "to our next merry meeting after the forest is purged of this knave."

"Here's to you," said the sheriff, with alacrity.

Now the sheriff had all the time been egging the soldier on to make him do that which he professed not to wish him to do.

Personally he had no particular wish even to engage in the pursuit of the outlaw again, but it mattered not to him, who was the instrument, so that the object was gained, the destruction of Robin Hood being to him any way a large pecuniary gain.

Those who wished his claim to the earldom of Nottingham to be defeated would pay him, while Prince John, who loved the chase and jealoused the outlaws for killing the deer, promised no end of rewards when he came to the throne, to him who should the outlaw slay.

This he did not wish the knight to know, who himself was actuated by sundry motives.

A desire, in the first place, to distinguish himself at once on his arrival in England.

Secondly, a dislike to any man who was patronised by the lion-hearted king.

There was a third motive.

He hated any body who was well spoken of by the common people. In general a good man is not much prized by the middle and wealthier classes.

Every true prophet, every reformer, every benefactor of his species, has had to seek for supporters and disciples from among the poor and humble.

The rich neither care, as a rule, for material nor for moral reform.

As a rule, when they propose them, or yield to them, it is from no better motive than fear.

"Now then, that I have made up my mind," resumed Sir Guy of Gisborne, "where is this scarecrow to be found?"

"Everywhere; but dear Guy——"

"Seek not to dissuade me."

"He is the best archer——"

"Hang him!"

"The best quarterstaff player."

"Curse him!"

"The best wrestler."

"A fico for him!"

"Oh, Sir Guy!"

"Owe me nothing, when you have told me where this mighty man is to be found."

"Well, Sir Guy, a wilful man will have his way. So it must be. People do say——"

"What?"

"That Robin Hood——"

"Well."

"Does usually hang out——"

"Where?"

"In Barnesdale wood."

"How far?"

"Two days march."

"Enough. Leave you him to me. Let all our men be combined under your command."

"Mine?"

"Yes, my doughty sheriff, or you are no longer friend of mine. Fear not——"

"Fear!"

"It looks like it."

"Sir Guy!"

"Let us not quarrel. You come after. I will go in advance, and shall not ask you to join me until I have slain this redoubtable boaster; when, at sound of my horn, you shall come and do your best to slay as many of the merry men, since so you call them, as you can. The rest we will take prisoners and hang as an example in Nottingham town."

The sheriff groaned. He would much have liked to see them hanging from gibbets, but he doubted.

"Another cup, to put some colour in your white face, my jolly master," said Sir Guy; "enough of business today. My friend Mondidier is awake again, and will be glad of our company."

"Ay, that will I," said the Norman *reitre*, turning round; "that last sleep has cooled the fever. Still I am athirst, and would like a cup of good sack."

"Sack!" * said the sheriff shaking his head.

"Aye, sack. The long-nosed apothecary who came just now would starve me. Nonsense, man; because I have a wound in my breech, wouldst have me play the woman and drink small beer?"

"You know best," said the sheriff.

"Does he!" exclaimed his wife, entering without ceremony. "I suspect you are about to kill him between you; here is some soup of herbs, which will do him more good than all your fiery mixtures."

The Norman captain made a wry face, but 'twas more to show his manhood than anything else, the *soupe aux herbes*, reminding him of his old mother in Normandy, who many a time and oft had cured him of his drunken frolics by the administration of some such simple remedies which to this day are justly popular in the various provinces of Gaul.

While the lady was administering to her patient, the sheriff and knight were laying their plans.

Ere they they had quite concluded, she summoned them to a banquet prepared with her own fair hands.

She insisted also that the wounded man should be left in peace for a couple of hours.

Those couple of hours were extended to eight by means of a narcotic in his broth.

CHAPTER XXIV.

IN THE GREEN WOOD.

MEANWHILE Robin Hood was far away, little aware of what was being plotted against him.

The forest of Sherwood, which we have already had so much occasion to notice, though at that time celebrated for its extent and the thickness of the woody parts thereof, was not even then what it once had been, and vestiges of its former vastness were found for many miles beyond the spots where the royal meres, or forest boundaries, were then placed. A space of cultivated country would intervene, meadows and fields would stretch out, with nothing but a hawthorn or a beech overshadowing them here and there; but then suddenly would burst upon the traveller's eye, a large patch of wood, of several miles in length, broken with the wild irregular savannahs, dells, dingles, banks and hills which characterised the forest he had just left behind.

This was especially the case to the north and east, but one of the largest tracts of woodland, beyond the actual meres, lay in the south-eastern part of Yorkshire. It was separated by some three or four miles of ground irregularly cultivated, and broken by occasional clumps of old trees, and even small woods, from Sherwood itself, and, being more removed from the highway between the southern portion of England and the northern border, was more wild and secluded than even the actual forest. In extent it was about five miles long, and from three to four broad, and had evidently, in former times, been

---

* Sack is a kind of wine, now brought chiefly from the Canaries.

a portion of the same vast woody region which occupied the whole of that part of England. No great towns lying in the country immediately surrounding it, and no lordly castle, belonging to any very powerful baron, this tract was without that constant superintendence which was exercised over the forest ground in the southern parts of the island, and the game was left open as an object of chase alike to the yeomen of the lands around, the monks of a neighbouring priory, and some of the inferior nobles, who held estates in that district. Under a yellow sandy bank, then, upon the edge of this wood with tall trees rising above, and the brown leaves of autumn rustling around, were three outlaws.

Robin Hood, who had been out hunting all the day before, had started with some of his companions on his way back to join his merrie men, leaving his wife to follow.

Tired after his midday meal as men will be, he fell into a sound slumber.

The spot was a pretty one, if we believe the ballad which revels in the tale.

When shaws are sheen and shrads full fair,
And leaves both large and long,
It is merry to walk in the fair forest
And hear the small bird's song.
The woodweele sang, and would not cease,
Sitting upon the spray;
So loud, he awakened Robin Hood
In the greenwood where he lay.

It appears that Little John and Will Scarlett had remained with their chief, and sat finishing a pleasant repast, lightened by wine and merry talk.

Will Scarlett was still in the heyday of his love; no black or brown or blue or grey eyes had weaned him from his fealty, even for a moment.

Little John, on all topics connected with love, was thoughtful as if his time had not come yet, and yet as if he wished that it would.

Hitherto he had been too busy to think of anything but the interests of his friends.

Little John was the most unselfish nature in the world.

Every one else first, and himself last.

Such was not only his theory, but his practice.

The chief of the outlaws, who lay recumbent on the ground, began to get uneasy.

"The woodweele sings loudly," said Will Scarlett.

"If I thought he troubled Robin I would drive him away."

Ere the other could reply, Robin leaped to his feet and rubbed his eyes.

"Is that you, my masters?"

"How now—what is it?"

"Not much," replied the outlaw, with a laugh; "but the truth is that I have dreamed a dream."

"Quotha!" cried Little John.

"And in this dream. I bethought me two strong yeomen overpowered me in fight, and beat me when they bound me. Something awoke me as they were about to slay."

"Hum!"

"If I meet two such yeomen, I shall think of my dream," continued Robin.

"Ah," said Little John, to whom these words were addressed, "those that mind freets, freets will follow, as Allan-a-Dale says."

"True, John," answered Robin Hood; "but I shall leave this place, nevertheless."

And the three put on their green frocks, and with their arrows at their backs walked out among the deer.

Until they came to the merry greenwood,
Where they had gladdest to be;
There they were aware of a wight yeoman,
That lean'd him against a tree.
A sword and a dagger he wore by his syde,
Of many a man the bane,
And he was clad in his capul hide,
Top, and tail, and mane.

He was alone, so as Robin scorned to attack one man unless he was alone, he first sent Will Scarlett to recounoitre in the direction of Mansfield.

He and Little John then crept forward to see who this wight was.

He was a rude looking yoekel enough, with a horse hide cloak, not uncommon even now among Yorkshire jockeys and horse-dealers.

He was by no means a pleasant fellow to meet, with money and a timid heart.

He looked as big a ruffian as he in reality was, and that said much.

"I will tackle that customer," said Robin, "he's a stranger about here, and looks no good. There is a down glance about him bodes ill.

"True master, but——"

"Hearken, Little John, that knave is one of those of which I dreamed, be sure."

It may surprise the thoughtful reader, who knows that dreams and omens are, like ghosts and haunted houses, the weak invention of silly minds that cannot distinguish between the palpable and impalpable, to hear Robin speaking in such a strange way.

But in those days of ignorance and benighted ideas, people did actually believe in the crude fancies which indigestion or nightmare or an uncomfortable position might arouse in their brains.

Just as people believed in ghosts, not understanding that that which is not, cannot be seen.

Those who believe in the possibility of seeing the spirit of the departed, should watch the breath when it leaves the body.

The one is as impalpable as the other.

"He looks a dog that will bite," said Little John, "however, he is a knave worth trouncing; if he has no business here I will trounce him well."

"He is waiting for something," continued Robin.

"Get thee behind yonder tree," said Little John, "while I go ask his business."

"Nay," replied Robin, "this man is mine. I saw him first, and he is my right."

"But he is a mountain of a fellow."

"Never mind. There is always some excuse for you to fight when we are together. I will have this man."

"As you will."

"Do you go and seek Will. If I want you I will sound my horn."

Now, if there was one person more devoted to another it was Little John to Robin Hood, but he was angry now, for the ruffian they had espied was a hulking brute, who might overcome the outlaw by sheer muscular force.

"Had I not better remain, in case he has comrades?" said the gigantic forester.

"Little John," replied the King of Sherwood, with something of dignity of manner, acquired from the Cœur de Lion, "when I give orders, I expect to be obeyed."

The big forester looked dumbfounded, and walked away without a word.

CHAPTER XXV.

SIR GUY.

IF the good-natured, good-hearted, and burly lieutenant of the outlaws could ever really have been angry, it was on the present occasion.

He wanted to fight the capul-hided ruffian.

Robin wouldn't let him.

He wanted to remain behind, a kind of army of reserve.

Robin wouldn't let him.

"I have a great mind to go and give myself up and be hanged," he muttered; "I'm no use. I am not worthy to be the friend of Robin—he snubbed me. I'll obey him no more—yes you will, you big Saxon ass—no—but won't the first chap who gives me a chance get a famous drubbing."

And with this satisfactory plaster upon his conscience he followed in the track of Will Scarlett.

His frown was dark, and his face was flushed, as he strode along with his arrows on his back and his huge quarterstaff in his hand.

He did not precisely know which way Will Scarlett had taken, but he was aware that it was in the direction of Mansfield.

By degrees the giant's serenity quite returned, and he strode along, humming to himself.

Suddenly he stopped.

He listened with all his ears.

It was the clang of weapons, the cries of men in mortal strife, with shouts of delight.

Little John's face became quite complaisant as he stepped out, a perfect colossus, not larding the lean earth, for he was of the William Banting school, but dashing aside branches and boughs until he reached the end of a large vista of the forest, where Will Scarlett and two of the merry men were engaged in a mortal conflict with seven opponents.

The two outlaws fell as Little John came in sight, and Will Scarlett, having done enough for honour, seemed inclined to save himself.

The ballad tells us that on Little John's approach,

> Scarlette he was flying afoote,
> Fast over stock and stone,
> For the proud sheriffe with seven score men
> Fast after him is gone.
>
> "One shoote now I will shoote," quoth John,
> "With Christ his might and mayne,
> I'll make yond sheriffe that wends soe fast,
> To stopp he shall be fayne."

But the forest Maypole, as some have called him, not inaptly, now dashed from the covert, and with a loud shout announced his presence.

"I will stop the pranks of this accursed sheriff," he said, in a towering passion, and hastily preparing his bow, he drew a long arrow to the head.

But no one should ever do anything in a passion, which is an emotion of the mind which, though sometimes useful, is often dangerous.

A learned pundit has said, speaking of anger. "In morality, and in preserving the order of the world, resentment is a powerful instrument. Not merely the hurt that anger prompts to, but the very expression and aspect of the passion, inspire dread, and make men exert themselves to avoid causing it. Our anger is a wall of fire around us. In the government of human beings, the display of angry feelings suffices very often to check disobedience."

But the abuse is very bad.

Now, though no man was more readily disposed never to let the sun go down upon his wrath, Little John was peppery and hot.

When he saw the sheriff his face became red and swollen, his brows were knit, his eyes started, while he pulled the string rapidly and, over doing it, the good bow broke, and the arrow fell useless to the ground.

"May the foul fiend take thee and the tree from which you were taken," said Little John.

At the same moment he picked up the bow which one of the dead outlaws had dropped, and with this once more took aim.

"Have at thee, rascal sheriff," he said, and then we'll hie for the forest."

This time either the outlaw was more careful, or the bow was better, or something, but the shaft was loosed.

The sheriff was coming full tilt at the outlaws; with his large *posse comctati* behind him, what had he to fear from two of the merrie men?

But he saw that shaft, and ere it was almost sped fell flat upon his horse, grasping the mane, and riding stirrupless, like one John Gilpin of later days, who hence was to acquire a reputation nearly as great as that of the burly forester.

Unfortunate act this for one of the men-at-arms.

The escort of the astute and cunning sheriff rode close together, and for one of them to have stooped to save himself would have been a most unpardonable and unsoldierly act.

The centre man then received it in his body and suffered death therefrom, it being notorious in all romances of chivalry, middle age romaunts, or histories, which are scarcely as credible, that whereas heroes, lords, knights, and people either of note, or necessary to the conduct of the narrative, die very hard, even after many deadly and mortal wounds coming to life again, the mere rag and bobtail, the *oi polloi*, the ragamuffins, are incontinently killed at once, and thus got rid of forthwith, which is a great saving of time to the reader and of trouble to the author.

There are historians, who go so far as to give the name of this worthy, which, seeing that he was not introduced before, and never can properly be brought in again, is almost a work of supererogation.

Still it is best to be minute, so we freely quote his biographer.

"His name was William-a-Trent, who had been very anxious to be of the expedition against Robin Hood, but it had been better for him—

> To have been abed with sorrow.
> Than to be that day in the greenwood glade,
> To meet with Little John's arrowe.

Requiescat in pace.

The fellows who had been pressing Will Scarlett so hard, and from whom, when left alone, he very wisely fled, had now got up to him; but the outlaw had a tree behind him, and though the town-bred knaves pressed him hard again, yet was our red-haired hero too much of an outlaw to yield.

With one eye on Little John, he gave loud blows, warded off others, and was soon relieved by the big forester, rushing in with his mighty club, with which two men were at once felled, a third maimed, and the whole party would have been routed but for reinforcements which suddenly came up, and hemmed both in.

Will Scarlett now fought under one oak-tree, Little John under the other.

The giant had the most assailants. His huge strength, his mighty frame, showed the leaders the necessity of a large force to overwhelm him.

Will Scarlett had five, which was of itself a compliment seldom paid to one man.

"You run," said Little John, "I'll make these pigmies hold an hour. Robin Hood is not far with a hundred bowmen—run to him for your life."

"I will not leave you," shouted Will.

"A malison on your chivalry," cried John; "if you mind not they will have us both."

Will Scarlett, small as he was, now combatted more like a madman that an ordinary being.

But the numbers against them were fearful.

A dozen men-at-arms and retainers were down.

Some old wary Norman soldiers were watching.

One or two of them gave whispered orders, and then a score of staves, spears, and sticks were thrown between the legs of the outlaws.

Both fell, and ere they could regain their footing they were overwhelmed and crushed by weight and numbers.

The sheriff rode up as soon as they were safe.

"Pick me out a good tree to hang me these knaves," he said, in a pompous tone.

"You dare not," cried Little John; "the forest is alive with true men. Lift but a hand and it shall be nailed to the tree you point at."

The sheriff looked warily round.

He had some experience of the outlaws, and hence his fear of them.

"Who are you?" he said.

"Little John."

"And you?"

"Will Scarlett."

"Ah! say you so? 'Tis well. My men, these are birds too precious to hang in the forest. They are nearly as great prizes as Robin Hood himself."

"Dastard," said Little John, "were the brave outlaw the favoured of your king, the rightful Earl of Huntingdon, whom you would rob, but here, you would go on your bended knees. You no more dare hang us while he lives, than you dare meet him alone in the forest."

"My insolent forest Maypole," said the sheriff, who, surrounded by a large force of his men, felt wonderfully brave and defiant, "I would hang you here on one of the forest trees, but that I am bound to show you an example to the good people of Nottingham."

"Capital," cried Little John; "I would as soon be in Nottingham as anywhere else, for then I can make love as Robin did, to your pretty wife."

"Silence, insolent knave!"

"How is the good dame?" said Will Scarlett, demurely. "I hear she favours red-haired men."

"Tie and gag those men, put sentries on all sides and watch. There will be news anon," and the plethoric sheriff, in a towering passion, walked away.

If you want a thing done do it yourself.

Had the sheriff even have seen it done, he might have had the outlaws gagged; but the men-at-arms, after civilly bidding them hold their tongues, tied them to two trees, without closing their mouths.

The fellows were Nottingham men, and had a very wholesome regard for their own skins.

The outlaws were not three feet apart.

They were surrounded by hundreds of troopers and men-at-arms.

But their faces were calm and serene enough.

The soldiers posted sentries, made fires, and the sheriff as usual began feasting.

In his cups he spoke, loud enough for them to hear, of the trap laid for Robin.

"Ah! ah! he is by this time the prisoner of he in the capul-hide," he said.

"Heaven shield us." whispered Little John.

"What is it?" asked Scarlett.

The outlaw told the story of their meeting with a suspicious character in the wood.

"There was an ambuscade no doubt," continued Little John, ruefully.

"I wish they'd hang me at once," said Will.

"So do I," whimpered Little John.

Then there came a blast from a distant horn, a signal agreed on between the sheriff and Sir Guy of Gisborne.

> "Oh hearken! oh hearken!" the sheriff said,
> "I hear now tidings good;
> For yonder I hear Sir Guy's horn blow,
> And he hath slain Robin Hood.
>
> Yonder I hear Sir Guy's horn blow,
> It blows so well in tide,
> And yonder he comes, that wight yeoman,
> Clad in his capul-hide."

Little John groaned aloud, and was nearer fainting than he had ever been in his life before.

He seemed to hear the knell sounded of his chieftain's life.

CHAPTER XXVI.

THE FIGHT.

Now all the boys, and all the girls for that matter, are so clever now-a-days, that it would be of no use our pretending to let them think Robin was killed, so we will not make any mystery of the matter.

As a clever historian properly observes of this adventure "it is right excellent."

The capul-hided knight marched as if to an assured conquest, nor doubted that he should either take Robin Hood or slay him.

But the ready wit and invention of the outlaw were always near when bravery failed, and fortune seems to have delighted in affording him opportunities of showing the ascendancy of his mind over his head.

When the stalwart Little John started off in a huff to join his comrades, Robin Hood waited until he was out of sight before he disturbed the stranger.

The ill-looking ruffian, in the capul-hide, was armed with dagger, sword, quarterstaff and bow.

He was a regular walking armoury, as things were in those days.

Presently Robin stood alone, listened attentively, made sure that none were near, and then entered the glade where Sir Guy of Gisborne stood, quietly and without any ostentation.

The man coolly leaned against the tree, scarcely taking notice of the youthful forester who came his way.

"I give you good-day, fellow," said Robin, in his haughty way, "thou should'st be a good archer, if I may judge by thy bow."

"I have missed my way," said Sir Guy, not answering the question, "being not acquainted with this wood, and have lost my day's work."

Robin looked at him keenly.

Was this simplicity or artfulness?

He did not look like a man who would easily lose his way in an English forest.

"You are not of these parts then?"

"I am not."

"I am, and can show you whatever you want to find," was the outlaw's reply.

> "I seek an outlaw," the stranger said,
> "Men call him Robin Hood;
> I'd rather meet him, that proud outlaw,
> Than forty pound so good."
>
> "Now come with me, thou wight yeoman,
> And Robin thou shalt see;
> But first let us some pastime find
> Under the greenwood tree."

Now when the stranger yeoman said unto Robin Hood that he was in search of himself, he at once made up his mind that if he were simply some fellow who, in a frolic, had boasted he would capture Robin Hood, he would let him go after he had a game with him; but that if he were one of the crafty agents of the detested sheriff, he should be punished severely.

"You seek Robin?"

"I do."

"What want you with him?"

"I wish to take him."

"So ho! Well, an' if you would find Robin Hood you must prove yourself a good archer. None others are admitted to his presence. I would not, for my head, present thee otherwise."

"Wilt show me this vaunting outlaw?"

"I will, on condition——"

"What condition?"

"That we shoot together in the greenwood glade."

"Agreed."

On this Robin cut two long wands, from which he removed all extraneous buds and leaves, and setting them threescore rods asunder, they prepared their bows to shoot.

It was evidently Robin's object to prove the skill of this venturous stranger, who had entered his dominions bow in hand, as if challenging him to a trial in the very art in which he excelled. Had the man been a skilful archer, or a more skilful archer than he proved, it is likely that Robin, instead of the awkward stroke which he bestowed on him, would have endeavoured to enlist him in his band.

"You see yon rods?"

"I do, of course."

"Well, an you hit one of them I shall account you a good archer."

"My good fellow, it cannot be done. I will not try that which is manifestly impossible; so lead the way and shoot, thyself."

> The first time Robin shot at the pricke
> He missed but an inch it fro;
> The yeoman he was an archer good,
> But he could never do so.

To descend to plain prose, Robin Hood, without taking the least aim, fired, and the arrow went within an inch of the wand.

"Hit, by heavens!"

"No," said Robin. "You can easily beat that."

The man shrugged his shoulders and took aim.

Three times the stranger tried, and three times he failed, not coming within a foot of the rods.

"Thou art nervous," said Robin, "and do not allow for the wind."

With that he cut a third wand, and placed close beside the other, within a foot, and laid a small piece of wood across.

"Cans't shoot between?" asked Robin.

"I will try," said the man in capul hide.

And taking more careful aim than before, his arrow passed between the two wands.

"Pretty fair; and now, my master, see me split the wands in twain."

"Impossible."

"One," said Robin.

And the arrow cleft the wand in twain.

"Two."

And the same result followed.

"A blessing upon thy heart," cried capul-hide. "Why my good yeoman,

> —— thy shooting is good,
> An thy heart be as good as thy hand,
> Thou wert better than Robin Hood.

Who and what art thou?"

"I am at home," replied Robin, "and you should, as a stranger, tell me who and what you are."

> "I dwell by dale and down," quoth he,
> "And Robin to take I'm sworn;
> And when I am called by my right name
> I am Guy of Good Gisborne."

"Ah," said the outlaw, musing, "a friend of the worthy sheriff of Nottingham."

"The same, my fine fellow; and once I had some goodly estates in the west, but the king—heaven's malison—took them from me, so that I must earn some fresh ones."

"Indeed."

"They say this outlaw fellow claims to be Earl of Huntingdon. If then, I slay him, I doubly gain, for I win renown and perhaps an estate."

"A traitor to his king," said Robin, musing.

"Fellow!"

"A friend of the accursed sheriff of Nottingham—coward, knave, and informer!"

"Churl!"

"A common thief-taker, who dares to call himself a knight!" continued the outlaw, speaking aloud, but to himself.

"Villain!"

"Thou hast a good estate," continued Robin, "but I have a better.

> "My dwelling is in this wood," says Robin,
> "By thee I set right nought;
> I am Robin Hood of Barnesdale,
> Whom thou so long hast sought."
> He that had neither been kith nor kin
> Might have seen a full fair fight,
> To see how together these yeomen went
> With blades both brown and bright.

CHAPTER XXVII.

THE RESULT.

WHEN the capul-hide clad knight heard the other announce in a cold, dignified manner that he was Robin Hood, his delight knew no bounds.

Sir Guy of Gisborne was one of those happily constituted people who have a high opinion of their own deserts and capabilities.

To be conquered by a simple yeoman was quite out of the question.

"Thou art Robin Hood?" he said.

"I am."

"Then by the foul fiend, from whose den you have come, you die!"

"Come on."

"You see this horn?" continued he of the capul-hide.

"Of course," said Robin, mimicking his adversary.

"There are those not far distant who wait to hear from it three *mots*, which will announce thy death."

"Boaster."

"One moment, be not in a hurry, my man. The sheriff of Nottingham with seven hundred men will capture me all your gang; ere this your lieutenants are taken, and now I shall ride with your head on my saddle bow. Let it be a combat unto death, and say thy prayers, for I have vowed by Sathanas to take thy mooncalf head, and I will."

"If," said Robin, still leaning on his bow, and allowing his sword to remain in its sheath, "you had shown one spark of feeling, if, despite your Norman origin, you had allowed me to see one sign of manliness, I had forgiven thy boasting. My men would have scourged thee from the wood, and all had been said."

"Have at thee, knave."

"But now, you have said no quarter, and as you have said so shall it be. I will not spare thee, even on thy bended knees, but will carry thy head on high where everybody may see it, on my bow point. Now say thy prayers, if thou knowest any, for in ten minutes your head will be low—*for so a little bird told me.*"

This remark of Robin Hood's is so far satisfactory, as pointing to the origin of a very mysterious phrase, which has often bothered the erudite.

Both now stood on the defensive.

Each man had drawn his sword, and with something of the theatrical air which good swordsmen often assume, looked at the point, passed his fingers along the edge, which, though neither so sharp as a razor nor as wide as a knife-back, was quite equal to the task of cutting off a man's head.

They were well matched, though common opinion might, on a cursory glance, have decided in favour of the knight.

He was a man of great personal strength, which, properly directed, is of great avail. He had learned the art of the swordsman in France from Spanish teachers, and he was as rugged-hearted as the most rugged-hearted Russian bear.

There was no chivalrous nicety about him, and he was always ready to take a mean advantage of an enemy.

Robin was slighter, shorter, and younger.

But a keen eye, which had noticed his clean limbs, his calm eye, his iron muscles, would have felt little fear for him in the conflict.

The knight, whose sword was longer than that of the outlaw, made a sudden dash at Robin.

The outlaw saw at once he had his match to deal with. He even in the first dash of the fight had to yield his ground.

The tactics of the knight were dark.

He always tried to *brusque* a victory.

The outlaw retreated slowly to have his back to a tree, and the sun out of his eyes.

"Ah! ah!" shouted Sir Grey, "I have you now."

"The holy Virgin forfend," replied Robin; "I would sooner be in the devil's keeping."

"That will come quick enough."

And while speaking still their swords struck sparks on all sides.

The clangour was great.

The birds fled afraid, the hares crouched in their forms, not a deer would remain within half a mile.

The blows aimed by Sir Guy were all such as, had they taken effect, would have been mortal.

His sword was a Toledo blade, which had seen service before; that of Robin was a gift of King Richard's.

Still the sledge-hammer strokes of the knight threatened to shiver it to pieces.

Robin began to weary of this state of things.

He now dashed at the knight, disdaining to guard himself, attacking instead.

But the experienced knight stood like a rock.

"Ah! ah!" he cried, "my springal! Getting tired, are you! I begin to believe you lied, when you called yourself Robin."

The outlaw now began to be extremely cautious, as he saw that the man was a far more practised swordsman than he expected.

The outlaw frowned darkly, for he liked not to find his match in his own forest, and while the combat still lasted, he was contriving some means of freeing himself from this audacious stranger.

Suddenly he made a desperate leap on one side, turned round and sought a more suitable position.

He was light and wary, but the Norman was a keen and "cunning traitour," so that he pressed Robin sorely, and lifted his sword to give him a blow, that, had it fallen on his head, must have certainly despatched him.

Robin Hood fell over the root of a tree, and thus received a slight wound in his side.

As has been sagely remarked, Sir Guy of Gisborne was not the man to throw such a chance away.

He flew at Robin, who, with the rapidity of thought, breathed a prayer to our Lady.

"Ay, dear Lady," he cried, addressing the Virgin, "let me not die before my time."

It was the belief in those days, that a prayer to the Madonna was of more avail than to the fount of religion.

They were ignorant, and followed blindly their clergy very much as we do ours, believing what they tell us, without taking the trouble to think for themselves.

But in this instance, some miracle seemed to have been worked in favour of Robin—it was probably his own faith in his prayer—for no sooner did he regain his feet, than he seemed endowed with double strength.

"Villain! that blow was thy last!" he cried.

"Villain thyself! Thus do I deliver——"

He did not finish his sentence, for the outlaw struck him on the neck, and the man fell back with a loud cry.

The knight gave a fearful gasp, groaned horribly, and died, upon which Robin rested.

As soon as this most desirable consummation for himself was perpetrated, Robin said a hearty and sincere prayer of thanks for his happy deliverance.

Then he thought him of the words which Sir Guy had used relative to himself, and how he had threatened to carry his head to the sheriff of Nottingham.

Robin accordingly cut his head off, gashed it so that no one might know whose it was, and stuck it on the end of his bow.

He then stripped the body, and taking off his own mantle of Lincoln green, exclaimed in the savage pleasantry of those times, " If thou hast had the worst strokes at my hand, thou shalt have the better cloth."

> Then Robin did off his gown of green
> And on Sir Guy did throw;
> And he put on the capul-hide
> That clad him top to toe.
> Thy bow, thy arrows, thy little horn
> Now with me I'll bear,
> For I'll away to Barnesdale
> To see how my men do fare.

Now Robin Hood, in an old capul-hide and as a jolly archer, was two very different fellows, as the following description of the latter by Chaucer will show :—

> And he was clad in coat and hood of green ;
> A sheaf of peacock arrows, bright and keen,
> Under his belt he bare full thriftily.
> Well could he dress his tackle yeomanly ;
> His arrows drooped not with feathers low,
> And in his hand he bare a mighty bow.
> His head was like a nut, with visage brown:
> Of woodcraft all the ways to him were known.
> An arm-brace wore he, that was rich and broad,
> And by his side a buckler and a sword ;
> While on the other side a dagger rare.
> Well sheathed, was hung ; and on his breast he bare
> A large St. Christopher of silver sheen.
> A horn he had, the baldric was of green,—
> A forester truly, was he, as I guess."

CHAPTER XXVIII.

THE RESCUE.

WE left Will Scarlett and Little John in the hands of the sheriff of Nottingham, tied to two trees within talking distance one of the other.

They both for a moment were almost inclined to believe that their chief and captain was taken.

They gazed with awe at the man who was coming on, and exchanged strange glances.

"Ah, ah! my knaves," said the sheriff, "so you see your power is broken for ever, for here comes he who has slain your chief."

"It was not done fairly," cried Little John, who foamed at the mouth with rage and hearty defiance; "he has been betrayed. I warned him of that knave in a capul-hide."

"Silence!"

"I will not. Let me free, and let me try my hand on this base churl who has slain the best blood in England."

"Silence—mind him not," cried the sheriff: "and now, Sir Gisborne, you have done that which will never be forgotten in England. Your country owes you a reward."

"Said I not?"

"You did ; but I believed it not. As it has been done, receive my thanks; and, as the representative of my native town, allow me to ask what will be the reward you will ask of me?"

"Base slave," cried Little John and Will Scarlett.

"I ask no gold," said the chief of the outlaws, speaking in a hollow tone out of the capul-hide ; "here is the head of the master ; let me have a crack at his knave, Little John, and his churl, Will Scarlett. That is the only recompense I ask here."

"But, Sir Guy," said the avaricious old sheriff and jeweller, who expected to make a good penny out of the town's present to the Norman, "you are simply mad. You have done a deed worth a knight's fee, but since you are pleased with little, go and take it."

"I ask no better," groaned Little John, while Will Scarlett was simply speechless.

The man in the capul-hide drew near Little John with a large open knife, and while the two glanced at him with fierce hatred and remorse, he waved the weapon before their eyes.

"Do you not know me, babes?" he said, in a low tone ; "do you think I am going to be killed by any Norman, though he wore ever so much capul-hide?"

"Now, I shall get loose as sure as there are saints in heaven," cried Little John.

"Amen," said Will Scarlett.

The ballad thus describes the rescue :—

> Robin pulled forth an Irish knife,
> And loosed John hand and foot,
> And gave him Sir Guy's bow in his hand,
> And bade him arise and shoot.
> Then John took Guy's bow in his hand,
> His bolts and arrows each one,
> When the Sheriff saw Little John bend the bow
> He ettled him to be gone.

But Will Scarlett and Robin Hood, too, bent the bow, and some hundred of outlaws who came rushing up to the joyous rescue.

"Now, sheriff, stay," said Robin; "this once more I spare your life. On the ground beside you is the head of your friend Guy of Gisborne ; but as sure as I catch you again in my dominions, worrying my people and confiscating their goods, I will slay you as I would a wild cat in my path ; now go, and quickly, for Little John here itches to let fly at your fat paunch, and if he does it's little good your ungodly guts will ever do you again."

The sheriff waited to hear no more, but, pale and trembling, rode off towards Nottingham, too happy to escape with his life from his ever victorious enemy.

* * * * *

Robin and his followers encamped on the ground, for all were glad, after the events of the day to obtain immediate rest.

They had all had their trials, but he himself had had a rude encounter, which he was not likely easily to forget.

At early dawn the merry men were again afoot, and having taken orders from their chief, departed on their several errands, having instructions to meet at the old trysting place in about ten days, when Robin informed Little John and Will Scarlett that he would be prepared to engage in fresh adventures, which were as necessary as food to his existence.

Little John and Will Scarlett were particularly glad to hear this, as they, too, were never more happy than when wandering about in search of the unexpected.

They were very much like gipsies in their tastes and habits, revelling in the greenwood, and always, in despite of weather, preferring the open air to the cover of houses.

Sir Ralph and his lady had returned to their home after a month's visit, though they, too, had promised to return at no very distant period, to accompany Robin in his visit to court, where he was determined to present himself, and have his rank acknowledged openly and triumphantly.

* * * * *

Robin about this time was thoughtful and moody. He appeared to have attained to the summit of human happiness, having unlimited command over brave and devoted men, having a bride that might have done honour to a prince.

What was it?

Well, the outlaw had been married more than a year without any prospects of descendants to take his title and estates, if he regained them.

He was the more moody and thoughtful that he strove to conceal his feelings from Maid Marian, who would, indeed, have been miserable had she suspected the nature of the feelings which made Robin so fond of solitude and retirement.

Happily she considered the death of his father the moving cause of his dullness of spirits, and tried hard to console him by taking care to have plenty both of employment and amusement for him.

There was, however, one who was even more bent than she was on occupying him, that was the sheriff.

This man looked upon Robin Hood as the bane of his existence.

THE WOUNDED FORESTER.

Continually, we may say, perpetually, defeated, he resolved that he would never rest until he was revenged.

His continual failures were made the subject of constant remark and jeering.

His friends and acquaintances were continually throwing his failures in his teeth.

Knowing that this would never cease until he gained the day, he resolved to try once more.

We shall see how Robin came to know of this, and how the brave outlaw punished him for his next attempt.

Meanwhile, until his merry men collected around him at the trysting place, he passed his time in hunting and hawking.

The latter pastime was a great source of delight to Maid Marian, who selected it in preference to any other game, because it enabled her to enjoy horse exercise.

The autumn was advancing, and on the day fixed for the festival, which took place every month, Robin and Maid Marian went out riding.

Maid Marian lead the way, for she had her reasons. At the end of one of the avenues in the forest, they came in sight of two other riders, one a lady the other a knight.

It was Sir Ralph and Agnes, with a number of friends behind, and also men-at-arms.

"How came they here?" said Robin.

"My dear good Robin," said Maid Marian, with a merry laugh, "you have been so dull lately that I thought you wearied of my company. I have therefore sent for your old friends to cheer you up."

"Beshrew me," cried Robin, "but you wrong me. I have not been well, but weary of my Marian—never!"

His wife smiled, but shook her head.

"Men are such fickle creatures," she said, "one knows not how to believe them. I verily believe to keep up their spirits they should woo a fresh lass every year, if only to keep up the excitement."

Robin laughed. He knew that Marian was but speaking to cheer him, so without continuing a discussion which might lead him too far he rode to greet his guests.

Sir Ralph and Lady Agnes Tressilian looked as well and happy as ever.

The episode of Lucy was fortunately a secret.

Such events are truly but episodes in a man's life, though to a woman they are so serious.

"Well met, my gallant Robin. I come in answer to the invitation of your worthy dame, for self and wife to spend a day or so in the forest, where I am always happier than elsewhere."

"Except," said Agnes, merrily, "when shooting by moonlight in your own park."

"'Tis a remnant of my forest learning," replied Ralph, blushing to the eyes. " I am half an outlaw."

Why did Ralph blush ?

Was it because Lucy dwelt in his village now, and sometimes roamed in the park at nights ?

Ah me ! Men will be deceivers ever.

As soon as the first greetings were over, Maid Marian, who had constituted herself hostess, rode forward until they reached a point of the wood whence a scene could be distinguished that called for a cry from Sir Ralph.

"What have we here," he said ; "you have made the forest as gay as a May-day bride !"

The words of Sir Ralph gave a good idea of the picture which was presented to his eye. It was, indeed, like a May-day pageant, or like one of those scenes which we now-a-days see upon the stage, but which are but feeble representations of those that in former times were constantly acted in reality.

Though, it is true, we form exaggerated images of many things which we do not behold, imagination presents but a very faint idea of the splendour and decoration of those ages—when sumptuary laws were enacted in various countries to prevent peasants from displaying gold and silver embroidery in their garments.

What may be called representation was a part of that epoch.

It was in every palace and in every castle, at the table of the grave citizen with his gold chain, in the arm-chair of the justice, in the hall of the franklin.

It sat upon the forked beard of Chaucer's merchant, it appeared in the party-coloured garments of the gallant of the court.

In short, a great part of everything in that day was effect ; it was one of the great objects of the age, and all classes of people had an eye for it.

Perhaps in everything, as in their great buildings, their taste was better than our own—in very few points could it be worse ; and in consulting what is bright and pleasing to the eye, what is exciting and dazzling to the imagination, they followed where nature led—nature who delights in striking contrasts, as much as in gentle harmonies.

If, indeed, we can form a very faint idea of the splendour of the court and the castle, our conception is still more inadequate of the picturesque decoration of humble scenes in those days.

We are apt to conceive that it was all rude or gross ; and we scarcely believe in the charms of the merry morrice dance, in the graces and attractions that sported round the May-pole, in the moonlight meetings which old Fitzstephen records, or in, and of, the sweeter or more gentle pleasures and pastimes of the peasantry of old England ; and yet all these things were true, all were enacted by living beings like ourselves upon every village green throughout the land, long before a feeble mockery of them crept into a close and stifling play-house.

Whether planted by accident or design I know not, but at the side of one of the little savannahs I have described, where the grass was short and dry, six old oaks came forward from the rest of the wood, three on either hand, at the distance of about forty feet apart, forming a sort of natural avenue.

Their long branches stretched across and nearly met each other, and under this natural canopy was spread out the long table, prepared for the knight's repast ; while from bough to bough above, crossing each other in various graceful sweeps, were innumerable garlands, forming a net-work of forest flowers.

The board, too—let not the reader suppose it was rude and bare, for it was covered with as fine linen as ever came from the looms of Ireland or Saxony.*

The board had a nosegay laid where every man was expected to sit, and the ground beneath was strewed with rushes and green leaves to make a soft resting-place for the feet.

Under the trees were gathered together various groups of stout archers in their peculiar garb, with many a country girl from the neighbouring villages, all in holiday apparel.

* We need not refer the learned reader to the curious investigations of M. Le Grand. The above, however, we may add, is strictly historical.

A number of young countrymen, too, were present, showing that the rovers of the forest were at no great pains to conceal their place of meeting ; for their lawless trade found favour in the sight of the many, and their security depended as much upon the confidence and goodwill of the lower orders as upon the dissensions and disunion of the higher classes.

The first sight of the knight and the outlaw caused not a little bustle amongst the companions of the latter. There was running here and there, and putting things in array ; and it was very evident, that although expected and prepared for, everything was not quite ready when the knight arrived.

"Give him good morrow—give the noble knight good morrow !" cried the forester, putting his horn to his lips, and waving his hand for a signal.

Every man followed his example, and in a moment the whole glades of the forest rang with the sound of the merry horn. Not a note was out of tune, no two were inharmonious, and, as with a long swell and fall the mellow tones rose and died away, the effect in that wild yet beautiful scene was not a little striking and pleasant to the ear.

"Yeomanly! yeomanly! right yeomanly done !" cried Robin Hood. "This is the way, my friend, that we receive a true friend to the English commons and the good old Saxon blood. Will you please to dismount, and taste our cheer ? If yonder cooks have not done their duty, and got all ready, I will fry them in their own grease, though I guess from yon blazing log that they are somewhat behindhand."

As he spoke he fixed his eye upon a spot, to which those of the knight followed them, where a scene not quite harmonious with the poetry of the rest of the arrangement was going on, but one very satisfactory to the hungry stomachs of the knight's retainers.

An immense pile of blazing wood, fit to have roasted a bullock, whole, was crackling, and hissing, and roaring so close to a distant angle of the wood, that the flames scorched the green leaves of the farther side.

Beside it were some five men, in clean white jackets, running hastily about, and basting sundry things of a very savoury odour, which, by the contrivance of small chains and twisted strings, were made to revolve before the fire.

Each man was glad enough to keep to windward of the blaze ! and, even then, full many a time were they forced to run to a distance for cool air and free breath, for the heat was too intense for any one to endure it long without suffering the fate of the immense masses of meat which were turning before it.

About fifty yards from this burning mountain was a lesser volcano, over which, upon primitive tripods of three long poles, hung sundry pots of vast dimensions, emitting steam very grateful to the nose : while in a cool spot under the trees appeared the no less pleasant sight of two large barrels, one twined round with a garland of young vine-leaves, and the other with a wreath of oak.

A host of drinking cups, fit to serve an army, lay near them, and a man with a mallet was busily engaged in driving a spigot and faucet to give discreet vent to the liquor within.

"Ho, where is Little John ?" cried Robin. "Ah ! ah ! I see him yonder, our jolly master of the revels, basting the cooks for not basting the capons. Hullo ! Little John !"

The tall forester here stepped forward.

He was now in his prime, quite six feet six, with shoulders which seemed as fit to carry a bull as a calf, a round head covered with nut-brown hair, and a face running over with fun and jest.

He had just returned from a journey to Nottingham, there to dispose of certain trifles picked up during the month.

In a few minutes more, by his aid and that of his lieutenants, all was ready.

About a third of those present found seats on the ground, while the rest placed themselves on stools round the table, and it is worthy of remark, that many of the village girls, who had come as guests, preferred the greensward, with a stout young bowman beside them, eating, as was then customary with lovers, out of the same dish.

As Robin gaily remarked, there was plenty of food for

all; for, besides two gigantic barons of beef, there was many a roasted pig of tender age, capons, and fowls and pigeons, a heron here and there, together with that most excellent of all ancient dishes, a bittern made into soup, while in the centre of the table was seen the peacock, with his majestic tail spread out.

Close to the herons, wherever they appeared, had been placed, by order of Little John, who would have his jest at the long-legged fowl, large dishes of magnificent trout.

"There," observed the master of Robin Hood's revels, "the ancient enemies sit down side by side peaceably, to show that man may make friends of all things."

There was no serving at the table of Robin Hood. The knight's good yeomen had fought side by side with the outlaws and fell as easily into the customs of Sherwood as their lord, sitting down pell-mell with the green-coated rangers, attacking the meat as soon as grace was said.

The cooks, themselves, as soon as their functions were done, and the dinner was dished up, took such places as they could find, and every man drawing forth anelace, or dagger, as the case might be, assailed the dish that was before him, and helped his neighbours and himself.

For some time a deep silence fell over the whole party, and less noise attended the proceeding than ever occurs now-a-days, for dishes and platters were all of wood, and the knives were encountered by no forks in those times, so that little clatter accompanied the operation either of carving or eating.

At the end of about ten minutes, some five or six of the younger men rose from various parts of the table, and made an excursion towards the barrels.

They returned loaded with large flagons, and the only act of ceremony which took place was, that Little John himself, with a large blackjack of strong ale in one hand and a stoup of wine in the other, approached Sir Ralph, while another of the band brought a large silver cup and offered him drink.

Thus refreshed, another attack upon the unresisting viands succeeded, after which more tankards of wine were set around for every one to help himself as he liked.

The juice of the grape soon had its effect so far as to quicken the movements of the tongue, and the jests and laughter, and it must be said, noise also, became great.

Such was a monster picnic in Sherwood forest in the days of our forefathers.

Presently dancing began, on which the principal guests adjourned to a small green knoll, whence they could see all that passed.

A merry jovial sight it was, and one to open the heart and make the soul glad to see so many truly enjoying themselves in a harmless and pleasant way.

Suddenly there was a momentary lull.

"Hush!" said Little John, "I heard the blast of a horn."

"I heard it," cried Robin.

"Whence comes it?"

A second horn sounded.

"That is Godfrey's blast at the hollow oak on Mostyn's Edge," said Little John; "a messenger with news."

At this intimation a few looked to their bows, while the country girls ran to the other side of the green.

In a few minutes a mounted man entered the arena.

It was Thomas-a-Gee.

He bowed low to Robin Hood, and intimated he had a word to say.

The outlaw waved his hand for the sports to continue, and then spoke aside.

"No bad news, I hope?" said Sir Ralph, when the short conference was over.

"Only my old friend, the sheriff, at me again. He will never rest until I teach him manners."

"What now?"

"I know not; but some trickery. This interview of the sheriff with Master Blount," said Robin Hood, addressing Little John, "bodes us no good."

"If I can aid you, command me," said Sir Ralph.

"I will give you the first chance," replied the outlaw, laughing; "but I know not yet the danger to be feared. Strike up, music, and you, Will Scarlett, attune your throat to harmony that may suit fair lady's ears."

Will Scarlett did as he was bid, and in this and other

ways the merry men kept up the festivities to a late hour. Next day Sir Ralph and Lady Tressilian left, delighted to see Robin cast off the black melancholy which had assailed him for some days.

The fact was, the outlaw saw a chance of action, which to him was a necessary of existence.

Maid Marian was happy at once, for like a true woman, she was a kind of weather-glass, influenced by her husband's health and spirits.

As soon as his friends had departed, Robin sent the outlaws throughout the forest to scatter abroad, and discover what new scheme was afoot on the part of the Sheriff of Nottingham.

CHAPTER XXIX.

THE SHERIFF AT WORK.

BUT leaving Robin Hood to his devices, we will return to his indefatigable enemy, who seemed unable to rest until such time as he rid the world of a man who had brought him to such constant shame.

Cowardice is ever revengeful, and none are so eager to get up expeditions and forays as those who are afraid to head them themselves.

Sir Thomas Beauchamp returned to Nottingham, to recount his defeat to the bold Captain Mondidier, with fire and fury in his words.

"So the brave Guy of Gisborne hath fallen," said the Norman *reitre*, now able to sit up in an easy chair, with cushions to keep his wounds from being made worse.

"He has fallen. The foul fiend ever fights on the side of this man," cried Sir Thomas.

"He is brave."

"Brave or not, I seek him no more in the forest; and never will I know rest until by some means I catch me this arrant knave, for fear of whom none can ride in forest or follow road."

"You have tried every means. What now?"

"I cannot yet think; but the thought will come. I hate not in vain. You will sup with me alone to-night. Good wine is often good counsel."

"There spake a man of sense."

The proud and purse-proud sheriff, wounded in his tenderest part—not physically, like Mondidier, but mentally—spent the rest of the day shut up in his private room, where, true to his tastes as a jeweller and banker, he often spent hours overhauling his books and making sure of what was owing to him by the various gentry about.

To this sanctum, some weeks after his retreat to Nottingham, he called one Thomas-a-Gee, a satellite of his, but strongly suspected of knowing more of the affairs of the outlaws than any other man in the town.

"So you have come at last," said the haughty sheriff, intending by this style of discourse to alarm the man.

"I came the moment you sent for me, Sir Thomas," said the man.

"Oh! Well, I have some questions to ask, which I wish answered truly."

"I will speak truly."

"When had you your dealings last with any of Robin Hood's gang?" he began.

"Sir!"

"No pretended astonishment. What I ask for I wish to know."

"I never have any dealings with outlaws, please your worship."

"Humph! A man may not be expected to commit himself, truly. Well, who has most dealings with Robin Hood, in all Nottingham town?" continued Sir Thomas.

"Your worship," said the man, with a faint grin.

"Sirrah!" fumed the sheriff.

"Pardon me, sir. I am sure you misunderstand me. Buys not your lordship much store of gold, silver, and precious stones of Master Blount for transmission to London?"

"I do."

"Well, Master Blount is banker-general to the outlaws, who bring him all their spoil."

"And all the precious stones?"

"Spoil."

"The gold?"

" Spoil."

" The silver ?"

" Spoil."

" Merciful heavens ! "

And the sheriff sank back in his chair, overpowered at the magnitude of the dealings which for several years he had been carrying on with the outlaws.

Ever since Robin Hood had commanded the outlaws it had been the practice of himself or one of his lieutenants to bring, under cover of the night, all their store of plunder to Master Blount, who, finding the quantity at times inconveniently large, was obliged to transfer them to the sheriff.

Sir Thomas, who knew how apt lords, ladies, and knights were to raise money on valuables, freely bought, the more that he was troubled with few scruples of conscience.

" The sordid knave ! I'll trounce him ! " cried the sheriff. " But art sure of this ? "

" As that I live."

" Well, keep your own counsel, and we will devise. Do the outlaws bring these things themselves ? "

" So 'tis said."

" Then will we trounce the knave. Say nothing of what I have spoken about, and you shall have rare sport anon."

The man bowed with a grin, satisfied that something had been done to draw suspicion from himself, and then retired.

" Ah ! ah ! we have you, Master Blount," said the sheriff, rubbing his hands, " so you tamper with our enemies, do you ? You shall pay for this, or my name is not Sir Thomas Beauchamp. To-night I will visit you, sirrah—and we shall see. Fines go to the treasury, but a good sop may silence me, Master Blount."

That evening the avaricious sheriff, who combined intense love of money with love of good cheer, feasted with Captain Montdidier, who, brave soldier though he was, was in no hurry to leave quarters where he found himself so comfortable.

The sheriff did not explain his views with regard to Blount to any one, reserving the narrative as a *bon bouche* on his return.

About eight, however, he summoned two serving men, and bidding the Norman and other friends not to spare the wine until his return, went forth, the servitors armed with staves, and he himself with a cloak cast over his rich dress, jewels, and gold chain of office.

The night was dark, but in Nottingham the word of the sheriff was law, and he feared not.

Who would attack a man who was judge and jury too, and who could hang a fellow at pleasure ?

Here, at all events, Sir Thomas could venture to show some little courage.

Walking on through some of the narrow streets, which then formed the lower part of the good town of Nottingham, with the projecting gables of the upper stories shading them from the sun, and nearly meeting overhead, they at length reached a curiously carved and ornamented wooden house, small and sunk in among the others, so as scarcely to be seen by any one passing hurriedly along, like a modest and retiring man jostled back from observation by the obtrusive crowd.

Here Sir Thomas Beauchamp paused, and one of the men was about to knock at the door, when a shrill and mysterious whistle was heard from the opposite side.

" Ah ! what have we here ? " cried the sheriff, while the two men raised their lanterns and clutched their staves.

On the opposite side appeared two ill-looking fellows driving a poor donkey before them.

" What do you here at this time ? " cried the pompous magistrate.

" Poor men whose donkey got loose," said one.

" But why whistle at a donkey ? "

" It's so cold," muttered the men.

" The man is a fool ; go your way, and do not be whistling in Nottingham streets after curfew."

" Certainly not, your worship."

And with these quiet words the men moved a little way on. They were in the dress of charcoal burners, and their animal doubtless served the purpose of bringing the fuel to market.

The servant knocked, and a man putting his head out of a little round window, was addressed by the sheriff.

" Is Master Blount in ? "

" Yes, but—"

" But me no buts, an' you would not stand in the stocks. I am the Sheriff of Nottingham, and must see your master on most important business."

The man closed the window, and after some delay was heard drawing the bolts and bars of the door.

" Why this delay ? " asked the sheriff, angrily.

" My master was about to retire to rest."

" Nonsense ; I dare say he takes his glass o'nights. Show me to his room, I may not tarry."

The old man bustled up stairs, leading the way to the first floor, where he knocked at the door of a large room.

The sheriff followed, leaving his men to keep good guard below.

The door of the apartment was opened.

It was large and ill-furnished. Whatever other tastes the man Blount might possess, he seemed not to care for rich furniture.

There was a bed without curtains.

An old table.

A couple of very wretched chairs, and a very small fire.

But report said that in other parts of the house, where Master Blount did not transact business, people might have found rich and handsome furniture, and young faces and pleasant forms to share his wealth.

Master Blount in every way bore a very ill character for morals, a very excellent one for wealth.

He himself was a thin, skinny anatomy, whose bones were ill covered with the flesh, which he strove to put upon them by daily applications to brawn, capons, and good wine.

" To what do I owe the pleasure of this visit ? " asked he, bowing and scraping as he handed the sheriff a chair. " Is it a pure honour you pay me, or is it business ? "

" That we shall all know anon, master. I must have some talk with you."

" With pleasure, Sir Thomas," said Master Blount, whose jaws, however, chattered.

" You have sold me much silver and gold and many precious stones of late ? " began the sheriff.

" I have."

" Whence came it all ? "

" From my many clients."

" And pray who may they be ? "

" I reveal no names, Sir Thomas ; it is not the custom of a discreet tradesman."

" Shall I tell you ? "

" An you will joke, your worship, you must."

" I joke not, good Master Blount. I am here in all the majesty of the law, and I say your trade is with the outlaws."

" The outlaws ! "

" Never be so astonished, man. I have it on certain authority."

" Pardon me, Sir Thomas—the fact is, I'm so astonished, so confounded, so bewildered ——"

" Hearken, friend Blount," said the sheriff, sternly, " this is a Star Chamber matter. If I mentioned it in my despatches to London you would be exchequered pretty heavily."

" I asseverate ! "

" No lies ! "

" Worthy sir—worshipful sir ——"

" Peace, and hear me. If you will confess that you have dealings with the outlaws I may pardon you."

" If I do may ——"

What form of oath the unfortunate dealer in bullion and diamonds might have taken we are unable to record, as at this moment a most formidable sneeze was heard, the door of a cupboard opened, and a huge figure stepped out half smothered with dust and laughter.

The money-man trembled, while the sheriff shook both with rage and fear.

" I couldn't stand your confounded cupboard any more," said the tall man.

Neither spoke.

" Sorry to disturb you, but must be going. How do ye, sheriff, and how's your friend Montdidier ? "

" Little John ! "

" So you've found your tongue, have you, most wise and potent worship ? "

"Villain, you shall hang for this!"

"Hearkee, friend sheriff; you and I are old acquaintances, and you know that what I say I mean. If you make one cry to alarm a peaceable town I will baste you till you shall be as sore as a hard-worked donkey's back. Sit you there while I go speak to my comrades without. By the mass, if you call out I will burn the house and you in it."

"My house!" cried Master Blount.

"I hope not. By the way, my worthy sheriff, that gold chain of office looks well;" and ere the astonished magistrate could say a word he whisked it off the other's neck on to his own, and descended the staircase, which creaked under his weight.

"The villain!" cried Sir Thomas.

"The monster!" said Master Blount.

"My chain!"

"My good name!"

By degrees, however, the magistrate calmed. He knew that the town would restore him his badge, for was it not lost while endeavouring to capture a notorious outlaw?

"It is no use crying over spilt milk, Master Blount," he said, severely. "I have ample evidence to hang you, now."

"Oh, Lord!"

"Felony without benefit of clergy."

"Mercy!"

"The least is forfeiture of all your goods to the state," went on Sir Thomas.

"Better die! My wife—my poor children!"

"But I am a merciful man," began the sheriff, "and will have regard to your family."

The jeweller groaned. Such mercy as he had to expect from the avaricious sheriff was vain indeed.

"Listen."

But their plan is best developed by subsequent events.

CHAPTER XXX.

FOREST GLIMPSES.

IN the days of Robin Hood there were no chroniclers save the bards and the monks.

As a rule these men sang and wrote only of love and chivalry.

Fortunately Robin Hood made himself such a name as penetrated even the thick skulls of those days, when peer and peasant bowed the knee to power.

We thus have authentic records of our hero's doings, which are, however, nearly all in the form of verse.

But all ancient history almost is contained in heroic verse. Homer told the siege of Troy, and most of us have memory of historic deeds from lays and poetic legends, being always glad to remember—

——that piece of song,
That old and antique song, we heard last night.

The ballads devoted to the exploits of Robin Hood and his bold company of outlaws are amongst the most popular of these interesting remembrances of the past. They breathe of the inflexible heart and honest joyousness of old England; there is more of the national character in them than in all the songs of classic bards or the theories of ingenious philosophers. They are numerous, too, and fill two handsome volumes.

Though Riton, an author ridiculously minute and scrupulous, admitted but eight-and-twenty into his edition, the number might be extended, for the songs in honour of bold Robin were for centuries popular all over the isle, and were they now out of print might be restored, and with additions, from the recitations of thousands, north as well as south.

Though modified in their language, during their oral transmission from the days of King John till the printing-press took them up, they are in sense and substance undoubtedly ancient.

They are the work, too, of sundry bards; some have a Scotch tone, others taste of the English border; but the chief and most valuable portion belongs to Nottinghamshire, Lancashire, Derbyshire, and Yorkshire; and all—and this includes those with a Scottish sound—are in a true and hearty English taste and spirit.

A few of these ballads are probably the work of some joyous yeoman who loved to range the green woods, and enjoy the liberty and licence which they afforded; but we are inclined to regard them chiefly as the production of the rural ballad maker, a sort of inferior minstrel, who, to the hinds and husbandmen, was both bard and historian, and cheered their firesides with those rhymes and ruder legends, in which the district heroes and romantic stories of the peasantry were introduced, with such embellishments as the taste of the reciter considered acceptable.

These ballads, graphic as they are, will, by some be pronounced rude; we must admit, too, that they are often inharmonious and deficient in that sequence of sound, which critics, in these our latter days desire; but the eye, in the times when they were composed, was not called, as now, to the judgment-seat; and the ear—for music accompanies without overpowering the words—was satisfied with anything like similarity of sound. The ballad-maker, therefore, was little solicitous about the flow of his words, the harmony of balanced quantities, or the clink of his rhymes. His compositions, delighting as they did our ancestors, sound rough and harsh in the educated ear of our own times, for our taste is delicate in matters of smoothness and melody. They are, however, full of incident and human character; they reflect the manners and feelings of remote times; they delineate much that the painter has not touched, and the historian forgotten; they express, but without acrimony, a sense of public injury or private wrong; nay, they sometimes venture into the regions of fancy, and give pictures in the spirit of romance. A hearty relish for fighting and fun; a scorn of all that is skulking and cowardly; a love of whatever is free and manly and warm-hearted; a hatred of all oppressors, clerical and lay; and a sympathy for those who loved a merry joke, either practical or spoken, distinguish the ballads of Robin Hood.

That adventure which we are now about to tell is one of the best authenticated and one of the most interesting in all Robin Hood's history.

The day after the interview between Master Blount and the sheriff, the latter was seated in his justice-room, attending to some such petty affair as slitting a poacher's ears or branding a deer-stalker, when a domestic whispered in his ears that a deputation of townsmen wished to see him.

"Show them in, show them in!" cried the sheriff, graciously, "let these knaves stand down. I am always at the beck and call of duty. What is it? some mischief afloat i'faith."

The deputation, a body of jolly citizens, here entered, headed by the cringing Blount.

"Give you good-day," said Sir Thomas. "What can I do for you, my friends?"

"Please, your worship," began the jeweller, "a few of us met this morning, and talking, some bragging was made of the shooting of Yorkshire lads."

"But surely they shoot not better than our Nottingham boys?"

"That has been the matter under discussion, and upon this rose much talk."

"Well?"

"We have therefore come to your worship to ask you to fix a day when there may be a grand shooting match on the borders of the two counties, and we townsmen will find the prize, which shall be an arrow with silver shaft, and head and feathers of gold."

"'Tis a right loyal and joyous proposition," said the sheriff. "And now let the court be adjourned, that we may offer refreshment to our worthy fellow-citizens. Let the men go back to prison—a pack of idle deer-killing knaves."

The poor unfortunates who, like those of later date, "must hang that jurymen may dine," were hurried away, and soon the justice-room became the scene of much feasting, during which the whole plan of the campaign was laid out, the sheriff, however, taking good care not to let out the real truth, which is quaintly enough told by the historian of the time.

"Now it happened that the Sheriff of Nottingham, desirous to seize Robin and some of his merry men, did cry a full fayre play of archery, aware that he would be present at a strife so much after his own heart."

The day was fixed for as soon as proclamation could

be made over the country side, there being no means but common rumour-talk to make such things known.

It was for about a fortnight after the notable plot was laid, and on a spot contiguous to both countries, between Barnesdale wood and Mansfield.

It was an excellent spot, and likely, from its proximity to the leading seats of archery, to attract many comers.

None can help grieving that amongst the many changes of this world, the forest world should have departed.

The green and bowery glades of the old forest, their pleasant places of sport and exercise, the haunts of the wild deer, the wolf, and the boar, the fairy-like dingles and dells, the woodcraft that they witnessed, the scenes and the characters that were peculiar to themselves, have now, alas! passed away from most of the countries of Europe, and have left scarcely a glen where the wild stag can find shelter, or where the contemplative man can pause under the shade of old primeval trees, to reflect upon the past or speculate upon the future.

The antlered monarch of the wood is now reduced to a domestic beast, in a walled park; and the man of thought, however he may love nature's unadorned face, however much he may feel himself cribbed and confined amongst the works of human hands, must shut his prisoner fancy within the bounds of his own solitary chamber, unless he is fond to indulge them by the side of the grand, but monotonous ocean.

The infinite variety of the forest is no longer his; it belongs to another age, and to another class of beings.

In the times I write of it was not so, and the greater part of every country in Europe was covered with rich and ancient wood; but, perhaps, no forest contained more to interest or to excite than that of merry Sherwood—comprising within itself, as the reader knows, a vast extent of very varied country, sweeping round villages, and even cities, and containing in its involutions many a hamlet, the inhabitants of which derived their sustenance from the produce of the forest ground.

The aspect of the wood itself was as different in places as it is possible to conceive.

In some spots the trees were far apart, with a wide expanse of open ground, covered by low brushwood, or the small shrubs bearing the bilberry; in others, you came to a wide extent, covered with nothing but high fern and scrubby hawthorn trees; but throughout a great part of the forest the sun seldom, if ever, penetrated during the summer months, to the paths beneath, so thick was the canopy of green leaves above, while those paths themselves were generally so narrow that in many of them two men could not walk abreast.

There were other and wider ways, indeed, through the wood, some of them cart roads, for the accommodation of woodmen and carriers, some of them highways from one neighbouring town to another, but the latter were not very numerous nor very much frequented—many a tale being told of travellers lightened of their baggage in passing through Sherwood; and, to speak the truth, no one could very well tell at that time who and what were the dwellers in the forest, or their profession, so that those who loved not strange company kept to the more open country if they could.

It was, however, a beautiful ride over almost any part of the woodland, offering magnificent changes of scene at every step, and the people of those times were not so incapable of enjoying it as has been generally supposed; but still, with all the tales of outlaws and robbers which were then afloat, it required a stout determination, or a case of great necessity, to impel any of the citizens of towns in the vicinity to make a trip across the forest in the spring or autumn of the year.

Those who did so, usually came back with some story to tell; and some of the wanderers, indeed, brought home stripes upon their shoulders and empty bags.

The latter, however, were almost always of particular classes.

Rich monks and jovial friars occasionally fared ill, the petty tyrants of the neighbouring shire ran a great risk if they trusted themselves far under the green leaf; the wealthy and ostentatious merchant might sometimes return rather lighter than he went, but the peasant, the honest franklin, the village curate, the young, and women of all degrees, had generally very little to relate, except that they had seen a forester here or a forester

there, who gave them a civil word, and bade God speed them, or who aided them in any case of need with skilful hands and a right good will.

CHAPTER XXXI.
THE TRIAL OF SKILL.

SUCH a spot as that we have endeavoured to photograph to our readers, was the one chosen for the celebration by means of which the sheriff hoped to entrap Robin.

He was, however, but ill-served if he thought that any such enterprise as that he contemplated could be carried out without the outlaw hearing of it.

Though he kept his real intentions secret, his malevolent hatred of the man he had injured was well known, and every act of his was canvassed and talked over in mead, meadow, and village alehouse.

No sooner did the cry go forth as to the match, than people began, naturally enough, to talk it over freely, and while warm discussions arose as to who were likely to be the victors, motives were also mentioned.

The connection of Master Blount with the outlaws was well-known, and yet his secret visits to the sheriff were suspicious.

In Nottingham town were many friends to the brave chief of Sherwood Forest.

Every rumour that got afloat was carried to him.

The "full fayre play" was one temptation, and the natural desire to carry off the palm from Yorkshire was another, and it behoved him to be cautious.

The sheriff was to take the leading part in the display. This of itself was suspicious.

But this would not prevent him from making the trial, though, for the sake of himself and his faithful people, he determined to take every precaution.

He accordingly selected six men to accompany him, whose names are variously given.

One very good authority says, George-a-Green, Reynold Greenleaf, Gilbert of the White Hand, Will Scarlett, Much, and Little John.

Now most of these were personally known to the sheriff, but the outlaw trusted first to their disguises and then to his own wit to extract himself from any difficulty.

His people, or as many of them as it was thought wise to take with them, were to be near at hand.

The day at length came, and from all parts came a large concourse of people to witness that, which in those days was considered far more interesting than a tournament.

Archery was the passion of the English people at that time.

With respect to the origin of archery we know nothing more than that it must have been practised at a very early period; for we are told that Hagar, in order not to see her son die, set herself down a good way off, as it were a bow-shot; and, soon after, it is said that Ishmael dwelt in the wilderness, and became an archer.

The bow and arrow are frequently mentioned in Scripture, more particularly in the accounts of the wars of the Jewish people. Indeed, down to the introduction of gunpowder, bows and arrows were implements of warfare among all nations.

Great dependence was usually placed upon the archers in war; and frequently the success of a battle has been properly attributed to them, as at Cressy, Poictiers, and Agincourt.

It is believed that the long-bow was common in England long before the Saxon invasion. The Saxons were expert archers, both in battle and in field sports. The Normans brought with them the arbalist, or crossbow; but from the reign of Edward II. the long-bow, the favourite national weapon, seems to have been fully established.

Edward III. directed the sheriffs of shires to see that the people exercised themselves in their leisure time in archery, in place of following useless or unlawful games or amusements.

Under Edward IV. a precept was issued, commanding that every Englishman should have a bow of his own height; and butts were ordered to be set up in every township for the inhabitants to shoot at, and if any one neglected the use of his bow he was subject to a fine.

The rifle has now superseded the bow, but as an amusement for the young the use of the latter weapon is unrivalled.

The day, we have said, was fine; and early in the day the butts were placed "under the greenwood shade," and the prize to the victor formally announced.

> "A right good bow he shall have,
> The shaft of silver white,
> The head and feathers of rich red gold;
> In England is none like."
> This then heard he, good Robin,
> Under his trystall tree:
> "Come, make you ready, my wight young men,
> That shooting will I see."

When the outlaw and his friends approached the spot where the trial was to take place all were ready for the strife.

The bold archers, handling their polished yews, stood around, and in the midst the sheriff, busy as sheriff could be.

There was a great array of force to keep the ground, and though the trumpeters announced freedom to all to come and go, even to the outlaws of the forest, Robin, who had small faith, it seems, in this proclamation of peace or assurance of fair play, thus addressed his men:

"Six of you, whom I have already chosen, shall shoot with me for the arrow with the golden head. The others must stand with their bows ready, lest all this should prove to be a plot."

The men acquiesced as in duty bound, and then the whole of the competitors mixed in the crowd as if they had been strangers one to the other.

The sheriff had a large tent, within which he sat, with a table by him, on which was the prize arrow.

A number of flagons and drinking-cups were there for himself and friends, amongst whom was Montdidier, who, though compelled from the peculiarity of his wounds to walk on crutches, still was unable to resist the joyous day, and came in a litter.

There were also numerous royal soldiers, who knew but one thing—duty.

By these the sheriff was safe to be obeyed.

But the scene of the contest being near the highway, a large body of troops was concealed ready for action.

Robin Hood had never been in such terrible peril of his life. Not one of his scouts had brought him news of this complication of the day's troubles.

The butts were set up at no great distance from the tent.

The contest began at the targets.

The Yorkshiremen began with six of their very best men, and all hit the target, but not the bull's-eye.

Six Nottingham boys followed.

The same result followed, the distance of a hundred and fifty yards making this very good shooting.

Will Scarlett stept in and hit the plum centre; behind him came Little John, who clove his arrow in twain, in which he was imitated by all his comrades, Robin alone not shooting.

The clamour was now great.

Fresh Nottingham men stood up, and with great success. Yorkshire men followed with the same.

The crowd began to shout and bet at a great rate.

Now the Nottingham men had the day, then the Yorkshire men.

Upon this all agreed to change the butt for the wand.

This was the signal for intense excitement, as it was now certain that none but the very best archers would venture to make the trial.

The outlaws had been the best shooters, so that the other Nottingham men, whose only desire was to win, allowed them to stand forward and shoot.

The Yorkshire people chose the best on their side. They shot first.

One hit it, two grazed, the rest were wide.

> Thrice Robin he shot about
> And always slit the wand;
> And so did good Gilberte
> With the white hand.
> Little John and Will Scarlett
> Were archers good and free;
> And Little Muche and good Reynold
> The worst they would not be.

But if Robin's men shot well, he hit the mark with every shaft he discharged. Indeed the best, ablest, and most concise of the outlaw's historians says, " It came to Robin's turn, and he discharged three arrows at the wand with such rapidity, that, but for seeing the three transfix it, and none else but him firing, they would not have credited it."

A fearful shout now arose; the Yorkshire men who would generally have allowed themselves defeated, had one or two among the lot who were greatly inclined to wrangle.

But those around the sheriff cried shame, and he was compelled to interpose his authority, and declare that the Nottingham men had won the prize.

"Let the one who shot last come up and take the silver arrow, for it is his rightfully," he said.

Robin spoke in whispers to his men, and then approached the spot where the sheriff's tent was situated.

All the competitors save the outlaws, followed, the Nottingham men making Robin Hood, who was unknown to them, their leader.

He wore a rich dress, as if he had been some nobleman fitted for the day, with a jewel in his cap, and walked with the commanding step of a free and undaunted Englishman.

The sheriff stood up impatient to see if his hopes were at last about to be realised.

The outlaw separated himself from his party and stood before the sheriff, his head bowed, as if with proud humility.

"This is the prize, fellow," he said.

"Thanks," replied Robin, placing the arrow in his belt.

"By the Holy Rood!" cried Sir Thomas Beauchamp, "'tis that rantipole knave, Robin Hood! Seize him!"

And there was great clamour, the sheriff causing great horns to blow.

"Silence!" said Robin, looking calmly round upon the throng, "the sheriff did cry a fayre play, and all, to the outlaws of the forest, were to come and go freely."

"Except thee, thou arrant knave."

"Let he who would take me come," said Robin.

"Down with the thief! Take his silver arrow from him!" cried some few of the defeated Yorkshiremen.

"Shame! shame!" cried the Nottingham men, "bilboes, bilboes."

A scuffle ensued, during which Robin, after severely punishing one or two who rashly tried to arrest him, made away and joined his men.

The sheriff was frantic, as it was clear he might escape if something were not done.

> Full many a bow there was ybent,
> And arrows there let glide;
> Full many a kirtle there was rent,
> And wounded many a side.
> Little John, he was hurt full sore
> With an arrow in the knee,
> That he might neither run nor ride;
> It was a great pitie.

The fact is, that while the rival Yorkshire and Nottingham men were indulging in the pleasures of an Irish row, the sheriff had ordered up his men-at-arms and bowmen, who were posted on all sides.

CHAPTER XXXII.

A HAVEN OF SAFETY.

ROBIN and his men, about seven score in number, retreated steadily; but that they would soon be overpowered was evident.

Only the masterly way in which the outlaw and his lieutenants managed their small forces enabled them to keep back their assailants.

Suddenly Robin Hood sounded a merry blast.

Then from the skirt of the forest rushed his reserve, who momentarily checked the pursuers.

This enabled the whole party to reach the forest.

From its skirts they poured such incessant flights of arrows as to force the enemy to reform.

This gave them a respite.

Now it was they discovered the bulky and brave lieutenant was wounded.

"Master mine," said Little John, when this did befal, "I can go no farther. Let not the proud sheriff find me alive, nor leave him a neck to hang me by. I conjure you, by the faithful service I have done you, to take out your broad sword rather, and strike off my head!"

The brave outlaw chief at once declined to do anything so harsh and cruel to his friend.

He, however, ordered a retreat as soon as the wound of Little John had been bound up.

"I shall only be a trouble to you," said Little John, as he found himself urged on by the support of Robin and Will Scarlett; "I pray you leave me."

"We will all perish first," said Robin.

A halt was now declared, that the chief might look about him and direct the line of march.

They were at the bottom of a valley, the sides of which were so thickly coated with trees that none could pass between them; while the bottom of the valley was the bed of a sparkling stream.

"Who lives hereabout?"

"I," said George-a-Green.

"Is this river deep?"

"I have walked down it fishing, many a time."

"'Tis well. Let every man post himself where he can at the first *mot* (pronounced *mo*) drop into the water. Hide all."

The outlaws obeyed; and when the sheriff with some hundred of his men came in sight, not an outlaw was to be seen.

Robin Hood, Will Scarlett, and some of the picked men of the party surrounded Little John, who had lost much blood, but whose awkward wound in the knee Friar Tuck was now carefully dressing.

The giant had lost more blood than he was used to, and it made him pale and weak.

He looked at the formidable array of the enemy.

"Robin," he said, "you were never so hard set in all your life. I shall only be a burden to you."

"Never. If we cannot take you, we will rather stay and fight it out—"

"Better cut my head off," murmured Little John.

"I would not that," said Robin then,
"John, that thou wert slawe,
For all the gold in merry England,
Though it lay there in a raw."
Up then he took him on his back,
And bore him well a mile,
And many a time he laid him down,
And shot another while.

As soon as the king of Sherwood had satisfied Little John that he would neither cut off his head nor leave him, he gave a low signal to his men, who, having ambushed themselves according to their individual tastes, gave the enemy so warm a reception as to lay many of them low.

Before they could respond to the volley of the outlaws, the bugle note was sounded, and the merrie men, by order of their leader, slipped into the stream and descended it in good order.

It was not very wide, so that a dozen men served as a good rear-guard; a large body of men-at-arms and bowmen following in their train.

They, however, did not attempt any further attack on the archers of Sherwood forest, but kept them in sight.

"Hem!" said Robin Hood.

"What is it?" asked Will Scarlett.

"I like not the look of things."

"Why?"

"These men are but a feint. There are not a hundred of them."

"The others?"

"Are in front."

"Oh!"

"We could cut through them easily, and thus outwit the main body, but first of all Little John must be thought of."

"No, no!" cried the wounded giant, "I will not be the cause of ruin to my king and lord."

"Silence," said Robin Hood; "I leave you not. I stand or fall by those who would stand or fall by me."

A low murmur of approval from the outlaws was the reward of this declaration.

"Will Scarlett!"

"Here!"

"Do you choose twenty picked men; the passage is narrow here—hold it, until I sound the retreat. Then haste to join me," continued Robin.

As soon as these words were spoken, Robin Hood, with the rest of his men, retreated about a hundred yards, and then gave a whispered order.

In a quarter of an hour a capital litter, made from two stout poles, with transverse pieces, and a bed of leaves, grass, and coats, was made, upon which Little John was placed.

Six stout outlaws then bore him along.

The chief then bade his followers guard the valiant giant with their lives, sounded the retreat for Will Scarlett, and with Much the miller and Thomas-a-Green, entered the forest and glided towards the front.

He was quite certain that Sir Thomas, with his cavalry and a large body of archers, had gone forward to waylay them from some cunningly devised ambuscade.

It was well that Robin Hood was a good general, for had he not acted thus prudently he might with his whole force have perished miserably.

The valley widened as they advanced, while the larger trees grew less densely together, though the underbrush was still thick.

Through this Robin made his way for some time, not a word being said by himself or his companions.

The outlaw was listening with the keen ear and quick sensitiveness of the Red Indian, whose acuteness in the forest and plain he so nearly rivalled.

At last the sound of horsemen at no great distance made him pause and look around.

In front of him there was a wooded slope, to his right the river and a wooded plain.

Over the trees towered a proud castle.

"Whose towers are those?" asked Robin.

"'Tis the castle of Sir Richard of the Lea," replied Thomas-a-Green.

"Nonsense!" cried the outlaw, "if this be his castle, how is it that he needed a loan of us?"

"Ah, but captain," said Thomas-a-Green, who was a rare frequenter of inns and collector of gossip, "since you befriended him he has become a rich man, at least his son has. His wife turned out to be a very great heiress, and this castle came to her in fief."

"By our lady, an men be not very much changed," replied Robin, "we have found a way out of this scrape."

"How, master?"

"I think we could hold yonder castle against the sheriff."

"Of course, if we could get inside."

"That I hope we may do."

"How so?"

"Go thou, Thomas-a-Green, and gain an entry. Tell Sir Richard of the Lea that Robin Hood, beleaguered by an overwhelming force in the forest, asks hospitality for himself and wounded."

"Excellent well, master."

"Wait."

"Speak, master."

"Say I can hold my post for some hours, until nightfall, in fact; but my men are weary, my wounded many, and all of us in great need of food—that will suffice. But add, that 'twill be best not to send an answer until dark. If we are hard pressed I will sound my bugle."

Thomas-a-Green bowed, and started down the stream to obey the orders of his captain.

In a very short time the whole body of outlaws came in sight, slowly retreating with their burthen.

Robin, as soon as they were close to him, so posted them that only a powerful hand-to-hand conflict could dislodge them.

In this way they waited for the night to come.

When Sir Thomas found that the outlaw had intrenched himself in the wood, he commanded every avenue to be guarded, satisfied that this time he had Robin Hood in a trap from which he could not hope to escape.

He then ordered some of his men to go round and levy supplies on franklin and peasant in the name of the law and the redoubtable sheriff of Nottingham.

JUSTICE! JUSTICE!

Upon the edge of the merry forest-land, on the side nearest to Derbyshire, not far from the little river Lind, and surrounded at that time by woods which joined the district on to Sherwood itself, there rose, in the days I speak of, a Norman castle of considerable extent. It had been built in the time of William Rufus, had been twice attacked in the turbulent reign of Stephen, had been partly dismantled by order of Henry II., and had been restored but recently. Being not far from Nottingham, it was frequently visited by noble and royal personages, and was often the scene of the splendid and ostentatious hospitality of the old baronage of England.

It has now crumbled down, indeed, and departed; the ploughshare has passed over most of its walls, and the voice of song and merriment is heard in it no more. The lower part of one of the square flanking-towers in the outer wall is all that remains of the once magnificent castle; and a dingley copse, where many a whirring pheasant rises before the sportsman, now covers the hall and the lady's bower.

In the days of which we speak, however, it was in its greatest splendour, having come into the possession of Sir Richard's son, through his wife, and being the favourite dwelling of the race. It was situated upon a gentle eminence, and the great gate commanded a view over some sixty or seventy acres of meadow-land, lying between the castle and the nearest point of the wood; and for the distance of nearly three miles on the Sherwood side, though there was no cultivated land, except, indeed, a few detached fields here and there, the ground assumed more the aspect of a wild chase than a forest, with the thick trees grouping together to the extent of an acre or two, and then leaving wide spaces between, as pasture for the deer and other wild animals, only broken by bushes and hawthorns.

This district was properly within the limits of Sherwood; but, as all persons know who are acquainted with the forest law, certain individuals frequently possessed private woods in the royal forest, which was the case with Sir Richard; and, whether or not he had originally any legal right of chase therein, such a privilege had been secured to the manor in the previous reign by the king's special grant and permission. His rights of vert and venison, as they were called, extended over a wide distance around; and it was reported that some disputes had arisen between himself and his sovereign, whether he had not extended the exercise of those rights somewhat beyond their legitimate bounds.

Except that they dressed differently, and used different weapons, nor knew ought of gunpowder, guns, electricity and a lot of other things, the result of scientific discovery, and without which, while the island was less thickly peopled, they seem to have done very well, our ancestors were very much like ourselves.

They had the same feelings, the same emotions, the same love of family, the same tenderness to women—all but the brutes, and they are not worth mentioning—which belong to us of a later date.

The home of an Englishman has ever been his castle, but also his delight, and that of which we must offer a few words, formed no exception to this good old rule.

The great hall of the castle was the favourite sojourn of the family. It was large, lofty, spacious, with more light than any other apartment, while all around its walls were the trophies of the chase, and above all a goodly collection of arms, such as spears, two-handed swords, war clubs, battle axes, and above all bows, strings, gloves and traces, self-bows and back bows, quivers, belts and arrows.

In a large arm-chair, on one side of the vast fireplace, whose huge gulf would have swallowed an ox, and whose handsome and fanciful andirons * could have supported the largest beam ever carted for fuel, sat Sir Richard of the Lea.

On the opposite side of the fireplace, in a similar arm-chair, sat his worthy dame, who, though the mother of a stalwart son, was still young looking and handsome.

Standing near his mother were her son and son's wife, the latter admiring the beautiful child of about a year old which the proud nurse held up for inspection with some of the usual small talk which appertains to nurses in all ages and times.

"Brave as his father, beautiful as his mother," she cried enthusiastically.

"Seems to me," said the young knight somewhat grimly, "that one can scarce tell him from any other baby at this age."

"Oh," said the mother.

"Fie,"

"I am shocked at you, son of mine," said the grandmother.

Well, if she felt so she only smiled.

"Well Gurtha," continued the father, "you know best. But take him now to his room. I will ride abroad an hour—what haste, Hardy?"

"A messenger from the forest."

"Admit him."

Thomas-a-Green at once stepped over the threshold, cap in hand, to where the happy group stood.

Despite themselves a gloom fell over the whole party.

"What message bring you, my man?"

"From Robin Hood."

"Speak it aloud, then," cried Sir Richard of the Lea, rising with haste and pleasure; "a message from the noble outlaw in this house is a command."

Thomas-a-Green bowed low, and delivered his message without further hesitation.

No sooner had the two men heard it, than, while the women looked alarmed and fearful, he and his son hastened to reply.

"All within this castle is your master's," said the former, "eh, my son?"

"My father has but spoken the truth. While you, Sir Richard, see the men prepared for defence, I will to join the merry men. You will accompany, master yeoman."

Nothing further was needed.

Gratitude for the past existed in a lively degree in the bosom of that family, and they would no more have thought of refusing shelter and protection to the out-

laws, at the peril of their lives, than of giving up the weekly dole paid out to the begger at their gate for charity.

Every castle in those days of rapine, slaughter, and intrigue, had its secret door.

It was a necessary part of the domestic economy of a chivalrous knight to be able to retire unnoted to the forest.

That by which the young knight led the outlaw opened into the forest, after crossing a moat.

They were thus able to reach the spot where the outlaws were in ambuscade without difficulty.

The meeting between the outlaw and the young knight was most cordial.

No time, however, was wasted in idle compliments.

Robin Hood had learned by means of his scouts, that the sheriff's forces were busy cooking and feeding.

Some sentries only guarded the lines.

None seemed to have been placed on the side of the small plain between the front of the castle and the wood.

The knight and Robin Hood soon, therefore, altered their plans.

The distance was small.

At the first approach of the outlaws the drawbridge would be lowered and the gates opened.

They would start the party with Little John at a quick trot in advance, and the main body would bring up the rear.

Before the enemy could recover from their surprise the merry men would be safely housed.

No sooner had this been decided on than it was put into action. Little John, who, though suffering acutely, bore his pain with all the coolness and energy of a Spartan boy, was lifted up, and at as rapid a pace as his bearers could assume, the litter was taken towards the castle.

A loud shout from the scouts at the top of the hill awoke the attention both of Sir Richard and Sir Thomas.

The royal and local troops began rushing to their arms, but those who were near enough to be reached, received such a volley as threw them into a state of utter confusion.

Robin made his men retreat in solemn order, not giving a step more than was absolutely necessary.

His eye was on the castle gates, to which the litter was being hurried.

Presently it disappeared.

With a joyous shout Robin Hood gave the signal to his men, who, one and all, took to their heels with a rapidity quite marvellous.

When the sheriff and his men arrived the gates were closed, the drawbridge up.

Nothing was to be seen but one sentinel on the look-out battlement.

The sheriff, furious at this disappointment, which capped all those which had ever occurred to him in connection with Robin Hood, now furiously hailed the castellan.

Sir Richard came to the battlements.

"Who hails so furiously?"

"I, Thomas Beauchamp, Sheriff of Nottingham, and representative of his majesty, I'd have you know."

"Then all I can say is, that his majesty has a very ill-mannered representative," was the calm reply.

A titter from the soldiers did not tend to the sheriff's good humour.

"Do I speak to Sir Richard?"

"You do."

"Then I demand, under threat of all the direst pains and penalties of the law, that you yield up an arch traitor who has just entered within your gates."

"A sick man, guarded and supported by his friends, has craved my hospitality, and I have given it."

"Do you know the man?"

"I never ask impertinent questions," said Sir Richard of the Lea with extreme dryness.

Fresh titter—fresh fury.

"You have given shelter to Robin Hood and Little John, thieves, murderers, and traitors."

"Indeed."

"If you do not surrender them, you will be punished severely."

"You had better come and take them," said Sir

---

* *Andiron*, a contrivance which was, in old English houses and halls, made use of to assist in the burning of the logs of wood placed upon the hearth. In old inventories of furniture, the term is frequently employed; and at the present time is sometimes used for what is more commonly called a fire-dog. The andirons were used in pairs, one on each side of the hearth. The logs of wood were placed upon the horizontal bars, the upright portion, or standard, being merely ornamental. The standard frequently bore the armorial bearings of its owner; and sometimes arabesques, or other designs, were traced upon it in silver, particularly in the reign of James I. At a later period, the upright portion of the andiron was often fashioned to represent a human figure. In the hall at Penshurst, Kent, a large andiron is still to be seen standing upon the hearth.

Richard hotly; "did I not know, that despite your low chapman manner you did disgrace the magistracy by being sheriff of Nottingham, I would put an arrow through you. Away! lest my forbearance cease."

The sheriff, with a quivering lip, choked with emotion, retreated somewhat, and then gave advice to his men to surround the castle on every side.

"I will have Robin out of that, if I tear it down stone by stone," he said.

Which promise conveying the idea of a long siege, his lieutenants suggested that they should eat and sleep upon the resolution, which the stout knight approving of, the whole party retreated.

They were now full seven hundred in number, and quite capable, therefore, of attacking even so well appointed a castle, but as night was fast approaching and all had the appetite of wolves, they were glad to surround the castle with a chain of sentries and then betake themselves to feasting.

CHAPTER XXXIII.

OF A WONDERFUL ADVENTURE THAT BEFEL LITTLE JOHN.

The reception which Robin Hood met with in the castle was all he could wish.

His loan of four hundred pounds had been the turning point in the fortunes of the family, and they knew it.

As a rule benefits conferred make enemies, or turn devoted into lukewarm friends, but never where the intellect is bright and clear and the true heart in the right place.

Then an act of kindness binds a man to you for aye!

The first thing done was to provide a bedroom for Little John, the exertions he had made having swollen his leg very much.

Fortunately the family chaplain was a bit of a leech.

In his hands, after every detail had been seen to, the patient was placed.

All this while the servants, cooks and others, had been at work preparing a banquet, Homeric in its character, for the famished outlaws.

The banquet took place in the huge banquetting hall of the castle—none of your little modern dining rooms, but with tables for a hundred and fifty.

Everything was on a gigantic scale in those days of giants.

The outlaws, less provident than our moderns, had taken no provision to their shooting match.

They were famished.

It was a sight to see the viands vanish before the hungry men. But the supply was greater than the demand, and the moment came when all cried enough.

Robin then retired with the family, leaving his men and officers to the kindness of the attendants.

The outlaw chief, after a pleasant hour with the women of the family, remained alone with the father and the son.

"My good friends," he said, after some indifferent discourse, "I wish now to explain my views."

"We listen with profound attention."

"If my dearest friend and most faithful companion, Little John, had not been wounded severely, I would never have done you so ill a turn as to come here."

"I should never have forgiven you if you had passed by."

"You speak like a hospitable host and a noble knight," continued Robin; "that I expected. But by acting as I have done, I have brought you into serious trouble."

"My friend, when I was in trouble, you did not hesitate to save me," replied Sir Richard.

"That was money," said Robin, laughing; "that matters not—a man's purse is not his castle."

"It is often dearer."

"True; but you have made an enemy—a bitter, savage, and unforgiving enemy."

"A fico!"

"One who will give you no peace by flood or field—who will haunt you at bed and board—a fiend in human shape."

"And what am I, Robin, that I should care for Sir Thomas Beauchamp?" said Sir Richard.

"A brave and stalwart knight, and a good servant of the king," replied Robin. "But you live in troublous times. This part of England is full of traitors and rebels, who will gladly make any excuse to injure you. Should this man by stratagem or force possess himself of your person, he will slay you."

"My friend, I am a soldier."

"And so am I; therefore listen to my plans."

"We listen."

"The sheriff will probably not use all his strength at once. He knows we are many. Let us then make a sturdy defence for a day,—say to morrow,—and then we will secretly glide from the castle, and scouts shall let the sheriff know. You will have thus done your duty to your friends, and at the same time we shall relieve you from further trouble by disappearing at night."

"Robin Hood," said Sir Richard of the Lee, with deep and earnest feeling, "me and mine feel to you as men rarely do feel to others. At a time when I had not a friend in the world you stepped in to save one wholly a stranger to you. I say then again, to put you wholly at your ease, command me, command all. Whatever you may decide is law."

"Then I command you to send the womenfolk to bed, and let me have that which I seldom do have—a jolly carouse," cried Robin, throwing his cap into the air.

The father and son laughed heartily, and going forth, told the dames what King Robin Hood had decided; at which, with many a wise shake of the head and look of virtuous indignation, the ladies went laughingly to bed, as good wives should do who love their lords and have tolerable faith in their discretion.

A few minutes later the table in the sitting hall was loaded with wine, and one or two plates-full of salt things by way of a relish, and all was ready for the carouse.

But the outlaw bethought him that they had not yet visited Little John; and fearful that the wine might make him make a hole both in his memory and his manners, he resolved to see the huge lieutenant.

Carrying out the orders which had been given, the worthy father who served as leech had visited the outlaw and reported favourably as to the patient, so that all went slowly and quietly to the corridor in which he slept, hoping to find him asleep.

Dark and gloomy was the passage which led from the more noisy part of the house to that quiet dormitory where Little John had been placed that he might sleep.

Entering upon its confines, Robin led the way, but at once distinguished a confused clamour of voices.

"Friar Tuck, by the Lord!" said the outlaw, in a low tone. "He is in hot disputation with your chaplain."

"Good sooth! they are well met," replied Sir Richard, "for they are equally fond of good liquor. There's my hedge priest would fain consume it all himself, while yours would dispense it."

"Hang that priest!" said Robin. "I'll bet a rose-noble he is trying to make Little John drink."

"I have no doubt of it," replied Sir Richard.

"John, my friend," they could hear the friar say, "am I not an old friend, and will you not take my advice? A jug of ale is the best remedy. Drink, boy, drink! That's the way!"

"Kenwood, the holy father, who has written on arrow wounds," replied the other priest, "hath said that ale hot, ale cold, ale spiced, ale in any shape, is bad."

"Lo! how he blasphemeth!"

"Many cooks spoil the broth," said Little John, "and many doctors kill the patient. Decide between you, for I have much need of rest."

On entering the room, the whole party found Little John lying on his bed with a woeful and somewhat comic countenance, gazing at the two monks, who, with clenched fists, were arguing violently one against the other, according to their several views.

"Pretty doctors, doctors of evil," said Robin, "what are you about with my patient? Begone, both of you, to the kitchen, and end me your quarrel there with quarter-staves if you please. Send some nice quiet girl to nurse Little John, and give him cooling drinks."

"Queer company for a sick man," quoth Friar Tuck.

"Rather say proper company. Avaunt!"

"So—this is the way I am treated," said Tuck, maundering.

To settle the matter, Robin pushed the two priests out of the room, and, after a short conversation with Little John, perceiving that the giant forester really was sleepy, left him, and returned towards the hall, where the most wonderful preparations had been made for their carouse.

Uncommonly large logs were piled on the huge andirons, while fruit, pastry, and salt meats had been placed beside the wine, such notable devices for promoting intoxication and dissipation being perfectly well known to the ancients, who excelled us, however, greatly in the quantity, if not the quality, of what they consumed.

Various wines graced the board, but the principal and favourite wine of all classes in those days was Burgundy.

Wine is a very good friend, but a bad enemy; on the present occasion, however, all were too glad to have met not to put aside every other consideration but that of enjoying themselves.

Xerotes, or a dry habit of body, should be an uncommon complaint in this country, as we seem to do all we can to cure it by means of imbibing good liquors.

Yeomen were the men who could do it, and in this, despite his claims to nobility, Robin was quite a yeoman.

Zealous were his friends, for they too on this occasion showed themselves true Englishmen, nor did the festivities cease until they were summarily interrupted in the morning by events which will be recorded in their proper place.

CHAPTER XXXIV.

OF A WONDERFUL ADVENTURE WHICH BEFEL LITTLE JOHN—(Continued.)

THE brave outlaw who gives his name to this narrative was never in his life so glad of anything as of the departure of the two drunken and quarrelsome priests.

He was tired, he was faint and wanted repose. The ladies of the house had seen to everything he could require, such as nourishing and refreshing broths, so that the effort made by the worthy friar to intoxicate him was a pure work of superorogation.

As soon, therefore, as the priests had retired, Little John closed his eyes and tried to sleep.

But sleep, alas, is one of those things which we cannot put around us like a cloak, when we will, but must be wooed, and coyly too, or else it flies hastily from our embraces.

Little John was in pain, and finding that he did not go off into a sudden sleep, but dozed only, began thinking of the events of the day. and then of the events of the week, and then of a lot of other events much older, until he began to find them very much muddled up and confused.

And then we suppose Little John slept.

Well, so we must suppose, though little John declared in strict confidence long after, when what happened was a very good joke, that he really had not all the while relapsed into unconsciousness.

However this may be, whether he was lying or not half asleep and half awake, or wholly awake, the stalwart outlaw felt unmistakably two warm lips pressed close to his own, which warm lips gave him a most unmistakable kiss, and then were removed.

Now Little John was as artful as a fox.

It occurred to him that if this kiss was given to him under the impression that he was asleep, if he opened his eyes or moved his lips, or in any way showed that he was aware of what had happened, he should not have the pleasure or satisfaction of having the event repeated.

Now Little John was ready to swear on his solemn oath, that the lips which had pressed his belonged to both a young and a pretty woman, and though under the circumstances young and pretty women may be bold enough, yet is there nothing they object to so much as being found out.

But though Little John lay still, the effect was not repeated, and after a while, he therefore slowly opened his eyes, and looked around.

The room which he occupied was large, with a window over-looking the private garden of Lady Lee.

Its window was stained.

The room was richly furnished, with numerous hangings of excellent tapestry.

There was a low fire in the large fireplace, which could have taken a cart-load of wood, if needed.

But at none of these did Little John look. His eyes were fixed on the dainty figure of a young woman or girl, who sat near a half distinguished lamp, musing.

That she was young, fresh, and handsome, Little John could have sworn, and yet that did not satisfy him, he must see her face.

The giant forester groaned.

Now he was not in any particular pain, so his groan was what the French call a *ruse*.

Of course he knew that the maiden fair was placed there to nurse him, and he was particularly desirous to see what kind of lips were those which had kissed him.

As soon as the artful outlaw uttered his moan of pain, the girl rose, poured out some drink from a vase, under which burnt a night light, and approached the bed.

As if to guard against the chill of a night watch, she wore a cloak and hood.

Envious cloak, envious hood.

She put her hand, it was a very soft one, under his head, and lifted it so that he might drink.

"Thank you," sighed the giant.

The maiden dropped his head, and raised the light. She saw at once that he was wide awake and better.

"Were you thirsty?"

"Very."

"Are you sleepy?"

"No."

"But you ought to be," she said; "I was told by the lady of the Lea not to let you talk."

"That voice!" cried Little John.

"Oh!"

"That voice!"

"Traitor!" she murmured.

"It is—it is my Rose."

"Yes; and a pretty one you have been, after all your promises in the forest, to neglect your Rose."

"I have been so busy——"

"Nonsense!"

"Fighting."

"Silly!"

"Seeing other people married and happy."

"Indeed!"

"And now I'm very bad."

"Poor fellow, so he is. Well, forgive me, if I am a little cross."

"On one condition," said Little John.

"What is that?"

"Do it again."

"What again?"

"Kiss me."

"Oh, you false, deceitful man! I thought you were quite sound asleep."

"It was so nice."

"Will you be very good," said Rose, one of whose hands the giant had firmly clasped in his.

"I will."

She stooped, and the lovers exchanged this time one passionate kiss.

"There now," said Rose, drawing away with a deep sigh, "you promised—so now you must be quiet and go to sleep."

"I am not sleepy."

"But you will be ill."

"Not a bit."

"What then?"

"Let us talk a bit. I want to know how you came here. I only knew from William Gammel, whom we call Will Scarlett, that you had gone away."

"Everybody else got married besides me, so I went into service again," pouted the girl.

"Rose."

"Little John."

"Do you know what I'll do, if you'll only give me another kiss like the last."

"I didn't give it. You took it."

"Well, if you'll only let me take another, what do you think I'll do?"

"I don't know."

"Marry you next week."

"Impudence. As if I'd have you—"

"Why did you kiss me then?"

Rose made no answer, but, somehow or other, it so happened that her head came rather nearer than was necessary to the bold outlaw, who vindicated his title to that appellation by taking that which was not given him.

It was to the giant the first kiss of love, no mean thing in a man's remembrance, if we believe the poet:—

> Away with your fictions of flimsy romance,
> Those tissues of falsehood which folly has wove;
> Give me the mild beam of the soul-breathing glance,
> Or the rapture which dwells in the first kiss of love.
> I hate you, ye cold compositions of art!
> Though prudes may condemn me, and bigots reprove,
> I court the effusions that spring from the heart,
> Which throbs with delight to the first kiss of love.
> Oh! cease to affirm that man, since his birth,
> From Adam till now has with wretchedness strove;
> Some portion of Paradise still is on earth,
> And Eden revives in the first kiss of love.

"And now," said Rose, behaving like a very sensible little woman, "I have permitted this because you are ill. So no more nonsense, or I shall be compelled to retire."

"Don't go away. I'll do whatever you tell me,"

"Take this potion, and do not speak until I address you."

The outlaw took the potion and closed his eyes. It was a sleeping or composing draught, left for the purpose of being given him, did he not otherwise woo slumber. It had its effect, and soon Little John slept soundly.

The grey light of dawn was in the sky when he awoke, and to his great satisfaction he found that his companion had not watched all night.

She slept soundly in a cosy arm-chair by the fire.

Little John fancied that he had never felt so happy in all his life. Though ill and suffering, he seemed to have forgotten all save the fact that he was loved by such a dear little woman. Like a good many others, he was young in love's mysteries, and had all his troubles to come.

Pleasant as it is, as a rule, it is not without its drawbacks; as the poet has truly said :—

> Alas! the love of woman! It is known
> To be a lovely and a fearful thing;
> For all of theirs upon that die is thrown;
> And if 'tis lost, life hath no more to bring
> To them but mockeries of the past alone,
> And their revenge is as the tiger's spring.
> Deadly, and quick, and crushing. Yet, as real
> Torture is theirs; what they inflict they feel.

No sooner did the outlaw move uneasily in his bed, however, than Rose came towards him, smoothed his pillow, and then, after a loverlike interchange of embraces, retired to see to the doctor and his breakfast.

The doctor's duty was brief.

Little John was incapable of being moved for some time, but apart from this, he was doing well enough.

He only wanted nursing, and that he had to perfection.

Robin Hood visited him after the morning meal, and it was with ill-concealed satisfaction that he heard Robin's decision to leave him there until he was quite recovered.

Little John was perfectly well aware that, wounded as he was, he was of no use to his friends, or he would have hesitated before leaving Robin.

"Get well as quick as you can," said Robin, with a sly glance at Rose; "and who knows but we may dance at your wedding before a month is over our heads?"

The big forester blushed, and Rose turned away. They were as yet novices in the tender fancies.

Then Robin shook his friend kindly by the hand and retired.

CHAPTER XXXV.
THE SHERIFF OUTWITTED.

THE whole of that day the outlaws remained within the castle, Sir Richard paying not the least attention to the summons of the sheriff, who several times offered him free pardon if he would but surrender the outlaws.

The sheriff had no means of carrying on a regular siege, being unprovided with battering rams and ladders; he therefore simply invested the fortress.

Robin employed his day in giving his men rest, seeing to their wounds, and in making arrows.

He was resolved to sally forth, cut his way through the enemy, and seek the shelter of his forest fortress until the sheriff should disband his forces.

During the whole of that day, Sir Richard and his family were lavish in their attentions to the outlaw chief, to whose former considerate kindness he owed so much of his present prosperity.

All that the castle had within its walls was placed at his disposal. As in all fortified mansions of that day, there was an armourer, and he was constantly at work.

The night promised to prove excessively dark; a night without a moon, and during which even that stars would not be visible, as heavy black clouds were piling themselves up upon the horizon.

The outlaw had arranged his plans long before night. Look-outs from the battlements had observed the position of all the invading force.

Robin called all his men an hour after dark into the courtyard, and gave his orders.

They were to follow him in Indian file, make the circuit of the camp, and then, if a favourable opportunity occurred, disperse in the forest, to collect only at the old trysting-place, where the others would not dare to follow.

Robin then parted from his friends, leaving Little John to their care.

All were armed with swords and shields, their bows and arrows, as not likely to be useful, being strapped on their backs.

Robin, with Will Scarlett close behind, led the van. He had taken mental note of the position of the enemy, and knew which way to go.

They walked upon the greensward noiselessly, like a line of shadows or Red Indians on the war trail.

Robin clutched a heavy battle-axe, which Sir Richard had made him a present of.

Not a single word was spoken.

There were sentries and prowlers on all hands. The slightest error might bring about an engagement against overwhelmingly superior forces.

From the castle they ascended a kind of slope, behind which the bulk of the enemy were camped.

They were compelled to take this way, as to cross the river was impossible without being discovered.

The wind howled fiercely through the trees, and everything was more calculated to inspire a desire for home comforts than for camping out in the cold and desolate night.

Hate and vengeance, however, are rare warmers of the human blood.

Coward as the sheriff was by nature, he was brave enough when surrounded by his numerous forces.

As soon as the head of the outlaw column came to the top of the slope, they became aware that they were close to the most important part of the camp.

Close to some very large fires in a hollow were collected the whole of the officers, while within hail was nearly all the army.

Robin raised his hand, and the outlaws sank out of sight.

He and Will Scarlett now examined the ground to see by what means they could hope to escape. As there were many wounded and the force against them was overwhelming, the outlaw wished to pass through without a contest.

And yet it seemed hardly possible.

Will Scarlett and Robin stood behind a tree out of sight of the soldiers, and sufficiently far off to be clear of the light.

On every side were bodies of men.

Towards the river, however, was a thicket apparently impenetrable. To reach this the men must crawl on their hands and knees along a low ridge nearly in sight of the sentries.

It was the only plan.

Robin gave his orders, and the defilé began. Every outlaw in his turn passed by their chief, standing erect in the gloom behind the green oak-tree.

Where he and Will Scarlett stood they could see their

great enemy the sheriff in earnest conversation with his officers.

Robin placed his finger on his lips.

"I must hear their plans," he whispered.

With this he stooped low and crawled forward until he was only separated from the enemy by three yards' distance and a low bush.

"How long will it be before the battering-ram and ladders will arrive?" said one.

"I hope by morning."

"I hope so, too. This is slow work. Arrows and bolts will avail nothing against those walls."

"If I remain here a month—aye, a year," said the sheriff, with a fierce oath, "I will have that rascal Robin. As long as he lives there will be no peace for me. The very boys in the streets make a laughing-stock of me."

The officers grinned, but said nothing.

"The knave is the bane of my existence. How long will it take to make a breach in the walls?" he then asked.

"The castle is stout," said a Norman soldier; "it may take us a day, or more."

Robin moved quickly back to where his lieutenant was secreted behind the oak-tree, and bade him follow the others, all of whom were out of sight.

Will Scarlett hesitated.

"Go—I follow."

The outlaw could delay no longer.

Robin Hood, with a dark frown on his face, slowly followed. The gloom was now so great that he could walk upright unperceived.

He reached a spot near the thicket and paused.

He faced the sheriff, who sat regaling himself under a tree. With a quiet and steady hand he tightened his bow.

The sheriff, to guard against the cold night air, wore an ermine cloak, with a fur cap of the same costly material.*

Robin knew that there was about two inches between the top of his head and the top of his hat.

He was determined to give him a fright he should remember.

The ermine cap was fastened under the chin by a leather strap.

Certain of his aim, Robin could have planted an arrow in his eye, and thence pierced the brain, but he never killed a man unnecessarily.

He had a great contempt but no personal animosity against the sheriff.

Then his arrow whizzed from his bow, and the sheriff's cap was nailed to the tree.

A bellow—for his vociferations were loud as those of any bull—was the answer to this attack.

In terror-stricken accents the wretched man asked for mercy.

He could not conceive but that he was wounded unto death, being, as he found, unable to move.

A scene of wild confusion followed, during which the outlaw retreated slowly to the thicket.

Then his bugle sounded merrily.

A terrible volley followed from all sides.

The soldiers ran about in wild confusion, while a ringing shout proclaimed the presence of the outlaws behind them.

Darkness had, however, set in so thoroughly that though the chiefs got their men together as rapidly as possible, not a trace of the outlaws was to be seen.

Glad of the excuse, Sir Thomas Beauchamp returned at once to Nottingham, where he took to his bed and was ill for quite ten days from the terrible fright of that arrow.

On his sick bed, however, one great thought occupied him, and that was the thought of speedy vengeance on Robin Hood.

The sheriff was cunning enough to know how to touch the outlaw in a tender place.

That was his heart, which, in men of his own kidney, is about the hardest thing about them.

* The ermine is an animal which is found in cold countries, and which very nearly resembles a weasel in shape, having a white pile, and the tip of the tail black, and furnishing a choice and valuable fur.

CHAPTER XXXVI.
JUSTICE! — JUSTICE!

ROBIN HOOD had been a month at home, and strange to say, there was no tidings of Little John, save the report of a messenger that he was getting slowly better.

As the outlaw-king knew that Rose was with him, he was not so much surprised as others might have been.

It was a bright summer's day, and Robin, who had dined, sat under his great trysting-tree with Maid Marian by his side, while all around were his chief lieutenants and officers.

The men were chiefly dispersed on their usual avocations. Convey, the wise it call. Steal! a fico for the phrase.

The King of Sherwood was in a better humour than he had been in for some time. The gloom imparted to him by the death of his father had passed away somewhat.

"I wonder that Little John has not returned before," said Maid Marian. "I call this playing the truant."

"There is a reason," said Robin, with a smile.

"A lass?" asked Maid Marian.

Like all women, she was quick in finding out a love-match!

"Alas!" said Robin, demurely.

"And why alas a lass?" asked Maid Marian, who was quick in understanding the euphuism of the time.

"Is not a lass the ruin of every proper man?" he replied.

"Treason to womankind!" cried Maid Marian, merrily.

At this moment a horn sounded in the distance one of those notes which indicated that an arrival of some importance might be expected.

Sentries were located all round the trysting-tree to see that none approached unobserved.

Robin rose and listened, but as the note was not repeated for some time, he and his people went on with their conversation, quite aware that ample warning would be given.

The subject, however, was changed, and men and women too, spoke of the adventures of the past.

Then came a second tra-la-la from the horns, and in a minute or two, there came in sight a small party of horsemen, two ladies accompanying them.

At the head rode one who was recognized at once.

It was Little John.

"Here comes the truant," said Robin.

Before, however, the big forester could reply one of the ladies dismounted, and rushing forward, cast herself at the knees of the monarch of Sherwood Forest.

"Justice! justice!" she cried.

"Rise, lady," said Robin, taking her by the two hands, "whoever you may be, I promise you justice if I can give it you, but cannot see a woman kneel to a man."

The lady threw back her veil and rising showed the well-known features of the Lady of Sir Richard.

"What has happened?" cried Robin.

"Sore sorrow," replied the lady, but as her words were somewhat incoherent from the greatness of her grief, we think it best to narrate what had happened in our own words.

When Sir Thomas Beauchamp, the sheriff, was a little recovered from his illness, instead of being thankful for the great mercy vouchsafed to him in his narrow escape from the unerring aim of Robin Hood, lay tossing himself on a bed of sickness, plotting and scheming how to injure Robin Hood and his friends.

At length a plan was hit upon, which promised to be easy of fulfilment.

A messenger was despatched to Prince John, who, though not openly acting as regent, was, in the absence of Richard, recognised as such by most of the northern chieftains.

Meanwhile Sir Richard, unsuspicious of the furious hate of the sheriff, and strong in a good conscience, pursued the usual avocations of a gentleman of the time, without troubling himself as to the designs of his enemy.

A country gentleman in those days was perhaps a little more useless than such persons are even now. In the time of which we speak, they had nothing to do except in war time but amuse themselves. Now, what else practically do they do, except blindly cheer or bark in the Commons the cunning leaders behind whom they sit, because they make laws in favour of the land, and against the millions whose birthright it is?

So much of communism as advocates the right of every born man to a bit of his native earth, is true and just.

But legislation and a banded troop of legislators allow no more to the millions than the hole in which they are cast at death.

Thanks to a revolution, which was the just retribution on a wicked, cruel, and vile aristocracy, and equally vile monarchy, the French people have acquired every man his own acre.

Now Sir Richard, born to good luck, to wealth and honour, like a good many others, thought, of course, it perfectly natural, and never suspected, more than any other owner of fat acres, that at best he only held them in trust for the community—and had not much thought but to enjoy that which was his.

Fortunately he was a good man, as rich men go—they are mostly much more grasping and selfish than the poor—and so his occupations and pleasures ever tended to the comfort and employment of the humbler folk.

He was above all fond of hawking, and whenever the weather suited and opportunity offered, went forth with a gay party.

His wife naturally followed in his wake, as did his son and daughter, but the last of all was at the moment too much wrapped up in her child, to be a fit companion.

It was two days before the visit of his lady to Robin, that the cavalcade went forth a hawking.

It was a bright and sunny day. as befitted a pleasure which of all others was the favourite of both sexes in England in that day.

Our ancestors were ever early risers, which is the case mostly even in these degenerate days with those who are fond of field sports, as our favourite poet insinuates when speaking of the chase :—

> He also had a quality uncommon,
> To early risers after a long chase,
> Who wake in winter ere the cock can summon
> December's drowsy day to his dull race.
> A quality agreeable to woman,
> When her soft liquid words run on apace,
> Who likes a listener, whether saint or sinner;
> He did not fall asleep just after dinner.

The day had been particularly fortunate; herons and many other fowls, with hares and other game.

They were riding towards the castle slowly, having breathed their horses pretty freely.

Presently they came to a high road which they had to to cross.

Sir Richard and his amiable wife rode in front.

"Who comes?" said the latter, lifting her gloved hand in the direction of a body of horsemen.

"Some rich traveller—some knight, who may demand our courtesy," said Sir Richard.

With a waive of his hand, the hospitable knight made his troops halt.

As a matter of necessary precaution in those days, every one looked to his arms.

No one was ever safe.

Banditti swarmed in the land, the discharged soldiers of both sides.

Civil war is ever painful, when it is but to gratify the ambition of rival princes, and the best thing a nation can do whose leaders are quarrelling for supremacy, is to thrust both on board a ship, send them to some desert island, and then let them fight as to which shall be Robinson Crusoe, and which Man Friday.

Much dreadful bloodshed, many innocent lives, and great social misery would be saved, by serving all rival claimants for a throne in this way.

No matter which wins, the masses are never gainers.

On the desert island let the best man win.

The cavalcade came trotting on towards the hawking party, nor halted until within twenty feet, when the main body halted, and one man in the garb of an officer came forward.

"May I ask if I speak to Sir Richard of the Lea?" he said, in a courteous way enough.

"I am Sir Richard."

"I regret to say that I have a warrant against yourself and son for high-treason," continued the pursuivant.

"Indeed!" said the knight, sarcastically, while his men frowned and the Lady Richard turned pale.

"I regret to say it is so," replied the man, "and that I have the pain to execute it."

"Hearkee, Mr. Pursuivant, we are about equal in number, and the result of a contest would be doubtful. But my wife is with me. Show me then your warrant that I may see by whom signed, and I will go freely if the warrant is good."

"Never!" cried his wife.

"Father, this is madness," said the son.

"The warrant!"

The pursuivant showed it, and the knight read the parchment, with a dark frown.

"The base knave," cried Sir Richard, "this cowardly sheriff, afraid to do his own dirty work, has got the prince to sign. I will to the latter at once and defy this knave."

"You know best," said the pursuivant, drily, "but my orders are to take you to Nottingham Castle, put you in a dungeon, and see you communicate with none. In your place I should fight—my men are not very hearty in the matter."

"You are a worthy fellow," cried Sir Richard, "and shall be rewarded properly."

"Too late," said the pursuivant.

"Fly all!" cried Sir Richard—and then he added to his wife in a low tone, "let Robin Hood know. Take Little John as a guide."

Then he and his son awaited calmly the approach of a large party of the sheriff's own guard, who came galloping up, and who at once surrounded and took the father and son prisoners.

They seemed scarcely to notice that the Lady of the Lea had disappeared with her attendants.

Now it was well known that the sheriff of Nottingham, though without any authority to try a knight, was one of those unscrupulous men who feared not to do an act of gross injustice.

He might have taken pattern by one of the many kings who have ruled us for our sins, and poisoned him secretly.

Murder seems to come natural to kings as measles does to common people.

The lady of the Lea accordingly hurried with all convenient speed back to her castle, where, though really quite recovered, Little John had slily enough remained behind.

And what think you Little John had done in the absence of the master and mistress of the house?

Got himself quietly married, by the two priests, the chaplain and Friar Tuck, who had remained with him.

The witnesses were the young lady of the Lea, and her own private female attendant.

It was late in the evening when Sir Richard's wife came in, and it being dark and stormy, she made all her preparations to start at daybreak.

A word was enough for Little John who, knowing the knight in danger, at once resolved to guide her to Robin Hood.

We have seen the result, and how the lady did mount her palfrey and ride a pace into Sherwood to claim for her husband the assistance of Robin Hood.

We have see how she fared.

CHAPTER XXXVII.

ON TO NOTTINGHAM.

> Up then starte he good Robin
> As man that had gone wode;
> O busk ye, busk ye, my merry men all,
> For him that died on rode.
> And he that this sorrow forsaketh,
> By him that died on tree,
> And by him that all things maketh,
> No longer shall dwell with me,

THE personal character as well as history of the bold outlaw is stamped on every verse. Against luxurious bishops or tyrannic sheriffs his bow was ever bent and his arrow in the string; he attacked and robbed and sometimes slew the latter without either compunction or remorse. In his more humorsome moods he contented himself with enticing them, in the guise of a butcher or a potter, with the hope of a good bargain, into the green wood, where he first made merry and then fleeced them, making them dance to such music as his forest afforded, or join with Friar Tuck in hypocritical thanksgiving for the justice and mercy they had experienced.

Robin's eye brightened and his language grew poetical when he was aware of the approach of some swollen pluralist—a Dean of Carlisle or an Abbot of St. Mary's—with sumpter-horses, carrying tithes and dining gear, and a slender train of attendants. He would meet him with great meekness and humility ; thank our Lady for having sent a man at once holy and rich into her servant's sylvan diocese ; inquire, too, about the weight of his purse, as if desirous to augment it ; but woe to the victim who, with gold in his pocket, set up a plea of poverty. " Kneel, holy man," Robin would then say, " kneel, and beg of the saint who rules thy abbey-stede to send money for thy present wants ;" and as the request was urged by quarterstaff and sword, the prayer was a rueful one, while the gold which a search in the prelate's mails discovered was facetiously ascribed to the efficacy of his intercession with his patron saint, and gravely parted between the divine and the robber.

Robin Hood differed from all other patriots—for patriot he was—of whom we read in tale or history. Wallace, to whom he has been compared, was a high-souled man of a sterner stamp, who loved better to see tyrants die than gain all the gold the world had to give ; and Rob Roy, to whom the poet of Rydal Mount has likened the outlaw of Sherwood, had little of the merry humour and romantic courtesy of bold Robin. This seems to have arisen more from the nature than the birth of the man. He was no lover of blood—nay, he delighted in sparing those who sought his life when they fell into his power ; and he was, beyond all example, even of knighthood, tender and thoughtful about women. Even when he prayed he preferred our Lady to all the saints in the calendar. Next to the ladies he loved the yeomanry of England. He molested no hind at the plough, no thresher in the barn, no shepherd with his flocks ; he was the friend and protector of husbandman and hind, and woe to the priest who fleeced or the noble who oppressed them. The widow, too, and the fatherless he looked upon as under his care ; and wheresoever he went some old women was ready to do him a kindness for a saved son or a rescued husband.

The personal strength of the outlaw was not equal to his activity ; but his wit so far excelled his might that he never found use for the strength which he had, so well did he form his plans and work out all his stratagems. If his chief delight was to meet with a fierce sheriff or a purse-proud priest "all under the green-wood tree," his next was to encounter some burly groom who refused to give place to the king of the forest, and was ready to make good his right of way with cudgel or sword. The tinker who, with his crab-tree staff, "made Robin's sword cry twang," was a fellow of this stamp. With such companions he recruited his bands when death or desertion thinned them ; and it seemed that to be qualified for his service it was necessary to excel him at the use of the sword or the quarterstaff. His skill in the bow was not so easily approached. He was a man, too, of winning manners and captivating address ; for his eloquence, united with his woodland heartiness, sometimes prevailed on the very men who sought his life to assume his livery, and try the pleasures which Barnesdale or Plompton afforded.

The good outlaw handed over the lady of the Lea to the charge of Maid Marian, or, as in prosaic language we should call her, Mrs. Robin Hood.

Little John would have accompanied his master, but the King of Sherwood objected.

"You have been twice wounded, my little forester," he said, "once in the knee, once in your heart. Stay at home and guard your own wife and mine. When the honeymoon is over you shall go with me."

The huge outlaw laughed, but it is to be well remarked that on this occasion he showed no such reluctance as when he wanted to execute dire vengeance on he in the capul hide.

More than seven-score archers bent their bows, and neither hedge nor ditch, nor dike nor stream stayed them till they were in sight of Nottingham town.

Then the whole body halted, and sent forth scouts to learn what was going on. The main body would wait for reinforcements.

Robin Hood was well aware that the object he had now in view was one not to be attained by so small a force. A very large number, a very fair proportion of the people of Nottingham would aid him, but all the royal troops, tipstaves and others, with the local constables and guard, would be against him.

He had therefore sent scouts and runners to scour the whole forest, with a view to collecting not only all the outlaws that could be found, but also such villagers as might be disposed to assist him.

Those who were sent into the town speedily returned with the information that a counsel had been hastily held, and though much had been done to pacify the blood-thirsty sheriff, the noble and good-hearted knight had been condemned to death.

His execution was to take place one hour after day-break.

Now this was news which irritated Robin Hood to the last degree, and made him, with a dark and gloomy brow, vow vengeance against the magistrate he had so long been lenient with.

Giving strict orders to his men to keep close, Robin made himself a goodly disguise, and walked slowly into the town, driving a couple of pigs before him.

It was early in the evening, and the town was too much agitated for any one to notice him with anything of suspicion.

His dress was in accordance with his calling, he not forgetting to keep up the illusion in speech and manners, in this not like a certain prince in a pantomine who, having a design on a baron's daughter, disguised himself as a drayman. The brewer is said to have

Be-frocked and be-whipped him,
And Otto, on his part, unsparingly tipped him,
Then started away,
With the wine in the dray,
Completely disguised in his drayman's array.
But pondering after
The baron's fair darter,
He failed to remember his <i>rôle</i> as a carter,
And nearly created the dickens's own " to do,"
For he knocked with a bang,
And he noisily rang,
As gentlemen visitors only are wont to do ;
Although I may tell
You, he knew very well
That a modest appeal at the area bell
Would, in his new line of life, better have fitted him,
As the flunkeys with justice remarked who admitted him.

Robin Hood found it easy to pass himself off for what he pretended to be, being, as he was, an excellent mimic.

He therefore entered an inn where he was not known and sat down, after trading away his pigs to the land-lord.

The worthy Boniface, finding that he had made a good bargain, joined his guest and talked very freely.

Naturally the talk of the hour was the coming execution of Sir Richard of the Lea, which the landlord seemed to think very cruel.

Politics were spoken in almost abject whispers in those days, when nobles and priests—weak and erring mortals—were allowed to think for the many.

" What be he a done ?" asked Robin.

" Well," said Boniface, scratching his head, " nothing pertikler."

" Murder ?"

" Noa."

" What then ?"

" Well, giv' a shelter to Robin Hood, the friend of the poor man."

" And he be to die for that ?" said the pig-drover ; " dom me—it aint right."

" But you musnt say so, my man. Shall I fill your tankard ?"

" With wine, and supper for two," continued the pig-drover.

" Wine ! You have plenty of money ?"

" More than I want ; so here is the price of the pigs back again."

ROBIN HOOD STOPS THE FRIAR.

"But 'twas a bargain."

"So it is now," continued the other; "but you said just now I was the friend of the poor man."

"Noa!"

"Yes."

"You—Robin?"

"Hush! My name mentioned in Nottingham to-night would cause a great crime. I came to save Sir Richard —and please Providence I will."

This was said with an earnestness that carried conviction to the ears of Boniface, who hastened to serve one with alacrity he so truly admired. In the course of the evening the outlaw gathered all the information he needed, and retired to his camp to prepare for action.

CHAPTER XXXVIII.

THE RESCUE.

BY threats of violence, by cunning sophistry, by urging the earnest desire of Prince John to rid himself of one who was an enemy to his regal pretensions, but above all by promising a share of his many possessions, the wily and inhuman and avaricious sheriff had contrived to make the head men of Nottingham and some

minor nobles join him in the illegal and cruel attempt to deprive Sir Richard of the Lea of his life.

That he was a friend of Robin Hood was enough.

Our noble outlaw, like every reformer who would serve the masses, was hated, feared, and detested by the middle and upper class.

They could not but hate one who would give rights and privileges to the commons.

It was therefore with less of hesitation that they implicated themselves in a crime every way illegal.

Such a tribunal had no right whatever to try a noble or a knight for any such supposed crime.

He had a right to appeal to his peers and to his king.

But when he asked for this it was coarsely and rudely denied him by the sheriff.

He was promised a priest at daybreak, and that was all the comfort he could obtain.

Sir Richard of the Lea was a brave soldier, and very much of a Christian gentleman, so that though like all sensible men he had no wish to die, he was far above any fear of death.

He would gladly have seen his wife and children again, and in an ordinary case would have asked leave to see them. But the manner of the sheriff, with his knowledge of his character, precluded the possibility of his so demeaning himself.

He retired at a late hour then to rest, after praying earnestly, and being fatigued and worn-out with many emotions, slept soundly.

Scarcely had the dim grey of dawn lit up the eastern sky, than the door of his dungeon creaked, and raising his head he saw the promised priest.

"So soon?"

"My son, one fleeting hour remains of life."

"Well, father, I hope it will not take so long to shrive me; that I am being atrociously murdered is something to set off against my sins."

"Do not blaspheme the law."

"Call you the cold-blooded vengeance of the vile sheriff of Nottingham legal, father? No; as I may die in peace with man, I say it is cruel, fearfully cruel murder. This man is about to avenge his own base conduct to one his superior in everything—the good, the brave, the noble Robin Hood."

"My son, how can you speak of one who is the enemy of the church?" said the priest, with pious horror.

"Forgive me," said Sir Richard, humbly, and recollecting how little time he had to make his peace with Heaven, he knelt in the vain and evil mood of confession, when to man we say that which belongs to God.

The praying machines of the Chinese are as rational.

The priest, however, who in all probability believed as much in his own power as spirit-rapping knaves do in theirs, gave him absolution.

Sir Richard had obtained one grace from the sanguinary sheriff. He was to be decapitated, not hung.

His rank and golden spurs spared him from this latter indignity.

A scaffold was erected in front of the prison. Such a sight had not been seen for years.

At dawn of day, the people began to collect in vast crowds, some attracted by curiosity, some by sympathy —for none were so ignorant as not to be aware that Sir Richard would die simply as a friend to Robin Hood.

Vague rumours of a rescue were heard on all sides, and yet none could tell whence they came. No one knew for certain that Robin Hood was in the town, though as usual there were plenty to declare they had really seen him.

But gossip should never be taken as matter of historic truth.

The number of troops collected was very great, as the occasion was one demanding serious consideration.

Robin had never yet been known to desert a friend, and had rescued many at the very last moment.

Sir Thomas Beauchamp would gladly have retired to his most private apartments, and there concealed himself during the execution, but no one would take the responsibility to command.

It wanted ten minutes to five.

Five was the hour named by the judge.

There he sat in state upon his war-horse, surrounded by a close body of his guard.

The open space before the prison consisted of a green, with here and there a mound, now crowded with spectators. The rest was the main road, which was lined with troops.

The whole shone gaily in the bright morning light— gaily, though the scene was a sad one. But what cares the sun, which shines for all: for rich, for poor, for high and mighty, for humble and weak?

The prison gates flew open.

All eyes a minute before had been fixed on the scaffold, in one corner of which stood the executioner.

It was a large, tall, bony man, masked and leaning on his axe, which was heavy and bright.

From association, the scaffold, soon to be dripping with human gore, was looked upon with awe.

But now the interest changed.

All eyes were fixed on the prisoner instead of on the scaffold, and though all could not see him many could. A loud cry arose from every quarter of the green.

"Long live brave Sir Richard!"

"Cut me down the rabble knaves!" said Sir Thomas.

At that moment a bugle sounded, to which a response was given from every part of the field, arrows were poured in heavy volleys on the guard.

Confusion reigned on all sides.

"A rescue! a rescue;" shouted the outlaws, pouring in on all sides, while hundred of apprentices and other Nottingham lads, catching up their clubs, made common cause with the outlaws.

No where was Robin to be seen.

But who comes bounding down a narrow street leading to the large open place where the execution was to have taken place?

Who comes thus with a powerful reinforcement?

It is the King of Sherwood, who at last, leaping over every impediment, gained a position near Sir Thomas.

"Speak to me, thou bold sheriff," exclaimed Robin; "I vow to God I have not run so far or so fast these seven years; judge ye if it is for your good."

"A thousand marks for his head!"

Fearful confusion existed on the field; but the military, seeing the power of the merry men, and the sympathy they met with from the citizens, acted on the defensive, which gave time and opportunity to the outlaws to form in favourable positions.

"Sir Sheriff," said Robin, with a cold smile, "release my friend, whom you hold against the king's law, and I may yet forgive you."

"Insolent!"

"I speak seriously. Once!"

The sheriff looked round the field, and saw a proud and showy military array, bound by law and duty to support him.

He trembled very much, and tried to bluster excessively, but it was a very bad show.

"Twice!" said Robin.

The sheriff waved his hand for the execution to proceed.

"Thrice!"

> Robin he bent a good yew-bow,
>   An arrow he drew at will,
> And he hit so sore the proud sheriff,
>   He on the street lay still.
> And before he might arise
>   Upon his feet to stand,
> There he smote off the sheriff's head
>   With his bright brand.
> Says, "Lie thou there, thou proud sheriff,
>   Evil mote thou thrive;
> There might no man in thee have trust
>   The whiles thou wert alive."

Thus ended the mortal career of one who up to this time had been the worst enemy that the outlaw-chief had yet known.

The troops and the officials of the town, seeing the death of Sir Thomas Beauchamp, and finding that victory was likely to go against them, at once agreed to yield up both the father and son, the latter of whom had been brought to a window to witness the execution of his parent.

A truce was then cried, after which Robin addressed the people, and explained the reasons which had induced him to act at last in a way so foreign to his usual habits.

As the sheriff was unpopular, very unpopular we may say, he was little mourned, though, of course, no one could say what sort of a person the next would prove to be.

His wife, however, mourned him. He was much older than she, and not particularly amiable, but he was her husband.

So that night she had a good cry.

She was also a whole month ere she consented to trust her lovely person and valuable fortune to another's keeping.

This time she married to please herself, as rich widows, who as young girls have married to please their parents, usually do.

Who shall say whether she blessed or cursed Robin?

As soon as the outlaw chief had retreated from the ancient city of Nottingham, and gained once more the shelter of the greenwood tree, then he called a council.

"Sir Richard," he said gravely, "we are now quits. You saved my life—I have yours."

"I know it. Come you then to my castle and receive the thanks of the dearest of women."

"She is in the forest, where you and yours will do well to be for some time to come," continued Robin; "Richard is away. The council in London hold the reins of power feebly against the Prince John; for what we have done both shall be outlawed. Rely upon it, for the death of the sheriff we shall suffer. My fastnesses, however, are impregnable. I can vanish in the earth, or with a blast of my bugle conjure up armies. Come you, then, you and yours, all women, children, and soldiers, to the green wood. Then shall one go to good Richard and explain all. With his written pardon in our hands we shall alone be safe."

Sir Richard of the Lea heard him and was convinced. What ensued therefrom will be seen.

CHAPTER XXXIX.

OF THE NEW SHERIFF OF NOTTINGHAM, AND WHAT BEFEL AT HIS TABLE.

Now Prince John, when he heard of what had happened in Nottingham, the thing being told him by the friends of the sheriff and the enemies of Robin Hood, determined to punish severely both the outlaw and the brave knight who had befriended him.

Though his position was not an official one, there were few who were inclined to dispute his rights during the absence of the king in foreign parts.

He therefore at once dispatched Sir Michael Rathdane, a rough and portly knight, with powers to wield the authority of sheriff until the king's return.

He himself with a large force intimated his intention to follow shortly, and make one more effort to destroy this royalty of Sherwood forest, which was such a thorn in his side.

It seemed incredible to the haughty prince how one man could so defy his fellows.

He then left York with a large retinue of nobles and knights, and took his way to Nottingham, as the ballad says: "And to take that gentle knight, and Robin Hood if he may."

By proclamation he confiscated the lands of the former, while on the head of the latter he set a price, and marched northward after his brother monarch.

And everywhere he went he found the trail of noble, worthy Robin Hood.

> All the pass of Lancashire,
> He went both far and near,
> Till he came to Plympton park,
> He missed many of his deer.
> There our prince was wont to see
> Of herds many a one;
> He hardly could find one fair deer
> That carried one good horn.

"I swear by the Holy Trinity," said the prince, who was by no means mealy-mouthed, "that I will give a knight's ransom for but a sight of this presumptuous outlaw; and on him who will bring me the head of that presumptuous outlawed rebel, Sir Richard of the Lea, I will bestow his castle and lands, I swear by St. Edward."

There were many among the cavaliers who seemed to think such offers very injudicious.

> Then up and spake a fair old knight,
> That was true in his fay,
> "Oh my liege lord, my sovereign king,
> One word I shall you say;
> There is no man in this countrie
> May hold that good knight's lands,
> While Robin Hood can ride or rise
> With a bent bow in his hand.
> That he shall not lose his land,
> The best ball in his hood;
> Give it no man, my lord the king,
> That you wish any good."

It is difficult to say with one so wayward and capricious as Prince John, what effect these words may have had; but certain it is, that he went on his way thoughtfully.

He patiently continued his search for Robin Hood for many other days, but though he came where he had slain his deer, and had held high carousal, he could never obtain either a sight of the outlaw or any of his merry men.

"By St. Edward and the holy rood! this fellow is invisible. We must on to Nottingham."

It will readily be believed that Sir Michael Rathdane, being wholly a creature of the cruel prince's, made gorgeous preparations to receive his patron.

Gold, silver, and precious stones, flags, banners, and men-at-arms were in those days the materials of popular and royal processions.

Unless the great man was popular the applause was wanting.

Genuine shouts from the *plebs* can only be won by great individual worth.

But the haughty prince, who could brook none to assume authority near him, and yet who had to bow his neck to the yoke of the barons, cared naught for popular applause.

His theory of government was that of certain modern governments—brute force.

When, therefore, he entered Nottingham, amid loud flourish of trumpets, and the people shouted not, he looked at them with the utmost scorn.

The crowds gazed moodily at him. It was not safe in those days to shout against the powers that existed, but the power of silence remained.

The cavalcade swept on, a goodly sight to see, and when the prancing nobles and knights had entered the town, there came the camp followers and servants.

In the rear of these, as if glad of the protection of so large a body, came two men, who, however, did not look as if they needed protection, or lacking it cared much for extraneous knights.

The populace of the good city had seen many a seedy knight, but none so drear and worn as this one.

His armour was battered, his surcoat torn, his helmet broken and patched, as if he came from one of the many well-fought fields of the Continent or Holy Land.

He did not hide his face, which was marked and peculiar, though so disfigured with grizzly beard on upper lip, on chin, over the eyes hanging like a pent-house, while the hair fell in thick and matted curls so as to disguise the real character of his face.

The horse he bestrode was better than might have been expected from the appearance of the master, being strong, heavy, and bony, and thus well suited to a heavy-weight.

His squire, a mere peasant, was as roughly used as his master, while he bestrode a horse of much less pretentious appearance, being in reality nothing more than a wiry pony.

The main body of the prince's followers went to the sheriff's house, which was of large dimensions, purposely for these gatherings.

Still the inns and ale-houses had their fair share.

To one of the latter went the knight and his squire, and descending from their horses, proceeded to make such ablutions as were necessary to clean them from the dust of the road.

Then the somewhat ill-favoured knight, with a pompousness which ill beseemed his appearance, bade his squire, no squire of dames, but a rough specimen of clod-hopping humanity, go to the sheriff's house, and say that Sir Harry Juder, a poor knight, desires to pay his devoirs to him.

Now it was not usual for any man, no matter what his rank, to refuse to receive a true knighted soldier, but the character of Prince John was known.

"What if he grow angry, master mine?"

"Let him get pleased again."

"But my shoulders may suffer if I am saucy."

"Your head will, if you do not go. Get speech of the prince if you can; if not, the sheriff will do."

The serving-man who knew his master to be quick in words and acts, went forth, and luckily finding the prince in the court-yard of the sheriff, that personage for a wonder was graciously pleased to accept the profferred homage of the old soldier.

Sir Harry Juder, as the stout man called himself, averring that he had no court garb to wear, went to the banquet in his armour: a proceeding which excited some few smiles, but no remarks, as every knight was liable to be under some vow.

When the iron-clad warrior entered the banquet-room the guests were taking their seats, and the stranger naturally obtained a seat only at the lower table, at a distance from Prince John.

The festivities at once commenced.

It was not the custom of the Normans to indulge so much in drink as the Saxon, but Prince John, himself a wine-bibber, found plenty of imitators.

If a king were to take off his shoe and drink out of it, his courtiers would follow suit.

As soon as the more solid viands were disposed of, and the wine circulated freely, the conversation also was free.

The expedition against Robin Hood was spoken of openly.

Various stories were told of the bold outlaw.

The prince repeated that he believed him to be invisible or an arrant coward.

"I am an old forester, as well as an old soldier," said Sir Harry Juder, in a deep voice, something like that of a ventriloquist, speaking in imitation of a ghostly personage, "and know the character, mind—I say the character—of Robin Hood well."

"Have you anything to advise?"

"I have, most noble prince."

John frowned. His flatterers always called him king in his brother's absence.

"If your majesty," continued the old knight, with a wily smile, "desires to see Robin Hood, you must do as I bid you, else he will continue invisible."

"And what then do you desire that I should do?" inquired the prince.

> "Take five of your ablest knights
>   That be in all your lede,
> And walk down to yon abbey,
>   And cleed ye in monk's weed.
> And I will be your leadsman,
>   And lead you on the way:
> And ere ye come to Nottingham
>   Mine head then dare I lay,
> That ye shall meet with Robin Hood
>   In life if that he be,
> And ere ye come to Nottingham
>   With een ye shall him see.

"Gramercy, good knight," said the prince, with whose humour this proposition did not jump, "I have no wish to put my head in the lion's mouth."

"It is an awkward place," replied Sir Harry Juder, in a peculiar tone of voice.

"Eh—what?" cried John, with a start, and then recovering himself, he added, "but if you know him so well, why not try the experiment yourself?"

"And what, most mighty prince, would you give me, if I went and brought him into Nottingham?"

"The first boon you asked, were it the richest in the land," replied the Prince.

"'Tis done," said the old knight thoughtfully; "tomorrow at morn, I will array me as a monk. An' five gallant knights will accompany me as my men-at-arms—I pledge my word as a man and a—hem—knight, that they shall return in safety—"

"Gads truth! but you are a doughty knight, and I will provide your escort."

Saying which, with a malicious smile, which so became his appearance and his character, he selected five stalwart youths, of those notoriously the least devoted to himself, to personate the men-at-arms of the old knight, so soon to be transformed into a fat prior.

The young men laughed and then agreed to go, being brave and noble fellows.

Prince John then agreed to wait in Nottingham the result of this most uncertain adventure, which he often declared would end in complete discomfiture—which it did, but not in the sense in which he meant it.

As soon as all was settled, the knight, pleading the necessity of early rising, retired to his hostelrie, taking his five confederates with him, nothing loth.

But the early rising was nothing but an excuse, as when Sir Harry Juder reached his inn, the revelry was renewed, nor did they break up until the five young men were completely overcome. The big and burly knight, whose stature somewhat resembled that of Little John, remained as untouched by liquor as if he had taken water.

CHAPTER XL.

IN THE GREENWOOD.

THERE was an abbey in Nottingham.

Now in those days religion was by no means made the thing of gloom and sorrow that fanatics would turn it in.

Because a man was religious he did not expect others to refrain from cakes and ale, but rather, doing his duty to Providence, in the way then understood, was all the more jolly—especially on Sunday.

When Sir Harry Juder made himself known in the abbey, where one of note recognised him as a personal friend, he found every assistance both for himself and companions.

He next day, then, clothed himself in monk's weeds, and had his men dressed as saintly men-at-arms, one, however, assuming the cord as well as himself.

Thus looking full grave and comely, they rode slowly on towards the forest.

Now certain ballad-mongers will have it that the adventure belonged to royalty.

> Our king was great above his cole
>   A broad hat on his crown,
> Right reverendly and abbot like
>   He rode towards the town.
> Stiff boots and large our king had on,
>   Forsooth as I you say;
> And he sang through the greenwood
>   The convent is clothed in grey.

Some time had elapsed, since Sir Richard of the Lea had elected to join Robin Hood, rather than be subject to the ill-usage of Prince John and his barons, and both the outlaw and his friend began to fancy that their daring assault was forgotten.

The deadly way in which Sir Thomas had persecuted Robin, was of course, to his mind and that of his friends, ample justification for all that he had done.

But in the eyes of the law the sheriff would be looked upon as right.

The merry monarch of Sherwood, therefore, took the precaution and filled the whole of the forest with scouts to let him know whether any one was coming.

The spot selected by the outlaw to receive the reports of his spies and scouts was a sweet grassy dell, where the birds sang pleasantly overhead, and where all his lieutenants and leading friends were collected, save Little John, whose absence was not much noted, as he was known to be in that state called love, which leaves a man quite at the mercy of the gentler sex.

Robin, however, blamed him not, when he looked into the eyes of his own dear Marian, knowing how many a time and oft he had abandoned adventure and neglected friendship, that he might gaze lovingly into her eyes.

The day was warm, and the outlaw chief preferred the society of their dames to chasing the wild deer, the more that the larders were full, and Robin never encouraged any unnecessary waste.

Every now and then Robin, who had Marian beside him, received a report, to none of which, however, did he pay much attention, until he was aroused by Allan-a-Dale.

"Master mine," said the poet and rhymester of the band, to whom, probably, we owe many of the ballads, "I think there is fish coming you would like to fry."

"Of what sort?"

"A fat and portly abbot, with five well-coated men-at-arms in his train."

"I will up and at them," cried Robin; "that is the sort of game for my money."

With these words the outlaw took his staff, and followed by a few of the men in Lincoln green, went to meet the disguised monk, who, at the head of his party, came ambling across a mead.

Now Robin, who had often in the dress of a beggar or a monk imposed on others, seems never to have imagined that a similar deceit might be practised upon himself. It is complimentary to the other's performance of the character of a monk that he fairly deceived the outlaw, who, on seeing him approach, advanced with a score of archers at his back, and stopped one who came desirous to be stopped; he did this with his usual courtesy.

> Robin he took the other's horse
>   Right hastily in that stede,
> And said, "Sir Abbot, by your leave,
>   Awhile ye must abide.
>
> "For we are yoemen of this forest,
>   Under the greenwood tree:
> And we live by our good king's deer,
>   For other shift have not we.

And ye have churches and rents both,
And gold full great plentye,
Give us, I pray you, of your spending,
For fair Saint Charitee."

"Fair sir, you are welcome to Sherwood," said Robin, doffing his cap; "how goes the abbey."

"Poorly," said the fat monk, from under his cowl.

"But the rents and revenues come in, do they not?"

"Slowly."

"You mean to say that you have little money."

"Little or none," said the other, whose fat sides seemed to shake with fear, or it might be laughter.

"How much?"

"I tell thee honestly, good yeoman," said the simulated monk, "I brought only forty pounds with me, but were it an hundred, thou and thy merry men should have it."

The outlaws smiled.

Robin took the forty pounds. He gave twenty to his men and bade them be merry. He took ten for himself, and returned ten to the traveller.

"Take this for your journey; we shall perhaps meet some other time," he said.

"Now, art thou Robin Hood?" said the other; "and if it be so, I am commanded by Prince John to bid you come to him to Nottingham, where he now holds his court; he sends his royal seal as a true token."

The outlaw shook his head.

"What mean you, yeoman?"

"A lift of the little finger of King Richard is worth the whole body of Prince John."

"Why."

"His word is not worth a tinker's oath."

"How so?"

"Such is my word, Sir Abbot; and you be friend of his, go thy ways. I am sorry I gave thee back the ten pounds."

"Worthy and staunch yeoman," said the false monk, with all the unctuousness of a fat priest, "would you go if you had Richard's word?"

"I would."

"Read this."

And the priest handed a small strip of parchment to the outlaw, who drew Allan-a-Dale to his side.

"Read out," said Robin.

"To worthy Robin, greeting. *Come to Nottingham in all security. I will be there to see justice done.* The bearer is a trusty soul, and my friend. RICHARD."

"And that is all?" asked Robin, gravely, as he peered into the false monk's face.

"No," said that worthy, with a smile, and he showed under his furred sleeve a signet ring.

The outlaw knelt as he recognised the token, which was always to be shown him with genuine messages from the monarch of England to the monarch of Sherwood forest.

He spoke—

I love no man in all the world
So well as I do my king.
Thrice welcome is my lord's seal;
And monk, for thy tidings,
Sir abbot, for thy tidings good
To-day shalt dine with me,
All for the love I bear my king,
Beneath my trysting tree.

There were, however, two opinions among the outlaws as to the truth and honesty of this messenger; some said he had a down and felon look, and had possessed himself of the signet in some nefarious manner; while even Maid Marian, she knew not why, looked at him with suspicion.

There seemed to her the faint echo of some memory connected with this grizzly monk, and as far as she could make it out, the memory was not pleasant.

Women have their strong likes and dislikes, prejudices if you will, but they are very often right.

Theirs is an instinct which, when those whom they love are in danger, rarely deceives them.

The monk meantime had been assisted to dismount by Robin, and his men given over to the outlaws of inferior rank by the chief.

The abbot, whose lofty stature and proud walk excited as much admiration as his grizzly and fierce countenance

excited fear, strode up to Maid Marian, and with courtly grace—your priest is after all your true courtier—paid his respects to the queen of Sherwood.

She received him coldly enough, which nowise discomposed the reverend father, who, casting himself on the grass beside her, began to chatter to her those pleasant nothings which assume in able hands such intrinsic importance.

During the course of conversation the abbot's discourse savoured somewhat of gallantry.

"Sir priest, I allow no man to flatter me but my husband," she said, proudly.

"Then thou art a rare wench."

"Wench, sir churchman! I'd have you know"——

"Know nothing," continued the impudent envoy.

Maid Marian blushed crimson, and a dark frown rose upon her brow.

"Before you get angry," said Sir Henry Juder, with an earnestness quite startling, "look me full in the face."

Marian looked, but still was puzzled.

The false monk whispered a short sentence.

The eyes of the maiden sparkled with fun.

"And so, having fooled the prince and his knights, you would fool my husband?" she said, with a pout.

"If you would help me."

"And that is how you got the signet?"

"Yes."

"Well, as it is but a joke," said Marian, "I will humour you. Besides, Robin is so sure of his penetration, that I shall not be sorry to give him a lesson. Men always fancy that they can see further than we women, but they often find themselves mistaken."

Whereupon the monk laughed, and proceeded to ply Maid Marian with questions as to the history of the late assault on Nottingham, which the outlaw's wife related, though with a sort of defiant way which seemed meant to convey that the other knew quite as much about it as she did.

While this was going on, Robin Hood came up.

"Oh! oh!" he said, with one of his merry laughs, "you seem like old friends."

"The holy father is so very gallant," began Maid Marian; and then she added, as if struck by a sudden thought, "where is that mountain, Little John?"

"Ah, poor fellow!" said Robin, with a deep sigh; "he has fallen into the nets of the fowler."

"How so?" asked the priest, whose old hoarseness seemed to have come back since Robin's return.

"A woman!" continued Robin; "he, the mighty and the great, has fallen into the toils of a girl."

"Ah, my son," said the abbot, shaking his head, "this is, I fear, a general failing of the men of Sherwood."

"We are partial to the sex," replied Robin, "but we know how to keep them in order."

Which observation obtained for the outlaw an imaginary box on the ear, after which Maid Marian retired to leave the two men in conference.

The suspicions of Allan-a-Dale had been communicated to Robin Hood, but the writing was authentic and the signet ring well known to him, so that apparently there could not be any deception.

It was, however, the duty of the outlaw chief to be cautious; and in the course of a conversation, which lasted some minutes, he took occasion to dive into the secrets of the envoy's heart.

Now the monarch of Sherwood noted well one thing, and that was that whenever he spoke to the abbot of the king's residence in the forest with him, the other knew mostly what had passed.

Things to all appearance which were a secret between Robin Hood, Maid Marian, Friar Tuck, Will Scarlett, and Little John especially, this stranger was familiarly acquainted with.

"There is deep design and treachery here," thought Robin; "or there is perfect truth and knowledge. I will believe the latter."

He accordingly turned the conversation, and gradually spoke of himself, his happiness in the woods, and his general disinclination for the life which would open to him as Earl of Huntingdon.

At which the envoy incontinently laughed.

"But, messire, I had forgotten—you stand in need of

refection. I never knew a priest yet but what thought of his belly before his matins."

On which the envoy laughed, and seated himself upon the grass.

CHAPTER XLI.

SPORTS AND PASTIMES.

No sooner had the monarch of Sherwood said the above words than he blew his horn, and at the blast appeared seven-score archers, who, at Robin's bidding, hastened east, west, north, and south, to collect what worthy Sancho Panza called "belly lumber," leaving a still perfect regal guard to wait upon the outlaw and his guests, and accompany them to the trysting tree, which grew in the depths of the forest.

As the day was warm and the weather pleasant, they walked slowly along under the greenwood arches, talking pleasantly by the way.

Robin Hood was by this time, being never of a suspicious disposition, quite satisfied, and yet he was puzzled at the frank intimacy between the priestly envoy and his wife Marian.

Not for one moment was Robin uncomfortable. She must be a faulty woman of whom a man is jealous, but Maid Marian certainly was not.

Let a man, however, once admit this subtle tempter to a grasp of his soul, and he will be miserable. Evade its insinuations as he liked, they would return, until Robin began to get quite angry with himself.

In this mood they reached the trysting tree, and found that, thanks to the delay in their progress, the tables were covered with venison, bread, and wine.

The abbot seated himself.

"By St. Austin," he said, addressing Maid Marian, "his men, too, are more at his bidding than my yeomen are at mine."

"Make good cheer, abbot," cried Robin, and he helped him to the fat meat and the choice venison and wine, "and for the news thou hast brought may thou be ranked among the blessed."

The abbot smiled, lifted up a cup of wine, and drank to the bright eyes of Maid Marian with such a strange expression, that the lady laughed, while Robin was half inclined to be angry.

But he was the host, and scorned to show any idle jealousy of a woman he so much loved as he did Marian.

He passed the glass round, nor would he cease the toasts and huge bumpers until his sensible partner seemed to think that they had nearly had enough.

Upon this Robin rose with a huge bumper—the churchman and his attendant knights had fully refreshed themselves—and signalled for a bumper to be handed to all present.

"I drink wassail to you," he said.

All lifted their goblets, and set them down empty.

"And now thou shalt see, sir abbot," said Robin, "the manner of life we lead, and pray thee possess the king with it."

And as he spoke he waved his hand.

> Up then rose his men in haste,
>   Their bows were smartly bent,
> The priest was never so sore aghast,
>   He weened to have been shent.
> Two slender wands were then set up,
>   And thereto gaun they gang;
> By fifty paces, our good priest said,
>   The marks they were too lang.

On one of these wands Robin hung a garland, and said,—

"Whoever shall fail to shoot within that garland shall forfeit his bow and shafts and receive a buffet."

There was great laughter at this, and all the best bowmen in the company stood forward.

The scene was now gay and lively in the extreme. The marks were at one end of the glade, the competitors at the other.

Behind, forming a group to themselves, was the family of Sir Richard of the Lea.

He himself was erect in his armour, an interested observer.

Much the Miller, Will Scarlett, Allan-a-Dale, and all the leaders began. The lieutenants shot, and so did all the men.

Whoever failed in his aim received such a buffet from the outlaw as made him reel.

All had the humiliation once.

Then came Robin's turn, and all rather hoped, than expected, that he would be a sufferer.

But the surest hand will sometimes fail: after shooting several times through the garland, and twice cleaving the wand, he missed the mark, perhaps wilfully, by three finger-breadths; on this his men called him to judgment.

"Stand forth, sir," said Gilbert with the White Hand, "and take your pay—you did not spare us."

> "If it be so," said bold Robin Hood,
>   "That better may not be,
> Sir Abbot, I give thee mine arrow,
>   I pray, sir, serve thou me."
>
> "It falleth not mine order," said the priest,
>   "Good Robin, by thy leave,
> All for to smite a good yeoman,
>   For doubt I should him grieve."
>
> "O smite on boldly," said Robin,
>   "I give to thee full leave;"
> Anon the good priest with that word
>   He folded up his sleeve.
>
> And such a buffet he gave Robin,
>   To the ground he gade full near.
> "I make mine avowe to God," quoth Robin,
>   "Thou art a stalworth friar."

Robin, as he spoke, looked at the other's arm and hand, and as he did so shook his head.

"That hand can shoot as well as smite," he said, and gazed wistfully in his face.

"Who art thou?"

"Our liege," said Sir Richard of the Lea, kneeling at the feet of the abbot, who thereupon cast off cloak, false hair, wig, and every atom of his disguise.

The outlaws, as was the fashion of the day, kneeled, and as their monarch looked proudly around, asked for mercy and pardon for all mistakes; which Richard, more than ever delighted with the frank and kindly manners of the king of Sherwood, freely granted.

"And now, my merry men, all rise, for I have business with your master; business which will not brook of any delay. I ask, therefore, that my presence among you be held a profound secret. Have I your promise—all?"

"All, all!"

"'Tis well. And now I think if Robin Hood were the hospitable person he professed to be, he would ask the King of England to pledge him in a bumper—eh, Maid Marian?"

"A pretty wife," said Robin, laughing. "I believe she knew you all the time."

"Women can keep a secret," laughed Richard, and the carouse recommenced.

Before, however, the glasses went round, with the song and the toast, Richard settled to be stopped four hours after sundown.

They would have to start at daybreak.

The five young knights to whom he had revealed himself had sufficiently proved their fidelity by keeping his secret.

While this arrangement was being made, a noise was heard at no great distance as of one singing.

All held their tongues.

The following were the words :—

> "Little John,
> A jolly brisk blade, right fit for his trade,
>   For he was a lusty young man.
> Tho' he was called Little, his limbs they were large,
>   And his stature was seven feet high;
> Wherever he came, they quaked at his name,
>   For he soon would make them to fly."

There was a loud laugh at this, for the words emanated from the ample chest of Little John himself.

"Oh, oh," whispered the king, laughing, "we are becoming braggarts in our old age. Lend me an old cloak, somebody."

One was easily found, fastened round the waist of the king, and the hood put over his head.

Scarcely had he done so, when Little John came in sight in the jolliest of humours.

"Who quakes at your name?" said Robin, drily.

"Why everybody. I make every boy and man run save you," replied Little John, who, though not intoxicated, was still fresh.

"Tush, you man mountain; 'tis but boasting. Here is an honest miller from Leicester will trounce you in a trice."

"Will he, by heavens!—have at him," and waving his huge club over his head, he shouted some lines of a ballad, probably written by Allen-a-Dale, which referred to one of Robin's earlier adventures.

"And about, and about, and about they went
    Like two wild boars in a chase;
Striving to aim, each other to maim,
    Leg, arm, or any other place.
And knock for know they lustily fought,
    Which held two hours or more,
That all the wood rang, at every bang,
    They played their work so sore."

"When yon fellow has done roaring like a bull, I am ready to begin," said the king.

"Ah, is this the tinker?" cried Little John, whirling his staff.

"Yes," said the king, laughing, "and a first-rate tinker too, for making holes in pots."

A roar followed the merry monarch's pleasantry, and the two began.

Richard was a first-rate hand in all trials of skill, but he knew that he had no mean player to contend against.

He accordingly put in requisition all his knowledge of the game, and found even then that he must exercise all his skill and caution to win.

He therefore, recognising all the skill of his antagonist, conceived it to be the best plan to act chiefly on the defensive, until he saw the proper time come to deliver the blow that should make him a winner.

At first there was scarcely any standing Little John's powerful and scientific blows, until at last the king commenced making a series of rapid feints that almost bewildered the love-sick forester.

Presently he planted a well-directed blow on the other's leg, which made the tall outlaw swear.

The rapidity no less than the science of his antagonist was startling.

Little John twirled his staff, dealt blows right and left, whirled it about, dashed it here and there with such speed and force, that Richard grew impatient.

Next instant, in an unguarded moment, Little John laid himself open, and ere he could recover, lay sprawling on the ground, with a broken and bleeding crown.

"A Richard! a Richard!—hurrah!" shouted the yeomen.

"What?" said Little John, rising, without regard to his severe wound—thought nothing of in those heroic days—"have I been pummelling my liege?"

"No," cried the monarch, taking him heartily by the hand, laughing all the while, "been pummelled by your king."

"'Tis all the same," replied the tall forester. "Give me a goblet, and I will drink your health, my noble liege."

And Little John took up about a quart of strong Burgundy, which glided down his throat as if it had been milk.

With this trifling interruption the festivities were continued to about eleven, when, by preconcerted arrangement, a horn sounded, and the king, who had been thoughtful for some time, retired to his couch.

CHAPTER XLII.
THE VESSEL.

At early dawn the two monarchs were again on foot. Their plans were ready laid. The five knights with three-score of archers were to follow the road to a given rendezvous, while Robin, Little John, and King Richard were to reach the same spot by quite a different route.

Their object was strict secrecy.

The king had confided to his friend that while abroad he had received full particulars of a conspiracy against his person, the betrayer of which was interested in its being true.

His communication appeared frank enough, while the particulars left no doubt of the existence of the plot.

But as his informant was a distant relative and would enjoy title and estates if the others were punished, he, King Richard, wished to act with perfect circumspection, having no desire to alienate friends from him by unnecessary suspicion.

"Sir Gilbert de Frontdebœuf," said the king, "has always appeared to me friendly and true. This missive, however, is plain enough. He has turned against me, and is about to be led into the trammels of the advisers of my brother."

"You have certain evidence?"

"Certain that he is incensed against me. Now, for what, is the secret I want to discover."

"Is he an honourable man?"

"I always thought him so."

"Then there is perhaps treachery afoot, and you will do right to unmask it."

"But I fear me there is double treachery. My informant is one who, educated for Mother Church, has avoided entering in the hope of succeeding to Sir Gilbert, who has an only son."

"Is the son in the conspiracy?" asked Robin.

"More hot and furious than the father."

"Does the nephew expect you?"

"Heaven forfend! He but gives me timely notice of that which I may expect. But I am firmly resolved to find out for myself."

"How propose you to do it?"

"You must do it. Here is a signet of my brother's, one he usually wears and seldom parts with. That and a line from his confessor will bid them trust the bearer. They will then explain, perhaps, why it is such old friends have deserted me."

They were advancing all the time through the green wood.

The morning had risen beautifully fine; the sky was one vast expanse of blue, and a delicious cool air played about, tempering the sun's heat.

Robin led them by those mysterious ways, dells, and paths, known almost wholly to himself, never stopping, even when conversation became animated.

In this way they reached a halting-place, where they were glad to rest their weary feet, and take refreshment.

Little John, who was an excellent purveyor, had taken upon himself to provide and carry provisions, which were laid out upon the green in a twinkling.

All of the party were hungry, but just as they were about to appease that most vulgar of human wants Little John raised his finger to his lips.

All were still and silent.

Then Little John rose and disappeared, reappearing in a few minutes with the almost insensible form of a beautiful youth.

"I do believe," said the huge forester, with a glow of honest indignation, "that the creature is dying of hunger."

And without more ado, he poured a good drop of wine down the throat of the pale-looking youth, which after first nearly choking him, brought back the colour to his cheeks.

He opened his eyes.

"Why did you not let me die?" he asked.

"Not exactly," replied Little John, "when you only complained of hunger and thirst."

The tall forester continued helping the youth, who was extraordinarily handsome, while Robin and the king looked on with a strange smile.

"Now then, another cup."

"No more, kind sir."

"Let the young lady be quiet," said Robin, demurely, "you are a rough nurse."

"Young lady!" cried Little John, with a start and a blush, as he reflected how roughly he had carried her.

"Yes," said the stranger, with downcast eyes, "I am a girl, and a most wretched one."

"Why?" asked Robin.

"Ah, sir, you look kind and good, but you know not the troubles which one of my sex has to go through in these times."

"I am a husband, and hope to be a father; you can

tell your tale to one who will sympathise with, and if need be, befriend you. I am Robin Hood."

With a shriek she fell on her knees.

" Then you will defend me against a cruel and bad king, and against my father.

Richard raised his finger to his lips.

" You surely, child, must be mistaken. Our king is a good and generous one."

" Why, then, did he steal an only child from her father?"

" Speak, child," said Robin, who, with the others, listened attentively and bewilderedly ; " tell your story."

" I am Elfrida, only daughter of Sir Gilbert de Front-deboeuf," she began.

The king's brow darkened. He began to suspect.

" Four month's ago King Richard, during the late rebellion, stayed at my father's house."

" Yes."

" He must, it appears, have seen me, for no ·sooner was he gone than an emissary of his, an ugly, impudent page, came fluttering about me with the most tempting proposals. The king had seen and loved me, and if I would leave my father, there was nothing he would not do for me."

" And what said you ?"

" Spurned him."

" Brave girl ; but why told you not your father ?"

" He loved the king, and I did not wish to pain him."

" Well."

" He went away, and I thought no more of it, even though my cousin John would flout me for refusing so good an offer."

" Ah !" gasped the king.

" I silenced him, and threatened to expose him. Alas ! he was a creature of the cruel king, and by his aid I was carried away to York, where I have since been detained."

" S'death !" muttered the king, biting his moustache.

" I remained in apartments more fitted for tamborine girls, they were so gay, than for a modest girl, until it became known to me that the monarch who had so honoured a poor innocent girl had arrived. I saw him, and I liked him not."

" What manner of man ?" asked Robin.

The girl described Prince John to a nicety.

" By the sainted mother of God ! " said the king in a terrible tone, " for this most wretched deceit that traitor shall die ! Girl, I am King Richard."

With a cry wild and grateful, the girl turned from the outlaw to the king.

" And will you take me home ?"

" I will. But we must forward now. Can you walk, pretty one ? Don't blush—I won't eat you. If you like it better, I'll say you are ugly and I don't like the look of you."

A coquettish blush tinged her cheek as she spoke.

" I can walk. Three days have I wandered in the wood, having lost my way ; but now I am quite strong and can walk."

" And if you can't, I can carry six like you," said Little John.

Everybody laughed, and then the whole party rising from the sward, hurried forward.

The king and Robin were in deep conference, while the girl remained behind with Little John, who took care that she should not too much fatigue herself in crossing over brooks and in ascending steep hill sides.

Both the king and Robin Hood now saw clearly to the bottom of the foul conspiracy by which a faithful servant of the king had been alienated from him, while Richard was made the cloak to screen the foulness of the others vices.

The meeting in the wood, however, was something so providential, that they saw clearly through it the means of escaping from the difficulty, restoring the allegiance of Sir Gilbert, and punishing, at all events, the petty traitor.

As they went along through the wood their plans were laid with minuteness, and almost every contingency provided against.

This done, King Richard, who was truly of those who hated dullness, and would, if he had known it, have sung cheerily,—

" Away with melancholy ! "

changed the conversation, nor alluded to it once more until they were in sight of the small fortaliced castle of Sir Gilbert.

CHAPTER XLIII.

THE CROW'S NEST.

THE castle, which be longed to the sturdy old Norman—irascible and quick in temper, like most of his race—from being perched upon a height, was called by the common people the Crow's Nest.

Such names often stick to both buildings and natural objects, from the mere circumstance that they are generally both picturesque and descriptive.

It was not a large castle, and yet he commanded many vassals, who, however, in time of peace were scattered over his rather wide domains.

At the foot of the hill, in a spot embowered by trees, was a village such as always were in those days beneath the shelter of the larger building.

To this village the wayfarers directed their steps.

In the woods nigh at hand were ambushed the five knights and the outlaws.

Here was a small hostelrie, which they at once entered, and found seats, at least Robin and Little John.

The abbot and page retreated to a smaller and less noisy apartment.

The outlaws seated themselves close to a large party of men who were drinking, and were rather noisy in their demeanour ; they were regular soldiers, and their garb bespoke them to be retainers belonging to Prince John ; they were talking very loudly, and were most clamorous in their actions ;' their conversation was of a disjointed and desultory nature, principally relating to feats of arms. As the subject was roughly handled, there being more talkers than listeners, neither of the new arrivals paid any attention to it ; they drank their ale, and conversed apart in a low tone ; they were nearly ready to depart, when one of the drinking party offered an observation which immediately attracted their attention, and induced them to pause.

" What does this gathering portend ? " said one.

" Humph ! every one has their own opinion."

" It smells to me very like another rising. They do say this stalwart old knight Sir Gilbert will join us as soon as the envoy from Prince John arrives. He is expected every minute."

Robin and John exchanged glances.

Rising carelessly and paying for their ale, they went back and told the king what they had heard.

" Heaven is delivering the traitors into our hands. But the envoy ?"

" My men will make short work with him."

Saying which Robin led the way into the open air, and as soon as they were a proper distance from the ale-house, gave a shrill and clear whistle, which brought four outlaws to his side.

" Be on the look out, my minions of the moon. Every man or woman either that shall come ambling from Nottingham town arrest them, and bring them here."

The outlaws bowed and departed, the king and his companions seating themselves under a broad oak.

They had not been there for more than about half an hour when a scuffle was heard, and then up came a party of outlaws with a serving-man in the livery of King John, with two inferior attendants.

These men were searched with an ability peculiar to the outlaws, and stripped of every scrap of money, paper, and other valuables.

Robin soon added to this their clothes, and after giving over the men to the care of the merry footpads, he dressed himself in the habiliments of the envoy, and taking two yeomen as servitors and the abbot and page as fellow-travellers, walked up the narrow winding path towards the castle.

The portcullis was up, the drawbridge down, and there hastened to the entrance a young man in knightly garb.

" You ride from Nottingham ? " he asked, eagerly.

" We do."

" From the prince ? "

" I bear his despatches."

" In then, in heaven's name ! for my uncle is raging like a bear. Who are these ? "

A ROYAL BUFFET.

"My servitors and a worthy churchman and his mass-boy, who had lost their way in the woods. I wish you to show them all kindness."

"That will I," cried the other cheerfully, and he led them into a small refectory, while Robin followed the passage leading to the hall, where Sir Gilbert and his son were.

The father and son, choleric and fiery Normans, had so chafed themselves into fury at the thought of dishonour cast upon their house, that they were ready for any act of treason.

"So, sir, you have come at last," said the two-faced knight, as the envoy entered.

"Yes: and am going quicker than I came, if you speak to me thus."

The two angry men looked at him with astonishment.

"Saw any one ever such an impertinent jackanapes?" began the knight.

"Sir!" said Robin Hood, sternly, "I have come here from motives of kindness to you, and on business connected with Prince John and King Richard."

"Name him not."

"I must. If you are too obstinate or foolish to hear me—it is well. I can go."

"Speak, and prove that you have something to say, or I will hang you on the battlements."

"Sir Gilbert," said the envoy, closing the door, taking a chair, and helping himself to a glass from a bowl of wassail, "I am here as an envoy first, but mostly as a friend. Will you answer me one question?"

"Yes," said the bewildered knight.

"Have you anybody in this house who, if you were driven to rebellion, and were attainted, would gain your title and estates?"

"Why of course: cousin John," fumed Sir Gilbert.

"And has it never struck you that this gentleman, in order to gain his ends, has fabricated a charge against our good and noble king?"

"You are an envoy of Prince John?"

"To that, Sir Choleric, we will come presently."

"If the foul story of King Richard seeing your daughter, and sending a pander for her were false—"

"Sir!"

"If it was the pure invention of cousin John—"

"One word."

"If cousin John had painted your daughter in such glowing colours to the prince, as to induce him to abduct her—"

"Impossible!"

"If he took her to York, and intended her evil of the worst kind, passing himself as King Richard—"

"'Death, sir!"

"If, terrified and alarmed, she fled to the woods, ere the snarer could ensnare—"

"Withont, there!"

"If, once having roused your anger, cousin John had sent a sly messenger to King Richard, to warn him of intended treason—"

"Son, gag me this ruffian!"

But the son listened.

"If King Richard, disbelieving the traitor, came in hot haste to give his old friend a chance of explaining himself, and voyaging in the wood, met your poor child distraught and dying—"

"Give me air!"

"If, I say, all this were told you, what would you do?"

"'Tis a lie, a juggle! Michael, summons my warders, call John."

"On your head be it—in the name of King Richard I arrest you," said Robin Hood, advancing, with a staff in one hand, and with the other putting his bugle to his lips, and winding a piercing blast.

The door flew open, and King Richard, surrounded by his knights and merry men, entered.

Cousin John, livid and pale, scarcely able to crawl, rushed forward and fell at his uncle's knees.

"Pardon! pardon!" he cried.

"Then all this fellow has told me is true?"

"Sir Gilbert, fellow not my trusty Robin, Earl of Huntingdon. Whatever he has told you, rely on it as true. And now, young man, there is a rope round your neck: speak truthfully and honestly if you can."

"I see it in his face—I have right of pit and gallows—hang him."

"All rights cease in presence of your sovereign," said King Richard, mildly; "but he has made full confession, and my judgment is, that when we have made him march to Nottingham and shame his employer, he go beyond the seas, knowing that, if ever he shows his face in England again, he shall hang."

"But my child?"

"I am here," said his daughter, stepping forward on the arm of mighty Little John, "thanks to this worthy yeoman, able once more to call you father."

The old knight paused a moment to conquer his emotion.

"My liege, by foul treachery and falsehood I had been led nearly into the trap dug for me by my enemies. I was to blame for being so hasty, and submit to any punishment that you may fix upon, for in thought I have been a traitor to my good and generous sovereign."

"Tut, man, you were deceived by black falsehood, and now away with the traitor; and if you will shake hands, old rugged bear, the only thing I shall think of punishing is your pantry, which your pearly-eyed daughter here, who has called me very hard names, will doubtless see provided."

The knight was gouty, the knight was ailing, but as his sovereign uttered these words, he rose to his feet, gave one or two wild and incomprehensible hunting cries, whirled round like a dervish, and then sank plump into his chair.

"All's well that ends well," he said; "please God I'll get drunk to-night."

"But the gout, 'father," replied his daughter, resuming her old position at his side.

"Away, you jade; if you dare to tease your old father, he'll perhaps want to know more about your adventures than you would like to tell in this presence."

At which words she fled, leaving only Robin Hood, Little John, and the king with the knight and his son.

"'Tis well," said the king, sternly, "that the innocent dove did escape the fowler's net, for had my brother have taken advantage of her weakness, his punishment should have indeed been condign."

"I thank you, sire. How I could have been so blind is a mystery to me—but it cannot be undone."

"Nor will I have a word said more; here, you lazy Little John, take off my helmet. Is your head better?"

"Quite well, sire."

Sir Gilbert de Frontdebœuf and his son, despite all their sorrows, could not but look so ludicrously puzzled at the presence in their castle, as sole guardians to the king of England, of a band of outlaws, that the expression was seen in their faces.

"You are surprised," said the king, gravely, "that I am surrounded by outlawed and banned men. Sir Gilbert, during many of the miserable days, which rebellion has made in this land, treachery and lust of dominion would have succeeded, and Richard would have lost his crown, but for the devotion, bravery, and noble-heartedness, of my faithful commons, Robin Hood, Little John, Will Scarlett, and the other merry men of Sherwood Forest."

"Gad zooks!" cried the astonished knight; "I should never have thought thieves had been such honest men."

And while yet the laughter was hot at his sally, the worthy knight held out his hand and shook Robin's hand.

"*Mort de ma vie!*" he added, "there is one in the strong-room who wears your cloth, I doubt, who was put there for killing a deer in my chase, cracking a keeper's crown, and kissing three wenches. We'll have him out—every outlaw in Sherwood shall be free of my deer."

"What manner of man?" asked Robin.

"Stout and burly, more like a priest than a minion of the moon," said Gilbert.

"My old friend, the friar! Have him up. Unbind him not, but let the clerk of Copmanhurst appear. Is he sober?"

"Well," cried the knight, scratching his head, "we have been so much occupied with our own affairs, that I am rather afraid he has been forgotten."

The son hurried away, and while the serving-men brought in goodly store of provisions for a feast, opened the friar's cell, and brought him to the light.

Friar Tuck had probably only fasted a number of hours likely to be beneficial to soul and body, but he did not think so, for the first thing his deliverer heard was a volley of abuse, followed by a lecture on the sinfulness of starving a man of God.

"A man of God," said a deep voice, as he entered the banquet-hall, "should behave as such, and neither steal venison, break noddles, nor kiss wenches."

"But that I think that is a voice I may not answer," cried the angry priest, "I would say many things."

"Shield not thyself thus. If the clerk of Copmanhurst is angry with his old guest, his arm is at his disposal."

"No, Sir Black Knight," replied Tuck, "I have tried the weight of your fist, and though maybe I may again, I hope it will not be fasting."

"So," said the knight, amazed at the king's varied acquaintances, "*this* is one of your friends?"

"Yes, I suppose I must own him," said the good-natured monarch, laughing.

"Well sirrah, why didn't you say so? If I had known you were a friend of the Lion-heart, you might have killed my deer, threshed my men, kissed my girls."

"Sir Gilbert."

"My liege."

"I don't think my name would have served me yesterday."

"Humph!" said the knight, making some such wry face as he was wont to get up when his toe gave its most gouty twinges.

And now, business being over, the five young faithful knights, who had been true to their king, were called in and the supper began in earnest.

All animosity, doubt, and political excitement were now placed on one side.

King Richard was never happier than when he quite put away every trace of state.

With those who knew his humour, and did not trench too much upon his goodnature, he was then the most charming of boon companions and drinkers.

Fond of good living, fond of his glass, fond of his song, there was no one who could bring out better the companionable qualities of his loyal subjects than King Richard.

It will therefore surprise none to hear that between them they contrived to make a very pleasant night of it.

CHAPTER XLIV.

A ROYAL FREAK.

MANY writers have urged that while King Richard was better than most other kings, he was but that useless character a knight errant.

From Alfred down to Queen Victoria, leaving those two out of the question, we have had nothing but detestably bad kings and queens—the Cœur de Lion being the only exception.

The grasping ambition of the aristocracy, the time-serving sycophancy of the clergy, and the gross ignorance of the people have, under these circumstances, been the sole reasons why monarchy has even been tolerated.

With an educated people, a Christian church, and a patriot aristocracy, monarchy could not have existed.

But Richard was rather a chivalrous soldier than a statesman. Born to rank, he accepted it as a thing of course, and his soul being attuned rather to war than diplomacy, he left poor England to be guarded over by a set of blood-suckers, princes, barons, and bishops, while he fought for glory.

It is only that characteristic, in which he resembled Don Quixotte, which made him undertake such extraordinary and singular adventures.

The one in which he was engaged was more like a school-boy's frolic, than anything else.

Next day, having secured his prisoner, and put both the gouty knight and his daughter into a litter under the charge of the alarmed envoy and the retainers of the prince, he himself, accompanied only by Robin, his followers, and the four knights, returned towards the trysting place, intending to take his departure for Nottingham from that point.

Robin himself ventured to remonstrate against the monarch's decision, but received for his pains a good rating, and like a loyal and obedient subject said no more.

First a courier was despatched to Prince John, to say that Sir Harry Juder had so far succeeded in his design that in two days he would enter Nottingham, bearing with him Robin Hood and his leading men in his train.

At this Prince John was overjoyed, as securing to him the person of one of the boldest and most useful adherents of his brother.

He was so delighted, that until the moment came when he should glut his eyes with such a prisoner, he did nothing but feast.

The sheriff's house was one with a noble presence, and having a large covered gallery in front. This the new sheriff, in honour of his guest, decked out most gaily.

All the citizens were ordered, on pain of high pains and penalties, and the strong displeasure of the prince, to treat it as a gala day, so that perforce more flags, arras and other adornments were seen than had been known for many a day.

The people, both gentle and simple, both those who sided with Robin—who, for his rough, rude, coarse day, was as true a patriot as Garibaldi—and those who hated and feared him, turned out in great array.

There was a strange mustering of soldiers, too, retainers of great nobles and others, some of whom Prince John cared not to see, as knowing them loyal to the crown.

But it was a festive day, and not one in which any political complications were like to arise.

But man proposes and heaven disposes.

The day was yet young; it was ten, and still Prince John was impatient already.

"I hope this old iron-cap is no braggart or trick-player," he said as he took his seat in the balcony.

"He would hardly befool your grace."

"I'd flay him alive, knight though he be, an' he flouted me," cried John.

Sir Gilbert de Frontdebœuf, who that morning had arrived, and sat erect on horseback near the gallery, coughed.

"Is anything the matter?" cried the prince; "why, if one jokes about a mailed sir, all the others back."

"I know Sir Harry Juder," replied Sir Gilbert, "and I beg to say that your highness would scarcely like to flay him, or even to speak of it."

"God's wounds!" cried the brutal prince, "he or any other man who stood in my way."

"Your grace can tell him so," said Sir Gilbert de Frontdebœuf, coldly; "here he is."

At the same moment a flourish of trumpets was heard, and five knights in gay apparel, preceded by five pursuivants-at-arms, appeared in the road.

Behind and around them was a cloud of archers in the well-known Lincoln green.

What came behind none could see.

The citizens began to run; some were alarmed, some caught up sword and spear, but others smiled.

"Foregad!" said Prince John, uneasily, "the outlaw seems to have caught the knight."

"'Tis passing strange."

"Ah! there rides the outlaw in Lincoln green. Is that huge fellow in green beside him Little John?"

"No, your grace, 'tis Sir Harry Juder, or if you like it better, King Richard, God bless him."

The prince turned white, and would have fled.

"Nay," said Sir Gilbert de Frontdebœuf, with a lowering frown, "I have his orders. My retainers guard every avenue. If you move I shall make you prisoner before all."

The guilty man shivered, and seating himself on his throne, awaited the brother's coming, more alive than dead.

By this time the truth was everywhere known that the lion-hearted king had returned in his usual mysterious way, and that having been the guest of Robin Hood, to do him honour and show his appreciation of his true worth and sterling honesty, had led aside his monkish garb, and dressed like one of the outlaws in Lincoln green.

The great majority of the people were delighted to find that, instead of being present at a gaol entry, they were to see a festival, and nearly all were rejoiced that Robin Hood had obtained life and grace.

And now the merry cavalcade approached, and Prince John, despite the splendour of the day, drew his miniver or ermine cloak around him as if he was cold.

As, indeed, he was, with the shivers of fear and dread for his own wickedness.

It was a marvel to see how the boldest and loudest talkers against their lord and master, the joint conspirators with the prince, now fell from him.

These were the loudest to wave their bonnets, and cry "God save King Richard."

He rode with a smiling face and serene brow, conversing amicably and unaffectedly with Robin Hood, as if he had been one of his courtiers.

Though not able when absent to defend Robin Hood, he threw the mantle of his friendship over him.

And that is much; for whom the king delighteth to honour, the servile multitude will too often applaud.

They were in front of the balcony, and Sir Richard of the Lee had called the king's attention several time to the prince.

"His grace bows to your majesty," said the staunch old courtier.

"He will have to bow his neck lower," replied the king, in a stern cold voice, without once turning round his head.

The mayor and burgesses now hurried forward to greet the king, and asked if it was his pleasure that Nottingham castle should hoist the royal flag?

"No; I am all for the commons to-day; and so, Mr. Mayor, if I shall not eat you out of house and home, we will hold our court in the house of your worshipful self."

A tremendous huzza arose upon this, the mayor being a sturdy stickler for popular rights.

And so without halting they went on to the mayor's residence, which was both picturesque and pleasant, he being a man of considerable wealth, earned by honest industry.

As soon as the archers had made a lane to keep off the exuberant loyalty of the crowd, the king alighted, and walking in his Lincoln green with a graceful step, not always compatible with armour, ascended the step, bowed to the crowd, and disappeared, leaning on the arm of Robin Hood.

Prince John sat dumbfounded, unable to speak.

"Whither do you take me?" he said, addressing Sir Gilbert de Frontdebœuf in a hollow tone.

"Where my cousin John already lies," replied the Norman knight, "in Nottingham castle."

And shortly after King Richard entered the mayor's residence, Prince John passed, under heavy escort, evidently a prisoner.

And none said God bless him.

CHAPTER XLV.

WHAT LAY UNDER THE STRAWBERRIES.

It was generally rumoured in Nottingham that the king, utterly disgusted with his brother, would, on this occasion, settle the matter by privately putting him to death—but rumour lied.

Richard was too generous, and though determined to keep a sharp lookout on his brother for the future, by no means put him under any very painful restraint.

His custodian in Nottingham castle was a man in whom Prince John himself had every reason to put confidence.

It was Sir Herbert Trent, a sworn friend of the king, but at the same time one wholly averse to bloodshed.

This is the description given of him at this time, in the history of those days.

He was in person about the middle height, rather above it than below, and at this period was not more than twenty-three years of age. His forehead was broad and fine, with short, dark hair curling round it; his features were small, except the eye and brow, the former of which was large and full, and the latter strongly marked. The mouth was very handsome, showing when half open in speaking, the brilliant white teeth, and giving to the whole countenance a look of playful gaiety: but when shut, there was an expression of much thoughtfulness, approaching perhaps to sternness, about it, which the rounded and somewhat prominent chin confirmed. The upper lip was very short; but, on either side, divided in the middle, was a short, black moustache, not overhanging the mouth, but raised above it; and the beard, which was short and black like the hair, was only suffered to grow in such a manner as to ornament, but not encumber the chin.

In form the cavalier was muscular, and powerfully made, his breadth of chest and shoulders giving the appearance of a more advanced period of life, than that at which he had yet arrived. He was evidently a soldier, for he was fully armed, as if having lately been or being still in scenes of strife and danger; and to say the truth, a man fully armed in those days was certainly more loaded with weapons, offensive and defensive, than was probably ever the case before or since.

"Armed at all points, I see," remarked Prince John, when his custodian announced that he was come to pay his respects.

"At *all* points," replied Sir Herbert, who laid very great stress upon this one word.

"Well, I suppose it will be but a day's wonder. As soon as my brother starts for France I shall be free again."

"Not, your grace, if I remain your jailer."

"Why so?"

"Does your highness wish to know?" said Sir Herbert, with cold and quivering lips.

"I do."

"I am the affianced husband of Elfrida Frontdebœuf, who so happily escaped from your kind custody at York."

The Prince groaned.

"But," he said, rallying, "that was only a political necessity."

"Indeed, my lord."

"I wished too well to the family to intend her any harm," continued the prince.

The keeper bowed.

"Does your highness require anything more?"

"No—yes."

"Which does your highness mean?"

"Well, am I to be starved, or poisoned, or stabbed?"

"Neither one nor the other. Your highness requires refection."

"Wine and a boon companion."

"I can offer you no one but myself," he replied.

"Thanks, that would be too gloomy. When you are in a better humour, I say not nay;" laughed the prince, always selfish and volatile.

Sir Herbert Trent bowed.

When Lord Belford be avenged himself for the intended insult put upon the wife, who afterwards lived thirty years honoured and respected by all.

King John expiated many of the wild escapades of the unprincipled prince.

The wine was soon brought, and presently, after some delay, Sir Herbert Trent returned, and said that a cousin of his, somewhat of a roysterer, would be happy if he were allowed to pay his respects to the prince.

"His name?"

"Reginald Markham."

"Oh! I know. He will drink, that will do."

Sir Herbert Trent smiled a cold sardonic smile as he bowed himself out.

Soon after Sir Reginald Markham, a young and handsome courtier, came strutting in.

Now the prince knew that his confederates and friends would not desert him, for one simple reason.

They knew him so false and treacherous, that if left to himself they knew he would revenge himself by betraying his co-rebels.

But Reginald was but a boon companion, so with him he only quaffed and joked and spoke of the scandal of the day.

Presently the conversation ceased. The prince became moody and thoughtful.

The courtier was too respectful to interrupt him.

The casement was open, and, seated in a large chair, with his feet resting on a stool, sat the captive prince, gazing down upon a part of the town and the meadows and orchards beyond.

The apple-trees were all in blossom, and every shrub in the manifold gardens had put on the blush of vegetable youth, promising rich fruit in the maturity of the year.

Beyond the meadows and the orchards came slopes and rising ground, and lines of deep wood, sheltering the intervening space, and then high hills were seen fading off into the sky.

On the left hand the scene was all open; but on the right an angle of the cathedral, as it then appeared, bounded the view, while the tower of another church of inferior dimensions rose up under the eye, and cut the long straight lines of the houses and other buildings.

The soft air of summer wafted to the window the scent of the blossoms from the fields beyond, and John thought it spoke of liberty.

Uprose from the streets and houses the manifold sounds of busy life, the buzz of talking multitudes, the call, the shout, the merry laugh of idle boyhood, and still to the captive's ears they spoke of liberty.

The bells joined in and rang complines, and turning his eyes thither, he thought how often he had heard those sweet tones, at even-close, in the happy days of early youth, returning from the chase, or any other of the free sports of the time. His sight wandered on, over tower and spire, round which the crows were winging their airy flight, to the deep woods and blue hills flooded with glory from the declining sun.

Still, still, it all spoke of liberty; and John's heart felt oppressed, his very breathing laboured, as he remembered the mighty blessing he had lost.

It was like the sight of a river to a man dying with thirst in the sands of Africa, without the strength to reach it.

He gazed, and perhaps for a moment might forget himself and his hard fate in a dream of enjoyment, but if he did it lasted not long—the dark reality soon came between him and the light of fancy—and letting his head droop, he turned away with a deep sigh, and gave up a brief space to bitter meditation.

The sun was going down when Reginald Markham entered the prince's chamber, and ere he had been there half an hour, the bright orb had sunk beneath the horison; but in these northern climes heaven has vouchsafed to us a blessing which brighter lands do not possess—the long soft twilight of the summer evening—and the sky was still full of light, so that one might have read with ease in the high chamber of the prince nearly half an hour after the star of day had disappeared. It was just at that moment that Reginald, who was sitting with his face towards the door, saw it open slowly and silently, and a beautiful girl, dressed in somewhat gay and sparkling attire, even for those gaudy times, entered with a noiseless step, bearing a small basket in her hand.

An expression of some surprise on the young man's countenance made John himself turn round, and the sight suddenly produced signs of greater amazement in his face than even in Reginald's. He rose instantly, however, saying—

"What would you, my fair lady?"

"Nothing, royal sir," replied the girl, "but to bring your grace this small basket of early strawberries. You will find the flavour good," she added, "especially at the bottom, where they have not been heated by the sun."

As she spoke she put down the basket on the table, and was retreating quickly, but John exclaimed—

"Stay—stay, pretty one! Tell me who you are, that I may remember in my prayers one who has thought upon her captive prince, and striven to solace him in his imprisonment."

"It matters not," replied the girl, curtseying low, and speaking evidently with a country accent; "it matters not. I promised not to stay a moment, but to give the strawberries and to come away. God send your grace a happy even, and a happy morning to boot!" Thus saying she retired, closing the door carefully behind her.

"This is strange," said the prince, taking up the basket, and turning towards Reginald.

But the young man was buried in deep meditation.

"You seem surprised?" said the prince; "and, faith, so am I too. I never saw the girl in all my life. Did you, Reginald?"

"Methinks I have," observed Reginald, "and that many a mile hence. But I will now leave you my prince, the gates will soon be shut."

"Nay, stay, and take some of this sweet food," said the prince, "which has been brought me, not by ravens, but by doves."

"He is right, he is right!" cried Reginald. "There is more than fruit in that basket, or I am much mistaken."

The prince laid his hand upon it firmly, and fixed a keen and searching glance upon the young man, saying, "Whatever there be in it is mine, and for mine eye alone."

But his companion passed round the table, bent one knee before him, and kissing his hand respectfully, said, "My noble and future king, you have mistaken me, but it is now time to tell you that I am no gaoler. If I be not very wrong, there are in that basket tidings which shall soon set you free as the wind. I have already asked permission for you to ride forth, accompanied by six gentlemen of my choosing, and followed by a train of spears. I said that it was the only means of you keeping in health. I might have added, had I pleased, and to liberty. Now, my prince, see what that basket does contain, and believe me, if it cost my head to keep your secret, I would not reveal it."

"Thanks, Reginald, thanks," replied the prince; "we often suspect the honest of being guilty, but this time suspicion has taken a different course, and I have long suspected thee of being honest. Now suppose all your hopes are false?" and he overturned the basket on the table.

Nothing fell from it except the fruit, but fastened to the bottom by a piece of wax, appeared, on closer inspection, a small billet, folded so as to take the form of the basket.

Prince John opened it hastily, and found, as he expected, that it was from one of the many who were implicated with him, and who were afraid that if he were brought to trial he might try to gain mercy by betraying his associates.

They said that there could be no doubt of obtaining leave for him to ride out under the guard of a dozen gentlemen or so, when an escape could be easily contrived.

They bade the prince trust Reginald Markham.

A plan which had been already spoken of would be the best, and he would best explain.

The prince read the letter, and then informed the other of its contents.

"What is your plan?"

"Your grace shall ride a race."

"A race?"

"Ay, my prince, a race that shall set you free."

"And my gaoler?"

"He must be kept out of the way."

"Why, is he so bitter?"

"Ah, my lord," said Reginald, with something of a flushed face, "it was not well to seek his bride as your leman."

"I never spoke to the girl."

"But your grace abducted her."

"I was wrong, fore gad!" cried John, who was the most coarse swearer of his day, "I was wrong. But I am ever thus. A pretty face will upset all my good resolutions."

"We all feel that way. But Elfrida was the daughter of a good knight, and the affianced wife of a good man."

"He will marry her?"

"Because he knows her virtuous, and because the king hath sworn to her truth."

"How met Richard with knowledge of her truth?"

"He and the outlaw found her in the forest, and she told them a strange story, not very pleasant to King Richard to hear."

"Ah! I see."

"They took her home to her father and explained."

"Was ever anything so unfortunate! That Robin Hood is my most bitter foe. He is ever baulking me in my hopes."

"Here it is fortunate," said Reginald, drily; "for had harm come to the girl, your grace might have suffered the fate of Rufus."

The prince turned pale, more with passion than fear.

"'Tis rude speaking thus to one who may be your king."

"Those who speak thus are your grace's truest friends," said Reginald. "Even a king may do that which nobles and commons may not bear."

"I misdoubt me," said John, gaily, "you will be a sturdy baron, one of the stiff-necked generation, if I come to be king."

"I will strive to do my duty to my conscience."

While this conversation was taking place Reginald Markham was putting back the strawberries.

Reginald had scarcely completed his task and set down the basket when there entered the room the guardian already alluded to, with a silver dish in his hand. His eye was stern, and his whole mien that of one suspicious of the slightest unusual thing.

"Seeing that a fair lady has carried you some strawberries, my lord," he said, "I have brought you a dish to put them in."

And taking up the basket he emptied it slowly into the silver plate.

"Thanks, sir, thanks," said the prince gaily, and with a look of total indifference as to what was done with the fruit. "Methinks if you had brought me some cream it would have been as well."

"Your lordship shall have it immediately," answered the other; "they are fine berries so early in the season."

"They will refresh me after my fever," said John, "for still my mouth feels dry."

"You shall then have the cream directly," replied the other, vexed at himself, having found nothing to confirm his suspicions.

He then left the room.

Prince John and Reginald Markham looked at each other with a smile, and the note was soon re-read and totally destroyed.

CHAPTER XLVI.

A RACE FOR FREEDOM.

KING RICHARD kept great state in Nottingham. It was not often he showed himself in England, being too fond of war in foreign parts; but now not only did his feudal vassals come crowding round him, but the people generally, who were glad to see the king of whom they had heard so much.

Robin Hood, though sorely against his genuine feelings, remained at court, putting off his forest garb and assuming the gay and showy apparel of a noble.

So Richard willed.

It was the king's intention to wait in Nottingham the arrival of his counsellors.

At last the good-natured monarch was quite angry, and determined that he would bring his brother to judgment.

He was not one of those who even thought of sending him to the block, but he wished to let him feel some punishment.

He was at the same time more anxious than he otherwise would have been from his extreme desire to return to Normandy, where a petty war was waging, to which he wished to put an end.

On one or two occasions he suggested that Robin Hood should accompany him, but the bold outlaw resolutely refused: he would never leave England, his Marian, and his outlaws.

The day came when couriers brought intelligence that the privy-council were at hand; and Richard, who had been passing the time in amusement, of which hawking was the favourite episode, hastened out to meet them.

He wished, before Prince John was formally brought before him, to warn the judges he himself had selected not to be too severe.

Meanwhile, events were occurring which were to alter very much his intentions.

About half an hour after these events had taken place John stood in the midst of the chamber already described, habited in a light riding suit, but armed only with his sword. He was gazing with a look of expectation at the door, when it opened, and his young companion Reginald entered in haste.

"Oh, yes," he said, with a well pleased smile, "he fully confirms the permission; and, indeed, Greenly, Hardy, and Arthur, with three or four more, are already waiting in the courtyard for your coming."

"Is my horse prepared, then?" demanded the prince.

"Why the foolish grooms, my prince," replied the young man, "had brought out the roan, alleging that the grey was lean, and not like a prince's horse; but I bade them saddle him, notwithstanding, saying that I had given him to your grace, and checking them for not obeying the order they had received; he is doubtless caparisoned by this time. But you are pale, my prince —the fever has weakened you; were it not as well to take a cup of wine before you ride forth?"

The prince shook his head.

"Not so," he said; "when I strike my spur into that horse's side the very thought of freedom shall give me better strength and courage than the best wine that ever France produced. However, let me have your arm; it will be well to seem a little weaker than I am. Do you go with me, Reginald?"

"No, my prince," answered his companion, "I am not one of those named, and to speak the truth, I did not seek the honour, for I might but embarrass you, and I must provide for my own safety here."

"Are you sure you can?" demanded the prince. "You must not risk your life for me, Reginald."

"Oh! fear not—fear not;" replied the young nobleman, "give me but one hour, and I will be beyond the reach of harm."

After a few more words, the prince took his arm, and slowly descended the stairs, at the foot of which they found a number of gentlemen assembled, with several servants holding the horses which had been prepared for their excursion.

The prince bowed familiarly to the various gentlemen present, and was received with every appearance of deference and respect.

"Good morning, Hardy," he said, "good morning, gentlemen; you are good judges of horses, and Reginald has given me one which he declares will make an excellent charger—God speed the mark. When shall I need a charger again? But here he comes, at least I suppose so. What think you of him?"

"Nay, no jesting, gentlemen!" cried Reginald, remarking a smile upon the lips of the rest; "that is a horse which, when well-fed and pampered highly, will do more service than a thousand sleek-coated beauties."

"To the latter appellation, at least, he has no title," replied one, looking at the horse as it was led forward, "but he has good qualities about him, nevertheless."

"He seems quiet enough," observed the prince, "and to say sooth, that is no slight matter with me to-day. I am not strong enough to ride a rough-paced, fiery charger. But let us mount, gentlemen, and go. Farewell, Reginald, I will not break your horse's wind."

"I defy your grace," answered Reginald, holding prince John's stirrup, as he mounted slowly. "I wish you a pleasant ride."

"If I can obtain many such rides," continued Prince John, "I shall soon be quite well. See how proud Arthur is of his horse! and yet I would bet a silver tankard against a pewter can, that Greenly would beat it for the distance of half a mile, or Hardy within."

Hardy, who was near, smiled, well pleased, and the other, to whom Prince John had spoken, exclaimed, "Do you hear what the prince says, Arthur—that Greenly's horse would beat yours for half a mile?"

"Greenly would not venture to try," answered Arthur, "I should think."

"Oh, I will try!" cried Greenly, "to please the prince, I will try with all my heart. Let us set off!"

"Nay, nay," rejoined John," let us wait till we get upon the turf on the higher ground. If I remember right, there is as fair a course there as any in England. We will make matches there for you, and I will give a golden drinking cup as a prize for the horse that beats all the rest. You shall run two and two at a time, and the gentlemen who remain with me will be the judges of each course."

"Agreed, agreed!" cried the whole party with one accord.

"I shall win the cup!" said Arthur.

"Not you!" shouted Hardy, in his loud, hoarse voice. "It is scarcely fair for me, however, for I am so much heavier than you are."

"But you have a stronger horse," replied Prince John, and thus passing the time in light conversation, they mounted slowly the first gentle slopes in the neighbourhood, and came upon some fine dry turf at the top.

As soon as they found an open space where there was grass enough Arthur and Greenly put their horses into a quick pace and galloped on, taking for the winning-post a tree that stood detached at the distance of about half a mile.

Arthur was the lighter man of the two, and he rode well, but Greenly's horse was decidedly superior, and he had already passed the tree when his competitor was two or three lengths behind. The prince seemed greatly to enjoy the sport, and cheered on the men and horses with his voice and hand. Two more competitors speedily succeeded the first, and still the whole party kept advancing over the wild, turfy sort of down, ever and anon choosing an open spot for their gay pastime.

"Now, Hardy," said the Prince, at length, "you must try with Arthur. As you are the heavier man you have some advantage in his horse being rather tired. We will give you a mile's course, too, so that your beast's strength will tell. There, up to that gate, with the little village church beyond; and if you beat him, I will fill the cup with silver pieces. He is so proud of his beast, it makes me mad to see him."

Arthur patted the arching neck of his proud charger with a self-satisfied smile, and at the given signal gave him his head. Away the two best horses in the party went, and ran the longer course before them with very equal speed, Arthur taking the lead at first, but Hardy's stronger beast gaining upon him afterwards. Arthur, however, was the first to reach the gate, but Hardy dared him to try his chance back again, and away they came once more at headlong speed. This time Hardy was first, till, at the distance of about three hundred yards from the Prince, his horse stumbled, and came down with a heavy fall. The rider and the charger were both upon their feet again in a moment, but the beast had struck his knee, although not severely, and went lame as he finished the rest of his course.

"I know not how we must award the prize here," said the Prince; "for had it not been for that accident——"

"Oh, it is mine—it is mine, fairly!" cried Arthur.

"Yes, my lord, I think he has won it," said several voices round.

"Oh, I have won it!" reiterated Arthur; but added, laughing, "unless his grace himself will ride a course with me upon his grey charger."

"It must be but a short one, Arthur," answered Prince John; "but I do not mind if I try for some hundred yards or two the metal of the beast. What say you to that little tree?"

"With all my heart," replied Arthur.

"On, then," cried the prince; and at the same moment he loosed the rein—at which his horse had been tugging for the last half-hour—and struck his spurs into the animal's sides. Like an arrow shot from a bow, the lean and bony charger darted forth, covering an immense space of ground at every stretch, and speedily leaving Arthur and his vaunted steed behind.

Spurring with all his might, the disappointed cavalier followed on John's track; but though the distance to the tree was certainly not more than five hundred yards, the prince was fully fifty in front when he passed it.

Seeing that it was in vain to make any further effort, Arthur slackened his speed; but to his astonishment the prince spurred on, gaining upon him every minute, and at the distance of about seventy or eighty yards, feeling the immense speed and power of the horse that he bestrode, Prince John turned gaily round in the saddle, and, waving his hand, exclaimed in a loud voice—

"All courteous things to my brother! Tell him he shall hear from me soon!"

At this moment King Richard and Robin Hood came up, cantering slowly along.

A dark frown crossed the monarch's face.

"How is this?" he said to one of the gentlemen.

Hardy candidly explained.

"He has the cunning of a fox," said Richard, quietly. "Well, in flight and exile he cannot do much harm. I will even back to Nottingham. Let him go."

And perhaps in his own heart glad to be off punishing one who was so nearly allied to him, he turned back towards the town, and when the privy council arrived simply gave them a grand banquet, leaving business to the next day.

CHAPTER XLVII.
ROUGH WOOING.

IT was a painful day for Robin when he took, what somehow he believed would be, his last interview with King Richard.

There are times when our feelings get the better of us, and despite common sense and reason we believe in omens.

Richard himself was never in heartier spirits, for he was once more going into battle against the enemies of his country.

With all his great qualities, Richard was even more a soldier than a statesman, and loved the clang of arms.

At length the monarch of Sherwood and the king of England parted; the one to march with his forces to the sea coast, there to embark for Normandy, the other to rejoin his men, who had preceded him on the way to the old trysting place.

Robin was thoughtful, and Robin was sad, so that he was glad to be alone.

He was one of those to whom at times his own company was very pleasant.

He had cast off the trappings of a court, and appeared once more in his costume of an English yeoman.

We will, however, leave him, and follow the fortunes of one of simpler rank.

Nottingham town was one of the strongholds of the outlaws; hence they had taken some of their best men, while Nottingham lasses were the favourites as wives.

If an artisan were illused by his master; if an apprentice were beaten; if parents were unkind, in fact, whenever the wild impulses of youth led men astray, they quietly walked off to the forest and joined Robin Hood.

Now Arthur-a-Bland was the son of a tanner in Nottingham.

He was a tall man of his inches, and handsome too.

But he was cousin to Little John.

His acquaintance with the tall forester was not very great, but he had met him once or twice at ale-houses, and his descriptions of forest life were entrancing.

For some time he had been inclined to leave the sober life of an artisan for the forest. He was in fact a wild unsettled lad, and loved the hide better when rough and warm on the bull's back, than in his own tan-pit, and in a fair way of becoming soles and uppers for boots and shoes. In his day there was no settled work for a tanner; husbandmen tanned the leather of their own shoes and horse-furniture in a way which science would scorn now, but tough withal and wearable; and this perhaps induced honest Arthur to think more of Barnesdale Wood and his cousin Little John than of toiling with raw hides in an unsavory solution of oak-bark and ditchwater.

But he was restrained by one feeling.

He loved the prettiest, most coquettish, laughing, bright-eyed little girl in all Nottingham.

He had every reason to think that she loved him.

But a girl of sixteen either does not know her own mind or will not surrender to the wishes of a lover quite so easily as more experienced damsels.

Arthur-a-Bland loved Mary Hardinge with all his heart and soul.

What the girl's thoughts might have been it was almost impossible to say.

She was courted on all hands, and when a girl has many lovers, she does not easily resign her liberty by selecting one.

The consequence was that Arthur was jealous.

It was after work hours, and Arthur-a-Bland, as was his wont of an evening, had gone down to drink his mug of ale at the ale-house.

There are few innkeepers but are aware of the attractions of a pretty face.

Hardinge was quite up to the influence of his daughter's bright eyes and ruddy cheeks.

As a matter of course, he was not very anxious to marry her.

The girl, too, was young, and attached to her rough father.

She therefore played with them all, not even allowing the chosen one to know too certainly his victory.

Mary was alone.

Her father was out.

Arthur came in as usual, took off his cap, and as was also usual when none were present, kissed her.

"Don't."

"Why?"

"I don't like it."

"What has come to you?"

"Nothing; don't be rude. Father Anselmo says girls should never allow themselves to be kissed."

"What then, were their lips made for?"

"I don't know."

And Mary flounced away in search of the usual mug of ale.

"Mary," said Arthur-a-Bland, when she returned, "I wish a word with you."

"Two."

"I saw Tom the blacksmith last night."

"Well?"

"Is he coming here to-night?"

"Yes."

"Then there will be murder. He kissed you last night, and you made no fuss."

"He's a friend of father's."

"And so am I; and more than that, always thought I was a friend of yours."

"I never told you so."

"You have as good as accepted me as a husband."

"Until some one better turns up."

"Mary?"

"Yes."

"We must come to an understanding to-night. I can't go on shilly-shallying any more. I am two-and-twenty, I have pretty good work, and why not marry at once?"

"I shall never marry until I am years older," said Mary, "and I don't think I could be fool enough to throw myself away upon you."

"Mind that you mean what you say," said the youth, tartly, "for I shall never ask you again."

"Just as you like."

Arthur-a-Bland, very pale and determined, rose, drank his ale, and held out his hand.

"Good-bye, Mary."

"I shan't shake hands with you," she replied; "if you go like this, I will never speak again."

"Then promise to marry me in a month."

"I will not be forced to anything. Ask me a year hence."

"Now or never!"

"Then no at once."

"You will be sorry some day," said Arthur-a-Bland, and went out without turning his head.

Mary's face was very flushed and hot, and a tear even stood in her eye. But she was resolved, and nothing could move her to call him back.

Arthur was dogged and angry. He had not the wit to see that all this was coquetry.

In this unsettled state of mind, and with a reputation for a broil, he walked into the forest prepared alike for mischief or for mirth, careless whether he met with a dun deer or an armed outlaw. In colours suited to his character the old minstrel has sketched him:—

> In Nottingham there lives a jolly tanner,
>   His name is Arthur-a-Bland:
> There's never a squire in Nottinghamshire
>   Dare bid bold Arthur stand.
> With a long pike-staff on his shoulder,
>   So well he can clear his way;
> By two and by three he makes them to flee,
>   For he hath no list to stay.

In his passion he asked nothing better than to meet some one whom he could trounce.

But as luck would have it, he met no one the first day, and so camped alone in a thicket, supping on his passion and temper.

He cast women to the wind, and thought that never again should he think of one.

But 'tis our destiny, and if one jilts us, there is another ready. There is as good fish in the sea as ever came out of it.

After bemoaning his sad fate for some time, he put his head on the grass and went to sleep.

When he woke at early morn, he was cooler, and he held a council of war with himself.

Should he give up father, mother, friends, and business for a girl's frown?

It was a serious consideration.

But there is a lurking devil in us all, which does more mischief than is generally believed.

It is pride.

And after, in the girl's presence, walking straight off to the wood, he could not reconcile to himself to go back.

So he determined to do something which should qualify him for an outlaw.

To shoot the king's deer and break the forest laws was the easiest way.

Now Arthur-a-Bland, in addition to his large pike, had a bow and quiver.

So he determined to have some sport.

Now as he looked at the red deer he chanced to meet Robin Hood, and not knowing him, resolved to have some sport.

"What makes you here so like a thief?" inquired the Tanner; "I am a keeper in this forest, and it is my duty to stay you."

"Hast any assistants, man?" inquired Robin: "it is not one man that stops me."

"Truly, friend," said the Tanner, "I have no better assistant than this good oak-graff, and it will do all I want."

> "For thy sword and thy bow I care not a straw,
>   Nor all thine arrows to boot;
> For an I get a knop at thy bare scap,
>   Thou canst as well spit as shoot.
> Speak gently, good fellow, said jolly Robin,
>   And give better terms to me;
> Else I'll thee correct for thy neglect,
>   In not speaking mannerly."

"Marry, guep with a wanion," exclaimed the tanner; "I regard not thy big looks."

Robin on this unbuckled his belt, laid aside his sword and bow, and, taking up a good quarterstaff of oak, said, "Let us measure staves, so that the play may be fair."

> "I care not for length," bold Arthur replied,
>   My staff is of oak so free;
> Eight foot and a half, it will knock down a calf,
>   And I hope it will knock down thee."
> Then Robin Hood could no longer forbear,
>   But bestowed on him such a knock
> That quickly and soon the blood came down,
>   Before it was ten o'clock.

Now the tanner was in that mood of mind when a man accepts no such favours without some return, and so he gave the outlaw a blow that brought the blood trickling down every individual hair of his head.

Now at the sight of his own blood, Robin's anger arose, and he struck lustily and well; but the tanner laid on as if he were cleaving wood.

All Barnesdale resounded with their blows.

"Hold thy hand," cried Robin, "thou hast done enough. I make thee free of the wood."

"Why gad a mercy," answered the tanner, "I may thank my staff, not thee, for that."

"Well, well, good fellow," continued the outlaw, "thy name and trade?"

> "Oh, I am a tanner," bold Arthur replied,
>   "In Nottingham long have I wrought;
> And if thou'lt come there, I vow and swear,
>   I will tan thy side for nought."
> "Gad a mercy, good fellow," said jolly Robin,
>   "Since thou art so kind, so free,
> An if thou'lt tan my hide for nought,
>   I will do as much for thee."

There was, of course, a pause in the strife during this conversation.

"I wish," said Robin, "that you would quit the tan-pits and live with me in the forest. As sure as my name is Robin Hood thou shalt not want gold and fee."

"Ah!" exclaimed Arthur-a-Bland, "if you are Robin Hood you can tell me where my kinsman Little John is. If we can find him we are not likely to part soon."

A blast on the horn brought Arthur's relative, who was ready as usual to take up his master's quarrel.

> But Robin Hood took them both by the hands,
>   And danced round the oak-tree;
> For three merry men, and three merry men,
>   And three merry men we be.

CHAPTER XLVIII.

A QUARREL AND A WEDDING.

An hour later the three men were seated in a most friendly way together.

Arthur-a-Bland had told his story, at which both Robin Hood and Little John laughed consumedly.

"Why don't you know," said the outlaw, laughing, "that women are ever thus?"

"How so?"

"The girl wanted to be courted. If you had remained all the evening she would have been willing enough."

"Dost think so?"

"What say you to a trudge back to Nottingham?" asked Robin; "and if you will be guided by me we will dance at your wedding in a week."

"How so?"

"You must leave everything to me, and speak only when spoken to."

"But what magic art, my master, do you possess to make a woman change her mind?"

"No magic art, my friend, but some experience of the sex."

"They are deceitful hussies."

"Not at all. They are the best of creatures, but they like to rule over us, and they like to be made much of until they surrender themselves as wives."

"Well, Mary might have had her own way."

"If she had agreed to marry you the day you wished."

"I dare say what you say is very true, so shall leave myself wholly in your hands."

"And you have done well," cried Little John. "If any one can set you right it is the master."

Now Little John's faith in Robin Hood was something marvellous. But from the testimony of all it was deserved.

The personal character of Robin Hood stands high in the pages of both history and poetry. Fordun, a priest, extols his piety; Major pronounces him the most humane of robbers; and Camden, a more judicious authority, calls him the gentlest of thieves; while in the pages of the early drama he is drawn at heroic length, and with many of the best attributes of human nature. His life and deeds have not only supplied materials for the drama and the ballad, but proverbs have sprung from them: he stands the demigod of English archery; men used to swear by his bow and his clemency; festivals were once annually held, and games of a sylvan kind celebrated in his honour, in Scotland as well as in England. The grave where he lies has still its pilgrims; the well out of which he drank still retains his name; and his bow and one of his broad arrows were within this century to be seen in Fountains Abbey, a place immortalized by his adventure with the Curtal Friar.

*   *   *   *   *

THE RESCUE OF MAID MARIAN.

We return to the humble hostelrie kept by Hardinge.

Mary his daughter, like a great many others of her sex, enjoyed nothing better than to have her own way. She was fond of flattery and admiration, and did not like being driven any faster than she thought proper.

Still she was sincerely attached to Arthur-a-Bland, and this not being the first lovers' quarrel in which she had known him indulge, was quite certain that she would see him back again the next day.

But when at early dawn a serving man of his father's came round to know why he had not been home all night, she began to be seriously alarmed.

Like most girls, she formed an exaggerated idea of the character of the outlaws, and believed that if Arthur-a-Bland had really gone to the woodlands he was lost to her for ever.

She, however, would not own to a "lover's quarrel," but simply stated that Arthur had been taking a drop of ale and then gone away.

The mother retired surprised and broken hearted.

Her son had never stopped out a whole night before.

When Mary was alone, she, too, fretted much, though trying to hide it from all observers. That day passed, and yet he came not.

Evening came.

The shadows fell long and heavy on the darkened ground.

Mary was attending to her household affairs.

Her father was attending to some of the out-door necessities of his little farm, no man in those days being without his bit of land.

Mary, after bustling about a good deal, sat down to her spindle, and from sheer habit began to sing in a monotonous and melancholy tone of voice.

As she did so, something darkened the door of the ale-house.

It was a man in the costume of a pedlar.

"Give you good day, my pretty lass," said the stranger.

"What's your will, sir?"

"A mug of your best October, my little one. But why so serious? Has your good man run away?"

"I never had a good man," she replied; "my father is master of this house."

"It shows the bad taste of the young people."

Mary tossed her head and went away. She knew that sweethearts were plenty enough.

But flighty as any girl may be, there is always one she prefers to all others in her secret heart of hearts.

The girl brought back the mug of ale and then, more from habit than anything else, asked the pedlar which way he had come.

"Through the forest," said the pedlar.

"What saw you?"

"Not much. The outlaws touch not poor men."

"Saw you anything else?"

"Yes. This morning I met a stout artisan lying on the banks of a small river, quite exhausted and faint. He seemed to me nearly out of his mind."

"What manner of man was he?"

"Good-looking enough, and by trade a tanner."

"What did he?"

"I believe the lad was mad, for he cut such capers as fairly frightened me, leaping about, and sighing like a furnace the name of some pitiless Mary, who had sent him to pasture with the wild beasts."

"Could'st find the place?" said Mary, quietly.

"Well, me thinks I could, but not at night."

"Could'st describe it, so that I should find it?" continued the girl.

"Why so?"

"I would find this man, and bring him back, poor fellow."

"Dost know him, lass?"

"I do; and I fear my cruelty has driven him beside himself."

"Are you his Mary?"

"I am," said the girl, humbly.

"Oh!"

"You blame me?"

"I don't know your story."

"He would have made me promise to marry him. But since my mother's death, father has none but me, so I would fain wait. Father is not rich. If in the next four years I could save a little money for father, then Arthur-a-Bland might have me and welcome."

"And if I had so told the youth?"

"You would have told the truth."

"And if I had persuaded him?"

"You would have done well."

"And if I had brought him here?"

"I should say welcome."

Next minute the pedlar vanished, and the tanner stood in his place.

When Robin Hood the false pedlar, re-entered the inn, it was with Harding, quite reconciled to his daughter's marriage.

The outlaw had arranged to give the girl a dowry, and the father a sum of money, with cows and oxen and pigs enough to make him as rich as many a small franklin.

As soon as matters were thus satisfactorily arranged, all sat down to supper, and it was surprising to note how quiet Mary was.

A number of her old admirers came in, but, though she was civil to them all, she behaved as one who knew her place, and was satisfied with the choice she had made.

Four days after they were married, and Arthur-a-Bland, despite all the efforts of his friends, went to the greenwood with Robin, of whom he became an attached and devoted follower, nor did either husband or wife ever regret their union.

Such was ever the plan of Robin Hood: to unite in the holy bonds of matrimony all true lovers, for which, no doubt, he had the thanks of many a generation.

CHAPTER XLIX.

THE FRIAR OF FOUNTAIN'S DALE.

We now approach a part of the history of Robin Hood, which, though always related and generally believed, is certainly a demand on the credulity of our readers.

To leave it out would be unfair.

Popular rumour gives it as true.

We give the tale as it is told to us.

"A north-country mile and an inch at a shot" is a rhyming instance of the strength and skill of Robin Hood in archery; nor are proofs in prose wanting. "The abbot of Whitby," says a Yorkshire tradition, "had heard that Robin Hood and Little John were famous for the distance as well as the accuracy of their shooting, and begged them after dinner to give him an example. He took them to the top of the abbey, whence each of them shot an arrow, which fell not far from Whitby-laths, in memorial of which the abbot set up a pillar where each of the arrows was found. The place where Robin's arrow fell is still called Robin Hood's Field, and the place where Little John's fell is called John's Field; the distance of these places from Whitby Abbey exceeds a measured mile."

If this be admitted as prose evidence of the distance to which Robin's bow could send a shaft, for the matchless accuracy of his aim there are in verse many examples; his arrows, like the stones of the Benjamite slingers, flew to a hair's breadth and did not miss.

Yet at this weapon he was once nigh overmatched; not indeed by human skill, but by the wondrous dogs of the Friar of Fountain's Dale, that caught the arrows in their mouths as they flew. It is to be feared that the breed of these dogs either became immediately extinct, or that they were trained by the skill, now lost, of a sorcerer. The adventure of the Friar and his curtal dogs is a rustic romance. That martial monk, by a species of scholastic magic known to the vulgar by the name of the Oxford Art, educated his dogs in a new kind of warfare, and with his sword and bow reigned for seven years the sovereign of Fountain's Dale. He might have continued longer on his throne had not his merits provoked the hostility of his brother-monarch of Sherwood.

The old ballad in which the friar's contest with Robin is related is both well imagined and well rhymed.

"It happened one summer's morn," says the legend, "that Little John performed a deed of archery much to the pleasure of his master.

> "Will Scarlett he did kill a buck,
> And Midge he kill'd a doe,
> But Little John kill'd a hart of grease,
> Five hundred foot him fro.
>
> Joy on that heart said Robin Hood,
> Shot such a shot for me,
> I'll ride my horse a hundred miles
> To find a match for thee."

(As we have no authority whatever for this narrative better than the ballads, we must freely quote.)

There was perhaps some envy in the laugh which Will Scarlett raised at this. "I know," said he, "a curtal friar in Fountain's Abbey who can fight you both." Now, in those days there were martial monks whose duties consisted in preaching to the Saracens, or in cutting their throats; they were peculiar to Asia; yet something of the same sort of animal was not uncommon in this country. England had prelates who, like Anthony Beck, Bishop of Durham, loved to fight in the van; or like Sinclair of Dunkeld, could draw the sword and lead to victory when his country was invaded. The same military taste descended lower; and the church had humbler servants of very questionable motality, like the curtal Friar. When Will Scarlett gave this insulting commendation to the Friar, he added:

> "The curtal Fryar in Fountain's Abbey
> Well can a strong bow draw:
> He will beat you and your good yeomen,
> If you set them all in a raw."
>
> Then Robin he swore a solemn oath,
> And it was by Mary free,
> That he would neither eat nor drink
> Till the Friar he did see.

Now Robin Hood knew full well that Will Scarlett was simply out of temper, and that in saying what he did, he merely gave vent to a little petulance, so that he at one moment thought also that his good lieutenant was but joking with him.

"You are sure that such a man as the Friar of Fountain's Dale really exists?"

"Master, I do."

"Then will I go forth to meet him."

The outlaw put on his best steel harness and a helmet which had resisted many a stroke; he likewise belted a sword by his side, and with a buckler on his shoulder and his trusty bow in his hand away he went into Fountain's Dale to achieve this new adventure.

> And coming into Fountain's Dale,
> No further would he ride ;
> There he was aware of the curtal Fryar
> Close by the water-side.

> The Fryar had on a harness good,
> On his head a cap of steel ;
> Broad-sword and buckler by his side,
> And they became him weel.

Will Scarlett pointed triumphantly to him. Robin stood a little while looking at the military monk. No man ever entered upon a combat with less consideration ; it was ever word and blow with him ; yet in the present case he saw the propriety of having a reason of some kind for rushing upon strife—a cause of offence was not long wanting.

> Robin Hood he lighted off his horse,
> And tied him to a thorn ;
> "Carry me o'er the water, thou curtal friar,
> Or else thy life's forlorn."

> The friar took Robin on his back,
> Deep water he did bestride,
> And neither spoke word good or bad
> Till on the other side

All as yet went smoothly ; the friar, with a meekness which he might have learned in Fountain's Abbey, obeyed the command of the imperious stranger, carried him over the stream, and placed him safely on the bank : but here his meekness and courtesy ended.

> Lightly leapt Robin from off his back,
> When the fryar he said again,
> "Now carry me back thou fine fellow,
> Or faith it shall breed thee pain."

> Robin took the fryar upon his back,
> Deep water he did bestride,
> And neither spake good word or bad
> Till he came to the other side.

This could not last long ; it endured, however, on Robin's side longer than on the friar's, who, desiring to bring the matter to an end, carried the outlaw to the middle of the stream, and, tossing him roughly in, told him to either sink or swim, at his pleasure. Robin preferred swimming to sinking, and reaching the bank, grasped his bow, and plucked out an arrow from his quiver :—

> One of his best shafts below his belt
> At the fryar he let fly,
> The curtal fryar with his steel buckler
> Did put the arrow by.

> "Shoot on, shoot on," the friar he said,
> "Shoot on as thou hast begun ;
> If thou shootest here for a summer's day
> Thy mark I will not shun."

How many arrows the steel buckler of the friar put aside the ballad neglects to say ; four-and-twenty was the usual number of shafts in an archer's quiver in those days ; at all events, Robin shot with his usual skill, but shot all his arrows away without injuring his invulnerable adversary. He then laid aside his bow, drew his sword, and, with his buckler on his arm, closed with the friar, who opposed him with equal arms and equal resolution :—

> They fought from ten o'clock o' the day
> Till four in the afternoon ;
> Then Robin Hood came to his knees,
> Of the fryar to beg a boon.

> "A boon, a boon, thou curtal fryar,
> I beg it on my knee ;
> Let me set my horn unto my mouth,
> And to blow out blasts three."

> "That will I do" said the curtal friar,
> "Of thy blasts I have no doubt ;
> I hope thou'lt blow so passing well,
> Till both thy eyes fly out."

It is probable that the friar was not aware of the importance of the boon which he so readily granted ; or it

may be that he was prepared for all emergencies, and relied for assistance on his reserve of "great ban-dogs," as fit to match the force of all Robin's forest chivalry. Be that as it may, no sooner were the blasts blown than fifty yeomen with bent bows in their hands came hastening to the aid of their leader.

"Whose men are these ?" inquired the friar.

"They are mine," replied Robin Hood.

> "A boon, a boon," said the curtal fryar,
> "The like I gave to thee :
> To set my fist thus to my mouth,
> And to whute out whutes three."

> "That will I do," said Robin Hood,
> "Or else I were to blame ;
> For three whutes in a fryar's fist
> Will make me glad and fain."

Robin seems not to have been prepared for the four-footed opposition which "three whutes on the friar's fist" were destined to call up. No sooner had he whooted thrice than half a hundred great ban-dogs came running to his side ; and the friar proceeded to lay down rules for the coming combat :—

> "Here is for every man a dog,
> And I myself for thee ;"
> "Nay, by my faith," said Robin Hood,
> "Good fryar, that must not be.

> Two dogs at once to Robin did go,
> One behind, the other before,
> And Robin Hood's mantle of Lincoln green
> Off from his back they tore.

This Robin may have expected ; but for the scene which followed no previous experience could have prepared him ; he had hitherto found nothing but steel to resist his shafts. His men turned their arrows at once on their four-footed adversaries :—

> But whether his men shot east and west
> Or they shot north and south,
> The curtal dogs, so taught they were,
> Caught the arrows in their mouth.

Little John was less amazed at this than his master.

"Take off thy dogs, friar," he exclaimed, "else evil will befall both them and thee."

"Who art thou ?" said the friar, emboldened by the battle having hitherto gone in his favour ; "whose man art thou that comes here to prate to me ?"

"I am Little John, and Robin Hood is my master," replied he ; and as he spoke he shot his arrows with such dexterity that half a score of the friar's dogs fell dead each by a single shaft.

"Hold thy hand, good fellow," cried the friar ; "thy master and I shall agree ; shoot no more, I pray thee."

> This curtal friar kept Fountain's Dale
> For seven long years and more,
> And there was never a knight nor lord
> Could make him yield before.

CHAPTER L.

ILL NEWS

It would not have been possible for the monks and ballad-mongers of that day to confine themselves to the possible or the probable ; hence the introduction of this narrative in a life, the principal details of which are perfectly true.

We, however, as chroniclers, anxious to do justice to the memoirs of a great hero, have felt ourselves bound to give the apochryphal with the real.

Before King Richard went away, he took such steps as were necessary to enable Robin Hood to prosecute his claims, not only to the title, but to the vast estates which were connected with the name of Huntingdon.

Robin, however, assured the monarch that unless he was to attend his court occasionally, he preferred remaining as he was.

"But you may have a son."

"In that case, my liege, I will prosecute my claim with vigour."

But there appeared, unfortunately, no chance of that

outlaw being a father, and though he did not wholly despair, yet was he lukewarm in the pursuit of the rights of his forefathers.

Like another hero of our own time, Robin Hood would have been out of place a constant dweller in palaces.

There was, however, one temptation which at length outweighed every other.

If he obtained his rank, possessions, and castle, his men, instead of living by levies on churchmen and Normans, would be clothed and fed from the revenues of their lord and master, Robin Earl of Huntingdon.

While Richard remained in England, which he did until he was re-crowned at Winchester, all went well.

His counsellors listened to the monarch's wishes, and promised to abide by his decision.

Then the king took his departure for France, to avenge himself on his rival and enemy, Philip.

No sooner was the king's back turned, Robin found how great was the power of money.

Those who held his estates were all rich men, and though if he had chosen to use force, there could be no doubt of his being able to take Huntingdon Castle, yet was such not his wish.

The chief opponent of the rights of Robin, and the one who held Huntingdon Castle, was in possession of other and enormous revenues.

The final decision of Robin's claim rested with Hubert Walter, one Bishop of Salisbury, afterwards Archbishop of Canterbury, Lord Chancellor, and Grand Justiciary.

Like all churchmen, he was greedy of gold.

Strange, but true is it, that those whose profession it is to preach humility to all men, and to explain the evils of avarice and the utter uselessness of gold as a means of happiness, are always personally fond of the loaves and fishes.

Even the very best have this defect, just as what are called pious people never give money in charity.

The crafty earl sent present after present to the churchman, and thus gained delay, now to collect some fresh evidence, now to prepare for removal.*

On the borders of Barnesdale, and where a soft, sweet spring rippled past, was a charming cottage, overgrown with creeping plants, and having a garden before it, which gave evidence of patient labour and refined tastes in its inmates.

Here reside at intervals a couple who were the admiration of the few villagers who ever passed that way.

None knew them, and though curiosity was rife enough, few cared to satisfy it when they saw two other inhabitants of the house.

One was the extraordinary dwarf Geruth, the other his bloodhound, Wolf.

The superior tenants of the cottage were Robin Hood and Maid Marian, who every now and then, putting aside the simple state of the forest monarch, here revelled in the pure delights of domestic love and retirement.

Like all men of his temperament, there were moments when repose was a relief, and when he was too glad to retire and let time glide past, like the great ever-rolling river that it is.

For Maid Marian these were times of unalloyed happiness, and it was because he felt this that he himself took so much pleasure in them.

They would work in their garden, sit and converse, sing, play the cithern, and generally pass the time like a couple to whom matrimony is ever a honeymoon.

Geruth kept watch, and thus kept off all too curious observers, who, had they known that even a sylvan monarch was so near at hand, would have given them little rest.

At times Geruth went to the village, as, though the caverns of the outlaws abounded with everything, the monarch chose here to live in strict incognito.

Geruth had been gone about an hour, and Robin and Marian were talking in the garden, secreted from view by a paling covered by honeysuckle, when they were aroused by the sound of horses' footsteps.

The outlaw looked out and saw that one, all covered with dust and mud, and having the appearance of having performed a long journey, had halted close to their cottage.

He was looking about like one who has lost his way.

"Sir Traveller," said Robin, courteously, "can I do anything to serve you?"

"Put me on the way which I have lost," replied the other, quickly; "and if you would but refresh my horse and self, the obligation would be deeper."

"Dismount, sir traveller, and both you and horse shall have all that you want."

The man obeyed, and evidently with some difficulty dismounted, just in time to give his horse to Geruth, then returning from the village.

"See to the horse, good Geruth; rub him down and feed him well," said Robin, at the same time ushering the traveller into his garden bower.

Scarcely was he seated when Maid Marian appeared with such a cold collation as might have made Friar Tuck's mouth water.

The traveller, having hurriedly spoken his thanks, began eating, with the air of one who has travelled far and fast.

"Have you far to go now?" asked Robin.

"To Nottingham."

"'Tis a good distance yet; your horse will need a good hour's rest,'" replied Robin.

"I may not tarry longer, though my news is but ill indeed. But that it is my duty, I would gladly not hurry," replied the courier.

"May I ask the ill news?"

"Aye! it will ring in England ere many hours, and cause grief to all, save traitors and tyrants."

"Speak, in God's name—it cannot be—"

"The King is dead—"

"Merciful heaven!" cried Robin, "the best king and pleasantest companion England ever knew. Oh! Marian, this is sad news!"

"It is. Heaven rest his soul and take pity on England, for now the bad prince will reign."

"If I mistake not," said the courier, respectfully, "I speak to Robin Hood and Maid Marian?"

"You do."

"Then you are highly honoured. The king's last words were: 'See that Robin, my trusty Saxon subject, has justice done him.'"

"May He in whose hands he is now, bless him! We ne'er shall see his like again. But we must away. There will be evil enough now, for King John hates all who bow not as slaves."

After some conversation the messenger departed, and Robin and Marian, locking up their cottage, went away to commence anew the life of a mere outlaw.

It is of this period that the historian speaks thus:—

"In these forests," says Ritson, "and with this company, he for many years reigned like an independent sovereign; at perpetual war with the King of England and all his subjects, with the exception, however, of the poor and the needy, or such as were desolate and oppressed, or stood in need of his protection." This wild life had for Robin charms of its own; it suited the taste of a high but irregular mind to brave all the constituted authorities in the great litigated rights of free forestry; the deer with which the woods swarmed afforded food for all who had the heart to bend a bow; and a ruined tower, a shepherd's hut, a cavern, or a thicket,

When leaves were sharp and long,

gave such shelter as men who were not scrupulous about bed or toilet desired; while wealthy travellers, or churchmen abounding in tithes supplied them, though reluctantly, with Lincoln-green for doublets, and wine for their festivals.

Robin Hood knew now that whatever might have been his hopes they were all over, and that he must be content to live and die an outlaw.

---

* The high blood of Robin seems to have been doubted by Sir Walter Scott, who, in the character of Locksley, makes the traditionary Earl of Huntingdon but a better sort of rustic, with manners rather of a franklyn than a noble. Popular belief is, however, too much even for the illustrious author of Ivanhoe, and bold Robin will remain an earl while woods grow and waters run. The strict historical fact appears to be that he was born in Nottingham in the year 1160, and during the reign of Henry II. In his youth he was extravagant and wild, dissipated part of his patrimony, and was juggled out of the remainder by the united powers of a sheriff and an abbot. This made him desperate, and drove him to the woods.

In his innermost heart there was very little regret.
He loved the greensward.
He loved his throne under the trysting tree.
He loved the society of his Maid Marian and he loved to sit surrounded by his outlaws, a very king indeed.
In the long evenings when, after a day well spent, he and his lieutenants sat under a splendid oak, it was his habit to sing or have tales told.
The latter were always popular in England.
The taste has survived to this day.

CHAPTER LI.

ROBIN HOOD'S STORY.

It was a May evening; some passing showers had made the forest bright, but under the spreading oak, with a large warm fire, there sat a dozen or more to enjoy themselves before they went to their cavern homes.

"What cheer to-day?" asked Little John, of his chief.

"Little," replied Robin Hood, "except that I heard a tale that amused me much."

"Tell it," said Maid Marian.

That was enough for the outlaw.

THE SUMMONER'S TALE.

A summoner, who was ever on the watch for prey, rode forth one morning to cheat a poor old woman, against whom he pretended to have a complaint. His track lay by a forest side; and it chanced that he saw before him, under the trees, a yeoman on horseback, gaily equipped, with a bow and arrows. The stranger was in a short green cloak; and he had a hat with a black fringe.

"Good-morrow, sir," quoth the summoner, overtaking him.

"The same to you," quoth the yeoman, "and to every other jolly companion. What road are you bound upon to-day through the green wood? Are you going far?"

"No," replied the summoner. "My business is close at hand. I'm only going about a rent that's owing to my master."

"Oh, what, you are a bailiff, then?" quoth the yeoman.

"Just so," returned the summoner. He had not the face to own himself what he was; the very name of summoner was such a disgrace.

"Well now; that's good," said the stranger: "for I'm a bailiff myself; and as I'm not very well acquainted with this part of the country, I shall be glad of your good offices, if you have no objection to my company. I have plenty of money at home; so if you travel into our parts, you shall want for nothing."

"Many thanks," cried the summoner; "I'm yours, with all my heart."

The new friends gave their hands to one another, and pushed on their horses merrily.

The summoner, who always had an eye to business, and was besides of an inquisitive nature, and as fond of poking his nose into everything as a woodpecker, lost no time in asking the stranger where he lived, in case he should come to see him.

The yeoman, in a tone of singular gentleness, answered, that he should be very glad of his visit; that he lived indeed a great way off, in the north; but that before they parted he would instruct him so well in the locality that it should be impossible for him to miss it.

"Good," returned the summoner. "And now, as we are of one accord and one occupation, pray let me into a secret or two, how I may prosper in my employment. Don't mince the matter as to conscience or sin, or any of that kind of nonsense; but tell me plainly how you transact business yourself."

"Why, to say the truth," answered the yeoman, "I have a very hard master and very little wages, and so I live by extortion. I take all that people give me, and a good deal more besides. I couldn't make both ends meet else: and that's the plain fact."

"Precisely my case," cried the summoner. "I take everything I can lay my hands on, unless it be too heavy or too hot. To the devil with conscience and repentance, say I. Catch me at confession who can. Well are we met, by the Lord. What is your name, my dear fellow?"

The yeoman began smiling a little at this question.

"Why, if you must know," quoth he, "my name, betwixt you and me, is Devil. I am a fiend, and live in hell; and I am riding hereabouts to see what I can get. Your business and mine are precisely the same. You don't care how you get anything, provided you succeed; nor do I. I'll ride to the world's end, for instance, this very morning, sooner than not meet with a prey."

"God bless me," cried the summoner, crossing himself, "the 'devil,' do you say? I thought you were a man like myself. You have a man's shape. Have you no particular shape, then, of your own?"

"Not a bit of it," quoth the stranger. "We take what likeness we please; sometimes a man's, sometimes a monkey's; nay, an angel's, if it suits us. And no marvel. For a common juggler can deceive your eyes in such matters; and it is hard if a devil can't do it better than a juggler."

"But why," inquired the summoner, "not be content with some one shape in particular?"

"Because," replied the other, "the more disguises the more booty."

"That is taking a great deal of trouble, is it not?" asked the summoner. "Why couldn't you take less?"

"For many reasons, good Master Summoner," quoth the devil. "But all in good time. The day wears, and I have got nothing yet; so I must attend to business. Besides, you couldn't understand the matter if I told it. You haven't wit enough for its comprehension. But if you must know why we trouble ourselves at all, you must know that God wills it, and that devils themselves are but instruments in his hands. We can do nothing at all, if he doesn't choose it; and do what we may, we can sometimes go no farther than the body. We are not always permitted to touch the soul. Witness the case of Job. Sometimes, on the other hand, we are permitted to torment a man's soul, and not his body; and all is for the best. Our very temptations are the cause of a man being saved, if he resists them. Not that we have any such good intention. Our design is to carry him away with us, body and soul. Sometimes we are even compelled to be servants to a man. Archbishop Dunstan had a devil for a servant, and I served an apostle myself."

"And have you a new body every time you disguise yourselves," inquired the summoner, "or is it only a seeming body?"

"Only a seeming body sometimes," answered the devil. "Sometimes, also, we possess a dead body, and give people as good substantial words as Samuel did to the witch; though some learned persons are of opinion that it was not Samuel whom she raised, but only his likeness. Be all this as it may, of one thing you may be certain, my good friend; and that is, that you shall know more of us by-and-by, and be able to talk more learnedly about it, than Virgil did when he was living, or Dante himself. At present let us push on. I like your company vastly, and will stick to you as long as you do not choose to forsake mine."

"Nay," cried the summoner, "never talk of that. I am very well known for respectability, and I hold myself as firmly pledged to you as you do yourself to me. We are to ride and prosper together. You are to take what people give you, I am to take what I can get; and if the profits turn out to be unequal we divide them."

"Quite right," said the devil; and so they push forward.

They were now entering a town, and before them was a hay-cart, which had stuck in the mud. The carter, who was in a rage, whipped his horses like a madman. "Heit, Scot! heit, Brok!" cried he to the beasts. "What! it's the stones, is it, that make you so lazy? The devil take ye both, say I. Am I to be thwacking and thumping all day? The devil take you, hay, cart, and all."

"Ho, ho!" quoth the summoner; "here's something to be got."

He drew close to his companion, and whispered him: "Don't you hear?" said he; "the carter gives you his hay, cart, and three horses."

" Not he," answered the devil. " He says so, but he doesn't mean it. Ask him if he does. Or wait a little, and you'll see."

The carter thwacked his horses again, and they began to stoop, and to draw. " Heit now !—gee up !—matthy wo !—ah,—God bless 'em !—there they come. That was well twitched, Grey, my old boy. God bless you ! say I, and Saint Elias to boot. My cart's out of the slough at last."

" There," said the devil; " you see how it is. The fellow said one thing, but he thought another. We must e'en push on. There's nothing to be got here."

The companions continued their way through the town, and were just quitting it, when the summoner, pulling his bridle as he reached a cottage door, said, " There's an old hag living here who would almost as soon break her neck as part with a halfpenny. I'll get a shilling out of her for all that, though it drive her mad. She shall have a summons else, and that 'll be worse for her. Not that she has committed any offence, God knows. That's quite another business. But mark me now, and see what you must do if you would get anything in these parts."

The summoner rattled the old woman's gate, crying, " Come out, old trot; come out. You've got some friar or priest with you."

" Who's there ?" said the woman. " Lord bless us ! God save you, sir ! What is your will ?"

" I've a summons for you," said the man. " You must be with the archdeacon to-morrow, on pain of excommunication, to answer to certain charges."

" Charges !" cried the poor woman. " Heaven help me ! There can be no charges against a poor sick body like me. How am I to come to the archdeacon ? I can't even go in a cart, it gives me such a pain in my side. Mayn't I have a summons on paper, and so get the lawyer to see to it ?"

" To be sure you may," answered the summoner, " provided you pay me down—let me see—ay, a shilling. That will be your quittance, and all. I get nothing by it, I assure you. My master has all the fees. Come, make haste, for I must be going. A shilling. Do you hear ?"

" A shilling !" exclaimed she. " Heaven bless us and save us ! Where, in all the wide world, am I to get a shilling ? You know I haven't a penny to save my life. It's myself, that ought to have a shilling given to me, poor wretch !"

" Devil fetch me then, if you won't be cast," said the summoner; " for I shan't utter a syllable in your favour."

" Alas !" cried she, " God knows I'm innocent ! I've done nothing in the world."

" Pay me," interrupted the summoner, " or I'll carry away the new pan I see yonder. You have owed me as much years ago, for getting you out of that scrape about your husband."

" Scrape about my husband !" cried the old widow. " What scrape ? You are a lying wretch. I never was in any scrape about my husband, or anything; nor ever summoned into your court in all my born days. Go to the devil yourself. May he take you and the pan together ?"

The poor old soul fell on her knees as she uttered these words, in order to give the greater strength to the imprecation.

" Now, Mabel, my good mother," cried the devil, " do you speak this in earnest ?"

" Ay, marry do I," cried she. " May the devil fetch him, pan and all; that is to say, unless he repents."

" Repent !" exclaimed the summoner : " I'd sooner take every rag you have on your bones, you old reprobate."

" Now, brother," said the devil, " calm your feelings. I'm very sorry, but you must e'en go where the old woman desires. You and the pan are mine. We must arrive to-night; and then you'll know more about us, all and our craft, than ever was discovered by doctor of divinity."

And with these words, sure enough, the devil carried him off. He took him to the place where summoners are in the habit of going.

Great laughter followed this narrative, and then, like true yeomen, they retired early to rest.

CHAPTER LII.

KING JOHN AND THE INNKEEPER.

ROBIN HOOD, as soon as the death of King Richard was well authenticated, was well aware that any hope of acquiring the earldom of Huntingdon for himself or for his successors was wholly out of the question.

King John was his inveterate enemy; and had he not been engaged in warfare with his barons, and in forcing the application of the game laws generally, there can be no doubt he would have devoted a large portion of his time to rooting out the outlaws.

But, like many other procrastinating personages, King John thought there was always time enough to do this.

Robin Hood, brave as he was, knew full well the difference between defying Prince John at the head of a faction and King John at the head of the kingdom.

He, accordingly, was satisfied to remain quiet for some months, simply walking in Watling Street, and taking a purse occasionally as circumstances required.

Be utterly quiet Robin could not, as we shall see by the present adventure.

Merry England ! Ah, merry England ! What a difference there has always been between thee and every other land ! What a cheerfulness there seems to hang about thy very name ! What yeoman-like hilarity is there in all the thoughts of the past ! What a spirit of sylvan cheer and rustic hardihood in all the tales of thy old times !

When England was altogether an agricultural land— when a rude plough produced an abundant harvest, and a thin but hardy and generous peasantry devoted themselves totally to the cultivation of the earth—when wide forests waved their green boughs over many of the richest manufacturing districts of Great Britain, and the lair of the fawn and the burrow of the cony were found where now appear the fabric and the mill—there stood, in a small town, or rather, I should call it, village, within the confines of Sherwood, a neat little inn, well known to all the wayfarers on the road as a comfortable resting-place, where they could dine on their journey to or from the larger city.

The house was constructed of wood, and was but of two stories; but let it not be supposed on that account that it was devoid of ornament, for manifold were the quaint carvings and rude pieces of sculpture with which it was decorated, and not small had been the pains which had been bestowed upon mouldings, and cornices, and lintels, and door-post, by the hand of more than one laborious artisan.

Indeed, altogether, it was a very elaborated piece of work, and had probably been originally built for other purposes than that which it now served : for many were the changes which had taken place in that part of the country, as well as over the rest of England, between the days we speak of and those of a century before.

It was, we have said, in the merry month of May, and in "Merrie England," as we are content to call it, though the Normans were apt to make it a very miserable England.

The inn which we have feebly and faintly described had been shut for some time.

A new landlord had, however, taken it.

A jolly landlord too, brown, whiskered, and handsome, with a handsome wife and two handsome handmaidens, which was a little more than circumstances seemed to require.

But John Hardy, as he called himself, started as if he expected rare custom.

He had the finest of Burgundies; ales that foamed in the tankard and still did not make the head ache.

Few seemed to know anything of the new landlord, and yet all were familiar with him.

He rose early. In this like the bird who will

-----Clap his wings, and call his family
To sacred rites ; and vex the ethereal powers
With midnight matins at unseal hours.
Nay, more, his quiet neighbours should molest
Just in the sweetness of their morning rest.
Beast of a bird, supinely when he might
Lie still and sleep, to rise before the light.
What if his dull forefathers us'd that cry;
Could he not let a bad example die ?

Long before any legitimate traffic was on the road he was afoot, his door was open, and himself gazing up and down the road, as if in expectation of customers.

A flagon of right good wine prepared him for a hearty breakfast, which his spouse prepared for him with her own fair hands, considering it unseemly that any one else should wait upon her lord and master.

In the days of which we speak early rising was the rule. All who were not invalids were afoot earlier even than our farm labourers and farmers, so that John Hardy's opening was not lost.

Custom soon came when it was found that he really did sell a good article.

Good wine needs no bush—that is, no sign, a large bush being to this day the indication of a *cabaret* on the continent.

It was about the fifth or sixth of May.

John Hardy, who only wanted the modern invention of a pipe to have attained perfect felicity, was seated in a bower on the opposite side to his house.

He had a flagon of wine, which he sipped with the air of one who knew that he had something good to drink.

His eye was cast casually down the road to where a traveller was advancing.

He was a yeoman. He was dressed in a green coat and hood, and had a sheaf stuck in his belt full of arrows with peacock feathers. Bright and keen were they. He had a right yeomanly hand at such tackle. His arrows never looked as if they were moulting; and in his hand he carried a mighty bow. His head was shaped like a nut, and his face sunburnt. He knew all about woods. His arm was defended by a showy bracer; he had a sword and buckler on one side; a fine dagger on the other, in capital condition; a bright silver image of St. Christopher on his breast; and he wore a horn by a green belt. A proper forester was he, you might be certain.

But he was tall as well as proper, and when the innkeeper saw him coming, he hastily rose, crossed the road, and called his wife.

"There comes one who can eat a breakfast," he said, with a sly aside wink, meant for her alone.

"I can see him," replied his wife, who glanced through a kind of loophole.

John Hardy nodded, drew his coat about him, put a hat on his head, went to the door, and began whistling.

The other way another traveller was coming.

This was a captain of a ship, who came a long way out of the west. I think he was from Dartmouth. He had got a horse upon hire, which he rode as well as he was able. He wore a *falding* that reached to his knee, with a dirk hanging under his arm from a string round the neck; and his skin was all tanned with the sun. A jovial companion was he. He had helped himself to many a swig of wine at Bourdeaux, while the merchant was asleep. Conscience was not in his line. If he got the better of a vessel at sea, he always sent the men home by water. As to his seamanship and his pilotage, his knowledge of rivers and coasts, of sun and moon, and his heavings of the lead, there wasn't such another from Hull to Carthage. He was both audacious and cautious. With many a tempest had his beard been shaken. He knew the soundings of every harbour from Gothland to Cape Finisterre, and every creek in Brittany and Spain. His vessel was called the *Magdalen*.

The innkeeper smiled.

This looked like business.

"How fares it, my honest friend?" said the innkeeper, as the forester came up, speaking in a muffled voice, as if his were thickened with wine.

"Middling," replied the forester, gruffly; "can a poor man break his fast?"

And he sighed deeply.

"I have breakfast ready for thee," continued the innkeeper. "It would have been a pity to pass my house without refreshment."

"I'm but a poor trencherman," said the tall forester.

The landlord grinned. He did not laugh outright, he didn't move a muscle, but his cachinnation was none the less effective.

He enjoyed it.

"What are you laughing at?" growled the surly one.

"Nothing, your worship."

"Then don't do it again, that's all."

"Certainly not, your worship," said mine host, who then led the way into the house.

The landlord's wife had provided a supper worthy of a prince.

Decidedly the tall forester had fallen upon fortunate days.

He sat down, heaved again a deep sigh, and began to eat, with the air, however, of a man who rather performs a duty than does a thing to please himself.

The landlord and the landlord's wife watched him with a covert smile.

By degrees he warmed to his work, and as a goodly flagon or two of ale warmed his inside, began sensibly to rouse.

The sea-captain had joined by this time.

He was a black-bearded, beetle-browed, individual, who did not prepossess one in his favour.

The innkeeper made, however, no difference in his treatment of one or the other.

He was speedily despatching the good things set before him, in a kind of friendly rivalry with the tall forester.

An hour by the clock did these two men feed.

There is a limit to all things, even to a good meal, and the two men were at length compelled to pause.

"Enjoyed your breakfast?" said the politic landlord, stepping in at the opportune moment.

"Splendid," said the big man.

"Princely," said the captain.

At this moment a clatter of horses was heard, and then human voices.

Then all was bustle and activity.

A gentleman of rank and fortune, to judge from the fussiness of his attendants, halted to refresh.

He was armed, that is, wore armour, but a rich furred pelisse and ermined bonnet concealed the steel.

The landlord received him with a chuff kind of hospitality very different from the genial manner he had shown to the yeoman and sea captain.

The gentleman frowned somewhat, as with ready despatch the board was cleared and then freshly laid.

The breakfast was as good as that provided for the others.

It was manifest, however, that the richer guest was less welcome than the others.

Women in general are attracted by show and glitter. Though the landlord's wife waited on her new guest, it was with reluctance.

"Do those bright eyes of yours come from the forest?" he said, with a round oath.

The woman, who was handsome enough to have been a queen, bowed her head, while the landlord frowned.

"Why you look as if you never saw a nobleman before," continued the other.

"I have seen many, from our late noble king to petty knights in the train of the prince."

"What prince?"

"Prince John."

"Sdeath, woman, he is how king."

"I beg his grace's pardon."

"By the Holy Mother of God—but you seem not much to like him in these parts!"

"Your worship," put in the innkeeper, "my wife is grateful for some small favours shown us when his grace was wandering in the forest, and she cannot easily forget the lion-hearted prince."

"Oh," said the other, with a peculiar grin, "then you know something I dare say about Robin Hood."

"A proper man, who has honoured me with his company many times," replied the innkeeper.

At which the forester opened his eyes to their utmost width.

"May the holy and eternal Virgin Mary, mother of God, curse him! May St. Michael, the advocate of holy souls, curse him! May all the angels and archangels, principalities and powers, and all the heavenly armies, curse him!" said the gentleman, furiously.

"Our armies swore terribly in Flanders," cried the captain, "but nothing to this. I couldn't find it in my heart to curse my dog so."

The attendants of the nobleman looked menacingly at the interrupter.

"And pray, sir, who may you be?" said the other, superciliously.

"Captain Josh Lambert."

"Well, then, Captain Josh Lambert, please to speak when you are spoken to. I want no observations from strangers."

The captain stood staring with open eyes, clutching his dirk with his fist, and fuming horribly.

"I allow no brawls in my house," said the landlord, stepping forward; "be it king, noble, or peasant, in my house all bow to my authority."

"Bravo, good host," laughed the gentleman, with a peculiar twinkle of the eye.

"As for Robin Hood, I see not why he should be cursed. He is the friend of the poor, and the enemy only of the oppressor and tyrant. But for him, this part of England would be miserable indeed."

"Why?"

"Men of rank fear to affront him, so treat their vassals with decency and consideration."

"For egad! if I caught the jackanapes, I'd make him shorter by the head. A time is coming, my good people, when to own to be Robin's friend will be bad."

"A bad time."

"A good time. And I, as a friend of my king's, and one not unconsidered in his councils, warn you of it. Even if every tree in Sherwood is felled to the ground he will find the outlaw, and hang him high as Haman."

Silence followed.

"It is resolved to root out the whole pestilent gang," continued the other.

"And this because of the best man heaven ever let live," said the tall forester. "The friend of woman, and one on whose time it might be written, 'Next to the ladies he loved the yeomanry of England; he molested no hind at the plough, no thresher in the barn, no shepherd with his flocks; he was the friend and protector of husbandman and hind, and woe to the priest who fleeced or the noble who oppressed them. The widow, too, and the fatherless, he looked upon as under his care, and wheresoever he went some old woman was ready to do him a kindness for a saved son or a rescued husband.'"

"You speak feelingly," sneered the nobleman; "mayhap you know him?"

"All do about here."

"A nice neighbourhood!" laughed the other. "Well, I care not what any of you think, but this I know: he must and will be uprooted. To horse!"

And throwing down a gold piece for the refreshment of himself and his tenants, he went out.

"Who was he?" asked the captain.

"King John," said the innkeeper, drily.

The sea captain stood still and scratched his head. The tall forester laughed.

"Ah!" continued mine host, "it is no laughing matter. If he had had more men with him it would have been a hanging matter."

"Humph! I wish I were on ship-board again," said Captain Lambert.

"Would that I could find Robin Hood," muttered the tall forester.

"Where is he, that he cannot be found?" asked mine host.

"This fortnight he has gone no man knows whither. In silly jest I said no disguise of his could hide him from my eyes; and here have I been wandering ten days in search of him, and every man I meet I think must be he."

"I dare say now you have met him and didn't know him," replied the innkeeper.

"That is impossible!"

"Pay your money, my poor Little John," said the innkeeper, laughing.

"Magic!" roared the tall forester. "Thou Robin Hood?"

"Even so; and our fair waitress here Maid Marian. You see, John, you have lost your wager."

"I've done best, after all," said the sea captain, plucking off his beard and revealing no less a countenance than that of Will Scarlett.

The merriment now was great; and scouts being stationed to give timely warning of any danger, it was agreed to keep up the joke for the remainder of the day.

Robin had already a customer to take his place at a moment's warning.

CHAPTER LIII.

JOHN'S VENGEANCE.

KING JOHN was not a man to be easily deceived. There was something in the manner of Robin Hood which led him to suspect that he was not what he seemed, while the stately dignity of Maid Marian was beyond her sphere.

She could not hide that.

Putting the two things together the monarch, who was equally licentious and vengeful, determined to visit the outlaw with punishment of a kind suited to his black heart.

As soon as they were four miles from the hostelrie, the king halted and called up his men.

They were three men-at-arms and six foot archers.

They were some of his most devoted followers, men whom he had trusted upon many occasions to do his dark behests.

The king dismounted.

"Herbert," he said, calling one of the archers aside, "you noticed that voluptuous beauty at the inn?"

"I did, my liege."

"She is a ward of the crown."

"Indeed."

"Unjustly detained from our guardianship by outlaws."

"Yes, my liege."

"Do you take two men and go slowly back. She surely must sometimes walk in the wood. Watch your opportunity and bring her on. Gag her, but otherwise do not hurt her—she is a dainty one, not fit for the rude forest."

"Is that all, Sire?"

"All—but mind, no brawls with the outlaws; you else will get more than you bargain for. They have a marvellous way of fitting a stick to a man's back, which is less pleasant than clever."

"We will take care of ourselves."

"I need not say be quick when you have done the deed; for if you tarry, the outlaws will hang you."

And with these cheerful words the king rode off, leaving his followers, but ill content.

Had the word Robin Hood been used instead of "the outlaws" they would probably have refused compliance.

This the king knew.

Herbert and his two archers were bold and reckless men, who, principally employed on such enterprises of the monarch's as would not bear the light, were always prepared to do his behests.

They were well paid, and the chink of gold was a salve to their consciences.

They did not return by the road, but, entering the forest, skirted it so as to keep out of sight.

In this way they soon came to a convenient spot in sight of the inn.

They saw that its occupants were busy, and hence had to expect some delay, so lay down on the grass.

It happened that about this time a great many carters, and drovers, and others had come up, keeping the whole of the inn staff fully occupied.

Robin had arranged with the man who really was the innkeeper to resign his post, as on reflection the walk to Barnesdale was best performed by day.

It so happened, therefore, that circumstances chimed in with the views of these secreted villains.

All were to leave the inn by a back door, without exciting any notice.

Maid Marian went first, taking her way towards the forest with that light and elastic step which showed how gladly she left the shelter of a roof tree for that of the forest.

She trod upon the grass and buttercups with a sense of keen delight.

She was about to join her sylvan court, and she was happy.

Suddenly three armed ruffians leaped upon her, and scarcely giving her time to utter one cry, seized and gagged her.

But that one cry was sufficient.

Robin Hood heard it and knew its import.

"That accursed king," he muttered, as he bounded over the sward in pursuit.

THE MARRIAGE OF LITTLE JOHN.

But nowhere could he see anything. The one cry, which had stricken to his heart, had been heard and then all was over.

.With a scared and terrified look he entered the forest, and rushing in the direction of the original sound, soon reached a ·spot where he could distinguish the mark of three forms upon the grass.

No Red Indian was ever quicker on a trail than Robin Hood. He soon saw that they had started off at a rapid rate through the forest, the way in which they had trampled down the grass proving this.

With a knit brow and an angry frown, that boded no good to the ravishers, Robin Hood, who had fortunately provided himself with sword and quarterstaff, dashed in pursuit, using, however, sufficient caution not to alarm the ruffians, and thus cause them to part company and baffle his pursuit.

Soon, however, he came in sight of the villains, one of whom bore Maid Marian rudely enough on his shoulder.

"Stop, ye villains and murderers," cried Robin Hood, "know ye what ye are doing?"

"Obeying orders," replied Herbert, who lagged behind.

"I'll have you strung up by the heels and roasted over a slow fire, as sure as I am Robin Hood."

The man who bore Maid Marian put her down, and the three ruffians with one accord rushed at the one man.

But Robin stepped on one side and snatched Maid Marian from their arms.

This was a sad hindrance to his means of defence..

The archers were three to one.

They were disciplined and experienced soldiers; but even then they would not have prevailed against the outlaw but for the cunning of Hubert in urging him to where he stumbled over a root.

Striking him a fearful blow on the head, the villain would have despatched him, but footsteps were heard in chase.

They snatched up Maid Marian; and when Little John and Will Scarlett came up it was to find their noble chief stunned and bleeding.

He was, however, soon brought to, and the chase renewed.

Will Scarlett, in his disguise of a captain, had brought with him his dog Fangs, which he had locked in the stable with his horse.

It was a bloodhound.

No sooner did he take up the trail of the Norman soldiers than, with a long, low howl, he lowered his head to the ground and started at a moderate pace on their track.

The three men followed, now pretty certain to restore their beloved lady.

A junction with the rest of the king's party was all they had to fear.

And even this contingency would not have restrained Robin Hood when his wife was in danger.

He had made up his mind.

The ravishers, however, swerved somewhat from the high road, so that it was only after some reflection that they found they were on their way to a small hunting box of the king's.

Here, in all probability, they would await the coming of the royal and revengeful profligate.

But Robin resolved that his wife should not be subject to the insolent attentions of the monarch, even if to prevent such a contingency, he had to take the king's life.

A woman's honour at any time is worth a monarch's existence.

Not for ten kings would Robin have seen her injured.

As soon as he was fully prepared all set forward at a rapid pace, the dog being held in leash that he might not get too forward, and thus lose them the track.

The day was fine and the track easy for the dog.

The intelligent animal fully understood what was required of him. He knew that he was on the track of Maid Marian.

Once or twice as they advanced they were met by outlaws, to whom they give quick and rapid orders.

Then the three continued on their way.

They required no assistance at present, though if they had to besiege the king's pleasure palace such an event might render a collection of all their forces within the bounds of probability.

They travelled some hours, and though the pace at which they travelled was a very rapid one, they never once came in sight of the archers.

Still the dog kept on at a steady and quiet pace.

As all of the party were well acquainted with the forest, there was little chance of their making a mistake as to their destination.

The archers having declined to advance by the main-road, could be taking no other direction but that of the hunting-box.

This had been the scene of more than one of King John's disgraceful orgies, where all considerations but those of voluptuousness and debauchery were lost sight of.

Monarchy is all very well when strongly restrained by the popular element, but in every other form it is an unmitigated curse.

In no form is it without its objections.

The stumbling-block to democracy in America is slavery—not any error in the only rational system of government.

About evening they came in sight of a small convent, which, being tenanted by women and a few old priests, was closed at an early hour.

Rapine and robbery were of daily occurrence on all hands.

There was, however, a small hamlet, with the usual accompaniment, an ale house.

Towards this the dog directed his steps at once, without a moment's hesitation.

Entering and glancing their eyes around, no sign of the men could be seen.

"What for you, my masters?" said the host.

"Three archers with a woman in their company have been here?" replied Robin.

"They have."

"Royal archers?"

"Yes."

"How long since they have left?"

"They hired horses and went away about an hour ago."

Robin Hood sank exhausted on a bench. Fatigue and painful disappointment had quite overcome him.

"Which way?" asked Little John.

The man pointed out.

"Can we have horses?" continued Robin.

The answer was in the negative, as the three were all that the poor inhabitants of the village could spare—indeed all they possessed.

"Will the dog trace them?" asked Robin.

"To-morrow, as well as to-day," replied the outlaw; "you must rest."

"What is your hurry?" asked the landlord.

Little John looked hard at him.

"Are your a friend to those in Lincoln green?" he asked.

"Ah! that am I," said the landlord, heartily. My son Will, of the Cleugh, has been with them these ten years. But why do you ask?"

"Because these ruffians have stolen away the wife of Robin Hood," cried Little John.

"Gad zooks! and what about my horses?" replied the host.

"Care not about them. How far can these archers go without halting?"

"There is no halting-place, until they reach Tristan's Bower—our king's lodge."

"And that——"

"Will take them two hours hard ride."

"But we will be up to them by morn. At all events nature can endure no longer," cried Robin Hood; "I must rest."

The landlord, at once, at a signal from Little John, proceeded to make ready a hearty supper, and prepare a room where they could snatch two or three hours sleep.

Robin confessed, that much as his feelings were concerned, he could not move without repose.

Excess of strong feeling had, of itself, incapacitated him from further exertion.

With a view to drown his own feverish impatience, he sat down to the supper as soon as prepared, and both ate and drank freely.

Little John undertook to wake him.

But as soon as he had put him to rest, he and Will Scarlett held an earnest conference.

"I am as fresh as a lark," said Little John.

"Well."

"What say you to my tracking the ruffians to their dens?"

"You cannot do it without the dog."

"Will he not go without you?"

"No."

"Then you must go yourself," sighed Little John, "while I remain to guard him."

Will Scarlett agreed, and about an hour later, having to a certain extent rested himself after his fatigue, looked to his arms, whistled to the dog, and went upon his way.

The faithful hound, who at once knew what was expected of him, trotted on almost at his master's side.

The night was dark and gloomy, but though stars might fade, and moon refuse to shine, the unerring instinct of the dog made up for all.

Will Scarlett was well aware that the horsemen could not follow any of the narrower paths of the forest; he, therefore, felt confidence as long as the hound kept to a kind of cross-road used by cattle, and drovers, and pigs, and at times by persons of a higher degree.

The village towards which the dog was leading him was exclusively composed of men who, while calling themselves charcoal burners, were in reality the worst set of bandits.

They were encouraged by King John when prince, because they were the enemies of Robin Hood.

Will Scarlett was well aware of the dangers he had to encounter, and how much caution he must use to avoid spoiling matters.

The spot was the centre of as fine hunting ground as any in the world, and hence had been chosen by the king.

Unfortunately, it was made the hiding-place for acts of iniquity far worse than hunting.

The king had found it in a curious way.

The charcoal-burners had, under circumstances of peculiar atrocity, murdered two of Robin Hood's men.

The outlaw determined to punish them.

The sun was nearly set behind the distant mountains when a few of the scattered and terrified inhabitants of the village of Hazledon—which had, four days before, been burned by a band of English outlaws—were now busied in repairing their ruined dwellings. One high tower in the centre of the village alone exhibited no appearance of devastation. It was surrounded with court walls, and the outer gate was barred and bolted. The bushes and brambles which grew around, and had even insinuated their branches beneath the gate, plainly showed that it must have been many years since it had been opened.

While the cottages around lay in smoking ruins, this pile, deserted and desolate as it seemed to be, had suffered nothing from the violence of the invaders; and the wretched beings who were endeavouring to repair their miserable huts against nightfall seemed to neglect the preferable shelter which it might have afforded them without the necessity of labour.

Before the day had quite gone down, a knight, richly armed, and mounted upon an ambling hackney, rode slowly into the village. His attendants were a lady, apparently young and beautiful, who rode by his side upon a dappled palfrey; his squire, who carried his helmet and lance and led his battle-horse, a noble steed, richly caparisoned. A page and four yeomen, bearing bows and quivers, short swords, and targets of a span breadth, completed his equipage, which, though small, denoted him to be a man of high rank.

He stopped and addressed several of the inhabitants, whom curiosity had withdrawn from their labour to gaze at him; but at the sound of his voice, and, still more, on perceiving the St. George's Cross in the caps of his followers, they fled, with a loud cry.

The knight endeavoured to expostulate with the fugitives, who were chiefly aged men, women, and children; but their dread accelerated their flight, and in a few minutes, excepting the knight and his attendants, the place was deserted by all.

He paced through the village to seek a shelter for the night, and, despairing to find one either in the inaccessible tower or the plundered huts of the peasantry, he directed his course to the left hand, where he spied a small, decent habitation, apparently the abode of a man considerably above the common rank. After much knocking, the proprietor at length showed himself at the window, and, speaking with great signs of apprehension, demanded their business. The warrior replied that his quality was that of an English knight and baron, and that he was travelling to the court of the king on affairs of consequence.

The knight asked news relative to the occurrence, and when he heard that Robin Hood had punished the murderers and burned their village, swore a round oath. "That villain will never rest until I hang him," he said; "but why is yonder tower shut up?"

"'Tis a long story and little known," replied the other; "but this I do know, it has been abandoned for twenty years."

"Then shall it be opened," said the knight, "and light let into it."

And he kept his word; the door was burst open, the tower repaired, the ditch made deep, and to this spot many a noble damsel and feeble dame was carried to satisfy the inordinate desires and love of pleasure not peculiar to this English prince.

Partly to conceal his vagaries, and partly out of dislike to the noble Saxon outlaw, here he would let none live save charcoal burners and a servant or two of his own.

Will Scarlett cared not, he knew that one sound of his bugle would probably bring him aid, and he was determined at any cost to succeed in tracing Marian.

About an hour after midnight he came in sight of the tower, but neither in village nor in castle was there the faintest sight of light.

The curfew law was well obeyed.

One thing was certain, that none others had come this way since the passage of the three archers and their captive.

Anywhere else, trusting to the prestige of the outlaw's name, he would have awakened mine host, but here any such proceeding was out of the question.

There remained the green sward, and with this, his dog crouching at his feet, he was content to be satisfied.

CHAPTER LIV.

THE KING'S FAVOURITE.

It was bright morn when Will Scarlett awoke, and when he did the birds sang merrily, the dew was light upon the grass, and nature in one of her most charming humours.

The outlaw rose to his feet.

All was still, save that in one or two huts the dwellers were busy making their morning fires.

The dog moaned lowly.

Will Scarlett looked warily around, and there, coming under the green arches of the forest, was Robin Hood and Little John.

Both had walked hard and fast, and when they took their seats beside Will Scarlett on the sward were scarcely able to crawl.

The events of twenty-four hours had much affected the bold outlaw.

He had a fearful dread upon his soul with regard to his beloved Maid Marian, which literally unmanned him.

"Hast seen anything?" he asked, in a hollow tone.

"No," said Will Scarlett, "not the faintest sign of anybody or anything."

"I must get within those walls," murmured Robin Hood.

"Impossible!"

"There is no impossibility."

"How?"

"We must keep close," said Robin, loudly, and with a strange fever in his eye; "if the base king comes before I can see Marian, there shall be wailing amid the Normans. Another Tyrrell shall be found for another Rufus."

"Hush!" said Will, who though obedient in all things to Robin, had the ignorant and popular prejudice in favour of kings, fostered by cunning knaves and sycophantish priests.

"I will not hush, my good Will. Which like you best, my good Will, that I and Marian die, or that this tyrant should suffer?"

"Perish a thousand kings!" said Will,

"'Tis well. Now listen to me!" continued Robin Hood. "I mean to enter that tower before this godless king does, I mean to witness his attempt on the virtue of my wife, and I mean to poignard him on the spot."

All listened awe-struck at the very emission of sentiments which are native to the soul with regard to tyrants.

"Do you, having aided me, go forth and bring up my men. If I have to kill this king there will be rare sport in England," he added, cruelly; "it shall go hard but we will find a Saxon heir to the throne."

"But how will you enter the castle?"

"Come this way," said Robin, diving into the wood, and leading them to where they could see the high wall of the garden.

It was not a well fortified tower, being only used as a hunting-box, when mostly it was guarded without from surprise.

"I must go over that wall."

"How?"

"We must cut down a tree, which Little John then must carry to the ditch; leave all the rest to me."

They acquiesced, and retiring further into the forest contrived to pick out and cut down a tall pine, which, denuded of boughs, cut short like stepping places, would easily enable him to climb the wall.

As soon as dark set in, the extempore ladder was carried to where it could be supported against a buttress.

Little John and Will Scarlett held it firmly.

With a stern brow Robin shook hands with his two devoted followers.

"If harm happens to you, master," said Little John, "I will pull the tower down stone by stone."

"You will never see me again, my friends, unless with my wife in all honour."

And with a gloomy brow he ascended, sat across the top of the wall, and looked down.

The descent was easy.

With a wave of the hand he bid farewell to his followers and leaped down.

The garden, in an age when flowers and fruits were not much cultivated, consisted chiefly of bushy walks.

As usual there was one shady well-covered walk, which was emphatically called the "king's walk."

In most royal palaces there was such a private retreat, where none were expected to penetrate save the favoured individual selected by his grace.

Along this Robin Hood took his way slowly and thoughtfully, until he reached the spot where the garden and yard were divided one from the other.

Here a heavy wooden gate separated the two, a gate, however, of bars.

Robin peered through, and saw several persons in the garden pursuing their usual avocations.

It was early, and though soon the curfew would compel all others to retire, yet within a royal dwelling place no such influence had any sway.

There no law save the will of the master prevailed.

There were several women and two or three men.

For these Robin did not care, but still at the same time, he preferred acting with circumspection.

Presently the attendants, having finished what they were about, went in.

Robin then tried the gate.

It was bolted on the other side, while in the centre was a ponderous lock.

Now for a man who used his hands pretty freely, Robin Hood had a small and feminine one.

Without much dificulty he contrived to pass it through, and to slip the bolts.

The key was another matter.

He had no contrivance to pick locks with, such department of the trade being unknown.

He felt the lock carefully all round.

He felt it all over.

To his great surprise the key was in it.

Next moment it was turned, and Robin was in the court-yard of the tower.

Circumspection was now needed, and the outlaw, who was armed with his *dague* and short sword, moved along slowly and gently.

In this way he soon reached the end of a wide passage to the left of which was the kitchen, where he could see that the three archers, four women, some serving men and others were collected, passing the time as merrily as might be.

The door of the dark passage was open, and the outlaw glided in.

Arrived at the foot of a wide staircase he found himself in total darkness.

But he held firmly by the rope, which then served the place of a bannister, and clambered up.

Soon he found himself in a long passage faintly illuminated.

Along this he walked slowly, examining each door.

At last he halted at one from beneath which came a faint light.

He peered through the keyhole.

Yes!

At a small table, pale but thoughtful and determined, sat Maid Marian.

Robin knocked gently.

She started.

He then tried the door.

It was locked on the outside.

In a moment more he had opened it, and was in the room.

"Why disturb me more?" she said, without raising her head.

"Hist! Marian, beware!" was the reply.

And she was clasped in her husband's arms.

In a few minutes all was explained, and the delight of the wife at the fidelity and devotion of her husband knew no bounds.

"But there is no time to love," exclaimed Robin.

"Hark! Some one comes. Conceal yourself."

Scarcely had he done so when a woman entered, while outside there stood the three archers.

"The castle is closed for the night, lady; we wish to retire. Is there anything we can do for you?"

"Supper," whispered Robin.

"I am faint and weary with my detestable journey," said Maid Marian, and would have refreshment."

"It is here."

And as she spoke she took a tray from the hands of a servant and brought it in.

She then retired.

The husband and wife laughed.

"We will sup of the king's fare and be merry, and then," grinned Robin, "we will sleep in the king's bed."

Marian smiled at the conceit, and having brought husband and wife to this point we there leave them.

CHAPTER LV.

A BOLD STRATAGEM.

A FLOOD of rich and glorious light poured into the chamber when they awoke.

Both sprang to the ground at once.

Action now became imperative, as the king's arrival might be momentarily expected.

Robin tried the door.

It was locked on the outside.

The windows, mere loopholes, were out of the question.

The outlaw walked up and down, and chafed somewhat like a wild beast in a cage.

Soon, however, the rustic attendants came again with the morning meal, and clearing away the one of the night before, looked somewhat amazed at the evidence there given of Marian's appetite.

But a king's favourite, even for a day, was not a person lightly to be talked to.

The remains were removed without a word.

Again the husband and wife were left alone.

A hearty breakfast was always a wise precaution to take before any forest adventures.

The pair regaled themselves freely on the king's pastry and wine and bread.

Both felt the better for it.

Now came the time for action.

To gain the garden was the grand object; for once there Robin could communicate with his friends.

The heavy door stood in their way.

Robin advanced to it, with his dagger.

No sooner, however, had he tried it than he found that it would resist any such means of exit.

What could he do then?

Circumstances decided for him.

A low musical blast of trumpets on the outside warned him that the king had arrived.

Now the whole matter had changed.

Death before dishonour, was his motto.

A rapid exchange of words took place, and then Robin selected a hiding-place behind the floating arras.

He did not need to retreat to it for a long time.

Though the noise and bustle announced that the king was in the castle, he did not make his appearance.

They rightly judged him to be carousing.

King John dearly loved the wassail-bowl, in which to drown care and remorse.

No man is so evil as never to be visited by the scorpion-whip of conscience, which lashes us for our good.

The middle of the day came.

Robin began to feel uncomfortable.

A general attack by his outlaws on the town appeared to be the only resource left him.

Then the door was again opened, and, with a message from the king, enters a trencher-man, with a repast both rich and rare.

His grace would do himself the honour shortly.

From behind the arras Robin Hood smiled grimly.

A deed was perhaps about to be done which might change the fortunes of all England.

But no thought of this interfered with the mid-day meal. There was glorious fun in eating at the amorous monarch's expense.

At last, a heavy, stately step was heard in the passage, and the outlaw prepared.

The door was opened, and King John entered, flushed with wine.

"Where is this queenly damsel," he said, as he closed the door behind him, "who consorts with outlaws?"

"I am here."

This was said calmly.

"Oh!" cried the king, "you are the *damoisel?* Well, I must say the thief has good taste. Come, kiss me, lass, that I may forgive thee for marrying a thief."

"I kiss no one but my husband. I obey not orders, who am in the habit of giving them."

"Well said, lass! Hast more wine there?"

And he staggered forward.

The king was drunk.

He nearly fell against Maid Marian as he pushed forward, and was clutched by the nervous hand of Robin Hood.

"Eh!"

"Silence!"

"Guards without!"

"Silence! or this dagger shall do its duty. One thrust of it, and there will be an end."

The king sank back in his chair, quite overcome.

"Wine!"

Maid Marian hastened to pour him out a large cup-full, which he drained off.

Then, without a murmur, he allowed the outlaw to unrobe him.

His habitual instincts made him believe that he was being put to bed by fair hands, and he muttered a refrain of his own all the time :—

> And then to bed,
> And then to bed,
> And then to bed, with Marian.

Upon which the outlaw's wife moved away with a smile of scorn upon her handsome lips.

But Robin Hood himself was the disrober and he cared not for his words.

"See there, Norman tyrant and sot; as far below the genial Richard who in his cups was generous, as a grunting hog is beneath a noble hart."

And then quite coolly he put on the king's boots, ermined cloak, and furred cap.

Marian screamed with laughter, though taking care not to make too much noise.

Soon, however, she became grave and serious as she thought of the extreme danger to Robin.

He threw open the door, and with a very good imita-of what the king's walk would have been, offered his arm to Maid Marian, and passed down the corridor.

Several varlets and others were to be seen at first, but all ran away.

The coast was quite clear.

Now what to do was a puzzler to Robin.

In these robes, to be seen clambering over the garden-wall in company with a lady would excite strange suspicions.

Robin resolved to walk openly out.

He saw just, when about to cross the court-yard, that a postern gate was open, and that an inferior warder and two archers stood in converse.

A loud hem from the supposed king startled them excessively.

They looked round, and saw, as they believed, King John advancing in conversation with a lady.

They moved on one side, pretending not to see the monarch, and entered the guard-house.

Robin, still walking with the utmost composure, moved on one side to let Marian pass.

He then followed, again taking her arm in his, and bending low to whisper to her, as he had seen many a court gallant do in his time.

He was whispering words of comfort to her all the while.

They took their way along the fosse in a direction which, while it ultimately would lead to the wood, was in a straight line from the windows.

Several were concealed on the ramparts.

Suddenly there arose a terrible uproar in the castle, just as Robin reached a thicket.

Out from the castle gates rushed archers and men-at-arms.

Robin turned slowly round.

His royal robes still encumbered him, but they did not prevent him from winding his bugle.

In a moment his most faithful followers and lieutenants were crowding round him in the utmost amazement.

Robin merely laughed.

"Send back that rabble," he said.

The very sight of some fifty men in Lincoln green sufficed for this.

On the ramparts, in a towering passion, was the king, before whose face Robin took off his royal robes, cast them to the ground, and turned away, quite satisfied to have taken his revenge mildly, where another would have had dire vengeance.

But this ever was Robin—making himself almost loved by his enemies for his gentleness.

As his historian truly says, (we quote this for those of our readers who believe Robin a myth) :—

"His popularity among the common people was universal, and has come down to us as fresh and untarnished as it must have been in his own day. There is not an authority but has a good word for him. Fordum, a writer and a priest in the fourteenth century, calls him ' *ille famosissimus siccarius,*' that most celebrated robber. Major styles him ' the most humane and the prince of all robbers.' He was compared by the author of a curious Latin Poem, dated *Julii* 1304, to William Wallace, the hero of Scotland. The renowned Camden speaks of him as ' the gentlest of thieves.' Shakespeare' in ' As You Like it,' in his discription of the Duke's mode of life, in allusion to its happiness, says, ' He is already in the Forest of Arden, a many merry men with him, and there they live like the Old Robin Hood of England * * * and fleet the time carelessly as they did in the Golden World.' Drayton, a charming poet, in his ' Polybion,' a work of extraordinary ability, thus characterises him :—

> What often times he took, he shared amongst the poor.
>   *   *   *   *   *
> The widow in distress he graciously reliev'd,
> And remedied the wrongs of many a virgin griev'd:
> He from the husband's bed no married woman wan,
> But to his mistress dear, his loved Marian,
> Was ever constant known.

Geoffrey Chaucer hath named him in kind terms: indeed, were we to enumerate all who have made mention of his name in their works, in strains of eulogy and tones of panegyric, we should exhaust the patience of our readers; we may sum them up in the words of a gentleman who has most ably edited a very handsome edition of the ' Robin Hood Ballads,' and whose title to his opinion, from his very close research into the subject, is unquestionable. In concluding his life, he says, ' He was a man who, in a barbarous age, and under a complicated tyranny, displayed a spirit of freedom and independence which has endeared him to the common people, whose cause he maintained (for all opposition to tyranny is the cause of the people), and in spite of the malicious endeavours of pitiful monks, by whom history was consecrated to the crimes and follies of titled ruffians and sainted idiots, to suppress all record of his patriotic exertions and virtuous acts, will render his name immortal."

CHAPTER LVI.

THE WEDDING.

For some time after this adventure Robin thought it wise to keep close.

There was very little hope now of his rightful claims to the earldom of Huntingdon being considered. So, after a somewhat severe mental struggle, which the hopes of being looked upon by his fellow-countrymen and friends as a noble without taint had created, he wisely determined to give up all such thoughts, and to live in the green wood in the old manner, and, if possible with equal happiness to that which he had so long enjoyed.

He summoned his people together, and told them his determination. "He concluded by saying that, taking everything into consideration, it was, perhaps, for the best, because they had been as a little community which was completely, as it were, isolated in society. They had lived together without mixing with any but those of the band, and did they go once more into society they would, probably, frequently have reflections cast upon their former mode of life; they would be disunited, and compelled to be subservient to laws and customs which a habit of living freely and simply in the green wood would render highly distasteful and oppressive. They had for years looked up to him, as a large family would look up to a loved and honoured head of the house; they had been accustomed to his sway, and ever cheerfully obey its dictates; they had been very happy as they had lived, and they might almost ensure, if they still followed the same mode of life, that they would still receive the same amount of happiness which they had hitherto experienced, and, therefore, they would live on in the old way, nor change their acts and manners in any one way but where they might be improved. There was still the same shelter—still the green leaves and flowers to dwell among; and he believed that, after a cool consideration, he should lay his head down with calmer contentment, and sleep more lightly, than he should have done had he made the change in his condition which he had expected."

Thus speaks the author of the "Life of Robin Hood and Little John."

His discourse is said to have had a great effect upon his followers—especially as he spoke to them in all the affectionate terms and endearing manner of a loving brother.

It was under the trysting tree.

His tones, look, and voice were those of some mighty monarch, resigning some minor distant empire, to devote himself solely to his own people.

How thoroughly and how truly they understood and appreciated his motives might have been seen by the tremendous shout with which his announcement was greeted.

The outlaws were, as a rule, glad that they were to remain in the old forest.

Here they were safe from their enemies.

And habit is a severe chain. To break through its thrall requires more courage than people generally think.

Habit and association made them love the green wood.

No one was more delighted than Little John, who once the monarch of Sherwood forest had made known his final resolve, also made up his mind.

To what?—

To get married.

This unexpected announcement certainly took the outlaws by surprise.

Their delight, however, was unbounded. Such an opportunity for a gala did not occur every day.

Robin Hood determined that it should be the occasion for a three days' holiday.

When April with his sweet showers has pierced the drought of March to the root, and bathed every vein in the balm that produces flowers; when Zephyr too, with his sweet breath, has animated the tender green buds in the woods and on the heaths; and the young sun has run half his course in the Ram; and the little winged creatures, that sleep all night with their eyes open, begin their music, (so irresistible in their hearts is nature) then did Little John fix on his marriage day.

We need scarcely say that the huge mountain of a man, with a heart big enough for three, had only room in it for one woman.

And that was Rose.

And Rose dearly loved him, though, like most little women, she dearly loved to tease her giant.

A fine time of it had Little John a month before the wedding in persuading Rose to keep to her promise.

"You won't make a fool of me before all the men." he would say.

"Well, I don't know."

"But you won't?"

"What mean you, fair sir?"

"That if you do not keep faith with me I shall fly to foreign parts and take service."

"Who'd have you?"

"Anybody."

"Well, I won't."

"Rose, you don't mean this," said big Little John, with a melancholy smile. "You can't."

"Well, perhaps I don't," replied Rose, stifling a laugh.

And then came the eventful day when, to the great delight of the tall forester, Rose formally placed herself in the hands of the bridesmaids.

It would be impossible to describe the delight of Little John. The dream of his life was about to be realised. He that could never understand a woman loving one so uncouth and rough as himself, was at last to have the peerless woman of his choice, all his own.

The general body of outlaws partook in his pleasure.

Next to Robin, he was the favourite.

There was so much heart in that big body.

Though the bride was fair indeed, none envied him; for there were fair women enough for all in merry England—land of the beautiful and the brave.

The altar was erected under an oak—symbol of England's power.

Friar Tuck was in full and new canonicals, provided for the occasion.

Robin Hood and Maid Marian wore the richest robes their almost inexhaustible treasury could supply them with.

All the young men who had not wives had provided themselves with partners.

Girls were to be found in abundance ready to trip it on the light fantastic toe.

Now, however, they were all collected round the altar, where, previous to the marriage ceremony, Friar Tuck, in the presence of bride and bridegroom, delivered what he called an allocution.

"Before we proceed let us speak of matrimony, which means the conjunction of man and wife.

"Who would be without a wife?

"A wife! Why bless my son, how can a man have any adversity that has a wife? Answer me that. Tongue cannot tell, nor heart think, of the felicity there is between a man and his wife. If he is poor, she helps him to work. She takes care of his money for him, and never wastes anything. She never says 'yes,' when he says 'no.' 'Do this,' says he. 'Directly,' says she.

"O blessed institution! O precious wedlock! thou art so joyous, and at the same time so virtuous, and so recommended to us all, and so approved by us all, that every man who is worth a farthing should go down on his bare knees, every day of his existence, and thank Heaven for having sent him a wife; or if he hasn't got one, he ought to pray for one, and beg that she may last him to his life's end; for his life, in that case, is set in security. Nothing can deceive him.

"A wife is the gift of Heaven: there's no doubt of it. Every other kind of gift, such as lands, rents, furniture, right of pasture or common—these are all gifts of fortune, that pass away like shadows on a wall; but you have to apprehend no such misfortune with a wife. Your wife will last longer, perhaps, even than you may desire.

"He has only to act by his wife's advice, and he may hold up his head with the best. A wife is so true—so wise. Oh! ever while you live take your wife's advice, if you would be thought a wise man."

Here Friar Tuck stopped for breath, and seeing one near him him with a flagon, he snatched it from him, and drank one deep draught to the health of the about to be married couple.

This course, as a matter of course, was very readily followed; one loud shout arising in their honour.

The ceremony then began by direction of Robin, who had no wish to see all the people elevated with drink before the business of the day was over.

To keep them sober afterwards was out of the question, as Friar Tuck would be the first to set the example.

Indeed, it was sufficiently clear that he could only just get through the ceremony.

He had been up early and had imbibed.

As soon as the two were made one, and Little John had publicly imprinted a kiss on his blushing bride's lips, the Friar, though in full canonicals, took a girl on each arm and led the way towards the banquetting ground, singing one of those absurd ditties which from the monkish schools have come down to modern times, to the delight of every young schoolboy:—

Amo, amas,
I love a lass
As cedar tall and slender;
Sweet cowslip's grace
Is her nominative case,
And she's of the feminine gender.

Rorum, corum,
Surt Divorum,
Harum scarum Divo;
Tag-rag, merry-derry, periwig, and hat-band,
Hic hoc aorum, genitivo.

The outlaws laughed all the more for not understanding, anything the friar said being considered witty.

The feast was the most gorgeous ever seen upon the sward of the old trysting place.

To describe minutely all that was upon the table would be to print a page of *menu*.

But by this time our readers are pretty *au fait* to what constituted a dinner in the time of King John.

As soon as the solids had been despatched, the drinking began in earnest.

Robin Hood proposed the health of the bride and bridegroom.

He was not one of the time-servers who think a dinner incomplete until they have screamed themselves hoarse with drinking a toast to royalty.

Robin Hood was a patriot.

And no patriot, as a patriot, can be a friend to monarchy.

Indeed, the view taken by one writer on this question, though not original, is, perhaps, nearer the truth than any other speculation concerning the famous hero which has yet been formed. It is, that he was the last Saxon who made a positive stand against the dominancy of the Normans; that, in fact, his predatory attacks upon them were but the national efforts of one who endeavoured to remove the proud foot of a conqueror from the neck of his countrymen.

His means were all unequal to accomplish this noble and daring design; but his efforts were unceasing, and must have been the source of constant alarm and harass to the Normans within his three counties, as well as of much uneasiness to the governments under which he lived.

We need not say with what applause the toast was greeted, nor how Rose laughed, nor how Little John rose, stammered, and sat down, all unable to make a speech.

Several other toasts followed, all of which increased the general hilarity.

At last, with a flushed and almost angry countenance, the friar rose.

His speech, though he was quite excited with drink, was sufficiently incoherent.

"In the old days of King Arthur, which the Bretons hold in such high estimation, this land was all full of fairies. The Elf-Queen, with her merry attendants, was always dancing about the green meads. Such at least was the opinion a long time ago—many hundred years. Nowadays we see them no longer; for the charity and piety of the begging friars, and others of their holy brethren, who make search everywhere by land and water, as thick as the motes in the sunbeams, blessing our halls, chambers, kitchens, bowers, cities, boroughs, towers, castles, villages, barns, dairies, and sheep-folds, have caused the fairies to vanish; for where the fairy used to be, there is now the friar himself. You are sure to meet him before breakfast and dinner, saving his matins and holy things, and going about with his wallet. Women may now go up and down in safety; for though they may see things in the bushes and under the trees, it's only the friar.

"What, then, is the reason my health has not been proposed, when my ability is patent?

"I propose my own health."

Roars of laughter followed this sally, which was highly applauded by Robin Hood.

Then, in order to check intemperence and insubordination, Maid Marian set the example of a dance, which all damsels approved of, and the more feasting was given up.

It would be impossible for any pen, however graphic, to describe the glorious scene of hearty English enjoyment which followed, as different from the stiff and stupid festivities which too often accompany a wedding now, as light is from darkness.

About dusk there was a general game of hide and seek, when Little John suddenly snatched up his little wife, and, despite her struggles, carried her off.

Nor could all the efforts of the discomfited outlaws succeed in discovering to what secret retreat he had carried her.

And thus ended the celebrated wedding of Little John, who, though not least, was married last.

CHAPTER LVII.

EVIL NEWS.

Yet thee to leave is death, is death indeed.

Clasp me a little longer on the brink
Of fate! while I can feel thy dear caress;
And when this heart hath ceased to beat—Oh! think—
And let it mitigate thy woes excess—
That thou hast been to me all tenderness,
And friend to more than human friendship just.
Oh, by that retrospect of happiness,
And by the hopes of an immortal trust,
God shall assuage thy pangs—when I am laid in dust!
CAMPBELL.

Lay me then, gently, in my narrow dwelling,
Thou gentle heart;
And though thy bosom should with grief be swelling,
Let no tear start;
It were in vain. MOTHERWELL.

Touch'd by the music and the melting scene,
Was scarce one tearless eye amidst the crowd.
Stern warriors, resting on their swords, were seen
To veil their eyes.
*   *   *
Then mournfully the parting bugle bid
Its farewell o'er the grave. CAMPBELL.

WE now approach a part of our narrative which we would willingly pass over, especially as there is very slight historical grounds for the story.

We are content, however, to rest upon the evidence of the modern historian who has made Robin Hood the subject of a special study.

Four happy years passed away, during which many adventures happened to the outlaws, too similar to those already recorded to be of interest to the reader.

The effect of King John's reign upon the people of England was tremendous.

Long before he became king, Prince John had succeeded in obtaining for himself the most decided hatred of the nation.

No sooner was it known that he was to have the crown, than it became the signal for outrage and violence over the whole kingdom.

The barons and nobles collected their vassals and filled their castles with armed men and provisions.

The peasantry and poorer classes, bursting from a long thrall like the French revolutionists, committed violence and devastation to a fearful extent.

It was difficult for those who commanded in the king's absence to prevent the kingdom from becoming one scene of anarchy, carnage, and devastation.

King John, copying his dead brother's example where least it should have been copied, sought glory in foreign war.

Blood and money were as nought.

Then, after some years of absence, he came back from Rouen to England for succours.

He had expended an enormous amount of human life and treasure in a useless war, carried on by his generals while he was wasting his substance and health in luxurious dissipation and debauchery at Rouen.

The king was expected every hour, and was to hold a court at Nottingham.

Now, Robin Hood had all this time been much molested by the king's orders, especially by the haughty churchmen who ruled fair England during the monarch's absence.

As many of them would naturally be on their way through the forest to join the court, Robin determined to have a brief return to his old ways.

He never wearied of them.

Robin was one of those who could not grow old.

It was not in the nature of his warm and generous heart to become callous or warped.

His men were now more than a thousand in number, and were, though generally scattered over the ground, easily collected together.

Robin Hood and several of his lieutenants collected a select party near one of the cross roads which continually were met with near the highway.

This done, he took the garb of a knight, with a squire and two men-at-arms, and posted himself so that he could see any that came from a small hostelry where he put up.

The day was fine.

It was charming weather at the sea side or near green fields and breezy heaths, but it burned the skin in the crowded thoroughfares.

As Robin watched, he saw one of his spies come up.

"Who comes?"

"The Abbot of Ramsay."

"Where to?"

"To York."

"How attended?"

"By fifty men-at-arms and as many archers."

"'Tis well. Go forward and bid Little John and Will Scarlett be ready."

The man obeyed and soon the outlaw saw the advance guard of the abbot's escort.

There were mounted men-at-arms and archers on foot.

The knight did not move, but sat erect upon his horse, watching the spectacle.

The van soon came up, and halted a little beyond the inn.

Behind were the sumpter mules.

Then came the fat abbot, a man of surly mien, who was surrounded by numbers of ecclesiastics.

"It is hot—I am athirst," said the abbot of Ramsay, wiping his purply face. "I wonder if they have any good ale.

"Capital," replied the supposed knight; "I will myself be your cupbearer, my lord abbot."

This courtesy from one of apparent rank, brought a smile on the priest's face.

Then Robin came out with his squire and men-at-arms who bore flagons of right strong ale.

He waited on the abbot, while the others did the same by the ecclesiastics.

The waiting men saw to the wants of the guard.

The ale was good, the day was hot, and the supply abundant. No one stinted themselves.

Then the abbot, who was too haughty and proud to be stingy, ordered his almoner to pay.

The innkeeper was happy.

The party had drunk more than his regular customers in a whole week.

Then they started forward still moving slowly for the benefit of the sumpter mules and the palfreys on which the fat monks rode.

The abbot of Ramsay much pleased with the courtesy of the knight, and finding him going the same way called him to his side.

Conversation ensued,

Presently they came to a shady part of the road, where the highway narrowed to very small limits.

"A pleasant shade," quoth the abbot.

"Pleasanter than safe," muttered the knight.

"Why so?"

"It is such spots the outlaws choose for their attacks."

The abbot shuddered.

"But Hubert Walter told me there was nothing to fear from them."

"Little, but then are you not Abbot of Ramsay, Baron of Broughton?"

"I am."

"You are passing through the territories of one who disputes your title to the rank of Earl of Huntingdon."

"The impudent knave. You have heard that story?"

"I have. I was in the field of battle when his father acknowledged him in the presence of King Richard."

"The man was mad. No evidence has been brought," said the abbot, coldly, "to prove his claim. But who are you who speak so glibly of him?"

"You shall call me what you will," replied the knight, with a smile, "here men call me Robin Hood."

"Treason!" shouted the abbot, "close round. The outlawed robbers are upon us!"

At the same moment Robin Hood backed into the bushes, and sounded his horn, when up rose from every tree, and briar, and hedge a flood of men in Lincoln green.

The escort of the greedy churchman was taken without a blow being struck.

Thus the man who originally held the title and lands of Huntingdon was a prisoner in his hands.

The abbot, utterly overwhelmed, demanded an instant interview with Robin Hood.

"You shall have it, sooner than you wot," said Little John, drily.

The tall forester walked at the head of his mule.

In this way they reached the forest, or rather a dense part of it, where the outlaw had retreated.

The common men had been disarmed and sent about their business.

None were kept prisoners but the monks and the sumpter mules.

Soon they were brought before Robin, who, with Maid Marian, was now clothed in all the insignia of their courtly rank.

They sat, however, upon their sylvan throne surrounded by outlaws.

"Welcome, sir abbot, to Sherwood!"

"Abbot and Baron of Broughton," began the haughty priest.

"Stay!" said Robin.

"Why?"

"Do you wish to be made a martyr of, and transfixed with arrows?"

"Not unnecessarily."

"Then let not my men hear you mention my title in their presence," said Robin Hood, in a low and warning tone of voice.

The abbot bowed, to hide his excited and angry feelings.

Little John and some such expeditious outlaws were now busy unloading the sumpter mules, as well as those of the almoner, which was richly supplied.

The abbot looked on with a dark and kindling brow at this summary proceeding.

The food was all placed out upon the ground, and the monks and their chief invited to partake.

The outlaws added a goodly supply of roast and boiled venison.

The Abbot of Ramsey, who was a great feeder, would have repeated the banquet, but his stomach was too much for him.

Sundry bottles of rare wine from his own stock, which he saw being opened, decided him.

Like the others he helped himself.

Robin Hood was in a grave and solemn humour, so that few spoke.

It was, however, his care that no distinction should be made between the proud and wealthy abbot and his meanest followers.

Many a junior monk, holding such a post as porter or the like, tasted a meal unknown to them before, and never to be forgotten.

It was rare fun for the outlaws to see the annoyance of the abbot.

He dared not say anything lest he should arouse the evil passions of men he had been taught to consider such terrible and dangerous fellows, men who cared not for human life.

But the worst was to come, the crowning misery of all.

The Abbot of Ramsay loved rank and power, but above all, money.

Money—not for what it would procure—but money for its own simple sake, to keep, to store up, to hide.

He was a miser.

Miser, which means miserable.

"And now, sir abbot," said Robin, "ere the dessert be brought on, allow me to inform you of one of our rules—a very stringent one."

"How can men out of the pale of the law make laws?"

"I am a king where I stand, and I make laws to suit my own purposes."

"Let me hear this one."

"It is that every guest entertained at my table shall pay for his entertainment according to his rank and means," was the reply.

ROBIN HOOD'S LAST SHOT.

"As your men have   en all I have what more can you expect?"

"Sir abbot, by foul and nefarious means you have robbed me of title and estates," said Robin, Hood drily. "I may not often have so good a chance of reprisal. For your repast you will pay me ten thousand gold pieces."

"Whence, monster, am I to take them?" cried the Abbot of Ramsay.

"Out of the rents of my estates," replied the outlaw, amid the laughter of the outlaws.

"And if I refuse?" asked the angry abbot, of Ramsey gloomily.

"You will never leave the forest alive," replied Robin. "It is not often I am cruel; but from you I have received nothing but injury, and I shall therefore require the full amount. I demand of you but a small part of that you have robbed me of."

"I robbed you?"

"King Richard has decided that the title and lands of Huntingdon are mine."

"King John has decided otherwise."

"Dare not compare the lion and the craven heart," said Robin, severely. "Will you or will you not pay the money?"

"I have not got it."

"Prepare the obstinate abbot's prison, Little John," said Robin Hood, severely. "Discharge all the inferior monks."

"I will pay the money. Send my almoner to me."

"Anything he has is already our own."

"I know that."

"What wilt do, then?"

"Write to the treasurer of my abbey. In two days you shall have the money."

"In the meantime you shall have all honourable treatment."

"I thank you, cousin."

"I hope you will recollect my hospitality."

"I shall."

"Favourably?"

"Very favourably."

"I doubt it not. Priests are always grateful."

The almoner was sent for ; but having been under the care and superintendence of Friar Tuck, he was not quite so clear in the head as he might have been.

"My tablets."

"Your reverence has them."

"You have been drinking."

"All have."

"Dare you, sir ?"

"I dare anything."

The abbot took the tablets from the almoner, and in a fierce and angry mood wrote an order on the treasury of the abbey for the large sum.

Little John, Friar Tuck, and the almoner were sent for it.

In two days the money came.

Robin Hood, with a grave and serious face, bade adieu to the Abbot of Ramsay.

"May we never meet again !"

"To our next merry meeting !" said the abbot.

"Pray we never do !" replied Robin : "for I should not have the same patience."

And thus they parted.

We have on the faith of the same historian an idea of what was the result.

It will readily be imagined that a man like the Abbot of Ramsay was not going to remain long unavenged.

CHAPTER LIX.

EVIL NEWS—(continued).

KING JOHN, who had immediate need of every noble or wealthy person he could command for a friend at this time, at once turned a listening and attentive ear to what the abbot related, and sent on a hundred men-at-arms, cased in steel, and commanded by Sir William de Gray, own brother to a John de Gray, his favourite minister, confident to rout Robin Hood from Sherwood Forest, and cut him and his people to pieces without the slightest quarter or mercy—ruthless king.

The knight, who was, of course, a Norman, his hireling band also being recruited from that country, vowed he would at once lay Robin Hood's head at the monarch's feet, and departed upon his perilous errand with the firm and settled purpose of putting his threat into immediate execution.

His men were, for the occasion, armed only with long Roman swords, and all fully expected to obtain a victory with the greatest ease imaginable ; but when they came to Nottingham town they were taught to expect a very different issue ; they, however, merrily laughed to scorn all they were told, and marched out with the greatest confidence to the green wood of the forest, banners flying and all certain of success.

Robin Hood, who fully knew of their threatened arrival in Nottingham, of their general intention and peculiar equipments, prepared in a certain part of the great wood to meet them as they deserved.

One of his faithful people, disguised as a peasant, offered, for a consideration, to guide the Norman troops to Robin's most private haunt, and his proffered services were accepted ; after leading them across the wood several miles, through almost one entire entanglement and maze of briar, bush, brake, swamp and covert, and fatiguing them out excessively, being encased in armour, they, at length, arrived at an open glade studded in all parts with tall beech and elm and oak trees, and there were posted Robin Hood and his men.

The stout and confident Normans gave a great and ringing shout as their eyes lighted upon their long-concealed enemy, and the merry men at once responded by a loud, insulting laugh of derision ; this inflamed the warlike Normans in a very high degree, and irritated at Saxon insolence, they rushed on to the attack with all the impetuosity their fatigued limbs would enable them.

To their utter surprise, the sturdy men came out, and opposed them with nothing but quarterstaves, and with such agility, that the troop found their swords of very little use, for they could not exercise an activity at all competent to cope with that always displayed by their bold adversaries, and the heavy quarterstaffs rattled with such uncommon vigour upon their casques and breastplates, that they grew utterly confused ; and when some of the men threw away their heavy helmets to enable them to act with greater freedom, they were at once so beaten about the head that they fell in dozens senseless to the ground.

Sir William de Gray, the bold general who directed the forward movements of his men-at-arms, grew at once enraged beyond description at the severe drubbing his men were there receiving, and perceived with his military eye at the same time that, encased in such a heavy weight of metal, they had not sufficient power to act, heartily cursed and condemned him who had advised him to go thus equipped, and thought it prudent at once to draw off his men, and retreat as well as he could upon Nottingham, with the intention of returning on the morrow in a very different guise, and then either conquering the foe or perishing on the battle-field.

He at once, therefore, blew a blast of his horn, and summoned his warriors to retreat, which they at once did in tolerable good order, Robin not suffering his men to pursue them, save a few scouts and outlyers, who followed them for the purpose of ascertaining that they really did quit the forest of Sherwood ; and this once ascertained he returned with his followers to the trysting tree, and there enjoyed a good repast after his morning's exertion.

But the battle was not over.

CHAPTER LX.

DEATH CLAIMS HIS OWN.

THE faithful chronicler, we find, thus continues his narrative.

Robin Hood anticipated that Sir William had not done with him, and the arrival of some of the men who had been sent to learn their movements, with intelligence of their intended attack on the morrow, proved he was right. On the morrow they came, clothed in the light dresses of archers ; they were good bowmen, and this time they were armed with bows and spears, and a lighter species of sword and buckler.

Robin Hood determined to meet him in the same spirit, and to read him a lesson. He drew up his men in the same place as he had the preceding day, and waited their coming.

Time passed on, however, and they came not ; Robin began to think they had altered their mind, when one of his people arrived, stating that the troop were in the wood—were on their way to attack him—and, by a singular circumstance, had missed their road, and stumbled upon the direct track to the trysting-tree, were all the females were assembled, waiting the issue of the conflict.

Not a moment was to be lost ; the men broke up their position, and at the top of their speed proceeded to check the further advance of the Normans. They had some distance to pass over, and notwithstanding their efforts, the Normans succeeded in getting close up to the glade, in the centre of which stood the trysting-tree. There they saw the females assembled, and with the ruthless barbarity of the time, the Norman, feeling satisfied he should inflict a bitter sting upon the outlaws, and gratify revenge for his previous defeat, seeing them unprotected, resolved to suffer his men to ill-use them first, and butcher them afterwards ; but the women, on seeing them, set up a shriek, and retreated with precipitancy ; and he noticed that many of them followed the directions of one who appeared a superior among them, and prevented a continuance of the heedless confusion into which they were at first thrown, and who was now with rapid steps leading the females away : he raised his bow, and taking a deliberate aim, fired. He was a good marksman—his arrow struck his victim, and she fell bleeding to the ground.

A shriek of agony filled the air, and she was borne by the maidens swiftly away.

There was one who saw her danger, who observed the Norman take his aim, and came bounding along in a series of frantic leaps, to throw himself within range of the arrow. He had his own bow bent, and fixed, he thought, in sufficient time to prevent the discharge of the other's arrow; but he was too late; the knight's arrow quitted his bow at the same moment Robin Hood's left his—for it was he who witnessed and strove to prevent the soldier's barbarous act.

Each sped to its course; Marian fell, mortally wounded; and the Norman, with a quivering shriek, leaped five feet in the air, and fell dead with an arrow through his heart.

Robin Hood knew it was Marian that fell, and was in a state of frenzy. Little John also knew that she had fallen, and to the men he communicated it, to animate them to revenge. Every man in the band had loved her as though she had been a dearly prized sister, and yet a queen. Her gentleness, her uniform sweetness, kindliness, and tender consideration, had won their esteem and love to the furthest extent human nature allowed them; and when they knew she had fallen by the cool and deliberate act of the men opposed to them, they uttered a short fierce shout, which, in its tone, told a terrible tale, and then they rushed on to the attack with a stern silence which, in all their actions, they had never before exhibited.

But they resolved that her memory should receive an oblation which should not easily be forgotten. They went to work like tigers, with a fury and deadly success that were frightful to behold.

Little John's exertions were terrific. With a huge sword—for, independent of the unfortunate event just related, they had expected the encounter to be a fierce one—he cut down every one who confronted him; every blow carried certain death with it. He slew and spared not; and stalked on, mowing down men as if they were briars in his path.

Robin Hood, too, fought with a fierce and desperate resolution. His brows were upon his eyelids, and his eyeballs were as round as marbles; while his teeth were clenched, his lips set firm, and his face pale to deathliness. His arm seemed nerved with a giant's strength. All who came within his reach, and stood up before him, met their death.

He seemed unconscious of all things but the deadly task he was pursuing with such tremendous success. Unwounded, he fought in the thickest of the fight. His sword flew in all directions, inflicting utter destruction upon whomsoever it alighted; and as he cut down each opposer he changed not, save to set his teeth still firmer; for, with all this horror around him, he had a thronging sense of the agony which was awaiting him in the glade.

Soon it grew understood there was no quarter given or taken; and each man fought actuated by the knowledge he was fighting for his life, and a resolve to sell it dearly. The conflict was of the most sanguinary nature. Fierce oaths and execrations mingled with the groans of the dead and dying.

The Normans fell in numbers. Man after man was cut down, wounded to the death, while the merry men seemed to bear a charmed life. But they were all expert swordsmen, powerful men, and frenzied by a burning desire of revenge and a deadly hatred of the Norman race. Their hands grasped their weapons firmer, and their arms seemed nerved with an additional strength, in being opposed to them.

For two hours fought they in this way; and at length a mere handful of Normans were left, and then they threw down their arms and fled, the merrie men pursuing them, cutting them down as they overtook them. Out of the hundred men who that morning had marched blithely from Nottingham, three only returned to relate the events of the fatal and bloody conflict.

When the conflict was ended by the flight of the Normans, Robin threw his sword from him and flew to the glade where he had seen Marian carried, and there he saw her lying extended upon the ground, and Maude, in a torrent of tears which blinded her, making ineffectual efforts to stanch the blood which was flowing from her side.

Robin threw himself by her side, his heart bursting with anguish, his tongue clove to the roof of his mouth, he felt choking and unable to articulate a word. At his approach Marian opened her eyes, and turned them upon him; she recognised him instantly, and scanned him hastily.

"Are you unhurt, dear Robin?" she articulated, in a feeble voice.

"I am—I am," he uttered, hoarsely, trying to force the words out.

"The Holy Mother be praised!" she exclaimed, a faint smile illumining her features; "I have prayed earnestly that you might, and the Blessed Virgin has heard my prayers. And has that terrible battle ceased, dear Robin?"

"It has, Marian; we have driven them from the wood. But, dear Marian, you—I—Holy Mother of God! I cannot endure this sight!" burst forth Robin, with agony, and buried his face in his hands.

"Nay, Robin, dear Robin, look up," faintly uttered Marian, trying to speak cheerfully; "I am not much hurt, indeed I am not. See—the arrow is out; it is only a flesh wound. You know, dear Robin, if the wound were mortal I should have died when I drew it forth—and I am smiling on thee. Look upon me, dear Robin!"

And she reached forward her hand to touch him; he raised his head at her words, and found that the exertion had caused her to faint away.

But her words had raised hopes in him; he saw it was as she had said, and he believed fondly that she still might be spared to him; he therefore prepared to stanch the blood by means in use among them, and which had ever proved effectual.

With the aid of Mhude, part of her dress was removed, the wound bathed, some bruised herbs applied, and then it was carefully bandaged. As the exertion of removing her might have a fatal effect upon her, a couch was brought, a large tent of leaves erected over her, and she was carefully watched until she came to her senses; after a little while she seemed better, and expressed a desire to sleep, and soon she fell into a deep slumber.

Robin then went to see the condition of his men. He found Little John actively employed with Much and Will Scarlett in binding up the wounds of those who had been maimed in the fray, and directing the burial of all who had fallen. He had the satisfaction of discovering that not one of his men was killed, and but seven badly wounded; the wounds of the remainder were of no moment, while the slaughter of the Normans was awful.

A deep pit was dug far from the scene of action, and their bodies were thrown in it. When this was completed, Robin returned to Marian, and sat by her side until she awoke; and when she had shaken the effects of her deep sleep from her eyelids, she turned her full dark eyes upon him, and smiled as she told him she felt no pain, and she was sure she should soon be better.

She said this more because she knew he would be happier to hear it than from any inward conviction she felt that such was the case; but she wished only to see him cheerful, whatever might be her own feelings, and she knew the nearer he deemed her recovery proportionably would his cheerfulness increase.

For some days she continued thus, but at length a change took place for the worse; inflammation ensued, and all hopes of her recovery fled. Robin scarce ever quitted her side.

At length, on the evening of the day succeeding inflammation commencing, she awoke from a deep sleep into which she had fallen, and her eyes lighted on Robin, who was kneeling by her side, and with his hands upraised was praying in passionate earnestness, while the big scalding tears were coursing each other down his pale cheeks; his words had no sound, but she could tell by the quivering emotion of his lip how enthusiastically fervent were the prayers he breathed.

She awaited silently until he had concluded; then she called in a faint, quiet tone to him.

"Dear Robin," she exclaimed, "my beloved husband, my first, dearest, and last love! the time has come when we must part; I feel the hand of death upon me, and I know that my time here with thee, thou dearly loved, is but brief. Before we part I would tell thee, with my expiring words, with what felicity I have dwelt with thee ever since we were united; I would tell thee how in my heart of hearts I have cherished the daily, hourly, exhibition of thy love for me, how I have felt in all things it has known no change, never, never! I would tell thee, Robin, how happy, how very happy, thou hast made me, and in the fullness of my heart would wish most earnestly I could coin my thankfulness into some visible shape, that you might see how I have appreciated thy love. That I have loved thee with the entire worship of a heart wholly engrossed by thee, the Holy Mother be my judge. I have tried to show thee as much, indeed I have; and if my acts have been inadequate to my wishes, it has arisen wholly from inability to express that which was so deeply engraven upon my heart. I have striven to discharge the duties of one who loved thee, and of a wife—"

"And have done so, dear Marian—have more than done so," interrupted Robin, trying hard to speak, without betraying the anguish his spirit was crushed beneath.

"And should have done so, dearest Robin," she continued, faintly smiling, "had it pleased heaven that we should have lived together until we laid down our lives, good old folk; however, such is not ordained, and I shall pass away from you happier, as I think you have appreciated my love to the extent it existed. Place your arm round me, dear Robin—so, and let me lay my head upon your shoulder; there, now I can breathe my last words into your ear, and my spirit will pass lightly and happily away, for I shall utter my last sigh upon thy breast."

"Beloved Marian, talk not so," cried Robin, in a voice of the keenest misery, "I cannot bear to hear thee speak of parting for ever. Holy Mother of God, it is too much! Oh, dear Lady of Heaven, if thou didst ever hear me, and serve me at my prayers, hear me now; spare her to me, spare her, or I am miserable for ever—for ever!"

"'Tis a vain wish, dear Robin," uttered Marian, gently pressing his hand with her hot parched fingers, "we must at some time part; it is bitter, God knows it is bitter to part; but it is the will of Him who ordains all things, and we should not repine or seek to change what he ordaineth. Think, dear Robin, that we shall meet again. Oh! yes, we shall again meet among trees and flowers, and sweet shining faces, and all fair things, and never part again, never! never!—a place where there is nought but sunshine, and nothing to alter the sweet nature of the beauty around.

"Just ere I awoke, Robin, I had a dream; I thought you and your people were all in the pleasant old wood, and you smiled and made merry, and the sun shone on the green leaves, and the blossoms and buds were in their brightest colours, and the trees were all garlanded, as on the happy, happy day that saw us united, dear love; and I thought, amid all this joy and delight, I was suddenly led away, and I seemed to be taken to some drear, dark place. I had no power to prevent being taken—I looked on you, and the smile I saw before still played on your features; the people appeared to grow gayer yet, and it seemed as if I was about to leave it all for ever, never again to look upon what I then beheld; in my anguish I covered my eyes with my hand and wept. While still in tears, a light hand was placed upon my shoulder; I turned my face to see who had touched me, and looked upon the placid, sweet features of my dear mother. 'Weep not, my dear child,' she exclaimed, 'weep not; thou'rt passing the ordeal we must all endure; thou hast but quitted a pleasant, yet a fleeting scene of happiness for one which is eternal—behold!' I looked and suddenly I found myself in a garden of surpassing beauty, the loveliest faces with the sweetest expression of kindness, and purity were beaming round me, the air was fragrant with the scent of the most delightful flowers, and the trees were so green and so fresh, and the birds warbled so beautifully, and the air was so cool, that I have no words to describe them; and, oh! dear Robin, what far exceeded all, I saw thee hastening towards me, looking upon me with loving eyes, and a face so happy that, with a cry of delight, I sprang towards thee, and my mother's soft voice sounded in my ears, saying, 'And this endureth for ever;' at that moment I awoke, and I knew that my hour was come.

"I feel that I am dying; I can feel myself each moment growing weaker and weaker; but, dear Robin, my head is pillowed on thy breast; thine eyes, which

have always turned upon me with the soft endearing expression of affection, are looking on me, if sadly, yet lovingly; thy arm is round me, and like a weary child upon its mother's bosom, I feel as if falling into a gentle slumber; my voice grows fainter, I can hear, and my sight is dimmer, for I cannot see thine eyes so plainly as before; kiss me, Robin."

He pressed his burning lips to hers, and she felt his hot tears raining on her face. She lifted her feeble hand, and with her finger traced the spot where a tear had fallen, and pressed it to her lips. Her voice became a whisper, and now her lips almost touched his ear. Again she spoke:—

"Robin, my best beloved, when I am away from thee, when thou hast only the memory of her who loved thee to live in thy heart, let not thy sad thoughts make each hour one of weariness and wretchedness; believe that I am happy, that my spirit is hovering round thy spirit, as it will if it be permitted, and that it will receive pleasure when it sees thee smile and look cheerful; and for the sake of those around thee, who so much honour and love thee, as I have most proudly seen and known, who look up to thee in all things, and take the tone of their actions from thy looks and temperament, and would be sad wert thou sad, even to the extent of thy sorrow; and for my sake, for thy Marian's sake, to lighten this dread hour of parting, turn not thy face from thy people, but be pleasant, and cheerful, and happy, as before. Promise me this, dear, dear Robin, and I shall die so happy."

"I will—I will strive—I—God help me! I know not what I shall do," sobbed Robin, weeping like a child.

"Bless you, Robin! May the Almighty bless thee, my beloved! And I have now one last request. You will grant it me, I know, sweet love. I would I could see thee smile, but all is dark around me, and I hear my mother's gentle voice summoning me away. I come—I—Robin, hour after hour have we sat beneath yon trysting tree, long before cruel men made thee a tenant in the wood. We were young hearts then, dear Robin, and sat beneath that tree, with its trembling leaves quivering over us, and the sweet delicate flowers waving round us, gazing upon each other with deep love, and thoughts which had no tongue, and hearts that throbbed and panted till we felt faint.

"One night, when the moon shone clearly over every leaf and flower, and there was no cloud to shade for an instant its gentle light, we wandered through the wood. It was before you told me that you loved me; yet I knew that you did, yet feared and doubted. We seated ourselves beneath that tree, and you said kind words, soft and low; and I felt a sweet languor steal over my senses. I thought it would be pleasant to weep, I knew not why; my head sunk upon your shoulder; the bright moonlight showed clearly all the beautiful things growing and waving silently around us; and then I thought how sweet it would be to be buried there among those flowers. And ever since we have dwelt in this wood I have cherished that hope, treasured it up, and now I would, dear Robin, be laid in that spot, for thou wilt be ever near me; and the flowers will not bloom less brightly, nor the grass be less green and fresh, because it is waving over the head of one who loved to look upon their tender beauty while living. I—let me hear thee say, Robin, I shall be laid there."

"You shall, dearest Marian! You shall, my sweet angel! And when my time shall come—God grant it may be soon!—if there is one true heart near me to do my last bidding, I will lie beside thee; and the green turf shall wave over us both, dear Marian, in death, as it did beneath us in life."

"Bless thee! bless thee! With my last breath I pray for thee; with my last words I bless thee. Farewell—let thy lips receive my last sigh, my beloved Robin—smile upon me—I cannot see thee, but I shall know if thou dost. I die happy—happy—I come—I—Robin—bless thee—dearest—bless——"

The words, which were barely beyond a whisper, ceased. Robin felt his lips receive a faint kiss as a low sigh left Marian's, his hand a gentle pressure, and then all was motionless. For a long time he remained in the same position, scarce daring to breathe. Then some one entered the tent. He looked up wildly. It was Maude. He turned his eyes rapidly upon Marian's face, and then suddenly depositing his slight burden upon the couch, he sprung up, with convulsively clenched hands, with a frantic madness in his eyes, and shrieked forth—falling senseless to the ground as he uttered the words—

"Holy Mother of God! She is gone for ever!—my best beloved!—my wife! MARIAN IS DEAD!"

CHAPTER LXI.

THE END OF ALL.

MANY days elapsed, until Robin had reached his fifty-fifth year and Little John his sixty-fifth, and yet both were as hale and strong as many who were their juniors twenty years. There was little necessity for them to pass such an active time as they had during John's reign, because the Earl of Pembroke, who was guardian to King Henry III., disliking bloodshed, did much to ameliorate the condition of the people. Probably from inactivity, Robin Hood began to feel dull and listless; the sudden cessation of excitement produced a reaction on his spirits, and again he was ever at the grave of Marian, and then wandering alone in the most solitary part of the wood; a presentiment was upon him that his time was near at hand, and much as he strove to shake it off, it clung with the utmost tenacity to him. Little John, who always tended him with the most affectionate earnestness, quickly perceived the melancholy change which had taken place, and applied himself at once to the task of arousing him from its influence; he traced it to its right source, and judged if a change was made in his system, that he would recover the healthful tone of spirits he had recently enjoyed.

Robin had more than ever excited the love of the people for him by his daring acts in their behalf, and could with safety traverse any part of the county of Nottingham alone.

An abbey which stood on the borders of the wood, called Kirkleys Abbey, had once received him when wounded in an attack upon a band of Normans; the prioress claimed a relationship, and tended him very carefully until he recovered. Little John now strenuously advised him to seek her and there be blooded, a remedy at that time for nearly all diseases of the frame or mind; and to gratify the strong desire Little John evinced, Robin complied with his wish. He sent word a day or so before, in order to prepare the prioress, and when he went there she received him with a smiling face and outstretched hands. She invited him to partake of some refreshment, which, however, he declined, and requested only that she would bleed him, a duty which she performed with much dexterity upon such members of the abbey as needed it, and he knew her skill, and had no hesitation in trusting her. She showed him into a small upper room, which she said she had prepared for him, and he laid upon a couch while she opened a vein in his arm; she then took such an enormous quantity of blood from him, that he refused to permit her to take any more; and then she smiled as before, bound up his arm, and leaving him to repose, quitted the room, carefully locked the door after her, put the key in her pocket, and descended the stairs with the smile still upon her countenance.

This prioress, although devoted to God, had an unsaintly love for a certain knight, who was very frequent in his visits to the abbey; he learned from her that the celebrated Robin Hood, her kinsman, was coming to her to be blooded,

¶ [This knight was a brother of Sir Guy of Gisborne, a mean dastardly, spiritless wretch; who, without the courage to meet our hero, worked upon this woman's fears, until he persuaded her to bleed Robin to death. The woman, of a weak mind, not possessing a spark of real virtue, suffered herself to be drawn into his views, and satisfied herself that she was doing a good act, in shortening the life of one who was an outlaw, and therefore a bad man; she had succeeded in drawing a great quantity of blood from her victim, but his resolution prevented her at that time from carrying her project into effect; but when darkness drew on she stole cautiously to the chamber, and found our hero in a deep sleep; she quietly removed the bandage from his arm, and having the satisfaction to see the wound break out afresh and the blood began to trickle down his arm, she carried the bandage away with her, locked the door as before, and descended, leaving him there alone to die.

The morning broke, and as it began to pour its beams into the little chamber, Robin opened his eyes, but experienced such a dreadful sensation of faintness that he could scarce move. For a short time he lay still, and he began to think of his young days, of green trees and blue skies; then he exerted himself to try and shake off the faintness, and then he discovered he was deluged with blood, that the bandage was removed, and, from the loss of blood he had experienced, he was on the verge of death. His first impulse was to spring up and try the door, but he fell to the ground in the attempt; he, however, crawled to it and found it fast. He then dragged himself to the window, but found he had not strength for the leap, and, as a last resource, he put his horn to his mouth, and blew three weak blasts. His dear old friend Little John was near at hand, as he ever was when his services were needed. He heard the summons, feeble as it was, for he was hovering round the abbey walls.

His blood ran cold as he heard the faint tones, and in an instant he suspected something was wrong. He called together a party of the merry men, rushed to the abbey, and demanded instant admittance. It was denied him, and his suspicions were confirmed.

He seized a large block of stone which lay near, which no two other men could have moved, and hurled it against the door. It dashed it open, and he rushed in. Again he heard the feeble notes of the horn. He followed the sound, flew up the stairs, and threw himself against the door of the room where Robin was confined, and burst it open, to see a sight which turned his heart cold. Robin, with scarce half an hour's life in him, was leaning against the casement: the couch was a mass of blood.

Thus ended the career of him whose life forms one of the most extraordinary features in the annals of this country. Thus passed away—the victim of one of a sex whom he had ever most highly honoured—one adored by the common people far and near; his memory revered for the open-handed generous-hearted charity with which he relieved wants, and the bold chivalric spirit with which he endeavoured to lift the wretched serfs out of the galling clutches of a dire oppression. He who at all times, and in all seasons, was at the service of those who needed his aid, at any risk, at any personal sacrifice, undaunted by appalling dangers, unmoved at the prospect of future punishments, was thus struck down, and by the hand of woman; her from whom, having exhibited such devotion, such true knightly feeling in her behalf, he could least have expected the blow. Thus he, who had faced the perils of fierce conflicts, encountered foes singly and in numbers, had withstood the desperate efforts of well-trained swordsmen, the chance bolts in a *melée*, or death-dealing weapons in a sanguinary fray;—he who had dared and escaped all these, now gave up the ghost, treacherously and wickedly deprived of life by means which added one strong pang to the regrets which he felt at parting with his old companions and the old familiar places for ever.

Thrice ten thousand times would he rather have fallen, with his bonnie yew bow in his hand, or his trusty sword, than thus steal out of the world, the victim of a malicious wanton, who, under the garb of saintly sanctity, covered sins of the most infamous description. But thus it was to be; and the "just, generous, benevolent, faithful, and beloved," quitted the scenes of his vicissitudes, trials, exploits, happiness, and sorrow, for a better world, leaving behind him a name which has come down to us intact, extolled by a priest for his piety, by the oldest historians for his humanity and gentleness, and universally honoured for the efforts which he made, as the last of his race, to shake off the oppressive yoke of the Norman conquerors.

THE END.